EXPLOSIVE PRAISE FOR ROBERT LUDLUM'S

THE SIGMA PROTOCOL

"Perfectly executed…. Packed with all the classic Ludlum elements…thunders forward at breakneck pace." —*People*

"[A] triumph…. Harkens back to the roller-coaster ride/thrill-a-minute *Bourne Identity*." —*Kirkus Reviews*

"Ludlum at his best." —*Sullivan County Democrat*

"Vintage Ludlum." —*Houston Chronicle*

"Dazzling…a clean launch of the '80s spy novel into a thrilling action/adventure web of intrigue meant for the twenty-first century." —*Publishers Weekly*

"It's amazing that ten pages before the end of the book, you still can't figure out how he's going to resolve the complex plot he's presented. Yet he does, and pretty satisfactorily." —*Colorado Springs Gazette*

"[Ludlum] shows that…his storytelling skill was still at an all-time high…provides no less suspense than his die-hard fans would expect." —*Bookreporter.com*

"An accomplished novel…classic Ludlum…moves at breakneck speed…with well-developed players and a fascinating stage, Ludlum has risen to some of his finest work in this clever and enjoyable novel." —*Chattanooga Times Free Press*

"Better than anything [Ludlum's] done in nearly twenty years…here is vintage Ludlum…the plot is rich with new insight." —*Gannett Newspapers*

W9-BXL-703

"Ludlum keeps things moving with plenty of gunplay and running about . . . quite good." —*Booklist*

THE PROMETHEUS DECEPTION

"His best thriller yet." —*Kirkus Reviews*

"Ludlum's latest is a spy thriller that should keep even the most experienced readers guessing....The pace is fast, the action plentiful.... A must-read." —*Booklist*

THE AMBLER WARNING

"Serves as a fine introduction for those unfamiliar with those works written by Ludlum during his lifetime." —*Bookreporter.com*

"An intense, powerful novel, rich in detail, complex plotting, and characterization...chilling...the rapid pace of this book and the exhilarating twists to the story make it next to impossible to put down...excellent." —*Affaire de Coeur*

THE MOSCOW VECTOR

"Plenty of excellent shootouts." —*Publishers Weekly*

THE LAZARUS VENDETTA

"A fast read and sure to delight fans of both espionage and the technothriller." —*Booklist*

"A solid intelligence, some really scary nanotechnology, and a writing style that always gets the job done." —*Publishers Weekly*

THE
PROMETHEUS
DECEPTION

THE
SIGMA
PROTOCOL

ROBERT LUDLUM

THE
PROMETHEUS
DECEPTION

THE
SIGMA
PROTOCOL

St. Martin's Griffin ☙ New York

www.stmartins.com

ISBN-13: 978-0-312-36687-2
ISBN-10: 0-312-36687-6

The Prometheus Deception was originally published
by St. Martin's Press in 2000.

The Sigma Protocol was originally published
by St. Martin's Press in 2001.

First St. Martin's Griffin Edition: September 2006

10 9 8 7 6 5 4 3 2 1

THE PROMETHEUS DECEPTION

Prometheus swept down from the heavens
bringing the gift of fire.

Wrong move.

PROLOGUE

Carthage, Tunisia
3:22 A.M.

The driving rain was unrelenting, whipped into a frenzy by howling winds, and the waves surged and crashed against the coast, a maelstrom in the black night. In the shallow waters just offshore, a dozen or so dark figures bobbed, clinging to their buoyant, waterproof haversacks like survivors of a shipwreck. The freak storm had caught the men unawares but was good; it provided better cover than they could have hoped for.

From the beach, a pinpoint of red light flashed on and off twice, a signal from the advance team that it was safe to land. *Safe!* What did that mean? That this particular stretch of Tunisian coastline was left undefended by the *Garde Nationale*? Nature's assault seemed far more punishing than anything the Tunisian coast guard could attempt.

Tossed and buffeted about by the heaving swells, the men made their way toward the beach, and in one coordinated movement clambered silently onto the sand by the ruins of the ancient Punic ports. Stripping off their black rubber dry suits to reveal dark clothing and blackened faces, they removed their weapons from their haversacks and began distributing their arsenal: Heckler & Koch MP-10 submachine guns, Kalashnikovs, and sniper rifles. Behind them, others now came ashore in waves.

Everything was precisely orchestrated by the man who had trained them so exhaustively, so tirelessly, for the last months. They were Al-Nahda freedom fighters, natives of Tunisia come to free their country from the oppressors. But their leaders were foreigners—skilled terrorists who also shared their faith in Allah, a small, elite cell of freedom fighters drawn from the most radical wing of Hezbollah.

The leader of this cell, and of the fifty or so Tunisians, was the master terrorist known only as Abu. Occasionally his full nom de guerre was used: Abu Intiquab. The father of revenge.

Elusive, secretive, and ferocious, Abu had trained the Al-Nahda fighters at the Libyan camp outside of Zuwarah. He refined their strategy on a full-scale model of the presidential palace and instructed them in tactics both more violent and more devious than anything they were used to.

Barely thirty hours ago, at the port of Zuwarah, the men had boarded a five-thousand-ton, Russian-built break-bulk freighter, a cargo ship that normally hauled Tunisian textiles and Libyan manufactured goods between Tripoli and Bizerte in Tunisia. The powerful old freighter, now battered and decrepit, had traveled north-northwest along the Tunisian coast, past the port cities of Sfax and Sousse, then swung around Cap Bon and entered the Golfe de Tunis, just past the naval base at La Goulette. Alerted to the schedule of the coast guard patrol boats, the men had dropped anchor five miles from the Carthage coast and swiftly launched their rigid-hulled inflatables, equipped with powerful outboard motors. Within minutes, they had entered the turbulent waters of Carthage, the ancient Phoenician city so powerful in the fifth century B.C. that it was considered Rome's great rival. If anyone in the Tunisian coast guard happened to be monitoring the ship on radar, he would see only a freighter pausing momentarily, then heading on toward Bizerte.

On the shore, the man who had flashed the red signal was hissing orders and cursing in a low voice with unquestioned authority. He was a bearded man in a military-issue rain anorak worn over a keffiyeh. Abu.

"Quiet! Keep it down! What do you want, to bring out the whole godforsaken Tunisian *Garde?* Quickly, now. Let's move it, *move* it! Clumsy *fools!* Your leader rots in jail while you dawdle! The trucks are waiting!"

Next to him stood a man wearing night-vision goggles and silently scanning the terrain. The Tunisians knew him only as the Technician. One of Hezbollah's top munitions experts, he was a handsome, olive-skinned man with heavy brows and flashing brown eyes. As little as the men knew about Abu, they knew even less about the Technician, Abu's trusted adviser. According to rumor, he was born to wealthy Syrian parents and raised in Damascus and London, where he was schooled in the intricacies of arms and explosives.

Finally the Technician spoke, quietly and calmly. He pulled his black, hooded waterproof garment tight against the torrential rain.

"I hesitate to say it, my brother, but the operation is going smoothly. The trucks loaded with matériel were concealed just as we had arranged and the soldiers encountered no resistance on the short drive along the Avenue Habib Borguiga. Now we have just received the radio signal from the first men—they have reached the presidential palace. The coup d'etat has begun." As he spoke he consulted his wristwatch.

Abu nodded imperiously. He was a man who expected nothing less than success. A distant series of explosions told Abu and his adviser that the battle was under way. The presidential palace would be seized im-minently, and in a matter of hours, the Islamic militants would control Tunis. "Let us not congratulate ourselves prematurely," Abu said in a low, tense voice. The rain was letting up now, and in a moment the storm passed just as suddenly as it had appeared.

Suddenly the silence on the beach was shattered by voices shouting at them in strident, high-pitched Arabic. Dark figures raced across the sand. Abu and the Technician tensed and reached for their weapons, but then saw it was their Hezbollah brethren.

"A zero-one!"

"An *ambush!*"

"My God! Mighty Allah, they're *surrounded!*"

Four Arab men approached, looking frightened and out of breath. "A zero-one distress signal," panted the one carrying a PRC-117 field radio on his back. "They were able to transmit only that they were surrounded by the security forces at the palace and taken captive. Then the transmission was killed! They say they were set up!"

Abu turned to his adviser in alarm. "How can this be?"

The youngest of the four young men who stood before them said, "The matériel left for the men—the antitank weapons, the ammunition, the C-4—all of it was defective! Nothing worked! And the government forces were lying in wait for them! Our men were set up from the *beginning!*"

Abu looked visibly pained, his customary serenity vanished. He beckoned his number-one adviser. "*Ya sahbee,* I need your wise counsel."

The Technician adjusted his wristwatch as he came close to the master terrorist. Abu put one arm around his adviser's shoulders. He spoke in a low, calm voice. "There must be a traitor in our ranks, an infiltrator. Our plans were leaked."

Abu made a subtle, almost undetectable gesture with a finger and thumb. It was a cue, and his followers immediately grabbed the Technician by the arms, legs, and shoulders. The Technician struggled mightily, but he was no match for the trained terrorists who held him. Swiftly, Abu's right hand shot out. There was a flash of metal and Abu plunged a serrated, hooked knife into the Technician's abdomen, yanking the blade down and then out to inflict the maximum damage. Abu's eyes were blazing. "The traitor is *you!*" he spat out.

The Technician gasped. The pain was obviously excruciating, but his face remained a stolid mask. "No, Abu!" he protested.

"*Pig!*" spat Abu, lunging at him again, his serrated knife aimed at the Technician's groin. "No one else knew the timing, the exact plans! No one! And you were the one who certified the matériel. It can be no one else."

Suddenly the beach was flooded with blindingly bright carbon-arc light. Abu turned and realized that they were surrounded and vastly outnumbered by dozens upon dozens of soldiers in khaki uniforms. The Groupement de Commando of the Tunisian *Garde Nationale,* machine guns pointed, had abruptly appeared from over the horizon; a thundering racket from above announced the arrival of several attack helicopters.

Bursts of automatic gunfire hit Abu's men, turning them into jerking marionettes. Their bloodcurdling screams were abruptly silenced, and their bodies toppled to the ground in strange and awkward positions. Another burst of gunfire, and then it stopped. The unexpected silence that followed was eerie. Only the master terrorist and his munitions specialist had not been fired upon.

But Abu seemed to have only one focus of attention, and he spun back around to the man he had branded a traitor, positioning his scimitar-shaped blade for another attack. Badly wounded, the Technician tried to ward off his assailant, but instead began to sink to the ground. The loss of blood was too great. Just as Abu lunged forward to finish him off, powerful hands grabbed the bearded Hezbollah leader from behind, slamming him down and pinning him to the sand.

Abu's eyes burned with defiance as the two were taken into custody by the government soldiers. He did not fear any government. Governments were cowards, he had often said; governments would release him under some pretext of *international law* and *extradition* and *repatriation.* Deals would be struck behind the scenes, and Abu would be quietly released, his presence in the country a carefully kept secret. No government wanted to bring on itself the full fury of a Hezbollah terror campaign.

The terrorist master did not struggle, but instead caused his body to go slack, forcing the soldiers to drag him away. As he was dragged past the Technician, he spat full in his face and hissed, "You are not long for this world, *traitor! Pig!* You will *die* for your treachery!"

Once Abu was taken away, the several men who had grabbed the Technician gently released him, easing him down onto a waiting stretcher. Obeying the instructions of the battalion captain, they backed away as the captain approached. The Tunisian knelt beside the Technician and examined his wound. The Technician winced but uttered not a sound.

"My God, it's a wonder you're still conscious!" said the captain in heavily accented English. "You have been badly injured. You have lost a great deal of blood."

The man who had been known as the Technician replied, "If your men had responded to my signal a little more speedily, this wouldn't have happened." He instinctively touched his wristwatch, which was equipped with a miniaturized high-frequency transmitter.

The captain ignored the barb. "That SA-341 up there," he said, pointing up to the sky, where a helicopter hovered, "will take you to a high-security government medical facility in Morocco. I'm not permitted to know your real identity, nor who your real employers are, so I won't ask," the Tunisian began, "but I think I have a good idea—"

Just then the Technician whispered harshly, "Get *down!*" He quickly pulled a semiautomatic pistol from the holster concealed under his arm and fired off five quick shots. There was a cry from a copse of palm trees, and a dead man toppled to the ground, his sniper rifle clutched in his hand. Somehow an Al-Nahda soldier had escaped the massacre.

"Mighty Allah!" exclaimed the frightened captain of the battalion as he slowly raised his head and looked around. "I think we're even now, you and I."

"Listen," the Arab-who-was-not-an-Arab said weakly, "tell your president his minister of the interior is a secret Al-Nahda sympathizer and collaborator who conspires to take his place. He's in league with the deputy minister of defense. There are others . . ."

But the loss of blood had been too great. Before the Technician could finish his sentence, he passed out.

PART ONE

CHAPTER
ONE

Washington, D.C.
Five weeks later

The patient was conveyed by a chartered jet to a private landing strip twenty miles northwest of Washington, D.C. Although the patient was the only passenger on the entire aircraft, no one spoke to him except to ascertain his immediate needs. No one knew his name. All they knew was that this was clearly an extremely important passenger. The flight's arrival appeared on no aviation logs anywhere, military or civilian.

The nameless passenger was then taken by unmarked sedan to downtown Washington and dropped off, at his own request, near a parking garage in the middle of an unremarkable block near Dupont Circle. He wore an unimpressive gray suit with a pair of tasseled cordovan loafers that had been scuffed and shined a few too many times, and looked like one of a thousand midlevel lobbyists and bureaucrats, the faceless, colorless staffers of a permanent Washington.

Nobody gave him a second look as he emerged from the parking garage, then walked, stiffly and with a pronounced limp, to a dun-colored, four-story building at 1324 K Street, near Twenty-first. The building, all cement and gray-tinted glass, was scarcely distinguishable from all the other bland, boxy low-rises along this stretch of northwest Washington. These were the offices, invariably, of lobbying groups and trade organizations, travel bureaus and industry boards. Beside its front entrance a couple of brass plaques were mounted, announcing the offices of INNOVATION ENTERPRISES and AMERICAN TRADE INTERNATIONAL.

Only a trained engineer with highly rarefied expertise might have noticed a few anomalous details—the fact, for example, that every window frame was equipped with a piezoelectric oscillator, rendering futile any attempt at laser-acoustic surveillance from outside. Or the high-frequency white-noise "drench" that enveloped the building in a cone of radio waves, sufficient to defeat most forms of electronic eavesdropping.

Certainly nothing ever attracted the attention of its K Street neighbors—the balding lawyers at the grains board, the grim-faced accountants in their ties and short-sleeved shirts at the slowly failing business consulting firm. People arrived at 1324 K Street in the morning and left in the evening and trash was deposited in the alley Dumpster on the appropriate days. What else did anybody care to know? But that was how the Directorate liked to be: hidden in plain view.

The man almost smiled to himself when he thought about it. For who would ever suspect that the most secretive of the world's covert agencies would be headquartered in an ordinary-looking office building in the middle of K Street, right out in the open?

The Central Intelligence Agency in Langley, Virginia, and the National Security Agency in Fort Meade, Maryland, were housed in moated fortresses that proclaimed their existence! *Here I am*, they seemed to say, *right here, pay no attention to me!* They virtually dared their opponents to breach their security—as inevitably happened. The Directorate made those so-called clandestine bureaucracies look about as reclusive as the U.S. Postal Service.

The man stood inside the lobby of 1324 K Street and scanned the sleek brass panel, on which was mounted a perfectly conventional-looking telephone handset beneath a dial pad, from all appearances the sort of arrangement that appears in lobbies in office buildings around the world. The man picked up the handset and then pressed a series of numbers, a predetermined code. He kept his index finger pressed on the last button, the # sign, for a few seconds until he heard a faint ring, signifying that his fingerprint had been electronically scanned, analyzed, matched against a preexisting and precleared database of digitized fingerprints, and approved. Then he listened to the telephone handset as it rang precisely three times. A disembodied, mechanical female voice commanded him to state his business.

"I have an appointment with Mr. Mackenzie," said the man. In a matter of seconds his words were converted into bits of data and matched against another database of precleared voiceprints. Only then did a faint buzzing in the lobby indicate that the first inner set of glass doors could be opened. He hung up the telephone receiver and pushed open the heavy, bulletproof glass doors, entered a tiny antechamber, and stood there for a few seconds as his facial features were scanned by three separate high-resolution surveillance cameras and checked against stored, authorized patterns.

The second set of doors opened onto a small, featureless reception area of white walls and gray industrial carpeting, equipped with hidden monitoring devices that could detect all manner of concealed weapons. On a marble-topped console in one corner, there was a stack of pamphlets emblazoned with the logo of American Trade International, an organization that existed only as a set of legal documents and registrations. The rest of the pamphlets were given over to an unreadable mission statement, filled with platitudes about international trade. An unsmiling guard waved Bryson past, through another set of doors and into a handsomely appointed hall, paneled in dark, burled walnut, where about a dozen clerical types were at their desks. It might have been an upscale art gallery of the sort one might find on Fifty-seventh Street in Manhattan, or perhaps a prosperous law firm.

"Nick Bryson, my main man!" exclaimed Chris Edgecomb, bounding from his seat at a computer monitor. Born in Guyana, he was a lithe, tall man with mocha skin and green eyes. He'd been at the Directorate for four years, working on the communications-and-coordination team; he fielded distress calls, figured out ways to relay information to agents in the field when it was necessary. Edgecomb clasped Bryson's hand warmly.

Nicholas Bryson knew he was something of a hero to people like

Edgecomb, who yearned to be field operatives. "Join the Directorate and change the world," Edgecomb would joke in his lilting English, and it was Bryson he had in mind when he said it. It was a rare event, Bryson knew, that the office staff saw Bryson face-to-face; for Edgecomb, this was an occasion.

"Somebody hurt you?" Edgecomb's expression was sympathetic; he saw a strong man who had been hospitalized until recently. Then he continued hastily, knowing better than to ask questions: "I'll pray to Saint Christopher for you. You'll be a hundred percent in no time."

The Directorate's creed, above all, was segmentation and compartmentalization. No one agent or staffer should ever know enough to be in the position to jeopardize the security of the whole. The organizational chart was shrouded even to a veteran like Bryson. He knew a few of the desk jockeys, of course. But the field personnel all operated in isolation, through their own proprietary networks. If you had to work together, you knew each other only by a field legend, a temporary alias. The rule was more than procedure, it was Holy Writ.

"You're a good man, Chris," Bryson remarked.

Edgecomb smiled modestly, then pointed a finger upward. He knew Bryson had an appointment—or was it a summons?—with the big man himself, Ted Waller. Bryson smiled, gave Edgecomb a friendly clap on the shoulder, and made his way to the elevator.

"Don't get up," Bryson said heartily as he entered Ted Waller's third-floor office. Waller did anyway, all six feet, four inches and three hundred pounds of him.

"Good Lord, look at you," Waller said, his eyes appraising Bryson with alarm. "You look like you came out of a POW camp."

"Thirty-three days in a U.S. government clinic in Morocco will do that to you," Bryson said. "It's not exactly the Ritz."

"Perhaps I should try being gutted by a mad terrorist someday." Waller patted his ample girth. He was even larger than the last time Bryson had seen him, though his avoirdupois was elegantly sheathed in a suit of navy cashmere, his bull neck flattered by the spread collar of one of his Turnbull & Asser shirts. "Nick, I've been tormenting myself since this happened. It was a serrated Verenski blade from Bulgaria, I'm told. Plunge and twist. Terribly low-tech, but it usually does the job. What a business we're in. Never forget, it's what you *don't* see that always gets you." Waller settled weightily back in the tufted-leather chair behind his oak desk. The early-afternoon sun filtered through the polarized glass behind him. Bryson took a seat in front of him, an unaccustomed formality. Waller, who was normally ruddy and seemingly robust, now looked pallid, the circles under his eyes deep. "They say you've made a remarkable recovery."

"In a few more weeks, I'll be as good as new. At least that's what the doctors tell me. They also say I'll never need an appendectomy, a side benefit I never thought of." As he spoke, he felt the dull ache in his lower-right abdomen.

Waller nodded distractedly. "You know why you're here?"

"A kid gets a note to see the principal, he expects a reprimand." Bryson feigned lightheartedness, but his mood was tense, somber.

"A reprimand," Waller said enigmatically. He was silent for a moment, his eyes settling on a row of leather-bound books on the shelves near the door. Then he turned back and said in a gentle, pained voice: "The Directorate doesn't exactly post an organizational chart, but I think you have some inkling of the command-and-control structure. Decisions, particularly ones concerning key personnel, do not always stop at my desk. And as important as loyalty is to you and to me—hell, to most of the people in this goddamned place—it's coldhearted pragmatism that rules the day. You know that."

Bryson had only had one serious job in his life, and this was it; still, he recognized the undertones of the pink-slip talk. He fought the urge to defend himself, for that was not Directorate procedure; it was unseemly. He recalled one of Waller's mantras: *There's no such thing as bad luck,* then thought of another maxim. "All's well that ends well," Bryson said. "And it did end well."

"We almost lost you," Waller said. "*I* almost lost you," he added ruefully, a teacher speaking to a prize student who has disappointed him.

"That's not pertinent," Bryson said quietly. "Anyway, you can't read the rules on the side of the box when you're in the field; you know that. You *taught* me that. You improvise, you follow instinct—not just established protocol."

"Losing you could have meant losing Tunisia. There's a cascade effect: when we intervene, we do so early enough to make a difference. Actions are carefully titrated, reactions calibrated, variables accounted for. And so you nearly compromised quite a few other undercover operations, in Maghreb and other places around the sandbox. You put other lives in jeopardy, Nicky—other operations and other lives. The Technician's legend was intricately connected to other legends we'd manufactured; you know that. Yet you let your cover get blown. *Years* of undercover work compromised because of you!"

"Now, wait a second—"

"Giving them 'defective munitions'—how did you think they wouldn't suspect you?"

"Damn it, they weren't *supposed* to be defective!"

"But they were. Why?"

"I don't *know!*"

"Did you inspect them?"

"Yes! No! I don't know. It never crossed my mind that the goods weren't as they were represented."

"That was a serious lapse, Nicky. You endangered years of work, years of deep-cover planning, cultivation of valuable assets. The lives of some of our most valuable assets! Goddamn it, what were you thinking?"

Bryson was silent for a moment. "I was set up," he said at last.

"Set up how?"

"I can't say for sure."

"If you were 'set up,' that means you were already under suspicion, correct?"

"I—I don't know."

" 'I don't *know*'? Not exactly words that inspire confidence, are they? They're not words I like to hear. You used to be our top field operative. What happened to you, Nick?"

"Maybe—somehow—I screwed up. Don't you think I've gone over it and over it in my mind?"

"I'm not hearing answers, Nick."

"Maybe there *aren't* any answers—not now, not yet."

"We can't afford such screwups. We can't tolerate this kind of carelessness. None of us can. We allow for margins of error. But we cannot go beyond them. The Directorate doesn't tolerate mistakes. You've known that since day one."

"You think there was something I could have done differently? Or maybe you think somebody *else* could have done it *better?*"

"You were the best we ever had, you know that. But as I told you, these decisions are reached at consortium level, not at my desk."

A chill ran through Bryson upon hearing the bureaucratese that told him Waller had already distanced himself from the consequences of the decision to let him go. Ted Waller was Bryson's mentor, boss, and friend, and, fifteen years ago, his teacher. He had supervised his apprenticeship, briefed him personally before the operations he worked on early in his career. It was an immense honor, and Bryson felt it to this day. Waller was the most brilliant man he'd ever met. He could solve partial differential equations in his head; he possessed vast stores of arcane geopolitical knowledge. At the same time his lumbering frame belied his extraordinary physical dexterity. Bryson recalled him at a shooting range, absently hitting one bull's-eye after another from seventy feet while chatting about the sad decline of British bespoke tailoring. The .22 looked puny in his large, plump, soft hand; it was so under his control that it might have been another finger.

"You used the past tense, Ted," Bryson said. "The implication being that you believe I've lost it."

"I simply meant what I said," Waller replied quietly. "I've never worked with anyone better, and I doubt I ever will."

By temperament and by training, Nick knew how to remain impassive, but now his heart was thudding. *You were the best we ever had, Nick.* That sounded like an homage, and homage, he knew, was a key element of the ritual of separation. Bryson would never forget Waller's reaction when he pulled off his first operational hat trick—foiling the assassination of a moderate reform candidate in South America. It was a taciturn *Not bad:* Waller had pressed his lips together to keep from smiling, and to Nick, it was a greater accolade than any that followed. It's when they begin to acknowledge how valuable you are, Bryson had learned, that you know they're putting you out to pasture.

"Nick, nobody else could have accomplished what you did in the Comoros. The place would have been in the hands of that madman,

Colonel Denard. In Sri Lanka, there are probably thousands of people who are alive, on both sides, because of the arms-trading routes you exposed. And what you did in Belarus? The GRU still doesn't have a clue, and they never will. Leave it to the politicians to color inside the lines, because those are the lines that we've drawn, that *you've* drawn. The historians will never know, and the truth is, it's better that way. But we know that, don't we?"

Bryson didn't reply; no reply was called for.

"And on a separate matter, Nick, noses are out of joint around here about the Banque du Nord business." He was referring to Bryson's penetration of a Tunis bank that channeled laundered funds to Abu and Hezbollah to fund the coup attempt. One night during the operation more than 1.5 billion dollars simply disappeared, vanished into cyberspace. Months of investigation had failed to account for the missing assets. It was a loose end, and the Directorate disliked loose ends.

"You're not suggesting that I had my hand in the cookie jar, are you?"

"Of course not. But you understand that there are always going to be suspicions. When there are no answers, the questions linger; you know that."

"I've had plenty of opportunities for 'personal enrichment' that would have been far more lucrative and considerably more discreet."

"You've been tested, yes, and you've passed with flying colors. But I question the method of diversion, the monies transferred through false flags to Abu's colleagues to purchase compromisable background data."

"That's called improvisation. It's what you pay me for—using my powers of discretion when and where necessary." Bryson stopped, realizing something. "But I was never debriefed about this!"

"You offered up the details yourself, Nick," said Waller.

"I sure as hell never—oh, *Christ*, it was *chemicals*, wasn't it?"

Waller hesitated a split-second, but just long enough that Bryson's question was answered. Ted Waller could lie, blithely and easily, when the need dictated, but Bryson knew his old friend and mentor found lying to him distasteful. "Where we obtain our information is compartmented, Nick. You know that."

Now he understood the need for such a protracted stay in an American-staffed clinic in Laayoune. Chemicals had to be administered without the subject's knowledge, preferably injected into the intravenous drip. "God*damn* it, Ted! What's the implication—that I couldn't be trusted to undergo a conventional debriefing, offer the goods up freely? That only a blind interrogation could tell you what you wanted to know? You had to put me under without my *knowledge?*"

"Sometimes the most reliable interrogation is that which is conducted without the subject's calculation of his own best interest."

"Meaning you guys thought that I'd lie to cover my ass?"

Waller's reply was quiet, chilling. "Once assessments are made that an individual is not one hundred percent trustworthy, contrary assumptions are made, at least provisionally. You detest it, and I detest it, but that's the brutal fact of an intelligence bureaucracy. Particularly one as reclusive—maybe *paranoid* is the more accurate word here—as we are."

Paranoid. In fact, Bryson had learned long ago that to Waller and his colleagues at the Directorate, it was an article of faith that the Central Intelligence Agency, the Defense Intelligence Agency, and even the National Security Agency were riddled with moles, hamstrung by regulation, and mired in an arms race of disinformation with their hostile counterparts abroad. Waller liked to call these, the agencies whose existence was emblazoned on Congressional appropriations bills and organization charts, the "woolly mammoths." In his earliest days with the Directorate, Bryson had innocently asked whether some measure of cooperation with the other agencies didn't make sense. Waller had laughed. "You mean, let the woolly mammoths know we exist? Why not just send a press release to *Pravda?*" But the crisis of American intelligence, in Waller's view, went far beyond the problems of penetration. Counterintelligence was the true wilderness of mirrors. "You lie to your enemy, and then you spy on them," Waller had once pointed out, "and what you learn is the lie. Only now, somehow, the lie has become true, because it's been recategorized as 'intelligence.' It's like an Easter-egg hunt. How many careers have been made—on either side—by people who have painstakingly unearthed eggs that their colleagues have just as painstakingly buried? Colorful, beautifully painted Easter eggs—but fakes nonetheless."

The two had sat talking through the night in the below-ground library underneath the K Street headquarters, a chamber furnished with seventeenth-century Kurdish rugs on the floor, old British oil paintings of the hunt, of loyal dogs grasping fowl in their pedigreed mouths.

"You see the genius of it?" Waller had gone on. "Every CIA adventure, botched or otherwise, will eventually come under public scrutiny. Not so for us, simply because we're on nobody's radar." Bryson still remembered the soft rattle of ice cubes in the heavy crystal glass as Waller took a sip of the barrel-proof bourbon he favored.

"But operating off the grid, practically like outlaws, can't exactly be the most practical way to do business," Bryson had protested. "For one thing, there's the matter of resources."

"Granted, we don't have the resources, but then we don't have the bureaucracy, either, the constraints. All in all, it's a positive advantage, given our particular purview. Our record is proof of it. When you work in ad hoc fashion with groups around the world, when you don't shy from extremely aggressive interventions, then all you need is a very small number of highly trained operatives. You take advantage of on-the-ground forces. You succeed by *directing* events, coordinating the desired outcomes. You don't need the vast overheads of the spy bureaucracies. All you really need is *brains*."

"And blood," said Bryson, who had already seen his share of it by then. "Blood."

Waller had shrugged. "That great monster Joseph Stalin once put it quite aptly: you can't make an omelet without breaking some eggs." He spoke about the American century, about the burdens of empire. About imperial Britain in the nineteenth century, when Parliament would debate for six months about whether to send an expeditionary force to rescue a general who had been under siege for two years. Waller and his colleagues at the Directorate believed in liberal democracy, fervently and unequivocally—but they also knew that to secure its future, you couldn't play, as Waller liked to say, by Queensbury rules. If your enemies operated by low cunning, you'd better summon up some good old low cunning of your own. "We're the necessary evil," Waller had told him. "But don't ever get cocky—the noun is evil. We're extra-legal. Unsupervised, unregulated. Sometimes *I* don't even feel safe knowing that we're around." There was another soft rattle of ice cubes as he drained the last drops of bourbon from the glass.

Nick Bryson had known fanatics—friendlies and hostiles both—and he found comfort in Waller's very ambivalence. Bryson had never felt he'd fully had the measure of Waller's mind: the brilliance, the cynicism, but mostly the intense, almost bashful idealism, like sunlight spilling through the edge of drawn blinds. "My friend," Waller said, "we exist to create a world in which we won't be necessary."

Now, in the ashy light of the early afternoon, Waller spread his hands on his desk, as if bracing himself for the unpleasant job he had to do. "We know you've been having a hard time since Elena left," he began.

"I don't want to talk about Elena," Bryson snapped. He could feel a vein throbbing in his forehead. For so many years she had been his wife, best friend, and lover. Six months ago, during a sterile telephone call Bryson had placed from Tripoli, she had told him she was leaving him. Arguing would do no good. She had clearly made up her mind; there was nothing to discuss. Her words had wounded him far worse than Abu's blade. A few days later, during a scheduled stateside debriefing—disguised as an arms-acquisition trip—Bryson arrived home to find her gone.

"Listen, Nick, you've probably done more good in the world than anybody in intelligence." Waller paused, and then spoke slowly, with great deliberateness. "If I let you continue, you'll start to subtract from what you've done."

"Maybe I screwed up," Bryson said dully. "Once. I'm willing to concede that much." There was no point in arguing, but he couldn't stop himself.

"And you'll screw up again," Waller replied evenly. "There are things we call 'sentinel events.' Early warnings signs. You've been extraordinary for fifteen years. Extraordinary. But *fifteen years*, Nick. For a field agent, those are like dog years. Your focus is wavering. You're burned out, and the scary thing is, you don't even know it."

Was what happened to his marriage a 'sentinel event,' too? As Waller continued to speak in his calm, reasonable, logical way, Bryson felt a rush of different emotions, and one of them was rage. "My skills—"

"I'm not talking about your skill set. As far as fieldwork is concerned, there's nobody better, even now. What I'm talking about is restraint. The ability *not* to act. That's what goes first. And you don't get it back."

"Then maybe a leave of absence is in order." There was an undertone of desperation in his voice, and Bryson hated himself for it.

"The Directorate doesn't grant sabbaticals," Waller said dryly. "You know that. Nick, you've spent a decade and a half making history. Now you can study it. I'm going to give you your life back."

"My life," Bryson repeated colorlessly. "So you *are* talking about retirement."

Waller leaned back in his chair. "Do you know the story of John Wallis, one of the great British spymasters of the seventeenth century? He was a wizard at decrypting Royalist messages for the Parliamentarians in the 1640s. He helped establish the English Black Chamber, the NSA of its time. But when he retired from the business, he used his gifts as professor of geometry at Cambridge, and helped invent modern calculus—helped put modernity on its track. Who was more important—Wallis the spy, or Wallis the scholar? Retiring from the business doesn't have to mean being put out to pasture."

It was a vintage Waller rejoinder, an arcane parable; Bryson almost laughed at the absurdity of it all. "What did you have in mind for *me* to do? Work as a rent-a-cop at a warehouse, guarding T-beams with a six-shooter and a nightstick?"

" '*Integer vitae, scelerisque purus non eget Mauris jaculis, neque arcu, nec venenatis gravida saggittis pharetra.*' The man of integrity, free of sin, doesn't need the Moorish javelin, nor the bow, nor the heavy quiver of hunting arrows. Horace, as you know. In the event, it's all arranged. Woodbridge College needs a lecturer in near-eastern history, and they've just found a stellar candidate. Your graduate studies and linguistic mastery make you a perfect match."

Bryson felt eerily detached from himself, the way he sometimes did in the field—floating above the scene, observing everything with a cool and calculating eye. He often thought he might be killed in the field: that was an eventuality he could plan for, take into account. But he had never thought he would be fired. And that it was a beloved mentor who was firing him made it worse—made it *personal*.

"All part of the retirement plan," Waller continued. "Idle hands are the devil's workshop, as they say. Something we've learned from hard experience. Give a field agent a lump sum and nothing to do, and he'll get himself into trouble, as night follows day. You need a *project*. Something real. And you're a natural teacher — one of the reasons you were so good in the field."

Bryson said nothing, trying to dispel a wrenching memory of an operation in a small Latin American province, the memory of looking at a face in the crosshairs of a sniper-scope. *The face belonged to one of his "students" — a kid named Pablo, a nineteen-year-old Amerindian he'd trained in the art of defusing, and deploying, high explosives. A tough but decent kid. His parents were peasants in a hillside village that had just been overtaken by Maoist insurrectionists: if word got out that Pablo was working with their enemies, the guerrillas would kill his parents, and most likely in cruel and inventive ways — that was their signature. The kid wavered, struggled with his loyalties, and decided he had no choice but to cross over: to save his parents, he'd tell the guerrillas all he knew about their adversaries, the names of others who had cooperated with the forces of order. He was a tough kid, a decent kid, caught in a situation where there was no right answer. Bryson peered at Pablo's face through the scope — the face of a stricken, miserable, frightened young man — and only looked away after he squeezed the trigger.*

Waller's gaze was steady. "Your name is Jonas Barrett. An independent scholar, the author of half a dozen highly respected articles in peer-reviewed journals. Four of them in the *Journal of Byzantine Studies*. Team efforts — gave our near-eastern experts something to do in their down time. We do know a thing or two about how to build a civilian legend." Waller handed him a folder. It was canary yellow, which signified that the card stock was interlaced with magnetic strips and could not be removed from the premises. It contained a legend — a fictive biography. *His* biography.

He skimmed the densely printed pages: they detailed the life of a reclusive scholar whose linguistic capacities matched his, whose expertise could be quickly mastered. The lineaments of his biography were easily assimilated — most of them, that was. Jonas Barrett was unmarried. Jonas Barrett never knew Elena. Jonas Barrett was not in love with Elena. Jonas Barrett did not ache, even now, for Elena's return. Jonas

15

Barrett was a fiction: for Nick to make him real meant accepting the loss of Elena.

"The appointment went through a few days ago. Woodbridge is expecting their new adjunct lecturer to arrive in September. And, if I may say so, they're lucky to have him."

"I have any choice in the matter?"

"Oh, we could have found you a position at any of a dozen multinational consulting firms. Or perhaps one of the behemoth petroleum or engineering companies. But this one is right for you. You've always had a mind that could handle abstractions as easily as facts. I used to worry it would be a handicap, but it turned out to be one of your greatest strengths."

"And if I don't *want* to retire? What if I don't *want* to go gently into that good night?" For some reason, he flashed back on the blur of steel, the sinewy arm plunging the blade toward him. . . .

"*Don't*, Nick," Waller said, his expression opaque.

"Jesus," Bryson said softly. There was pain in his voice, and Bryson regretted letting it show. Bryson knew how the game was played: what got to him wasn't the words he had been listening to so much as the man who was speaking them. Waller hadn't elaborated, hadn't needed to. Bryson knew he wasn't being offered a choice, and knew what lay in store for the recalcitrant. The taxicab that swerves suddenly, hits a pedestrian, and disappears. The pinprick a subject may not even feel as he makes his way through a crowded shopping mall, followed by the open-and-shut diagnosis of coronary failure. An ordinary mugging gone awry, in a city that still had one of the highest rates of street crime in the nation.

"This is the line of work that we have chosen," said Waller gently. "Our responsibility supersedes all bonds of kinship and affection. I wish it were otherwise. You don't know how much. In my time, I've had to . . . sanction three of my men. Good men gone bad. No, not even bad, just unprofessional. I live with that every day, Nick. But I'd do it again in a heartbeat. *Three men.* I'm begging you—don't make it four." Was it a threat? A plea? Both? Waller let his breath out slowly. "I'm offering you life, Nick. A very good life."

But what lay ahead for Bryson wasn't life, not just yet. It was a sort of fugue state, a shadowy half-death. For fifteen years, he had devoted his whole being—every brain cell, every muscle fiber—to a peculiarly hazardous and strenuous endeavor. Now his services would no longer be required. And Bryson felt nothing, just a profound emptiness. He made his way home, to the handsome colonial-style house in Falls Church that barely seemed familiar any longer. He cast his eyes over the house as if it were a stranger's, taking in the tasteful Aubussons that Elena had picked out, the hopeful pastel-painted room on the second floor for the child they never had. The place was both empty and full of ghosts. Then he poured himself a water tumbler full of vodka. It was the last time he would be fully sober in weeks.

The house was full of Elena, of her scent, her taste, her aura. He could not forget her.

They were sitting on the dock in front of their lakeside cabin in Maryland, watching the sailboat. . . . She poured him a glass of cold white wine, and as she handed it to him she kissed him. "I miss you," she said.

"But I'm right here, my darling."

"Now you are. Tomorrow you'll be gone. To Prague, to Sierra Leone, to Jakarta, to Hong Kong . . . who knows where? And who knows for how long?"

He took her hand, feeling her loneliness, unable to banish it. "But I always come back. And you know the expression, Absence makes the heart grow fonder."

"Mai rărut, mai drăgut," she said softly, musingly. "But you know, in my country, they say something else. Celor ce duc mai mult dorul, le pare mai dulce odorul. *Absence sharpens love, but presence strengthens it."*

"I like that."

She raised an index finger, wagged it in his face. "They also say something else. Prin depărtare dragostea se uită. *How do you say—long absent, soon forgotten?"*

"Out of sight, out of mind."

"How long before you forget me?"

"But you're always with me, my love." He tapped his chest. "In here."

He had no doubt the Directorate had him under electronic surveillance; he hardly cared. If they assessed him as a security risk, they would certainly sanction him. Perhaps with enough vodka, he thought grimly, he might even save them the trouble. Days passed, and he saw and heard from no one. Maybe Waller interceded at consortium level to cut him slack, because he knew it wasn't just the severance that caused him to fall apart. It was Elena's departure. Elena, the anchor of his existence. Acquaintances would sometimes say how *calm* Nick always seemed, but Nick seldom felt calm: calm was what Elena had provided. What was Waller's phrase for her? A *passionate serenity*.

Nick hadn't known he was capable of loving somebody as much as he loved her. In the vortex of lies where his career played out, she was his one true thing. At the same time, she too was a spook: she would have had to have been for them to build a life together. In fact, she was cleared almost all the way to the top, because she worked in the Directorate's cryptography division, and you never knew what sort of thing they'd come across. The typical hostile intercept often contained morsels of intelligence about the United States; decrypting them meant the possibility of being exposed to your own government's innermost secrets — information most of the agency's division heads weren't even cleared for. Analysts like her lived desk-bound lives, the computer keyboard their only weapon, and yet their intellects roamed the world as freely as any field agent.

God, how he loved her!

In a sense, Ted Waller had introduced them, though in fact they had met in the least promising of circumstances, a result of an assignment Waller had given him.

It was a routine package transport, which Directorate insiders sometimes called the "coyote run," referring to the smuggling of human beings. The Balkans were on fire in the late 1980s, and a brilliant Romanian mathematician was to be exfiltrated from Bucharest with his wife and daughter. Andrei Petrescu was a true Romanian patriot, an academician at the University of Bucharest specializing in the arcane mathematics of cryptography. He had been pressed into service by Romania's notorious secret service, the Securitate, to devise the codes used in the innermost circles of the Ceauşescu government. He wrote the cryptographic algorithms, but he refused their offer of employment: he wanted to remain in the academy, a teacher, and he was revolted by the Securitate's oppression of the Romanian people. As a result, Andrei and his family were kept under virtual house arrest, forbidden from traveling, their every movement watched. His daughter, Elena, said to be no less brilliant than her father, was a graduate student in mathematics at the university, hoping to follow in her father's footsteps.

As Romania reached a boiling point in December of 1989, and popular protests began to break out against the tyrant Nicolae Ceauşescu, the Securitate, the tyrant's Praetorian guard, retaliated with mass arrests and murders. In Timisoara, a huge crowd gathered on Bulevardul 30 Decembrie, and demonstrators broke into Communist Party headquarters and began throwing portraits of the tyrant out of the windows. The army and the Securitate fired on the unruly crowd throughout the day and night; the dead were piled up and buried in mass graves.

Disgusted, Andrei Petrescu decided to do his small part to fight the tyranny. He possessed the keys to Ceauşescu's most secret communications, and he would give them away to the tyrant's enemies. No longer could Ceauşescu communicate in secret with his henchmen; his decisions, his orders, would be known the moment he uttered them.

Andrei Petrescu wrestled with the decision. Would this imperil the lives of his beloved Simona, his adored Elena? Once they had discovered what he had done—and they would know, for no one else outside the government knew the source codes—Andrei and his family would be rounded up, arrested, and executed.

No, he would have to get out of Romania. But to do that he needed to enlist a powerful outsider, preferably an intelligence agency such as the CIA or the KGB, that had the resources to get the family out.

Terrified, he made cautious, veiled inquiries. He knew people; his colleagues knew people. He made his offer, and his demand. But both the British and the Americans refused to get involved. They had adopted a hands-off policy toward Romania. His offer was rebuffed.

And then very early one morning he was contacted by an American, a representative of another intelligence agency, not the CIA. They were interested; they would help. They had the courage the others lacked.

The operational details had been designed by the Directorate's logistical architects, refined by Bryson upon consultation with Ted Waller. Bryson was to smuggle out of Romania the mathematician and his family, along with five others, two men and three women, all of them intelligence assets. Getting into Romania was the easy part. From Nyírábrány, in the east of Hungary, Bryson crossed the border by rail into Romania at Valea Lui Mihai, carrying an authentic Hungarian passport of a long-haul freight driver; with his drab overalls and his callused hands, he was given barely a once-over. A few kilometers outside Valea Lui Mihai he found the truck that had been left for him by a Directorate contact. It was an old Romanian panel truck that belched diesel. It had been ingeniously modified in-country by Directorate assets: when the back of the truck was opened, the cargo bay seemed to be stacked with crates of Romanian wine and *tzuica*, plum brandy. But the crates were only one row deep; they concealed a large compartment, taking up most of the cargo area, in which all but one of the Romanians could be hidden.

The group had been instructed to meet him in the Baneasa forest, five kilometers north of Bucharest. Bryson found them at the designated rendezvous point, a picnic spread out before them, looking like an extended family on an outing. But Bryson could see the terror in their faces.

The leader of the eight was obviously the mathematician, Andrei Petrescu, a diminutive man in his sixties, accompanied by a meek, moon-faced woman, apparently his wife. But it was their daughter who arrested Bryson's attention, for he had never met a woman so beautiful. Twenty-year-old Elena Petrescu was raven-haired, petite, and lithe, with dark eyes that glittered and flashed. She wore a black skirt and dove-gray sweater, a colorful babushka tied around her head. She was silent and looked at him with profound suspicion.

Bryson greeted them in Romanian. "*Buna ziua*," he said. "*Unde este cea mai apropiata statie Peco?*" Where is the nearest gas station?

"*Sinteti pe un drum gresit,*" responded the mathematician. You are on the wrong road.

They followed him to the panel truck, which he'd parked in the shelter of a copse of trees. The beautiful young woman joined him in the cab, as was the preordained arrangement. The others took their seats in the hidden compartment, where Bryson had left sandwiches and bottled water to get them through the long journey to the Hungarian border.

Elena said nothing for the first several hours. Bryson attempted to make conversation, but she remained taciturn, though whether she was shy or just nervous he could not tell. They passed through the county of Bihor and neared the frontier crossing point at Bors, from where they would cross over to Biharkeresztes in Hungary. They had driven through the night and were making good time; everything seemed to be going smoothly—too smoothly, Bryson thought, for the Balkans, where a thousand little things could go wrong.

So it did not surprise him when he saw the flashing lights of a police car, a blue-uniformed policeman inspecting oncoming traffic, about eight kilometers from the border. Nor did it surprise him when the policeman waved them over to the side of the road.

"What the hell is this?" he said to Elena Petrescu, forcing a blasé tone as the jackbooted policeman approached.

"Just a routine traffic stop," she replied.

"I hope you're right," Bryson said, rolling down the window. His Romanian was fluent but the accent was not native; the Hungarian passport would explain that. He prepared himself to quarrel with the cop, as would any long-haul truck driver annoyed by some petty inconvenience.

The policeman asked him for his papers and the truck's registration. He inspected them; everything was in order.

Was something wrong? Bryson asked in Romanian.

Officiously, the policeman waved a hand toward the truck's headlights. One of them was burned out. But he would not let them go so easily. He wanted to know what was in the truck.

"Exports," replied Bryson.

"Open," said the policeman.

Sighing with annoyance, Bryson got out of the cab and went to unlock the tailgate. A semiautomatic pistol was holstered at his back, concealed inside his gray muslin work jacket; he would use it only if he had to, for killing the policeman was enormously risky. Not only was there the chance of being seen by a passing motorist, but if the officer had radioed in the truck's license plate numbers while he was pulling them over, his dispatcher would be waiting for a further communication. If none came, others would be called in, the truck's plates flagged at border control. Bryson did not want to have to kill the man, but he realized he might not have any choice.

As he pulled open the rear door, he could see the cop eyeing the crates of wine and *tzuica* greedily. Bryson found that reassuring: perhaps a bribe of a case or two of spirits would be enough to satisfy the man and send him on his way. But the policeman began pawing through the crates as if inventorying them, and he quickly reached the false wall, a mere two feet or so in. Eyes narrowed in suspicion, the Romanian tapped at the wall, heard the hollowness.

"Hey, what the fuck is this?" he exclaimed.

Bryson slipped his right hand around to the holstered pistol, but just then he saw Elena Petrescu saunter around the back of the truck, one hand placed saucily on her left hip. She was chewing gum, and her face was heavily made up with too much lipstick, mascara, and rouge: she must have applied it while she sat waiting in the cab. She looked like a vamp, a prostitute. Working her jaw up and down, she leaned in very close to the policeman and said, *"Ce curu' meu vrei?"* What the fuck do you want?

"Fututi gura!" said the policeman. Fuck you! He reached behind the crates with both hands, running them along the false back, obviously feeling for a pull or knob or lever to open it. Bryson's stomach plummeted as the man gripped the indentation that opened the secret compartment. There was no explaining the seven concealed passengers; the policeman would have to be killed. And what the hell was Elena doing, antagonizing him further?

"Let me ask you something, comrade," she said in a quiet, insinuating voice. "How much is your life worth to you?"

The cop whirled around, glaring at her. "What the fuck are you talking about, whore?"

"I ask you, how much is your life worth? Because you're not just about to end a good career. You're about to buy yourself a one-way ticket to the psychiatric prison. Maybe to some pauper's grave."

Bryson was aghast: she was destroying everything, she had to be stopped!

The policeman opened the canvas pouch that hung around his neck and took out a bulky, old, military-style field telephone, which he began to dial.

"If you're making a call, I suggest you make it directly to the Securitate headquarters, and ask for Dragan himself." Bryson stared incredulously: Maj. Gen. Radu Dragan was the second-in-command at the secret police, notoriously corrupt and said to be sexually "dissolute."

The policeman stopped dialing, his eyes searching Elena's face. "You threaten me, bitch?"

She snapped her gum. "Hey, I don't care what you do. If you want to interfere with Securitate business of the highest and most confidential nature, be my guest. I just do my job. Dragan likes his Magyar virgins, and when he's done with them, I always drop my girls off across the border like I'm supposed to. You want to get in my way, fine. You wanna be the hero who makes Dragan's little weakness public, it's up to you. But I sure as hell wouldn't want to be you, or anyone who knows you." She rolled her eyes. "Come on, dial Dragan's office." She recited a number with a Bucharest area code and exchange.

Slowly, dazed, the policeman punched out the numbers, then put the handset to his ear. His eyes widened and he quickly disconnected the call: he had obviously connected with the Securitate.

He turned around quickly, striding away from the truck, muttering profuse apologies as he got into his cruiser and drove off.

Later, as the border guards waved them through, Bryson said to Elena, "Was that really the Securitate's phone number?"

"Of course," she said indignantly.

"How did you—?"

"I'm good with numbers," she said. "Didn't they tell you that?"

At the wedding, Ted Waller was Nick's best man. Elena's parents had been relocated, under new identities, to Rovinj, on the Istrian coast of the Adriatic, under Directorate protection; for reasons of security, she was not allowed to visit them, a proscription she accepted, with a heavy heart, as a terrible necessity.

23

She had been offered work as a cryptographer in Directorate headquarters doing code-breaking and signals-intercept analysis. She was immensely gifted, perhaps the finest cryptographer they'd ever had, and she loved the work. "I have you, and I have my work—and if only I had my parents near me, my life would be perfect!" she once said. When Nick first told Waller that things were getting serious between the two, he felt almost as if he were asking permission to get married. A father's permission? An *employer's* permission? He wasn't sure. A life in the Directorate meant that there were no sharp boundaries between matters private and professional. But he had met Elena on Directorate business, and it seemed appropriate to let Waller know. Waller had seemed genuinely overjoyed. "You've finally met your match," he said, grinning broadly, and he instantly produced an iced bottle of vintage Dom Perignon, like a magician extracting a nickel from a child's ear.

Bryson thought back to their honeymoon, spent in a tiny, verdant, nearly uninhabited island in the Caribbean. The beach was pink sand; a ways inland were almost magical groves of tamarisk beside a little brook. They went exploring there for the sole purpose of getting lost, or pretending to, and then losing themselves, losing themselves in each other. Time out of time, she'd called it. When he thought of Elena, he recalled their setting out to get lost—it was a minor ritual of theirs—and reminding themselves that so long as they had each other, they were never lost at all.

But now he had lost her for real, and felt lost himself, rootless, anchorless. The big empty house was silent, but he could hear her bruised voice over the sterile line as she said, quietly, that she was leaving him. It was a thunderbolt, yet it shouldn't have been. No, it wasn't the months of separation, she insisted; it was far deeper than that, far more fundamental. *I don't know you anymore,* she had told him. *I don't know you, and I don't trust you.*

He loved her, goddamn it, he *loved* her: wasn't that enough? His pleas were clamorous, impassioned. But the damage had been done. Falseness, hardness, coldness—they were traits that kept a field operative alive, but they were also traits that he'd started to bring home, and no marriage could survive that. He had kept things from her—one incident in particular—and for that he felt enormously guilty.

And so she was going to leave, to rebuild her life without him. Request transfer out of headquarters. Her voice on the sterile line sounded both as close as the next room and eerily distant. She said nothing heatedly, and yet her very lack of expression was what was so hard to bear. Seemingly, there was nothing to discuss or debate: it was the tone of someone pointing out a self-evident fact—that two plus two was four, that the sun rose in the east.

He remembered the stricken sensation that came over him. "Elena," he said, "do you know what you *mean* to me?"

Her response—leaden, beyond hurt—still echoed in his mind: "I don't even think you know who I am."

Once he returned from Tunisia and found her gone from their house, all her things gone, he'd tried to track her down, implored Ted Waller to help, with whatever resources were at his disposal. There were a thousand things he wanted to say to her. But it was as if she had vanished from the face of the earth. She did not intend to be found, and she would not be found, and Waller would not violate that. Waller was right about her; he'd met his match.

Alcohol, in sufficient quantities, is Novocain for the mind. The trouble is that when it wears off, the throbbing pain returns, and the only remedy is more alcohol. The days and weeks that followed his return from Tunisia became mere shards, fractured images. Images in sepia. He would take out the garbage and notice the sound, the bright clinking of glass liter bottles. The phone would ring; he never picked it up. Once the doorbell rang: Chris Edgecomb was at his door, in violation of every Directorate stricture. "I got worried, man," he'd said, and he looked it, too.

Bryson didn't want to think about what he himself might look like to a visitor—haunted, unkempt, unshaven. "They send you?"

"Are you kidding? They'd have my ass if they knew I was here."

Bryson supposed this was what was called an intervention. He couldn't remember the words he spoke to Edgecomb, only that he'd pronounced them with emphatic finality. The kid wouldn't come again.

Mostly, Bryson remembered waking up after a binge, twitching and blinking, his nerves feeling peeled raw; he had the vanilla stench of bourbon, the juniper acridity of gin. Staring at his morning face in the mirror, all inflamed capillaries and dark hollows. Trying to force down some scrambled eggs, and gagging at the smell.

A few isolated sounds, a few scattered images. Not a lost weekend; a lost three months.

His neighbors in Falls Church evinced little interest, perhaps out of politeness or indifference. He was, what, a corporate accounting exec for some industrial supplies firm, wasn't he? Guy must have got laid off. He'd either pull out of it, or he wouldn't. The professional-managerial casualties of the Beltway economy seldom invite compassion; besides, the neighbors knew better than to make inquiries. In suburbia you kept your distance.

Then one day in August, something shifted within him. He saw the purple asters start to bloom, flowers that Elena had planted the year before, pushing through with defiance, as if nurtured by neglect. He would do likewise. The trash bags no longer clinked as he toted them to the curb. He began to eat real food, three times a day, even. He still moved shakily at first, but a couple of weeks later he slicked his hair down, shaved carefully, got into a business suit, and made his way to 1324 K Street.

Waller tried to mask his relief with professional detachment, but Bryson could see it in his glittering eyes. "Who was it who said there are no second acts in American lives?" Waller said quietly.

Bryson returned the gaze steadily, calmly. Waiting, at peace with himself at last.

Waller smiled, just barely—one would have had to know him well to recognize it as a smile—and handed him the canary file folder. "Let's call this a third act."

CHAPTER
TWO

Five years later

Woodbridge College, in western Pennsylvania, was a small school, but it exuded a sense of quiet prosperity, of exclusivity beyond the norm. One saw it in the manicured *greenness* of the place: the emerald lawns and perfect flower borders of an institution that could pay lavishly for aesthetic incidentals. The architecture was the brick-and-ivy, collegiate-Gothic style typical of so much university construction from the twenties. From a distance, it might have passed for one of the ancient colleges of Cambridge or Oxford—if the college was taken out of those shabby, light-industrial towns and placed in the middle of Arcadia. It was a sheltered, secure, conservative establishment, a place to which America's richest and most powerful families had no anxieties about sending their impressionable scions. The campus convenience stores and eateries did a brisk business in latté and focaccia. Even during the late sixties, the college remained, as its then-president had once famously joked, a "hotbed of rest."

"Jonas Barrett," to his own surprise, turned out to be a gifted lecturer, his courses far more popular than the subjects he taught would normally have justified. Some of the students were bright, and almost all of them more studious and better behaved than he'd ever been in his own college days. One of his faculty colleagues, a wry, Brooklyn-bred physicist who used to teach at the City College of New York, had observed to him, shortly after he'd settled in, that the place made you feel like an eighteenth-century live-in tutor, responsible for educating the children of an English lord. You lived amid splendor, but it wasn't exactly yours.

Still, Waller had told the truth: this was a good life.

Now Jonas Barrett looked out over a packed auditorium, at a hundred expectant faces. He'd been amused when the *Campus Confidential* had called him, after only his first year of teaching at Woodbridge, an "icily charismatic lecturer, more Professor Kingsfield than Mr. Chips," and re-marked on his "stone-faced, slyly ironic visage." Whatever the reasons, his course on Byzantium was among the most popular classes in the history department.

He glanced at his watch: it was time to wrap up the lecture and gesture toward the next. "The Roman Empire had been the most astonishing political achievement in human history, and the question that has haunted so many thinkers is, of course, why it fell," he intoned in a high professorial manner laced with a tincture of irony. "You all know the sad tale. The light of civilization flickered and dimmed. The barbarians at the gate. The destruction of humanity's best hope, right?" There was murmured assent. "*Horseshit!*" he exclaimed suddenly, and a surprised titter was followed by a sudden hush. "Pardon my Macedonian." He looked around the lecture hall, his arched-brow expression challenging. "The Romans, so called, lost their claim to the moral high ground way before they lost their claim to empire. It was the Romans who avenged an early set-to with the Goths by taking Goth children they'd seized as hostages, marching them into the public squares of dozens of towns, then slaughtering them one by one. Slowly and painfully. As far as sheer cal-culated bloodthirstiness, nothing the Goths ever did could compare. The western Roman Empire was an arena of slavery and bloodsport. By con-trast, the *eastern* Roman Empire was far more benign, and it survived the so-called fall of the Roman Empire. 'Byzantium' is only what the West-erners called it—the Byzantines always knew themselves as the true Roman Empire, and they safeguarded the scholarship and the humane values we cherish today. The west succumbed not to enemies from without, but rot from within—this much is true. And so civilization didn't flicker and dim. It just moved east." A pause. "You can come by and pick up your papers now. And enjoy your weekend, as much as you deem wise. Just remember Petronius: Moderation in all things. Including moderation."

"Professor Barrett?" The young woman was blond and fetching, one of those students who listens gravely and always sits in the front rows. He had stowed away his lecture notes and was fastening the straps of his battered leather satchel. He barely listened as she talked, complaining about a grade received, the tone urgent, the words banal, utterly familiar: *I worked so hard . . . I feel I did my very best . . . I really, really tried. . . .* She followed as he walked toward the door, then to the parking lot outside the classroom building, until he reached his car. "Why don't we discuss this during office hours tomorrow?" he suggested gently.

"But Professor . . ."

Something's wrong.

"I guess I feel it's the grade that was wrong, Professor."

He hadn't realized he'd spoken aloud. But his antennae were buzzing. Why? Out of some sudden, baseless paranoia? Was he going to end up like one of those Vietnam posttraumatics who jump whenever they hear a car backfire?

A *sound*, something definitely out of place. He turned toward the student, but not to look at her. Instead, to look *past* her, beyond her, to whatever had flickered in his peripheral vision. Yes, there *was* something amiss in the general vicinity. Strolling too casually in his direction, as if enjoying the spring air, the verdant setting, was a broad-shouldered man in a charcoal flannel suit, white shirt, and perfectly knotted rep tie. That wasn't academic garb at Woodbridge, not even for administrators, and the weather was too warm for flannel. This was indeed an outsider, but one feigning—*attempting* to feign—that he belonged.

Bryson's field instincts were signaling wildly. His scalp tightened and his eyes began scanning from side to side, like a photographer testing different focal points in rapid succession: the old habits were returning, unbidden and somehow atavistic, rudely out of place.

But *why?* Surely there was no reason to be alarmed over a campus visitor—a parent, an official from Washington's educational bureaucracy, maybe even some high-level salesman. Bryson did a quick assessment. The man's jacket was unbuttoned, and he caught a glimpse of maroon braces holding the man's trousers up. Yet the man was also wearing a belt and the trousers were cut long, breaking deeply over the man's black, rubber-soled shoes. A surge of adrenaline: he'd worn similar attire himself, in a previous life. Sometimes you needed to wear a belt as well as suspenders because you were carrying a heavy object in one or both of your front pockets—a large-caliber revolver, say. And you needed the cuffs a little too long to ensure that your ankle holster was well concealed. *Dress for success,* Ted Waller used to advise, explaining how a man in evening dress could conceal a veritable arsenal if the fabric was tailored just right.

I'm out of the game! Leave me in peace!

But there was no peace; there never would be any peace. Once you were in you could never get out, even if the paychecks stopped and the health benefits expired.

Hostile parties around the world thirsted for revenge. No matter what precautions you took, no matter how elaborate the cover, how intricate the extraction. *If they really wanted to find me, they could.* To think otherwise was delusional. This was the unwritten certainty among the Directorate's operatives.

But who's to say they're not from the Directorate itself, doing a full sterilization, in that cynical phrase—removing the splinters, mopping up? Bryson had never met anyone who had retired from the Directorate, though surely such retirees did exist. But if someone at the consortium level in the Directorate came to doubt his loyalties, he, too, would be the victim of a full sterilization. It was a virtual certainty.

I'm out, I've put it behind!

Yet who would believe him?

Nick Bryson—for he *was* Nick Bryson now, Jonas Barrett gone by the wayside, discarded like a snake's shed skin—looked closely at the man in the suit. The man's salt-and-pepper hair was brush cut, the face broad and ruddy. Bryson tensed as the interloper approached, smiling as he did so and showing small white teeth. "Mr. Barrett?" the man called from halfway across the emerald lawn.

The man's face was a mask of reassurance, and that was the final giveaway, the mark of a professional. A civilian hailing a stranger always exhibited at least some tentativeness.

Directorate?

Directorate personnel were better than this, smoother and less obvious.

"Laura," he said quietly to the student, "I need you to leave me and go back into Severeid Hall. Wait at my office upstairs."

"But—"

"*Now!*" he snapped.

Speechless and scarlet, Laura turned and hurried back toward the building. A change had come over Professor Jonas Barrett—as she would explain it to her roommate that evening, he suddenly seemed different, *scary*—and she quickly decided she'd better do what he told her.

Soft footsteps were audible from the opposite direction. Bryson spun. Another man: redheaded, freckled, younger, wearing a navy blazer, tan chinos, and bucks. More plausible as a campus costume, except for the buttons on the blazer, which were too bright and brassy. Nor did the blazer lie quite flat over his chest: a bulge was visible where you'd expect to find the shoulder holster.

If not Directorate, then who? Foreign hostiles? Others from the more overt U.S. agencies?

Now Bryson identified the noise that had alerted him in the first place: the sound of a car that was idling, quietly and continuously. It was a Lincoln Continental with dark tinted windows, and it wasn't in a parking space but parked in the lane where he'd left his own car, blocking it.

"Mr. Barrett?" The larger, older man made eye contact with him, his loping stride swiftly decreasing the distance between them. "We really need you to come with us." The accent was bland, Midwestern. He stopped barely two feet away and gestured toward the Lincoln.

"Oh, is that right?" Bryson said, his delivery cold. "Do I know you?"

The stranger's reply was nonverbal: hands on hips, chest out to display the contours of his holstered handgun beneath his suit jacket. The subtle gesture of one professional to another, one armed, the other not. Then abruptly the man doubled over in agony, his hands grabbing at his stomach. With lightning speed, Bryson had driven the steel nib of his slim fountain pen into the man's muscled belly, and the professional responded with an unprofessional, if wholly natural, move indeed. *Reach for your weapon, never the wound:* one of Waller's many axioms, and though it meant countermanding a natural instinct, it had saved Nick's life more than a few times. This man was not top-rank.

As the stranger's hands flailed at the ruined flesh, Bryson plunged his hands into the man's jacket and retrieved the small but powerful blue-steel Beretta.

Beretta — not Directorate issue; then whose?

He slammed the butt against the man's temple — heard the sickening crunch of bone against metal, heard the senior agent slump to the ground — and with the weapon pointed, spun to face the redheaded man in the blue blazer.

"My safety's *off,*" Nick shouted to him, urgent and demanding. "Yours?"

The play of confusion and panic on the young man's face gave away his inexperience. He had to have calculated that Nick would easily be able to squeeze off the first shot the instant he heard the click of the safety release. *Bad odds.* But the inexperienced could be the most dangerous, precisely because they didn't react in a rational and logical manner.

Amateur hour. His gun aimed steadily at the redheaded field man, Bryson backed up slowly in the direction of the idling vehicle. The doors would be unlocked for immediate access, of course. In one fluid motion, all the while keeping the Beretta leveled at the redheaded novice, he yanked open the car door and slid into the driver's seat. With a glance he knew the vehicle's windows and windscreen were bulletproof, as they had to be. Bryson had only to throw the gearshift out of park, and the car lurched forward. He heard a bullet strike the back of the car — the license plate, he judged from the clatter. And then another struck the rearview window, pitting it but doing no further damage. They were firing at the car's tires, hoping to stop his flight.

In a matter of seconds he was roaring through the tall, ornamental wrought-iron gates of the campus. Barreling down the tree-lined main drive, one assailant down and the other firing wildly yet ineffectually, his mind raced. He thought: *Time's up.* And: *Now what?*

If they'd really intended to kill me, I'd be dead.

Bryson sped down the Interstate, his eyes scanning the lanes ahead and behind for pursuers. *They caught me unarmed and unaware, deliberately so.* Which meant that they were up to something else. But what? And how did they find him in the first place? Could someone have gained access to a 5-1 classified Directorate database? There were too many variables, too many unknowns. But Bryson felt no fear now, only the icy calm of the seasoned field operative he had once been. He wouldn't drive to any of the airports, where they'd certainly be expecting him; instead, he'd drive directly back to his house on campus, the least expected place to go. If this was inviting another confrontation, so be it. Confrontation meant exposure of limited duration: flight could go on indefinitely. Bryson no longer had the patience for protracted flight: Waller had been right about that, at least.

Turning down the campus road to his residence on Villier Lane, he heard, then saw, a helicopter raking the sky, making its way toward the small campus helipad atop the science building tower donated by a software billionaire, the tallest building on campus by far. It was normally used only by major donors, but this chopper had federal markings. The helicopter was a follow-on; it had to be. Bryson pulled up in front of his house, a ramshackle Queen Anne–style dwelling with a mansard roof and plaster facade. The place was empty, and he knew from the alarm system, which he had installed himself, that no one had entered the house since he'd left it that morning.

Entering, he verified that the system hadn't been tampered with. The strong sun streamed through a parlor window onto the wide pine floorboards, giving rise to a resinous, evergreen smell. That was the chief reason why he'd bought the house: the scent reminded him of a happy year he'd spent in a half-timbered house outside Wiesbaden when he was seven and his father was stationed at the military base there. Bryson was no typical army brat—his father was, after all, a general, and the family was usually provided with comfortable living quarters and a household staff. Still, his childhood was all about learning how to pick up stakes and put them down again in some other part of the world. Transitions were helped by his natural facility with languages, which others always marveled at. Making new friends didn't come quite as easily, but in time he developed a skill at that, too. He'd seen too many army brats who styled themselves as surly outsiders to want to join their ranks.

He was home now. He would wait. And this time the meeting would be on his territory, on his terms.

It didn't take long.

Only a few minutes elapsed before a black government Cadillac sedan, complete with a small U.S. flag flying from the antenna, pulled into his driveway. Bryson, watching from the house, realized that the very overtness of the display was meant to provide reassurance. A uniformed government driver got out and opened the vehicle's rear door, and a short, wiry man stepped out. Bryson had seen him before—a fleeting face from C-SPAN. Some sort of intelligence official. Bryson stepped out onto his porch.

"Mr. Bryson," the man said in a husky voice, the accent New Jersey. He was in his mid-fifties, Bryson estimated, with a thatch of white hair, the face narrow and creased; he wore an unstylish brown suit. "You know who I am?"

"Somebody with a lot of explaining to do."

The government man nodded, his hands raised in a gesture of contrition. "We fucked up, Mr. Bryson, or Jonas Barrett if you prefer. I take full responsibility. Reason I've come up here is to apologize to you personally. And also to explain."

An image from a TV screen came to Bryson, white letters beneath a talking head. "You're Harry Dunne. Deputy chairman of the CIA." Bryson remembered watching him testify to a Congressional subcommittee once or twice.

"I need to talk to you," the man said.

"I've got nothing to say to you. I wish I could direct you toward your Mr. Breyer or whatever his name is, but I'm drawing a blank."

"I'm not asking you to *say* anything. I'm just asking you to *listen*."

"Those were your goons, I take it."

"Yes, they were," Dunne admitted. "They overstepped the bounds. They also underestimated you—they figured, wrongly, that after five years out of the field you'd gone soft. You've also taught them a couple of key tactical lessons that will no doubt come in handy for them down the road. Especially Eldridge, once he gets stitched up." There was a dry rattle in his throat when he laughed. "So now I'm asking you nice as I can. All aboveboard." Dunne walked slowly over to the porch where Bryson was leaning against a wooden column, his arms folded behind his back. Taped to his upper back was the Beretta, which he could mobilize in an instant if he had to. On television, on the Sunday-morning talking-head shows, Dunne possessed a somewhat commanding presence; in person, he seemed almost shrunken, a little too small for his clothes.

"I have no lessons to teach," Bryson protested. "All I did was defend myself against a couple of men who were in the wrong place and didn't seem to wish me well."

"The Directorate trained you well, I'll say that much."

"I wish I knew what you were talking about."

"You know full well. Your reticence is to be expected."

"I think you've got the wrong man," Bryson said quietly. "A case of mistaken identity. I don't know what you're referring to."

The CIA man exhaled noisily, followed by a rattling cough. "Unfortunately, not all of your former colleagues are as discreet, or maybe the correct word is *principled*, as you. Oaths of fealty and secrecy tend to loosen their holds when money changes hands, and I do mean serious money. None of your former colleagues came cheap."

"Now you've really lost me."

"Nicholas Loring Bryson, born Athens, Greece, the only son of General and Mrs. George Wynter Bryson," the CIA man recited, almost in a monotone. "Graduated from St. Alban's School in Washington, D.C., Stanford, and Georgetown's School of Foreign Service. Recruited while at Stanford into an all-but-invisible intelligence agency known to the very few who know about it as the Directorate. Trained in fieldwork, fifteen highly successful and secretly decorated years of service, with operations ranging from—"

"Nice bio," Bryson interrupted. "Wish it were mine. We academics sometimes like to imagine what it might be like to live an active life outside these cloistered, ivied walls." He spoke with some bravado. His legend was designed to evade suspicion, not withstand it.

"Neither one of us has any time to waste," Dunne said. "In any case, I do hope you realize that we intended no harm."

"I realize no such thing. You CIA boys, from everything I've read, have a long menu of ways to inflict harm. A bullet in the brain, for one. Twelve hours on a scopolamine drip, for another. Shall we talk about poor Nosenko, who made the mistake of defecting to our side? He got the red-carpet treatment from your gentlemen, didn't he? Twenty-eight months in a padded crypt. Whatever it took to break him, you were all too willing to do."

"You're talking ancient history, Bryson. But I understand and accept your suspicion. What can I do to allay it?"

"What's more suspicious than the need to allay suspicion?"

"If I really wanted to take you down," Dunne said, "we wouldn't be having this conversation, and you know that."

"It might not be quite as easy as you think," Bryson said, his tone blasé. He smiled coldly to let the CIA man pick up on the implied threat. He had given up the pretense; there seemed little point.

"We know what you can do with your hands and your feet. No demonstrations are required. All I'm asking you for is your ears."

"So you say." *How much did the Agency really know about him, about his Directorate career? How could the security firewall have been breached?*

"Listen, Bryson, kidnappers don't supplicate. I guess you know I'm not a man who makes house calls every day. I've got something to tell you, and it won't be easy to hear. You know our Blue Ridge facility?"

Bryson shrugged.

"I want to take you there. I need you to listen to what I've got to tell you, watch what I've got to show you. Then, if you want, you can go home, and we'll never bother you again." He gestured toward the car. "Come with me."

"What you're proposing is sheer madness. You do realize this, don't you? A couple of third-rate thugs show up outside my class and try to strong-arm me into a car. Then a man I've seen only on TV news shows— a high official in an intelligence agency with little credibility to speak of, frankly — shows up on my front lawn trying to entice me with a titillating combination of threats and lures. How do you expect me to respond?"

Dunne's gaze did not waver. "Frankly, I expect you'll come anyway."

"What makes you so sure?"

Dunne was silent for a moment. "It's the only way you'll ever satisfy your curiosity," he said at last. "It's the only way you'll ever know the truth."

Bryson snorted. "The truth about *what?*"

"For starters," the CIA man said very quietly, "the truth about yourself."

CHAPTER
THREE

In the Blue Ridge mountains of western Virginia, near the borders with Tennessee and North Carolina, the CIA maintains a secluded area of hardwood forest interspersed with northern spruce, hemlock, and white pine, about two hundred acres in all. Part of the Little Wilson Creek wilderness, within the Jefferson National Forest, it is a rugged territory of a wide range of elevations, dotted with lakes, streams, creeks, and waterfalls, far removed from the main hiking trails. The nearest towns, Troutdale and Volney, are none too close. This wilderness preserve, enclosed by electric security fence and topped with concertina wire, is known within the Agency by the generic, colorless, and quite forgettable name of the Range.

There, certain exotic forms of instrumentation, such as miniaturized explosives, are tested amid the rocky outcroppings. Various transmitters and tracking devices are put through their paces there, too, their frequencies calibrated away from the surveillance range of hostile parties.

It is entirely possible to spend time on the Range and never notice the low-slung concrete-and-glass building that serves as combination administrative headquarters, training and conference facility, and barracks.

This building is situated a hundred yards or so from a helipad clearing that, owing to peculiarities of elevation and vegetation, is nearly impossible to find.

Harry Dunne had said little during the trip there. In fact, the only opportunity for chat had been the brief limousine ride to the campus helipad; during the helicopter trip to Virginia, both men, accompanied by Dunne's silent aide-de-camp, wore protective noise-insulating headphones. Debarking from the dark green government helicopter, the three men were met by an anonymous-looking assistant.

Bryson and Dunne, the assistants in tow, passed through the facility's unremarkable-looking main lobby and descended a set of stairs into a subterranean, spartan, low-ceilinged chamber. On the smooth, white-painted walls were mounted, like blank rectangular canvases, a pair of large, flat, gas-plasma display monitors. The two men took their seats at a gleaming table of brushed steel. One of the silent assistants disappeared; the other took a seat at a station just outside the closed door to the chamber.

As soon as Dunne and Bryson were seated, Dunne began to speak without ceremony or preface. "Let me tell you what I believe you believe," he began. "You believe you're a fucking unsung hero. This is in fact the central unshakable conviction that has enabled you to endure a decade and a half of tension so brutal, any lesser man would have cracked long ago. You believe you spent fifteen years in the service of your country, working for an ultraclandestine agency known as the Directorate. Virtually nobody else, even at the highest levels of the U.S. government, knows of its existence, with the possible exception of the chairman of the President's Foreign Intelligence Advisory Board and a couple of key players in the White House who've been cleared up the wazoo. A closed loop—or rather, as close as you can come to a closed loop in this fallen world."

Bryson took measured breaths, determined not to betray his emotions by any visible display of shock. Yet he was shocked: the CIA man knew of matters that had been cloaked with extraordinary thoroughness.

"Ten years ago, you even received a Presidential Medal of Honor for services rendered above and beyond," Dunne went on. "But, your operations being so hush-hush, there was no ceremony, no president, and I bet you didn't even get to keep the medal." Bryson flashed back to the moment: Waller opening the box and showing him the heavy brass object. Of course, it would have put operational secrecy unacceptably at risk if Bryson had been invited to the White House for the presentation; still, he'd swelled with pride all the same. Waller had asked him if it bothered him—the fact that he'd achieved the highest civilian honor in America and nobody would ever know. And Bryson, moved, told him honestly no—Waller knew, the president knew; his work had made the world just a little safer, and that was enough. He'd meant it, too. That, in a nutshell, was the ethos of the Directorate.

Now Dunne pressed a sequence of buttons on a control panel embedded in the steel-topped table, and the twin flat screens shimmered into vibrant display. There was a photograph of Bryson as an undergraduate at Stanford—not an official portrait, but a candid, taken without his knowledge. Another of him in a mountain region of Peru, clad in fatigues; this dissolved into an image of him with dyed skin and grizzled beard, impersonating one Jamil Al-Moualem, a Syrian munitions expert.

Astonishment is an emotion impossible to sustain for any length of time: Bryson felt his shock gradually ebbing into sharp annoyance, then anger. Obviously he'd been caught in the middle of some interagency squabble over the legality of Directorate methods.

"Fascinating," Bryson interjected dryly, finally breaking his silence, "but I suggest you take up these matters with others better placed to discuss them. Teaching is my only profession these days, as I assume you know."

Dunne reached over and gave Bryson a comradely pat on his shoulder, no doubt intended to reassure. "My friend, the question isn't what we know. It's what *you* know—and, more to the point, what you *don't*. You believe you've spent fifteen years in the service of your country." Dunne turned and gave Bryson a penetrating stare.

Quietly, steely, Bryson answered, "I know I did."

"And you see, that's where you're wrong. What if I told you that the Directorate in fact isn't part of the United States government? That it never was. Quite the fucking contrary." Dunne leaned back in his chair and ran a hand through his rumpled white mane. "Ah, shit, this isn't going to be easy for you to hear. It's not easy for me to say, I'll tell you that. Twenty years ago, I had to bring a guy in. He thought he'd been spying for Israel, and was a real zealot about it. I had to explain to him that he'd been false-flagged. It was Libya that was paying for his services. All the contacts, the controls, the hotel-room rendezvous in Tel Aviv—all part of the setup. Pretty flimsy one, at that. Fucker shouldn't have been double-dealing anyway. But even I had to feel sorry for him when he learned who his real employers were. I'll never forget his face."

Bryson's own face was burning hot. "What the hell does that have to do with anything?"

"We were supposed to arraign him in a sealed Justice Department courtroom the next day. Guy shot himself before we had the chance." One of the gas-plasma screens dissolved into another image. "Here's the guy who recruited you, right?"

It was a photograph of Herbert Woods, Bryson's adviser at Stanford and an eminent historian. Woods had always liked Bryson, admired the fact that he spoke a dozen languages fluently, had an unsurpassed gift for memorization. Probably liked the fact that he was no slouch as an athlete either. Sound mind, sound body—Woods was big on that.

The screen went blank, then flared with a grainy photo of a young Woods on a city street that Bryson immediately recognized as the old Gorky Street in Moscow, which after the end of the Cold War became Tverskaya once again, its pre-Revolutionary name.

Bryson laughed, bitterly, not bothering to hide his ridicule. "This is insanity. You're going to 'reveal' to me the 'damning' fact that Herb Woods was a commie when he was young. Well, sorry: everyone knows that. He never hid his past. That's why he was such a staunch anti-Communist: he knew firsthand how seductive all that foolish utopian rhetoric could be once upon a time."

Dunne shook his head, his facial expression cryptic. "Maybe I'm getting ahead of myself. I told you before that all I wanted you to do was listen. You're a historian now, right? Well, bear with me while I give you a quick history lesson. You know about the Trust, of course."

Bryson nodded. The Trust was widely regarded as the greatest espionage ploy of the twentieth century, bar none. It was a seven-year sting operation, the brainchild of Lenin's spymaster, Feliks Dzerzhinksi. Shortly after the Russian Revolution, the CHEKA, the Soviet intelligence organization that grew into the KGB, secretly founded a fake dissident group involving a number of supposedly disaffected high-ranking members of the Soviet government who believed, or so the word was quietly put out, that the collapse of the USSR was imminent. In time, anti-Soviet groups in exile were drawn into working with the Trust; in fact, Western intelligence units grew dependent upon the information—entirely fraudulent, of course—it provided. Not only was the hoax brilliantly designed to mislead those governments around the world who sought the Soviet Union's demise, it was, further, a superbly effective way for Moscow to penetrate the networks of its chief enemies abroad. And it worked phenomenally well—so well, in fact, that the Trust became a case study of the perfect deception operation, taught within intelligence agencies the world over.

By the time the nature of the subterfuge was exposed, in the late twenties, it was too late. Exiled leaders had been kidnapped and murdered, networks of collaborators destroyed, would-be defectors within Russia executed. The in situ forces of opposition to Soviet rule never recovered. It was, in the words of one eminent American intelligence analyst, "the deception operation upon which the Soviet state was built."

"Now you're the one talking ancient history," Bryson said in disgust, shifting in his seat impatiently.

"Never discount the power of inspiration," Dunne said. "In the early sixties, you had a small circle of brainiacs at the GRU—Soviet military intelligence, if you don't consider that a contradiction in terms." He chuckled. "These guys concluded that their intelligence agencies were all neutered, ineffectual, feeding out of the same trough of disinformation each one had created—or, to put it another way, a whole lot of ink and not much squid. The way these guys figured it—and they were geniuses, understand, IQs off the charts, the real deal—the intelligence agencies were spending most of their time chasing their own tails. These guys, they called themselves the *Shakhmatisti*, the chess players, chess club. They despised their own clumsy Russky operatives, and they had utter contempt for the sort of Americans who cooperated with them: sad sacks and losers, in their book. So they took another look at the Trust and tried to see if there was a lesson to be learned. They wanted to recruit the best and the brightest within their enemy's camp, same as us, and they figured out a way to get them. Same as us. Recruit them for a life of adventure."

"I'm not following."

"Neither were we, until very recently. It was only in the last few years that the CIA learned of the Directorate's existence. And, far more crucial, what the Directorate meant."

"Try talking sense."

"We're talking about the greatest espionage gambit in the entire twentieth century. The whole thing was an elaborate ruse, do you see? Like the Trust. These GRU geniuses, their masterstroke was to establish a penetration operation right on enemy soil—our soil. A super-secret spy agency staffed by a lot of gifted people who had no idea as to the identities of their real bosses, known only as the consortium, and who were instructed to conceal their work from any and all U.S. government officials. Now, that's the beauty part. You can't tell anybody else, especially not the government you're ostensibly working for! I'm talking about good, red-blooded Americans who got up in the morning and drank their Maxwell House coffee and toasted their Wonder Bread and drove to work in their Buicks and Chevys, and went out into the world and risked their lives—yet never knew who their real employers were. It went like clockwork—like a classic 'big store' con of old."

Bryson couldn't endure this litany any longer. "Goddamn you, Dunne! Enough! This is all lies, a goddamn pack of lies. If you really think I'd fall for this crap, you're out of your goddamn mind." He stood up abruptly. "Get me the hell out of here. I'm tired of your little low-rent theatrical production."

"I hardly expected you to believe me—not at first," Dunne said calmly, barely even shifting in his seat. "Hell, I wouldn't believe it either. But bear with me for a sec." He gestured toward one of the screens. "Know this guy?"

"Ted—Edmund Waller," Bryson breathed. He was looking at a photograph of Waller as a much younger man, stocky but not yet obese, wearing a Russian Army dress uniform at what appeared to be some kind of ceremonial occasion in Red Square. Part of the Kremlin was visible in the background. Scrolling up to the side of the image were biographical details. Name: GENNADY ROSOVSKY. Born 1935 in VLADIVOSTOK.

Childhood chess prodigy. Trained in American English, by a native speaker, since age seven. Certificates in ideology and in military science. A list of medals and other military honors followed.

"Chess prodigy," Bryson muttered to himself. "What the hell is this?"

"They say he could have beat Spassky and Fisher both, if he'd wanted to make a career of it," Dunne said, a harsh edge in his voice. "Too bad he decided to play for bigger game."

"Pictures can be doctored, pixels manipulated digitally—" Bryson began.

"Are you trying to convince me or yourself?" Dunne said, cutting him off. "Anyway, in a lot of cases we've got originals, and I'd be happy to have you inspect them. I can assure you we've been over everything with a microscope. We might never have known about the operation. Then our luck changes. *Mirabile* fucking *dictu*, Professor, we got access to the Kremlin archives. Money changed hands; buried archives were unearthed. There were one or two scraps of paper with pretty tantalizing stuff in them. Which would have told us nothing, to be honest, except for the lucky break of a couple of midlevel defectors, who gave us all they had. In isolation, their debriefings were meaningless. Taken together, with the Kremlin documents thrown in, patterns began to emerge. Which was how we learned about you, Nick. But it wasn't a whole lot, since apparently the inner circles kept the whole operation incredibly segmented, the way terror cells operate.

"So we started to wonder about what we didn't know. It's been a top-priority project for the past three years. We've got only the foggiest idea of who the real principals are. Except, of course, for your friend Gennady Rosovsky. He's got a sense of humor, got to hand him that. You know who he named himself after? Edmund Waller was the name of an obscure and extremely slippery seventeenth-century poet. He ever talk to you about the English civil war?"

Bryson swallowed hard and nodded.

"You'll get a laugh out of this, I know you will. During the interregnum, this Edmund Waller wrote praise poems for Cromwell, the Lord Protector. But, you see, he was also a secret conspirator in a Royalist plot. After the Restoration, he was honored at the Royal Court. That make any kind of sense to you? Guy calls himself after the great double-agent of English poetry. Like I said, I'm sure it's a laugh riot to you highbrows."

"So you're claiming that I was recruited at college into some . . . some kind of cat's-paw organization, that everything I did after that was a sham, is that what you're saying?" Bryson spoke bitterly, skeptically.

"Only the machinations didn't start then. They started earlier. A lot earlier."

He tapped a sequence on the control panel, and another digitized image came to life on the screen. On the left, he saw his father, Gen. George Bryson, robust, handsome, and square jawed, next to Nick's mother, Nina Loring Bryson, a soft-spoken, gentle woman who taught the piano, followed her husband to his postings around the world, and never breathed a word of complaint. On the right, another image—a grainy image from the police files—showed a crumpled vehicle on a snowy mountain road. The remembered pain slammed Bryson in the gut; after all these years, it was still almost unbearable.

"Let me ask you something, Bryson. Did you believe this was an accident? You were fifteen, already a brilliant student, terrific athlete, prime of American youth, all that. Now both your parents are suddenly killed. Your godparents take you in . . ."

"Uncle Pete," Bryson said tonelessly. He was in a world of his own, a world of shock and pain. "Peter Munroe."

"That was the name he took, sure, not the name he was born with. And he made sure you went to college where you did, and made a lot of other decisions for you besides. All of which pretty much guaranteed that you'd end up in their hands. The Directorate's, I mean."

"You're saying that when I was fifteen, my parents were murdered," Bryson said numbly. "You're saying my entire life has been some kind of . . . immense deception."

Dunne hesitated, wincing. "If it makes you feel any better, you weren't alone," he said gently. "There were dozens just like you. It's just that you were their most spectacular success."

Bryson wanted to press the point, argue with the CIA man, show the essential illogic of his reasoning, point out the flaws in his case. But instead he found himself overcome by an intense feeling of vertigo, a harrowing sense of guilt. If what Dunne said was correct, even anywhere near correct, then what in his life was real? What had ever been true? Did he even know who he was himself? "And Elena?" he asked stonily, not wanting to hear the answer.

"Yes, Elena Petrescu, too. Interesting case. We believe she was recruited out of the Romanian Securitate, assigned to you by the Directorate in order to keep tabs on you."

Elena . . . no, it was *inconceivable*, she wasn't Securitate! Her father was an enemy of the Securitate, a brave mathematician who turned against the government. And Elena . . . he had rescued her and her parents, they had built a life together. . . .

They were horseback riding along an endless stretch of deserted sandy beach in the Caribbean. Coming off a full gallop, they slowed to a trot. The moonlight was silvery, the night cool.

"Is this island all ours, Nicholas?" she exulted. "I feel like we're all alone here, that we own everything we see!"

"We do, my darling," Bryson said, infected by her playful exuberance. "Didn't I tell you? I've been diverting funds from discretionary accounts. I've bought the island."

Her laugh was musical, joyful. "Nicholas, you are terrible!"

" 'Nick-o-las'—I love the way you say my name. Where did you learn to ride so well? I didn't know they even had horses in Romania."

"Oh, but they do. I learned to ride on my grandmother Nicoleta's farm in the foothills of the Carpathian mountains, on a Hutsul pony. They're bred to work in the mountains, but they're so marvelous for riding, so lively and strong and sure footed."

"You could be describing yourself."

The waves crashed loudly behind them, and she laughed once more. "You never really saw my country, did you, my dear? The Communists made Bucharest so ugly, but the countryside, Transylvania and the Carpathians, is so beautiful and unspoiled. They still live in the old way, with the horse-drawn wagons. Whenever we tired of university life we would stay with Nicoleta in Dragoslavele, and every day she'd make us mamagliga, *fried cornmeal mush, and* ciorba, *my favorite soup."*

"You miss the homeland."

"A little. But mostly I miss my parents. I miss them so terribly. It's such agony for me not to be able to see them. The sterile phone calls maybe twice a year—it's not enough!"

"But at least they're safe. Your father has many enemies, people who would kill him if they knew his whereabouts. Securitate remnants, professional assassins who blame him for giving away the codes that led to the downfall of the Ceaușescu government that kept them in power. Now they're in hiding themselves, inside Romania and abroad, and they haven't forgotten. There are teams of them, called sweepers, who track down their old enemies and execute them. And they desperately want revenge against the man they consider the worst turncoat of all."

"He was a hero!"

"Of course he was. But to them he was a traitor. And they will stop at nothing to extract their vengeance."

"You frighten me!"

"Only to remind you how important it is that your parents remain in hiding, protected."

"Oh God, Nicholas, I pray nothing ever happens to them!"

Bryson pulled on the reins, bringing his horse to a stop as he turned to face Elena. "I promise you, Elena. Anything I can humanly do to keep them safe, I will."

A minute of silence passed, and then another. Finally, Bryson, blinking hard, said, "But it doesn't make any sense. I did goddamned valuable work. Time and again I—"

"—fucked us up the ass but good," Dunne interrupted, toying with a cigarette but not lighting it. "Every one of your great successes was a devastating setback to American interests. And I say this with the greatest professional respect. Oh, let's see. That 'moderate reform candidate' you protected? He was in the pay of the Sendero Luminoso, the Shining Path terrorists. In Sri Lanka, you pretty much destroyed a secret coalition that had been on the verge of brokering a peace between the Tamils and the Sinhalese."

Another image was downloaded onto the high-resolution screen, as a spray of pixels scrambled into colors and contours. Bryson recognized the face while it was still half a blur.

It was Abu.

"Tunisia," Bryson said, breathing hard. "He—he was going to stage a coup, he and his followers—fanatics. I moved in, leveraged some opposition groups, figured out who in the palace was playing both sides. . . ." It was not an episode he remembered altogether fondly: he would never forget the carnage along the Avenue Habib Borguiga. Nor the moment when Abu unmasked him and nearly took his life.

"Let's see now," Dunne said. "You burned him. Took him down, and handed him over to the government."

That was true. He'd turned Abu over to a trusted group of government security men, who jailed him along with dozens of his henchmen.

"Then what happened?" Dunne prompted, as if he was testing.

Bryson shrugged. "He died in captivity a few days later. I won't tell you I shed any tears."

"I wish I could say the same," Dunne said, his voice suddenly hard. "Abu was one of ours, Bryson. One of mine, I should say. I trained him. He was our chief asset in the whole region. I'm talking the entire god-damn sandbox."

"But the attempted coup . . ." Bryson put in feebly, his mind whirling. Nothing was making any sense!

"A bullshit cover story, to keep up his bona fides with the lunatics. He was leading the Al-Nahda, all right—right off the fucking cliff. Abu worked deep, deep cover. Needed to if he was going to survive the day. You think it's easy penetrating terrorist cells, especially Hezbollah, the big kahuna? They're all so goddamned suspicious. If they haven't known you and your family your entire goddamned life, they want to see you shed blood by the gallon, the blood of Israelis, otherwise they never trust you. Abu was a slick bastard who played rough, but he was *our* slick bastard. And he had to play rough. Thing is, he was getting close to Khadafy. Very close. Khadafy figured if Abu took Tunisia, he could make it a Libyan province, more or less. Abu was getting to be an asshole buddy of his. We were on the verge of having a direct feed to every Islamic terror group north of the Sahara. Then the Directorate sandbagged him, planted phony munitions—and by the time our people discovered we'd been stung, it was too late. Pretty much set back our whole network about twenty years. Brilliant work. Got to hand it to those *Shakhmatisti* whiz kids. Brilliant, really fucking brilliant, to have one American spy agency undoing the work of the other. You want me to go on? Tell you about Nepal and what you really accomplished? What about Romania, where you guys probably thought you helped get rid of Ceauşcscu? What a farce. Just about everyone from the old regime changed clothes one day and became the new government, you know that! Ceauşescu's underlings had been plotting the bastard's downfall for years—they delivered their boss to the wolves so they could stay in power. Which was just what the Kremlin wanted. So what happens? There's a fake coup d'etat, the dictator and his wife try to escape in a helicopter that suddenly develops 'engine trouble' so they can't escape, they get arrested and tried in a closed, kangaroo court, and face a firing squad on Christmas Day. The whole thing was a goddamned setup, and who benefited? One by one, all the Eastern European satellites were falling like dominoes, kicking out the old Party apparatchiks, going democratic, breaking away from the Soviet bloc. But Moscow wasn't going to lose Romania, too. Ceauşescu had to go, he was bad PR. The guy was a goddamned pain in Moscow's ass anyway, always was. Moscow wanted to keep Romania, maintain the security apparatus, install a new puppet. And who's there to do their dirty work? Who else but you and your good friends in the Directorate? Jesus, man, how much do you really want to know?"

"Damn it!" Bryson shouted. "This makes no sense! How ignorant do you think I am? The goddamn GRU, the Russians—that's all the past. Maybe you Cold War cowboys at Langley haven't yet heard the news—the war's over!"

"Yes," Dunne replied raspily, barely audible. "And for some baffling reason the Directorate is alive and well."

Bryson stared at him mutely, unable to get any words out. He felt his brain working, spinning in circles, circuits overheating, sparks flying.

"I'll level with you, Bryson. There was a time when I wanted to kill you, kill you with my bare hands. That was before we'd figured out the whole story, the way the Directorate worked. Nah, let's be straight with each other, I'd be bullshitting you and me both if I said we have anything remotely approaching the whole story. We still hardly know more than

ROBERT LUDLUM

isolated segments. For decades there had been rumors, no more substantial than dandelion wisps. Once the Cold War's over, the whole operation falls into quiescence, as best as we can figure. It's like the old parable of the blind man and the elephant. We can feel a trunk here, a tail there, but on the highest levels, we still don't know what kind of beast we're dealing with. What we do know—and we've had you under surveillance for the past few years—is that you were one deluded piece of shit. Which is why I'm talking to you real nice and not wrapping my hands around your throat." Dunne laughed bitterly, and the laugh turned into a cough—a smoker's hack. "See, here's what we speculate. Seems like after the Cold War, the organization broke off from its original masters. Control shifted into other hands."

Warily, sullenly, Bryson ventured: "Whose?"

Dunne shrugged. "Don't know. Five years ago, the organization apparently went into a period of relative dormancy: you weren't the only agent to be terminated—a whole lot of people were let go. Maybe the place was being shut down; it's impossible to say with any certainty. But now we've got reason to think it's being reactivated."

"What's that supposed to mean, 'reactivated'?"

"Not sure. That's why we decided to bring you in. We hear stuff. Your old masters appear to be accumulating arms, for some reason."

"For some reason," Bryson repeated dully.

"You could say they're poised to foment global instability—anyway, that's how our overeducated analysts might phrase it, in their Locust Valley lockjaw. But I ask myself, for what? What are they after? And I don't know. Like I say, what scares me is the stuff I don't know."

"Interesting," said Bryson sardonically. "You hear 'rumors,' you 'speculate,' you give me a goddamned digital slide show like some corporate consultant, yet you don't have the faintest clue what you're really saying."

"That's why we need you. The old Soviet system may be down, but the generals aren't down for the count. Look at General Bushalov—he's looking like a strong challenger on the political scene in Russia. Say something bad happened that he could blame on the United States—my prediction is, he'd be catapulted into power. Deliberative democracy? Plenty of Russkies would say, Good riddance to that. In Beijing there's a powerful reactionary cabal within both the National People's Congress

50

and the Central Committee. Not to mention the Chinese Army, the PLA, the People's Liberation Army, which is a force unto itself. No matter how you look at it, a lot of yuan are at stake, and a lot of power is, too. One school of thought has remnants of *Shakhmatisti* teaming up with a handful of their Beijing brethren. But I'm just blowing smoke out my ass. Because nobody really knows but the bad guys, and they ain't saying."

"If you really believe all this, truly think that I was some kind of chump in the biggest con game of the last century, what the hell do you need me for?"

The two men locked eyes for a long while. "You apprenticed with one of their masterminds, one of their founders, for Christ's sake. Gennady Rosovsky—back in Russia his nickname was apparently *Volshebnik*, 'the Sorcerer.' Know what that makes you?" Dunne's laugh turned into a hacking cough again. "The sorcerer's apprentice."

"Damn you!" Bryson exploded again.

"You know how Waller's mind works. You were his best student. You do realize what I'm asking you to do, don't you?"

"Yeah," Bryson replied sardonically. "You want me to get back inside."

Dunne nodded slowly. "You're our best bet. I could appeal to your patriotism, to the better angels of your being. But goddamn if you don't owe us one."

Bryson's mind was reeling. He did not know what to think, what to say to the CIA man.

"Don't take offense," Dunne told him, "but if we're trying to scent them out, then at least we should send out the best bloodhound we can find. I mean, how can I put this?" He'd been toying with the unlit cigarette so long that tobacco crumbs were beginning to spill from it. "You're the only one who knows what they smell like."

CHAPTER
FOUR

The strong midday sunlight bleached the buildings along this particular block of K Street, shimmered and glared against the plate-glass windows of the office buildings. Across the street, Nicholas Bryson intently watched 1324 K Street, a building at once deeply familiar and profoundly strange. Sweat rolled down his face, dampening his white dress shirt. He stood at the window of a deserted office space, tiny binoculars discreetly held to his face, curled in, and concealed by one hand. No doubt the commercial real-estate agent who had given him the keys to the vacant rental space thought it was strange that this international businessman wanted to spend a few minutes alone in what might be his office, in order to get a *feel* for it, the feng shui and all. The real-estate agent surely thought Bryson was another one of those touchy-feely New Age businessmen, but at least he'd left him alone for a while.

His pulse raced, his temples throbbed. There was nothing comforting or welcoming about the modern office building that served as the head-quarters of his employer, that for so long had been home base, a place of sanctuary and renewal, an island of continuity and calm reassurance in his ever-shifting, violent world. He watched from the dark, empty office suite for a good quarter of an hour, until a knock at the door came; the real-estate agent was back and curious to know the verdict.

It was immediately apparent that 1324 K Street had changed, though the transformations were subtle. The plaques on the front of the building, announcing its occupants, had been replaced with others, though just as banal-sounding as the previous ones. Harry Dunne had told him the K Street headquarters had been abandoned, but Bryson refused to accept his assurance on face value. The Directorate was also great at hiding in plain sight. "Naked is the best disguise," Waller used to say.

So was it indeed gone? THE AMERICAN TEXTILE MANUFACTURERS BOARD and THE UNITED STATES GRAINS PRODUCERS BOARD sounded just as plausible as the other notional organizations whose plaques had been put there by some creative camouflage artists within the Directorate, but what necessitated the change? Too, there were other alterations at 1324 K Street. In a quarter-hour of discreet surveillance, Bryson had seen an unusually high number of people pass through its front doors. Far too many, certainly, to be Directorate employees or blind contractors. So something different was going on here.

Maybe Dunne was right after all. But his early-warning system had been triggered. *Accept nothing at face value; question everything you're told.* Another of Ted Waller's lines. That went for Waller and Dunne and everyone else in the business for that matter.

The matter of how to get into the building without alerting its occupants was one he had been wrestling with for hours. He approached the issue as yet another fieldwork conundrum to be solved; in his mind, he had worked out dozens of ingenious methods of entry. Yet all of them carried risks without commensurate odds of success. Then he recalled one of Waller's—*damn it, Gennady Rosovsky's*—truisms: *When in doubt, go in the front door.* The best and most effective stratagem would be to enter the building openly, brazenly.

Yet duplicity was a necessary part of the game plan; it would always be so. He thanked the real-estate agent, told him he was interested, and asked him to prepare a leasing agreement. He handed over one of his false business cards, and then told the man he had to rush off to another appointment. He approached the building's front entrance, his senses hyperalert to any sudden movements, any shifts in crowd patterns or coloration, that might signal a threat.

So where was Ted Waller?

Where was the truth? Where was sanity?

The jarring traffic noises swelled all around him, the cacophony overwhelming. *"It's the only way you'll ever know the truth."*

"The truth about what?"

"For starters, the truth about yourself."

But where was the truth? Where were the lies?

"You believe you're a fucking unsung hero. . . . You believe you've spent fifteen years in the service of your country, working for an ultraclandestine agency known as the Directorate."

Stop it! This was madness!

Elena? You, too? Elena, the love of my life, now departed from my life as abruptly as you first appeared?

"You believe you've spent a decade and a half in the service of your country."

The blood I spilled, the gut-wrenching fear, the innumerable occasions I almost lost my life, extinguished the lives of others?

"We're talking about the greatest espionage gambit in the entire twentieth century. The whole thing was an elaborate ruse, do you see?"

*"You're saying my entire life has been some kind of . . . immense decep-*tion!"

"If it makes you feel any better, you weren't alone. There were dozens just like you. It's just that you were their most spectacular success."

Insanity!

"You're the only one who knows what they smell like."

Someone crashed into him, and Bryson spun in a crouch, hands flat and stiff at his side, ready to attack. It was no professional, but instead a tall, athletic-looking executive carrying a gym bag and a squash racquet. The man fixed Bryson with a scowl contorted with fear. Bryson apologized; the executive glared and moved on, quickly, nervously.

Face it, face the past, face the truth!

Face Ted Waller, who was *not* Ted Waller! This much Bryson knew by now. He still had his own sources from the old KGB, the old GRU, men living in retirement or gone into new lines of work in a mercenary post–Cold War world. Inquiries were made, records checked, data confirmed. Telephone calls placed, false names used, meaningless-sounding but in fact highly significant phrases employed. Men were contacted, men whom Bryson had known in a past life, a life he was sure he had left behind. A diamond dealer in Antwerp; an attorney-businessman in Copenhagen; a highly paid international trade "consultant" and "fixer" in Moscow. Once key sources all, former Soviet GRU officers who had since emigrated, left behind the spy world as Bryson thought he had. All of whom maintained records in safe-deposit boxes, stored on encrypted magnetic tape, or simply archived in their formidable brains. All of whom were surprised, some unnerved, frightened even, to be contacted by a man who had attained legend status in their former trade, who had once paid them generously for their information, their assistance. Separately, identifications were provided, checkable and confirmable several times over.

Gennady Rosovsky and Edmund Waller were one and the same. There was no doubt about it.

Ted Waller—Bryson's best man, boss, confidant, employer—was indeed a GRU sleeper agent. Once again the CIA man, Harry Dunne, was correct. *Madness!*

Arriving in the outer lobby, he noticed that the intercom panel where he had once entered a coded, constantly changing series of numbers had been removed; in its place was a glass-encased directory of law firms and lobbying organizations located within. Below each firm name was a list of its chief officers and their office numbers. He was surprised to find that the front door opened with no annunciation apparatus, no locks or barriers of any sort. Anyone could come in and out.

Beyond the glass doors, which now appeared to be of regular window glass, not bulletproof, the inner lobby looked little changed—a standard reception area with one security guard/receptionist seated behind a tall half-moon of curved marble counter. A young black man in a blue blazer and red tie looked up at him with little interest.

"I've got an appointment with—" He hesitated but a split-second as he called to mind a name from the directory in the outer lobby—"John Oakes of the American Textiles Manufacturers Board. I'm Bill Thatcher from Congressman Vaughan's office." Bryson affected a slight Texas twang; Congressman Rudy Vaughan was a powerful ranking member from Texas whose opinion, and committee chairmanships, no doubt meant quite a bit to the textile board.

The usual preliminaries were gone through. The director of the lobbying board was telephoned by security; his executive assistant had no record of any scheduled visit by Congressman Vaughan's chief legislative aide but was more than happy to accommodate such an important figure. A sprightly young woman with frosted blond hair came down and escorted Bryson into the elevator, apologizing all the while for the mix-up.

They got off on the third floor and were met right at the elevator by a blond man whose hair looked a little "refreshed," wearing an expensive suit, looking a little too polished. Mr. Oakes all but ran up to Bryson, arms outstretched. "We're grateful for Congressman Vaughan's support!" the lobbyist exclaimed, shaking Bryson's hand with both of his. In a confiding voice he added, "I know Congressman Vaughan understands the importance of keeping America strong, free of cheap, underpriced imports. I mean, *Mauritanian fabrics*—that is not what this country is about! I know the Congressman understands that."

"Congressman Vaughan is interested to learn more about the international labor standards bill that you're supporting," Bryson said, looking around as the two of them strode down the hallway that was once so familiar. Yet there were none of the old personnel, no Chris Edgecomb nor any of the others whom Bryson knew only by face. None of the communications workstations or modules, the global satellite monitors. Nothing was the same, including the office furniture. Even the floor plan had been altered, as if the entire floor had been gutted. The old small-arms storeroom was gone, replaced by a conference room with smoked-glass walls and expensive-looking mahogany table and chairs.

The too-well-dressed lobbyist led Bryson into his corner office and invited him to sit. "We understand the Congressman is up for reelection next year," the man said, "and we consider it *vital* to support those members of Congress who understand the importance of keeping America's economy strong."

Bryson nodded absently, looking around. This was the office that had once belonged to Ted Waller. If there had been even an inkling of doubt, that was now vanished. This was no notional organization, no cover.

The Directorate had vanished. There was no trace of Ted Waller, the only man who could confirm—or deny—the truth of CIA man Harry Dunne's account of the truth behind the Directorate.

Who's lying? Who's telling the truth?

How could he reach his old employers when they had vanished off the face of the earth as if they'd never existed?

Bryson had hit a wall.

Twenty minutes later, Bryson had returned to the parking garage, returned to his rented vehicle, and ran through all the checks that had once been second nature to him. The tiny pressure-sensitive filament he had pressed into place along the door handle on the driver's side was still in place, as was the filament on the passenger-side door handle; anyone who had attempted to pick the lock or otherwise gain entry to the car would have dislodged the indicators without knowing it. He knelt quickly and did a brief visual survey of the underside of the automobile, confirming that no devices had been placed there. He had not been aware of any attempts to follow him to K Street or into the parking garage, but he could no longer satisfy himself with such counter-surveillance efforts. As he started the car he felt the old familiar knot in his stomach, the ganglion of tension that hadn't been there for several years. The moment of truth passed uneventfully; there was no ignition-triggered detonation.

He drove down through several levels to the garage exit, where he inserted his magnetic-striped ticket into the card reader that controlled the liftgate arm. The ticket popped back out, rejected. *Damn it,* he muttered to himself. It was almost amusing—almost, but not quite—that for all his precautions, he would be delayed by a simple mechanical glitch. He inserted the card again; still, it failed to activate the arm. The bored-looking parking attendant came out of his booth, came up to Bryson's open window, and said, "Let me give it a try, sir." The attendant inserted the ticket into the machine, but still it was rejected. He glanced at the blue paper ticket, nodded with sudden understanding, and approached the car window.

"Sir, is this the same ticket you were issued when you entered?" the attendant asked, handing it back to Bryson.

"What's that supposed to mean?" Bryson said irritably. Was the attendant questioning whether this was in fact Bryson's vehicle, whether Bryson might be trying to take someone else's? He turned to look at the attendant and was immediately bothered by something, some aspect of the man's hands.

"No, sir, you're misunderstanding me," the attendant said, leaning in. Bryson suddenly felt the cold hard steel of a gun barrel pressed against his left temple. The attendant held a small-caliber, snub-nosed pistol to Bryson's temple! It was *insane!* "I'm saying, *sir*, that I want you to keep both of your hands on the steering wheel," said the attendant in a low, steady voice. "I'd rather not have to use this thing."

Jesus Christ!

That was it! The hands, the manicured nails—they were the soft, well tended hands of a man who took inordinate care with his appearance, who likely traveled in exclusive, moneyed circles and had to fit in—not the hands of a parking-garage attendant. But the realization had come an instant too late! The attendant abruptly opened the car's rear door and leaped into the backseat, the gun once again to Bryson's temple.

"Let's *go! Move* it!" shouted the fake attendant, just as the barrier lifted. "*Don't* remove those hands from the wheel. I'd hate to slip, pull the trigger by accident, you know? Let's go for a little drive, you and me. Get some fresh air."

Bryson, having stowed his weapon in his glove compartment, had no choice but to drive out of the garage and onto K Street, following the false attendant's directions. As the car entered traffic, Bryson felt the gun barrel cut into the flesh of his left temple, and he heard the low, steady, conversational banter of the man behind him.

"You knew this day was going to come, didn't you?" the professional said. "Odds are it'll happen to all of us at some point. You overstep, go a little too far. Push when you should have pulled. Stick your nose into something that's no longer your business."

"Care to fill me in on where we're going?" Bryson said, trying to keep his voice light. His heart hammered, his mind raced. He added, as an aside, "Mind if I put on the news . . . ?" He casually reached out his right hand for the radio knob, then felt the pistol's barrel slam into his head as the hit man roared, "*Goddamn* you, get those hands back on the *wheel!*"

"Jesus!" Bryson exclaimed as the pain spread. "Watch it!"

The killer had no idea that Bryson's Glock was nestled against the base of his spine, in his rear waist holster. But he was not going to take any chances.

Then how to retrieve it? The hit man—for he *was* a hit man, Bryson knew, a professional, whether on the Directorate payroll or a contract employee—insisted that Bryson keep his hands visible at all times. Now he had to follow instructions, waiting for a moment of distraction on the part of the hit man. The earmarks were in everything about the man: the confident plan of action; the quick, efficient moves; even the glib speech.

"Let's just say we're going someplace outside the Beltway, someplace where a couple of guys can talk freely." But *talking*, Bryson realized grimly, was the last thing on the hit man's agenda. "A couple of guys in the same business who just happen to be on different ends of a gun, that's all. It's nothing personal, I'm sure you realize that. Strictly business. One minute you're looking through the sights, next minute you're looking at the barrel. Happens. The wheel's always turning. I'm sure you were very good in your time, which is why I have no doubt you're going to take this like a man."

Bryson, considering his options, didn't reply. He'd been in roughly similar circumstances countless times before, though never, except during his early training days, on the other side of a pistol. He knew how the man in the seat behind him was thinking right now, the way the flow chart was patterned: *if* A, *then* B . . . How a sudden move on Bryson's part, a direction ignored, the steering wheel spun in the wrong direction, would initiate a countermeasure. The hit man would try to avoid pulling the trigger while they were in traffic, for fear the vehicle might careen out of control, imperiling both men. This familiarity with the options available to his enemy was one of the few cards Bryson had to play.

Yet at the same time Bryson was quite aware that the man would not hesitate to fire directly into Bryson's head if he had to, lunging forward to grab and steady the steering wheel. Bryson didn't like the odds.

Now they were crossing the Key Bridge. "*Left*," the man barked, indicating the direction of Reagan National Airport. Bryson obeyed, careful to seem compliant, resigned, the.better to put the other man off his guard.

"Now take this exit," the killer resumed. The exit would take them toward the area immediately outside the airport where most of the rental-car agencies had offices.

"You could have done me back there at the parking garage," Bryson muttered. "You *should* have, actually."

But the hit man was too skilled to be drawn into a discussion of tactics or to allow Bryson to challenge his competence. Obviously the expert had been fully briefed as to the nature of Bryson's mind, how Bryson would likely react in such a circumstance. "Oh, don't even try that," the professional said with a low chuckle. "You saw all the videocams back there, the potential witnesses. You know better than that. You wouldn't have done it there either, I'll bet. Not based on what *I* hear about your skills."

A slip there, Bryson reflected. The man was definitely a contract employee, an outsider, which meant any backup was unlikely. He would be operating on his own. A Directorate staffer would be protected by others. This was a valuable piece of data to store away.

Bryson steered the car into a deserted, vacant parking area, the far end of what was once a used-car lot. He parked as instructed. He turned his head to his right to address the other man, then felt the barrel of the gun grind painfully into his temple: the professional made no secret of his displeasure. "Don't *move*," came the steely voice. Turning his head back around, staring straight ahead, Bryson said, "Why don't you at least make this quick?"

"So now you're feeling the way the other guys felt," said the professional, amused. "The fear, the sense of futility, of hopelessness. Of resignation."

"You're waxing entirely too philosophical for me. I'll bet you don't even know who's issuing your checks."

"Beyond the fact that they clear, I don't really care."

"No matter who they are, what they do," said Bryson quietly. "No matter whether they're working *against* the U.S. or not."

"Like I said, so long as the checks clear. I don't do politics."

"That's a pretty short-term way of thinking."

"We're in a short-term business."

"It doesn't have to be." Bryson let a moment of silence pass. "Not if we come to mutually agreeable terms. We all lock some away; it's *expected* of us. Discretionary accounts, reimbursed expenses, overstated of course—a percentage of our expense allowance salted away, laundered clean, invested in the market. Put your money to work for you. I'm willing to put some of it to work for me right now."

"To buy your own life," the professional said solemnly. "But you seem to forget that my livelihood goes beyond one transaction. You may be one account, but they're the entire goddamned bank. And you don't bet against the house."

"No, you don't bet against the house," Bryson agreed. "You just report back that the mark was even better than you'd been led to believe, more skilled. Managed to escape, *Jesus*, the guy's good. They're not going to doubt you on that; it's what they *want* to believe anyway. You'll still keep your retainer, your deposit, and I'll double the contract amount. Sound business practice, my friend."

"Accounts are watched very carefully these days, Bryson. It's not like when you were in the game. Money is digital, and digital transactions leave tracks."

"Cash doesn't leave tracks, not if it's unsequenced."

"Everything leaves tracks these days, and you know it. Sorry, I've got a job to do. And in this case, it's facilitating suicide. You have a history of depression, you know. You had no personal life to speak of, and the groves of academe could never compare to the excitement of spy work. Your clinical depression was diagnosed by a top-rank psychiatrist and psychopharmacologist—"

"Sorry, the only shrinks I've ever seen were government-issue, years ago."

"A few *days* ago, according to your health-insurance records," replied the killer, a grim smile in his voice. "You've been seeing a shrink for over a year."

"That's *bullshit!*"

"Anything's possible in this day and age of the computerized database. Pharmacy records, too—antidepressants prescribed for you, purchased by you, along with antianxiety drugs, sleeping pills. It'll all be there. A suicide note left on your home computer, too, I'm told."

"Suicide notes are almost always handwritten, never typed or computer generated."

"Granted—we've both set up hits to look like suicides, I'm sure. But believe me, no one's ever going to dig into this that far. There'll be no postmortems for you. You have no family to request an autopsy."

The professional's words, though no doubt prescripted, still wounded, because they were the truth: he had no family, not since Elena had left. *Not since my parents were killed by the Directorate,* he added to himself bitterly.

"But let me say, I'm honored to be given this assignment," the hit man resumed. "They say you were one of the top field men, after all."

"Why do you think you were assigned?" Bryson said.

"I don't know, and I don't care. A job's a job."

"You think you're expected to survive it? You think they want you around telling tales? Who knows how much I might have told you? You think you're going to survive this last job?"

"I don't really give a shit," said the man unconvincingly.

"No, I don't think your employers ever planned to let you live," Bryson went on, grimly. "Who the hell knows *what* I spilled to you?"

"What are you trying to say?" asked the hit man after a moment of uncomfortable silence. He seemed to hesitate for an instant; Bryson could feel the grinding pressure of the pistol barrel momentarily let up. It was all the opportunity he needed, this second or two of genuine indecision on the part of his intended assassin. Quietly, he slipped his left hand off the steering wheel and slithered it down around to his back. He had the Glock! With lightning speed he pointed it toward the back of his seat and, firing blind, squeezed the trigger again and again in quick succession. Three rapid explosions filled the car's interior as the large-caliber bullets pierced the seat cushions, the noise ear-shattering. Had he hit the man? In an instant he got his answer as the barrel of the pistol fell away from the back of his head. Bryson spun around, whipping his pistol around, too, as he did so, and he realized that the man was dead, half of his forehead blown away.

They met at Langley this time, in Dunne's seventh-floor office in the Agency's new building. Standard security procedures were bypassed; Bryson was admitted to CIA headquarters with a minimum of ceremony.

"Why does it not surprise me the Directorate boys declared you beyond salvage?" Harry Dunne said with a hoarse laugh that became a sustained hacking cough. "I just think they must have forgotten who they were dealing with."

"Meaning what?"

"Meaning that you're better than anyone they can send after you, Bryson. For Christ's sake, you'd think those fucking cowboys would know that by now."

"They also know they don't want me in this office, in this *building*, spilling my guts."

"Wish you had anything to spill," replied Dunne. "But they knew how to keep all of you isolated, atomized. You don't know real names, just legends, and a fat lot of good that does us. Legends that are, or were, internal to the Directorate yield nothing in our own in-house data search. Like this 'Prospero' you keep mentioning."

"I told you, that's all I knew him as. Plus, it was over fifteen years ago. In the field, that's a geological era. Prospero was, I believe, Dutch, or at least of Dutch origins. Very resourceful operative."

"The best Agency sketch artists have produced a drawing based on your description, and we're trying to match the image against stored photographs, sketches, verbal descriptions. But the artificial-intelligence software still hasn't advanced enough yet. It's arduous, hit-or-miss work. So far we've had just one hit, as the digital hard-disk jockeys like to say. A fellow you said you worked with in Shanghai on a particularly sensitive exfiltration case."

"Sigma."

"Ogilvy. Frank Ogilvy, of Hilton Head, South Carolina. Or maybe I should say, *late* of Hilton Head."

"Moved? Transferred?"

ROBERT LUDLUM

"A crowded beach, a hot day. Seven years ago. Keeled over from a massive heart attack, apparently. Caused a minor commotion on the boardwalk that day, one witness told us, so crowded and all."

Bryson sat quietly for a moment, examining the windowless walls of Dunne's office, contemplating. Abruptly he said, "If you're looking for ants, go find yourself a picnic."

"Come again?" Dunne was once again absently shredding a cigarette.

"That was one of Waller's sayings. *If you're looking for ants, go find yourself a picnic.* Instead of looking for them where they *were*, we need to figure out where they *are*. Ask yourself: What do they need? What kind of spread are they in the *mood* for?"

Dunne put down the ruined cigarette and looked up, suddenly alert. "Weaponry, the word is. Seems they're trying to stockpile an arsenal. We think they're instigating some kind of turbulence in the southern Balkans, although their ultimate target is elsewhere."

"Weaponry." Something was turning in Nick's mind.

"Guns and ammo. But sophisticated stuff." Dunne shrugged. "Things that go boom in the night. When the bombs and bullets start flying, your own generals always start to look more appealing. Whatever they're hatching, we've got to put an end to it. By whatever means."

" 'Whatever means'?"

"You and I understand the definition. Though a straight-shooter like Richard Lanchester never could. A whole lot of good intentions, but where does all that idealism get you in the end? Notice all the saints are dead." The venerable and revered Richard Lanchester was chairman of the National Security Council in the White House. "Dick Lanchester believes in rules and regulations. But the world doesn't play by rules. Anyway, sometimes you gotta break 'em to save 'em."

"Can't play by Queensbury Rules, is that it?" Bryson said, recalling Ted Waller's words.

"Tell me how you used to get hold of weaponry. You sure weren't using U.S. government requisitions. You pick up stuff on the street, or what?"

"Actually, we were always particular about our 'instruments,' as we called them. The munitions. And you're right—given the restrictions, the deep secrecy, we had to round up the stuff ourselves. We couldn't exactly drive up to an army warehouse with a transfer order. Take a fairly typical ordnance-intensive operation—like the one in the Comoros, in 'eighty-two, where the idea was to stop a band of Executive Outcome mercenaries from overtaking the place."

"They were CIA," Dunne put in, almost wearily. "And all they were after was a dozen Brits and Americans that some loony-tunes named Colonel Patrick Denard had kidnapped and was holding for ransom."

Bryson flinched, but pressed on. "First, a few hundred Kalashnikov assault rifles. They're cheap, reliable, lightweight, and they're made in about ten different countries, so they're hard to trace. You'd want a smaller number of sniper rifles with night-vision scopes—preferably a BENS 9304 or Jaguar Night Scope. Rocket launchers, and rocket grenades, preferably CPAD Tech. Stinger missiles can come in handy—the Greeks make a lot of them under license, and they're easy to come by. You've got your Kurdish guerrillas, the PKK, raising cash by selling them to the Tamil Tigers, the LTTE."

"You're losing me."

Bryson sighed impatiently. "Where you're routing arms illegally, there's always substantial quantities that go astray. Somehow they lose a few with every truckload."

"Fall off the back of the truck."

"In a manner of speaking, yes. Then, of course, you want to stockpile ammunition rounds. That's where the amateurs would always go wrong—they end up with more guns than ammo."

Dunne looked at him strangely. "You *were* good, weren't you." It wasn't a question, and it wasn't a compliment either.

Bryson stood up suddenly, his eyes wide. "I know where to find them. Where to start, anyway. Right around this time of year"—he looked at the date on the face of his digital watch—"hell, in about ten days' time or so, there's going to be an annual floating arms bazaar off the Costa da Morte—in international waters off Spain. It's something like a twenty-year institution, as regular an event as the Macy's Thanksgiving Day parade. An immense container ship filled with major-league munitions, and a lot of major-league gunrunners to keep them company." Bryson paused. "The ship's registered name is the *Spanish Armada*."

"The picnic," Dunne said with a sly smile. "Where the ants gather. Sure. Not a bad idea."

Bryson nodded, his thoughts far away. The thought of returning to his old line of work—especially now that he realized how he was deceived into it—filled him with repugnance. Yet there was something else, too, another emotion: rage. The desire for revenge. And one more emotion as well, a quieter one: a need to *understand*, to delve into his own past. To force his way through all the secrets and lies to something like truth. A truth he could live with. "That's right," Bryson added wearily. "For any group, whether outlaw or deep-undercover governmental, that's interested in acquiring arms without official scrutiny, the *Spanish Armada* is always a picnic."

CHAPTER
FIVE

Atlantic Ocean
Thirteen nautical miles SW of
   Cabo Finisterre, Spain

The immense ship seemed to materialize out of the fog, looming vast
and unlovely, as long as a city block, maybe several city blocks. It was a
thousand feet long, its black hull sunk deep in the water. The supercarrier
was loaded with cargo, multicolored, corrugated metal containers stacked
three high and eight across, maybe ten rows from bridge to bow, each
box twenty feet long and nine feet high. As the Bell 407 helicopter circled
the ship and then hovered directly above the forecastle, Bryson did a
quick calculation. Two hundred and forty giant boxes, and that was just
on deck; belowdecks, in the hold, he knew, the ship could carry three
times the number of containers above. It was an immense load of cargo,
made all the more ominous by the bland sameness of the metal boxes,
the contents of each a mystery.

   The helicopter's lights garishly illuminated the flat, cleared deck; all
the way at the stern end of the ship, the tall superstructure towered above

the rows of containers, white with dark windows, its bridge bustling with modernistic-looking radar and satellite antennae. The deckhouse looked as if it belonged to another type of vessel entirely, a luxury yacht, not a freighter. For this was no mere container ship, Bryson reflected as the helicopter gently landed atop the giant H in a circle that was painted on the forecastle deck.

No, this was the *Spanish Armada*, a legend in the shadowed world of terrorists and covert operatives and other illegal, or semilegal, operators. The *Spanish Armada*, though, was no armada, no fleet: it was just the moniker of one immense ship packed with weaponry both exotic and mundane. No one knew where Calacanis, the mysterious lord of this floating arms bazaar, obtained his wares, but it was whispered that he purchased many of them quite legally from the stores of nations with too many arms and not enough cash, countries like Bulgaria and Albania and other Eastern European states; from Russia, from Korea and China. Calacanis's customers came from all over the world, or really the underworld: from Afghanistan to Congo, where dozens of civil wars raged, conflagrations stoked by illegal arms purchased by representatives of legally elected governments who came to pay their calls on this very ship, anchored thirteen nautical miles off the Spanish coast, above the relatively shallow continental shelf yet outside Spanish territorial waters, and thus free to do business, constrained by no country's laws.

Bryson removed his headset when the other three passengers did the same. He had flown to Madrid, then took a connecting flight on Iberian Airlines to La Coruña, in Galicia. He and another had boarded the helicopter at La Coruña, then made a quick stop at the harbor town of Muros, forty-seven miles southwest, and from there flew the thirteen miles to the ship. They had said little to one another beyond polite, meaningless banter. Each assumed the others were coming to shop, to strike deals with Calacanis; nothing needed to be said. One of them was Irish, probably Provo; another appeared Middle Eastern; the third Eastern European. The pilot was a sullen, equally taciturn Basque. The interior of the helicopter was luxurious, with leather seats and bubble door windows: Calacanis seemed to spare no expense anywhere.

Bryson wore a stylish Italian suit, far flashier than the conservative clothes he normally wore, purchased and tailored just for the occasion at

Agency expense. He was traveling under an old Directorate legend that he had himself created some years ago.

John T. Coleridge was a shady Canadian businessman known to be deeply involved in some dirty business deals, acting as a middleman for several crime syndicates in Asia and a few outlaw states in the Persian Gulf, occasionally even a procurer for assassinations. Although Coleridge was an elusive figure, his name was known in certain circles, and that was the important thing. True, Coleridge hadn't been seen for seven years, but that wasn't so rare in this strange business.

Harry Dunne had insisted that Bryson use a new legend specially created for him by the wizards of the CIA's technical services division, graphic arts reproduction branch — master forgers who specialized in what was euphemistically called "authentication and validation." But Bryson refused. He wanted no leaks, no bureaucratic paper trails of any kind. Whether he could trust Harry Dunne was an open question; he *knew* he didn't trust Dunne's organization. Bryson had spent too many years watching and hearing tales about CIA leaks and gaffes and indiscretions to trust them. He'd provide his own cover, thank you very much.

But Bryson had never met Calacanis before, never once set foot on the *Spanish Armada*, and Basil Calacanis was famously careful about who he was willing to meet with. In his business it was too easy to get burned. So Bryson had prepared the way to ensure his acceptance here.

He had brokered an arms deal. Money hadn't changed hands — it hadn't gone that far, the deal hadn't been consummated — but he established contact with a German arms broker he had met a few times as Coleridge, who lived in a luxury hotel in Toronto and who had recently been ensnared in a web of bribes he had paid to leaders of Germany's Christian Democratic Party. Now the German was living in Canada, in fear of being extradited to Germany, where he would surely stand trial. He was also known to be badly in need of funds. So Bryson was not surprised that the German had been extremely interested in John Coleridge's proposal that they do a little business together.

Bryson made it known that, in the guise of Coleridge, he represented a consortium of generals in Zimbabwe, Rwanda, and Congo who desired to purchase some high-powered, hard-to-procure, and very expensive weaponry — which only Calacanis could provide. But Coleridge was re-

alistic enough to know that he could hardly broker the deal without
entrée to Calacanis's arms bazaar. If the German, who had done quite a
bit of business with Calacanis, would make that introduction, he would
get a piece of the action, a decent chunk of the commission for doing
little more than sending a fax of introduction to Calacanis's ship.

As Bryson and the other passengers got out of the helicopter, they were
met by a young, powerfully built, balding redheaded man who shook
their hands and smiled obsequiously. He did not say their names aloud,
but introduced himself as Ian.

"Thank you so much for coming across," Ian said in an upper-class
British accent, as if they were old companions come to help a sick friend.
"You've picked a fine night to pay us a visit—calm seas, full moon,
couldn't ask for a more glorious evening. And you're all just in time for
dinner. Please, step over this way." He indicated a spot just off the landing
pad where three bulky guards toting submachine guns stood waiting. "I'm
dreadfully sorry to make you go through this, but you know Sir Basil."
He smiled apologetically, shrugged. "Terribly security-conscious, you
know. Sir Basil can't be too careful these days."

The three swarthy guards expertly frisked the four new arrivals, glowering at them suspiciously. The Irishman was outraged and snapped at
the man frisking him but made no move to stop him. Bryson had expected this ritual, and so he had brought no weapon. The guard who
patted him down checked all the usual places and some of the unusual
ones besides, but of course found nothing. He then asked Bryson to pop
open his briefcase. "Papers," the guard said in an accent he determined
was Sicilian.

The guard grunted, mollified.

Bryson looked around, noticed the Panamanian flag at the bow, saw
the Class One/Explosives labels plastered over many of the containers.
Certain privileged buyers were permitted to inspect the goods they were
buying, actually look into the containers. But nothing was offloaded here.
The *Spanish Armada* would later call at selected safe harbors, such as
the port of Guayaquil, in Ecuador, which was believed to be Calacanis's
home base; or Santos, in Brazil—the two ports were the most corrupt
pirates' dens in the entire hemisphere. In the Mediterranean the ship
would call on the Albanian port of Vlorë, one of the world's greatest

smuggling centers. In Africa, there were the ports of Lagos in Nigeria, and Monrovia in Liberia.

Bryson had passed.

He was in.

"This way, please," Ian said, gesturing toward the deckhouse, where the crew's quarters, the bridge, and, Calacanis's staterooms and offices surely were. As the four passengers walked, they were shadowed at a discreet distance by the armed guards. The helicopter lifted off, and as they reached the superstructure, the racket subsided. Now Bryson could hear the familiar sounds of the sea, the gulls, the lapping waves, and he could smell the saline odor of the sea mixed with the powerful, acrid smell of the ship's diesel fuel. The moon shone brightly over the Atlantic waters.

The five men just barely fit in the small elevator that lifted them from the main deck level to the 06 deck.

When the elevator opened, Bryson was astonished. He had not seen such luxury in the yachts of the most extravagant billionaires. No expense had been spared. The floors were marble-tiled; the walls, dark mahogany paneling; the fittings, gleaming brass. He passed an entertainment center and screening room, a fitness center equipped with the most elaborate machinery, a sauna, a library. Finally they came to an enormous saloon, the owner's stateroom, which faced aft and to port. It was two levels high, and it was outfitted with an opulence rarely seen in the grandest of grand hotels.

There were four or five other men standing by a bar, which was tended by a bartender in black tie. A white-uniformed stewardess, a dazzlingly beautiful blonde with stunning green eyes, offered him a flute of Cristal champagne and smiled shyly. Bryson took the champagne, thanked her, and looked around, trying not to be too obvious about it. The marble floors were mostly covered with oriental rugs; plush sofas were arranged in seating areas; several walls were lined with books that, upon closer inspection, proved to be fake. There were crystal chandeliers. The only peculiar touches were large fish, stuffed and mounted on the walls, evidently trophies from game fishing.

Looking at the other guests, some of whom were chatting with one another, he realized that he recognized a few of them. But who were they? His head spun; his prodigious memory was being taxed to its limit.

71

Gradually, dossiers attached themselves to vaguely familiar faces. A Pakistani middleman, a highly placed officer in the Irish Provisional Army, a businessman and arms trader who had done more than perhaps anyone to stoke the Iran-Iraq war. These and others were middlemen, retailers, here to acquire their goods wholesale. He went cold with tension, wondering whether any of these men had met him in his previous life. Did anyone here know him, whether as Coleridge or by another one of his many identities? There was always the risk of being unmasked, being hailed by one name when he had identified himself by another. The risk went with the job; it was one of the many occupational hazards; he always had to be on the alert for such a possibility.

Still, no one gave him more than a curious glance, the sort of look cast by fellow predators who want to know their competition. None seemed to recognize him. Neither did he get that prickly feeling at the back of his head that told him he was supposed to have known any one of the men here. Slowly he felt the tension subside.

He overheard one of them muttering something about a "multimode Doppler radar," someone else mentioning Scorpions, Czech-made Striela antiair missiles.

Bryson caught the blond waitress stealing a glance at him, and he smiled pleasantly. "Where's your boss?" he asked.

She looked embarrassed. "Oh," she said. "Mr. Calacanis?"

"Who else could I mean?"

"He will be joining his guests for dinner, sir. May I offer you caviar, Mr. Coleridge?"

"Never liked the stuff. Al-Biqa?"

"Pardon me?"

"Your accent. It's a Levantine dialect of Arab, from the Bekaa Valley, am I right?"

The waitress blushed. "Nice party trick."

"I see Mr. Calacanis draws from all over. Sort of an equal-opportunity employer."

"Well, the captain is Italian, the officers are Croatian, the crew Filipino."

"It's like a model U.N. here."

She smiled bashfully.

"And the clients?" Bryson persisted. "Where do they come from?"

Her smile faded at once, her manner suddenly cold. "I never ask, sir. Please excuse me."

Bryson knew he had pushed too far. Calacanis's staff would be friendly but above all discreet. It would not do to ask about the man himself, of course, but between Dunne's briefing and his own time with the Directorate, he had managed to put together a profile. Vasiliou Calacanis was a Greek born in Turkey to a good family, was sent to Eton with a son of one of England's most powerful arms-manufacturing families, and somehow thereafter—no one knew for sure how—established an alliance with the classmate's family, then went into business selling arms on behalf of the British family to the Greeks fighting the Cypriots. Somewhere along the way, powerful British politicians were paid off, potent connections established, and Vasiliou became Basil and then Sir Basil. He belonged to the best London clubs. His ties to the French were even stronger; one of his main residences was an enormous château on the Avenue Foch in Paris where he entertained regularly the powers from the Quai d'Orsay.

After the collapse of the Berlin Wall, he did a major trade in surplus Eastern European weaponry, particularly dealing with Bulgaria. He profited immensely from selling to both sides of the Iran-Iraq war, shipping scores of helicopters to both. He struck major deals with the Libyans, the Ugandans. From Afghanistan to Congo, several dozen civil wars raged, ethnic and nationalist conflagrations, which Calacanis had fueled by providing easy access to assault rifles, mortars, pistols, land mines, and rockets. He had furnished his yacht-cum-freighter with the blood of hundreds of thousands of innocents.

One of the stewards began to speak discreetly to each of the guests one by one. "Dinner is served, Mr. Coleridge," he said.

The dining room was even more opulent, more outlandishly extravagant, than the stateroom from which they came. On each wall was painted a fantasy mural of the sea, so that it appeared as if they were dining alfresco, on a calm ocean during a bright afternoon, surrounded by graceful sailboats. The long table was covered in a white linen cloth, set with crystal and candles, beneath a great crystal chandelier.

One of the stewards escorted Bryson to a seat near the head of the table, next to a very large barrel-chested man with a close-cropped gray beard and olive complexion. The steward inclined his head toward the great bearded man, whispering something.

"Mr. Coleridge," said Basil Calacanis in the deep rumble of a Russian basso profundo. He extended his hand to Bryson. "Pardon me if I don't get up."

Bryson shook Calacanis's hand firmly as he took his seat. "Not at all. It's a pleasure to meet you. I've heard so much about you."

"Likewise, and likewise. I'm surprised it's taken us so long to meet."

"It's taken me altogether too long to eliminate the middleman," Bryson said wryly. "I got tired of paying retail." Calacanis responded with a booming laugh. As the others were seated around the table, they pretended not to be eavesdropping upon the exchange between their host and his mysterious, favored guest. Bryson noticed one of the dinner guests who seemed to be listening intently, a guest he had not seen at the bar. This was a stylishly dressed man in a pinstriped double-breasted suit with a shoulder-length mane of silver hair. Bryson felt himself go cold with foreboding; the man was familiar to him. Though they had never met each other, Bryson knew the face from surveillance videos and photographs in dossiers. He was a Frenchman who moved nimbly in these circles, a renowned contact for extremist terrorist groups. Bryson could not recall the name, but he knew the longhaired man was an emissary from a powerful, far-right French arms dealer named Jacques Arnaud. Did that mean that Arnaud was supplying Calacanis, or the other way around?

"Had I but known how pleasant it is to shop here, I'd have come long ago," Bryson continued. "This is an extraordinary ship."

"You flatter me," the arms dealer said dismissively. " 'Extraordinary' is hardly the word I would use for this old rust bucket. She's just barely seaworthy. Though you should have seen her when I bought it a good ten years ago from the Maersk shipping line. They were retiring the old tub, and I'm never one to pass up a bargain. But I'm afraid Maersk got the best of me there. The damned boat was badly in need of repair and repainting. Plus about a ton of rust had to be scraped off." He snapped his fingers in the air, and the beautiful blond stewardess appeared with a bottle of Chassagne-Montrachet, pouring a glass for Calacanis and then for Bryson. She barely acknowledged Bryson's presence. Calacanis lifted his glass in Bryson's direction and said with a wink, "To the spoils of war." Bryson toasted as well. "Anyway, the *Spanish Armada* sails at a decent clip—twenty-five, thirty knots—but she gulps two hundred and fifty tons of fuel a day. This is what you Americans call overhead, hmm?"

"I'm Canadian, actually," Bryson said, suddenly alert. Calacanis did not seem the sort of man who made such slips. He casually added, "I doubt she came furnished like this."

"The damned living quarters looked like an old city hospital." Calacanis was looking around the table. "They never come with the amenities one requires. So, Mr. Coleridge, I understand your clients are Africans, is that right?"

"My clients," Bryson said with a polite smile, the avatar of discretion, "are highly motivated buyers."

Calacanis gave another wink. "The Africans have always been some of my best customers—the Congo, Angola, Eritrea. You've always got one faction battling another one down there, and somehow there always seems to be plenty of money on both sides. Let me guess: they're interested in plain-vanilla AK-47s, crates of ammo, landmines, grenades. Maybe rocket-propelled grenades. Sniper rifles with night-vision sights. Antitank weapons. Am I barking up the right tree?"

Bryson shrugged. "Your Kalashnikovs—they're genuine Russian?"

"Forget Russian. That stuff's crap. I've got boxes of Bulgarian Kalashnikovs."

"Ah, nothing but the best for *you*."

Calacanis smiled in appreciation. "Quite so. The Kalashnikovs made by Arsenal, in Bulgaria, are still the finest ones around. Dr. Kalashnikov himself prefers the Bulgarian make. How do you know Hans-Friedrich again?"

"I helped him broker a number of big sales of Thyssen A. G. Fuchs tanks to Saudi Arabia. I introduced him to some oil-soaked friends in the Gulf. Anyway, as for the Kalashnikovs, I'll certainly defer to your expertise," Bryson said graciously. "And assault rifles—"

"For those you simply can't do better than the South African Vektor 5.56mm CR21. Terribly sleek. Once they've tried it, they'll never use anything else. Its integral Vektor reflex optical sight can enhance the probability of a first-time hit by sixty percent. Even if you don't know what the hell you're doing."

"Depleted uranium shells?"

Calacanis arched an eyebrow. "I may be able to dig some up for you. Interesting choice. Twice as heavy as lead, the best antitank weapon you can find. Slices through tanks like a hot knife through butter. And radioactive besides. You say your clients are from Rwanda and Congo?"

"I don't believe I said." The back-and-forth was stretching Bryson's nerves to the breaking point. It was not a negotiation, it was a gavotte, a highly orchestrated dance, each partner watching the other closely, waiting for a misstep. There was something about Calacanis's manner that seemed to indicate he knew more than he was letting on. Did the wily arms merchant accept John T. Coleridge at face value? What if his web of contacts extended deeply, *too* deeply, into the intelligence world? What if somehow, in the years since Bryson had left the Directorate, the Coleridge legend had been rolled up, exposed as fiction by a hypercautious — or vengeful — Ted Waller?

A tiny cellular phone on the table next to Calacanis's dinner plate suddenly rang. Calacanis picked it up and said harshly, "What is it? . . . Yes, Chicky, but he has no credit line with us, I'm afraid." He disconnected the call and placed the phone back on the table.

"My clients are interested in Stinger missiles as well."

"Ah, yes, these are very much in demand. Every terrorist and guerrilla group seems to want a crate of them these days. Thanks to the U.S. government, there's quite a decent inventory of them floating around. The Americans used to pass them out to their friends like candy. Then in the late 1980s some of them found their way onto Iranian gunboats and shot down U.S. Navy helicopters in the Gulf, and suddenly the U.S. was in the embarrassing position of having to buy them back. Washington's offering a hundred thousand dollars for the return of each Stinger, which is four *times* their original cost. Of course, I pay better." Calacanis fell silent, and Bryson realized that the blond stewardess was standing to the Greek's right, bearing a covered serving tray. When Calacanis nodded, she began to serve him a breathtakingly elaborate timbale of salmon tartare with pearly black caviar.

"I take it Washington's a good customer of yours as well," Bryson suggested quietly.

"They have, how do you say, deep pockets," Calacanis murmured vaguely.

"But in certain circles one hears that the *pattern* of buying is being stepped up recently," he went on in a low tone of voice. "That certain organizations in Washington, certain covert agencies that have the latitude to operate without oversight, have been acquiring rather . . . *heavily* from you."

Bryson tried to affect a casual tone, but Calacanis saw right through it and gave Bryson a sidelong glance. "Are you interested in my wares, or in my clients?" the arms dealer said coldly.

Bryson felt himself go numb, realizing how badly he'd miscalculated.

Calacanis started to get up. "Will you excuse me, please? I believe I'm neglecting my other . . . guests."

Quickly, in a low, confiding voice, Bryson said, "I ask for a reason. A *business* reason."

Calacanis turned to him warily. "What sort of business can you possibly have with government agencies?"

"I have something to offer," Bryson said. "Something that might be of interest to a major player not officially connected with a government but who has, as you put it, deep pockets."

"*You* have something to offer *me*? I'm afraid I don't understand. If you wish to transact your own business, you certainly don't need me."

"In this case," Bryson said, lowering his voice yet further, "there's no other acceptable conduit."

"*Conduit?*" Calacanis seemed exasperated. "What on *earth* are you *talking* about?"

Bryson was almost whispering now. Calacanis bent his head to listen. "Plans," Bryson muttered. "Blueprints, specifications that may be worth a great deal of money to certain parties with, shall we say, unlimited budgets. But in no way can my fingerprints be on this. I can't be connected in any way. Your services as conduit, as middleman, for want of a better word, will be remunerated quite handsomely."

"You intrigue me," Calacanis said. "I think we should continue this discussion in private."

Calacanis's library was furnished in delicate French antiques that were invisibly bolted to the floor. Roman blinds and curtains covered two glass walls; the other walls were decorated with framed antique nautical charts and maps. In the middle of one wall was a paneled oak door; where it led, Bryson had no idea.

That the Greek had been so quick to leave his own dinner party was testament to the allure of the blueprints and specification sheets Calacanis now held in his hand. They had been prepared by the graphic artists of the Agency's technical services division, designed to pass close inspection by an arms dealer with long experience in reading such plans.

Calacanis made no attempt to hide his excitement. He looked up from the blueprint, his dark eyes gleaming with avarice. "This is a new generation of the JAVELIN antitank weapon system," he said in hushed awe. "Where the *hell* did you get this?"

Bryson smiled modestly. "You don't divulge trade secrets, and neither do I."

"Lightweight, man-portable, fire-and-forget. The round's the same—the 127-millimeter-diameter missile, of course—but the command launch unit appears to have gotten far more sophisticated, highly resistant to countermeasures. If I'm reading this right, the hit rate's now almost one hundred percent!"

Bryson nodded. "So I'm given to understand."

"Do you have the source codes?"

Bryson knew he meant the software that would allow the weapon to be reverse-engineered. "Indeed."

"There will be no shortage of interested parties; the only question will be who has the resources. This will fetch quite a price."

"I take it you have a customer in mind."

"He's on board the ship at this very moment."

"At dinner?"

"He very politely turned down my invitation. He prefers not to mingle. At the moment he's inspecting the goods." Calacanis picked up his cellular phone and punched out a number. As he waited for it to ring, he remarked, "This gentleman's organization has been on quite the buying spree of late. Massive quantities of mobile armaments. A weapon such as this will interest him, I have no doubt of it, and money seems to be no object for his employers." He paused and said into the phone, "Can you ask Mr. Jenrette to stop by the library, please?"

The interested party, as Calacanis had identified him, appeared at the door of the library barely five minutes later, escorted by the balding red-headed man named Ian who had first greeted Bryson at the helicopter.

His name was Jenrette, but Bryson knew at once that "Jenrette" was only the latest in a series of cover identities. As the middle-aged, tired-looking man with the scraggly gray hair crossed the study to Calacanis's desk, his eyes met Bryson's.

Kowloon.

The rooftop bar at the Miramar Hotel.

Jenrette was a Directorate operative he knew as Vance Gifford.

"This gentleman's organization has been on quite the buying spree of late. Massive quantities of mobile armaments. A weapon such as this will interest him, I have no doubt of it, and money seems to be no object for his employers."

Money no object . . . this gentleman's organization . . . quite the buying spree.

Vance Gifford was still attached to the Directorate, which meant that Harry Dunne was right: the Directorate still lived.

"Mr. Jenrette," said Calacanis, "I'd like you to meet a gentleman who has an interesting new toy I think you and your friends might like to purchase." Ian the bodyguard and aide-de-camp stood with his back erect against the doorjamb, watching in silence.

Vance Gifford stared in shock for the briefest instant before his expression softened, and he gave a smile that Bryson immediately recognized as false. "Mr. — Mr. Coleridge, is it?"

"Please call me John," Bryson said casually. His body was paralyzed; his mind raced.

"Why do I have a feeling we've met somewhere before?" said the Directorate man, feigning joviality.

Bryson chuckled, causing his body to relax. But it was a feint, a ruse,

for he was studying the man's eyes, the minute changes in facial mus-
culature that signaled the truth beneath the lie. *Vance Gifford is an active,
present Directorate operative.* Bryson was sure of it.

He was active when they met eight or nine years ago in East Sector,
a strictly scheduled rendezvous in the Miramar bar in Kowloon. *We
barely knew each other, spent maybe an hour talking business, covert funding and dead drops and the like. Given the compartmentalization, neither
one of us had any idea what the other really did in the organization.*

And Gifford had to be active still, otherwise Calacanis wouldn't have
summoned him here to inspect the prototype—the lure.

"Was it Hong Kong?" Bryson asked. "Taipei? You look familiar as
well." Bryson acted blasé, even amused by the unspecified, unexplained
mix-up in identities. But his heart was racing. He felt perspiration break
out on his brow. His field instincts were still there, still finely honed; but
his psychology, his emotions, were no longer in the proper, hardened
condition. *Gifford's playing it straight,* Bryson realized. *He knows who I
am, but he doesn't know why I'm here. Like a seasoned field man, he's
rolling with it, thank God.* "Anyway, wherever and whenever it was, it's
good to see you again."

"I'm always in the market for a new toy," the Directorate man said
offhandedly. Gifford/Jenrette's eyes were keen; they regarded Bryson furtively. *Surely he knows I'm out.* When a Directorate agent was burned,
the word was circulated at lightning speed, to prevent infiltration attempts
on the part of the disenfranchised one. *But how much does he know of
the circumstances of my termination? Does he regard me as a hostile? Or
as a neutral? Will he assume that I've gone private, like so many covert
operatives did after the end of the Cold War, gone into military procure-
ment? Yet Gifford's smart: he knows he's being offered stolen top-secret
technology, and he knows that's hardly an ordinary business deal, even in
this strange world of black-market arms dealing.*

*One of several things can happen now. He may assume he's being set
up, offered bait with a hook in it. If he does, then he'll conclude I've gone
over—to another government agency, even another side! Baited hooks were
a classic recruitment technique employed by the main foreign intelligence
services.* Bryson's mind whirled. *Maybe he'll assume I'm part of some interagency, internecine bureaucratic battle, a sting of some sort.*

Or worse—what if Gifford suspects me of being an impostor, of running an operation against Calacanis, maybe even against Calacanis's clients?

This was madness! There was no way to anticipate Gifford's response, no way to be sure. The only thing was to be prepared for anything.

Calacanis's face betrayed nothing. The Greek beckoned the Directorate man to his desk, across which he had spread out the blueprints and specs and source codes for the sophisticated weapon design. Gifford walked over and bent down to inspect the plans with great intensity.

Gifford's lips barely moved while he whispered something to the arms merchant without looking at him.

Calacanis nodded, looked up, and said blandly, "Will you please excuse us, Mr. Coleridge? Mr. Jenrette and I should like to confer privately."

Calacanis rose and opened the oak paneled door, which Bryson now saw led to a private study. Jenrette followed, and the door closed behind them. Bryson sat on one of Calacanis's antique French side chairs, frozen like an insect trapped in amber. Outwardly he was waiting patiently, a middleman greedily contemplating great riches from a deal about to be consummated. Inwardly his mind was spinning, desperately trying to anticipate the next move. It all came down to how Jenrette decided to play it. What had the man whispered? How could Jenrette reveal how he knew Bryson without telling Calacanis about his work with the Directorate? Was Jenrette prepared to do that? How much could be divulged? How deep was Jenrette's cover? These were unknowable things, fundamentally. Too, the man who called himself Jenrette had no idea what Bryson was doing here. For all he knew, Bryson had indeed gone private and was selling weapons designs; how could Jenrette/Gifford know otherwise?

The study door opened, and Bryson looked up. It was the blond stewardess, holding aloft a tray of empty glasses and a bottle of what looked like port. Obviously she had been summoned by the Greek and had entered Calacanis's private study by means of another passage. She seemed not to notice Bryson as she retrieved used champagne flutes and wineglasses from the desk Calacanis had been using, then approached Bryson. Briefly stooping to pick up a large glass ashtray, laden with the remains of Cuban cigars, from the small end table next to Bryson, she suddenly spoke, her words low and almost inaudible.

"You're a popular man, Mr. Coleridge," she murmured without even giving him so much as a glance. She placed the ashtray on her serving platter. "Four friends of yours await you in the next room." Bryson looked up at her, saw her eyes dart to the oak paneled door on the other side of the library. "Try not to bleed on the Heriz runner. It's quite rare, and one of Mr. Calacanis's favorites." Then she was gone.

Bryson stiffened, his body surging with adrenaline. Yet he knew enough to keep still, betray nothing.

What did this mean?

Was an ambush being set up in the adjacent study? Was she part of the setup? If not—why had she just warned him?

The door to Calacanis's study suddenly opened again. It was Calacanis himself, with Ian, his bodyguard, looming just behind him in the doorway. Gifford/Jenrette stood farther in the background.

"Mr. Coleridge," Calacanis called out, "won't you join us, please?"

For a split-second Bryson stared, trying to assess the Greek's intentions. "Certainly," he replied, "in a moment. I think I left something important in the bar."

"Mr. Coleridge, I'm afraid we really have no time to waste," Calacanis said in a loud, harsh voice.

"This won't take a minute," Bryson said, turning toward the exit door that led to the dining room. It was blocked, he now saw, by another armed guard. But instead of staying put, Bryson continued his stride toward the exit as if nothing were wrong. Now he was but a few feet away from the stocky bodyguard who had just arrived.

"I'm sorry, Mr. Coleridge, we really must have a word, you and I," Calacanis said with a slight nod that was clearly a signal to the guard at the door. Bryson's body surged with adrenaline as the stocky bodyguard turned to secure the door.

Now!

He lunged forward, slamming the bodyguard against the hard wooden doorframe of the open door, the sudden movement catching the bodyguard unprepared. The guard struggled, reaching for his weapon, but Bryson hammered his right foot into the man's abdomen.

An alarm suddenly went off, ear-piercingly loud, clearly triggered by

Calacanis, who was shouting. As the bodyguard momentarily lost his balance, Bryson took advantage of the brief moment of vulnerability to sink his right knee into the man's midsection, at the same time gripping the face with his right hand and forcing him to the floor.

"Stop right there!" thundered Calacanis.

Bryson turned quickly and saw that Ian, the other bodyguard, had assumed a marksman's stance, leveling a gun, a .38 caliber pistol, with both hands.

In that instant, the stocky bodyguard beneath him managed to rear up, screaming, exerting all of his strength, but Bryson leveraged that motion against his adversary, pushing the man up and over, his right hand clawing the bodyguard's eyes, so that the man's head was a shield of sorts, right in front of his own face. Ian would never fire with such a high probability of striking another guard.

Suddenly there was an explosion, and Bryson felt the spray of blood. A dark red hole appeared in the middle of the bodyguard's forehead; the man slumped, dead weight. Ian had, surely by accident, killed his own colleague.

Now Bryson pivoted, arced his body suddenly to one side, just missing the explosion of another bullet, and spun through the open door and into the hallway. Bullets exploded behind him, splintering wood and pockmarking the metal bulkheads. With alarms shrieking all around him at deafening volume, he broke into a run down the corridor.

Washington, D.C.

"Let's face it. You're not going to be deterred whatever I say, isn't that right?" Roger Fry looked at Senator James Cassidy expectantly. In the four years that Fry had been his chief of staff, he had helped draft policy statements for the Hill and speeches for the hustings. The Senator had turned to him whenever a thorny issue arose. Fry, a slight, red-haired man in his early forties, was someone he could always depend upon for an instant electoral read. Price supports for dairy farmers? City advocates could cry bloody murder if you took one position, while the agribusiness lobby would come after you if you took the other. Often enough, Fry would say, "Jim, it's a wash—vote your conscience," knowing that Cassidy had made a career of doing so anyway.

The late-afternoon sun streamed through the venetian blinds, casting slats of shadows on the floor of his Senate office and bringing out the glow from Cassidy's burnished mahogany desk. The senator from Massachusetts looked up from his briefing papers and met Fry's gaze. "I hope you realize how valuable you are to me, Rog," he said, a smile playing at his lips. "It's because you're so good at looking after the pragmatic, temporizing, horse-trading side of this business that, every once in a while, I can actually get on my hind legs and say what I believe."

Fry was always struck by how distinguished, how damned *senatorial* Cassidy looked: the coifed mane of wavy silver hair, the chiseled features. A little over six feet, the senator was photogenic with his broad face and high cheekbones, but up close, the eyes were what made him: they could grow warm and intimate, making constituents feel as if they'd found a soul mate, or turn cool and unsparing, drilling through a squirrelly witness who'd come before his committee.

"Every once in a while?" Fry shook his head. "Too damn often, if you ask me. Too damned often for your own political health. And one of these days, it's going to catch up with you. The last election wasn't a walk in the park, if I may remind you."

"You worry too much, Rog."

"Somebody has to, around here."

"Listen, the constituents care about these things. Did I show you this letter?" It was from a woman who lived on Massachusetts's north shore. She had sued a marketing company and discovered they had thirty single-spaced pages of information on her, going back fifteen years. The company knew, and was in the business of selling, more than nine hundred separate items of information about her—including her choice of sleeping aids and antacids and hemorrhoid ointments and the soap she used when she showered; it itemized her divorce, medical procedures, credit ratings, her every traffic infraction. But there was nothing unusual about this; the company had similar dossiers on millions of Americans. The only thing unusual was that she found out about it. That letter, and a few dozen like it, was what first aroused Cassidy's concern.

"You forget, Jim, I answered that letter personally," replied Fry. "I'm just saying you don't know what you're stirring up this time around. This goes to the heart of the way business works today."

"That's why it's worth talking about," said the senator quietly.

"Sometimes it's more important to live and fight another day." But Fry knew what Cassidy was like when he had a bee in his bonnet: moral outrage would trump the cool calculation of political interest. The senator wasn't a saint: he sometimes drank too much and, especially in his early years when his hair was a glossy black, slept around too freely. At the same time, Cassidy had always maintained a core of political integrity: all things being equal, he did try to do the right thing, at least where the rightness of the thing was as clear as the political cost of doing so. It was a strain of idealism that Fry railed against and, almost despite himself, respected.

"You remember how Ambrose Bierce defined a statesman?" The senator winked at him. "A politician who, as a result of equal pressure from all sides, remains upright."

"I was in the cloakroom yesterday and found out you've got a new nickname," Fry said, smiling thinly. "You'll like this one, Jim: 'Senator Cassandra.' "

Cassidy frowned. "Nobody listened to Cassandra—but they should have," he grunted. "At least she could say she told 'em so. . . ." He broke off. They'd been through it; they'd had this conversation. Fry was being protective of him, and Cassidy had heard him out. But on this subject, there wasn't anything left to talk about.

Senator Cassidy was going to do what he was going to do, and there was no stopping him.

No matter what it cost.

CHAPTER SIX

Footsteps thundered behind him on the steel deck as Bryson raced toward the center stairwell. Spying the elevator, he paused but a split-second before he rejected that option; the elevator moved slowly, and once inside it, he would be in a vertical coffin, easy prey for anyone able to shut off the elevator mechanism. No, he would take the stairs, noisy as they were. There was no other way out of the superstructure. He had no choice. *Up or down?* Up toward the wheelhouse, the bridge, would be an unexpected move, yet it risked his getting trapped on an upper deck with few egresses. No, that was a bad idea; down was the only way that made sense, down to the main deck and escape.

Escape? How? There was only one way off the ship, and that was off the main deck and into the water—whether by jumping, which was suicide in these cold Atlantic waters, or down the gangplank, which was too slow and too exposed a descent.

Jesus! There was no way out!

No, he mustn't think that way; there had to be a way out, and he would find it.

He was like a rat in a maze; that he didn't know the layout of this immense ship put him at a distinct disadvantage to his pursuers. Yet the very size of the vessel guaranteed endless passages in which to lose the chasers, hide if needed.

He vaulted to the stairs and began taking them two and three at a time, while above him came shouts. One of the bodyguards was dead, but there were no doubt quite a few others, alerted and summoned by the various alarms and by two-way radios. The footsteps and shouts grew increasingly loud and frantic from the stairwell. His pursuers had increased in number, and it was likely a matter of just seconds before others emerged from other parts of the ship.

The ship's whistles and alarms sounded in a cacophony of raucous whoops and metallic grunts. A landing led to a short passageway that seemed to open onto an outside section of a deck. Quietly he opened the door, closed it behind him silently, ran straight ahead, and found himself on the aft deck, open to the elements. The sky was black, the waves lapped gently at the stern. He ran to the railing, looking for the welded steel grips and steps one sometimes found on the side of ships that were used for emergency escape. He could climb down to another level of the ship, he quickly thought, and lose them that way.

But there were no steel grips on the hull. The only way out of here was down.

Suddenly there came the explosion of gunfire. A bullet ricocheted off a metal capstan with a high-pitched pinging sound. He spun away from the railing and into the shadow behind a steel mooring winch on which the steel hawse cable was wound around capstan drums, like some giant spool of thread, then dove behind it for cover. Another round of bullets pitted the metal just a few feet from his head.

They were firing without restraint here, and he realized that with the open sea behind him they could fire heedlessly without fear of damaging any of the ship's delicate navigational equipment.

Inside the ship they would have to be more careful when firing rounds. And that was his protection! They would not hesitate to kill him, but they would not want to damage their ship — or its precious cargo.

He would have to get out of the open areas and back into the belly of the ship. Not only would hiding places be numerous there, but he could take advantage of their hesitance to fire freely.

But now what? Here he was, trapped out in the open, with only a great steel capstan as protection. This was the most hazardous place for him on the entire ship.

There seemed to be two or three gunmen here, no more and no less. Clearly he was outnumbered. He needed to divert them, misdirect them, but how? Looking around wildly, he spotted something. Behind an iron bollard, a tall cylinder rising several feet from the deck, he noticed a paint can, left there no doubt by a deckhand. He crawled forward along the deck and grabbed the can. It was almost empty.

There was a sudden burst of gunfire as he was spotted.

He drew back quickly, grasping the handle of the can, then immediately hurling it forward toward the railing, where it struck the hawse pipe. He peered around the barricade, saw both men turn toward the source of the clatter. One of them ran toward it, away from where Bryson had concealed himself. The other spun around in a classic marksman's position, looking from one side to another. As the first man raced toward the starboard side of the ship, the second circled around toward the port side, his weapon pointed toward the mooring winch the whole time. This man saw through the ruse, suspected Bryson of having caused the diversion, believed Bryson was still huddled behind the winch.

But he did not expect Bryson to come around the winch toward him. Now Bryson was just a few feet away from the second security guard. A sudden shout came from the first man, a declaration that Bryson was not there, an unprofessional move. The second man, just inches away from Bryson, turned, distracted.

Move!

Now!

Bryson lunged and tackled the man to the deck, slamming his knee into the man's stomach. The man gasped as the air left his lungs, and as he reared up, Bryson slammed his elbow into the man's throat. He could hear the crunch of cartilage as he vised the man's throat in a hammerlock. The man roared in pain, which gave Bryson the opportunity he needed to grab the security man's gun, try to wrench it out of his hand. But the security guard was a professional, and he would not give his weapon up so easily; despite the great pain Bryson was inflicting, Calacanis's soldier struggled, refusing to yield the pistol. Gunfire came from the other side of the deck, fired by the first gunman as he ran toward his colleague, which was jarring his aim. Bryson twisted the weapon around until the man's wrist cracked; the ligaments tore audibly, and the gun now turned back toward the man's own chest. His index finger jabbed at the trigger, finally grabbed it, and Bryson bent his wrist and fired.

The soldier arched backward, his chest punctured. Bryson's aim was perfect, even in the confusion of the struggle; he had hit the man's heart.

Grabbing the weapon from the limp fingers, he sprung to his feet and began firing wildly in the general direction of the running man, who stopped to fire back, knowing that firing while running made for terrible aim. That instant's pause was the window Bryson needed. He let loose a volley of semiautomatic fire, one round piercing his attacker's forehead. The man toppled to one side, crumpled against the railing, dead.

For a few seconds he was safe, Bryson calculated. But he could hear footsteps on the deck, growing louder and coming closer, and he heard the accompanying shouts, and that told him he was hardly safe at all.

Now where?

Immediately up ahead he saw a door marked DIESEL GENERATOR ROOM. This had to lead to the engine room, which at the moment seemed the best place to escape. He raced across the deck, yanked open the door, and ran down a steep, narrow set of metal stairs painted green. He was in a large, open area that was deafeningly loud. The auxiliary diesel generators here were in operation, providing power for the ship, since its engine was off. With several large strides he ran across a railing that circled the room above the mammoth generators.

Through the rumble he could hear that his pursuers had followed him down here, and in a moment he saw several silhouetted figures racing down the metal steps, visible only as shadows in the dim light with its sickly green cast.

There were four of them, running down the steep stairways with a stiffness, an awkwardness, that puzzled him for a moment, until he saw that two of them were wearing night-vision goggles, the others carrying sniper rifles outfitted with night-vision scopes. The outlines were unmistakable.

He raised the stolen pistol, quickly aimed at the first man down the stairs, and—

Suddenly all was darkness!

The lights in the room had been extinguished, probably from some central control room. No wonder they carried such equipment! By eliminating all light they hoped to gain the advantage provided by their sophisticated weaponry. On a ship such as this, a floating arsenal, there would be no shortage of such matériel.

But he fired anyway, into the darkness, in the direction toward which he had been aiming just a second or two ago. He heard a cry, then a crash. One man was down. But it was insanity to just keep firing into the darkness, using up precious ammunition when he had no idea how many rounds remained in the weapon and had no way to obtain any more.

It was what they wanted him to do.

They expected him to respond like a cornered animal, a drowning rat. To flail away desperately. To fire into the darkness with abandon. Use up the ammunition pointlessly, foolishly. And then, aided by their night vision, they would easily hunt him down.

Blinded in the darkness, he extended his arms, felt around for obstacles, both to avoid and to hide behind. The men wearing infrared monocular night-vision units, the lenses strapped against their eyes by means of a head harness and helmet mount, were doubtless also carrying handguns. The others had rifles fitted with advanced infrared weapon sights. Both allowed the user to see in total darkness by detecting the differentials in thermal patterns given off by animate and inanimate objects. Short-range thermal-imaging scopes had been used with great success during the Falklands war in 1982, in the Gulf in 1991. But these, Bryson recognized, were state-of-the-art RAPTOR night-vision weapon sights, lightweight, super accurate, with extreme long-range accuracy. They were often used by combat snipers, mounted on their .50 caliber sniper rifles.

Oh, dear God. The playing field was hardly level, as if it ever was. The noise of the generator seemed, in the darkness, even louder.

In the pitch blackness he saw a tiny, dancing red dot flit across his field of vision.

Someone had located him and was aiming directly at his face, his eyes!

Triangulate! Estimate the sniper's location based on the direction from which the infrared reticule was aiming at him. This wasn't his first time as the target of a sniper with a night-vision scope, and he had learned to estimate the distance of the shooter.

But every second he paused to aim gave his enemy, who saw him as a green object against a darker green or black background, time to aim as well. And his enemy knew for certain where he was located, whereas Bryson was relying on luck and rusty experience. And how could he possibly aim at blackness? What was there to aim at?

He squinted to bring up available light, but there really was none to be summoned into his eyes. Instead, he raised his pistol and fired.

A scream!

He had hit someone, though how well he couldn't yet tell.

But a second or two afterward, a bullet spat against the machinery to his left, pinging loudly. Night vision or no, his enemies had missed. They did not seem to care whether their rounds struck the generator or not. The machinery was encased in steel, heavy-gauge and durable.

That meant they did not care what they hit, or whether they missed. So how many more were there? If the second man was indeed down, that meant two remained. The problem was that the generator was so loud he could not hear footsteps approaching, nor the ragged breathing of a wounded man. He was in effect both blind *and* deaf.

As he raced down the catwalk, one hand outstretched before him to protect him from striking unseen objects, the other grasping his weapon, he heard gunfire again. One round whizzed so close to his head he could feel the gust of wind against his scalp.

Then his searching hand struck something hard—a bulkhead. He had come to a wall at one end of the cavernous room. He swung his weapon first to one side, then to the other, each time striking steel railing.

He was trapped.

Then he became aware of the dancing red bead in the darkness, as one of the snipers aimed at the green oval that was, in the night-vision scope, his head.

He thrust the pistol into the air in front of himself, prepared to aim at nothing again. Then he shouted: "Go ahead! If you miss me, you risk damaging the generator. That's a lot of delicate electronic equipment there, microchips easily shattered. Kill the generator, and you kill all the power in the ship—and see what Calacanis thinks about that."

A split-second of silence. He even thought he saw the red dot waver, though he knew he might be imagining things.

There was a low chuckle, and the infrared reticule passed across his field of vision again, steadied, and then—

The spit of a silenced weapon, and then three more spits, and then came a scream and the sound of another body crashing to the steel floor of the catwalk.

What?

Who had fired at his enemy? Someone had done it—Bryson knew it hadn't been him! Someone had fired a round of shots using a silenced pistol.

Someone had fired at his pursuers—and perhaps even eliminated them!

"Don't move!" Bryson shouted into the darkness at the one remaining gunman he calculated had to be out there. His cry made no sense, he knew—why should any of his adversaries, equipped as they were with night-vision goggles or sights, pay any attention?—but such a shout, unexpected and even illogical, could buy him a few seconds of confusion.

"Don't shoot!" came another voice, faint against the deafening noise of the generators.

A woman's.

It was the voice of a woman.

Bryson froze. He thought he had seen only men descend the metal stairs into the room, but the bulky equipment could easily disguise a female silhouette.

But what did she mean, *don't shoot?*

Bryson shouted, "Put down your weapon!"

Suddenly he was blinded by a flash of light, and he realized that the lights in this room had suddenly gone on! Brighter than they'd been before.

What was going on?

In a second or two his eyes readjusted to the light, and there, standing on a catwalk high above, he could make out the shape of the woman who had been speaking to him. The woman wore a white uniform—the uniform of Calacanis's steward from the dinner that seemed so much a part of the distant past.

On her head she wore a helmet and head-harness, the lens of an infrared monocular night-vision unit obscuring half her face. Yet Bryson recognized her as the beautiful blonde he had exchanged a few words with before dinner, and who had spoken a few hasty words to him just before the violence had begun—words he now recognized as indeed a genuine warning.

And here she was, crouched in a marksman's stance, gripping the butt of a Ruger with a long silencer attached, moving it from one side to another, steadily back and forth. He realized, too, that there were four bodies sprawled at different points around the generator room—two from the deck close to the generator, one at the beginning of the catwalk on which he was standing, and a fourth lying a mere six feet away, alarmingly close.

And he saw that the woman was not aiming at him. She was covering him, aiming everywhere else, protecting him against others! The stewardess was standing by a small bank of controls and switches; that was where she had turned the lights on. "Come on!" she shouted over a dull roar. "This way!"

What the hell was going on?

Bryson stared in bafflement.

"Come on, let's go!" the woman shouted angrily. Her accent was definitely Levantine.

"What do you want?" Bryson shouted back, more to stall for time than to elicit any response. For what could this be but a trap—a clever one but a trap nonetheless?

"What the hell do you think?" she shouted, turning her gun toward him, returning to the marksman's stance. He aimed his gun directly at her, and just as he was about to pull the trigger, he saw her shift the barrel a few inches to her right, heard the cough of another silenced round.

And at the same instant he both heard a crash and saw a body topple from the catwalk just above him.

Another sniper with a night-vision-equipped rifle. Dead.

She had just killed him.

The sniper had stolen silently up to him, about to kill him, and she had dropped him first.

"Move it!" the woman shouted to him. "Before any others come here. If you want to save your own life, move your ass!"

"Who are you?" Bryson shouted back, stunned.

"What does it matter right now?" She pushed the night-vision monocular up and off her face, so that it rested on the top of her head. "Please, there's no time! For God's sake, look at your situation, calculate your odds. What the hell *choice* do you have?"

CHAPTER SEVEN

Bryson stared at the woman.

"Come *on!*" she called, her voice rising in desperation. "If I wanted to kill you, I would have done so already. I've got the advantage, I've got the infrared—not you."

"You don't have the advantage now," Bryson called back, his grip steady on his stolen weapon, lowered at his side.

"I know this ship inside and out. Now, if you want to stay here and play games, be my guest. I have no choice now but to get off the ship. Calacanis's security force is large—there are plenty of others, probably on the way right now." With her free hand she pointed toward an object mounted high on one of the bulkheads near the ceiling of the generator room. Bryson recognized it as a surveillance camera. "He has much of the ship on camera, but not all. So you can follow me and save your life, or you can stay here and be killed. The choice is yours!" She turned quickly and raced down the catwalk and up a short set of metal stairs to a hatch cover. Unlatching it, she glanced back and jerked her head toward the opening, signaling him to follow.

Bryson hesitated no more than a few more seconds before he did so.

His mind spun; he tried to make sense of the woman. *Questions!* Who *was* she? What was she doing, what did she want, why was she here?

The woman was obviously no mere ship's steward.

So who *was* she?

She beckoned; he came through the hatchway behind her, all the while gripping his weapon.

"What are you —?" he began.

"*Quiet!*" she hissed. "Sound carries far here." She shut the hatch door behind him and slid home a large deadbolt. The painfully loud noise of the generator room was gone. "This is an antipirate ship, fortunately for us. Specially constructed so passages can be closed, locked."

He caught her eyes, momentarily distracted by her remarkable beauty. "You're right," he said quietly yet forcefully, "I don't have much choice right now, but you'd better tell me what's going on here."

She gave him a stare that was at once forthright and defiant and whispered, "No *time* for explanations right now. I'm undercover here, too. Following arms transfers to certain parties that want to blast Israel back to the Stone Age."

Mossad, he told himself. But her accent told him she was Lebanese, from the Bekaa Valley; something wasn't quite right. Would a Mossad field operative be Lebanese, not Israeli?

She cocked her head as if hearing some distant noise he could not perceive.

"This way," she said abruptly, vaulting up the steel stairs. He followed her to a landing, then out a hatch that opened into a long, empty, dark corridor. She paused for a moment, looked both ways. As his eyes adjusted to the dim light, he saw that the tunnel went on and on, as far as he could see. It seemed to run the entire length of the ship, from bow to stern; it appeared to be a little-used service alley. "Come!" she hissed, suddenly breaking into a run.

Bryson followed, lengthening his strides to adjust to the woman's lightning-fast pace. He observed that her tread was odd: springy and light, virtually silent. He emulated her, realizing that she was attempting to minimize the reverberation against the steel surface — both to keep from being heard and to be able to listen to any followers, he guessed.

Within a minute, when they had run a few hundred feet down the dark tunnel, he thought he heard a muffled noise coming from the aft end, behind them. He turned his head, noticed a shift in the pattern of the shadows at the far end. But before he could say anything to her, he saw her swerve to the right and flatten herself against the steel bulkhead, behind a vertical steel girder. He did the same, though not a second too soon.

There was an explosion, a burst of automatic gunfire. Bullets spat into the bulkhead, ringing, clattering against the deck.

Whipping his head to his left, he saw a plume of flame shooting from a machine gun at the far end of the tunnel, the shooter shadowy and indistinct. There came another burst of gunfire, and then the killer was running down the corridor toward them.

The woman was struggling with a hatch cover. "Shit! It's painted shut!" she whispered. With a quick glance back down the long, dark passage at the approaching assassin, she said, "This way!" Suddenly leaping forward, away from the protective shelter of the bulkhead and its steel girders, she raced ahead. She was right to move; otherwise, they would be trapped here, obvious targets. He peered quickly around the girder, looked back, and saw the shooter slow his pace, raise his Uzi submachine gun, and aim it directly at the woman.

Bryson did not hesitate. He pointed his pistol toward the killer, squeezed the trigger twice in succession. One round exploded; the second squeeze of the trigger produced nothing more than a small click. The chamber was empty, as was the magazine.

But the shooter was down. The pursuer's Uzi crashed to the deck as he tumbled awkwardly to one side. Even from this distance Bryson could see the man was dead.

The steward turned back with a grim, fearful expression and saw what had happened. She gave Bryson a quick look of what might have been appreciation, but said nothing. He raced to catch up with the woman.

For the moment they were safe. Now, suddenly, she veered off to the right and stopped abruptly at another section of bulkhead, also divided by vertical girders. She leaned over, grabbed a bar that was mounted over an oval opening in the bulkhead the size of a manhole, and agilely swung her feet into the hole like a child playing on monkey bars. In an instant she had disappeared. He did the same, though somewhat more awkwardly: as physically agile as he was, he lacked her apparent familiarity with the ship.

They were in a box-shaped, low-ceilinged compartment that was almost totally dark, the only light coming from the dim service alley. When his vision adapted to the dark, he realized they were in a square space that connected to another one, by means of another manhole, and then another, and another. He could see clear across to the other side of the ship. This was a thwartships passage, he realized, the sections separated by heavy steel girders. She was peering into the next compartment, then without warning she grabbed on to the bar and swung her body inward, feet first.

He followed suit, but the moment he got to his feet, he heard her whisper, "Shh! *Listen!*"

He could hear the distant hammering of footsteps on steel. The sound seemed to be emanating from the service alley from which they had come, and also from a level above. It sounded like at least half a dozen men.

She spoke quickly, in a low voice. "I'm sure they've found the one you killed. Which tells them you're armed, probably a professional." Her English was heavily accented but remarkably fluent. Her intonation seemed to be questioning, though he couldn't see her facial expression. "Although it's obvious you are, if you've survived this far. They also know you—we—can't have gotten too far yet."

"I don't know who you are, yet you're risking your life for me. You don't owe me anything, but an explanation would be appreciated."

"Look, if we get out of here, we'll have time to talk. Right now we don't. Now, do you have any other weapon on you?"

He shook his head. "Just this damn thing, and it's empty."

"Not good. We're way outnumbered. There are enough of them to fan out, search every passage, every hold. And as we've just seen, they're equipped with some serious weaponry."

"There's no shortage of it on this ship," Bryson remarked. "How far are we from the containers?"

"Containers?"

"The boxes. The cargo."

Even in the semidarkness he could see a white flash of smile as she realized what he was saying. "Ah, yes. Not far at all. But I don't know what's in them."

"Then we'll just have to look. Do we have to go back out to the service alley?"

"No. There's a passageway cut into the floor of one of these box girders. But I don't know which one, and without lights, we run the risk of just stepping down into it."

Bryson reached into a pocket, retrieved a book of matches, lit one. The compartment instantly lit up with a feeble amber light. He walked over to the next opening, the rush of air extinguishing the flame, and he lit another. She ran alongside and looked into the adjoining space. "There it is," she said. Bryson waved the match out just before it burned down to his finger. She reached out her hand to take the matchbook; he handed it over, understanding that, since she was in the lead, she had the more immediate need.

As soon as the darkness returned, she grabbed the steel bar, lifted her feet, and thrust them through. As she pulled herself erect by means of another handhold mounted inside the next compartment, she tapped her feet against the deck, searching out solid steel. "Okay. Careful."

He swung himself through the manhole, alighting carefully, keeping to the edges of the compartment floor. She was already descending into the vertical passage by means of a steel ladder that was welded in place. As Bryson waited to follow her down, he heard loud footsteps approaching, accompanied by shouts; then he could see a beam of light from a powerful flashlight illuminate the service alley they'd come from. He ducked down to the steel floor just as a flashlight beam shone directly at them. The light moved from side to side slowly.

He froze, his face pressed against the cold steel. He was aware of the loud ship's Klaxons, still blaring ceaselessly, but strangely, they had become almost background noise against which he could now hear other, more subtle, sounds.

He held his breath. The light moved to the center of the passage, then stopped, as if they had located him. He felt his heart hammer so loudly he swore it was audible. Then the beam moved off to one side and was gone.

The loud footsteps seemed to be passing by. "Nothing here!" a voice called out.

He waited a full minute before allowing himself to move. It seemed an eternity. Then he gingerly felt around for the smooth round edges of the opening in the floor until his fingers encountered the jutting steel of the ladder.

In a few seconds he, too, was climbing down the ladder.

They seemed to be descending for hundreds of feet, though he knew it had to be less than that. Finally the ladder came to an end, and the two of them were crawling through a long, dark horizontal tunnel whose floor was damp and smelled of bilge water. The tunnel was so low that they could not stand erect. The footfalls of the pursuers were now so distant and muffled they were all but inaudible. The woman moved rapidly through the tunnel, bent over, almost crab-walking, and Bryson found himself doing the same. Then the tunnel branched to the right, and she grabbed hold of another vertical metal ladder and began climbing nimbly upward. Bryson followed, but this ascent was a brief one; it led to what looked like another alley. The woman lit a match, whose flame revealed that on either side of the alley were steep, high corrugated-steel walls; in a moment, he realized that the walls were in fact the ends of steel shipping containers packed closely together. The walkway ran between two long rows of containers.

She stopped, knelt, lighted another match, and inspected a label plastered at the end panel of one container. "Steel Eagle 105, 107, 111 . . ." she read quietly.

"Knives. Field-grade, tactical-ops. Keep looking."

She moved on to the next container. "Omega Technologies—"

"Electronic warfare components. Jesus, they've got everything here. But that's not going to do us any good."

"Mark-Twelve IFF Crypto—"

"Crypto systems for transponders or interrogators. Try the next bay. Hurry!"

Meanwhile, Bryson was squatting in front of a container in the row opposite, trying to make out the label by the dim light emitting from the woman's match a few feet away. "I think we got something here," he said.

"XM84 stun grenades, nonlethal, nonfragmentation. Flash-and-bang." He muttered to himself, "I'd prefer something lethal, but beggars can't be choosers."

Quietly, she continued to read aloud: "AN/PSC-11 SCAMP."

"Several-Channel Anti-Jam Man-Portable. Keep going."

She waved out one match and lit another. "ANFATDS?"

"Army Field Artillery Tactical Data System. Not going to help us much either."

"AN/PRC-132 SOHFRAD?"

"Special Operations High Frequency Radio. Nope."

"Tadiran—"

He cut her off. "Israeli telecommunications and electronics maker. From your homeland. Nothing we can use."

Then he noticed the label on the adjoining container: M-76 grenades, and M-25 CS riot grenades, used by the military and police for crowd control. "Here we go," he said excitedly, though restraining the volume. "This is exactly what we need. Now, do you know how to open these things?"

She turned back toward him. "All we need is a bolt-cutter. These containers are high-security-sealed to prevent pilferage—they're not really locked in any serious way."

The first container came open easily once the high-security seal was snapped off. The metal lashing gear crisscrossing the front end of the nine-foot-high container slid out quickly, and then a door opened. Inside were stacked wooden crates of grenades and other armaments: a veritable Aladdin's cave of weaponry.

Ten minutes later they had assembled a pile of assorted arms. Once they had familiarized themselves with how to use them and how to keep them from going off accidentally, Bryson and the woman began stuffing the smaller objects, the grenades and ammunition and the like, into the pockets of their Kevlar body armor plates. The larger objects, they secured to their shoulders and backs by means of makeshift holsters, rucksacks, and slings of rope; the largest ones they would simply carry. Each wore Kevlar helmets with attached face shields.

Suddenly there came an enormous crash from directly overhead, then another. The screech of metal scraping against metal. Bryson slipped into the narrow gap between two containers and wordlessly signaled to the woman to do the same.

A sliver of bright light appeared above as a trapdoor in the ceiling appeared to open, actually an opening in the hatchway covering this bay of the cargo hold. The light came from high-intensity flashlights, several of them, in the hands of three or four of Calacanis's soldiers. Behind them, beside them, there were others, many others, and even from this angle, diagonally below, Bryson could see they were heavily armed.

No! He was expecting a confrontation, but not here, not so soon! There had been no opportunity to formulate a strategy, to coordinate with the nameless blond woman who had for some reason become his accomplice.

He seized the grip of the Bulgarian-made Kalashnikov AK-47 assault rifle and slowly angled it upward, mentally running through his options. To fire at the men from here would be the equivalent of sending up a flare confirming his location. Calacanis's men couldn't be certain that Bryson and the woman were here.

Then Bryson caught a glimpse of the array of large weapons that lay abandoned on the steel walkway floor. That told his enemies that they had guessed right, or rather, that they had accurately pinpointed the sounds from below—that their quarry was either here or had just been here.

But why weren't they firing?

When you're outnumbered, go on the offensive. His instincts told him to fire first, to pick off as many of his pursuers as he could, whether it gave away their positions or not.

He raised the Kalashnikov, peered through the low-light, variable-intensity illuminated sight to zero the reticle, and squeezed the trigger.

An explosion, followed instantly by an agonized scream, and one of Calacanis's soldiers toppled from the ramparts above all the way down to the steel ramp a few feet away. Bryson's aim was precise; the man, struck in the forehead, was dead.

Bryson pulled into the shadows of the recess between containers, bracing for the full-automatic explosion of gunfire that he knew would be the response.

But nothing came!

There was a shout from above, a barked command. The men drew back and assumed firing stances, but did not fire!

Why the hell not?

Baffled, Bryson raised his weapon again and squeezed off two more carefully aimed shots. One of the men went down right away, dead; another sagged to his feet, screaming in pain.

Suddenly Bryson realized: they had been ordered to hold their fire!

They could not risk firing their weapons so near the containers! The corrugated-steel shipping crates were filled with the most explosive, highly flammable arms—not all of them, of course, but enough to make it dangerous. One misplaced round that penetrated the thin steel skin of a container might detonate a cache of bombs, of C-4 plastic explosives, or who knows what else, setting off a conflagration so immense that it might sink the vast ship.

As long as he sought cover between containers, then they would not fire. Yet the instant he or the woman emerged and were safely away from the containers, a sharpshooter would attempt to take them out. This meant that Bryson was safe as long as he remained in position here—but there was no escape, no way out, and his enemies surely knew that. They could wait him out, wait for him to blunder.

He released his hold on the Kalashnikov, let it dangle by its strap at his side. From here he could see that the blonde was crouched between two containers twenty feet away or so, watching him, waiting to see what he would do. Bryson jabbed his thumb first to the left, then to the right, an unspoken question: *Which way out?*

Her reply was immediate, also signaled by means of hand gestures: the only way out was to emerge from the shelter of the containers, and take the ramp back in the direction from which they had come. Shit! They had no choice but to expose themselves! Bryson pointed to himself, telling her that he would go first. Then he raised his other major tactical weapon, a South African–made Uzi submachine gun. At the same time he began to sidle out from the protective alley, keeping his back against one of the containers, until he was out in the open, the Uzi pointed toward the guards above. As swiftly as they could, given the burden of the load of weaponry they were saddled down with, they moved toward their only escape.

Slowly the woman emerged, too, and now both of them sidled down the ramp, their backs against the enormous steel boxes. Several powerful, crisscrossing beams of light shone directly at them, in their eyes, illuminating their every move. In his peripheral vision Bryson could see several of the shooters shifting positions, aiming at them from oblique angles so they could fire at them without fear of striking the containers. But it would take precise marksmanship.

And Bryson did not intend to allow them the opportunity.

He shifted the Kalashnikov toward the shooters, and as he released the safety, he heard a loud clattering from behind. He turned quickly to look and saw men clambering out of the hatch that had been their escape route! These men, at much closer range, their aim therefore more reliable, might not be so hesitant to fire. Now they were surrounded, their sole means of escape gone!

A sudden hailstorm of machine-gun fire. It was coming from the woman, who then ducked back between the shelter of two containers. There were shouts, screams, and several of the advancing men collapsed to the ground, wounded or dead. Taking advantage of the gunfire, Bryson reached into the pocket of his flak jacket, retrieved a burst-fragmentation grenade, pulled out the pin, and hurled it up toward one group of Calacanis's men above. A chorus of shouts arose and the men scattered just as the grenade exploded, sending an immense shower of shrapnel everywhere, knocking several of the men out. Metal fragments clattered against Bryson's own face shield.

Another round of machine-gun fire from the woman, just as several of the men who had just emerged from the hatch advanced toward them, fanning out, pistols drawn. Bryson pulled out another grenade and hurled it upward; this one exploded much more quickly, with equally devastating results. He then fired a burst from the Uzi at the approaching soldiers. Several were hit; two of them, equipped with bulletproof vests, kept moving. Bryson fired at them again. The impact of the rounds even against the Kevlar vests was sufficiently powerful to knock one of them over. Bryson fired one long sustained burst and hit the other man in an exposed portion of the throat, killing him instantly.

"Come!" the woman shouted. He saw that she was backing up farther into the narrow passage between containers, deeper into the darkness.

She seemed to have another route in mind; he would have to trust her, take on faith that she knew what she was doing, where she was going. Wildly firing off another long burst of artillery as cover, Bryson dove out from his protective cover to the open ramp. As he ran he was firing all around him, seemingly crazily. But it worked: he made it to the passage across the way, just in time to see her disappear to the left in a crawlspace between the ends of several containers, dragging a long heavy object behind her.

He recognized the weapon. Just before he turned, he pulled out another grenade and hurled it back toward Calacanis's men — at least, those who remained standing.

It was insanity! The woman was lugging this oversized, rifle-shaped weapon that was slowing down their escape!

"Go on," he whispered to her. "I can get it."

"Thank you."

He grabbed the weapon, swung it over his shoulder, pulling the canvas strap around his chest. Now she was climbing down a railing that led to the next row of containers below. He climbed down as well, then followed close behind as she shimmied between another set of containers. Now he could hear footsteps all around, though chiefly above and behind, and he deduced that their pursuers were splitting up into small teams. Where was she going? Why did she insist on their carrying this goddamned weapon?

She was weaving a strange, jagged path — between containers, then climbing down the railing to the next level down. There were eight or so levels of containers belowdecks, below the hatch covers, and who knew how many rows, which provided a great maze. That's what she was doing: she was trying to lose them in the maze! He was disoriented; he had no idea which way she was going, but she was moving quickly and seemingly with purpose, so he continued to follow her, his agility somewhat impaired by having to carry the weapon.

At last they came to another vertical tunnel with a steel ladder mounted within. She vaulted up it almost as if running. Bryson was starting to feel winded. The additional thirty or forty pounds he was carrying didn't help. The woman was in peak physical condition, he observed. This tunnel rose fifty feet or so and stopped at a dark, horizontal tunnel that was tall enough to stand up in. As soon as he had come through, she shut the hatch door behind him and bolted it shut.

"This is a long tunnel," she said. "But if we can make it to near the end, to the oh-two deck, we're out of here."

She broke into a run, her stride long, hurried; Bryson followed close behind.

A sudden loud, echoing, clicking sound, and they were instantly plunged into absolute darkness.

Bryson threw himself onto the steel deck by force of habit, learned from long years of field ops, and he heard the woman do the same.

The explosion of a gunshot was followed immediately by the sound of steel hitting steel as a round hit the bulkhead just inches away. The aim was too good, too close, to be anything but enhanced by a thermal night-vision scope. Another explosion, and Bryson was immediately struck in the chest!

The bullet tore into his Kevlar vest with the impact of a powerful fist slamming him in the chest. Bryson had no night-vision; that had not been among the Aladdin's cave of armaments they had managed to turn up in their quick forage through the shipping containers. But the Lebanese woman did.

Didn't she?

"I don't have it!" she whispered harshly, as if reading his thoughts. "I dropped it somewhere back there!"

Now they could hear footsteps coming closer and closer in the blackness—not running but briskly walking, with great determination. The determination of someone who can see in the dark, can see his target as clearly as if it were high noon. The confident stride of a killer approaching in order to improve his sight lines.

"Stay down!" Bryson hissed as he took out the Uzi and fired off a burst in the general direction of the killer. But it did nothing; the killer was advancing toward them steadily, Bryson could sense.

In the left pocket of his flak jacket was a jumble of hand grenades. M651 CS teargas grenades, which would be a mistake, because in this contained space it would get them, too: they had no protection. M90 pyrotechnic smoke grenade dischargers, which generate thick smoke screens, would do no good either, since thermal scopes could see through it.

But there was another one, he knew: a high-tech species of hand grenade that might do the trick.

There had been no time to explain to the woman what he was about to do. He had simply grabbed a few of the weapons from Calacanis's store. Now what? He needed to tell her without the killer, or killers, understanding.

Just move!

He found the grenade, identifying it by its unusual contours, its smooth body. Swiftly he pulled out its pin, waited the requisite few seconds, and lobbed it a few feet short of where he estimated Calacanis's soldier had reached.

The explosion was brief but blindingly bright, phosphorus-white, and it illuminated the killer in freeze-frame like a trick of the camera. Bryson could see the man, submachine gun hoisted in firing position, jerk his head up in astonishment. But the light disappeared just as quickly as it had appeared, and Bryson could feel the air fill at once with burning-hot smoke. The killer was caught off guard, taken by surprise, and Bryson seized the moment to scoop up the long steel projectile and then propel himself forward, coming at the woman with great velocity. As he did so, he called to her in Arabic, "Run! Straight ahead! He can't see us now!"

Indeed, the American-made M76 smoke grenade, once detonated, had released a thick smoke screen laced with hot brass flakes that floated in the air and descended to the ground very slowly. It was a high-tech obscurant, specifically designed to block detection of infrared waves by thermal imaging systems. The hot metal fragments confounded the killer's scope, so it could no longer distinguish the heat of the human body from the cooler background. Now the air was filled with a hot metallic haze; the assassin's field of vision was now nothing more than a densely speckled cloud.

Bryson rushed onward, the woman racing just ahead of him. By the time their enemy recovered a few seconds later and began firing madly, indiscriminately, Bryson and the woman were well beyond him down the corridor. Artillery exploded everywhere, clattering against the steel bulk-heads aimlessly.

He felt a hand reach out to make contact with him: the blond woman was guiding him through a hatchway, pulling him up onto a steel ladder until he had his bearings and was able to make his way up the rungs in the utter darkness. From behind he could hear another hailstorm of bullets as the soldier fired away blindly, and then the barrage abruptly stopped. *He's out of ammunition*, Bryson thought. *He'll have to reload.*

But he won't have time.

The woman opened a hatch cover, and suddenly he could see. In the same instant as he felt the welcome, cold night air hit his lungs, he saw that they were outside, in the open, on a small, starboard section of deck. She closed the hatch behind them and slid home the deadbolt. The sky was dark and starless, cloudy, but it seemed almost bright by contrast.

They were on the 02 deck, one level above the main deck. Bryson noticed that the Klaxons had ceased; the alarms had stopped ringing. Nimbly making her way around several large piles of greasy cables, like tangles of snakes, the woman took several quick strides toward the bulwark.

She knelt and untied a cable from a pelican hook, which released a boom, a davit arm, which now swung outward. Secured to the davit cradle was a twenty-seven-foot-long rescue boat, a Magna Marine patrol craft, one of the fastest speedboats made.

Then the two of them climbed into the boat, which swayed unsteadily on its bridle rig. She yanked at a line, releasing the brake, and abruptly they plummeted downward, the boat crashing into the water, free of all restraints.

She powered it up and the motor came on with a throaty roar, and then the boat lurched forward, almost flying over the surface of the water. The woman took the steering wheel while Bryson maneuvered the long steel tube, the immense missile he had lugged throughout the ship. They barreled full-throttle ahead at a speed of around sixty miles per hour. Calacanis's immense ship loomed as large as a skyscraper, its tall black hull ominous.

The loud noise emitted by the Magna patrol boat seemed to have alerted Calacanis's security forces, for suddenly the black sky was lit up with blindingly bright beams of light, thunderously loud explosions. Security men now ringed the bulwarks, standing on the railings and various other perches, their submachine guns and sniper rifles blazing. They were ineffective; Bryson and the woman were out of range.

They had escaped, and they were safe!

But then Bryson noticed the rocket launchers being hoisted onto the deck, targeted directly at them.

They're going to blow us out of the water.

He became aware of the whine of an outboard motor, which crescendoed into a powerful roar. Directly ahead, coming around the ship's stern, was a Boston Whaler patrol boat, twenty-seven-foot Vigilant class, with mounted machine guns. This was no Spanish coast guard vehicle; it was clearly private.

And as it raced toward them, growing closer and closer, its machine guns were firing nonstop.

The woman heard, then saw, and she didn't need to be prompted. She opened the throttle even further, accelerating to maximum speed. The boat they were on had no doubt been chosen by Calacanis for maximum speed, but so had the approaching patrol boat.

They were speeding toward the shore, but there was no certainty that they would win any contest. Now the pursuing patrol boat was almost within firing range, its guns blazing all the while. It was a matter of seconds before it overtook them. The sea was flecked, churned, by the hailstorm of bullets from the machine guns.

And the huge rocket launchers on board the *Spanish Armada* were clearly about to fire; the missiles were within range.

"Fire it!" the woman shouted. "Before they blow *us* up!"

But Bryson had already raised the Stinger to his shoulder, the gripstock in his right hand, launch tube in his left, canvas strap around his chest. He peered through the sight, squinting his other eye. The Stinger's super-advanced software made for extreme accuracy, using a passive infrared seeker. They were well beyond the recommended minimum distance of two hundred meters.

Bryson aligned the target in the optical sight, hit the override on the Identification Friend or Foe interrogation function, then actuated the missile function.

The audible tone signaled that the missile had locked on the target. He fired.

There was an explosion of astonishing force, a recoil that knocked him backward as the dual-thrust rocket motor ignited, propelling the missile forward. The disposable missile launch tube dropped into the water.

And the heat-guided missile soared into the air, tracing a long arc toward the patrol boat, trailing a long plume of smoke like a hasty scrawl in the night sky.

A second later the patrol boat exploded into a fireball, a sulphurous cloud of smoke spewing upward. The ocean was roiled, huge waves rushing toward them even as they raced on ahead.

The air was pierced by a long, loud blast of the *Spanish Armada*'s emergency whistle, followed by a series of short blasts and then one long one.

The woman had turned around, staring in horrified fascination. Bryson could feel a wave of intense heat on his face. He lifted the second missile—the only remaining one, which had been bundled with the first—and shoved it into the firing apparatus. Then he turned the missile-launcher to his left and fixed in the infrared sights the superstructure of the *Spanish Armada* itself. It began to beep, indicating that it had locked onto the target.

Heart pounding, holding his breath, he fired.

The missile streaked toward the enormous container ship, swerving as it corrected its own path, headed right for the very heart of the ship.

An instant later came the explosion, which seemed to begin within the bowels of the ship and expand outward. Pieces of the ship flew upward amid the black smoke and thrusting flame, and then, in some sort of peculiar sequence, there came another blast, even louder.

And then another. And another.

One by one the containers had superheated, detonating their highly flammable contents.

The sky was filled with fire, an immense rippling sphere of flame and smoke and detritus. The noise hurt their ears. A black oil slick spread into the water, and that, too, immediately burst into flames, and everything was smoke and fire and crashing waves.

Calacanis's huge vessel, now a ruined hulk, listed to one side, the wreckage all but hidden in an acrid black cloud, and it began to sink deep into the ocean.

The *Spanish Armada* was no more.

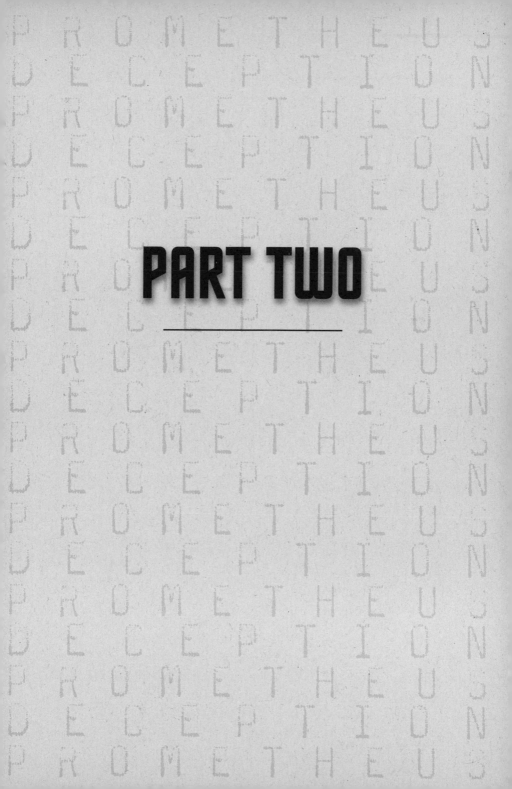

PART TWO

CHAPTER
EIGHT

They came ashore at a narrow, rocky spit of land, buffeted by violent waves crashing against the steep cliffs. This was the *Costa da Morte*, the Coast of Death, so named for the uncounted legions of ships wrecked upon the perilous, harsh coastline.

Wordlessly, they pulled the rescue boat as far up the sandbar as they could, stashing it in a hidden cove, away from the searchlights of the coast guard and the avaricious eyes of smugglers; at least the boat would not be washed away by the next big wave. He unstrapped the two large weapons from around his chest, the AK-47 and the Uzi, and hid them beside the boat, concealing them with sand, rocks, pebbles, and an arrangement of smaller boulders so that they could not be seen even from close up. It would not do to be observed walking around like a couple of mercenaries, and besides, they had plenty of other, smaller weapons stuffed in their vests.

The two maneuvered awkwardly among the rocks, weighed down by the artillery that filled every pocket, was slung around their shoulders and their backs. Their clothes were drenched, of course—her white uniform, his Italian suit—and they shivered from the cold of the icy water.

Bryson had some idea of where they had landed, having studied detailed Agency maps of the Galician coast of Spain, the stretch of land nearest the point at which the *Spanish Armada*, according to surveillance satellite reports, had dropped anchor. He believed they had come ashore at, or near, the village of Finisterre, or Fisterra, as the Galegos call it. Finisterre: the end of the world, just about Spain's most westerly point. Once the westernmost limit of the known world to the Spaniards, the place where untold numbers of smugglers met their gruesome, but mercifully sudden, end on the barnacle-encrusted rocks.

The woman was the first to speak. Sinking down on the edge of a boulder, visibly shivering, she placed her hands on her head, inserted her fingers into her hair, and tugged off a blond wig, revealing short auburn hair. She took out a sealed plastic pouch and removed from it a small, white plastic case, a holder for contact lenses. Swiftly, she touched her fingers against her eyes and removed the colored contact lenses, placing first the right, then the left, into the case. Her dazzling green eyes had become a deep brown. Bryson watched in fascination but said nothing. Then she took from the plastic pouch a compass, a waterproof map, and a tiny pinpoint flashlight. "We can't stay here, of course. The coast guard will be combing every inch of shoreline. My *God*, what a *nightmare!*" She switched on the penlight, cupping a hand around it as she examined the map.

"Why do I have the feeling you've been through nightmares like this before?"

She looked up from the map, regarded him sharply. "Do I really owe you an explanation?"

"You owe me nothing. But you risked your life to save me, and I'd like to understand. Also, I think I like you better as a brunette than as a blonde. Earlier you said you were 'following arms transfers,' presumably for Israel. Mossad?"

"In a sense," she said cryptically. "And you—CIA?"

"In a sense." He had always adhered to the principle of need-to-know and saw no need to divulge more.

"Your target—your area of interest?" she persisted.

He hesitated for a moment before he spoke. "Let's just say that I'm up against an organization that's vastly more far-reaching than anything you might have in your sights. But let me ask you this: Why? Why did you do it? Scrap the entire infiltration, then put your own life on the line?"

"Believe me, it wasn't my choice."

"Then whose choice was it?"

"It was the circumstances. The way things worked out. I made the foolish mistake of warning you, failing to take into account the surveillance cameras Calacanis has everywhere."

"How do you know you were observed?"

"Because after the madness began I was pulled away from my duties and told that a Mr. Boghosian wanted to see me. Boghosian is—*was*— Calacanis's head thug. When he asks to see you, well, I knew what that meant. They had checked the surveillance tape. At that point I knew I had to escape."

"But that begs the question of why you warned me in the first place."

She shook her head. "I saw no reason to let them claim more victims. Especially since my ultimate purpose was to prevent the spilling of innocent blood by the terrorists and fanatics. And I didn't think it would place my own operational security at stake. Obviously I miscalculated." She resumed studying the map, all the while shielding the penlight with a cupped hand.

Touched by the woman's candor, Bryson said gently, "Do you have a name?"

She looked up again, gave a half-smile. "I'm Layla. And I know you're not Coleridge."

"Jonas Barrett," he said. He let the question of what he was doing here hang in the air. Let her probe, he thought. Information will be exchanged when, *if*, the time was right. Lies, legends, cover names all came so easily to his tongue now, as they once had. *Who am I really?* he wondered mutely: the melodramatic question of the adolescent, strangely transposed to the maddened consciousness of an ex–field operative who'd found himself very lost. Waves crashed noisily around them. There was the mournful sounding of a foghorn from a lighthouse perched high above the sea. The famous lighthouse at Cabo Finisterre, Bryson knew. "It's not clear you miscalculated," he said, appreciatively, almost under his breath.

She gave him a quick, sad smile as she switched off her penlight. "I need to charter a helicopter or private plane, something that will get me—us—out of here, and quickly."

"The most likely place to do that is Santiago de Compostela. About sixty kilometers east-southeast of here. It's a major tourist destination—a pilgrimage town, a holy city. I believe there's a small airport outside the city that has some direct international flights. We may be able to charter a plane or a helicopter there. Certainly worth a try."

She gave him a hard stare. "You know this area."

"Barely. I've studied the map."

A sudden, powerful beam of light lit up the beach just yards away, propelling them both to the ground, their instincts honed by field experience. Bryson threw himself behind a large boulder and froze; the woman who called herself Layla flattened herself beneath a ledge. Bryson felt the sand on his face, cold and wet; he could hear her steady breathing a few feet away. Bryson had not worked with many female operatives in the course of his career, and it was his belief, rarely vocalized, that the few women who actually made it over the obstacles placed there by the spymasters, almost all of whom were men, had to be exceptional. About this mysterious Layla he knew virtually nothing except that she was one of the exceptional ones, highly skilled and calm under pressure.

He could see the searchlight sweep down the beach, its beam pausing for a moment at just about the point where he had concealed the boat in the hidden cove, providing additional cover with rocks gathered from the sand. Perhaps experienced eyes could discern the disruption he had caused in the natural pattern of the rocks, seaweed, and other jetsam and flotsam. From behind the boulder that shielded him from the searchers, Bryson was able to peer around. The search craft was moving parallel to the coastline, a pair of high-powered beams moving back and forth along the jagged cliffs. No doubt powerful magnifying binoculars were being employed by the searchers as well. At such a distance, night-vision scopes were useless, but he did not want to take a chance by getting up prematurely, simply because the searchlights had moved on. Often the extinguishing of the search beams was merely the prelude to the *real* search: only when the lights went out did the creatures scuttle forth from under their rocks. So he remained in place for five minutes after the beach had gone dark again; he was impressed that he did not have to urge Layla to do the same.

When they finally emerged from their hiding places, shaking the cramps from their limbs, they began scrambling up the rock-strewn hillside, dense with scraggly pines, until they came to a narrow gravel road on the ridge of the cliff. Along the road was a succession of high, massive granite walls enclosing tiny plots of land and dominated by ancient stone houses covered with moss. Each had the same granary built high on pillars, the same conical hayrack, the same trellis overgrown with green grapes, the same collection of gnarled trees heavy with fruit. This was a territory, Bryson realized, whose denizens lived and worked the land as they had always done, for generations upon generations. It was a place where the intruder was not welcome. A man on the run would be regarded with the utmost suspicion, strangers sighted and reported.

There was a sudden scuff of feet on the gravel not more than a hundred feet behind them. He spun around, a pistol in his right hand, but saw nothing in the darkness and fog. Visibility was extremely limited, and the road bent around so that whoever was approaching could not be seen. He noticed that Layla, too, was aiming a weapon, a pistol with a long perforated silencer screwed onto the barrel. Her two-handed marksman's stance was perfect, almost stylized. The two of them froze in place, listening.

Then there was a shout from the sandbar below. There were at least two of them; there had to be more. But where had they come from? What were their precise intentions?

Another sudden noise: a gruff voice nearby, speaking a language Bryson did not immediately understand, then another scuff of feet on gravel. The language, he quickly realized, was Galego, the ancient language of Galicia that combined elements of Portuguese and Castilian Spanish. He could make out only isolated phrases.

"*Veña! Axiña! Que carallo fas aí? Que é o que che leva tanto tempo? Móvete!*"

With a quick glance at each other, they each silently advanced along a stone wall toward the source of the noise. Low voices, thuds, a metallic clatter. When they rounded a bend in the wall, Bryson could see two

ROBERT LUDLUM

silhouetted figures loading crates into an ancient panel truck. One was in the cargo bay of the truck, the other lifting crates from a stack and handing them to him. Bryson glanced at his watch: a little after three o'clock in the morning. What were these men doing here? They had to be fishermen, that was it. Peasant fishermen gathering the local crop, *percebes*, barnacles scooped from the waterline, or perhaps harvesting mussels from the *mejillonieras*, the rafts floating in the water just offshore.

Whoever they were, the men were locals hard at work and no direct threat. He put away his weapon and pantomimed to Layla to do the same. Pointed guns would be a mistake; confrontation would be unnecessary.

Upon closer examination, Bryson could see that one of the men looked middle-aged, the other not long out of his teenage years. Both looked rough, peasant laborers; they also looked like father and son. The younger was the one inside the truck's cargo bay; the older one was handing him cartons to stack.

The elder one spoke to the younger: "*Veña, móvete, non podemos perde-lo tempo!*"

Bryson knew enough Portuguese from countless operations in Lisbon, and a few in São Paulo, to understand what the men were saying. "Come on, move it!" said the elder. "We're on a tight schedule. No time to waste!"

He gave Layla a quick glance and then shouted in Portuguese, "*Por favor, nos poderían axudar? Metímo-lo coche na cuneta, e a miña muller e máis eu temos que chegar a Vigo canto antes.*" Can you please help us? Our car ran off the side of the road, and my wife and I are trying to get to Vigo as soon as possible.

Both men looked up suspiciously. Now Bryson could see what they were loading, and it was not crates of barnacles or mussels. It was sealed cartons of foreign cigarettes, mostly English and American. These were not fishermen. They were smugglers, bringing in contraband tobacco to sell at grossly inflated prices.

The older man set down a carton on the gravel road. "Foreigners? Where do you come from?"

"We drove down from Bilbao. We're on holiday, seeing the sights, but the damned rental car turned out to be a piece of crap. The transmission gave out and we went into a ditch. If you could give us a lift, we'd make it worth your while."

"I'm sure we can help," said the older man, signaling to the younger, who then jumped out of the back of the truck and began approaching them from at an angle, moving noticeably closer to Layla. "Jorge?"

Suddenly the younger one had a revolver out, an ancient Astra Cadix .38 Special, which he leveled at Layla. Taking a few steps closer to her, he screamed, "*Vaciade os petos! Agora mesmo!* Empty your pockets. *All* of them! Quick, everything, and don't try anything fancy! *Now!*"

Now the older one had a revolver out, too, this one pointed at Bryson. "You, too, my friend. Drop your wallet, and kick it toward me," he barked. "That expensive-looking watch, too. *Move* it! Or your lovely wife gets it, and then you!"

The young man lurched forward, grabbing Layla by the shoulder with his left hand, jerking her toward him, his revolver at her temple. He did not seem to notice that Layla's facial expression had not changed, that she did not cry out or seem moved in any way. Had he noticed the calmness of her demeanor, he would have had cause for alarm.

She caught Bryson's eye; he nodded all but imperceptibly.

With a sudden jerking motion, she produced two handguns at once, one in either hand. In her left was a .45, a Heckler & Koch USP compact; in her right was a massive, extremely powerful .50 caliber Israeli Desert Eagle. At the same time, Bryson whipped out a Beretta 92 and leveled it at the older smuggler.

"Back!" Layla suddenly shouted in Portuguese at the teenager, who stumbled backward in sudden fright. "Drop the gun right now or I'll blow your head off!" The teenager regained his footing momentarily, hesitated as if considering how to respond, and she immediately squeezed the trigger on the enormous Desert Eagle. The explosion was astonishingly loud, all the more terrifying because it went off so near the young man's ear. He dropped his ancient Astra Cadix, flung his hands into the air, and said, "*Non! Non dispare!*" The revolver clattered to the ground but did not go off.

Bryson smiled, advancing toward the older man. "Put the gun down, *meu amigo*, or my wife will kill your son or nephew or whoever he is, and as you've just seen, she's a woman who's not able to control her impulses very well."

"*Por Cristo bendito, esa muller está tola!*" the middle-aged smuggler spat out as he knelt down and gently dropped his gun to the gravel. Christ almighty, she's a crazy woman! He put his hands in the air, too. "*Se pensan que nos van toma-lo pelo, están listos! Temos amigos esperando por nós ó final da estrada.*" If you're planning to rip us off, you're an idiot. We have friends waiting for us down the road—

"Yeah, yeah," Bryson said impatiently. "We have no interest in your cigarettes. We just want your truck."

"*O meu camión? Por Deus, eu necesito este camión!*" Good Christ, I *need* this truck!

"Well, you just ran into a patch of bad luck," Bryson said.

"Kneel!" Layla ordered the teenager, who did so at once. The boy was red-faced and shivering like a frightened child, wincing each time she waved her Desert Eagle.

"*Polo menos nos deixarán descarga-lo camión? Vostedes non necesitan a mercancía!*" pleaded the old man. At least will you let us unload the truck? You don't need the merchandise!

"Go ahead," Layla said.

"No!" Bryson interrupted. "There's always another weapon concealed inside, in case of hijacking. I want both of you to turn around and start walking back down the road. And don't stop until you can't hear the truck anymore. Any attempts to run after us, to fire a weapon, to place a phone call, and we'll turn right around and come at you with weapons you've never even seen before. Believe me—you don't want to test us."

He ran toward the truck's cab, indicating with a jerk of his head that Layla should get in on the other side. With the Beretta trained on the two Galegos, he ordered, "*Move* it!"

The two smugglers, young and old, rose unsteadily, their hands still raised, and began walking away down the gravel road.

"No, wait," she said suddenly. "I don't want to take any chances."

"What?"

She jammed the smaller-caliber pistol into a pocket of her flak jacket and pulled out another gun, this one strange-looking, which Bryson recognized at once. He nodded and smiled.

"*Non!*" the young smuggler screamed, turning back.

The older one, presumably the father, shouted, "*Non dispare! Estamos facendo o que nos dicen! Virxen Santa, non imos falar, por que íamos?*" Don't shoot! We're doing what you say! Mother of God, we're not going to talk, why should we?

The two men each broke into a run, but before they got more than a few yards, there were two loud pops as Layla fired a shot at each one. With each shot, a powerful carbon dioxide charge propelled a syringe of a potent tranquilizer into each man's body. This short-range projector was designed for overpowering wild animals without killing them; the tranquilizer would last, in a human being, perhaps thirty minutes. The two men toppled to the ground, their bodies writhing briefly before they passed into unconsciousness.

The old truck rattled and clattered as its arthritic engine strained against the steep grade of the winding mountain road. The sun was coming up the jagged cliffs, painting the horizon with pastel brushstrokes and casting a strange pale glow on the slate roofs of the fishing villages they passed.

He thought about the beautiful, remarkable woman sleeping in the front seat next to him, her head leaning against the vibrating window.

There was something tough and flinty about her, yet at the same time vulnerable, even melancholy. It was in fact an appealing combination, but his instincts warned him away for a multitude of reasons. She was too much like himself, a survivor whose tough exterior shielded a supremely complicated interior that at times seemed at war with itself.

And there was Elena, always Elena—a spectral presence, a mystery in her own way. The woman he never really knew. The promise of searching her out had become for him a beckoning siren, elusive and treacherous.

Layla meant at most a strategic partnership, an alliance of simple convenience. She and Bryson were using each other, assisting each other; there was something almost clinical, tactical about their relationship. It was nothing more than that. She was a mere means to an end.

Exhaustion was now overcoming him, and he pulled the truck over into a copse and dozed for what he thought was twenty minutes or so; he awoke with a jolt several hours later. Layla was still sleeping soundly.

He cursed silently to himself; it was not good to lose this much time. On the other hand, bone-tiredness usually caused miscalculations and misjudgments, so maybe the sacrifice had been worth the cost.

Pulling back onto the highway, he noticed the road was becoming crowded with people walking in the direction of Santiago de Compostela. What had been an isolated few pedestrians had become a line of them, even a throng of them. Most were walking, though a few were on old bicycles, even a few on horseback. Their faces were sunburned; many of them walked with crook-necked sticks, wore simple, rough clothing, and had backpacks with scallop shells tied to them. The scallop shell, Bryson recalled, was the symbol of the pilgrim along the *Camino de Santiago*, the pilgrim's road of some one hundred kilometers from the pass at Roncesvalles in the Pyrenees to the ancient shrine of Saint James in Santiago. It usually took a month to make the journey on foot. Here and there along the roadside were pushcarts, gypsy vendors selling souvenirs — postcards, plastic birds with flapping wings, scallop shells, brightly colored cloths.

But soon he noticed something else, something for which he had no easy explanation. A few kilometers before Santiago, the traffic was becoming increasingly congested. Cars and trucks moved more slowly, almost bumper to bumper. Somewhere up ahead was an obstruction, perhaps a traffic jam. Road work?

No.

The wooden barricades and flashing lights from the cluster of official vehicles, which became visible as he rounded a turn, supplied the answer. It was a police roadblock. Spanish police were inspecting vehicles, surveying drivers and passengers. Cars seemed to be waved through quickly, but trucks were being detained, pulled over to one side as licenses and registrations were checked. The throngs of pilgrims passed by with curious looks, unhindered by the police.

"Layla," he said. "Quick, wake up!"

She jerked awake, startled, immediately alert. "What — what is it?"

"They're looking for our truck."

She saw at once what was going on. "Oh, God. Those bastards must have come to, filed a report with the police . . ."

"No. Not them, not directly. People like that tend to avoid the authorities whenever possible. Someone must have got to them, offered them a handsome bribe. Someone with direct lines to the Spanish police."

"*Guardacostas?* Unlikely to be any of Calacanis's people, even if any of them survived."

He shook his head. "My guess is that it's another entity entirely. An organization that knew I was on board the ship."

"A hostile intelligence organization."

"Yes, but not in the way you may think." *Hostile isn't the word*, he thought. *Diabolical, maybe. An organization with tentacles reaching high into the governments of several world powers. The Directorate.* He suddenly swerved the truck over to the side of the road, locating a gap in the stream of pilgrims. There were shouted protests from pushcart vendors, the honking of car horns.

Hopping out, he quickly unscrewed the license plates with the screwdriver blade of a pocket knife, then returned with them to the front seat. "Just in case any of the search party is stupid enough to look only for the license plate. The trick is going to be us: they'll be looking for a couple, a man and a woman together matching our description, perhaps wearing disguises quickly thrown together. So obviously we'll have to split up, and go on foot, but we'll have to do more. . . ." Bryson's voice faded as he caught sight of one of the pushcarts nearby. "Hold on."

A few minutes later he was conversing, in Spanish, with a rotund gypsy woman selling shawls and other native costumes. She expected this customer—a native Castilian, from the fluency of his Spanish and the lack of accent—to drive a hard bargain and was surprised when the man all but threw down a wad of peseta notes. Moving quickly from cart to cart, he assembled a pile of clothing and returned with it to the truck. Layla's eyes widened; she nodded, then said solemnly, "So now I'm a pilgrim."

Chaos, utter chaos!

Car horns blared, angry drivers yelled and cursed. The stream of pilgrims grew into a throng, a crowd of strikingly diverse people whose only commonality was their devout faith. There were old men with walking sticks who looked as if they could barely take another step, old women garbed entirely in black, black headscarves revealing only the upper part of their faces. Many wore shorts and T-shirts. Some walked with bicycles. There were weary-looking parents carrying squalling infants, their older children squealing with delight and weaving in and out of the crowds. There was the odor of sweat, onions, incense, a whole range of human smells. Bryson was dressed in a medieval cassock with a crook-handled walking stick, monk's garb from a distant past that was still worn in certain isolated orders. Here, it was being peddled as a souvenir. It had the advantage of having a hood that Bryson put up, concealing some of his features, the rest obscured by shadow. Layla, fifty yards or so behind him, wore a peculiar shift fashioned of a coarse fabric that looked like muslin, with a gaudy sweater covered with sequins, and on her head, a bright red kerchief. As strange as she looked, she blended in with the rest of the crowd perfectly.

The wooden barricades just ahead had been arranged to allow a broad passage for pedestrians to move through; two uniformed police officers stood on either side of the barricades perfunctorily examining faces as they passed. On the other half of the road, cars and trucks were being admitted one at a time. Those on foot were moving at a normal pace, hardly slowed at all, Bryson was relieved to observe. As he passed the policemen, Bryson walked unsteadily, leaning hard on the stick, the gait of a man nearing the end of a brutally long journey. He neither glanced at the faces of the policemen nor pointedly ignored them. They seemed to pay him no attention. In a few seconds, he was safely through the barricades, buffeted along by the stream of people.

A flash of light. It was the strong morning sunlight glinting off something reflective nearby; he turned his head to see a pair of high-powered binoculars being held up to the face of another uniformed policeman, who was standing atop a bench. Like his colleagues manning the barricades, he was also scrutinizing the faces of those entering the city along Avenida Juan Carlos I. He was a backup, or perhaps a second filter, and he was scanning the crowd with a methodical regularity. The sun was already beating down, though it was early morning, and the man's pale complexion was flushed.

Bryson did a double-take, puzzled by the paleness of the man's skin, the blond hair beneath the visored cap. Blonds were not common in this part of Spain, but they were not unheard of. Yet that wasn't what drew his attention. It was the pale skin, almost white. No policeman or border guard could last for long in this climate without his face tanning, or at least turning ruddy, from the powerful sun. Even a desk-bound official couldn't avoid being out in the sun on his way to work or at lunchtime.

No, this was not a local, not a native. Bryson doubted the man was even a Spaniard.

The blond policeman was sweating profusely, and he briefly lowered his binoculars to mop his face with a crooked elbow, and that was when Bryson first saw the man's facial features.

The sleepy-looking gray eyes that belied the ferocious concentration, the thin lips, the chalky skin, the ash-blond hair. The man was familiar. Khartoum.

The blond man had been posted as a technical expert from Rotterdam, visiting the Sudanese capital with a group of European specialists advising Iraqi officials on the construction of a ballistic-missile plant and taking orders for turnkey equipment that could be used to assemble Scud missiles. The blond man was in fact an interloper, an infiltrator, a penetration agent. He was Directorate. He was also a dispatch agent, an expert in the quick-kill. Bryson had been in Khartoum to install surveillance, obtain hard evidence that could later be used against the Iraqis. He had done a brush-pass exchange with the blond killer, providing him with microdot dossiers of the desired targets, including information on where they were staying, their schedules, the presumptive holes in their security. Bryson didn't know the blond man's name; he knew only that the man was a stone killer, one of the best in the trade: supremely skilled, probably a sociopath, the perfect dispatch agent.

The Directorate had sent one of their best here to kill him. Now there could be no doubt his former employers had marked him "beyond salvage."

Yet how had they found him? The smugglers must have talked, angry about their stolen truck, eager to earn a no-doubt generous bribe. There were not many roads in this part of the country, very few routes from Finisterre, therefore easily scrutinized by air if they had quick access to a helicopter. Bryson had not heard or seen a helicopter, but there had been that stretch of time when he had been asleep. Also, the old farm truck had been so loud that a helicopter could have passed directly over-head and he would not have heard it.

It had to be the hastily abandoned truck, which served as a veritable beacon to their pursuers, evidence that he and Layla were in the immediate vicinity. And there were only two ways to go on that road: into Santiago de Compostela, or away from it. No doubt both possibilities had been covered, roadblocks placed at points of convergence.

He wanted to turn back, confirm that Layla was still behind him, still safe, but he could not risk doing so.

Bryson's pulse quickened. He looked away, but it was too late. He had seen the instant of recognition in the killer's eyes. *He saw me; he knows me.*

Yet to run, to make any sudden moves that made him stand out from the crowd, was to throw up a flag, confirm the killer's suspicions. For the dispatch agent could not be sure at that distance. Not only had it been years since Khartoum, but the hooded cassock Bryson was wearing obscured his face, and the killer would not fire indiscriminately.

Time had slowed almost to a stop as Bryson's mind raced. His body surged with adrenaline, his heart pounded, yet he restrained himself from accelerating his pace. He could not stand out from the crowd.

In his peripheral field of vision Bryson saw the killer turn toward him, his right hand moving toward the holstered weapon at his waist. The crowd of pilgrims was so thick that it almost carried Bryson along, but at a rate that was excruciatingly slow. How can the killer be sure I'm the man he wants? With this hood . . . and then Bryson had the sickening realization that it was the very fact that he was wearing a hood that made him stand out from the crowd; in the brutally hot sun, some of the men wore caps to shield their heads from the rays of the sun, but a hood trapped in the heat and was unbearably hot; none of those who had hoods on their old-fashioned monastic garb wore them up. He stood out.

Though he did not dare turn to look, he became aware of the sudden, jerking motion in his peripheral vision, the glint of light on a metal object that was surely a gun. The killer had his weapon out; Bryson sensed this almost instinctually.

Suddenly he sagged to his feet, feigning heat stroke, causing those immediately around him to stumble. Shouts of annoyance; a woman's cry of concern.

And then a split second later came the deadly cough of a silenced weapon. Screams, shrill and terrified. A young woman just a few feet to his left crumpled, the top of her head blown off. Blood sprayed in a radius of six feet or so. The crowd began to stampede; cries of fear, shouts of anguish went up. Dirt exploded nearby as bullets sprayed the ground. The killer was firing rapidly, in semiautomatic mode. Having spotted his target, he no longer cared whether he struck the innocent.

Amid the pandemonium, Bryson found himself nearly trampled by the frenzied, stampeding crowd; he struggled to his feet, his hood down, only to be knocked to the earth again. All around him were the screams and cries of the wounded and the dying, and those surrounding them. Managing to gain a foothold, he lurched forward, enduring repeated impact from those trying to flee the madness.

He had guns, but to take one out, to return fire, would be suicide. He was certainly far outnumbered; the moment he squeezed the trigger, he was in effect sending up a flare, advertising his location to the single-minded killers sent here by the Directorate. Instead, he rushed forward, keeping his head down, low to the ground, camouflaged by the tangle of bodies.

A fusillade of bullets ricocheted off the steel of a street sign ten feet away, indicating that the blond killer had lost sight of him, disoriented by the surging crowd. Twenty feet ahead, there was another scream, and the body of a man on a bicycle arched as he was struck in the back. The blond was firing at phantoms now; this only served Bryson's purpose, creating a maximum disturbance into which he could disappear. He risked a glance around, as so many others were straining to see the source of the gunfire, and was astonished to see the blond killer suddenly propelled forward as if shoved from behind. He had been hit by a bullet! The marksman twisted his torso, then toppled off the fence, either dead or seriously wounded. But who had gotten off the shot? A flash of scarlet: a bright red kerchief, which then disappeared into the crowd.

Layla.

Relieved, he turned back around and kept moving with the crowd, like a piece of driftwood borne on a powerful current. He could not move toward her, against the stream, if he wanted to; he certainly dared not flash her a signal. He knew how the Directorate staged high-priority hits, of which this was certainly one. They did not stint on manpower. A dispatch agent was like a cockroach: where you found one, there was certain to be others. But where? The blond marksman from Khartoum seemed to be operating like a lone asset, which meant that the others were backup. Yet no backup was visible. Bryson knew the Directorate's methodology too well to believe that the blond was acting alone.

The crowd of pilgrims was now out of control, a riot, a seething, teeming mass of frightened people, some trying to run down the *avenida*, others running in the opposite direction. What had been ideal cover but a few moments ago had become dangerous, violent. He and Layla would have to detach themselves from the panicked throng, disappear into Santiago, and find a way to the airport at Labacolla, eleven kilometers to the east.

He pulled out of the stream of pedestrians and cycles, nearly side-swiped by an unsteady bicyclist, and grabbed hold of a street lamp to steady himself against the onrush while he waited for Layla to emerge. He searched the passing crowd for her face, but mostly for her scarlet kerchief. Alert, too, for other anomalies: flashes of steel, police uniforms, the unmistakable look of a hired killer. Bryson knew he must have been a strange sight: he was attracting stares. One pilgrim in particular, clutching what seemed to be a Bible beneath the folds of his brown monk's outfit, seemed to be peering at him with undisguised curiosity from across the swarming Avenida Juan Carlos I. Bryson caught the monk's eye just as the man pulled out his Bible, but the object was long, blue steel.

A gun.

In the split second that his brain processed what his eyes were seeing, Bryson lurched to his right, crashing into a bicyclist and causing it to topple, its middle-aged male rider frantically trying to steady himself while shouting angrily.

A spit; an explosion of blood that spattered Bryson's face. The bicyclist's temple had been blown off, leaving only a gaping wound, a sickening mass of crimson. Screams erupted anew from all around. The man was dead, the shooter a man in a monk's cassock fifty feet away, his gun still pointed, still firing.

It was insanity!

Bryson rolled over, enduring kicks to his head and back inflicted by the panicked, stampeding crowd. He grabbed a holstered weapon, the Beretta, yanked it out.

A man screamed: *"Unha pistola! Ten unha pistola!"* He's got a gun!

Bullets struck the iron street lamp, ringing loudly, and spit into the ground a few yards away. Bryson scrambled to his feet, steadied himself, located the monk-killer, squeezed the trigger.

The first shot hit the assassin in the chest, causing his gun to drop; the second shot, squarely to the center of his chest, knocked the man over entirely.

Off to his left, glinting in his peripheral vision, was an object that Bryson's instincts told him was another weapon. He turned just in time to see another man, also in the guise of a pilgrim, leveling a small black pistol at him from less than twenty feet away. Bryson spun to the right, out of the line of fire, but the sudden explosion of pain in his left shoulder, shooting lines of fire down his chest, told him he had been hit.

He lost his footing, his legs collapsing beneath him. He crumpled to the pavement. The pain was excruciating; he felt blood hotly soaking his shirt, his left arm going numb.

Hands grabbed at him. Disoriented, seeing through a scrim of haze, Bryson reflexively pummeled his attacker just as he heard Layla's voice. "No, it's me. *This* way. This way!"

She was clutching his good shoulder, his elbow, helping him to stand erect, supporting him.

"You're all right!" Bryson shouted with relief, amid the chaos — illogically, for it was *he* who had been shot.

"I'm fine. Come *on!*" She pulled him toward one side, across the stampede of frenzied pilgrims whose panic had now reached fever pitch. Bryson forced himself to move, quickening his stride, moving through the pain. He caught sight of another monk watching him from a few feet away, also clutching something. Jolted into action, Bryson raised his pistol, pointing it, just in time to see the monk lift the oblong object — a

Bible—to his lips, kissing it, praying aloud amid the violence, the madness.

They were entering a large park, broad and spacious, with manicured gardens and rows of eucalyptus trees. "We must find a place to let you rest," Layla said.

"No. The wound is superficial—"

"The *blood!*"

"I think it's more of a graze. Obviously it nicked blood vessels, but it's nowhere near as serious as it may look. We can't afford to rest here; we have to keep moving!"

"But where?"

"Look. Straight ahead—across the road—a cathedral, a square. The Praza do Obradoiro—it's jammed with people. We have to stay with the crowds, disappear into them whenever we can. Whatever we do, we can't stand out." He sensed her momentary hesitation and added, "We'll take care of my wound later. Right now it's the least of our problems."

"I don't think you know how much blood you're losing." With an almost clinical detachment, she unbuttoned the top few buttons of his shirt and delicately pulled the blood-matted cloth away from the skin of his shoulder; he felt a twinge of pain. She gently palpitated the wound; the pain intensified, a jagged bolt of lightning. "All right," she pronounced, "we can tend to it later, but we have to stanch the blood flow." Whipping the red scarf from her head, she tied it firmly around his shoulder, anchoring it at the underarm, fashioning a sort of tourniquet that would do for the time being. "Can you move your arm?"

He lifted it, winced. "Yeah."

"It hurts? Don't be a hero."

"I'm not. I never ignore pain; it's one of the most valuable signals the body gives us. And yes, it does hurt. But I've suffered a lot worse, believe me."

"I believe you. Now, there's a cathedral up the hill—"

"The main Cathedral of Santiago. The square surrounding it, the Praza do Obradoiro, sometimes called Praza de Espana, is the endpoint of the pilgrim's journey, always crowded. A good place to lose our pursuers, find a vehicle. We have to get out of this open area immediately."

They started up the eucalyptus-lined path. Suddenly a pair of bicyclists zoomed by, veering around them just a few inches away, then continued up the path. Entirely innocent, presumably a couple of pilgrims heading for the center of town, but it startled Bryson. Perhaps the loss of some blood had dulled his reactions. The assassins sent by the Directorate were disguised, with diabolical cleverness, as religious pilgrims. Anyone they passed, anyone in a crowd, could be a killer sent to terminate him. At least in a minefield the trained eye could distinguish the mine from the field. Here, there was no such distinction.

Except the familiarity of the faces.

Some—not all, but some of the dispatch agents, the leaders—were men Bryson knew, had had dealings with in the past, however casual or distant. They had been sent because they could more easily find him in a crowd. But the sword was double-edged: if they recognized him, he would recognize them. If he remained alert, watchful, he would see them before they saw him. It was not much of an advantage, but it was all he had, and he would have to exploit it to its maximum extent.

"Wait," he said abruptly. "I've been spotted, and so have you. They may not know who you are, not yet. But me, they know. And there's the bloodstained shirt, the red tourniquet. No, we can't give them that."

She nodded. "Let me get us another change of clothes."

They were thinking along the same lines. "I'll wait here—no, strike that." He pointed to a small, moss-covered ancient cathedral surrounded by gardens planted with exotic species of flora. "I'll wait inside *there.*"

"Good." She hurried up the path toward the main square while he turned back toward the church.

He waited anxiously in the dim, cool, deserted cathedral. A few times the heavy wooden doors to the church opened; each time it was a genuine pilgrim or tourist, or so they appeared. Women with children, young couples. Watching from a concealed alcove off the narthex, he studied each one. One could never be sure, but none of the signs were present, nothing that alerted his internal alarms. Twenty minutes later the doors opened again; it was Layla, holding a paper-wrapped bundle.

They changed, separately, in the cathedral's restrooms. She had accurately estimated his size. Now they were dressed in the plain garb of middle-class tourists: a simple skirt and blouse for her with a broad-brimmed, gaily decorated sun hat; khaki pants, a white short-sleeved knit shirt, and a baseball cap for him. She had managed to locate a couple of large bandages and an iodine-based disinfectant to temporarily cleanse the wound. She had even provided them with cameras—a cheap video camera, sans film, for him; an even cheaper 35mm camera on a neck strap for her.

Ten minutes later, each of them wearing modish sunglasses, walking hand in hand like honeymooners, they entered the immense, bustling Praza do Obradoiro. The square was filled with pilgrims, tourists, students; vendors hawked postcards and souvenirs. Bryson stopped before the cathedral, pretending to take some video footage of the baroque eighteenth-century facade, the centerpiece of which was the Pórtico de la Gloria, the astonishing Spanish Romanesque twelfth-century sculpture crowded with the likenesses of angels and demons, monsters and prophets. As he looked through the telephoto lens of the viewfinder, he moved the camera from the portico, sweeping across the facade of the cathedral, then panning across the crowd of tourists and pilgrims, as if capturing the entire scene on video, an amateur cinematographer.

Putting down the video camera, he turned to Layla, smiling and nodding like a proud tourist. She touched his arm, the two of them engaged in an exaggerated pantomime of honeymooner affection in order to deflect the suspicions of any who might be watching. His disguise was minimal, but at least the peak of the baseball cap cast a shadow across his face. Perhaps it would be enough to induce uncertainty, raise doubts in any watchers.

Then Bryson became aware of a movement, a synchronized shifting, on several points in the distance. Everywhere around him was filled with motion, but against that background was a coordinated, symmetrical movement. The perception would not have registered with anyone who had not had his extensive field experience. But it was there, he was sure of it!

"Layla," he said quietly, "I want you to laugh at something I just said."

"Laugh . . . ?"

"Right now. I've just told you something hysterically funny."

Abruptly she laughed, throwing her head back in abandon. It was an utterly convincing act that Bryson, even though he had requested it, expected it, found unnerving. She was a skilled performer. She had instantly become the entranced lover who found her new husband's every witticism hugely entertaining. Bryson smiled in modest, yet gratified, acknowledgment of his own cleverness. As he smiled, he picked up the video camera and looked through the viewfinder, panning it over the crowd around them as he had done a moment ago. But this time he was looking for something specific.

Through her smile, Layla's voice was tense. "You see something?"

He found it.

A classic triad formation. At three points around the square, three persons stood very still, peering through binoculars in Bryson's direction. Individually, none of them was remarkable or worthy of attention; each might have been a tourist taking in the sights. But together, they represented an ominous pattern. On one side of the *praza* was a young woman, with flaxen hair worn up, wearing a blazer that was too warm for such a hot day, though it would serve to conceal a shoulder holster. On another side, representing the second point of an isosceles triangle, was a fleshy-faced, bearded man of chunky build, garbed in black clerical vestments; his high-powered binoculars seemed jarring, not the sort of optical equipment likely to be used by a man of the cloth. At the third leg of the triangle was another man, of sinewy build and swarthy complexion, in his early forties; it was this man who tugged at Bryson's memory, demanded closer inspection. Bryson touched the button for the zoom lens, tightening the shot, moving in for a close-up of the swarthy man.

He felt his insides go cold.

He knew the man, had dealt with him several times on some high-priority assignments. He had in fact hired the man on behalf of the Directorate. He was a peasant named Paolo from a village outside of Cividale. Paolo always operated in tandem with his brother, Niccolo. The two of them had been legendary game hunters in the remote hill country of northwestern Italy where they had grown up, and so they had easily become highly skilled hunters of human beings, assassins of rare talent. The brothers were much-sought-after bounty hunters, mercenaries, killers for hire, jobbers. In his past life, Bryson had hired them for the occasional odd job, including a dangerous infiltration of a Russian firm called Vector, which had been rumored to be involved in bioweapons research and manufacture.

Where Paolo went, so did Niccolo. That meant there was at least one other, positioned somewhere outside the legs of the triad.

Bryson's heart thudded; his scalp went prickly.

But *how* had they located him and Layla so easily? They had lost the pursuers, he had been sure; how had they been found once again, in a crowd of this size, particularly having changed outfits, altered the configuration?

Was it something about the clothes—too new, too bright, somehow not quite right? But Bryson had taken pains to scuff up his brand-new leather loafers on the pavement outside the church where they had stopped, and had seen to it that Layla did the same. He had even soiled their clothes with a light sprinkling of dust.

How had they been found?

The answer came to him in a slow, sickening realization, a terrible certainty. He felt the warmth of blood on his left shoulder, which had oozed out from the bandage; he did not have to look at it, or touch it, to be sure. The gunshot wound had continued to bleed steadily, profusely, seeping into the fabric of his knit shirt, turning a large area of his yellow shirt crimson. The blood had been the giveaway, the beacon, negating all the precautions they had taken, penetrating their disguise.

His pursuers had finally located him, and now they were moving in for the kill.

Washington, D.C.

Senator James Cassidy could feel the eyes of his colleagues on him—some bored, some wary—as he stood up heavily, spread his thick, spotted hands on the well-rubbed wooden rail, and began to speak in a rich, dulcet baritone. "In our chambers and committee rooms, we go on a great deal, all of us, about scarce resources and endangered species. We talk about how best to manage our diminishing natural resources in an era when everything seems to be for sale, when everything has a price tag and a bar code. Well, I'm here to say something about another kind of endangered species, a vanishing commodity: the very notion of privacy. In the papers, I read an Internet maven who says, 'You already have zero privacy. Get over it.' Well, those of you who know me know I'm sure as hell *not* one to get over it. Stop and look around you, I say. What do you see? Cameras and scanners and mammoth databases of a reach that defies human comprehension. Marketers can follow every aspect of our lives, from the first phone call we make in the morning to the time our security systems say we have left our houses, to the video camera at the toll booth and the charge slip we get at lunch. Go on-line, and every transaction, every 'hit,' is tracked and recorded by so-called infomediaries. Private companies have been approaching the Federal Bureau of Investigation with the proposal that the Bureau sell them their records, their information, as if *information* were just another government asset to be privatized. This is the beginning of something troubling: the naked republic. The surveillance society."

The senator looked around and realized that he was experiencing a rare moment: he actually had his colleagues' attention. Some of them appeared transfixed, others skeptical. But he had their attention.

"And I ask you one question: Is this a place you want to live in? I see no reason to hope that the cherished notion of privacy has a ghost of a chance against the forces arrayed against it—overzealous national and international law-enforcement bodies, marketers and corporations and insurance companies and the new managed-care conglomerates and the million tentacles of every enmeshed corporate and governmental concern. The people who want to maintain order, the people who want to squeeze every penny they can out of you—the forces of order and the forces of commerce: that's a formidable alliance, my friends! That's what privacy, *our* privacy, is up against. It is a pitched, yet terribly one-sided, battle. And so my question, my question for my distinguished colleagues on either side of the aisle, is simple: *What side are you on?*"

CHAPTER
NINE

"Don't look," Bryson commanded softly, still panning the crowd and peering through the magnifying viewfinder. "Don't turn your head. It's a triad, as far as I can tell."

"What distance?" She spoke quietly, intensely, while at the same time grinning, the effect bizarre.

"Seventy, eighty feet. An isosceles triangle. At your three o'clock, a blond woman in a blazer, hair up, oversized round sunglasses. At six o'clock, a big bearded man in a black priest's getup. At nine o'clock, a slender man, late thirties, swarthy complexion, dark short-sleeved shirt, dark pants. All of them have small binoculars, and I'm sure each has a gun. Okay?"

"Got it," she said almost inaudibly.

"One of them's the team leader; they're waiting for his signal. Now, I'm going to point something out and ask you to look through the video camera. Tell me when you've located them."

He abruptly gestured at the cathedral's portico with an open, flat hand, like some amateur cinematographer, holding the video camera out for

THE PROMETHEUS DECEPTION

her. "Jonas," she said, alarmed. It was the first time she had called him by name, though it was a cover name. "Oh, my God, the *blood!* Your shirt!"

"I'm fine," he said shortly. "Unfortunately, it's what drew their attention."

She instantly turned her look of alarm into a bizarre, inappropriate grin, followed by a giggle, play-acting for an audience of three, the effect bizarre. She leaned in, peering through the viewfinder as he rotated it in a slow arc around the square. "The blond woman, check," she said. A few seconds later, she added, "The bearded priest in black, check. The younger guy in the dark shirt, check."

"All right." He smiled, nodded, continuing the performance. "I suspect they're trying to avoid a repeat of what happened by the barricades. Obviously they're not averse to killing innocent bystanders if need be, but they'd rather avoid it if possible, if only because of the political fallout. Otherwise, they'd have already taken a shot at me."

"Or they may not be certain it's you," she pointed out.

"Their positioning indicates that if they were uncertain a few minutes ago, they no longer are," Bryson said in a hushed tone. "They've moved into place."

"But I don't understand: Who are they? You seem to know something about them. These are not just faceless pursuers to you."

"I know them," Bryson said. "I know their methods; I know they work."

"How?"

"I've read their field manual," he said cryptically, deliberately so, unwilling to elaborate.

"If you know them, then you must have an idea of what kind of risks they'll take. You say 'political fallout'—are you saying these are government operatives? Americans? Russians?"

"I think transnational is the best description. None of the above, or maybe all of the above—neither Russian nor American nor French nor Spanish, but an organization that operates between the cracks, operating on a subterranean level where borders aren't delineated. They work with governments but not for them. It appears as if they're watching, waiting for a clearing to form around me. Given their distance, they want a space

139

large enough to allow for a standard margin of error. But if I make any sudden movements, appearing as if I'm about to bolt, they'll simply fire away, bystanders be damned."

They were surrounded by tourists and pilgrims, jammed up against them so closely it was hard to move. He continued: "Now, I want you to cover the woman, but be very subtle about taking out your gun, because they can observe your every move. They may not know who you are, but they know you're with me, and that's all they need to know."

"What does that mean?"

"It means they consider you at the very least an accessory, if not an outright accomplice."

"Great," Layla moaned, then flashed a discordant smile.

"I'm sorry—I didn't ask you to get involved."

"I know, I know. I made the choice."

"As long as we're hemmed in like this by all these people, you're free to move your hands below waist level. But you should assume they can see all movements from mid-torso up."

She nodded.

"Tell me when you have your gun out."

She nodded again. He could see her reach into her large woven handbag.

"Got it," she said.

"Now, with your left hand, lift the camera from around your neck and take a picture of me with the cathedral behind me. Go for a wide-angle shot; that'll allow you to see the blond woman at the same time. Take your time doing it: you're an amateur photographer, and you're not good with cameras. No hurried motions, nothing smooth or professional."

She put the camera up to her face, squinted her right eye.

"All right, now I'm going to seem to be joking around with you, pretending to take a video of you taking a picture of me. As soon as I hold the video camera to my face, you will react with annoyance; I'm ruining your perfect frame. You whip the camera away from your face with unexpected force, a sudden movement that will distract and confuse the watchers. Then, aim right and squeeze off a shot. Take down the blond woman."

"At *this* distance?" she said incredulously.

"I've seen your accuracy. You're one of the best I've seen; I have confidence. But don't wait for a second go; dive right for the ground."

"And you? What will you be doing?"

"Aiming at the bearded guy."

"But there's a *third*—"

"We *can't* cover all three, that's the maddening thing about this damned arrangement."

She gave another disconcerting false smile, then put the 35mm camera up to her face, clutching her Heckler & Koch .45 in her right hand at about waist level.

He smiled impishly as he drew the video camera to his face. At the same instant, with a small, barely detectable movement, he reached his free hand around to the small of his back and pulled the Beretta from his waistband. His hands were trembling; he could hardly breathe.

Directly behind her, visible through the video camera lens and some fifty to eighty feet distant, the bearded false priest lowered his binoculars. What did that mean: that they had decided to hold their fire, confused by Bryson's ruse? That they did not want to fire indiscriminately with innocent bystanders just inches away? If so, they had just bought themselves a little time.

If not . . .

Suddenly the bearded man shook his wrist, ostensibly an innocent gesture designed to restore circulation in a tired hand, but clearly a sign to the others. A signal, delivered moments before Bryson had anticipated it would come. *No!*

They had *no* time.

Now!

He dropped the video camera just as he swooped the gun upward, squeezing off three rapid shots just over Layla's shoulder.

At the exact same moment, she let her camera drop from its neck strap, whirled her .45 magnum up and over, and fired over the heads of the crowd.

What followed was a bewildering sequence of explosions, shot answering shot in rapid-fire fashion, provoking terrified screams from all around. As Bryson dove to the ground, he was able to catch a glimpse of the bearded man staggering, sinking, obviously hit. Layla threw herself downward, tumbling against Bryson, slamming against the limbs of those surrounding them, knocking a young woman over. Someone very near had been struck by a stray round, wounded but not fatally so, a collateral injury.

"She's down!" Layla gasped as she rolled to her side. "The blonde— I saw her go down."

The gunfire ceased as abruptly as it had begun, but the shouts, the horrified clamor, continued to rise.

Two of Bryson's would-be assassins were down, perhaps permanently so; but at least one certainly remained standing: Paolo, the assassin from Cividale. And surely there were others as well; Paolo's brother was almost certainly in the vicinity.

Running feet kicked at them, others tripped over them, stumbled. Once again a crowd had become a stampede, and as they plunged into the middle of the chaos, Bryson and Layla managed to get to their feet, rushing headlong with the others, disappearing into the maddened crowd.

Weaving in and out of the onrushers, Bryson saw a narrow cobblestone street, almost a lane, coming off the *praza*. It was little more than a lane, barely big enough for one car to pass through it. He ran toward it, weaving around human obstacles, determined to follow it as far as he could until they lost the Italian brothers or whoever else was chasing him. It appeared likely that there would be small, ancient houses on this street, perhaps small courtyards, alleys leading to other alleys. Mazes in which to lose themselves.

His shoulder wound was once again throbbing, blood oozing thick and hot; what had begun to heal had been wrenched open. The pain had become incredible. Yet he forced himself to run faster. Layla kept up easily. Their footsteps echoed in the empty street. As he ran, he was searching the narrow, shadowed street, searching for a courtyard, a shop, any place into which they could duck. There was a small, Romanesque church tucked between a couple of even older stone buildings, but it was locked; a handwritten sign pasted on one heavy wooden door declared that it was closed for repairs. In this town of churches and cathedrals, the smaller houses of worship, which did not attract tourists, probably got little attention and less funding.

Approaching the church, he stopped short, grabbing a massive iron door handle and rattling it.

"What are you *doing?*" Layla asked, alarmed. "The *noise*—come on, let's keep going!" She was breathing hard, her chest heaving, her face flushed. Footsteps echoed in the street, approaching.

Bryson did not reply. He gave the door handle one last, mighty tug. The padlock was small and rusted, and it looped through an even rustier hasp, which easily came off the door with a splintering sound. People did not break into churches as a rule; the lock was mostly symbolic, all that was required in this town of the devout.

He yanked the door open and entered the dark central portal. Layla, giving a small grunt of frustration, followed, shutting the door behind them. Now the only light in the dim narthex came from small, dusty quatrefoil windows high above. There was a dank, mildewy smell here, and the air was chilly. Bryson looked around briefly, then leaned back against a cold stone wall. His heart was pounding from the exertion, and he felt weak from the searing pain of his wounded shoulder, and from loss of blood. Layla was pacing the length of the nave, presumably looking for exits or hiding places.

After a few minutes he had caught his breath, and he returned to the entrance doors. The broken lock would draw the attention of anyone who knew the town; either it should be reassembled so that it looked intact, or it should simply be removed entirely. As he reached for the handle to pull the door open, he listened for any approaching footsteps.

There *was* the sound of running feet, and then a voice, a shout in a strange language that was neither Spanish nor Gallego. He froze, glancing at the floor, at the narrow bands of light that came in through a small louver at the bottom of the door. Kneeling, he put his ear against the slats and listened.

The language was oddly familiar.

"*Niccolò, o crodevi di velu viodût! Jù par che strade cà. Cumò o controli, tu continue a cjalà la 'plaza'!*"

He recognized it, understood the words. *I thought I saw him, Niccolo!* the voice was saying. *Down the street. You watch the plaza!*

It was an obscure, dying language called Friuliano, a tongue he had not heard in years. Some said it was an ancient dialect of Italian; others believed it was a language in its own right. It was spoken only in the northeast corner of Italy near the Slovenian border, by a dwindling number of peasants.

Bryson, whose facility with languages had often proved as useful a survival mechanism as his ability with firearms, had taught himself Friuliano a decade or so ago, when he had hired two young peasants from the remote mountains above Cividale, remarkable hunters, assassins. Brothers. When he had hired Paolo and Niccolo Sangiovanni, he had made it a point to learn their strange tongue, largely so that he could keep close tabs on the brothers, listen to what they said to one another, though he never let on that he understood what they were saying.

Yes. It was Paolo, who had indeed survived the shootout in the Praza do Obradoiro, shouting to his brother, Niccolo. The two Italians were superb hunters and had never failed him in any assignment he had given them. They would not be easy to evade, but Bryson did not intend to evade them.

He heard Layla approach, and he looked up. "I need you to find us some rope or cable," he whispered.

"Rope?"

"Quickly! There must be a door off the chancel, maybe leading to a rectory, a supply closet, something. Please, *right away!*"

She nodded and ran back down the nave toward the sanctuary.

He stood quickly, opened the door a crack, and called out a few words in Friuliano. Since Bryson's ear for languages was almost pitch-perfect, he knew the accent would closely approximate that of a native. But more than that, he pitched his voice higher, tightening his throat to match Paolo's timbre. His mimicry was uncanny, he knew; it was one of his most useful talents. A few snatches of muffled, shouted phrases, heard at a distance and distorted by echoes, would sound to Paolo like his own brother. *"Ou! Paolo, pessèe! Lu ai, al è jù!"* Hey! Paolo, come quick! I've got him—he's down!

The response came rapidly. *"La setu?"* Where are you?

"Ca! Lì da vecje glesie—cu le sieradure rote!" This old church—the broken lock!

Bryson got to his feet quickly, spun to one side of the portico, flattening himself against the doorframe, the Beretta gripped in his left hand.

The footsteps accelerated, slowed, then approached. Paolo's voice now came from just outside the church door. "Niccolo?"

"*Ca!*" Bryson shouted, muffling his voice in the cloth of his shirt. "*Moviti!*"

A brief hesitation, then the door was flung open. In the sudden flood of light, Bryson saw the swarthy skin, the lean, sinewy build, the tight black curls of the close-cropped hair. Paolo squinted his eyes, his expression fierce. He entered warily, looking from side to side, his weapon down at his side.

Bryson sprung forward, slamming into Paolo with the full force of his body. His right hand was a rigid claw, smashing against the cartilage of the Italian's throat, twisting the larynx enough to disable, not to kill. Paolo let out a loud scream of pain and surprise. Simultaneously, with his left hand, Bryson cracked the Beretta against the back of Paolo's head, aiming with precision.

Paolo slumped to the floor, unconscious. Bryson knew the concussion was minor, that Paolo would be out no more than a few minutes. He grabbed the Italian's weapon, a Lugo, and quickly searched his body for any concealed weapons. Since Bryson had trained the Sangiovannis in field tactics, he knew there would be another weapon, and he knew where to find it: strapped to the left calf, under loose-fitting slacks. Bryson took that, too, and then removed a jagged fishing knife from a scabbard on the Italian's belt.

Layla was watching, stunned, but now she understood. She threw Bryson a large spindle of insulated electrical wire. Not ideal, but it was strong, and in any case it would have to do. Working quickly, the two of them bound the Italian's hands and feet so that the more he struggled, the tighter the knots would become. The design was of Layla's invention, and it was a clever one. Bryson tugged at the knots, satisfied that they would hold, and then he and Layla carried the assassin into a sacristy off the north transept. Here it was even dimmer, but their eyes had by now become accustomed to the low light.

"He's an impressive specimen," Layla said dispassionately. "Powerful — almost like a coiled spring."

"Both he and his brother were supremely gifted natural athletes. Hunters, both of them, with the innate skills, the instincts, of mountain lions. And just as ruthless."

"He once worked for you?"

"In a past life. He and his brother. A few brief assignments and one major one, in Russia." She looked at him questioningly; he saw no reason to hold out. Not now, not after everything she had put herself through for him. "There's a Russian institute known as Vector, in Koltsovo, Novosibirsk. In the mid- to late 1980s, rumors circulated in American intelligence circles that Vector was no mere research institute, but was involved in the research and production of agents of biological warfare."

She nodded. "Weaponized anthrax, smallpox, even plague. There were rumors . . ."

"According to a defector who came over in the late eighties—the former deputy chief of the Soviet biological warfare program—the Russians were targeting major U.S. cities for a biological first strike. Technical intelligence told us very little. A compound of low-rise buildings surrounded by high electrified fences and patrolled by armed guards. That was all the conventional U.S. intelligence agencies had, CIA or NSA. Without concrete evidence, neither the U.S. nor any other NATO government was willing to act." He shook his head. "Typically passive response on the part of the intelligence bureaucrats. So I was sent in to do a high-risk, dangerous penetration no other intelligence agency would ever dare. I assembled my own team of black-bag specialists and muscle, which included these boys. My employers had a shopping list—high-res photographs of containment facilities, air locks, fermentation vats for growing viruses and vaccines. And most of all, they wanted actual samples of the bugs—Petri dishes."

"My God . . . Your employers—but you said 'no other intelligence agency' would ever attempt such a thing. . . . Did CIA . . ."

He shrugged. "Leave it at that." He thought, *But what's the point of withholding anything, anymore?* "These fellows, the Sangiovanni brothers, were there to overpower night sentries, take out armed guards swiftly and silently. So they were muscle, of a rarefied sort." He smiled grimly.

"How'd they do?"

"We got the goods."

While they waited for Paolo to come to, Layla went to the church's front door and reassembled the broken hasp and padlock so that it appeared unbroken. Meanwhile, Bryson stood watch over the Italian assassin. In about twenty minutes, Paolo began to stir, his eyes shifting beneath his closed lids. He groaned slightly, and then his eyes came open, unfocused.

"*Al è pasât tant timp di quand che jerin insieme a Novosibirsk,*" Bryson said. It's been a long time since Novosibirsk. "I always knew you were devoid of any allegiances. Where's your brother?"

Paolo's eyes widened. "Coleridge, you bastard." He tried to pull his hands up, grimaced as the thin wires cut into his wrists. He snarled through bloody teeth, "*Bastard, tu mi fasis pensà a che vecje storie dal purcìt, lo tratin come un siôr, a viodin di lui, i dan dut chel che a voe di vè, e dopo lu copin.*" Bryson smiled and translated for Layla's benefit. "He says there's an old Friulian peasant proverb about the hog. They treat it like a prince, cater to it, serve its every need—until the day they slaughter it for meat."

"Who's the hog supposed to be?" asked Layla. "You or him?"

Bryson turned back to Paolo, speaking in Friuliano. "We're going to play a little game here called truth or consequences. You tell me the truth, or you face the consequences. Let's start with a simple question: Where's your brother?"

"Never!"

"Well, you've just answered one of my questions—that Niccolo came here with you. You almost killed me back in the square. What kind of gratitude is that to show your old boss?"

"*No soi ancjmò freât dal dut!*" Paolo bellowed. I'm not done yet! He struggled against the restraints, wincing.

"No," Bryson said with a smile. "Neither am I. Who hired you?"

The Italian spit a gobbet of saliva, which hit Bryson's face. "*Fuck you!*" he shouted in English, one of the few phrases he knew.

Bryson wiped at the spittle with his sleeve. "I'll ask you one more time, and if I don't get a truthful answer—the operative word being *truthful*— I'll be forced to use this." He held up the Beretta for display.

Layla approached, spoke quickly in a low voice. "I'm going to keep watch at the door. All this shouting may attract some unwanted attention."

ROBERT LUDLUM

Bryson nodded. "Good idea."

"Go ahead and kill me," the assassin taunted in his native language. "It makes no difference to me. There are others, *many* others. My brother may have the pleasure of killing you himself—it would be my dying gift to him."

"Oh, I have no intention of killing you," said Bryson coolly. "You're a brave fellow; I've seen you face down death fearlessly. Death doesn't frighten you, which is one of the things that make you so good at what you do."

The Italian's eyes narrowed in suspicion as he attempted to puzzle out the meaning. Bryson could see him shifting his ankles, his wrists, testing the restraints for weaknesses. But there were none.

"No," Bryson continued, "instead, I would rather take away the only thing that means anything to you: your ability to hunt, whether it's *cinghiale*, your beloved wild boar, or human beings placed 'beyond salvage' by the liars who control the secret arms of government." He paused, aimed the Beretta at the assassin's kneecap. "The loss of one knee, of course, won't keep you from walking—not with all the advanced prosthetic joints that are available these days—but you certainly won't be able to run very well. The loss of both of your knees—well, that will certainly deprive you of your livelihood, don't you think?"

The assassin's face went ashen. "You goddamned sellout," he hissed.

"Is that what they tell you? And who do they say I sold out *to?*"

Paolo stared defiantly, but his lower lip quivered.

"So I ask you one more time, and consider very carefully before you either refuse to answer or attempt to lie to me: *Who hired you?*"

"*Fuck you!*"

Bryson fired the Beretta. The Italian screamed, and blood drenched his pants at the knee. Most if not all of the kneecap was probably gone. He would not likely hunt prey, human or animal, again. Paolo writhed in pain. At the top of his lungs he shouted a string of curses in Friuliano.

Suddenly there came a crash at the church door, followed by a male voice shouting and a throaty cry in Layla's voice. Bryson whirled around to see what had happened—had she been struck? He rushed to the entrance just in time to see two silhouetted figures struggling in the dark-

148

ness. One of them had to be Layla; who was the other? He leveled his gun and shouted, "Stop or you're dead!"

"It's all right," came Layla's voice. He felt a surge of relief. "Bastard put up a nasty fight."

It was Paolo's brother, Niccolo, his arms trussed behind his back. A wire that hung loosely around his neck was all that remained of a garrote she had evidently used to pull tight around his throat the second he burst in. A thin, crimson line at the base of his neck was the telltale evidence of his near-strangulation. She had had the advantage of surprise, and had utilized it well; she had fashioned the restraint ingeniously so that the harder Niccolo pulled his arms, the harder the wire cut into his throat. His legs, however, were unbound, and though he sprawled on the floor, he kept kicking, wheeling around to try to gain his footing.

Bryson leaped atop Niccolo's chest, slamming his feet down to knock the wind out of him, and at the same time holding him down, enabling Layla to toss a loop of wire around his knees and ankles and bind them tightly. Niccolo bellowed like a gored ox, joining the bloodcurdling screams of his brother from the sacristy fifty feet away.

"Enough," Bryson said disgustedly. He ripped a length of cloth from Niccolo's khaki shirt, and, bunching it up, jammed it into Niccolo's mouth to muffle the bellowing. Layla produced a roll of strong packing tape she had located somewhere, probably in the supply closet where she had found the electrical wire, and she used it to secure the gag over Niccolo's mouth. Bryson ripped off another piece of Niccolo's shirt, handed it to Layla, and asked her to gag the brother as well.

While she did that, he dragged Niccolo down the nave to another alcove, shoving him into a confessional booth. "Your brother's just been shot, badly," Bryson told him, waving the Beretta. "But as you can hear, he's still alive. He won't be walking again."

Niccolo whipped his head back and forth, roaring through the gag. He bucked his legs up and down against the stone floor in a mute, animal-like display of defiance and anger.

"Now, I'm going to make this as simple for you as I can, my old friend. I want you to tell me who hired you. I want the complete verbal dossier, the codes, the contact names and procedures. Everything. As soon as I remove your gag, I expect you to begin talking. And don't even *contemplate* fabricating anything, because your brother has already told me a good deal, and if anything you say doesn't jibe with what he said, I'm going to assume that *he's* the one who's lying. And I will kill him. Because I really don't like liars. Are we clear?"

Niccolo, who had stopped bucking his legs, nodded frantically, his eyes wide, searching Bryson's face. The threat was obviously effective; Bryson had located the killer's single area of vulnerability.

From the other side of the church, Bryson could hear Paolo whimpering and groaning, muffled by the gag Layla had put in his mouth.

"My partner is across the aisle with Paolo. All I have to do is give her the signal, and she'll fire one single round into his forehead. Are we clear?"

Niccolo's nodding became even more frenzied.

"All right, then." He ripped the wide plastic tape off Niccolo's mouth, leaving a red stripe on the skin that had to have been extremely painful. Then he grabbed the bunched-up wet rag and yanked it out.

Niccolo took several deep, ragged breaths.

"Now, if you make the serious mistake of lying to me, you'd better hope your brother has already told me the exact same lie. Or you'll have killed him, just as if you yourself squeezed the trigger against his temple, understand?"

Niccolo gasped, "Yes!"

"But if I were you, I'd stick to the truth. The odds are much better. And bear in mind, I know where your families live. How's *nonna* Maria? And your mother, Alma—does she still have her boarding house?"

Niccolo's eyes were at once fierce and wounded. "*I am telling you the truth!*" he screamed in Friuliano.

"As long as we're clear about that," Bryson replied blandly.

"But we don't *know* who hired us! The procedures are the same as when we worked for you! We are the *mus*, the beasts of burden! They tell us *nothing!*"

Bryson shook his head ruminatively. "Nothing is ever sealed in a vacuum, my friend. You know that as well as I. Even when you deal with a cutout, you know your contact's cover name. You can't help but pick up bits and pieces of information. And they may not tell you *why* you're doing a particular operation, but they always tell you *how* to do it, and that can be quite revealing as well."

"I told you, we don't *know* who our employers are!"

Bryson raised his voice, speaking with controlled fury. "You worked with a team, under a team leader; you were issued instructions; and people *always* talk. You damned well know who hired you!" He turned toward the aisle as if preparing to call out a signal.

"No!" cried Niccolo.

"Your brother—"

"My brother doesn't know either. I don't know what he said to you, but *he doesn't know!* You know how the lines, the—compartments—how this works! We're only the hired help, and they pay us in cash!"

"Language!" Bryson demanded.

"*Che . . .* language?"

"The team you're working with here. What *language* do they speak to one another?"

Niccolo's eyes were wild. "Different languages!"

"The team *leader!*"

"Russian!" he shouted desperately. "He's a *Russian!*"

"KGB, GRU?"

"What do we know of these things?"

"You know faces!" Bryson spat out. Louder, he called: "Layla?"

Layla approached, understood Bryson's gambit. "Would you like me to use a silencer?" she inquired in a matter-of-fact way.

"No!" Niccolo thundered. "I tell you what you want to know!"

"I'll give him another sixty seconds," Bryson said. "Then, if I don't hear what I want to hear, fire away—and yes, actually, a silencer might be a good idea." To Niccolo, he said, "They hired you to kill me because you know me, know my face."

Niccolo nodded, his eyes closed.

"But they knew you once worked for me, and they wouldn't just hire you to kill your old employer without a plausible cover story. No matter how little loyalty you two have. So they told you I was a sellout, a traitor, is that right?"

"Yes."

"A traitor to what, to whom?"

"They only said you were selling names of agents, that we and everyone else you'd ever worked with would be identified, flushed out, executed."

"Executed by *whom?*"

"Hostile parties . . . I don't know, they didn't say!"

"Yet you believed them."

"Why would I not believe them?"

"Was a bounty placed on my head, or was this a straight job price?"

"Yes, a bounty."

"How much?"

"Two million."

"Lire or dollars?"

"Dollars! Two million *dollars.*"

"I'm flattered. You and your brother could have retired to the hills and hunted *cinghiale* to your hearts' content. But the problem with offering a bounty to a team is that it diminishes the incentive for the team to coordinate; everyone wants to make the hit separately. Bad strategy, self-defeating. The bearded one was the team leader?"

"Yes."

"Was he the Russian-speaker?"

"Yes."

"You know his name?"

"Not directly. I hear someone call him Milyukov. But I know the face. He's like me, like us—he does assignments."

"Freelance?"

"They say he works for a—a plutocrat, a Russian baron. One of the secret powers behind the Kremlin. A very rich man who owns a conglomerate. Through it, they say he secretly runs Russia."

"Prishnikov."

There was a glint of recognition in the Italian's eyes. He had heard the name before. "Maybe, yes."

Prishnikov. Anatoly Prishnikov. Founder and chairman of the mammoth, shadowy Russian consortium Nortek. Immensely rich and powerful and, indeed, the power behind the throne. Bryson's heart began beating rapidly. Why would Anatoly Prishnikov have sent someone to eliminate Bryson?

Why?

The only logical explanation seemed to be that Prishnikov was controlling the Directorate, or was among those controlling it. Harry Dunne of the CIA had said that the Directorate had been founded and, from its beginning, been controlled by a small cabal of Soviet GRU 'geniuses,' as he put it.

"What if I told you that the Directorate in fact isn't part of the United States government?" Dunne had said. *"That it never was . . . The whole thing was an elaborate ruse, do you see? . . . A penetration operation right on enemy soil—our soil."*

And then, after the Cold War ended, as the Soviet intelligence services fell into collapse, control of the Directorate *shifted into other hands*, he had said. Agents were terminated.

I was set up, then pushed out.

And Elena? She had disappeared—meaning what? That she was deliberately separated from him? Could that explain it? That the masters had to keep the two of them apart from each other for some reason? Because they knew things, could put things together?

". . . Now we've got reason to think it's being reactivated," Dunne had said. *"Your old masters appear to be accumulating arms, for some reason. . . . You could say they're poised to foment global instability. . . . Seems they're trying to stockpile an arsenal. We think they're instigating some kind of turbulence in the southern Balkans, although their target is elsewhere."*

Their ultimate target is elsewhere.

Generalities, blanket statements, vague assertions. The outlines remained murky and uncertain. Facts were all he had to work with, and there were altogether too few of them.

Fact: A team of assassins made up of Directorate operatives—past or present ones, he had no idea—had been trying to kill him.

But *why?* Calacanis's security forces may simply have considered him an interloper, a penetration agent to be eliminated. But the assassin-squads here in Santiago de Compostela seemed too well organized, too orchestrated, to be simply a reaction to his appearance on Calacanis's ship.

Fact: The Sangiovanni brothers had been hired to kill him even before his appearance on the *Spanish Armada*. The controllers of the Directorate had decided he was a threat prior to that. But how, and why?

Fact: The leader of the assassin squad was also in the employ of Anatoly Prishnikov, an immensely wealthy private citizen. Thus, Prishnikov had to be one of the controllers of the Directorate—but why would an ostensibly private citizen be running a rogue intelligence outfit?

Did this indicate that the Directorate had gone private—had been the object of a hostile takeover, co-opted by Anatoly Prishnikov? Had it become a private army of Russia's most powerful, most secretive mogul?

But something else occurred to him. "You said the team spoke other languages," he said to Niccolo. "You mentioned French."

"Yes, but—"

"But nothing! Which member of the squad spoke French?"

"It was the blonde."

"The blond woman in the plaza—her hair was up."

"Yes."

"And what are you holding back about her?"

"Holding *back?* Nothing!"

"I find this very interesting, because your brother was much more talkative on the subject." The bluff was audacious, but made with enormous certitude and therefore quite convincing. "*Much* more talkative. Perhaps he *invented* things, made up a story—is *that* what you're telling me?"

"*No!* I don't know what he told you—we just overheard things, little scraps. Maybe names."

"Maybe names?"

"I heard her speaking in French to another agent who was aboard the arms ship that blew up. The *Spanish Armada.* The agent was a Frenchman who was there to make some kind of arms deal with the Greek."

"A deal?"

"This Frenchman is—*was*—a double, I heard them say."

Bryson recalled the longhaired, elegantly dressed Frenchman from Calacanis's dining room. The Frenchman was known to be an emissary from Jacques Arnaud, France's wealthiest and most powerful arms dealer. Was he with the Directorate as well, or at least working with or for them? What did it mean that Jacques Arnaud, the extreme-right-wing French arms merchant, was somehow in league with the Directorate—and therefore in league, too, with the richest private citizen in Russia?

And if it was true that two powerful businessmen, one in Russia and one in France, were controlling the Directorate, using it to foment terrorism around the world—what was their objective?

They left the two Italian brothers bound and gagged in the old cathedral. Bryson asked Layla, who had had paramedic training, to attempt to stanch the blood flow from Paolo's ruined knee, using a tightly fastened rag to compress the wound.

"But how can you be so considerate to a man who tried to murder you?" she asked later, genuinely puzzled.

Bryson had shrugged. "He was just doing his job."

"This is not how we work in the Mossad," she protested. "If a man has tried to kill you and failed, you must never let him get away. It is an inviolable rule."

"I have a different set of rules."

They spent the night in an anonymous, small *hospedaje* outside Santiago de Compostela, where she immediately set to work dressing his shoulder wound, cleansing it with peroxide she had purchased at a *farmacía*, suturing it and applying an antibacterial ointment. She worked quickly, with the practiced skill of a medical professional.

Appraising his shirtless torso, she ran her finger along a long, smooth welt. The wound inflicted by Abu in Tunisia, on Bryson's last assignment, had been repaired by a top-flight surgeon on contract with the Directorate. No longer did it throb painfully, though the memory remained, as traumatic as ever.

"A memento," he said grimly, "from an old friend." Outside the small window, the rain was coming down in sheets over the moss-stained cobblestone.

"You nearly died."

"I had some good medical care."

"You have been attacked often." She fingered a much smaller wound, a dime-size area of puckered flesh on his right biceps. "This?" she inquired.

"Another memento."

The memory of Nepal came flooding back, overpoweringly so, of a fearsome adversary named Ang Wu, a renegade officer in the Chinese Army. Now Bryson wondered what had *really* happened in that exchange of gunfire. What had he really been sent to do, and on whose behalf? Had he really been only a pawn of a malevolent conspiracy he still didn't understand?

So much blood spilled; so many lives wasted. And for what? What had his life meant? The more he learned, the less he understood. He thought of his parents, of the last time he saw them alive. Was it truly possible they had been killed by the masterminds behind the Directorate? He thought about Ted Waller, the man he had once admired more than anyone in the world, and he felt a surge of rage.

What was it that Niccolo, the Friulian assassin, had called himself and his brother—beasts of burden? They were hired muscle, pawns in the service of an odious game whose rules were never explained to them. Now it occurred to Bryson that there was no difference between him and the Italian brothers. They were all no more than instruments used by shadowy forces. Nothing better than pawns.

She had been sitting on the edge of the bed; now she got up and went to the tiny bathroom, returning a moment later with a glass of water. "The pharmacist gave me a few antibiotic pills. I told him I'd be getting a prescription in the morning, so he was willing to give me enough to tide you over." She handed him a few capsules and the glass. A flash of the old suspicion spoke to him silently, warningly: What were these unmarked pills she was giving him? Until the more rational voice in his head: *If she wanted to kill you, she's had plenty of opportunities to do it, more directly, in the last twenty-four hours. More than that, she simply didn't have to risk her own life to save yours.* He took the capsules from her and washed them down with a swallow of tap water.

"You seem distant," Layla said as she packed up the medical supplies. "Far away. You're thinking of something troubling."

Bryson looked up, nodded slowly. Sharing a room with a beautiful woman—even though the sleeping arrangements were quite chaste, she in the bed, he on the sofa—was something he had not done since Elena's sudden departure, years ago. The opportunities had presented themselves time and time again, but he had remained monastic, for some reason punishing himself for whatever he had done to send her away.

What *had* he done?

How much, he wondered, of their life together had been set up, stage-managed by Ted Waller?

And he thought back to the one time, the one important time, that he had lied to her. He had lied to protect her. He had concealed something from her. Waller was fond of quoting Blake: "We are led to believe a lie," he would orate, "when we see not through the eye."

But Bryson had not meant for Elena to see, to know, what he had done for her.

Now he searched his mind, recalling that evening in Bucharest that he had kept from her.

What was the truth? *Where* was the truth?

For all its paranoia and mayhem, the underworld of the black-operations specialist is a small one, and word travels fast. Bryson had received intelligence through several reliable contacts that a team of ex-Securitate "sweepers" was offering serious money for any leads that might unearth the location of one Dr. Andrei Petrescu, the mathematician and cryptologist who had betrayed the revolution by leaking the Ceauşescu government's ciphers. Among the disaffected former members of the notorious secret service there was great bitterness about the coup d'etat that had unseated their patron's government and removed them from power. They would never forgive or forget the traitors and were determined to hunt them down, whatever the cost, however much time it took. They had targeted several turncoats, Petrescu among them. Scores were to be settled, vengeance won.

Through a blind relay, Bryson arranged a meeting in Bucharest with the chief of the sweepers, the former number-two in the Securitate. Though Bryson's cover identity was not known to the Securitate man, his bona fides were established. The message was relayed that Bryson had urgent information that would undoubtedly be of great interest to the sweepers. He would come to the rendezvous site alone, verifiably so; the Securitate man was to do the same.

For Bryson, this was personal. He had made arrangements without the Directorate's knowledge. Such an off-the-books meeting would never have been approved; the potential ramifications were too serious. Yet Bryson could not risk having the contact vetoed; this was too important to Elena, and therefore to him. So he notified headquarters that upon the conclusion of an operation in Madrid he would be taking a much-needed, if altogether too brief, vacation, a long weekend in Barcelona. Permission was, of course, granted; he had long been owed vacation time. He was acting in direct contravention of Directorate policy, yes, but he had no choice. This had to be done. He purchased flight tickets in cash under an assumed name that appeared nowhere in Directorate databanks.

Neither did he tell Elena what he was doing, and here the deception was most important, for she would never have approved his meeting with the head of the team who sought to kill her father. Not only would she deem it far too dangerous to her husband, but she had made it abundantly clear on several occasions that under no circumstances was he to freelance in matters involving her parents. She was terrified of losing both her husband and her parents, of stirring up the hornet's nest of Securitate vengeance. Were it up to her, he would never have made such an appointment. And until now, he had respected her wishes. But this was an opportunity not to be passed up.

Bryson met the ex-Securitate man at a dark, subterranean bar. As promised, he had indeed come alone, although he had laid careful plans in advance. Favors had been called in, bribes paid.

"You have information on the Petrescus," said Major General Radu Dragan as Bryson joined him at a dimly lit booth.

Dragan knew nothing about Bryson, but Bryson, drawing upon his network of sources, had done his homework. Elena had first mentioned his name on the night of the exfiltration from Bucharest, to scare off the policeman who had been so interested in what was in the truck; as it turned out, she knew the man's name and phone number so well because Dragan had been the one who had enlisted her father's help; Andrei Petrescu's betrayal of the Securitate was therefore a very personal matter to Dragan.

"I certainly do," said Bryson. "But first we should discuss terms."

Dragan, a craggy, sallow-faced man of sixty, raised his brows. "I am *happy to discuss 'terms,' as you put it, once I learn the nature of what you have to tell me."*

Bryson smiled. "Absolutely. The 'information' I have to give you is quite simple." He slid a sheet of paper across the table; Dragan picked it up and scrutinized it in puzzlement.

"What—what is this?" asked Dragan. "But these names—"

"—are the names of every single member of your extended family, all relatives by blood or by marriages, along with their private addresses and telephone numbers. You, who have taken such security precautions to protect those near and dear to you, should recognize what immense resources I must have access to in order to have been able to unearth that information. Therefore you must know how easy it would be for me and my colleagues to track down each and every one of them, even if you were able to hide them all once again."

"Nu te mai piş a impráş tiat!" barked Dragan. Don't piss at me! "Who the hell are you? How dare you talk to me like this!"

"I simply want your reassurance that all your sweepers will be called off immediately."

"You think that because one of my men sells information to you, you can make threats?"

"As you are well aware, none of your men has access to this information; even your most trusted aide knows but a few names and vague locations. Believe me, my information comes from sources far more reliable than any of your circle. Purge them all, execute them all; it will make no difference. Now, listen to me. If you, or anyone who works with or for you or is connected to you in any way whatsoever, harms a hair on the Petrescus' heads, my associates will personally maim and then murder every member of your family."

"Get out of here! Leave at once! Your threats are of no interest to me."

"I am giving you the opportunity to call off the sweepers right this very minute." Bryson glanced at his watch. "You have exactly seven minutes to issue the order."

"Or?"

"Or someone you care about very much will die."

Dragan laughed and poured himself more beer. "You are wasting my time. My men are in this pub watching me, and all I have to do is signal

ROBERT LUDLUM

and they will take you away before you have a chance to make a single phone call."

"Actually, it's you who are wasting time. The fact is, you want me to make a phone call. You see, my associate is in an apartment on Calea Victoriei at this very moment, with a gun to the head of a woman named Dumitra."

Dragan's already pale face went even paler.

"Yes, your mistress, who strips at the Sexy Club on Calea 13 Septembrie. Not your only mistress, but she has lasted several years already, so you must have at least some kindly feelings toward her. My associate is waiting for my telephone call to come in over his cell phone. If he does not receive it in"—Bryson glanced again at his watch—"six, no, five minutes, he has been instructed to put a bullet through her brain. All I can say is, you had better hope my phone is working, and his, too."

Dragan scoffed, but in his eyes Bryson could see the anxiety.

"You can save her life by rescinding the execution order on the Petrescus right now. Or you can do nothing, and she will die, and the blood will be on your hands. Here, you can use my cell phone if you don't have one with you. Just take care not to use up the battery—you really do want me to be able to reach my friend."

Dragan took a long sip of beer, feigning casualness.

But he did not speak, and four minutes passed by quickly.

With barely one minute remaining before the execution deadline, Bryson called the Calea Victoriei.

"No," he said when the phone was answered. "Dragan refuses to rescind the order, so I'm afraid this call is just to ask you to go ahead. But do me a favor, and hand the phone to Dumitra so she can make a last-minute plea to her rather coldhearted lover." Bryson waited until he could hear the woman's desperate voice on the other end of the line, and then he handed the phone to Dragan.

Dragan took it, said a brusque hello, and even across the table Bryson could hear the mistress's shrieked pleas. Dragan's face began twitching, but he said nothing. Yet it was obvious that he recognized Dumitra's voice and knew this was no hoax.

"Time's up," said Bryson, glancing for a last time at his wristwatch.

Dragan shook his head. "You have bought the bitch off," he said. "I

THE PROMETHEUS DECEPTION

don't know how much you paid her to act out this little farce, but I'm sure it wasn't much."

The first shot exploded out of the earpiece; Bryson could hear it four feet away, followed instantly by the strangled scream. There was another shot, but this time there was no scream.

"Is she that good an actress? No?" Bryson stood up and took the phone back. "Your stubbornness and skepticism just cost the life of your woman. Your people will confirm for you what has just happened, or you can go to her apartment and see for yourself if you can stand to do it." He was sickened and horrified by what he'd had to do, but he knew there was no other way to prove that he was serious. "There are forty-six names on that piece of paper, and one of them will be murdered every day until your entire family is extinct. The only way you can stop it is by rescinding the orders on the Petrescus. And once again, let me remind you that if anything happens to them, anything at all—your family will be executed en masse at once."

He turned around and walked out of the pub and never saw Dragan again.

But within an hour the word went out that the Petrescus were not to be touched.

Bryson said nothing about it to either Elena or Ted Waller. When he returned home several days later, Elena asked him about his trip to Barcelona. Normally, they each respected the partitions between their lives and work, avoiding asking each other questions about what each other was doing; she had never before asked about his travels. But this time she studied his face as she asked him questions about Barcelona, far too many questions. He lied easily and persuasively. Was she jealous, was that it? Did she suspect him of meeting a lover on Las Ramblas? This was the first time he had ever detected such a note of jealousy on her part and it made him wish even more that he could tell her the truth.

But did he even know the truth?

"I know almost nothing about you," he said, getting up from the bed and sitting down on the sofa. "Except for the fact that you've saved my life several times in the last twelve hours."

161

"You need to get some rest," she said. She wore a pair of gray sweat-pants and a loose-fitting, oversized man's undershirt that emphasized, rather than concealed, the swell of her breasts. There were no clothes to pack, no busy work to occupy her hands, so she sat on the edge of the bed, folding her long, firm legs and crossing her arms across her breasts. "We can talk in the morning."

He sensed she was evading his questions, so he persisted:

"You work for the Mossad, yet you come from the Bekaa valley, speak with an Arabic accent. Are you Israeli? Lebanese?"

Looking down, she said quietly, "Neither. Either. My father was Is-raeli. My mother is Lebanese."

"Your father's dead."

She nodded. "He was an athlete, a superb athlete. He was murdered by Palestine terrorists at the Olympic Games in Munich."

Bryson nodded. "That was 1972. You must have been a baby."

She continued looking down, her face flushed. "I was not much more than two years old."

"You never knew him."

She looked up. Her brown eyes were fierce. "My mother kept him alive for me. She never stopped telling stories about him, showing us pictures."

"You must have grown up hating the Palestinians."

"No. The Palestinians are a good people. They are displaced, home-less, stateless. I despise the fanatics who think nothing of killing the in-nocent for the sake of lofty ideals. Whether they're Black September or the Red Army Faction; whether they're Israeli or Arab. I hate zealots of any kind. When I was barely out of my teens, I married a fellow soldier in the Israeli Army. Yaron and I were deeply in love as only the very young can be. When he was killed in Lebanon, that was when I decided to work for Mossad. To fight the zealots."

"Yet you don't consider Mossad a band of zealots?"

"Many of them are. Yet some are not. Since I freelance for them, I can pick and choose my assignments. That way I can be sure that the work I'm doing is for a cause I believe in. Many jobs I turn down."

"They must think highly of you to give you such latitude."

She bowed her head modestly. "They know my deep-cover skills and my connections. Maybe I'm the only one foolish enough to accept certain assignments."

"Why *did* you accept the assignment on the *Spanish Armada?*"

She cocked her head at him, looking surprised. "Why else? Because that's where the fanatics buy the weapons without which they could not kill the innocent. Mossad had good information that agents of the Jihad National Front were stocking up there—feeding at the trough. Placing me there was a two-month operation."

"And if it weren't for me, you'd still be there."

"And what about you? You told me you're CIA, but you're not, are you?"

"What makes you say that?"

She touched her nose with the tip of her index finger. "Something smells wrong," she said with a knowing smile.

"Something about me?" Bryson said, amused.

"Well, actually, something about your enemies, your pursuers. The assassin squads—that violates standard accepted protocol. Either you're a freelancer like me, or you're with some other agency. But not CIA, I don't think."

"No," he admitted. "Not CIA, exactly. But I'm working for them."

"Freelance?"

"In a way."

"But you've been in the business a long time. The scars on your body give it away."

"It's true. I *was* in the business a long time. But I was forced out. Now they've brought me back in for one last assignment."

"Which is—"

He hesitated. How much to tell her? "It's a counterintelligence mission, in a sense."

" 'In a sense' . . . 'in a way' . . . If you don't want to tell me anything, fine, so be it." Her nostrils flared as she spoke with quiet intensity. "We'll each get on our separate aircrafts out of Spain first thing in the morning and never see each other again. When we get home and do the inevitable paperwork, we'll each file contact reports on each other, debrief as completely as we can what we know about the other's work, and that'll be the extent of it. Inquiries will be made, then dropped. A sealed file will be added to the Mossad's archives on CIA, another one added to CIA's Mossad files, mere drops of water in the ocean."

"Layla, I'm grateful to you for everything—"

"No," she interrupted. "I don't want your gratitude. You misunderstand me. You don't *know* me at all. I have my own reasons for interest—selfish reasons, if you wish. We're both following an arms trail—to different places, different endpoints. But the trails intersect, overlap. Now, it's obvious to me that whoever it is who wants you dead, they're not fringe actors. Their resources and access to information is too good. They're probably governmental."

Bryson nodded. She had a point.

"Now, I'm sorry, but I won't lie to you. The acoustics in the church were such that I could easily overhear your interrogation of the Italian, without even trying. If I wanted to double-deal you, I wouldn't have admitted that to you, but it's a fact."

He nodded again. Also true. "But you don't understand Friuliano, do you?"

"I understand names. You mentioned Anatoly Prishnikov, a name that's well known to everyone in our line of work. And Jacques Arnaud—less well known, perhaps, but a provider of arms to many of Israel's enemies. He stokes the fires of the Middle East and gets enormously rich in the process. I know him, and I detest him. And I may have a way to get to him."

"What are you talking about?"

"I don't know where the trail leads you next. But I can confirm for you that one of Arnaud's agents was on the ship, selling weapons to Calacanis."

"The one with the long hair, double-breasted suit?"

"That's the one. He uses the name Jean-Marc Bertrand. He travels often to Chantilly."

"Chantilly?"

"The location of the château where Arnaud lives and entertains regularly, and quite lavishly." She stood, went briefly to the bathroom, and emerged a few minutes later, patting her face dry with a towel. Without her makeup her features were even more exquisite. Her nose was strong yet delicate, her lips full, and all dominated by wide brown eyes that were at once warm and intense, intelligent and playful.

"You know something about Jacques Arnaud?" Bryson asked.

She nodded. "I know a good deal about the man's world. The Mossad has had Arnaud in its sights for quite some time now, so I've been to Chantilly, as a guest at several of his parties."

"Under what sort of cover?"

She removed the coverlet from the bed. "As a commercial attaché at the Israeli embassy in Paris. Someone whose influence must be courted. Jacques Arnaud does not discriminate. He sells to the Israelis as readily as he sells to our enemies."

"Can you get me to him, do you think?"

She turned around slowly, her eyes wide. She shook her head. "I don't think that's a wise idea."

"Why not?"

"Because I can't risk compromising my operation any further."

"But you just said that we're on the same trail."

"That's *not* what I said. I said our trails intersected. That's a very different thing."

"And your trail doesn't lead to Jacques Arnaud?"

"It may," she acknowledged. "Or it may not."

"In any case it may be useful to you to go to Chantilly."

"In your company, I assume," she said teasingly.

"Obviously that's what I'm asking you. If you already have diplomatic contacts in Arnaud's social set, that would facilitate my entry."

"I prefer to work alone."

"A beautiful woman like you, on a social outing—wouldn't it be entirely plausible that you'd be accompanied by a male?"

She blushed again. "You flatter me."

"Only to twist your arm, Layla," Bryson said dryly.

"Whatever works, is that it?"

"Something like that."

She smiled, shook her head. "I'd never get clearance from Tel Aviv."

"Then don't request it."

She hesitated, dipped her head. "It would have to be a temporary alliance, which I may be forced to jettison at any moment."

"Just get me inside the château, and you can abandon me at the front door if you want. Now tell me something: Exactly *why* does Mossad have Jacques Arnaud in its sights?"

She gave him a look of surprise, as if the answer were so obvious it was scarcely worth saying. "Because in the last year or so, Jacques Arnaud has become one of the world's leading suppliers of arms to terrorists. This is why I found it interesting that the man who was summoned to see you—what was his name, Jenrette?—came aboard the ship in the company of Arnaud's agent, Jean-Marc Bertrand. I assumed this American named Jenrette was buying for terrorists. So I was quite intrigued to see that *you* were meeting with Jenrette. I must say, for much of the evening I wondered what you were doing."

Bryson fell silent, his mind working feverishly. Jenrette, the Directorate operative he knew as Vance Gifford, had come aboard with Jacques Arnaud's agent. Arnaud was selling weapons to terrorists; the Directorate was buying. Did that mean—by logical extension—that the Directorate was sponsoring terrorism around the globe?

"It's vital that I get to Jacques Arnaud," Bryson said very quietly.

She shook her head, smiling ruefully. "But we may get nothing out of it, either one of us. And that's really the least of our worries. These are very dangerous men who will stop at nothing."

"I'm willing to take that chance," Bryson said. "It's all I have right now."

The team of professional killers followed the screams. They had been assigned to mop up, which entailed searching the narrow, cobblestone streets that radiated off the Praza do Obradoiro in Santiago de Compostela. Now that it had been conclusively determined that their subject had eluded all location attempts, their next order of business was to locate all stray team members. The dead had been loaded into unmarked vehicles and brought to a cooperating local *mortuorio* where falsified papers would be drawn up, certificates of death stamped, the bodies buried in unmarked graves. Next of kin would be compensated handsomely and knew not to ask questions; this was standard operating procedure.

When the wounded and the dead had been rounded up and accounted for, there still remained two team members at large: the Friulian-speaking peasant brothers from the remote corner of northwestern Italy. A quick sweep of the streets turned up nothing; no emergency codes had been received. The brothers were not responding to repeated radio calls. They were presumed killed, but that was not a certainty, and black-operations procedures stipulated that the wounded were either to be extracted or finished off. So one way or another, the brothers had to be checked off on a list.

Finally it was a report of muffled screams emanating from a side street that drew the mop-up team's attention. They traced the sounds to an abandoned, boarded-up church. Once they burst in, they located first one brother, then the other. Both were manacled, tied up, and gagged, though one of the brother's gags was loose, which was fortunate: that had enabled his screams to be heard, and the brothers thereby located.

"Christ, what took you so long?" gasped the first brother in Spanish, through the loosened gag. "We could have died here! Paolo's lost a huge amount of blood."

"We couldn't permit that to happen," said one of the mop-up team. He took out his semiautomatic pistol and fired twice into the Italian's head, killing him instantly. "Weak links are unacceptable."

By the time he found the second brother, crouched in a fetus position, pale and shaking and surrounded by a large pool of blood, he could see that the brother knew what to expect. It was in Paolo's wide, unblinking eyes. Paolo did not even whimper before the two shots came.

CHAPTER
TEN

Chantilly, France

The magnificent Château de Saint-Meurice was situated thirty-five kilo-meters from Paris, a vast seventeenth-century manse whose splendor was dramatically illuminated by scores of artfully placed spotlights. No less dramatic or magnificent were its surroundings, great sculpted gardens lit this evening like a stage set. This was most appropriate, for the Château de Saint-Meurice was indeed a stage on which the rich and powerful promenaded, making their skillfully timed entrances and exits, exchanging carefully scripted banter. The actors and the audience, however, were one and the same. All were there to impress each other; all knowingly played their roles within the artificial confines of an elaborate masque.

Although the evening's occasion was a gathering of European trade ministers, an offshoot of the annual G-7 Conference, the cast of characters did not change much from party to party at the Château de Saint-Meurice. The beautiful people of Paris and its environs were all there, *tout le beau monde,* or at least everyone who mattered. Clad in their finest evening wear, their tuxedoes or evening gowns, the women glittering with jewels normally sequestered in a safe or bank vault, they arrived in their sparkling, chauffeured Rolls Royces or Benzes. There were *comtes* and *comtesses, barons* and *baronnes, vicomtes* and *vicomtesses;* there were royalty from the corporate world and celebrities from the world of the broadcast media and the theater; they came from the highest levels of the Quai d'Orsay, from the most rarefied circles in which high society intersected with high finance.

Across the drawbridge and up the front steps of the château, the walkway lined with hundreds of candles whose flames danced in the gentle evening breezes, came elegant men with silver hair, but also inelegant men, squat and balding, whose coarse appearance belied the immense power and influence they wielded, some of whom wore on their arms their flashiest accoutrements, long-legged, glamorous mistresses to be displayed before one and all.

Bryson wore a tuxedo from Le Cor de Chasse, and Layla wore a spectacular strapless black gown obtained at Dior. Around her neck was a simple choker of pearls whose understated elegance did not detract from her extraordinary beauty. Bryson had been to many a function like this in his previous life, and had always felt like an observer rather than a participant, though he was meant to fit in as one of them—as he inevitably did. The semblance of poise came naturally to him, though not the sense of belonging.

Layla, however, seemed entirely at ease. A few traces of makeup, deftly and subtly applied—little more than eyeliner and lip gloss—accentuated her natural beauty, her olive skin, her large liquid brown eyes. Her wavy chestnut hair was pinned up, with just a few strands deliberately unrestrained, emphasizing her lovely swan neck; the risqué though tasteful décolletage of her gown highlighted her magnificent breasts. She could, and did, pass for either Israeli or Arab, being in fact both. She smiled easily, laughed merrily, her eyes inviting and withholding all at once.

She was greeted by several people, all of whom seemed to know her in her legend as an Israeli diplomatic functionary from the Foreign Ministry in Tel Aviv with mysterious clout and connections. Layla seemed to be known, yet not known, which was the perfect situation for a covert operative to be in. She had placed a call, earlier the day before, to a casual acquaintance at the Quai d'Orsay known to have close ties to

Jacques Arnaud, the master of the Château de Saint-Meurice and a fixture at Arnaud's many parties. The acquaintance, who served as one of the arms manufacturer's social antennae, was *delighted* to hear that Layla was in Paris for a few days, *mortified* that she had not been directly invited to this fête, which was *surely* an oversight, and had insisted that Layla by all means *must* come; Monsieur Arnaud would be *most* offended, *appalled*, if she did not. And by all means, she must bring an escort, for the acquaintance knew that the lovely Layla was rarely without one.

Bryson and Layla had talked late into the night, strategizing their visit to Arnaud's château. For it was a supremely risky venture, after the destruction of the *Spanish Armada*. Obviously there were no survivors who might recognize either of them, but powerful men like Calacanis and any others aboard the ship, including the emissaries and agents sent by powerful men, simply did not perish in a fiery inferno without alarms going off in boardrooms and inner offices all around the world. Powerful men engaged in nefarious and hugely profitable enterprises would be on a heightened state of alert. Jacques Arnaud had lost one of his conduits, and therefore he had to be concerned for his own safety; who knew whether the obliteration of Calacanis's tanker had been merely the first shot fired in a campaign being waged against black-market arms dealers worldwide? As France's leading arms manufacturer, Jacques Arnaud would always be careful about possible threats to his life and livelihood; in the aftermath of the explosion off the Cabo Finisterre, he would be extra-cautious.

Layla had been a green-eyed blonde, so at least her appearance had been radically altered. Bryson, however, could not take the chance that he would not be recognized. If surveillance video had been uplinked from the ship via satellite at any time before the ship's destruction, then video stills of his likeness would have been circulated among private security forces with enormous resources.

So Bryson had purchased certain products at a stage-costume-supply shop near the Opera, and by the next day his appearance had been altered dramatically. His hair was now silver-gray, with the variegated tones of a blond man who had gone gray. The technical services wizards at the Directorate had tutored Bryson well in the black arts of disguise. Cheek inserts had turned his face jowelly; the application of spirit gum had put latex pouches under his eyes, as well as wrinkles and fine lines around the eyes and mouth. Subtlety was paramount, as Bryson had learned from years of disguise: minor changes could have major effects yet raise no suspicions. He now looked easily twenty years older, a distinguished older gentleman who fit right in with the other men of accomplishment and position who frequented the Château de Saint-Meurice. He had become James Collier, an investment banker and venture capitalist from Santa Fe, New Mexico. As was not uncommon among certain venture capitalists who preferred to work away from the glare of public scrutiny, he would say little about what he actually did, turning away polite inquiries with self-deprecating wit.

Bryson and Layla were staying at a small, moderately priced, anonymous hotel on rue Trousseau. Neither one of them had stayed there before; its chief distinction was its very mediocrity. Each of them had arrived in Paris by a different route from Labacolla Airport—Bryson via Frankfurt, and Layla via Madrid. There had been a certain awkwardness about the sleeping arrangements, no doubt unavoidable. They were traveling as a couple, which usually meant sharing a bed or at least a room. Yet Bryson had requested that the hotel put them in separate bedrooms in an adjoining suite. A bit out of the ordinary, perhaps, but it did bespeak a certain level of propriety on the part of the unmarried couple, an old-fashioned discretion. In truth, Bryson knew the temptations of the flesh threatened to overwhelm him. She was a beautiful, highly sexual woman, and he had been solitary for far too long. But he did not want to destabilize an already tenuous working relationship, he told himself. Or perhaps he feared losing a necessary wariness. Was that it? Was it that he *wanted* to keep his distance so long as Elena remained a question mark in his life?

Now, as Layla guided him across the crowded room, smiling and nodding to social acquaintances, she kept up a lilting patter. "The story is that the château was built in the seventeenth century by one of Louis the Fourteenth's ministers. It was so grand that the king became jealous, had the minister arrested, stole his architect and landscaper and all the furniture, and then, inspired by a fit of envy, started construction on Versailles, determined never to be outdone."

Bryson smiled and nodded, maintaining the appearance of a moneyed guest suitably impressed by his surroundings. As Layla spoke, his eyes roamed the crowd, ever alert for the familiar face, the quickly averted glance. He had done this sort of thing countless times before, but this time was different, nerve-racking: he had stepped into the unknown. Also, his plan was vague, a necessary improvisation based on his own finely honed instincts.

Exactly what *was* the connection, if any, between Jacques Arnaud and the Directorate? The team of assassins dispatched to kill him had been working with Arnaud's man on the *Spanish Armada*. The assassins—the Friulian brothers—were Directorate hires, which strongly indicated that Arnaud himself was at least affiliated with the Directorate in some mysterious, unspecified capacity. More than that, a man known by Bryson to be Directorate—Vance Gifford, or, as he'd styled himself, Jenrette—had been aboard the ship, having arrived in the company of Arnaud's emissary.

It was all highly circumstantial, but taken together, the pieces of circumstantial evidence created a mosaic that was highly suggestive. Jacques Arnaud was one of the shadowy powers who now controlled the Directorate.

What Bryson needed was *proof.* Hard, incontrovertible evidence.

It was here somewhere, but *where?*

According to Layla, the Israelis believed that Jacques Arnaud's firm was involved in laundering enormous sums of money for criminal elements that included the Russian *mafiya*. The Mossad's surveillance suggested that Arnaud often received and placed business-related calls here, at his château, and repeated attempts by the Mossad and other intelligence services to tap his phones had proven useless. His communications were undecipherable, protected by hard encryption. This strongly suggested to Bryson that somewhere in the château there had to be specialized telecommunications equipment, "black" telephones at least, capable of encrypting, and decrypting, telephonic signals—phone calls, faxes, and E-mails.

As they maneuvered through the crowds, from room to room, Bryson noticed the paintings that crowded the walls, and that gave him an idea.

In a small room upstairs, two men in business suits sat in semidarkness, their faces illuminated only by the eerie bluish flicker from the banks of video monitors. The stainless steel and brushed chrome, the fiber-optic cables and cathode-ray tubes, made up a peculiar modern-art installation mounted on the ancient stone walls. Each monitor displayed a different angle in a different room below. Miniaturized cameras concealed in the walls, in fixtures and fittings, unseen and unnoticed by the myriad guests, relayed high-resolution video images to the security men huddled before the monitors. The clarity was such that the watchers could zoom in on any face that was of interest or concern, pulling in tight for a close-up that took up an entire screen. Images could be digitized, electronically compared against other images stored in a vast off-site data bank known as the Network. Any questionable persons could be identified and discreetly invited to leave, if need be.

Buttons were pushed; a face was enlarged on one monitor, the features screened onto a grid and scrutinized by the two men. It was the silver-haired, slightly jowelly, sun-lined face of a man whose name, furnished in advance to Arnaud's security people, was James Collier of Santa Fe, New Mexico.

What drew the attention of the two men was not that they recognized the man's face. Instead, it was the fact that they did not recognize the face. The man was an unknown quantity. To Arnaud's ever-vigilant security force, the unknown was always a cause for concern.

Jacques Arnaud's wife, Giséle, was a tall, imperious woman of aristocratic bearing, with an aquiline nose and gray-streaked black hair. Her hairline was unnaturally high, her facial skin too taut, unmistakable evidence of regular visits to a "clinic" in Switzerland. Bryson spotted her holding court in a corner of the book-lined library, a small crowd hanging on her every word. Bryson recognized her face from her regular appearances in the society pages of *Paris Match*, several years of which he had pored over in the Bibliothèque Nationale de France.

The hangers-on seemed dazzled by her cleverness, her every aperçu received with uproarious merriment. Accepting two flutes of champagne from a waiter and handing one to Layla, Bryson pointed to a canvas that hung near where Madame Arnaud was holding forth. Striding up to it eagerly, thereby positioning himself within earshot of the hostess, Bryson remarked in a voice just loud enough to be overheard by the adjacent gathering, "Fantastic, isn't it? Ever see his portrait of Napoleon? Extraordinary—he turns Napoleon into a Roman emperor, posing him frontally like a statue, a living icon."

His gambit worked; the proud owner could not resist turning her head toward a conversation she found more intriguing, since it concerned one of her own works of art. Bestowing upon Bryson a gracious smile, she said in fluent English, "Ah, and have you ever seen a stare as hypnotic as the one Ingres gives Napoleon?"

Bryson returned the smile, glowing as if he had found a soul mate. He bowed his head and extended his hand. "You must be Madame Arnaud. James Collier. A wonderful evening."

"Pardon me," she announced to her gathering, gently dismissing them. Moving closer, she said, "I see you're an admirer of Ingres, Mr. Collier."

"I would say I'm an admirer of *yours*, Madame Arnaud. Your collection of pictures demonstrates a truly discriminating eye. Oh, may I introduce my friend, Layla Sharett, of the Israeli embassy."

"We've met before," said the hostess. "So good to see you again," she said, taking Layla's hand, though her attention remained riveted on Bryson. In her prime, Bryson saw, she must have been a woman of striking beauty; even as a woman in her early seventies, she was a coquette. She had the courtesan's talent for making a man feel he was the most fascinating man in the room, that no other man or woman existed. "My husband tells me he finds Ingres *boring*. He is not the connoisseur of art you seem to be."

Bryson, however, did not want to seize this potential opening to be introduced to Jacques Arnaud. On the contrary, he preferred not to be called to the arms tycoon's attention. "If only Ingres had been so fortunate as to have you as a subject for one of his portraits," he said, shaking his head wistfully.

She affected a scowl, though Bryson could see she was secretly pleased. "Please! I would *hate* to have my portrait done by Ingres!"

"He did take forever on some of his portraits, didn't he? Poor Madame Moitessier had to sit for twelve years."

"And he turned her into a Medusa, her fingers into *tentacles!*"

"But an extraordinary portrait."

"Claustrophobic, I think."

"They say he may have used a *camera lucida* to produce some of his compositions—in effect, spying on his subjects before he captured them, you might say."

"Is that right?"

"Still, as much as I admire his paintings, nothing compares to his drawings, don't you agree?" Bryson knew that the Arnauds' private collection included some of Ingres's drawings, displayed in less public rooms of the château.

"I couldn't agree more!" Giséle Arnaud exclaimed. "Though he himself considered his drawings to be potboilers."

"I know, I know—while he lived in poverty in Rome, he was forced to support himself by drawing pictures of visitors and tourists. Some of the greatest paintings were done by artists working just to keep food on the table. The fact is, Ingres's drawings are his best work by far. The use of white, of negative space, the way he captures light—they're truly masterpieces."

Madame Arnaud lowered her voice and said confidentially, "Actually, we have a few of his drawings hanging in the billiards room, you know."

The ruse had worked. Madame Arnaud had invited Bryson and his guest to stroll into parts of the house that were not open to the other guests. She had offered to show him the drawings herself, but Bryson had declined, refusing to steal her away; but if she really didn't mind, perhaps they could take a quick look by themselves?

As he and Layla wandered through halls and more intimate, less public rooms, whose walls were hung with less impressive works by lesser French artists, Bryson oriented himself. He had prepared well: he had located the collection of blueprints of historically important châteaux, maintained at the Bibliothèque Nationale de France, and had studied the layout of the Château de Saint-Meurice. He knew it was highly unlikely that the Arnauds would have done anything to alter Château de Saint-Meurice's floor plan; the only variable was the use they made of the rooms, the location of the bedrooms and offices, particularly Arnaud's private office.

Bryson walked idly arm-in-arm with Layla down one hallway, turning left into another. As they rounded a corner, they heard low, muffled, male voices.

They froze. The voices gradually became more audible and more distinct. The words were in French, but one speaker's French had a definite foreign accent, which Bryson quickly placed as Russian, probably from Odessa.

". . . to return to the party," the Frenchman was saying.

The Russian said something that Bryson couldn't quite make out. Then the Frenchman replied, "But once Lille happens, the outrage will be enormous. The way will be clear."

Signaling Layla to stay back, Bryson flattened himself against the wall and inched forward, his tread silent, all the while listening, concentrating. Neither the voices nor the footsteps seemed to be approaching. He took from the breast pocket of his tuxedo what looked like a silver ballpoint pen, then pulled from one end a long, thin, glasslike wire, telescoping it to its maximum eighteen-inch length. He bent the tip of the flexible fiber-optic periscope cable, then nudged it along the wall until it jutted out no more than half an inch beyond the wall's end. Looking into the small eyepiece, he was able to see the two men clearly. One, a trim, compact man with heavy black glasses, entirely bald, was clearly Jacques Arnaud. He was conferring with a tall, florid-faced man whom Bryson did not immediately recognize. A few seconds later the man's identity came to him: Anatoly Prishnikov.

Prishnikov. The mogul widely believed to be the true power behind the figurehead currently occupying the president's office in the Kremlin.

Shifting the fiber-optic periscope slightly, Bryson was startled to discover another man, much closer, seated just around the corner. A guard, clearly armed, stationed at the beginning of the corridor. Shifting the scope yet again revealed another seated figure, another armed guard, stationed halfway down the hall, where the men were standing, in front of a large, steel-paneled door.

Arnaud's private office.

They were in a part of the château that had no windows; ordinarily, it would be an unlikely location for an office. But Arnaud's chief concern was security, not views.

The two men made the sort of final gestures that indicated they were finished talking, and fortunately they headed down the hall in the other direction. There was no need for Bryson and Layla to disappear.

Withdrawing the fiber-optic periscope and collapsing it back into its pen case, he turned toward Layla and nodded. She understood without his saying anything. They had located their target, the locus of Jacques Arnaud's business activities within the Château de Saint-Meurice.

Swiftly, his tread silent, he backtracked until he found the open door to a room they had just passed. The sitting room was, as he had previously noted, dark and sparsely furnished, evidently rarely used. He consulted the luminous radium dial of his Patek Philippe watch. After a full minute had elapsed, he signaled to Layla, then ducked into the room, waiting in its dark recesses.

Layla began weaving down the hall toward the room that had to be Arnaud's private, secure office, staggering as if drunk. Suddenly she let out a whoop of laughter and said to herself, though loudly enough to be heard by at least the first guard, just around the corner, "There's *got* to be a bathroom around here *somewhere!*"

Turning the corner unstably, she came upon the armed guard, seated in a delicate antique chair. He straightened, stared at her with hostility. "*Puis-je vous aider?*" May I help you? he demanded stiffly in French, in a voice that commanded her to go no further. He was barely out of his twenties, with crew-cut black hair, heavy eyebrows, a pudgy, round face, and a five o'clock shadow. His small red mouth was turned down in a pugnacious frown.

She giggled and continued to stagger toward him. "I don't know," she replied provocatively, "*can* you help me? Why, what do we have here? *Un homme, un vrai*—a *real* man. Not like those *pédés*, those young fairies and old goats out there."

The guard's stern expression softened somewhat, his posture relaxed as he sized her up to be no threat to the security of Jacques Arnaud's sanctum. His cheeks reddened visibly. There was no doubt he was quite taken with Layla's voluptuous body, the swell of her breasts revealed by the low-cut black gown. "I'm sorry, mademoiselle," he said nervously, "please, stay right there—you must go no further."

Layla smiled coyly, bracing herself against the stone wall with one outstretched hand. "But why would I *want* to go any further?" she said huskily, suggestively, as she inched closer to him. "Looks like I've found what I've been looking for." She moved her hand along the wall, slinking ever closer to him, jutting her breasts forward.

The young guard's smile was uncomfortable. He cast a nervous glance down the hall at the other sentry, who seemed to be paying him no attention. "*Please*, mademoiselle—"

She lowered her voice. "Maybe you can help me . . . to find a bathroom."

"Back down the hall you came," he replied, attempting a businesslike tone, though without much success, "there is a restroom."

Her voice became even more breathy and suggestive. "But I keep losing my way around here, and if you wouldn't mind showing me . . ."

The guard again glanced uneasily at his compatriot, who was too far down the hall to take notice.

"Perhaps," she added, arching her brows, "a little guided tour. It needn't take long at all, hmm?"

Flush-faced and awkward, the guard rose from his chair. "Very well, mademoiselle," he said.

There were now, Layla calculated, several possible avenues the guard could pursue. If he happened to take her into the room in which Bryson was concealed, the guard would be taken down, the element of surprise a weapon as deadly as Nicholas Bryson's hands.

But the guard instead guided her into another room, this one a *chambre de fumeur*, comfortably furnished. He was, she noticed, quite unmistakably aroused. He gave a wolfish grin as he pulled the door closed.

It was time to put Plan B into effect. She turned to him, her face full of anticipation.

Silently, Bryson rushed into the hallway, turned the corner, and then slowed his pace, sauntering toward the sole remaining guard, who kept a solitary vigil before the closed steel-paneled door of Arnaud's presumably empty office.

Now it was Bryson's turn to feign drunkenness, though to a very different end. The guard looked up as Bryson approached with a loose-limbed, swaying walk.

"Monsieur," the guard said brusquely, part greeting and part warning.

As he sashayed closer to the guard, Bryson held up his gold Zippo lighter, shaking his head disgustedly. In English, he said, "The damnedest thing! Can you believe this? I remember my lighter, but it's the damned cigarettes I forget!"

"Sir?"

In French, Bryson said, "*Vous n'auriez pas une cigarette?*" He kept waving the Zippo and shaking his head. "You're a Frenchman—you *must* have one."

The guard obligingly reached into his jacket pocket at the same instant that Bryson flicked the Zippo's striker, which jetted forward not a tongue of flame but a quick spray of a powerful neural incapacitant. Before the guard even had a chance to reach for his gun, he was at once blinded and frozen in place; a few seconds later he slumped forward, unconscious.

Working quickly, Bryson propped the guard back on his chair like a mannequin, folding the man's hands in his lap. The guard's eyelids were closed, so Bryson, knowing from long experience that they could not be forced open, left him as he was. From a distance, one would assume the guard was on duty; a passerby who came near would assume the guard had fallen asleep.

The incapacitating spray was not the only item of security equipment Bryson had purchased in Paris; he also had with him an array of other small devices, including infrared- and RF-code scanners and grabbers and a security-gate scanner. But a quick inspection of the steel door confirmed that only one piece was necessary. No doubt Arnaud employed the usual alarms and intrusion detectors when he planned to be gone from his home for any lengthy period of time. This evening, however, having just stopped into his office and perhaps intending to return again within the next few hours, he had simply allowed the door to close behind him. Although the door locked automatically, it was by means of nothing more elaborate than a conventional pin-tumbler door lock. Bryson took out a small black device, a lock-pick gun that he had learned to use over the years and had found far speedier than a manual lock-pick set. He inserted it into the lock, then pulled the plunger back and forth a few times until the tumblers turned and the heavy door popped open.

Shining his small pen flashlight around the dark room, he was taken aback at how spare it was. There appeared to be no file cabinets, no locked credenza. In fact, the office had a barrackslike spareness. There was a small seating area with a couch, two chairs, and a coffee table, and a completely bare mahogany table used as a desk. On the desk were a Tensor lamp and two telephones. . . .

The phone.

The phone in question was there, a flat, charcoal-gray box about a foot square, apparently nothing more than a desk telephone with a lid. But Bryson recognized it at once. He had seen countless models, though few as sleek and compact: the latest generation of satellite encryption phone. The lid contained both the antenna and the RF. Built into the device was a chip containing the encryption algorithm, which used nonlinear-phase signal encryption, fixed-length convolver, unlimited 128-bit keys. Wiretapping the line would do no good, since the encryption key was never transmitted. An intercepted call would sound like garbled nonsense, the voices both highly encrypted and scrambled. The phone's satellite uplink capacity meant that it could work even from remote corners of the earth.

Bryson worked quickly, deftly dismantling the telephone. The door was locked behind him, and the guard would be out for at least half an hour, but there was a definite risk that Jacques Arnaud would return suddenly. If he did, and found one guard missing and the other passed out, he might simply attribute the wayward behavior to the party's carnival atmosphere, which had somehow infected his household staff. Of course, that was only if Layla had managed to keep the lustful young guard occupied. Somehow Bryson did not doubt her ability to do so.

There was nothing more he could do now than work as swiftly as he could.

Spread out before him on the burnished, bare surface of Arnaud's desk were the electronic guts of the telephone. Unseating the special read-only chip from the circuitry, he held it up, examining it in the strong light of the Tensor lamp.

It was precisely what he had hoped to find. The cryptochip was relatively bulky, as such proprietary chips typically were, having been produced in very small quantities to link a small cadre of conspirators while ensuring zero-knowledge encryption. The mere fact that Arnaud had such a piece of equipment sitting on his desk revealed that he was part of a tightly linked group, international in scope, that required absolute secrecy. Could he in fact be one of the hidden principals of the Directorate?

Bryson removed from his dinner jacket an object that looked like a miniature transistor radio. In the coin-size slot at one end he inserted the cryptochip, then switched the device on. An indicator light changed from green to red and then, some ten seconds later, back to green again. A signal had pulsed through the chip, capturing the data. He listened for any voices in the hallway or approaching footsteps; then, satisfied there were none, he ejected the cryptochip and replaced it in the satellite phone's circuitry. In a few minutes he had the phone reassembled. In the chip reader he now had stored all the specifications of the chip's "key," vast sequences of binary digits and algorithmic instructions. The encryption scheme changed each time the phone was used, never once repeating itself. It was a high-tech version of a self-replenishing one-time pad. Fortunately, he now had every single combination recorded. Making use of this information was a daunting task, but there were others who specialized in this highly specialized area.

Moments later Bryson was striding down the hall back toward the party. The guard in the corridor by the office door, he took note, was still out. When he came to, in ten minutes, he would quickly recall what had happened to him, but the odds were great he would do nothing, summon no help, for to reveal that he had been overpowered by one man was surely to ask for abrupt termination.

In the *chambre de fumeur*, the young guard stood with his trousers gathered around his feet, his shirt unbuttoned and hanging open, as he prepared for final gratification. Layla stroked his bare abdomen, kissing his neck. She had protracted things for just about as long as she plausibly could. Glancing at the sweep second hand of her tiny gold wristwatch, she took mental note of the time. According to their plan, it was just about time that . . .

A scuff on the stone floor outside.

Bryson's prearranged signal. He was precisely on schedule.

She stooped to grab her small black velvet evening bag, then gave the guard a quick, friendly peck on the check. "*Allons,*" she said crisply, rushing to the door. The guard gaped at her, his face flushed crimson, eyes half-maddened with desire. "*Les plus grands plaisirs sont ceux qui ne sont pas réalisés,*" she whispered as she glided out of the room. The highest pleasures are the unrealized ones. Just before she shut the door, she said, "But I will never forget you, my friend."

Layla's purse was heavier than it had been previously: it now contained his snub-nosed Beretta. She knew that the guard, however angry and frustrated he might be, would never say a word about her, for to do so would be to confess to an unforgivable security lapse. She checked her makeup in a compact mirror, reapplied her lip gloss, and then returned to the party, entering through the banquet room. Bryson, she saw, was himself just arriving.

A small string ensemble was playing chamber music in the banquet room, while coming quite audibly from the adjoining parlor were the thumping beat and blaring synthesizer sounds of rock music. The two sounds clashed bizarrely, the elegant strains of Mozart's eighteenth-century music easily overwhelmed by the jarring, earsplitting cacophony of the twenty-first.

Bryson placed an arm around Layla's slender waist and said to her quietly, "I hope you enjoyed yourself."

"Very funny," she murmured. "I'd much rather have traded places with you. Mission accomplished?"

As Bryson was about to reply, he noticed the balding head of Jacques Arnaud in a distant corner of the room. He seemed to be conferring with another man in a dinner jacket whose earpiece indicated that he was part of Arnaud's security team. Arnaud nodded, looking around the room.

Then another man rushed up to the two, his gestures and facial expressions revealing great urgency. There was a brief, huddled consultation; then Bryson saw Arnaud's gaze flicker in his direction. Suspicions had been aroused, security breaches reported, a warning sounded. Bryson had little doubt that Arnaud was looking directly at him, and wondered whether the Frenchman had been tipped off by surveillance cameras in the vicinity of his office. Bryson knew there would be cameras. But everything at this point was calculated risk. In fact, to do nothing was the gravest risk of all.

The answer came a second or two later, when the two security men Arnaud had been huddling with suddenly broke away and began threading their way through the crowd, each taking a different path around the room toward Bryson and Layla. In their singleminded haste, the guards collided with several guests. Then a third raced into the room, and it became immediately evident what they were doing: all three exits from the room were now covered, and Bryson and Layla could not escape.

Closed-circuit surveillance cameras had indeed captured their movements through the halls of the château outside of the party. Bryson's surreptitious entry into Jacques Arnaud's office had been observed; or perhaps, given the delay in response time, only his exit from the office had been seen.

And now they were surrounded.

Layla squeezed his hand with almost painful pressure, a silent alert; she, too, saw the vise they were in. Their options were severely restricted. Guns would not be fired if it were at all avoidable; Arnaud's people would try to apprehend Bryson and Layla quietly without alarming the other guests. Appearances were to be preserved if possible. But Bryson had little doubt of the ruthlessness of the host and his security team. If shots had to be fired, they would be. Explanations could be offered later, lies furnished, the true circumstances covered up.

Bryson's head spun as he watched the security men race toward him, slowed only by the obstacle presented by the other guests, in addition to Arnaud's preference to maintain some semblance of propriety. He felt Layla jabbing something into his hand and realized she was trying to hand him her black velvet handbag. But why? He had seen the bulge and had guessed that she had disarmed the guard in the *chambre de fumeur*, stolen his weapon. But surely she knew he had a weapon of his own.

The jabbing continued, and finally Bryson took the handbag from her, opening it, and realized at once what she had been so insistently trying to pass to him. He put the bag behind his back, slipped out the small canister, a leftover from the *Spanish Armada*, and yanked the lever before he dropped it to the floor. The grenade rolled a good distance along the ancient stone before it started spewing out dense gray smoke. Within seconds, a cloud of thick smoke began rising from the floor, along with an acrid, sulphuric odor.

Screams immediately erupted in the crowd, cries of *"Au feu!"* and "Run!" Arnaud's guards were a good six to eight feet away when the panic arose. Soon the separate cries were joined by others, male and female, the frenzy growing, hysteria overtaking the room as it filled with smoke. The proper, dignified party guests had become terrified lemmings, rushing toward the exits with shouts of fear. Alarms were clanging, presumably set off by smoke detectors. The music in both adjoining rooms had stopped; the chamber group and the rock group had joined the evacuation. The surging crowd was utter pandemonium, and Layla and Bryson disappeared into the stampede, unseen by Arnaud's security forces.

Guests screamed, clung to one another, elbowed others out of their way. As the two of them rushed through the main door, plunging through the flailing, panicked crowd, Bryson grabbed Layla and pulled her off in the direction of the elaborate topiary that surrounded the château. Within the thick hedges Bryson had concealed a motorcycle. He jumped astride the high-powered BMW and kick-started it, signaling for her to climb on.

Moments later they were roaring through the confusion and madness, leaving behind guests spilling out of the château's front doors, limousines pulling up to the château, summoned to rescue their frantic passengers. Within three minutes they were speeding down the A-1 highway toward Paris, passing car after car.

But they were not alone.

As they left other cars far behind, Bryson soon became aware of a small, high-powered black sedan accelerating, closing in on them, coming closer and closer, leaving other vehicles far behind. One hundred feet, fifty feet, twenty . . . and then Bryson saw, in the motorcycle's rear-view mirror, that the sedan was not just approaching, it was swerving madly, fishtailing back and forth. But it was not a car out of control; its bizarre movements were controlled, apparently deliberate.

It was trying to run Bryson off the road!

As Bryson opened the throttle fully, accelerating to the motorcycle's maximum capacity, he spotted an exit up ahead and abruptly changed lanes, veering toward the exit. The black sedan followed, cutting across several lanes of traffic, protesting horns blaring in its wake. Bryson could feel Layla's hands on his shoulders, her grip tightening. He winced; the pain was great, the shoulder wound exquisitely sensitive.

Bryson pulled on to the exit ramp, the car now less than ten or fifteen feet behind and gaining. "Hold on tight!" he shouted, and he felt Layla's hands squeeze even tighter in acknowledgment. He emitted an involuntary cry of agony.

Suddenly he spun off to the left, executing a one-hundred-and-eighty-degree "bootlegger's turn" in such a confined area that the motorcycle almost flipped over, but he somehow managed to regain balance, wheeling around until he was headed back down the ramp along the narrow shoulder, leaving the sedan still barreling up the exit.

Now, roaring down the highway the wrong way, he kept to the shoulder, which broadened somewhat. Headlights flashed furiously, horns blared. He glanced in the small rearview mirror. They had lost the black sedan; it had been forced by the cars behind it to continue up the ramp and off the highway.

Now the BMW's throttle was fully open; the engine straining, giving off a blatting noise. They were virtually flying along the side of the A-1, against traffic.

But they were still not in the clear, for rushing toward them was a single headlight of a motorcycle, speeding even faster than the other vehicles on the road, and Bryson knew it had to be another pursuer dispatched from the Château de Saint-Meurice.

There was a squealing of brakes, car horns honking, and suddenly the other motorcycle, too, had reversed direction and was just behind them. In the rearview, Bryson could see it gaining on them; though he could not see the make of the cycle, the engine roar told him that it was even more powerful than the BMW he had rented in Paris, capable of attaining even greater speeds.

Suddenly Bryson felt something slam into them. It was the other motorcycle, deliberately crashing into the rear wheel, almost knocking them over! Above the motorcycle's roar he could hear, very near his ear, Layla screaming in terror.

"Are you all right?" he shouted.

"Yes!" she screamed in reply. "But *move* it!"

He tried to put on another burst of speed, but the motorcycle was already traveling at its maximum.

Another impact sent the motorcycle veering off the side of the road. Just off the shoulder was a long flat meadow, cleared farmland interspersed with wooden boxes used to collect hay or other crops. Bryson righted the vehicle, then accelerated off the asphalt and onto the grass and dirt, the pursuing motorcycle right behind. No gunshots, which told him that the driver needed to use both hands for maneuvering and could not spare a hand to use a weapon.

Pursue your pursuer.

This had been one of Ted Waller's oft-repeated aperçus.

In the end, you will decide who is predator and who is prey. The prey survives only by becoming the predator.

Bryson now did the unexpected, circling around the meadow, carving deep ruts in the soft earth, until he was charging straight at the other motorcycle.

The other motorcyclist, obviously taken aback by this change in strategy, tried to spin out of the way, but there was no time. Bryson crashed into him, and the driver was flung from his vehicle.

Slamming on his brakes, the cycle spewing dirt into the air, he came to a stop. Layla leaped off, then he did, flinging the bike to the ground.

The other driver was running away, and as he ran he was obviously reaching for a weapon, but Layla already had hers out, and she fired the Beretta three times in rapid succession.

With a scream, the pursuer tumbled to the ground, but he had managed to wrest his weapon from its holster, and he fired back. His aim was off; bullets spit into the ground near them. Layla fired again, then Bryson had his gun out and fired, hitting their enemy in the chest.

He flew backward, sprawled on the ground, dead.

Bryson raced toward him, flipping the prone body over, rummaging through the man's pockets for identification.

He pulled out a wallet. He was not surprised to find one; the pursuer had been given no notice, and thus no time to rid himself of identifying documents.

What he saw, however, he was not prepared for. It was beyond a surprise; the shock was deep, stunning, taking his breath away.

The detritus of bureaucracy, in this case, was straightforward. Documents could be forged, but Bryson was an expert at recognizing fake documents, and this was not one of them. There was no doubt. He examined it carefully in the bright moonlight, turning it over, locating the requisite fibers and irreproducible markings.

"What is it?" Layla asked. He handed it to her; she saw at once.

"Oh, my *God!*" she said, her voice hushed.

Their pursuer had been no mere rent-a-cop, nor even a French citizen on Arnaud's security payroll.

He was a U.S. citizen, employed at the Paris station of the CIA.

CHAPTER
ELEVEN

The secretary had been with the Central Intelligence Agency for seventeen years, but she could count on the fingers of one hand the number of times anyone had tried to bypass her and barge into the office of her boss, Harry Dunne. Even on the few occasions when the Director of Central Intelligence dropped by his deputy's office unannounced (Harry almost always went to the director's office), and the matter was urgent, the director had at least waited for her to buzz Harry.

Yet this man had ignored her entreaties, her protestations and warnings, her firm insistence that Mr. Dunne was out of town, and had just done the unthinkable. He had stormed past her and had gone right into her boss's office. Marjorie knew the mandated security procedures; she pressed the emergency button mounted underneath her main desk drawer, thereby summoning Security, and only then had she frantically warned Harry Dunne over the intercom that, despite her best efforts, this lunatic was coming through.

Bryson knew there were only two choices now: retreat or confrontation, and he preferred confrontation, the only option that had a chance of eliciting spontaneous revelation, forcing unplanned truths. Layla had urged him to stay away from the Agency, counseling that survival was more important now than whatever information he could obtain. But to Bryson there was really no choice at all: to penetrate the lies, to finally learn the truth about Elena, about his entire life, he had to face Dunne.

Layla remained in France, trying to work her contacts, to learn what she could about Jacques Arnaud and his recent activities. He had not told her anything about the Directorate; it was still best to keep her in the dark. She said good-bye to him at Charles de Gaulle airport, surprising Bryson with the ardency of her hug, her kiss that was more than the farewell kiss of a friend, immediately after which she turned away in flushed embarrassment.

Harry Dunne was standing at his plate-glass window, jacket off, smoking a cigarette on a very long ivory holder. Smoking in the headquarters building was, Bryson knew, against Agency regulations, but as deputy director, Dunne was unlikely to be called on it by anyone. He turned as Bryson entered, Marjorie right behind him.

"Mr. Dunne, I'm so *sorry*, I tried to *stop* this man!" Marjorie called frantically. "Security's on the way."

For an instant Dunne seemed to be examining him, his narrow, creased face compressed into a frown, the small bloodshot eyes glittering. Bryson had taken care to disguise himself, alter his appearance just enough to confound any video face-matching equipment. Then Dunne shook his head as he exhaled a plume of smoke with a loud, hacking cough. "Naw, it's all right, Margie, call off Security. I can deal with this fella myself."

Bewildered, the secretary looked from her boss to the intruder, then, straightening, she backed out of the room, closing the door behind her.

The white-haired Dunne took a step toward Bryson, visibly enraged. "All Security would do would be to restrain me from killing you with my bare hands," he snapped, "and I'm not sure I want that. What kind of game are you playing here, Bryson? You think we're fools, is that it? You think we don't get constant field reports, satellite feeds? I guess it's true what they say: once a traitor, always a traitor." Dunne snubbed out his cigarette in an overflowing glass ashtray on the edge of his desk. "I have no idea how the hell you got into the building, with all our vaunted security procedures. But I expect the surveillance video will tell the tale."

Bryson was jolted by the man's unbanked fury, and it caused him to hesitate. Fury was the last thing he expected on the part of Harry Dunne. Fear, defensiveness, bluster—but not anger. Through gritted teeth, Bryson said, "You sent out your henchmen to kill me. Low-level Paris-station flunkies."

Dunne snorted with derision as he pulled another cigarette from the jacket pocket of his rumpled gray suit. He inserted it in the ivory holder and lighted it, waving out the match and dropping it into the ashtray. "You can do better than that, Professor," Dunne said, shaking his head as he turned back to the picture window that looked over the verdant Virginia countryside. "Look, the facts are simple. We sent you out to worm your way back into the Directorate. Instead, all you seem to have done is blow up some of our most promising links to the Directorate. Then you disappeared, went to ground. Sort of like a mob hit man blowing away witnesses." He turned back to Bryson, exhaled a cloud of smoke into his face. "We thought you were ex-Directorate. I guess that's where we made our biggest mistake, huh?"

"What the hell are you trying to say to me?"

"I'd like to ask you to take a polygraph, but that's one of the first things they teach you boys, isn't it—how to beat the box?"

Disgusted, Bryson slapped a stiff blue plastic-laminate card onto the only bare spot of mahogany visible on Harry Dunne's desk. The Agency ID card he had pulled from the wallet of the dead motorcyclist outside of Paris, the pursuer dispatched from Jacques Arnaud's château. "You want to know how I got in here?"

Dunne picked it up, immediately examined the hologram: holding it up to the light, tipping it to bring out the three-dimensional CIA seal, finding the magnetic foil sandwiched between the plastic layers. It was an everyday object at the CIA, but only at the CIA—a high-tech, high-security identification card, virtually impossible to fake. Dunne slid it into a desktop card reader. On his large blue computer screen, a face popped up, along with an employee's basic personnel information. The face wasn't Bryson's, but at the moment, Bryson's altered and disguised face fairly closely resembled the one up on the monitor.

"Paris station. Where the *hell* did you get this?" Dunne demanded.

"You going to listen to me now?"

Dunne's face was wary. He exhaled twin plumes of smoke through his nostrils as he sank into his desk chair. He snubbed out the cigarette, prematurely. "At least let me call Finneran in here."

"Finneran?"

"You met him at Blue Ridge. My aide-de-camp."

"Forget it."

"He's my goddamned institutional memory—"

"Forget it! Just you and me and the listening devices."

Dunne shrugged. He pulled out another cigarette, but instead of placing it into the holder, he began toying with it between nicotine-stained fingers. Through the threadbare fabric of Dunne's blue button-down shirt, Bryson could see the outlines of an array of nicotine patches along his shoulders and biceps.

As Bryson recounted the events of the past few days, Dunne became grave. When he finally spoke, his voice was hushed. "A two-million-dollar bounty on your head, placed even *before* you showed up on Calacanis's ship. Somehow the word was out on the street that you were back in the game."

"You seem to forget they tried to dispatch me in Washington. They seemed to know I'd be coming back, looking for the old Directorate headquarters. That points to a leak in the pipes right here, in this building." Bryson inscribed a small circle in the air with an index finger.

"Christ!" shot back the deputy director, tearing the cigarette in half and flinging the pieces toward the ashtray. "The whole goddamned thing was off the books, the only record of your involvement your name in the Security data bank for purposes of clearing you in and out of the building."

"If the Directorate is wired into CIA, that's enough to do it."

"Come *on*, man, it wasn't even a true name! You were Jonas Barrett— a cover alias used in the Security logs being, incidentally, against every fucking rule in the playbook. You don't lie to Security. Never lie to Mother."

"Expense vouchers, equipment requisitions—"

"Buried, all messaging text in proprietary cipher, all need-to-know, all DDCI priority. Look, Bryson, I covered my ass, what the hell you think? You were a huge goddamned risk on my part, I gotta tell ya. I don't know what stress they put you under, how they might have burned you out. Put a guy's red-bordered folder under a fucking microscope, you still don't know shit about what's in his head. I mean, look, they put you out to pasture in your little cow-town college—"

"*For God's sake*," thundered Bryson, "do you think I *volunteered* for this? Your goons came and wrenched me out of retirement. I was just beginning to heal, and you came to tear open the scab! I'm not here to defend myself—I assume you boys did your homework on me. I want to know what the hell CIA was doing, following me outside Paris in order to kill me. I hope to hell you have a good explanation, or at least a convincing lie."

Dunne glowered. "I'm going to ignore that last dig, Bryson," he said quietly. "Think this through, wouldya? According to what you're telling me, you were recognized by this Directorate operative you worked with in Kowloon, Vance Gifford—"

"Yes, and according to the Sangiovanni brothers, I was also identified by Arnaud's man aboard the ship. That's obvious and beyond dispute. It's not hard to walk back the cat and see how Santiago de Compostela happened. I'm talking about Chantilly, about Paris! About one CIA operative I happened to flush out because he was sloppy enough to leave his ID papers on his person. And where there's one, there's always more, you know that as well as I. So what are you going to tell me—that the Agency is out of control? It's either that or you're double-dealing me, and I want to know which it is, *now!*"

"*No!*" Dunne shouted hoarsely, his voice then dissolving in a series of hacking coughs. "Those aren't the only possible explanations!"

"Then what are you trying to sell me?"

Dunne drew his own circle in the air with an index finger, mimicking Bryson's, signaling the room bugs. He scowled. "I'm saying I want to check some things out. I'm saying I think we ought to continue this discussion at another time and place." His face seemed even more lined, the hollows deeper, and for the first time his eyes looked haunted.

The Rosamund Cleary Extended Care Facility was, in plain English, a nursing home. It was a handsome, low-slung red-brick facility surrounded by a few acres of wooded land in Dutchess County, in upstate New York. Whatever it was called, it was an expensive, well-managed place, a last home for the financially privileged who needed medical attention that relatives and other loved ones could not give them. For the last twelve years it had been the home of Felicia Munroe, the woman, who, with her husband, Peter, had taken the teenaged Nicholas Bryson in after Bryson's parents had been killed in an automobile crash.

Bryson had loved the woman, had always had a close and loving relationship with her, but he had never thought of her as his mother. The accident had happened too late in his life for that. She was just Aunt Felicia, the doting wife of Uncle Pete, who'd been one of his father's best friends. They had taken loving care of him, welcomed him into their home, even paid his way through boarding school and then college, for which he was eternally grateful.

Peter Munroe had met George Bryson at the Officers Club in Bahrain. Colonel Bryson, as he was then, had been supervising construction of a major new barracks, and Munroe, a civil engineer for a multinational construction firm, had been a bidder on the project. Bryson and Munroe had become fast friends over too many beers—the specialty of the club in that nonalcoholic nation—and yet, when the bids were submitted, Colonel Bryson recommended *against* Pete Munroe's firm. He had no choice, really; another construction company had underbid them. Munroe took the bad news in good spirit, took Bryson out for a round of drinks on him, and said he didn't really give a shit—he'd gotten more out of this fucking country than he'd ever expected to—a friend. Only later—too late, as it turned out—did the senior Bryson learn why the winning bidder came in so low: dishonesty. The firm tried to stick the army with millions of dollars in cost overruns. When George Bryson tried to apologize, Munroe refused to accept his apology. "Corruption's a way of life in this business," he said. "If I really wanted the job, I would have lied, too. *I* was the naïve one." The friendship between George Bryson and Pete Munroe, however, was sealed.

But was that the truth? Was there really more to it? Was Harry Dunne telling him the truth? Now that he had concrete evidence that an active CIA operative on the Agency payroll had attempted to kill him in France, everything was in question. For if Dunne had had anything to do with that, was anything else he said to be trusted? In some ways Bryson regretted not coming here first, before flying off to the *Spanish Armada*. He should have found old Aunt Felicia and questioned her before agreeing to do Dunne's dirty work. Bryson had visited Felicia twice before, once with Elena, but not in several years.

Dunne's words to him that day in the Blue Ridge Mountains, the day that changed his life, still echoed in his head. He would not soon forget them.

"Let me ask you something, Bryson. Did you believe this was an accident? You were fifteen, a brilliant student, terrific athlete, prime of American youth, all that. Now both your parents are suddenly killed. Your godparents take you in—"

"Uncle Pete . . . Peter Munroe."

"That was the name he took, sure. Not the name he was born with. And he made sure you went to college where you did, and made a lot of other decisions for you besides. All of which pretty much guaranteed that you'd end up in their hands. The Directorate's, I mean."

Bryson found Aunt Felicia sitting in front of a television set in a spacious public sitting room tastefully appointed with Persian rugs and massive mahogany antiques. Several other elderly people were scattered about the room, a few reading or crocheting, several dozing. Felicia Munroe appeared to be watching golf with rapt fascination.

"Aunt Felicia," Bryson said heartily.

She turned to look at him, and for a fleeting instant recognition seemed to dawn on her face. But it immediately gave way to a foggy bewilderment. "Yes?" she said sharply.

"Aunt Felicia, I'm Nick. Remember me?"

She stared at him with incomprehension, squinting. He realized that the traces of senility he had seen in her years ago had grown into something far deeper and more serious. After staring for an uncomfortably long time, she gave a slow smile. "It *is* you," she breathed.

"Remember? I lived with you—you took care of me . . . ?"

"You've come back," she whispered, finally seeming to comprehend. Tears sprang to her eyes. "My heavens, how I've missed you."

Bryson's heart lifted.

"My darling George," she trilled. "My dearest darling George. How long it's been."

For a moment he was perplexed, and then he understood. Bryson was about the same age that his father, Gen. George Bryson, was when he died. In Aunt Felicia's confused mind—a mind that probably could recall clearly events of half a century ago, yet could not remember her own name—he *was* George Bryson. And indeed the resemblance was strong. He was often startled to see how much he was coming to look like his father, the older he got.

Then, as if she had suddenly grown bored with her visitor, she turned her gaze back to the television set. Bryson stood, shifting his weight from foot to foot, unsure what to do next. In a minute or so, Felicia seemed to become conscious of his presence, and she turned to look at him again.

"Why, hello there," she ventured tentatively. Her face looked worried, the expression rapidly turning frightened. "But you—but you're *dead!* I thought you were dead!"

Bryson simply looked at her neutrally, not wanting to disturb the illusion. *Let her believe what she wants to believe; perhaps she will say something. . . .*

"You died in that terrible accident," she said. Her face was racked with tension. "Yes, you did. That terrible, terrible accident. You and Nina both. What an awful thing. And you leaving poor young Nicky an orphan. Oh, I don't think I stopped crying for three days. Pete was always the strong one—he got me through it." The tears glistened in her eyes once again, and they began to course down her cheeks. "So much Pete didn't tell me about that night," she continued, her voice almost a singsong. "So much he couldn't tell me, *wouldn't* tell me. How the guilt must have eaten him up inside. For years he wouldn't talk to me about that night, about what he did."

A chill ran down Bryson's spine.

"And he'd *never* talk to your little Nicky about it, you know. What a thing to carry with you, what a terrible, terrible thing!" She shook her head, dabbing at her eyes with the frilly cuff of her white blouse. Then she turned back to the television.

Bryson strode to the TV, shut it off, and stood right in front of her. Though the poor woman's short-term memory had been destroyed by the effects of senility, or perhaps Alzheimer's disease, it appeared that many of her long-term memories might have been spared.

"Felicia," he said gently, "I want to talk to you about Pete. Pete Munroe, your husband."

The direct stare seemed to unnerve her; she studied the pattern on the carpet. "He used to make me a whiskey sling when I had a cold, you know," she said. She seemed lost in the memory, her manner now relaxed. "Honey and lemon juice and just a *wee* bit of bourbon. No, more than a wee bit. You'll be better in no time."

"Felicia, did he ever talk about something called the Directorate?"

She looked up at him blankly. "An untreated cold can linger for a week. But with treatment, it will pass in seven days!" She giggled, waggling her finger. "Peter always said an untreated cold can linger for a week . . ."

"Did he ever talk about my father?"

"Oh, he was a great talker. Told the funniest stories."

At the other end of the room, one of the patients had had an accident, and two janitors appeared with mops. The two custodians chattered to each other in Russian. A Russian phrase, spoken loudly, was audible. *Ya nye znayu,* one of them said brusquely: I don't know. The accent was Muscovite.

Felicia Munroe had heard it, too, and she perked up in response. "*Ya nye znayu,*" she repeated, then giggled. "Gibberish! Gibberish!"

"Not really gibberish, Aunt Felicia," Bryson put in.

"Gibberish!" she replied defiantly. "Just the sort of nonsense Pete would say in his sleep. *Ya nye znayu.* All that craziness. Whenever he talked in his sleep, he'd talk in that funny language, and he just *hated* when I teased him about it."

"He talked like that in his sleep?" Bryson said hollowly, his heart thudding in his rib cage.

"Oh, he was a terrible sleeper." For a moment she seemed lucid. "Always talked in his sleep."

Uncle Pete spoke Russian in his sleep, the one time when you can't control your utterances. Was Harry Dunne right: was Peter Munroe an associate of Gennady Rosovsky's, a.k.a. Ted Waller? Could it be true? Was any other explanation even *possible?* Bryson was dumbstruck.

But Felicia kept talking. "Particularly after you died, George. He was so sorry. He tossed and turned, he yelled and cried in his sleep, and always talking that *gibberish!*"

The area of Rock Creek Park in Washington, on the northern part of Beach Drive, was a good location for the rendezvous with Harry Dunne very early the next morning. Bryson had chosen it; Dunne had invited him to select the meeting point not out of deference to Bryson's field skills—after all, Dunne's experience as an operative with the Agency's clandestine division had been over twice as long as Bryson's with the Directorate—but more likely as a courtesy extended by a host to his honored guest.

The CIA deputy director's request to meet off site, outside Agency walls, was alarming to Bryson. It was hard to believe that Dunne, the number-two man in the Agency, feared his own office was bugged; that fact itself gave credence to the theory that the CIA had been penetrated by the Directorate—that Bryson's old handlers had somehow managed to extend their tentacles into the highest reaches of the CIA. Whatever information Dunne might have been able to collect, the mere fact that he insisted on continuing their discussion in a neutral, secure location was unnerving proof that something was very wrong.

Still, Bryson would take nothing at face value. *Trust no one,* Ted Waller used to say with a cackle, words now grotesquely appropriate: Waller himself had turned out to be the cardinal betrayer of trust. Bryson would not let down his guard; he would trust no one, Dunne included.

He arrived at the designated location a full hour early. It was barely four o'clock in the morning, the sky dark, the air cold and damp. Passing cars were few, spaced far apart in time: night-shift workers going home, their replacements arriving. The business of government was round-the-clock.

The silence was strange, unaccustomed. Bryson became aware of the sounds of twigs crackling underfoot as he paced the dense woods surrounding the clearing he had chosen, noises that would ordinarily be masked by the ambient roar of nearby traffic. He wore the crepe-soled shoes he favored for field work because they minimized such noise.

Bryson surveyed the location, searching for points of vulnerability. The wooded ridge overlooked a small patch of meadow, next to a small, asphalt-paved parking area, at the edge of which was a concrete, bunkerlike restroom facility, half sunken below ground, in which they had agreed to meet. Rain had been forecast, and though the forecast had turned out wrong, a sheltered location had seemed desirable. Too, the facility's thick concrete walls would provide protection in the event of ambush from without.

But Bryson was determined that there would be no ambush. He made a circuit around the wooded ridge, through the dense trees overlooking the meadow, checking for recently made footsteps or branches broken in a suspicious pattern, as well as for scopes, mounts, or other devices that might have been emplaced in advance. A second sweep revealed all possible avenues of approach; nothing would be left to chance. After two more sweeps, each from different directions and covering different vantage points, Bryson was satisfied that no ambush was already in place. That did not rule out any future arrivals, but at least he would be able to authoritatively detect subtle changes in background, divergences otherwise ignored.

At precisely five o'clock in the morning, a black government sedan pulled off Beach Drive and into the parking area. It was a Lincoln Continental, unmarked except for generic government license plates. Watching through small, high-powered binoculars from a blind he had chosen in a dense copse of trees, Bryson could make out Dunne's regular driver, a slender African American in a navy blue uniform. Dunne sat in the backseat clutching a file folder. There appeared to be no one else in the vehicle.

The limousine pulled up to the restroom and came to a stop. The driver got out and went to open the door for his boss, but Dunne, impatient as always, was already halfway out of the car. He was scowling, his habitual expression. Glancing briefly to either side, he descended the short flight of steps, his face illuminated garishly by the sulphurous fluorescent lights, and then disappeared into the small building.

Bryson waited. He watched the driver, waiting for any suspicious moves—furtive phone calls placed on a concealed cellular phone, quick signals to passing vehicles, even the loading of a gun. But the driver simply sat behind the wheel, waiting with the calm, still patience his boss lacked.

After a good ten minutes had elapsed, and Bryson was sure that Dunne was probably fed up by now, he came down the hillside, following a path that kept him concealed from passersby, winding around to the back of the restroom, which was even with the ground level. Putting on a sudden burst of speed, he raced to the building, confident that he had not been observed. Now he leaped down into the moat that surrounded the bunker and circled around to the entrance, unseen.

The fluorescent lights flickered as he approached. The building reeked of urine and excrement, with an astringent overlay of cleaning solution, woefully insufficient. He listened at the door for a moment until he heard Dunne's signature hacking cough. He entered swiftly, closing the heavy steel door behind him and locking it with the strong padlock he had brought.

Dunne was standing at a urinal. He turned his head slowly when Bryson entered. "Nice of you to saunter in," he muttered. "Now I see why those Directorate fuckers fired your ass. Punctuality ain't your strong suit."

Bryson ignored the jabs. Dunne knew exactly why he was ten minutes late. Dunne zipped up, flushed, and went to the sink. They looked at each other in the mirror. "Bad news," Dunne said, his voice echoing, as he washed his hands. "The card's legit."

"The card?"

"The Agency ID card you took off the motorcyclist's body in Chantilly. It's not doctored paper. The guy was detailed to the Paris station for over a year as an operative *in extremis*—for when the real dirty stuff had to be done."

"Trace the personnel records, the name on the assignment authorization, even how he was recruited."

Dunne scowled again, radiating disgust. "Why didn't I think of that," he said with heavy irony. He shook his hands dry—there were no paper towels, and he refused to use the automatic hand-drying machine—then wiped them on his pants. He fished a crumpled Marlboro pack out of his breast pocket and fumbled out a partly crushed cigarette, which he placed in his mouth. Without lighting it, he went on, "I ordered a Code Sigma–priority search through all the computer banks, down to the last firewall. Nothing."

"What do you mean, nothing? You keep thick personnel files on every-one, from the director on down to the lady who cleans the washrooms in the imaging center."

Dunne grimaced. The unlit cigarette dangled from his lower lip.

"And you guys don't leave anything out. *Anything*. So don't tell me you turned up nothing in the guy's personnel file."

"No, I'm telling you the guy had no file. As far as Langley central is concerned, he didn't exist."

"Come on! There's health coverage, insurance, paychecks—a bunch of administrative and bureaucratic horseshit that Personnel bombards every single employee with. You telling me he wasn't getting *paychecks?*"

"*Christ's* sake, you're not fucking *listening!* The guy didn't exist! It's not unheard of—the real serious wetworkers, we don't like to have a paper trail on them. Files are buried, requisitions deep-sixed after payments are authorized. So the precedent is there. Thing is, someone knew how to play the system, keep the guy's name off all the books. He was like a *ghost*—there but not there."

"So what does this mean?" Bryson asked quietly.

Dunne was silent for a moment. He coughed. "It means, buddy, that the CIA may not be the best agency to investigate the Directorate. Es-pecially if the Directorate has its moles inside, which we have to assume."

Dunne's words, though not unexpected, came as a bolt of lightning because of the finality with which the CIA man uttered them. Bryson nodded. "Not easy for you to admit," he said.

Dunne tipped his head to one side in acknowledgment. "Not partic-ularly," he conceded, an obvious understatement. The man was shaken, though obviously reluctant to admit it. "Look, I don't want to believe the goddamned Directorate might have reached out and touched my own people. But I didn't get where I did by indulging in wishful thinking. See, I never went to one of your hoity-toity universities—I got into St. John's by the skin of my ass. I don't speak a dozen languages like you do, either—just English, and that none too good. But what I had, see— and still do, I like to think—was something that's a scarce commodity in the intelligence business, and that's horse sense. Or whatever the hell you want to call it. Look at what's happened to this goddamned country in the last forty years, from the Bay of Pigs to Vietnam to Panama to what- ever's the latest fuckup in the *Washington Post* this morning. All brought to you by the so-called Wise Men, those 'best and the brightest' with their fancy Ivy League sheepskins and their trust funds, who keep getting us into all these scrapes. They got education, but no common sense. Me, I can *smell* when something's off, I got an instinct for it. And I don't go whistling past graveyards. So I can't dodge the possibility—and it's only a possibility, mind you—that someone on my team is involved. I'm not going to bullshit you. I don't want to have to play my last card, but I may have to."

"Which is?"

"What the fuck does the *Washington Post* call him, the 'last honest man in Washington'? Which isn't saying much in this corrupt city."

"Richard Lanchester," Bryson said, recalling the epithet often applied to the president's national security adviser and chairman of the White House National Security Council. He knew of Lanchester's unequalled reputation for probity. "Why is he your last card?"

"Because once I play it, it's out of my control. He may be the one man in government who can head this thing off, circumvent corrupted channels, but once I involve him, it's no longer contained in the intel- ligence community. It's all-out internecine war, and frankly, I don't know whether our government could survive it."

"Jesus," Bryson breathed. "You're saying the Directorate's reach is that high?"

"That's what it smells like to me."

"Well, I'm the one whose life is on the line out there. From now on, I communicate only with you, *directly* with you. No intermediaries, no

E-mail that can be cracked or faxes that can be intercepted. I want you to isolate a sterile line at Langley, routed through a lockbox, sequestered and segregated."

The CIA man nodded his acquiescence.

"I also want a code-word sequence so I can be certain you're not speaking under duress, or that your voice is being falsified. I want to know it's you, and that you're speaking freely. And one more thing: all communications go directly between you and me—not even through your secretary."

Bryson shrugged. "Point taken, but you're overreacting. I'd trust Marjorie with my life."

"Sorry. No exceptions. Elena once told me about something called Metcalf's Rule, which says that the porosity of a network increases as the square of the number of nodes. The nodes, in this case, refers to anyone who's knowledgeable about the operation."

"Elena," said the CIA man with heavy derision. "I guess she knows something about deception, huh, Bryson?"

The remark stung, despite everything that had happened, even despite his own bitterness over her unexplained disappearance. "Correct," Bryson returned. "Which is why you've got to help me get to her—"

"You think I sent you out there to save your marriage?" Dunne interrupted. "I sent you out there to save the goddamned world."

"Damn it, she *knows* something, she has to. Maybe quite a bit."

"Yeah, and if she's involved—"

"If she's involved, she's involved in a central way. If she's a dupe like I was—"

"Wishful thinking, Bryson, I *warned* you—"

"*If she's a dupe like I was,*" Bryson thundered, "then her knowledge is *still* invaluable!"

"And of course she'll happily spill all the fucking beans to you out of, what, nostalgia? Remembrance of all the good times past?"

"If I can *get* to her," Bryson shouted, then he faltered. Quietly, he went on, "If I can get to her . . . damn it, I *know* her, I can tell when she's lying, when she tries to shade the truth, what she's trying to avoid discussing."

"You're dreaming," said Harry Dunne flatly. He coughed, a painful-sounding, rattling, liquid cough. "You think you know her. You pretend you know her, *knew* her. You're so sure, aren't you? Just like you were so sure you knew Ted Waller, a.k.a. Gennady Rosovsky. Or Pyotr Aksyonov—alias your 'uncle' Peter Munroe. Did your little visit to upstate New York enlighten you further?"

Bryson couldn't hide his astonishment. "God*damn* you to hell!" he shouted.

"Get real, Bryson. You think I haven't maintained a cordon of surveillance on that nursing home ever since I learned about the Directorate? Poor old biddy's so addled, our men could never get much out of her, so I could never be sure whether she knew the truth about her husband, or how *much* she knew. But there was a chance that she might be contacted by someone connected with her late husband."

"Bullshit!" Bryson shot back. "You don't have the resources to keep a team of watchers on her twenty-four hours a day, seven days a week, until she dies!"

"Christ," Dunne said impatiently. "Obviously not. One of the administrators there earns a nice chunk of change on the side from Felicia's 'dear old cousin Harry,' who's fiercely protective. Anyone calls for Felicia, arranges to come by, even drops by, an administrator named Shirley gives me a call first thing. She knows I like to protect sweet addle-brained Felicia from gold diggers or people who might upset her. I take care of my cousin. Shirley always has my phone number wherever I am. So I always know who Felicia's in touch with. No surprises. Point is, you work with what you've got; you cover what you can. Most of the others just seem to have disappeared without a fucking trace. Now we gotta stand here in this stinking shithole all day?"

"I don't like it much either, but it's remote, secluded, and safe."

"Aw, Christ. You care to tell me why you went to see Jacques Arnaud?"

"As I told you, his emissary, his agent on Calacanis's ship, was clearly working with both the Directorate and with Anatoly Prishnikov in Russia. Arnaud had to be a key node."

"But for what? You wanted to reach out to Arnaud directly?"

Bryson paused. Ted Waller's words—Gennady Rosovsky's—came back to him, as they did so often: *Tell no one anything they don't absolutely need to know. Even me.* He hadn't yet told Dunne about the cryptochip he had copied from Arnaud's secure satellite phone, and he would not. Not yet.

"I considered it," he lied. "At least to observe those around him."

"And?"

"Nothing. A waste of time." *Always hold back a card.*

Dunne took out from his battered leather portfolio a red-bordered manila envelope, from which he drew a batch of eight-by-ten photographs. "We've gone through the names you gave us in the debriefing, ran them through every available database, including every top-secret code-word proprietary. Wasn't easy, given how clever and thorough your friends at the Directorate seem to be—selecting and rotating aliases using computer algorithms, all that shit I don't really understand. Directorate operatives get reassigned, uprooted, their biographies rewritten, networks detached and reassembled. It was mind-numbing work, but we do have a few candidates for you to look at." He displayed the first black-and-white glossy.

Bryson shook his head. "Nope."

Dunne frowned, took out another.

"No recollection."

Dunne shook his head, showed him another.

"Doesn't register. You've got some dummies in here, don't you—known fakes, hoping to trip me up."

A smile seemed to play at the corners of Dunne's lips. He coughed. "Always testing, huh?"

Dunne didn't reply. He pulled out another photograph.

"Nope—hey, wait a minute." Bryson was looking at a photograph of an agent he recognized. "This one I know. That Dutchman, cover name Prospero."

Dunne nodded as if Bryson had finally answered the question right. "Jan Vansina, a senior official at the International Red Cross headquarters in Geneva. Director of management for international emergency relief coordination. Brilliant cover for traveling easily around the world, especially to crisis spots, and it gives him access even to places where foreigners are normally barred—North Korea, Iraq, Libya, and so on. You had a good relationship with him."

"I saved his life in Yemen. Warned him off an ambush, even though the standard operating procedure required me to contain what I knew, whether it meant his execution or not."

"Not big on following orders either, I see."

"Not when I think they're stupid. Prospero was quite impressive. We worked together once, jointly laying a snare for a NATO engineer and double agent. What's Vansina doing here? It looks like indoor surveillance cameras."

"Our people caught him in Geneva, at Banque Geneve Privée. Authorizing the rapid-sequence transfer of a total of five-point-five billion dollars through separate and commingled accounts."

"Laundering, in other words."

"But not for himself. He was apparently acting as a conduit for an immensely well-funded organization."

"You didn't get all this background from a hidden video camera."

"We have sources throughout the Swiss banking industry."

"Reliable?"

"Not all, to be sure. But in this case, it was somebody pretty damned plugged in. An ex–Directorate operative who traded confirmable information in exchange for the elimination of a long prison sentence." He glanced at his wristwatch. "Extortion usually works."

Bryson nodded. "You think Vansina's still active?"

"This photograph was taken two days ago," Dunne said quietly, taking a pager from his belt and pressing a button on it. "Sorry, I should have signaled Solomon, my driver, twenty minutes ago. Our agreement is that I'd send him a page when you showed up, if he wasn't able to establish visual confirmation. Which he didn't, since you made one of your Harry Houdini appearances."

"What's the point of signaling your driver? To let him know you're okay—that I didn't do you harm, is that the point?" Bryson's voice rose in annoyance. "You really don't trust me, do you?"

"Solomon just likes to keep close tabs on me."

"You can never be too cautious," Bryson said.

There was a sudden loud banging on the restroom door.

"You lock it or something?"

Bryson nodded.

"So who's the too-cautious one?" Dunne said derisively. "Christ, let me go assure my worrywart driver that everything's jake."

Dunne went to the restroom door, tugged at the padlock, and shook his head. "I'm alive," he called out hoarsely. "No guns to my head or anything."

A muffled voice from the other side of the door said, "You're needed out here, sir, please."

"Cool your jets, Solomon. I said I'm fine."

"That's not it, sir. It's something else."

"What is it?"

"A call just came in, immediately after you paged me. On the car phone, sir—the one that you said only's supposed to ring if it's National Security Maximum."

"Oh, Christ," said Dunne. "Bryson, would you mind . . . ?"

Bryson approached the side of the concrete doorjamb, reaching for his weapon at the same time that he inserted a key in the padlock, springing it open. He flattened himself against the wall, out of sight, gun drawn.

Dunne watched Bryson's preparations with undisguised incredulity. The door came open, and Bryson was able to confirm that it was the same slender African-American man he'd seen behind the wheel of Dunne's government-issue car. Solomon seemed abashed, ill at ease. "I'm sorry to disturb you, sir," he said, "but it really does sound important." He was looking at his boss, his hands empty at his sides, no one else beside or behind him. The driver appeared not to have seen Bryson, who leaned against the wall, out of the intruder's line of sight.

Dunne nodded and, looking rankled, headed out toward the limousine, his driver following.

Suddenly the driver spun back around toward the open door, lunging with extraordinary, unexpected agility diagonally into the restroom toward Bryson, a large Magnum pistol in his right hand.

"What the hell—?" shouted Dunne, turning around with amazement.

The explosion thundered in the small interior, fragments of concrete flying everywhere, piercing Bryson's flesh as he dodged to his right, just missing the bullet. Several more came in rapid succession, shattering the walls, the floor inches from his head. The suddenness of the attack had caught Bryson off guard, forcing him to focus his energies on leaping out of the way, momentarily keeping him from leveling his own gun. The chauffeur was wild, firing madly, his face contorted with an animal-like fury. Bryson sprung forward, his gun extended, just as another explosion came, louder than any that had come before. A gaping red hole appeared at the center of the driver's chest, an explosion of blood, and the man tumbled forward, clearly dead.

Harry Dunne stood fifteen feet away, with his blue-steel Smith & Wesson .45 aloft, still pointed at his own chauffeur, a wisp of smoke curling from the barrel. He looked dazed, his expression almost crestfallen. Finally, the CIA man broke the silence. "Jesus Christ," he said, coughing so hard he almost doubled over. "Jesus Christ almighty."

CHAPTER TWELVE

The light in the Oval Office was eerie, silvery-gray, lending a somber cast to a gathering that did not need any more gloom. It was twilight, the end of a long, overcast day. President Malcolm Stephenson Davis sat in the small white sofa at the center of the seating area where he preferred to conduct his most serious meetings. In chairs on either side of him sat the directors of the CIA, the FBI, and the NSA; immediately next to him, at his right hand, was the special assistant to the president for national security affairs, Richard Lanchester. It was rare for such a senior collection of administration officials to gather outside the official confines of the Cabinet Room, the Situation Room, or the National Security Council. But the very unusual venue of the occasion underscored its gravity.

The reason for the meeting was abundantly clear. A little over nine hours earlier a powerful blast in the Dupont Circle station of the Washington Metro had killed twenty-three people and injured easily three times that; the fatality list grew longer as the day went on. The nation, though inured to tragedy, terrorist bombings, school shootings, was in a state of shock. This had happened in the very heart of the nation's capital—a mile from the White House, as CNN's commentators kept repeating.

A bomb left in what appeared to be a laptop computer case had gone off during the height of the morning rush hour. The sophisticated nature of the bomb, the details of which were being kept from the public, seemed to indicate the involvement of terrorists. In this age of all-news-all-the-time cable channels and radio stations, and the lightning-fast communications of the Internet, the terrible story seemed to reverberate, get worse by the minute.

Viewers seemed particularly fascinated by the most gruesome details—the pregnant woman and her three-year-old twin daughters, killed instantly; the elderly couple who had saved up for years to come to Washington from Iowa City; the group of nine-year-old elementary schoolchildren.

·"It's more than a nightmare, it's a disgrace," the president said grimly. The other men shook their heads in silent assent. "I'm going to have to reassure the nation in an address either tonight, if we can coordinate it in time, or tomorrow. But I sure as hell don't know what I'm going to say."

"Mr. President," said FBI Director Chuck Faber, "I want to assure you that we have no fewer than seventy-five special agents on the case even as we speak, combing the city, coordinating the investigations as lead agency with the local police and ATF. Our materials analysis unit, the explosives unit—"

"I have no doubt," the president cut him off sharply, "that you folks are all over this like a cheap suit. I mean in no way to disparage the Bureau's capabilities, but you do seem to be quite good at handling terrorist events after the fact. I'm just curious why you never seem to be able to *prevent* them."

The FBI director's face flushed. Chuck Faber had won his reputation as the take-no-prisoners district attorney in Philadelphia, later becoming Pennsylvania's attorney general. He made no secret of the fact that he wanted to run Main Justice, wanted the attorney general's job, considered himself far more qualified than the current incumbent. Faber was probably the most skilled bureaucratic games player in the room. He was famously confrontational, but he was also too politically savvy ever to confront the president.

"Sir, respectfully, I think that's not quite fair to the men and women of the Bureau." The quiet, calm voice was that of Richard Lanchester, a tall, fit man with silver hair and aristocratic features whose understated suits were custom-tailored in London. Most White House correspondents, whose notion of high fashion tended to be the Euro-extremes of Giorgio Armani, mistakenly described Lanchester as an "unfashionable" or even "frumpy" dresser.

Lanchester, however, rarely paid much attention to such personal descriptions in the newspapers or on television news. In fact, he preferred to steer clear of journalists altogether, since he strongly opposed leaking, which seemed to be a varsity sport in Washington. Somehow, though, he was admired by the Washington press corps anyway. Perhaps this was precisely because he refused to cultivate them, something most of them had never witnessed before. The label bestowed on him by *Time* magazine, "The Last Honest Man in Washington," was so often repeated in columns and on the Sunday-morning talking-head shows that it had become something of a Homeric epithet.

"It's just that their prevention efforts tend to go unheralded," Lanchester went on. "It's usually impossible to ascertain what *might* have happened were it not for any particular intervention."

The FBI director gave a grudging nod.

"There are news reports that we—that is, the U.S. government—could have prevented this tragedy," intoned the president. "Is there any truth to this?"

There was a moment of awkward silence. Finally, the director of the National Security Agency, Air Force Lt. Gen. John Corelli, replied. "Sir, the problem is that the target fell between the cracks. As you know, our charter forbids us from operating domestically, as does the CIA's, and this was a U.S.-based operation."

"And we're hamstrung by the legalities, sir," put in FBI Director Faber. "That is, we need probable cause to obtain a court-ordered wiretap, but unless we *know* to request such authorization, why in the world would we ask for it?"

"And as for the myth that the NSA is continuously sweeping for telephone calls, faxes, signals . . . ?"

"*Myth* is the word, sir," said NSA Director Corelli. "Even with the enormous capacity we've got at the Fort Meade campus, we can't possibly sweep every phone conversation in the world. Plus, we're not permitted to listen to conversations within the U.S."

"Hallelujah for that," said Dick Lanchester softly.

The FBI director turned to face Lanchester with an expression of purest contempt. "Really? And I suppose you applaud our inability to monitor encrypted conversations, whether over the phone or fax or over the Internet."

"You may not be aware of a little thing called the Fourth Amendment to the Constitution, Chuck," replied Lanchester dryly. "The right of the people to be protected against unreasonable searches and seizures—"

"And what about the right of the people to catch a subway train without being killed?" put in CIA Director James Exum. "I somehow doubt the framers contemplated digital telephony."

"The fact remains," said Lanchester, "that Americans don't want to sacrifice their privacy."

"Dick," the president said quietly, firmly. "The time for that discussion is over and done. The argument is moot. The treaty should pass the Senate any day now, creating an international surveillance agency that will protect us from such mayhem. And damn it, not a moment too soon, either."

Lanchester shook his head in sorrow. "This international agency is effectively going to expand the power of government a thousandfold," he said.

"No," the NSA director put in curtly. "It's going to level the playing field, that's all. For God's sake, the NSA isn't allowed to listen in on the conversations of Americans without a court order, and our British counterpart, the GCHQ, is similarly hamstrung by the legal restriction forbidding it to tap domestic calls in Britain. You seem to forget, Richard, that if the Allies didn't have the ability to read enemy messages during the Second World War, the Germans might well have won."

"We're not in a war."

"Oh, but we are," said the CIA director. "We're in the middle of a global war against terrorists, and the bad guys are winning. And if you're suggesting that we all just pack it in—"

A low tone sounded from the telephone on the small table next to where the president was sitting. The men in the room knew that the president's intercom went off only in the case of an urgent situation, as per Davis's explicit instructions. President Davis picked up the handset. "Yes?"

His face went ashen. He put the phone down, then looked around at the others. "That was the Situation Room," he said gravely. "An American jetliner just went down three miles from Kennedy Airport."

"What?" gasped several of the men at once.

"Blown out of the sky," President Davis murmured, eyes closed. "A minute or so after takeoff. A flight to Rome. One hundred and seventy-one passengers and crew members—all of them dead." He placed his hands over his eyes, massaging them with his fingers. When he removed his fingers, his eyes shone with tears, but the expression in them was fierce, even ferocious. His voice shook. "Jesus Christ, I will not go down in history as the Commander in Chief who sat by idly while terrorists seized control of our world. Goddamn it, we have *got* to *do* something!"

CHAPTER
THIRTEEN

The glass office tower on rue de la Corraterie, just south of Place Bel-Air in the heart of Geneva's commercial and banking district, was the deep blue of the ocean, and it glistened in the afternoon sun. On the twenty-seventh floor were the offices of the Banque Geneve Privée, where Bryson and Layla waited in the small but luxuriously appointed waiting room. With its mahogany wainscoting, Oriental rugs, and delicate antiques, the bank was an island of nineteenth-century elegance perched twenty-seven floors above the ground within one of Geneva's most modernistic skyscrapers. The subliminal message it seemed to project was one of old-world civility in harmony with high technology. Its setting could not have been more apt.

Bryson had arrived at Geneva-Cointrin Airport, checked in to Le Richemond, and then met Layla's train, the Paris-Ventimiglia express, from Paris a few hours later at Gare Cornavin. There had been a warmth in their greeting, as if no time had elapsed since Bryson's Paris departure. She was excited, which she displayed in her quiet, vibrant way; she had dug quite a bit and uncovered only a few tiny nuggets, but they were, in her opinion, nuggets of gold. Still, there was no time for a debriefing; he took her to the hotel, where they checked into separate rooms; she changed into a suit, fixed her hair, and they immediately proceeded to rue de la Corraterie for the meeting Bryson had arranged with a Swiss banker.

They were not kept waiting long; this was Switzerland, where punctuality was holy writ. A matronly woman of middle age, with gray hair worn up in a bun, appeared in the waiting room at the exact time of their appointment.

She addressed him by his CIA-supplied cover name. "You must be Mr. Mason," she said haughtily. It was not the tone customarily used with favored clients; she knew he was from the U.S. government and therefore to be considered an annoyance. She then turned to Layla. "And you are—?"

"This is Anat Chafetz," Bryson said, using one of her Mossad-furnished aliases. "Mossad."

"Monsieur Bécot is expecting both of you? I had been told there would just be you, Mr. Mason." The assistant was perturbed.

"I assure you that Monsieur Bécot will want to see both of us," Bryson said, matching her hauteur.

She nodded brusquely. "Excuse me."

She returned a minute later. "Please come with me."

Jean-Luc Bécot was a compact, bespectacled man whose precise, economical movements revealed the precision of the man. He had short silver-gray hair, gold wire-rimmed glasses, and wore a tailored gray suit. He shook their hands politely but warily and asked them if they would like coffee.

Another assistant, this one a young man in a blue blazer, came in a moment later bearing three tiny cups of espresso on a gleaming silver tray. He silently set down two cups on the coffee table next to where Layla and Bryson sat, and then placed the third on the glass-topped desk behind which Jean-Luc Bécot was stationed.

Bécot's office was decorated in the same opulent style as the rest of the bank's offices, the same assemblage of delicate antiques and Persian carpets. One entire wall was a plate-glass window that looked over Geneva, the view breathtaking.

"Now then," Bécot said, "I am sure you both appreciate that I am a busy man, and so forgive me for asking you to come right to the point. You alluded to financial irregularities in the handling of one of our accounts. Let me assure you that Banque Geneve Privée permits no such irregularities. I am afraid you have come here in vain."

Bryson smiled tolerantly throughout the banker's opening remarks, tenting his fingers. When Bécot came to a halt, Bryson said, "Monsieur Bécot, the very fact that you are meeting with me indicates that you or one of your associates placed a call to Central Intelligence Agency headquarters in Langley, Virginia, to check on my bona fides." He paused, saw the unspoken acknowledgment in the banker's face. Bryson had no doubt that his phone call a few hours earlier had raised all sorts of alarm. The CIA had sent one of its operatives to Geneva to question a Swiss banker in connection with an account—all of Banque Geneve Privée was surely up in arms by now; there would have been frantic calls made, hurried consultations. There was a time when any self-respecting Swiss banker would simply have refused to see an officer of American intelligence: the secrecy of bank accounts was paramount. But times had changed, and although money laundering still continued in Switzerland on a massive scale, the Swiss had succumbed to international political pressure; they were much more cooperative these days. Or at least they were eager to give the appearance of cooperation.

Bryson resumed. "You know that I would not be here were it not a situation of some gravity—one that involves your bank directly, and that threatens to entangle your bank in a nasty legal mess, which I'm sure you wish to avoid."

Bécot gave an ugly, prim little smile. "Your threats will not work here, Mr.—Mr. Mason. And as for why you brought with you a Mossad officer, if this is your clumsy attempt to increase the pressure—"

"Monsieur Bécot, let us speak plainly," said Bryson, adopting the tone of an international law-enforcement agent who held all the cards. "Under the 1987 Convention of Diligence, neither you nor your bank can claim ignorance of an account holder or of any account holder's use of your bank to launder money for criminal purposes. The legal ramifications are quite serious, as you well know. Representatives of the intelligence agencies of two world powers have come before you to seek your assistance in a major international money-laundering investigation; you can either help us, as you are required to do by law, or you can turn us away, in which case we will be forced to report this suspected criminal activity to Lausanne."

The banker stared at Bryson impassively for a moment, his coffee untouched. "What, precisely, is the nature of your investigation, Mr. Mason?"

Bryson sensed the man's vacillation; it was time to thrust. "We are examining the activities in Banque Geneve Privée account number 246322, held by one Jan Vansina."

Bécot hesitated for an instant. The name, if not the number, had registered immediately. "We never divulge the names of our clients—"

Bryson glanced at Layla, who took her cue. "Substantial monies have been wire-transferred into this account from a fictitious *Anstalt* in Liechtenstein, as you're well aware. From here the funds have been wired to an array of accounts: several different shell companies in the Isle of Man, and Jersey, in the Channel Islands; to the Caymans, Aguilla, the Netherlands Antilles. From there the funds have been split and routed to the Bahamas and San Marino—"

"There is nothing illegal about wire transfers!" snapped Bécot.

"Unless they are done to launder illicit monies," she said with equal vehemence. Bryson had filled her in with the few details Harry Dunne had provided on Vansina's bank account; the rest was sheer embellishment. Bryson was impressed. "In this case, these laundered funds have been used to fund the purchase of arms used in the activities of known terrorists around the world."

"This sounds suspiciously like a fishing expedition," said the Swiss.

"A fishing expedition?" repeated Layla. "More like an international criminal investigation undertaken by Washington and Tel Aviv simultaneously, which should be evidence enough of how seriously this is being taken at the highest levels. But I can see we are wasting Monsieur Bécot's time." She rose, and Bryson did the same. "Obviously we are not dealing on a high enough level here," she said to Bryson. "Monsieur Bécot either does not have the decision-making capability or is deliberately concealing his own criminal role. I am sure that the bank's director, Monsieur Etienne Broussard, will have a more enlightened view—"

"What is it that you want?" interrupted the banker, desperation now evident in his face, his voice.

Bryson, still standing, said, "Quite simply, we want you to telephone the account holder, Mr. Vansina, immediately, and request that he come into the bank at once."

"But Monsieur Vansina is never to be directly approached, that is the stipulation of his account! He contacts *us*, that is the way it is done. Besides, I have no contact number for him!"

"False. There are always contact numbers," said Bryson. "If you are doing business as you should, you have photocopies of his passport and other identification papers, addresses and telephone numbers of his home and place of work—"

"I cannot *do* that!" cried Bécot.

"Come, Mr. Mason, we are wasting time here. I'm sure Monsieur Bécot's superior will understand the gravity of the situation," said Layla. "Once the request is made through diplomatic liaison and the courts in Washington, Tel Aviv, and Lausanne, the Banque Genève Privée will be publicly named as an accomplice in the funding of international terrorism and money laundering, and—"

"No! Sit down!" the banker said, all pretense at bankerly gravitas abandoned. "I will call Vansina."

Concealed in the small, stuffy, closet-size room, lined with video screens, where the bank's surveillance cameras were monitored, Bryson perspired heavily. The plan he had devised called for him to remain in hiding while Layla met with Vansina in Bécot's office, still in the guise of a Mossad officer investigating money laundering. She would interrogate Vansina, elicit whatever useful information she could, and then Bryson would appear suddenly, drawing upon the tactical value of surprise.

Layla remained in the dark about the Directorate and Bryson's relationship to it. As far as she was concerned, Bryson was simply uncovering a trail in the illicit arms trade. She knew a fragment of the whole; she did not yet need to know more. The time would come when Bryson would fill her in, but it was not yet.

Bryson had intended to secrete himself anywhere in the vicinity of Bécot's office—a neighboring office, a broom closet, whatever. He had not counted on the serendipity of discovering this surveillance station. From here he was able to observe the comings and goings in and out of the office building's lobby; several other feeds came from hidden cameras inside each elevator; two more covered the twenty-seventh-floor lobby area adjacent to the elevator bank and the bank's waiting room. Too, there were views of the main corridors on the twenty-seventh floor. There was no camera within Bécot's office, or any other office for that matter, but at least he would be able to view Vansina's arrival as well as the Dutchman's movements in the elevator. Vansina was a top-notch field operative and took nothing for granted. He would assume, for instance, that there were closed-circuit cameras concealed in the elevators, as there were in many modern office buildings. But he would likely also assume, as would Bryson, that such cameras were being watched by incurious, underpaid security staff looking only for obvious signs of violent crime. Vansina might use the semiprivate occasion to adjust a gun holster or a monitoring device taped to his chest. Then again, he might do nothing suspicious at all.

The call to Vansina had been placed in Bryson and Layla's presence, and then Layla had remained by the banker's side to ensure that he did not make any follow-up calls to Vansina, warning him off, or anything of the sort.

Bryson knew that Jan Vansina would respond quickly, and indeed, within twenty minutes the Directorate operative arrived in the main lobby. Vansina was a slight, hunch-shouldered man with a full but close-trimmed gray beard and tinted wire-rimmed spectacles. Between his unassuming physical presence and his benign cover as director of emergency medical assistance for the International Red Cross, he was not a man anyone would suspect of being the extremely clever killer that he was. Vansina's greatest attribute, in fact, was that he was constantly underestimated. A casual observer might in fact think Vansina kindly, even harmless. Bryson, however, knew well that Vansina was a powerful, ruthless man of great skill and wily intelligence. He knew better than to underestimate him.

Vansina shared an elevator with a young woman, who got off on the twenty-fifth floor, at which point he was alone for a few seconds. Yet Bryson found him impossible to read, neither apprehensive nor particularly tense. If the man's suspicions were at all aroused by this emergency summons from his private banker, his expression did not indicate it.

Bryson watched him emerge from the elevator and check in with the receptionist; Vansina was ushered in at once. Bryson saw him accompanied down the corridor by Bécot's matronly assistant, then into Bécot's office, at which point the surveillance ended.

No matter: Bryson knew the script that Layla was following, since he had designed it himself. He waited for the signal from Layla indicating that it was time for him to make his appearance. She would place a call to his cell phone, let it ring twice, then terminate the call.

Her interrogation of Vansina would last anywhere from five to ten minutes, depending on the degree of truculence Vansina presented. He looked at his watch, his eyes on the sweep–second hand, and waited.

Five minutes passed slowly, feeling like an eternity. There were two backup emergency signals, neither of which she had employed. The first would be to dial his cell phone, letting it ring. After the second ring, he would know the situation was urgent. In the alternative, she would open Bécot's office door, which he would be able to observe on the surveillance monitor.

Yet no emergency signals came.

As focused as he was on the matter at hand, he could not keep his mind from dwelling on the agent he knew as Prospero. What was it that Dunne had said? Vansina had been acting as a conduit, presumably for the Directorate, laundering over five billion dollars. Laundered funds were an everyday necessity for intelligence agencies, but almost always they were relatively small sums, untraceable payments to agents and contacts. *Five billion dollars*, however, was an order of magnitude beyond payments to assets. Such a quantity of money had to be funding something large. If Dunne's information was accurate — and it seemed less and less likely that the CIA man was deliberately misleading him, not when he had killed his own bodyguard to protect him — the Directorate was channeling money to, and in fact orchestrating, terrorist organizations. But which ones, why, and to what end? Perhaps the cryptochip that he had copied from Jacques Arnaud's secure phone would yield the answer, but whom could he trust with that crucial piece of evidence?

And if Jan Vansina was directly involved in the cycling of diverted funds, Bryson doubted the Dutchman was acting as a blind conduit. Vansina was far too skilled, and too senior, to act in such an innocent capacity. Vansina would *know*. For all Bryson knew, Vansina was one of the Directorate's principals by now.

Suddenly the door to the closet swung open, flooding the small room with light, and for an instant Bryson was blinded, unable to see who was there.

Within a few seconds Bryson could make out the shape, then the face. Jan Vansina, grim faced, eyes blazing. In his right hand a gun was pointed directly at Bryson; in his left hand he gripped a briefcase.

"Coleridge," Vansina said. "A flash from the past."

"Prospero," said Bryson, startled. Unprepared for the intrusion, he reached for the pistol holstered inside his suit jacket, then froze when he heard the click of the safety being released.

"*Don't* move," barked Vansina. "Hands at your side! I will not hesitate to use this. You know me, so you know I speak the truth."

Bryson stared, slowly lowered his hand. Vansina would indeed have no compunction about killing him in cold blood; why he had not done so already was a mystery.

"Thank you, *Bryson*," the Dutchman went on. "You wish to talk with me; we will talk."

"Where's the woman?"

"She is safe. Bound and locked in a storage closet. She is a strong and clever woman, but she must have expected this to be a, how do you say, cakewalk. I must say, her Mossad paper appears quite genuine. Your backstoppers are excellent."

"It *is* genuine, because she *is* Mossad."

"Even more intriguing, Bryson. I see you have established new alliances. New alliances for changing times. This is for you." He tossed the briefcase at Bryson, who made the split-second decision to catch it, not dodge it.

"Good catch," said Vansina jovially. "Now, please hold it out in front of you with both hands."

Bryson scowled. The Dutch operative was as quick-witted as ever.

"Come, let us talk," said Vansina. "Walk straight ahead, keeping the briefcase in front of you at all times. Any sudden moves, and I will shoot. Drop it, and I will shoot. You know me, my friend."

Bryson obeyed, silently berating himself. He had fallen into Vansina's trap by underestimating the wily old operative. How had he turned the tables on Layla? There had been no sound of gunfire, but perhaps he had used a silencer. Had he killed Layla? The thought tore at him, filled him with anguish. She had been serving as his accomplice; although Bryson had tried to dissuade her from working with him further, and she had insisted, he still felt responsible for whatever happened to her. Or had Vansina spoken the truth and bound and locked Layla up? He marched forward, urged along by the waving of Vansina's gun, crossing the narrow hall into an empty conference room. Although the lights in the room were off, there was still plenty of afternoon sun flooding in through the plate-glass window. The view of the city of Geneva from this high up was even more spectacular than that from Bécot's office window: the famous plume of the Jet d'eau and the Parc Mon Repos clearly visible from here, though not a sound from the city was audible.

Holding the briefcase, he was unable to retrieve his gun. Yet if he dropped the briefcase to go for his weapon, even that brief second would be time enough for Vansina to fire into the back of his head.

"Sit," commanded the Dutchman.

Bryson sat at the head of the table, placing the briefcase down on the table in front of him, still clutching it in both hands.

"Now place your left hand flat on top of the table, followed by your right. In that order, please. No sudden motions—you know the drill."

Bryson did so, his hands flat on the table on either side of the briefcase. Vansina sat at the other end of the table, his back to the plate-glass window, his weapon still aimed at Bryson.

"Move a hand to rub your nose, I shoot," said Vansina. "Move a hand to take a cigarette from your breast pocket, I shoot. Those are the ground rules, Mr. Bryson, and I know you understand them well. Now then, tell me this, please: Does Elena know?"

Stunned, Bryson tried to make sense of the question. *Does Elena know?* "What are you talking about?" he whispered.

"Does she know?"

"Does she know *what?* Where is she? Have you *spoken* with her?"

"Please don't affect to be concerned about the woman, Bryson—"

"Where *is* she?" Bryson interrupted.

The bearded man hesitated but a second before replying, "I am asking the questions here, Bryson. How long have you been with the Prometheans?"

Dully, Bryson repeated, "The Prometheans?"

"*Enough.* No more games! How long have you been in their employ, Bryson? Were you double-dealing while you were on active duty? Or perhaps you grew bored as a college professor, in search of adventure? You see, I'd really like to understand the inducement, the lure. An appeal to misbegotten idealism? Power? You see, we have so much to talk about, Bryson."

"Yet you insist on leveling a gun at me as if you've completely forgotten Yemen."

Vansina, looking amused, shook his head. "You are still a legend in the organization, Bryson. People still retell stories of your operational skill, your linguistic talent. You were a great asset—"

"Until I was shoved out the door by Ted Waller. Or should I say Gennady Rosovsky?"

Vansina paused a long while, unable to conceal the astonishment in his eyes. "We all have many names," he said at last. "Many identities. And sanity lies in the ability to distinguish among them, to keep them separate. Yet you seem to have lost that ability. You believe one thing, then another. You don't know where reality ends and fantasy begins. Ted Waller is a great man, Bryson. Greater than any of us."

"So he has you deceived still! You believe him, you believe his lies! You don't *know*, Prospero? We were puppets, drones—automatons, programmed by the overseers! We acted blindly, not understanding who our real masters were, what the *real* agenda was!"

"There are circles within circles," Vansina said solemnly. "There are things we know nothing about. The world has changed, and we must change with it, must adapt to the new realities. What have you been told, Bryson? What lies have *you* been fed?"

"The 'new realities,' " Bryson began hollowly, not understanding. He was stunned, baffled to the point of momentary speechlessness, when he saw the enormous shape suddenly looming in the plate-glass window, abruptly appearing from out of nowhere. He recognized it as a helicopter only at the instant that the fusillade of bullets riddled the glass, the automatic machine-gun fire shattering the glass into a crystalline hailstorm.

Bryson dove to the floor, tumbled beneath the long conference table, but Vansina, at the head of the table and therefore much closer to the window, had no such opportunity. His hands flew out to his side like a bird attempting flight, and then his entire body danced, animated grotesquely, almost prancing like some marionette. The bullets penetrated his face, his chest, blood erupted from his twitching body in scores of tiny geysers, and his bloodied face contorted in a horrible scream, a full-throated bellow that was entirely masked by the deafening racket of the hovering helicopter, the ear-splitting thunder of gunfire. As the wind howled through the conference room, the mahogany table was split, chewed up by a thousand bullets, the carpet crisscrossed, pitted. From his shelter under the thick tabletop, Bryson saw Vansina seem almost to rise into the air before crumpling against the gray carpet, red-spattered from his blood, limbs splayed unnaturally, his eyes hollow red cavities, his face and beard a horrifying bloodied pulp, the entire back of his head missing. Then, as suddenly as it had appeared, the helicopter lunged out of sight and was gone. The cacophony had abruptly ceased, the only sounds the faint traffic noises from the street hundreds of feet below, and the moaning of the wind as it whistled through stalactites of glass, whirling around the slaughterhouse of a room now gone eerily silent.

CHAPTER FOURTEEN

Racing from the conference room, from the nightmarish scene of blood and machine-gun rounds and broken glass, Bryson ran through a hall choked with horrified bystanders. There were screams, shouts in *Schweizerdeutsch* and French and English.

"Oh, *Jesus Christ!*"

"What happened, was it snipers? Terrorists?"

"Are they inside the building?"

"Call the police, an ambulance, *quickly!*"

"My God, the man's dead—he's, oh *God*, he's been *massacred!*"

As he ran, he thought of Layla. *Not her, too!* Could the helicopter have circled the building, locating targets in windows on the twenty-seventh floor?

And he thought: *Jan Vansina was the object of the freakish attack.* Not me. Vansina. It *had* to be. He ran through the kaleidoscopic images in his mind, sorting through them, recalling angles of fire. Yes. Whoever was manning the machine gun or guns from within the helicopter had been *deliberately aiming for Jan Vansina.* This was no random attack, nor a generalized attempt to kill whoever was present in the conference room. The gunfire had been aimed precisely, from at least three different and precise angles, at the Directorate operative.

But *why?*

And who? The Directorate could not have been killing its own, could it? Perhaps fearing that Vansina was meeting with an old friend, sharing information . . .

No, it stretched the imagination too far, made too little sense. The reasons, the logic behind the attack remained obscure. But the fact remained, Bryson was convinced, that the man who was supposed to be killed had in fact been killed.

These thoughts spun through his mind in a matter of seconds; he located Bécot's office, yanked open the closed door—and found it empty.

Neither Layla nor the banker was here. Turning to leave, he noticed a china espresso cup overturned on the floor beside the coffee table, a few papers scattered near the desk. Signs of either a hurried departure or a brief struggle.

Muffled sounds came from somewhere within the room or very nearby, thumping noises, cries. His eyes quickly searched the room, found the closet door. He ran to it, opened it. Layla and Jean-Luc Bécot were bound in ropes, gagged. Polyurethane "humane restraints," as strong as leather, secured their wrists and ankles. The banker's wire-rimmed glasses lay bent on the closet floor beside him, his tie askew, his shirt torn, hair wild. Through the wadded cloth gag stuffed in his mouth he tried to shout, his eyes bulging. Next to him, Layla was bound even more thoroughly, expertly, the gag tight in her mouth. Her gray Chanel suit was ripped; one of her matching gray high-heeled shoes had come off. She, too, had vinyl restraints around her wrists and ankles. Her face was bloodied and bruised; obviously she had struggled fiercely but had been overwhelmed by the superior strength of the man who had been Prospero.

The brute *animal* who had been Prospero, Jan Vansina. Bryson swelled with rage at the dead man. He pulled the gag from her mouth, then from the banker's; both captives took deep, gulping breaths, filling their lungs with much-needed air. Bécot gasped, cried out. Layla gasped, too: "Thank you. My God!"

"He didn't kill you, either of you," Bryson remarked as he worked quickly to untie the ropes. He searched for a knife or other blade to sever the strong plastic restraints; seeing nothing, he ran to the banker's desk and spied a silver letter opener, quickly rejecting it since it had a point but no blade. In a side desk drawer he found a small but sharp pair of scissors, ran back to the closet, and used it to release them both.

"Call Security!" the banker said through gulps of air.

Bryson, who could already hear the sirens of the approaching emergency vehicles growing steadily louder, said, "The police are on their way, I suspect." He took Layla by the arm, helped her to her feet, and the two of them ran from the room.

Passing the open conference room door, in front of which a crowd had gathered, she stopped.

"Come on," hissed Bryson. "There's no *time!*"

But she peered inside, saw the crumpled body of Jan Vansina surrounded by jagged shards of glass, the shattered window. "Oh, my God!" she breathed, horrified, quivering. "Oh, my *God!*"

Not until they reached the crowded Place Bel-Air did they come to a stop.

"We have to leave," Bryson said. "Travel separately—we can't be seen together, not any longer."

"Travel—but where?"

"*Out* of here—out of Geneva, out of Switzerland!"

"What are you saying—we can't just—" She stopped in midsentence when she realized that Bryson's attention was riveted on a newspaper displayed in a kiosk. It was a copy of *La Tribune de Genève*.

"My God," said Bryson, moving closer. He grabbed it from a tall stack, riveted by the large black banner headline above a photograph of some sort of terrible accident.

TERROR STRIKES FRANCE:
HIGH-SPEED PASSENGER TRAIN
DERAILED IN LILLE

LILLE—A powerful bomb blast derailed and tore apart the high-speed passenger train Eurostar about thirty miles south of Lille early this morning, killing hundreds of French, British, American, Dutch, Belgian, and other business travelers. Although emergency workers and volunteers worked frantically throughout the day, searching the wreckage for survivors, French authorities fear that the death toll may exceed 700. An official at the crash site, who preferred to remain anonymous, speculated that the incident was the work of terrorists.

According to records made available by railroad officials, the train, Eurostar 9007-ERS, left the Gare du Nord in Paris, bound for London, at approximately 7:16 A.M., with nearly 770 passengers on board. At approximately 8:00 A.M., the 18-car train passed through France's Pas-de-Calais region, where a series of high-powered explosions, reportedly buried beneath the tracks, went off below the train's front and rear sections simultaneously. Although there was no immediate claim of responsibility, sources in the French security service, the Sûreté, have already compiled a list of possible suspects. Several anonymous sources in the Sûreté have confirmed rampant speculation that both the French and the British governments had received repeated warnings of an impending attack on the Eurostar in the last several days. A Eurostar spokesman would neither confirm nor deny a report provided to *La Tribune de Genève* that the intelligence services of both countries had leads pointing to suspected terrorists planning to blow up the train but were unable to intercept or monitor telephone conversations between the alleged terrorists because of legal constraints.

"This is an outrage," declared French National Assembly member Françoise Chouet. "We had the technical ability to prevent this sickening carnage, yet our police are hamstrung by our laws from doing anything about it." In London, Lord Miles Parmore renewed his call in Parliament for passage of the International Treaty on Surveillance and Security. "If the governments of France and England had the ability to keep this sabotage from happening, it is simply criminal that we sat there and did nothing about it. This is a national—no, an international—disgrace."

The United States national security adviser, Richard Lanchester, attending a NATO summit in Brussels, issued a statement denouncing the "slaughter of innocents." He added, "In this period of mourning, we must all ask ourselves how to make sure something like this never happens again. With great reluctance and sadness, the Davis administration joins its allies and good friends England and France in calling for worldwide passage of the International Treaty on Surveillance and Security."

Lille.
Bryson's blood ran cold.

He remembered the low, conspiratorial voices of two men emerging from Jacques Arnaud's private office in the Château de Saint-Meurice. One was the arms merchant himself, the other Anatoly Prishnikov, the Russian tycoon.

"Once Lille happens," Arnaud had said, "the outrage will be enormous. The way will be clear."

Once Lille happens.

Two of the world's most powerful businessmen, one an arms dealer, the other a mogul who no doubt secretly owned or controlled large segments of the Russian defense industry—Bryson would have to obtain a complete dossier—had foreknowledge of the devastation at Lille, the attack that killed seven hundred people.

Quite likely the men were among those who planned it.

Both of them principals of the Directorate. The Directorate was behind the nightmare at Lille; there was no question about it.

But to what *end?* Senseless violence was not the Directorate's way; Waller and the other overseers had always prided themselves on their strategic genius. Everything was strategy, everything served an ultimate end. Even the murder of Bryson's parents, even the massive deception that had become his life. The murder of a few field operatives might be justified by nothing more than the need to remove an encumbrance, an obstacle, a threat. But the wholesale murder of seven hundred innocent

THE PROMETHEUS DECEPTION

travelers was in another category entirely, moved from low-level tactics to higher strategy.

The outrage will be enormous.

The public outcry over the derailing and destruction of the Eurostar train was indeed great, as it would inevitably be over such a preventable tragedy.

Preventable tragedy.

The key was preventable. Prophylaxis. The Directorate *wanted* this outrage, *wanted* to spur calls for prevention of any future terrorism. Yet *prevention* could mean any number of things. A treaty to fight terrorism was one thing, no doubt little more than window dressing. But surely any such treaty would lead to the bolstering of national defenses, the acquisition of weapons intended to protect public safety.

Arnaud and Prishnikov, merchants of death with a vested interest in world chaos, because chaos was a form of marketing—the marketing of their goods, their weapons, the increasing of demand. These two moguls were presumably behind Lille and . . .

And what else? Standing there on the street, he was oblivious to the bustle of passing pedestrians. Layla was reading the article over his shoulder, saying something to him, but he did not hear her. He was retrieving remembered news stories in the filing cabinet of his mind. Several recent incidents that he had read about, seen television coverage about, terrible things that at the time did not register as directly applicable to his own life, his mission.

Just a few days ago there had been a devastating explosion in a Washington, D.C., metro station during the morning rush hour that had killed dozens of people. And later that same day—he remembered because the timing was so unfortunate—an American jetliner had blown up just after taking off from Kennedy Airport, en route to Rome. One hundred fifty, one hundred seventy people had been killed.

The outcry in America had been anguished, clamorous. The president had issued a call for passage of the international security treaty, which had previously been stalled in the Senate. After Lille, the European nations would surely join the Americans in pushing for strong measures to restore sanity to a world spinning out of control.

Control.

Was this the "higher purpose," the underlying reason behind the Directorate's madness? A rogue intelligence agency, once a small but powerful behind-the-scenes player known to no one, making a bid to seize control where the rest of the world had failed?

Damn it, it was all vaporous speculation, theory upon theory, conclusions drawn from tentative suggestions. Unprovable, shadowy, insufficient. But an answer to Dunne's initial question, the reason why the CIA man had plucked Bryson from a contented retirement and all but forced him to investigate, was beginning to suggest itself. It was time to level with Harry Dunne, present him with a scenario, with hypotheses. To wait for firm, undeniable documentation of the Directorate's agenda would be to let another Lille happen, and that was morally repugnant. Did the CIA really need another seven hundred innocent people to die before it decided to do something?

And yet . . .

Yet the biggest piece of the puzzle remained missing.

"*Does Elena know?*" Vansina had asked. The implication being that the Directorate did not know where she was, or where her loyalties resided. It was more important than ever that she be located: the very question—*does Elena know?*—implied that she had to know something crucial. Something that would not only explain her disappearance from his life but also reveal the pattern, the key to the Directorate's true intentions.

"You know something about this." Layla's voice: a statement, not a question.

He realized that she had been speaking to him for a while. He turned to look at her. Had she not overheard Arnaud's remark about Lille at the château? Evidently not.

"I have a theory," he said.

"Which is?"

"I need to make a call." He handed her the newspaper. "I'll be right back."

"A call? To whom?"

"Give me a few minutes, Layla."

She raised her voice. "What are you *hiding* from me? What are you really up to?"

He saw in her beautiful brown eyes bewilderment, but something more: hurt, anger. She was justified in being angry. He had been using her as an accomplice while telling her almost nothing. It was more than hurtful, it was unacceptable, particularly to a field agent as skilled and knowledgeable as she was.

He hesitated, then spoke. "Let me make a phone call. When I return, I'll fill you in — but I warn you, I know a lot less than you must think I do."

She put a hand on his arm, a quick, affectionate gesture that said any number of things — thank you, I understand, I'm here for you. He was moved to kiss her, lightly and on the cheek: nothing sexual, but a moment of human contact, an expression of gratitude for her bravery and support.

He walked quickly to the end of the block, taking a side street off Place Bel-Air. There was a small *tabac* that sold, in addition to cigarettes and newspapers, prepaid telephone cards. He purchased one, located an international telephone in a booth on the street. He dialed 011, then 0, then a sequence of five numbers. There was a low electronic tone; then he dialed seven more digits.

It was a sterile line, a number that Harry Dunne had given him; it rang directly through to Dunne's CIA office and at Dunne's private study at home. Dunne had guaranteed that he, and only he, would answer it.

The phone rang once.

"Bryson."

Bryson, about to speak, caught his breath. The voice was unfamiliar; it did not sound like Dunne. "Who is this?" he said.

"It's Graham Finneran, Bryson. You — I think you know who I am."

Dunne had mentioned Finneran when they had last met in his CIA office. Dunne had identified Finneran as his aide-de-camp, one of the men who had accompanied Dunne to the CIA's Blue Ridge Mountains facility, one of Dunne's few trusted aides.

"What is this?" said Bryson guardedly.

"Bryson — I — Harry's in the hospital. He's quite ill."

"Ill?"

"You know he's got a terminal case of cancer — he won't talk about it, but it's obvious — and he collapsed yesterday and had to be taken to the hospital in an ambulance."

"You're saying he's dead, is that it?"

"No—thank God, no, but I don't know how long he's got, to be honest. But he's briefed me fully on your . . . your project. I know he was worried, frankly—"

"Which hospital?"

Finneran hesitated, barely a second or two, but it was too long. "I'm not sure I should say just yet—"

Bryson disconnected the call, his heart pounding, the blood rushing in his ears. His instincts commanded him to get off the line at once. Something was not right. Dunne had assured him that no one else would answer this telephone, and he would not violate protocol, even on his deathbed. Dunne knew Bryson, knew how Bryson would react.

No. Graham Finneran—if it *was* Graham Finneran; Bryson wouldn't recognize his voice in any case—would never have answered the phone. Dunne would never have permitted it.

Something was terribly wrong, and it was more than the health of the CIA man.

Had the Directorate finally reached its chief adversary within the Agency, finally neutralized the last institutional bulwark against their growing power?

He raced back through the Place Bel-Air, found Layla still standing by the news kiosk. "I have to go to Brussels," he said.

"What? Why Brussels? What are you *talking* about?"

"There's a man there—someone I need to reach."

She looked at him questioningly, beseechingly.

"Come on. I know of a pension in the Marolles. It's rundown and shabby, and it's not in a particularly pleasant part of town. But it's safe and anonymous, and it's not where anyone would think to look for us."

"But why *Brussels?*"

"It's a last resort, Layla. Someone who can help out, someone extremely highly placed. A person some people consider the last honest man in Washington."

CHAPTER
FIFTEEN

The headquarters of the Systematix Corporation comprised seven large, gleaming glass-and-steel buildings on a sylvan, beautifully landscaped campus—twenty acres in all—outside Seattle, Washington. There were dining rooms and exercise rooms in each building; the corporation's employees, who were renowned for their loyalty and discretion, had little reason to leave while they labored away. They were a closely knit community, recruited from the best training programs around the world and compensated generously. They realized, too, that they had thousands of colleagues elsewhere whom they would never meet. Systematix, after all, had offices around the world, and owned controlling stakes in many more companies, though the extent of these holdings remained a matter of avid conjecture.

"I have a feeling we're not in Kansas anymore," Tony Gupta, the jovial chief technology officer of InfoMed, told his boss, Adam Parker, as the two were escorted to the meeting room. Parker smiled thinly. He was the CEO of a nine-hundred-million-dollar company, but even he had to feel some slight trepidation as he arrived at the fabled Systematix campus.

"Ever been here before?" Parker asked. He was a rangy man with salt-

and-pepper hair who used to run marathons before a knee injury forced him to stop. Now he rowed and swam and, even with the bad knee, played tennis with a ferocity that made it hard for him to keep his partners for more than a few games. He was an intensely competitive man, a quality that enabled him to build his company, which specialized in medical "informatics" and data warehousing. But he knew when he was outmatched.

"Once," Gupta said. "Years ago. I was up for a job as a software engineer, but at the interview there was a brainteaser that I flunked. And just to get that far, I had to sign three nondisclosure agreements. They were fanatical about secrecy." Gupta adjusted his tie, which he'd knotted too tightly. He wasn't accustomed to wearing one, but then this was no ordinary occasion; Systematix wasn't known to indulge the self-conscious informality that was de rigeur among so many New Economy corporations.

Parker didn't have a good feeling about the impending acquisition, and had made no secret about it to Gupta, who was the man he trusted most among his colleagues. "The board isn't going to let me stop the deal," Parker said softly. "You realize that, don't you?"

Gupta looked at their escort, a blond, lithe woman and shot his boss a warning glance. "Let's just listen to what the great man has to say," he replied.

Moments later, they took their seats along with twelve other men and women on the top floor of the largest building, with a breathtaking view of the surrounding hills. This was the centerpoint of the seemingly diffuse and decentralized company that was Systematix. For most of the assembled—the directors of InfoMed—it was their first time face-to-face with Systematix's legendary founder, chairman, and chief executive officer, the reclusive Gregson Manning. In the past year, as Adam Parker knew, Manning had acquired dozens of such companies in cash transactions.

"The great man," Gupta had called him, and though the words were arch, they were not ironic. Gregson Manning *was* a great man, almost everyone agreed. He was one of the richest men in the world, had created from nothing a vast corporation that manufactured much of the infrastructure of the Internet. Everyone knew his story—about how he dropped out of CalTech when he was eighteen, lived in a communal house with his techie friends, started Systematix out of a garage. Now it was hard to think of a single company anywhere that didn't rely upon Systematix technologies for some part of their operations. Systematix was, as *Forbes* once said, an industry unto itself.

Manning had also emerged as a major philanthropist, albeit a controversial one. He had given hundreds of millions of dollars to help bring inner-city schools on-line, to use modern technology to help further educational goals. Parker had heard rumors, too, that Manning had anonymously given billions to help underprivileged children in the form of scholarships to institutions of higher learning.

And, of course, the business press idolized him. For all his vast wealth, he always came across as unassuming and unpretentious; he was depicted not as reclusive so much as retiring. *Barron's* once dubbed him the "Daddy Warbucks" of the Information Age.

But Parker could not shake his feeling of unease. Yes, some of it had to do with the unpalatable prospect of relinquishing control—damn it, he'd nurtured InfoMed as if it was his own child, and it pained him to think of it being reduced to a tiny component of a giant conglomerate. But there was something more than that: it was almost a clash of cultures. At the end of the day, Parker was a businessman, plain and simple. His chief investors and advisers were businessmen. They talked the language of finance: of return on invested capital, market value added. Of cost centers and profit centers. Maybe it wasn't high-minded, but it was honest and Parker could understand it. Yet that wasn't how Manning's mind seemed to work. He thought and spoke in sweeping terms—about historical forces, global trends. The fact that Systematix was immense and exceedingly profitable seemed almost incidental to him. "Look, you've never cared for visionaries," Gupta once said to Parker, after one of their marathon strategy sessions, and no doubt he was on to something.

"I'm so pleased you could come, all of you," Gregson Manning told his visitors, shaking their hands firmly. Manning was tall, well built, and slender, his hair dark and glossy. He was ruggedly handsome, square-jawed and broad shouldered, with an unmistakably patrician air. His features were fine, his nose aquiline and strong, his skin unlined, nearly poreless. He radiated health, self-assurance, and, Parker had to admit to himself, charisma. He wore khakis, an open-necked white shirt, and a lightweight, cashmere blazer. He gave a warm smile, revealing white, perfect teeth. "I wouldn't be here if I didn't respect what InfoMed has accomplished, and you wouldn't be here if . . ." Manning trailed off, his smile widening.

"If we didn't appreciate the forty percent premium you're offering for our shares," the rumpled, big-bellied chairman of the InfoMed board, Alex Garfield, interjected, laughing. Garfield was a venture capitalist of limited imagination who happened to have provided a much-needed infusion of cash during InfoMed's infancy. His interest in the company didn't go much beyond the terms for which he could swap his equity stake. Adam Parker didn't admire Garfield, but he always knew where he stood with him.

Manning's eyes sparkled. "Our interests converge."

"Mr. Manning," Parker said, "I do have some concerns—they may be moot in light of such financial considerations, but I may as well voice them."

"Please," said Manning with a tilt of his head.

"When you acquire InfoMed, you're not only acquiring a vast medical database, you're acquiring seven hundred dedicated employees. I'd like a sense of what's in store for them. Systematix is one of those companies that people know everything and nothing about. It's privately held, tightly controlled, and a lot of what it does is pretty damned mysterious. And the obsession with privacy can be a little unsettling, at least if you're outside it."

"Privacy?" Manning tilted his head, his smile fading. "I think you have things precisely backward. And I would very much regret if you found our larger aims here to be mysterious."

"I don't think anyone exactly understands your organization chart," Parker said testily. Looking around the room, sensing the awe with which the others regarded Gregson Manning, Parker realized that his remarks were less than welcome; he also realized that this was his last opportunity to voice them.

Manning fixed him with a stare, forthright yet not unfriendly. "My friend, I do not believe in the regalia of the traditional organization, the partitions and barriers and 'dotted-line reporting' relations. I think everyone here knows that. The key to our success at Systematix—our not inconsiderable success, I think I can say without immodesty—has been to jettison the old ways of doing things."

"But there's a logic to any corporate structure," Parker said, pressing the point, as the other men in the room looked at him with unfriendly stares. Even Tony Gupta reached over and put a cautioning hand on his arm. Still, Parker wasn't used to holding his tongue and he was damned if he was going to start now. "Subsidiary divisions and whatnot, there's a reason for flowcharts, I hate to say it. I just want to know how you intend to integrate the acquisition."

Manning spoke to him as if to a slow child. "Who invented the modern corporation? Men like John D. Rockefeller of Standard Oil, and Alfred Sloan of General Motors. In the postwar era of economic expansion, you had Robert McNamara at Ford and Harold Geneen at ITT, Reginald Jones at General Electric. It was the heyday of multiplex managerial strata, with chief executives assisted by staffs of planners and auditors and operations strategists. Rigid structures were necessary to conserve and manage the scarcest resource of all, the most *valuable* asset of all: information. Now, what happens if information becomes as free and copiously available as the air we breathe or the water we drink? All that becomes unnecessary. All that gives way."

Parker recalled a quote of Manning's that had once appeared in *Barron's*—something to the effect that the goal of Systematix was "to replace doors with windows." And he had to admit that the man was mesmerizing, as supernally articulate as his reputation had suggested. Still, Parker stirred in his seat uneasily. *All that gives way.* "Gives way to what?"

"If the old way was vertical hierarchy, the new way is the forging of horizontal networks, cutting across organizational boundaries. We're about building a network of companies that we can *collaborate* with, not direct from above. The boundaries are down. The logic of networking puts a premium on self-monitoring, information-driven systems. Continual monitoring means we eliminate risk factors within the organizational structure and outside of it, too." The setting sun behind Gregson Manning cast an aura around his head, adding to his unsettling intensity. "You're an entrepreneur. Look ahead of you, and what do you see? Atomized capital markets. Radically dispersed labor markets. Pyramidal organization yielding to fluid, self-organizing means of collaboration. All of which requires that we exploit connectivity, not just internally but externally as well, arriving at common strategies with our partners, extending control beyond the purview of ownership. Informational channels are recombinant. There must be transparency at all levels. I'm merely giving words to an inkling, an intuition I think we've all had about the future of capitalism."

Parker was baffled by Manning's words. "The way you're talking, it sounds as if Systematix isn't really a corporation at all."

"Call it what you like. When boundaries are truly permeable, there isn't anything so localizable as a traditional firm. But we've already lived through an era of managerialism answerable to no one. Ownership can only be fragmented, risk disaggregated only for so long. The poet Robert Frost said good fences make good neighbors. Well, I don't believe that. Porosity, walls you can see through, walls you can move whenever you need—that's what the world requires these days. To succeed, you've got to be able to walk through walls." Manning paused briefly. "Which is easier when there aren't any."

Alex Garfield turned toward his CEO. "I don't pretend to follow all this, but, Adam, the record speaks for itself. Gregson Manning doesn't have to defend himself to anyone. I think all he's saying is he doesn't believe in a collection of sealed-off business units. He's talking about integration in his own way."

"The walls have to fall," Manning said, sitting up very straight. "That's the reality behind the rhetoric of reengineering. You might say we're turning back the Industrial Revolution. The Industrial Revolution was about the division of work into tasks; we're trying to go from tasks to *process*, and to do so in a domain of absolute visibility."

Frustrated, Parker pursued his line of questioning. "Yet so many of the technologies you've been investing in—these networking technologies and the rest—well, I don't understand the thinking behind it," Parker said. "And then there's that FCC report that Systematix is about to launch another fleet of low-earth-orbit satellites. Why? There's already so much bandwidth available. Why *satellites?*"

Manning nodded as if pleased by the question. "Maybe it's time to raise our sights."

There were grunts of assent and laughter around the room.

"I've been talking about business," Manning went on. "But think about our own lives, too. You mentioned privacy earlier. The conventions of privacy treat the private sphere as a domain of personal freedom." Now Manning's expression became grave. "But for many, it may be the sphere of intimate violation and abuse, neither free nor personal. The housewife who is raped and robbed at knifepoint, the man whose home has been invaded by armed marauders—ask them about the value of privacy. Information in its full amplitude means *freedom from*—freedom from violation, freedom from abuse, freedom from harm. And if Systematix can move society toward that goal, then we are talking about something we've never had before in human history—something very near to *total security*. To some degree, surveillance has played a larger part in our lives, and I'm proud of the role we've had in that—the cameras in elevators and subways and parks, the Nannycams and all the rest of it. And yet truly sophisticated surveillance systems, what you might call panic buttons: these things currently remain the luxuries of the rich. Well, let's *democratize* them, I say. Bring everyone into view. Jane Jacobs wrote about 'eyes on the street,' and we can go even beyond that. The rhetoric about the global village has been just that, rhetoric, but it can be *real*, and technology can make it so."

"That's a lot of power for one organization to take on."

"Except that power, too, is no longer a discrete location, but a *web* of sanctions throughout society. In any case, I think you're looking at it too narrowly. Once truly meaningful safety and security become pervasive, all of us end up finally having power over our own lives."

Manning was interrupted by a knock; his personal assistant stood at the door looking concerned.

"Yes, Daniel?" Manning asked, surprised by the intrusion.

"A phone call, sir."

"Not a good moment." Manning smiled.

The young assistant coughed quietly. "The Oval Office, sir. The president says it's urgent."

Manning turned to the assembled. "You'll forgive me, then. I'll be right back."

In his large, hexagonal office, sun-bathed yet cool, Manning settled into his chair and put the president on the speakerphone. "I'm here, Mr. President," he said.

"Listen, Greg, you know I wouldn't bother you if it weren't important. But we need a favor. There's a pattern to the terrorism, and we've got a missing link in the skies over Lille, in France. A dozen American businessmen were killed in that tragedy. Yet none of our satellites were overhead at the right time. The French government's been hammering us for years to stop the overflights, stop invading the privacy of their citizens, so the eyes are usually switched off over that segment of the continent. Or so my experts tell me, it's all Greek to me. But they're telling me that Systematix satellites were in position. They'd have the imagery we need."

"Mr. President, you recognize that our satellites haven't been approved for photo reconnaissance. They're strictly licensed for telecommunications, digital telephony."

"I know that's what your people told Corelli's guys."

"But it was your administration that decided to restrict nongovernmental surveillance instrumentation." As Manning spoke, his eyes drifted toward a photograph of his daughter on his desk: a sandy-haired girl with a dreamy, giddy smile, as if she were laughing at a private joke.

"If you want me to eat crow, Greg, I will. I'm not too proud to beg. But goddamn it, this is serious. We need what you've got. For Chrissakes, cut me some slack. I haven't forgotten what you've done for me in the past, and I won't forget this."

Manning paused, allowing a few seconds of silence to elapse. "Have your NSA techies call Partovi at my office. We'll transmit whatever we've got."

"I appreciate it," President Davis said hoarsely.

"I'm just as concerned about the problem as you are," Manning said, his eyes lingering again on the sandy-haired little girl. He and his wife had named her Ariel, and she had indeed been a creature of magic. "We've all got to pull together."

"Understood," the president said, awkward in his importuning. "Understood. I knew you'd come through for me."

"We're all in this together, Mr. President."

Ariel's laugh had been like the tinkle of a music box, he remembered, and his mind, usually so tightly focused, began wandering.

"Good-bye, Gregson. And thank you."

It occurred to Manning, as he switched off the speakerphone, that he'd never heard President Malcolm Davis sound so strained. A taste of misfortune could do that to a man.

CHAPTER
SIXTEEN

The pension was in a seedy area of Brussels, the Marolles, a refuge for the city's poor and disenfranchised. Many of the seventeenth-century buildings were crumbling, collapsing bit by bit. The impoverished residents of the tenements were mostly Mediterranean immigrants, many of them Maghrebis. A stout, suspicious Maghrebi woman was the proprietor of the pension La Samaritaine, perched glumly behind a desk in the dark, malodorous warren that served as the hotel's lobby. Her customary clientele were transients and petty criminals and destitute immigrants; she regarded the too-respectable-looking man who arrived in the middle of the night with minimal luggage, wearing good clothes, as peculiarly out of place here, and therefore suspect.

Bryson had arrived by rail, at the Gare du Nord, and had grabbed a quick late-night dinner of soggy *moules et frites* and watery pilsener at a snack bar on the way. He asked the dour proprietress for the room number of his female friend who had, he believed, checked in earlier. She raised her eyebrows insinuatingly and divulged the number with a smirk.

Layla had arrived a few hours earlier, via a Sabena flight into Zaventem Airport, having purchased a ticket at the last minute. Although it was after midnight, and he expected she was as bone-tired as he was, he noticed the light seeping through the crack between her door and the filthy carpet, and he knocked. Her room was as dismal, as dingy, as his.

She poured them each a Scotch, neat, from a bottle she had picked up near the Vieux Marché. "So who is this 'honest man' from Washington you want to meet here?" She added impishly: "It can't be anyone from your CIA—unless you've actually found one honest man at Langley." The bruises on her face from the struggle with Jan Vansina were bluish-purple, nasty looking.

Bryson took a sip, took a seat in a rickety armchair. "No one from the Agency."

"Well?"

He shook his head. "Not yet."

"Not yet what?"

"I'll fill you in when the time is right. Just not yet."

Sitting in a mismatched, but equally rickety, chair on the other side of a small table whose wood-grain veneer was flaying off, she set down her drink. "You're withholding from me—you're continuing to withhold, really—and that's not the deal."

"There was no deal, Layla."

"Did you really think I would join you blindly, in a mission I don't understand?" She was angry, and it was more than the alcohol or the exhaustion.

"No, of course not," he said wearily. "Quite the opposite, Layla. Not only did I not ask your help, I've tried to discourage you, push you away. Not because I didn't think you'd be helpful—you've been remarkable, invaluable—but because I couldn't assume the responsibility of endangering your life the way I'm endangering my own. But this is my battle to fight, my mission. If there's a subsidiary benefit to you, if whatever we end up learning serves your purpose, too, so much the better."

"That's so coldhearted."

"Maybe I am coldhearted. Maybe I have to be."

"But there's a gentle, caring side to you as well. I can sense it."

He didn't reply.

"Also I think you've been married."

"Oh? What makes you say that?"

"You have, yes?"

"Yes," he admitted. "But why do you say it?"

"Something about the way you are with me, the way you are with women. You are wary, of course—you don't *know* me, after all—yet at the same time you're comfortable with me, yes?"

Bryson smiled, amused, but said nothing.

She continued, "I think that most men in our . . . our line of work are unsure how to treat women field operatives. Either we are neuters, sexless, or we are potential romantic conquests. You seem to understand that it is more complex than that—that a woman, like a man, can be both, or neither, or something else entirely."

"You speak in riddles."

"I don't mean to. I just think—well, I suppose I'm saying that we are man and woman . . ." She tipped her glass toward him, a strange sort of salute.

He understood what she was hinting at, yet he pretended not to. She was an extraordinary woman, and the truth was that he was strongly attracted to her, increasingly, the more time he spent with her. But to pursue the attraction was to be selfish, to raise expectations he did not intend to meet, *could* not meet, until he finally understood what had happened between himself and Elena. The physical pleasure might well be considerable, but it would be momentary, fleeting; and it would simply end up confusing them, altering their relationship, introducing a destabilizing element.

"You seem to speak from experience," he said. "About how some men don't understand women who do the sort of work you do. Your husband—you said you married an Israeli soldier—was he one of those men who didn't understand?"

"I was a different person then. Not even a young woman—I was a girl, half formed."

"Was it his death that changed you?" asked Bryson gently.

"And my father's death, even though I never knew him." She looked pensive, and took another sip.

He nodded.

Her head bowed, she said, "Yaron, that was my husband, he was stationed at Kiryat Shmona during the *intifada*, helping to defend the village. One day the Israeli Air Force launched a rocket attack on a Hezbollah terrorist base in the Bekaa Valley, not too far from where I lived as a child, and by accident they killed a mother and all five of her children. It was a nightmare. Hezbollah retaliated, of course, by launching their Katyusha rockets against Kiryat Shmona. Yaron was helping get villagers into bomb shelters. He was hit by one of the rockets, his body incinerated almost beyond recognition." She looked up, tears in her eyes. "So tell me, who was in the right? Hezbollah, whose sole mission seems to be to kill as many Israelis as they can? The Israeli Air Force, which was so determined to eliminate a Hezbollah camp that they didn't care if they killed the innocent?"

"You knew the mother who was killed with her five children, didn't you?" said Bryson quietly.

She nodded, finally losing her composure, biting her lip as the tears flowed. "She was my sister, my . . . my older sister. My little nieces and nephews." For a few moments she could not speak. Then she said, "You see, it is not always the men who fire the Katyushas who are the guilty ones. Sometimes it's the men who supply the Katyushas. Or the men who sit in their bunkers with their charts and plan the attack. A man like Jacques Arnaud, who owns half of the French National Assembly and grows rich selling to the terrorists, the madmen, the fanatics of the world. So I want you to know that when you finally decide you can trust me, when you finally tell me why you are risking your life, and what it is you hope to find . . . I want you to know who it is you'll be telling." She stood, kissed him on the cheek. "And now I need to go to sleep."

•

Bryson returned to his room, his mind working feverishly. It was vital that he reach Richard Lanchester as soon as possible; in the morning he would begin to make telephone calls to reach the national security adviser. He realized that he still had far too little information, and too little time. With Harry Dunne mysteriously vanished, for whatever reason, Lanchester was the one man in government with both the power and the independence of mind to do something about the Directorate's metastasizing power. Although Bryson had not met the man, he knew the rudimentary biography: Lanchester had made millions on Wall Street but gave up business in his midforties to pursue a life of public service. He had run his friend Malcolm Davis's successful presidential election campaign and in return had been named as Davis's national security adviser, where he rapidly distinguished himself. His probity and intelligence made him an anomaly among the grandstanding and corruption of the Beltway; he was notable for his fair-mindedness and an unassuming, amiable brilliance.

According to the newspaper account about the carnage at Lille, Lanchester was visiting Brussels on what was billed as a largely ceremonial visit to SHAPE, the Supreme Headquarters Allied Powers Europe; there, he was consulting with the secretary general of NATO.

It would not be easy to reach Lanchester, particularly in the environs of NATO's world headquarters.

But there might be a way.

Shortly after five in the morning, having passed a tense and restless night punctuated by the ceaseless cacophony of traffic and the shouts of all-night revelers, Bryson awoke, bathed in cold water since there seemed to be no hot, and drew up a plan.

He dressed quickly, went out to the street, located a newsstand that stayed open all night and sold a good selection of international newspapers and magazines, heavily favoring European. As he expected, many of the papers, from the *International Herald-Tribune* to the *Times* of London, from *Le Monde* and *Le Figaro* to *Die Welt*, published extensive coverage of the Lille attack. Many of them cited Richard Lanchester, often using the same quotation; a few of them ran longer, sidebar interviews with the White House adviser. Bryson bought an array of newspapers and took them to a café, ordered several strong cups of black coffee, and began reading through the articles, marking them up with a pen.

Several newspapers mentioned not only Lanchester but his spokesman, who was also the spokesman for the National Security Council, a man named Howard Lewin. Lewin was in Brussels as well, accompanying his boss and the White House delegation on their visit to NATO headquarters.

Press spokesmen like Howard Lewin had to be available at all times to handle urgent inquiries from journalists. Returning to his hotel room, Bryson was able to reach the spokesman in just one phone call.

"Mr. Lewin, I don't believe we've ever spoken before," said Bryson in an urgent, hard-bitten voice. "I'm Jim Goddard, European bureau chief for the *Washington Post*, and I'm sorry to disturb you so early in the morning, but we've got a bombshell on our hands, and I'm going to need your help with it."

He had Lewin's attention at once. "Absolutely—uh, Jim?—what's up?"

"I wanted to give you a heads-up. We're about to go to press with a full-dress, above-the-fold, front-page story on Richard Lanchester. Banner headline, the works. I'm afraid you folks aren't going to be very happy with it. In fact, let me be blunt about it, it may well be the end of Lanchester's career. It's devastating stuff—the culmination of a three-month investigation."

"*Jesus!* What the hell are we talking about here?"

"Uh, Mr. Lewin, I ought to tell you, I've been getting major pressure from the top to just run with the damned thing, not let a word of it leak before it comes off the press, but personally, I see this series as hugely damaging not only to Lanchester but potentially to national security as well, and I . . ." Bryson let his voice trail off for a moment, to let his words sink in. Then he offered the lifeline, which the spokesman had no choice but to grab at. ". . . I wanted to give your boss an opportunity to at least respond to this—maybe even, hell, stall it for a while. I'm trying not to let my personal feelings, my admiration for the man, get in the way of my newsroom responsibilities here, and maybe I shouldn't have even made this call, but if I can get the great man himself on the horn, maybe I can finesse this thing—"

"Do you know what *time* it is in Brussels?" Lewin stammered. "This—this last-minute notice—this is a goddamned setup, it's *completely* irresponsible on the *Post's* part—"

"Look, Mr. Lewin, I'm going to make this your judgment call, but I want us to be *absolutely* clear that I gave you the opportunity to put out this fire, that this is all going to be on your head—hold on a second"—he shouted across the room to an imaginary colleague, "No, *not* that photo, the *head shot* of Lanchester, you idiot!" and then resumed speaking into the phone—"but you tell your boss I need to hear from him on this cell number in the next ten minutes or we're running with this thing, including the line 'Mr. Lanchester declined to comment,' are we *clear?* Tell Lanchester—I'd advise you to use these exact words—that the brunt of the piece concerns his relationship with a Russian official named *Gennady Rosovsky,* got that?"

"Gennady . . . *what?*"

"Gennady Rosovsky," Bryson repeated, giving the Washington number of his cell phone, which would give no indication that he was in Brussels. "Ten minutes!"

Bryson's phone rang barely ninety seconds later.

Bryson recognized the cultured baritone, the mid-Atlantic accent, at once. "This is Richard Lanchester," the national security adviser said in a tone just short of frantic. "What the *hell's* going on here?"

"I assume your spokesman filled you in on the piece we're running with."

"He mentioned some Russian name I've never heard before—Gennady something-or-other. What's this all about, Mr. Goddard?"

"You know damned well Ted Waller's real name, Mr. Lanchester—"

"Who the hell is Ted Waller? What *is* this?"

"We need to talk, Mr. Lanchester. Immediately."

"Well, talk away! I'm here. What kind of hatchet job is the *Post* preparing? Goddard, I don't know you, but as I'm sure you're well aware, I do have your publisher's home number, I see her socially, and I won't hesitate for a second to call her!"

"We have to talk in person, not over the phone. I'm in Brussels; I can be at SHAPE headquarters in Mons in an hour. I want you to call ahead to the front-gate security post, so I can pass right through, and the two of us can have a heart-to-heart."

"You're in *Brussels?* But I thought you were in Washington! What the hell—?"

"One hour, Mr. Lanchester. And I suggest you make not a single phone call about this between now and the time I arrive."

He knocked softly at Layla's door. She opened it quickly; she was already dressed, freshly bathed, fragrant of shampoo and soap. "I passed by your room a few minutes ago," she said as he entered. "I overheard you talking on the phone. No, don't tell me—I won't ask; I know: 'when the time is right.' "

He sat down in the same rickety chair where he had sat last night. "Well, I think the time is right, Layla," he said, and he immediately felt a burden begin to lift, almost a physical sensation, of finally being able to breathe deeply after so long being deprived of oxygen. "I need to tell you this, because I'm going to need your help, and I'm certain they're going to try to take me out."

"They . . . ?" She touched his arm with her hand. "What are you telling me?"

Choosing his words carefully, he spoke, telling her of things he had not spoken of to anyone except the now-disappeared CIA deputy director Harry Dunne. He confided that he had just one mission, which was to infiltrate, and then destroy, a shadowy organization known, to the very few who knew about it, as the Directorate; and he told her of his desperate hope to involve Richard Lanchester in the effort.

She listened, wide-eyed, taking it all in; then she got to her feet and began pacing the room. "I don't think I completely understand. This is not an American agency—it's international, multilateral?"

"That's one way of putting it. When I worked for them, they were based in Washington, though their headquarters appear to have moved. Where, I don't know."

"What are you saying—they've just disappeared?"

"Something like that."

"Impossible! An intelligence agency is like any other bureaucracy—it has telephone numbers and faxes and computers, not to mention office staff. It's like—what's the expression in English, trying to hide an elephant in the middle of a room!"

"The Directorate, when I worked for it, was lean, bare-bones, agile. And skilled at various forms of camouflage. The way the CIA is able to disguise its proprietaries as benign-seeming private corporations, or the Soviets used to create so-called Potemkin villages, false fronts, turning biological-warfare facilities into laundry-soap factories or even colleges."

Pensive, she shook her head in disbelief. "And do you mean to say they *compete* with CIA and MI-6 and Mossad and the Sûreté? With the *knowledge* of the other agencies?"

"No, that's not it at all. Its members are given to understand that they do operations the more mainstream agencies are not permitted to do, whether by charter or by governmental policy."

She nodded, unsmiling. "Yet at the same time they are able to keep their own existence secret? How can this be? People gossip, secretaries have friends . . . there are congressional oversight committees . . ." She went to the dressing table and, visibly distraught, began fumbling with her small black leather handbag, rummaging through it, finally pulling out a lipstick. She applied a dab of color, blotted her lips with a tissue, put the lipstick back.

"But that's the ingenious thing! Through a combination of extremely tight compartmentalization and careful recruitment — members are chosen carefully, drawn from all around the world, their backgrounds especially conducive to this line of work, to maintaining a code of silence. The compartmentalization ensures that no one operative ever gets to know another more than fleetingly; no one ever works with more than one handler. My handler was a legend in the agency, one of the founders, a man named Ted Waller. A man I came to idolize," he added regretfully.

"But surely the president must know!"

"To be honest, I have no idea. I believe the existence of the Directorate has always been kept from whoever occupies the Oval Office. Partly to protect the president from knowing too much about wet work and other sordid business, to provide him with plausible deniability. That's standard operating procedure in intelligence outfits worldwide. And partly, I'm sure, because the president is considered by the permanent intelligence community to be a mere tenant of the White House. A renter. He moves in for four years, maybe eight if he's lucky, buys new china, redecorates, hires and fires, gives a bunch of speeches, and then he's gone. Whereas the spies remain. *They're* the permanent Washington, the true inheritors."

"And you think the one person in government most likely to know about its activities is the chairman of the president's Foreign Intelligence Advisory Board, yes? The group that meets in secret to oversee the NSA and the CIA and all the other American spy agencies?"

"Correct."

"And the chairman of this intelligence oversight is Richard Lanchester."

"Exactly."

Nodding, she said, "This is why you want to meet with him."

"Correct."

"But for *what?*" she cried. "To tell him *what?*"

"To tell him what I know about the Directorate, about what I think it's up to. This was the big question, the reason I was brought back from retirement: Who's controlling the Directorate now? What is it really doing?"

"And you think you have the answers?" She seemed belligerent, almost outright antagonistic.

"No, of course not. I have theories, backed up by evidence."

"What evidence? You have nothing!"

"Whose side are you on, Layla?"

"I'm on *yours!*" she shouted. "I want to protect *you*, and I think you're making a mistake."

"A mistake?"

"You go to see this man Lanchester with . . . with wisps of nothing, crackpot accusations—he'll dismiss you at once. He'll think you're crazy!"

"Quite possibly," conceded Bryson. "But it's my job to make him think otherwise, and I believe I can."

"And what makes you think you can trust him?"

"What choice do I have?"

"He could be one of the enemies, one of the liars! How can you be sure he's *not?*"

"I'm sure of *nothing* anymore, Layla. I feel like I'm in a maze, I'm lost. I don't know where I am, *who* I am anymore."

"What makes you so sure you can believe what this CIA man told you? What makes you so sure he's not one of them, one of the liars?"

"I'm not *sure*, I told you that! This is not a matter of certainty, it's a matter of calculation, of odds."

"Then you believed it when he told you your parents were killed?"

"My stepmother—the woman who was sort of my guardian after my parents were killed—pretty much confirmed it, though she's ill, I think she has Alzheimer's, her mind is going. The fact is, the only people who really know the truth are the people I'm desperate to find—Ted Waller, and Elena."

"Elena is your ex-wife."

"Officially not an ex-wife. We never divorced. She disappeared. I suppose you'd say we're separated."

"She *abandoned* you."

Bryson sighed. "I don't know what happened. I wish I knew; I badly *want* to know."

"She just disappeared, she never got in touch? One day there, next day gone?"

"Right."

She shook her head in disapproval. "Yet I think you love her still."

He nodded. "It's—it's just so hard for me to think straight about her, to know what to believe. Did she ever love me, or was she assigned to me? Did she run away from me in despair, or out of fear, or because she was forced to? What is the truth, *where* is the truth?" Had his secret mission to Bucharest somehow backfired? Had Elena been reached by the sweepers, frightened into hiding somehow? But if so, wouldn't she have left word for him to explain her actions? Another possibility: Had she somehow discovered that he had lied to her about his whereabouts that weekend? Had she found out that he hadn't been in Barcelona? She might feel violated, betrayed, but would that really drive her away without raising it with him first?

"And somehow you think you'll learn this truth by flying everywhere, looking for Directorate operatives? It's *insanity!*"

"Layla, once I track these wasps to their nest, they're over. They must know that I've got the goods on them. I have a detailed knowledge of operations going back twenty years, transgressions of just about every national and international law."

"And you will present all this to Richard Lanchester, and you hope he will expose them, put a stop to it?"

"If he's as good a man as people say he is, that's exactly what he'll do."

"And if he's not?"

Bryson was silent; she went on, "You'll bring a weapon."

"Of course."

"Where is yours? You don't have it on you."

He looked up, startled. She had a quick, discerning eye. "It's in my luggage, still disassembled so I could get it through airport security."

"Well, then," she said. She removed a .45 from her purse, the Heckler & Koch USP compact.

"Thanks, but I'll take the Beretta." He smiled. "Of course, if you still have that .50 caliber Desert Eagle . . ."

"No, Nick, I'm sorry."

"*Nick?*" He felt a hollow thudding in his chest; she knew his true name, though she had never before uttered it, and he had never told her. My God, what *else* did she know?

She was pointing it at him from halfway across the room. It took him a moment to realize what was going on. He was frozen in the chair, his normal split-second reactions dulled by disbelief.

Her eyes were doleful. "I can't let you meet with Lanchester, Nick. I'm truly sorry, but I can't."

"What the hell are you doing?" he demanded.

"My job. You've left us no choice. I never thought it would come to this."

He felt as if the air had gone out of the room. His body went cold; he registered the shock viscerally.

"No," he said hoarsely, the chair in which he sat spinning slowly a million miles away. "Not you. They've gotten to you, too. When did they—"

And he exploded from the chair with the force of a tightly coiled spring, lunging at her with a suddenness that startled her, causing her instinctively to draw back to brace herself, defensively repositioning herself, her fierce concentration broken for the barest instant. Thrown off-balance, she fired, the explosion filling the small room, percussive and deafening. Bryson felt the projectile whiz by his left cheek, the gunpowder searing his face and temple, heard the cartridge casing spit onto the floor, and at almost the same moment he vaulted into the air, knocking her body to the floor, sending the gun clattering across the floor.

But she was no longer the woman he'd thought he knew; she'd been transformed into a tigress, a wild-eyed jungle predator crazed by bloodlust. Layla reared up, her right hand a rigid claw jabbing into his throat, while she simultaneously slammed her left elbow into his solar plexus, knocking the wind out of him.

Still, he managed to rise, swinging a fist at her, but she suddenly ducked under and shot upward, wedging her right shoulder into his right armpit as she vised her right arm around his neck, and with a loud grunt she grabbed her own left biceps and pulled in toward herself, choking him.

He had fought hand-to-hand with some of the fiercest, most dangerous and highly trained assassins in the world, but she was in another league entirely. She was brutally strong, as untiring as a machine, and she fought with a ferocity he had never seen before. Somehow managing to free himself from the headlock, he reared up again, swinging at her, but she jumped backward, deflecting his blow with her left arm, then sank suddenly to the floor and slammed a fist into his stomach, guarding her face with her left hand. .

Bryson gasped, grappled for the soft flesh at the base of her neck, but she was too quick: she delivered a hard kick to the back of his right knee, causing him to sag. Striking the back of his head with her elbow, she almost succeeded in knocking him to the ground, but Bryson forced himself to ignore the blinding pain, summoning all of his considerable strength along with combat techniques learned decades ago that now returned to him like ancient hindbrain reflexes.

He spun out of her way, then launched his body at her frontally, hurling all of his weight against hers while simultaneously throwing a left-handed punch into her right kidney. She screamed, a shrill, full-throated cry not of pain but of rage. Leaping into the air and pivoting, she thrust out her right leg, scissoring it into his abdomen with astonishing force. Bryson groaned; she landed with her right leg forward and threw her right hand back-knuckle against his face with the impact of steel; then, grabbing his shoulders, she drove her left knee into his groin. As he doubled over in agony, she raised her right elbow and drove it into his spine, the pain staggering, then reached for the left side of his face, wrenching his head clockwise as she took him down.

With one last surge of desperate energy, he thrust his hands out, blindly grasping for her legs, slamming the bony side of his hand hard against the nerve center just above her left knee, clutching at it, forcing her down as well, and as she stumbled backward, he thrust his knee into her midsection, cracking his elbow against the side of her neck. She screamed, loosening the grip of her right hand, reaching for something, and he saw what it was: the Heckler & Koch was just feet away; he could *not* let her regain control of it! He shifted slightly, then jammed his elbow into the cartilage of her throat. She gagged, instinctively reaching with her right hand to dislodge his elbow and protect the vulnerable area, and that was enough to allow him to grab the pistol with his left hand, spinning it around and crashing it against the top of her head, the blow carefully calculated neither to kill her nor seriously cripple her.

She crumpled to the floor, her eyes half open, only the whites visible. He felt her throat for a pulse and found it; she was alive, though she would be out for several hours. Whoever she was, *whatever* she was, she had had the chance to kill him at the outset, when she had the gun trained on him, but she hesitated; either she could not do it or she found it almost impossible to bear the thought of doing so. She, like he, was probably a pawn, lied to and manipulated, recruited to an assignment about which she was carefully kept in the dark. In a way she was a victim, too.

A victim of the Directorate?

It seemed likely, even probable.

And he needed to question her, find out everything she knew. But not now; there was no time.

He searched the tiny closet, where she had hung her few items of clothing and stowed a couple of pairs of shoes, for a rope or something similar to tie her up. Kneeling down, he felt along the floor, grabbing something that he realized was the spike heel that had somehow come loose from her gray shoes, the ones she had worn to the bank in Geneva. Something extremely sharp at one end of the heel lanced his finger. Wincing, he picked up the two-inch-long gray object and saw a small, razor-sharp blade protruding from the end that was intended to attach to the sole of the shoe. He inspected it more closely: the narrow blade, like an artist's X-Acto knife, fit into the base of the shoe, the heel threaded so that it screwed in.

He looked back at Layla. The whites of her eyes were still exposed, her jaw slack; she was still unconscious.

Her spike-heeled shoes, he suddenly understood, had been ingeniously outfitted with a razor blade, which was accessible by twisting off the heel. He examined the other shoe, which had been adapted the same way. It was a brilliant little trick.

And then it struck him.

The image of her in the closet off the banker's office, bound with brightly colored polyurethane "humane restraints," the sort normally used by law-enforcement agents to transport dangerous prisoners. Jan Vansina, Directorate operative, had fettered her with strong plastic handcuffs— *which she could easily have cut her way out of.*

Geneva had been a setup.

Layla had been in cahoots with Vansina, both of them Directorate. Vansina had only pretended to attack her; she had cooperated. At any time she could have freed herself.

What did this mean?

There was a small, two-person elevator at the end of the dark hall, the kind that was operated by opening or closing an accordion inner gate. Fortunately, there seemed to be no one else on the floor. Bryson had seen no one else go in or out of rooms on the floor; likely, they were the only ones.

He hoisted her—though she was not big, she was now deadweight and quite heavy—and, putting her head on his shoulder, grasped her beneath the buttocks and carried her, as if she were a drunken spouse, to the elevator. Bryson had readied a rueful joke about his wife's perennial inebriation, but never had a chance to use it.

He took the elevator down to the hotel's basement, which stank of flooded sewage, and set her down on the gritty concrete floor. After searching for a few minutes, he found a storage closet, removed the buckets and mops, and placed her inside. With a length of old clothesline, he carefully bound her wrists and ankles with several tight knots, winding the rope around and around her legs and torso, looping it and tying it into slip knots, then tested the restraints to make sure she could not get out of them if she came to before he returned. The rope was secure— and she was barefoot, with no hidden blade anywhere.

Then, taking one more precaution—if she did become conscious un-expectedly soon, she might yell for help—he stuffed a gag in her mouth and tied it tight, checking to see that she could still breathe.

He turned the lock on the closet door, which would serve only to keep her in—he was convinced, however, that she would never have the op-portunity to open the door herself—and not keep someone out.

Then Bryson returned to his hotel room to prepare to meet Richard Lanchester.

In a dark room halfway across the world, three men huddled around an electronic console, their tense faces bathed in the cool green light emitted by diodes.

"It's a digital relay feed direct from Mentor, one of our space-based satellites in the Intelsat fleet," intoned one of them.

The reply was urgent, the tone revealing long hours of stress. "But the voice-pattern ID—how reliable is Voicecast?"

"Within a tolerance of between ninety-nine and ninety-nine-point-nine-seven degrees," the first man said. "Extremely reliable."

"The identification is affirmative," remarked the third man. "The com-munication was initiated by a GSM cellular phone on the ground whose coordinates indicate Brussels, Belgium, the recipient based in Mons." The third man adjusted a dial; the voice that emerged from the console was astonishingly clear.

"*What is this?*"

"*We need to talk, Mr. Lanchester. Immediately.*"

"*Well, talk away! I'm here. What kind of hatchet job is the Post pre-paring? Goddard, I don't know you, but as I'm sure you're well aware, I do have your publisher's home number, I see her socially, and I won't hesitate for a second to call her!*"

"*We have to talk in person, not over the phone. I'm in Brussels; I can be at SHAPE headquarters in Mons in an hour. I want you to call ahead*" to the front-gate security post, so I can pass right through, and the two of us can have a heart-to-heart."

"You're in Brussels? But I thought you were in Washington! What the hell—?"

"One hour, Mr. Lanchester. And I suggest you make not a single phone call about this between now and the time I arrive."

"Order an interception," one of the watchers said.

"The decision must be taken at a higher level," replied another, clearly his superior. "Prometheus may prefer to continue gathering information on the target's activities, on how much the target knows."

"But if the two meet in a secure facility—what kind of penetration can we expect?"

"Good Christ, McCabe! Is there anywhere we can't penetrate? Relay the sound file. Prometheus will decide the course of action."

PART THREE

CHAPTER
SEVENTEEN

The president's national security adviser sat across the burnished mahogany conference table from Bryson, tension creasing his high forehead. For over twenty minutes Richard Lanchester had listened in rapt absorption to Bryson's account, nodding, taking notes, interrupting only for occasional clarifications. Every question he asked was not only pertinent but incisive, piercing through layers of ambiguity and confusion right to the crux of the issue. Bryson was impressed by the man, by his brilliance, his quick intelligence. He listened closely, concentrating deeply. Bryson spoke as he would debrief a handler or a case officer, just as he used to brief Waller after a field operation: calmly, objectively, coolly assessing probabilities while not injecting conjecture without basis. He tried to provide a context in which the revelations could be meaningfully placed. It was difficult.

The two men sat in a special secure facility located within the NATO secretary general's command-and-control center, an acoustically insulated room-within-a-room known informally as the "bubble." Its walls and floor were actually one module separated from the surrounding concrete walls by foot-thick rubber blocks that kept all sound vibrations from emanating outward. Technical surveillance countermeasures were employed daily to ensure that the bubble remained secure, free of any taps or listening devices. Security officers swept the room and its immediate environs daily. There were no windows, and thus no risk of laser or microwave bounces that could read the vibrations from human voices. Then there was an elaborate system of fallbacks: a spectral correlator was used at all times to detect surveillance using a spectrum analyzer, and an acoustic correlator used passive sound-pattern matching to automatically detect and classify any listening device. Finally, an acoustic noise generator was constantly on, generating an audio blanket of pink noise designed to defeat wired microphones inside walls, contact microphones, and any audio transmitters located in electrical outlets. Lanchester's insistence that they meet within the extraordinarily secure walls of the bubble was testimony to the seriousness with which he regarded Bryson's urgently imparted information.

Lanchester looked up, visibly shaken. "What you're telling me is preposterous, the sheerest madness, yet somehow it has the ring of truth. I say that because bits and pieces of what you say precisely confirm what little I know."

"But you *must* know about the existence of the Directorate. You're chairman of PFIAB; I'd have thought you'd know all about it."

Lanchester removed his rimless spectacles, polished them thoughtfully with a handkerchief. "The existence of the Directorate is one of the most closely held secrets in the government. Shortly after I was named to PFIAB I was briefed about it, and I must say at first I thought my briefer— one of those nameless, anonymous, behind-the-scenes intelligence officers who are part of the permanent establishment around Washington— had taken leave of his senses. It was one of the most fantastic, most implausible things I'd ever heard. A covert intel agency that operated entirely out of sight, without controls, without accountability or oversight—outlandish! If I'd dared to suggest the idea to the president, he'd have had me committed to St. Elizabeth's immediately, and quite justifiably so."

"Then what is it you find so implausible? You're referring to the true nature of the Directorate, the deception within the deception?"

"Actually, no. Harry Dunne did give me a briefing some months ago, when he'd apparently uncovered only part of the story. He told me of his belief that the Directorate's founders and principals were all Soviet GRU, that Ted Waller was a man named Gennady Rosovsky. What he told me was alarming, deeply astonishing, and by its very nature his findings had to be kept extremely protected: our government would be thrown into turmoil, security vulnerabilities exposed, shaken to its very foundations. That's why your mention of that name drew my immediate attention."

"Yet you must have been skeptical of what he told you."

"Oh yes, deeply so. I won't say I dismissed him, Dunne's credentials are too heavy to be ignored—but the notion of such a mammoth deception operation—it's difficult to accept, frankly. No, what I find most troubling is your assessment of the Directorate's present-day activities."

"Dunne must have kept you informed about all this."

He shook his head slowly, the barest movement. "I haven't spoken with him in weeks. If he was compiling this sort of dossier, by rights he should have kept me apprised. Perhaps he was waiting until he had more, until he'd amassed a substantive, incontrovertible file."

"You must have a way to reach him, locate him."

"I have no tricks up my sleeve. I'll make calls, see what I can do, but people don't just vanish from the seventh floor of the CIA. If he's been taken hostage, or if he's dead, I'll be able to find it out, Nick. I'm fairly confident I can track him down."

"When we spoke last, he was concerned about infiltration within the Agency—that the Directorate had extended its reach inside."

Lanchester nodded. "I'd say the identification you pulled off the would-be killer in Chantilly speaks volumes. It's always possible that the paper was simply stolen, or that the fellow was turned, hired locally. But I'd have to agree with both you and Dunne. We can't rule out the possibility that the CIA's been infiltrated pretty deeply. I'm flying back to Washington in a few hours, and I'll put in a call to Langley en route, speak with the Director myself. But let me be brutally frank with you, Nick. Look at the totality of what you're telling me. An overheard exchange at a French arms dealer's chateau, the implication that he and Anatoly Prishnikov were involved in planning the catastrophe at Lille. I don't doubt it's true, but what do we have, really?"

"The word of an intelligence operative of almost two decades," said Bryson quietly.

"An operative for this same, bizarre agency that we now know to be a hostile power operating on American soil against American interests. I'm sorry to be so brutal, but this is the way it reads. You're a defector, Nick. I don't doubt your honesty for a second, but you know how our government has always treated defectors—with the highest suspicion. For God's sake, look at what we did to the poor defector Nosenko, who broke from the KGB to warn that the Russians were behind the Kennedy assassination and that our own CIA had been penetrated by a high-level mole. We locked him up in solitary, in a prison cell, and interrogated him for years. James Jesus Angleton, the CIA counterintelligence chief back then, was certain this was a Soviet dangle, an attempt to manipulate us, mislead us, and he'd have none of it. Not only did he not believe the most significant KGB defector we'd ever had—even after Nosenko had passed polygraph after polygraph—but he brutalized the man, broke him. And Nosenko had specific names of agents, operations, controls. You're giving me rumors, overhears, suggestions."

"I'm giving you more than enough to act on," snapped Bryson.

"Nick, listen to me. Listen, and understand. Say I go to the president and tell him that there's some sort of *octopus*—a faceless, nebulous organization whose existence I can't definitively establish, can't substantiate, and whose aims I can only *guess* at. I'll be laughed out of the Oval Office, or worse."

"Not with your credibility."

"My credibility, as you put it, is based on my unwillingness to be alarmist, my insistence on having the goods before we act. Good Lord, if someone else spoke up at the National Security Council, or in the Oval Office, with such allegations without basis, I'd be furious."

"But you *know*—"

"I *know* nothing. Suspicions, inklings, those patterns we imagine we see. That isn't knowledge. In the jargon of international law, they don't constitute evidentiary warrant. It's insufficient—"

"You propose to do *nothing*?"

"I didn't say that. Listen, Nick, I believe in the rules. People chide me all the time for being a stickler. But that doesn't mean I'm going to sit back and let these *fanatics* take the world hostage. What I'm saying is that I need more. I need *proof.* I will mobilize every form of state authority we can muster, but to do that I need you to come back to me with something."

"Damn it, there's no *time.*"

"Bryson, *listen* to me!" Bryson saw the harrowed look in Lanchester's face. "I need more. I need specifics. I need to know *what they're planning!* I'm counting on you. We all are."

"I'm counting on you. We all are." Lanchester's voice came from the speaker console in the darkened room thousands of miles away. *"Now, how can I help? What resources can I place at your disposal?"*

The listener picked up a telephone handset and pressed a button. In a moment he spoke, his voice hushed. "So he's made contact. As we expected."

"It fits the profile, sir," came the voice at the other end of the line. "He goes straight to the top. I'm surprised only that he didn't attempt blackmail or other threats."

"I want to know exactly who he's working with, who he's working for."

"Yes, sir. Unfortunately, we don't know where he's going next."

"Don't worry. The world is a very small place today. He can't get away. There's no place to go."

Bryson left the rented car a few blocks from the Marolles and approached the pension on foot, alert for any disruptions in pattern, anyone who seemed not to belong. There was nothing out of the ordinary, but his mind was not set at ease. He had been manipulated, deceived too often. Richard Lanchester had not dismissed him out of hand, but neither had he been roused to immediate action. Did that mean he, too, was to be suspected? Paranoia bred upon itself; Bryson knew that that way lay madness. No, he would take Lanchester at face value, as a man who seemed genuinely concerned yet quite reasonably needed hard facts upon which to order action. It was a setback, but in another sense it was a step forward, because he had enlisted a powerful ally. Or if not an ally, at least a sympathetic ear.

Once past the glum woman at the front desk, Bryson took the stairs to the basement, to the storage closet. From the outside he could see it was still locked; that was a relief. But he put nothing past Layla anymore; he pulled his weapon out from his belt, concealed by his suit jacket, and stood to one side as he silently turned the lock, then suddenly whipped open the door.

She did not spring out; there was only silence.

From where he stood he could see that the closet was empty. The clothesline had been severed, pieces discarded on the floor.

She was gone.

She could not have escaped without outside assistance. There was no way she could have slipped the knots or severed them; she had no blade or other tool. He had made sure of that.

Now he was certain: *she had been working with others nearby.*

Her accomplices were likely in the vicinity now; they knew where he was staying, and if she had hesitated momentarily before firing her gun, they would not. Returning to his room was therefore out of the question, a risk he must not take.

He mentally ran through the contents of his suitcase upstairs. Over twenty years he had learned to travel with the minimum, to assume that his hotel room would be searched. Habitually, he arranged his things in such a way that he would inevitably be able to tell if someone had gone through them, information that often proved useful. Since he assumed his suitcase would be rifled, he had learned not to leave anything irreplaceable behind, unattended. He learned, too, to separate valuables into two broad categories: those with monetary value, and those of strategic value. It was items in the first category that were most likely to be stolen by casual thieves, larcenous maids and the like: money, jewelry, small electronics that looked expensive. Those in the second category—things like passports real and forged, identity papers and licenses and other documents, canisters of film, videotapes or computer disks—were least likely to be stolen by simple thieves, yet if pilfered often could not be replaced.

For that reason, Bryson was more likely to leave cash and such in his luggage, but take with him his false passports. True to habit, he had on his person all of his papers, his weapon, and the downloaded cryptographic key from Jacques Arnaud's secure phone, a tiny microchip he had been carrying with him for quite some time now. If he abandoned his hotel room and never returned, he would survive. He would need money, though that was fairly easily arranged. But he could continue.

But to where? Simple penetration of the Directorate was out of the question now. They knew of his hostile intent. The only remaining strategy was a frontal one: to try to locate Elena by using his standing as her former husband as a lure.

They didn't know what he knew, what he might have learned from her.

Whether she was assigned to him or not, whether tasked to manipulate him, keep him in the dark, she nevertheless might have told him things, inadvertently or intentionally. He had been her husband, however fraudulent the marriage was designed to be; there had been, of necessity, moments of intimacy, times when the two of them were entirely alone.

The deception could be doubled back, turned back on them as well. Why not? What if he let it be known that he had learned things from Elena, deliberately or not—facts they would not want him to know? Information that could be locked away, used as a bargaining chip, left with an attorney to be released in the event of death?

He had something here. A husband knew things about his wife that no one else did. They didn't know what she might have passed on to him, intentionally or not. He would *use* the uncertainty, the ambiguity— use it as a bright, shining beacon, a lure.

Exactly how he would use it was still unclear, the plan inchoate. But there still remained agents he had had brief dealings with, operatives in Amsterdam and Copenhagen, Berlin and London, Sierra Leone and Pyongyang. He would begin the methodical, painstaking process of contacting them, or whichever ones of them whose names and contact information still functioned, using them as conduits to pass on the message to Ted Waller.

To do this he would need money, but that was fairly easily arranged. He had his hidden accounts in Luxembourg and Grand Cayman, as yet untouched; the necessity of hiding contingency funds was virtually a law of nature among Directorate operatives, a matter of survival. He would arrange wire transfers, secure the funds he needed to travel freely, now that he could no longer trust the CIA.

And then he would begin to contact former colleagues, using them to pass on the threat. And a demand: an insistence upon a meeting with Elena. A condition that, if not met, would result in the release of information he had until now held in reserve. Blackmail, pure and simple. Ted Waller would understand; it was mother's milk to him.

He closed the storage-closet door and searched for another way out of the hotel, an exit that didn't require going through the lobby. After circling the dark basement warrens for a few minutes, he found a little-used service exit, an iron door that was all but rusted shut. He struggled with it until he managed to loosen the handle; a little while later he wrenched it open. It gave on to a narrow, trash-strewn cobblestone alley, barely passable and evidently rarely used.

A side street, really little more than a parking area for residents of the neighboring tenements, led to the main thoroughfare, where he disappeared into the crowds of pedestrians. His first stop was a shabby department store, where he purchased an entirely new outfit of clothing, changing in the fitting room and discarding his old clothes there, to the bafflement of the clerk. He also picked up a knapsack, an assortment of other casual clothes, and a cheap airline carry-on bag.

Searching for a branch office of a large international bank, he passed the window of an electronics shop, dominated by a row of television sets all tuned to the same broadcast. The sight was immediately familiar: he recognized the landmarks of Geneva; it seemed to be a travel advertisement for Switzerland, then he realized it was actually news footage, and then he felt his legs go weak at what he saw next.

It was the Hôpital Cantonal in Geneva. The camera panned through its corridors, across its emergency room, jammed with people on stretchers, corpses in body bags. The camera panned across a hellish scene: bodies stacked up in preparation for carting away. The caption on the screen read: "Geneva, yesterday."

Yesterday? What catastrophe could possibly have just happened?

He turned back to the street, spotted a newsstand, saw the banner headlines: GENEVA. ANTHRAX. OUTBREAK. ATTACK.

He grabbed an *International Herald-Tribune*, noting the headline that ran across the top in thirty-six-point type: ANTHRAX VICTIMS CONTINUE TO FILL GENEVA HOSPITALS AS INTERNATIONAL AUTHORITIES SEARCH FOR ANSWERS; UP TO A THOUSAND DEATHS EXPECTED.

Reeling, he read with horror.

> GENEVA—A sudden, widespread outbreak of anthrax has turned into an epidemic here, as the city's hospitals and clinics fill with stricken residents. An estimated 3,000 have been infected by the deadly disease, with some 650 persons already declared dead. Hospital administrators have instituted emergency procedures to prepare their facilities for what many fear will be an overwhelming influx of anthrax cases in the next 48 hours. City officials have ordered businesses, schools, and all governmental offices closed and have warned tourists and business visitors to stay away from Geneva until the source of the infection can be determined. The city's mayor, Alain Prisette, expressed his shock and grief, while warning residents and visitors alike to remain calm.
>
> Patients began pouring into Geneva's hospitals and clinics yesterday in the predawn hours complaining of severe flulike symptoms. By five o'clock in the morning, over a dozen cases of anthrax had been diagnosed at the Hôpital Cantonal. By noon yesterday the victims numbered in the thousands.
>
> City and health officials have been working around the clock to determine the source of the outbreak. Sources here refused to speculate on reports that the deadly disease may have been released by a truck driving through the city with a truck-mounted aerosolized dispenser emitting a cloud of spores.
>
> Anthrax has a mortality rate as high as 90%. After expo-

sure, the victim develops severe respiratory distress, followed by the rapid onset of shock and subsequent death within 36 hours.

Although inhalation anthrax can be treated with a repeated course of penicillin, authorities here point out that hospital staff must take protective measures or risk infection themselves. Anthrax spores can remain present for decades.

As Swiss authorities continue their investigation into the source of the infection, health officials estimate that by the end of the week victims will number in the tens of thousands.

The question many are asking here is, why? Why was Geneva targeted, and how? Speculation centers on the fact that Geneva serves as the headquarters of a number of powerful transnational organizations, including the World Health Organization. The mayor refused to comment on widespread speculation that the outbreak was the result of a biological weapon wielded by an unnamed terrorist organization that had been planning such an attack for weeks, if not months.

Bryson looked up from the newspaper, blood draining from his face. If this report was accurate, and there was no reason to suppose it was not, a biological-weapons attack had occurred in Geneva while he was still there, or immediately afterward.

An American jet blown out of the sky . . . the Eurostar train blown up in Lille . . . a bomb detonated in the Washington Metro during morning rush hour . . .

He was seeing a pattern of terrorism, increasing in frequency, the commonalities evident. Each was designed to incite chaos, wide-ranging public injury, and resulting fear. These were classically designed terrorist paradigms, except for one thing.

No one had claimed responsibility.

It was customary, though not inevitable, for terrorists to claim responsibility for their deeds, assert a justification. Otherwise, the incident had no purpose except random demoralization.

Since Bryson knew the Directorate had been behind Lille, it was by no means impossible that the Directorate had had a hand in the Geneva attack. In fact, it was likely.

But why?

What was the objective? What did the Directorate hope to accomplish? Why was a conspiracy of extremely powerful private citizens banding together to instigate a wave of terror in various sites around the world? To what end?

Bryson no longer accepted the theory that private arms dealers were trying to create an artificial demand for their goods. Uzis were useless against an outbreak of anthrax. There was more to it; there was another pattern, another logic. But *what?*

He had just come from Geneva, had been very close to Lille only days before. *In both cases, he had been there.* True, he had come to Geneva because of a report that Jan Vansina, a Directorate operative, was there. He had gone to Chantilly—not Lille, but close to it—to track the activities of Jacques Arnaud.

Was it possible that he was being set up? Terrorist outbreaks in places he had just visited—would he somehow be tied in because he had been in the vicinity?

He thought about Harry Dunne and his insistence that he go to Geneva to confront Jan Vansina. In that case, Dunne had encouraged him to go there; Dunne could have had a hand in setting him up. But Chantilly? Dunne hadn't known in advance . . .

Layla had. In that case, Layla had let him know about Arnaud's château in Chantilly. She had been reluctant to take him there—or had *feigned* reluctance—but it was she who let him know about Chantilly. In effect, she had waved the red flag at the bull.

Harry Dunne had encouraged him to visit Geneva; Layla had induced him, subtly, to Chantilly. In both places, there had been terrorist strikes immediately afterward. Was it possible that Dunne and Layla had been working together, both on behalf of the Directorate, to manipulate him, set him up to take the fall for a series of devastating attacks?

Jesus, what was the *truth?*

He folded up the newspaper to take it with him, and that was when he noticed a small article, accompanied by an equally small photograph. It was the photograph that first caught his eye.

Bryson recognized the face at once: it was the florid-cheeked man he had seen emerging from Jacques Arnaud's private office at the château in Chantilly. Anatoly Prishnikov, chairman and CEO of the mammoth Russian conglomerate Nortek.

ARNAUD JOINT VENTURE ANNOUNCED, the headline read. Jacques Arnaud's far-flung corporate empire had just announced a joint business venture with the Russian conglomerate, which itself represented the consolidation of a number of industries that formerly belonged to the Soviet military.

The nature of the business venture was unspecified, but the article took note of Nortek's growing presence in the European market, mentioning its role in a wave of mergers in the electronics industry. A pattern was beginning to emerge, but what was it exactly? A worldwide coalescence of major corporations, each of which was—*or could be*—a defense contractor.

Under the control of the Directorate, if his information was accurate. Did this mean that the Directorate was attempting to seize control of the defense establishments of the world's great powers? Could that have been what Harry Dunne was so fearful of?

Had Dunne been maneuvering to set him up as a dupe, a fall guy? Or was Dunne himself—if he was still alive—the dupe?

Now, at least, it was clear where he would have to go to look for answers.

There was a theatrical supply shop on rue d'Argent, two blocks north of the Theatre de la Monnaie, where Bryson made several purchases. Then he entered the branch office of an international bank, where he initiated a sequence of wire transfers from his Luxembourg account. By the end of the afternoon he had, discounting transaction fees, almost a hundred thousand dollars, mostly in American dollars, but also in a range of European currency as well.

He stopped into a travel agency and signed on as a last-minute member of a charter tour. Then he found a sporting-goods store and bought a few more items.

Departing from Zaventem Airport the next day was a leased, decrepit Aeroflot plane whose passengers were a motley, rowdy group of backpackers who had paid bargain-basement prices for the "Moscow Nights" package tour of Russia—three nights and four days in Moscow, followed by an overnight train to St. Petersburg, where they would spend two nights and three days. The accommodations would be inexpensive, which was a polite term for squalid, and all meals were included, which was not necessarily a plus.

One of the backpackers was a middle-aged man wearing green fatigues, a baseball cap, and a bushy brown beard. He was traveling alone but he joined in the general hilarity. His new, instant friends knew him as Mitch Borowsky, a bookkeeper from Quebec who had backpacked all around the world, and happened to be in Brussels when the urge to go to Moscow had struck him. He was lucky enough to get one of the last remaining empty seats on the charter flight. It was totally last-minute, he explained to his new comrades, but Mitch Borowsky liked to do things at the last minute.

CHAPTER
EIGHTEEN

It was 10:00 A.M. in the Map Room, on the ground level of the White House, and an "impromptu" had been convened — an unscheduled meeting of agency heads and their deputies. It was at such irregular meetings that emergent situations were dealt with, fires extinguished and, at times, set. At such meetings, the incremental decisions that collectively produced the policies and doctrines of state were reached.

Rapid events required rapid responses: the needed consensus could only be reached in a free-form setting unencumbered by snail-paced bureaucracy, cabinet-level politicking, and endless second-guessing of timid analysts. Success in the executive branch meant mastery of one basic tenet. One did not present the commander in chief with problems; one presented him with solutions. It was at the impromptus — in the White House or the adjacent Old Executive Office Building — that solutions were crafted.

There were eight chairs around a long mahogany table, a white notepad in front of each seat. A rose damask sofa stood against one wall, a picture of orphaned gentility; above it, framed, was the last situation map used by President Roosevelt, who had overseen the American conduct of

World War II from here. It was hand-labeled with a date: APRIL 3, 1945. Roosevelt had died a little more than a week later. In subsequent years, the once-top-secret command center had been converted to a storage area. Only in the current administration had the windowless room once more come into active use. Even so, the redolence of its history lent solemnity to the proceedings.

Richard Lanchester sat at one end of the table, looking around curiously at his colleagues. "I'm still not clear about the agenda this morning. Urgency was conveyed in the message I got, but very little content."

NSA Director John Corelli spoke first. "I would have thought you were in the best position to appreciate the significance of what has happened," Corelli said, meeting Lanchester's level gaze. "He's made contact."

"*He?* Sorry?" Lanchester raised an eyebrow. He had taken a night flight from Brussels, had barely had a chance to shower and shave before the meeting was convened, and the wearing schedule told on his lined face.

Morton Culler, the senior intelligence officer at the NSA and a twenty-year veteran of the agency, exchanged glances with his boss. Culler's thinning hair was slicked back with gel, his slate eyes unblinking behind the thick lenses of his aviator-style glasses. "Nicholas Bryson, sir. We're talking about the visit he paid you in Brussels."

"Bryson," Lanchester repeated the name, his face impassive. "You know who he is?"

"Of course," Culler said. "It's all exactly as we'd expected. It fits his profile, you see. He goes straight to the top. Did he try to blackmail you? Use threats?"

"It wasn't like that," Lanchester protested.

"And yet you agreed to see him face-to-face."

"Anyone in public life accumulates a protective armamentarium, a Praetorian guard of receptionists and press officers and functionaries. He got past all that using deception. But he got my attention by revealing his knowledge of something very few of us know about."

"And did you find out what he wanted from us?"

Lanchester paused. "He talked of the Directorate."

"He admitted his allegiance, then," the CIA director, James Exum, said precisely.

"On the contrary. He described the Directorate as a global threat. He seemed impatient that we hadn't taken effective action against it. He alluded to patterns of deceptions, to a shadowy supranational organization. It sounded mad, much of it. And yet . . ." Lanchester fell silent for a moment.

"And yet?" Exum prompted.

"Frankly, a certain amount of what he said made sense. It scared me."

"He's a master at that, sir," Culler said. "A real spinner of tales. A genius at manipulation."

"You seem to know a great deal about this man," Lanchester said tartly. "Why don't you fill me in?"

"That's precisely what we intend to do," Corelli said. He nodded toward the two unfamiliar faces in the room. "Terence Martin and Gordon Wollenstein, from the joint intelligence task force we've assembled for the purpose. I've asked them here to brief everyone present."

Terence Martin was a tall man in his midthirties with a dry manner and a trace of Maine in his accent. His military background was evident from his ramrod posture. "Nicholas Bryson. Son of George Bryson, a one-star general in the United States Army before he died. Bryson was in the Forty-second Battalion, Mechanized, in North Korea, and later served in Vietnam, during the first phase of the engagement. A kit bag full of combat honors. Glowing fitness reports and officers' evaluations, all the way up. Nicholas, his only child, was born forty-two years ago. At that point, George Bryson was regularly on the move, with rotating posts around the world. Nina Bryson, his wife, was an accomplished pianist, taught music. Quiet, unassuming. Followed him from place to place. Young Nicholas spent his childhood in a dozen different countries. At one point, eight countries in the course of four years: Wiesbaden, Bangkok, Marrakech, Madrid, Riyadh, Taipei, Madrid, Okinawa."

"Sounds like a recipe for isolation," Lanchester said, nodding slowly. "It must have been easy to lose your bearings in that kaleidoscope of cultures. You pull into yourself, into a shell, withdraw from the people around you."

"Only here's where things get interesting," Gordon Wollenstein interjected politely. He was red-haired and ruddy, with a deeply creased face, and a tieless, slightly disheveled appearance. Only his quiet, observant manner suggested his disciplinary expertise in psychology. His Berkeley doctoral thesis on new-generation techniques of psychological profiling was what had first brought him to the attention of certain experts in the U.S. intelligence community. "You've got a child who, every time he gets settled, has to pull up stakes. Abruptly, and with little warning. And yet at every posting, he acquired perfect native command of the cultures, the customs, and the language of the locale. Not the army base, not the American cohort, but the *natives*, the people in whose land he was living. Presumably from contact with his parents' servants. Four months after he arrived at Bangkok, at the age of eight, he spoke fluent, accentless Thai. Shortly after arriving at Hanover, none of his German classmates would have guessed he was an American. Same with Italian. Chinese. Arabic. Even Basque, for God's sake. Not just the official languages, but the local dialectal variants—the language of the playground as well as of the radio broadcasts. It was as if he'd spent his whole life in the place. He was a sponge, a human chameleon, with a really astonishing capacity to, well, 'go native.' "

"We've confirmed that his test scores were remarkable, always at the top of his class," Terence Martin put in. He distributed a summary sheet to the others in the room. "Extraordinary intelligence, extraordinary athletic skills. Not a freak of nature, but close. Still, it's clear something happened to him during his adolescence." Martin nodded at Wollenstein, giving him the signal to proceed.

"Adaptability is a funny thing," Wollenstein said. "We talk about 'code switching,' when people grow up multilingual—effortlessly able to think and express themselves in many tongues. More troubling is the ability to adopt and discard different value systems. To exchange one code of honor for another. What if there's no bright line between being adaptable and being unmoored? We believe that Bryson changed after his parents were killed, when he was fifteen. Once the ties to those parental values were severed, violently, he became susceptible to other influences. Adolescent rebelliousness, steered and manipulated by interests hostile to ours, turned him into a very dangerous man indeed. We're talking about a man with a thousand faces. A man who may have cultivated grievances against the authorities that once governed his life. His father spent his life in the service of his nation. On some prerational level, he may blame the United States government for his father's death. This is not a man you want as an enemy."

Martin cleared his throat. "Unfortunately, we've never had the luxury of choosing our enemies."

"And in this case, he seems to have chosen us." Wollenstein paused. "A man whose powerful abilities to adapt to circumstance verge on something like multiple personality disorder. I'm frankly speculating here. But my team and I have grown convinced that multiplicity is the key to Nicholas Bryson. It isn't like dealing with one man with a stable set of habits and traits. Think of a one-man consortium, if you will."

"It's important that you understand what Gordon has been telling us," Martin said. "All the evidence suggests that he's been turned into a very dangerous man indeed. We know of his involvement in something called the Directorate. We know that 'Coleridge' is one of his field names. We know that he has been highly trained—"

Lanchester cut him off. "I told you, he spoke to me about the Directorate. Said he was trying to destroy it."

"Classic disinformation ploy," Corelli said. "He *is* the Directorate, for all intents and purposes."

Terence Martin opened a large manila envelope and withdrew a set of photographs, which he distributed to the assembled. "Some of these are grainy, some less so. You're seeing a lot of high-res satellite surveillance product. I'd direct your attention to the photograph labeled 34-12-A." The image showed Nicholas Bryson onboard a vast container vessel. "Spectroscopic analysis tells us he's holding a quartz container of 'red mercury,' so-called. An extremely efficient high explosive. The Russkies came up with it. Nasty stuff."

"Just ask the good citizens of Barcelona," Corelli said. "That's what was used in the recent explosion there."

"Photograph 34-12-B is grainy, but I think you can make it out," Martin went on. "We took it from a security camera in the Lille station. Bryson again." He held up another image, an aerial view of the landscape just ten miles east of Lille. It was a scene of destruction, twisted rails and train cars in disarray, like the playthings of a bored child. "Again, we've got forensic trace-evidence confirmation that the explosive used was red mercury. Probably ten cc's would have done the trick."

Martin passed out another image: Bryson in Geneva. "You can just make him out from a cluttered street scene — outside the Temple de la Fusterie."

"We figured he kept a stash in one of the Geneva banks," Morton Culler said. "But he was up to something else there. We didn't know until a few hours ago."

"It wasn't until we learned about the release of weaponized anthrax there," Martin said. "Precisely in the sector of the Old Town where we'd photographed him. Presumably there were confederates, but they may have been unwitting. He's the one who orchestrated it, that much is clear."

Lanchester leaned back in his chair, his face drawn. "What are you telling me?"

"Call it what you like," Corelli said. "But I'd say your man is the Typhoid Mary of global terror."

"At whose behest?" Though Lanchester's gaze was fixed in the middle distance, his voice was insistent.

"That's the trillion-dollar question, isn't it?" Exum said, with his deceptive Southern languor. "John and I have some disagreements on this issue."

John Corelli glanced at Martin, prompting him. "I'm here because Lieutenant General Corelli asked me here in an advisory capacity," Martin said. "But there's no secret as to my own recommendation. However formidable Bryson is, he can't be acting alone. I say we follow him covertly, see where he leads us. Follow the hornet to the hive." He smiled, exposing small, off-white teeth. "Then apply a blowtorch."

"John's people are saying wait until we learn more," Exum said, in a tone of exquisite courtesy. He leaned across the table and picked up the photograph of the Eurostar disaster. "*This* is my answer." Abruptly, his voice grew hard. "It's too dangerous to delay any further. Forgive me, but this isn't a goddamn *science fair*. We cannot have another *massacre* while the NSA boys wait until they've finished the crossword puzzle. And on this I think the president and I are on the same page."

"But suppose he's our one lead to a larger conspiracy..." Corelli began.

Exum snorted. "And if you can just get seven across, you'll figure out ten down. Five letters, starts with E ..." He shook his head gravely. "John, Terence, I have the greatest respect for your gamesmanship. But you and your whiz kids forget one simple thing. *There's no time.*"

Lanchester turned to Morton Culler, the NSA ace. "Where do you come out?"

"Exum's right," Culler said heavily. "Let me be more precise. Bryson must be apprehended immediately. And if apprehension poses any difficulties, he must be terminated. We've got to dispatch the Alpha squad. And make their assignment very explicit. We're not talking about a guy who owes library fines for overdue books. We're talking about someone responsible for mass murder, and who seems to have an even bigger game afoot. So long as he's alive and out there, none of us can relax our vigilance."

Lanchester shifted uncomfortably. "The Alpha squad," he said quietly. "It isn't supposed to exist."

"It *doesn't* exist," Culler said. "Officially."

Lanchester placed his hands flat on the polished table. "Listen, I need to know how certain you are in this analysis," Lanchester said. "Because I'm the one man in this room who's met with Bryson, face-to-face. And—I just have to say it—that's just not the vibe I got from him. He struck me as a man of honor." Lanchester paused, and for a few moments, nobody spoke. "Still, I've been fooled before."

"Alpha will be dispatched immediately," Morton Culler said, and waited until his colleagues nodded in agreement. Disagreements having been aired, the consensus decision was joined. They all understood the significance of the order. The Alpha squad was composed of trained killers, equally skilled at sniper fire and hand-to-hand combat. To mobilize them against someone was to impose an almost certain death sentence.

"Good *Christ*. Wanted dead or alive," Lanchester said grimly. "It's uncomfortably like the Old West."

"We're all conscious of your *sensitivities*, sir," Culler said, his voice betraying a hint of sarcasm. "But this is the only way to handle it. Too many lives are at stake. He would have killed you in an instant if he judged that it suited his purposes, *sir*. For all we know, he may still try."

Lanchester nodded slowly, looking pensive. "This isn't a decision to be made lightly. It may be that my judgment has been impaired by my personal encounter. And I have to worry that—"

"You're doing the right thing, sir," Culler said quickly. "Let's just hope we're not too late."

CHAPTER
NINETEEN

The nightclub was hidden on a tiny *pereulok*, an alley off Tversky Bul'var, near Moscow's Ring Road. It was truly concealed, like some speakeasy in 1920s America. Unlike an illicit liquor joint of Prohibition days, though, the Blackbird was secreted away not from the eyes of government liquor authorities but from the riffraff, the masses. For the Blackbird was meant to be a private oasis of wealth and vice for the elite, the select: the rich, the beautiful, and the heavily armed.

It was located in a shambling brick structure that looked like the abandoned factory it was: in pre-Revolutionary times, Singer sewing machines had been manufactured here. Its windows were blacked out, and there was a single door, of black-painted wood, though with steel-plate reinforcement, and on the door, in peeling, antique Cyrillic letters, were the Russian words *Shveiniye Mashini*: Sewing Machines. The only indication that anything was to be found within was the long line of black Mercedes limousines extending down the narrow alley, looking out of place, as if they had all somehow ended up in the wrong place, the whole lot of them.

Shortly after arriving at Sheremetyevo-2 Airport, and then, for appearance's sake, checking into the Intourist Hotel with the rest of his raggedy tour group, Bryson had placed a call to an old friend. Thirty minutes later a midnight-blue Mercedes sedan had pulled up in front of the Intourist, and a uniformed driver ushered him into the backseat of the car, where a single envelope had been placed.

It was twilight, but the traffic along Tverskaya Ulitsa was heavy, the drivers manic, changing lanes abruptly, ignoring any rules of the road, even driving up on the sidewalk in order to pass slower-moving vehicles. Russia had gone mad, chaotic and furious, since Bryson had last been there. Though much of the old architecture remained in place—the wedding-cake Stalinist Gothic skyscrapers and the mammoth Central Telegraph facility; a sprinkling of the old shops, like Yeliseyevsky's food emporium and the Aragvi, once the only decent restaurant in town— there were incredible changes. High-priced shops glittered along the once-somber avenue that had been, before the collapse of the Communist state, Gorky Street: Versace, Van Cleef & Arpels, Vacheron Constantin, Tiffany. Yet along with the visible signs of plutocratic wealth were evidence of far-reaching poverty, of a social system that had broken down. Soldiers openly begged for alms, *babushki* sold moonshine or fruits and vegetables, or else they pleaded with you to tell you your fortune for a few rubles. Peroxide hookers were more brazenly in evidence than ever before.

Bryson got out of the chauffeured sedan, took the small plastic card from the envelope that had been left for him, and inserted it in a slot like that of an automatic teller mounted on the splintering wooden door, the card's magnetized strip facing out. The door buzzed open, and he entered a completely dark area. Once the door had closed behind him, he felt around for the second door, which the driver had told him, in barely serviceable English, would be there. Grasping the cold steel knob, he pulled the next door open, revealing the bizarre, garish world within.

Purple and red and blue beams of light floated and rippled on clouds of white fog and bounced off alabaster Greek columns and plaster Roman statuaries, black marble counters and high stainless-steel stools. Spotlights spun from high above in the dark recesses of what had once been the factory floor. Rock music of a sort Bryson had never heard before, a kind of Russian techno-pop, thundered at earsplitting volume. The odor of marijuana mingled with strong, expensive French perfume and bad Russian aftershave.

He paid his admission fee, the equivalent of $250, and sidled through a dense, gyrating crowd of mobsters in gold chains and huge, gaudy Rolexes who were somehow talking on cell phones over the deafening music, accompanied by their molls and other women who were either hookers or trying to look like them, in low-cut tops and short-hemmed skirts that left nothing to the imagination. Burly, shaven-headed bodyguards glowered; the club's security guards skulked around the periphery, uniformed like ninjas in black fatigues with billy clubs. High above the pulsating, spastic throng was a glass-and-steel gallery, where spectators could watch, through a glass floor, the cavorting below, as if it were some exotic, otherworldly terrarium.

He climbed the steel spiral staircase to the gallery, which was revealed to be another world entirely. The chief attraction on this level were the strippers, mostly platinum blond, though a few of them were ebony-skinned, their outsized busts all obviously silicone-enhanced. They danced under bright spotlights, positioned throughout the gallery.

A hostess in a filmy, revealing outfit, wearing a telephone headset, stopped him; she spoke a few, quick words in Russian. Bryson replied wordlessly by slipping her a few twenty-dollar bills, and she escorted him to a steel-and-black-leather banquette.

As soon as he was seated, a waiter brought several trays of *zakuski*, Russian appetizers: pickled beef tongue with horseradish sauce, red and black caviar and blini, mushrooms in aspic, pickled vegetables, herring. Though Bryson was hungry, none of it looked particularly appetizing. A bottle of Dom Perignon appeared—"compliments of your host," the waiter explained. Bryson sat alone, watching the crowd, for a few more minutes until he spotted the elegant, slim figure of Yuri Tarnapolsky gliding toward the table, both hands extended in exuberant welcome. Tarnapolsky seemed to have materialized out of nowhere, though Bryson now realized that the wily ex-KGB man had in fact entered the gallery from the kitchen.

"Welcome to Russia, my dear Coleridge!" Yuri Tarnapolsky exulted. Bryson stood, and the two embraced.

Although Tarnapolsky had chosen an unlikely venue for their rendezvous, he was a man of exquisite and very expensive tastes. As usual, the ex–KGB agent was impeccably dressed in an English bespoke suit and foulard tie. It had been seven years since he and Bryson had worked together, and though Tarnapolsky was now well into his fifties, his tanned face was smooth and unlined. The Russian had always taken good care of himself, but he appeared to have been the beneficiary of some high-priced cosmetic surgery.

"You look younger than ever," said Bryson.

"Yes, well, money can buy anything," replied Tarnapolsky, sardonic and amused as ever. He gestured for the waiter to pour the Dom Perignon, along with small glasses of Georgian wine, a white Tsinandali and a red Khvanchkara. As Tarnapolsky raised his glass in a toast, a stripper approached the table; Yuri slid a few crisp, large-denomination ruble notes into her G-string and politely urged her in the direction of a table of dark-suited businessmen.

He and Bryson had worked a number of extremely sensitive jobs together, which Tarnapolsky had always found highly lucrative; the Vector operation had only been the most recent. International arms-inspections teams had been unable to find evidence to support the rumors that Moscow was illegally producing bioweapons. Whenever the inspectors made "surprise," unannounced visits to the Vector laboratory facilities, they turned up nothing. Their "surprise" visits were no surprise. So the Directorate controllers had instructed Bryson that in order to get hard evidence of Russian work in germ warfare, he would need to break into Vector's central laboratory in Novosibirsk. As resourceful as Bryson was, that was a daunting proposition. He needed assistance on the ground, and the name of Yuri Tarnapolsky had come up. Tarnapolsky had recently retired from the KGB and was in the private sector, meaning that he was for sale to the highest bidder.

Tarnapolsky had proved to be worth every kopek of his exorbitant fee. He had obtained for Bryson the blueprints of the laboratory facility, even arranged for the street sentry to be diverted to a "reported burglary" at the residence of the chairman of the city's governing council. Using his KGB identification to browbeat and intimidate the institute's internal security guards, Tarnapolsky had gotten Bryson into the third-containment-level refrigerated tanks, where Bryson was able to locate the ampules he needed. Then Tarnapolsky had arranged to have the ampules spirited out of the country by a circuitous route, concealed in a shipment of frozen lamb en route to Cuba. Bryson, and the Directorate, had thereby been able to prove what dozens of arms inspectors could not: that Vector, and therefore Russia, was involved in making biological weapons. They had the irrefutable proof in the form of seven ampules of weaponized anthrax, an extraordinarily rare strain.

At the time Bryson had been pleased with his success, with the ingenuity of the operation, and indeed, he had been highly lauded by Ted Waller. But the news from Geneva of the sudden outbreak of a rare strain of anthrax—precisely the same strain that he had pilfered from Novosibirsk—had now turned everything inside out. Now he felt sickened by the way he had been manipulated. There could be little question that the anthrax he had stolen years earlier had just been used in the Geneva attack.

Tarnapolsky smiled broadly at him. "You are enjoying our black-skinned beauties from Cameroon?" he inquired.

"I'm sure you understand the importance of telling no one about my visit," said Bryson, struggling to make himself heard over the cacophony.

Tarnapolsky shrugged, as if to say the question need not have been raised. "My friend, we all have our secrets. I have a few of my own, as you might imagine. But if you are in town, may I assume you are not here to take in the sights—unlike the rest of your group?"

Bryson explained the nature of the delicate operation for which he wished to hire Tarnapolsky. As soon as Bryson uttered the name Prishnikov, however, the KGB man's composure was quite clearly disturbed.

"Coleridge, my dear, I am not one to look a gift horse, as you say, in the mouth. As you know, I have always enjoyed our joint ventures." He gave Bryson a somber, even shaken, look. "The prime minister one fears less. You see, there are stories about this man. This is not an American-style businessman, this you must understand. When you are 'downsized' by Anatoly Prishnikov, you do not collect welfare checks. No, you are far more likely to end up as part of the cement that one of his companies manufactures. Perhaps you will end up as a component of the pigment in the lipstick another one of his companies sells. Do you know what you call a gangster who has, through graft and extortion, acquired ownership of large sectors of your country's industry?" Tarnapolsky gave a wan smile and answered his own question. "You call him CEO."

Bryson nodded. "A difficult target deserves handsome remuneration."

Tarnapolsky sidled close to Bryson in the banquette. "Coleridge, my friend, Anatoly Prishnikov is a dangerous and ruthless man. I am sure he has his confederates in this very club, if he doesn't own it outright."

"I understand, Yuri. But you are not a man to shy from a challenge, as I recall. Perhaps we can work something out to our mutual satisfaction."

Over the next several hours, at the Blackbird and then continuing at Tarnapolsky's immense apartment on Sadovo-Samotechnaya, the two men worked out both the financial terms and the highly complex arrangements. The assistance of two others would be required, and Tarnapolsky would supply them. "To get to Anatoly Prishnikov, blood will certainly be shed," Tarnapolsky warned. "And who's to say that some of it will not be our own, hmm?"

By the early hours of the morning, they had devised a plan.

They had given up on any direct approach to Prishnikov, who was far too well defended, far too dangerous a target. The point of vulnerability, Tarnapolsky concluded, after making a few highly discreet telephone calls to former KGB colleagues, was Prishnikov's senior deputy, a small, weedy man named Dmitri Labov. Prishnikov's longtime lieutenant, Dmitri Labov was known in certain circles as *chelovek kotory khranit sekrety*—the man who keeps the secrets.

But even Labov would hardly be a simple target. Tarnapolsky's research had determined that the deputy was driven every day between his heavily guarded residence and the heavily guarded Nortek office, in suburban Moscow near the old Exhibition of Economic Achievements of the USSR on Prospekt Mira.

Labov's chauffeured vehicle was a bullet- and bomb-resistant Bentley—there were, Bryson knew, no truly bulletproof or bomb-proof vehicles—with almost two tons of armoring on the chassis. It was practically a tank, a Level IV armored vehicle, the highest level of protection that exists, capable of withstanding super-powered military ammunition including 7.62 NATO rounds.

During stints in Mexico City and South America, he had acquired a familiarity with such fully armored vehicles. They were usually fabricated with a quarter-inch of 2024-T3 aluminum as well as a high-performance synthetic composite, typically aramid and ultrahigh-molecular-weight polyethylene. Mounted inside the 19-gauge steel car doors would be a 24-ply sheet of high-strength fiberglass-reinforced plastic, half an inch thick, capable of stopping a .30-carbine slug fired from five feet away. The glass would be a polycarbonate/glass laminate; the fuel tank would be self-sealing, antiexplosive even when directly hit; a special dry-cell battery would keep the engine running after an attack. "Run-flat" tires would enable getaways at high speeds for up to fifty miles even when the tires were shot through by gunfire.

Labov's Bentley would have been modified specifically for Moscow, where gangs were likely to use AK-47 assault rifles. It would probably also be able to withstand grenades and small pipe bombs, probably even armor-piercing ammunition, high-velocity, full-metal-jacket rounds.

But there were always vulnerabilities.

For one, there was the driver, who was probably not professionally trained. For some reason, the Russian plutocrats tended to use their own personal assistants as drivers, not trusting professional ones and not bothering to have them trained in something they probably considered common sense, though it was not.

And there was one more vulnerability—around which Bryson had devised his plan.

Every morning at exactly seven o'clock in the morning Dmitri Labov left his apartment building just off the Arbat, a very exclusive, recently renovated nineteenth-century building that had once been reserved for ranking Central Committee officials and Politburo members. The apartment complex, now home to Russia's nouveaux riches, mostly *mafiya*, was sealed off and well guarded.

This consistency in schedule, the information obtained by Tarnapolsky, was an example of the slipshod security combined with flamboyantly showy protective measures that was peculiar to large-scale criminal enterprises, Bryson had learned. Security professionals knew the importance of varying their charges' schedules, ensuring that nothing was predictable.

Just as Tarnapolsky had been informed, Labov's Bentley pulled out of the newly built underground parking garage beneath Labov's apartment building and traveled a short distance before pulling onto Kalinin Prospekt. Bryson and Tarnapolsky, in a nondescript Volga, tailed the Bentley as it traveled the Ring Road all the way to Prospekt Mira. Shortly after the Bentley had passed the titanium-clad Sputnik obelisk, which soared majestically into the sky, it turned left onto Eizensteina Ulitsa, then proceeded three more blocks to the refurbished baronial palace that provided the headquarters for Nortek. There, Labov's car entered another underground parking garage.

It would remain there for the entire day.

The only somewhat unpredictable element to Labov's schedule concerned the time of his return home. He had a wife and three children and was known to be a family man who never missed dinner at home unless there was an emergency at work or Prishnikov summoned him back in. Most days, however, his limousine left the Nortek garage by seven or seven-fifteen in the evening.

This evening, Labov was clearly intent on getting home in time for dinner with the family. At five minutes after seven o'clock, his Bentley emerged from the Nortek garage. Tarnapolsky and Bryson were waiting, in a grimy white package-delivery panel truck across the street, and Tarnapolsky immediately radioed ahead to his confederate. The timing would be tight, but it should be manageable. Most important, it was still rush hour in this congested city.

Tarnapolsky, who had spent years in the early part of his career tailing dissidents and petty criminals around Moscow, knew the city intimately. He drove, following the Bentley at a discreet distance, only pulling up fairly close when the traffic was heavy enough to provide cover.

When the Bentley turned left onto Kalinin Prospekt, it ran into a serious traffic jam. A large truck was jackknifed and stalled across all lanes of traffic, halting all cars in either direction. Truck horns blared, car horns honked repeatedly; there were loud shouts as frustrated drivers stuck their heads out of their car windows to hurl epithets at the obstruction. But there was nothing to be done; the traffic was frozen.

The filthy white panel truck was stopped immediately ahead of Labov's Bentley, cars hemming them in on all sides. Tarnapolsky's confederate had abandoned his eighteen-wheeler truck, taking the keys with him, on the pretense of searching for help. Traffic would not move for a good long while.

Bryson, dressed in black jeans and a black turtleneck and wearing black leather gloves, crouched on the floor inside the truck and released the hinged trapdoor. There was enough clearance to the ground that he was able to drop to the pavement and belly under the panel truck and then under Labov's Bentley. In the extremely unlikely event that traffic somehow was able to move a few feet, the Bentley could not, since it was blocked by the delivery truck.

Moving quickly, his heart racing, Bryson slid under the Bentley's chassis until he located the precise spot he was looking for. Although the undercarriage was mostly one solid mass of molded steel, aluminum, and polyethylene, there was a small perforated area where the air-intake filter was located. This was the second vulnerability: after all, even passengers of armored vehicles had to breathe. Swiftly, he pressed an adhesive-backed aluminum-alloy filter panel over the vent, a specially designed, radio-controlled device Tarnapolsky had been able to acquire from contacts in the private-security industry in Moscow. Once he assured himself it was securely in place, he wriggled out from under the car and, still undetected, back under the panel truck, the hinged trapdoor still open. He lifted himself up and into the truck and shut the trapdoor behind him.

"*Nu, khorosho?*" asked Tarnapolsky. Everything okay?

"*Ladno,*" replied Bryson. It's fine.

Tarnapolsky called the driver of the jackknifed truck, ordering him to return to his abandoned truck and get it moving again, just as police sirens began to sound.

Traffic started moving a few minutes later, the blaring horns stopped, the cursing came to an end. The Bentley roared ahead, gunning its engine, passing the paneled delivery truck as it resumed its course down

Kalinin Prospekt. Then it made its customary left turn, onto the quiet side street, essentially retracing its morning path.

It was then that Bryson pressed the switch on the transmitter he gripped in his hand. As Tarnapolsky maneuvered down the street after the Bentley, they could see an immediate reaction. The limousine cabin filled at once with thick, white tear gas. The Bentley veered crazily from one side to another before pulling over to the side of the deserted street; the driver had obviously been overcome. Both front and back doors of the limousine were flung open as both driver and Labov emerged, coughing and wretching, hands pressed over their stinging eyes. The driver clutched a handgun uselessly at his side. Yuri Tarnapolsky veered the truck over to the side of the road as well, and the two men jumped out. Bryson fired a projectile at the driver, who toppled at once. The short-acting tranquilizer dart would knock him out for hours; the amnesiac effect of the narcotic would ensure that he had little or no recollection of the evening's events. Then Bryson rushed over to Labov, who had collapsed on the sidewalk, coughing and temporarily blinded. Meanwhile, Tarnapolsky hoisted the driver back into the driver's seat of the Bentley. Taking out a bottle of cheap vodka he had bought on the street, he spilled a good quantity into the chauffeur's mouth and over his uniform, leaving the half-filled bottle on the seat beside him.

Bryson looked around to confirm that there was no one on the street who could see what they were doing; then he hustled Labov, half-dragging the small man, into the nondescript panel truck, a boxy vehicle like hundreds in the area, which would never be identified, particularly since its license plates, covered in mud, were illegible.

By just before eight o'clock in the evening, Dmitri Labov was bound, in a seated position, to a hard metal chair in a large deserted warehouse in the Cheryomushki district, not far from the wholesale fruit-and-vegetable market. The city government had confiscated it from a Tatar clan that had been caught selling produce on the black market to restaurants without paying the requisite tribute to city officials.

Labov was small and bespectacled, with receding, straw-colored hair and a round, pudgy face. Bryson stood before him and spoke in perfect Russian with a slight St. Petersburg accent, the legacy of his Directorate Russian-language tutor. "Your dinner is getting cold. We'd love to get you home before your wife gets frantic. In fact, if you play your cards right and cooperate fully, no one ever has to know you were abducted."

"What?" spat Labov. "You deceive yourself. Everyone already knows. My driver—"

"Your driver is passed out in the front seat of your limousine, parked by the side of the road. Any passing *militsiya* will simply assume he's dozing, drunk like half of Moscow."

"If you plan to drug me, go ahead," Labov said, at once frightened and defiant. "If you plan to torture me, go ahead. Or just go ahead and kill me. If you dare. Do you have any *idea* who I am?"

"Of course," said Bryson. "That's why you're here."

"Do you have any idea what the consequences will be? Do you *know* whose wrath you are incurring?"

Bryson nodded slowly.

"Anatoly Prishnikov's anger knows no bounds! It is not impeded by national borders!"

"Mr. Labov, please understand, I wouldn't think of harming a hair on your head. Or that of your wife, Masha. Or little Irushka. I won't have to—there'll be nothing left of them after Prishnikov is through."

"What the fuck are you saying?" Labov shouted, red-faced.

"Let me explain," Bryson said patiently. "Tomorrow morning I will personally drive you to Nortek headquarters. You may still be a little woozy from the tranquilizers, but I will help you into the building. And then I will leave. But everything will be recorded on the security cameras. Then your boss will become extremely interested in who I am, and why you were in my company. You will tell him that you told me nothing." Bryson paused. "But do you think he will believe you?"

Outraged, Labov screamed, "I have been a loyal aide to him for twenty years! I have been nothing but loyal!"

"I don't doubt that. But can Anatoly Prishnikov afford to believe you? I ask you—you know him better than anyone. You know what kind of man he is, how deep-rooted is his suspicion."

Labov had begun to tremble.

"And if Prishnikov thought that there was even the slightest chance that you had betrayed him, how long do you think he would let you live?"

Labov shook his head, his eyes wide with terror.

"Let me answer my own question. He would let you live just long enough to know that your loved ones had died horribly. Long enough for you and everyone in the firm to be reminded of the price of betrayal—of *weakness*."

Yuri Tarnapolsky, who had been watching from the sidelines, stroking his chin idly, put in: "You remember poor Maksimov."

"Maksimov was a traitor!"

"Not according to Maksimov," Tarnapolsky said gently. He toyed with his service revolver, polishing its barrel with a soft white handkerchief. "Do you know he and Olga had an infant son? One would think that Prishnikov would spare the young and the innocent—"

"No! *Stop!*" gasped Labov, ashen-faced. He was having difficulty breathing. "I know much less—much less than you must think. There is a great deal I don't know."

"Please," said Bryson warningly. "Evasion will simply waste our time and will add to the length of time you are gone—the period of missing time you must somehow account for. I want to know about Prishnikov's alliance with Jacques Arnaud."

"There are so many deals, so many arrangements. They accelerate. There are more than ever now."

"Why?"

"I think he is preparing for something."

"For what?"

"Once, I heard him speaking on his secure phone to Arnaud and saying something about the 'Prometheus Group.'"

The name chimed in Bryson's head. He had heard it before. Yes! Jan Vansina had used the phrase in Geneva, wondering whether he was "with the Prometheans."

"What is the Prometheus Group?" Bryson demanded urgently.

"Prometheus—you have no idea. No one has any idea. I hardly know. They are powerful—immensely powerful. It is not clear to me whether Prishnikov follows their orders, or whether he gives them orders."

"Who are 'they'?"

"They are important, powerful people—"

"You've said that already. *Who are they?*"

"They are everywhere—and nowhere. Their names are not to be found on mastheads, on letterheads, on papers of incorporation. But Tolya—Prishnikov is among them, this I am sure of."

"Arnaud is one of them," prompted Bryson.

"Yes."

"Who else?"

Labov shook his head in defiance. "You know, if you kill me, Prishnikov will leave my family alone," he said reasonably. "Why don't you kill me?"

Tarnapolsky looked over, a wry smile on his face. "Do you know how they found Maksimov's child, Labov?" He approached Labov, still menacingly polishing his revolver with the handkerchief.

Labov jerked his head back and forth like a child unwilling to listen. Had his hands been free he would surely have clapped them over his ears. Quivering, he blurted out, "The Jade Master! He is making arrangements with . . . with the man they call the Jade Master."

Tarnapolsky gave Bryson a sharp look. They both knew whom the moniker referred to. The so-called Jade Master was a powerful general in the Chinese military, the People's Liberation Army. General Tsai, based in Shenzhen, was famously corrupt and had facilitated the efforts of certain international conglomerates to establish a foothold in the immense Chinese market—in exchange, of course, for certain considerations. General Tsai was also world-renowned as a collector of precious imperial Chinese jade and was known to sometimes accept blandishments in the form of valuable jade carvings.

Labov saw the look between the two men. "I don't know what you hope to accomplish," he said contemptuously. "Everything is about to change, and you cannot stop it."

Bryson turned back to Labov quizzically. "What do you mean, 'everything is about to change'?" he demanded.

"Days remain—only days," Labov said cryptically. "Only a few days I am given to prepare."

"To prepare *what*?"

"The machinery has already been put into place. Now power is about to be transferred fully! Everything will come into view."

Tarnapolsky finished polishing his revolver, pocketed the handkerchief, and then pointed the gun a few inches away from Labov's face. "Are you referring to a coup d'etat?"

Bryson interrupted, "But Prishnikov is already the power behind the throne in Russia! Why the hell would he want something like that?"

Labov laughed dismissively. "Coup d'etat! How little you know! How narrow is your view! We Russians have always been happy to give up our freedom for safety and security. You will, too, all of you. Every last one. For now the forces are too great. The machinery is already in place. Everything is about to come into view!"

"What the hell are you talking about?" thundered Bryson. "Prishnikov and his colleagues—do they now aspire higher than the corporate world—do they aim to take over governments now, is that it? Have they become besotted with their own wealth and power?"

"We would appreciate some specifics, my friend," Tarnapolsky said, lowering his revolver, the threat no longer necessary.

"Governments? Governments are outdated! Look at Russia—what kind of power has the government? None! The government is powerless. It's the corporations that make the rules now! Maybe Lenin was right after all—it *is* the capitalists who control the world!"

Suddenly, with the speed of a cobra, Labov's right hand lunged out a few inches, the maximum play allowed by the constraints. It was just enough for him to grab Tarnapolsky's revolver, which was almost next to him. Tarnapolsky reacted swiftly, grabbing Labov's hand, twisting it hard to loosen Labov's grip on the revolver. For a moment, the gun was pointing upward and back, right at Labov's own face. Labov seemed to be staring at the muzzle, hypnotized by it, a strange, sweet smile on his face. Then, just before Tarnapolsky was able to wrench it away, Labov pointed it between his own eyes and squeezed the trigger.

CHAPTER
TWENTY

The suicide of Anatoly Prishnikov's longtime aide-de-camp was a grim turn of events; Labov may have been a ruthless corporate functionary, the fax and the phone his deadly weapons, but he was no killer, and his death had meant the shedding of unnecessary blood. More than that, it was a complication, a deviation from their carefully laid-out plan.

Labov's driver would return to consciousness within the hour; whether or not he would have any specific recall of the Bentley filling with tear gas, his memory would be disjointed, hazy. He would awake to find his uniform reeking of cheap vodka, a bottle on the seat beside him, his passenger and charge gone; he would panic. No doubt he would place a call to Labov's home; that angle had to be covered as well.

Among the papers in Dmitri Labov's wallet, Yuri Tarnapolsky had turned up Labov's home phone number. From his cell phone—Moscow these days seemed to be overrun with mobile phones, Bryson had noticed—Tarnapolsky then placed a quick call to Masha, Labov's wife.

"*Gospozha* Labova," he said in the obsequious tones of a low-level office functionary, "this is Sasha from the office. Sorry for the interruption, but Dmitri wanted me to call to say he'll be somewhat delayed, he's on an urgent phone call to France that can't be interrupted, and he sends his apologies." Lowering his voice, he added confidentially, "It's just as well, since his regular driver seems to have hit the bottle again." He gave an aggrieved sigh. "Which means I'll have to make alternative arrangements. Ah, well. Good evening." And he hung up before the wife could ask any questions. It would do; such delays were unavoidable in Labov's line of work. When and if the chauffeur called in a state of agitation and disorientation, the wife would respond with anger or annoyance and would dismiss him at once.

All this was reasonably straightforward. Labov's suicide, however, was a loose end that had to be tied up as best they could. Bryson and Tarnapolsky were limited in what they could do, because the ex-KGB man was absolutely unwilling to place any calls to the Nortek office; assuming that all calls incoming or outgoing were recorded, he did not want a tape of his voice to be found. A solution had to be quickly improvised, an explanation for the suicide that might be accepted without too much follow-up investigation. It was Tarnapolsky who came up with the idea of planting various suspect items on Labov's person and in his briefcase: a package of Vigor brand Russian-made condoms, a few soiled, dog-eared cards from less-than-reputable Moscow clubs known for the sexual hijinks that took place in private back rooms — Tarnapolsky had a small collection of such *cartes de visite* — and, the crowning touch, a half-used tube of ointment customarily used to treat the topical manifestation of certain more benign sexually communicable diseases. Quite likely such escapades were entirely alien to such a proper, work-oriented man as Labov; but it was precisely such a man who might react so violently to finding himself in the middle of a sordid embarrassment. Alcohol, tawdry sex: these were normal, everyday vices.

Now it was a race: against time, against the likelihood that, one way or another, Prishnikov would learn that Nortek had been penetrated. Far too much could go wrong, Bryson knew. Labov's limousine, with its semi-conscious driver, could be identified by a vigilant *militsiyoner* and reported to Nortek headquarters. Labov's wife could call his office back, for one reason or another. The risks were enormous, and Prishnikov would be quick to react. Bryson had to get out of Russia as soon as possible.

Tarnapolsky drove his Audi at top speed to Vnukovo Airport, thirty kilometers southwest of Moscow. This was one of Russia's domestic airports, serving all regions of the country but particularly the south. He had arranged with one of the new private aviation firms for an emergency, late-night flight to Baku for one of his wealthy clients, a businessman with extensive financial interests in Azerbaijan. Tarnapolsky had not gone into detail, of course, except to mention a sudden eruption of labor unrest at a factory, the factory director taken hostage. Given the suddenness of the booking, a substantial outlay of cash was required. Bryson had it, and was glad to pay it. Customs Control had to be paid off, as well, for expedited paperwork; this required another hefty sum.

"Yuri," said Bryson, "what's in it for Prishnikov?"

"You're talking about the Jade Master, I take it. Yes?"

"Yes. I know you're well versed in the Chinese military, the PLA—you did your time in the KGB's China sector. So what exactly would Prishnikov hope to gain from establishing an alliance with General Tsai?"

"You heard what Labov said, my friend. Governments are powerless now. It's the corporations that make the rules. If you're an ambitious titan like Prishnikov and you want to control half of the world's markets, there are few better partners than the Jade Master. He's a ranking member of the PLA's General Staff, the one most responsible for turning the People's Liberation Army into one of the world's largest corporations, and the man in charge of all of its commercial ventures."

"Such as?"

"The Chinese military controls an astonishingly complex web of businesses, interlocking enterprises, vertically integrated. I mean, from automobile factories to airlines, from pharmaceuticals to telecommunications. Their real-estate holdings are vast—they own hotels all over Asia, including Beijing's showpiece, the Palace Hotel. They own and operate most of China's airports."

"But I thought the Chinese government had begun cracking down on the military—that the Chinese premier issued an executive decree ordering the army to begin divesting itself of all its businesses."

"Oh, Beijing tried, but the genie was already out of the bottle. What do you Americans say, the toothpaste was out of the tube? Perhaps it is better to talk of Pandora's box. The fact is, it was too late. The PLA has become the most powerful force in China by far."

"But haven't the Chinese slashed their defense budget a number of times in recent years?"

Tarnapolsky snorted. "And then all the PLA has to do is go out and sell a few weapons of mass destruction to rogue nations. It's like having a bake sale, or do you call it a yard sale? My dear Coleridge, the PLA's economic might is simply beyond imagining. Now they've begun to recognize the strategic importance of telecom. They own and launch satellites; they own China's largest telecommunications company; they've been working with the giants of the West—Lucent, Motorola, Qualcomm, Systematix, Nortel—to develop immense mobile phone and paging networks, information systems. It is said that the PLA now owns the skies over China. And the one true owner, the man in charge, the man behind it all—is the Jade Master. General Tsai."

As Tarnapolsky's Audi pulled up to the airstrip, Bryson saw a small plane, a brand-new Yakovlev-112, waiting on the runway. He could see at once that it was a single-engine prop four-seater. It was tiny, surely the smallest craft in the company's fleet.

Tarnapolsky saw Bryson's surprise. "Believe me, my friend, this was the best I could do on such notice. There are far bigger, far nicer planes—they mentioned their YAK-40, their Antonov-26—but all were in use."

"It'll do, Yuri. Thanks. I owe you."

"Let's just call it a business gift. . . ."

Bryson cocked his head. He heard the squealing of brakes not far off; when he turned to look, he saw a massive, wide Humvee, black and glossy, roaring down the airstrip toward them.

"What the hell is this?" exclaimed Yuri. The Humvee's doors flew open, and three black-clad men jumped out, wearing black face masks and the black Kevlar-and-nylon garb of commandos.

"Get down!" shouted Bryson. "Shit! We have no *weapons!*"

Tarnapolsky, diving to the floor of the Audi, pulled out a tray mounted under the front seat. It held several weapons and piles of ammunition. Yuri handed Bryson a Makarov 9mm automatic pistol, then pulled out a large Kalashnikov Bizon submachine gun, a Russian Spetsnaz weapon. There was a sudden hail of bullets, and the Audi's windscreen turned white with starburst cracks. The glass, Bryson realized, was at least partially bullet-resistant. He crouched down. "This car isn't armored, is it?"

"Light," replied the KGB man as he shouldered the weapon and took a deep, slow breath. "Level One. Use the doors."

Bryson nodded; he understood. The doors were reinforced with either high-strength fiberglass or a synthetic composite, meaning he could use them as shields.

Another burst of ammunition, and the commandos, visible through the side window, assumed firing stance. "Special delivery from Prishnikov," Tarnapolsky said, almost under his breath.

"The wife called," Bryson said, the instant he realized it. But how did Prishnikov know where to dispatch his commandos? Perhaps the answer was simple: the fastest way out of Russia was by air, and anyone foolish enough to take down Prishnikov's most valued assistant had better escape the country without delay. Moreover, there were just a few airports near Moscow, only two of them having the facilities to handle private planes. A last-minute booking, made urgently . . . Prishnikov had made a calculated guess, and he had guessed right.

Tarnapolsky sprang his door open, sprang to the ground, crouching behind it, and fired off a burst of machine-gun fire. "*Yob tvoyu mat!*" he growled: Fuck your mother.

One of the marksmen fell, taken out by Tarnapolsky.

"Good shot," Bryson said. A line of shots moved across the opaque-white windshield, spraying tiny pebbles of tempered glass at Bryson's face. He unlatched the car door on his side, got directly behind it, and fired off a few rounds at the two remaining commandos. At the same time, Tarnapolsky got off another burst of fire, and a second man sprawled to the paved landing strip.

One more remained—but where?

Bryson and Tarnapolsky scanned the dark field on either side, searching for movement. The landing lights illuminated the blacktop but not the surrounding fields, where the third man had to be concealed, lying in wait, weapon at the ready.

Tarnapolsky fired off a round at what appeared to be movement, but there was no response. He stood up, wheeled around, aiming the Bizon toward the dark area on the other side of the landing strip, nearest Bryson. *Where the hell was he?*

Prishnikov's men were surely outfitted with rubber-soled boots, enabling them to move silently, stealthily. Gripping the Makarov in both hands, he moved it around in a slow circuit, starting from his far right and moving steadily counterclockwise.

By the time he saw the tiny, dancing red dot on the back of Tarnapolsky's head, it was too late for Bryson to do anything but cry out.

"Get down!" he shouted.

But an exploding bullet had entered Yuri Tarnapolsky's head, blowing his face off.

"Oh, *Christ!*" Bryson shouted in horror as he spun around. He caught a flicker of reflected light, saw a tiny movement on or near the plane, several hundred feet away. The third sniper had positioned himself against the aircraft, using it as protection. Bryson repositioned the Makarov, exhaled slowly, and squeezed off one precisely aimed shot.

There was a distant cry, the clatter of a weapon on the tarmac. The third commando, the one who had killed Yuri Ivanovich Tarnapolsky, was dead.

Casting a look back at the corpse of his friend, Bryson leaped out of the Audi and ran toward the plane. Others would be on the way, in greater numbers; his only chance of survival was to get on board the aircraft and pilot it himself.

He ran to the Yakovlev-112, jumped onto the wing, and swung into the pilot's seat, closing the hatch behind him. He strapped himself in, sat back against the seat, closed his eyes. *Now what?* Flying the plane itself was not a problem; he had sufficient hours in the air and had performed numerous emergency departures in his Directorate years. The problem, instead, would be navigating in Russian air space without clearance, without support from the tower. But what choice was there? Returning to Tarnapolsky's car meant heading back into the jaws of Prishnikov's commandos, and that was not an acceptable option.

He inhaled, held his breath, then turned the ignition key. The engine caught right away. He checked the instruments and began slowly taxiing toward the end of the runway.

He couldn't ignore the tower, he knew. To take off without being in contact with the air-traffic controller was not only risky, even potentially fatal, but it would be viewed by the Russian Air Force as a deliberate provocation. Measures would be taken.

He keyed the microphone and spoke in English, the language spoken by international flight controllers. "Vnukovo Clearance, Yakovlev-112, RossTran three niner niner foxtrot. Number one for runway three, straight-out departure. Ready for clearance to Baku."

The reply came back after a few seconds, staticky yet brisk: "*Shto?* What? Did not copy, say again."

"RossTran three niner niner foxtrot," he repeated. "Ready for departure via Vnukovo three, ready to taxi."

"You have no flight plan, RossTran three nine nine!"

Undeterred, Bryson persisted. "Vnukovo Ground, RossTran three niner niner foxtrot, ready for taxi. Climb and maintain ten thousand. Expect flight level two hundred fifty ten minutes after departure. Departure frequency one-one-eight point five five. Squawk four six three seven."

"RossTran, hold, I repeat, hold! You have no authorization!"

"Vnukovo Ground, I'm flying certain high-ranking Nortek executives on an emergency visit to Baku," he said, assuming the characteristic above-the-law arrogance of Prishnikov's minions. "The flight plans should have been filed. You have my serial number; you can call Dmitri Labov to verify."

"RossTran—"

"Anatoly Prishnikov would be *extremely* unhappy to learn that you are interfering with the administration of his businesses. Perhaps, Comrade Air Traffic controller, you could tell me *your* name and identification."

There was a pause, several seconds of radio silence. "Go ahead," the voice snapped. "Fly at your own risk."

Bryson applied the throttle, accelerated toward the end of the runway, and the plane lifted off.

CHAPTER TWENTY-ONE

Monsignor Lorenzo Battaglia, Ph.D. — senior curator at the Chiaramonti Museum, one of the many specialized collections within the Monumenti Musei e Gallerie Pontifice, the Vatican museums, in the Citta del Vaticano — had not seen Giles Hesketh-Haywood for many years, and he wasn't exactly overjoyed to see him again.

The two men were meeting in a magnificent, damask-walled reception room off the Galleria Lapidaria. Monsignor Battaglia had been a curator at the Vatican museums for twenty years, and his connoisseurship was respected around the world. Giles Hesketh-Haywood, his effete English visitor, had always struck him as a faintly absurd, even comical, creature, with those oversized round tortoise-shell spectacles, those bright silk neckties that swelled flamboyantly from a very tight knot, the checkered vests, those gold horseshoe cufflinks, the old briar bowl stuck jauntily in his breast pocket, the posh accent. He reeked of golden cavendish tobacco. His charm was boundless, if oily. Hesketh-Haywood was an upper-class twit, in some ways — so *teddibly* English — but his trade was an unsavory one. Ostensibly, he was a dealer in antiquities, but really he was nothing more than a high-end fence.

Hesketh-Haywood, part connoisseur, part out-and-out crook, was the sort of shady fellow who vanishes for years at a time before showing up on the yacht of some Middle Eastern oil sheik. Though he was steadfastly vague about his past, the Monsignor had heard all the rumors: that his family was once of the high-living English gentry but fell on hard times in the postwar Laborite era. That Hesketh-Haywood had been educated among the scions of great wealth, but by the time he got out of school, his family had nothing left but a mountain of debt. Giles was a scamp, a rogue, a delightfully unscrupulous fellow who started out smuggling archaeological antiquities out of Italy, no doubt bribing the export licensing board. He was very gray-market, but some extraordinary artifacts had passed through his hands. If you didn't want to know how they came into his possession, you knew enough not to ask. Men like Hesketh-Haywood were tolerated in the art world only because of those rare occasions on which they could be useful—he had in fact once proved useful to the Monsignor, conducting a certain "transaction" that the Monsignor prayed the world would never learn about—but the cordiality displayed by the Monsignor was now paper-thin. For the favor that Hesketh-Haywood was now asking him was astonishing, appalling.

Monsignor Battaglia closed his eyes for a moment to summon the words he needed, and then he leaned forward and spoke gravely to his visitor. "What you propose is out of the question, Giles. It is far more than a 'prank.' It is an outright scandal."

The Monsignor had never seen Hesketh-Haywood's supreme self-satisfaction waver, and it wasn't wavering now. "A *scandal*, Monsignor?" Giles Hesketh-Haywood's eyes, magnified behind the thick lenses, looked both owlish and amused. "But there are so *many* kinds of scandal, are there not? For instance, the intelligence that a senior Vatican official, a world-renowned expert in the art and artifacts of the ancient world, an ordained *priest* to boot—that this gentleman maintains a mistress on Via Sebastiano Veniero—well, some people aren't quite so enlightened as *we* are about such things, isn't that so?"

The Englishman leaned back in his chair and waggled a long, slender finger in the air. "But it's the *money*, not the women, that may cause the greater dismay. And sweet young Alessandra continues to enjoy her comfortable *demaine*, I trust. Comfortable—some might say *lavish*, especially given the rather modest salary of the Vatican curator who supports her." He sighed, shook his head contentedly. "But I like to think that I've made my contribution to that worthy cause."

Monsignor Battaglia could feel his face turn red. A vein on his temple started to throb.

"Perhaps there is an accommodation that we might reach," Battaglia said at last.

Those thick-lensed round spectacles were starting to give Bryson a splitting headache, but at least he had achieved what he'd come to Rome to do. He was exhausted, having landed the small plane at an airfield outside of Kiev, safely outside of Russian airspace, and taken two connecting flights on a commercial airliner to Rome. The call he had placed to the Monsignor had been answered right away, as he knew it would be, for the curator was almost always interested in what Giles Hesketh-Haywood had to offer.

Giles Hesketh-Haywood, one of Bryson's many carefully manufactured legends, had often come in useful in his previous career.

As a connoisseur of, and dealer in, antiquities, he naturally had reason to travel to places like Sicily, Egypt, Sudan, Libya, and elsewhere. He deflected suspicion by *prompting* suspicion: an elementary exercise in misdirection. Since alert officials assumed he was a smuggler, it never crossed their minds that he might be a spy. And most of them, of course, were only too happy to accept his bribes: if they didn't, after all, others surely would.

The small item appeared the very next morning in *L'Osservatore Romano*, the official Vatican newspaper, with over five million copies sold worldwide. OGGETTO SPARITO DAI MUSEI VATICANI? ITEM STOLEN FROM VATICAN COLLECTION? the headline read.

According to the account, the Vatican museum had discovered, in their annual inventory, that it was missing a rare Sung Dynasty chess set made of carved jade. The exquisite jade set had been brought back from China by Marco Polo in the early fourteenth century and presented to the Doge of Venice. Cesare Borgia acquired the set in 1500, and after his death, it was presented to one of the Medici Popes, Leo X, who cherished it; it even appears in the background of one of his great portraits. In 1549, Pope Paul III used it to play a match against the legendary chess master Paulo Boi and was defeated.

The newspaper article quoted a spokesman for the Vatican museum emphatically denying the charge. At the same time, however, the museum refused to offer proof that it still possessed the rare chess set. There was a brief, indignant quote from senior curator Monsignor Lorenzo Battaglia to the effect that the Vatican museum had hundreds of thousands of distinct items in its catalogs, and that, given the vastness of its holdings, it was inevitable that some objects might be temporarily mislaid; there was no reason in the world to jump to the conclusion that an act of theft had taken place.

Over caffe latté in his suite at the Hassler, Nick Bryson read the piece with professional satisfaction. He hadn't asked that much of the Monsignor. The denials, after all, were true. The legendary Sung Dynasty jade chess set still safely reposed in one of the Vatican's hundreds of storage vaults; like most of the immense Vatican holdings, it was never displayed. It had not been displayed for over forty years, in fact. It had not been stolen—but anybody reading the paper would conclude otherwise.

And Bryson was certain that the right people would be reading this article.

He picked up the phone and called an old acquaintance in Beijing, a Chinese civil servant named Jiang Yingchao, now highly placed in the foreign ministry. Jiang had had dealings with Giles Hesketh-Haywood a decade ago; he recognized Giles's honking tones immediately.

"My English friend," exclaimed Jiang. "What a pleasure it is to hear from you, after so long a silence."

"You know I don't like to impose upon our friendship," Bryson replied. "But I trust our last transaction was . . . helpful to your career. Not that you needed it, of course: your ascent up the ranks of the diplomatic corps has been most impressive."

Giles did not need to remind his Chinese diplomat friend: Jiang had been a low-level cultural attaché in the Chinese embassy in Bonn when he had first been introduced to Giles Hesketh-Haywood. It was not long after they had lunch together that Giles made good on his promise, obtaining for Jiang an extremely valuable ancient Chinese artifact at a cost that was far below what it would fetch if it ever hit the open market. The miniature, red-pottery walking horse from the Han Dynasty had made a very special gift from Jiang to the ambassador, no doubt greasing the wheels of his career. Over the years, Hesketh-Haywood had furnished a number of priceless objects to his diplomat friend, including ancient bronzes and a Qing Dynasty vase.

"And what have you been up to all these years?" asked the diplomat.

Bryson gave a long, aggrieved sigh. "I'm sure you saw that absolutely *scurrilous* article in *L'Osservatore Romano*," he remarked.

"No, which article might that be?"

"Oh, dear, forget I even *mentioned* it. Anyway, an *extraordinary* object has just *happened* to fall into my possession, and I thought a *branché* chap such as yourself might know of someone who might be interested in it. I mean, there's a *terribly* long list of extremely interested potential buyers, but just for old times' sake I thought I'd call you first. . . ." He began to describe the jade chess set, but Jiang cut him off.

"I will call you back," Jiang said sharply. "Let me have your number."

There was a delay of half an hour before Jiang Yingchao called on a sterile line. No doubt he had located the Vatican newspaper and then made a few rapid, excited calls first.

"You do understand, my dear fellow, that this isn't the sort of thing that comes up very often," said Giles. "But it's positively frightful how careless some of these great institutions are about their treasures, isn't it? Positively *frightful*."

"Yes, yes," Jiang interrupted impatiently. "There would be a great deal of interest, I'm sure. If we're talking about the same thing—the Sung Dynasty jade chess set—"

"I'm speaking *hypothetically*, my dear Jiang, of course. You do realize that. I'm saying that if such a *marvelous* set happened to become available, you might want to put out the word. *Discreetly*, of course. . . ."

The coded language was clear; it was like waving a red flag at a bull. "Yes, yes, I do know of someone, yes indeed. There is a general, you know, who is known to collect such things, these Sung Dynasty masterpieces of carved jade. It is the general's consuming passion. You may know his nickname, his moniker—the Jade Master."

"Hmm. Not sure I do, Jiang. But you think he might have any interest?"

"General Tsai is most interested in repatriating looted imperial trea-sures, bringing them back to the motherland. He is a fervent nationalist, you know."

"So I am given to understand. Well, I would need to know quite soon if the general has any interest, because I'm about to tell the hotel operator to *hold* all my *calls*—those *loathsome* oil sheiks from Oman and Kuwait simply won't stop *calling!*"

"No!" Jiang blurted out. "Give me two hours! This masterpiece *must* be returned to China!"

Bryson did not have to wait that long. The diplomat called back barely an hour later. The general was interested.

"Given the extraordinary nature of this property," Bryson said firmly, "I absolutely insist on meeting my customer face-to-face." At this point, Bryson knew he could pretty much set his own terms for the meeting with General Tsai.

"But—but of course," sputtered Jiang. "The . . . customer would re-quire nothing less. He needs to have every assurance of the item's au-thenticity."

"Naturally. All certificates of provenance will be provided."

"Of course."

"The meeting must be immediate. I can accept no delay."

"That is not a problem. The Jade Master is in Shenzhen, and he looks forward to meeting with you as soon as possible."

"Good. I'll take the first flight to Shenzhen, and then the general and I will have an initial conversation."

"What do you mean, an *initial conversation . . .* ?"

"The general and I will pass a convivial hour or two, I'll show him photographs of the chess set, and if I feel we've established a comfort level, we'll proceed to the next step."

"Then you won't be taking the set with you to your meeting with the general?"

"Oh, good *Lord*, no. After all, such a customer would be in a position to expose me if he wanted to. Can't be too careful these days. You know my motto: I never deal with strangers." He chortled. "After I meet this chappy, of course, we won't be strangers anymore, now will we? If everything's in order—if everything *feels* right—we can discuss importation, filthy lucre, all those *boring* humdrum details."

"The general will insist on inspecting the jade chess set, Giles."

"Certainly, but not at first. Oh, no. China's terra incognita to me, I don't know the chappies in charge. I guess I feel a smidgen vulnerable there. Wouldn't want your General Whosit to *confiscate* the thing and bundle me off to one of those *cabbage* farms or what have you."

"The general is a man of his word," Jiang objected stiffly.

"My antennae have served me awfully well these last twenty years, old friend. Wouldn't want to ignore them at *this* late date. Fella can't be too careful with you inscrutable Orientals, you know." He chuckled; there was silence on the phone. "And you know me—a jigger of rice wine and I'm *anybody's!*"

Flamboyantly attired in a yellow kid-skin vest and a silk-and-cashmere checked suit, Giles Hesketh-Haywood arrived at Shenzhen's Huangtian Airport and was met by an emissary of General Tsai wearing the dark-green, rankless uniform of the Chinese People's Liberation Army, the standard red metal enamel star at the front of his standard-issue "Mao" cap. The emissary, a stony-faced middle-aged man who offered no name, whisked Bryson through customs and immigration. The way had been prepared; the airport personnel were deferential and inspected nothing.

That was left to General Tsai's men. Once they were clear of immigration, the emissary wordlessly hustled Bryson through an unmarked door where two other green-uniformed soldiers were waiting. One of them unceremoniously rifled through his luggage, leaving nothing unopened or unchecked. Meanwhile, the other began frisking him systematically, from head to foot, even slicing the insoles in the costly English leather shoes. Bryson was not surprised at the search, though he emitted squawks of indignation befitting his legend's prissy persona.

He had not arrived unarmed, though. Anticipating that he would be searched before being permitted to meet with the general, he had left behind any firearms, or in fact anything that would be out of character for Giles Hesketh-Haywood to carry. The risk of being caught, and therefore sabotaging the entire legend, was too great.

But concealed in Hesketh-Haywood's glove-soft leather belt was a weapon so well concealed that it was worth the risk. Sewn between two layers of the finest Italian cordovan leather was a long, flexible metal strip about an inch wide by twelve inches long, made of an aluminum-vanadium alloy, a razor-sharp blade down most of its length. The blade was easily and quickly removed from the belt by opening one snap and pulling hard. It was difficult to use without wounding oneself, but if employed properly, the blade would slash human skin down to the bone with virtually no pressure. And if that was insufficient, Bryson was confident that he could rely, as he often did, on his ability to improvise, to find weapons where others saw none. But he hoped weapons would not be needed. The uniformed soldier ordered Bryson to remove his belt; he ran it cursorily between his fingers and detected nothing.

A black, late-model Daimler limousine was idling in front of the terminal exit doors, a military chauffeur at the wheel, also in the green rankless uniform of the Chinese Army, with a bland, unreadable face, his chin tucked toward his chest in a gesture of humility.

The dour emissary opened the passenger's door for Bryson, placed the suitcase in the trunk, then got into the front seat. He did not speak a word; the driver steered the Daimler away from the curb and onto the airport access road toward Shenzhen.

Bryson had been to Shenzhen once, years before, but he scarcely recognized it. What was a tiny, sleepy fishing village and border town barely twenty years ago had exploded into a clamorous and chaotic metropolis of hastily paved roads, slapdash apartment complexes, and belching factories. From the rice paddies and virgin farmland of southern China's Pearl River Delta had sprouted the skyscrapers and power plants and industrialized sectors of the Special Economic Zone. The chaotic skyline bristled with construction cranes, the sky an ugly gray polluted haze. The bustling population of some four million people settled on the banks of the fetid Shenzhen River were mostly *mingong*, or peasant workers, lured from their rural provinces with the promise of jobs at subsistence wages.

Shenzhen was a megalopolis in a hurry, a boomtown city going at a furious pace twenty-four hours a day, running at full blast on the high-octane fuel that was the most profane of words in all of Communist China: capitalism. But it was capitalism at its brashest and cruelest, the dangerous hysteria of a frontier city, crime and prostitution rampant and evident. The glittering heights of consumer excess, the lurid billboards and flashing neon, the swanky shops of Louis Vuitton and Dior, were, Bryson knew, nothing more than a veneer. Behind it lay concealed the desperate poverty, the squalor of the *mingong*'s grim daily existence, the metal sheds housing dozens of migrant laborers with no plumbing, scrawny chickens running around tiny, filthy yards.

The traffic was thick, choked with late-model automobiles and bright red taxis. Every single building was new, tall, modernistic. The streets bustled with blinking signs, all of them in Chinese with the rare exception of an English letter here and there—an M for McDonald's, a KFC. Everywhere seemed to be lavish colors, gaudy restaurants, and stores selling consumer electronics—camcorders and digital cameras and computers and televisions and DVDs. Street merchants peddled roasted pigs and ducks and live crabs.

The crowds were dense, shoulder-to-shoulder, with almost everybody carrying a mobile phone. But unlike Hong Kong, twenty miles to the south, there were no elderly people practicing tai-chi in the parks; in fact, there were no old people here at all. The maximum length of stay in the Special Economic Zone was fifteen years, and only the able-bodied were welcome.

The emissary turned around in the front seat and began speaking. "*Ni laiguo Shenzhen ma?*"

"Pardon?" said Bryson.

"*Ni budong Zhongguo hua ma?*"

"Sorry, no speakee the lingo," Bryson drawled. The emissary had asked him if he understood Chinese, whether he had been here before; Bryson wondered whether he was being crudely tested.

"English?"

"I am, and I speak it, yes."

"This is your first time here?"

"Yes, it is. Charming place, though—wish I'd discovered it earlier."

"Why do you meet the general?" The emissary's expression had turned outright hostile.

"Business," Bryson said shortly. "That *is* what the general does, right?"

"The general is in charge of the Guandong Sector of the PLA," the emissary upbraided him.

"Well, there sure seems to be a lot of business going on here."

The driver grunted something, and the emissary fell silent, then turned around.

The Daimler crawled through the unbelievable congestion of the streets, the strange cacophony: the hysterical shrieks of high-pitched voices, the blaring of truck horns. In front of the Shangri-La Hotel the traffic finally came to a standstill. The chauffeur turned on his siren and flashing red light and veered up onto a crowded sidewalk, barking shrill orders through the car's loudspeakers, scattering the frightened pedestrians like so many pigeons. Then the Daimler zipped ahead of the knot of traffic.

Finally they came to a checkpoint, the entrance to a highly industrialized sector that appeared to be under the direct control of the military. Bryson assumed that it was here that General Tsai had his primary residence, perhaps maintained his headquarters. A soldier holding a clipboard leaned in and gestured rudely to the emissary, who quickly got out. The car continued down the street, past drab residential buildings into a more industrial-looking area, predominately warehouses.

Bryson was instantly wary. He was not being taken to the general's residence. But where was he being driven?

"*Neng bu neng gaosong wo, ni song wo qu nar?*" he demanded in a deliberately heavy British accent, the syntax that of a speaker ill at ease with the language. Care to tell me where you're driving me?

The driver did not reply.

Bryson raised his voice, now speaking with his customary fluency, that of a native speaker. "We're nowhere near the general's barracks, *siji!*"

"The general does not receive visitors at his residence. He keeps a very low profile." The driver spoke impertinently, even disrespectfully, not as a Chinese speaker of his station would address a superior, not using *shifu* for "master." It was disconcerting.

"General Tsai is famous for living extremely well. I advise you to turn this car around."

"The general believes that the truest power is exercised invisibly. He prefers to remain behind the scenes." They had pulled up before a large industrial warehouse, next to military-drab Jeeps and Humvees. Without turning around, the engine still running, the driver continued, "Do you know the story of the great eighteenth-century Emperor Qian Xing? He believed it was important for a ruler to have direct contact with those he ruled, without his subjects knowing. So he traveled throughout China disguised as a commoner."

Realizing what the driver was saying, Bryson jerked his head to the side, for the first time focusing on the driver's face. He cursed himself. The driver *was* General Tsai!

Suddenly the Daimler was surrounded by soldiers, and the general was barking out commands in Toishanese, his regional dialect. The car door opened, and Bryson was hustled out. He was grabbed by both arms, a soldier restraining him on either side.

"*Zhanzhu!* Stand still!" shouted one of the soldiers, training his side-arm at Bryson as he commanded him to keep his hands at his sides. "*Shou fang xia! Bie dong!*"

The general's window electrically rolled down; the general grinned. "It was very interesting speaking with you, Mr. Bryson. Your facility with our language grew stronger the longer we chatted. It makes me wonder what else you may be concealing. Now I suggest you meet your inevitable death with serenity."

Oh, Jesus! His true identity was known! How? And for how long?

His mind raced. Who could have revealed his true identity? More to the point, who *knew* about the Hesketh-Haywood ruse? Who knew he was coming to Shenzhen? Not Yuri Tarnapolsky. Then who?

Photographs of his face had been faxed, connections made. But it made no *sense!* There had to be someone close to the general who recognized his face, was able to penetrate the facade of the English high-end fence. Someone who knew him; no other explanation was logical.

As General Tsai drove off, the Daimler emitting a cloud of exhaust smoke in his face, Bryson was shoved and pulled toward the warehouse entrance. The handgun was still trained on him from behind. He calculated his odds, and they were not good. He would have to free a hand, preferably his right, and grab the vanadium blade from the sheathing of his belt in one rapid, smooth movement. In order to do that, though, he would need to arrange for a diversion, a distraction. For the instructions from the general were clear: he was to meet his "inevitable death." They would not hesitate to fire on him, he was sure, if he made any sudden attempt to break free. He did not want to test their orders.

Then why was he being brought into this warehouse? He looked around, seeing the immensity of the cavernous facility, clearly intended for the delivery and storage of motor freight. At one end was an enormous freight elevator large enough to accommodate a tank or a Humvee. The air was acrid with the smell of motor oil and diesel fuel. Trucks and tanks and other large military vehicles were stored in serried ranks, very close together, across the expanse of the warehouse floor. It looked like the storage area for a prosperous, high-volume car or truck dealership, though the concrete walls and floors were grimy with spilled motor oil and the residue of exhaust fumes.

What was going on? Why was he being brought here, when they could just as easily have executed him outside, where there were no nonmilitary witnesses?

And then he realized why.

His eyes were riveted on the man who stood in front of him. A man who was armed to the teeth. A man he knew.

A man named Ang Wu.

One of the few adversaries he'd ever encountered whom he'd have to describe as physically intimidating on every level. Ang Wu, a renegade officer in the Chinese Army, attached to Bomtec, the trading arm of the PLA. Ang Wu had been the local PLA representative in Sri Lanka; the Chinese had been shipping arms to both sides of the conflict, sowing dissent and suspicion, vending the highly flammable fuel for the region's smoldering resentments. Outside Colombo, Bryson and the ad hoc band of commandos he'd assembled for the task had headed off a lethal caravan of munitions under Ang Wu's direct control. In an exchange of gunfire, Bryson had shot Ang Wu in the gut, taking him down. His enemy was helicoptered out, reportedly back to Beijing.

But had there been more to the incident, an underlying meaning, an unexplained plan in which he had been merely a pawn? What *really* lay behind the exercise?

Now, Ang Wu stood before Bryson, a Chinese AK-47 machine gun hanging from his shoulders on a diagonal nylon sling. On each hip was holstered a handgun. Draped around his waist like a belt were bandoliers of machine-gun rounds, and sheathed at his side and ankles were gleaming knives.

The grip on each of Bryson's shoulders tightened. He could not free his hand to grab his belt, at least not without being shot down in the interim. *Oh, God!*

His old nemesis looked happy. "So many ways to die," Ang Wu said. "I always knew we would meet again. For a long time I am looking forward to our reunion." With a fluid motion he unholstered one of the handguns, a Chinese-made semiautomatic, hefting it, seemingly enjoying its solidity, its power to extinguish life. "This is General Tsai's gift to me, his generous reward for my years of service. A simple gift: that *I* get to kill you myself. It will be very—how do you say—up close and personal."

There was a glacial smile, an array of very white teeth. "Ten years ago in Colombo, you took my spleen—did you know that? So we start with that first. Your spleen."

In his mind, the enormous warehouse had collapsed into a very small space, a narrow tunnel, with Bryson at one end and Ang Wu at the other. There was nothing else but his adversary. Bryson took a slow, deep breath. "It hardly seems a fair fight," he said with a forced, artificial calm.

The Chinese assassin smiled and, extending his arm, aimed the pistol at the lower left region of Bryson's torso. As his enemy thumbed the safety, Bryson suddenly lurched forward and twisted his body in an attempt to dislodge himself from his captors' grips, and then—

There was a small coughing noise, more like a spit, and a tiny red hole, like the beginning of a teardrop, appeared in the very center of Ang Wu's broad forehead. He slid to the floor very gently, like a drunk passing out.

"*Aiya!*" screamed one of the guards, whirling around, just in time to catch a second silenced round in his head as well. The second guard shrieked, reached for his weapon, then abruptly crumpled to the ground, the side of his head blown away.

Suddenly free, Bryson flung himself to the floor, at the same time spinning around and looking up. On a steel catwalk twenty feet above, a tall, portly man in a navy-blue business suit stepped from behind a concrete pillar. In his hand was a .357 Magnum, a long perforated cylinder attached to its barrel, a wisp of cordite curling from its end. The man's face was momentarily in shadow, but Bryson would know the heavy tread anywhere.

The portly man tossed the Magnum high into the air toward Bryson. "Catch," he said.

Bryson, thunderstruck, grabbed the weapon as it dropped.

"Glad to see your skills haven't gone completely rusty," said Ted Waller as he began descending a steep set of steps. He gave Bryson a look of what could be mistaken for amusement; he sounded out of breath. "The hard part's coming up."

CHAPTER
TWENTY-TWO

Senator James Cassidy saw the headline in *The Washington Times*—saw the reference to his wife, her drug arrest, allegations of possible obstruction of justice—and read no more. So it was out, at last, all in the open—a source of profound personal anguish, something he had desperately sought to keep from the hard, raptor eyes of the media. A buried secret had been unearthed. But how?

Arriving at his office at six in the morning, hours before he usually appeared, he found his top staff already assembled, looking as ashen and enervated as he felt. Roger Fry spoke without preamble. "*The Washington Times* has been gunning for you for years. But we're already had more than a hundred phone calls from all the other media outlets. They're trying to track down your wife, too. This is out-and-out carpet bombing, Jim. I can't control this. None of us can."

"Is it *true?*" asked Mandy Greene, his press secretary. Mandy was forty, and had been with him for the last six years, but stress and anxiety made her seem older than she'd ever looked before. Cassidy couldn't remember her ever losing her composure. But this morning her eyes were red-rimmed.

The senator exchanged glances with his chief of staff; it was clear Roger had told the others nothing. "What exactly are they saying?"

Mandy picked up the newspaper, then tossed it angrily across the office. "That four years ago your wife was arrested for buying heroin. That you made phone calls, called in favors, and had the charges dropped, the arrest expunged. 'Obstruction of justice' is the phrase they're bandying about."

Senator Cassidy nodded, wordlessly. He sat down in his large leather office chair and turned away from his staffers for a moment, looking out the window into the gray light of a cloudy Washington morning. There'd been phone calls from the reporter yesterday, calls both for him and for his wife, Claire, but they went unanswered. He'd had a bad feeling about it, had slept little.

Claire was at their family home in Wayland, Massachusetts. She had her problems; many politicians' wives did. But he remembered how it started—the minor skiing accident that led to back surgery, the fused vertebrae, the Percodans she'd been given for the operative pain. Soon she started to crave the narcotic for more than the cessation of pain. The doctors wouldn't renew her prescription. They referred her to a "pain management" group, which specialized in counseling. But the narcotics had introduced Claire to a kind of sweet oblivion, a place protected from the stresses and strains of public life, from a private life that didn't provide the comfort she required. He could blame himself for that—for not having been there, by her side, when she needed him. He'd come to understand how inimical his world was to her. It was a world that, ultimately, relegated her to the sidelines, and Claire, so beautiful, so accomplished, so loving, had not been raised to sit out life on the bleachers. For Cassidy, there were too many Beltway engagements, too many colleagues to romance and inveigle and bully and cajole into doing the right thing. And Claire was lonely; she experienced a pain that was not merely physical. He never really knew which was the real injury, the isolation or the accident, but he'd come to suspect that the spiral of depression and dependency to which she'd succumbed had merely been precipitated by her hospitalization.

Desperate after she could no longer obtain her prescription narcotics, desperate for a form of relief she knew was fleeting yet somehow seemed to make things endurable, she went to a corridor park near Eighth and H Streets in Washington and tried to buy a quantity of street heroin. The man she met there was encouraging, sympathetic, made it easy. He gave her two small glassine bags of the stuff. She paid him with crisp large bills freshly dispensed from an ATM.

And then he flashed a badge and took her down to the station. When the precinct captain discovered who she was, he called the assistant D.A., Henry Kaminer, at home. And Henry Kaminer called his law-school class-mate Jim Cassidy, who happened to be serving as the chairman of the Senate Judiciary Committee. That's how he found out. Cassidy remembered the phone call, the hesitance, the awkward small talk that preceded the shattering revelation. It was among the worst moments of his life.

Claire's delicate, drawn face filled his mind, and the words of a poem he'd once read echoed in his mind: *not waving but drowning*. How could he have been so blind to what was happening in his own household, his own marriage? Could a public life make a man so out of touch with his private one? Yet there was Claire: *not waving but drowning*.

Cassidy turned around to face his staff. "She wasn't a felon," he said stonily. "She needed *help*, damn it. She needed treatment. And she got it. Six months in rehab. Discreetly, quietly. Nobody needed to know. She didn't want the pitying glances, the knowing looks. The special scrutiny that comes with being a senator's wife."

"But your career . . ." Greene began.

"My goddamn *career* was what drove her to it in the *first* place! Claire had dreams, too, you know. Dreams of having a real family, with kids and a father who loved them and her, who made his wife and kids his first and last priority, the way a man should. Dreams of having a *normal life*—it probably didn't seem too much to ask. She wanted a *home*, that was all. She gave up her dreams so I could be—what did *The Wall Street Journal* call me last year?—the 'Polonius of the Potomac.'" Bitterness entered his voice.

"But how could she have jeopardized everything you'd worked for, everything you'd *both* worked for?" Mandy Greene could not conceal the flare of anger and frustration.

Cassidy shook his head slowly. "Claire was in agony, knowing that everyone would look at her as the woman who might have destroyed a senator's career. You'll never understand the sort of hell she went through. But she went *through* it; in a sense, we both did. And damn it, we came out the other side! Until now. Until this." He looked over at the receptionist's twelve-line telephone, all brightly lit and ringing nonstop in an electronic purr. "*How*, Roger? How did they find out?"

"I'm still not sure," Roger said. "But what they've got is incredibly detailed. An electronic record of the arrest record, somehow retrieved despite the fact that it was officially expunged. Claire's sizable cash withdrawal the evening in question. Municipal phone exchange records, itemizing a flurry of phone calls made between your home and Henry Kaminer's on the night of the arrest. More calls between Kaminer's private line and the precinct captain. Phone logs between the arresting officer and the station house. Even the electronic records of the payments you made to Silver Lakes for her rehabilitation."

Cassidy looked grim, but forced a wry grin. "No one person could have leaked all that. The most private, personal records have been breached. It's what I was warning about, I suppose. The surveillance society."

"Well, that's not how it's going to play," Mandy Greene said brusquely, regaining her air of professionalism at last. "It's going to look as if you were campaigning for privacy because of the skeletons in your *own* closet. You know that better than anyone."

Roger Fry started pacing around the office. "It's bad, Jim, I'm not going to minimize it. But I honestly think we can ride this thing out. It'll get worse before it gets better, but the people in Massachusetts know you're a good man, and your colleagues, whether they like you or not, know you're a good man. Time is the great healer, in politics as in everything else."

"I don't intend to find out, Rog," Cassidy said, gazing out the window again.

"I know it looks bad now," Fry said. "They'll try to crucify you. But you're strong. You'll show them."

"You don't understand, do you?" Cassidy spoke severely but not unkindly. "It isn't about me. It's about Claire. The first sentence of every news story refers to Claire Cassidy, the wife of Senator James Cassidy. That may continue for days, weeks, who the hell knows? I cannot subject her to this. I cannot put her *through* this. She will not survive it. And there's only one way to take this off the table: There's only one way to take this off the front pages and the talk shows and the news hours and the gossip columns." He shook his head, speaking in the mock-stentorian tones of a newsreel reader: "*Senator Cassidy braces for Senate investigation, Senator Cassidy fights to keep his seat, Senator Cassidy denies wrongdoing, Senator Cassidy's disgrace, did judiciary chair abuse office? Senator married to junkie.* Now, that's page-one news, and it can go on and on and on. *Senator Cassidy resigns in wake of damaging allegations* is a story, yes, but a two-day story. The travails of Jim and Claire Cassidy, private citizens, soon get buried somewhere after the wire reports from Somaliland. Five years ago, I made a solemn promise to my wife that we would put this behind us, whatever it took. Now that promise has come due."

"Jim," Fry said delicately, trying to keep his voice steady, "there's simply too much uncertainty now to make any binding decisions. I beg you to hold off." .

"Uncertainty?" The senator laughed bitterly. "But I've never been more certain of anything in my life." He turned to Mandy Greene. "Mandy, it's time for you to earn your paycheck. You and I are going to draft the press release. *Now.*"

CHAPTER
TWENTY-THREE

Bryson froze, barely able to breathe. He was in shock, his mind numb. It was as if a bolt of lightning had streaked down from the sky, searing his consciousness, tearing apart the filaments of reason. He gasped. Everything was madness, illogic; he could barely suppress a scream.

Ted Waller!

Gennady Rosovsky!

The great manipulator, the magician of the dark arts who had turned his life into a great and unthinkable deception.

Bryson grasped the semiautomatic pistol he'd just been thrown, felt it settle into his grip as if it were an appendage, a part of his body. He pointed it back at the man who had just given it to him, realizing that with one well-aimed shot he could kill Ted Waller, and *it would not be enough!*

It would not answer the questions that tormented him, nor would it satisfy his need for vengeance against the liars and manipulators who had made his life a lie. Still, he trained the weapon on Waller, aiming at his old mentor's face, overcome by fury yet roiled with questions, *so many questions!*

What came out, in a tight, strangled voice, was the first question that leaped into the forefront of his mind. "Who the hell *are* you?"

He thumbed back the safety, squeezed the trigger back until the gun clicked into automatic mode. A twitch of his index finger and he could discharge ten rounds into Ted Waller's head, and the liar would topple from his perch on the catwalk to the warehouse floor twenty feet below. Yet Waller, that finest of shots, aimed no weapon back at him. He simply stood there, an obese old man with a cryptic smile on his face.

Waller spoke, his voice echoing in the cavernous space. "Let's play True or False," he said, invoking his old pedagogical exercise.

"Fuck you," said Bryson in cold fury, his voice trembling with banked rage. "Your real name is Gennady Rosovsky."

"True," Waller replied, his face impassive.

"You attended the Moscow Institute of Foreign Languages."

"True." A smile flickered. *"Pravil'no. Otlichno."* That's correct. Excellent.

"You're GRU."

"True-ish. To be accurate, the verb tense is past. I *was*."

Bryson raised his voice until he was shouting. "And it was all *horseshit*, all that *shit* you told me about how we were saving the world! When all the time you were working for the other side!"

"False," said Waller, his voice clear and loud.

"Enough lies, you son of a bitch! *Enough lies!*"

"True."

"Goddamn you to hell, I don't know what the hell you're doing here—"

"At the risk of sounding like General Tsai: when the student is ready, the teacher appears."

"I don't have time for your Buddhist bullshit!" he thundered.

Bryson heard the footfalls, the clanking of weaponry, and he spun around. A pair of green-uniformed guards had entered the warehouse, carbines at the ready. Bryson squeezed off several shots, and at the same instant he heard the explosion of gunfire coming from above and behind, from the direction of Waller. The two guards were hit; they tumbled forward, sprawling to the ground. Bryson dove to the floor, atop Ang Wu's body, and he turned over the limp body, grabbed the dead assassin's submachine gun, yanking the sling from around his neck, gripping it in both hands and angling it upward as he dropped Waller's gun. He expected to see another set of guards, but there was none.

Then he tugged the handgun from Ang Wu's hand and shoved it into the front pocket of his ridiculous Hesketh-Haywood suit. Ang Wu had strapped hunting knives to each ankle; Bryson grabbed each, knife and scabbard together, and carefully tucked each one under his belt. His belt! He suddenly remembered the aluminum-vanadium blade—but now he had weaponry that was far more effective.

"This way!" called Waller, turning around and disappearing into the dim recesses of the concrete-walled balcony. "Building's surrounded."

"Where the hell are you going?" shouted Bryson.

"Some of us have done our homework. Come *on*, Nick!"

What choice was there? Whoever, *whatever* Ted Waller actually was, he was surely right: the warehouse was surrounded by PLA guards; if there was another exit at the ground level, as there almost certainly was, it would simply lead him into the ranks of his enemy. Of his *immediate* enemy. Waller raced up the steel steps just in time to see the fat man disappearing into a large open stairwell, just beyond long rows of parked military vehicles. Weaving between the serried ranks of Jeeps and Humvees and Chinese-manufactured trucks, Bryson ran to the stairwell just in time to see Waller climbing the stairs with speed and agility, the almost balletic grace that had always surprised him. Still, Bryson was fleeter of foot, and he caught up with Waller in a matter of seconds. "To the roof," Waller muttered. "Only way out."

"The *roof*?"

"No alternative. They'll be piling in momentarily, if they aren't already." Waller was short of breath. "One stairwell. One freight elevator, but it's frightfully slow."

By the time they had reached the third-floor landing, they could already hear shouts from below, running footsteps.

"Shit," said Waller. "Now I wish I hadn't had the paté last night. You go ahead."

Bryson shot ahead up the stairway, rounding the wide bends until he reached what was obviously the top floor. He emerged into the night air, the broad expanse of a parking lot, row upon row of tanks and trucks.

What the hell now? What did Waller have in mind? To goddamned *jump* from the top of the building? Leap across the ten- or twenty-foot chasm to the next building?

"Burn the bridges," Waller panted as he came out of the stairwell, and Bryson understood what his ex-mentor was saying. Block the path of their pursuers—but *how?* With *what?* There were no doors to lock or barricade. . . .

There were *vehicles* galore, hundreds, *thousands* of them. He ran to the nearest row, tried the door handle, found it locked. *Shit!* He ran to the next; it was locked as well. There was no *time* for this!

Spying a row of soft-top Jeeps, he ran over to them. Pulling one of Ang Wu's hunting knives from its scabbard, he slashed at the canvas top, then poked his hand in and opened the locked door from inside. The key was in the ignition, which made sense in such a well-guarded warehouse, where separating each vehicle from its key would be a logistical nightmare. Waller was standing clear of the stairwell, a cell phone to his mouth, talking. Bryson keyed the ignition, revved the Jeep's engine, and drove it straight ahead, at top speed, toward the open stairs. As he approached, he saw that the Jeep was too wide to fit through the opening, but that would suit his purposes nicely. With a great crash, the Jeep smashed into the concrete wall, its front end jutting into the opening, then sank a few feet as the front tires dropped down to the second or third step before stopping. He could just manage to force open the driver-side door, and he squeezed out between the Jeep and the abutting concrete wall.

But it would be nothing more than a delay: several men pushing together could dislodge the vehicle. It wasn't enough! Searching the adjacent rows of vehicles, he spotted what he desperately hoped to find: a fifty-five-gallon heavy-gauge-steel fuel drum. Tipping it slowly to the ground, he rolled it toward the Jeep, now obstructing the exit onto the roof. He tugged at the plastic bung-hole seal, turned it, and popped it off. Gasoline began pouring out, forming a puddle on the concrete floor around the vehicle. He rolled it further, tipping the bottom up so that the fuel poured out even faster, a flood of it, torrents running around the Jeep's tires, rivers of gas advancing to the top of the stairwell, then seeping around the Jeep and down the steps. The gasoline odor was overpowering.

In short order he had emptied the drum down the stairwell, just as he heard thundering footsteps, the guards running up the stairs to the roof.

No *time!*

Grabbing his tie, he yanked it free; dropping it into the puddle of fuel until it was soaked, he jammed it into the bung hole of the now-empty fuel drum. It was empty of liquid fuel, but full of gasoline vapor — or, more precisely, a mix of air and gasoline vapor. The proportions might not be ideal, but he knew from long experience that it would do. He took out Giles Hesketh-Haywood's brass lighter and touched the flame to the improvised fuse. The flame roared to life, and Bryson tossed the steel drum over the Jeep and down into the stairwell, then jumped backward and ran as fast as he could.

The explosion was immense, deafeningly loud. The entire stairwell had become a fireball, a roaring yellow inferno. Waller, seeing what he had done, raced across the rooftop as well. In a few seconds, there came another, fantastically loud explosion as the Jeep's fuel tank was ignited. The flames were dazzlingly bright, painful to look at: rolling, shimmering waves of fire, now billowing clouds of black smoke. Bryson came to a halt when he was halfway across the roof, and Waller loped up to him, flushed and sweat-soaked.

"Nicely done," Waller said, looking up at the sky. From the stairwell there came loud, agonized screams, but in a moment they were blotted out by a louder noise, a thundering racket from overhead: the sound of helicopter rotor blades. An armored helicopter, painted green with camouflage spots, roared directly above, hovering into place over a clearing free of vehicles, and slowly descended to the roof.

Bryson gasped. "What the *hell* —?"

The helicopter was an AH-64 Apache, clearly marked as U.S. Army, painted with an official army tail code.

Waller ran toward it, instinctively ducking his head though there was no need to do so. Bryson hesitated for just a moment before he, too, ran toward the mammoth helicopter. The pilot was clad in U.S. Army fatigues. How could it be? If the Directorate was GRU, how had Waller arranged for a U.S. Army combat helicopter?

As he clambered on, he saw Waller spin around, looking past Bryson with alarm. Waller cried out, said something that Bryson could not make out. Bryson turned, saw the dozens of PLA soldiers pouring out of the freight elevator no more than a hundred feet away, on the opposite side of the roof from the inferno that had been the stairwell. He clambered into the helicopter and suddenly felt an explosion of pain in his back, a crushing blow to the right side of his ribcage. He had been struck! The pain was immense, inconceivable. He screamed; his legs buckled, and Waller grabbed him by the arm and pulled him into the chopper as it lifted into the air. As they rose, he could see the massed troops below, the amber blaze, the billows of sooty black smoke.

Bryson had been shot before, a number of times, but this was worse than anything he had experienced earlier. The pain grew instead of subsiding; a nerve had been struck. He was losing volumes of blood, he was sure of it. As if from far away he could hear Waller saying, "... a U.S. Army chopper, they won't dare try to blast us out of the sky ... international incident, and General Tsai isn't so foolish as to ..."

Waller's voice was fading in and out, like a radio with poor reception. He felt ice-cold one moment, then feverishly hot the next.

He heard "... okay there, Nicky? ..."

And: "... first-aid kit but there's an infirmary in the Hong Kong airport ... long flight and I don't want to delay ..."

And then: "... the eighteenth-century physicians might have been on to something, you know, Nicky. It's probably good to be bled from time to time...."

He passed in and out of consciousness, through a kaleidoscope of images. There was a landing on a helipad somewhere; he was helped onto a stretcher.

He was brought into a modern building, hurried down a long hallway. A white-coated female nurse or doctor attended to him, stripping him to the waist, stitching the wound ... the flare-up of pain, astonishing and white-hot, followed by the steep and rapid descent into the darkness of a deep, drugged sleep.

"Truth? I just want to nail the guy." Adam Parker was steamed and didn't mind if Joel Tannenbaum, his longtime attorney, knew it. The two were meeting for lunch, as they did every month or so, at Patroon, an upscale, beef-and-claret restaurant on East Forty-seventh Street. The walls were paneled in dark wood and festooned with Kips engravings. Parker had reserved a private room where the two men could smoke Romeo y Juliets with their martinis. Parker prided himself on his physical condition, but whenever he was in Manhattan, he gravitated toward places like this one, redolent of a bygone Establishment and its venial excesses.

Tannenbaum tucked into his grilled veal chop. He'd been on the Law Review at Columbia, ran the corporate litigation department at Swarthmore & Barthelme, but beneath his high-powered credentials and hightoned affiliations, he was a street fighter, a scrappy kid who'd grown up in the Bronx and always gave as good as he got. "Guys like that don't like being nailed. They eat guys like you as an after-dinner mint. Sorry, Adam. I'm not going to start lying to you at this late date. You know the old joke about the mouse trying to screw an elephant? Trust me, you don't want to climb up Jumbo's back."

"Give me a break," Parker said. "We've made mischief before, you and me. I'm just asking you to file a few papers. An injunction."

"Saying what?"

"Enjoin them from commingling data from InfoMed with those other informational resources—we've got all these confidentiality agreements that have got to be honored. Charge that we've got prima facie evidence that they're conducting themselves in violation of these covenants as entered and agreed upon blah blah blah."

"Adam, you've got *bubkes*."

"Sure, yeah, but I just want to tie them up. I don't want to make it easy on them. They think they can swallow me in one easy gulp, and I want to give 'em a hairball they won't forget."

"Jumbo's not going to notice. They've got army battalions of lawyers on staff. They'll have it thrown out in two minutes."

"Nothing involving the law takes two minutes."

"Five."

"I'll take what I can get. Thing is, I'm not going to go quietly."

"Am I supposed to be moved by your poeticism?"

"Given the size of your retainer, yes." Parker laughed ruefully.

"Adam, I've known you for, what, fifteen years? You were my best man. . . ."

"Marriage lasted eight months. I should have asked for my present back."

"Believe me, some people did." Tannenbaum took a careful sip of his martini.

"You were saying."

"Adam, you're an asshole, a prick, an arrogant, hypercompetitive, know-it-all son of a bitch without a trace of humility or any sense of your own limitations. That's probably why you've done so well for yourself. But this time? For once in your life, you're out of your league."

"Screw you."

"I'm a lawyer. I screw other people." Tannenbaum shrugged. "All I'm saying is, punch your own weight, Adam."

"That what they taught you at Columbia Law School?"

"If only they had. Look, you don't need me for this. You're here because you want my advice. So hear what I'm trying to tell you. Every law firm that's worth a damn has got some sort of relationship with Systematix or one of its affiliates. Look around you and what do you see? Expense-account lunches on every four-top. A sizable portion of which is ultimately defrayed by everybody's favorite client, vendor, or customer: Systematix."

"They think they're the goddamn Standard Oil of information."

"Don't even reach for historical analogies. Systematix makes Standard Oil look like the Little Pie Company. But does anybody make trouble for them? It's like you always say—life isn't fair. Fact is, the Department of Justice acts like their wholly owned subsidiary. That company's got its tentacles everywhere."

"You're shitting me."

"I swear on my mother's grave."

"Your mother lives in Flatbush."

"My point remains. They bought your company. You took their money. Now you're acting like a dog in the manger. Listen to yourself."

"No, you listen to *me*. They're going to be sorry they fucked with Adam Parker. If you won't do the papers, I'll find somebody who will. Sure, I took the money, but I didn't exactly have a choice. It was a hostile take-over."

"Adam. You really don't want to mess with these people. You know me. Not a lot scares me in this life. But this . . . well, trust me when I say it isn't business as usual. They follow their own rules."

Parker finished the martini and signaled for another. "I may be an asshole, and I may be an arrogant son of a bitch, but I am not a patsy," he said, undeterred. "Tell you one thing. Those Systematix drones are going to remember my name."

"We have your usual room ready for you, Mr. Parker," the concierge said as soon as Parker appeared at the St. Moritz that evening. The concierge knew Parker liked the assurance, liked knowing that they'd made a note of his usual preferences.

But on his infrequent visits to Manhattan, Adam Parker also liked to indulge in some unsual preferences indeed. That morning, he'd made a phone call to Madame Sevigny, as she styled herself, who'd promised "two *jeunes filles*, our very finest." Madame Sevigny advertised in no publication; all her clients—they were mostly men of great wealth and power who lived in other parts of the country—had to have been properly introduced to her. For her part, she guaranteed absolute discretion. Her girls knew that a lapse of discretion was more than their lives were worth. They also knew that if they abided by Madame Sevigny's exacting rules, they could put away a sizable nest egg in just a couple of years. Madame Sevigny had a physician on retainer who conducted regular blood tests and pelvic examinations of the *jeunes filles*, ensuring that their health and hygiene were beyond reproach. All of them maintained exercise schedules and dietary regimens that would put a professional gymnast to shame, and before they kept their appointments, Madame Sevigny conducted her own private inspections. As she deemed necessary, eyebrows would be tweezed, skin exfoliated and moisturized, feet pumiced, eyelashes tinted, legs waxed, nails filed; every bodily crevice would be irrigated and perfumed. "It is so difficult to be a natural beauty," Madame Sevigny would sigh, as she gave her *jeunes filles* a final inspection.

At ten P.M. precisely, a phone call from the St. Moritz lobby announced the girls' arrival. Parker, lounging in his opulently appointed suite in a white terrycloth bathrobe, felt a sensation of warmth rise within him. All this stress he'd been under since the Systematix takeover—*God*, but he needed this. It had been too long. He was always quite precise in his instructions to Madame Sevigny—as the old semiconductor plutocrat who first sized him up and told him about Madame's special services had explained, there was no point in beating around the bush with Madame S. What he had in store this evening was the sort of thing that his wife—a horsey, *wholesome* woman—simply couldn't be expected to understand. It wouldn't have surprised him, though, if the semiconductor mogul understood something of his pleasures.

The knock on the door came minutes later.

"My name is Yvette," the striking, statuesque brunette said breathily.

"And my name is Eva," the lithesome blonde said. They closed the door behind themselves. "You like?"

Parker grinned widely. "Very much," he said. "But I thought Madame Sevigny said it would be Yvette and Erica."

"Erica took ill," Eva said. "She sent me instead and asked me to send her regrets. We are like sisters. I think maybe you will not be disappointed."

"I'm sure I won't," Parker said, eyeing with dry-mouthed anticipation the flat, gray briefcase Yvette carried. "Can I get you girls anything?"

The two girls exchanged glances and shook their heads. "We begin, *allons-y?*" Yvette said.

"Please," Parker said.

An hour later, Parker was bound to the brass bedposts with black silk scarves, moaning with pleasure as the two girls took turns spanking and stroking his reddened flesh. They were expert; every time he came too near to climaxing, they would move their attentions elsewhere, massaging his arms and chest with fingers that were as soft and as hard as anything he could image. Yvette now caressed his body with her soft breast and moist crotch as Eva readied the hot wax.

The fragrant beeswax dripped on his body with intensely erotic heat, in equal measure painful and pleasurable. "Yes," he panted, nearly delirious. "Yes." His torso was laced with sweat.

Finally, Yvette mounted him, taking his manhood into herself, enveloping him in her warmth. The silk bonds had been loosened enough to allow him to sit part of the way up, and now Eva clasped his chest from behind. Her fingers massaged his shoulders, and now his throat.

"And, I think, a final pleasure for you," Eva whispered in his ear. He barely saw a glint of the razor-sharp wire before she had looped it around his neck.

"Oh God," he groaned before the wire sliced through cartilage, fascia, and vessels, subtending his carotid arteries, trachea, and esophagus, and he spoke no more.

Yvette, her eyes closed, lost now in her own pleasure, noticed first the waning of turgor within her. Her eyes opened, and she saw the gentleman's head slumped forward, and the other girl, the girl who called herself Eva, holding a shiny metal loop. Was this some new plaything?

"And now, I think, it is your turn," Eva said breathily, and encircled Yvette's neck with the shiny wire. Only then did Yvette notice the blood around the gentleman's neck, like a bright red cravat, and just moments later she was conscious of absolutely nothing at all.

CHAPTER TWENTY-FOUR

He awoke slowly, aching all over, his head throbbing. He was sitting in a recliner seat in a small, luxurious executive jet, a blanket over him, a fluffy pillow behind his head. The windows were black; the noise and vibration indicated that they were in flight. The cabin was empty except for two other passengers. A fortyish man in a navy-blue flight-attendant's uniform, blond crew cut, dozed in shadows at the rear of the cabin. And seated in a wide leather seat across the aisle from Bryson was Waller, reading a leather-bound volume under a small, bright circle of light.

"*Nu, vot eti vot, tovarishch Rosovsky, dobri vecher,*" Bryson said in Russian. "*Shto vyi chitayete?*" His speech was slurred; he felt drugged.

Waller looked up, gave a slight smile. "I really haven't spoken that beastly language in decades, Nicky. I'm sure I'm quite rusty." He closed his book. "But in answer to your question, I'm rereading Dostoyevsky. *The Brothers K.* Just to confirm my recollection that he's really quite a bad writer. Lurid plotting, heavy-handed moralizing, and prose out of *The Police Gazette.*"

"Where are we?"

"Somewhere over France by now, I imagine."

"If you used chemicals on me, I hope you got whatever you wanted."

"Ah, Nick," Waller exhaled, "I'm sure you believe you have no reason to trust me, but the only chemical you received was a painkiller of some kind. Fortunately there's a half-decent, well-equipped emergency clinic for travelers at Chek Lap Kok. But that's a nasty little bullet wound you sustained. Apparently your second in a matter of weeks, the last being a superficial graze wound in the left shoulder. You always were a quick healer, but you're starting to get a little long in the tooth, you know. It's really a young man's game, like American football. I told you that when I pulled you out five years ago."

"How'd you find me?"

Waller shrugged, settled back in his seat. "We have our sources, both electronic and human. As you well know."

"Pretty audacious to use a U.S. military chopper in foreign airspace."

"Not especially. Unless you really believe Harry Dunne's fabrications about our being some sort of rogue elephant."

"You're claiming it's not true?"

"I'm not claiming anything, Nick."

"You've already admitted you're Russian-born. Gennady Rosovsky, born in Vladivostok. Trained as a GRU sleeper penetration agent, a *paminyatchik*, by the Soviet Union's top spymasters, specialists in the English language, American culture and way of life, right? And a chess prodigy. Yuri Tarnapolsky confirmed all this for me. Even in your youth you had a reputation—some called you the Sorcerer."

"You flatter me."

Bryson gazed at his old mentor, who was now stretching his legs, his hands interlaced behind his neck. Waller—that was how he knew him, inasmuch as he *did* know him—looked supremely comfortable.

"Somewhere in the back of my mind," Waller went on, "I always knew there was the remote, theoretical chance that my GRU file might somehow, someday, make its way out of a safe in cold storage to U.S. intelligence. The way a long-buried corpse might wash up from its grave in a flood. But who'd ever have predicted it, really? Not even us. Everyone mocks the CIA for not anticipating the sudden collapse of the Soviet

Union, and I'm hardly no defender of theirs, but I always thought that unfair—even *Gorbachev* didn't see it coming, for God's sake."

"Aren't you dodging the great unasked question here?"

"Why not ask it?"

"Are you a *paminyatchik*, a GRU sleeper, or not?"

"'Am I now or have I ever been,' to paraphrase the buffoon Senator McCarthy? I *was*; I am *not*. Is that unambiguous enough?"

"Unambiguous, but vague."

"I defected in place."

"To our side."

"Naturally. I was an illegal here seeking to make it legal."

"When?"

"Nineteen fifty-six. I had arrived in 1949 as a boy of fourteen, when legends were plentiful and not thoroughly vetted. By the midfifties I saw the light and terminated my ties to Moscow. By then I'd seen, and heard, enough of Comrade Stalin to shatter whatever youthful illusions I'd once had about the radiant future of a communist world. After the Cuban Missile Crisis, I wasn't alone in realizing the idiocies, the follies, the essential flabbiness of the CIA. That was when I and Jim Angleton and a few others founded the Directorate."

Bryson shook his head, mulling. "A GRU sleeper defects in place, there are consequences. His handlers in Moscow will be greatly displeased, retaliation threatened and inevitably carried out. Yet you're maintaining that your true identity remained cloaked for *decades*. I find it hard to believe."

"Completely understandable. But do you imagine I simply sent them a Dear Ivan letter—'Oh, and you can stop sending those paychecks, because I'm switching sides'? Not bloody likely. I took some care with it, as you can imagine. My controller was a greedy bastard and not a little careless. He liked to live well and supported his habit by double-dipping and feeding from the expense-account trough a little too often."

"Translation: he embezzled."

"Indeed. In those days, that was grounds for either the gulag or a bullet in the neck in the Lubyanka courtyard. And with what I knew, and could pretend to know, I forced him to write me off the books. I disappear, he stays alive, everyone goes home happy."

"Then Harry Dunne's story *wasn't* a fabrication, was it?"

"Not one hundred percent, no. An ingenious pastiche of truths and half-truths and outright falsehoods. Like the very best lies."

"What part of it isn't true?"

"What did he tell you?"

Bryson's heart began to pound slowly. His adrenaline surged, combating whatever narcotic was in his bloodstream. "That the Directorate was founded in the early 1960s by a small cell of fanatics at the GRU, or maybe VKR, brilliant strategists known as the *Shakhmatisti*, the chess players. Inspired by the classic Russian deception operation, the Trust, from the twenties. A penetration operation on American soil, the most brazen intelligence ruse of the twentieth century, far eclipsing the ambitions of the Trust. Controlled by a tight inner circle of directors, the Consortium, with all officers and staff outside that circle deluded into the belief that they were working for a maximum-security American intelligence unit—and constrained by zealous compartmentalization and gradated code-word secrecy from revealing anything, to anyone, about their work."

Waller smiled, his eyes closed.

"And according to Dunne, the true origins of the Directorate in Moscow would never have been discovered were it not for the collapse of the Soviet Union. Which resulted in the dissemination of a few stray documents inadvertently revealing code-name operations that didn't fit into known KGB or GRU structures; a contact name here and there; then the entirety confirmed by midlevel defectors."

Waller's grin broadened. He opened his eyes. "You almost have *me* convinced, Nick. Alas, Harry Dunne is in the wrong line of work. He should have written fiction; he has a wild imagination. His tale is at once outlandish and quite persuasive."

"What part of it is fiction?"

"Where do I begin?" Waller sighed petulantly.

"How about with the goddamned *truth?*" exploded Bryson, unable to tolerate his coyness any longer. "If you even *know* it anymore! How about starting with my *parents?*"

"What about them?"

"*I spoke with Felicia Munroe, Ted!* My parents were *murdered* by you goddamned fanatics! To put me under the direct control of Pete Munroe, to bring me into the Directorate."

"By murdering your parents? Come *on*, Nicky!"

"You're denying that Pete Munroe was secretly Russian-born, like you? Felicia as good as confirmed for me Harry Dunne's version of the 'accident' that ended their lives."

"Which was *what*, precisely?"

"That my 'Uncle Pete' did it—that he was wracked with guilt afterward."

"The poor old woman is senile, Nicky. Who's to say what the hell she meant?"

"You're not going to dismiss it that easily, Ted. She said that Pete talked Russian in his sleep. Dunne said that Pete Munroe's actual name was Pyotr Aksyonov."

"He's right."

"Oh *Jesus!*"

"He *was* Russian-born, Nick. I recruited him. Fanatically anticommunist. His family disappeared in the purges of the nineteen-thirties. *But he didn't kill your parents.*"

"Then who did?"

"They weren't killed, for God's sake. *Listen* to me." Waller studied the circular pool of light on his tray-table. "There are things I never told you, for reasons of compartmentalization—things I thought it better for you not to know—but I'm sure you already know the basic contours. The Directorate is, and was, a supranational agency established by a small cadre of enlightened members of U.S. and British intelligence, as well as a few high-level Soviet defectors whose bona fides were beyond reproach, yours truly included."

"When?"

"In nineteen-sixty-two, shortly after the Bay of Pigs debacle. We were determined to see that such a disgrace never happened again. It was my idea initially, if you'll allow me a brief immodesty, but my dear friend James Jesus Angleton of the CIA was my earliest and most vociferous supporter. He felt, as did I, that American intelligence was being eviscerated by amateurs and bumblers—the so-called Old Boys, really a bunch of overprivileged Ivy League frat boys—patriotic perhaps, but laughably arrogant, convinced they knew what they were doing. A Wall Street clique who basically ceded Eastern Europe to Stalin out of a simple failure of nerve. A bunch of elitist corporate lawyers who lacked the *cojones* to do things the way they had to be done, who lacked the necessary ruthlessness. Who didn't *understand* Moscow as I did.

"Remember, not long after the Bay of Pigs, a KGB officer named Anatoly Golitsyn defected and laid it all out for Angleton in a series of debriefings—how the CIA was riddled with moles—penetrated, corrupted, to its very core. And the less said about the British, with Kim Philby and his ilk, the better. Well, that about did it for Angleton. He not only provided the Directorate's initial black-box funding and set up the covert funding channels, but he also approved the basic, cellular organizational structure. He helped me devise the box-within-a-box strategy, the decentralization and internal segmentation, as a way of maintaining maximum secrecy. He emphasized the necessity of keeping our very *existence* unknown from all but the heads of the governments we served. Only by cloaking its very existence could this new organization hope to escape the mire of penetration, disinformation, and politics to which spy agencies on both sides of the Cold War had been held hostage."

"You don't expect me to believe that Harry Dunne was so far off base, so *misinformed* about the Directorate's true origins."

"Absolutely not. He wasn't misinformed. Harry Dunne was a man on a mission. He constructed a straw man. An *argumentum ad logicam*, a brilliant caricature, plausible-sounding and laced with shards of the truth. An imaginary garden filled with real toads, as it were."

"To what end?"

"To point you toward us, urge you to go after us and, if possible, destroy us."

"*To what end?*"

Waller sighed in exasperation, but before he could speak, Bryson went on: "Are you going to sit there and *deny* that you tried to have me terminated?"

Waller shook his head slowly, almost sadly. "There are others I might try to deceive, Nicky. You are far too clever."

"In the parking garage in Washington, after I went to K Street and found headquarters gone. *You* were behind that."

"Yes, that was our hire. It's not easy to find top-notch talent these days. Why did it not surprise me that you bested the fellow?"

But Bryson, not so easily mollified, stared at him furiously. "You ordered a sanction on me because you were afraid I'd expose the *truth!*"

"Actually, no. We were alarmed by your behavior. All external signs seemed to indicate that you'd gone bad, that you'd joined forces with Harry Dunne and had turned against your old employers. Who can fathom the human heart? Were you embittered by your early termination? Did Dunne turn your head with his lies? We couldn't know, and so we had to take protective measures. You knew far too much about us. Even despite all the compartmentalization, you knew *far* too much. Yes, a beyond-salvage order went out."

"*Christ!*"

"Yet all the while I remained skeptical. I know you better than perhaps anyone, and I was unwilling to accept the dossier, the analysts' assessments, at least without further corroboration. So I deployed one of our finest new recruits to cover you on Calacanis's ship, monitor your activities until I could be sure one way or the other. I handpicked her to watch you, check up on you, report back."

"Layla."

Waller nodded once.

"She was assigned as a limpet?"

"Correct."

"That's *horseshit!*" Bryson shouted. "She was far more than a god-damned limpet. She tried to *kill* me in Brussels!"

Bryson watched Waller's face for telltale signs of deception, but of course it was unreadable. "She acted on her own, in contravention to my orders. I'm not denying that, Nick. But you have to consider the chronology."

"This is *pathetic*. You're weaving back and forth, backing and filling, desperately trying to cover the holes in your story!"

"*Listen* to me, please. At least give that much to the man who saved your life. Part of her charge was to watch out for you too, Nick. To presume innocence on your part unless and until we learned otherwise.

When she saw that you were about to be ambushed on Calacanis's ship, she warned you off."

"Then how do you explain *Brussels?*"

"A regrettable impulse on her part. Her intention was essentially a protective one. To protect the Directorate and our mission. When she learned you were about to meet with Richard Lanchester in order to blow apart the Directorate, she tried to talk you out of it. And when you persisted, she panicked; she took matters into her own hands. She assumed there simply wasn't time to contact me for instructions; she had to move at once. It was a bad decision, a miscalculation. It was unfortunate, and impulsive, and she tends to be impulsive. No one is perfect. She's a fine operative, one of the best to come out of Tel Aviv, and she's beautiful. A rare combination. One tends to overlook the faults. She's doing fine, incidentally. Thank you for asking."

Bryson ignored the sarcasm. "Let me get this straight: you're saying she *wasn't* tasked with killing me?"

"As I said, her mission was observation and reporting, protection where needed, not termination. But at Santiago de Compostela it became evident that termination orders had been taken out against you by others. Calacanis had been killed, his security forces decimated; it seemed unlikely to have originated with him, given the rapid sequence of events. I deduced that you were being exploited as a cat's paw; the question was, by whom?"

"Ted, I *saw* some of the agents arrayed against me—I *recognized* them! A blond operative, a dispatch agent from Khartoum. The peasant brothers from Cividale I used in the Vector operation. These were *Directorate hires!*"

"No, Nick. The killers at Santiago de Compostela were freelancers who sell their talent to the highest bidders, not exclusively for us—and they'd been hired to do the job at Santiago precisely *because* they knew your face. Presumably they were told you were a sellout, that you might give up their names. Self-survival is a powerful incentive."

"That and a two-million-dollar bounty on my head."

"Indeed. I mean, for heaven's sakes, you were traveling around the world using an old Directorate legend. I could have rolled you up in a second. Did you seriously assume we didn't have 'John T. Coleridge' in our database?"

"Then who hired them?"

"The possibilities are numerous. You had put out so many feelers by then; you spoke to old KGB sources to verify my true identity. You think they don't talk? Or *sell* information, to be exact, the mercenary bastards?"

"You're not going to argue it was CIA, I hope. Harry Dunne obviously wasn't sending me out to do his dirty work while at the same time ordering me killed."

"Granted. But presumably a team was monitoring the situation on the *Spanish Armada*, and when the vessel was destroyed, a decision was made that you were a hostile."

"A decision made by *whom?* Dunne kept the whole operation off the books, no records maintained, only my 'Jonas Barrett' alias recorded in the Security data banks."

"Expenses, perhaps."

"Buried, encrypted. All requisitions DDCI-need-to-know Priority."

"The place leaks like a sieve, you know that. Always has. That's why we exist."

"Richard Lanchester agreed to see me as soon as I mentioned your true name. He made it clear he knew about the Directorate's origins — as outlined by Harry Dunne. Are you saying Lanchester was lying too?"

"He's a brilliant man, but he's vain, and vain men are easily gulled. Dunne might have debriefed him as artfully as he did you."

"He wanted me to probe further."

"Naturally. As would you, if you were in his position. He must have been a frightened man."

Bryson's head was spinning; he was overcome by vertigo. Too many pieces didn't *fit!* Too much remained unexplained, inconsistent. "Prospero — Jan Vansina — kept asking me whether Elena 'knew' something. What was he talking about?"

"I'm afraid some suspicion fell on Elena at the same time we were wondering about your defection to the enemy. Vansina needed to determine whether she was complicit. I maintained that you'd been false-flagged, and of course I was proven correct."

ROBERT LUDLUM

"And what about the roster of operations you devised or controlled—
Sri Lanka, Peru, Libya, Iraq? Dunne said that they were all secretly designed to defeat American interests abroad—but under such a deep cloak
of secrecy that even the participants didn't see the chess moves because
we were too close to the board."

"Poppycock."

"What about Tunisia? Was Abu not a CIA asset?"

"I don't know everything, Nicky."

"It looks as if your whole elaborate penetration operation, ostensibly
to defeat a coup, was engineered to unmask and neutralize a key CIA
asset. To eliminate an Agency direct feed into a network of Islamic terrorist cells throughout the region—one hand undoing the work of the
other!"

"Twaddle."

"And the Comoros, in 1982—you sent us to foil an attempt by mercenaries from Executive Outcome to take over. But according to Dunne,
they were CIA hires attempting to free British and American hostages.
What's the truth?"

"Check the records. The hostages were only freed later, after our operation. Check the employment records if you can locate them. Unwind
the sequence. These weren't CIA hires, they were underwritten by nationalist elements. Do your homework, my boy."

"*Goddamn you!* I was *there*, you know. And I was on board the *Spanish
Armada*, ostensibly carrying a blueprint of a new-generation Javelin antitank missile as a bargaining chip. Calacanis knew immediately who the
interested buyer would be, and it was *your man!* It was Directorate—
Vance Gifford or whatever his real name is. Calacanis himself confirmed
the pattern of increased acquisition out of Washington."

"We're not Washington-based anymore, Nicky, you know that. We had
to relocate; we were penetrated."

"And why the hell was your operative so interested in acquiring the
blueprint? For your personal *collection*, was that it?"

"Nicky—"

"And why did he arrive on the ship in the company of Jacques Arnaud's man, Jean-Marc Bertrand? Are you pretending you weren't acquiring weapons?"

342

"Gifford was doing his *job*, Nick."

"His job being *what*, exactly? According to Calacanis, the man was on a spending spree."

"In this world, as you know better than most, you don't just inspect the goods without buying. Browsers are quickly detected and dispatched."

"The same way Prospero—Jan Vansina—laundered five billion dollars in Geneva? A penetration ruse?"

"Who told you that—Dunne?"

Bryson didn't reply, but simply stared at his old mentor, his heart pounding. He felt his right ribcage begin to throb; the painkiller had obviously begun to wear off.

Ted Waller went on in a voice rich with sarcasm, "Did he tell you this off-site? Wouldn't talk in his office? Told you he feared wiretaps?"

When Bryson didn't reply, Waller continued. "The deputy director of Central Intelligence doesn't have the power to have his own office swept, Nick?"

"Bugs come in plastic, too. Sweeping won't detect them—nothing will, short of tearing apart the plaster."

Waller snorted softly. "It was a show, Nicky. A goddamned piece of *theater*. An attempt, successful as it turned out, to persuade you that he was the good guy, the forces of darkness arrayed against him—the forces, in this case, being the entire CIA. In which he's the number two." Waller shook his head sadly. "Really."

"I gave him an Agency ID card I took off the body of one of the black-operatives who tried to terminate me outside Chantilly."

"And let me guess. He had the card tested and found it to be fake."

"Wrong."

"Maybe he was unable to turn up any records. He did a Code Sigma, found that it had been assigned to an operator in extremis, and there the trail went cold. He couldn't trace the name."

"That's not exactly far-fetched. Agency extremis operators don't leave tracks, you know that. Dunne admitted to me the CIA wasn't the best agency to investigate the Directorate."

"Ah, and it made you trust him all the more, didn't it. I mean, trust him *personally*."

"You're saying he was trying to have me terminated while at the same time he was directing me to investigate the Directorate's activities? That's not just illogical, that's *insane!*"

"Directing complex field operations is always a shifting calculation. My guess? Once he saw you had survived the attack, he realized you could be reprogrammed, redeployed against another lead. But it's time to return your seat to an upright and locked position, as they say. We're there."

Waller seemed to be speaking from a great distance, and Bryson didn't understand what he meant; he could feel everything receding, and the next thing he knew he was aware of a bright white light. He opened his eyes and saw that he was in a room that was all white and steel. He was lying down in a tightly made bed between heavy linens; his eyes ached from the brightness of the light; his throat was parched and his lips were dry, cracked.

Before him were figures silhouetted against the light, one of them unmistakably Waller, the other much thinner and smaller, presumably a nurse. He heard Waller's rich baritone: ". . . he's coming to even as we speak. Hello there, Nicky."

Bryson grunted, tried to swallow.

"He must be thirsty," came a female voice that was quite familiar. "Can someone get him some water?"

It couldn't be. Bryson blinked, squinted, tried to get the room into focus. He could see Waller's face, then hers.

His heart began hammering. He squinted again; he was sure he was imagining things. He looked again, and then he was sure.

He said, "Is that you, Elena?"

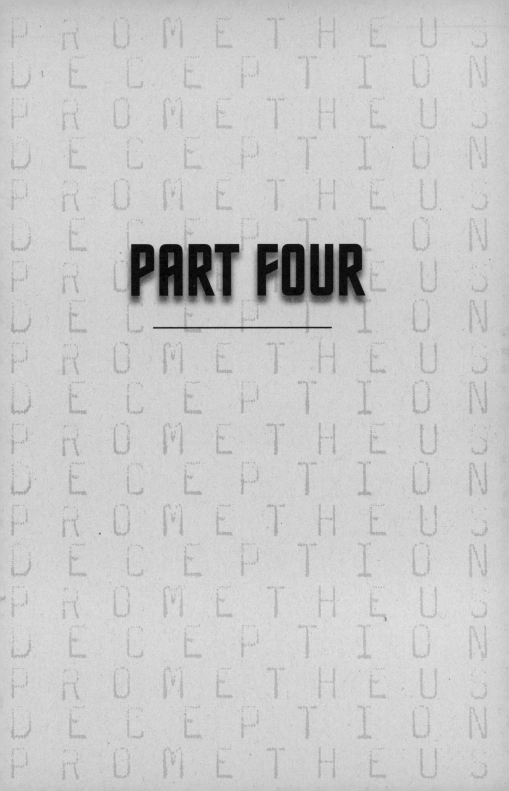

PART FOUR

CHAPTER
TWENTY-FIVE

"Nicholas," she said, coming closer. She came into focus. It was Elena, still ravishingly beautiful, though she had changed: her face had gotten thinner, more angular, which made her eyes seem even larger. She looked wary, even frightened, but her voice was matter-of-fact. "It's been so long. You've aged so."

Bryson nodded, managed to rasp, "Thanks."

Someone handed him a plastic cup of water: a nurse. He took it, gulped it down, handed back the cup. The nurse refilled it and gave it to him again. He drank greedily, gratefully. Elena sat beside the bed, close to him. "We must talk," she said, suddenly urgent.

"Yes," he said. His throat was raw; it hurt to speak. "There's—there's so much to talk about, Elena—I don't know where to begin."

"But there's so little time," she said. Her voice was brusque and businesslike.

There's no time, her voice echoed in his head. There's no time? For five years I've had nothing *but* time, time to ponder, to agonize.

She went on, "We need to know everything you've learned, everything

ROBERT LUDLUM

you have. Any way in to Prometheus. Any way we can break the crypto-graphic perimeter."

He looked at her in astonishment. Was he hearing her right? She was questioning him about cryptography, about something called "Prome-theus" . . . She had disappeared from his life for five years and she wanted to talk about *cryptography?*

"I want to know where you went," Bryson said hoarsely. "*Why* you vanished."

"Nicholas," she said briskly, "you told Ted that you took the key from Jacques Arnaud's encrypted phone. Where is it?"

"I . . . I did? When did I . . . ?"

"On the plane," said Waller. "Have you forgotten? You said you had a disk or a chip, some such thing. You took it, or copied it, from Arnaud's private office—you weren't entirely clear about it. And no, you weren't under the influence of chemicals. Though you were somewhat delirious, I must say."

"Where am I?"

"In a Directorate facility in the Dordogne. France. That IV in your arm is just for rehydration and antibiotics to ward off sepsis from your wounds."

"A Directorate . . ."

"Our headquarters. We've had to move here in order to maintain operational security. Washington was breached; we had to take evasive action, we had to leave the country in order to do our work."

"What do you want with me?"

"We need whatever you have, and we need it immediately," said Elena. "If our calculations are right, we have just a few days, perhaps only *hours.*"

"Before *what?*"

"Before Prometheus takes over," said Waller.

"Who is Prometheus?"

"The question is, *what* is Prometheus, and we don't have the answer. That's why we need the cryptochip."

"*And I want to know what happened!*" thundered Bryson. He gasped; he felt as if his throat would split. "With *you,* Elena! Where you went—*why* you went!"

348

He could see by the set of her jaw that she was determined not to be diverted from her line of questioning. "Nick, let us please talk about these personal matters another time. The time is very short—"

"What *was* I to you?" Bryson said. "Our marriage, our life together—what was that to you? If that's ancient history, if that's the past, you at least owe me an explanation—what happened, why you had to leave!"

"No, Nick—"

"I know it had something to do with Bucharest!"

Her lower lip seemed to be trembling, her eyes brimmed with tears.

"It did, didn't it?" he said in a softer voice. "If you know *anything*, you must know that what I did, I did for you!"

"Nick," she said desperately. "Please. I'm trying to hold myself together here, and you're not helping things."

"What do you think happened in Bucharest? What lies were you told?"

"*Lies?*" she suddenly exploded. "Don't talk to me about lies! You lied to me, you lied straight to my *face!*"

"Excuse me," said Waller. "You two need privacy." He turned and left the room, and then the nurse did too, and they were alone.

Bryson's head ached, his throat was so raw it felt as if it were bleeding inside. But he talked through the pain, desperate to communicate, to arrive at the truth. "Yes, I lied to you," he said. "It was the biggest mistake I ever made. You asked me about my weekend in Barcelona, and I lied. And you know that—you *knew* that. At the *time* you knew that, didn't you?"

She nodded, tears spilling down her cheeks.

"But if you knew I was lying, you must have known *why* I lied! You must have known I went to Bucharest because I loved you."

"I didn't know *what* you did, Nick!" she cried, looking up at him.

He ached for her, for the intimacy they had once shared. He wanted to throw his arms around her, but at the same time he wanted to grab her by the collar, shake the truth out of her. "But you know *now*, don't you?"

"I—I don't know *what* I know, Nick! I was terrified, and I felt so hurt, so horribly betrayed by you—so frightened for my life, for my parents—that I had to disappear. I know how good you are at finding people, so I had to leave without a trace."

"Waller knew where you were all along."

She looked up at the ceiling, and he followed her eyes to a tiny red dot: a video surveillance camera; there was no doubt that if this were a Directorate facility there were cameras throughout. What did that mean, that Waller was likely watching, listening? If he was, then he was; so what?

She was clenching and unclenching her hands. "It was just a few days after you said you were going to Barcelona for the weekend. In·the normal course of my work—processing the 'harvest,' the signals-intercept prod-uct—that I came across a report that a Directorate operative had made an unscheduled appearance in Romania, in Bucharest."

"Oh, *Jesus.*"

"You know, I was just doing my job, and so of course I followed up the lead and found that it was you. I was—I was devastated, because I knew you were supposed to be in Barcelona. I knew this wasn't any cover story: it was such a rare thing for you to have a weekend off, and you had coordinated all your plans in an entirely overt way. And well—you know me, I'm very emotional, I feel things so strongly—I went to see Ted and told him what I had found. *Demanded,* really, that he level with me. He could see at once he was dealing with a distraught wife, a *jealous* wife, and yet he didn't attempt to cover for you. It was a relief yet not a relief. If he had tried to cover for you, I would have been angry, *terribly* angry. Yet the fact that he wasn't trying to do so told me that this was news to him—this information had taken him by surprise. And that was even more of a·worry for me. Even Ted didn't know you were in Bucharest."

Bryson covered his eyes with a hand, shaking his head. Good God, he had been under surveillance the entire time! He had been so thorough in his "dry-cleaning," so careful to shake any tails. How could this have happened? What did this mean?

"Did he investigate?" Bryson asked. "Or have you investigate?"

"Both, I'm sure. I downlinked the photo-reconnaissance, so now I had a photo of you in Bucharest, which somehow made it more concrete, more awfully true. Then a separate and independent source, an agent code-named Titan, corroborated the information and added more. This was the intelligence that nearly did me in. Titan reported that you had

had a secret meeting with Radu Dragan, the head of the ex-Securitate's vengeance squad."

"God, *no!*" Bryson cried out. "You must have thought—since I was being so secretive, you must have thought I was doing something underhanded, something I had to keep hidden from you!"

"Because I knew through Ted that you were meeting with Dragan without Directorate knowledge! You had to be making a deal, one you weren't proud of, one you had to conceal. But I gave you a chance. I asked you one day—asked you point-blank."

"You had never asked me before about anything I did when I wasn't home."

"You could tell how important the answer was to me, I'm sure. Yet you continued to lie! Baldly!"

"Elena, darling, I was protecting you! I didn't want to alarm you, I knew you would object if I'd given you advance notice. If I'd told you after the fact you'd have worried endlessly, you couldn't have *taken* it!"

She shook her head. "I know this now. But then Titan reported that you had cut a deal with Dragan, that you had given up my parents' location in exchange for some larger concession—"

"That was a *lie!*"

"But I didn't *know* that at the time!"

"How could you have thought I was capable of selling them out? How could you have accepted that?"

"Because you had *lied* to me, Nicholas!" she screamed. "You gave me no reason to think otherwise! You *lied!*"

"Dear God, what you must have thought of me."

"I went to Ted and demanded that he get me out of the country. Hide me somewhere, somewhere *safe!* Somewhere you could never track me down. And I wanted my parents moved as well—at once—which was an enormous expense because of the security cordon that was in place. Ted agreed this was for the best. I was wounded to—to the marrow by your betrayal, and most of all I was desperate to protect my parents. Waller moved me here, to the Dordogne facility, and settled Mama and Papa an hour or so from here."

"Waller believed that I'd done this?"

"Waller knew only that you'd lied to him as well, that you were doing something off the books."

"But he never raised it with me, never once mentioned it!"

"Does that surprise you? You know how he keeps things close to the vest. And I begged him not to say a thing to you, not to alert you."

"But don't you know what I *did?*" Bryson shouted. "Don't you *know?* Yes, I *did* make a deal with the sweepers—a deal to protect your parents! I threatened them, I made it clear that if ever anyone so much as laid a finger on your parents, Dragan's entire extended family would be wiped out. That this was personal for me! I knew that only the threat of a Sicilian-style revenge would get his attention."

Now Elena was sobbing. "In the years—the years since—I've wondered. Papa died two years ago, and Mama last year. Without him she had no will to live. Oh, God, Nicholas. I thought you were a monster!"

His arms went up to embrace her, though he could barely sit up. Weeping, she fell forward, collapsing into his arms. She touched the bandaged wound, hit a nerve; the pain almost took off the top of his head. But his arms closed around her, patting her gently, reassuring her. She seemed fragile, her beautiful eyes liquid, bloodshot. "What I did," she moaned. "What I assumed of you, what I assumed you did . . . !"

"Compounded by my failure to trust you, be honest with you. But Elena, this was not just a simple misunderstanding—you were deliberately and systematically misled by this agent code-named Titan. Why? To what *end?*"

"It must be Prometheus. They know we're on to them, closing in on them. And they must have seized upon the circumstance to poison the well, to spread a fog of uncertainty and dissension within our ranks. To set one against another, husband against wife in this case. False reports were filed in order to exploit the vulnerability—to hobble us where they could."

" 'Prometheus' . . . you and Waller both keep mentioning it. But you must know *something*, have some notion as to what it is, its objectives . . ."

Elena caressed his face, looked into his eyes. "How I've missed you, my darling." She sat up, took his hand in hers and squeezed, then slowly she got up off the bed. She began pacing as she spoke, just as she had always done whenever puzzling out a particularly complex problem. It was as if the physical activity, the repetitive motion catalyzed something in her thought processes.

"Prometheus is a name we first encountered only some twenty months ago," she said slowly, distantly. "It appears to refer to some sort of international syndicate, perhaps a cartel, and as best we can make out the Prometheus Group involves a consortium of technology companies and defense contractors, and their agents highly placed in governments around the world."

Bryson nodded. "Jacques Arnaud's vertically integrated defense corporations, General Tsai's PLA-owned defense contractors, Anatoly Prishnikov's extensive holdings throughout the old Soviet Union, the new Russia. Corporate alliances being established on a global scale."

She looked at him sharply, stopped pacing for a moment. "Yes. Those three cardinal among them. But there seem to be many participants, acting in concert."

"Acting *how?* Doing *what?*"

"Corporate acquisitions, mergers, consolidation—all seem to be accelerating."

"Mergers, consolidations in the defense sector?"

"Yes. But with an emphasis on telecommunications and satellites and computers. And it's more, *much* more than the amassing of a corporate empire. Because in the last five months there has been an epidemic of terrorist incidents, from Washington and New York to Geneva and Lille. . . ."

"Prishnikov and Arnaud both knew about Lille in advance," Bryson said suddenly. "I overheard this, saw them discussing Lille a few days before. 'The way will be clear,' they said. 'The outrage will be enormous.' "

" 'The way will be clear,' " she mused aloud. "Defense industry insiders, owners fomenting chaos in order to boost the value of their stock . . ." She shook her head. "No, that doesn't track. The most direct way to increase demand for armaments is to foment *war*, not isolated, individual terrorist attacks. It's one of the theories behind the massive arming that led to World War Two, that international cartels of arms dealers built up the young Nazi Germany knowing that not too far down the line there would be a global war."

ROBERT LUDLUM

"But this is a different era—"

"Nicholas, think this through. Key players in Russia, China, and France—at least, and surely there are others—in a position to pit their nations against one another, sound the drumbeats of coming war, the need to strengthen national defenses. . . . *That's* how it *should* be done."

"There's more than one way to spur calls for 'defense readiness.'"

"But if you hold the levers of power, there must be a good reason why you don't pull them. No, we're not seeing a global arms race. That's not the pattern at all. Separate incidents, that's what we're seeing. Individual acts of terrorism, unclaimed, unattributed. All happening on an accelerating schedule. But *why?*"

"Terrorism is another form of war," Bryson said slowly. "War by other means. A *psychological* war whose intent is to demoralize."

"But a war requires at least two sides."

"The terrorists and those who fight them."

She shook her head. "It still doesn't track. 'Those who fight them'—that's too nebulous."

"Terrorism is a form of theater. It's committed by an actor for an audience."

"So the desired end result is not the destruction itself, but the publicity caused by the destruction."

"Exactly."

"The publicity almost always helps attract attention to some cause, some group. But this recent wave of terrorism had no known authors, no cause or group. So we have to examine the publicity, the news, to see what links them all. What do these terrorist incidents all have in common?"

"That they could have been prevented," said Bryson abruptly.

Elena stopped and turned toward him with a curious smile. "What makes you say that?"

"Go back over the newspaper accounts, the transcripts of the television and radio coverage. Every time, after each incident, a comment appeared in the stories—usually attributed to some unnamed government official—to the effect that had adequate surveillance measures been in place, the tragedy would certainly have been prevented."

354

"Surveillance measures," she repeated.

"The treaty. The International Treaty on Surveillance and Security, which has just been agreed to by most of the countries of the world."

"The treaty creates a sort of international watchdog agency, right? A sort of super-FBI?"

"Right."

"Which would require the investment of billions and billions of dollars in new satellite equipment, police equipment, and the like. Potentially very lucrative for the companies . . . like Arnaud's, Prishnikov's, Tsai's . . . maybe that's it. An international treaty that serves as a mask, a cover for massive buildups in defense. So that we're all armed, protected against terrorists — terrorism being the new, post–Cold War threat to peace. And all the members of the U.N. Security Council have signed it and ratified it by now, isn't that right?"

"All but one. Great Britain. That's supposed to happen any day now. The main agitator there is Lord Miles Parmore."

"Yes, yes. He's a — how do you say, he's a blowhard, but he's been quite effective at organizing support for the treaty. Never underestimate the man who's willing to put himself out there. Remember the Reichstag in 1933."

Bryson shook his head. "That's not how the Prometheans operate. Lord Parmore has been brilliantly effective, but I suspect he's not a brilliant man. I'll bet the controlling intellect is elsewhere. It's what our fearless leader likes to say — 'follow the brawn, look for the brains.' "

"You're saying there are puppetmasters in London directing the Parliamentary debate?"

"Count on it."

"But who? If we could find out . . ."

"I'm going to have to go there, meet with Parmore, question him, dig as deeply as I can."

"But can you go? Are you well enough?"

"If you get these damned tubes out of my arm, I'm fine."

She fell silent for a moment. "Nicholas, normally I'd be the over-protective wife, insisting you stay in bed and get better. But if you honestly feel well enough — time is of the essence — "

"I can go to London. I *want* to go. As soon as we can get a flight there."

"I'll make a call, arrange for them to get the private jet ready for a departure in six hours or so, assuming Ted doesn't need it."

"Good. The airstrip is close."

"A very short drive." She nodded, stopped in midpace. "So now Cassidy makes sense."

"Cassidy? Senator Cassidy?"

"Right."

"What about him? He was forced out of office because of revelations having to do with—what was it, his wife was caught dealing drugs or something?"

"Well, it's a little more complicated than that, but those are the basic outlines of the story. Years ago his wife was addicted to painkillers, and she bought drugs from an undercover police officer. Senator James Cassidy was able to get her police record expunged, then he got her into a treatment program."

"What does that have to do with the treaty?"

"First of all, he was the Senate's leading opponent of the treaty. He saw it as marking the end of individual privacy. In fact, he was the loudest voice in Washington warning of the steady erosion of privacy in the age of the computer. Many commentators saw irony in the fact that a senator so obsessed with privacy would be brought down because of something hidden in his past—they sniggered that he obviously had something to hide, that's why he was so obsessed with privacy."

"There may be something to that."

"That's not the point. The thing is, he's the ninth member of Congress in the last few months to either resign or announce he wasn't going to run again."

"It's a difficult time to be a politician, that's all."

"No question. But you know me—I'm trained to look for patterns where others don't necessarily see them. I noticed that among those nine were five who resigned under a cloud, you might say. In disgrace. And those five had been outspoken opponents of the international treaty on surveillance. Surely that was no coincidence—and it doesn't take an expert in elliptic curve cryptography or asymmetric key cryptosystems to see that. Private information had been leaked. Information that somehow became public — mental-health treatment in one case, extensive use of antidepressant medication, renting pornographic videos, a check written to an abortion clinic . . ."

"So supporters of the treaty are playing rough."

"More than that. Supporters of the treaty with access to the most private records."

"Some renegade elements within the FBI?"

"But the FBI generally doesn't *have* such information on people, you know that! Certainly not since the days of J. Edgar Hoover. Maybe when they do an in-depth investigation of a criminal suspect, but otherwise they don't."

"Then who, or what?"

"I began to look for the deeper pattern to see whether there might be a controlling intelligence behind this pattern of exposure. What did these congressmen all have in common? I inputted extensive biographies on them, whatever I could get, whatever financial information I could gather on the Internet — and, as you know, there's quite a bit out there as long as you can get a Social Security number, which is simple to get. And a curious fact turned up. Two of the disgraced congressmen had mortgages from a Washington, D.C., bank, First Washington Mutual Bancorp. And then I found the link: *all five of them* were clients of First Washington."

"So either the bank is somehow complicit in the blackmail, or somehow someone managed to access the bank's records."

"Right. Bank records, checks, money transfers . . . which can lead to health-insurance records, then medical records."

"Harry Dunne," Bryson said.

"Another Prometheus member. The CIA's deputy director of central intelligence."

"*Dunne* is?"

"Yes, yes, or so we speculate," she said hastily. "Go on, what about him?"

"Dunne was the one who plucked me out of retirement, yanked me from my quiet life and all but forced me to investigate the Directorate. By then you were already on the track of Prometheus, and Dunne wanted to find out what you knew, presumably to neutralize you. Because the CIA is behind this treaty — they want to see increased surveillance around the world."

"It may be, yes. For a variety of reasons, not least being the CIA's need for a mission, a reason to survive now that the Cold War's over. And yes, I have been on the track of Prometheus, but I still haven't been able to get a clear sense of its outlines. I've been using the Directorate's computers here, hacking away at Prometheus signals. We've identified certain members, like Arnaud, Prishnikov, Tsai, and Dunne; we're also able to record communications between and among them. But everything is encrypted, of course. We can see the *pattern* of transmissions, but we can't see the *content*. It's sort of like a hologram—you need two 'data spaces' to be able to read the signals in the clear. I've been struggling with that long and hard, and so far without success. But if you have code information, *anything* . . ."

Bryson sat up in the hospital bed. He was feeling stronger; his legs felt crampy and needed to be exercised. "Hand me my phone, could you? It's right there, on the table."

"Nicholas, it's not likely to work well here—we're underground, and the signal—"

"Just hand it to me." She gave him his small silver GSM mobile phone. He turned it over and pulled something out of its battery compartment. It was a tiny black oblong. "This may help you."

She took it. "It's—a chip, a silicon chip . . . ?"

"An encryption chip, to be precise," he said. "Copied from Jacques Arnaud's office phone."

CHAPTER
TWENTY-SIX

She took him down a long subterranean passage that led from the clinic to another wing of the facility. The floors were highly polished stone, the walls white, the low ceilings acoustically insulated. There was no sunlight, no window; they could have been anywhere in the world.

"This facility was built a decade ago or so as the Directorate's European base of operations," she explained. "And I've been working here since — well, since I left the States." She left unspoken: *since I left you.* "But when it became clear that our U.S. operations had been breached — likely a result of our investigation into Prometheus — Waller ordered the entire Washington office transferred here, which necessitated additional construction. As you'll see, very little is visible from the outside; it appears to be nothing more than a posh little research facility built into the side of a mountain."

"I'll take your word for it that we're in the Dordogne," Bryson said. His legs were fine; the only discomfort came from the wound in his side, which shot daggers of pain up and down his back as he walked.

"Well, you'll see soon enough when I take you for a walk outside. We'll probably have a little downtime waiting for the chip to process."

They came to a brushed-steel double-door where Elena entered a code on a small pad and then placed her thumb on a sensor. The doors slid open. The air inside was cool and dry.

The walls of the low-ceilinged room were lined with racks of super-computers, workstations, television monitors. "We believe this is the most powerful supercomputer center in the world," Elena said. "We have Crays with petaflops of processing power, capable of *quadrillions* of op-erations per second. There are linked IBM-SP nodes, multithreaded-architecture computers, an SGI Onyx Reality Engine system. There's a mass-storage system with a hundred and twenty gigabytes of on-line ca-pacity, a twenty-terabyte robotic tape server."

"You're losing me, darling."

But her excitement was palpable; she could barely contain it. She was in her element here, the Romanian graduate student who'd learned ad-vanced mathematics on blackboards and rudimentary 1970s-era comput-ers and now suddenly found herself in wonderland. She had always been like this, as long as he'd known her — transported by her work, bewitched by the technology that made it all possible.

"Don't forget the seventy-five miles of fiber-optic cable that's here, Elena." It was Chris Edgecomb, the tall, slender, green-eyed Guyanan with mocha skin. "Man, every time I see you, you look rougher and rougher!" Chris threw his arms around Bryson, hugged him hard. "They brought you back."

Bryson winced but smiled, happy to see the computer specialist again after so long a time. "I guess I can't stay away."

"Well, I know your wife must be glad to see you again too."

"I don't think 'glad' is a strong enough word," said Elena.

"Saint Christopher seems to take good care of you, though," said Chris. "No matter what you go through. I'm not going to ask where you've been or what you've been doing, of course. But it's good to see you. I've been helping Elena on the software side of things, trying to crack the Prometheus message traffic. But it's a bear. *Strong* crypto. And we've got *toys* here, man — a serious, high-speed connection to the Internet backbone for distributed computing. An all-digital, gigabit-capacity communication satellite oper-ating in the K- and Ka-frequency bands, in geosynchronous orbit, with the ability to carry digital communications at fiber-optic data rates."

Elena inserted the cryptochip in a port in one of the Digital Alpha machines. "You see, stored on tape here are five months of encrypted communications among the Prometheans," she explained. "We've been able to pick it up by means of simple phone taps and satellite sweeps, but we haven't been able to crack them—we haven't been able to read them, listen to them, to *understand!* The encryption is too strong. If this is really a bug-free copy of the Prometheus algorithmic 'key,' we may have a breakthrough."

"How quickly will you know?" asked Bryson.

"It might be an hour, maybe several hours. Or maybe less, depending on a number of factors, including what level the key is from. Think of it as a key to an apartment building: the key may be a master, the kind that opens every door in the whole building. Or maybe it just opens the door to an individual unit. We'll see. Either way, it's exactly what we've needed to break Prometheus."

"Why don't I give you a page or a call when I have a hit?" Chris said. "In the meantime I think Ted Waller wants to see you two."

Waller's spacious, though windowless, office was furnished identically to his old one on K Street—the same seventeenth-century Kurdish rugs on the floor, the same British oil paintings of dogs grasping fowl in their mouths.

Waller was sitting behind his same massive French oak desk. "Nicky, Elena, I have a morsel of information that might be of interest to you. Elena, I don't believe you've met one of our most talented and redoubtable field operatives, who's honoring us with an all-too-infrequent visit home." A large, high-backed chair that had been facing Waller's desk swiveled around slowly. It was Layla.

"Ah, yes," Elena said, taking Layla's hand icily. "I've heard quite a bit about you."

"And I of you," Layla replied, her tone no warmer. She did not get up. "Hello, Nick."

Bryson nodded. "I believe last time we saw each other you were trying to kill me."

"Oh, that," Layla said, blushing. "Nothing personal, you understand."

"Of course."

"In any case, I thought you might want to know that it seems as if our friend Jacques Arnaud may be taking himself out of the picture," Layla said, regarding them both with a clear, confident gaze.

"How do you mean?" Bryson asked.

"He's taking steps to liquidate all his holdings. The actions, I'd have to say, of a frightened man. This isn't an orderly retreat, or the migration of assets from one sector to another. Not business as usual, so to say. The merchant of death is putting himself out to pasture."

"But that makes no sense!" Bryson said. "I don't see the logic—do you?"

"Well," Layla said, almost smiling, "that's why we have analysts like Elena. To make sense of what operatives like you and I work so hard to collect."

Elena had been silent, her lips forming a thoughtful moue. Now her eyes focused. "Your source, Layla?"

"One of Arnaud's great rivals. A man nearly as estimable, and every bit as amoral, as Arnaud himself—a brother in malevolence—and yet he despises him with the enmity Cain felt for Abel. His name is Alain Poirier. It will not be new to you, I am sure."

"So you've just learned from Arnaud's great rival about the incipient dissolution of Arnaud's enterprises," Elena said.

"That's pretty much the shape of it," Layla said. "In English, anyway. You'd no doubt find it more memorable couched in the language of algorithms. I'm sure your methods are unfathomably obscure."

Waller watched the jousting between the two women as if at Wimbledon.

"Actually," Elena replied, "they begin with a pretty commonplace axiom: consider the source. For instance, you believe that Poirier is an enemy of Arnaud's. This is a natural assumption. They have depicted themselves in that light. In fact, they have done so all too assiduously."

"What are you trying to say?" Layla said coolly.

"I think if you investigate further, you'll discover that Poirier and Arnaud are actually business partners. Principals in a series of interconnected, widely dispersed holding companies. The rivalry is a ruse, pure and simple."

Layla narrowed her eyes. "You're saying the information I have is worthless?"

"Not at all," Elena said. "The fact that you've been 'rumbled'—identified and fed a line—is very useful intelligence indeed. Obviously Arnaud wishes us to believe this about him. We must attend not to the falsehood so much as the attempt to propagate the falsehood."

Layla fell silent for a moment. "You may have a point," she conceded sullenly.

"If Arnaud is trying to discourage our scrutiny," Bryson said, "the natural conclusion is that he's part of an enterprise that must elude scrutiny to succeed. They want us off our guard, to sow confusion. Something is happening, and soon. We can't let anything escape us now. Christ, we're dealing with forces that have marshaled an unprecedented degree of power and knowledge. Our best hope is that they underestimate us."

"My fear," Layla said ruefully, "is that they'll be right to."

Waller had left Directorate headquarters for an urgent meeting in Paris, and in the meantime Bryson and Elena had to wait. They passed the time by going for a long hike outside, down the mountainside, through hedges of rosemary, along the banks of the Dordogne. They were indeed in France, as Bryson realized once they'd emerged from the subterranean tunnels of the Directorate facility. The main entrance and exit seemed to be through an ancient stone villa built into the mountain face. Observers and passersby would see only the villa, which was large enough to plausibly contain offices and research facilities for an American think tank, presumably an off-site boondoggle for American scientists. It would explain the traffic in and out of the facility, the flights arriving and departing from the local airstrip. No one would have any idea of how large and far-ranging the facility really was, how deeply carved into the mountain.

Bryson walked more carefully than he otherwise might have, favoring his wounded right side, from time to time grimacing at the pain. They descended the craggy cliffs, walking along an old pilgrim path through a valley of walnut farms that hugged the Dordogne River, that ancient watercourse that wound its way past Souillac and down to Bordeaux. These were the farms of solid peasants, the salt of the earth and the dour custodians of the French countryside, though some of the simple stone cottages had over the years become the homes of Englishmen who couldn't afford to vacation in Provence or Tuscany. Higher on the cliffs were the local wine châteaux that made good *vin du pays*. In the distance, the verdant landscape north of Cahors was dotted with medieval hill towns where the small restaurants served up humble but serious *cuisine du terroir* to the large peasant families on Sundays. Bryson and Elena wended their way through the woods, with their famous truffles hidden away beneath the roots of ancient trees, whose secret locations are passed down in families from generation to generation, kept secret even from the very owners of the land.

"It was Ted's idea to relocate here," Elena explained as they walked, hand in hand. "You can see why a man who so loves to eat would fall in love with the countryside, with the chevres and the walnut oil and the truffles. But it's quite practical as well. We're quite well hidden here, the cover is plausible, the airstrip convenient. And there are fast, efficient highways in every direction—north to Paris, east to Switzerland and Italy, south to the Mediterranean, west to Bordeaux and the Atlantic. My parents loved it here." Her voice became soft, pensive. "They missed the homeland, of course, but it was such a wonderful place to spend their last years." She pointed to a cluster of stone cottages far off in the distance. "We lived in one of those little houses there."

" 'We'?"

"I lived with them, took care of them."

"I'm happy for you. My loss was their gain."

She smiled, squeezed his hand. "You know, the old saying is true. *Mai rǎrut, mai drǎgut.*"

"Absence makes the heart grow fonder," he translated. "And what did you always used to say—*celor ce duc mai mult dorul, le pare mai dulce odorul?* Absence sharpens love, but presence strengthens it, right?"

"Nicholas, it's been hard for me, you know. Very hard."

"And for me. More so."

"I've had to rebuild my life without you. But the ache, the sense of loss, never went away. Was it the same for you?"

"I suspect it was much harder for me, because of the uncertainty.

Because of never knowing *why*—why you disappeared, where you went, what you *thought.*"

"Oh, *iubito! Te ador!* We were both victims—victims, hostages to a world of distrust and suspicion."

"I was told you were 'assigned' to me as a watcher."

"*Assigned?* We fell in love, and that quite by accident. How can I ever prove to you I was *not?* I was in *love* with you, Nicholas. I still am."

He took her through Harry Dunne's lies, the tale of a young man selected for his athletic and linguistic abilities, then recruited blind, manipulated, his parents killed.

"They are very clever, the Prometheans," she said. "With an organization that is so cloaked in layers of secrecy like ours, it is not difficult to construct a plausible lie. Then they made it seem that you were a hostile, that you were trying to destroy us—so you could not check on the accuracy of what they told you."

"But did you know about Waller?"

"About—"

"About his . . ." Bryson spoke tentatively. "His background."

She nodded. "About Russia. Yes, he briefed me. But not long ago, just recently. I think only because he was planning to bring you in, and he knew we would talk."

Her phone rang. "Yes?" Her face brightened. "Thank you, Chris."

Hanging up, she said to Bryson, "We have something."

Chris Edgecomb handed Elena a pile of red-bordered folders, each thick with printouts. "Man, when this code cracked, it *cracked.* We had five high-speed laser printers smoking, printing out all this stuff. The main thing that slowed us down was the artificial-intelligence transcript agent— converting the spoken word to the printed one requires huge computing power and a lot of time, even at the speed of our processors. And we're still nowhere close to done. I tried to winnow out anything extraneous, but I decided to err on the side of being inclusive, and leave the main decisions to you as to what's important and what's not."

"Thanks, Chris," she said, taking the folders and laying them out on the long table in the conference room adjacent to the supercomputer center.

"I'll have coffee brought in for you two. I have a feeling you're going to need it."

They divided up the pile of printouts and began poring over them. By far the most valuable product was the decrypts of telephone conversations among the principals, of which there were many, some extensive, some conference calls. Since the exchanges were encrypted, the participants tended to speak freely. Some of them—the more canny ones, including Arnaud and Prishnikov—remained circumspect. They used coded language, references that the other would understand without having to resort to explicitness. Here, Elena's knowledge of speech patterns, her ability to discern deliberate concealment even in plain speech, was crucial. She flagged quite a few transcripts with sticky pads. And since Bryson was more familiar with the players and their backgrounds, as well as with the specifics of certain operations, he was able to pick up on different references, other meanings.

Barely had they started reading through the papers than Bryson said, "I'd say we've got the goods on them. It's no longer a matter of hearsay. Here, Prishnikov is actually planning the Geneva anthrax attack, fully three weeks in advance."

"But they're clearly not running the show," Elena said. "They're deferring to another—really, to two others, possibly Americans."

"Who?"

"So far they don't use the names. There's a reference to West Coast time, so one of them may be either in California or somewhere on the Pacific Coast of the U.S."

"What about London? Any idea who the puppetmaster might be there?"

"No. . . ."

Chris Edgecomb suddenly came into the room, holding aloft a few sheets of paper. "This just broke," he said, excitement evident in his face. "It's a pattern of funds-transfer traffic into and out of the First Washington Mutual Bancorp—I think you might find it interesting." He handed Elena several sheets of paper, each covered with columns of figures.

"That's the bank in Washington used by a majority of members of Congress, isn't that right?" said Bryson. "The one you suspect was involved in blackmailing—leaking personal information on opponents of the treaty?"

"Yes," said Elena. "These are proprietary transfers."

Edgecomb nodded.

"The cycles, the periodicity—it's unmistakable."

"What is it?" asked Bryson.

"This is a sequence of authorization codes characteristic of a wholly owned entity. A trail, as it were."

"Meaning what?" Bryson demanded.

"This Washington bank appears to be owned and controlled by another, larger financial institution."

"That's not uncommon," Bryson said.

"The point is, there's a pattern of deliberate obfuscation going on here—that is, the ownership is elaborately concealed, carefully hidden."

"Is there a way to find out who the secret owner is?" Bryson asked.

Elena nodded, distracted, as she studied the figures. "Chris, the recurring number here has to be the ABA routing code. Do you think you can run it down, identify which—"

"I'm one step ahead of you, Elena," he said. "It's a New York–based firm called Meredith Waterman . . . ?"

"My God," she said. "That's one of the oldest, most respected investment banks on Wall Street. It makes Morgan Stanley or Brown Brothers Harriman look like upstarts. I don't understand—why would Meredith Waterman be involved in blackmailing senators and congressmen into supporting the International Treaty on Surveillance and Security . . . ?"

"Meredith Waterman is probably privately held," said Bryson.

"So?"

"So it may itself be a holding company, in a sense—a front. In other words, maybe it's being used by another institution or an individual or a group of individuals—say, the Prometheus Group—to mask their true holdings. So if there's a way to get a list of all past and present partners in Meredith Waterman, maybe also majority owners . . ."

"That shouldn't be hard at all," said Edgecomb. "Even privately held firms are strictly regulated by the SEC and the FDIC, and they're required to file all sorts of documents which we should be able to access."

"One or more of those names may indicate Prometheus ownership," said Bryson.

Edgecomb nodded and left the room.

Bryson suddenly thought of something. "Richard Lanchester was a partner at Meredith Waterman."

"What?"

"Before he left Wall Street and went into public service, he was a big star in investment banking. Meredith Waterman's golden boy. That's how he made his fortune."

"Lanchester? But he—you said he was sympathetic, he was helpful to you."

"He lent a sympathetic ear, yes. He seemed genuinely alarmed. He listened, but in reality he did nothing."

"He said he wanted you to come back to him with more evidence."

"Which is just a variant of what Harry Dunne wanted—to use me as a cat's paw."

"You think Richard Lanchester could be part of Prometheus?"

"I wouldn't rule him out."

Elena returned to the transcript she'd been scrutinizing, and then she looked up suddenly. "Listen to this," she said. " 'The transfer of power will be complete forty-eight hours after the British ratify the treaty.' "

"Who's speaking?" asked Bryson.

"I—I don't know. The call originates in Washington, routed through a sterile pipeline. The unnamed caller is speaking to Prishnikov."

"Can you get a voice ID?"

"Possibly. I'd have to listen to the actual recording, determine whether the voice was altered, and if so, how well it was altered."

"Forty-eight hours . . . the 'transfer of power' . . . *to* whom, *from* whom. Or to *what, from* what? Jesus, I've got to get to London right away. When is the jet scheduled to leave?"

She looked at her watch. "Three hours and twenty minutes from now."

"Not soon enough. If we drove . . ."

"No, it would take far too long. I suggest we just go out to the airstrip and invoke Ted Waller's name, pull all the strings we've got, ask them to fly out as soon as absolutely possible."

"It's just as Dmitri Labov said."

"Who?"

"Prishnikov's deputy. He said, 'The machinery has just about fallen into place. *Power is to be transferred fully!* Everything will come into view.' He said that only days remained."

"This must be the deadline he was talking about. My God, Nick, you're right, there's no time to waste."

As she stood up, the lights in the room seemed to flicker briefly, the interruption a fraction of a second at most.

"What was that?" she asked.

"Is there an emergency generator in the facility somewhere?"

"Yes, of course, there must be."

"It just went on."

"But it would only go on in case of a true emergency," she said, puzzled. "Nothing has happened, as far as I can tell—"

"*Move!*" shouted Bryson suddenly. "*Out of here!*"

"What?"

"*Run!* Elena, *move* it—*now!* Something's been patched into the power grid. . . . Where's the nearest exit to outside?"

Elena turned, pointed to the left.

"*Jesus,* Elena, *let's go!* I'll bet the doors lock automatically, sealing intruders in as well as out. I know that's what's going on!"

He raced down the hallway; Elena scooped up several computer diskettes from the table and then ran after him.

"Which *way?*" he screamed.

"Straight through those doors!"

She led the way, and he followed. In a matter of seconds they had come to a set of steel doors marked EMERGENCY EXIT; a red crash-bar at the middle of the doors was used to force the doors open, probably setting off an alarm at the same time. Bryson slammed himself against the crash bar; the double-doors opened outward into the dark night as an alarm rang. A rush of cold air came at them. No more than two feet in front of them was a floor-to-ceiling gate constructed of steel bars. The gate was slowly closing, automatically, from left to right.

"Jump!" shouted Bryson, diving through the steadily narrowing space. He spun around and grabbed Elena, dragging her through the gap between the gate and the stone wall, her body just barely clearing it. They were on the steep hillside next to the old stone villa, the electric gate concealed by tall hedges.

Bryson and Elena ran directly ahead, away from the villa and down the hill. "Is there a car around here somewhere?" asked Bryson.

"There's an all-terrain vehicle parked right in front of the villa," she replied. "It's—there it is!"

A small, boxy, four-wheel-drive Land Rover Defender 90 glinted in the moonlight twenty yards ahead. Bryson ran toward it, jumped into the front seat, and felt for the key. It wasn't in the ignition. Jesus, where the hell was it? In a remote setting like this, wouldn't it be left in the car? Elena leaped into the car. "Under the mat," she said.

He reached down, felt the key under the rubber floor mat. Inserting the key in the ignition, he started it; the Land Rover roared to life.

"Nick, what's happening?" Elena cried out as the car lurched forward and down the steep path away from the compound.

But before Bryson had a chance to speak, there was an immense, dazzlingly bright flash of white light, and a rumbling explosion that seemed to come from deep in the mountain. In a second or two the blast surfaced, the sound terrifyingly loud, deafening, all-enveloping. As Bryson steered the Land Rover around a sharp twist, crashing into and then through vegetation, he could feel the heat sear his back, exactly as hot as if he'd leaned right back into the fire.

Elena turned back, gripping the handrails to steady herself. "Oh, my God, Nick!" she screamed. "The facility—the compound—it's been completely destroyed! Oh, God, Nick, look at that!"

But Bryson would not turn around; he did not dare. They had to keep moving. There was not a second to lose. The wheels spun through the underbrush as he accelerated, faster and faster, and he thought just one thing: *My love—you're safe.*

You're safe, you're alive, you're with me.

For now.

Dear God, for now.

CHAPTER
TWENTY-SEVEN

They arrived in London, both of them, by ten o'clock in the evening, by which point it was too late to accomplish what they had to do. They spent the night together in a hotel in Russell Square, in the same bed for the first time in five years. They were strangers to each other, in a sense, but each found the other's body immediately familiar—reassuringly yet excitingly so. For the first time in five years they made love, the passion urgent, almost desperate. They fell asleep entangled in each other, exhausted both from the lovemaking and from the enormous strains that had impelled them there.

In the morning they spoke of the nightmare they had both witnessed, sifting details, trying to make some sense of the penetration.

"When you called the airstrip to reserve the jet," asked Bryson, "you probably didn't use a sterile line, did you?"

She shook her head slowly, her face taut with anxiety. "The airstrip wasn't equipped with a scrambler on its end, so there was no point. But calls originating in the Directorate facility were generally considered safe, since our internal communications center was beyond the reach of out-

ROBERT LUDLUM

side interference. If we phoned London or Paris or Munich, say, we usually used the sterile channels—but only to protect the other end."

"But calls made across such a distance—a hundred miles or more, for instance—generally are routed from landlines to microwave towers, and it's the microwave transmission that's penetrable by satellite surveillance, right?"

"That's right—landlines can be tapped into, but not by satellite. It has to be by conventional means—phone taps placed on the wires and such. And that requires knowing exactly where the calls originated."

"Prometheus obviously knew the details of the Dordogne center," Bryson said quietly. "For all Waller's precautions, the comings and goings, into and out of the airfield, must have been observed, noted. And the airstrip was an easy target for a conventional phone tap."

"Waller—thank God, he was gone! But we have to reach him."

"Jesus. I'm sure he knows. But Chris Edgecomb—"

She covered her eyes with her hand. "Oh, dear God, Chris! And Layla!"

"And dozens of others. Most of them I didn't know any longer, but you must have had quite a few friends among them."

She nodded silently, removed her hand from her eyes, which were flooded with tears.

After a moment's silence, Bryson resumed. "They must have patched into the power grid and planted explosives—plastique—throughout and *beneath* the facility. Without inside resources—without human beings who'd been turned—they could never have done it. The Directorate was on the verge of unraveling the Prometheus Group's plans, and so it had to be neutralized. They sent me—and others, I'm sure—and when those efforts didn't pan out, they went for the direct approach." He closed his eyes. "Whatever secrets, plans they're protecting, we have to assume they're of monumental importance to the men behind Prometheus."

A direct, frontal approach to the treaty's most vocal proponent, Lord Miles Parmore, was therefore doomed to fail: it would only alert their enemies without yielding information; such men were well guarded, well prepared for deception, misdirection. Moreover, Bryson's instinct told him that Lord Parmore was not their man. He was a figurehead, a very public figure, closely watched, incapable of maneuvering behind the

372

scenes. He could not be a Prometheus control. The true control would have to be someone affiliated with Parmore, connected to him in a tangential way. But connected *how?*

The Prometheus conspirators were too clever, too thorough, to allow connections to remain visible. Records would be altered, erased. Even close scrutiny would not reveal the hidden controls, the puppetmasters. The only giveaway would be what was *not* there, records missing, obviously deleted. Yet the search for such gaps would be the proverbial search for a needle in a haystack.

Finally, it was Bryson's idea that they dig more deeply, dig into the past. It had been his experience that the truth could often be discerned there, in old files and books—records rarely accessed, too dispersed, too difficult to alter convincingly.

It was a theory, but only a theory, and it took them that morning to the British Library at St. Pancras, which lay sprawled across a landscaped square off Euston Road, its orange, hand-molded Leicester brick shimmering in the bright morning sun. Bryson and Elena made their way through the plaza, past the large bronze of Newton by Sir Eduardo Paolozzi, and into the spacious entrance hall. Bryson scanned the faces of the people he passed, attuned to the slightest sign of recognition. He had to assume that the Promethean networks had been alerted to him, perhaps even to their presence in London, though so far there was no sign of it. Inside the library, a broad flight of travertine steps took them to the main reading room—an expanse of oak desks with individual desk lamps—and they walked through the discreet paneled doors that led to the carrels. The double carrel they had reserved was private but not cramped, its round-backed oak chairs and green leather-topped desks creating a slightly clubby feeling.

Within an hour, they had gathered most of the necessary volumes, starting with selections from the official proceedings of Parliament— heavy, large volumes with rugged, black library bindings. Many had been unopened for years, and gave off a musty smell of decay when the pages were turned. Nick and Elena went through them with intense and single-minded focus. Had there been earlier debates about civil threats and civil liberties—other decisions with implications for civilian surveillance? On a pad, they each jotted down errant facts—unexplained references, names, sites. These were areas where the marks of the sculptor's chisel might be in evidence.

It was Elena who first spoke the name aloud. *Rupert Vere*. A low-key, soft-spoken, and highly expert maneuverer, the embodiment of political moderation but also—the chronicles made this clear over the years—a master of procedural cunning. Was it possible? Was the intuition worth checking out?

Rupert Vere, Member of Parliament from Chelsea, was Britain's foreign secretary.

Bryson followed the intricate tracery of the Chelsea MP's career through the smaller regional papers, which were more attuned to incidental details, less preoccupied with the official significance of events. It was painstaking, even stupefying work, the matter of collating a hundred tiny articles in dozens of local gazettes and circulars, the paper often yellowed and brittle. At times, Bryson was seized with exasperation—it seemed like madness to think that they'd find clues to the most concealed of conspiracies right out there in the open, in the public record.

But he persevered. They both did. Elena made the analogy to her signals-intercept work: within the cascade of noise, the abundance of useless information, might be a signal somewhere—if only they could make it out. Rupert Vere had graduated with a first from Brasenose College, Oxford; he had a reputation for laziness, which was quite likely a cunning subterfuge. He also had a distinct gift for cultivating friendships, a *Guardian* columnist noted: ". . . and so his influence goes beyond the formal ambit of his authority." A picture was coming gradually into focus: for years, Foreign Secretary Rupert Vere had been working behind the scenes to prepare the way for passage of the treaty, calling in political debts, inveigling friends and allies. And yet his own pronouncements were temperate, his ties to the firebrands nowhere in evidence.

Finally, it was a seemingly trivial piece of data that caught Bryson's attention. In the yellowing pages of the *Evening Standard*, there was an account of the 1965 rowing races in Pangbourne, on the Thames, where nationally ranked teams from secondary schools around the country competed. In small agate type, the paper reported on the teams. Vere, it appeared, rowed for Marlborough, where he was a sixth-former. The language was stilted, the account seemingly innocuous.

At the Pangbourne Junior Sculls, a number of the quads and doubles distinguished themselves. In particular, the J18 quad from Sir William Borlase School recorded the fastest time of the day (10m 28s), but were pressed quite close by the crews in the strong J16 class where St George's College Crew (10m 35s), with the GBv France double scullers Matthews and Loake aboard, were chased hard by Westminster. In both the J14 classes the Hereford Cathedral School doubles proved outstanding (12m 11s, and 13m 22s). There were also some high-class performers among the J16 singles. At the front Rupert Vere (11m 50s) had 13 seconds on his Marlborough team mate Miles Parmore, while David Houghton (13m 5s) finished almost half a minute clear of his pursuers. Showing real promise, Parrish of St George's (12m 6s) and Kellman of Dragon School (12m 10s) headed the MJ16 class, finishing fourth and fifth overall. The younger age groups race over a 1500m distance at Pangbourne. The WJ13 winner, Dawson of Marlborough (8m 51s), had finished a creditable second-equal in the morning's WJ14 race and now finished fifth overall, behind MJ13 winner Goodey.

He reread the item and soon found a couple of similar ones. Vere had rowed for Marlborough, in the same eight as Miles Parmore.

Yes. The British Foreign Secretary and MP from Chelsea, an early champion of the treaty, had been a teammate and longtime friend of Lord Miles Parmore.

Had they found their man?

The New Palace of Westminster—better known as the Houses of Parliament—was, in its very blend of antiquity and modernity, a quintessentially British institution. As far back as the Viking King Canute, a royal palace existed on these grounds. But it was Edward the Confessor and William the Conqueror in the eleventh century who enlarged the ancient dream of royal munificence and splendor. The historical continuities were as real as the Magna Carta; the discontinuities were greater still. And when the structure was rebuilt in the mid-nineteenth century, it represented the height of the Gothic Revival style, an enduring legacy to the ingenuity of its architects—a vision of an artificial, invented antiquity, which would be reinvented once more when a World War II blitzkrieg destroyed the Commons Chamber. Carefully restored, albeit in a more subdued interpretation of late Gothic, it was a replica of a replica.

Even as it opened onto one of London's busiest centers of traffic, Parliament Square, the Houses of Parliament themselves remained aloof and protected by their eight-acre arcadian redoubt. The "new palace" itself was a whirlpool of human traffic. It had almost twelve hundred rooms, and fully two miles of passages. The areas of the buildings that members routinely used, that tourists routinely saw, were impressive indeed, but there was much more, the plans for which were, for reasons of security, not readily accessible. But they, too, could be found in the historical archives. Bryson had given himself two hours to learn and master their details. A series of shifting orthogonal forms arranged themselves in his mind into a layout that had a visceral immediacy to him. He knew precisely how the Peers' Library related to the Prince's Chamber; he knew the distance between the Speaker's Residence and the Sergeant-at-Arms residence, knew how long it would take to go from the Commons Lobby to the first of the Minister's rooms. In an era without central heating, it was essential to have some special chambers that were protected from the exterior wall by unused, insulating spaces. Moreover, any vast public work would, it was understood, be in constant need of repair and refurbishment, and there had to be passageways for workmen to go about their tasks without disturbing the grandeur of the public spaces. Like government itself, its functioning required complex spaces and relays that were invisible to the citizenry.

Elena, meanwhile, scoured every recorded detail of Rupert Vere's life. Another tiny detail had caught her attention: when Vere was sixteen, he'd won a *Sunday Times* crossword puzzle competition. He was a gamesman, which seemed somehow apt: yet the game he was playing was anything but trivial.

At five o'clock in the morning, a backpacker in a leather flight jacket and black plastic glasses walked around the perimeter of the Houses of

Parliament, like a sleepless tourist trying to walk off a hangover. Or at least Bryson hoped he would be taken for one. He stopped before the black statue of Cromwell, near St. Stephen's Entrance, and read the carefully lettered sign: PACKAGES LARGER THAN A4, OTHER THAN FLOWERS, MUST BE DELIVERED VIA THE BLACK ROD'S GARDEN ENTRANCE. He walked past the Peer's Entrance, noting its precise location vis-à-vis the others; then made his way through the small stand of horse-chestnut trees and noted the location of each security camera, invariably posted high in white enameled hoods. The Metropolitan Police of London, Bryson had learned, maintains a network of traffic cameras, three hundred of them fixed on posts and high buildings across the city. Each has a number, and if an authorized person types in the number, he or she can call up a clear, color image of London. It is possible to rotate the camera and zoom it in. It is possible to follow police chases, moving from camera to camera, and to follow a motorist or pedestrian without being detected. It would not be wise to spend much time on surveillance here, he decided; this would have to be brief.

He took in the four-tiered structure of the main gallery, mapping the physical structure itself with the mental representations he had formed, turning the abstract metrics into concrete perceptions. It was essential to transmute data into intuition, which could be accessed instantly and unreflectively, without calculation and consideration. That was one of Waller's early lessons to him, and among the most valuable. *In the field, the only maps that matter are in your head.*

St. Stephen's Tower, the clock tower at the north end of the Parliament building, was three hundred and twenty feet tall. The Victoria Tower, on the opposite end of the complex, was wider but nearly as high. Between the towers, the roofing was garlanded with scaffolding; the process of exterior repair work was almost unceasing. External stairs surmounted the roof twenty feet from the Victoria Tower. And then he ambled toward the Thames and scanned the far side of the complex, which abutted directly onto the Thames. By the galleries, there was a fifteen-foot terrace, but at the towers to either end, the drop was sheer, a plumb line. Across the river, he saw a few anchored boats. Some were designated for sightseeing trips, others for maintenance purposes. One was stenciled FUEL AND LUBRICATION SERVICE. He took note of it.

The plan was set, the schedule determined. Bryson made his way back to their hotel and changed, and then he and Elena went over the plan twice more. Yet his concerns were not allayed. The plan had too many moving parts; he knew the probability of a mishap grew geometrically as the sequence of constituent events lengthened. But there was no choice now.

Smartly attired in a double-breasted, pin-striped suit and round horn-rimmed glasses, Bryson — or rather, as his pass attested, Nigel Hilbreth — ascended the stairs from the lower waiting hall to the upper waiting hall of the Chamber of Commons and took his seat in the gallery. His face was composed into a mask of bland disinterest, his sandy hair neatly parted, mustache tidy. He was every inch a midlevel civil servant, including even the fragrance — Penhaligon's Blenheim, purchased on Wellington Street. A simple expedient perhaps, but in some ways equally as effective as the dye, glasses, and adhesive-backed facial hair. It was originally Waller, too, who first alerted him to the rarely discussed olfactory aspects of camouflage. When Bryson had an assignment in East Asia, he would abstain from meat and dairy products for several weeks: Asians, with their diets of fish and soy, found Westerners to have a characteristically "meaty" smell, their skin proteins affected by their beef-rich diet. He made similar dietary accommodations preceding assignments in the various Arabic regions. An adjustment in fragrance was a trivial change, but Bryson knew that it was often through such subliminal clues that we detect the strangers among us.

"Nigel Hilbreth" sat quietly observing the tense parliamentary deliberations, a small black briefcase by his feet. Below, on the long, green leather-upholstered benches, the MPs sat with an unusual measure of attentiveness, their documents lit by the small capsule lamps that dangled just above their heads, suspended on long wires from a vaulted ceiling. It was an ungainly solution to a problem that admitted no elegant one. The ministers of the current government sat on the front bench to the right side; the opposition faced them to the left. The gallery benches, paneled with precisely incised dark-brown woodwork, rose steeply above them, in balcony formation.

Bryson had arrived in the middle of the emergency session, but he knew precisely what was being bruited about: it was the issue that was at the forefront of every organ of governmental deliberation in the world right now, or had been only recently: the Treaty on Surveillance and Security. In this instance, however, the precipitating incident was the horrendous damage wrought by a recidivist splinter faction of Sinn Fein, which had detonated a shrapnel bomb in the middle of Harrods during one of its busiest hours, wounding hundreds. *Was that, too, secretly funded and instigated by the Prometheus Group?*

For the first time, he was able to see Rupert Vere in the flesh. Foreign Secretary Vere was a deceptively wizened-looking man, seemingly older than his fifty-six years, but one could tell that his small, darting eyes missed little. Bryson glanced at his watch—another subtle prop, an old tank watch from McCallister & Son.

Half an hour earlier, Bryson had, adopting the blasé manner of a Whitehall civil servant, asked a messenger to deliver a note, presumably official and semiurgent Whitehall business, to the foreign secretary. Any minute now it would be brought to Vere by one of his assistants. Bryson wanted to study his reaction when he opened the note and read its contents. The note—a simple, almost childish contrivance that Elena, a lover of puzzles, had devised—was framed like an English crossword-puzzle clue:

> *Put yourself between support and a definite article, then add*
> *a couple. Puzzled? See you at your alcove suite during the*
> *intersession.*

It had been Elena's inspiration to put, in the form of a clue, the one watchword that he could not ignore.

As a member of the Opposition held forth on the threats to civil liberties posed by the prospective treaty, Rupert Vere was handed an envelope. He opened it, scanned the note, and then looked up into the gallery directly at Bryson. He had an intent yet nearly unreadable expression. It was all Bryson could do not to flinch; long seconds passed before he realized the foreign secretary was merely gazing up into the middle distance, that his eyes weren't focusing on anyone at all. Bryson struggled to maintain his placid, bored expression, but it was not easy. If he attracted notice, he was done for: that had to be the operating assumption. The sentries controlled by the Prometheus Group undoubtedly knew exactly what he looked like. But there was a good chance that they hadn't been notified about Elena, or that if they knew about her, they would assume she had been killed in the destruction of the Directorate's Dordogne headquarters.

It was Elena, therefore, who would have to make the direct approach. The session would adjourn in ten minutes. What happened next would determine everything.

Members of the British cabinet typically have offices on Whitehall and other nearby streets; the foreign secretary is the titular head of the Foreign and Commonwealth Office, and his official quarters are on King Charles Street. But Bryson knew that because of his hours negotiating with members of parliament, Rupert Vere also maintained quarters beneath the sloping roof of the Palace of Westminster. The suite was a mere five-minute walk from the Commons chambers, and provided a discreet meeting area for matters that required sensitivity and immediacy.

Would Vere do what the note had suggested, or would he surprise them with another response altogether? Bryson believed that Vere's primary reaction would be curiosity, that he would indeed return directly to his office under the eaves. But in case Vere panicked, or decided for some reason to go elsewhere, Bryson had to tail him. Having identified the foreign secretary, he was able to follow him out of the Commons Chambers by picking him out of the crowd of Parliament members. He shadowed Vere as he made his way up the stone committee staircase, past busts of prime ministers past, to his Parliamentary office, until he could follow him no longer without attracting attention.

Rupert Vere's personal secretary was Belinda Headlam, a thickset woman in her early sixties who wore her gray hair in a tight bun. "This lady says you're expecting her," she murmured to the foreign secretary as he entered the antechamber. "She says she's left you a note?"

"Yes, well," Vere replied, and then he saw Elena sitting on the tufted leather sofa outside his office. She had taken care to project the right image: her navy suit revealed décolletage, though not inappropriately so; her glossy brown hair was pulled back; her lips were painted in eggplant gloss. She looked stunning, yet at the same time professional.

Vere raised his eyebrows and smiled rapaciously. "I don't believe we've met," he said. "But you've certainly got my attention. Your note, that is." He beckoned her to follow him into his small, dim, but exquisitely appointed office built in the eaves beneath the Parliament building's vast slate roof. He sat behind his desk and indicated that she should sit in a leather chair a few feet away.

For a moment, he shuffled his correspondence. Elena was conscious of Vere sizing her up—less, it almost seemed to her, as an adversary than as a potential conquest.

"You must be a puzzler, too," he said at last. "The answer is 'Prometheus,' is that right? A rather crude clue, though. *Me* between *pro* and *the*, plus *us*." He paused, his eyes boring into hers. "To what do I owe the pleasure of your company, Miss . . . ?"

"Goldoni," she replied. She had not lost her accent, so it would have to be a foreign name. She watched him closely but could not read him. Rather than pretending he didn't understand what she was hinting at, he had immediately acknowledged the word Prometheus—yet his bland reaction revealed no alarm, no fear, not even any defensiveness. If he was acting, he was skilled, though that would not have surprised her: he had not gotten as far as he had without some talent at dissembling.

"I assume your office is sterile?" Elena said. He gave her a look of puzzled incomprehension, but she persisted. "You know who sent me. You'll have to excuse the irregularity of this means of making contact, but then that's the reason for my visit. The matter is urgent. The existing channels of communication may have been compromised."

"I beg your pardon," he said haughtily.

"You must not use the existing codes," Elena said, watching his face closely. "This is of utmost importance, particularly with so little time remaining before the Prometheus plan goes into force. I will be in touch with you soon to indicate when the channels have been normalized."

Vere's tolerant smile faded. He cleared his throat and got to his feet. "You're starkers," he said. "Now, if you'll please excuse me—"

"*No!*" Elena interrupted in an urgent whisper. "All cryptosystems have been compromised. Their integrity *cannot* be relied upon! We are changing all the codes. You must await further instructions."

All of Vere's professional charm had vanished; his face grew hard. "Get out of here at once!" he demanded in a loud, clipped voice. Was that panic in his voice? Was he using indignation to cover his fear? "I'll be reporting you to the constabulary, and you'll be making a grave mistake if you ever try to enter these halls again."

Vere reached over to press his intercom button, but before he could do so, the door to his chambers swung open. A slim, tweedy man entered, shutting the door behind him. Elena recognized the face from her recent researches: it was Rupert Vere's longtime deputy, Simon Dawson, the seniormost member of Vere's staff, who was charged with formulating policy.

"Rupes," Simon Dawson said in an almost languorous drawl. "I couldn't help overhearing. Is this woman being tiresome?" Dawson's pale brown hair, apple cheeks, and lanky figure gave him the unsettling look of a middle-aged schoolboy.

Vere was visibly relieved. "As a matter of fact, Simon, yes," Vere said. "She's nattering at me all kinds of hogwash—about something called Prometheus, about crypto-something-or-other, 'Prometheus plans being in force'—utter madness! The lady must be reported to MI-5 at once—she's a public danger."

Elena took a few steps away from Vere's desk, her gaze shifting from one man to the other. Something was very wrong. Dawson had closed the heavy oak door behind him, she noticed. That made no sense. Unless . . .

Dawson withdrew a flat, silenced Browning from his Harris tweed jacket.

"Crikey, Simon, what are you doing with a pistol?" Vere asked. "That really shouldn't be necessary. I'm sure this woman has the sense to leave at once, don't you?" She studied the shifting expressions of Vere's face, a rapid sequence of puzzlement, dismay, and fear.

The civil servant's long, tapered fingers rested by the trigger with practiced ease. Elena's heart was pounding, her eyes darting wildly around the room hoping to find an opportunity for disruption or escape.

Dawson looked into her eyes, and she returned the stare, boldly, brazenly, almost daring him to fire. Suddenly Dawson squeezed the trigger. Frozen with terror, she watched as the pistol bucked slightly in his hand. There was a spitting sound of a silenced bullet, and then a splotch of crimson spread across Foreign Secretary Rupert Vere's heavily starched white shirt, and he collapsed onto the oriental carpet.

Dawson turned to Elena with a faint, glacial smile. "Now, that was unfortunate, wasn't it? Having to cut short such a distinguished career. But then you really left me no choice. You told him far too much. He's a clever man, and he'd easily put things together, and that wouldn't do at all. That's something you can understand, can't you?" He moved closer to her, then closer still, until she could feel the clammy moisture of his breath. "Rupes may have been an indolent fellow, but he wasn't dim. What did you think you were up to, chatting to him about Prometheus? This really isn't on. But let's talk about *you*, shall we?"

My God! Simon Dawson! It was another name she'd come across in the old Pangbourne news clips, the name of a younger classmate she'd assumed had later become Vere's protégé.

Wrong.

Dawson was the control.

The same logic that had ruled out Miles Parmore should have ruled out Rupert Vere: he was too visible. The real puppetmaster was the faceless deputy, working through his oblivious superior.

"So you kept him in the dark all along," Elena said, half to herself.

"Rupes? There was no need for him to know. He's always trusted my advice implicitly. But nobody had his charm. One needed the charming stooge. *Needed*, past tense. He's not exactly necessary any longer, is he?"

She took a step back. "You mean because Britain's now a signatory to the treaty."

"Exactly. As of ten minutes ago. But who are you? I fancy we haven't been introduced properly." The Browning still rested comfortably in Dawson's right hand. He pulled a flat metallic case from his breast pocket, evidently some sort of wireless personal digital assistant. "Let's see what the Network has to say," Dawson murmured. He held the device up in the air and pointed it toward her. An image of her face immediately appeared on the square LCD screen. Then the screen began to flicker as hundreds of faces flashed by almost in a blur, until a match was found.

"Elena Petrescu," he said. He read from an electronic file. "Born in 1969, Bucharest, Romania. Only daughter of Andrei and Simona Petrescu, Andrei having been Romania's leading specialist in cryptography. Ah, *most* intriguing. Exfiltrated from Bucharest just before the 1989 coup d'etat by . . . Nicholas Bryson." He looked up. "You're *married* to Nicholas Bryson. Now it comes together. Directorate employees, both of you. Separated for five years . . . in the year before you left, you bought, let's see, three ovulation kits—obviously trying to get pregnant. Hmm . . . didn't happen, I take it. Regular weekly sessions with a psychotherapist—I wonder, were you dealing with the difficulty of being a political defector in a strange country, or working at an agency as secret as the Directorate, or was it the crumbling marriage?"

There was something about the disjunction between what he was saying and his casual tone that made Elena shudder. She noticed that although he was still holding his Browning, he was paying it little attention.

"Your plans have leaked, you should know that," Elena said.

"It really doesn't concern me," Dawson replied airily.

"I doubt that. You were concerned enough about Rupert Vere knowing and informing MI-5 that you killed him."

"The CIA and MI-6 and MI-5 and all the other three-letter spy agencies have all been neutralized. The Directorate took us longer—perhaps by virtue of your paranoid structure—though the very secrecy that insulated you from penetration also made it that much easier for us to paralyze you, funnily enough. It's strange how long it's taken you people to realize that time has passed you by, that there's simply no need for you any longer! The NSA is overwhelmed with the sheer volume of traffic—the E-mails and cell-phone calls it struggles to vacuum up, all the Internet traffic. Good God, it's a Cold War relic—it thinks the Soviet Union never went away! And to think that there was once a time when the NSA was the crown jewel of American intelligence, the biggest, the best! Well, encryption has pretty much ended that reign. And the CIA—the folks who accidentally had us bomb the Chinese embassy in Belgrade, who had no *idea* India had nuclear weapons! The ineptitude! The less said of them, the better. Intelligence agencies are a thing of the past. No wonder you all try so hard to block the rise of Prometheus—you're like dinosaurs impotently raging against the inevitability of evolution! But by this weekend, your demise will be evident to the entire world. On the shores of the lake, a new global order will be assured, and the welfare of the human race will be secure as it's never been before." He turned his attention to the Browning once again, pointing it at her. "Sometimes the few must be sacrificed at the altar of the many. I can already see the headlines in the *Telegraph*—FOREIGN SECRETARY VERE SLAIN BY SUICIDAL STALKER. And in the *Sun*, something like SLAYS CAB MIN, THEN SELF. They'll probably intimate some sordid sexual angle. And the gun and the powder spray will positively identify you as the killer."

As Dawson spoke, he was unscrewing the silencer from the Browning; then, as tightly coiled as a mountain cat, he took two long, rapid steps toward Elena. With a grip of iron, he placed the gun in her hand, crushing her fingers around it, then bent her arm so that the barrel pressed hard against her temple. Elena started thrashing violently, convulsively: if nothing else, she would spoil the tableau he had planned. She screamed at the top of her lungs. She felt as if another force altogether had taken possession of her body, the concentrated will to survive transmuting into a primal muscular response. She writhed and flailed, and when she heard another voice it seemed to come from a great distance.

Nick Bryson's voice.

"Dawson, what on earth are you doing? She's one of *ours!*" Bryson shouted. The door to the closet opened, and Bryson stepped out, disguised as a Whitehall civil servant with hairpiece, mustache, and glasses; only upon close examination did he bare any resemblance to Nicholas Bryson. The shoulders of his suit were flecked with wood splinters and dust, evidence that he had made his way into the office through a crawl space. "She was dispatched personally by Jacques Arnaud!" Bryson warned.

"What—who the hell are you?" gasped Dawson, spinning around to look at the intruder with mingled astonishment and uncertainty; in so doing, he momentarily loosened his grip on Elena, who suddenly lunged to one side. In one violent motion she was able to wrench the pistol, which Dawson had been forcing into her hand, away from him. Elena hurled it toward Bryson, who dove into the air and retrieved it.

Bryson gripped it in both hands, aiming it at Vere's deputy. "*Don't* move," he said sharply. "Or there'll be two bodies on the floor."

Dawson froze, staring malevolently at Bryson, then shifting his eyes toward Elena.

"Now, we have a few questions for you," Bryson said, advancing toward Dawson, the gun still pointed. "And you'd be wise to answer them as completely and truthfully as you can."

Dawson shook his head in disgust, backing up slowly. "You're sadly mistaken to think that you can threaten me. Prometheus has been in the planning for over a decade. It's larger than any one person, any one *nation* for that matter."

"Freeze!" Bryson shouted.

"You can kill me," said Dawson, still backing up, edging closer and closer to Elena, "but it's not going to change a thing, or even slow anything down. The gun in your hands was used to kill my dear friend there; if you're so foolish as to kill me too, you'll have two homicides on your head. And it's only fair to warn you that this office is equipped with electronic eavesdropping devices; the moment your friend here entered the foreign secretary's office and I saw what she was really up to, I placed a call to the Alpha squad, Grosvenor Square detachment. I'm sure you know about the Alpha squad."

Bryson only stared.

"They'll be here any moment now. They're probably entering the building already, you goddamned son of a *bitch!*" And as he raised his voice, he leaped toward Elena, grabbing her by the throat, his thumbs squeezing the cartilage in a death grip. Elena's screams quickly became gagging, strangulated sounds.

There was a thunderous explosion as the bullet was fired from the unsilenced Browning in Bryson's hands. At the top of his forehead, near the hairline, a tiny oval wept blood. Dawson, his face oddly immobile, slumped face forward onto the floor.

"Quick!" Bryson said. "Grab his pocket computer, his wallet, whatever else is in his pockets."

Her face wrinkled with distaste, she searched the dead man's pockets, taking keys, wallet, Palm Pilot, and assorted scraps of paper. Then she followed him through the open closet door and saw where Bryson had removed the plywood backing.

Belinda Headlam's experience in Foreign Secretary Rupert Vere's employ had taught her the supreme importance of discretion. She knew that he conducted negotiations of exquisite sensitivity in his alcove suite, and she had her suspicions that it might also be his lair for the occasional assignation, as well. Last year, the young woman from the agricultural ministry had seemed ever so slightly flushed and dishabille when she'd had to interrupt their conversation with the urgent summons from the prime minister. Foreign Secretary Vere had been just a little short with her for a few days afterward, as if he had been embarrassed by the interruption and displeased at her. But all that passed and she tried to put the episode out of her head. Men had their weaknesses, she knew; they all did.

Yet the foreign secretary was a most eminent man, one of the most capable members of the government, as the leader page of the *Express* often repeated, and she was honored that he had handpicked her as his personal assistant. But *surely* something was wrong. She wrung her hands, agonized about what to do, and finally decided she couldn't dither any longer. The foreign secretary's office was well soundproofed—he had insisted on that—but that noise, muffled though it was, sounded terribly like a gunshot. Could that be? And if it *were* a gunshot and she'd done nothing—why, then what? What if the foreign secretary were wounded and in dire need of help? Then there was the fact that Simon Dawson, his deputy, had joined them, and it wasn't like him to stay for so long. There was, furthermore, something *peculiar* about the tarted-up woman who'd passed him a note. Mrs. Headlam had an inkling of what Foreign Secretary Vere's appraising look might mean, but the woman didn't seem as if she were there on such . . . *business.*

Something was dodgy.

Belinda Headlam stood up and rapped sharply on the secretary's door. She waited five seconds and rapped again. Then, saying, "I'm so terribly sorry," she pushed open the door. And then she screamed.

The sight was so shattering it took her almost half a minute before she had enough sense to notify security.

Sergeant Robby Sullivan of the Palace of Westminster Division of the Metropolitan Police kept himself lean and taut with an hour of hard jogging each morning, and he looked askance at his colleagues who, as the years wore on, allowed themselves to—well, get a little podgy. You might have thought they didn't take the beat seriously. Robby had been assigned to Westminster Division for seven years, charged with policing the halls of Parliament, ousting intruders, and generally keeping the peace. Though the time had passed with relatively few incidents, years of IRA threats had given him much practice at responding to alarms.

Still, nothing had prepared him for the scene in the foreign secretary's suite. He and Police Constable Eric Belson, his young redheaded deputy, radioed New Scotland Yard for immediate backup, but in the interim they sealed off Vere's chambers and used the existing detail to station an officer by every major stairwell. From Mrs. Headlam's account, there was likely a killer on the loose in the building—a woman, at that. Though how she'd managed to get out of the office without going past Mrs. Headlam was a puzzlement. She would not be permitted to escape from the building, he was determined—not on his watch. He'd gone through regular drills, knew all the requisite moves and maneuvers. Of course, this time it was the real thing. The adrenaline reminded him of that.

The air in the long, dark passageway was musty, dead, and stifling, evidently having been undisturbed for years. Bryson and Elena moved quickly yet silently through the gloom, crawling on hands and knees in some places, walking erect with an awkward, stoop-shouldered gait where space allowed. Bryson carried with him the briefcase he had brought into the Parliament building, an encumbrance but perhaps a vital asset. The only light came from the daylight that filtered in through cracks in the mortise work or ceiling molding. The ancient wood flooring creaked alarmingly as they passed between offices and public spaces and supply rooms. Voices on the other side of the wall were muffled, louder in some places than in others. At one point Bryson noticed something, a peculiar noise pattern, and he stopped. Their eyes were beginning to get used to the dark; he could see Elena turn to him quizzically, and he put a finger to his lips as he peered through a crack.

He saw the boots, then the fatigues, of U.S. Marines. The secret Alpha squad had arrived and had dispersed to search the building. The welcoming committee. He guessed that the Marines were ordinarily assigned to the American embassy in Grosvenor Square, interspersed among the regular contingent whose job it was to guard the building and the ambassador. Their lethal presence was alarming in the extreme: the highly trained hit squad would be mobilized only upon top-secret-code-word orders dispatched at the highest levels of the U.S. government. Oval Office authority was required. Whatever the terrifying agenda of Prometheus—he had overheard part of Dawson's rant, which seemed in some way to concern a new generation of governmental espionage—it was being put into place with the cooperation of the White House, knowingly or not.

Madness! This was no mere bureaucratic transformation, no simple governmental shift. The Prometheus killers seemed instead to be front men of some kind of officially sanctioned power struggle, an epochal transfer of power. But what could it be?

Immediately ahead of them, the crawlspace was interrupted by a metal enclosure: an air duct. Feeling with his fingertips, he located a hinged access door for maintenance purposes. Panels of air filters were tightly lodged in place. Bryson pulled out a long, flat screwdriver from the briefcase and worked the filters loose from their frames until the passageway was unblocked. Now he and Elena entered the square-sided steel enclosure, shimmying and sliding down a steep decline through a narrow space of ribbed steel, which vibrated with regular bursts of cold air. "This leads to a space over the Chancellor's Gate," Bryson said, his voice echoing and metallic, "and then to Victoria Tower. But we're going to have to play this by ear."

However large the Alpha squad detachment, it would not be numerous enough to search the immense Palace of Westminster, which contained, in seven acres, the two houses of Parliament—twelve hundred rooms, more than a hundred staircases, over three kilometers of passages. There would undoubtedly be others in plainclothes searching for them who would be no less lethal: field operatives in the employ of the Prometheus Group. They could be anywhere. Bryson's mind was a whirl of memorized maps and plans; he needed to simplify, to find the order in the chaos. If he and Elena were to survive, he'd have to trust his instincts, and the training that shaped them. It was all they had.

Their pursuers would, he was sure, examine all possible means of egress, of escape, from Rupert Vere's office; that would determine the avenues of their search. Calculations would be made, search routes decided, based upon a fixed set of variables. The window was one obvious way out, but that was high above the ground, and no evidence would be found of any ropes or climbing apparatus. Vere's personal secretary, who guarded the entrance to the office suite, would assert that no one had run past here, though it was possible that she had been absent, away from her desk, for some period of time, in which case that route could not be ruled out.

That left one more avenue that had to be searched by their pursuers, and it would not take the killers long to realize that the plywood panel at the back of the closet was loose, though propped back into place. This meant that several killers from the Alpha squad or Prometheus were likely to be already finding their way through the crawlspace. Bryson and Elena's only hope was that the searchers might be confounded by the maze of hidden passages.

But a few seconds after they emerged from the steel air duct, Bryson could hear footsteps whose proximity seemed to indicate that they were coming from within the crawlspace, and not from outside. There was a certain echoing tonality, accompanied by a wooden creak. *Yes.* Bryson was now sure of it. Someone was following them through the concealed passage.

He felt Elena grab his shoulder, put her mouth to his ear, and whisper, "Listen!"

He nodded: *I hear.*

His mind raced. He had Dawson's Browning, with whatever ammunition was loaded in the chamber and magazine, and he had several implements in the briefcase that would be less effective in hand-to-hand combat. But the dismal fact was, there would be no hand-to-hand, close-range struggle. If they were spotted, guns would be fired, whether silenced or not.

Bryson stopped suddenly at another crack of light that seeped through the mortise work, and he peered through. He was looking into a fluorescent-lit utility room, its floors covered with old green linoleum. Looking more closely, he could make out shelving on one end stacked with what appeared to be cleaning supplies. Though the room was lit, it also appeared to be empty. He felt along the walls of the crawlspace until he found the detachable plywood panel that likely covered an egress into a closet that gave onto the utility room. With a small Phillips-head screwdriver he took from his briefcase, he unscrewed the panel and then pulled it loose. The wood squeaked and groaned as it came off. Indirect light shone through the opening; they could make out the outlines of the small closet, illuminated by a narrow slit of light that came in where the closet door met the linoleum floor.

Quietly, they squatted down and squeezed through the low, small opening. Bryson went first into the cluttered closet, and Elena followed. There was a sudden, jarring sound: Elena had knocked against a bucket, sending the wooden handle of a mop or broom clattering against the wall. They froze. Bryson held a hand in the air, signifying a command to halt. They listened, waited. Bryson's heart thundered.

After an endless minute, Bryson was satisfied that the noise had not attracted attention, and they resumed. Slowly, carefully, he opened the closet door. The utility room was indeed empty, though the lights were on; it was likely that someone had been here only recently, a cleaning person, who would therefore be returning at any time.

They raced silently across the room to the door that had to lead to a hallway. It was open a crack. Bryson pushed it open just enough to get his head through; he looked to either side down the dim hall. He saw no one. He whispered to Elena, "Stay here until I signal that it's safe to come out."

Bryson passed a vending machine and an old brown bucket in which stood a wet-mop, and then a figure appeared. He stopped short, reached for the Browning, which he had jammed into his waistband.

But it was only an old lady, a slow-moving cleaning woman pushing a metal cart. Relieved, Bryson continued down the hall toward her, mentally preparing a response in case he was asked questions. He was a civil servant, as his clothing—though dust-covered—indicated. Yet he was mindful that the old woman could become a resource as well, and they could afford to bypass no resources.

"Excuse me," Bryson said as he approached, dusting off his shoulders with a flick of his hand.

"Lost, are you?" the cleaning woman said. "Can I help you, dearie?" She had a kindly, wrinkled face, her white hair thin and wispy. She seemed old to be doing such manual labor, and she moved with such apparent physical exhaustion that she stirred Bryson's sympathy. Yet her eyes regarded him shrewdly.

Lost? But wasn't it a natural question: dressed as he was, Bryson appeared to be out of place in this service corridor. Had the word been circulated so quickly that one—or more—fugitives were roaming the building? He thought rapidly.

"I'm with Scotland Yard," Bryson replied in a flawless English lower-middle-class accent. "Some security breaches in the area. Maybe you've heard . . . ?"

"Aye," the old lady said wearily. "I don't ask questions. Be more than my job's worf, it would." She wheeled the cart down the hall toward them and parked it against the wall. "Lot of rumors flying around." She mopped her careworn brow with an old faded-red kerchief as she waddled up to him. "But you mind answerin' me just one question?"

Guardedly, Bryson said, "What's that?"

The ancient cleaning lady gave a perplexed look as she sidled up to Bryson and continued in a low, confiding voice, "What the hell are you doing *still alive?*" She whipped out a large blue-steel gun from the folds of her smock, pointed it at Bryson, and squeezed the trigger. Lightning-fast, Bryson swung his Kevlar-lined briefcase upward in a sharp arc, crashing it *hard* into her forearm. The gun clattered to the floor, skidding across the linoleum down the hall, away from him.

With a shrill scream, the harridan crouched and then sprang forward, her face contorted, her hands extended like claws, like deadly instruments. She slammed into him, knocking him to the floor just as he was reaching for the concealed gun. The wound in his side ached. *She's a goddamned old lady!* Bryson thought, then realizing—as she clawed at his eyes—that she was no old lady, she was far younger, far stronger, something more akin to a wild beast than a woman. She jabbed one thumb directly into his eye socket, the pain immense, blinding him, while she slammed her knee into his crotch, connecting at once with his genitals. Bryson roared with agony and determination, summoning his considerable strength, and slammed her to the floor. His right eye was bloodied, but he could still see through it, and what he saw made an eel of fear wriggle in his belly. She had pulled out a flashing blade, a long, thin stiletto. It gleamed wetly, as if coated with a viscous fluid. He knew at once that the blade must be coated with the alkaloid toxiferene, which made it an extremely dangerous weapon. The slightest nick or scrape would lead to immediate paralysis and a suffocating death.

Bryson could smell the blade and its acrid poison as it whisked millimeters from his face: he had jerked his head back just in time to save his life. Now the crazed woman reared up and lunged, and again Bryson's evasive action was only just sufficient; a button from his shirt was sliced off and went flying into the air. He went at her with both hands, with all of his strength, unable to risk reaching for the gun. The stiletto flashed in a blur near Bryson's face, but now Bryson lashed out with his left arm, like a cobra, directly *toward* the blade—a counterintuitive move, because it meant rising up and greeting the instrument of death, or the appendage that held it, rather than retreating from it—and as he seized the wrist of the hand holding the stiletto, the harridan was clearly taken by surprise.

But only for an instant. Bryson's strength would normally be far superior, but he was no longer in peak physical condition, nowhere close to it. He was, he was now realizing, badly weakened by the gunshot wound in Shenzhen; he had not given himself time to recover. And she had a mastery of moves he had never seen before. As her arm struggled against Bryson's grip, the long blade trembling, her left foot, clad in a steel-toed leather shoe, swung around, striking him again in the genitals. He groaned as he felt the pain radiating coldly through his testicles; he felt sick to his stomach. He shoved her again, slamming her back to the floor and knocking her white wig off her head, revealing close-cropped black hair and the lines of a latex face mask.

They were locked in struggle. She screamed again, her eyes wild. She was powerful and extraordinarily coordinated, and she lashed back and forth like a rabid beast. She tried to kick at him again, using her other foot, but Bryson had anticipated the move and rolled onto her, locking her legs in place, using his greater body mass, still holding her wrist, the stiletto blade still pointed at him. He had to move carefully around it, keeping all skin, all appendages clear of its lethal point. She was bucking violently, but he concentrated his strength, his energy, on angling her wrist back at her, directing the slickly gleaming stiletto toward her neck. Her arm shook with all the muscular resistance she could summon, but it was not enough: Bryson commanded more brute strength. Inch by inch, he pushed the tremulous blade back toward the soft exposed skin of the rabid woman's neck. Her eyes, hooded with latex skin folds, widened in terror as the blade gently creased her skin.

The effect was immediate. Her lips spread into a contorted rictus, spittle coming from her mouth, and she suddenly went limp against the floor and began to thrash wildly, her mouth opening again and again like a fish out of water, in soundless gasps. Then, as the deadening paralysis spread through her body, all respiration ceased; only a few muscles continued to twitch spasmodically.

Bryson pulled the blade from the dead woman's slackened grip, located the leather scabbard in the folds of her smock, and replaced the stiletto inside, then slid the scabbard into the breast pocket of his suit jacket. He gasped for breath, touched the sticky blood that covered his right eye. He heard a cry: Elena rushed forward from the utility room, placing her hands on either side of his face, her panicked eyes searching his face. "Oh, God, my darling!" she whispered. "I think your eye looks worse than it actually is. Was that a poison of some sort?"

"Toxiferene."

"She could have killed you, so easily!"

"She was strong, and very, very good."

"Alpha, do you think?"

"Almost certainly Prometheus. Alpha units are marines or navy SEALs. She was some sort of an exotic, probably hired from Bulgaria or the old East Germany—one of the defunct Eastern-bloc services."

"I hated staying back there, doing nothing!"

"You would have just gotten hurt, and she might have used you against me. No, I'm glad you did."

"Oh, Nicholas, I'm *useless*. I know *nothing* about combat, about fighting! *Draga mea*, we have to get out of here. They want to kill you and me both!"

Bryson nodded, gulped. "I think we should separate —"

"*No!*"

"Elena, by now they know there are two of us, a man and a woman. Their surveillance is too good, too complete. The foreign secretary of England has been assassinated, and all forces are going to be on alert, not just Prometheus and Alpha."

"There must be a thousand people in this building. Surely there's safety in numbers."

"Crowds are better for killers than their targets, especially when the killers know what the marks look like. These are people who will *not* be deterred by normal considerations of prudence."

"I can't! I'm sorry — on my own I can't fight, you know that! I can help you in many ways, but . . . please!"

Bryson nodded; she was terrified, and he couldn't send her off on her own in such a state. "All right. But we're going to have to take back hallways wherever we can find them, service corridors, that sort of thing. The crawlspaces and air ducts are no longer safe — they're probably crawling with agents by now. Somehow we have to get to the east side of the building if our escape plan's going to have any chance of succeeding."

Standing to one side of the utility room window so that he could not be seen from outside, Bryson saw at once that it was worse than he'd imagined. He counted six men in fatigues — members of the Alpha squad. Two of them were patrolling the state officer's courtyard; two others were checking building exits, and two were walking along the roof, surveying the area with binoculars.

He turned back to Elena. "Well, that's just modified the plan. We're going to have to go out to the hallway and look for a freight elevator."

"To the ground floor?"

He shook his head. "That's going to be crawling with police — and others. First or second floor, and then we'll look for an alternative way out." He walked quickly to the door and listened for a few seconds. He heard nothing; no one had come by even during his struggle with the crone. Obviously this was a little-used area. But the fact was, the Prometheus decoy had been circulating here, obviously expecting one or both of them to come by. That told him two things: that this was probably near a convergence point, where various routes came together and led to an exit from the building; and that there would be others not too far away. The sooner they were out of this section, the better.

He opened the door a crack, peered out, then looked to either side; it was clear. He signaled to Elena. They raced down the empty service corridor to the left, and when they reached a turning, Bryson stopped, looked right, spotted an elevator. He ran toward it, Elena close behind. It was an old-fashioned type of elevator with a tiny diamond-shaped glass window and a folding accordion gate inside. This was good: it meant that it was not likely to require a key to operate, since it predated such security precautions. He pressed the call button, and the cab whined slowly up, its compartment dimly illuminated. It was empty. He pulled the gate open, and they got in. He pressed the button marked 2.

For a moment he closed his eyes, visualizing the map. Obviously this would open on to a back service hall, used for cleaning and maintenance, but exactly where it led he wasn't certain. The layout of the Parliament building was exceedingly ornate; he had managed to memorize the main routes, though not all of them.

The elevator stopped on the second floor. Bryson looked out, surveying as much as he could of the area, which also looked clear. He pushed the door open, and they got out. Turning to the right, he saw an old green-painted door, with a scuffed crashbar mounted at hip-height. He approached it and pushed it open easily. Now they were in an ornate, marble-tiled hallway lined with mahogany doors labeled with gilt numerals. This was not a public, ceremonial area, nor was it grand enough for Parliament members, and there were no names or titles on the doors. Apparently these were offices belonging to committee staff—office clerks, executive officers, audit officers, secretaries, and other support staff. It was long and dimly lit; several people, presumably civil servants, walked unhurriedly into and out of offices. None of them seemed to glance at Bryson or Elena, nor did anything about their body language suggest that they were watchers or undercover operatives. *Instinct*, again: Bryson had nothing else to go on.

He stopped for a moment, trying to orient himself. The eastern end of the building was to the right; that was therefore the direction in which they should head. A well-dressed woman strode down the hall toward them, her heels clicking against the marble and echoing in the long hallway. Instinctively he looked at her, sizing her up; she approached them and passed with a curious stare. He suddenly remembered that, though he was still nominally attired as a respectable clerk, he had to be a frightful sight: one eye was bloodied, perhaps blackened, and his clothes were torn and disheveled from doing battle with the decoy cleaning lady. Elena's clothes were disheveled as well. Both of them looked decidedly out of place, their physical appearance drawing attention, which was exactly what he did not want. There was no time to look for a restroom in which to clean themselves up; now they would have to rely on a combination of speed and good luck. But luck was something he never liked to count on; luck inevitably ran out just when you took it for granted.

He continued down the hall, his head down as if deep in thought, walking quickly, holding Elena's hand, pulling her along. Here and there an office door was open and clusters of people stood talking quietly. If they glanced at the two of them, at least they might not see his bloodied face.

But something was not right here; he was overcome by anxiety. He felt the hairs on the back of his neck become prickly. The noises were *wrong*. The normal pattern of ringing telephones was absent; instead, the phones seemed to be ringing in sequence, at different offices and on different sides of the hallway. He could not rationally articulate why this bothered him, and he knew it was possible that he was beginning to imagine things. Too, he noticed that people engaged in conversation seemed to fall silent as he passed. Was he being *paranoid?*

He'd spent fifteen years in the field, and he had learned above all that one's instinct was the most valuable weapon one had. He did not ignore feelings that others might dismiss as delusional or paranoid.

They were being watched.

But if they were really being watched, why was nothing happening?

Pulling Elena's hand, he quickened his stride. He no longer cared whether his actions stood out or attracted attention; the situation was beyond that now.

About seventy-five yards ahead of them was a small leaded stained-glass window of the sort usually seen in a medieval cathedral. He knew that the windows here overlooked the Thames. "Straight ahead and to the left," he said to Elena under his breath.

She squeezed his hand in silent response. In a few seconds the corridor ended, and they turned left. Elena whispered, "Look—a committee room—it's probably empty. Do you think we should duck into there?"

"Excellent idea." He did not want to turn around to see whether they were being followed, but he heard no footsteps close behind. On their right was a massive, arched, oak double-door labeled, on a frosted-glass pane, COMMITTEE TWELVE. If they were able to enter it quickly, they might be able to lose any followers, or at the very least confuse them for a while. The doorknob turned freely; the door was unlocked, but the lights—two massive crystal chandeliers—were switched off and the immense room was vacant. It was an amphitheater, with several raised seating areas of leather-backed, brass-studded wooden chairs above a depressed center floor, which was of highly decorated, brightly colored encaustic tile. At the center of the room was a long wooden conference table, topped with green leather, and behind it two long, tall wooden pews—the benches for the committee members. Light came in through two large, tall leaded windows on the opposite side of the room facing the doors, a long rectangular shade running down the middle of each to block the direct sunlight that reflected off the Thames. Even in repose the room was at once solemn and grand. The vaulted ceiling was at least thirty feet high; the walls were wainscoted in dark wood more than halfway up, and above the wainscoting was elaborate burgundy wallpaper of a Gothic pattern. Several large, dreary nineteenth-century oil paintings hung on each wall: battle scenes, portraits of early kings commanding troops at sea, swords poised, Westminster Abbey crowded with nineteenth-century subjects mourning a casket draped with the Union Jack. The only touches of modernity were jarring: several microphones that dangled on long wires from the ceiling, and a television monitor mounted on one wall and labeled HOUSE OF COMMONS ANNUNCIATOR.

"Nicholas, we're not going to be able to hide in here," Elena said quietly. "At least not for long. Are you thinking of—the windows?"

He nodded, setting down his briefcase. "We're three flights above ground level."

"Such a drop!"

"It's not without risks," he agreed. "But it could be worse."

"Nick, I'll do it if you insist, if you really think we have no choice. But if there's any way—"

There was a noise in the hallway immediately outside. The doors flung open, and Bryson dropped to the ground, pulling her down after him. Two men entered, dark silhouettes, then two more. Bryson saw at once that they were *policemen*, wearing the blue uniforms of the Metropolitan Police!

And Bryson knew he and Elena had been spotted. "Freeze!" one of the policemen shouted. "Police!"

The men, unusual for British police, were carrying sidearms, aimed at them.

"Hold it right there!" another man shouted.

Elena screamed.

Bryson whipped out his Browning but did not draw. He calculated: four policemen, four handguns. It was far from impossible to take them on, using the wooden chairs as shields, as obstacles.

But *were* they in fact policemen? He could not be certain. They looked resolute, their expressions fierce. *But they did not fire*. Prometheus killers would probably not have hesitated. Would they?

"That's the buggers!" one of the policemen shouted. "The assassins!"

"Drop the weapon," called the one who appeared to be in charge. "Drop it at once. You got nowhere to go now." Bryson turned around, saw that they were indeed trapped; they were fish in a barrel. The four police constables continued to advance into the room, closer and closer, spreading out so that they had Bryson and Elena surrounded.

"*Drop it!*" the same one repeated, now shouting. "Drop it, you scum. Get to your feet, hands in the air. *Move it!*"

Elena looked at Bryson, desperate, unsure what to do. Bryson considered his option. To surrender was to give themselves up to a questionable authority, to police who might in fact *not* be police, might be Prometheus killers in disguise.

And if they were legitimate members of the Metropolitan Police? If so, he could not kill them. Yet if they were true police constables, they believed they were on the verge of apprehending a couple of assassins, a man and a woman who had just killed the foreign secretary. They would be taken into custody and questioned for hours—hours they could not spare. With no certainty that they would be released.

No, they could not surrender to them! Yet to do anything else was *madness*, was *suicide!*

He inhaled deeply, closed his eyes for a moment, and when he opened them again, he got to his feet. "All right," he said. "All right. You've got us."

CHAPTER
TWENTY-EIGHT

One of the men seemed clearly to be in charge: a tall, fit man whose name tag said SULLIVAN.

"All right, drop the gun and put your hands in the air, and you won't get hurt," Sullivan said steadily. "There's four of us and only two of you, but I guess you've already figured that out."

Bryson held his pistol up, though not directly pointed at anyone. *Were they really who they said they were?* That was his greatest concern right now.

"Agreed," Bryson answered with forced calm. "But I first want to see some identification."

"Shutcher gob!" bellowed one of the policemen. "Here's *my* identification right *here*, you sod." He indicated his pistol. "Try me."

But Sullivan replied, "Fine. As soon as you're cuffed you'll have all the time in the world to study our warrant cards."

"No," Bryson said. He raised the Browning ever so slightly, still pointed at no one in particular. "I'll be happy to cooperate once I'm confident you are who you say you are. But there are teams of mercenaries and assassins roaming the halls of Parliament, operating in violation of about a dozen British laws. Once I'm satisfied you're not one of them, I'll drop the gun."

"Take the arsehole down," growled one of the men.

"We fire when I give the order, Constable," Sullivan said. Then, addressing Bryson: "I'll show you my warrant card, but be warned—you've killed the foreign secretary, you bastard, so you're probably fool enough to try for one of us blokes. If you're lucky enough to squeeze off a shot, it'll be the last thing you ever do, so don't fuck with us, you hear me?"

"Understood. Take it out with your left hand, *slowly*, and display it for me, palm open. Got it?"

"Got it," Sullivan said, following Bryson's instructions. The leather folding wallet lay open in his left hand.

"Good. Now slide it across the floor to me—toss it slowly, *gently*. No quick moves—don't startle me or I'm likely to fire in self-defense."

Sullivan flicked his left wrist, sending the wallet across the floor. It stopped right at Bryson's feet. As Bryson leaned to pick it up, he became aware of one of the men—the one who was obviously itching to fire—advancing on him from the left side. Bryson whirled around, gun pointed directly at the constable's face. "Don't move, you *idiot*. I meant what I said. If you believe I really murdered the foreign secretary in cold blood, then you surely don't think I'd hesitate to blow you away, do you?" The trigger-happy man froze, backed up a few steps, but kept his gun still leveled at Bryson.

"That's it," said Bryson. He sank slowly to his knees to retrieve the wallet, all the while keeping the gun level, shifting it back and forth from man to man. He quickly snatched the leather wallet from the floor, opened it, and glanced at the silver badge on the right flap in the form of the Metropolitan Police crest. Inside the plastic sleeve on the left side was a white laminated card with Sergeant Robert Sullivan's photograph, in uniform, along with his warrant number, rank, serial number, and signature. It certainly looked legitimate, though it was easily within the Prometheus team's capabilities to obtain genuine or cleverly forged police identification. The name, Sullivan, matched the leader's name tag, and the collar number on the epaulet of his navy blue sweater matched the number on the warrant card. Sullivan was identified as a member of the Special Operations Unit, meaning that he, and presumably the others, were allowed to carry weapons. It was possible, of course, that they had simply been thorough about these details. In truth, very little could be determined conclusively from the badge, in fact, except for the fact that there *was* one and, upon quick examination, it checked out. An under-cover team of assassins assembled on such short notice was not likely to have every detail of their disguises straight, yet so far he had not spotted a gaffe.

His instincts told him the policemen were legitimate. He based this assessment on a whole range of minor details, behavioral cues, attitudes, and, most important, the fact that they had held their fire. They could easily have killed him, but they had not done so. In the end it was that simple fact that led Bryson to drop his gun and raise his hands in the air, and Elena did the same.

"All right, nice and easy now, move toward that wall, the both of you, and put your hands flat against it," said Sullivan.

They walked slowly to the closest wall and placed their hands against it. Bryson kept alert for any departure from expected behavior patterns. Weapons were now lowered; that was good. Two members of the team approached, quickly locked handcuffs on their wrists, then patted both of them down for concealed weapons. Another scooped up Bryson's gun.

"My name is Police Sergeant Sullivan. You're both under arrest in connection with the murder of Foreign Secretary Rupert Vere and Un-dersecretary Simon Dawson." Sullivan flipped a switch on his two-way pocket radio and detailed his location, calling for backup.

"I understand the necessity for going through established procedures," said Bryson, "but a careful ballistic examination will reveal that it was Dawson who murdered the foreign secretary."

"Murdered by his own deputy? Bloody likely."

"Dawson was a control, an agent of an international syndicate with a significant interest in passing the surveillance treaty. He was far too careful, I'm sure, to leave any evidence in plain sight linking him to this group, but there *will* be evidence—altered phone logs, visitors admitted to the Parliament building to see him yet not recorded in his own records—"

Suddenly the great arched doors banged open again, and two large, heavily muscled, uniformed men carrying automatic submachine guns came rushing into the room. "Ministry of Defense, Special Forces!" called the taller of the two men in a husky baritone.

Officer Sullivan turned in surprise. "We weren't notified of your participation, sir."

"Nor we of yours. We'll take over from here," the tall man said. He had steel-gray brush-cut hair and cold blue eyes.

"That won't be necessary," Sullivan said. His tone was calm, but there was no mistaking his resolve. "We've got everything under control."

Bryson turned with alarm, his hands cuffed. The machine guns were Czech, nothing that would have been issued by the British Ministry of Defense. "No!" he shouted. "Mother of *Christ*, they're not who they say!"

Baffled, Sullivan looked from Bryson to the crew-cut man. "You're Ministry of Defense, you say?"

"Right," the man replied brusquely. "We've got the situation under control."

"*Get down!*" Bryson screamed. "They're *killers!*"

Elena dove to the floor, screaming, and Bryson dove next to her, a row of wooden chairs the only barrier between them and the intruders.

But it was too late. Even before he finished speaking, the hall echoed with the deafening thunder of automatic fire as the gray-haired killer and his cohort sprayed bullets into the four police constables, *riddled* their bodies with bullets. Stray rounds pinged against the stone floor and chewed into the mahogany wainscoting. Caught off guard, their sidearms holstered, the genuine policemen were easy targets. A few of them reached, seconds too late, for their weapons. They staggered, their bodies twisting from side to side, almost dancing in a pathetic but vain attempt to dodge the bullets before they crumpled to the floor.

Elena shrieked, "Oh, my *God! Oh, my God!*"

Horrified and sickened, Bryson watched, powerless to do anything.

The air was acrid with cordite, with the coppery smell of blood. The brush-cut Promethean killer consulted his wristwatch.

Bryson understood what had just happened and why. The Prometheus Group would never countenance the risk of letting the two of them be taken into official custody: the dangers posed by what they might divulge could not be gauged with precision. Rather, the Promethean hirelings would themselves want to interrogate them, and only then kill them. That was the only possible explanation for why they were still alive.

Now the tall killer spoke in a deep voice. His accent, which on first hearing had sounded British, now seemed to be Dutch, Bryson decided. "We're going to have a few hours of fun together," the Prometheus killer said. "Chemical interrogation has become quite advanced in recent years, as you'll see."

On the floor, Bryson struggled, quietly and discreetly, with the handcuffs, but without a key, or something he could use as a key, it was no use. He looked around; the policemen who lay dead, their bodies riddled with bullets, were no closer than six to eight feet away. He would not be able to take a handcuff key off one of their bodies without being seen doing so; he would never get away with it. But to stay here meant to face chemicals, probably administered inexpertly and in such quantities that they would sustain serious and irreversible damage.

No, he corrected himself. *After the chemicals will be death.*

Robby Sullivan had felt the impact across his midriff like the kick of a horse, and the next thing he knew he was slumped to the floor. His shirtfront was soaked with blood; he couldn't get his breath. A bullet must have punctured a lung, because he felt as if he were slowly drowning. His breathing was shallow, labored. And all the while, his mind fought for some semblance of comprehension. What was going on? The couple who had surrendered appeared to be unharmed, even while his loyal and devoted men, good men all of them with girlfriends or wives and families, had been brutally mowed down. They had all been trained to expect such a possibility, but in reality their jobs in the Westminster Division could not have been more peaceful. What had happened to his men was ghastly, *unthinkable! And me too,* he thought ruefully. *I'm not long for this world either.* But he didn't understand: had the armed men come to *rescue* the assassins? Then why had the handcuffed man tried to warn him? He stared at the ceiling, his gaze moving in and out of focus, steadily weakening, wondering how much longer he would remain conscious.

He had been unable to get his gun out in time, but who on God's green earth would have expected soldiers from the Ministry of Defense to suddenly turn on them with machine guns? They weren't, of course, from the Ministry. The uniforms—their uniforms weren't Ministry of Defense . . . something was definitely off. The handcuffed man was right, which might well mean that the protestations of innocence were justified. Things were happening beyond his ability to understand, but this much seemed clear: the handcuffed man had surrendered peacefully, his protests plausible; and the intruders with machine guns were unquestionably cold-blooded killers. Robby Sullivan felt reasonably certain that he was dying, that he was just minutes from death, and he prayed to the Lord Jesus Christ that He would allow him just one more chance to set things right. Slowly, through a haze, he felt around for his gun.

"You are wanted internationally, as I'm sure you know," said the Dutchman matter-of-factly.

Elena was weeping, her cuffed hands up to her face. "No, please," she moaned softly. "Please."

He noticed that the second man, who had the slightly thickened features of a pugilist, had shifted position and was moving in closer, his machine gun clutched in one hand and what looked like a hypodermic needle in the other.

"The assassination of a British cabinet member is a most serious crime. But we simply want to talk to you—we want to know why you are so determined to interfere, to instigate such trouble."

Bryson's keen ears heard a faint sound from a few feet away. He allowed himself to glance quickly and saw that the constable named Sullivan was moving his hand, reaching . . .

Bryson moved his eyes back to the brush-cut killer, staring at him fiercely. *Don't let him see what I just saw.*

"The Directorate is no longer, I'm sure you know that," continued the gray-haired man. "You have no support, no backup—no resources. You are alone, and you are tilting at windmills, as the saying goes."

Keep him occupied! Don't let his attention stray, don't let him hear . . .

"We're far from alone," Bryson said intensely, his eyes flashing. "Long before you destroyed the Directorate, we had put out the word. You and your coconspirators have already been found out, and whatever the hell you're attempting to pull off is already finished."

The police constable's fingertips were brushing the barrel of the handgun, clawing at it, flailing at it; it was mere inches beyond his reach!

The crew-cut man continued as if he hadn't heard a word Bryson said. "There's really no reason for any more blood to be shed," he said reasonably. "We simply want to have an honest, heart-to-heart conversation with you. That's all."

Bryson did not dare look again, but he heard the tiniest scrape of metal against the stone floor. *Distract him! Engage his attention elsewhere—he must not hear, must not notice!* Bryson abruptly raised his voice. "What is it that's worth all the destruction, the terrorism?" he shouted. "The *bombs?* What is it that justifies blowing an airliner out of the sky that's packed with hundreds of people—with innocent men and women and children?"

"But you see, we believe that the few must be sacrificed at the altar of the many. The lives of a few hundred mean *nothing* compared to the safety and security of millions—of *billions*—the protection of untold generations of . . ." The Prometheus killer's words trailed off as his face creased with suspicion. He cocked his head to one side, listening. "Tomas!" he called.

The two gunshots were nearly deafening, twin explosions, one immediately following the other. The policeman had done it! He had lifted his pistol and, summoning a strength and resolve that momentarily banished the shock and lethargy of extreme blood loss, had fired two very well-aimed shots. There was a spray of blood as the large-caliber bullet drilled through the Promethean's head and exited at the back, the round freezing him in midturn, his expression a combination of fury and surprise. His shorter cohort twitched spasmodically before sinking to his knees: the bullet had passed through his neck, obviously having intersected with both his spinal cord and a major artery.

Elena had rolled out of the way, frightened by the sudden gunfire and not understanding where it had come from. When the explosions stopped, she waited a few seconds and then raised her head, and this time she did not scream; the shock was too great, and she was probably numbed by now to all the violence. Eyes wide and liquid with tears, she murmured a low prayer, clasping her cuffed hands.

The police constable who had done it, Sergeant Sullivan, was breathing noisily, a death rattle. He'd been wounded badly in the torso, a sucking wound. Bryson looked over and saw that the sergeant had probably a few minutes left.

"I don't know . . . who you are . . ." the policeman said weakly. "Not who we thought . . ."

"We're not killers!" Elena called. "You know that, I *know* you do!" In a trembling voice she added, quietly, "You've just saved our lives."

Bryson heard the jangle of metal on the floor right by his head: Sullivan had tossed him his key ring.

Must hurry, he thought. *How much time remained before others would arrive, attracted by the explosions? Two minutes? One? Seconds?*

Bryson reached over with his manacled hands and grabbed the key ring, quickly locating a handcuff key. With a little maneuvering, Bryson worked the small key into Elena's cuffs, springing them open; she then took the key and swiftly unlocked his. One of the policeman's two-way radios crackled to life: "Jesus, what's going on?" a tinny, staticky voice demanded.

"Go," the sergeant told the two in a faint whisper.

Elena saw Bryson racing toward the right-hand arched window. "We can't leave this man here—not after what he's done for us!" she protested.

"He's not answering his radio," Bryson replied quickly as he unhooked the long shade and threw it, clatteringly, to the floor, then began working loose a bolt on the window frame. "They'll locate him quickly, and they'll be able to do more for him than we could do." *But there's nothing they can do for him,* he thought but didn't say. "Come *on!*" he shouted.

Elena rushed to the window, tugged at a sliding bolt until it came free. Bryson turned, saw Sullivan slump back on to the floor, now silent and still. *The man turned out to be a hero,* Bryson thought. *There aren't many of them.* He yanked at the window, hard. It seemed not to have been opened in years, perhaps decades. But after another hard tug it yielded, admitting a rush of cold air into the room.

This side of the Palace of Westminster, the east side, fronted directly onto the Thames, the length of the building running nearly nine hundred feet. Most of it, about seven hundred feet, was taken up by a terrace, furnished with chairs and tables, where members of Parliament had tea or entertained; but on either side of the terrace two narrow, somewhat taller sections of the building jutted out, with just a short stone embankment and a low steel fence, and then water. They were in one of the two protruding ends, as Bryson had planned; the river was directly below them, almost a straight plumb line down.

Elena looked out, turned to Bryson with a frightened expression, but then, to Bryson's astonishment, she said, "I'll go first. I'll—I'll pretend I'm diving off the highest diving board in Bucharest."

Bryson smiled. "Protect your head and neck from the impact. Better to cannonball it, tuck your head and neck into your arms as you drop. And jump out as far as you can so you're sure to hit the water."

She nodded, bit her lower lip.

"I see it—the boat," he said.

She looked, nodded again. "At least that much I did right," she said with a wan smile. "Thames River Cruises was happy to rent a speedboat to my boss, a rich and eccentric unnamed Member of Parliament who wanted to impress his latest lady friend by taking her directly from the Parliament embankment to the Millennium Dome in the fastest boat they had. That was the easy part. But their boats are moored at the Westminster pier—to get one of them to rope it up right in front of the palace required a rather sizable bribe. In case you wonder where all the cash went."

Bryson smiled. "You did great." He could see the boat bobbing in the water about twenty feet to the left, tied to the steel fence in front of the terrace. Elena took a short step from the floor to the bottom of the window, Bryson assisting her. He looked around, saw no sharpshooters on this section of the roof, nor any patrolling the terrace, this hardly being a logical or expected escape route. Valuable resources had to be expended carefully, priorities assessed, men assigned where they were deemed to be most needed.

She stood on the ledge of the open window, took a deep breath. Her left hand squeezed his shoulder. Then she leaped straight out into the air, tucking herself into a ball, and dropped the fifty feet into the water with a loud splash. He waited for her to give him the thumbs-up signaling that she was fine, and then Bryson climbed onto the window ledge and jumped.

The water was cold and murky, the current powerful; when he surfaced, he saw that Elena, a strong swimmer, had almost reached the boat. By the time he had swum to it, she had started the motor. He climbed up and jumped into the cockpit and within seconds they were speeding across the water, away from Parliament, from the teams of killers.

Within a few hours they were in their hotel room on Russell Square. Bryson had gone shopping, with a highly specific list Elena had provided, and returned with the equipment she needed: the fastest and most powerful laptop computer he could buy, equipped with an infrared port; a fast modem; a variety of computer cables.

She looked up from the laptop, which was connected by telephone wire to the phone jack, and from there to the Internet. "I think I need a drink, darling."

Bryson poured her a Scotch, neat, from the room's bar, then poured one for himself. "You're downloading something?" he asked.

She nodded and took a grateful sip. "Password-recovery software — shareware. Dawson took precautions — his handheld device was password-protected. Until and unless I can crack that, we're not going to get a thing. But once we get past the password, I'll bet we're in."

He picked up Dawson's billfold. "Anything here?"

"Just credit cards, some cash, a bunch of papers. Nothing useful — I've checked." She turned back to the laptop. "This may be it." She entered a password into Dawson's personal digital assistant. A moment later her face lit up. "We're in."

Bryson took a celebratory drink. "You're a remarkable woman."

She shook her head. "I am a woman who loves her work. You, Nicholas, are the remarkable one. I've never known a man like you."

"You must not know many men."

She smiled. "I've known my share. Maybe more than my share. But no one like you — no one as brave and as . . . *stubborn*, I would say. You never gave up on me."

"I don't know if that's quite true. Maybe for a while — in my deepest, darkest depression, when I was drinking far too much of this stuff"—he held up his glass, toasted her—"maybe then I did. I was angry—hurt and confused and angry. But I was never sure, I was never certain—"

"About what?"

"About the reasons why you left. I had to know. I knew I'd never be satisfied until I knew the truth, even if it tore the heart out of me."

"You never asked Ted Waller?"

"I knew better than to ask him. I knew that if he knew anything—or if he wanted to tell me anything—he would."

She looked distant, vaguely troubled, and she began tapping at the device with a small black stylus. "I've often wondered," she said, her voice trailing off. "Oh, my."

"What?"

"There's an entry here in his date book. 'Call H. Dunne.' "

Bryson looked up suddenly. "Harry Dunne. *Jesus*. Is there a phone number?"

"No. Just 'Call H. Dunne.' "

"When is the entry?"

"It's—it's three days ago!"

"*What?* My God, of course—of course he's still around—still reachable by those who he's willing to talk to. Does that thing have phone numbers or an address book?"

"It seems to have everything—an enormous amount of data." She tapped again at the screen. "Shit."

"Now what?"

"It's encrypted. Both the telephone and address-book database, and something else that's labeled 'transfers.' "

"Shit."

"Well, that's good and bad."

"How is that good?"

"You only encrypt something valuable, so there must be something interesting here. The locked room is the one you want to go into."

"That's one way of looking at it."

"The problem here is limited resources. This is a top-of-the-line note-book computer, but it doesn't have a fraction of the computing power of the supercomputers we had in the Dordogne. Now, this is a 56-bit DES encryption algorithm, fortunately—it doesn't use 128-bit keys, thank God—but it's still strong."

"Can you crack it?"

"Eventually."

"Eventually meaning . . . hours?"

"Days or weeks with this computer, and that's only because I know these utilities, these systems, inside out."

"We don't even have *days*."

She was silent for a long time. "I know," she said at last. "I suppose I can try to improvise—basically, parcel out the work to different hacker sites on the Internet, distribute the chore of crunching billions of number combinations. And see if we get anything that way. It's sort of like that old saying about how an infinite number of monkeys with typewriters will eventually come up with Shakespeare."

"Sounds dubious."

"Well, I'll be frank—I'm not very hopeful."

Three hours later, when Bryson returned with carry-out Indian food, Elena looked careworn and gloomy.

"No luck, huh?" Bryson said.

She shook her head. She was smoking, something Bryson had not seen her do since first escaping Romania. Popping out from the computer's floppy drive one of the diskettes she had rescued from the Dordogne facility, containing decrypted Prometheus information, she put out her cigarette and went to the bathroom. She returned with a wet washcloth plastered on her forehead, then sank into an armchair. "My head hurts," she said. "From thinking too much."

"Take a break," Bryson said. He set down the paper bags of food and came around to the back of her chair, then began massaging her neck.

"Oh, that feels great," she murmured. After a moment, she said, "We have to reach Waller."

"I can try one of the emergency relay channels, but I have no idea how deeply the Directorate has been penetrated. I can't even be sure he'll get it."

"It's worth a try."

"Yes, but only if it doesn't compromise our own security. Waller would understand that, approve of it."

THE PROMETHEUS DECEPTION

"Our security," she mumbled. "Yes."

"What are you saying?"

" 'Security' made me think of passwords and encryption."

"Naturally."

"And that made me think of Dawson, and how an obviously busy and careful man like that keeps track of all his passwords. Because someone like that never uses just one password—it's not secure."

"How would he keep track?"

"There would be a list somewhere."

"It's always been my experience that the weakest link in computer security in an office is always the secretary who keeps the password taped in her desk drawer because she can never remember it."

"I'm sure Dawson was more cunning than that. Yet the cryptographic 'key' is a long series of numbers—truly impossible to memorize. So he has to keep it . . . can you hand me his Palm Pilot?"

Bryson retrieved it from her work station and gave it to her. She turned it on and tapped at the screen with the stylus. For the first time in hours she smiled. "There's a list here, all right. With the mysterious label '*Tesserae.*' "

"If I remember my high school Latin, that's plural for *tessera*, meaning 'password.' Is the list in the clear?"

"No, it's encrypted, but it's a light encryption utility—it's called 'secure information management software.' A password protector. This is not difficult at all. It's sort of like locking the front door but leaving the garage door open. I can use the same password-recovery software I downloaded earlier. Child's play."

Her usual energy and enthusiasm having been restored, she returned to the work table. Ten minutes later, she announced that she had broken the code. She was able to read through all of the data Dawson had so carefully locked away.

"Dear *God*, Nick. The file marked 'Transfers' is a record of wire-transfer payments made into a long list of London bank accounts. Amounts ranging from fifty thousand to a hundred thousand pounds, in some cases triple that!"

"Who are the recipients?"

"These names! This is like a Who's Who of Parliament—members of

413

the House of Commons across the whole political spectrum—Labor, Liberal Democrat, Conservative, even Ulster Unionists. He's got names, dates of receipt, amounts, even times and locations of his meetings with them. A complete documentary record."

Bryson's pulse was racing. "Bribery *and* blackmail. The two cardinal elements of illicit political influence-peddling. It's an old Soviet technique for blackmailing Westerners—they'd pay you some token amount for your services as a consultant, perfectly legitimate-seeming, and then they'd have you—they had proof of Soviet payments into your bank account. So Dawson not only paid off members of Parliament, but he kept the proof of it, as potential blackmail, in case anyone wavered. *That's* how Simon Dawson exerted power. That's how he became the secret control behind Rupert Vere, his boss, the foreign secretary. And probably behind Lord Parmore, and no doubt behind dozens of other influential voices in Parliament. Simon Dawson was the secret *paymaster*. If you want to influence a political debate as charged and as crucial as the debate over the surveillance treaty in Parliament, money certainly helps grease the wheels. Payoffs. Bribes to unscrupulous politicians, to those whose votes are for sale."

"Apparently most of the most influential politicians in Parliament were selling their votes."

"I'm willing to wager there was more to some of those cases than simple bribery. If we were to go through the British press in the last year or so, I'll bet we'd find a pattern similar to what happened in the Congress in the U.S.—leaks of sensitive, private information, embarrassing and damaging secrets, human weakness revealed to the world. I'll bet the most diehard opponents of the treaty were forced out of office, just as Senator Cassidy was forced out in America. And the others were warned, compromised—and then given the carrot, a nice, fat 'campaign contribution.' "

"In laundered funds," Elena said. "Untraceable."

"Is there any way to determine the source of the funds?"

She popped one of the diskettes from the Dordogne facility into the computer. "Dawson's record is so complete it even has the bank codes for the originating bank. He doesn't list the bank name, just the code."

"You're comparing it against the data Chris Edgecomb downloaded?"

Her face seemed to cloud at the mention of Edgecomb's name; it had obviously recalled the nightmare. She didn't answer, but instead peered at the screen, at the long columns of numbers flashing by. "We have a match."

"Let me guess," Bryson said. "Meredith Waterman."

"That's right. The same firm that secretly owns the, uh, First Washington Mutual Bancorp. The place where you say Richard Lanchester made his fortune."

He inhaled sharply. "An old-line investment banking house has somehow become the conduit of illicit funds into Washington and London."

"And maybe other world-power centers as well—Paris, Moscow, Berlin . . ."

"No doubt. Meredith Waterman in effect owns Congress and Parliament."

"You said Richard Lanchester got very rich there."

"Right, but the story is that he left all that behind to go to Washington. That he severed all formal ties, all financial connections."

"I learned as a child never to believe what I read in the Bucharest papers. I was taught always to distrust the official story."

"A useful lesson, I'm sorry to say. You're speculating that Lanchester still has influence there, and that's how he's able to use his old bank to channel massive amounts of bribes?"

"Meredith Waterman is a privately held bank—a limited partnership, from what I've learned. It's basically owned by ten or twelve general partners. Do you think it's possible that he's still a partner there?"

"No. Can't be. Once he started working in the government, he would have had to give all that up—resign his partnership and put any assets there into a blind trust. To work at the White House requires full financial disclosure."

"No, Nick. Financial disclosure to the FBI, not *public* disclosure. He's never had to go through a Senate confirmation, has he? *Think* about it— maybe this is the reason why he refuses to accept the president's nomination to become secretary of state! Maybe it's *not* some kind of modesty—maybe he just doesn't want to go through the additional public attention, the scrutiny, that would come with it. Maybe he has things to hide—skeletons in his closet."

"Well, you're right that a national security adviser doesn't have to go through the same baptism by fire that the secretary of state does," Bryson conceded. "But White House officials are still under the microscope no matter who they are, their every move scrutinized, everyone always looking for financial improprieties."

Elena seemed impatient; she was a mathematician comfortable with abstract principles most of all, and she was developing a theory that he insisted on poking holes in. "I want you to consider this about Lanchester. In the last few months I've been watching closely what's happening with this International Treaty on Surveillance and Security. In our line of work, we're naturally very interested, right?"

He nodded.

"And, well, once this treaty is ratified, it will create an international executive, a new, global law-enforcement body with sweeping powers. And *who's going to head this new agency?* In the last few weeks, if you've been reading the newspaper reports very closely, you'd always find the same few names mentioned—always deep into the article, always couched as speculation—as possible directors. The term they always use is 'czar'—a word that always makes me nervous. You know how we Romanians felt about the Russian czar."

"The czar being Lanchester."

"His name is being floated—what do they call that, a 'trial balloon'?"

"But that makes no sense—he's known to be opposed to the treaty! He's supposed to be one of the voices in the White House who lobbied hardest *against* it, believing that such a worldwide law-enforcement agency could be abused, could infringe upon fundamental personal freedoms . . ."

"And how do we *know* he's opposed to it? Leaks, right? Isn't that how it works? But leaks to the press always have a hidden motive—people have reasons for making things known, for influencing public perceptions. Maybe Richard Lanchester wanted to sort of cloak his ambitions because he actually *wants* to be named to this position—which he would then reluctantly accept!"

"*Jesus.* I suppose it's possible he's been engaged in some sort of diversion for some reason."

"That 'some reason' being that at the same time he's behind the Prometheus conspiracy, and it's important to him that he not seem to be connected to any such maneuverings. Think of that game that is played with the shells and little ball, where you move the shells around and people try to guess which shell the ball is under. A shell game, yes? So this is a diversion, as you put it—a deflection. We all watch the public battle over legislation, over laws—while behind the scenes the *real* battle is being waged. The one involving immense amounts of money and power! A battle waged by wealthy and powerful private citizens who stand to become ten *times* as wealthy and powerful."

Bryson shook his head. Much of what she was saying was logical, made sense. Yet a national security adviser to the president, a White House official—a man in such a goldfish bowl simply could not orchestrate such a massive conspiracy. The risks were too great, the danger of exposure too grave. That did *not* make sense. And then there was the question of motive. The drive for money and power was as old as human civilization itself—older, perhaps. But . . . all of this simply to ensure that Lanchester was named to another bureaucratic position? *Ludicrous.* It couldn't be.

Yet he was now convinced that Richard Lanchester was the key to Prometheus—a vital link in the chain that *led* to Prometheus. "We have to get inside," he whispered urgently.

"Inside Meredith Waterman?"

Bryson nodded, deep in thought.

"In New York?"

"Right."

"But to do what?"

"To find out the truth. To find out what the exact connection is between this Richard Lanchester and Meredith Waterman and the Prometheus conspiracy."

"But if you're right—if Meredith Waterman is really the node, the locus of massive payments around the world—then it's going to be locked as tight as a drum. It's going to be well guarded, every file cabinet triple-locked, every computer code word protected, the files encrypted."

"That's why I want to get you inside."

"Nicholas, that's *crazy!*"

He chewed at his lower lip. "Let's think this through fully. To adapt one of your metaphors, if the door is locked, go in through the window."

"What's the window?"

"If we want to find out how a reputable old merchant bank got into the money-laundering business, I guarantee we're not going to dig up records in the expected places. Because, as you say, it'll be locked tight as a drum. All contemporary records will be sealed, locked away, unreachable. So we have to look at *yesterday*—at the *old* Meredith Waterman, the prestigious investment bank, back in its glory days. At the *past*."

"What are you saying?"

"Look, Meredith Waterman used to be one of those old-shoe Wall Street partnerships—a bunch of doddering old inbred geezers who made all the decisions around a coffin-shaped conference table under oil paintings of their ancestors. So when—*how*—did they start channeling money for bribes? And who did it? How did it happen, and when?"

She shrugged. "But where do you look for such records?"

"The archives. Every old-line bank with a sense of history stores its old files, archives, saving every damned scrap of paper, filing them away, labeling them for posterity. They had a true sense of history, these old guys, a sense—no doubt inflated—of their own immortality. The new owners would be unlikely to discard the old records, considering them essentially benign, since they came from the days before all the secret funds transactions. And *that's* our window, the soft underbelly. The place where security is most likely to be lax. Now, can you book us a couple of plane tickets on that thing?"

"Of course. To New York, right?"

"Right."

"Tomorrow?"

"*Tonight*. If you can find two seats tonight, grab them, on any airline, together or not, it makes no difference. We have to get to New York as soon as possible."

To the Wall Street headquarters of a venerable old investment bank, he thought. *A once-reputable bank that is now a vital link to the Prometheus deception.*

CHAPTER
TWENTY-NINE

The headquarters of the eminent investment bank Meredith Waterman was located on Maiden Lane in southernmost Manhattan, just a few blocks from Wall Street, in the shadow of the World Trade Center. Unlike the mock-Renaissance palazzo of the Federal Reserve Bank of New York nearby, where much of the nation's gold reserve was stored in five underground floors, the Meredith Waterman building was unassuming yet proud, quietly elegant. It was a graceful, four-story neoclassical building with a mansard roof and brick-and-limestone façade, constructed a century earlier in the style of the French Second Empire; it seemed to belong to a different place, a different era—to Paris in the time of Napoleon, when the French dared to dream of a world empire.

Surrounded by the new skyscrapers of the financial district as it was, the landmark Meredith Waterman building radiated a serene confidence borne of its aristocratic pedigree, for Meredith Waterman was the oldest private bank in America. It was famous for its genteel reputation, for managing the fortunes of generations of America's wealthiest families, its clients the oldest of old money. The name Meredith Waterman called to mind its legendary mahogany-paneled partners' room, yet at the same time it had a global reach. Articles and profiles in financial publications from *Fortune* to *Forbes* to *The Wall Street Journal* talked of the privately held bank's clubbiness, of the fact that it was owned by fourteen general partners whose families traced their roots back to the very founding of Manhattan, that it was the last remaining private partnership among America's large investment banks.

Bryson and Elena had spent a few hours in preparation. She had done considerable on-line research on Meredith Waterman, using the Internet facilities of the New York Public Library. Very little financial information about the bank was available: since it was not a publicly held corporation, it was required to divulge relatively little about its operations. About the general partners she was able to pull up considerably more, though largely in the realm of straightforward biography. Richard Lanchester was not among the listed partners; he had resigned shortly after being named the President's national security adviser. Since then he seemed to have no ties at all to his old employer.

And what about *social* ties, personal ones, friendships dating back to school days, family connections? Elena searched and searched, and found nothing. Lanchester's social circles seemed not to overlap with those of his old partners; neither had he gone to the same schools. If there was a Lanchester connection, it was not overt.

In the meantime, Bryson gathered information in the way in which he was most comfortable: by foot, by eye, by telephone call. He spent several hours walking around the neighborhood, posing as a telephone repairman, as a software salesman, as an entrepreneur in search of office space to rent, chatting up computer specialists who worked out of neighboring buildings. By the late afternoon he had amassed a decent amount of information about Meredith Waterman's physical plant, its computer systems, even its old corporate records.

Then in a final sweep of the area before his rendezvous with Elena, he walked past the building, directly in front of it, with the casual curiosity of a tourist from out of town. The main entrance was at the top of a broad, steep granite staircase. Inside, the oval marble lobby was illuminated dramatically, the centerpiece a large bronze statue on a pedestal. It appeared, at first glance, to be a Greek mythological figure; it looked familiar. Bryson had seen it somewhere before. Then he remembered: the skating rink at Rockefeller Center.

Yes. It appeared to be modeled after the famous gilded bronze statue in Rockefeller Center.

The statue of Prometheus.

It was five o'clock in the afternoon; they had completed their preparations, yet Bryson's surveillance indicated that they should not attempt a covert entry until after midnight. At least seven hours from now.

So long a wait, yet so short a time. Time was a scarce commodity, not to be wasted. Others had to be reached, chief among them Harry Dunne. Yet he was not to be found, no information offered as to his whereabouts beyond a vague statement that the deputy director of Central Intelligence was "on leave" for unspecified "family reasons"; rumors circulated that "family" was coded language for "medical," that the senior intelligence official was seriously ill.

Elena had done searches, made inquiries, yet turned up nothing.

"I tried the front-door approach," she said. "I called his home number, but the person who answered, a housekeeper, said he was very ill, and no, she had no information as to where he was."

"I don't believe she doesn't know."

"I don't either. But she was obviously very well briefed, and she was very quick to get off the phone. So that's a dead end."

"But obviously he *is* reachable—if we're correctly interpreting that note in Simon Dawson's Palm Pilot from a few days ago."

"I went through Dawson's PDA, and there's no phone number for Harry Dunne. Not even encrypted. Nothing."

"What about on-line records searches—medical records?"

"Easier said than done. I tried all the conventional medical-records searches using his name and social-security number, but nothing came up. I even tried a little outright deception, which I was fairly sure would work. I called the CIA personnel office pretending to be a White House secretary—I said the president wants to send flowers to his old friend Harry Dunne, and I needed an address to send them."

"That's nice. Didn't work?"

"Unfortunately, no. Dunne obviously doesn't want to be found. They insisted they had no information. Whatever his reasons, he's got a pretty effective cordon of privacy."

Cordon of privacy. A realization dawned on Bryson. What was the term Dunne had used once, in connection with Aunt Felicia? A 'security cordon'? "There may be another way," he said softly.

"Oh? How so?"

"There's an administrator at the nursing home where my Aunt Felicia lives—a woman named Shirley, as I recall—who always knows how to reach Harry Dunne. Always has his phone number so she can call him whenever anyone calls or visits Felicia."

"What? Why would Harry Dunne care who sees Felicia Munroe? The last time we saw Felicia together, wasn't she in very bad shape, mentally?"

"Sadly, yes. But Dunne obviously thinks it's important to keep a careful watch on her—*a security cordon*, he called it. Dunne wouldn't have placed a security cordon on her unless he feared she had something to reveal. Presumably whatever she knows—whether she's aware of its importance or not—had to do with the fact that Pete Munroe was in the Directorate."

"He *was?*"

"There's so much to tell you—more than we have time for now. We'll talk on the way."

"On the way where?"

"To the Rosamund Cleary Extended Care Facility. We're going to take a little drive upstate, to Dutchess County. To pay an unannounced, unscheduled visit to my Aunt Felicia."

"When?"

"*Now.*"

They arrived at the well manicured, beautifully landscaped grounds of the Rosamund Cleary Extended Care Facility shortly after six-thirty. The air was cool, fragrant of flowers and newly mown lawn and the end of a long, hot day.

Elena entered first and asked to speak to an administrator. She was driving by—she was staying with friends in town—and she had heard such wonderful things about the facility. It sounded like the perfect environment for her ailing father. Of course, it was late in the day, but was there maybe someone who worked there named Shirley? One of her friends had mentioned a Shirley. . . .

A short while later, Bryson entered and asked for Felicia Munroe. Since Elena was monopolizing Shirley's time, and Shirley was Dunne's contact, it was possible that a call might *not* be placed to Dunne. That would make things easier, but Bryson was not counting on that. For there was nothing wrong, really, with misleading Dunne into thinking that Bryson remained preoccupied with his own past. Perhaps it would falsely reassure the Prometheans that Bryson was on the wrong path, that he was therefore not that immediate a threat.

Let them think that I am dwelling on the past, on my own history. Let them think I'm obsessed.

But I am.

I am obsessed with unearthing the truth.

He prayed that Felicia would be in a lucid state.

She was eating dinner when Bryson was shown in, sitting by herself at a small, round mahogany table in the handsome dining room, where other residents sat by themselves or with one another at similar round tables. She looked up as he approached, and it was as if she were seeing someone she had just been speaking to five minutes earlier. Her eyes displayed no surprise. Bryson's heart sank.

"George!" she trilled, delighted. She smiled, her pearly dentures smeared with lipstick. "Oh, but this is so very confusing. You're dead!" Her tone became scolding, as if lecturing a naughty child. "You really shouldn't *be* here, George."

Bryson smiled, gave her a peck on the cheek, and sat across the table from her. She still mistook him for his father. "You caught me, Felicia," Bryson said sheepishly, his tone lighthearted. "But tell me again—how *did* I die?"

Felicia's eyes narrowed shrewdly. "George, none of that! You know very well how it happened. Let's not rehash all that. Pete feels bad enough, you know." She took a forkful of mashed potatoes.

"Why does he feel bad, Felicia?"

"He wishes it were him instead. Not you and Nina. He just berates himself over and over again. Why did George and Nina have to die?"

"Why *did* we have to die?"

"You know very well. I don't need to tell you."

"But *I* don't know why. Perhaps you can tell *me*."

Bryson looked up and was surprised to see Elena. She put her arms around Felicia, then sat down next to her, clasping in her two hands Felicia's bony, liver-spotted hand.

Did Felicia recognize Elena? It was impossible, of course; they had seen each other on only one occasion, years earlier. But there was something about Elena's manner that Felicia found comforting. Bryson wanted to catch Elena's eye, to find out what had happened, but Elena was devoting all her attention to Felicia.

"He really shouldn't be here," Felicia said, giving Bryson a sidelong glance. "He's dead, you know."

"Yes, I know that," said Elena gently. "But tell me what happened. Wouldn't it make you feel a little better to talk about what happened?"

Felicia looked troubled. "I always blame myself. Pete always says he wishes they didn't have to die—he wishes it were him. George was his best friend, you know."

"I know. Is it too painful for you to talk about? What happened, I mean? How they were killed?"

"Well, it's my birthday, you know."

"Is it? Happy birthday, Felicia!"

"Happy? No, it's not happy at all. It's so very, very sad. It's such a terrible night."

"Tell me about that night."

"Such a beautiful, snowy night! I made dinner for us all, but I didn't care if dinner got cold! I *told* Pete that. But no, he didn't want to spoil my birthday dinner. He kept telling George to hurry, *hurry!* Drive faster! And George didn't want to, he said the old Chrysler couldn't handle the icy roads, the brakes were bad. Nina was upset—she wanted them all to pull over and wait out the storm. But Pete kept *pushing* them, urging them on! *Hurry, hurry!*" Her eyes grew wide and filled with tears; she looked at Elena desperately. "When the car went out of control and

George and Nina were killed . . . oh, my Pete was in the hospital for over a month, and the whole time he kept saying, over and over and over again, 'It should have been me who was killed! Not them! It should have been *me!*' " The tears were spilling down her cheeks as the painful memory emerged from deep in the confused mind of a woman for whom the past and the present were a mingled palimpsest. "They were best friends, you know."

Elena put a comforting arm around the old woman's fragile shoulders. "But it was an accident," she said. "It was an accident. Everyone knows that."

Bryson reached over and hugged Felicia, blinking back tears himself. She was tiny, birdlike in his embrace.

"It's all right," he said soothingly. "It's all right."

"It must be such a relief for you," said Elena, sitting beside Bryson in the rented green Buick.

Bryson nodded as he drove. "I think I needed to hear it—even given the circumstances, even given the confused state of her mind."

"There's a certain observable consistency to her thoughts, even given the confusion, the thought disorder. Her long-term memory is sharp: that usually remains intact. She might not remember where she is at any given moment, but she'll clearly remember her wedding night."

"Yes. I suspect Dunne was counting on her advanced senility in the event that I contacted her for confirmation of his carefully constructed lies. As the sole surviving witness to the events, she's as unreliable as they come; Dunne knew that, knew she wouldn't be able to effectively contradict his fraudulent version."

"Though she just did," Elena pointed out.

"She did. But it took a degree of trust, of patience and persistence, of *gentleness* that I doubt Dunne's CIA men possess. Well, thank God for you, is all I can say. You're the one with the gentleness, and I think she picked up on it. Who'd ever have thought that such a gentle creature could have the makings of a deep-cover operative?"

She smiled. "You mean the phone number?"

"How'd you get it, and so quickly?"

"For one thing, I simply thought about where I'd put it if I were her, a place where I could get it quickly. I also figured that if Harry Dunne wanted the administrator to think he was a concerned relative, he wasn't at the same time going to insist on security precautions."

"Where was it, in her Rolodex, right on her desk?"

"Close. A list of 'emergency' contact numbers taped to the top lefthand corner of her desk blotter. I spotted it as soon as I sat down, so I 'accidentally' left my purse on the chair next to her desk, and as we were leaving for a tour, I suddenly remembered. I went to pick it up, spilled out its contents all over her desk and the floor. As I picked things up I took a glance and memorized it."

"And if it hadn't been right there?"

"Plan B would have required me to leave the purse there longer and retrieve it during her cigarette break. She's a heavy smoker."

"Was there a Plan C?"

"Yes. You."

He laughed, a rare moment of much-needed levity relieving the prevailing tension. "You give me too much credit."

"I don't think so. Now it's my turn, though. The reverse-number lookup has gotten easy these days, thanks to the Internet. I won't even have to do it myself—I can E-mail it to one of a hundred search services that'll get me the address in half an hour or less. Even call it in."

"The area code is eight-one-four—where is that? There are so many area codes these days."

"The note she scrawled beside it said 'PA'—Pennsylvania, I assume, right?"

"*Pennsylvania?* Why would Harry Dunne be there?"

"Maybe he's originally from there? A childhood home?"

"His accent is purest New Jersey."

"Relatives, then? I'll do a reverse-number lookup; that much should be easy to find out."

At one o'clock in the morning there was only a skeleton staff on duty at the Meredith Waterman building: a handful of security guards and one information technology staffer.

The tough-looking female security guard stationed at the employees' entrance at the side of the building was in the middle of reading a Harlequin romance, and she did not look happy about being disturbed.

"You're not on the admit list," she said dourly, her long-nailed index finger holding her place in the book.

The short-haired man in the aviator glasses and the shirt with MCCAF-FREY INFORMATION STORAGE SERVICES stitched on it just shrugged. "Hey, fine. I'll just head back to New Jersey and tell 'em you wouldn't let me in. Makes my job easier, and I still get paid."

Bryson turned around, readying his next riposte, when the guard relented somewhat. "What's the purpose of your—"

"Like I told you. Meredith is one of our clients. We do the off-site backup—it's an after-hours download. But we're getting digital collation errors. Doesn't happen a lot, but it happens. And it means I gotta check the routers on site here."

She sighed in irritation and picked up the phone, punching a number. "Charlie, do we have a contract with a McCaffrey"—she examined the stitching on Bryson's shirt—"Information Storage Services?"

She listened in silence. "The guy says he has to check on something here because of errors or something."

She listened again. "All right, thanks." She hung up, a superior smirk on her face. "You're supposed to call ahead," she said with a reproving scowl. "The service elevator's on the right down the hall. Take it down to B."

As soon as he reached the basement level, he raced to the freight-delivery entrance, which he had located during his earlier surveillance. Elena was waiting there, wearing the identical uniform and carrying an aluminum clipboard. The corporate records center was one large below-ground room, with a low acoustic-tiled ceiling, buzzing fluorescent lights, and row upon row of open steel warehouse shelves that held endless-seeming lines of identical, tall gray archive boxes. The boxes were arranged chronologically, with just a few entries for 1860, the year it was founded by Elias Meredith, an erstwhile trader in Irish linen. Each succeeding year took up more linear shelf space, until 1989—the last year whose paper files were stored here—which occupied an entire row. Each year was broken down into various categories—client records, personnel records, minutes of partners' and committee meetings, consent resolutions, amendments to bylaws, and so on. Folders were color-coded, with end tabs and bar codes.

Time was extremely limited: they knew they could not stay down here for much more than an hour before Security would begin to wonder what was taking so long. They divided up responsibilities, with Bryson surveying the paper files and Elena sitting at the computer terminal and examining the records-management database. This was an electronic records-tracking and inventory-management system, up-to-date though not password-protected. There would be no reason for it to be protected, since it was set up for ease of use by the bank's record clerks.

It was laborious work, made even more difficult by the fact that they had no idea exactly what they were looking for. Client records? But which clients? Records of large money transfers to offshore accounts? But how could they distinguish between a wire transfer that was nothing more shady than the semilegitimate parking of clients' assets offshore to avoid scrutiny by the IRS, or by a divorcing wife—and one that might be the beginning of a long sequence of transfers from one offshore bank to another, eventually ending up in the pocket of a senator? Elena came up with the idea of using the computer to search for them—by feeding in key words and pulling up file references. Yet after an hour they still had nothing.

In fact, they began to find documents missing, whole sections of them. After 1985, there were no partners' income records or earning statements to be found. It was not as if the documents had been removed. Elena was able to confirm, by poring over the electronic database manager, that not a single document pertaining to monies brought in by the partners was to be found after 1985.

Frustrated, increasingly tense as the minutes ticked by, Bryson finally decided to narrow his focus to just one partner: Richard Lanchester. He proceeded to examine all the Lanchester files—personnel, compensation, clients. The story they told was, just as the Lanchester myth had it, one of the genesis of a Wall Street whiz. He started at Meredith Waterman immediately after graduation from Harvard, and did not do grunt work for long. Within a very few years he emerged as an aggressive bond trader, generating huge income for the firm. He soon headed the department.

Then he added another specialty—currency speculation and investment. The money he made there made what he was doing before look like begging for pocket change. Richard Lanchester had become, in ten years, the biggest earner in the bank's history.

The Wall Street whiz kid had become a financial powerhouse, making himself and the other general partners extremely rich through his deals, and most of all through a complex series of financial trades. He had apparently mastered the delicate art of trading in financial instruments called derivatives, placing immense, multibillion-dollar wagers on stock-index futures and interest-rate futures. Essentially he was gambling on a massive scale, the casino being the global capital markets. He kept winning and winning and winning; no doubt, like a true gambler, he believed his luck would never run out.

It was late in 1985 when his luck ran out.

In 1985, everything changed. With rapt fascination, sitting on the cold concrete floor of the records room, Bryson came upon a thin folder of internal auditors' reports that described a reversal of fortune so abrupt, so devastating, that it was almost impossible to believe.

One of his immense bets, on Eurodollar futures, went bad. Overnight, Lanchester had lost the bank three *billion* dollars. This exceeded the bank's assets many times over.

Meredith Waterman was insolvent. It had survived a century and a half of financial crises, even the Great Depression; and then Richard Lanchester lost a bet, and America's oldest private bank was broke.

"My *God*," Elena breathed as she looked through the auditors' reports. "But . . . none of this was ever made known to the public!"

Bryson, as astonished as she, shook his head slowly. "Nothing. Never. Not an article, not a mention in the press—*nothing.*"

"How can this be?"

Bryson glanced at his watch. They had been down here for almost two hours; they were pressing their luck.

Suddenly he looked at her, eyes wide. "I think I understand now why we couldn't find any partners' income records after 1985."

"Why?"

"Because they found a benefactor. Someone to bail them out."

"What do you mean?"

He got up, found the gray file box that was marked, blandly, PART-NERSHIP INTEREST ASSIGNMENTS. He had seen it but hadn't bothered to open it; there was far too much to look through and that seemed unlikely to yield anything interesting. He opened the box and found only one thin manila file folder inside. The folder contained fourteen thin, stapled legal documents of no more than three pages each.

Each was headed PARTNERSHIP INTEREST ASSIGNMENT. He read the first one with a racing heart. Although he knew what it would say, it was nevertheless stunning, even terrifying, to see on the page.

"Nicholas, *what?* What is it?"

He read phrases aloud as he skimmed. "The undersigned agrees to sell all rights, title, and interest in my interest as a partner in the partnership. . . . In consideration thereof . . . succeed to all rights and liabilities associated with that interest."

"What are you reading? Nicholas, what *are* these documents?"

"In November of 1985, each of the fourteen general partners in Meredith Waterman signed a legal document selling their stake in the partnership," Bryson said. His mouth was dry. "Each of the partners was directly and personally responsible for the more than three billion dollars of debt that Lanchester had run up. Obviously they had no choice; they were all backed into a corner. They had to sell out."

"But . . . I don't understand—what was there left to sell?"

"Just the name. An empty shell of a bank."

"And the buyer got—what?"

"The seller paid fourteen million dollars—one million to each partner. And they were extraordinarily lucky to get that. Because the buyer was now saddled with billions of dollars of debt. Fortunately for him, he could afford it. Part of the condition of the sale was that each partner was required to sign a side confidentiality agreement—a nondisclosure agreement. A vow of secrecy. Enforceable by the threat of having their payment—the money disbursed over five years—revoked."

"This is . . . it's so *bizarre*," she said, shaking her head. "Am I understanding this right? Are you saying that in 1985 Meredith Waterman was *secretly* sold to one person? And no one knew it?"

"Exactly."

"But who was the buyer? Who'd be crazy enough to make such a deal?"

"Someone who wanted to become the secret owner of a prestigious, highly regarded investment bank—which he could then use as a vehicle. A front for illicit payments around the world."

"But who?"

Bryson gave a small, wan smile, and he too shook his head in puzzlement. "A billionaire named Gregson Manning."

"Gregson Manning—Systematix . . . ?"

Bryson paused. "The man behind the Prometheus conspiracy."

There was a quiet scuffing noise, which jolted Bryson—the sound of a leather shoe scraping against the concrete floor. He looked up from the files, which were spread out on a small table before them, and saw the tall, stout man in a blue security-officer's uniform. The man was staring at them with undisguised hostility. "You—hey, what the goddamned hell . . . ? You're—you're supposed to be from the computer company. *What the hell are you doing here?*"

CHAPTER
THIRTY

They were nowhere near the main bank of computers, the server on the other side of the large room. A file box, clearly labeled, stood in front of them; the fourteen legal documents spread out like a fan on the table.

"What the hell took you so long?" said Bryson in disgust. "I've been calling up to security for the last half hour!"

Gimlet-eyed, the security man regarded them with suspicion. His two-way radio crackled. "What the hell you talking about? I didn't get any calls."

Elena got up, waving her clipboard. "Look, without the service contract, we're just wasting our time! It's supposed to be left for us in the same place each time! We're not supposed to dig around for it—do you have any *idea* how much data's going to be lost?" She gesticulated wildly, thrusting an index finger toward his chest.

Bryson watched her, impressed; he followed her lead. "Security must have shut down the system," he said with a petulant shake of the head, getting up slowly.

"Hey lady," the guard protested, facing her, "I don't know what the hell you're talking—"

Bryson's hands shot out like the strike of a cobra, grabbing the security man's throat from behind with his left hand, and striking, with the hard edge of his rigid right hand, the brachial plexus nerve bundle at the base of the neck. The man went suddenly limp, slumping into Bryson's arms. He set the unconscious guard down on the floor gently, dragging him the short distance to the warehouse shelving, propping him up in the aisle between two rows of shelves. He would be out for at least an hour, possibly more.

As soon as they exited the bank through the freight entrance, they ran to the rented car, parked down the block and across the street. Not until they were several blocks away did either of them say anything. They were each in a state of shock. Exhaustion would be tolerated; there was nothing to do about that now except to grab sleep when they could; otherwise, they were surviving on caffeine and adrenaline.

It was three-twenty in the morning, the streets dark and deserted. Bryson drove through the empty streets of lower Manhattan, and when he reached the area of the South Street Seaport he found a narrow side street and pulled over to the curb.

"It's amazing," Bryson said quietly. "One of the richest men in the country—in the *world*—and America's most respected political figure. 'The last honest man in Washington,' or whatever the hell they call him. A partnership sealed years ago, in conditions of absolute secrecy. Manning and Lanchester never appear in public together, they're never mentioned in the same sentence; they seem to have no connection."

"Appearances are important."

"Crucial. For all kinds of reasons. I'm sure Manning wanted to preserve Meredith Waterman's impeccable reputation—it was far more valuable to him that way, as a paragon of old-line Wall Street that he could secretly use to control political leaders the world over. Now he had the perfect cover, the camouflage of unimpeachable respectability, concealing his conduit for bribes and other illegal funds channeled to Parliament and Congress, probably to the Russian Duma and Parliament, the French General Assembly—you name it. And he had a front that could in turn buy stakes in other banks, other companies, without his name ever being associated. Like the Washington bank where most Congressmen do their banking. It's all there—bribery, the potential for blackmail by using the most sensitive personal information . . ."

"And of course the White House," she put in. "Through Lanchester."

"Certainly Manning has major influence on U.S. foreign policy through him. That's why it was equally important to both men that not a word of how Manning bailed out Meredith Waterman ever leak. Richard Lanchester's reputation had to remain intact. If the word got out that he had single-handedly brought down America's oldest private bank with reckless speculation, he'd have been ruined. Instead, he was able to preserve the mystique of his financial genius. The brilliant but ethical man who made a fortune on Wall Street, who became so rich he was incorruptible, was willing to give it all up to work on behalf of his country. In 'public service.' How could America *not* be honored to have such a man in the White House assisting the president?"

A moment of silence passed. "I wonder whether Gregson Manning actually *sent* Lanchester to the White House? That maybe was one of the conditions of his saving Meredith Waterman."

"Interesting. But don't forget, Lanchester already knew Malcolm Davis before Davis announced his run for the presidency."

"Lanchester was one of his key supporters on the street, right? In politics, money buys friendship rather easily. And then he volunteered to run Davis's campaign."

"No doubt Manning secretly helped out there too—shoving a lot of money Davis's way, from Systematix, from his employees and friends and associates, and who knows how else. Thereby making Lanchester look good, look damned *invaluable*, in fact. So Richard Lanchester, who stared ruin in the face, who saw his illustrious career crash and burn, was suddenly a major player on the world stage. His career went supernova."

"And he owed it all to Manning. We have no way in to Manning, do we?"

Bryson shook his head.

"But you know Lanchester—you met in Geneva. He'll see you."

"Not now, he won't. By now he knows everything he needs to know about me—enough to know that I'm a threat to him. He'll never agree to see me."

"Unless you make that threat explicit. And demand a meeting."

"For what? Meet with him for what, to accomplish *what?* No, a direct, unmediated approach to him is just too blunt an instrument. As I see it, the best way in is Harry Dunne."

"Dunne?"

"I know the guy's temperament. He won't be able to resist an approach from me; he knows what I know. He'll *have* to see me."

"Well, I don't know about that, Nicholas. He may not be in any shape to meet with anyone."

"What are you talking about?"

"That telephone number we got at the nursing home—it's a town called Franklin, Pennsylvania. The phone number is listed as belonging to a small, private, very exclusive medical facility. A hospice. Harry Dunne may be in hiding—but he's also dying."

There were no direct flights to Franklin, Pennsylvania; the fastest way was to drive. But they desperately needed rest, even if only for a few hours. It was vital that they remained alert: there was still much to do, Bryson was sure of it.

Three or four hours of sleep, however, turned out to be worse than none at all. Bryson awoke groggy—they had found a motel about half an hour outside of Manhattan that looked suitably anonymous—to the sound of the tapping of computer keys.

Elena looked rested, apparently having showered, and she sat in front of her notebook computer, which was plugged into the phone jack in the wall.

She spoke without turning around, obviously having heard him stir. "Systematix," she said, "is either the most impressive evidence of unrestrained global capitalism, or the most frightening corporation that ever existed. It depends on how you look at it."

Bryson sat up. "I need coffee before I can look at it."

Elena pointed to a carry-out cardboard cup next to his side of the bed. "I went out about an hour ago. It might be cold by now; I'm sorry."

"Thank you. Cold is just fine. Did you sleep at all?"

She shook her head. "I got up after half an hour or so. Too much on my mind."

"Tell me what you found."

She turned around to face him. "Well, if knowledge is power, then Systematix is the most powerful corporate entity on the face of the earth. Their corporate motto is 'The Knowledge Business,' and that seems to be the only organizing principle—the only element that unites its immense holdings."

Bryson took a sip of coffee. It was indeed cold. "But I thought Systematix was a software company—one of Microsoft's chief rivals."

"Software and computers—that turns out to be a fraction of its real business. But it's extraordinarily diversified. We already know it owns Meredith Waterman, and through them the First Washington Mutual Bancorp. I can't *prove* it controls the banks in Great Britain where most members of Parliament have their accounts, but I strongly suspect it."

"Based on what? Given the elaborate precautions Manning took to conceal his ownership of Meredith, it can't be any easier to connect him to British banks."

"It's the *law* firms—the foreign law firms it has on retainer—that tell the story. And those firms, whether in London or Buenos Aires or Rome, are known to have close relationships to certain banks. That's how I can connect the dots."

"That's an impressive line of reasoning."

"Now, through Systematix, Manning has major stakes in the military-industrial giants. And recently it's launched a fleet of low-earth-orbit satellites. But listen to this: Systematix also owns two of America's three major credit-reporting agencies."

"Credit . . . ?"

"Think of how much information a credit company has on you. It's staggering. An incredible amount of highly personal information. And there's more. Systematix owns several of the largest health-insurance firms—and it also owns data-management firms that maintain the *records* for those insurance companies. It owns the medical data companies that manage the medical records for virtually all of the country's HMOs."

"My *God*."

"As I said, the one element that unites all these entities, or at least many of them, is information. What they know. The information they have access to. Just step back and look at it—life insurance and health insurance records, medical records, credit and banking records. Through its web of corporate holdings, Systematix has access to the most intimate, most private records on what I estimate to be ninety percent of the citizens of the United States."

"And that's just Manning."

"Hmm?"

"Manning is just one member of the Prometheus Group. Don't forget about Anatoly Prishnikov, who probably has similar holdings in Russia. And Jacques Arnaud in France. And General Tsai in China. Who knows what personal information this group has control over?"

"This is really frightening, Nicholas, you know that? For a girl who grew up in a totalitarian state, with the Securitate, with every other person informing on you—the possibilities are terrifying."

Bryson stood up, folded his arms. He could feel his body tense; he had the eerie and uncomfortable sensation of headlong *movement*, of plunging through an endless tunnel. "What Prometheus has managed to do in Washington—obtaining personal information that no one should ever have, then releasing it or threatening its release—it has the ability to do around the world. Systematix may be about information, but *Prometheus*—Prometheus is about *control*."

"Yes," Elena said, her voice seeming to come from very far away. "But for *what*? To *what end*?"

Control is about to be transferred . . . We see clearly now . . .

"I don't know," Bryson replied. "And by the time we learn the answer, it may well be too late."

Shortly after noon they pulled their rented car into the semicircular drive of a Georgian red-brick building that appeared to have once been a grand private home. It was marked with discreet brass letters on a low brick wall: FRANKLIN HOUSE. Elena waited in the car.

Bryson wore a white doctor's coat, purchased at a medical supply house on the way, and identified himself as a pain-management specialist from the University of Pittsburgh Medical Center, called in for a consult by the family of a hospice patient. Bryson relied on the generally unsuspicious environment of hospitals and other medical establishments, and he was not disappointed. No one asked to see identification. He struck an attitude of professional detachment, though with the appropriate air of concern: the family had contacted him through a colleague and asked them for any help he might suggest to ease the dying man's last days. With amused chagrin, Bryson showed them a pink "While You Were Out" message slip with the phone number on it.

"My secretary didn't write down the patient's name," he said, "and I'm embarrassed to say I left my office without the fax. . . . Do you have any idea who this might be?"

The receptionist glanced at the number and looked it up on her list of extensions. "Certainly, Doctor. That'd be a Mr. John McDonald in 322."

Harry Dunne looked like a cadaver on life support. His narrow face was now sunken; most of his white hair was gone; his skin looked unnaturally bronzed, though blotchy. His eyes bulged. An oxygen tube was in his nose; he was hooked up to an intravenous drip as well as an array of monitors that recorded his respiration and heart rate, tracing irregular green squiggles on the screen behind him, beeping audibly.

There was a direct phone line, even a fax machine, but both were silent.

He looked up when Bryson entered the room. He seemed woozy but alert, and after a few seconds he grinned, a cadaver's horrific smile. "You come to kill me, Bryson?" Dunne said with a mordant laugh. "That'd be a laugh. They got me on fucking life support. Keep the corpse breathing. Just like the goddamned CIA. No more of that shit."

"You're not an easy man to find," Bryson said.

"That's 'cause I don't want to be found, Bryson. I got no relatives to visit me on my deathbed, and I know what happens over at Langley when they hear you're sick—they're already breaking the seal on your safe, pawing through your files, moving you out of your office. Like the good old Soviet Union—the premier goes on vacation to Yalta, comes back to find his stuff in banker boxes on the street outside the Kremlin." He gave a guttural, rattling cough. "Got to cover your flanks."

"For how much longer?" Bryson's question was pointed and ruthless, meant to provoke. Dunne stared for a long time before he replied.

"Six weeks ago I was diagnosed with metastatic lung cancer. Did a last-ditch course of chemo, even radiation. The shit's in my stomach, in my bones—my goddamned hands and feet even. You know they're ordering me to stop fucking *smoking?* That's a hoot. I said, shit, maybe I should just go on a high-fiber diet, for all the good it's gonna do me."

"You really set me up well," Bryson said, not bothering to hide his anger. "Spun a whole elaborate lie about my past, about the Directorate, about how it began and what it was up to. . . . Was the point just to use me like your own personal cat's paw? Do your dirty work, get me back inside the Directorate to find out what we . . ." He paused, wondering about his use of the pronoun 'we.' *Is that how I think of me, of them? I'm part of 'we,' once more part of an agency that doesn't exist?* ". . . what we knew about the Prometheus group? Because we were the only intelligence agency in the world who'd managed to find out what was going on?"

"And what did you find out, after all that? Chicken shit." He smiled grimly, lapsed into another coughing spell. "I'm like goddamned Moses. Never gonna live to see the Promised Land. Just point the way, that's all."

"The Promised Land? *Whose* 'promised land'? *Gregson Manning's?*"

"Forget about it, Bryson," Dunne said, closing his eyes, a contorted smile on his face.

Bryson looked over at the pouch of clear liquid hanging on Dunne's IV stand. It said Ketamine. A painkiller, but it also had other uses. In the right quantities it could induce euphoria and delirium; it had even been used, upon occasion, as a crude truth serum by both Directorate and CIA. He strode quickly over to it, found the stopcock, and turned it to increase the flow.

"The hell are you doing?" Dunne said. "Don't shut me off. Morphine stopped working for me, they had to move me to harder stuff."

The increased flow of the opioid had an immediate effect. Dunne flushed, began perspiring heavily. "You don't get it, do you?"

"Get *what?*"

"You ever hear what happened to his kid?"

"Whose kid?"

"Manning's."

Elena had downloaded Manning's biography. "He had a daughter who was kidnapped, didn't he?"

"Kidnapped? That's not the half of it, Bryson. Guy was divorced, had an eight-year-old daughter who was the whole fucking world to him." His words began to slur. "He's visiting Manhattan, being honored . . . some big charity thing, daughter Ariel's in his apartment at the Plaza with the au pair . . . returns home that night, finds the au pair murdered, daughter's gone . . ."

"Jesus."

"Some wiseguys . . . make a little cash . . ." His words trailed off. "Paid the ransom . . . nothing . . . they took her to some remote cabin . . . Pennsylvania." Dunne broke out into another coughing fit. "Manning . . . not fuck around . . ." His eyes fell shut.

Bryson waited a moment. Had he overdone the dose? He stood up, readjusted the IV valve just as Manning's eyes were opening again. "The guy owns a whole fuggin' electronics empire . . . offered to help out the FBI . . . crack it . . . We got satellites, only we can't use 'em—they're shuttered . . . fuggin' Executive Order 1233—whatever the hell . . ."

Dunne's eyes were becoming more focused again. "Assholes over at Justice won't approve wiretap . . . cell phones of the kidnappers . . . Whole thing fucked up by bureau—bureaucratic bullshit. Protecting the privacy of criminals. Meanwhile, this pretty little eight-year-old girl . . . buried alive in a coffin three feet underground . . . asphyxiating slowly."

"Dear God . . . What a nightmare."

"Manning never the same after that. Saw the light."

"What—what was 'the light'?"

Dunne shook his head, smiled strangely.

Bryson stood up. "Where's *Lanchester*?" he demanded. "They say he's on vacation in the Pacific Northwest. It's a bunch of crap—not at this time he's not. Where *is* he?"

"Where they all are. The whole Prometheus gang, except yours truly. The hell you think? Lakeside."

"Lakeside . . . ?"

"Manning's house. On that lake outside Seattle." His voice was getting progressively weaker. His eyes closed. "Now go away, Bryson. I don't feel so good."

"What's the objective?" demanded Bryson. "What's the *point?*"

"It's a fucking freight train bearing down on you, brother," said Dunne. He stopped and hacked for almost a full minute. "Can't be stopped. You're too late. So you might as well get out of the fucking way."

Bryson noticed someone approaching from down the corridor: a slim black man, a male nurse, somehow familiar. *But from where?*

Abruptly he rose and left the room; his instincts warned him of impending trouble. He strode quickly, an overscheduled doctor perennially late for his next appointment.

As he reached the end of the corridor, he glanced back and saw the black man entering Dunne's room. The man was definitely familiar. All too familiar. *But who was he?*

Bryson ducked into a lounge filled with vending machines and Formica-topped tables, and he wracked his brain. From where, from what operation, from what country? Or was it from his civilian life, his teaching days?

A few minutes later he stuck his head into the hall and looked down toward Dunne's room. Seeing nobody in the area, he walked toward it, intending to glance into the room as he passed, try to catch a glimpse of the male nurse.

He approached Dunne's room. The door was open. He glanced inside; no one was there except Dunne, sleeping.

No.

The single unbroken tone from the heart-rate monitor caused him to look over. The EKG, normally jagged, was a flat line. Dunne's heart was no longer beating. He was dead.

He rushed into the room. Dunne's face was chalky white; he was unquestionably dead. Turning to the IV stand, he saw that the valve on the ketamine had been turned all the way, and the pouch of liquid was just about empty.

The nurse had turned the spigot. *He had killed Dunne.*

They had been under surveillance the entire time. The 'nurse'—whoever it was, he was not a nurse—had killed Dunne.

For talking?

Bryson raced from the hospice.

"Sir, we have a sighting."

The atrium was filled with banks of flat monitors, displaying constantly shifting, high-resolution images relayed from geosynchronous satellites. It was located in an upper level of a strip mall in Sunnyvale, California, above a diet center, the immense electronic capabilities well concealed as a result.

The young communications specialist pointed toward monitor 23A, striding quickly toward it. His middle-aged supervisor, wearing a lightweight telephone headset, approached the screen, squinting.

"Right there—a green Buick," said the younger man. "License plates match. Driver is the male, passenger the female."

"Facial recognition software?"

"Positive, sir. A confirmation. It's them."

"What's the direction?"

"South."

The supervisor nodded. "Dispatch Team 27," he ordered.

Elena drove.

They had to get to Seattle immediately, had to find the closest airport, and from there find a commercial flight—or charter one. Lakeside. Gregson Manning's house on the lake. Outside Seattle.

The Prometheus Group was assembling there, all of them. Meeting—to do what?

Whatever they were doing, they were all in one place. He had to get there at once.

"The male nurse," Bryson began. He had recalled to Elena this oddly familiar person. He stopped short.

Suddenly Bryson's head was reeling. Vividly recalled images flashed by. A concrete bunker at Rock Creek Park. Dunne's driver bursting in, demanding to see his boss. A *slender, lithe, well-muscled black man.* Solomon. Firing at him, his eyes cruel, almost sadistic; the same man lying dead, crumpled on the cement floor, blood erupting from bullet wounds in his chest after being shot down by his boss.

The realization dawned, sickeningly.

"That was Dunne's chauffeur. Obviously a Prometheus control."

"But—but I thought you said he was *dead*, that Dunne *killed* him!"

"Christ, what was I thinking! We all have special-effects wizards on staff—blood packs, those little explosive charges triggered by battery—squibs, I think they're called. The rigged wardrobe. The whole bag of tricks! I was straying, and Dunne had to do something dramatic to get me back into the fold. . . . Wait . . . *listen.*"

She cocked her head. "What do you hear?"

It was definitely there, the distant whump-whump of a helicopter. They were not near any helicopter facilities; there was no airstrip nearby.

"It's a chopper, but one of those extremely quiet models. It's got to be directly overhead. Do you have a makeup mirror, a compact, in your purse?"

"Of course."

"I want you to lower your window and hold it up, catch a reflection of the sky above. Look without letting anyone see that you're looking."

"You think it's following us?"

"For the last few minutes the sound has been fairly constant, neither louder nor softer. It's been right above us for miles now."

She opened her compact and thrust it out the open window. "There *is* something, Nicholas. Yes. A helicopter."

"Son of a bitch," Bryson muttered. A sign they had just passed indicated a rest stop a mile ahead. He accelerated, got into the right lane, following a beat-up, rust-bucket El Dorado into the rest area parking lot. The car's body was perforated by rust, part of the tail pipe dragged almost touching the ground, and the hood was secured with twine. He watched the car's driver get out, a scruffy-looking, bleary-eyed, longhaired man in grungy jeans, a black beret, and a black Grateful Dead T-shirt under a green canvas army jacket. A stoner, Bryson thought. A pothead.

"What are you doing?" Elena asked.

"Countermeasures." Bryson grabbed some papers from the glove compartment of the rented car. "Follow me. Take your purse and whatever else you've got with you."

Bewildered, she got out.

"You see that guy who just got out of that wreck of a car?"

"What about him?"

"Remember his face."

"How can I forget it?"

"I want you to wait right here until he comes out."

Bryson walked through the fast-food restaurant and saw that the driver of the El Dorado was neither in line nor seated at a table. *Either the vending machines, buying cigarettes or candy or soda, or else the restroom,* Bryson thought. The stoner wasn't at the vending machines, but he was in the men's room. Bryson recognized the man's ratty black sneakers under the door of one of the toilet stalls. He relieved himself, then stood by the sink, washing his hands. Finally, the man came out of the stall and went up to the sink. That in itself was a surprise; Bryson hadn't figured him for being much on cleanliness.

Bryson caught the stoner's eye in the mirror. "Hey," he said, "lemme ask you a favor."

The stoner glanced over at him suspiciously, didn't answer for a few seconds as he soaped his hands. Without catching Bryson's eye, he said with hostility, "What?"

"I know this might seem bizarre, but I need you to check outside for me, see if my wife's out there. I think she followed me."

"Sorry, man, I'm kinda in a hurry here." He shook off his hands and looked around for the paper-towel dispenser.

"Look, I'm desperate," Bryson said. "I wouldn't ask you if I wasn't. I'm willing to compensate you for your time." He pulled out a wad of bills and peeled off a couple of twenties. *Not too much money or it'll seem suspicious.* "Just look out there, that's all. Tell me if you see her."

"Aw, man. No fuckin' paper towels. I hate those fuckin' hot-air things." He shook the water off his hands, then he took the proffered bills. "This better not be no setup, man—I'll fuck you up but good."

"On the level, man. Totally on the level."

"What does she look like?"

"Brunette, early thirties, red blouse, tan skirt. Real pretty. You can't miss her."

"I get to keep this even if she's not there?"

"Oh, yeah, of course. Man, I *hope* she's gone." Bryson thought for a moment. "Come back and tell me and then I'll double it."

"Jeez, I don't know what the hell you're up to, man," the stoner said, shaking his head as he left the men's room.

He walked through the vending-machine area to the outside and looked around. Elena was stationed nearby, acting the part they had worked out, her arms folded, head swiveling from side to side, a furious expression on her face.

In a minute he returned to the men's room. "Yeah, I see her. That's one pissed-off chick."

"*Shit*," Bryson said, handing the man another couple of twenties. "I gotta shake that bitch. I'm a desperate man." He pulled out the roll of bills, this time removing hundred-dollar bills. When he had counted out twenty banknotes, he fanned them. "She's like a fucking stalker now, really making my life a total nightmare."

The stoner eyed the hundreds greedily. Distrustfully, he said, "What now? I'm not doin' anything illegal or anything—nothin' that gets me in trouble."

"No, no, of course not. Don't misunderstand me. Nothing like that."

Another man came into the rest room and glanced at the two of them warily before using the urinal. Bryson fell silent until the man left.

Then he said, "Your car that old El Dorado?"

"Yeah, it's a piece of shit—what about it?"

"Let me buy it from you. I'll give you two thousand bucks."

"No way, man, I got twenty five hundred bucks into it, with the new shocks."

"Make it three thousand." Bryson held up the keys to the Buick. "You can take mine."

"That better not be hot."

"Don't worry about it."

"Hey, that's a rental," he said suspiciously, seeing the Hertz key fob.

"Right. I'm not a *total* idiot. It's just a set of wheels to get you wherever you need to go. It's all paid for, and you can drop it wherever you want, I'll take care of it."

The stoner thought for a minute. "I don't want you coming back to me and complaining about the car being a piece of shit and all. I already told you that. She's got a hundred seventy-five thousand miles on her."

"Not to worry. I don't know you, I don't even know your name. You'll never see me again. All I care is, your car gets me away from my wife. It's worth it to me."

"Is it worth thirty-five hundred to you?"

"Yeah, yeah," Bryson said with feigned irritation.

"I got stuff in there."

"So go get it and come back with your stuff."

The stoner went to the parking lot, took a green army duffel bag from the trunk and filled it with old clothes, bottles, newspapers and books, a Walkman, a broken set of headphones. He came back to the men's room.

"I'll throw in another hundred for your beret and jacket." Bryson took off his expensive blue blazer and handed it to the man. "Take my jacket. You definitely got the better end of this deal. Plus you sold your car for three times what it's worth."

"It's a good car, man," he said sullenly.

Bryson handed him the hundred-dollar bill, then one more. "Wait for me to drive out of here before you take off, okay?"

The stoner shrugged. "Whatever."

Bryson took the keys to the El Dorado and shook the man's hand.

The stoner stood by the plate-glass windows of the vending-machine area until he saw his crappy old El Dorado drive slowly by. The car stopped, and then the man saw, to his astonishment, the pretty brunette wife in the red blouse run up to the car and jump in, and then the car drove away.

No freaks like suburban freaks, he thought, shaking his head in disbelief. *Shit.*

The Bell 300 helicopter hovered directly above the rest stop.

"We have a positive visual ID," said the observer in the front passenger's seat, peering through binoculars and speaking into his headset. He watched the man in the blue blazer get into the late-model Buick.

"Roger that," the voice replied. "We're going to satellite feed now, so give me the Buick's license plate again."

The observer dialed up the binoculars until he could read the license plate, then he read off the numbers. "Christ, will you look at the way

that guy's driving? Guy must have stopped off for a couple of drinks—
no wonder it took him so long."

The staticky voice came over the headset again. "You got a positive
on the woman?"

"Uh, that's a negative," the observer replied. "There wasn't any woman
with him. Think he might have left her there?"

The stoner in the black Grateful Dead T-shirt and elegant French blue
blazer couldn't believe his luck. First he unloads the piece-of-shit El
Dorado he hadn't been able to sell for five hundred bucks last summer
for thirty-five hundred. Then he gets a free rental, with what looked like
no time limit. And between selling his foul army jacket and beret, and
poking his head outside to ogle some fucked-up guy's chick, he'd made
more in half an hour than he'd made all month. Whatever the hell that
idiot's trip was, paying all that money to get away from his wife and then
letting the bitch back in the car, who cared.

He had the radio blasting and was cruising at almost ninety when all
of a sudden he saw the huge tractor-trailer bearing down on him from
the left, pulling up even with him . . .

And then forcing him to the side of the road!

What the hell was this? The pothead swung the wheel hard to
the right as the eighteen-wheeler forced him off the road and onto the
shoulder.

"The fuck—!" he bellowed as he leapt out of the car, waving his fist
at the truck driver. "What the *fuck* you think you're doin', you *fuck?*"

A man got out of the passenger's side of the truck's cab, a well-muscled
man of around forty with a crew cut. He walked around the car, looking
in the windows, then rapped his knuckles on the trunk lid. "Open it,"
he commanded.

"Who the *fuck* you think you are, you gas-guzzling fascist son—" the
stoner screamed, stopping short when he saw the flat silver pistol pointed
at his eyes. "Oh, shit."

"Open the trunk."

Trembling, the stoner went right to the car, opened the door, and fumbled around looking for the lever on the floor. "Shoulda known I'd get fucked," he muttered.

The crew-cut man inspected the trunk, then looked again in the backseat. He opened the back door and prodded the large green duffel bag. Just to be safe, he fired two shots into it, then another couple of shots into the front and rear seat cushions just for good measure.

The stoner just looked, still shaking, terrified.

The crew-cut man asked a few quick questions and then he put away his gun. "Get a haircut—and get a job," he grunted as he returned to the truck.

"What the hell happened?" barked the supervisor in the surveillance control center in Sunnyvale, California.

"I—I'm not sure," faltered the technician.

"What's that in the rear seat? Zoom it in."

"That there. It's a big bundle—a bag, a sort of duffel bag. Where'd that come from?"

"I didn't see it before, sir."

"Replay the feed from sector S23-994, time fourteen-eleven." He turned to the adjacent monitor. In a few seconds, he saw the strange man in the black T-shirt carrying the big green duffel bag out of the rest area and over to the late-model Buick.

"Same object," the supervisor said. "Switcheroo."

"Rewind it. Where'd that bag come out of?"

In a few seconds they could see the longhaired man gathering what looked like trash from the trunk and front and backseats of the rusty El Dorado.

"Shit. All right, do a capture of that vehicle—quick, now, just cut and paste the image and run a search on the visual signature."

"Got it."

Within thirty seconds there was a chime, and the El Dorado came into focus on the live satellite feed. "Zoom it," the supervisor said.

"Driver is a male, passenger female," said the technician. "We've got a confirmation. Subject in view again, sir."

The El Dorado belched clouds of oil smoke as Elena and Bryson roared down the highway.

It's still there. We didn't lose them.

A large, square wooden sign on the lefthand side of the road about fifty feet ahead announced, in letters crudely formed out of twigs, CAMP CHIPPEWAH. The entrance was little more than a gap in the trees, a rutted dirt road leading somewhere off into the woods.

Bryson looked more closely and saw a smaller sign hanging from the larger one on which was painted CLOSED.

The racket from above gradually became louder: the helicopter was changing altitude, descending.

Why?

He knew why. The road was sufficiently deserted; the helicopter was shifting into position.

He suddenly veered off the highway and onto the dirt road. It would likely lead to a wooded area.

"Nicholas, what are you doing?" Elena cried.

"The leaf canopy should help us evade detection," Bryson explained. "Maybe give us the opportunity to lose the chopper."

"We didn't lose it back at the rest stop, then . . . ?"

"Only for a while."

"It's not just following us, is it?"

"No, honey. I think they've got other plans for us."

The steady drone told him that the helicopter had easily spotted the turn off and was moving accordingly. The rutted dirt road led to a clearing, and then to a dirt path, apparently not meant for cars. He drove at top speed. The car was not suited to the terrain; the low-hanging undercarriage scraped continuously against the rocks. Tree branches on either side of the narrow lane scraped against the body of the car.

Then, just up ahead, he could see the helicopter hovering, slowly dropping into view. There was a clearing about a hundred feet ahead, the car speeding through the woods directly toward it. He slammed on the brakes; the car fishtailed, crashing into trees on either side. Elena screamed involuntarily and grabbed hold of the dashboard to brace herself.

Can't turn around — no room here to maneuver!

Just as the El Dorado entered the grassy clearing, with several small wooden cabins scattered around, the helicopter dropped down until it hovered not more than twenty feet above the ground, its front end tipped down.

"Use your gun!" Elena shouted.

"Won't do any good — it's bulletproof, and too far off, anyway."

He stole a lightning-fast glance at the chopper, searching for the gun turret, and instead saw a rocket launcher. He just narrowly missed plowing into a cabin, veered suddenly around it.

Suddenly there was an immense explosion: the cabin had turned into a fireball. They were firing incendiary devices, some kind of missiles!

Elena screamed again. "They're aiming at us! They're trying to kill us!"

With steely concentration, Bryson caught a peripheral glance at the helicopter, saw it shift again. He spun the wheel crazily to the right, sending the car careering, its wheels spinning noisily in the dirt.

Another blast! Just feet from the car, another cabin erupted in flames an instant after a missile streaked into it.

Focus! Don't be distracted, don't look — focus!

Need an escape, but what — where? Must get out of this clearing, out of the path of the missiles!

Bryson's thoughts were frantic. *Nowhere to go, nowhere out of range, nowhere a missile can't reach us!*

Jesus Christ! A missile streaked by so closely he could see it almost brush against the hood of the car, then hit a large oak tree, where it exploded. Fire was raging all around them now, the grassy meadow ablaze. The two destroyed cabins roared with pluming flames, pillars of fire.

"My God!" he heard himself shouting. He was nearly crazed with terror, overwhelmed by the sense of futility, the *madness* of the situation!

Then he spotted a bridge. Just across the burning field, a short path led down to a wide, muddy river, a rickety-looking, old wooden beam bridge across it. Flooring the accelerator, he drove straight ahead at top speed. Elena screamed, "What are you *doing?* You can't — the bridge won't hold us — it's not for cars!"

The trees just ahead exploded into orange flames, as another missile narrowly missed its mark. They plunged ahead straight into the inferno. For a second or two everything was orange-white as flames licked the glass, blackening it, and then they emerged on the other side of the conflagration, propelled forward onto the wooden bridge. It swayed perilously ten feet above the slow-moving river of mud.

"No!" Elena screamed. "*It won't hold us!*"

"Quick, roll down your window," Bryson shouted as he did the same. "And take a deep breath."

"What . . . ?"

The helicopter's blades thundered ever closer, a sound Bryson could feel more than hear.

He floored the accelerator once more, and the car lurched forward, crashing through the wooden parapets.

"No! *Nicholas!*"

The sensation was one of slow motion, as if time had almost come to a stop. The car teetered forward, then plunged into the river. Bryson roared, clutching the wheel and the dashboard; Elena clung to him, screaming as well.

The splash was enormous. The El Dorado plunged bumper first into the water, hurtling down. In the seconds before they were submerged in the opaque waters, Bryson heard a blast just behind them; he turned to see the bridge collapse in a starburst of flame.

Their world was dark, murky; the car sank; the brown water rushed into the windows, rapidly filling the interior. Bryson could see just a short distance ahead underwater. Holding his breath, he unbuckled the seat belt and helped Elena out of her seat belt, then out of the car, moving slowly, balletically, through the shadows, the billowy murk. Pulling her with all of his strength, they moved along just beneath the surface of the brackish water, carried along by the current, until he could no longer hold his breath and they came to the surface, surrounded by reeds and marsh grass.

They each gasped for air, gulping it in. "Stay down," he panted. They were surrounded by tall reeds, shielded from view. He could hear, but not see, the helicopter; he pointed toward the water, and Elena nodded, then they filled their lungs with air and went under again.

The instinct for survival is a potent source of energy: it urged them along, allowed them to stay under for a longer time than they might otherwise have done, made them swim with greater endurance. When they came up for air again, still camouflaged by reeds and grass, the helicopter roar seemed to have diminished; it seemed to be farther away. Keeping his head down, Bryson looked skyward and saw that the chopper had gained altitude, likely to survey a broader area.

Good; they're not sure where we've gone, whether we were trapped in the car to drown slowly . . .

"Again," Bryson said. They took deep breaths, filling their lungs to the bottom, then plunged. There was a rhythm now, a pattern to their flight; they swam, let the current carry them downstream, and when they couldn't hold their breath any longer they came up, sheltered by the wild aquatic vegetation.

They went down again, and up, then down again, and soon half an hour had gone by, and Bryson looked at the sky and saw that the helicopter had left. There were no signs of life to be observed; the watchers had lost their targets, no doubt hoping that the targets were dead.

Finally they reached a place where the river got shallow and they could stand and rest. Elena shook the muddy water from her hair, coughing a few times before she was able to catch her breath. Their faces were mud-covered; Bryson could not help laughing, though more from relief than from amusement.

"So this is what your life was like," she said, the analyst speaking to the field operative. She coughed again. "You're welcome to it."

Half smiling, he said, "This is nothing. You haven't lived until you've had to take a dive into the canals of Amsterdam. Three meters deep. A third of that's muck and filth. Another third's a layer of abandoned bicycles—they're sharp and rusty, and when they scrape you it hurts like hell. Then you stink for about a week. As far as I'm concerned, this is a refreshing dip in a nature preserve."

They climbed up onto the riverbank, the water draining from their soaked clothing. A cold breeze was blowing, rippling the reeds and chilling them both. Elena had begun shivering, and Bryson held her close, warming her as best he could.

About three-quarters of a mile from Camp Chippewah was a bar and restaurant. Sodden and cold, mud-encrusted, they sat at the bar, sipping hot coffee, talking quietly and ignoring the looks from the bartender and the other patrons.

A television mounted on the wall was blaring a soap opera, which had just begun; the bartender pointed a remote at it, changing the channel to CNN.

Richard Lanchester's patrician face occupied the entire screen, file footage from one of his numerous appearances before Congress. An announcer's voice came on in midsentence: ". . . sources say will be named to head the new international security agency. The reaction in Washington has been overwhelmingly favorable. Lanchester, who is reportedly enjoying a rare working vacation in the Pacific Northwest, was unavailable for comment. . . ."

Elena went rigid. "It's happening," she breathed. "They're not even bothering to hide anything any longer. Dear God, what is it, what are they doing—what is it *really?*"

Two hours later they had chartered a private plane to Seattle.

Neither one slept; they spoke quietly, urgently. They planned, strategized; they held each other, neither able to vocalize what they both feared, what the dying Harry Dunne had taunted Bryson with: *they were too late.*

CHAPTER
THIRTY-ONE

Their suite at the Four Seasons Olympic Hotel in Seattle—the busy hotel, situated conveniently near the Interstate 5 Expressway, seemed their best bet for escaping notice—was converted into a command center: it was strewn with maps, computer equipment, cables, modems, and printouts.

The tension was almost palpable. They had found the nerve center of a shadowy organization known as Prometheus, the site of a meeting this evening of enormous consequence. Harry Dunne's ravings had been confirmed by a variety of means. The city's limousine services all reported they had nothing available; there was a "function" tonight requiring quite a few cars. Most were discreet, though one owner could not resist dropping the name of the host: Gregson Manning. Flights were arriving throughout the day at Seattle-Tacoma Airport, pickups of VIPs arranged, many with security escorts. Yet not a single name of an arriving guest was revealed. The cordon of secrecy was extraordinarily tight.

So too was the secrecy that seemed to surround the life and career of Gregson Manning. It was as if two or three sanitized accounts of his personal life had been doled out to fatuous journalists, published prominently, and then recycled endlessly. The result was that although much was written about Manning, little was known.

They had more success in obtaining information about Manning's famous mansion on the shores of a lake outside of Seattle. The building of this digital fortress, this so-called "smart house," had taken years and was accompanied by much press coverage, a great deal of voyeuristic speculation. Apparently, after a period of trying to suppress reporting on his house, Manning had shifted to trying to control the reporting. That he had managed well. The mansion was described in tones of breathless astonishment, in "tours" published in such magazines as *Architectural Digest* and *House & Garden*, as well as in various wire-service reports and in *The New York Times Magazine* and *The Wall Street Journal*.

Many of the articles were accompanied by photographs; a few even included rudimentary plans which, though no doubt incomplete, allowed Elena and Bryson to note the approximate layout and the purpose of many of the rooms. The futuristic, hundred-million-dollar estate was cut so deep into the steep hillside that much of it was underground. There was an indoor pool; a tennis court; an art deco, state-of-the-art theater. There were conference rooms, exercise facilities with a trampoline room, bowling alley, shooting range, basketball court, a putting green. The mansion's front lawn, Bryson was careful to note, was directly on the shores of the lake, with two boat docks. Deep under the front lawn was a giant concrete-and-steel parking garage.

But what Bryson found most intriguing about Manning's house was that it was a fully digital house: all its electronic devices, all its appliances, were networked and controlled both locally and remotely, from the Seattle campus of Systematix. The house was programmed to serve the every want of its residents and guests. Every visitor was given an electronic badge programmed with their likes and dislikes, their tastes and preferences, from art to music, from lighting to temperature. Signals were relayed from the badge to hundreds of sensors. Wherever they moved throughout the house, the lights would dim or brighten according to their wishes, temperatures would adjust, their favorite music would come on the concealed sound system. Video screens were embedded in the walls, disguised as picture frames; they displayed a constantly changing selection of artwork from some twenty million images and pieces of art to which

Manning had quietly acquired the rights. Visitors to the house would therefore see the walls hung with only the art they loved, whether it was great Russian icons or Van Gogh, Picasso or Monet, Kandinsky or Vermeer. Apparently the resolution of the video monitors was so fine that guests were astonished to realize they were not viewing actual canvases.

But very little existed in the public record about the security of Gregson Manning's high-tech Xanadu. All Bryson could turn up was that the security system was, of course, redundant; that there were hidden cameras everywhere, even secreted within the interior stone walls; and that the electronic badges that all visitors and staff wore did more than change the music and the lighting: they also kept track of every visitor's whereabouts to within six inches. The system was said to be monitored at the Systematix campus. The place was said to be more heavily guarded than the White House. *No surprise*, thought Bryson grimly. *Manning has more power than the president.*

"It would be a big help if we could get the building plans," Bryson said after he and Elena had gone through the piles of articles photocopied from the public library and downloaded from the Internet.

"But how?"

"They're supposedly on file at city hall, blueprints occupying seven drawers. Under lock and key. But I have a strong impression that they've been 'lost.' Men like Manning frequently arrange to have municipal copies of sensitive documents 'misplaced.' And the architect, unfortunately, lives and works in Scottsdale, Arizona. Presumably he has the stamped originals, but there's no time to fly to Arizona. So we'll just have to wing it."

"Nicholas," she said, turning to him with anxiety in her face, "what do you intend to do?"

"I need to get inside. It's the seat of the conspiracy, and the only way to blow it, and them, out of the water is to confront and *witness*."

"Witness?"

"Witness, observe the members. See who they are, the ones whose names we don't know. Take photographs, record video evidence. Shine daylight into the darkness. It's the only way."

"But Nicholas, it's like trying to infiltrate Fort Knox, isn't it?"

"In some ways easier, in some ways harder."

"But even more dangerous."

"Yes. Even more dangerous. Especially without the Directorate as backup. We're on our own."

"We need Ted Waller."

"I don't know how to raise him, how to locate him."

"If he's still alive, he'll want to contact us." •

"He knows how to. The telephone numbers are still answered by answering services, coded messages taken and given to the right caller. I keep checking, but he still hasn't surfaced. He's a man who's skilled at disappearing without a trace if circumstances require it."

"But to try to enter the Manning estate on your own—"

"Will be difficult. But with your help—your expertise at computer systems—we may have a chance. One of the articles mentioned that the security at Manning's house is monitored both locally and at Systematix headquarters."

"That doesn't really help us—Systematix is probably even more secure than Manning's residence."

Bryson nodded. "No doubt. But the point of vulnerability may be the link. How would the house be connected to the company?"

"I'm sure they'd use the most secure method possible."

"What's that?"

"Fiber-optic line. Buried in the ground and physically connecting the two locations."

"Can fiber-optic lines be tapped?"

She looked up suddenly, startled, and then a slow smile started across her face. "Just about everyone believes it's impossible."

"And you?"

"I *know* it's possible."

"How do you know?"

"We've done it. A few years ago the Directorate devised several clever techniques."

"You know how to do it?"

"Of course. It takes some equipment, though nothing you can't get at a decent computer store."

Bryson kissed her. "Terrific. I have a lot of equipment to buy, and I need to conduct some surveillance on Manning's house and property. But first I need to make a phone call to California."

"Who's in California?"

"A company in Palo Alto I've dealt with before, in one of my Directorate aliases. Founded by a Russian émigré, Victor Shevchenko, an optics genius. He's got a Pentagon contract and yet he used to sell a fair amount of obscure, classified equipment on the black market, which is how I got to know him, during an international sting operation. I left him in place, didn't report his activities to Justice, because I figured he'd be more useful as a lead to much bigger fish. He was deeply grateful for my forbearance — and now it's time to collect. Victor is one of the very few sources for the instrument I need, and if I get to him now he may just have the time to air-freight it to us by this evening."

Bryson spent the next hour conducting discreet surveillance of Manning's estate, using small but high-powered binoculars, from the national forest land that adjoined it. The lakeside property occupied five acres. On the other side was a far more modest house on about an acre and a half.

The security, or at least as much as Bryson could observe, was extremely sophisticated. The chain-link perimeter fence was eight feet high, with fiber-optic stress-sensor line enmeshed throughout it. This ruled out climbing over the fence or attempting to cut through it. The bottom of the fence was buried in concrete, which made digging underneath difficult. Buried under the topsoil in front of the fence was a distributed pressure–sensor system, also fiber-optic lines, which detected the footsteps of intruders above a certain preset weight: pressure on the sensors disturbed the light flow and set off an alarm. In addition, the entire area was watched by surveillance cameras mounted on poles along the fence. Getting in this way had to be ruled out.

But every security system had its vulnerabilities.

For one thing, there was the forest that adjoined the Manning property, where he now stood. Then there was the lake, which seemed to Bryson to present the best opportunity to infiltrate undetected. He returned to the rented Jeep, hidden among the trees and far from the nearest road. As he drove down the access road he passed a small white van that was turning into the gated Manning estate. It was painted with the words Fabulous Food. Caterers, no doubt preparing for the evening's festivities. He caught a glance of the van's passengers.

Another possibility had just suggested itself.

There were errands to run, purchases to make, and far too little time remaining. Bryson had no difficulty locating a sporting-goods store specializing in mountain climbing, not in this capital of the Pacific Northwest. It was a large and well-stocked shop that also catered to the diverse need of hunters, which eliminated the need to make two other stops. But scuba-diving equipment had to be obtained at a separate dive shop. The yellow pages identified for him the location of an industrial safety products supply house, which serviced construction companies, telephone linemen, window washers, and the like; there, he found precisely what he needed: a portable electric winch, battery operated and quiet, in lightweight aluminum housing with a self-retracting lifeline — two hundred and twenty-five feet of galvanized steel cable, a controlled descent device, and a centrifugal braking mechanism.

An elevator parts supply company had exactly what he needed, as did a military surplus warehouse, where an employee recommended a decent shooting range close by. There he bought a .45 semiautomatic pistol for cash from a young, grubby-looking man practicing with it, who shared Bryson's vocal disgust with the goddamned gun-control laws and the goddamned waiting period, especially when a guy just wanted to pick up a piece for recreational purposes on the way out of town for a camping trip.

Batteries and bell wire were easily found at an ordinary hardware store, but he expected it to be far more difficult to find a decent theatrical supply house than it turned out to be. Hollywood Theatrical Supply, on North Fairview Avenue, sold and rented a complete range of equipment for stage and motion-picture industry use; Hollywood studios and production companies often went on location in the northwest and needed a local supplier.

All that remained was the single exotic piece of classified military equipment. Victor Shevchenko, the inventor of the virtual cathode oscillator, had been reluctant to part with one of them, but relented when Bryson let him know that there was no statute of limitations on violations of U.S. national security law. That, and fifty thousand dollars wired into the scientist-entrepreneur's Grand Caymans account, was enough to twist his arm.

By the time Bryson returned to the Four Seasons, Elena had purchased what she needed. She had even downloaded a U.S. geological-survey topographical map of the national forestland abutting Manning's estate.

After he explained what he had observed on his visit to the area surrounding the Manning estate, she asked, "Wouldn't it be much simpler for you to get in as a caterer, or maybe a florist?"

"I don't think so. I've thought it over, and my calculation is that the florists are probably accompanied in, they do their work, and they're accompanied out. Even assuming I could somehow enter with them, which I wouldn't count on, it would be next to impossible for me to disappear into the house—to not leave with the others—without putting the whole place on alert."

"But the caterers—they come in, they stay throughout the festivities . . ."

"The caterers may well turn out to be useful to me. But from what little I've read about Manning's security paranoia, we can assume that all of the caterer's employees are going to be background-investigated, photographed and fingerprinted, and issued electronic security passes only upon arrival. Getting into the house as a caterer will be next to impossible. I've rented a boat; it's the only way to get up on shore."

"But . . . but then what? I'm sure he has the front lawn protected!"

"No question about it. But from everything I can tell, it's the least secure entry point. Now, what have you learned about the security system link between Manning's house and Systematix?"

"I'm going to need a van," she said.

Outside of Seattle the U.S. Department of Agriculture maintains a garage facility where the Seattle-area employees of the U.S. Forest Service kept their government vehicles. In the adjacent open-air parking lot were several small green trucks marked with the forest service pine-tree shield. The security was virtually nonexistent.

Bryson drove Elena into the woods adjoining the Manning property. She was attired in green pants and shirt purchased at an army-navy surplus store, the closest thing they could get to a U.S. Forest Service uniform on such short notice.

Four hours remained before their strike time of nine o'clock P.M.

They walked through the forest near the high-security chain-link fence that marked the boundary of Manning's estate, careful to keep back far enough from the cameras and the pressure-detection alarm system next to the fence. Elena was looking for a buried fiber-optic cable that ran from the Manning mansion through a small area of the national forest.

She knew it was there. Manning's house was approximately three miles from Systematix headquarters, the communications linked by fiber-optic cable. During the construction of the house, Manning's contractor had filed an official request with the U.S. Department of Agriculture for an easement to run just twenty feet of fiber-optic line between his house and the public road. The form, which was a matter of public record and easily obtained on-line, mentioned one detail that especially intrigued Elena: the need to put down a device called an optical repeater. This was a box that served in effect as an amplifier, to boost the signal along the way, since there was always some leakage over long distances.

A repeater could easily be tapped into, if you knew what you were doing. Most did not; Elena most certainly did.

The only question was: where was the line?

A few minutes later she punched out a Seattle telephone number for the contractor listed in the easement request, the one who had installed the miles of cable.

"Mr. Manzanelli? My name is Nadya; I'm calling from the U.S. Geological Survey. We're taking soil samples to test for acidification, and we want to make sure we don't accidentally cut any fiber-optic cable out here. . . ."

When she explained what section of the national forest she was digging in, the contractor replied, "Jesus Christ, come on! Doesn't anyone there remember the hassle you folks gave us over digging the trench through government land?"

"I'm sorry, sir, I'm not familiar—"

"Goddamned Forest Service wouldn't permit it, and Mr. Manning was willing to kick in half a million bucks for new plantings and everything! But no—we had to run an above-ground conduit right along the fence!"

"Sir, I'm terribly sorry to hear that—I'm sure our new administrator would happily have granted Mr. Manning's request."

"You have any idea what kind of money Manning pays in property taxes alone?"

"At least there's no chance of our severing one of Mr. Manning's lines. Next time you speak with him, you tell him that all of us here at the U.S. Geological Survey appreciate what he's done for the country."

She disconnected the call and turned to Bryson. "Good news. We've just saved ourselves more than three hours."

At shortly after four o'clock P.M., Bryson was notified by Pacific Air Freight that a delivery had been received at the Seattle-Tacoma Airport. There was a problem, however: it could not be trucked into Seattle until the next morning.

"You gotta be kiddin' me," Bryson roared into the phone. "I need it at the quality-control lab *tonight*, and I got a fifty-thousand-dollar contract ridin' on it!"

"I'm sorry, sir, but if there's anything we can do to help you out in the meantime . . ."

At a few minutes before six o'clock, Bryson pulled the rented U-Haul van into the Pacific Air Freight terminal at the airport, where the thousand-pound machine was loaded onto the van by means of a hoist and the assistance of three apologetic employees.

Within an hour he drove the van deep into the thickly forested area next to the Manning property, a hundred yards from the green forest-service truck. He backed the van up so that its tail end faced the chain-link perimeter fence, though far enough away that it would not be detected by the security cameras. He slid the van door up and then positioned the machinery so that it had a direct line-of-sight to the Manning compound. The numerous trees and dense foliage that blanketed Manning's property and concealed his estate were no problem at all. Quite the opposite: they helped camouflage the Russian scientist's device.

Then he took a knapsack full of small round disks, each one connected to a firing pod that would detonate when it received a signal from a wireless transmitter. He hiked almost a quarter of a mile through the woods, back toward the main road. Then, strolling along the property line, out of sight of the cameras and removed from the pressure-triggered intrusion-detection system, he began tossing the disks over the fence, one by one, each separated from the other by approximately two hundred feet. The cartridges were small enough that they would attract no notice. If anyone happened to be monitoring the cameras—which was unlikely; the cameras were mostly there to provide a set of eyes in case one of the perimeter alarms went off—he would see nothing more than a blur, something presumably dropped by a bird, perhaps an insect. Nothing worth a second look.

Inside the cargo bay of the green forest-service truck, Elena quickly assembled her tools. Her laptop was now connected to the optical repeater by means of a twenty-foot cable that ran undetectably under the truck, concealed by dirt and leaves, and right to the junction box. She had a tap in place, at first just listening and watching, not transmitting anything. She had come prepared with loads of software, both commercial and specially written for the occasion. She did what was called a "stealth scan" to fingerprint the system, see what sort of intrusion-detection software was present; and she inserted a prewritten script designed to overload the system with an unexpectedly large quantity of data—create a buffer overflow. Then she ran a network packet sniffer to map out the systems on the security network, to find out what kind of network traffic was being sent and received, what the basic organization looked like.

Within the space of a few seconds she "owned the box," as the hackers liked to say. Though she was no hacker, she had long ago made it a point to learn the hacker's trade, just as a good field operative would learn the burglar's methods, the safecracker's techniques.

The training had paid off. She was in.

The fourteen-foot aluminum fishing boat was powered by a quiet, forty-horsepower Evinrude outboard motor. Bryson moved quickly across the lake, buffeted gently by the swells. The sound was minimal, carried away from the Manning property by a prevailing wind. As soon as he saw the string of bright orange barrier floats that demarcated the protected waters before Manning's dock and front lawn, he reduced speed and then cut the engine, which coughed and died. Theoretically he could have charged the line of floats, but he had to assume, even if he didn't know for sure, that Manning had some sort of security in place to detect the approach of intruder craft.

Even from here he could see the mansion, illuminated by floodlights, low-slung and hugging the hillside. Most of it was underground, making the structure appear more modest than it actually was. He dropped anchor, mindful of keeping the skiff in place as an escape option, if he was so fortunate as to be able to escape. He had told Elena, *assured* her, that his plan provided for a way out, but it was not true; he wondered if she secretly suspected it. He would win and survive, or he would lose and be killed. There was nothing in between.

Quickly, he began to assemble his equipment. Although he needed to travel as light as possible, he also had to provide for dozens of different obstacles that he simply could not foresee, which meant a range of equipment. It would be unfortunate to blow the entire operation for want of the right lockpick set. His tactical vest was heavy with various weapons, neatly folded clothing, and other objects, all sealed in plastic.

He radioed Elena on the secure two-way communicator.

"How's it going?"

"Good." Her voice was strong and clear, sounding upbeat. "The eyes are open."

She had succeeded in penetrating the video surveillance feed through the fiber-optic line. "How far can the eyes see?" Bryson asked.

"Uh, there are clear areas and areas that are not so clear."

"What's not so clear?"

"Private, residential areas and the like. They seem to be monitored locally." She meant that the cameras in the nonpublic parts of the house were watched not at Systematix headquarters but within Manning's house itself. Manning obviously wanted at least *some* semblance of privacy.

"That's unfortunate."

"True. But there is some good news. There are some good reruns on TV." She had located yesterday's video feed and had figured out how to pipe it back to the video monitoring system so that it appeared to be today's!

"That's excellent news. But wait until after stage one is completed. All right, now I'll be back in touch after I've gone for a swim."

The lightweight black Nomex bodysuit he preferred for infiltrating the residence was water absorbent, so he wore a scuba wetsuit over it. He felt overheated, but the cold lake water would soon cool him down. Over the tac vest he now fastened his inflatable BC, or buoyancy compensator, which was already strapped to the tank, adjusted the quick-release buckles, adjusted the weight belt, donned his silicone dive mask, put the second-stage regulator into his mouth. After a quick double-check of his equipment, he knelt on the side of the boat and plunged in, headfirst.

There was a splash, and he was floating on the surface of the lake. He looked around, oriented himself, and started deflating his vest. He sank slowly beneath the surface of the water, which was cold and crystalline. As he descended, he noticed that the water became steadily muddier and more opaque. He stopped to equalize the air pressure, felt his ears pop. When he had reached a depth of about sixty feet, it was hard to see much farther than ten or twenty feet ahead. This was not good; he would have to proceed carefully, slowly. Feeling weightless, he began swimming in the direction of the shore.

He listened for the distinctive, bass-toned moan of sonar, but he heard only silence—which was reassuring in one sense, nerve-racking in another: there *had* to be some sort of security system in place.

And then he saw it.

There, floating no more than ten feet ahead of him, swaying in the water like some marine predator. Netting.

But no mere netting. An underwater alarmed security barrier. Webbing with fiber-optic mesh woven into the structure, linked fiber-optic panels that formed alarm zones, sensors connected to electronic control units via optical fiber–communications cables. This was an intrusion-detection system of unusual sophistication, used to protect military marine installations.

The Aquamesh was rigged to a series of buoys and anchored to the lakebed by means of weights. He could not swim through it, of course; nor could he cut or tear it without setting off the alarm. He deflated his BC until he was standing on the lakebed, then approached it, examined it. He had in fact set something like this up in Sri Lanka, and he knew that false alarms were not uncommon. It was prone to chafing and breaking, since water is constantly moving, and underwater creatures, whether fish or crabs, might wriggle through, get caught, even nip into the cables. It was not a perfect system by any means.

But he could not take the chance of setting it off. Manning's security personnel would be on heightened alert tonight, of all nights. They were likely to respond to any alarms.

He found that he was breathing shallowly, a reaction to fear, and this was causing him to feel unpleasantly short of breath, as if he could not fill his lungs; he felt a momentary panic. He closed his eyes for a moment, forced himself to be calm until his breathing became steady.

This is designed for boats, for underwater craft, he remembered. Not for divers, not swimmers.

He settled to his knees, inspected the sinkers that held the netting down. The lake floor was silt, a soft muddy sediment that yielded as soon as he touched it. He pushed at the silt, then began digging with his fingers, his hands cupped like spades. A cloud arose all around him, turning the water opaque. Swiftly, and with remarkable ease, he had dug an elongated trench beneath the bottom of the mesh, through which he was able to half wriggle, half slither. As he passed by, the movement of the water rippled the sensor net. But that could not possibly be enough to set it off: the water in the lake was always moving.

He was on the other side now: in Manning's water. He listened again for the lowing of an active sonar system, but he still heard nothing.

And if I'm wrong?

If I'm wrong, he thought, *I'll know soon enough.* Speculation would do no good now. He swam onward with single-minded determination until he approached the pilings beneath the dock, mossy with algae. Maneuvering around to the far side of the dock, where he knew the boathouse was situated, he came closer and closer, the water increasingly shallow; now his feet touched bottom, the surface of the lake just two feet above. He deflated his vest completely, walking across the lake floor until his head emerged from the water and he was directly beneath the dock. He removed his mask, listened, peered around as far as he could see, and was satisfied that there was no one in sight; then he unbuckled the BC vest and attached tank of air and hoses, placing the scuba gear securely on a broad support beam. There he hoped it would remain in case he needed it again.

If I'm so lucky.

Then he grabbed the side of the dock and lifted himself up.

The boathouse blocked his view of the house; it also served to conceal him from anyone who happened to be looking out the front windows. The lawn was dark, the only illumination spilling onto the grass nearest the house from the tall arched windows. Sitting on the edge of the dock, he took off the tac vest, peeled off the wetsuit, and put the vest back on over the black Nomex bodysuit. One by one he removed the weapons and other instruments from the vest, pulled them out of their plastic bags, and replaced them. He crawled the length of the dock and got to his feet in front of the boathouse. It was dark, seemingly empty. If he had miscalculated, he had the snub-nosed .45 handy in one of the front pockets of his vest. He pulled it out and gripped it as he walked toward the main expanse of lawn.

So far, so good. But there was more to come, much more, and the security precautions would no doubt intensify as he approached the residence itself. He could not allow himself to relax his vigilance. He took out a black knit balaclava and pulled it down over his face. From another pocket of the utility vest he took the Metascope, the night-vision monocular that detected infrared light, and put it to his right eye.

He saw the beams at once.

The lawn was crisscrossed with them, motion-detector beam sensors, probably connected to infrared cameras. Anyone walking across the front lawn would break a beam and trigger the alarm.

But they went no lower than approximately three feet, in order to keep from being set off by small animals.

Dogs?

It was possible. It was, in fact, likely that there were guard dogs as well, though he had not heard or seen any.

The Metascope came with a head-mount assembly, allowing hands-free operation. He would need his hands free. He strapped the monocular on, the eyecup securely in place. Now he would be able to traverse the lawn while evading the infrared beams.

But as he dropped to his hands and knees, crawling under the level of the lowest beam, he heard something that made him freeze.

A low whine, a canine growl. He looked up, saw several dogs trotting across the lawn, their pace quickening. Not house pets: Dobermans. Bullet-headed, trained, vicious.

He felt his stomach tighten. Good Christ.

They galloped, stiff-legged, like horses, barking wildly, throatily, sharp teeth bared. Twenty yards off, he estimated, but gaining rapidly. From his tac vest he whipped out the tranquilizer dart gun, which looked like a pistol; he aimed, heart thudding, and fired. Four short coughs, and the carbon-dioxide-powered short-range projector shot four four-inch tranquilizer darts, the first one wide of the mark, the remaining three hitting their targets. It was a silent business: two of the dogs sagged to the ground almost instantly, the largest one continuing on unsteadily for another few yards before wobbling and then crashing. Each syringe injected 10 cc's of a fentanyl-based neuromuscular incapacitant, which worked immediately.

He was perspiring heavily, trembling involuntarily. Although he had prepared for the contingency, he had almost been caught unawares with neither dart gun nor .45 at the ready; a matter of seconds, and he would have been surrounded, powerful jaws at his throat, his groin. He lay flat on the dewy lawn, waiting. There might be other dogs, a second wave. The barking might have attracted the attention of the security guards. That was likely. But even highly trained dogs could have false alarms; if their barking stopped, attention would be turned elsewhere.

Thirty, forty-five seconds of silence. The black Nomex suit and black balaclava over his face enabled him to blend into the dark night. There were no other dogs in the vicinity; in any case, he could not afford to wait any longer. Built into the front lawn, as required by state building code, would be several grates, ventilation for the underground parking garage immediately below. One of the accounts he had read of the travails of constructing the mansion had alluded to a minor battle with the building inspector over the placement of the garage, invariably and inevitably called the Bat Cave because Manning and his guests entered it via an access ramp carved deep into the hillside on the other side of the house. Under the heat of public scrutiny, Manning had made concessions, adding ventilation shafts that opened unobtrusively into the front lawn.

Bryson resumed crawling across the lawn, moving to the left, careful to stay below the lower shaft of focused infrared light. He saw nothing. He crawled straight ahead another ten feet or so up the gradual slope toward the house, and then he felt it: the steel grille of a ventilation grate. He grabbed at the grating, prepared to unbolt it if need be, but it loosened after a few tugs.

The opening was not large, maybe eighteen by twenty-four inches, but it was enough for him to enter. The only question was, how far down? The inner walls of the ventilation shaft were smooth concrete: nothing to grip on to, no handholds. He had hoped for an easier descent, though he had prepared for the situation he now found. He had learned over twenty years of field operations to prepare for the worst; it was the only guarantor of success. The collar of the shaft, into which the grate was seated, was steel; at least that was something of a relief.

Peering through the night-vision monocular into the shaft, he satisfied himself that there were no infrared beams here. He finally removed the head-mounting apparatus of the night-vision monocular, which had begun to chafe uncomfortably, and pocketed it.

Taking out the two-way radio, he radioed Elena. "I'm going in," he said. "Cue the effects. Ignition stage one."

CHAPTER
THIRTY-TWO

The security guard stared at the image, dumbstruck. "John, will you take a look at this?" The room in which they sat was round, the smooth walls a mosaic of views, yet unbroken by individual monitors. Each rectangle represented the feed from a different camera.

The second guard in the control room swiveled around in his chair and did a double-take. There was no mistaking it. A fire was raging on the border of the property. Cameras 16 and 17, stationed on the western perimeter fence, showed flames shooting up from the woods, thick smoke.

"Shit," said the second man. "That's a goddamned brushfire! Some damned fool camper must have left a cigarette burning in the forest, and it's spreading!"

"What's the protocol? I've never had one of these before."

"What the hell do you think, asshole? First things first. Call the fire department. Then notify Mr. Manning."

As soon as Bryson gave her the word, Elena had pressed the button on the small wireless transmitter, which emitted a signal that instantly detonated the firing pods Bryson had wired to each of the twelve theatrical flash cartridges and the four flame-projector tubes. The flash cartridges, which nestled among the leaves and low foliage just over the perimeter fence on Manning's property, immediately generated thick plumes of dense brushfire smoke, mushroom clouds of grayish and black smoke; the flame-projector tubes produced flames that shot eight feet into the air, lasting only a few seconds. Bryson had timed them to go off in sequence, simulating the effect of a wildly spreading brushfire. These were props, special effects used in theatrical and film productions to imitate forest fires convincingly yet safely, without actually causing one. He had no interest in burning down national forestland; there was no need to do so.

"Seattle Fire Department Dispatch, go ahead."

"This is Security at Gregson Manning's estate. Get over here right away—we've got a huge fire that seems to have started in the national forest—"

"Thank you, but we're already on the way."

"*What?*"

"We've already been notified."

"You *have?*"

"Yes, sir. By one of your neighbors. The situation appears to be quite serious. We advise complete evacuation of the residence immediately."

"That's out of the *question!* Mr. Manning is in the middle of an *extremely important* function, with guests invited from all around the world, *important* guests—"

"Then it's all the more *crucial*, sir, that you evacuate your *important* guests to safety," snapped the dispatcher. "*Now!*"

Working at top speed, Bryson hooked the compact mechanical winch on to the steel collar at the head of the ventilation shaft. The double-locking snaphook at the end of the galvanized steel cable he connected to a carabiner, which hooked on the full body harness sewn into the tactical vest.

ROBERT LUDLUM

Built into the portable winch was a controlled descent device, user-controlled, with an auto-lock cam that gripped the rope as it was pulled through the spring-loaded reel, regulating the speed of the descent. It allowed him to lower himself down the shaft at a steady, metered rate.

As he lowered himself, he reached over and replaced the grate, shoving it up against the sturdy black thermoplastic casing of the winch, which would not be obtrusive at a distance. Then he resumed his descent down the dark, seemingly endless duct. In the distance he thought he could hear the warbling sirens of fire engines; they had responded even more speedily than he had anticipated. As the line continued its metered pay-out, he reflected that he was about to enter the zone of heaviest surveillance. The mock brushfire would raise all sorts of alarms, diverting the precious resources of Manning's security complement. Attention would be riveted on the threat of an enveloping forest fire, a far more immediate concern than any theoretical intrusion. Any alarms Bryson inadvertently set off would be attributed to the arrival of firefighters on the property. Confusion would reign, controlled panic: the ideal cover for his infiltration. Bryson had been careful to plant the smoke-generating cartridges sufficiently distant from Elena's truck that her presence would not create suspicion; still, she had to remain alert for questions. Bryson was confident she could handle them.

As the cable continued to spool out from the specially designed pulley far above, Bryson marveled at the distance, the astonishing *depth!* When he saw the red end-of-travel indicator near the cable's end, he knew that he had descended almost 225 feet, the maximum length of the line. Finally the line jerked to a stop. He looked down; another five or six feet remained. He dropped down to the polished concrete floor, his crouch absorbing the impact of the fall. He left the line dangling, in place in case it was needed.

Capt. Matthew Kimball of the Seattle Fire Department, an African-American man of imposing height and girth, planted both feet before Gregson Manning's chief of security, a stocky man in a blue blazer named Charles Ramsey who was only a few inches shorter.

"There's no evidence whatsoever of any brushfire," the firefighter said.

"Well, two of my men saw it on the cameras," Ramsey replied defiantly.

"Did you see it with your own eyes?"

"No, but—"

"Did *any* of your men see the fire with their own eyes?"

"That I don't know. But the cameras don't lie."

"Well, someone was in error," Captain Kimball grumbled, turning back to his crew.

Charles Ramsey glanced at the security man next to him, his eyes narrowing. "I want a head count of every single firefighter who entered the property," he snapped. "Something's definitely suspicious here."

Bryson found himself in a spacious parking garage whose floors were of concrete polished to the sheen of marble. There had to have been more than fifty vehicles here: antiques, collector's cars—Duesenbergs, Rolls-Royces, Bentleys, classic Porsches. All Manning's, he was sure. At the far end was an elevator, which went to the main house directly above.

Depressing the talk button on the two-way communicator, Bryson said quietly, "Everything okay?"

Elena's voice was faint but audible. "Fine. The last of the fire trucks has left. The flames and the smoke dissipated long before they arrived, leaving no trace."

"As planned. Now, as soon as all exterior activity returns to normal, I want you to . . . go to reruns." It was far too risky to feed in yesterday's surveillance video as long as there was activity outdoors, movement whose absence would be noticed by anyone watching the monitors. "And as soon as I'm in the house, I'm going to need you in close radio contact to guide me through the minefields."

Bryson became conscious of a movement in the shadows to his left, a shifting between the rows of automobiles. He turned, saw a blue-jacketed guard with a gun pointed.

"Hey!" shouted the guard.

Bryson spun out of the guard's line of sight, then dropped to the floor. The gun fired, the explosion reverberant in the chasmlike bunker. A round hit the concrete inches from his head, ricocheting, the spent cartridge clattering to the floor. Bryson whipped out the .45, aimed with split-second timing, then fired. The guard attempted to dodge the bullet, but caught it in his chest. He bellowed, his body twisting; Bryson fired again, and the man was down.

Bryson raced to the fallen man. The guard's eyes were wide, staring, his face contorted and frozen in pain. Clipped to the lapel of his blazer was a security pass. Bryson took it, examined it carefully. The house's security system was structured into zones, Bryson concluded, and controlled by means of a conditional-access system. The entrance to each separate zone would be equipped with a proximal scanner, much like the electric eyes of supermarket doors that opened automatically as you approached. The security pass, worn on the breast pocket of a shirt or blazer, was scanned, the unseen computer noting the wearer's ID as well as his location and the time and date, and checking which level of access the individual was allowed. For unauthorized persons, doors would not open, and alarms would sound. The system kept track of where everyone was at all times.

But Bryson also knew that penetrating the house's security had to be more complex than simply stealing a guard's security pass. Either there was a backup, biometric system—fingerprints or handprints, retinal scans and the like—or codes would have to be entered by the person seeking entrance.

The guard's security pass might in fact do nothing to help him get into the house. He would soon know for sure.

The elevator was his way into the house, the *only* way. He raced toward it. He would have to move quickly now, for where there was one guard there would be others; the slain guard's failure to answer a routine, radioed question would raise alarms—alarms that could not be masked by diversionary measures.

The elevator doors were brushed steel, with a call button and keypad mounted on the wall beside them. He pressed the button, but it did not light up. He pressed again, and again no response: a code had to be entered on the key pad in order to summon the elevator—probably a series of four numbers. Unless the sequence was entered, the call button did not function. The security badge he had taken from the guard and clipped to the front of his tactical vest would do no good here.

He inspected the walls nearest the elevator, looking for concealed cameras. It was almost certain that there were in fact security cameras here, but Elena had spoofed them by substituting yesterday's surveillance footage in the system. If for some reason she had been unable to do that, or she had reason to believe that her ruse was not working, she would have radioed him already. She was his eyes and ears; he had to rely on her thoroughness, her skill. And he did; he always had.

The elevator doors could, of course, be forced open by brute force and a crowbar, but that would be a mistake. Modern elevators, even those of rudimentary technology, ran on electronic circuitry, like so much else these days. Prying the doors open by ax or crowbar would break the elevator interlocks and stop the elevator from running; as long as any door on the shaft was open, the elevator would not run. That was a safety feature common to almost all elevators built in the last quarter century. And if the elevator did not run, Bryson ran the risk of drawing the attention of security personnel. Though by then he might already be inside, he did not want to alert security to his intrusion, raise an alarm. An effective covert entry required that tracks be covered.

For that reason he had brought a special tool called an interlock key, used by licensed elevator repairmen for emergency entry. It was a six-inch length of stainless steel about half an inch wide, flat and hinged at the top. He inserted it at the top of the brushed-steel doors, just inside the head door jamb, the flat steel frame around the doors, and moved it to the right. Between three and six inches in, just inside the frame and atop the right door panel, was the mechanical interlock. The hinged interlock key moved easily until it hit an obstruction: the protruding oblong of the interlock. The hinged flap of the key slid to the right, knocking the interlock to the right as well, and the doors slid smoothly open.

Cold air emerged from the dark, empty shaft. The elevator cab had been parked somewhere on an upper floor. Bryson took out a halogen penlight and shone it into the shaft, moving the small, bright circle of light from side to side, up and down. What he found was not encouraging. This was not a conventional residential elevator with a drum-and-winch system, nor was it traction-operated, with cables and counterweights. That meant he could not hope to use the cables to grab on to and pull himself up, using mountain-climbing techniques—there *were*

ROBERT LUDLUM

no cables to grab! All there was inside the steel-enclosed shaft was one large rail on the right side, along which the elevator was raised and lowered by hydraulic pressure. And that rail was slippery, highly lubricated; he could not grab it and pull himself up.

He had expected the worst, and he had gotten it.

Elena had already located the archive for past surveillance feeds. They were stored in flash memory in the database back at Systematix, easily reachable on this system. Ten days' worth of digitized video was stored, each by date, then further broken down by sector. It was a simple matter to retrieve a copy of yesterday's video and rename it with today's date. Then she inserted it into the video monitoring system. Now, instead of viewing live footage, Security was watching yesterday's archived footage, at the exact same time of day, just twenty-four hours earlier. Of course, this would work only for cameras one through eighteen, the outside and certain interior areas where foot traffic was light or nonexistent.

In the rear pockets of Bryson's tac vest were small, lightweight magnetic gripper devices that were customarily used for bridge and tank inspections, as well as underwater examinations of ships' hulls and offshore oil rigs. He strapped one onto each boot, then onto both hands, and he began to climb, scaling the smooth steel wall slowly: releasing and repositioning hands, feet, moving upward pace by pace, release and reposition. It was arduous work and slow going. As he mounted the wall, he remembered the distance he had dropped to enter the garage: over 225 feet, and that was from ground level, down the hill from the mansion. There would be at least one or two underground levels at which the elevator would stop, but he needed to go to the main level of the residence.

At last he saw, by the halogen beam of the penlight, the first of the basement elevator landings. He was conscious at all times that the elevator might be called to the parking level, that it would descend quickly toward him; in such an event, if he did not release the magnetic grippers quickly and flatten himself into the eighteen-inch clearance space between shaft and elevator car, he would be killed instantly. So he had to remain constantly alert for the sound of the machinery starting up.

Now only ten feet or so remained before he reached the level marked ONE where, inconveniently, the elevator car was stopped. Inconvenient, but not unexpected. Bryson sidled over, shifting hands and feet one by one, until he was directly underneath the cab. Then, turning around methodically, he placed the hand grippers one by one, with a metallic clang, onto the lower edge of the steel-sided car. Now he hung from the car itself, his feet dangling into the empty expanse of the seemingly bottomless shaft. He looked down for a moment, which was a mistake: the drop was some two hundred and fifty feet to a concrete floor. If anything went wrong, if the magnetic grippers somehow malfunctioned, that was it. He was not acrophobic, but neither was he immune to the fleeting sensation of terror. This was not a time to slow down, not when the elevator might be summoned at any moment. Moving as swiftly as he could manage, he began climbing up the side of the cab, sandwiched between the cab and the steel wall of the shaft with mere inches of wiggle room.

Don't let it move, he thought. *Don't let it move, don't let anyone call it. Not now, not at this moment.*

Reaching the top of the cab, he rested there for a moment, unfastening the grippers, jamming them back into the pockets of his vest. Then he swung over, grabbed the interlock at the top inside of the doors, and slid it to the left.

The doors opened.

And if someone's on the other side?

He hoped not. But he was prepared for that, too.

He was looking down at a dimly lit, elegantly furnished lobby in what seemed to be the main part of the house. He looked down, saw no one in the vicinity, then grabbed hold of the steel beam inside the doorframe and swung himself down, landing on a burnished marble floor.

The lights went on, subdued lighting from several sconces along the wall, probably activated by the security guard's badge.

He was in.

———

The two men in the Security Control room went through the tedious laundry list, the regular security check they performed countless times throughout the day.

"Camera one?"

"Clear."

"Camera two?"

"Clear."

"Camera three?"

"Cl—wait, yeah, it's clear."

"What's the problem?"

"I thought I saw some movement through the big picture windows, but it was just rain."

"Camera four?"

"Charlie, hold on a second. Jesus, it's really coming down out there— just like yesterday. And it was beautiful, really sunny, when my shift started. Fucking Seattle weather. You mind if I take a quick break?"

"A *break?*"

"Yeah, I brought the Mustang convertible and I left it open."

"You didn't park in the underground lot?"

"Got here sort of late," the guard admitted sheepishly. "So I used the front outside lot. I just want to run out there and put up the top before the leather gets ruined."

Charles Ramsey, head of security, sighed with irritation. "Christ, Bain, if you'd get here on time . . . all right, take a break, but make it fast."

Heart pounding from the exertion and from the tension, he sprang to his feet and turned back to the gaping elevator shaft. He approached, reaching carefully up for the interlock to close the doors, aware of the depth of the dark shaft. A fall would be fatal. Strangely, only now that he was out of the shaft did he fully appreciate that.

The movement was almost imperceptible, a quick flickering of lights in his peripheral vision. Bryson pivoted, saw the guard almost on top of him, about to tackle Bryson to the floor. When Bryson slammed the guard with all his weight, the guard threw a lunging punch, which Bryson blocked, grabbing the guard's right forearm while, at the same time, kicking the back of his knee with a steel-toed boot. The guard groaned, sagged for only an instant, then immediately regained his balance as he reached for his gun, struggling with the waist holster.

A mistake not to have the gun at the ready, Bryson thought. A mistake we both made. He took advantage of the man's momentary lapse and delivered a hard kick to the guard's groin. The guard bellowed, knocked backward maybe a foot or two from the open elevator shaft. Still, he somehow managed to get his pistol out, aimed, and prepared to fire. Bryson lunged to the left, confusing the guard's aim, and then spun back toward his enemy, kicking at the gun and sending it flying out of his hand.

"Goddamned bastard," the guard shouted as he leaped backward, arms extended, in an attempt to retrieve the gun; there was a look of almost indignant surprise on his face as he realized that there was no floor beneath him, nothing to break his fall as he threw himself backward, his feet up in the air, higher than his head. The expression of surprise immediately became terror: arms flailing in the air in a vain attempt to clutch on to something, anything, his feet scrambling; he let out an enormous scream of horror, which echoed metallically in the air shaft as he plunged quickly out of sight. The scream was long and sustained, gradually diminishing in volume as he fell away, ever more distant, then stopping abruptly as the body hit bottom.

The security guard, a sandy-haired young man, exited the house through the service entrance, emerging outside not far from the outdoor parking lot. He looked around, bewildered. Just minutes ago it was pouring rain—torrential rain, same as yesterday—and now it was a totally clear night, warm, with not a trace of precipitation anywhere.

Not a trace of rain.

No puddles on the ground, not even wet leaves on the trees.

Ten minutes ago he had seen rain coming down like some biblical flood; now it was a dry, warm night with no evidence that it had ever rained today.

"What the holy hell . . . ?" he exclaimed, taking out his handheld radio and calling Ramsey back in Control.

Ramsey exploded, as he knew the guy would. A string of profanities ensued, but when Ramsey finally got a grip on himself, he began issuing orders all around. "We got a perimeter breach," he said. "They're checking back at corporate, so now we got to follow the fiber-optic line from right outside the gates, see if there's a break."

Sweat poured down Bryson's face; his black Nomex suit itched. He took several deep breaths, then stepped forward toward the shaft, reached up to the interlock, flicked it closed. The steel doors closed silently.

Now he needed to orient himself, to determine which direction to move in order to find the security control room. That was the first order of business. It would tell him what he needed to know, where everything was. It was also the eyes of the enemy, and therefore it needed to be shut down.

He pressed the talk button on the communicator. "I'm at the main level," he said softly.

"Thank God," came Elena's voice. Bryson smiled: she was unlike any field backup he had ever worked with. Instead of being briskly, coldly professional, she was emotional, caring, concerned.

"Now which way to Control?"

"If you're facing the elevator, it's left. There's a long corridor running to either side . . . ?"

"Check." She was working off an array of video surveillance images, going by sight rather than by blueprint.

"Take the one to your left. When it ends, left again. There it widens out into a sort of long portrait gallery. That looks like the most direct route."

"Okay, roger. How are the eyes?"

"Shuttered."

"Great. Thanks."

He turned to the left and ran down the hall. Fiber-optic cables were threaded through the walls and foundations of this house, Bryson was certain. Miles and miles of the stuff, connected to miniature lenses whose pinhole apertures probably dotted the walls and ceilings. Unlike visible security cameras of old, these could not be detected, so they could not be spray-painted or duct-taped over. Were it not for Elena's ability to replace the actual feeds with yesterday's, Bryson would have been observed everywhere he went, with nothing to do about it. Now at least he could move freely, unseen. The security pass he had taken from the guard in the underground garage had so far done him no good at all. It hadn't admitted him to the elevator, though it had switched on the lights once he entered the house. It seemed to be more for keeping track of its wearer than for penetrating security; it had to go. He unclipped it and placed it on the floor of the corridor, against the wall, as if it had been lost by the person to whom it had been issued.

Elena put down the two-way communicator when she heard the crunch of footsteps right outside the truck. It was going too smoothly, she thought. The forest patrol is going to ask questions, and she would have to be persuasive in her answers.

She slid open the back of the van and let out a scream when she saw the muzzle of the pistol pointed at her eyes.

"Let's go!" shouted the man in the blue blazer.

"I'm with the U.S. Geological Survey!" she protested.

"Tapping into our security line? I don't think so. Hands down at your side, and no fucking around! We've got some questions to ask you."

Bryson had reached the long, rectangular room that Elena had called the portrait gallery. It was a peculiar-looking chamber, lined with ornate gilded frames like a room in the Louvre, except that each frame was empty. Or, rather, each frame held a flat grayish monitor, which probably turned into a high-resolution reproduction of a classic oil portrait, the picture changing according to the tastes of the person passing through, as broadcast by the electronic badge.

Bryson was about to step into the gallery when he noticed a line of tiny black beads running up the wall in a vertical line between frames. Every four feet or so another line of these minuscule black dots ran up one wall of the gallery. It almost looked ornamental, like part of the décor, except that it was ever so slightly discordant with the flocked wallpaper, the French Renaissance style. Bryson stood at the entrance of the gallery without entering. The black dots began about eighteen inches from the floor and ended about six feet up. He was fairly sure he knew what they were, but in order to make certain, he took out the night-vision monocular and put it to one eye.

Now he could see row upon row of thin filaments strung across the width of the long room every few feet, starting a few feet from the floor. What looked like glowing green strings were, he knew, laser beams in the infrared frequency: point-to-point sensors with columnated beams of light, invisible to the naked eye. But when the beams were broken by someone passing through—someone unauthorized—an alarm would be set off. They started eighteen inches off the floor, Bryson figured, so that they would not be triggered by any house pets.

The only way to traverse the room was by moving along the floor, staying below eighteen inches at all times so as not to break the lowest infrared-laser beam. And there was no clean and easy way to do it, either. He fastened the monocular on to the head-mounting apparatus; then, when it was securely in place, he dropped to the floor and began sliding on his back, pushing off with his boots. The whole while he was looking up, making sure he did not cross the beam. The Nomex suit was slick enough to allow rapid, smooth movement. Although the cameras had been digitally blinded, the rest of the systems were live; the slightest misstep would trigger an alarm. Yet the greatest threat came not from technology at all but from human beings: the possibility of a guard coming upon him during rounds, as had already happened twice.

He slid under a third, a fourth, a fifth infrared-laser beam. No beam was broken, no alarms triggered, not here.

Finally he slipped under the last light beam. He paused, still on his back, and peered closely around to make sure there were no others. Satisfied, he sat up, then got carefully to his feet. Now he was not far from the security control room; Elena would guide him in the right direction.

He depressed the talk button. "Passage successful," he whispered. "Where to now?"

No answer, so he spoke again, a bit louder.

Again, no response, just staticky dead air.

"Elena, come in."

Nothing.

"Elena, come in. I need guidance."

Silence.

"Which way, damn it?"

Christ, no! Were the communicators malfunctioning? He spoke again and received no response. Was there some jamming technology in place here, keeping her from receiving his signal, him from receiving hers?

But his people had to communicate! There was no way to jam all possible radio frequencies but the one you wanted to use yourself. That was an impossibility.

Then where was she?

He radioed her again, and again. No answer, no answer, nothing.

She was gone.

Had something happened to her? That was a possibility he had not seriously considered.

He felt a cold dread come over him.

But he could not stop, he could not expend any time figuring out where she was or what had happened to their communications. He had to move.

Bryson didn't need radioed instructions to tell him where the caterer's kitchen was. He could smell it down the hall, the enticing aroma of the hot hors d'oeuvres. A door slid open at the far end of the hall and a caterer came through, dressed in black pants and a long-sleeved white shirt, with a large, empty silver tray at his side. Bryson ducked back into the gallery, though not so far as to set off an alarm. There was enough room here, sufficiently removed from infrared beams, for him to change clothes. He quickly removed the tactical vest, then stripped off the black body suit. Taking a neatly folded set of black dress pants and a white shirt from a plastic-sealed package in the tac vest, he got into them at once, then changed his combat boots for rubber-soled black dress shoes.

Sticking his head into the hall that led to the kitchen, he heard laughter, bantering conversation, the metallic clink of pans and utensils. He stepped back into the gallery, waited until he heard the sound of the kitchen's double-doors swing open, then emerged stealthily. The same waiter who had come in five or so minutes earlier was now holding aloft a large tray loaded with appetizers.

Treading silently along the hallway, Bryson stole up behind the waiter. He knew the man would be an easy mark, yet he could not afford noise, could not afford to attract attention. When he was just a few feet behind the caterer Bryson lunged, clapping one hand over his mouth, crooking his elbow around the neck, forcing the man to the floor while, at the same time, grabbing the tray of food. The waiter tried to scream, his cry muffled behind Bryson's hand. Bryson set the tray down carefully and, with his free hand, squeezed hard at the nerve bundle under the man's jaw. The waiter slumped to the floor, unconscious.

Quickly dragging the body back into the gallery, he pushed the waiter into a seated position, hands folded, head down, as if grabbing a quick catnap. Then he ran back down the hall and grabbed the tray of food.

Move it, he told himself. At any moment another waiter could enter the hall and see his face, not recognize him. He knew the security control room was nearby, but where?

He turned into another hall, the door sliding automatically, initiated by electric eye. No: this led directly to the formal dining room, which tonight was unused. He turned around, heading back in the direction of the kitchen, then retraced the path the waiter had taken when first approaching the kitchen. Another set of electronically operated doors slid open to a corridor that he could see led to the main reception hall, but another hall intersected long before then, branching off to the right. Perhaps. He took the right, walked about fifty yards, saw a door marked:

SECURITY
AUTHORIZED PERSONNEL ONLY!

He stopped before it, took a deep breath to calm himself, then knocked on the door.

No answer. He noticed a small inset button on the doorjamb, which he pushed once.

In ten seconds, just when he was about to push the button again, a voice came over a speaker mounted on the wall outside the room. "Yes?"

"Hi, it's catering—I've got your dinner," Bryson said in a singsong voice.

A pause. "We didn't order anything," the voice said suspiciously.

"Okay, fine, you don't want any, no problem. Mr. Manning said to make sure his security people got fed tonight, but I'll just tell him you didn't want any."

The door flew open. The man who stood there in the blue blazer was stocky, his hair dyed brown with an unfortunate orange tint. The name badge on his lapel said *Ramsey*. "I'll take that," the man said, reaching for the tray.

"Sorry, I'm going to need the tray back—it's a big crowd out there! I'll set it up for you." Bryson stepped forward into the security room; Ramsey relaxed somewhat and let him through.

Bryson looked around, saw that there was just one other guard there monitoring. The room was round, high-tech to the point of being futuristic, its walls smooth and unbroken by individual monitor screens, yet dozens of individual panels showed different views in and around the property.

"We've got smoked duck breast, caviar, *gougere*, smoked salmon, tenderloin . . . Do you have a surface where I can set this up for you? This room seems awfully crowded."

"Put it anywhere," the man named Ramsey said, turning his attention back to the images on the wall. Bryson set down the tray gingerly on a bare area of console, then reached over to his left ankle as if to scratch. He quickly pulled out the tranquilizer gun and fired off two quick shots. Two sharp coughing sounds, and each of the security guards was struck, one in the throat, one in the chest. Both would be out for hours.

Now he rushed to the computer keyboards that controlled the images. Pictures could be enlarged, moved around, brought to the center. He located the set of images that represented the views of the main reception hall.

The reception hall, where a banquet was taking place. A meeting of the Prometheus Group on the eve of its takeover.

But a takeover of what?

And by whom?

He tapped at the keyboard, quickly figuring out how to manipulate the images. By moving a computer mouse, he realized, he was able to move a security camera, basically pan it from side to side, up or down, even move in for a close-up.

The reception hall was immense, several stories high, ringed with several balconies overlooking the atrium. Around dozens of elaborately set tables, covered in white tablecloths, with flowers, crystal, bottles of wine, were dozens of people—no, over a hundred people. Faces, familiar faces.

At one end of the room was a great, dazzling, gilded-bronze sculpture, twice life-size, of Joan of Arc astride her horse, sword drawn and pointing straight up, leading her countrymen into the battle of Orléans. Strange but somehow fitting for the crusader who was Gregson Manning.

And at the other end of the room, standing at a sleek, minimalistic podium, was Gregson Manning himself, wearing an elegant black suit, hair brushed back. He clutched the sides of the podium, his fervor evident even without any sound. Most remarkable was the wall behind him, which was lined with twenty-four giant video screens, each broadcasting a live image of Manning speaking. It was the sort of egomaniacal display one expected of a Hitler, a Mussolini.

Bryson moved the mouse to zoom in on the audience, the seated guests, and what he saw stunned him, paralyzed him.

He did not recognize all the faces by far, but many of those whom he did recognize would be known anywhere in the world.

There was the head of the FBI.

The Speaker of the House.

The chairman of the Joint Chiefs of Staff.

Several leading United States senators.

The secretary general of the United Nations, a soft-spoken Ghanaian admired for his civility and statesmanship.

The head of Britain's MI-6.

The head of the International Monetary Fund.

The democratically elected head of Nigeria. The chiefs of the militaries and security services in another half-dozen third-world nations, from Argentina to Turkey.

Bryson stared, jaw agape, gasping.

The CEOs of quite a few multinational technology corporations, some of whom he recognized quickly, some vaguely familiar. All of them, dressed in black tie, the women in formal evening gowns, were listening to Manning with riveted attention.

Jacques Arnaud.

Anatoly Prishnikov.

And . . . Richard Lanchester.

"My God . . . !" he breathed.

He found the volume knob and dialed it up.

Manning's voice came over the speakers, velvety smooth.

". . . a revolution in global surveillance. I'm also pleased to announce that Systematix facial-recognition software will also be ready for use in all public places. With the CCTV capabilities already in place, we will now have the ability to scan crowds and match faces against a stored, *international* database. And this is only possible because of the cooperation of all of us, representatives of forty-seven nations and growing daily—all of us *working together*."

Manning raised his hands as if delivering a benediction to the crowd.

"What about vehicles?" The accent was African; the speaker a dark-skinned man in a dashiki.

"Thank you, Mr. Obutu," Manning replied. "Our neural network technology allows us to not only recognize vehicles instantly but track them around the cities, around countries. And we can record and store that information for future use. You see, I like to think that we are not only widening the net, we're narrowing the *mesh*."

Another question, which Bryson couldn't make out.

Manning smiled. "I know my good friend Rupert Smith-Davies of MI-6 will heartily agree with me when I say that it's long past time that both the NSA and GCHQ must struggle with legal handcuffs. How ridiculous that, until now, the British could monitor the Americans but not themselves, and vice versa! Were Harry Dunne, our CIA coordinator, well enough to be here, I know he would stand up and tell us all a tale or two in his inimitably profane way."

There was general laughter.

Another question: a woman, her accent Russian. "When will the International Security Agency's powers become effective?"

Manning glanced at his watch. "The same moment that the treaty takes effect—which is in approximately thirteen hours. The esteemed

Richard Lanchester will be its director—global security czar, you might say. Then, my friends, we will all bear witness to a true New World Order, one in which we can take pride in having created. No longer will the citizens of the world be hostage to drug cartels and drug smugglers, terrorists and violent criminals. No longer will public safety be forced to take a backseat to the *privacy 'rights'* of child pornographers, pedophiles, and kidnappers."

A deafening round of applause.

"No longer will we all live in fear of another Oklahoma City bombing, another World Trade Center, another downed airliner. No longer will the U.S. government have to *beg* courts for *permission* to place wiretaps on the phones of kidnappers and terrorists and drug lords. To those who will complain—and there will always be complainers—that their individual liberties are being abridged, we will simply tell them this: those who do not break the law will have nothing to fear!"

Bryson did not hear the door to the control room open until he heard the familiar voice.

"Nicky."

He whirled around. "Ted! What the hell are you doing here?"

"The same question might be asked of you, Nicky. It's always what you don't see that gets you, hmm?"

Bryson took in Waller's attire, his tuxedo and black tie.

Ted Waller was a guest.

CHAPTER
THIRTY-THREE

"You're—you're one of them!" Bryson whispered.

"Oh, Nicky, good Lord—what's all this talk of *sides?* This isn't some schoolyard game—shirts and skins, Jets and Sharks!"

"You *bastard!*"

"What did I tell you about the need for a continual reappraisal and reassessment of strategic alliances? Adversaries? Allies? Such terms are, finally, meaningless. If I've taught you nothing else, at least I've taught you that."

"What are you *doing?* This was your battle, you enlisted all of us, for *years . . .*"

"The Directorate has been destroyed. You know that—you saw it happen."

"Has this been some sort of deception all along?" Bryson said, raising his voice to a shout.

"Nicky, Nicky. Prometheus is now our best chance, really—"

"Our best *chance?*"

"And besides, are our goals really all that different? The Directorate was a dream—a fond dream, which we actually had the good fortune to realize for a few years, against all odds. Ensuring global stability, protecting it from the crazies, the terrorists, the madmen. As I always say, the prey survives only by becoming the predator."

"This—this is no last-minute conversion," Bryson said, his voice hushed. "You've been behind this for years."

"I've been a supporter of the possibility."

"A supporter . . . wait. Wait a second! Those assets I once found missing from that offshore bank . . . a billion dollars—but you were never interested in amassing personal wealth. It *was* you! You helped *create* Prometheus, didn't you?"

"Seed money, I believe they call it. Sixteen years ago Greg Manning was a bit overextended, and the Prometheus project needed an immediate infusion of cash. You might say I became a principal stakeholder."

Bryson felt as if he had been kicked in the stomach. "But it makes no sense—if Prometheus were the enemy . . ."

"Survival of the fittest, my dear. Have you never entered two competitors in the same race? It's backup contingency planning—redundancy that assures victory. Communism had fallen, and the Directorate had lost its sense of purpose. I looked around and examined the options, and I knew that conventional spycraft was doomed. Either we were the way of the future or Prometheus was. One horse had to win."

"And so you went with whichever horse won, morality be damned. It made no difference to you what the different objectives were, did it?"

"Manning was one of the most brilliant men I ever met. It occurred to me that his idea was worth incubating, worth nurturing as a contingency."

"You *hedged* your goddamned *bets!*"

"Think of it as political arbitrage. It was the only prudent course. I've always told you, Nick, spycraft isn't a team sport. And I know you have the talent ultimately to recognize the good sense in my reasoning."

"Where's Elena?" Bryson shot back.

"She's a smart woman, Nick, but she didn't plan on being discovered, apparently."

"Where *is* she?"

"Manning's people have her here somewhere in the residence; I'm assured she's being treated with the respect you and I both know she deserves. Nick, do I really have to ask you outright? Is it that important to you that I put the question so bluntly? Will you join us—can you recognize the way of the future?"

Bryson raised his pistol, pointing it at Waller, his heart racing. *Why did you make me do this?* he pleaded inwardly. *Why, damn it?*

Waller saw the gun but did not flinch. "Ah, I see. I have my answer. I didn't think so. Alas."

The door flew open again, and a small army of Manning's security guards entered, guns pointed, outnumbering him some twelve to one. Bryson spun, saw others pouring in through another, concealed door in the round wall, and as his back was turned, he was grabbed from behind. He felt the cold steel of the muzzle against the back of his head, another gun to his right temple. He turned back, much more slowly this time, and Ted Waller was gone.

"Hands in the air," a voice commanded. "And don't even think about making any sudden movements. Don't try to grab the gun out of anyone's hands. You're a smart guy—you know about smart guns."

Electronic pistols, Bryson realized. Developed by Colt, by Sandia, by several European weapons firms . . . Capable of firing three shots with a single pull of the trigger.

"Hands up! Move it!"

Bryson nodded, thrust his hands in the air. There was nothing more to do, probably no hope of saving Elena either. The technology had been developed at the request of law enforcement, to keep police officers from being killed with their own firearms, when the gun is grabbed from them in a confrontation. There were fingerprint sensors on the trigger, each gun personally programmed so that only the authorized user could fire it.

He was marched, half-pushed, down the hallway outside the control room, down another short corridor. Guns at his temple, at the back of his head, he was frisked, the .45 caliber discovered and taken from him. One of the guards pocketed his snub-nosed pistol with ill-disguised triumph. He was disarmed totally, they had missed nothing. He had his hands, his instincts, his training, but it was all useless in the face of such an overwhelming artillery.

But why had they not killed him? What were they waiting for?

A door was opened, and he was shoved through it. He was in another oblong room, its dimensions similar to the portrait gallery. The lighting was dim, but he was able to make out the books lining the walls: russet leather-bound volumes in mahogany shelves that went from floor to a twenty-foot ceiling. A beautiful, grand library such as might be found in an English manor. The floor was parquet, perfectly worn.

Bryson stood, alone, inspecting the bookshelves, filled with a sense of foreboding, a sense that something was about to happen.

And suddenly the library disappeared: the book-lined walls glimmered, went silvery gray. It was an illusion! Like the portraits in the gallery, the books were a digital phantasm. He stepped forward to touch the smooth, yet slightly sandpapery gray walls, and then they lit up, this time bright, filled with *hundreds* of different images!

He stared in horror. The images were of himself! Film, video footage.

Of himself strolling on the beach with Elena. In bed with Elena, making love. Showering, shaving, urinating.

Arguing with Elena. Kissing her. Sitting in Ted Waller's office, shouting.

Elena and him riding horseback.

Bryson and Layla running through the passages of the *Spanish Armada*, evading Calacanis's gunmen. Hiding in the abandoned cathedral in Santiago de Campostela. Furtively searching Jacques Arnaud's private office. Meeting with Lanchester. Meeting with Tarnapolsky in Moscow. Running.

Meeting with Harry Dunne.

Scene after scene — surveillance video, taken from a distance, from close up, Bryson the star of each one. Scenes from his life, from the most intimate moments of his life. The most secret field operations. Nothing, not a single moment of the last ten years had gone unfilmed. The images were kaleidoscopic, flickering, horrifying.

Even footage of him lowering himself into the garage and climbing the elevator shaft. *They had seen him infiltrating the house, just moments ago.*

They had seen everything.

Bryson was dazed. His head spun; he felt overcome by vertigo; he felt violated, raped, sick to his stomach. He dropped to his knees and was sick, retching and retching until there was nothing more in his stomach, yet the dry heaves did not stop.

The whole thing was a setup. They knew he was coming; they wanted to observe; he had been under surveillance the entire time.

"Prometheus, you may recall, stole the gift of fire from the gods and gave this great gift to downtrodden mankind," said a calm voice, a soothing voice, amplified by hidden speakers throughout the room.

Bryson looked up. At the far end of the room, standing in a marble alcove, was Gregson Manning.

"They say you're a formidable linguist. You must know, then, the etymological derivation of the name Prometheus. It means fore-seeing, or fore-thinking. It seemed an apt name for us. Prometheus, according to the classical tradition, gave man civilization—language, philosophy, mathematics—and brought us from savagery to civility. This was the meaning of the gift of fire—light, illumination, knowledge. Making visible what had been concealed in the shadows. Prometheus, that Titan, willfully and knowingly committed a crime when he brought fire down from the heavens and taught the mortals how to use it. It was treason! He was threatening to put humans on an equal footing with the gods themselves! But in so doing he created civilization. And it is our task to make its continued existence secure."

Bryson walked a few steps closer to Manning. "So what do you have in mind?" he said. "Stasi on a global scale?"

"Stasi?" Manning replied scornfully. "Organize half the populace to spy on the other half, no one trusting anyone? I hardly think so."

"No," Bryson said, taking another few steps closer to the marble alcove. "The East Germans' technology was strictly Iron Age, wasn't it? No, you have supercomputers and miniaturized fiber-optic lenses. You have the ability to put *everybody* under the microscope. You and everyone in that hall out there—they've all bought into your nightmare vision. The Treaty on Surveillance and Security is merely a cover for a system of global surveillance that will make Big Brother seem benign—isn't that right?"

"Come now, Mr. Bryson. We teach our children when they're toddlers about Santa Claus—'he knows if you've been bad or good, so be good for goodness sake.' Whether you acknowledge it or not, the ethical principle has always been linked to what is *known* about us. The all-seeing eye. Good conduct tracks with transparency. When everything is visible, crime disappears. Terrorism becomes a thing of the past. Rape, murder, child abuse—all gone. Mass murders—wars—gone. As will be the fear that grips every man, woman, and child, our inability to leave our houses, to walk through our cities, to simply live our lives *as we want to live them*, free from *fear!*"

"And who will be watching?"

"The computer. Massively parallel computational systems around the globe, girded with evolutionary algorithms and neural networks. There's never been anything like it."

"And at the center of it all is the despot-voyeur, Gregson Manning, orchestrating your computers into a billion virtual Peeping Toms."

Manning smiled. "Do you know about the Igbo people, in eastern Nigeria? They live surrounded by the tumult and corruption of Nigeria, but they are free of it. Do you know why? Because their culture prizes what they call the transparent life. They believe that there is nothing about an upright person that his fellow villagers should not be allowed to know. Any sort of exchange is conducted in front of witnesses. They abhor any form of secrecy or concealment, even solitude. The ideal of total transparency is so highly developed that if a scintilla of distrust develops between two people, they may resort to a curious ritual known as *igbandu*, wherein each drinks the blood of each other. An idealistic but rather cumbersome regime, in the logistics of it, you'll concede. The Promethean networks produce the same results with an altogether bloodless technique."

"Irrelevant tales!" Bryson shouted, taking a few steps closer. "That has nothing to do with us!"

"You must be aware that, over the last decade, the crime rate in the United States, particularly in the major cities, dropped to a fraction of what it once was. Now, why do you think that was?"

"What the hell do I know?" Bryson snapped. "I suppose you have a theory."

"No theory. I *know*. Our social scientists come up with theory after theory, but they fail to explain it."

"You're not implying . . ." Bryson said slowly.

Manning nodded. "It was a pilot study of our outdoor surveillance capabilities. Years before we had our current capacities and resources, but you have to start small, don't you?" A ten-foot-square section of the wall to his left went blank for a moment, and then a map of midtown Manhattan snapped into view. Small blue dots peppered the street grid. "Those are the hidden rotational cameras that we installed," Manning went on, pointing toward the dots. "It starts with anonymous tips to the police. Suddenly, the arrest record begins to improve, mysteriously. And, for the first time in decades, crime doesn't seem to pay anymore. The police crow about their new methods, criminologists talk about the ebbs and flows of the crack wars, yet *nobody* talks about the cameras that record everything. The safety blanket of surveillance we've unfolded over the city. Nobody talks about the fact that the crime-ridden alleys are now a panopticon. Nobody talks about the Systematix pilot project, because *nobody wants to know.* Are you beginning to understand what we're capable of doing for humanity? Poor *homo sapiens.* First they have to live through millennia of marauding tribalisms, and when the Enlightenment arrives, the Industrial Revolution hunkers down. Industrialization and urbanization bring a whole new wave of social disruptions, unleashing ordinary crime on a scale never before seen in human history. Two world wars, more atrocities on and off the battlefield. And when there are no wars, hand-to-hand combat breaks out in urban war zones. Is that any way to live? Is that any way to *die?* The members of the Prometheus Group come from every rank in every country of the world, but they all understand the paramount importance of security."

Bryson took another few steps closer to Manning.

"And this is your idea of freedom." *Must keep him talking.*

"Real freedom is freedom *from.* We seek to create a world in which its citizens can live their lives free from the fear of the sadistic wife-beater, the drug-addicted car-jacker, or any of a thousand other threats to life and limb. That, Mr. Bryson, is *true* freedom. Where people are free to be at their best behavior—the way they are when they *know* somebody is watching."

Another two, three steps closer. Casual. Keep talking. "And so goes our privacy," Bryson said. He was now no more than ten or fifteen feet from where Manning stood talking. He glanced at his watch.

"The real problem with privacy is that we have too much of it. It's a luxury we can no longer afford. Now, thanks to Systematix, we have a powerful worldwide surveillance system in place — satellites orbiting the globe, millions of video cameras. Even, soon, implantable microchips."

"None of this will bring your daughter back," said Bryson softly.

Manning's face colored briefly. The walls went dark, plunging the room into a sepulchral gloom. "You know nothing about it," he hissed.

"No," Bryson admitted. Suddenly he leaped toward Manning, his hands extended to clutch Manning's throat in a powerful vise, *crush* his throat. At once he found himself falling through thin air, through nothingness! He slammed against the marble floor of the alcove, stunned, his jaw cracking hard against the stone, the pain immense. He spun around, looked for Manning — and then he saw the array of laser diodes lining the interior of the alcove. He had been witnessing a three-dimensional laser holographic projection — a high-resolution, lifelike image, the volumetric 3-D illusion created by lasers projecting video images onto microscopic particles in the air.

It was a hoax, an illusion. A *phantom*.

Bryson heard slow clapping, the clapping of one pair of hands, from the far side of the room, the side through which he had entered moments ago. It was Manning, walking toward him as he clapped, a phalanx of guards surrounding him.

"Well, if that's the way you feel," Manning said, a half-smile on his face. "Guards?"

The security guards rushed toward him, smart guns extended, and once again he was enclosed by them. He struggled, but they had his arms, his legs.

Manning paused on his way out the door. "Most men in your line of work die ignominious deaths. A bullet in the back of the head, the assailant unseen, unknown. Or one of a thousand possible accidents in the field. Nobody will be surprised to learn of the deaths of two more operatives, a man and a woman, killed in a foolhardy attempt to assassinate an assemblage of world leaders. An unexplainable attempt that will never be explained, because men and women like you, who live lives of secrecy and darkness, always die in secret, in the dark. Now, if you'll excuse me, I must rejoin my guests." And Manning was gone from the room.

As he struggled with the guards, Bryson sneaked a glance at his watch. Now! It should have happened by now! Or did they move the U-Haul van as well?

Smart guns were pressed against his forehead, his temple, the back of his head. He saw his confiscated snub-nosed .45 in the holster of a guard just a few feet away.

Suddenly the dim lights in the room were extinguished, and they were plunged into absolute darkness. At the same instant came a series of clicks, and he could hear the locked doors to the library slide half-way open.

It had happened.

Bryson lurched forward and grabbed his .45 from the guard's holster. A clutch of security guards pummeled him to the floor. "One more move and you're dead!" shouted one of them.

"Go ahead," Bryson screamed. He saw them point their guns at him, saw the triggers being squeezed—

And nothing.

Nothing happened. The guns were dead. The electronic brains had been incapacitated, fried, along with all of the electronics in Manning's house.

There were bewildered shouts, screams, as Bryson fired a few shots into the air with his mechanically operated pistol, warning them to back off. They did back away from him, all twelve of them, realizing that somehow they were powerless, impotent, their guns dead in their hands.

Bryson ran to the half-open door, his gun still blazing, and slipped out into the hallway.

He had to get out, had to get to Elena—but where was she?

And how long would his ammunition last?

Some of the guards pursued him; he fired at them, now aware of the need to conserve ammunition, and they backed away. He was fairly sure he had another round in the chamber, maybe one in the magazine as well, but rather than stop for a second to check, he had to run, it was vital to *run*. He ran through the house, through corridors once lined with great oil paintings and covered in the finest wallpaper, now gone silvery-gray, like the dusty wings of dead moths. Everywhere doors were half-open.

The Russian scientist's device had worked, just as Bryson had heard it did. The virtual cathode oscillator was invented by Soviet scientists in the 1980s as a means of targeting the electronic circuitry of American nuclear weapons. Soviet nuclear bombs were far more primitive; this was a way of turning an advantage into a disadvantage. The Soviets were, as a result, far ahead of the Americans when it came to what was called radio-frequency weapons. When activated, the device emitted a high-powered electromagnetic pulse no longer than a microsecond—long enough, how-ever, to burn out all electronic circuitry, heat up the microscopic junc-tions inside computers, and burn them up. All computers, everything with circuit boards and microchips within a quarter mile, would be affected. There were rumors that such a weapon had been used by terrorists to bring down several international plane flights.

Cars and trucks with electronic circuitry would not start, smart guns were struck dumb, and Manning's entire digital mansion had become inert.

And there was more.

The tiny fires in thousands of circuits throughout the house had caught on. Fires were burning in hundreds of places around Manning's house, smoke accumulating, wafting everywhere. Bryson remembered that the KGB had used this weapon to start a fire inside the U.S. Embassy in Moscow in the 1980s.

Bryson could hear screams from the reception hall. *Could she be there?* he wondered.

He flung open the doors to the banquet facility, found himself on a balcony overlooking the great hall. Fire had begun to rage below, flames licking the walls. Smoke was everywhere; panicked guests were running to the exits, tugging at doors that would not open, shouting, screaming. For some reason, whether it was a malfunction in the electronic equip-ment or some sort of security precaution, all the doors to the hall seemed to have locked automatically.

Was Waller down there? Was Manning?

Was Elena?

"Elena!" he shouted into the din.

No response.

She was not down there, or she had not heard him.

"Elena!" he shouted again, hoarsely.

Nothing.

He felt the cold steel of the blade at the exact same moment as the hot breath in his ear, the whispered Arabic words. The seven-inch combat knife pressed against the soft skin and delicate cartilage of his throat, the high-carbon-steel blade sharper than a brand-new razor. It slid slowly, the silky pain at once cold and hot, the sensation delayed for a second; but when it came his entire body screamed in agony.

And the whisper: "The rope of lies is always too short, Bryson."

Abu.

"I should have finished the job in Tunisia, traitor," the Arab terrorist hissed. "Now I will not waste the opportunity I am given."

Bryson went rigid, flooded with fear, with adrenaline. "If you'll *listen . . .*" Bryson replied, almost under his breath, the remark intended to distract for a second or two. At the same time he gripped the .45 at his side, placed his finger on the trigger, and then in one swift arc lifted the weapon and fired backward at his enemy.

There was only a muted click. *The gun was empty.*

Abu batted the gun away with a flick of his left hand; it went flying off to one side, clattering to the floor, useless.

Bryson had lost valuable seconds in reaction time. The blade sliced across the skin of his neck just as Bryson jammed the fingers of his right hand upward and under the handle. He grabbed the knife handle, twisting it violently to loosen Abu's grip; at the same time, he slammed the heel of his left foot into the back of Abu's right knee to knock him off balance. Abu grunted, and Bryson suddenly sank to the ground, lowering his center of gravity while still twisting the knife blade and Abu's wrist with it.

The knife clanged against the floor.

Bryson reached for it, but Abu, quicker, scooped it up. Clutching the knife in his fist like a dagger, Abu plunged it downward, sinking it into the soft meat of Bryson's left shoulder.

Bryson gasped; the pain was shattering, forcing him to his knees. He swung his right arm toward Abu's head; Abu sidestepped the punch easily, moving around him effortlessly, almost dancing. He didn't seem to break a sweat. He shifted his weight from foot to foot, his knees slightly bent, his stance soft and comfortable, the blood-slicked knife blade glittering in his right hand. Bryson staggered to his feet, kicked his right foot toward the inside of Abu's knee. But Abu sidestepped the kick, backing off just enough to cause Bryson to lose his balance, then catching the kicking leg and yanking it hard, forcing Bryson down again.

Abu seemed to know Bryson's moves before they happened. Bryson shot his arms forward to grab Abu's legs, but Abu simply slammed an elbow into Bryson's neck, trapping Bryson's head between his knees, and slammed him into the ground. Bryson's teeth cracked against his lips; he could taste blood, and he thought he might have lost a couple of teeth. Weakened by the knife wound in his shoulder, Bryson's reactions were slowed, delayed. He groaned, thrust out his right arm, and grabbed his enemy's ankle; then, locking it in his crooked elbow, he turned it until Abu bellowed in pain.

Suddenly Abu's arm shot out, the knife aimed directly at Bryson's heart. Bryson dodged, but not quite in time: the knife plunged into his side, between his ribs; the pain was searing, white-hot.

Bryson looked down, saw what had happened, and grabbed the knife handle. He yanked at it; it tugged horribly at his viscera, but it came out. Bryson hurled it over the balcony, groaning in pain: it was much better to be rid of a weapon that Abu was so skilled with. The knife dropped down into the inferno, clanking a second later against the floor far below.

Now they were both disarmed. But Bryson, down on the floor and badly weakened, was at a disadvantage. Moreover, Abu was immensely strong, all muscle, a coiled python. His movements were relaxed, fluid, flowing one into another. Bryson rolled back away from Abu; Abu kicked him, hard, in the abdomen. Bryson felt the wind come out of him; he almost passed out, but he struggled to his feet, swinging wildly.

Abu's face was blank, unreadable. When Bryson threw a punch at Abu's head, Abu's hands shot out, lightning-fast, and grabbed his wrists, twisting hard. Bryson tried to force Abu to relieve the hold by thrusting his knees into Abu's abdomen, but Abu jammed him with his own knees first, sending Bryson crashing to the floor, while at the same time twisting his wrists.

Bryson attempted to get up, but Abu threw his weight on top of him, flattening him against the floor; then, jumping into the air, he stomped up and down on Bryson's chest, putting all of his considerable weight into it. Bryson moaned; he could feel, actually *hear*, several ribs crack.

Abu went at him again, flipping him over so that his face cracked to the floor again. Now Abu wrapped one arm around his throat, pushing down on the back of his neck with his elbow in a rear choke-hold. At the same time Abu went down on his right knee and folded his left leg so that he was in a one-legged kneeling position, extremely stable. He began pulling Bryson back toward his left leg. Bryson tried to rise, but each time he did, Abu pushed him back with his elbow. He had no leverage! He was losing consciousness, his strength was fading. The air-flow to his brain was cut off; he began to see black-and-purple spots.

Part of him wanted to succumb to unconsciousness, a comfortable defeat, but he knew that any defeat would mean death. He screamed, summoned his last reserves of strength, flung his hands into Abu's face, and jabbed his fingers into his enemy's eye sockets.

Abu involuntarily released some of the pressure on Bryson's throat—not much, but just enough to allow Bryson to swing his fists around in an arc, one of them connecting hard with the brachial plexus nerve bundle in Abu's right underarm area. Bryson felt Abu's right arm go slack, momentarily paralyzed. He took advantage of the brief pause to grab a handful of Abu's groin, yanking hard. The choke-hold was broken.

Bryson tilted his right shoulder down and body-slammed Abu up against the balustrade overlooking the inferno. Bryson was now moving almost by instinct; his oxygen-starved brain felt distant from his hands, which seemed to move of their own volition. But fueled by rage and revenge, Bryson managed to force Abu's head and shoulders over the edge of the balcony. The two men were entwined, pushing and pulling at each other on the ledge, their muscles trembling. Abu's right arm was dead, the paralysis lasting longer even than Bryson had hoped. Bryson pushed, shoved as hard as he could, forcing Abu's shoulders out over the balcony, while Abu scissored both legs around Bryson's, locking the two men together. Bryson was feeble but determined; Abu had lost the use of one arm. They seemed evenly matched. Bryson straight-armed Abu's neck downward, but Abu came back up; Bryson straight-armed him again, this time keeping him down with all of his strength, the muscles in his right arm straining, trembling. Abu's eyes were fierce. He began hammering his good fist into Bryson's abdomen. For a few seconds Bryson held him down, clutching Abu's throat and squeezing with all his strength, trying to cut off the air, trying to compress the nerves and induce paralysis, but he was fading; he could no longer summon the strength; the pain from the stab wound radiated, depleting his power further. His hands trembled. Bryson summoned one last, superhuman surge of energy, his entire body an instrument of anger and revenge, but it was not enough; he didn't have the strength.

Abu roared, his crimson face contorted in pain and rage, spittle flying from his purpled lips, and he began to rise—

The explosion seemed to come out of nowhere, the bullet lodging itself in his enemy's right upper arm. Abu's legs loosened their viselike grip on Bryson's as he lost his balance and plummeted over the balcony.

Bryson stared as his enemy fell, wriggling in space, landing with a crash on top of the massive bronze equestrian sculpture, impaling himself on the sharpened point of the sword. As the bronze blade came out of his abdomen, Abu's scream was shrill, almost inhuman, and then it came to an abrupt, gargling stop.

Dazed, sickened, Bryson turned and saw the source of the gunshot. Elena was holding the pistol he had given her; staring at it as if it were some alien object, she lowered it slowly. Her eyes were wide.

Bryson staggered to his feet, made it a few steps, and collapsed into her arms. "You escaped," he panted.

"The room they locked me in was no longer locked."

"The gun . . ."

"The smart guns don't work, but their bullets are still good, aren't they?"

"We need to get out of here," he said, out of breath. "*Must* get out of here."

"I know," she said. She shifted her arms, putting one arm around his shoulders tenderly, supporting him as they walked out of the balcony and through the smoke-filled corridor toward the exit.

EPILOGUE

The New York Times, page 1.

SCORES OF WORLD LEADERS KILLED IN
FREAK HOUSE FIRE IN WASHINGTON STATE
Blamed Laid to Faulty Wiring in
'Digital San Simeon'

SEATTLE, Wash.—A glittering conference on the New
Global Economy at the high-tech lakeside mansion belonging to Systematix founder and CEO Gregson Manning
ended in tragedy today as dozens of prominent officials from
around the world were trapped in a blaze that burned the
$100-million-dollar estate to the ground.

A Seattle Fire Department spokesman, speaking to reporters early this morning, speculated that the fire may have
begun within the delicate electronic circuitry hidden in the
walls of this entirely computerized home, the residence of
the computer pioneer and host of the conference. According

ROBERT LUDLUM

to the spokesman, malfunctioning computer chips may have caused exit doors in the banquet hall where a gala dinner was taking place to seal automatically.

The body count is believed to number over one hundred. Among them is reportedly the Speaker of the House of Representatives . . .

MANNING TAKEN IN FOR QUESTIONING

WASHINGTON (AP)—Systematix chairman Gregson Manning, whose Seattle mansion burned to the ground overnight, trapping over one hundred government officials from around the world, was taken into custody at noon today at the Justice Department. Sources in the Attorney General's office insist that Mr. Manning's arraignment, on unspecified charges of national security violations, was unrelated to this morning's tragedy. Mr. Manning is said to have been under suspicion for several weeks.

Although a sealed courtroom is highly unusual, it is not unheard of. In cases involving matters of government secrecy, the Attorney General has the legal right to convene a special national security court, not open to the public. . . .

The Wall Street Journal, page 1.

PRESIDENT'S NATIONAL SECURITY ADVISER, RICHARD LANCHESTER, A SUICIDE AT 61

Richard Lanchester, the widely respected White House adviser and director of the National Security Council, took his own life yesterday afternoon, according to White House sources.

Said to be inconsolable over the loss of several close friends who perished in the recent fire that destroyed the residence of Systematix chief Gregson Manning and 102 prominent officials attending a conference there, and suffering as well from clinical depression and a failing marriage, Mr. Lanchester . . .

One year later

Getting the morning paper was a ritual, her ritual. Not because she liked to read the news; she didn't. That was Nicholas's habit, his need to stay in touch with the developments in the world they had left behind. It was a habit she disapproved of, precisely *because* they had left the world behind, at least the world of violence and weapons and lies.

But getting the paper from town was the way she liked to start the day. She would arise early and go for a swim—their bungalow was just up the bluff from one of the most beautiful, bluest, and most isolated beaches they had ever seen—and then she would ride her horse into the tiny collection of ramshackle huts that passed for a village here. Along with the groceries flown in from a nearby, larger island, the proprietor of the general store always received a small stack of newspapers from the U.S.; she always set aside one for the lovely woman with the lilting foreign accent who came riding in each morning.

Then Elena would gallop back along the deserted beach, the mile and a half to their bungalow. By that time, Nicholas was usually sitting on the stone patio he had laid himself, drinking coffee and reading. After breakfast they would go for another swim. So passed their days. It was paradise.

Even when the blood test administered by the island's sole doctor confirmed what she'd been feeling for several days, that she was pregnant, Elena continued to ride, though more carefully. They were overjoyed, planning for the arrival of a son or a daughter, discussing for hours how their lives would change and yet not change, their love deepening by the day.

Money was not a concern. The government had provided them a generous lump-sum settlement which, invested carefully, yielded more than enough to live on. Rarely did they discuss what had brought them here, why it was so important for them to escape, why they had to live here under new identities. It was understood between them: that was the past, a terribly painful episode, and the less said about it the better.

The mini-DVD she had recorded from Manning's surveillance system that night had provided them with all the protection they needed. Not because it afforded them the opportunity to blackmail, strictly speaking— but because the explosive secrets it contained were secrets everyone preferred to remain buried. It could only be destabilizing for the world to know how close it had come to a bloodless coup, a nonviolent takeover by a group of individuals who believed that governments were obsolete— yet were on the verge of creating a supranational security administration that would have made Stalin's U.S.S.R. or Hitler's *Bundesrepublik* seem lax.

Most of those individuals had perished in the fire at Manning's San Simeon, burned alive in a terrible end. Yet there were others who had aided and abetted those men and women; and so arrests were made. Quietly and discreetly, the reasons understood without being made explicit, deals were struck. Gregson Manning was believed to be in a special federal facility in North Carolina, serving time for unspecified violations of section 1435 of the National Security Act, said to involve economic espionage; he was rumored to be isolated from all contacts or means of communication. Powerful voices in the Senate called for a recall vote on the treaty, renouncing votes made in haste. Some blamed Richard Lanchester for manipulating the process. Without American backing, the treaty agreement fell apart. The truth never had to come out.

So sixteen copies of the DVD were made; one was couriered to the White House, using a code that Bryson knew marked it for the President's eyes only; a second went to the Attorney General of the United States. Others went to London, Moscow, Beijing, Berlin, Paris, and other world capitals. Heads of state had to know what had almost transpired, or else the virus would endure.

Of the three copies that remained, one was deposited with a lawyer Bryson knew to be trustworthy above and beyond, another was sealed in a safe-deposit box, and a third went with them, hidden somewhere on the island, insulated and protected. They were insurance policies. Bryson and Elena hoped they'd never have to collect on them.

This morning, about an hour after bringing the morning paper, Elena emerged from the perfect water to find Bryson absorbed in the newspaper, which rippled and crinkled in the wind.

"Only when you finally give up that nasty habit will you finally be free," she scolded him.

"You make it sound like smoking."

"It's almost as bad."

"And probably almost as hard to give up. But if I do, what excuse will you have for your morning ride?"

She chuckled. "Milk? Eggs? I'll think of something."

"*Jesus.*" He was leaning close over the paper.

"What is it?"

"Buried on page D-16. The business section."

"What does it say?"

"It's a tiny item — reads like nothing more than a rewritten press release from the Systematix Corporation in Seattle."

"But . . . but Manning's in prison!"

"He is. His company's being run by certain of his deputies in the interim. This dispatch says that the National Security Agency has just acquired a fleet of low-orbit surveillance satellites manufactured by Systematix."

"They try to bury the news, but it's really not very subtle, is it? Where are you going?"

Bryson had got up from his beach chair and was bounding up the dune to their bungalow. She followed him up. The wind carried the sound to her, so that she knew he had the television on. Another terrible habit she wanted to break him of: he had rigged up a satellite dish so that he could watch the news, though he had promised to keep that to a minimum.

Bryson was watching CNN, but was frustrated that there was no news, just some fashion segment. He turned toward her. "Ted Waller didn't die in that fire, you know. I saw the forensic reports, everything out of the Seattle Medical Examiner's office, and all the bodies were identified. Waller wasn't among them."

"I *know* that. We've known that for a year. What are you saying?"

"I'm saying that I see Waller's hand in this. Wherever he went, wherever he disappeared to, he has to be involved in this. I'm certain of it."

ROBERT LUDLUM

"Trust your instincts, I always say," came the voice from the television.

Elena screamed, pointed at the television. Bryson whirled around. His heart was thudding rapidly. Ted Waller's face filled the screen.

"What is this?" Elena gasped. "Is this a *show . . . ?*"

"Call it reality TV," said Waller.

"We were assured we'd be left alone!" Bryson thundered. "However you managed this satellite-feed interruption, it's a *violation!"* Bryson started pressing buttons on the remote, changing channels frantically. Waller's face was on each one, staring out at them phlegmatically.

"I still regret that we weren't able to say good-bye properly," Waller said from the TV screen. "I really do hope there's no bad blood."

Speechless, Bryson scanned the small living room frantically. Microscopic surveillance devices could be planted absolutely anywhere and everywhere, undetectable . . .

"I'll be in touch when the time is right, Nicky. Now may be premature." Waller looked off into the distance as if about to add something, and a hint of a smile came to his lips. "Well, I'll be seeing you."

"Not if I see you first, Ted," Bryson said acidly, and now he settled back in his chair. "We have a great deal of evidence in safekeeping, evidence we won't hesitate to release."

On the screen, Waller's gaze turned wary.

"Remember, Ted—it's what you don't see that always gets you."

Abruptly, Waller's image disappeared, replaced by a game show.

A move had been made. And countered. Bryson felt fury, outrage at the violation—and yet, after so many years in the service of the great game, oddly stirred as well. If Elena caught a glimpse of this, she kept it to herself. She still went for her early-morning rides, and they still spent much of the day outdoors, either on the shimmering white beach or on their wooden deck, surrounded by bougainvillea and shaded by young palm trees that undulated gently in the breeze.

Bryson had made a complete break from his past life, while he and Elena prepared to nurture the new life that was on its way. In the sun, his scars faded, and there were days when—the air fragrant with frangipani and lime and salt water—the dull ache from his old wounds grew imperceptible, like memories just out of reach. At moments, he almost thought he had left the world behind.

Almost.

THE
SIGMA
PROTOCOL

CHAPTER ONE

Zurich

"May I get you something to drink while you wait?"

The *Hotelpage* was a compact man who spoke English with only a trace of an accent. His brass nameplate gleamed against his loden-green uniform.

"No, thank you," Ben Hartman said, smiling wanly.

"Are you sure? Perhaps some tea? Coffee? Mineral water?" The bellhop peered up at him with the bright-eyed eagerness of someone who has only a few minutes left to enhance his parting tip. "I'm terribly sorry your car is delayed."

"I'm fine, really."

Ben stood in the lobby of the Hotel St. Gotthard, an elegant nineteenth-century establishment that specialized in catering to the well-heeled international businessman—*and, face it, that's me*, Ben thought sardonically. Now that he had checked out, he wondered idly whether he could tip the bellhop *not* to carry his bags, *not* to follow his every move a few feet behind, like a Bengali bride, *not* to offer unceasing apologies for the fact that the car that was to take Ben to the airport had not yet arrived. Luxury hotels the world over prided themselves on such coddling, but Ben, who traveled quite a bit, inevitably found it intrusive, deeply irritating. He'd spent so much time trying to break out of the cocoon, hadn't he? But the cocoon—the stale rituals of privilege—had won out in the end. The *Hotelpage* had his number, all right: just another rich, spoiled American.

Ben Hartman was thirty-six, but today he felt much older. It wasn't just the jet lag, though he had arrived from New York yesterday and still felt that sense of dislocation. It was something about being in Switzerland again: in happier days, he'd spent a lot of time here, skiing too fast, driving too fast, feeling like a wild spirit among its stone-faced, rule-bound burghers. He wished he could regain that spirit, but he couldn't. He hadn't been to Switzerland since his brother, Peter—his identical twin, his closest friend in all the world—had been killed here four years ago. Ben had expected the trip to stir up memories, but nothing like this. Now he realized what a mistake he'd made coming back here. From the moment he'd arrived at Kloten Airport, he'd been distracted, swollen with emotion—anger, grief, loneliness.

But he knew better than to let it show. He'd done a little business yesterday afternoon, and this morning had a cordial meeting with Dr. Rolf Grendelmeier of the Union Bank of Switzerland. Pointless, of course, but you had to keep the clients happy; glad-handing was part of the job. If he was honest with himself, it *was* the job, and Ben sometimes felt a pang at how easily he slipped into the role, that of the legendary Max Hartman's only surviving son, the heir presumptive to the family fortune, and to the CEO's office at Hartman Capital Management, the multibillion-dollar firm founded by his father.

Now Ben possessed the whole trick bag of international finance—the closet full of Brioni and Kiton suits, the easy smile, the firm handshake, and, most of all, the gaze: steady, level, concerned. It was a gaze that conveyed responsibility, dependability, and sagacity, and that, often as not, concealed desperate boredom.

Still, he hadn't really come to Switzerland to do business. At Kloten, a small plane would take him to St. Moritz for a ski vacation with an extremely wealthy, elderly client, the old man's wife, and his allegedly beautiful granddaughter. The client's arm-twisting was jovial but persistent. Ben was being fixed up, and he knew it. This was one of the hazards of being a presentable, well-off, "eligible" single man in Manhattan: his clients were forever trying to set him up with their daughters, their nieces, their cousins. It was hard to say no politely. And once in a while he actually met a woman whose company he enjoyed. You never knew. Anyway, Max wanted grandchildren.

Max Hartman, the philanthropist and holy terror, the founder of Hartman Capital Management. The self-made immigrant who'd arrived in America, a refugee from Nazi Germany, with the proverbial ten bucks in his pocket, had founded an investment company right after the war, and relentlessly built it up into the multibillion-dollar firm it was now. Old Max, in his eighties and living in solitary splendor in Bedford, New York, still ran the company and made sure no one ever forgot it.

It wasn't easy working for your father, but it was even harder when you had precious little interest in investment banking, in "asset allocation" and "risk management," and in all the other mind-numbing buzz-words.

Or when you had just about zero interest in money. Which was, he realized, a luxury enjoyed mainly by those who had too much of it. Like the Hartmans, with their trust funds and private schools and the immense Westchester County estate. Not to mention the twenty-thousand-acre spread near the Greenbriar, and all the rest of it.

Until Peter's plane fell out of the sky, Ben had been able to do what he really loved: teaching, especially teaching kids whom most people had given up on. He'd taught fifth grade in a tough school in an area of Brooklyn known as East New York. A lot of the kids were trouble, and yes, there were gangs and sullen ten-year-olds as well armed as Colombian drug lords. But they needed a teacher who actually gave a damn about them. Ben did give a damn, and every once in a while he actually made a difference to somebody's life.

When Peter died, however, Ben had been all but forced to join the family business. He'd told friends it was a deathbed promise exacted by his mother, and he supposed it was. But cancer or no cancer, he could never refuse her anyway. He remembered her drawn face, the skin ashen from another bout of chemotherapy, the reddish smudges beneath her eyes like bruises. She'd been almost twenty years younger than Dad, and he had never imagined that she might be the first to go. *Work, for the night cometh*, she'd said, smiling bravely. Most of the rest she left un-spoken. Max had survived Dachau only to lose a son, and now he was about to lose his wife. How much could any man, however powerful, stand?

"Has he lost you, too?" she had whispered. At the time, Ben was living a few blocks from the school, in a sixth-floor walk-up in a decrepit tenement building where the corridors stank of cat urine and the lino-leum curled up from the floors. As a matter of principle, he refused to accept any money from his parents.

"Do you hear what I'm asking you, Ben?"

"My kids," Ben had said, though there was already defeat in his voice. "They need me."

"*He* needs you," she'd replied, very quietly, and that was the end of the discussion.

So now he took the big private clients out to lunch, made them feel important and well cared for and flattered to be cosseted by the founder's son. A little furtive volunteer work at a center for "troubled kids" who made his fifth-graders look like altar boys. And as much time as he could grab traveling, skiing, parasailing, snowboarding, or rock-climbing, and going out with a series of women while fastidiously avoiding settling down with any of them.

Old Max would have to wait.

Suddenly the St. Gotthard lobby, all rose damask and heavy dark Viennese furniture, felt oppressive. "You know, I think I'd prefer to wait outside," Ben told the *Hotelpage*. The man in the loden-green uniform simpered, "Of course, sir, whatever you prefer."

Ben stepped blinking into the bright noontime sun, and took in the pedestrian traffic on the Bahnhofstrasse, the stately avenue lined with linden trees, expensive shops, and cafés, and a procession of financial institutions housed in small limestone mansions. The bellhop scurried behind him with his baggage, hovering until Ben disbursed a fifty-franc note and gestured for him to leave.

"Ah, thank you so *much*, sir," the *Hotelpage* exclaimed with feigned surprise.

The doormen would let him know when his car appeared in the cobbled drive to the left of the hotel, but Ben was in no hurry. The breeze from Lake Zurich was refreshing, after time spent in stuffy, overheated rooms where the air was always suffused with the smell of coffee and, fainter but unmistakable, cigar smoke.

Ben propped his brand-new skis, Volant Ti Supers, against one of the hotel's Corinthian pillars, near his other bags, and watched the busy street scene, the spectacle of anonymous passersby. An obnoxious young businessman braying into a cell phone. An obese woman in a red parka pushing a baby carriage. A crowd of Japanese tourists chattering excitedly. A tall middle-aged man in a business suit with his graying hair pulled back in a ponytail. A deliveryman with a box of lilies, attired in the distinctive orange and black uniform of Blümchengallerie, the upscale flower chain. And a striking, expensively dressed young blonde, clutching a Festiner's shopping bag, who glanced generally in Ben's direction, and then glanced at him again—quickly, but with a flicker of interest before averting her eyes. *Had we but world enough and time*, thought Ben. His gaze wandered again. The sounds of traffic were continuous but muted, drifting in from the Löwenstrasse, a few hundred feet away. Somewhere nearby a high-strung dog was yipping. A middle-aged man wearing a blazer with an odd purple hue, a tad too stylish for Zurich. And then he saw a man about his age, walking with a purposeful stride past the Koss Konditerei. He looked vaguely familiar—

Very familiar.

Ben did a double-take, peered more closely. Was that—could that really be—his old college buddy Jimmy Cavanaugh? A quizzical smile spread over Ben's face.

Jimmy Cavanaugh, whom he'd known since his sophomore year at Princeton. Jimmy, who'd glamorously lived off-campus, smoked unfiltered cigarettes that would have choked an ordinary mortal, and could drink *anybody* under the table, even Ben, who had something of a reputation in that regard. Jimmy had come from a small town in western upstate New York called Homer, which supplied him with a storehouse of tales. One night, after he taught Ben the finer points of downing Tequila shots with beer chasers, Jimmy had him gasping for breath with his stories about the town sport of "cow tipping." Jimmy was rangy, sly, and worldly, had an immense repertory of pranks, a quick wit, and the gift of gab. Most of all, he just seemed more *alive* than most of the kids Ben knew: the clammy-palmed preprofessionals trading tips about the entrance exams for law school or B-school, the pretentious French majors with their clove cigarettes and black scarves, the sullen burn-out cases for whom rebellion was found in a bottle of green hair dye. Jimmy seemed to stand apart from all that, and Ben, envying him his simple ease with himself, was pleased, even flattered by the friendship. As so often happens, they'd lost touch after college; Jimmy had gone off to do something at the Georgetown School of Foreign Service, and Ben had stayed in New York. Neither of them was big on college nostalgia, and then distance and time had done their usual job. Still, Ben reflected, Jimmy Cavanaugh was probably one of the few people he actually felt like talking to just now.

Jimmy Cavanaugh—it was *definitely* Jimmy—was now near enough that Ben could see that he was wearing an expensive-looking suit, under a tan trench coat, and smoking a cigarette. His build had changed: he was broader-shouldered now. But it was Cavanaugh for sure.

"Jesus," Ben said aloud. He started down the Bahnhofstrasse toward Jimmy, then remembered his Volants, which he didn't want to leave unattended, doormen or no doormen. He picked the skis up, hefted them over one shoulder, and walked toward Cavanaugh. The red hair had faded and receded a bit, the once-freckled face was a little lined, he was wearing a two-thousand-dollar Armani suit, and what the hell was he doing in Zurich of all places? Suddenly they made eye contact.

Jimmy broke out in a wide grin, and he strode toward Ben, an arm outstretched, the other in the pocket of his trench coat.

"Hartman, you old dog," Jimmy crowed from a few yards away. "Hey, pal, great to see you!"

"My God, it really *is* you!" Ben exclaimed. At the same time, Ben was puzzled to see a metal tube protruding from his old friend's trench coat, a *silencer*, he now realized, the muzzle pointing directly up at him from waist level.

It had to be some bizarre prank, good old Jimmy was always doing that kind of thing. Yet just as Ben jokingly threw his hands up in the air and dodged an imaginary bullet, he saw Jimmy Cavanaugh shift his right hand ever so slightly, the unmistakable motions of someone squeezing a trigger.

What happened next took a fraction of a second, yet time seemed to telescope, slowing almost to a halt. Reflexively, abruptly, Ben swung his skis down from his right shoulder in a sharp arc, trying to scuttle the weapon but in the process slamming his old friend hard in the neck.

An instant later—or was it the same instant?—he heard the explosion, felt a sharp spray on the back of his neck as a very real bullet shattered a glass storefront just a few feet away.

This couldn't be happening!

Caught by surprise, Jimmy lost his balance and bellowed in pain. As he stumbled to the ground, he flung out a hand to grab the skis. *One hand.* The left. Ben felt as if he'd swallowed ice. The instinct to brace yourself when you stumble is strong: you reach out with both hands, and you drop your suitcase, your pen, your newspaper. There were few things you wouldn't drop—few things you'd still clutch as you fell.

The gun was real.

Ben heard the skis clatter to the sidewalk, saw a thin streak of blood on the side of Jimmy's face, saw Jimmy scrambling to regain his orientation. Then Ben lurched forward and, in a great burst of speed, took off down the street.

The gun was real. And Jimmy had fired it at him.

Ben's path was obstructed by crowds of shoppers and businessmen hurrying to lunch appointments, and as he wove through the crowd he collided with several people, who shouted protests. Still he vaulted ahead, running as he'd never run before, zigzagging, hoping that the irregular pattern would make him an elusive target.

What the hell was going on? This was madness, absolute madness!

He made the mistake of glancing behind him as he ran, inadvertently slowing his pace, his face now a flashing beacon to a once-friend who for some unfathomable reason seemed bent on killing him. Suddenly, barely two feet away, a young woman's forehead exploded in a mist of red.

Ben gasped in terror.

Jesus Christ!

No, it couldn't be happening, this wasn't reality, this was some bizarre nightmare—

He saw a small scattering of stone fragments, as a bullet pitted the marble facade of the narrow office building he was racing past. Cavanaugh was on his feet and running, now just fifty feet or so away from Ben, and though he had to fire in midstride, Cavanaugh's aim was still unnervingly good.

He's trying to kill me, no, he's going to kill me—

Ben feinted suddenly to the right, then jerked to the left, leaping forward as he did. Now he ran flat out. On the Princeton track team, he was an eight-hundred-meter man, and, fifteen years later, he knew his only chance for survival was to find a surge of speed inside him. His sneakers weren't made for running, but they'd have to do. He needed a destination, a clear goal, an endpoint: that was always the key. *Think, dammit!* Something clicked in his head: he was a block away from the largest underground shopping arcade in Europe, a garish, subterranean temple of consumption known as Shopville, beneath and adjacent to the main train station, the Hauptbahnhof. In his mind's eye, he saw the entrance, the bank of escalators at the Bahnhofplatz; it was always quicker to enter there and walk underneath the square than to fight through the crowds that typically thronged the streets above. He could seek refuge underground in the arcade. Only a madman would dare chase him down there. Ben sprinted now, keeping his knees high, his feet ghosting along with great soft strides, falling back into the discipline of the speed laps he used to devour, conscious only of the breeze at his face. Had he lost

Cavanaugh? He didn't hear his footsteps anymore, but he couldn't afford
to make any assumptions. Single-mindedly, desperately, he *ran*.

The blond woman with the Festiner's bag folded up her tiny cellular
phone and placed it in a pocket of her azure Chanel suit, her pale glossy
lips compressed in a small moue of annoyance. At first everything had
gone like—well, like clockwork. It had taken her a few seconds to decide
that the man standing in front of St. Gotthard was a probable match.
He was clearly in his mid-thirties, with an angular face and strong jaw,
curly brown hair flecked with gray, and hazel-green eyes. A pleasant-
looking fellow, she supposed, handsome, even; but not so distinctive that
she had been able to ensure a definite identification from this distance.
That was of no consequence. The shooter they'd chosen could make the
identification; they'd made sure of that.

Now, however, matters seemed less than perfectly controlled. The target was an amateur; there was little chance he would survive an encounter with a professional. Still, amateurs made her uneasy. They made
mistakes, but erratic, unpredictable ones, their very naïveté defying rational prediction, as the subject's evasive actions had demonstrated. His
wild, protracted escape attempt would merely postpone the inevitable.
And yet it was all going to take time—the one thing that was in short
supply. Sigma One would not be pleased. She glanced at her small, be-
jeweled wristwatch, retrieved the phone, and made one more call.

Winded, his starved muscles screaming for oxygen, Ben Hartman paused
at the escalators to the arcade, knowing he had to make a split-second
decision. 1. UNTERGESCHOSS SHOPVILLE read the blue overhead sign. The
down escalator was crowded with shoppers laden with bags and strollers;
he'd have to use the up escalator, which had relatively few riders. Ben
charged down it, elbowing aside a young couple who were holding hands
and blocking his path. He saw the startled looks his actions had pro-
voked, looks that mingled dismay and derision.

Now he raced through the underground arcade's central atrium, his
feet scudding along the black rubberized floor, and he allowed himself a
glimmer of hope before he realized the error he'd made. From all around
him arose screams, frenzied shouting. Cavanaugh had followed him here,

into this enclosed, contained space. In the mirrored facade of a jewelry store, he caught a glimpse of muzzle fire, a burst of yellow-white. Instantly, a bullet tore through the burnished mahogany panels of a travel bookstore, exposing the cheap fiberboard beneath. Everywhere was pandemonium. An old man in a baggy suit a few feet away clutched his throat and toppled like a bowling pin, blood drenching his shirtfront.

Ben dove behind the information station, an oblong concrete-and-glass structure perhaps five feet wide, on which was mounted a list of stores, elegant white lettering on black, a shoppers' guide in three languages. A hollow explosion of glass told him that the information box had been hit. Half a second later, there was a sharp crack, and a piece of concrete fell heavily from the structure, landing near his feet.

Inches away!

Another man, tall and stout in a camel-hair topcoat and a jaunty gray cap, staggered a few feet past him before collapsing to the floor, dead. He'd been shot in the chest.

Amid the chaos, Ben found it impossible to distinguish Cavanaugh's footsteps, but, gauging his position from the reflected muzzle flash, he knew no more than a minute remained before he would be overtaken. Remaining in position behind the concrete island, he stood, to his full six feet, and peered around wildly, looking for new refuge.

Meanwhile, the screams crescendoed. Ahead, the arcade was crowded with people, shrieking, crying out hysterically, crouching and cowering, many of them trying to hide their heads beneath folded arms.

Twenty feet away there were escalators marked 2. UNTERGESCHOSS. If he could close the distance without being shot, he could get to the level below. His luck might change there. It couldn't get any worse, he thought—then he changed his mind as he saw a widening pool of blood flowing from the man in the camel-hair coat a few feet away. Dammit, he had to *think!* There was no way he could close the distance in time. Unless . . .

He reached for the dead man's arm and dragged him over. Seconds remained. He yanked off the dead man's tawny coat and grabbed the gray cap, conscious of baleful eyes upon him from shoppers cowering near the Western Union. This was no time for delicacy. Now he shrugged into the roomy overcoat, pulled the cap down hard on his head. If he was to remain alive, he would have to resist the urge to dart toward the second-level escalators like a jackrabbit: he had gone hunting enough to know that anything that moved too abruptly was likely to be shot by an itchy-fingered gunman. Instead, he clambered slowly to his feet, hunched, staggering, weaving like an old man who had lost blood. He was now visible and supremely vulnerable: the ruse had to last just long enough to get him to the escalator. Maybe ten seconds. So long as Cavanaugh thought he was a wounded bystander, he wouldn't waste another bullet on him.

Ben's heart was hammering in his chest, his every instinct screaming at him to break into a sprint. *Not yet.* Hunched over, shoulders rounded, he staggered on with an unsteady gait, his strides as long as he could make them without exciting suspicion. Five seconds. Four seconds. Three seconds.

At the escalator, which had emptied out, abandoned by the terrified pedestrians, the man in the bloodied camel-hair overcoat seemed to crumple face forward, before the movement of the stairs took him out of view.

Now!

Inaction had been as strenuous as exertion, and, every nerve in his body twitching, Ben had broken his fall with his hands. As quietly as he could, he raced down the remaining stairs.

He heard a bellow of frustration from upstairs: Cavanaugh would now be after him. Every second had to count.

Ben put on another burst of speed, but the second below-ground level of the arcade was a virtual maze. There was no straight route of egress to the other side of the Bahnhofplatz, just a succession of byways, the wider walkways punctuated with kiosks of wood and glass that sold cellular phones, cigars, watches, posters. To a dilatory shopper, they were islands of interest—to him, an obstacle course.

Still, they reduced the number of sight lines. They lessened the chance of the long-distance kill. And so they bought him time. Perhaps enough time for Ben to secure the one thing he had on his mind: a shield.

He ran past a blur of boutiques: Foto Video Ganz, Restseller Buchhandlung, Presensende Stickler, Microspot. Kinderboutique, with its window crammed with furry stuffed animals, the display framed by green-and-gold-painted wood with an incised ivy pattern. There was the chrome and plastic of a Swisscom outlet . . . All of them festively plying their goods and services, all utterly worthless to him. Then, straight ahead, to his right, next to a Credit Suisse/Volksbank branch office, he spotted a luggage store. He looked through the window, heaped high with soft-sided leather suitcases—no good. The item he was after was inside: a large, brushed-steel briefcase. No doubt the gleaming steel cladding was as much cosmetic as functional, but it would serve. It would have to. As Ben darted in the store, grabbed the article, and ran out, he noticed that the proprietor, pale and sweating, was jabbering hysterically in *Schweitzerdeutsch* on the telephone. No one bothered to run after Ben; word of the insanity had already spread.

Ben had gained a shield; he had also lost precious time. Even as he sprang out of the luggage store, he saw its display window transformed into an oddly beautiful spiderweb in the instant before it disintegrated into shards. Cavanaugh was close, so close Ben didn't dare look around to try to locate his position. Instead, Ben charged forward into a crowd of shoppers emerging from Franscati, a large department store at one end of the cruciform plaza. Holding up the briefcase, Ben lunged forward, tripping on someone's leg, regaining his footing with difficulty, losing a few precious moments.

An explosion inches from his head: the sound of a lead bullet slamming into the steel briefcase. It jolted in his hands, partly from the impact of the bullet, partly from his own muscular reflex, and Ben noticed a bulge on the steel casing facing him, as if it had been stuck by a small hammer. The bullet had penetrated the first layer, had almost penetrated the second. His shield had saved his life, but only just.

Everything around him had gone blurry, but he knew he was entering the teeming Halle Landesmuseum. He also knew that carnage was still trailing him.

Throngs of people were screaming—huddled, cringing, running—as the horror, the gunfire, the bloodshed came closer.

Ben plunged into the frenzied crowd, was swallowed up by it. For a moment the gunfire seemed to have stopped. He tossed the briefcase to the floor: it had served its purpose, and its gleaming metal would now make him too easy to pick out of the crowd.

Was it over? Was Cavanaugh out of ammunition? Reloading?

Jostled one way, then another, Ben scanned the labyrinthine arcade for an exit, an *Ausgang*, through which he could disappear unseen. *Maybe I've lost him*, Ben thought. Yet he didn't dare look back again. No going back. Only forward.

Along the walkway that led to the Franscati department store, he spotted a fake-rustic sign of dark wood and gilt lettering in shrift: KATZKELLER-BIERHALLE. It hung above an alcove, an entrance to a deserted restaurant. GESCHLOSSEN, a smaller sign read. Closed.

He raced toward it, his movement camouflaged by a frenzied rush of people in that general direction. Through a faux-medieval archway beneath the sign, he ran into a spacious, empty dining room. Cast-iron chains from the ceiling supported enormous wooden chandeliers; medieval halberds and engravings of medieval nobility adorned the walls. The motif continued with the heavy round tables, which were crudely carved in keeping with someone's fantasy of a fifteenth-century arsenal.

On the right side of the room was a long bar, and Ben ducked behind it, gasping loudly for breath, as desperately as he tried to remain silent. His clothes were soaked with sweat. He couldn't believe how fast his heart was thudding, and he actually winced from the chest pain.

He tapped the cabinetry in front of him; it made a hollow sound. Obviously fashioned from veneer and plaster, it was nothing that could be relied upon to stop a bullet. Crouching, he made his way around a corner and to a protected stone alcove, where he could stand and catch his breath. As he leaned back to rest against the pillar, his head cracked into a wrought-iron lantern mounted on the stone. He groaned involuntarily. Then he examined the light fixture that had just lacerated the back of his head, and he saw that the whole thing, the heavy black iron arm attached to the ornamental housing that held the bulb, could be lifted right out of the mounting bracket.

It came out with a rusty screech. He managed to get a firm grip and held it against his chest.

And he waited, trying to slow the beating of his heart. He knew something about waiting. He remembered all those Thanksgivings spent at the Greenbriar; Max Hartman was insistent that his sons learn how to hunt, and Hank McGee, a grizzled local from White Sulfur Springs, was given the job of teaching them. *How hard could it be?* he remembered thinking: he was an ace at skeet shooting, had reason to be proud of his hand-eye coordination. He let this slip to McGee, whose eyes darkened: *You think the hunt's really about shootin'? It's about waitin'.* And he fixed him with a glare. McGee was right, of course: the waiting was the hardest part of all, and the part he was temperamentally least suited for.

Hunting with Hank McGee, he had lain in wait for his quarry.

Now he *was* the quarry.

Unless . . . somehow . . . he could change that.

In a few moments, Ben heard approaching footsteps. Jimmy Cavanaugh entered stealthily, tentatively, glancing from side to side. His shirt collar was grimy and torn and bloodied from a gash on the right side of his neck. His trench coat was soiled. His flushed face was set in a determined grimace, his eyes wild.

Could this really be his friend? What had Cavanaugh become in the decade and a half since Ben had last seen him? What had turned him into a killer?

Why was this happening?

In his right hand Cavanaugh gripped his blue-black pistol, the ten-inch-long tube of a sound suppressor threaded to its barrel. Ben, flashing back on target-practice memories from twenty years ago, saw that it was a Walther PPK, a .32.

Ben held his breath, terrified that his gasping would give him away. He drew back into the alcove, clutching the iron light fixture he had just torn from the wall, flattening himself out of sight as Cavanaugh made a sweep of the restaurant. With a sudden but sure movement of his arm Ben flung the iron lantern fixture, smashing it into Cavanaugh's skull with an audible thud.

Jimmy Cavanaugh screamed in pain, his cry high-pitched like an animal's. His knees buckled, and he squeezed the trigger.

Ben could feel a flare of heat, a fraction of an inch away from his ear. But now, instead of drawing back farther, or attempting to run, Ben lunged forward, slamming himself into his enemy's body, pummeling him to the ground, Cavanaugh's skull cracking against the stone floor.

Even badly wounded, the man was a powerhouse. A rancid miasma of sweat arose from him as he reared up and vised a massive arm around Ben's neck, compressing his femoral artery. Desperately, Ben reached for the gun, trying to grab it but succeeding only in wrenching the long silencer up and back toward Cavanaugh. With a sudden ear-shattering explosion the gun went off. Ben's ears rang with a sustained squeal; his face stung from the blowback.

The grip on Ben's throat loosened. He twisted his body around, free of the chokehold. Cavanaugh was slumped on the ground. With a jolt Ben saw the dark red hole just above his old friend's eyebrows, a horrific third eye. He was suffused with a mixture of relief and revulsion, and the sense that nothing would ever be the same.

CHAPTER TWO

Halifax, Nova Scotia, Canada

It was still early in the evening, but already it was dark, and an icy wind roared along the narrow street, down the steep hill toward the roiling waters of the Atlantic. Fog had settled over the gray streets of this port town, blanketing it, closing it in. A miserable drizzling rain had begun to fall. The air had a salty tang.

A sulfurous yellow light illuminated the ramshackle porch, the worn front steps of a large, gray clapboard house. A dark figure in a yellow hooded oilcloth slicker stood under the yellow light, jamming his finger against the front door buzzer insistently, over and over and over. Finally there came the clicks of the safety bolts, and the weathered front door came slowly open.

The face of a very old man appeared, peering out angrily. He was wearing a stained pale blue dressing gown over rumpled white pajamas. His mouth was caved in, the baggy skin of the face pallid, the eyes gray and watery.

"Yes?" the elderly man demanded in a high, raspy voice. "What do you want?" He spoke with a Breton accent, a legacy of his French Acadian forebears who fished the seas beyond Nova Scotia.

"You've got to *help* me!" cried the person in the yellow slicker. He shifted his weight anxiously from one foot to the other. "Please! Oh, God, please, you've got to *help!*"

The old man's expression became clouded with confusion. The visitor, though tall, looked to be in his late teens. "What are you talking about?" he said. "Who are you?"

"There's been a horrible accident. Oh, *God!* Oh, Jesus! My dad! My dad! I think he's *dead!*"

The old man pressed his narrow lips together. "What do you want from me?"

The stranger flung a gloved hand toward the handle of the storm door, then dropped it. "Please just let me make a call. Let me call an ambulance. We had an accident, a terrible accident. The car is totaled. My sister—badly hurt. My dad was driving. God, my *parents!*" The boy's voice broke. Now he seemed more a child than a teenager. "Oh, Lord, I think he's dead."

Now the old man's glare seemed to soften, and he slowly pushed open the storm door to let the stranger in. "All right," he said. "Come in."

"Thank you," the boy exclaimed as he entered. "Just for a moment. Thank you so much."

The old man turned around and led the way into a dingy front room, flicking on a wall switch as he entered. He turned to say something just as the boy in the hooded rain slicker came closer and with both hands, clasped the man's own hand, seemingly a gesture of awkward gratitude. Water ran down from the sleeve of his yellow slicker onto the old man's dressing gown. The boy made a sudden, jerking movement. "Hey," the old man protested, confused. He pulled away, then slumped to the floor.

The boy stared down at the crumpled body for a moment. He slipped off his wrist the small device that held a tiny retractable hypodermic needle and put it in an inside pocket of his slicker.

Quickly he surveyed the room, spotted the ancient television, and turned it on. An old black-and-white movie was playing. Now he set about his task with the confidence of someone much older.

He went back to the body, set it carefully on a shabby orange lounge chair, arranging the arms and head so that it looked as if the old man had fallen asleep in front of the TV.

Pulling a roll of paper towels from inside his slicker, he swiftly mopped up the water that had pooled on the wide pine boards of the entrance hall. Then he returned to the front door, which was still open, glanced around outside, and when he was satisfied, stepped out onto the porch and closed the door behind him.

The Austrian Alps

The silver Mercedes S430 wound up the steep mountain road until it arrived at the clinic gates. A security guard in the booth by the gate came out, saw who the passenger was, and said with great deference, "Welcome, sir." He did not bother to ask for identification. The chief of the clinic was to be admitted with dispatch. The car turned onto the ring drive through a sloping campus where the vibrant green of well-tended grass and sculpted pines contrasted with drifting patches of powdery snow. Towering in the distance overhead were the magnificent white crags and planes of the Schneeberg peak. The car drove around a dense stand of tall yews, and over to a second, hidden security booth. The guard, who had already been alerted to the director's arrival, pressed the button that raised the steel bar and, at the same time, touched the switch that lowered the steel spikes set into the pavement, which would ruin the tires of any vehicle that entered without being cleared through.

The Mercedes drove up a long narrow road that led only to one place: an old clock factory, formerly a *Schloss* that had been built two centuries ago. A coded remote signal was sent, an electronic door opened, and the car pulled into the reserved parking space. The driver got out and opened the door for his passenger, who strode quickly into the entrance. There another security guard, this one behind bulletproof glass, nodded and smiled a welcome.

The director entered the elevator, an anachronism in this ancient Alpine structure, inserted his digitally encoded identification card to unlock it, and made his way to the third, and top, floor. There he passed through three sets of doors, each unlocked by means of an electronic card reader, until he came to the conference room, where the others were already seated around the long burnished mahogany table. He took his place at the head of the table and looked around at the others.

"Gentlemen," he began, "only days remain before the fulfillment of our dream so long deferred. The long gestation period is nearly over. Which is to say, your patience is about to be rewarded, and beyond the wildest dreams of our founders."

The sounds of approval around the table were gratifying, and he waited for them to subside before continuing. "As for security, I have been assured that very few of the *angeli rebelli* remain. Soon there will be none. There is, however, one small problem."

Zurich

Ben tried to stand, but his legs would not support him. He sank to the ground, on the verge of becoming violently ill, feeling at once cold and prickly-hot. Blood roared in his ears. An icicle of fear was lodged in his stomach.

What had just happened? he asked himself. Why in the hell was Jimmy Cavanaugh trying to kill him? What kind of madness was this? Had the man's mind snapped? Had Ben's sudden reappearance after a decade and a half triggered something in a disturbed brain, a rush of twisted memory that for some reason had propelled him to murder?

He could taste liquid, brackish and metallic, and he touched his lips. Blood was seeping from his nose. It must have happened in the struggle. He'd gotten a bloody nose, Jimmy Cavanaugh a bullet in the brain.

The noise from the shopping arcade outside was subsiding. There were still shouts, the occasional anguished cry, but the chaos was diminishing. Steadying himself with his hands on the floor, he pushed himself up, managed to get to his feet. He felt dizzy, vertiginous, and knew it was not from any loss of blood; he was in shock.

He forced himself to look at Cavanaugh's body. By now he'd calmed down enough to think.

Somebody I haven't seen since the age of twenty-one turns up in Zurich, goes insane and tries to kill me. And now he lies here dead, in a tacky medieval-themed restaurant. No explanation to offer. Maybe there'd never be an explanation.

Carefully avoiding the pool of blood around the head, he went through Cavanaugh's pockets, first the suit jacket, then the pants, then the pockets of the trench coat. There was absolutely nothing there. No ID cards, no credit cards. Bizarre. Cavanaugh seemed to have emptied his pockets, as if in preparation for what happened.

It had been premeditated. *Planned.*

He noticed the blue-black Walther PPK still clutched in Cavanaugh's hand and considered checking the magazine to see how many rounds were left. He pondered taking it, just slipping the slim pistol into his pocket. What if Cavanaugh wasn't alone?

What if there were others?

He hesitated. This was a crime scene of sorts. Best not to alter it in any way, in case there was legal trouble down the line.

Slowly, he got up and made his way, dazed, into the main hall. Now it was mostly deserted, apart from a few clusters of emergency medical technicians tending to the wounded. Someone was being carried on a stretcher.

Ben had to find a policeman.

The two cops, one clearly a rookie and one middle-aged, looked at him dubiously. He'd found them standing by the Bijoux Suisse kiosk, near the Marktplatz food court. They wore navy-blue sweaters with red shoulder patches that read *Zürichpolizei*; each had a walkie-talkie and a pistol holstered to the belt.

"May I see your passport, please?" the young one asked after Ben had spoken for a few minutes. Evidently the older one either didn't speak English or preferred not to.

"For God's sake," Ben snapped in frustration, "people have been killed. A guy's lying dead in a restaurant down there, a man who tried—"

"*Ihren Pass, bitte,*" the rookie persisted sternly. "Do you have identification?"

"Of course I do," Ben said, reaching for his billfold. He pulled it out and handed it over.

The rookie examined it suspiciously, then gave it to the senior man, who glanced at it without interest and thrust it back at Ben.

"Where were you when this happened?" the rookie asked.

"Waiting in front of the Hotel St. Gotthard. A car was supposed to take me to the airport."

The rookie took a step forward, uncomfortably close to him, and his neutral gaze became frankly mistrustful: "You are going to the airport?"

"I was on my way to St. Moritz."

"And suddenly this man fired a gun at you?"

"He's an old friend. *Was* an old friend."

The rookie lifted an eyebrow.

"I hadn't seen him in fifteen years," Ben continued. "He recognized me, sort of came toward me as if he was happy to see me, then suddenly he pulls out a gun."

"You had a quarrel?"

"We didn't exchange two words!"

The younger cop's eyes narrowed. "You had arranged to meet?"

"No. It was pure coincidence."

"Yet he had a gun, a loaded gun." The rookie looked at the older cop, then turned back to Ben. "And it was outfitted with a silencer, you say. He must have known you would be there."

Ben shook his head, exasperated. "I hadn't talked to him in years! He couldn't possibly have known I'd be here."

"Surely you must agree that people do not just carry around guns with silencers unless they mean to use them."

Ben hesitated. "I suppose that's right."

The older policeman cleared his throat. "And what kind of gun did you have?" he asked in surprisingly fluent English.

"What are you talking about?" Ben asked, his voice rising in indignation. "I didn't have a gun."

"Then forgive me, I must be confused. You say your friend had a gun, and that you did not. In which case, why is he dead, and not you?"

It was a good question. Ben just shook his head as he thought back to the moment when Jimmy Cavanaugh leveled the steel tube at him. Part of him—the rational part—had assumed it was a prank. But obviously part of him had not: he'd been primed to react swiftly. Why? He replayed in his mind Jimmy's easy lope, his wide welcoming grin . . . and his cold eyes. Watchful eyes that didn't quite match the grin. A small discordant element that his subconscious mind must have registered.

"Come, let us go to see the body of this assassin," the older policeman said, and he placed a hand on Ben's shoulder in a way that was not at all affectionate but instead conveyed that Ben was no longer a free man.

Ben led the way across the arcade, which now swarmed with policemen, reporters snapping pictures, and made his way down to the second level. The two *Polizei* followed close behind. At the KATZKELLER sign Ben entered the dining room, went to the alcove, and pointed.

"Well?" demanded the rookie angrily.

Astonished, Ben stared, wide-eyed, at the spot where Cavanaugh's body had been. He felt light-headed, his mind frozen in shock. There was nothing there.

No pool of blood. No body, no gun. The lantern arm had been replaced in its fixture as if it had never been removed. The floor was clean and bare.

It was as if nothing had ever happened there.

"My God," Ben breathed. Had he snapped, lost touch with reality? But he could feel the solidity of the floor, the bar, the tables. *If this was some elaborate stunt* . . . but it wasn't. He had somehow stumbled into something intricate and terrifying.

The policemen stared at him with rekindled suspicion.

"Listen," Ben said, his voice reduced to a hoarse whisper, "I can't explain this. I was here. *He* was here."

The older policeman spoke rapidly on the walkie-talkie, and soon they were joined by another officer, stolid and barrel-chested. "Perhaps I am easily confused, so let me try to understand. You race through a busy street, and then through the underground shopping arcade. All around you, people are shot. You claim that you are being chased by a maniac. You promise to show us this man, this American. And yet there is no maniac. There is only you. A strange American spinning fairy tales."

"*Goddammit*, I've told you the *truth!*"

"You say a madman from your past was responsible for the bloodshed," the rookie said in a quiet, steely voice. "I see only one madman here."

The older policeman conferred in *Schweitzerdeutsch* with his barrel-chested colleague. "You were staying at the Hotel St. Gotthard, yes?" he finally asked Ben. "Why don't you take us there?"

Accompanied by three policemen—the barrel-chested one walking behind him, the rookie ahead of him, and the older policeman close by his side—Ben made his way through the underground arcade, up the escalator, and down the Bahnhofstrasse toward his hotel. Though he was not yet cuffed, he knew that this was merely a formality.

In front of the hotel, a policewoman, whom the others had clearly sent ahead, was keeping a custodial watch over his luggage. Her brown hair was short, almost mannish, and her expression was stony.

Through the lobby windows, Ben caught a glimpse of the unctuous *Hotelpage* who'd attended to him earlier. Their eyes met, and the man turned away with stricken look, as if he'd just learned he'd toted bags for Lee Harvey Oswald.

"Your luggage, yes?" the rookie asked Ben.

"Yes, yes," Ben said. "What of it?" Now what? What more could there be?

The policewoman opened the tan leather hand luggage. The others looked inside, then turned to face Ben. "This is yours?" the rookie asked.

"I already said it was," Ben replied.

The middle-aged cop took a handkerchief from his pants pocket and used it to lift an object out of the satchel. It was Cavanaugh's Walther PPK pistol.

CHAPTER THREE

Washington, D.C.

A serious-looking young woman strode briskly down the long central corridor of the fifth floor of the United States Department of Justice Building, the mammoth Classical Revival structure that occupied the entire block between Ninth and Tenth Streets. She had glossy dark brown hair, caramel-brown eyes, a sharp nose. At first glance she looked part-Asian, or perhaps Hispanic. She wore a tan trench coat, carried a leather briefcase, and might have been taken for a lawyer, a lobbyist, maybe a government official on the fast track.

Her name was Anna Navarro. She was thirty-three and worked in the Office of Special Investigations, a little-known unit of the Justice Department.

When she arrived at the stuffy conference room, she realized that the weekly unit meeting was already well under way. Arliss Dupree, standing by a whiteboard on an easel, turned as she entered and stopped in midsentence. She felt the stares, couldn't help blushing a little, which was no doubt what Dupree wanted. She took the first empty seat. A shaft of sunlight blinded her.

"There she is. Nice of you to join us," Dupree said. Even his insults were predictable. She merely nodded, determined not to let him provoke her. He'd told her the meeting would be at eight-fifteen. Obviously it had been scheduled to start at eight, and he would deny ever having told her otherwise. A petty, bureaucratic way of giving her a hard time. They both knew why she was late, even if nobody else here did.

Before Dupree was brought in to head the Office of Special Investigations, meetings were a rarity. Now he held them weekly, as a chance to parade his authority. Dupree was short and wide, mid-forties, the body of a weight lifter in a too-tight light gray suit, one of three shopping-mall suits he rotated. Even across the room she could smell his drugstore aftershave. He had a ruddy moon face the texture of lumpy porridge.

There was a time when she actually cared what men like Arliss Dupree thought about her and tried to win them over. Now she didn't give a damn. She had her friends, and Dupree was simply not among them. Across the table, David Denneen, a square-jawed, sandy-haired man, gave her a sympathetic glance.

"As some of you may have heard, Internal Compliance has asked for our colleague here to be temporarily assigned to them." Dupree turned to her, his eyes hard. "Given the amount of unfinished work you've got here, I'd consider it less than responsible, Agent Navarro, if you accepted an assignment from another division. Is this something you've been angling for? You can tell us, you know."

"This is the first I've heard of it," she told him truthfully.

"That right? Well, maybe I've been leaping to conclusions here," he said, his tone softening a bit.

"Quite possibly," she replied, dryly.

"I was making the assumption that you were wanted for an assignment. Maybe you *are* the assignment."

"Come again?"

"Maybe you're the one under investigation," Dupree said in a mellower tone, evidently pleased by the idea. "It wouldn't surprise me. You're a deep one, Agent Navarro." There were laughs from some of his drinking buddies.

She shifted her chair to get the light out of her eyes.

Ever since Detroit, when the two of them were staying on the same floor of the Westin and she turned down (politely, she thought) Dupree's drunken, highly explicit proposal, he'd been leaving condescending little remarks, like rat droppings, in her performance evaluation folder: . . . *as best she can given her obviously limited interest . . . errors a result of inattention, not incompetence . . .*

He described her to a male colleague, she'd heard, as "a sexual harassment suit waiting to happen." He tarred her with the most vicious insult you can give someone in the Bureau: *not a team player.* Not a team player meant she didn't go out drinking with the boys, including Dupree, kept her social life separate. He also made a point of papering her files with mentions of mistakes she'd made—a few minor procedural omissions, nothing at all serious. Once, on the trail of a rogue DEA agent who'd been turned by a drug lord and was implicated in several homicides, she'd neglected to submit an FD-460 within the required seven days.

The best agents make mistakes. She was convinced that the best ones in fact made more minor gaffes than average, because they were focused more on following the trail than on following every single procedure in the manual of rules and regs. You could slavishly observe every last ridiculous procedural requirement and never crack a case.

She felt his stare on her. She looked up, and their eyes locked.

"We've got an unusually heavy caseload to deal with," Dupree went on. "When somebody doesn't do their share, it means more work for everyone else. We've got a midlevel IRS manager suspected of organizing some pretty complicated tax scams. We've got a rogue FBI guy who seems to be using his shield to pursue a personal vendetta. We've got some ATF shit-heel selling munitions from the evidence vaults." That was a typical array of cases for the OSI: investigating ("auditing" was the term of art) misconduct involving members of other government agencies—in essence, the federal version of internal affairs.

"Maybe the workload here is a little much for you," Dupree said, pressing. "Is that it?"

She pretended to jot down a note and didn't reply. Her face was prickly warm. She inhaled slowly, struggling to tamp down her anger. She refused to give in to his baiting. Finally she spoke. "Look, if it's inconvenient, why don't you refuse the request for interdepartmental transfer?" Anna asked it in a reasonable tone of voice, but it wasn't an innocent question: Dupree lacked the authority to challenge the highly secretive, all-powerful Internal Compliance Unit, and any reference to the limits of his authority was bound to infuriate him.

Dupree's little ears reddened. "I'm expecting a brief consult. If the spook hunters at ICU knew as much as they pretend, they might realize that you aren't exactly cut out for that line of work."

His eyes shone with what she imagined was contempt.

Anna loved her work, knew she was good at it. She didn't require praise. All she wanted was not to have to spend her time and energy trying to hang on to her job, clinging by her fingernails. Again she kept her face a mask of neutrality. She felt the tension localize itself in her stomach. "I'm sure you did your best to make them understand."

A beat of silence. Anna could see he was debating how to reply. Dupree glanced at his beloved whiteboard, at the next item on his agenda. "We'll miss you," he said.

Shortly. after the meeting broke up, David Denneen sought her out in her tiny cubbyhole of an office. "The ICU wants you because you're the best," he said. "You know that, don't you?"

Anna shook her head wearily. "I was surprised to see you at the meeting. You're in operations oversight now. Doing great, by all accounts." Word was he was on the fast track for a position in the AG's office.

"Thanks to you," Denneen said. "I was there today as divisional representative. We take turns. Got to keep an eye on the budget numbers. And on you." Gently, he placed a hand on hers. Anna noticed that the warmth in his eyes was mixed with concern.

"It was good to see you there," Anna said. "And send my best to Ramon."

"I'll do that," he said. "We'll have to have you over for paella again."

"But there's something else on your mind, isn't there?"

Denneen's eyes didn't leave hers. "Listen, Anna, your new assignment, whatever it is, isn't going to be like getting a new call sheet. What people say around here is true—the ways of the Ghost are mysterious to man." He repeated the old jest with little humor. The Ghost was an in-house nickname for the longtime director of the Internal Compliance Unit, Alan Bartlett. During closed hearings before the Senate subcommittee on intelligence, back in the seventies, a deputy attorney general had referred to him, archly, as "the ghost in the machine," and the honorific had stuck. If Bartlett wasn't ghostly, he was a legendarily elusive figure. Seldom seen, reputedly brilliant, he ruled over a rarefied dominion of highly classified audits, and his own reclusive habits made him emblematic of its clandestine ways.

Anna shrugged. "I wouldn't know. I've never met him, and I don't think I know anyone who has. Rumors thrive on ignorance, Dave. You of all people know that."

"Then take a word of advice from an ignoramus who cares about you," he said. "I don't know what this ICU thing is about. But be careful, O.K.?"

"Careful how?"

Denneen just shook his head, uneasily. "It's a different world over there," he said.

Later that morning, Anna found herself in the immense marble lobby of an office building on M Street, on her way to her appointment at the Internal Compliance Unit. The unit's workings were obscure even within the department, and its operational purview was—or so certain senators had occasionally charged—dangerously undefined. *It's a different world over there*, Denneen had said, and so it seemed.

The ICU was located on the tenth floor of this modern office complex in Washington, isolated from a bureaucracy it was sometimes obliged to scrutinize, and she tried not to gawk at the splashing indoor fountain, the green marble floors and walls. She thought: *What kind of government agency gets fitted out like this?* She got on the elevator. Even that was trimmed with marble.

The only other passenger on the elevator was a too-handsome guy around her age in a too-expensive suit. A lawyer, she decided. Like just about everyone else in this city.

In the mirrored elevator walls she saw him giving her The Look. If she caught his eye, she knew he'd smile and say good morning and strike up a banal Elevator Conversation. Even though he was no doubt well intentioned and probably just wanted to flirt politely, Anna found it mildly annoying. Nor did she respond well when men asked her why a woman as beautiful as she was had become a government investigator. As if what she did for a living were the special province of the homely.

Normally, she pretended not to notice. Now, however, she threw him a scowl. He looked away hastily.

Whatever it was that the ICU wanted from her, it had come at a damn inconvenient time; Dupree was right about that. *Maybe you are the assignment*, he'd said, and though Anna had shrugged off the suggestion, it nagged at her, absurdly. What the hell was that supposed to mean? No doubt Arliss Dupree was in his office right now, gleefully sharing his speculation with some of his drinking buddies on the staff.

The elevator opened onto a lavishly appointed, marble-lined hall that could have been the executive floor of a high-priced law firm. Off to the right she spotted the seal of the Department of Justice mounted on one wall. Visitors were instructed to buzz for admittance. She did so. It was 11:25 A.M., five minutes before her scheduled appointment. Anna prided herself on her punctuality.

A female voice demanded her name, and then she was buzzed in by a handsome dark-skinned woman with a squared-off haircut—almost too chic for government work, Anna thought to herself.

The receptionist assessed her coolly and directed her to take a seat. Anna detected a very faint Jamaican accent.

Within the office suite, the trappings of the swanky building gave way to a setting of utter sterility. The pearl-gray carpet was immaculate, like no government carpet she'd ever seen. The waiting area was brightly lighted with an array of halogen bulbs that left virtually no shadows. Photos of the President and the Attorney General were framed in lacquered steel. The chairs and the coffee table were of hard blond wood. Everything looked brand new, as if it had been freshly uncrated, unsoiled by human habitation.

She noticed the foil hologram stickers on both the fax machine and the telephone on the receptionist's desk, government labels indicating that these were secure lines, employing officially certified telephony encryption.

At frequent intervals, the phone purred quietly, and the woman spoke in a low voice using a headset. The first two calls were in English; the third must have been in French, because the receptionist responded in that language. Two more in English, gently eliciting contact information. And then another in which she spoke in a language, sibilant and clicky, that Anna had a hard time identifying. Anna glanced at her watch again, fidgeted in the hard-backed chair, and then looked at the receptionist. "That was Basque, wasn't it?" she said. It was something more than a guess, but less than a certainty.

The woman responded with a fractional nod and a demure smile. "It won't be much longer, Ms. Navarro," she said.

Now Anna's eye was drawn to the tall wooden island behind the receptionist's station, which extended all the way to the wall; from the legally required exit sign, she realized that the wooden structure concealed the entrance to a staircase. It was artfully done, and it allowed ICU agents or their guests to arrive and depart unnoticed by anyone in the official waiting room. What kind of outfit was this?

Another five minutes went by.

"Does Mr. Bartlett know I'm here?" Anna asked.

The receptionist returned her gaze levelly. "He's just finishing up with someone."

Anna returned to her chair, wishing she'd brought something to read. She didn't even have the *Post*, and clearly no reading material would be allowed to soil the pristine waiting area. She took out an automatic-teller-machine slip and a pen and started making a list of things to do.

The receptionist placed a finger on her ear and nodded. "Mr. Bartlett says he'll see you now." She emerged from her station and guided Anna down a series of doors. No names were posted; only numbers. Finally, at the end of a hallway, she opened a door marked DIRECTOR and took her into the tidiest office she had ever seen. On a far table, stacks of paper were perfectly arrayed in equidistant piles.

A small, white-haired man in a crisp navy suit came out from behind a vast walnut desk and extended a small, delicate hand. Anna noticed the pale pink moons of his perfectly manicured nails and was surprised by the strength of his grip. She noticed that the desk was barren, save for a handful of green file folders, and a sleek, black telephone; mounted on the wall just behind it was a velvet-lined glass display case containing two antique-looking pocket watches. It was the one eccentric touch in the room.

"I'm so terribly sorry to keep you waiting," he said. His age was indeterminate, but he was probably in his early sixties, Anna decided. His eyes were owlish through his glasses, large round lenses in flesh-colored frames. "I know how busy you are, and you were so very kind to have come by." He spoke softly, so softly that Anna found herself straining to hear him over the white noise of the ventilation system. "We're very grateful for your making the time."

"If I may speak candidly, I didn't know we had a choice when ICU called," she said tartly.

He smiled as if she had said something amusing. "Please do sit down."

Anna settled into the high-backed chair opposite his desk. "To tell you the truth, Mr. Bartlett, I'm curious about why I'm here."

"You weren't inconvenienced, I hope," Bartlett said, interlacing his small fingers in a prayerful tent.

"It's not a matter of inconvenience," Anna replied. In a strong voice, she added, "I'm happy to answer whatever questions you may have."

Bartlett nodded encouragingly. "That's rather what I'm hoping. But I'm afraid these answers won't be easy to come by. In fact, if we could even frame the questions, we'd be halfway home. Am I making any sense to you?"

"I return to my own question," Anna said with banked impatience. "What am I doing here?"

"Forgive me. You're thinking that I'm being maddeningly elliptical. Of course you're right, and I apologize for it. Occupational hazard. Too much time shut away with paper and more paper. Deprived of the bracing air of experience. But that must be your contribution. Now let me ask you a question, Ms. Navarro. Do you know what it is that we do here?"

"The ICU? Vaguely. Intragovernmental inquiries—only, the classified kind." Anna decided that the query called for reticence; she knew a little more than what she volunteered. She was aware that behind its bland title was an extremely secretive, powerful, and far-reaching investigative agency charged with highly classified audits and examinations of other U.S. government agencies that couldn't be done in-house, and which involved highly sensitive matters. ICU officials were deeply involved, it was said, in scrutinizing the CIA's Aldrich Ames fiasco; in investigating the Reagan White House's Iran-Contra affair; in examining numerous Defense Department acquisitions scandals. It was the ICU, people whispered, that had first uncovered the suspicious activities of the FBI's counterintelligence agent Robert Philip Hanssen. There were even rumors that the ICU was behind the "Deep Throat" leaks that led to Richard Nixon's downfall.

Bartlett looked off into the middle distance. "The techniques of investigation are, in their essentials, everywhere the same," he said, finally. "What changes is the bailiwick, the ambit of operations. Ours has to do with matters touching on national security."

"I don't have that kind of clearance," Anna put in quickly.

"Actually"—Bartlett allowed himself a small smile—"you do now."

Had she been cleared without her knowledge? "Regardless. It's not my terrain."

"That's not strictly the case, is it?" Bartlett said. "Why don't we talk about the NSC member you did a Code 33 on last year?"

"How the *hell* do you know about that?" Anna blurted. She gripped the arm of her chair. "*Sorry*. But how? That one was strictly off the books. By the direct request of the AG."

"Off *your* books," Bartlett said. "We have our own way of keeping tabs. Joseph Nesbett, wasn't it? Used to be at the Harvard Center for Economic Development. Got a high-level appointment at State, then on to the National Security Council. Not *born* bad, shall we say? Left to his own devices, I suspect he'd be all right, but the young wife was a bit of a spendthrift, a rather grasping creature, wasn't she? Expensive tastes for a government employee. Which led to that lamentable business with the offshore accounts, the diversion of funds, all of it."

"It would have been devastating had it come out," Anna said. "Damaging to foreign relations at a particularly sensitive moment."

"Not to mention the embarrassment to the Administration."

"That wasn't a primary consideration," Anna retorted sharply. "I'm not political that way. If you think otherwise, you don't know me."

"You and your colleagues did precisely the right thing, Ms. Navarro. We admired your work, in fact. Very deft. Very deft."

"Thank you," Anna said. "But if you know so much, you'll know that it was far from my usual turf."

"My point remains. You've done work of genuine sensitivity and displayed the utmost discretion. But of course I know what your daily fare consists of. The IRS man guilty of peculation. The rogue FBI officer. The unpleasantness involving Witness Protection—now, that was quite an interesting little exercise. Your background in homicide forensics was indispensable there. A mob witness is killed, and you single-handedly proved the involvement of the DOJ case officer."

"A lucky break," Anna said stolidly.

"People make their own luck, Ms. Navarro," he said, and his eyes were unsmiling. "We know quite a bit about you, Ms. Navarro. More than you might imagine. We know the account balances on that ATM slip you were writing on. We know who your friends are, and when you last called home. We know you've never padded a travel-and-expense report in your life, which is more than most of us can say." He paused, peering at her closely. "I'm sorry if any of this causes you disquiet, but you realize that you relinquished any civil rights to privacy when you joined the OSI, signed the disclaimers and the memoranda of agreement. No matter. The fact is that your work has invariably been of a very high caliber. And quite often extraordinary."

She raised an eyebrow, but said nothing.

"Ah. You look surprised. I told you, we have our own way of keeping tabs. And we have our own fitness reports, Ms. Navarro. Of course, what immediately distinguishes you, given our concerns, is your particular combination of skills. You have a background in the standard 'audit' and investigative protocols, but you also have an expertise in homicide. This makes you, may I say, unique. But to the matter at hand. It's only fair to let you know that we've done the most thorough background check on you imaginable. Everything I'm going to tell you—anything I state, assert, conjecture, suggest, or imply—must be regarded as classified at the topmost level. Do we understand each other?"

Anna nodded. "I'm listening."

"Excellent, Ms. Navarro." Bartlett handed her a sheet of paper with a list of names on it, followed by dates of birth and countries of residence.

"I'm not following. Am I supposed to contact these men?"

"Not unless you've got a Ouija board. All eleven of these men are deceased. All passed from this vale of tears within the past two months. Several, you'll see, in the United States, others in Switzerland, in England, Italy, Spain, Sweden, Greece . . . All apparently of natural causes."

Anna glanced at the sheet. Of the eleven, there were two names she recognized—one a member of the Lancaster family, a family that once owned most of the steel mills in the country, but was now better known for its foundation grants and other forms of philanthropy. Philip Lancaster was, in fact, somebody she'd assumed had died long ago. The other, Nico Xenakis, was presumably from the Greek shipping family. To be honest, she knew the name mainly in connection to another scion of the family—a man who had made a tabloid name for himself as a roué back in the sixties, when he'd dated a series of Hollywood starlets. None of the other names rang any bells. Looking at their dates of birth, she saw that all of them were old men—in their late seventies to late eighties.

"Maybe the news hasn't reached the ICU whiz kids," she said, "but when you've had your three score and ten . . . well, no one gets out alive."

"In none of these cases is exhumation possible, I'm afraid," Bartlett continued implacably. "Perhaps it's as you say. Old men doing what old men will do. In those instances, we cannot prove otherwise. But in the last few days, we've had a stroke of luck. In a pro forma way, we put a roster of names on the 'sentinel list'—one of those international conventions that nobody seems to take any notice of. The most recent death was of a retiree in Nova Scotia, Canada. Our Canadian friends are sticklers about procedures, and that's how the alarm was sounded in time. In this instance, we have a body to work with. More precisely, *you* do."

"You're leaving something out, of course. What is it that connects these men?"

"To every question, there's a surface answer and a deeper one. I'll give you the surface answer, because it's the only one I have. A few years ago, an internal audit was conducted of the CIA's deep-storage records. Was a tip received? Let's say it was. These were nonoperational files, mind you. They weren't agents or direct contacts. They were, in fact, clearance files. Each was marked 'Sigma,' presumably a reference to a codeword operation—of which there seems to be no trace in the Agency's records. We have no information as to its nature."

"Clearance files?" Anna repeated.

"Meaning that some time long ago each man had been vetted and cleared—for something, we don't know what."

"And the source of origin was a CIA archivist."

He didn't reply directly. "Each file has been authenticated by our top forensic document experts. They're old, these files. They date as far back as the mid-forties, before there even *was* a CIA."

"You're saying they were started by OSS?"

"Exactly," Bartlett said. "The CIA's precursor. Many of the files were opened right around the time the war was ending, the Cold War beginning. The latest ones date from the mid-fifties. But I digress. As I say, we have this curious pattern of deaths. Of course, it would have gone nowhere, a question mark in a field full of question marks, except that we began to see a pattern, cross-checked and correlated with the Sigma files. I don't believe in coincidences, do you, Ms. Navarro? Eleven of the men named in these files have died in a very short interval. The actuarial odds of this happening by chance are . . . remote at best."

Anna nodded impatiently. As far as she could see, the Ghost was seeing ghosts. "How long is this assignment for? I've got a real job, you know."

"This *is* your 'real' job now. You've already been reassigned. We've made the arrangements. You understand your task, then?" His gaze softened. "This doesn't seem to quicken your pulse, Ms. Navarro."

Anna shrugged. "I keep coming back to the fact that these guys are all in the graduating class, if you know what I mean. Old guys tend to pop off, O.K.? These were old guys."

"And in nineteenth-century Paris, getting trampled by a carriage was pretty commonplace," Bartlett said.

Anna furrowed her brow. "Excuse me?"

Bartlett leaned back in his chair. "Have you ever heard of the Frenchman Claude Rochat? No? He's someone I think about quite a bit. A dull, unimaginative, plodding, dogged fellow, who, in the 1860s and 1870s, worked as an accountant in the employ of the *Directoire*, France's own bureau of intelligence. In 1867, it came to his attention that two low-level clerks at the *Directoire*, apparently unacquainted, had both been killed in the course of a fortnight—one the victim of an apparent street robbery, the other trampled to death by a mail coach. It was the sort of thing that happened all the time. Quite unremarkable. But still he wondered, especially after he learned that at the time of death, both of these humble clerks had on their persons costly gold pocket watches—in fact, as he confirmed, the two watches were *identical*, both with a fine cloisonné landscape on the inside of the watchcase. A small oddity, but it arrested his attention, and, to the exasperation of his superiors, he spent the next four years trying to figure out why, and how, this small oddity had come about. In the end, he uncovered a spy ring of extraordinary intricacy: the *Directoire* had been penetrated and manipulated by its Prussian counterparts." He registered her darting glance and smiled: "Yes, those pocket watches in the case are the very ones. Exquisite craftsmanship. I acquired them a couple of decades ago at an auction. I like having them nearby. It helps me to remember."

Bartlett closed his eyes for a contemplative moment. "Of course, by the time Rochat completed his investigations, it was too late," he went on. "Bismark's agents, through a cunning diet of misinformation, had already tricked France into declaring war. 'À Berlin' was the great cry. The result was disastrous for France: the military dominance it had enjoyed since the Battle of Rocroi in 1643 was completely destroyed, in just a couple of months. Can you imagine? The French army, with the Emperor at its head, was led straight into an ingenious ambush near Sedan. And that was the end, needless to say, for Napoleon III. The country lost Alsace-Lorraine, it had to pay staggering reparations, and it had to submit to two years of occupation. An extraordinary blow, it was—one that shifted the whole course of European history irreversibly. And just a few years earlier, Claude Rochat was tugging at a little thread, not knowing where it would lead, not knowing whether it would lead anywhere. It was just those two lowly clerks and their matching pocket watches." Bartlett made a sound that wasn't quite a laugh. "Most of the time, something that looks trivial really *is* trivial. *Most* of the time. My job is to worry about such matters. The tiny threads. The boring little discrepancies. The trivial little patterns that just might lead to larger patterns.

The most important thing I do is the least glamorous thing imaginable."
An arched eyebrow. "I look for matching pocket watches."

Anna was silent for a few moments. The Ghost was living fully up to
his reputation: cryptic, hopelessly obscure. "I appreciate the history lesson," she said slowly, "but my frame of reference has always been the
here and now. If you really think these deep-storage files have ongoing
relevance, why not simply have the CIA investigate?"

Bartlett withdrew a crisp silk pocket square from his suit jacket and
began to polish his eyeglasses. "Things get rather awkward around here,"
he said. "The ICU tends to get involved only in cases where there's a real
possibility of internal interference or anything else that might preclude
a thorough inquiry. Let's leave it at that." There was a hint of condescension in his voice.

"Let's not," Anna said sharply. It wasn't a tone to take with the head
of a division, especially one as powerful as the ICU, but subservience
wasn't in her skill set, and Bartlett might as well know at the outset
whose services he had engaged. "With respect, you're talking about the
possibility that someone in, or retired from, the Agency may be behind
the deaths."

The director of the Internal Compliance Unit blanched slightly. "I
didn't say that."

"You didn't deny it."

Bartlett sighed. "Of the crooked timber of humanity, nothing straight
was ever made." A tight smile.

"If you think Central Intelligence might be compromised, why not
bring in the FBI?"

Bartlett snorted delicately. "Why not bring in the Associated Press?
The Federal Bureau of Investigation has many strengths, but discretion
isn't among them. I'm not sure you appreciate the sensitivity of this
matter. The fewer people who know about it, the better. That's why I'm
not involving a team—just an individual. The right individual, I dearly
hope, Agent Navarro."

"Even if these deaths really are murders," she said, "it's highly unlikely
you'll ever find the killer, I hope you know that."

"That's the standard bureaucratic response," Bartlett said, "but you
don't strike me as a bureaucrat. Mr. Dupree says you're stubborn and
'not exactly a team player.' Well, that's precisely what I wanted."

Anna forged ahead. "You're basically asking me to investigate the CIA.

You want me to examine a series of deaths to establish that they are murders, and then—"

"And then to amass any evidence that would allow us to conduct an audit." Bartlett's gray eyes shone through his plastic-rimmed glasses. "No matter who's implicated. Is that clear?"

"As mud," Anna said. A seasoned investigator, she was used to conducting interviews with witnesses and suspects alike. Sometimes you simply needed to listen. Sometimes, however, you needed to goad, to provoke a response. Art and experience came in knowing when. Bartlett's story was perforated with elisions and omissions. She appreciated the need-to-know reflexes of a wily old bureaucrat, but in her experience, it helped to know more than you strictly needed to. "I'm not going to play blindman's bluff," she said.

Bartlett blinked. "I beg your pardon?"

"You must have copies of these Sigma files. You must have scrutinized them closely. And yet you claim you have no idea what Sigma was about."

"Where are you going with this?" His voice was cool.

"Will you show me these files?"

A rictuslike smile: "No. No, that won't be possible."

"Why not?"

Bartlett put his glasses on again. "I'm not under investigation here. As much as I admire your tactics of interrogation. Anyway, I believe I've been clear on the relevant points."

"No, dammit, that's not good enough! You're fully acquainted with these files. If you don't know what they add up to, then at least you've got to have your suspicions. An educated hypothesis. Anything at all. Save your poker face for your Tuesday-night card game. I'm not playing."

Bartlett finally erupted. "For Christ's sake, you've seen enough to know that we're talking about the reputation of some of the major figures of the postwar era. These are *clearance* files. By themselves, they prove nothing. I had you vetted before our conversation—did that implicate you in my affairs? I trust your discretion. Of course I do. But we're talking about prominent individuals as well as obscure ones. You can't simply go stomping around in your sensible shoes."

Anna listened carefully, listened to the undertone of tension in his voice. "You talk about reputations, yet that's not what you're really concerned about, is it?" she pressed. "I need more to go on!"

He shook his head. "It's like trying to fashion a rope ladder out of gossamer. Nothing that we've ever been able to pin down. Half a century ago, something was hatched. *Something.* Something that involved vital interests. The Sigma list encompasses a curious collection of individuals—some were industrialists, we know, and there are others whose identity we haven't been able to figure out at all. What they have in common is that a founder of the CIA, someone with enormous power in the forties and fifties, took a direct interest in them. Was he enlisting them? *Targeting* them? We're *all* playing blindman's bluff. But it would seem that an undertaking of enormous secrecy was launched. You asked what connects these men. In a real sense, we simply don't know." He adjusted his cuffs, the nervous tick of a fastidious man. "You might say we're at the pocket-watch stage."

"No offense, but the Sigma list—that goes back half a *century!*"

"Ever been to the Somme, in France?" Bartlett asked abruptly, his eyes a little too bright. "You ought to go—just to look at the poppies growing among the wheat. Every once in a while, a farmer in the Somme cuts down an oak tree, sits down on the trunk, and then sickens and dies. Do you know why? Because during the First World War, a battle had taken place on that field, a canister of mustard gas deployed. The poison gets absorbed by the tree as a sapling, and decades later it's still potent enough to kill a man."

"And that's Sigma, do you think?"

Bartlett's gaze grew in intensity. "They say the more you know, the more you know you don't know. I find the more you know, the more unsettling it is to come across things you don't know about. Call it vanity, or call it caution. I worry about what becomes of unseen little saplings." A wan smile. "The crooked timber of humanity—it always comes down to the crooked timber. Yes, I appreciate that all this sounds like ancient history to you, and perhaps it is, Agent Navarro. You'll come back and set me straight."

"I wonder," she said.

"Now, you'll be making contact with various law-enforcement officials, and as far as anyone knows, you'll be conducting a completely open homicide investigation. Why the involvement of an OSI agent? Your explanation will be terse: because these names have cropped up in the course of an ongoing investigation into the fraudulent transfer of funds, the details of which nobody will press you to disclose. A simple cover, nothing elaborate required."

"I'll pursue the sort of investigation I've been trained to do," Anna said warily. "That's all I can promise."

"That's all I'm asking for," Bartlett replied smoothly. "Your skepticism may be well founded. But one way or the other, I'd like to be sure. Go to Nova Scotia. Assure me that Robert Mailhot really did die of natural causes. Or—confirm that he *didn't*."

CHAPTER FOUR

Ben was driven to the headquarters of the *Kantonspolizei,* the police of the canton of Zurich, a grimy yet elegant old stone building on Zeughausstrasse. He was led in through an underground parking garage by two silent young policemen and up several long flights of stairs into a relatively modern building that adjoined the older one. The interior looked like it belonged in a suburban American high school, circa 1975. To any of his questions, his two escorts answered only with shrugs.

His thoughts raced. It was no accident that Cavanaugh was there on Bahnhofstrasse. Cavanaugh had been in Zurich with the deliberate intent to murder him. Somehow the body had disappeared, had been removed swiftly and expertly, and the gun planted in his bag. It was clear that others were involved with Cavanaugh, professionals. But who—and, again, *why?*

Ben was taken first to a small fluorescent-lit room and seated in front of a stainless-steel table. As his police escorts remained standing, a man in a short white coat emerged and, without making eye contact, said, *"Ihre Hände, bitte."* Ben extended his hands. It was pointless to argue, he knew. The technician pumped a mist from a plastic spray bottle on both sides of his hands, then rubbed a cotton-tipped plastic swab lightly but thoroughly over the back of his right hand. Then he placed the swab in a plastic tube. He repeated the exercise for the palm, and then did the same with Ben's other hand. Four swabs now reposed in four carefully labeled plastic tubes, and the technician took them with him as he left the room.

A few minutes later, Ben arrived at a pleasant, sparely furnished office on the third floor, where a broad-shouldered, stocky man in plainclothes introduced himself as Thomas Schmid, a homicide detective. He had a wide, pockmarked face and a very short haircut with short bangs. For some reason Ben remembered a Swiss woman he'd once met at Gstaad telling him that cops in Switzerland were called *bullen*, "bulls," and this man demonstrated why.

Schmid began asking Ben a series of questions—name, date of birth, passport number, hotel in Zurich, and so on. He sat at a computer terminal, typing out the answers with one finger. A pair of reading glasses hung from his neck.

Ben was angry, tired, and frustrated, his patience worn thin. It took great effort to keep his tone light. "Detective," he said, "am I under arrest or not?"

"No, sir."

"Well, this has been fun and all, but if you're not going to arrest me, I'd like to head on back to my hotel."

"We would be happy to arrest you if you'd like," the detective replied blandly, the barest glint of menace in his smile. "We have a very nice cell waiting for you. But if we can keep this friendly, it will all be much simpler."

"Aren't I allowed to make a phone call?"

Schmid extended both hands, palms up, at the beige phone at the edge of his crowded desk. "You may call the American consulate here, or your attorney. As you wish."

"Thank you," Ben said, picking up the phone and glancing at his watch. It was early afternoon in New York. Hartman Capital Management's in-house attorneys all practiced tax or securities law, so he decided to call a friend who practiced international law.

Howie Rubin and he had been on the Deerfield ski racing team together and had become close friends. Howie had come to Bedford several times for Thanksgiving and, like all of Ben's friends, had particularly taken to Ben's mother.

The attorney was at lunch, but Ben's call was patched through to Howie's cell phone. Restaurant noise in the background made Howie's end of the conversation hard to make out.

"*Christ*, Ben," Howie said, interrupting Ben's summary. Someone next to him was talking loudly. "All right, I'll tell you what I tell all my clients who get arrested while on ski vacations in Switzerland. Grin and bear it. Don't get all high and mighty. Don't play the indignant American. No one can grind you down with rules and regulations and everything-by-the-book like the Swiss."

Ben glanced at Schmid, who was tapping at his keyboard and no doubt listening. "I'm beginning to see that. So what am I supposed to do?"

"The way it works in Switzerland, they can hold you for up to twenty-four hours without actually arresting you."

"You're kidding me."

"And if you piss them off, they can throw you in a dirty little holding cell overnight. So don't."

"Then what do you recommend?"

"Hartman, you can charm a dog off a meat truck, buddy boy, so just be your usual self. Any problems, call me and I'll get on the phone and threaten an international incident. One of my partners does a lot of corporate espionage work, point being we've got access to some pretty high-powered databases. I'll pull Cavanaugh's records, see what we can find. Give me the phone number where you are right now."

When Ben had hung up, Schmid led him into an adjoining room and sat him at a desk near another terminal. "Have you been to Switzerland before?" Schmid asked pleasantly, as if he were a tour guide.

"A number of times," Ben said. "Mostly to ski."

Schmid nodded distractedly. "A popular recreation. Very good for relieving stress, I think. Very good for letting off tension." His gaze narrowed. "You must have a lot of stress from your work."

"I wouldn't say that."

"Stress can make people do remarkable things. Day after day they bottle it up, and then, one day, *boom!* They explode. When this happens, they surprise themselves, I think, as much as other people."

"As I told you, the gun was planted. I never used it." Ben was livid, but he spoke as coolly as he could. It would do no good to provoke the detective.

"And yet by your own account, you killed a man, bludgeoned him with your bare hands. Is this something you do in your normal line of work?"

"These were hardly normal circumstances."

"If I were to talk to your friends, Mr. Hartman, what would they tell me about you? Would they say you had a temper?" He gave Ben an oddly contemplative look. "Would they say were . . . a violent man?"

"They'd tell you I'm as law abiding as they come," Ben said. "Where are you going with these questions?" Ben looked down at his own hands, hands that had slammed a lamp fixture against Cavanaugh's skull. *Was* he violent? The detective's imputations were preposterous—he'd acted purely in self-defense—and yet his mind drifted back a few years.

He could see Darnell's face even now. One of his fifth-graders at East New York, Darnell had been a good kid, an A student, bright and curious, the best in his class. Then something happened to him. His grades dropped, and before long he stopped handing in homework altogether. Darnell never got in fights with the other kids, and yet from time to time welts would be visible on his face. Ben talked to him after class one day. Darnell couldn't look him in the eye. His expression was cloudy with fear. Finally he told him that Orlando, his mother's new boyfriend, didn't want him to waste time on schoolwork; he needed him to help bring in money. "Bring in money how?" Ben had asked, but Darnell wouldn't answer. When he telephoned Darnell's mother, Joyce Stuart, her responses were skittish, evasive. She wouldn't come into the school, refused to discuss the situation, refused to admit anything might be wrong. She, too, sounded scared. A few days later, he found Darnell's address from student records and paid a visit.

Darnell lived on the second floor of a building with a ruined facade, a stairwell festooned with graffiti. The buzzer was broken, but the apartment door was unlocked, and so he traipsed up the stairs and knocked on 2B. After a long wait, Darnell's mother appeared, visibly battered—her cheeks bruised, her lips swollen. He introduced himself and asked to come in. Joyce paused, then led him toward the small kitchen, with its deeply gouged countertops of beige Formica and yellow cotton drapes flapping in the breeze.

Ben heard yelling in the background before the mother's boyfriend strode over. "Who the fuck are you?" demanded Orlando, a tall, powerfully built man in a red tank top and loose jeans. Ben recognized a convict's physique: an upper body so overdeveloped that the muscles looked draped over his chest and shoulders like a lifejacket.

"He's Darnell's schoolteacher," Darnell's mother said, the words cottony from her bruised lips.

"And you—are you Darnell's guardian?" Ben asked Orlando.

"Hell, you could say I'm his teacher now. Only, I'm teaching him shit he needs to know. Unlike you."

Now Ben saw Darnell, fear making him look even younger than his ten years, padding into the kitchen to join them. "Go away, Darnell," his mother said in a half-whisper.

"Darnell don't need you filling his head with bullshit. Darnell needs to learn how to move rocks." Orlando smiled, revealing a gleaming gold front.

Ben felt a jolt. *Moving rocks:* selling crack. "He's a fifth-grader. He's ten years old."

"That's right. A juvenile. Cops know he ain't worth arresting." He laughed. "I gave him the choice, though: he could either peddle rocks or peddle his ass."

The words, the man's casual brutality, sickened Ben, but he forced himself to speak calmly. "Darnell has more potential than anyone in his class. You have a duty to let him excel."

Orlando snorted. "He can make his living on the street, same as me."

Then he heard Darnell's treble voice, shaky but resolute. "I don't want to do it anymore," he told Orlando. "Mr. Hartman knows what's right." Then, louder, bravely: "I don't want to be like you."

Joyce Stuart's features froze in a preemptive cringe: "Don't, Darnell."

It was too late. Orlando lashed out, cracking the ten-year-old in the jaw, the blow propelling him out of the room. He turned to Ben: "Now get your ass out of here. In fact, let me help you."

Ben felt himself stiffen as rage coursed through his body. Orlando slammed his open hand against Ben's chest, but instead of staggering backward, Ben lunged toward him, pounding a fist into the man's temple, then another, pummeling his head like a speedbag. Stunned, Orlando froze for a crucial few moments, and then his powerful arms banged uselessly against Ben's sides—Ben was too close for him to land a punch. And the frenzy of rage was an anaesthetic, anyway: Ben didn't even feel the body blows until Orlando slid limply to the floor. He was down, not out.

Orlando's eyes flicked at him, the leering defiance replaced by fear. "You crazy," he murmured.

Was he? What had come over him? "If you ever touch Darnell again," Ben said, with a deliberate calm he did not feel, "I will kill you." He paused between each word for emphasis. "Do we understand each other?"

Later, from his friend Carmen in social services, he'd find out that Orlando left Joyce and Darnell later that day, never to return. If Ben hadn't been told, though, he soon would have guessed from the dramatic improvement in Darnell's grades and general demeanor.

"All right, man," Orlando had said at the time, in a subdued tone, gazing up at him from the kitchen floor. "See, we just had a misunderstanding." He coughed. "I ain't looking for more trouble." He coughed again and murmured, "You crazy. You crazy."

"Mr. Hartman, can you please put your right thumb here?" Schmid indicated a small white oblong marked IDENTIX TOUCHVIEW, on top of which a small oval glass panel glowed ruby red.

Ben placed his right thumb on the glass oval, then did the same with his left. His prints appeared immediately, much enlarged, on a computer monitor angled partly toward him.

Schmid tapped in a few numbers and hit the return key, setting off the high-pitched screech of a modem. He turned toward Ben and said apologetically, "This goes right to Bern. We will know in five or ten minutes."

"Know what?"

The detective rose and gestured for Ben to follow him back to the first room. "Whether there is already a warrant for your arrest in Switzerland."

"I think I might remember if there was one."

Schmid stared at him a long time before he started to speak. "I know your type, Mr. Hartman. For rich Americans like you, Switzerland is a country of chocolates, banks, cuckoo clocks, and ski resorts. You'd like to imagine that each of us is your *Hausdiener*, your manservant, yes? But you do know Switzerland. For centuries, every European power wished to make us its duchy. None ever succeeded. Now maybe your country, with its power and wealth, thinks it can do the same. But you are not— what is your expression—'calling the shots' here. There is no chocolate for you in this office. And it is not up to you to decide when, or whether, you are released." He leaned back in his chair, smiling gravely. "Welcome to Switzerland, Herr Hartman."

Another man, tall and thin, in a heavily starched white lab coat, came into the room as if on cue. He wore rimless glasses and had a small bristle mustache. Without introducing himself, he pointed to a white-tiled section of the wall marked with metric gradations. "You will please to stand there," he ordered.

Trying not to show his exasperation, Ben stood with his back flat against the tiles. The technician measured his height, then led him to a white lab sink, where he turned a lever that extruded a white paste and instructed Ben to wash his hands. The soap was creamy yet gritty and smelled of lavender. At another station, the tech rolled sticky black ink onto a glass plate and had Ben place each hand flat onto it. With long, delicate, manicured fingers, he rolled each of Ben's fingers first on blotter paper, then carefully onto separate squares on a form.

While the technician worked, Schmid got up and went into the adjoining room, then returned a few moments later. "Well, Mr. Hartman, we did not get a hit. There is no warrant outstanding."

"What a surprise," Ben muttered. He felt oddly relieved.

"Still, there are questions. The ballistics will come back in a few days from the *Wissenschaftlicher Dienst der Stadtpolizei Zürich*—the ballistics lab—but we already know that the bullets recovered from the platform are .765 Browning."

"Is that a kind of bullet?" Ben asked innocently.

"It is the sort of ammunition used in the gun that was found during the search of your luggage."

"Well, what do you know," Ben said, forcing a smile, then tried another tack: bluntness. "Look, there's no question the bullets were fired by the gun in question. Which was planted in my luggage. So why don't you just do whatever that test is on my hands that tells you whether I fired a gun?"

"The gunshot residue analysis. We've already done it." Schmid mimed a swabbing motion.

"And the results?"

"We'll have them soon. After you are photographed."

"You won't find my fingerprints on the gun either." *Thank God I didn't handle it*, Ben thought.

The detective shrugged theatrically. "Fingerprints can be removed."

"Well, the witnesses—"

"The eyewitnesses describe a well-dressed man of about your age. There was much confusion. But five people are dead, seven seriously injured. Again, you tell us you killed the perpetrator. Yet when we look there is no body."

"I—I can't explain that," Ben admitted, aware of how bizarre his account sounded. "Obviously the body was removed and the area cleaned. That just tells me that Cavanaugh was working with others."

"To kill you." Schmid regarded him with dark amusement.

"So it appears."

"But you offer no motive. You say there was no grudge between the two of you."

"You don't seem to understand," Ben said quietly. "I hadn't seen the guy in fifteen years."

The phone on Schmid's desk rang. He picked it up. "Schmid." He listened. In English, he said, "Yes, one minute, please," and handed the receiver to Ben.

It was Howie. "Ben, old buddy," he said, his voice now as clear as if he were calling from the next room. "You did say Jimmy Cavanaugh was from Homer, New York, right?"

"Small town midway between Syracuse and Binghamton," Ben said.

"Right," Howie said. "And he was in your class at Princeton?"

"That's the guy."

"Well, here's the thing. Your Jimmy Cavanaugh doesn't exist."

"Tell me something I don't know," Ben said. *He's dead as a doornail.*

"No, Ben, listen to me. I'm saying your Jimmy Cavanaugh *never existed.* I'm saying there *is* no Jimmy Cavanaugh. I checked with alumni records at Princeton. No Cavanaugh, first or middle initial J, ever enrolled in the school, at least not in the decade you attended. And there have never been any Cavanaughs in Homer. Not anywhere in that county. Not at Georgetown, either. Oh, and we checked with all sorts of hifalutin databases, too. If there were a James Cavanaugh that came close to matching your description, we'd have found him. Tried every spelling variant, too. You have no idea how powerful the databases are they've got these days. A person leaves tracks like a slug, we all do. Credit, Social Security, military, you name it. This guy's totally off the grid. Weird, huh?"

"There's got to be some mistake. I *know* he was enrolled at Princeton."

"You *think* you know that. Doesn't seem possible, does it?"

Ben felt sick to his stomach. "If this is true, it doesn't help us."

"No," Howie agreed. "But I'll keep trying. Meantime, you got my cellular, right?"

Ben replaced the receiver, stunned. Schmid continued: "Mr. Hartman, were you here on business or holiday?"

He forced himself to focus, and spoke as civilly as he could. "Ski vacation, as I said. I had a couple of bank meetings, but only because I was passing through Zurich." *Jimmy Cavanaugh never existed.*

Schmid clasped his hands. "The last time you were in Switzerland was four years ago, yes? To claim the body of your brother?"

Ben paused a moment, unable to stop the sudden flood of memories. *The phone call in the middle of the night: never good news. He'd been asleep next to Karen, a fellow teacher, in his grubby apartment in East New York. He grumbled, rolled over to answer the call that changed everything.*

A small rented plane Peter was flying solo had crashed a few days earlier in a gorge near Lake Lucerne. Ben's name was listed on the rental papers as next-of-kin. It had taken time to identify the deceased, but dental records made a definitive identification possible. The Swiss authorities were ruling it an accident. Ben flew to Lake Lucerne to claim the body and brought his brother home—what was left of him after the fuselage had exploded—in a little cardboard carton not much bigger than a cake box.

The entire plane flight home he didn't cry. That would only come later, when the numbness began to wear off. His father had collapsed, weeping, upon hearing the news; his mother, already confined to bed because of the cancer, had screamed with all of her strength.

"Yes," Ben said quietly. "That was the last time I was here."

"A striking fact. When you come to our country, death seems to accompany you."

"What are you getting at?"

"Mr. Hartman," Schmid said, in a more neutral tone of voice, "do you think there is any connection between your brother's death and what happened today?"

At the headquarters of the Swiss national police, the *Stadtpolizei*, in Bern, a plump middle-aged woman with heavy black horn-rimmed glasses glanced up at her computer screen and was surprised to see a line of text begin to flash. After staring at it for a few seconds, she remembered what she had long ago been instructed to do, and she jotted down the name and the long series of numbers after the name. Then she knocked at the glass-paned door of her immediate supervisor.

"Sir," she said. "A name on the RIPOL watch list was just activated." RIPOL was an acronym for *Recherche Informations Policier*, the national criminal and police database that contained names, fingerprints, license plate numbers—a vast range of law-enforcement data used by the federal, canton, and local police.

Her boss, a priggish man in his mid-forties who was known to be on the fast track at the *Stadtpolizei*, took the slip of paper, thanked his loyal secretary, and dismissed her. Once she had closed his office door, he picked up a secure phone that was not routed through the main switch-board, and dialed a number he rarely ever called.

A battered old gray sedan of indeterminate make idled down the block from *Kantonspolizei* headquarters on Zeughausstrasse. Inside, two men smoked and said nothing, weary from the long wait. The sudden ringing of the cellular phone mounted on the center console startled them. The passenger picked it up, listened, said, *"Ja, danke,"* and hung up.

"The American is leaving the building," he said.

A few minutes later they saw the American emerge from the side entrance and get into a taxi. When it was halfway down the block, the driver pulled the car into the early-evening traffic.

CHAPTER FIVE

Halifax, Nova Scotia

When the Air Canada pilot announced they were about to land, Anna Navarro removed her files from the tray table, lifted it closed, and tried to focus her mind on the case ahead of her. Flying terrified her, and the only thing worse than landing was taking off. Her stomach flip-flopped. As usual she fought an irrational conviction that the plane would crash and she would end her life in a fiery inferno.

Her favorite uncle, Manuel, had been killed when the clattering old cropduster he worked in dropped an engine and plummeted. But that was so long ago, she'd been ten or eleven, and a deathtrap cropduster had no resemblance to the sleek 747 she was in now.

She'd never told any of her OSI colleagues about her anxiety, on the general principle that you should never let them see your vulnerabilities. But she was convinced that somehow Arliss Dupree knew, the way a dog smells fear. In the last six months he'd forced her to practically live on planes, flying from one lousy assignment to another.

The only thing that allowed her to keep her composure was to spend the flight immersed in her case files. They always absorbed her, fascinated her. The dry-as-dust autopsy and pathology reports beckoned to her to solve their mysteries.

As a child she'd loved doing the intricate five-hundred-piece puzzles her mother brought home, the gifts from a woman whose house her mother cleaned and whose kids had no patience for puzzles. Far more than seeing the glossy image emerge, she loved the sound and feel of the puzzle pieces snapping into place. Often the old puzzles were missing pieces, lost by their careless original owners, and that had always irritated her. Even as a kid she'd been a perfectionist.

On some level, this case was a thousand-piece puzzle spilled on the carpet before her.

During this Washington-Halifax flight she had pored over a folder of documents faxed from the RCMP in Ottawa. The Royal Canadian

Mounted Police, Canada's equivalent of the FBI, was, despite its archaic name, a top-notch investigative agency. The working relationship between DOJ and RCMP was good.

Who are you? she wondered, staring at a photograph of the old man. Robert Mailhot of Halifax, Nova Scotia, the kindly retiree, devout member of the Church of Our Lady of Mercy. Not the sort of person you'd expect to have a CIA clearance file, deep-storage or no.

What could have connected him to the vaporous machinations of long-dead spymasters and businessmen that Bartlett had stumbled on? She was certain that Bartlett had a file on him, but had chosen not to give her access to it. She was certain, too, that he wanted her to find out the relevant details for herself.

A provincial judge in Nova Scotia agreed to issue a search warrant. The documents she wanted—telephone and credit-card records—had been faxed to her in D.C. in a matter of hours. She was OSI; nobody thought to question her vague cover story about an ongoing investigation into fraudulent international transfer of funds.

Still, the file told her nothing. The cause of death, recorded on the certificate in the crabbed and almost illegible handwriting of a physician, presumably the old man's doctor, was "natural causes," with "coronary thrombosis" added in brackets. And maybe it was only that.

The deceased had made no unusual purchases; his only long-distance calls were to Newfoundland and Toronto. So far, no traction. Maybe she'd find the answer in Halifax.

Or maybe not.

She was intoxicated by the same strange brew of hope and despair she always felt at the beginning of a case. One minute she knew for sure she'd crack it, the next it seemed impossible. This much she knew for sure: the first homicide in a series she investigated was always the most important. It was the benchmark. Only if you were thorough, if you turned over every rock, did you have any hope of making connections. You'd never connect the dots unless you saw where all the dots were.

Anna was wearing her travel suit, a navy-blue Donna Karan (though the cheaper line), and a white Ralph Lauren blouse (not couture, of course). She was known around the office for dressing impeccably. On her salary she could scarcely afford designer labels, but she bought them anyway, living in a dark one-bedroom apartment in a lousy part of Washington, taking no vacations, because all her money went to clothes.

Everyone assumed she dressed so nicely to make herself attractive to men, because that was what young single women did. They were wrong. Her clothes were body armor. The finer the outfits, the safer and more secure she felt. She used designer cosmetics and wore designer clothes because then she was no longer the daughter of the dirt-poor Mexican immigrants who cleaned the houses and tended the yards of rich people. Then she could be anyone. She was self-aware enough to know how ridiculous this was in rational terms. But she did it anyway.

She wondered what it was about her that rankled Arliss Dupree more—that she was an attractive woman who'd turned him down, or that she was a Mexican. Maybe both. Maybe in the world according to Dupree, a Mexican-American was inferior and therefore had no right to reject him.

She had grown up in a small town in Southern California. Both her parents were Mexicans who'd escaped the desolation, the disease, the hopelessness south of the border. Her mother, soft-spoken and gentle, cleaned houses; her father, quiet and introverted, did yardwork.

When she was in grade school she wore dresses sewn by her mother, who also braided her brown hair and put it up. She was aware that she dressed differently, that she didn't quite fit in, but it didn't bother her until she was ten or eleven, when the girls started forming iron cliques that excluded her. They'd never associate with the daughter of the woman who cleaned their houses.

She was uncool, an outsider, an embarrassment. She was invisible.

Not that she was in a minority—the high school was half-Latino, half-white, the lines rarely crossed. She got used to being called "wetback" and "spic" by some of the white girls and guys. But among the Latinos there were castes, too, and she was at the bottom. The Latino girls always dressed well, and they mocked her clothes even more viciously than the white girls did.

The solution, she decided, was to dress like all the other girls. She began to complain to her mother, who didn't take her seriously at first, then explained that they couldn't afford to buy the kind of clothes the other girls had, and anyway, what was the difference, really? Didn't she like her mother's homemade clothes? Anna would snap, "No! I hate them!" knowing full well how much the words hurt. Even today, twenty years later, Anna could barely think about those days without feeling guilt.

Her mother was beloved by all her employers. One of them, a genuinely rich woman, began donating all of her children's castoffs. Anna
wore them happily—she couldn't imagine why anyone would throw
away such fine clothes!—until she gradually came to realize that her
clothes were all last year's fashions, and then her ardor cooled. One
day she was walking down the hall at school and one of the girls in a
clique she very much wanted to join called her over. "Hey," the girl
said, "that's my skirt!" Blushing, Anna denied it. The girl stuck a probing finger under the hem and turned it over to reveal her initials inked
on the tag.

The RCMP officer who picked her up at the airport, Anna knew, had
spent a year at the FBI Academy learning homicide investigation techniques. He was not the sharpest knife in the drawer, she'd heard, but a
good sort.

He stood outside the security gate, a tall, handsome thirtyish man in
a blue blazer and red tie. He flashed a pearly smile, seemingly genuinely
happy to see her. "Welcome to Nova Scotia," he said. "I'm Ron Arsenault." Dark-haired, brown-eyed, lantern jaw, high forehead. Dudley Do-
Right, she thought to herself.

"Anna Navarro," she said, shaking his hand firmly. Men always expect
women to shake like a dead fish, so she always gave them her firmest
handshake; it set the tone, let them know she was one of the guys. "Nice
to meet you."

He reached out for her carry-on garment bag, but she shook her head,
smiled. "I'm O.K., thanks."

"This your first time in Halifax?" He was obviously checking her out.

"Yeah. It looks beautiful from above."

He chuckled politely as he guided her through the terminal. "I'll be
liaising with the Halifax locals for you. You got the records O.K.?"

"Thanks. Everything but the bank records."

"Those should be in by now. If I find them I'll drop them by your
hotel."

"Thanks."

"Sure thing." He squinted at something: contact lenses, Anna knew.
"Tell you the truth, Miss Navarro—Anna?—some folks back in Ottawa
can't quite figure why you're taking such an interest in the old geezer.

Eighty-seven-year-old man dies in his home, natural causes, you gotta expect that, you know?"

They had reached the parking lot.

"The body's in the police morgue?" she asked.

"Actually, in the morgue of the local hospital. Waiting in the fridge for you. You got to us before the old guy was planted, that's the good news."

"And the bad news?"

"Body had already been embalmed for burial."

She winced. "That might screw up the tox screen."

They got to a dark blue, late-model Chevrolet sedan that screamed "unmarked police vehicle." He opened the trunk and put her bag in.

They drove for a while in silence.

"Who's the widow?" she asked. It wasn't in the file. "French-Canadian, too?"

"A local. Haligonian. Former schoolteacher. Tough old biddy, too. I mean, I feel bad for the lady, she's just lost her husband, and the funeral was supposed to be tomorrow. We had to ask her to put it off. She had relatives coming in from Newfoundland, too. When we mentioned autopsy she wigged out." He glanced over at her, then back to the road. "Given how it's evening, I thought you could settle in, and we can get started bright and early tomorrow morning. ME's going to meet us at seven."

She felt a pang of disappointment. She wanted to go right to work. "Sounds good," she said.

More silence. It was good to have a liaison officer who didn't seem to resent an emissary from the U.S. government. Arsenault was as friendly as could be. Maybe too much so.

"Here's your inn. Your government doesn't exactly spend the big bucks, hey?"

It was an unlovely Victorian house on Barrington Street, a large wooden building painted white with green shutters. The white paint had been soiled to a dirty gray.

"Hey, so let me take you out to dinner, unless you've got other plans. Maybe Clipper Cay, if you like seafood. Maybe catch some jazz at the Middle Deck . . . ?" He parked the car.

"Thanks, but I've had a long day," she said.

He shrugged, his disappointment obvious.

The inn had a faintly musty smell, as from a baseboard dampness that never quite went away. An old-fashioned carbon was made of her credit card and a brass key provided; she was prepared to tell the beefy guy at the front desk that she didn't need help with her bags, but none was volunteered. The same slight mustiness pervaded her room, on the second floor, which was decorated in floral patterns. Everything in it looked worn, but not objectionably so. She hung her clothes in the closet, drew the curtains, and changed into gray sweats. A nice run would do her good, she decided.

She jogged along the Grand Parade, the square on the west side of Barrington Street, then up George Street to the star-shaped fortress called The Citadel. She stopped, panting, at a newsstand and picked up a map of the city. She found the address; it wasn't far at all from where she was staying. She could reach it in her run.

Robert Mailhot's house was unremarkable but comfortable-looking, a two-story gray clapboard with a gabled roof, practically hidden in a wooded patch of land behind a chain-link fence.

The blue light of a television flickered behind lace curtains in a front room. The widow, presumably, was watching TV. Anna stopped for a moment across the street, watching intently.

She decided to cross the narrow street to take a closer look. She wanted to see if it was indeed the widow, and if so, how she was behaving. Did she appear to be in mourning or not? Such things couldn't always be intuited simply by observing at a distance, but you never knew what you might pick up. And if Anna positioned herself in the shadows outside the house, she might not be seen by suspicious neighbors.

The street was deserted, though music played from one house, a TV from another, and a foghorn sounded in the distance. She crossed toward the house—

Suddenly, a pair of high-intensity headlights appeared out of nowhere. They blinded her, growing larger and brighter as a vehicle roared toward her. With a scream, Anna lunged toward the curb, unseeing, desperately trying to jump out of the way of the insane, out-of-control car. It must have been gliding down the street, lights off, its quiet engine noise masked by the ambient street noise, until it was but a few feet away, then suddenly switched on its lights.

And now it was barreling toward her! There was no mistaking it, the
car wasn't slowing, wasn't moving straight down the road like an automobile simply going far too fast. It veered toward the shoulder of the
road, toward the curb, heading right at her. Anna recognized the vertical
chrome grill of a Lincoln Town Car, its flattened rectangular headlights
somehow giving it a predatory, sharklike appearance.

Move!

The car's wheels squealed, the engine at full throttle, as the maniacal
car bore down on her.

She turned around to see it hurtling at her just ten or twenty feet
away, the headlights dazzling. Terrified, screaming, a split-second away
from death, she leaped into the boxwood hedge that surrounded the
house next to the widow's, the stiff, prickly branches scraping at her
sweatpants-covered legs, and rolled over and over on the small lawn.

She heard the crunch of the car hitting the boxwood, then the loud
squeal of tires as she looked up to see the car veer away from her, spraying mud everywhere, the powerful engine racing down the narrow dark
road, and then the headlights vanished just as abruptly as they had appeared.

The car was gone.

What had just happened?

She jumped to her feet, her heart thudding, adrenaline flooding
throughout her body, the terror weakening her knees so that she could
barely stand up.

What the hell was that all about?

The car had headed right for her, quite deliberately targeting her, as if
trying to run her down.

And then . . . it had unaccountably disappeared!

She noticed several faces looking through windows on either side of
the street, some of them closing drapes as soon as she noticed them.

If the car had for some reason been aiming for her, trying to kill her,
why hadn't it finished the job?

It was entirely illogical, maddeningly so.

She walked, panting deeply, coughing painfully, drenched with sweat.
She tried to clear her head, but the fear would not leave her, and she
remained unable to make sense of the bizarre incident.

Had someone just tried to kill her, or not?

And if so—why?

Could it have been a drunk, a joyrider? The car's motions had seemed far too deliberate, too elaborately choreographed for that.

The only logical answers required a paranoid mind-set, and she adamantly refused to allow her thoughts to go in that direction. *That way madness lies.* She thought of Bartlett's ominous words about decades-old plans hatched in utmost secrecy, old men with secrets to hide, powerful people desperate to protect reputations. But Bartlett was a man who, by his own admission, sat in an office surrounded by yellowed paper, far removed from reality, a setting all too conducive to the weaving of conspiracy theories.

Still, was it not possible that the incident with the car had been an attempt to frighten her off the case?

If so, they had picked the wrong person to try such a technique on. For it served only to stiffen her determination to find out what the real story was.

London

The pub, called the Albion, was located on Garrick Street, at the edge of Covent Garden. It had low ceilings, rough-hewn wooden tables, and sawdust floors, the sort of place that had twenty real ales on tap and served bangers and mash, kidney pudding, and spotted dick, and was jammed at lunchtime with a stylish crowd of bankers and advertising executives.

Jean-Luc Passard, a junior security officer for the Corporation, entered the pub and saw at once why the Englishman had chosen this place to meet. It was so dense with people that the two of them would certainly go unnoticed.

The Englishman was sitting alone in a booth. He was as described: a nondescript man of about forty, with bristly, prematurely gray hair. On closer inspection, his face was smooth, almost tight, as if from surgery. He wore a blue blazer and white turtleneck. His shoulders were broad, his waist narrow; he looked, even at a distance, physically imposing. Yet you would not pick him out in a lineup.

Passard sat down at the booth, put out his hand. "I'm Jean-Luc."

"Trevor Griffiths," the Englishman said. He shook hands with barely any pressure at all, the greeting of a man who did not care what you thought of him. His hand was large, smooth, and dry.

"It's an honor to meet you," Passard said. "Your services to the Corporation over the years are the stuff of legend."

Trevor's dead gray eyes showed nothing.

"We wouldn't have brought you out of your . . . retirement if it weren't
absolutely necessary."

"You screwed up."

"We had bad luck."

"You want a backup."

"An insurance policy, so to say. An added safeguard. We really can't
afford to fail."

"I work alone. You know this."

"Of course. Your record puts your methods beyond second-guessing.
You will handle the matter as you see best."

"Good. Now, do we know the target's whereabouts?"

"He was last spotted in Zurich. We're not certain where he's headed
next."

Trevor cocked an eyebrow.

Passard flushed. "He is an amateur. He surfaces periodically. We will
pick up his trail again soon."

"I will require a good set of photographs of the target from as many
angles as you have."

Passard slid a large manila envelope across the table. "Done. Also, here
are the encoded instructions. As you'll understand, we want the job to
be done quickly and untraceably."

Trevor Griffiths's stare reminded Passard of a boa constrictor. "You have
already brought in several second-raters. Not only have you thereby lost
both money and time, but you have alerted the target. He is now fearful,
cautious, and no doubt has been frightened into depositing documents
with attorneys to be mailed in the event of his demise, that sort of thing.
He will therefore be considerably more difficult to take out. Neither you
nor your superiors need to advise me on how to do my job."

"But you're confident you can do it, yes?"

"I assume that was why you came to me?"

"Yes."

"Then please don't ask foolish questions. Are we done here? Because
I have a busy afternoon ahead of me."

Anna returned to her room at the inn, poured a tiny screw-top bottle of white wine from the minibar into a plastic cup, downed it, and then ran a bath, making the water as hot as she could stand. For fifteen minutes, she soaked herself, trying to think calming thoughts, but the image of the Town Car's vertical chrome grill kept intruding on her consciousness. And she remembered the Ghost's soft-spoken remark: *"I don't believe in coincidences, do you, Ms. Navarro?"*

Slowly, her sense of self-possession returned to her. These things happened, didn't they? Part of her job was to know where significance might lie, but it was an occupational hazard to impute significance where there was none.

Presently, she slipped into a terry-cloth robe, feeling much calmer and now ravenously hungry. Slipped beneath the door of her room was a manila envelope. She picked it up and sank into a floral-upholstered armchair. Copies of Mailhot's bank statements going back four years.

The phone rang.

It was Sergeant Arsenault.

"So is half past ten going to be all right for our visit with the widow?" Around him she could hear the bustle of a police station in the evening.

"I'll meet you there at ten-thirty," Anna replied crisply. "Thanks for the confirmation." She debated whether to tell him about the Town Car, her brush with death, but held back. Somehow she was afraid that it would diminish her authority—that she would sound vulnerable, fearful, easily spooked.

"Right, then," Arsenault said, and there was a hesitation in his voice. "Well, I guess I'll be heading home. I don't suppose—I'll be driving by your way, so if you have any second thoughts about grabbing a bite . . ." He spoke haltingly. "Or having a nightcap." He was obviously trying to keep it light. "Or whatever."

Anna didn't reply immediately. In truth, she wouldn't have minded company just then. "That's nice of you to offer," she said finally. "But I'm really tired."

"Me, too," he said quickly. "Long day. All right, then. See you in the morning." His voice had subtly shifted: no longer a man talking to a woman, but one professional talking to another.

She hung up with a slight sense of emptiness. Then she closed the curtains to the room and started sorting through her documents. There was still plenty of stuff to work through.

She was convinced that the real reason she hadn't yet gotten married, had veered away from any relationship that seemed to be getting too serious, was that she wanted to control her own surroundings. You get married, you're accountable to someone else. You want to buy something, you have to justify it. You can no longer work late without feeling guilty, having to apologize, to negotiate. Your time is under new management.

At the office people who didn't know her well called her the "Ice Maiden" and probably a lot worse, mostly because she dated infrequently. It wasn't just Dupree. People didn't like to see attractive women unattached. It offended their sense of the natural order of things. What they failed to realize was that she was a genuine workaholic and seldom socialized, hardly had time to meet men anyway. The only pool of men she could draw from were in the OSI, and dating a colleague could only mean trouble.

Or so she told herself. She preferred not to dwell on the incident in high school that still shadowed her, but she thought of Brad Reedy almost daily, and with ferocious hatred. On the Metro she'd catch a whiff of the citrus cologne Brad used to wear and her heart would spasm with fear, then reflexive anger. Or she'd see on the street a tall blond teenage boy in a red-and-white-striped rugby shirt, and she'd see Brad.

She had been sixteen, physically a woman and, she was told, a beauty, though she didn't yet know it or believe it. She still had few friends, but she no longer felt like an outcast. She quarreled with her parents almost daily because she could no longer stand to live in their tiny house; she felt claustrophobic, she couldn't breathe.

Brad Reedy was a senior and a hockey player, and therefore a member of the school's aristocracy. She was a junior and couldn't believe it when Brad Reedy, *the* Brad Reedy, had stopped by her locker and asked if she wanted to go out sometime. She thought it was a joke, that he'd been put up to it or something, and she scoffed, turning away. Already she'd begun to develop a protective layer of sarcasm.

But he persisted. She flushed, went numb, said I guess, maybe, sometime.

Brad offered to pick her up at her house, but she couldn't bear the thought of his seeing how humble it was, so she pretended she had errands to do downtown anyway and insisted on meeting at the movie theater. For days before, she pored over *Mademoiselle* and *Glamour*. In a *Seventeen* magazine feature on "How to Catch His Eye" she found the perfect outfit, the sort of thing a rich, classy girl might wear, the kind of girl Brad's parents would approve of.

She wore a Laura Ashley tiny floral-print dress with a high ruffled collar she'd bought at Goodwill, which she realized only after she bought it didn't fit quite right. In her matching lime-green espadrilles and lime-green Pappagallo Bermuda bag and lime-green headband, she suddenly felt ridiculous, a little girl dressing up for Halloween. When she met Brad, who was wearing a ripped pair of jeans and a striped rugby shirt, she realized how overdressed she was. She *looked* like she was trying too hard.

She felt as if the entire theater were watching her enter, this over-dressed fake preppy with this golden boy.

He wanted to go out to the Ship's Pub for pizza and a beer afterward. She had a Tab and tried to play mysterious and hard to get, but she already had a wild crush on this teenage Adonis and still couldn't believe she was on a date with him.

After three, four beers, he began to get coarse. He drew close to her in the booth and put his hands on her. She pleaded a headache—it was the only thing she could think of on the spur of the moment—and asked him to drive her home. He took her out to the Porsche, drove crazily, and then made a "wrong turn" into the park.

He was a two-hundred-pound man, incredibly strong, fueled by just enough alcohol to make him dangerous, and he forcibly removed her clothes, put his hand over her mouth to muffle her screams, and kept chanting, *"Aw, you want it, you wetback bitch."*

This was her first time.

For a year afterward she went to church regularly. The guilt burned inside her. If her mother ever found out, she was sure, it would destroy her.

It haunted her for years.

And her mother continued to clean the Reedys' house.

Now she remembered the bank records, tented on the armchair. Couldn't ask for more compelling reading material during a room-service dinner.

After a few minutes, she noticed a line of figures, then looked at it again. How could this be right? Four months ago, one million dollars had been wired into Robert Mailhot's savings account.

She sat down in the chair, looked more closely at the page. She felt a rush of adrenaline. She studied the column of numbers for a long time, her excitement growing. An image of Mailhot's modest clapboard house popped into her head.

A million dollars.

This was becoming interesting.

Zurich

The streetlights flashed by, illuminating the backseat of the taxi like the jittery flashes of a strobe light. Ben stared straight ahead, looking at nothing, thinking.

The homicide detective had seemed disappointed when the lab results showed that Ben hadn't fired the weapon, and processed his release papers with a show of reluctance. Obviously, Howie had managed to pull some strings to get his passport returned.

"I'm releasing you on one condition, Mr. Hartman—that you get out of my canton," Schmid had told him. "Leave Zurich at once. If I ever find out you've returned here, it will not go well for you. The inquiry concerning the Bahnhofplatz shootings remains open, and there are enough unanswered questions that I would have reason to swear out a warrant for your arrest at any moment. And if our immigrations office, the *Einwanderungsbehörde*, gets involved, you should remember that you can be held in administrative detention for one year before your case reaches a magistrate. You have friends and connections, very impressive ones, but they will not be able to help you next time."

But more than the threats, it was the question the detective had put so casually that haunted Ben. *Did* the Bahnhofplatz nightmare have anything to do with Peter's death?

Ask it another way: What were the odds it *didn't* have anything to do with Peter's death? Ben always remembered what his college mentor, the Princeton historian John Barnes Godwin, used to say: Calculate the odds, and recalculate, and recalculate again. And then just go with your gut instinct.

His gut told him this was no coincidence.

Then there was the mystery surrounding Jimmy Cavanaugh. It wasn't just the body that had disappeared. It was his identity, his entire existence. How could such a thing happen? And how had the shooter known where Ben was staying? It made no sense, none of it did.

The disappearance of the body, the planting of the handgun—that confirmed that the man he knew as Cavanaugh had been working with others. But with *whom?* Working on *what?* What possible interest, what possible *threat*, could Ben Hartman be to anyone?

Of course it had to do with Peter. That *had* to be it.

You see enough movies, you learn that bodies are "burned beyond recognition" only when something's being covered up. One of Ben's first, desperate thoughts upon hearing the unbearable news had been that maybe there'd been a mix-up, that it wasn't really Peter Hartman who'd died in that plane. The authorities had made a mistake. Peter was still alive, and he'd call, and they'd laugh over the bungle in a grim sort of way. Ben had never dared suggest this to his father, not wanting to raise false hopes. And then the medical evidence arrived, and it was irrefutable.

Now, however, Ben began to focus on the real question: Not *was* it Peter, but *how* had he died? A plane crash could be an efficient way to conceal evidence of murder.

And then again, maybe it had been a genuine accident.

After all, who could have wanted Peter dead? Murdering someone and then crashing a plane—wasn't that a ludicrously elaborate cover-up?

But this afternoon had redefined what was within the realm of plausibility. Because if Cavanaugh, *whoever* he was, had tried to kill him, for whatever unfathomable reason, wasn't it likely he—or others connected with Cavanaugh—had also killed Peter four years ago?

Howie had mentioned databases accessed by a colleague of his who did corporate espionage work. It struck Ben that Frederic McCallan, the aged client he was supposed to meet at St. Moritz, might be helpful in this regard. McCallan, in addition to being a serious Wall Street player, had served in more than one administration in Washington; he'd have no shortage of contacts and connections. Ben took out his multistandard Nokia phone and called the Hotel Carlton in St. Moritz. The Carlton was a quietly elegant place, opulent without being ostentatious, with a remarkable glassed-in pool overlooking the lake.

His call was put right through to Frederic McCallan's room.

"You're not standing us up, I hope," old Frederic said jovially. "Louise will be devastated." Louise was his allegedly beautiful granddaughter.

"Not at all. Things got a little hectic here, and I missed the last flight to Chur." Strictly speaking this was true.

"Well, we had them set a place for you at dinner, figuring you'd show up eventually. When can we expect you?"

"I'm going to rent a car and drive up tonight."

"Drive? But that'll take you *hours!*"

"It's a pleasant drive," he said. And a long drive was precisely what he needed to clear his head right now.

"Surely you can charter a flight if you have to."

"Can't," he said without elaborating. The fact was, he wanted to avoid the airport, where others—if there *were* others—might be expecting him. "I'll see you at breakfast, Freddie."

The taxicab took Ben to an Avis on Gartenhofstrasse, where he rented an Opel Omega, got directions, and set off without incident on the A3 highway, heading southeast out of Zurich. It took a while to get the feel of the road, the great speed at which Swiss drivers raced along their main highways, the aggressive way they signaled that they wanted to pass by pulling up right behind you and flashing their high beams.

Once or twice he had a flash of paranoia—a green Audi seemed to be following him but then disappeared. After a while he began to feel as if he'd left all that madness behind in Zurich. Soon he'd be at the Carlton in St. Moritz, and that was inviolable.

He thought about Peter, as he'd done so often in the last four years, and he felt the old guilt, felt his stomach tighten, then flip over. Guilt that he'd let his brother die alone, because in the last few years of Peter's life he'd barely even talked to him.

But he knew Peter wasn't alone at the end. He'd been living with a Swiss woman, a medical student he'd fallen in love with. Peter had told him about it on the phone a couple of months before he was killed.

Ben had seen Peter exactly twice since college. Twice.

As kids, before Max had sent them off to different prep schools, they'd been inseparable. They fought constantly, they wrestled each other until one could claim, *You're good, but I'm better.* They hated each other and loved each other, and they were never apart.

But after college Peter had joined the Peace Corps and gone to Kenya. He had no interest in Hartman Capital Management either. Nor would he take anything out of his trust fund. What the hell do I need it for in Africa? he'd said.

The fact was that Peter wasn't just doing something meaningful with his life. He was escaping Dad. Max and he had never gotten along. "Christ!" Ben had exploded at him once. "You want to avoid Dad, you can live in Manhattan and simply not call him. Have lunch with Mom once a week or something. You don't need to live in some goddamned mud hut, for God's sake!"

But no. Peter had returned to the States twice: once when their mother had her mastectomy, and once after Ben had called to tell him that Mom's cancer had spread and she didn't have long to live.

By that time Peter had moved to Switzerland. He'd met a Swiss woman in Kenya. "She's beautiful, she's brilliant, and she still hasn't seen through me," Peter had told him over the phone. "File that one under 'strange but true.'" That was a favorite boyhood expression of Peter's.

The girl was returning to medical school and he was going with her to Zurich. Which was what had first got the two of them talking. You're tagging along with some chick you met? Ben had said scornfully. He was jealous—jealous that Peter had fallen in love, and jealous, on some crazy brotherly level, that he'd been replaced at the center of Peter's life.

No, Peter had said, it wasn't just that. He'd read an article in an international edition of *Time* magazine about an old woman, a Holocaust survivor, living in France, desperately poor, who'd tried without success to get one of the big Swiss banks to give back the modest sum her father had left for her before he'd perished in the camps.

The bank had demanded her father's death certificate.

She'd told them that the Nazis hadn't issued death certificates for the six million Jews they'd murdered.

Peter was going to get the old woman what was due her. Dammit, he said, if a Hartman can't wrest this lady's money from the greedy paws of some Swiss banker, who can?

No one was as stubborn as Peter. No one except Old Max, maybe.

Ben had little doubt Peter had won the battle.

He began to feel weary. The highway had become monotonous, lulling. His driving had fallen naturally into the rhythm of the road, and other cars no longer seemed to be trying to pass him quite so often. His eyelids began to droop.

There came a blaring car horn, and he was dazzled by headlights. With a jolt he realized that he'd momentarily fallen asleep behind the wheel. He reacted quickly, spinning the car to the right, swerving out of the oncoming lane of traffic, just barely missing a collision.

He pulled over to the side of the road, his heart pounding. He let out a long, relieved sigh. It was the jet lag, his body still on New York time, the length of the day, the madness at the Bahnhofplatz finally catching up with him.

It was time to get off the highway. St. Moritz was maybe a couple of hours away, but he didn't dare risk driving any longer. He had to find a place to spend the night.

Two cars passed by, though Ben did not see them.

One was a green Audi, battered and rusty, almost ten years old. Its driver and sole occupant, a tall man of around fifty with long gray hair pulled back in a ponytail, turned to inspect Ben's car, parked on the side of the road.

When the Audi had traveled about a hundred meters beyond Ben's car, it, too, pulled over to the shoulder.

Then a second car passed Ben's Opel: a gray sedan with two men inside. *"Glaubst Du, er hat uns entdeckt?"* the driver asked the passenger in Swiss-German. You think he's spotted us?

"It's possible," the passenger replied. "Why else would he have stopped?"

"He could be lost. He is looking at a map."

"That could be a ruse. I'm going to pull over."

The driver noticed the green Audi at the side of the road. "Are we expecting company?" he asked.

CHAPTER SIX

Halifax, Nova Scotia

The next morning Anna and Sergeant Arsenault drove up to the house belonging to Robert Mailhot's widow and rang the bell.

The widow opened the front door a suspicious few inches and stared out at them from the dark of her front hall. She was a small woman of seventy-nine with snow-white hair in a neat bouffant, a large, round head, an open face but wary brown eyes. Her wide flat nose was red, evidence either of weeping or booze.

"Yes?" She was, unsurprisingly, hostile.

"Mrs. Mailhot, I'm Ron Arsenault from the RCMP, and this is Anna Navarro from the United States Department of Justice." Arsenault spoke with a surprising tenderness. "We wanted to ask you some questions. Could we come in?"

"Why?"

"We have some questions, that's all."

The widow's small brown eyes shone fiercely. "I'm not talking to any police. My husband's dead. Why don't you just leave me *alone*?"

Anna sensed the desperation in the old woman's voice. Her maiden name, according to the documents, was Marie LeBlanc, and she was just about eight years younger than her husband. She didn't have to talk with them, though she probably didn't know that. Everything now turned on the dance of persuasion.

Anna hated dealing with the families of murder victims. Pestering them with questions at such a terrible time, days or even hours after the death of a loved one, was unbearable.

"Mrs. Mailhot," Arsenault said in an official voice, "we have reason to believe someone may have killed your husband."

The widow stared at them for a moment. "That's ridiculous," she said. The space between front door and jamb narrowed.

"You may be right," Anna said softly. "But if anyone did anything to him, we want to know about it."

The widow hesitated. After a moment, she scoffed, "He was old. He had a bad heart. Leave me alone."

She felt sorry for the old woman, having to undergo interrogation at such a terrible time. But the widow could kick them out any minute, and she couldn't allow that to happen. In a gentle voice she said, "Your husband could have lived longer than he did. You two could have had more time together. We think someone may have taken that away from you. Something no one had the right to take. If anyone did that to you, we want to find out who it was."

The widow's stare seemed to relent.

"Without your help, we'll never know who took your husband from you."

Slowly the space widened and the screen door came open.

The front parlor was dark. Mrs. Mailhot switched on a lamp, which cast a sulfurous light. She was wide-hipped and even shorter than she had first appeared to be. She wore a neat gray pleated skirt and an ivory fisherman's sweater.

The room was gloomy but immaculate, and it smelled of lemon oil. Recently cleaned—perhaps because Mrs. Mailhot expected relatives at her husband's funeral. Hair and fiber would be a problem. The "crime scene," such as it was, was not exactly preserved.

The room, Anna noticed, was furnished with great attention to detail. Lace doilies adorned the arms of the tweedy sofa and armchairs. All the white fringed silk lampshades matched. On little end tables silver-framed photographs were placed just so. One of them was a black-and-white wedding picture: a plain, vulnerable-looking bride, the groom dark-haired, sharp-featured, proud.

Atop the walnut television cabinet was a line of identical little ivory elephant figurines. Tacky, yet touching.

"Oh, aren't those *exquisite*," Anna said, pointing the elephants out to Arsenault.

"Sure are," Arsenault said unconvincingly.

"Are they Lenox?" Anna asked.

The widow looked surprised, then gave a proud little smile. "You collect them?"

"My mother did." Her mother had neither the time nor the money to collect anything except her meager paychecks.

The old woman gestured. "Please sit down."

Anna took a seat on the couch, Arsenault in the adjoining arm-chair. She remembered this was the room in which Mailhot had been found dead.

Mrs. Mailhot sat in an uncomfortable-looking ladder-back chair all the way across the room. "I wasn't here when my husband died," she said sadly. "I was visiting my sister like I do every Tuesday night. I just feel so terrible he died without me here."

Anna nodded sympathetically. "Maybe we can talk a little about the way he passed . . ."

"He died from heart failure," she said. "The doctor told me that."

"And he may have," Anna said. "But sometimes a person can be killed in such a way that it doesn't look like murder."

"Why would anyone want to kill Robert?"

Arsenault gave Anna a quick, almost undetectable glance. There was something about the woman's intonation: it wasn't a rhetorical question. She sounded as if she really wanted to know. The approach they took now would be crucial. The two had been married since 1951—half a century together. She surely had some inkling of whatever it was, if any-thing, that her husband might have been involved in.

"You two retired here a few years ago, is that right?"

"Yes," the old woman said. "What does this have to do with his death?"

"You lived on your husband's pension?"

Mrs. Mailhot raised her chin defiantly. "Robert took care of the money. He told me never to worry about those things."

"But did he ever tell you where the money was coming from?"

"I told you, Robert took care of everything."

"Did your husband tell you that he had one point five million dollars in the bank?"

"We can show you the bank records if you'd like," Arsenault put in.

The old widow's eyes betrayed nothing. "I told you, I know very little about our finances."

"He never talked to you about receiving money from anyone?" Arsen-ault asked.

"Mr. Highsmith was a generous man," she said slowly. "He never for-got the little people. The people who had helped him."

"These were payments from Charles Highsmith?" Arsenault prompted. Charles Highsmith was a famous, some would say notorious, media baron. With holdings even more extensive than his competitor Conrad

Black's, he owned newspapers, radio stations, and cable companies across North America. Three years ago, Highsmith had died, evidently having fallen overboard from his yacht, although the precise circumstances of the incident remained a matter of some controversy.

The widow nodded. "My husband was in his employ for most of his life."

"But Charles Highsmith died three years ago," Arsenault said.

"He must have left instructions for his estate. My husband didn't explain such things to me. Mr. Highsmith made sure we always had enough. That's the kind of man he was."

"And what did your husband do to inspire such loyalty?" Anna asked.

"There's no secret about that," the widow replied.

"Until he retired fifteen years ago, he worked for him as a bodyguard," Arsenault said. "And factotum. Someone who did special errands."

"He was a man Mr. Highsmith could trust implicitly," the old woman said, as if echoing an overheard accolade.

"You moved here from Toronto right after Charles Highsmith's death," Anna said, glancing at her file.

"My husband . . . had certain ideas."

"About Highsmith's death?"

The old woman spoke with obvious reluctance. "Like many people, he wondered about it. About whether it was an accident. Of course, Robert was retired by that point, but he still consulted on security. Sometimes he blamed himself for what happened. I think that's why he was a little . . . funny about it. He convinced himself that if it wasn't an accident, then maybe Highsmith's enemies would come after him one day. It sounds crazy. But you understand, he was my husband. I never questioned his decisions."

"That's why you moved here," Anna said, half to herself. After decades in major cities like London and Toronto, her husband had rusticated himself—had, in fact, gone into hiding. He moved to the place his ancestors and hers had once made a home, a place where they knew all the neighbors, a place that seemed safe, where they could keep a low profile.

Mrs. Mailhot was silent. "I never really believed it. My husband had his suspicions, that was all. As he aged, he became more anxious. Some men are like that."

"You thought it was an eccentricity of his."

"We all have our eccentricities."

"And what do you think now?" Anna said gently.

"Now I don't know what to think." The old woman's eyes grew moist.

"Do you know where he kept his financial records?"

"There are checkbooks and all that sort of thing in a box upstairs." She shrugged. "You can look if you want."

"Thank you," Anna said. "We need to go through with you the last week or so of your husband's life," Anna said. "In detail. His habits, where he went, any place he traveled. Any calls he might have placed or received. Any letters he got. Any restaurants you went to. Any repairmen or workers who might have come to the house—plumbers, telephone repairmen, carpet cleaners, meter readers. Anything you can think of."

They interviewed her for the next two hours, stopping only to use the toilet. Even when it was clear the widow was becoming weary, they forged ahead, determined to push her as hard as she'd let them. Anna knew that if they were to stop and ask to come back in the morning, she might change her mind in the meantime about speaking to them. She might speak to a friend, a lawyer. She might tell them to go to hell.

But two hours later they knew little more than when they began. The widow gave them permission to inspect the house, but they found no signs of forced entry at the front door or any of the windows. Likely the killer—if indeed the old man *had* been murdered—got into the house by means of subterfuge, or was an acquaintance.

Anna found an old Electrolux vacuum cleaner in a closet and removed the bag. It was full, which meant it probably hadn't been changed since Mailhot died. Good. She'd have the crime-scene people do a fresh-bag vacuum when they arrived. Maybe there would be some trace evidence after all.

Maybe they'd even turn up footprints, tire tracks. She would order elimination prints from the widow and anyone else who visited regularly, and have all the usual surfaces printed.

When they returned to the front parlor, Anna waited for the widow to sit and then chose a chair near her. "Mrs. Mailhot," she began delicately, "did your husband ever tell you *why* he thought Charles Highsmith might have been the victim of foul play?"

The widow looked at her a long time, as if deciding what to reveal. *"Les grands hommes ont leurs ennemis,"* she said at last, ominously. "Great men have great enemies."

"What do you mean by that?"

Mrs. Mailhot did not meet her gaze. "It's just something my husband used to say," she replied.

Switzerland

Ben took the first exit he came to.

The road went straight for a while, cutting through flat farmland, and then, after crossing over a set of train tracks, it began to twist through hilly terrain. Every twenty minutes or so, he'd pull over to consult his road map.

He was approaching Chur on the A3 highway, south of Bad Ragaz, when he began to focus on the dark blue Saab behind him. He didn't have the road to himself and he didn't expect to. Perhaps the Saab was carrying another lot of ski-happy vacationers. But there was something about the car, something about the way its pace seemed to synchronize with his. Ben pulled over to the side of the road, and the Saab drove right past him. There—he had been imagining things.

Now he resumed his drive. He was being paranoid, and after what he'd been through, who could blame him? He thought once more about Jimmy Cavanaugh, and then abruptly reeled his thoughts in: it filled him with vertigo, like staring into an abyss—a mystery piled upon a mystery. For his own sanity, he could not allow himself to dwell on it. There would be time to sort things out later. Right now, he needed *motion*.

Ten minutes later, images of carnage in the Shopville started to crowd his mind once more, and he reached for the radio dial to distract himself. Speed would help, too, he figured, and he stepped on the accelerator hard, felt the gears mesh smoothly and the car push faster up the sloping highway. He glanced at his rearview mirror and saw a blue Saab—the same blue Saab, he was certain. And as he accelerated, the Saab accelerated, too.

A knot formed in his stomach. At higher speeds, drivers intuitively leave greater distances between themselves and the next car, but the Saab had maintained precisely the same distance behind him as before. If it had wanted to pass him, it would have turned into the passing lane, which meant that its passengers had something else in mind. Ben peered in the rearview again, tried see through the other car's windshield, but it was hard to make out anything more than shadows. He could see only that there were two people in the front. *What the hell were they up to?* Now Ben fixed his attention on this road ahead of him. He wasn't going to let on that he was even aware of them.

But he had to lose them.

There would be plenty of opportunities in the tangle of roads around Chur; God knows he'd gotten lost there himself the last time he'd visited. Now he made a last-minute hairpin turn, veered onto the exit to the narrower Highway Number 3 going south toward St. Moritz. A few minutes later, the familiar blue Saab returned, perfectly centered in his rearview mirror. Driving too fast, Ben hurtled past Malix and Churwalden, making sharp ascents and sudden descents that made his stomach plunge. He turned onto poorly paved byways, taking them at speeds they weren't meant for, and the combination of the rough surfaces and the Opel's overstrained suspension system caused the car to shudder and jolt. Once, he could hear the car's chassis scrape loudly against a bulge in the pavement, and he saw sparks in the rearview mirror.

Had he shaken his pursuers? The Saab would disappear for long intervals, but never long enough. Time and again, it reappeared, as if linked to him by a strong invisible coil. Ben sped through a series of tunnels cut into gorge faces, past limestone cliffs and old stone bridges spanning deep ravines. He was driving recklessly, his mounting terror overcoming anything like caution; he had to count on his pursuer's prudence and sense of self-preservation. That was his only chance.

As he headed toward the narrow mouth of a tunnel, the Saab suddenly shot ahead of him and into the tunnel. Ben was puzzled: Had it been following another car all along? Only when Ben tried to emerge from the short tunnel did he see, in the yellowish mercury lights, what was happening.

Fifty feet ahead, the Saab was now parked laterally across the narrow road, blocking the egress.

Its driver, in a dark overcoat and hat, was holding up a hand, signaling him to halt. It was a barricade, a roadblock.

Then Ben became aware that another car was following from the rear. A gray Renault sedan. A car he'd caught glimpses of before without focusing on. One of *them*, whoever they were.

Think, dammit! They were trying to wedge him in, trap him inside the tunnel. *Oh, Christ!* He couldn't allow that to happen! Ordinary caution told him to slam on the brakes before hitting the barrier ahead, but

these weren't ordinary circumstances. Instead, following some mad impulse, Ben barreled ahead, flooring the gas pedal, his Opel sedan ram-
ming into the left side of the stationary two-door Saab. The Saab was a
sports car, built for speed, he knew, but it was probably eight hundred
pounds lighter, too. He saw the driver jump out of the way just before
the collision propelled the Saab to one side. The sudden deceleration
caused Ben to lurch forward against his straining seat belt and shoulder
strap, the taut fabric cutting into his flesh like bands of steel, but the
impact had cleared just enough room for him to scrape through, with a
horrifying scrape of metal against metal. The car he was driving—its
front end partly crumpled, viciously banged up—no longer resembled
the gleaming model he'd rented, but the wheels still turned, and he
roared ahead down the road, not daring to look back.

From behind him, he heard an explosion of gunfire. *Oh, dear Christ!
It wasn't over. It would never be over!*

Galvanized by a fresh surge of adrenaline, Ben found his every sense
gaining laser-like focus. The old gray Renault, the one that had come
up from behind him in the tunnel, had somehow made its way through
the wreckage, too. In his rearview, Ben could see a weapon thrust
through the passenger's side window, *aiming* at him. It was a submachine
gun, and, seconds later, it began firing off a nonstop fusillade of automatic fire.

Move!

Ben sped down an old stone bridge spanning a gorge so narrow there
was barely room for traffic in either direction. Suddenly there came a
hollow pop, an explosion of glass a few feet away. His rearview mirror
had been shot out; bullets spiderwebbed the rear windshield. They knew
exactly what they were doing, and soon he would be dead.

There was a muted explosion, like a dull popping noise, and the car
suddenly lurched to the left: one of his tires had blown out.

They were firing at his tires. Trying to disable him. Ben remembered
the security expert who'd lectured the senior executives at Hartman Capital Management about kidnapping risks in third-world countries, drilling them on a list of recommended countermeasures. They seemed
laughably inadequate to the reality, then as now. *Don't get out of the car*
was one of the pointers, he remembered. It wasn't clear he was going to
have much of a choice.

Just then, he heard the unmistakable wail of a police siren. Through a jagged hole in the opaque rear windshield, he saw that a third vehicle was coming up fast from behind the gray sedan, this one a civilian unmarked car with a flashing blue light on its roof. That was all he could see: it was too far away to make out the model. Confusion filled Ben's mind again, but abruptly the gunfire ceased.

He watched as the gray sedan made a sudden 180-degree turn over the shoulder of the road, zooming back on the narrow embankment and taking off past the police car. The Renault, his pursuers inside, had gotten away!

Ben brought his car to a halt just after the stone bridge, lolling his head back in his shock and exhaustion, waiting for the *Polizei* to arrive. A minute went by, and then another. He craned his neck back to the lethal stretch of road.

But the police car was gone now, too. The crumpled Saab had been abandoned.

He was alone, the only sound the ticking of his car's engines, and the hammering of his own heart. He pulled his Nokia from his pocket, remembered his conversation with Schmid, and made a decision. *They can lock you up for twenty-four hours without any cause*, Howie had told him. Schmid had made it clear that he was looking for an excuse to do just that. He would put off calling the *Polizei*. He couldn't think straight anymore.

As the adrenaline ebbed, panic gave way to a sense of profound depletion. He badly needed to rest. He needed to refuel, to take stock.

He drove his ruined Opel, the engine straining, the shredded tires making for a bone-jarring ride, a few miles up a hilly road to the nearest town, although really it was a village, a *Dorf*. Its narrow streets were lined with ancient stone buildings, progressing from tiny dilapidated structures to larger, half-timbered houses. A few lights were on, but most of the windows were dark. The street was unevenly paved, and the car's undercarriage, now low to the ground, regularly bumped and scraped against the cobblestone.

The narrow road became a main street soon enough, lined now with great gabled stone houses and rows of slate-shingled buildings. Now he came to a large cobblestoned square, marked RATHAUSPLATZ, dominated by an ancient Gothic cathedral. At the center of the square was a stone fountain. He appeared to be in a seventeenth-century village built upon much older ruins, its buildings a peculiar hodgepodge of architectural styles.

Across the town square from the cathedral was a seventeenth-century manor house with crow-stepped gables, marked with a small wooden sign identifying it as the *Altes Gebäude*, the Old Building, though it looked newer than most of the other buildings in town. Lights blazed from its small-mullioned windows. It was a tavern, a place to get food and drink, to sit and rest and *think*. He parked his wreck alongside an old farm truck, where it would be largely concealed from view, and went in, his trembling, twitching legs barely supporting his weight.

Inside, the place was warm and cozy, lit by a flickering fire in an immense stone hearth. It smelled of wood smoke and fried onions and roasted meats, wonderful and inviting. It looked like a traditional Swiss *Stübli*, an old-style restaurant. One round wooden table was obviously the *Stammtisch*, the place reserved for the regulars who came in every day to drink beer and play cards for hours. Five or six men, mostly farmers or laborers, regarded him with hostile suspicion, then went back to their cards. Sprinkled throughout the room were others having dinner or drinking.

Ben realized only now how famished he was. He looked around for a waiter or waitress, saw none, and sat down at an empty table. When a waiter arrived, a small round man of early middle age, Ben ordered something typically Swiss, heavy and reliable: *Rösti*, roasted potatoes, with *Geschnetzeltes*, or bits of veal in cream sauce, with a *Vierterl*, a quarter-liter carafe of local red wine. When the waiter returned ten minutes later, balancing several plates on his arm, Ben asked in English: "Where's a good place to spend the night?"

The waiter frowned and set down the dinner plates in silence. He moved aside the glass ashtray and the red *Altes Gebäude* matchbook, poured the deep red wine into a stemmed glass. "The Langasthof," he said, in a heavy Romansch accent. "It's the only place for twenty kilometers around."

While the waiter gave him directions, Ben tucked into his *Rösti*. They were brown and crisp, onion-tangy, delicious. He continued wolfing down his dinner, glancing through the partly fogged window at the small parking area outside. Another car was parked alongside his, obstructing his view. A green Audi.

Something twanged at the back of his mind.

Wasn't a green Audi behind him for a good stretch of A3 out of Zurich? He remembered having seen one, worrying whether he was being followed, dismissing it as a figment of an overactive imagination.

Turning his gaze, he thought he saw, in his peripheral vision, someone staring at him. Yet when his eyes swept the room, there was no one giving him so much as a casual glance. Ben set down his wineglass. *What I need is some black coffee*, he thought, *not more wine. I'm starting to see things that aren't there.*

Most of his dinner was gone, downed in record time. Now it sat heavily in his stomach, a leaden mass of greasy potatoes and cream sauce. He looked around for the waiter to order a strong coffee. Once again he got that creepy sensation of someone looking over at him, then looking away. He turned to his left, where most of the scarred wooden tables were empty, but a few people sat in dark booths, deep in shadow, next to a long, ornately carved wooden bar that was dark and unoccupied, the only object on its surface an old-fashioned white rotary-dial telephone. One man was sitting alone in a booth, drinking coffee and smoking, a middle-aged man in a worn brown leather bomber jacket with long graying hair pulled back into a ponytail. *I've seen him before*, Ben thought. *I know I've seen him before.* But where? Now the man casually brought an elbow to the table, leaned forward, and rested his head on the outstretched palm, the hand cradling the side of his face.

The gesture was too studied. The man was trying to hide his face, trying too hard to be casual about it.

Ben remembered a tall man in a business suit, sallow complexion, long gray hair worn in a ponytail. But from where? He had caught a quick glance of such a man, thinking in passing how ridiculous, how dated, a ponytail looked on a businessman. How . . . eighties.

The Bahnhofstrasse.

Ponytail man had been among the crowd milling around the pedestrian shopping district just before he spotted Jimmy Cavanaugh. Now he was certain of it. The man had been in the vicinity of the Hotel St. Gotthard; later, he'd followed Ben in a green Audi; now he was here, looking decidedly out of place.

Dear Christ, he's tailing me, too, Ben thought. *Since this afternoon, he's been watching me.* He felt his stomach tighten.

Who was he, and why was he here? If, like Jimmy Cavanaugh, he wanted to kill Ben—for whatever reason Cavanaugh had tried—why hadn't he done so already? There had been plenty of opportunities. Cavanaugh had pulled out a gun in broad daylight right on the Bahnhofstrasse. Why would Ponytail hesitate to fire at him in a mostly empty tavern?

He signaled the waiter, who bustled over with a questioning look. "Could I have a coffee?" Ben asked.

"Certainly, sir."

"And where's your rest room, your WC?"

The waiter pointed toward a dimly lit corner of the room, where a small corridor was barely visible. Ben pointed in that direction too, confirming the rest room's location in as broad a gesture as possible.

So Ponytail could see where he was going.

Ben slipped some money under his plate, pocketed one of the restaurant's matchbooks, got up slowly, and made his way toward the rest room. It was located just off the small corridor, on the other side of the dining room from the kitchen. Restaurant kitchens usually had service entrances from the outdoors, Ben knew, so they made good escape routes. And he didn't want Ponytail thinking he was trying to leave the restaurant through the kitchen. This rest room was small and windowless; he couldn't leave this way. Ponytail, presumably some sort of professional, would likely have already checked out the means of egress.

He locked the rest room door. There was an ancient toilet and equally ancient marble sink basin, and it smelled pleasantly of cleaning liquid. He pulled out his digital phone and dialed the telephone number of the *Altes Gebäude*. Ben could hear the faint sound of a telephone ringing somewhere in the restaurant. Probably the old rotary-dial phone he'd seen on the bar near Ponytail's booth, or one in the kitchen, if there was one there. Or both.

A man's voice answered, "*Altes Gebäude, guten Abend.*" Ben was fairly sure it was the waiter.

Making his voice deep and gravelly, Ben said, "I need to speak to one of your customers, please. Someone who's having dinner there tonight. It's urgent."

"*Ja?* Who is that?"

"Someone you probably don't know. Not a regular. It's a gentleman with long gray hair in a ponytail. He's probably wearing a leather jacket, he always does."

"Ah, yes, I think I know what you mean. A man of about fifty years?"

"Yes, that's the one. Can you please ask him to come to the phone. As I said, it's urgent. An emergency."

"Yes, at once, sir," the waiter said, responding to the tension Ben had put in his voice. He set the phone down.

Leaving the line open, Ben slipped his phone into the breast pocket of his sport coat, left the rest room, and returned to the dining room. Ponytail was no longer sitting at his booth. The telephone was at the bar, which was situated in such a way that it couldn't be seen from the entrance to the restaurant—Ben hadn't seen it until he was seated at his table—and no one standing or sitting at it could see either the entrance or the area of the restaurant roughly between the rest room and the entrance. Ben moved quickly to the entrance and out the door. He had bought himself maybe fifteen seconds during which he could leave, unseen by Ponytail, who was at the moment talking into the telephone's handset, hearing nothing but silence, wondering what had happened to the caller who had identified him so carefully.

Ben grabbed his bags from the ruined sedan and raced to the green Audi; a key was in the ignition, as if the driver had made preparations for a rapid getaway. Theft was probably unknown in this sleepy village, but there had to be a first time. Besides, Ben had a strong suspicion that Ponytail wasn't in a position to notify the police about his vehicle's disappearance. This way, he gained a working vehicle while depriving his pursuer of one. Ben leaped in and started it up. There was no sense in trying to be quiet now; Ponytail would hear the ignition of the engine. He threw the car into reverse, then, with a squeal of rubber, barreled over the cobblestoned expanse and, at top speed, out of the *Rathausplatz*.

Fifteen minutes later, he pulled up near a half-timbered stone building in a remote, wooded area off the small country road. A small sign in front read LANGASTHOF.

He tucked the car away discreetly behind a dense stand of pine trees and walked back to the front door of the guest house, where a small sign said EMPFANG, reception.

He rang the bell, and waited a few minutes before a light came on. It was midnight, and obviously he had awakened the proprietor.

An old man with a deeply lined face opened the door and, with a put-upon air, led Ben down a long, dark hall, switching on little wall sconce lights as he went, until he came to an oak-plank doorway marked 7. With an old skeleton key, he unlocked the door and switched on a small bulb, illuminating a snug room dominated by a double bed on which a white duvet was neatly folded. The diamond-patterned wallpaper was peeling.

"This is all we have," the proprietor said gruffly.

"It'll do."

"I'll put the heat on. It will take a good ten minutes."

A few minutes later, after he'd unpacked only what he needed for the night, Ben went into the bathroom to run the shower. The setup looked so alien, so complicated—four or five knobs and dials, a telephone-style hand-shower hanging on a hook—that Ben decided it wasn't worth it. He splashed cold water on his face, unwilling to wait for hot water to find its way through the pipes, brushed his teeth, and undressed.

The duvet was luxurious and lofty with goose down. He fell asleep almost immediately.

Some time later—hours, it seemed, though he couldn't be sure, since his travel alarm clock was still in his suitcase—he heard a noise.

He sat upright, his heart racing.

He heard it again. It was a soft but audible squeak, floorboards beneath the carpet. It came from near the doorway.

He reached over to the end table and grabbed the brass lamp at its base. With the other hand, he slowly yanked the cord out of its wall socket, freeing the lamp to be swung.

He swallowed hard. His heart hammered. He quietly swung his feet free of the duvet and over to the floor.

He lifted the lamp slowly, careful not to disturb anything else on the end table. When he had a good grip on it, he quietly, quietly, hoisted it up above his head.

And sprang suddenly off the bed.

A powerful arm reached out, grabbed at the lamp, wrenched it from his hands. Ben lunged toward the dark shape, turned his shoulder, and jammed it into the intruder's chest.

But in the same instant a foot swung out, catching Ben at the ankles, knocking him down. With all his strength, Ben tried to rear up and pummel his attacker with his elbows, but a knee rammed into his chest and his solar plexus, and the wind was knocked out of him. Before he had the chance to attempt another move, the intruder's hands shot forward, slamming Ben's shoulders down, pinning him to the floor. As soon as his breath came back, Ben let out a great bellow, but then a large hand clapped his mouth shut and Ben found himself looking into the haunted face of his brother.

"You're good," Peter said, "but I'm still better."

CHAPTER SEVEN

Asunción, Paraguay

The rich Corsican was dying.

He had been dying for three or four years, however, and probably had a good two years or more left in him.

He lived in a grand Spanish Mission-style villa in a wealthy suburb of Asunción, at the end of a long drive lined with palm trees, surrounded by acres of beautifully landscaped property.

Señor Prosperi's bedroom was on the second floor, and though it was flooded with light, it was so choked with medical equipment that it looked like an emergency room. His much younger wife, Consuela, had slept in her own bedroom for years.

When he opened his eyes this morning, he did not recognize the nurse.

"You're not the regular girl," he said, his voice a phlegm-laden croak.

"Your regular nurse is ill this morning," said the pleasant-looking blond young woman. She was standing at the side of his bed, doing something to his IV drip.

"Who sent you?" Marcel Prosperi demanded.

"The nursing agency," she replied. "Please calm down. It will do you no good to be upset." She turned the valve on the drip fully open.

"You people are always pumping me full of things," Señor Prosperi grumbled, but this was all he was able to get out before his eyes closed and he lost consciousness.

A few minutes later the substitute nurse checked his pulse at the wrist and found there was none. Casually she turned the IV valve back to its usual setting.

Then, her face suddenly contorted by grief, she ran to break the terrible news to the old man's widow.

Ben sat up on the carpeted floor, felt the blood drain from his head, then fell forward onto his knees.

He was overcome by vertigo, felt as if his head were spinning while his body was frozen, as if his head were disconnected from his body.

He was overcome by memories, of the funeral, of the burial ceremony at the small cemetery in Bedford. Of the rabbi chanting the Kaddish, the prayer for the dead: *Yisgadal v'yiskadash shmay rabbo* . . . Of the small wooden casket that held the remains, his father's composure suddenly cracking as the casket was lowered into the hole, crumpling to the ground, fists clenched, his hoarse wail.

Ben squeezed his eyes shut. The memories kept flooding his overloaded mind. The call in the middle of the night. Driving out to Westchester County to break the news to his parents. He couldn't do it over the phone. *Mom, Dad, I have some bad news about Peter.* A beat of silence; do I really have to go through this, what else is there to say? His father had been asleep in the immense bed, of course: it was four o'clock in the morning, an hour or so before the old man normally awoke.

His mother in her mechanized hospital bed in the adjoining room, the night nurse dozing on the couch.

Mom first. It seemed the right thing. Her love for her boys was uncomplicated, unconditional.

She whispered simply, *"What is it?"* and stared at Ben uncomprehending. She seemed to have been yanked from deep in a dream: disoriented, still half in the dream world. *I just got a call from Switzerland, Mom,* and Ben, kneeling, put a gentle hand on her soft cheek as if to cushion the blow.

Her long hoarse scream awakened Max, who lurched in, one hand outstretched. Ben wanted to hug him, but Dad had never encouraged such intimacy. His father's breath was fetid. His few strands of gray hair were matted, in wild disarray. *There's been an accident. Peter* . . . At times like these we speak in clichés and mind it not a bit. Clichés are comforting; they're well-worn grooves through which we can move easily, unthinkingly.

Max had at first reacted not at all as Ben had expected: the old man's expression was stern, his eyes flashed with anger, not grief; his mouth came open in an O. Then he shook his head slowly, closing his eyes, and tears coursed down his pale lined cheeks as he shook his head and then collapsed to the floor. Now he seemed vulnerable, small, defenseless. Not the powerful, formidable man in the perfectly tailored suits, always composed, always in control.

Max didn't go to comfort his wife. The two wept separately, islands of grief.

Now, like his father at the funeral, Ben squeezed his eyes shut, felt his extremities give out, unequal to the task of supporting him. He toppled forward, hands outstretched, touching his brother as he crumpled into his arms, feeling him to see if this phantasm were real.

Peter said, "Hey, bro'."

"Oh, my God," Ben whispered. "Oh, my God."

It was like seeing a ghost.

Ben took in a deep gulp of air, embraced his brother, and hugged him hard. "You bastard . . . You *bastard! . . .*"

"Is that the best you can do?" Peter asked.

Ben released the hold. *"What the hell—"*

But Peter's face was stern. "You have to get out of here. Get out of the country as fast as you can. Immediately."

Ben realized that his eyes were flooded with tears, which blurred his vision. "You bastard," he said.

"You have to get out of Switzerland. They tried to get me. Now they're after you, too."

"What the hell . . . ?" Ben repeated dully. "How could you . . . ? What kind of twisted, sick joke? Mom died . . . she didn't want to . . . You *killed her.*" Anger surged into his body, his veins and arteries, flushing his face. The two of them sat on the carpeted floor, staring at each other: an unconscious reenactment of their infancy, their toddler days, when they'd sit facing each other for hours, babbling in their invented language, the secret code no one else could understand. "What the hell was the *idea*?"

"You don't sound happy to see me, Benno," Peter said.

Peter was the only one who called him Benno. Ben rose to his feet, and Peter did the same.

It was always strange, looking into his twin brother's face: all he ever saw were the differences. How one of Peter's eyes was slightly larger than the other. The eyebrows that arched differently. The mouth wider than his, downwardly curved. The overall expression more serious, more dour. To Ben, Peter looked completely different. To anyone else the differences were microscopic.

He was almost bowled over by the sudden realization of how much he'd missed Peter, what a gaping wound his brother's absence had been.

He couldn't help thinking of Peter's absence as a form of bodily violence, a maiming.

For years, for all of their childhood, they had been adversaries, competitors, antagonists. Their father had brought them up that way. Max, fearing that wealth would make his boys soft, had sent them to just about every "character-building" wilderness school and camp there was—the survival course where you had to subsist for three days on water and grass; camps for rock-climbing and canoeing and kayaking. Whether Max intended to or not he pushed his two sons to compete against each other.

Only when the two were separated during high school did the competitiveness wane. The distance from each other, and from their parents, finally allowed the boys to break free of the struggle.

Peter said, "Let's get out of here. If you checked into this place under your own name, we're screwed."

Peter's pickup truck, a rusty Toyota, was caked with mud. The cabin was littered with trash, the seats stained and smelling of dog. It was hidden in a copse a hundred feet or so from the inn.

Ben told him about the horrific pursuit on the roadways near Chur. "But that's not all," he went on. "I think I was followed most of the way here by another guy. All the way from Zurich."

"A guy driving an Audi?" Peter asked, gunning the old Toyota's arthritic engine as he pulled onto the dark country road.

"Right."

"Fiftyish, long hair sort of tied back, kind of an old hippie?"

"That's the one."

"That's Dieter, my spotter. My antenna." He turned to Ben, smiled. "And my brother-in-law, sort of."

"Huh?"

"Liesl's older brother and protector. Only recently has he decided I'm good enough for his sister."

"Some surveillance expert. I picked up on him. Stole his car, too. And I'm an amateur."

Peter shrugged. He looked over his shoulder as he drove. "Don't underestimate Dieter. He did thirteen years in Swiss army counterintelligence in Geneva. And he wasn't trying to stay out of *your* sight. He was doing *counter*surveillance. It was just a precaution, once we'd learned that you'd arrived in the country. His job was to see if anyone was following you. To watch you, follow you, make sure you weren't killed or abducted. It wasn't a police car that saved your ass on Highway Number 3. Dieter put on the cop siren to fake them out. It was the only way. We're dealing with highly skilled professionals."

Ben sighed. " 'Highly skilled professionals.' *'They're* after you.' *'They.'* Who's *they?* Jesus!"

"Let's just say the Corporation." Peter was looking in the rearview mirror. "Who the hell *knows* who they really are."

Ben shook his head. "And I thought *I* was imagining things. You're out of your goddamned mind." He felt his face flush with anger. "You *bastard*, that accident . . . I always thought there was something fishy about it."

When Peter spoke after a moment, he seemed distracted, his words disjointed. "I was afraid you'd come to Switzerland. I've always had to be so careful. I think they were never really convinced I was dead."

"Will you *please* tell me what the hell is going on?" Ben exploded.

Peter looked straight ahead at the road. "I know it was a terrible thing to do, but I had no choice."

"Dad's never been the same since, you bastard, and Mom . . ."

Peter drove for a moment in silence. "I know about Mom. Don't . . ." His voice turned steely. "I really don't give a damn what happens to Max."

Surprised, Ben looked at his brother's face. "Well, you proved that, all right."

"It's you and Mom I felt . . . sick about. What I knew it would do to you two. You have no idea how much I wanted to contact you, tell you the truth. Tell you I was alive."

"Now do you want to tell me why?"

"I was trying to protect you, Benno. I would never have done it otherwise. If I thought they'd just kill me and that would be the end of it, I'd have gladly let them do it. But I knew they'd go after my family, too. Meaning you and Mom. Dad—as far as I'm concerned, Dad died to me four years ago."

Ben was at once thrilled to see Peter and furious at the deception, and he was finding it hard to think logically. "What are you talking about? Will you tell me a straight story already?"

Peter glanced over at what looked like a lodge set back from the road, a halogen light flooding its front entrance.

"What is it, five in the morning? But it looks like maybe someone's awake here." A light was on above the inn's front door.

He pulled the truck into a hidden clearing in the trees near the auberge and shut off the engine. The two men got out. The predawn morning was cold and quiet, with just the faint rustle of a small animal or bird from the woods behind the inn. Peter opened the front door, and they entered a small lobby. A reception desk was lit by a flickering fluorescent light, but no one was there. "The light's on, but nobody's home," Peter said. Ben smiled in appreciation: that was one of their father's favorite insults. He reached out to tap the small metal bell on the counter, but stopped when a door behind the counter opened, and a rotund woman emerged, cinching a bathrobe around her belly. She was scowling, blinking in the light, angry at being awakened. *"Ja?"*

Peter spoke quickly, fluidly in German. *"Es tut mir sehr leid Sie zu stören, aber wir hätten gerne Kaffee."* He was sorry to disturb her, but they wanted some coffee.

"Kaffee?" the old woman scowled. *"Sie haben mich geweckt, weil Sie Kaffee wollen?"* They'd woken her because they wanted coffee?

"Wir werden Sie für ihre Bemühungen bezahlen, Madame. Zwei Kaffee bitte. Wir werden uns einfach da, in Ihrem Esszimmer, hinsetzen." They would pay her for her trouble, Peter assured her. Two coffees. They'd simply like to sit in her dining room.

The disgruntled innkeeper shook her head as she hobbled over to a nook next to a small dark dining room, switched on the lights, and turned on a large red metal coffeemaker.

The dining room was small but comfortable. Several large curtainless windows, which in the daytime probably gave diners a beautiful view of the forest in which the auberge was nestled, were utterly black. Five or six round tables were covered with starched white tablecloths and already set for breakfast, with juice glasses and coffee cups and metal trays heaped with brown sugar cubes. Peter sat down at a table for two against the wall, near the window. Ben sat across from him. The innkeeper, foaming a pitcher of milk in her nook, was staring at the two of them, as people so often stared at identical twins.

Peter moved aside the plate and the silverware to make room for his elbows. "You remember when that whole thing erupted over the Swiss banks and Nazi gold?"

"I sure do." *So that's what this was about.*

"That was just before I moved here from Africa. I followed it pretty closely in the newspapers there—I guess I was particularly interested because of Dad's time in Dachau." There was a sardonic twist to his mouth now. "Anyway, a whole cottage industry suddenly sprang up. Lawyers and other shysters who got the bright idea to take advantage of elderly Holocaust survivors who were trying to track down their families' missing assets. I think I told you I read somewhere about an old woman in France, a survivor of the concentration camps. Turned out she'd been bilked of her entire life's savings by some French scumbag lawyer who said he had information about a dormant Swiss bank account belonging to her father. The lawyer needed money, though, up front, to do the investigative work, take on the Swiss bank, all that bullshit. Of course the old lady paid—an amount like twenty-five thousand dollars, her entire savings, money she needed to live on. The lawyer vanished, along with the twenty-five thousand. That got me worked up—I couldn't stand hearing about a defenseless old lady being taken advantage of that way— and I contacted her, offered to look for her father's Swiss account for free. She was understandably suspicious, having just been ripped off, but after we talked awhile she gave me permission to go ahead and look. I had to convince her I had no interest in her money."

Peter, who had been staring at the tablecloth as he spoke, now looked up directly at Ben. "Understand, these survivors weren't motivated by greed. They were seeking closure, justice, a connection to their dead parents, to the past. Money to get by on." He turned to glance at one of the windows. "Even as a legal representative of the old lady, I had all kinds of trouble dealing with the Swiss bank. They said they had no records of any such account. The usual story. These goddamned Swiss bankers—it's amazing, they're such anal-retentive record keepers, they keep every damned scrap of paper since time began, but now they're saying, Oops, they happened to lose a bank account. Uh huh, right. But then I heard about this security guard at the bank where the lady's father opened his account. The guard had gotten fired because he stumbled onto a shredding party—bank employees destroying heaps of documents from the forties in the middle of the night—and he rescued a pile of documents and ledgers from the shredder."

"I vaguely remember that," Ben said. The innkeeper came over with a tray and sullenly set down a metal pitcher of espresso and another one of steamed milk, then left the dining room.

"The Swiss authorities didn't like that. Violation of bank privacy, all kinds of sanctimonious bullshit. Never mind the shredding of documents. I tracked the guy down, outside of Geneva. He'd kept all the documents, even though the bank was trying to get them back, and he let me go through them to see if there was any record of the father's account."

"And?" Ben was tracing patterns on the white tablecloth with the tines of a fork.

"And nothing. I didn't find anything on it. Never did, by the way. But in one of the ledgers I found a piece of paper. Pretty eye-opening. It was a fully executed, legally valid, notarized and certified *Gründungsvertrag*—articles of incorporation."

Ben said nothing.

"In the waning years of the Second World War, some sort of corporation was established."

"Some sort of Nazi thing?"

"No. There were a few Nazis involved in it, but the majority of the principals weren't even German. We're talking about a board comprising some of the most powerful industrialists of the era. We're talking Italy, France, Germany, England, Spain, the U.S., Canada. Names you've heard of, even *you*, Benno. Some of the real big shots of world capitalism."

Ben tried to concentrate. "You said *before* the end of the war, right?"

"That's right. Early in 1945."

"*German* industrialists were founders of this corporation as well?"

Peter nodded. "It was a business partnership that cut clear across enemy lines. Does that surprise you?"

"But we were at war . . ."

"What do you mean 'we,' Kemosabe? The business of America is business, didn't anybody tell you?" Peter leaned back, his eyes bright. "I mean, let's just talk about what's on the public record. You had Standard Oil of New Jersey basically carving up the map with I. G. Farben, figuring out who'd get which oil and chemical monopolies, doing patent sharing, the whole thing. For God's sake, the entire war effort ran on juice from Standard Oil—it wasn't as if anyone in the military could afford to interfere. What if the company started having 'production problems'? Besides, John Foster Dulles himself had been a board member of Farben. Then there's the Ford Motor Company. All those five-ton military trucks that were the mainstay of German military transportation? Ford built those. The Hollerith machines that enabled Hitler to round up 'undesirables' with such incredible efficiency? All manufactured and serviced by Big Blue, good ol' IBM—hats off to Tom Watson. Oh, then there's ITT—a big stakeholder in Focke-Wulf, the company that made most of the German bombers. Want to hear something sweet? After the war was over, it sued the U.S. government for monetary compensation, given that Allied bombers had damaged those Focke-Wulf factories. I could go on and on. But that's just the stuff we know about, obviously a tiny fraction of what really went on. None of these characters gave a damn about Hitler. They owed their allegiance to a higher ideology: profit. To them, the war was like a Harvard-Yale football game—a momentary distraction from more serious matters, like the pursuit of the almighty dollar."

Ben shook his head slowly. "Sorry, bro'. Just listen to yourself. It all sounds like the usual counterculture rap: property is theft, never trust anyone over thirty—all that overheated, dated conspiracy crap. Next you're going to tell me they were responsible for Love Canal." He set his cup of coffee down sharply, and it clanked loudly against the saucer. "Funny, there was a time when anything having to do with business bored you stiff. I guess you really *have* changed."

"I don't expect you to take it in all at once," Peter said. "I'm just giving you the background. Context."

"Then tell me something real. Something *concrete*."

"There were twenty-three names on this list," his brother said, suddenly quiet. "For the most part, captains of industry, as they used to be called. A few blue-blooded statesmen, back when people thought there was such a thing. We're talking about people who shouldn't even have known each other—people any historian would swear never even *met*. And here they are, all linked together in some sort of business partnership."

"There's a step missing," Ben said, half to himself. "Obviously something drew your attention to this document. Something made you pull it out. What are you leaving out?"

Peter smiled mordantly, and the haunted look returned. "A name jumped out at me, Ben. The name of the treasurer."

Ben's scalp began to prickle, as if ants were swarming over it. "Who was it?"

"The treasurer of the corporation was a young financial whiz kid. An *Obersturmführer* in Hitler's SS, to boot. You may be familiar with the name: Max Hartman."

"Dad." Ben had to remember to breathe.

"He was no Holocaust survivor, Ben. *Our father was a goddamned Nazi.*"

CHAPTER EIGHT

Ben closed his eyes, inhaled deeply, and shook his head. "That's preposterous. Jews weren't members of the SS. The document's obviously a forgery."

"Believe me," Peter said quietly. "I've had plenty of time to study this document. It's no forgery."

"But then . . ."

"In April of 1945, our father was supposedly in Dachau, remember? Liberated by the U.S. Seventh Army at the end of April '45?"

"I don't remember the exact timing—is that right?"

"You were never very curious about Dad's background, were you?"

"Not really, no," Ben admitted.

Peter smiled grimly. "That's probably the way he preferred it. And lucky for you that you weren't. It's nice to live in a state of innocence. Believing all the lies. The story, the legend Dad created about the Holocaust survivor who came to America with ten bucks in his pocket and built a financial empire. Became a great philanthropist." He shook his head, snorted. "What a fraud he is. What a myth he created." With a sneer he added: "The great man."

Ben's heart began to pound slowly. Dad was difficult to get along with; his enemies called him ruthless. But a *fraud?*

"Max Hartman was a member of the *Schutzstaffel*," Peter repeated. "The SS, okay? File it under 'strange but true.' " Peter was so damned earnest, so convincing, and Ben never knew him to lie to his face. But this was so patently false! He wanted to scream, *Stop it!*

"What kind of corporation was it?"

Peter shook his head. "Possibly a front, a sort of dummy corporation, established with millions and millions of dollars in assets pooled by the principals."

"For what? To what *end?*"

"That I don't know, and the document doesn't specify."

"Where is this document?"

"I've got it hidden away safely, don't worry. This corporation, head-quartered in Zurich, Switzerland, in early April 1945, was called Sigma AG."

"And did you tell Dad you'd found this?"

Peter nodded and took his first sip of coffee. "I called him, read it aloud to him, asked him about it. He blew up, as I knew he would. Claimed the thing was a fake, like you did—as I knew he would. Got angry, defensive. Started shouting, screaming. How could I believe such slander? With all he'd been through, blah blah blah, how could I possibly believe such a lie? That sort of thing. I never expected to get anything out of him, but I wanted to gauge his reaction. So I started asking around. Looking into corporate records in Geneva, in Zurich. Trying to find out whatever happened to this firm. And then I was almost killed. Twice. The first time it was a 'car accident,' a near miss. A car swerving onto the pavement on the Limmatquai, where I was walking. The second time it was a 'mugging' on Niederdorfstrasse that was no mugging. I managed to escape both times, but then I was warned. If I persisted in digging around in things that were none of my business, next time I'd be killed. No more near misses. I was to hand over all pertinent documents. And if any of the details about this corporation got out, I'd be dead, along with everyone in our family. So don't think about phoning in a tip to the newspapers, they said. Dad I didn't care about, obviously. It was you and Mom I was protecting."

That sounded so much like Peter—he was no less fierce a protector of their mother than Ben had been. And he was levelheaded, not at all prone to paranoia. He *had* to be telling the truth.

"But why were they so concerned about what you knew?" Ben persisted. "Look at it objectively. A corporation was set up more than half a century ago. So *what?* Why the secrecy *now?*"

"We're talking about a joint partnership across enemy lines. We're talking about the risk of public exposure, and thus public disgrace, of some of the most powerful, revered figures of our time. But that's the least of it. Consider the nature of the enterprise. Mammoth corporations, Allied and Axis alike, establishing a joint entity in order to enrich all of them. Germany was blockaded at the time, but then, capital doesn't respect national boundaries, does it? Some people would call it trading with the enemy. Who knows what international laws might have been violated? What if there was some chance that the assets could be frozen or confiscated? There's no way of gauging the magnitude of those assets. A lot can happen in half a century. We could be talking about staggering sums of money. And even the Swiss have been known to waive the secrecy laws under international pressure. Obviously, some people came to the conclusion that I might just know enough to jeopardize their cozy arrangement."

" 'Some people'? Who was it who threatened you?"

Peter sighed. "Again, I wish I knew."

"Come on, Peter, if there's anyone else alive who was involved in setting up this corporation, they'd have to be ancient."

"Sure, most of the ones who were in high positions are gone. But some are still around, believe me. And some aren't all that old—in their seventies, even. If only two or three guys on the board of this company are still alive, they may be sitting on a fortune. And who knows who their successors might be? It's obvious they've got enough money to keep their secret buried, you know? By any means necessary."

"So you decided to disappear."

"They knew way too much about me. My daily schedule, the places I went, my unlisted home phone number, names and locations of family members. Financial, credit information. They were making a point, loud and clear, that they had extensive resources. So I made a decision, Benno. I had to die. They'd left me no other choice."

"No other *choice?* You could have given them their stupid document, agreed to their demands—moved on as if you'd never found the thing."

Peter grunted. "That's like trying to unring a bell, put the toothpaste back in the tube—can't be done. They were never going to let me live, now that I knew what I knew."

"So what was the purpose of the warning?"

"Keep me quiet while they determined how much I knew, whether I'd told anyone. Until they got rid of me."

Ben could hear the old woman moving about in the other room, the floorboards squeaking. After a while, he said, "How'd you do it, Peter? The death, I mean. It can't have been easy."

"It wasn't." Peter leaned back in his chair, resting the back of his head against the window. "I couldn't have done it without Liesl."

"Your girlfriend."

"Liesl's a wonderful, remarkable woman. My lover, my best friend. Ah, Ben, I never thought I'd be so lucky as to find someone like this. I hope someday you find someone even half as terrific as her. It was her idea, really. I'd have never been able to put the plan together. She agreed I had to disappear, and she insisted it had to be done right."

"But the dental records—I mean, Christ, Peter, they identified your body positively, beyond any doubt."

Peter shook his head. "They matched the body's teeth with the dental records back home in Westchester, the assumption being that those were really my dental X-rays in Dr. Merrill's office."

Ben shook his head, perplexed. "Whose body . . . ?"

"Liesl got the idea from the prank that the medical students at the University of Zurich pull almost every year at the end of the spring semester. Some joker always steals the cadaver from the gross anatomy class. It's sort of a morbid springtime ritual, medical-student humor— one day their cadaver just disappears. It's always reclaimed, sort of ransomed. Instead, she arranged to have an unclaimed body stolen from the hospital morgue. Then it was a simple matter to pull the dead guy's medical records, including dental records—this is Switzerland, everyone's documented."

Ben smiled in spite of himself. "But to switch the X-rays . . . ?"

"Let's just say I hired someone to do a simple, low-risk breaking-and-entering job. Dr. Merrill's office isn't exactly Fort Knox. One pair of films was substituted for another. No big deal. When the police came to him requesting my dental records, they got the substituted ones."

"And the plane crash?"

Peter explained, leaving out no significant detail.

Ben watched him as he spoke. Peter had always been soft-spoken, quiet, the deliberate, thoughtful one. But you'd never call him calculating or devious, and deviousness was what this plan had required. How frightened he must have been.

"A few weeks earlier, Liesl applied for a position at a small hospital in the canton of St. Gallen. Of course they were delighted to hire her—they needed a pediatrician. She found us a small cabin in the countryside, in the woods by a lake, and I joined her. I posed as her Canadian husband, a writer working on a book. All the while I maintained a network of contacts, my antennae."

"People who knew you were alive—that must have been risky."

"*Trusted* people who knew I was alive. Liesl's cousin is an attorney in Zurich. He was our listening post, our eyes and ears. She trusts him completely, and therefore so do I. An attorney with multiple international interests has his contacts in the police, in the banking community, among private investigators. Yesterday he learned about the bloodbath at the Bahnhofplatz, about a foreigner who was brought in for questioning. But as soon as Dieter had told me about the murder attempt on you, I realized what had happened. They, the inheritors, whoever on that list is still around, have probably always been suspicious that my death was faked. They've always been on the alert—either for my reappearance in Switzerland, or else for some sign that you were carrying on my investigations. I know for a fact that they've got a lot of Swiss policemen in their pocket, a bounty on my head. They practically *own* half the cops. I assume the bank where you had a meeting that morning, UBS, was the tripwire. So I had to come out of hiding to warn you."

Peter risked his life for me, Ben thought. He felt the sting of tears coming to his eyes. Then he remembered Jimmy Cavanaugh, the man who wasn't there. Hurriedly, he filled Peter in on the mystery.

"Incredible," Peter said, and he took on a faraway look.

"It's like they're trying to gaslight me. You do remember Jimmy Cavanaugh?"

"Of course. He spent Christmas with us at Bedford a couple of times. I liked the guy, too."

"What could he have had to do with the Corporation? Did they turn him, somehow, make every trace of his existence disappear at some point?"

"No," Peter said, "you're missing the point. Howie Rubin must have been right. There is no Jimmy Cavanaugh and there never was." He began speaking more quickly. "In a twisted way, there's a logic to this. Jimmy Cavanaugh—let's call him that, whatever his real name was—was never turned. He was working for them all along. Here's a kid who's older than the rest of the class, lives off campus, and before you know it, he's your asshole buddy. Don't you see, Benno? That was the plan. For whatever reason, they must have decided it was important to keep a close eye on you at that point. It was a matter of taking precautions."

"You're saying Cavanaugh was . . . *assigned* to me!"

"And probably somebody was assigned to me, too. Our dad was one of the principals. Did we learn something that might jeopardize the organization? Were we going to be a threat to them in some way? Did they need to worry about us? Maybe they needed to be sure. Until you went off to your ghetto and I went off to Africa—basically put ourselves out to pasture, as far as they were concerned."

Ben's mind reeled, and all this talk of *they* only made matters worse.

"Doesn't it make sense for a group of industrialists to bring in an operative, a killer, whose highly specific qualifications included knowing you by sight?"

"Hell, Peter, I suppose . . ."

"You *suppose?* Benno, if you think about it—"

The sound of shattering glass.

Ben gasped, saw the jagged hole that suddenly appeared in the windowpane. Peter seemed to bow his head, leaning forward deliberately onto the table in an oddly comic gesture, as if kowtowing exaggeratedly, genuflecting, giving a courtly salaam. In that same freeze-frame moment it was the expulsion of breath, the throaty *haaah*, that made no sense, until Ben saw the obscene crimson exit wound in the middle of Peter's forehead, the flecks of gray tissue and splinters of white bone fragments that sprayed over the table, on the plates and silverware.

"Oh, my *God!*" Ben keened. "*Oh, my God. Oh, my God.*" He toppled backward in his chair, tumbling to the floor, his head slamming against the hard oak floorboards. "*No,*" he moaned, barely aware of the volley of silenced gunfire exploding everywhere in the small dining room. "Oh no. Oh, my God." He was frozen, paralyzed by terror and shock and disbelief, so unfathomable was the horror in front of him, until some primitive signal of self-preservation emerged from deep within his hindbrain, propelling him to his feet.

Now he looked out of the shattered window, saw nothing but blackness, and then, illuminated by a muzzle flash preceding another gunshot, there was a face. The image lasted no longer than a split second, but it was emblazoned indelibly in his mind. The assassin's eyes were dark and deep-set, his face pale and unlined, the skin almost tight.

Ben leaped across the small dining room as, behind him, another windowpane shattered, another bullet pitted the plaster in the wall not a foot away.

The assassin was aiming at him now, that was clear. Or was it? Was he still aiming at Peter, this shot just wildly astray? Had he seen him, too? *Did* he see him?

As if in answer to his unspoken question, a bullet splintered the doorframe just inches from his head as he vaulted through it into the dark corridor that connected the dining room to the entrance area. From ahead, in the foyer, came a female shout, presumably the innkeeper yelling in anger or in fear; suddenly she loomed directly in his path, arms flailing.

He knocked her aside as he bounded into the foyer. The innkeeper squawked in protest.

He was barely thinking now, he was moving fast and frantically, dazed and numb and robotic, not having to think about what had just happened, not thinking about anything now except survival.

His eyes adjusting to the near-darkness—a small lamp in the far corner of the room, behind the reception counter, cast a tiny circle of light— he saw there was only the front door and another hallway that led to the guests' rooms.

A narrow staircase off the hallway, visible from here, led to more rooms upstairs. There was no window in the room he was now standing in, which meant it was a safe haven from incoming bullets, at least for a few seconds.

On the other hand, the lack of a window meant he was unable to see whether the shooter had run around to the front of the building. Peter's killer would have realized he had missed one of his targets, and so he'd have run either to the front *or* the back of the inn. Front entrance or back, unless there were others Ben didn't know about. That gave Ben a fifty-fifty chance of making it out through the front door.

Fifty-fifty.

Ben didn't like the odds.

And what if there were more than one of them?

If there were several, they'd have fanned out to stake out all entrances, all exits from the building. Either way, one or several killers out there, escaping through the front *or* the back was out of the question.

A scream issued from the dining room: the innkeeper had no doubt just discovered the sickening carnage.

Welcome to my world, madame.

From the floor above Ben could hear the heavy tread of footsteps. Other guests awakening.

Other guests: How many were staying here?

He rushed toward the front door, turned the heavy steel safety lock.

Rapid footfalls thundered from the staircase on the other side of the room, then a hulking figure of a fat man appeared at the foot of the stairs. He was wearing a blue bathrobe, looking as if it had been hastily thrown on. The man's face was fearful. *"Was geht hier vor?"* he cried.

"Call the police," Ben yelled back in English. *"Polizei*—telephone!" He pointed at the phone behind the reception desk.

"The police? What—is someone hurt?"

"Telephone!" Ben repeated angrily. "Go! Someone's been killed!"

Someone's been killed.

The fat man lurched forward clumsily as if he'd been pushed. He rushed to the reception desk, picked up the telephone, listened for a brief moment, then dialed.

The fat man was now speaking in German, loudly and quickly.

Where was the gunman—gunmen?—now? He'd burst inside and look for him and do to him what he'd done to Peter. There were other guests here, others who would get in the way ... but that wouldn't stop him, would it? He remembered the massacre in the Zurich arcade.

The fat Swiss hung up the phone. *"Sie sind unterwegs,"* he said. "Police—is coming."

"How far away are they?"

The man looked at him for a moment, then understood. "Just down the road," he said. "Very near. What happened—who was killed?"

"No one you know."

Again Ben pointed, this time toward the dining room, but the woman innkeeper burst through the doorway, shrieking, *"Er ist tot! Sie haben ihn erschossen! Dieser Mann dort draussen—Dein Bruder, er wurde ermordet!"* Somehow she'd concluded that Ben had killed his own brother. Insanity.

Ben felt his stomach turn over. He'd been in a haze, a deadened stupor, and suddenly the reality of it, the horror, was sinking in. The guest shouted something at her. Ben ran toward the hall that he guessed led to the rear of the house.

The woman was screaming at his back, but Ben kept running. The high caterwauling of a police siren joined the innkeeper's shrill hysteria, then grew louder as the police car came closer. It sounded like a single siren, a single car. But that was enough.

Stay or go?

They own half the cops, Peter had said.

He ran down the hall, turned sharply to the right, then saw a small painted wooden door. He flung it open: wooden shelves piled with linens.

The siren grew louder, now accompanied by the crunch of a car's wheels on gravel. The police were arriving at the front of the building.

Ben ran toward another wooden doorway at the end of the hall. A small louvered window next to it told him the door led to the outside. He turned the knob and pulled at the door. It stuck; he pulled again, harder, and this time it yielded and the door came open.

The area outside had to be safe by now: the police sirens would have scared the gunmen away. No one would be lurking in the dense woods back here for fear of getting caught. He leaped forward into the under-brush, his foot snagging on a vine, knocking him painfully to the ground.

Christ! he thought. *Must hurry.* The police had to be avoided at all costs. *They own half the cops.* He scrambled to his feet, lunged forward into the pitch-black.

The siren had gone silent, but now there were shouts, both female and male, the crunch of feet on the gravel. Running forward, he pushed branches away from his face, but still one scraped him, just missing an eye. He kept going, not slowing for a second, turning this way, juking that, through the close vegetation, the narrow tunnels, under canopies formed by interlaced branches. Something tore at his pants. His hands were scraped and bloodied. But he kept plowing through the trees, ma-chinelike, unthinking, until he came to the hidden clearing where Peter's truck was still parked.

He opened the driver's side door—unlocked, thank God—and of course there was no key in the ignition. He felt under the floor mat. Nothing. Under the seat. Nothing.

Panic overcame him. He inhaled sharply several times to try to calm himself. Of course, he thought. *I've forgotten what I know.*

He reached into the mess of wires beneath the dash, pulled them out to inspect the tangle by the weak overhead light. *Hot-wiring,* their beloved family groundskeeper, Arnie, had told him and Peter one summer morn-ing. *This is a skill you may never have a use for. But if you do, you'll sure be glad you got it.*

In a few moments he'd paired the two wires, and the ignition turned over, roared to life. Slamming the gearshift into reverse, he backed out of the clearing onto the dark road. No headlights in either direction. He shifted into drive; the old truck balked, but then lurched ahead, surging down the deserted highway.

CHAPTER NINE

Halifax, Nova Scotia

The next morning was cold and dreary. Fog had settled gloomily over the port, visibility no more than ten feet ahead.

Robert Mailhot lay on a steel examination table, clothed in a blue suit, his face and hands rosy with the funeral home's garish makeup. The face was bronze-tinted but heavily lined, angry, the thin mouth sunken, the nose a prominent beak. He looked to be five foot ten or eleven, which meant he'd probably been six feet tall as a young man.

The medical examiner was a corpulent, ruddy-faced man in his late fifties named Higgins: a thatch of white hair, small suspicious gray eyes. He was perfectly cordial, while at the same time guarded, neutral. He wore a green surgical gown. "So you've got reason to believe this was a homicide?" he said jovially, his eyes watchful. He was dubious and made no attempt to mask it.

Anna nodded.

Sergeant Arsenault, in a bright red sweater and jeans, was subdued. Both of them were rattled by their long and difficult interview with the widow. In the end, of course, she had given permission for the autopsy, saving them the headache of having to ask for a court order.

The hospital morgue reeked of formalin, which always made Anna uneasy. Classical music played tinnily from a portable radio on the stainless-steel counter.

"You're not expecting to find any trace evidence on the body, I hope," Higgins said.

"I assume the body was pretty thoroughly washed at the funeral home," she said. Did he think she was an idiot?

"What are we looking for, then?"

"I don't know. Puncture marks, bruises, wounds, cuts, scratches."

"Poison?"

"Could be."

She and Higgins and Arsenault together removed Mailhot's clothing, and then Higgins swabbed the body's hands and face clean of makeup, which could hide marks. The eyes had been sutured shut at the funeral home; Higgins cut the stitches and inspected for petechial hemorrhages— tiny pinpoints of blood under the skin—that might indicate strangulation.

"Any bruising inside the lips?" Anna asked.

The mouth, too, had been sutured closed. The medical examiner quickly sliced through the twine with a scalpel, then poked around inside the mouth with a latex-gloved finger. When someone is smothered with a pillow with enough pressure to stop the flow of air, Anna knew, you usually find bruises where the lips were forced against the teeth.

"Uh-uh," he said. "None that I can see."

All three began inspecting the shriveled body with magnifying glasses, inch by inch. With an old person this is difficult work: the skin is covered with dings and bruises, moles and broken capillaries, the marks and accretions of age.

They looked for needle marks in all the usual places: the back of the neck, between fingers and toes, the backs of the hands, the ankles, behind the ears. Around the nose and cheeks. Injection marks could be disguised with a scratch, but nothing turned up. Higgins even checked the scrotum, which was large and loose, the penis a tiny stub nestled on top. Pathologists rarely checked the scrotum. The guy was thorough.

They spent over an hour at it, then turned Mailhot over and did the same. Higgins took photographs of the body. For a long time no one spoke; there was just the staticky crackle of a clarinet, the lush swell of strings, the hum of refrigerators and other machinery. The formalin smell was unpleasant, but at least there was no smell of decay, for which Anna was thankful. Higgins checked the fingernails for tears or rips—did the deceased fight an assailant?—and scraped under the nails, putting the scrapings into small white envelopes.

"Nothing on the epidermis out of the ordinary, far as I can see," Higgins declared at last.

She was disappointed but not surprised. "Poison could have been ingested," she suggested.

"Well, it'll turn up in the tox," Higgins said.

"Maybe not," she said. "There's no blood."

"May be some," Higgins said. If they were lucky. Usually, when the funeral home prepared the body, the blood was completely removed except for small residual pockets, and replaced with embalming fluid. Methanol, ethanol, formaldehyde, dyes. It broke down certain compounds, poisons, rendering them untraceable. Maybe there'd be some urine remaining in the bladder.

He cut the usual Y-shaped incision from the shoulder down to the pelvis, then reached inside the thoracic cavity to remove the organs and weigh them. This was one of the aspects of an autopsy Anna found particularly repellent. She worked with death regularly, but there was a reason she hadn't become a pathologist.

Arsenault, looking pale, excused himself to get a cup of coffee.

"Can you take some samples of brain, some bile, kidney, heart, and so on?" she said.

Higgins smiled tartly: don't tell me my business.

"Sorry," she said.

"I'd wager we'll find arteriosclerosis," Higgins said.

"No doubt," she said. "The man was old. Is there a phone around here I can use?"

The pay phone was down the hall next to a vending machine that dispensed coffee, tea, and hot chocolate. The front of the machine was a large oversaturated color photograph of cups of hot chocolate and coffee, intended to look appetizing, but actually greenish and awful. As she dialed she could hear the buzz of the Stryker saw as Higgins cut through the rib cage.

Arthur Hammond, she knew, normally got to work early. He ran a poison-control center in Virginia and taught toxicology courses at a university. They'd met on a case and liked each other instantly. He was shy, spoke with an intermittent hesitation that hid an old stammer, rarely looked you in the eyes. Yet he had a wicked sense of humor. He was a scholar of poisons and poisonings back to the Dark Ages. Hammond was far better than anyone in the federal labs, better than any forensic pathologist, and certainly far more willing to help. He was not only brilliant but intuitive. From time to time she had brought him in as a paid consultant.

She caught him at home, on his way out the door, and explained.

"Where are you?" he asked.

"Uh, up north."

He gave a short nasal snort of amusement at her secrecy. "I see. Well, what can you tell me about the victims?"

"Old. How do you kill someone undetectably?"

A throaty chuckle. "Just break up with him, Anna. You don't have to kill him." This was his way of flirting.

"What about the old bolus of potassium chloride?" she said, politely ignoring his joke. "Stops the heart, right? Barely changes the body's over-all potassium level, so it's undetectable?"

"Was he on an IV?" Higgins asked.

"I don't think so. We didn't find any of the usual puncture marks."

"Then I doubt it. It's far too messy. If he wasn't on an IV, you'd have to inject it right into a vein, and you'd find blood spewed all over the place. Not to mention signs of a struggle."

She took notes in her tiny leather-bound notebook.

"It was sudden, right? So we can rule out long-term heavy metal poi-soning. Too gradual. Do you mind if I go get a cup of coffee?"

"Go ahead." She smiled to herself. He knew this stuff cold.

He returned in less than a minute. "Speaking of coffee," he said. "It's either something in their drink or their food, or else an injection."

"But we didn't find any puncture marks. And believe me, we went over that body carefully."

"If they used a 25-gauge needle you won't see it, probably. And there's always sux."

She knew he meant succinylcholine chloride, synthetic curare. "Think so?"

"Famous case back in '67 or '68—a doctor in Florida was convicted of murdering his wife with sux, which I'm sure you know is a skeletal muscle relaxant. You can't move, can't breathe. Looks like cardiac arrest. Famous trial, baffled forensic experts around the world."

She jotted a note.

"There's a long list of skeletal muscle relaxants, all with different prop-erties. Of course, you know, with old folks, anything can tip 'em over the edge. A little too much nitroglycerin will do it."

"Under the tongue, right?"

"Usually . . . But there's ampules of, say, amyl nitrite that could kill you if inhaled. Poppers. Or butyl nitrite. You get a major vasodilator response, drops their blood pressure, they keel over and die."

She wrote furiously.

"There's even Spanish fly," he said with a cackle. "Too much can kill you. I think it's called cantharidin."

"The guy was eighty-seven."

"All the more reason he might need an aphrodisiac."

"I don't want to think about that."

"Was he a smoker?"

"Don't know yet. I guess we'll see from the lungs. Why do you ask?"

"There's an interesting case I just worked on. Some old folks in South Africa. They were killed with nicotine."

"Nicotine?"

"You don't have to give that much."

"How?"

"It's a liquid. Bitter taste, but it can be disguised. Can also be injected. Death comes within minutes."

"In a smoker you can't tell, is that it?"

"You gotta be clever. I figured this out. The whole issue is the amount of nicotine in the blood versus its metabolites. What nicotine turns into after a while—"

"I know."

"In a smoker, you see a lot more of the metabolites than pure nicotine. If it's acute poisoning, you'll see a whole lot more nicotine and a lot less metabolites."

"What should I expect from the tox?"

"A normal toxicology screen is set up to detect drugs of abuse. Opiates, synthetic opiates, morphine, cocaine, LSD, Darvon. PCP, amphetamine. Benzodiazepines—Valium—and barbiturates. Sometimes tricyclic anti-depressants. Ask 'em to do the full tox screen plus all these others. Chloral hydrate's not on the screen, order that. Placidyl, an old sleeping drug. Screen for barbiturates, sleeping drugs. Fentanyl's extremely hard to detect. Organophosphates—insecticides. DMSO—dimethyl sulfoxide—used on horses. See what you come up with. I assume they're going to be doing G.C. Mass. Spec."

"I don't know. What's that?"

"Gas chromatography, mass spectrometry. It's the gold standard. How rural are you?"

"A city. Canada, actually."

"Oh, RCMP is good. Their crime labs are far better than ours, but don't quote me on that. Just make sure they check for anything in the local water or wells that might skew the tox. You said the body's embalmed, right? Have 'em get a sample of the embalming fluid and subtract it out. Ask 'em to do a full tox—blood, tissue, hair. Some proteins are fat soluble. Cocaine stores in the heart tissue, keep that in mind. The liver's a sponge."

"How long are all these tests going to take?"

"Weeks. Months."

"No way." Her exhilaration over talking with him suddenly waned. Now she was depressed.

"It's true. Then again, you might get lucky. Could be months, or it could be a day. But if you don't know exactly what poison you're looking for, odds are you're never going to find it."

"There's every evidence he died naturally," Higgins announced when she'd returned to the lab. "Cardiac arrhythmia, probably. Arteriosclerosis, of course. An old MI there."

Mailhot's face had been pulled down from the top of the scalp, like a latex mask. The top of his head was open, the pink ridges of brain visible. Anna thought she might be sick. She saw a lung on a hanging scale. "How heavy?" she asked, pointing.

He smiled in appreciation. "Light. Two hundred forty grams. Not congested."

"So he died quickly. We can rule out a CNS depressant."

"As I said, it looks like a heart attack." Higgins seemed to be running out of patience.

She told him what she wanted from the toxicology screen, reading off her notes. His eyes widened in disbelief. "Do you have any idea how costly this is going to be?"

She exhaled. "The U.S. government will pick up the cost, of course. I need to do this one thoroughly. If I don't find it now, it's likely I never will. Now I need to ask a favor."

He looked at her steadily. She sensed his annoyance.

"I'm going to ask you to flay the body."

"You're kidding me, aren't you?"

"I'm not."

"May I remind you, Agent Navarro, that the widow wants an open-casket funeral?"

"All they see are the hands and face, right?" To flay the body meant to remove all the skin, in large chunks so it could be sewn back together.

This enabled you to examine the subcutaneous skin. Sometimes this was the only way to discover injection marks. "Unless you object," she said. "I'm just a visiting fireman."

Higgins's face flushed. He turned to the body, jabbing in the scalpel a bit too violently, and began removing the skin.

Anna felt light-headed. Once again she was afraid she might be sick. She left the morgue and returned to the corridor in search of the rest room. Ron Arsenault approached, clutching a giant cup of take-out coffee. "Are we still slicing and dicing in there?" he asked, his good humor seemingly restored.

"Worse than ever. We're flaying the skin."

"You can't take it either?"

"I'm just using the little girl's room."

He looked skeptical. "No luck so far, I take it."

She shook her head, frowned.

He shook his head. "Don't you Yanks believe in old age?"

"I'll be right back," she said coolly.

She splashed her face with cold water from the sink, realizing too late that there were no paper towels here, only one of those hot-air hand dryers that never worked. She groaned, went to a stall, pulled a length of toilet paper off the roll, and blotted her face with the tissue, leaving white shreds here and there on her face. She looked in the mirror, noticed the dark circles under her eyes, flecked off the strings of toilet paper, reapplied her makeup and returned to Arsenault feeling refreshed.

"He's asking for you," Arsenault said, excited.

Higgins held up a leathery yellow sheet of skin about three inches square as if it were a trophy. "You're lucky I did the hands, too," he said. "I'm going to catch hell from the funeral-home director, but presumably they've got makeup they can cake on to cover the mending."

"What is it?" she asked, heartbeat accelerating.

"The back of the hand. The web of the thumb, the abductor pollucis. Take a look at this."

She came closer, as did Arsenault, but she saw nothing. Higgins pulled the magnifying glass from the examination table. "You see this little purplish-red flare, about half an inch long? Sort of flame-shaped?"

"Yeah?"

"There's your injection mark. Believe me, that's not where any nurse or doctor puts a syringe. You may have something, after all."

CHAPTER TEN

Bedford, New York

Max Hartman sat in his high-backed leather desk chair, in the book-lined library where he usually received visitors. It was strange, Ben thought, the way his father chose to sit behind the barrier of his immense leather-topped mahogany desk, even when meeting with his own son.

In the tall chair the old man, once tall and strong, looked wizened, almost gnomelike, surely not the effect he'd intended. Ben sat on a leather chair facing the desk.

"When you called, you sounded as if you had something you wanted to talk to me about," Max said.

He spoke with a refined mid-Atlantic accent, the German long submerged, barely detectable. As a young man recently arrived in America, Max Hartman had taken speech training and elocution lessons, as if he'd wanted to banish all traces of his past.

Ben peered at his father closely, trying to make sense of the man. *You were always an enigma to me. Distant, formidable, unknowable.* "I do," he said.

A stranger seeing Max Hartman for the first time would notice the large bald head, speckled with age spots, the prominent fleshy ears. The eyes, large and rheumy, grotesquely magnified behind the thick lenses of his horn-rimmed glasses. The jutting jaw, the nostrils permanently flared as if he were smelling a bad odor. Yet for all that age had wrought, it was evident that this was a man who'd once been quite handsome, even striking.

The old man was dressed, as he always was, in one of his bespoke suits, tailored for him on Savile Row, London. Today's was a splendid charcoal, with a crisp white shirt, his initials monogrammed on the breast pocket; a blue and gold rep tie, heavy gold cuff links. Ten in the morning on a Sunday, and Max was dressed for a board meeting.

It was funny how your perceptions were shaped by your history, Ben reflected. At times he could observe his father as he was now, old and fragile, yet at other moments he couldn't help seeing him through the eyes of an abashed child: powerful, intimidating.

The truth was, Ben and Peter had always been slightly afraid of their father, a little nervous around him. Max Hartman intimidated most people; why should his own sons be the exception? It took real effort to be Max's son, to love and understand him and feel tenderness toward him. It was like learning a complex foreign language, one that Peter couldn't, or wouldn't, learn.

Ben suddenly flashed on Peter's terrible, vindictive expression when he revealed what he'd discovered about Max. And then that image of Peter's face gave way to a flood of memories of his adored brother. He felt his throat constrict, his eyes fill with tears.

Don't think, he told himself. *Don't think of Peter. Here, in this house where we played hide-and-seek and pummeled each other, conspired in whispers in the middle of the night, screamed and laughed and cried.*

Peter's gone, and now you've got to hang in there for him too.

Ben had no idea how to begin, how to broach the subject. On the plane out of Basel he'd rehearsed how he was going to confront his father. Now he'd forgotten everything he'd planned to say. The one thing he'd resolved was not to tell him about Peter, about his reappearance, his murder. For what? Why torture the old man? As far as Max Hartman knew, Peter had been killed years ago. Why should he be told the truth now that Peter really was dead?

Anyway, confrontation wasn't Ben's style. He let his father talk business, ask about the accounts Ben was managing. Man, he thought, the old guy is still sharp. He tried to change the subject, but there really wasn't any easy or elegant way to say, By the way, Dad, were you a Nazi, if you don't mind my asking?

Finally, Ben took a stab at it: "I guess being in Switzerland made me realize how little I know about, about when you were in Germany..."

His father's eyes seemed to grow larger behind the magnifying lenses. He leaned forward. "Now, what inspires this sudden interest in family history?"

"Really, I think it was just being in Switzerland. It reminded me of Peter. This was the first time I'd been back there since his death."

His father looked down at his hands. "I don't dwell on the past, you know that. I never did. I only look ahead, not behind."

"But your time at Dachau—we've never talked about that."

"There's really nothing to say. I was brought there, I was fortunate enough to survive, I was liberated on April 29, 1945. I will never forget the date, but it's a part of my life I prefer to forget."

Ben inhaled, then launched in. He was keenly aware that his relationship with his father was about to be altered forever, the fabric about to be torn. "Your name isn't on the list of prisoners liberated by the Allies."

It was a bluff. He watched his father's reaction.

Max stared at Ben for a long moment, and then to Ben's surprise he smiled. "You must always be wary of historical documents. Lists thrown together at a time of enormous chaos. Names spelled wrong, names omitted. If my name is missing from some list compiled by some U.S. Army sergeant, so what?"

"But you weren't at Dachau, were you?" Ben asked quietly.

His father slowly swiveled his chair around, turning his back to Ben. His voice, when it came, was reedy, somehow distant. "What a strange thing to say."

Ben felt his stomach flutter. "But true, right?"

Max swiveled back around. His face was expressionless, blank, but a blush had appeared on his papery cheeks. "There are people who make a profession out of denying that the Holocaust ever happened. So-called historians, writers—they publish books and articles saying the whole thing was a fake, a conspiracy. That millions of Jews weren't murdered."

Ben found his heart thudding, his mouth dry. "You were a lieutenant in Hitler's SS. Your name is on a document—a document of incorporation listing members of a board of directors of a secret company. You were the treasurer."

When his father replied, it was in a terrible whisper. "I won't listen to this," he said.

"It's true, isn't it?"

"You have no idea what you're talking about."

"It's why you never spoke about Dachau. Because it was all a fiction. You were never there. You were a Nazi."

"How can you *say* such things?" the old man rasped. "How can you possibly believe this? How *dare* you insult me this way!"

"That document—it's in Switzerland. Articles of incorporation. The whole truth is there."

Max Hartman's eyes flashed. "Someone showed you a fraudulent document, designed to discredit me. And you, Benjamin, chose to believe it. The real question is why."

Ben could feel the room revolving around him slowly. *"Because Peter told me himself!"* he shouted. "Two days ago in Switzerland. He found a document! He found out the truth. Peter found out what you had done. He tried to protect us from it."

"Peter—?" Max gasped.

The expression of his father's face was terrible, but Ben forced himself to keep going.

"He told me about this corporation, who you really were. He was telling me everything when he was *shot dead.*"

The blood had drained from Max Hartman's face, the gnarled hand that rested on his desk visibly trembling.

"Peter was killed *before my eyes.*" And now Ben almost spat the words: "My brother, your son—another one of your victims."

"Lies!" his father shouted.

"No," Ben said. "The truth. Something you've kept from us all our lives."

Abruptly, Max's voice became hushed and cold, an arctic wind. "You speak of things you cannot possibly understand." He paused. "This conversation is over."

"I understand who *you* are," Ben said. "And it sickens me."

"Leave," Max Hartman shouted and he raised a quivering arm toward the door. Ben could picture that same arm raised in an SS salute, in a past that was distant but not distant enough. Never distant enough. And he recalled some writer's often quoted words: *The past isn't dead. It isn't even past.*

"Get out!" his father thundered. "Get out of this house!"

Washington, D.C.

The Air Canada flight from Nova Scotia arrived at Reagan National in the late afternoon. The taxi pulled up to Anna's Adams-Morgan apartment building just before six. It was already dark.

She loved coming home to her apartment. Her sanctuary. The only place where she felt utterly in charge. It was a small one-bedroom in a bad neighborhood, but it was her own perfectly realized world.

Now, as she got out of the elevator on her floor, she met her neighbor, Tom Bertone, who was heading down. Tom and his wife, Danielle, were both lawyers, both a little effusive, a little *too* neighborly, but pleasant enough. "Hey, Anna, I met your kid brother today," he said. "I guess he'd just gotten into town. Really nice guy." And the elevator doors closed behind him.

Brother?

She had no brother.

At the door to her apartment, she waited a long moment, trying to calm her racing heart. She fished out her gun, a government-issue 9 mm Sig-Sauer, holding it in one hand as she turned the key with the other. Her apartment was dark, and, recalling her early training, she went into standard E&S, evasion and search, tactics. That meant flattening yourself against a wall with a pistol drawn, then shifting to an orthogonal wall, and repeating the process. They drilled it into field agents with the training sets, but she never imagined she'd be doing it in her own apartment, her home, her *sanctuary*.

She closed the door behind her. Silence.

But there was *something*. A barely detectable odor of cigarettes, that was it. Too faint to be from an actual lighted cigarette; it had to be the residue from the clothing of someone who smoked.

Someone who had been in her apartment.

In the dim light provided by the streetlights outside, she could see something else: one of the drawers of her file cabinets was slightly ajar. She always kept them neatly shut. *Someone had been searching through her belongings.*

Her blood ran cold.

There was a draft from the bathroom: the window had been left open.

And then she heard a sound, quiet but not quiet enough: the almost inaudible squeak of a rubber-soled shoe on the bathroom tile.

The intruder was still there.

She flipped on the main overhead light, wheeled around in a crouch, her 9 mm drawn, the weight of it balanced in her two hands. She was grateful that it was a Sig factory short trigger, which fit her hands better than the standard model. The intruder wasn't visible, but the apartment was small and there weren't many places he could be. She straightened up and, adhering to the perimeter rule—*hug the walls*, the E&S instructors liked to say—she made her way toward the bedroom.

She felt the movement of air an instant before the gun was dislodged from her hands by a powerful kick from seemingly out of nowhere. Where had he come from? Behind the bureau? The filing cabinets? The gun clattered as it hit the sitting room floor. *Retrieve it, whatever you do.*

Abruptly she was slammed backward by another kick, and she sprawled against the bedroom door, her back hitting it with a dull thud. She froze in place as the man took a few steps back.

Except that he was hardly a man. He had the slender frame of an adolescent. As powerful as he was—sinewy muscles flexed under a tight black T-shirt—he looked no older than seventeen. *It didn't make sense.*

Slowly, carefully, she got to her feet and began moving, with feigned casualness, toward the oatmeal-colored sofa. The blue-gray butt of her Sig-Sauer protruded from under its plaited hem, just barely visible.

"Burglary's a real serious problem in this neighborhood, isn't it?" the man-boy said in a tone of rich irony. His glossy, black hair was cut short, his skin looked as if he'd only recently started to shave, and his features were small and regular. "The statistics are *shocking.*" He scarcely sounded like the typical delinquents who haunted Southeast Washington. If she had to guess, she'd say he wasn't a native of this country; she thought she detected a trace of an Irish brogue.

"There's nothing of value here." Anna tried to sound calm. "You must know that by now. Neither of us wants any trouble." She realized her hand was still numb from the blow. Keeping her gaze on him, she took another step toward the sofa. Trying for a light tone, she added, "Anyway, shouldn't you be in school or something?"

"Never send a man to do a boy's work," he replied agreeably. Suddenly he unleashed another roundhouse kick and she reeled backward against her small wooden bureau. The blow had landed squarely on her stomach, and she found herself gasping for breath.

"Did you know," the young intruder continued, "that as often as not it's the *owners* of handguns who are killed by them? Another statistic that bears thinking about. You really can't be too careful."

He wasn't a burglar, that much was obvious. He didn't *talk* like one either. But what was he after? She squeezed her eyes shut for a moment, mentally taking an inventory of her sparsely furnished apartment, her paltry belongings, the clothes, the lamps, the humidifier, the clothes . . . *the M26. Must try to find the M26!* No doubt he'd searched the place thoroughly, but this was an item whose function would not be obvious to those unfamiliar with it. "I'll get you money," she said loudly, and turned to the bureau, opening drawers. "I'll get you money," she repeated. Where had she kept the device? And would it still work? It had been at least two years. She found it in the large central drawer, next to several red cardboard boxes of checkbooks. "All right," she said, "here it is."

When she turned around to face him, she had the M26 Tasertron firmly in her grasp, switched it on, a high-pitched whine indicating that the device was fully charged.

"I want you to listen to me carefully," she said. "This is an M26 Taser, the most powerful one they make. Move away from me now, or I will use it. I don't care what kind of martial arts you know—twenty-five thousand volts will take the starch out of you."

The intruder's expression was blank, but he began to walk away from her, backing into the bathroom.

The instant the stun gun was activated, the cartridge would fire off the contactors, two fine conducting wires ending in quarter-inch needle points. The electricity discharged would be of a voltage sufficient to immobilize him for a spell, perhaps even knock him out.

She followed him toward the bathroom. He *was* inexperienced; by backing up into the small room, he had allowed himself to be cornered. A bad move, an amateurish slip. She switched the Taser on maximum; there was no point in taking any risks at this point. The device in her hand hummed and crackled. A blue arc of electricity played between two visible electrodes. She would aim for his midriff.

Suddenly she heard an unexpected sound, that of water running, the roar of the tap turned up full. *What the hell was he up to?* She lunged into the bathroom, aiming the Taser, and saw the man-child wheel around with something in his hands. Too late, she realized his gambit. It was the nozzle of her handheld shower, which propelled a drenching blast of water in her direction. Water that would ordinarily have been harmless. She dropped the primed M26 an instant too late. A bolt of electricity arced from it toward her drenched torso, a blue bolt of agony. As her major muscle groups spasmed, she collapsed to the floor, only the pain cutting through her dazed state.

"It's been a blast," the young man said tonelessly. "But I'm already running late. Catch you later." He winked, in a caricature of affection.

She watched, helpless, as he clambered out the bathroom window and disappeared down the fire escape.

By the time she was able to call the municipal police, she had verified that nothing was missing from the apartment. But that was the only question she'd been able to answer. The cops, when they arrived, asked the usual questions, debated whether to classify the incident as a home invasion or a burglary, and then seemed to run out of ideas. They'd do the crime-scene workup—they understood that she was some kind of fed, that she seemed to know what she was talking about. But it would take several hours. And in the meantime?

Anna glanced at her watch. Eight P.M. She called David Denneen's home number. "I'm sorry to bother you," she said, "but is that guest room of yours free? It seems my apartment has just turned into a crime scene."

"A crime . . . *Jesus*," Denneen said. "What happened?"

"I'll explain later. Sorry to spring this on you."

"Have you eaten yet? Come on over now. We'll set an extra place."

David and Ramon lived in a prewar apartment near Dupont Circle, a fifteen-minute cab drive away. It wasn't grand, but it was nicely appointed, with high ceilings and leaded windows. From the savory aromas she inhaled when she came in—chile, anise, cumin—she guessed that Ramon was cooking one of his moles.

Three years ago, Denneen was a junior agent under her command. He was a fast learner, did good work, and was responsible for several breaks; he'd tailed a White House special assistant to the Qatar Embassy, a lead that resulted in a major corruption investigation. She'd filed glowing reports in his personnel file, but soon she learned that Arliss Dupree, as the unit director, had been appending "fitness" evaluations of his own. They were vague but damning in intent: Denneen "wasn't government material." He "lacked the fortitude" expected of an OSI investigator, was "soft," "possibly unreliable," "flighty." His "attitude was problematic." All of it was nonsense, the bureaucratic camouflage of a visceral hostility, a reflexive prejudice.

Anna had become friends with both David and Ramon, had met them as a couple when she'd stopped in Kramerbooks, on Connecticut Avenue, and saw them shopping together. Ramon was a small, open-faced man with an easy smile, his white teeth dazzling against his dark complexion.

He worked as an administrator for the local Meals on Wheels program. He and Anna warmed to each other immediately; Ramon insisted that she dine with them that evening, as a spur-of-the-moment thing, and she agreed. It was a magical occasion, partly because of the excellence of Ramon's paella, partly because of the relaxed conversation and easy banter, none of which ever touched upon office matters; she envied them their easy intimacy and affection.

David, with his square jaw and sandy hair, was a tall, ruggedly handsome man, and Ramon noticed the way she looked at him. "I know what you're thinking," he confided to her at one point, when David was across the room with his back to them, fixing drinks. "You're thinking, 'What a waste.' "

Anna laughed. "It's crossed my mind," she said.

"All the girls say that." Ramon grinned. "Well, he ain't wasted on me."

A few weeks later, Anna had lunch with David and explained to him why he hadn't received a promotion from E-3 grade. On paper, he reported to Anna, but Anna reported to Dupree. "What would you like me to do?" Anna asked.

Denneen responded quietly, with less outrage than Anna felt on his behalf. "I don't want to make a big deal of this. I just want to do my work." He looked at her. "Truth? I want to get the hell out of Dupree's division. I happen to be interested in operations and strategy. I'm only E-3, so I can't arrange it. But you might be able to."

Anna pulled a few strings. It meant doing an end-run around Dupree, which didn't exactly endear her to OSI management. But it worked, and Denneen never forgot it.

Now she filled in Denneen about what had happened at her apartment, and between Ramon's chicken mole and a bottle of a velvety Rioja, she felt some of her tension ebb. Soon she found herself joking grimly about having been "trounced by a member of the Back Street Boys."

"You could have been killed," Denneen said solemnly, not for the first time.

"But I wasn't. Which proves that wasn't what he was after."

"And what might that have been?"

Anna just shook her head.

"Listen, Anna. I know you probably can't talk about it, but do you think there's any chance it has to do with your new assignment at ICU?

Old Alan Bartlett has kept so many secrets over the years, there's no telling what he's got you up against."

"*El diablo sabe más por viejo que por diablo,*" Ramón muttered. It was one of his mother's proverbs: The devil knows more because he is old than because he is the devil.

"Is it a coincidence?" Denneen persisted.

Anna looked at her wineglass and shrugged, wordlessly. Were others interested in the death of the people in the Sigma files? She couldn't think about this right now, and didn't want to.

"Have some more *carnitas,*" Ramón said helpfully.

The following morning at the M Street building, Anna was summoned to Bartlett's office the instant she arrived.

"What did you learn in Nova Scotia?" Bartlett asked, not wasting any time on social niceties this time.

She'd earlier decided against mentioning the intruder in her apartment; there was no reason to think it was related, and she worried, vaguely, that the episode would undermine his confidence in her. She told him about what was clearly relevant: the puncture mark in the old man's hand.

Bartlett nodded slowly. "What kind of poison did they use?"

"Haven't gotten the toxicology results back yet. It takes time. Always does. If they find something, they call you right away. If they don't, they keep testing and testing."

"But you really believe Mailhot might have been poisoned." Bartlett sounded nervous, as if uncertain whether this was good news or bad.

"I do," she said. "Then there's the money question. Four months ago the guy got a wire transfer of a million bucks."

Bartlett knit his brows. "From?"

"No idea. An account in the Cayman Islands. Then the trail disappears. Laundered."

Bartlett listened in perplexed silence.

She went on. "So I got the bank records going back ten years, and there it is, regular as clockwork. Every year Mailhot got a chunk of money, wired into his account. Steadily increasing amounts."

"A business partnership, perhaps?"

"According to his wife, these were payouts from a grateful employer."

"A very *generous* employer."

"A very rich one. And a very *dead* one. The old man spent most of his life working as a personal assistant to a wealthy press baron. A body-guard, a factotum, a lifelong gofer, best I can figure it."

"To whom?"

"Charles Highsmith." Anna watched Bartlett's reaction carefully. He nodded briskly; he'd already known this.

"The question, of course, is why the offshore payments," he said. "Why not a straightforward transfer from Highsmith's estate?"

Anna shrugged. "That's just one of many questions. I suppose one way to answer it is to trace the funds, see if they really did originate with Charles Highsmith's estate. I've done work before on laundered drug money. But I can't be optimistic."

Bartlett nodded. "What about the widow . . . ?"

"No help. She may be covering something up, but as far as I can tell, she didn't know much about her husband's business. Seemed to think he was in the grip of paranoia. Apparently, he was one of those who thought Highsmith's death might not have been an accident."

"Is that right?" Bartlett said, with a tincture of irony.

"And you're another one, aren't you? Obviously you knew about Highsmith's connection to Mailhot. Was there a Sigma file on him, too?"

"That's immaterial."

"Forgive me, but you'll have to let me be the judge of that. I have a sense that not much I'm reporting comes as news to you."

Bartlett nodded. "Highsmith was Sigma, yes. Both master and servant were, in this case. Highsmith seems to have placed great trust in Mailhot."

"And now the two are inseparable," Anna said grimly.

"You did superb work in Halifax," Bartlett said. "I hope you know that. I also hope you didn't unpack. It appears that we've got a fresh one."

"Where?"

"Paraguay. Asunción."

A fresh one. The words were, she had to admit, intriguing as well as chilling. At the same time, the Ghost's high-handed way with information filled her with frustration and a deep sense of unease. She studied the man's face, half-admiring its complete opacity. What precisely did he know? What wasn't he telling her?

And why?

CHAPTER ELEVEN

St. Gallen, Switzerland

Ben Hartman had spent the last two days traveling. From New York to Paris. From Paris to Strasbourg. At Strasbourg he had taken a short commuter flight to Mulhouse, France, near the borders of Germany and Switzerland. There he had hired a car to drive him to the regional Aéroport Basel-Mulhouse, very close to Basel.

But instead of crossing into Switzerland, which was the logical point of entry, he instead chartered a small plane to take him to Liechtenstein. Neither the charter operator nor the pilot had asked him any questions. Why would an apparently prosperous-looking international businessman be seeking to enter the duchy of Liechtenstein, one of the world's centers of money-laundering, in a manner that was undetectable, and frankly irregular, avoiding official border crossings? The code among them was understood: *don't ask.*

By the time he had arrived in Liechtenstein, it was almost one in the morning. He spent the night in a small pension outside Vaduz, and then set off in the morning to find a pilot who would be willing to cross the Swiss border, in such a way that his name would appear on no manifests or passenger lists.

In Liechtenstein, the plumage of an international businessman—the Kiton double-breasted suit, the Hermès tie, and the Charvet shirt—was protective coloration, nothing more. The duchy distinguished sharply among insiders and outsiders, among those who had something of value to offer and those who had not, among those who belonged and those who did not. It was emblematic of its clannishness that foreigners who sought to become citizens had to be approved by both the parliament and the prince.

Ben Hartman knew his way around places like these. In the past, that fact had filled him with moral unease, his permanent, ineradicable air of privilege burning like the mark of Cain. Now it was merely a tactical advantage to be exploited. Twenty kilometers south of Vaduz was an airstrip where businessmen with private jets and helicopters sometimes disembarked. There he had a conversation with a gruff, older member of the ground maintenance crew, referring to his requirements in terms that were both vague and unmistakable. A man of few words, he looked Ben over and scrawled a phone number on the back of a manifest ledger. Ben tipped him generously for the recommendation, though when he called the number, he reached a groggy-sounding man who begged off, saying he had another job today. He *did*, however, have a friend, Gaspar . . . Another call. It was afternoon before he finally met with Gaspar, a dyspeptic middle-aged man, who sized Ben up quickly and spelled out his exorbitant terms. In truth, the pilot made a handsome living flying businessmen over the border into Switzerland without leaving a trace in the computers. There were times when certain drug lords or African potentates or Middle Eastern operators needed to do some banking in both countries without the authorities watching. The pilot, who seemed to wear a perpetual sneer, assumed that Ben was up to something similar. Half an hour later, preparing for their departure, Gaspar had learned of a storm over St. Gallen and wanted to cancel the flight, but several more hundred-dollar bills had persuaded him otherwise.

As the light twin-engine propeller plane bounced through the turbulence over the eastern Alpine ranges, the taciturn pilot became almost voluble. "There's a saying where I come from. *Es ist besser reich zu leben, als reich zu sterben.*" He chuckled. "It's better to live rich than to die rich . . ."

"Just fly," Ben said dully.

He wondered whether his precautions were overly elaborate, but the truth was that he had no idea what the reach was of the people who had murdered his brother, or who had assigned the man he'd known as Jimmy Cavanaugh to try to kill him in Zurich. And he did not intend to make things easy for them.

In St. Gallen, Ben had hitched a ride with a farmer delivering vegetables to the markets and restaurants. The farmer surveyed him with bafflement; Ben explained that his car had broken down in the middle of nowhere. Later on, he rented a car and drove to the remote farming community of Mettlenberg. If the flight had been bumpy, the drive wasn't much better. The rain poured down, sheeting the windshield of the rented car. The car's wipers flicked back and forth quickly but uselessly, for the rain was too hard. It was late afternoon, and already it was

dark. Ben could barely see a few feet in front of him. It was probably
fortunate that the traffic in both directions on this small rural road was
heavy, inching along.

He was in a remote, sparsely populated area in the northeastern part
of Switzerland, in the canton of St. Gallen, not far from Lake Constance.
From time to time, when the rain momentarily abated, he was able to
see the large working farms on either side of the road. Herds of cattle,
flocks of sheep, acres of cultivated land. There were large primitive buildings containing stables and barns and evidently living quarters as well,
all under one large double-thatched roof. Beneath the eaves were wood-
piles stacked with geometric precision.

As he drove he experienced a whole range of emotions, from fear to
the deepest sadness to an almost violent anger. Now he was approaching
a cluster of buildings in what had to be the village of Mettlenberg. The
rain had slowed to a drizzle. Ben could see the ruins of a once fortified
medieval town. There was an old granary and an early sixteenth-century
church of St. Maria. There were picturesque, well-preserved stone houses
with decorated timber faces, gables, and half-hipped red roofs. It was
barely a village at all.

Peter had said that Liesl, his lover, had applied for an opening at a
small hospital here. He had checked; there was only one hospital for
kilometers around: the *Regionalspital Sankt Gallen Nord.*

A short distance past the "town center" was a relatively modern building of red brick, cheaply constructed, Ben guessed, in the 1960s. The
regional hospital. He found a Migros gasoline station where he parked
the car and made a call from the pay phone.

When the hospital switchboard operator answered, Ben said slowly, in
English, "I need to speak to the pediatrician. My child is ill." There
seemed little point in using his tourist German, since he wouldn't be
able to disguise his American accent, anyway, and a Swiss operator would
know English.

Peter had said that the hospital had hired Liesl because they "needed
a pediatrician," as if they had none other. Then again, maybe there were
others, but Ben doubted it, not in a hospital as small as this one.

"I will connect you with the, eh, the *Notfallstation,* sir. The emergency—"

"No," Ben interrupted quickly. "Not the emergency room. I need to
speak directly with the pediatrician. Is there more than one on staff?"

"Just one, sir, but the doctor is not in at this time."

Just one! Inwardly, Ben exulted; had he found her?

"Yes, a woman named Liesl-something, right?"

"No, sir. There is no Liesl on the staff here as far as I know. The pediatrician is Dr. Margarethe Hubli, but I tell you, she is not in the hospital. Let me connect—"

"I must be mistaken. That was the name I was given. Was there a doctor by the name of Liesl who left recently?"

"Not that I know of, sir."

Strike out.

He had a thought. There was a chance that Dr. Hubli would know Liesl, know who she was, where she had gone. This *had* to be the hospital where Liesl had gotten a job.

"Is there a number where I can reach Dr. Hubli?"

"I'm afraid I can't give out her home number, sir, but if you bring your child into the hospital—"

"Can you page her for me?"

"Yes, sir, I can do that."

"Thank you." He gave the number of the pay phone and a false name.

Five minutes later the phone rang.

"Mr. Peters?" a woman's voice asked in English.

"Thank you for calling, Doctor. I'm an American staying with friends here, and I'm trying to reach a doctor who I believe was on the staff of the regional hospital. I'm wondering whether you might know her—a woman named Liesl?"

There was a pause—*too* long a pause. "I don't know any Liesl," the pediatrician said.

Was she lying to protect Liesl? Or was he simply imagining it?

"Are you certain?" Ben persisted. "I was told there was a pediatrician named Liesl there, and it's urgent that I reach her. It's a family matter."

"What sort of 'family matter'?"

Bingo. She had to be protecting Liesl.

"It concerns her . . . her brother, Peter."

"Her—brother?" The pediatrician seemed confused.

"Tell her my name is Ben."

Another long silence passed.

"Where are you?" the woman asked.

Barely twenty minutes went by before a small red Renault pulled into the gas station.

A petite woman enrobed in a large military-green rain poncho, wearing mud-caked jeans and boots, got out tentatively before slamming the car door shut. She spotted him and approached. She was a real beauty, Ben could see. Not what he had expected, for some reason. Under the poncho hood he could see her short glossy dark brown hair. She had luminous blue eyes and a milky-white complexion. But her face was drawn, pinched: she looked scared.

"Thanks for coming," he said. "You obviously know Liesl. I'm her husband's twin brother."

She kept staring at him. "Good Lord," she breathed, "you look just like him. It's, it's like seeing a *ghost*." Her face, a mask of tension, suddenly crumpled. "Dear God," she gasped, breaking out in sobs, "he was so careful! So . . . many years . . ."

Ben looked at the doctor, confused.

"He didn't come back that night," she went on in a panicked rush. "I stayed up late, worried, terrified." She covered her face with her hands. "And then Dieter came by and told me what had happened . . ."

"Liesl," Ben breathed.

"Oh, *God!*" she wailed. "He was such a—such a good man. I loved him so much."

Ben wrapped his arms around her, sustaining her in a great hug of assurance, and he too felt his tears begin to flow.

Asunción, Paraguay

Anna was stopped at Customs by a fleshy-faced Paraguayan official in a short-sleeve blue shirt and tie. From his hair and complexion she could tell he was, like most Paraguayans, a mestizo, of mixed Spanish and Indian ancestry.

He sized her up, then tapped her carry-on bag, indicating that he wanted her to open it. He asked her a few questions in heavily accented English, then, glowering with apparent disappointment, waved her through.

She felt furtive, like a criminal casing a joint. Normal federal regulations required a visiting agent to check in with the local embassy, but she would do no such thing. The risk of a leak was too great. If trouble resulted, she'd deal with the protocol breach later.

She found a pay phone in the crowded airport lobby. It took her a minute or two to figure out how to use her calling card.

A message from Arliss Dupree, demanding to know when she would be returning to the OSI unit. And a message from Sergeant Arsenault of the RCMP. The toxicology results were in. He didn't say what they were.

When she reached RCMP headquarters in Ottawa, she was put on hold for a solid five minutes while they chased down Ron Arsenault.

"How're you doin' there, Anna?"

She could tell from his voice. "Nothing, huh?"

"I'm sorry." He didn't sound sorry. "I guess you wasted your time here."

"I don't think so." She tried to mask her disappointment. "The injection mark is significant. You mind if I talk to the toxicologist?"

He hesitated a moment. "I don't see why not, but it's not going to change anything."

"I'd just feel better about it."

"Hey, why not?" Arsenault gave her a Halifax number.

The airport was loud and chaotic. It was hard to hear the voice on the phone.

The toxicologist's name was Denis Weese. His voice was high and hoarse and ageless—he could have been in his sixties or in his twenties.

"We ran every single test you requested and then some," he said defensively.

She tried to imagine him: small and bald, she decided. "I'm grateful to you."

"They were extremely costly, you know."

"We're paying for them. But let me ask you this: Aren't there substances, toxins, that cross the blood-brain barrier, and then don't cross back?" Arthur Hammond, her poison expert, had suggested such a scenario in passing.

"I suppose there are."

"Which might be found only in the spinal fluid?"

"I wouldn't count on it, but it's possible." He was grudging: he didn't appreciate her theories.

She waited, and when he didn't go on, she asked the obvious: "How about a spinal tap?"

"Can't."

"Why not?"

"For one thing, it's just about impossible to do a spinal tap on a dead body. There's no pressure. It won't come out. For another, the body's gone."

"Buried?" She bit her lower lip. Damn.

"The funeral's this afternoon, I think. The body's been moved back to the funeral home. Burial's tomorrow morning."

"But you could go there, couldn't you?"

"Theoretically, but what for?"

"Isn't the eye—the ocular fluid—the same as the spinal fluid?"

"Yeah."

"You can draw *that*, can't you?"

A pause. "But you didn't order it."

"I just did," she said.

Mettlenberg, St. Gallen, Switzerland

Now Liesl had fallen silent. The tears, which had coursed down her cheeks, dampening her denim workshirt, were beginning to dry.

Of course it was she. How could he not have known?

They were sitting in the front seat of her car. Standing on the asphalt island of the gas station was too exposed, she said, after she'd regained her composure. Ben remembered sitting in the front seat of Peter's truck.

She looked ahead, through the windshield. There was only the sound of the occasional car roaring by, a truck's deep-throated horn.

At last she spoke. "It is not safe for you to be here."

"I took precautions."

"If anyone sees you with me—"

"They'll think it's Peter, your husband—"

"But if the people who killed him, who know he is dead, have somehow tracked me down—"

"If they'd tracked you down, you wouldn't be here," Ben said. "You'd be dead."

She was silent for a moment. Then: "How did you get here?"

He told her in detail about the private planes and cars, his circuitous route. He knew she would find his caution reassuring. She nodded appreciatively.

"I imagine those kinds of security precautions became second nature to you and Peter," he said. "Peter told me it was you who devised his fake death. That was brilliant."

"If it was so brilliant," she said mordantly, "they'd never have found him again."

"No. I blame myself for that. I should never have come to Switzerland, brought them out of the woodwork."

"But how could you have *known?* You didn't think Peter was *alive!*" She turned to face him.

Her skin was pale, almost translucent, her hair chestnut with golden highlights. She was slender, with perfect smallish breasts under a simple white blouse. She was extravagantly beautiful.

No wonder Peter had been willing to give up everything else in his life to spend it with her. Ben felt a powerful attraction, but he knew he would never act on it.

"You don't go by your real name," he said.

"Of course not. All of my friends here know me by another name. It's legally changed. Margarethe Hubli was the name of a great-aunt, actually. All they knew about Peter was that he was a boyfriend, a Canadian writer I was supporting. They knew him under a different name, too . . ."

Her words trailed off, and she fell silent, once again staring out the window. "He kept up some of his contacts, though, the ones he trusted. He called them his 'early warning system.' And then a few days ago, when he got a call telling him about the bloodbath at the Bahnhofstrasse . . . He understood what had happened. I begged him not to do anything. But no, he insisted on it! He said he had no choice." Her face had twisted into an expression of contempt, her voice a wail. Ben's heart was squeezed.

She went on in a small, choked voice, "He had to protect you. Persuade you to get out of the country. He had to save your life even if it meant putting his own in danger. Oh, God, I warned him not to go. I begged, *pleaded* with him."

Ben took her hand. "I'm so sorry." What could he say, really? That he was anguished beyond words that Peter had to die instead of himself?

That he wished it was the other way around? That he had loved Peter for far longer than she had?

She said softly, "I can't even claim his body, can I?"

"No. Neither of us can."

She swallowed. "Peter loved you so much, you know."

It was painful to hear. He winced. "We fought a lot. I guess it's like that law of physics, about how every action has an equal and opposite reaction."

"You two didn't just look alike, you *were* alike."

"Not really."

"Only a twin would say that."

"You don't know me. Temperamentally, emotionally, we were totally different."

"Maybe in the way that two snowflakes are different. They're still snowflakes."

Ben smiled appreciatively. "I'm not sure I'd call the two of us snowflakes. We were always too much trouble."

Something in that set her off again. Now she was weeping, her agony heartbreaking. "Oh, God, why did they have to kill him? For *what*? To what *end*? He would never talk, he was no fool!"

Ben waited patiently until she found some composure. "Peter told me he found a document, a list of names. Twenty-three names of high-ranking statesmen and industrialists. 'Companies you've heard of,' he said. He said it was an incorporation document, setting up some organization in Switzerland."

"Yes."

"You saw the document."

"I did."

"It seemed genuine to you?"

"From what I could tell, yes. All the markings, even the typewriting, looked like papers I've seen from the 1940s."

"Where is it now?"

She pursed her lips. "Just before we left Zurich for good, he opened a bank account. He said it was mostly for the vault the bank would rent him. He wanted to keep papers in it. I don't know for sure, but I'd guess he must have put it there."

"Is it possible he hid it at home, in your cabin?"

"No," she said quickly, "there is nothing hidden in our cabin."

Ben made a mental note of her reaction. "Did he leave a key to this vault?"

"No."

"If the account was in his name, wouldn't these, these bad guys have ways of learning about its existence?"

"That is why he didn't open it in his name. It's in the name of an attorney."

"Do you remember who?"

"Of course. My cousin, Dr. Matthias Deschner. Actually, he's my second cousin. A distant relative, distant enough that no one would connect him with us—with me. But he's a good man, a trustworthy man. His office is in Zurich, on St. Annagasse."

"You trust him."

"Totally. I trusted him with our lives, after all. He never betrayed us; he never would."

"If people today, people with influence and power and far-reaching contacts, are so desperate to get this document, it must be extremely important." Ben's mind abruptly filled with a horrific image of Peter's crumpled body gouting blood. His chest was so tight he couldn't breathe. He thought: *Peter was in the way, and they killed him.*

"They must be afraid their names will get out," she said.

"But which of them can be alive after all these years?"

"There are also the inheritors. Powerful men can have powerful successors."

"And some who aren't so powerful. There must be a weak link somewhere." Ben broke off. "It's *madness*, all of this. The idea that anyone would care about a corporation set up half a century ago—it just sounds *insane!*"

Liesl laughed, bitterly, without mirth. "It's all relative, isn't it, this question of what makes sense and what does not. How much of your own well-ordered life makes sense any longer?"

A week ago, he was spending his days in the "development" department of Hartman Capital Management, cultivating old clients and new prospects, flashing on his charm like high beams. It was no longer a world he could inhabit; so much of what he'd grown up knowing was a lie, part of a larger deception he could scarcely hope to penetrate. *Cavanaugh was assigned to you*, Peter had said. The Corporation—this

Sigma group, whatever it was—seemed to have operatives everywhere. Was that why his mother had been so insistent that he return to the family firm after Peter's death? Had she believed that he would be safer there, protected from dangers, from threats, from *truths* he could only begin to fathom?

"Did Peter ever learn anything more about this Sigma Corporation? About whether it had an ongoing existence?"

She pushed her hair back nervously, her bracelets jingling. "We learned very little that was concrete. So much remained conjecture. What we believe—*believed*—is that there are shadowy corporations and private fortunes that are devoted to erasing their origins. They're ruthless, these firms, as are the men funded by these companies. They're not troubled by such details as morality. Once they learned, somehow, that Peter had a paper that could reveal their involvement in Sigma, or that of their fathers—maybe expose these complicated corporate arrangements that were made during the war—once they learned this, they didn't hesitate to kill him. They will not hesitate to kill you, or me. Or anyone else who threatens to expose them or stop them, or who simply *knows* too much about their existence. But Peter also came to believe that these individuals had gathered together for larger purposes. To . . . orchestrate matters in the world at large."

"But when Peter and I spoke, he merely speculated that some of the old board members were protecting their own fortunes."

"If he had had time, he would have told you more of his theories."

"Did he ever talk about our father?"

She grimaced. "Only that he was a hypocrite and a world-class liar, that he was no Holocaust survivor. That he was actually a member of the SS." She added sardonically: "Apart from that, of course, Peter loved him."

He wondered whether the irony didn't conceal a kernel of truth. "Listen, Liesl, I need you to tell me how to get in touch with your cousin, the lawyer. Deschner—"

"Matthias Deschner. But for what?"

"You know why. To get the document."

"I said, for *what*?" She sounded bitter. "So you can be killed too?"

"No, Liesl. I don't plan to be killed."

"Then you must have some idea of why you must have this document that I can't possibly think of."

"Maybe so. I want to expose the killers."

He braced himself for an angry barrage, but was surprised when she answered quietly, serenely: "You wish to avenge his death."

"Yes."

Tears sprang to her eyes. Her mouth was contorted, twisted downward, as if to hold back another spell of weeping. "Yes," she said. "If you'll do it—if you're careful—as careful as you were in coming here—nothing would make me happier. Expose them, Ben. Make them pay." She pinched her nose between thumb and forefinger. "Now I must go home. I must say good-bye."

She seemed outwardly serene, but Ben could still detect the underlying fear. She was a strong and remarkable woman, a rock. *I'll do it for me and for you, too,* he thought.

"Good-bye, Liesl," Ben said, kissing her on the cheek.

"Good-bye, Ben," Liesl said as he got out of the car. She looked at him for a long time. "Yes, make them pay."

CHAPTER TWELVE

Asunción, Paraguay

The taxi from the airport was a rattling old Volkswagen Beetle, not as charming as it had first appeared. It seemed to have no muffler. They passed graceful Spanish colonial mansions before entering the traffic-choked downtown, tree-lined streets crowded with pedestrians, antique yellow trolley cars. There were more Mercedes-Benzes than she'd ever seen outside of Germany, many of them, she knew, stolen. Asunción seemed frozen in the 1940s. Time had passed it by.

Her hotel downtown was a small, shabby place on Colón. Her guidebook had awarded it three stars. Evidently, the guidebook's author had been paid off. The reception clerk warmed to her considerably when she began speaking to him in fluent Spanish.

Her room had high ceilings and peeling walls, and, since its windows opened on to the street, was incredibly loud. At least she had a private bathroom. But if you wanted to keep a low profile, you didn't stay where the gringos stayed.

She drank an *agua con gas* from the "honor bar," a minuscule refrigerator that barely cooled its contents, then called the number she'd been given for the *Comisaria Centrico*, the main police station.

This was no official contact. Captain Luis Bolgorio was a homicide investigator for the Paraguayan *policía* who had sought the American government's help by telephone on a few murder cases. Anna had obtained his name, outside channels, from a friend in the FBI. Bolgorio owed the U.S. government a few favors; that was the extent of his loyalty.

"You are in luck, Miss Navarro," Captain Bolgorio said when they spoke again. "The widow has agreed to see you, even though she's in mourning."

"Wonderful." They spoke in Spanish, the language of business; the everyday language here was Guaraní. "Thanks for your assistance."

"She's a wealthy and important lady. I hope you'll treat her with the greatest respect."

"Of course. The body . . . ?"

"This isn't my department, but I'll arrange for you to pay a visit to the police morgue."

"Excellent."

"The house is on the Avenida Mariscal López. Can you find your way there in a taxi, or do you need me to pick you up?"

"I can get a taxi."

"Very well. I'll have the records with me that you asked for. When shall we meet?"

She arranged with the concierge for a cab, then spent the next hour reading through the file on the "victim"—though she had difficulty thinking of such a criminal as a victim.

She knew that the manila file folder Alan Bartlett had provided her was probably all the information she was going to get. Captain Bolgorio was helping only because the occasional technological assistance he got from the U.S. government's NCAV bolstered his own success here, made him look good. One hundred percent quid pro quo. Bolgorio had arranged to have Prosperi's body held in the morgue.

According to Bartlett, Paraguay was notoriously uncooperative on extradition cases and had been a popular refuge for war criminals and other international fugitives for decades. Its odious and corrupt dictator, "President for life" General Alfredo Stroessner, had seen to it. There had been some hope for improvement after Stroessner was toppled in 1989. But no. Paraguay remained unreceptive to extradition requests.

So it was an ideal place of residence for an aging villain like Marcel Prosperi. A Corsican by birth, Marcel Prosperi essentially ran Marseilles during and after World War II, controlling the heroin, prostitution, and weapons dealings there. Shortly after the war ended, as the ICU file detailed, he escaped to Italy, then Spain, and later Paraguay. Here, Prosperi set up the South American distribution network for heroin out of Marseilles—the so-called "French connection" responsible for putting snow-white Marseilles heroin on the streets of the United States, in collaboration with the American Mafia drug-kingpin Santo Trafficante, Jr., who controlled much of the heroin traffic into the U.S. Prosperi's accomplices, Anna knew, included some of Paraguay's highest officials. All of this meant that he was a very dangerous man, even after death.

In Paraguay, Prosperi maintained a respectable front business—the ownership of a chain of automobile dealerships. For the last several years, however, he had been bedridden. Two days ago, he had died.

As she dressed for her meeting with the widow Prosperi, Anna mulled over the details of the Prosperi and Mailhot cases. Whatever she found out from the widow, or from the autopsy, she was willing to bet that Marcel Prosperi didn't die of natural causes, either.

But whoever was murdering these men was resourceful, well connected, clever.

The fact that each of the victims had been in Alan Bartlett's Sigma files was significant, but what did it reveal? Were there others who had access to the names attached to those files—whether in the Justice Department, in the CIA, or in foreign countries? Had the list somehow been leaked?

A theory was beginning to emerge. The killers—for there had to be more than one—were probably well financed and had access to good intelligence. If they weren't acting on their own, then they'd been hired by someone with money and power—but with what *motivation*? And why now, why so suddenly?

Once again, she was back to the question of the list—who exactly had seen it? Bartlett had spoken of an internal CIA audit, and of the decision to bring in the ICU itself. That suggested researchers, government officials. What about the Attorney General himself—had he seen it?

And there still remained several salient questions.

Why were the murders disguised as natural deaths? Why was it so important to keep the fact of the murders secret?

And what about— .

The phone rang, yanking her out of her reverie. The taxi was here.

She finished applying her makeup and went downstairs.

The taxi, a silver Mercedes—probably stolen, too—hurtled through the crowded streets of Asunción with apparent disregard for the sanctity of human life. The driver, a handsome man in his late thirties with his olive complexion nicely set off by his white linen tropical-weight shirt, brown eyes, and close-shaven hair, glanced back at her periodically as if hoping for eye contact.

She pointedly ignored him. The last thing she needed was some Latin Lothario taking an interest in her. She stared out the window at a street vendor selling fake Rolexes and Cartiers, holding up his goods for her as they stopped at a light. She shook her head. Another vendor, an old woman, was peddling herbs and roots.

She hadn't seen a single gringo face since she'd arrived here. Maybe that was to be expected. Asunción was not exactly Paris. A bus in front of them belched foul-smelling smoke. There was a burst of instrumental music.

She noticed the traffic had thinned, the streets were wider, tree-lined. They were on the outskirts of town, it appeared. She had a city map in her handbag, but didn't want to unfold it if it wasn't necessary.

She remembered Captain Bolgorio mentioning that Prosperi's house was on Avenida Mariscal López, which was in the eastern sector on the way back to the airport. She had traveled down it on the way into town, the street with all the beautiful Spanish Colonial mansions.

But the streets she saw out the window didn't look at all familiar. She certainly hadn't seen this part of town before.

She looked up at the driver and said, "Where are we going?"

He didn't reply.

She said, "Hey, listen to me," as he pulled the car over to the shoulder of a quiet, untrafficked side road.

Oh, Jesus.

She didn't have a weapon. Her pistol was locked in her drawer at the office. Her training in martial arts and self-defense would scarcely—

The driver had turned around and was pointing a large black .38 at her.

"Now we talk," the man said. "You arrive at the airport from America. You wish to visit the estate of Señor Prosperi. Do you understand why some of us might find you interesting?"

Anna focused on remaining calm. Her advantage would have to be psychological. The man's one disadvantage was the limits of his knowledge. He did not know who she was. Or did he?

"If you are a DEA whore, then I have one set of friends who would enjoy entertaining you . . . before your final, unexplained disappearance. And you won't be the first. If you are an American *político*, I have other friends who will enjoy engaging you in, let us say, conversation."

Anna composed her features into a look of boredom mixed with contempt. "You keep speaking of 'friends,' " she said, and then hissed in her fluent Spanish: *"El muerto al hoyo y le vivo al bollo."* Dead men have no friends.

"You do not wish to choose how you will die? It is the only choice most of us ever get."

"But *you* will have to choose first. *El que mucho habla, mucho yerro.* I feel sorry for you, taking on an errand and making such a botch of it. You really don't know who I am, do you?"

"If you're smart, you'll tell me."

She curled her lips in scorn. "That is the one thing I will not do." She paused. "Pepito Salazar would not want me to."

The driver's expression froze. "*Salazar,* you said?"

Navarro had mentioned the name of one of the most powerful cocaine exporters of the region, a man whose trading enterprise outstripped even that of the Medellín kingpins.

Now the man looked suspicious. "It is easy to invoke the name of a stranger."

"When I return to the Palaquinto this evening, it is *your* name I will be invoking," Anna said provocatively. The Palaquinto was the name of Salazar's mountain retreat, a name known only to the few. "I regret we were not formally introduced."

The man spoke with a tremor in his voice. To make trouble for a personal courier of Salazar was more than his life was worth. "I have heard stories of the Palaquinto, the faucets of gold, the fountains of champagne . . ."

"That's only for parties, and if I were you, I wouldn't count on any invitations." Her hand dipped into her small purse for her hotel keys.

"You must forgive me," the man said urgently. "My instructions came from people with incomplete knowledge. None of us would dream of dishonoring any member of Salazar's entourage."

"Pepito knows that mistakes will be made." Anna watched the .38 dangling loosely in his right hand, smiled at him encouragingly, and then, in a swift movement, dug her keys into his wrist. The jagged steel stabbed through flesh and fascia, and the gun dropped into Anna's lap. As the man howled in agony, she scooped it up in one deft movement and placed the muzzle at the back of his head.

"*La mejor palabra es la que no se dice,*" she said through gritted teeth. The best word is the one that is not said.

She ordered the man out of the car, made him walk fifteen paces into the scrubby roadside vegetation, then got into his seat and roared off. She could not afford the time, she told herself, to replay the terrifying encounter; nor could she allow panic to seize her instincts and intellect. There was work to do.

The house that had belonged to Marcel Prosperi was set back from the Avenida Mariscal López. It was an immense Spanish Colonial mansion surrounded by extravagantly landscaped property, and it reminded her of the old Spanish missions back home in California. Instead of a simple lawn, though, the expanse of land was terraced with rows of cacti and lush wildflowers, protected by a high wrought-iron fence.

She parked the silver Mercedes some distance down the road and walked toward the entrance, where a taxicab was idling. A short, pot-bellied man emerged from it and ambled toward her. He had the dark skin of a mestizo, a drooping black *bandito* mustache, black hair combed straight back with too much hair goo. His face gleamed with oil or per-spiration, and he looked pleased with himself. His short-sleeved white shirt was translucent in places where sweat had soaked through, revealing a mat of dark chest hair.

Captain Bolgorio?

Where was his police cruiser? she wondered as his cab drove away.

He approached her, beaming, and enveloped her hand in his two large clammy ones.

"Agent Navarro," he said. "A great pleasure to meet such a beautiful woman."

"Thanks for coming."

"Come, Señora Prosperi is not used to being kept waiting. She is very rich and very powerful, Agent Navarro, and she is accustomed to getting her way. Let's go right in."

Bolgorio rang a bell at the front gate and identified themselves. There was a buzz, and Bolgorio pushed the gate open.

Anna noticed a gardener hunched over a row of wildflowers. An el-derly female servant was walking down a path between ledges of cacti holding a tray of empty glasses and open bottles of *agua gaseosa*.

"We're all set to go to the morgue after this interview?" Anna said.

"As I said, this is really not my department, Agent Navarro. A mag-nificent house, is it not?" They passed through an archway into cool shade. Bolgorio rang the doorbell at the side of an ornately carved blond wooden door.

"But you can help arrange it?" Anna asked, just as the door opened. Bolgorio shrugged. A young woman in a servant's uniform of white blouse and black skirt invited them in.

Inside was even cooler, the floor tiled in terra-cotta. The servant led them to a large, open room that was sparely decorated with woven primitive rugs and earthenware lamps and pottery. Only the recessed lighting in the stucco ceiling seemed out of place.

They sat on a long, low white sofa and waited. The maid offered them coffee or sparkling water, but both of them declined.

Finally a woman appeared, tall and thin and graceful. The widow Prosperi. She looked around seventy but very well taken care of. She was dressed entirely in mourning black, but it was a designer dress: maybe Sonia Rykiel, Anna thought. She wore a black turban and outsized Jackie Onassis sunglasses.

Anna and Bolgorio both rose from the low sofa.

Without shaking their hands, she said in Spanish, "I don't see how I can help you."

Bolgorio stepped forward. "I am Captain Luis Bolgorio of the *policía*," he said with a bow of his head, "and this is Special Agent Anna Navarro of the American Department of Justice."

"Consuela Prosperi," she said impatiently.

"Please accept our deepest condolences on the passing of your husband," he continued. "We simply wanted to ask you a few questions, and then we'll be on our way."

"Is there some sort of problem? My husband was sick for a long time, you know. When he finally passed away it was surely a great relief for him."

Not to mention for you, too, Anna thought. "We have information," she said, "indicating that your husband may have been killed."

Consuela Prosperi looked unimpressed. "Please sit down," she said. They did, and she sat in a white chair facing them. Consuela Prosperi had the unnaturally tight skin of a woman who has had too many face-lifts. Her makeup was too orange, her lipstick glossy brown.

"Marcel was ill for the last several years of his life. He was confined to bed. He was in extremely poor health."

"I understand," Anna said. "Did your husband have enemies?"

The widow turned to her with an imperious glance. "Why would he have enemies?"

"Señora Prosperi, we know all about your husband's past endeavors."
Her eyes flashed. "I am his third wife," she said. "And we did not
speak of his business affairs. My own interests lie elsewhere."

This woman could hardly be ignorant of her husband's reputation,
Anna knew. She also did not seem to be much in mourning.

"Did Señor Prosperi have any regular visitors?"

The widow hesitated but an instant. "Not while we were married."

"And no conflicts that you know about with his international 'trading'
partners?"

The widow's thin lips compressed, revealing a row of vertical age lines.

"Agent Navarro means no disrespect," Bolgorio put in hastily. "What
she means to say is—"

"I'm quite aware of what she means to say," Consuela Prosperi
snapped.

Anna shrugged. "There must have been many people over the years
who wanted your husband apprehended, arrested, even killed. Rivals.
Contenders for territory. Disgruntled business partners. You know that
as well as I."

The widow offered no response. Anna noticed her thick orange pan-
cake makeup cracking over her sun-lined face.

"There are also people who sometimes provide early warnings," Anna
went on. "Intelligence. Security. Do you know if anyone ever contacted
him to warn him of any possible threats?"

"In the nineteen years we were married," Consuela Prosperi said, turning away, "I never heard anything of this."

"Did he ever express to you the fear that people were after him?"

"My husband was a private man. He was an absentee owner of his
automobile dealerships. He never liked to go out. Whereas I enjoy going
out quite a bit."

"Yes, but did he say he was afraid to go out?"

"He didn't *enjoy* going out," she corrected. "He preferred to stay in
and read his biographies and histories."

For some reason, Ramon's muttered words ran through her head. *El
diablo sabe más por viejo que por diablo*. The devil knows more because
he is old than because he is the devil.

Anna tried a different tack. "You seem to have very good security
here."

The widow smirked. "You do not know Asunción, do you?"

"There is great poverty and crime here, Agent Navarro," Captain Bolgorio said, turning to her with outspread hands. "People of the Prosperis' means must always take precautions."

"Did your husband have any visitors at all in the last few weeks of his life?" Anna went on, ignoring him.

"No, my friends came over quite a bit, but none of them ever went upstairs to see him. He really had no friends in the last years. He saw only me and his nurses."

Anna looked up suddenly. "Who supplied his nurses?"

"A nursing agency."

"Did they rotate—did the same ones come regularly?"

"There was a day nurse and an evening nurse, and yes, always the same ones. They took very good care of him."

Anna chewed at the inside of her lower lip. "I'm going to have to examine certain of your household records."

The widow turned to Bolgorio with an expression of indignation. "I don't have to put up with this, do I? This is a grotesque invasion of my privacy."

Bolgorio tented his hands as if in supplication. "Please, Señora Prosperi, her only interest is to determine whether there was any possibility of homicide."

"Homicide? My husband's heart finally gave out."

"If we must, we can obtain them at the bank," Anna said. "But it would be so much simpler if—"

Consuela Prosperi got up and suddenly stared at Anna, nostrils flared, as if the American were a rodent that had made its way into her house. Bolgorio spoke in a low voice. "People like her, they do not tolerate invasions of their privacy."

"Señora Prosperi, you say there were two nurses," Anna said, soldiering on. "Were they very reliable?"

"Very."

"But were they never sick or absent?"

"Oh, from time to time, of course. Or they would ask for a night off when there was a holiday. *Año Nuevo, Día de los Trabajadores, Carnaval,* that sort of thing. But they were very responsible, and the agency was good about bringing in replacements without my ever having to worry.

And the replacements were every bit as well trained as the regular nurses. Even on Marcel's last night, the substitute nurse did everything she could to try to save him—"

Substitute nurse. She sat upright, suddenly alert. "There was a substitute nurse on the night he died?"

"Yes, but as I said, she was as well trained—"

"Had you ever seen her before?"

"No . . ."

"Can you give me the name and phone number of the nursing agency?"

"Of course, but if you're implying that this nurse killed Marcel, you're being foolish. He was ill."

Anna's pulse quickened. "Can you call this agency?" she asked Bolgorio. "And I'd like to go to the morgue right now—could you please call ahead and arrange to have the body prepared for us."

"The *body*?" Consuela Prosperi said, alarmed, rising to her feet.

"My deepest apologies if we must delay the funeral," Anna said. "We'd like your permission to do an autopsy. We can always get a court order, but it would be simpler and faster if you'd give us permission. I can guarantee you, if you're having an open-casket service, no one will ever be able to tell—"

"What are you talking about?" the widow said, genuinely puzzled. She walked to the immense fireplace and lifted an ornate silver urn from the mantel. "I just received my husband's ashes a few hours ago."

CHAPTER THIRTEEN

Washington, D.C.

Justice Miriam Bateman of the United States Supreme Court got up with great effort from her massive mahogany partners' desk to greet her visitor. Leaning on her gold-handled cane, she made her way around the desk and, smiling warmly despite the great pain from her rheumatoid arthritis, took her visitor's hand.

"How nice to see you, Ron," she said.

Her visitor, a tall black man in his late fifties, leaned over to give the diminutive Justice a peck on the cheek. "You look wonderful as always," he said in his deep, clear baritone, his enunciation precise.

"Oh, rubbish." Justice Bateman hobbled over to a high-backed wing chair by the fireplace, and he took the matching one next to her.

Her visitor was one of Washington's most influential private citizens, a widely respected, extraordinarily well-connected attorney in private practice who had never held a government job, yet had been a confidant of every President, Democrat and Republican, since Lyndon Johnson. Ronald Evers, famous, too, for his splendid wardrobe, was wearing a beautiful charcoal pin-striped suit and a subdued maroon tie.

"Madame Justice, thank you for seeing me on such short notice."

"For God's sake, Ron, it's Miriam. How long have we known each other?"

He smiled. "I believe it's thirty-five years . . . Miriam, give or take a decade. But I still keep wanting to call you *Professor* Bateman."

Evers had been one of Miriam Bateman's star students at Yale Law School, and he had been instrumental behind the scenes in getting Justice Bateman nominated to the High Court some fifteen years earlier. He hunched forward in his chair. "You're a busy lady, and the Court's in session, so let me get right to the point. The President has asked me to sound you out on something that must not leave this room, something he's been giving a lot of thought to. Please understand, this is highly preliminary."

Justice Bateman's piercing blue eyes radiated keen intelligence behind the thick lenses of her eyeglasses. "He wants me to step down," she said somberly.

Her directness caught her visitor unprepared. "He has enormous respect for your judgment and instincts, and he'd like you to recommend your successor. The President hasn't much more than a year left in office, and wants to make sure the next Supreme Court vacancy isn't filled by the other party, which looks awfully likely at this point."

Justice Bateman replied quietly, "And what makes the President think my seat's going to be vacant any time soon?"

Ronald Evers bowed his head, his eyes closed as if in prayer or deep contemplation. "This is a delicate matter," he said gently, like a priest in a confessional, "but we've always spoken openly with one another. You're one of the finest Supreme Court Justices this nation has ever seen, and I have no doubt you'll be mentioned in the same breath as Brandeis or Frankfurter. But I know you'll want to preserve your legacy, and so you have to ask yourself a very hard question: how many more years do you have left?" He lifted his head, and looked directly into her eyes. "Remember, Brandeis and Cardozo and Holmes all outstayed their welcome. They lingered at the Court well past the time when they could do their best work."

Justice Bateman's gaze was unyielding. "Can I get you some coffee?" she asked unexpectedly. Then, lowering her voice conspiratorially, she said, "I've got a *Sachertorte* I've just brought back from Demel's in Vienna, and the doctors tell me I really shouldn't have any."

Evers patted his flat midriff. "I'm trying to be good. But thank you."

"Then let me return bluntness with bluntness. I'm familiar with the reputation of just about every judge with any stature in every circuit in the country. And I have no doubt the President will find someone highly qualified, extremely bright, a legal scholar of range and breadth. But I want to let you in on something. The Supreme Court's a place that takes years to learn. One can't simply show up and expect to exert any influence. There's simply no substitute for seniority, for length of service. If there's one lesson I've learned here, it's the power of *experience*. That's where real wisdom comes from."

Her guest was prepared for this argument. "And there's no one on the Court as wise as you are. But your health is failing. You're not getting any younger." He smiled sadly. "None of us is. It's a terrible thing to say, I know, but there's just no way around it."

"Oh, I don't plan to keel over any time soon," she said, a glint in her eye. The telephone beside her chair suddenly rang, startling both of them. She picked it up. "Yes?"

"I'm sorry to disturb you," came the voice of her longtime secretary, Pamela, "but it's a Mr. Holland. You asked me to put him right through whenever he calls."

"I'll take it in my hideaway office." She put down the phone and stood with difficulty. "Will you excuse me for a moment, Ron?"

"I can wait outside," Evers said, getting to his feet and helping her up.

"Don't be silly. Stay right here. And if you change your mind about that *Sachertorte*, Pamela's right outside."

Justice Bateman closed the door to the study and laboriously made her way to her favorite chair. "Mr. Holland."

"Madame Justice, forgive this intrusion," said the voice on the phone, "but a difficulty has arisen that I thought you might be able to help us with."

She listened for a few moments and then said, "I can make a call."

"Only if it's not too great an inconvenience," said the man. "I would certainly never disturb you if it weren't extremely important."

"Not at all. None of us wants this. Certainly not at this time."

She listened as he spoke some more, then said, "Well, we all trust you to do the right thing."

Another pause, and she added, "I'll see you very soon," and then hung up.

Zurich

An icy wind blew down the Limmatquai, the quay on the banks of the Limmat River. The Limmat cuts through the heart of Zurich before it flows into the Zurichsee, splitting the city into two distinct halves, one the Zurich of high finance and high-priced shopping, the other the *Altstadt*, the quaint medieval Old Town. The river twinkled in the soft early-morning sunlight. It wasn't even six in the morning, but already people were striding to work, armed with briefcases and umbrellas. The sky was cloudy and overcast, though rain didn't appear imminent. But the Zurichers knew better.

Ben advanced tensely along the promenade, past the thirteenth-century *Zunfthausen*, the old guildhalls, with their leaded-glass windows, that now housed elegant restaurants. At Marktgasse he turned left, heading into the warren of narrow cobbled streets that was the Old Town. After a few minutes he found Trittligasse, a street lined with medieval stone buildings, some of which had been converted into dwellings.

Number 73 was an ancient stone townhouse that was now an apartment building. A small brass frame mounted beside the front door held only six names, white letters embossed in black plastic rectangles.

One of them was M. DESCHNER.

He kept walking without slowing down, careful to evince no particular interest. Perhaps it was baseless paranoia, but if there was any chance that spotters for the Corporation were keeping a lookout for him, he did not want to jeopardize Liesl's cousin by simply arriving at the door. The appearance of a strange visitor by itself might arouse curiosity. However remote the possibility that watchers were in place, rudimentary precautions would have to be taken.

An hour later, a deliveryman in the distinctive orange and black uniform of Blümchengallerie rang the bell of Number 73 Trittligasse. The Blümchengallerie was Zurich's most upscale florist chain, and its colorfully clad deliverymen were not an uncommon sight in the city's wealthiest neighborhoods. The man held a sizable bouquet of white roses. The roses did, in fact, come from the Blümchengallerie; the uniform from the charity bazaar of a Catholic parish across town.

After a few minutes, the man rang again. This time a voice crackled out of the speaker: "Yes?"

"It's Peter Hartman."

A long pause. "Again, please?"

"Peter Hartman."

An even longer silence. "Come to the third floor, Peter."

With a buzz, the front door lock released, and he found himself in a dark foyer. Depositing the flowers on a marble side table, he climbed the worn stone stairs, which rose steeply through the gloom.

Liesl had given him Matthias Deschner's home and office addresses and phone numbers. Instead of calling the lawyer at his place of work, however, Ben had decided instead to appear unannounced at his home, early enough so that the attorney presumably wouldn't have left for the office. The Swiss, he knew, are supremely regular in their business hours, which usually begin between nine and ten. Deschner would surely be no different.

Liesl had said she trusted him—"totally," she said—but he could not assume anything anymore. Therefore he had insisted that Liesl not call ahead to introduce him. Ben preferred to surprise the attorney, catch him off guard, observe his genuine, unrehearsed first reaction to meeting a man he believed to be Peter Hartman—or would Deschner already know of Peter's murder?

The door opened. Matthias Deschner stood before him in a green plaid bathrobe. He was small, with a pale craggy face, thick wire-rimmed glasses, reddish hair that frizzed out at the temples. Age fifty, Ben supposed.

His eyes were wide with surprise. "Good God," he exclaimed. "Why are you dressed this way? But don't stand there—come in, come in." He closed the door behind Ben and said, "May I offer you coffee?"

"Thank you."

"What are you *doing* here?" Deschner whispered. "Is Liesl—?"

"I'm not Peter. I'm his brother, Ben."

"You—*what?* His *brother?* Oh, my *God!*" he gasped. Deschner pivoted around and stared at Ben with sudden dread. "They found him, didn't they?"

"Peter was killed a few days ago."

"Oh, Lord," he breathed. "Oh, Lord. They found him! He was always so afraid it would happen someday." Deschner stopped suddenly, a look of terror striking his face. "Liesl—"

"Liesl's unharmed."

"Thank God." He turned to Ben. "I mean, what am I saying—"

"That's all right. I understand. She's your blood relative."

Deschner stood before a small breakfast table and poured Ben a china cup of coffee. "How did this happen?" he asked gravely. "*Tell* me, for God's sake!"

"Surely the bank where you had a meeting the morning of the Bahn-hofstrasse incident was the tripwire," Deschner said. The two of them faced each other intently across the table. Ben had peeled off the baggy orange and black uniform to reveal his ordinary street clothes. "The Union Bank of Switzerland is a merger of several older banks. Maybe there was an old, sensitive account that was flagged, being watched. Perhaps by one of the parties you met with. An assistant, a clerk. An informer who'd been given a watch list."

"Placed there by this corporation Liesl and Peter were talking about, or one of its offshoots?"

"Quite possibly. All of the giant firms have long-standing, cozy relationships with the important Swiss banks. The complete list of founders will give us the names of suspects."

"Did Peter show you the list?"

"No. At first he didn't even tell me why he wanted to open an account. All I knew was that the account was monetarily insignificant. What he was really interested in was the vault that came with it. To keep some documents, he said. Do you mind if I smoke?"

"It's your house."

"Well, you know, you Americans are such fascists about smoking, if you'll pardon the expression."

Ben smiled. "Not everyone."

Deschner pulled a cigarette from the pack of Rothmans next to his breakfast plate, lit it with a cheap plastic lighter. "Peter insisted that the account not be in his name. He was afraid—correctly, as it turned out—that his enemies might have contacts in the banks. He wanted to open it under a false name, but that's no longer possible. The banks have tightened up here. A lot of pressure from the outside, mostly America. Back in the seventies our banks started demanding a passport when you opened an account. You used to be able to open an account by mail. No more."

"So did he have to open it under his real name?"

"No. In *my* name. I'm the account holder, but Peter was what they call the 'beneficial owner.' " He exhaled a plume of smoke. "We had to go in together to open the account, but Peter's name appeared on one form only, known only to the account adviser. The Establishment of the Beneficial Owner's Identity, it's called. This form is kept locked away in the files." In another room a telephone rang.

"Which bank?"

"I chose the Handelsbank Schweiz AG because it's small and discreet.

I've had clients who've happily done business with the Handelsbank, clients whose money is, shall we say, not entirely clean."

"So does this mean you can get into Peter's vault for me?"

"I'm afraid not. You'll have to accompany me. As the specified beneficiary and heir of the beneficial owner."

"If it's at all possible," Ben said, "I'd like to go to the bank straightaway." He remembered Schmid's icy warnings that he was not to return—warnings that if he violated that agreement, he would be persona non grata, subject to immediate arrest.

The phone kept ringing. Deschner crushed out his cigarette in a saucer. "Very well. If you don't mind, I'd like to answer that phone. Then I must make a call or two, reschedule my nine-thirty appointment."

He went into an adjoining room, his study, and returned a few minutes later. "All right then, no problem. I was able to reschedule."

"Thank you."

"Certainly. The account adviser—that's the banker, a senior vice president of the bank, Bernard Suchet—has all the relevant papers. He has a photocopy of Peter's passport on file. They believe he has been dead for four years. So far as anyone knows, the recent . . . *tragedy* has not been reported. Your own identity will be easy to establish."

"My arrival in this country came through somewhat irregular means," Ben said, choosing his words carefully. "My legal presence here cannot be verified through the normal passport, customs, and immigration systems. What happens if they alert the authorities?"

"Let's not think of all that can go wrong. Now, if I may finish dressing, we're in business. Then let us go at once."

CHAPTER FOURTEEN

Anna whirled around to Captain Bolgorio. "What? The body was *cremated? We had an *agreement*, dammit . . . !"

The Paraguayan detective shrugged, hands spread, eyes wide with apparent concern. "Agent Navarro, please, let us discuss these things later, not in front of the bereaved—"

Ignoring him, Anna turned back to the widow. "Were you told there would be an autopsy?" she demanded.

"Don't raise your voice to me," Consuela Prosperi snapped. "I'm not a criminal."

Anna looked at Bolgorio, livid. "Did *you* know her husband's body was going to be cremated?" *Of course he knew, the bastard.*

"Agent Navarro, I told you, this is not my department."

"But did you know this or *not?*"

"I have heard things. But I am a low man on the totem pole, please understand."

"Are we finished here?" Consuela Prosperi asked.

"Not yet," Anna said. "Were you pressured into a cremation?" she demanded of the widow.

The widow said to Bolgorio. "Captain, please remove her from my house."

"My apologies, madame," Bolgorio said. "Agent Navarro, we must go now."

"We're not finished here," Anna said calmly. "You were pressured, weren't you?" She addressed Señora Prosperi. "What were you told— that your assets would be frozen, locked up, made inaccessible to you, unless you went along with this? Something like that?"

"Remove her from my house, Captain!" the widow commanded, raising her voice.

"Please, Agent Navarro—"

"Señora," Anna said, "let me tell you something. I happen to know that a significant portion of your assets is invested in hedge funds and other investment partnerships and equities in the U.S. and abroad. The U.S. government has the power to seize those assets if it suspects you of being part of an international criminal conspiracy." She stood and walked toward the door. "I'm getting on the phone to Washington right now, and that's precisely what I'm going to order."

From behind her, she heard the widow cry out, "She can't do this, can she? You assured me my money was safe if I—"

"Keep quiet!" the homicide detective barked suddenly. Startled, Anna turned back, and saw Bolgorio standing face to face with the widow. His obsequiousness had vanished. "I'll handle this."

He strode toward Anna and grabbed her arm.

Outside the front gates of the Prosperi estate, Anna demanded, "What are you covering up?"

"You'd be wise to leave things alone here," Bolgorio said. There was malevolence in his voice now, a gleaming assuredness she hadn't seen before. "You're a visitor here. You are not in your own country."

"How was it done? Were morgue orders 'lost' or 'misfiled'? Did someone pay you off, is that how it happened?"

"What do you know of the way things work in Paraguay?" Bolgorio said, moving uncomfortably close to her. She could feel his hot breath, the spray of spittle. "There are many things you don't understand."

"You *knew* the body had been destroyed. From the moment I called you, I had a feeling. You knew there was no body waiting for me in the morgue. Just tell me this: were you ordered, or were you paid? Where did the request come from—from outside the government, or from above?"

Bolgorio, unfazed, said nothing.

"*Who ordered the body destroyed?*"

"I like you, Agent Navarro. You're an attractive woman. I do not want anything to happen to you."

He intended to frighten her, and unfortunately it was working. But she gave him only a blank look. "That's not a very subtle threat."

"This is not a threat. I truly don't want anything to happen to you. You need to listen to me, and then leave the country at once. There are people high up in our government who protect the Prosperis and others like them. Money changes hands, a great deal of it. You'll accomplish nothing by putting your own life in peril."

Oh, she thought, *you don't know who you're dealing with. Threatening me that way is like waving a red flag at a bull.*

"Did you order the cremation personally?"

"It happened, that's all I know. I told you, I'm not a powerful man."

"Then someone must know that Prosperi's death wasn't natural. Why else would they destroy the evidence?"

"You are asking me questions I don't know the answer to," he said calmly. "Please, Agent Navarro. Please take care of your own safety. There are people here who prefer to keep things quiet."

"Do you think *they*—these 'people who prefer to keep things quiet'— had Prosperi killed and didn't want that revealed?"

Bolgorio looked away, as if in contemplation. "I'll deny I ever told you this. I called the nursing agency before you got here. When I knew you were investigating Prosperi's death. That seemed to me the obvious place to ask questions."

"And?"

"The substitute nurse—the one who was with Prosperi the night he died—she has vanished."

She felt her stomach plummet. *I knew it was too easy*, she thought.

"How did this nurse come to the agency?"

"She came with excellent credentials, they said. Her references checked out. She said she lived within walking distance of here, and if they had any assignments nearby . . . She did three different assignments, all in this area, and all very well. Suddenly, the regular night nurse assigned to Prosperi fell ill, and the substitute was available, and . . ."

"They have no way to reach her?"

"As I said, she disappeared."

"But her paychecks, her bank account—"

"She was paid in cash. Not unusual in this country. Her home address was false. When we looked closely, everything about her was false. It was as if she had been created just for this occasion, like some stage set. And when the job had been accomplished, the set was struck."

"Sounds like a professional backstopping job. I want to talk to the nursing agency."

"You'll learn nothing. And I will not help you do that. I've already told you too much. Please, leave at once. There are so many ways for an

overly inquisitive foreigner to be killed here. Especially when very powerful people do not want things uncovered. Please—go."

She knew he was completely serious. This wasn't just a threat. She was
more stubborn than anyone she knew, and she hated giving up. *But
sometimes you just have to move on*, she told herself. *Sometimes the most
important thing is just to stay alive.*

Zurich

By the time Ben Hartman and Matthias Deschner were walking down
the Löwenstrasse, it had begun to drizzle. The sky was steel gray. The
linden trees that lined the street rustled in the wind. A steeple clock
struck the hour of nine o'clock in a melodious chime. Trams passed by
down the middle of the street—the 6, the 13, the 11—each stopping
with a squeal. FedEx trucks seemed to be everywhere: Zurich was a world
banking capital, Ben knew, and banking was a time-sensitive business.
Bankers hurried to work beneath umbrellas. A couple of Japanese girls,
tourists, giggled. Unpainted wooden benches sat unoccupied beneath the
lindens.

It drizzled, it stopped, it drizzled again. They came to a busy crosswalk
where Lagerstrasse crossed the Löwenstrasse. A building that housed the
Société de Banque Suisse stood empty, undergoing construction or ren-
ovation.

A pair of stylishly unshaven Italian men in identical black leather jackets passed by, both smoking. Then a matron wafting Shalimar.

On the next block Deschner, who was wearing an ill-fitting black raincoat over an ugly checked jacket, stopped at a white stone building,
resembling a townhouse, on the front of which was mounted a small
brass plaque. Engraved on it in graceful script were the words HANDELS-
BANK SCHWEIZ AG.

Deschner pulled open the heavy glass door.

Directly across the street, someone with the slender build of an adolescent
was sitting at a café, under a red Coca-Cola parasol. He was wearing
khaki cargo pants, a blue nylon backpack, and an MC Solaar T-shirt,
and he was drinking an Orangina from the bottle. With languid move-

ments, he flipped through a copy of a music magazine while speaking on a cell phone. From time to time he glanced at the entrance to the bank across the street.

A set of glass doors slid open electronically. They stood for a moment between thick doors, and then with a low buzz, the next set slid open.

The lobby of the Handelsbank was a large marble-floored chamber, completely empty except for a sleek black desk at the far end. A woman sat behind it, wearing a tiny wireless telephone headset, speaking quietly. She looked up as they entered.

"Guten morgen," she said. *"Kann ich Ihnen helfen?"*

"Ja, guten morgen. Wir haben eine Verabredung mit Dr. Suchet."

"Sehr gut, mein Herr. Einen Moment." She spoke softly into her mouthpiece. *"Er wird gleich unten sein, um Sie zu sehen."*

"You will like Bernard Suchet, I think," Deschner said. "He's a very good sort, a banker of the old school. Not one of these hustle-and-bustle young men in a hurry you see so much of in Zurich these days."

At this point, Ben thought, *I don't care if he's Charles Manson.*

A steel elevator pinged and slid open, and a round-shouldered large man in a tweed jacket strode up to them and shook hands first with Deschner, then with Ben. *"Es freut mich Dich wiederzusehen, Matthias,"* he exclaimed, and then, turning to Ben, "I am very pleased to make your acquaintance, Mr. Hartman. Please, come with me."

They rode up together in the elevator. There was a camera lens mounted discreetly on the ceiling. Suchet wore a permanent pleasant face. He had heavy rectangular-framed glasses, a double chin, and a large potbelly. His shirt was monogrammed with his initials on the pocket. A pocket square in his jacket matched his tie. A senior officer, Ben thought. Tweed jacket, not a banker's suit: he's above such things as dress code.

Ben watched him closely, waiting for any signs of suspicion. But Suchet seemed all business as usual.

The elevator opened on a waiting area covered in a wall-to-wall oatmeal deep-pile rug and furnished with antiques, not reproductions. They moved through the waiting area to a door, where Suchet inserted a badge that he wore on a chain around his neck, into an electronic card-reader.

Suchet's office was just down the hall, a spacious, light-flooded room. A computer was the only object on his long glass-topped desk. He sat behind it, while Deschner and Ben sat across from him. A middle-aged woman entered with two espressos and two glasses of water on a silver tray and set them down on the desk before the two visitors. Then a young male came in and handed Dr. Suchet a file.

Suchet opened it. "You are Benjamin Hartman, of course," he asked, moving his owlish gaze from the file to Ben.

Ben nodded, his stomach tightening.

"We have been provided with ancillary documentation certifying that you are the sole heir to the 'beneficial owner' of this account. And you affirm that you are, correct?"

"That's correct."

"Legally I am satisfied with your documentation. And visually—well, it is clear you are indeed Peter Hartman's twin brother." He smiled. "So what can I do for you this morning, Mr. Hartman?"

The Handelsbank's vaults were located in the basement of the building, a fluorescent-lit, low-ceilinged area that was nowhere near as sleek and modern as the upstairs. There were several numbered doors off a narrow corridor, presumably room-sized vaults. Several larger alcoves off the hallway appeared from a distance to be lined with brass, which upon closer inspection Ben saw were safe-deposit boxes of various sizes.

At the entrance to an alcove numbered 18C, Dr. Suchet stopped and handed Ben a key. He did not indicate which of the hundreds of vaults in this area was Peter's. "I assume you would like privacy," he said. "Herr Deschner and I shall leave you now. You can call me on this phone here"—he indicated a white phone on a steel table in the center of the room—"when you are finished."

Ben looked at the rows upon rows of vaults, and didn't know what to do. Was this a test of some sort? Or did Suchet merely assume that Ben would know the number of his vault? Ben glanced at Deschner, who seemed to sense his discomfort but, curiously, said nothing. Then Ben looked again at the key and saw a number embossed on it. *Of course. The obvious place.*

"Thank you," he said. "I'm all set."

The two Swiss left, chatting. Ben noticed a surveillance camera mounted high in the room, where the ceiling met the wall. Its red light was on.

He located vault 322, a small box at about eye level, and turned the key to open it.

Oh, God, he thought, heart thrumming, *what could be in here? Peter, what did you hide here that was worth your life?*

Inside was what looked like an envelope made of stiff wax paper. He pulled it out—the document inside was dismayingly thin—and opened it.

There was only one item inside, and it was not a piece of paper.

It was a photograph, measuring about five inches by seven.

It took his breath away.

It showed a group of men, a few in Nazi uniforms, some in 1940s suits with overcoats. A number of them were immediately recognizable. Giovanni Vignelli, the great Italian industrialist out of Turin, automotive magnate, his massive plants supplying the Italian military, diesel engines, railroad cars, airplanes. The head of Royal Dutch Petroleum, Sir Han Detwiler, a xenophobic Dutchman. The legendary founder of the first, and greatest, American airline. There were faces that he could not identify but had seen in the history books. A few of the men wore mustaches. Including the handsome, dark-haired young man standing next to an arrogant Nazi official with pale eyes who looked familiar to Ben, though he knew little of German history.

No, please, not him.

The Nazi, whose face he'd seen before, he could not identify.

The handsome young man was unquestionably his father.

Max Hartman.

A typewritten caption on the white border at the bottom of the photograph read: ZURICH, 1945. SIGMA AG.

He returned the photograph to the envelope and slipped it into his breast pocket. Felt it burn against his chest.

There could no longer be any doubt that his father had lied to him, had lied all his adult life. His head reeled. Abruptly a voice penetrated Ben's stupor.

"Mr. Hartman! Mr. Benjamin Hartman. There is a warrant for your arrest! We must take you into custody."

Oh, Jesus.

It was the banker, Bernard Suchet, speaking. He must have contacted the local authorities. A swift search of the country's arrival records would reveal that he had no documented arrival. Schmid's chill, understated words returned to him: *If I ever find out you've returned here, things will not go well for you.*

Suchet was flanked by Matthias Deschner and two security guards, their weapons drawn.

"Mr. Hartman, the *Kantonspolizei* have informed me that you are in this country illegally. Which means that you are perpetrating a fraud," the banker said. Deschner's face was a mask of neutrality.

"What are you talking about?" Ben said indignantly. Had they seen him slip the photo into his jacket?

"We are to detain you until the authorities arrive, momentarily."

Ben stared at him, speechless.

"Your actions put you in violation of the Swiss Federal Criminal Code," Suchet continued loudly. "You seem to be implicated in other offenses as well. You will not be permitted to leave except in the custody of the police."

Deschner was silent. In his eyes Ben could see what appeared to be fear. Why was he saying nothing?

"Guards, please escort Mr. Hartman to Secure Room Number 4. Mr. Hartman, you will take nothing with you. You are hereby detained awaiting official arrest."

The guards approached, weapons still pointed at him.

Ben got to his feet, his hands open at his side, and began walking down the corridor, the two guards falling in beside him. As he passed Deschner, he saw the attorney give the tiniest shrug of his shoulders.

Peter's words of caution: *They practically* own *half the cops.* Schmid's words of menace: *the* Einwanderungsbehörde *can hold you in administrative detention for a year before your case reaches a magistrate.*

He couldn't allow himself to be taken in. What galvanized him wasn't the chance that he would be killed or locked up, but the fact that in either case his investigations would come to an end. Peter's efforts would have been in vain. The Corporation would have won.

He couldn't let that happen. Whatever the price.

Secure Rooms, *die Stahlkammern*, were, Ben knew, where items of intrinsic value—gold, gemstones, bearer bonds—were displayed and assessed whenever an owner requested an official audit of his stored possessions. Though lacking vault-like impregnability, they were indeed secure, with reinforced steel doors and closed-circuit surveillance systems. At the entrance of *Zimmer Vier*, one of the guards waved an electronic reader by a blinking red light; when the door unlocked, he gestured Ben to enter first, and the two guards followed him. Then the door closed with a series of three audible clicks.

Ben looked around him. The room was brightly lit and sparely furnished; it would be difficult to lose, or hide, a single gemstone in this space. The slate-tiled floor was polished to a dark sheen. There was a long table of perfectly clear Plexiglas, and six folding chairs of gray painted metal.

One of the guards—burly and overweight, his red, fleshy face suggesting a steady diet of beef and beer—gestured for Ben to sit down on a chair. Ben paused before complying. The two guards had reholstered their sidearms, but made it abundantly clear that they wouldn't hesitate to use cruder physical means if he were less than cooperative.

"And so we wait, *ja?*" said the second guard, in heavily accented English. The man, his light brown hair brush cut, was leaner and, Ben judged, probably much faster than his cohort. Doubtless mentally swifter as well.

Ben turned to him. "How much do they pay you here? I'm a *very* rich man, you know. I can give you a very nice life if I choose. You do me a favor, I'll do you one." He made no effort to disguise his naked desperation; they would either respond or they would not.

The leaner guard snorted and shook his head. "You should speak your proposal louder, to be sure that the microphones pick it up."

They had no reason to believe that Ben would be good for his word, and there were no assurances he could make, while in captivity, to persuade them otherwise. Still, their amused contempt was encouraging: his best chance now was to be underestimated. Ben stood up, groaning, and clutched his midriff.

"Sit *down*," the guard commanded firmly.

"The claustrophobia . . . I can't take the . . . small, enclosed places!" Ben spoke in a tone that was increasingly frantic, verging on hysteria.

Both guards looked at each other and laughed scornfully—they would not be taken in by such an obvious ploy.

"No, no, I'm serious," Ben said with growing urgency. "My God! How explicit do I have to be? I have a . . . a nervous stomach. I have to get to a bathroom immediately or I'll . . . have an accident." He was playing the role of the flighty, flaky American to the hilt. "Stress brings it on much more quickly! I need my pills. Dammit! My Valium! A sedative. I have terrible claustrophobia—I can't be in enclosed spaces. *Please!*" As he spoke he started to gesticulate wildly, as if having a panic attack.

The lean guard just regarded him with an amused contemptuous half-smile. "You will have to take it up with the prison infirmary."

With a manic, stricken expression, Ben stepped closer to him, his gaze flicking toward the holstered gun and then back at the lean man's face. "Please, you don't understand!" He waved his hands even more wildly. "I'll have a panic attack! I need to go to the bathroom! I need a *tranquilizer!*" With lightning speed, he thrust both hands into the guard's hip holster and retrieved the short-barreled revolver. Then he took two steps back, holding the piece in his hands, his performance abruptly over.

"Keep your hands at shoulder level," he told the thickly built guard. "Or I fire, and you both die."

The two guards exchanged glances.

"Now one of you will take me out of this place. Or both of you will die. It's a good deal. Take it before the offer expires."

The guards conferred briefly in *Schweitzerdeutsch.* Then the lean one spoke. "It would be extremely stupid of you to use this gun, if you even know how, which I doubt. You will be imprisoned for the rest of your life."

It was the wrong tone: wary, alarmed, yet without terror. The guard was not at all unnerved. Perhaps Ben's earlier performance of weakness had been *too* effective. Ben could see that a measure of skepticism remained in their expressions and posture. At once, he knew what he must say. "You think I wouldn't fire this gun?" Ben spoke in a bored voice, only his eyes blazing. "I killed five at the Bahnhofplatz. Two more won't weigh on my mind."

The guards suddenly grew rigid, all condescension having instantly evaporated. "*Das Monster vom Bahnhofplatz,*" the fleshy one said hoarsely to his partner as a look of horror crossed his face. The blood drained from his florid complexion.

"You!" Ben barked at him, seizing the advantage. "Take me out of here." Within seconds, the thickset guard used his electronic reader to open the door. "And if you want to live, you'll stay behind," he told the leaner, evidently cleverer one. The door closed behind him, the three muffled clicks verifying that the bolts had electronically slid into place.

Frog-marching the guard in front of him, Ben traveled swiftly down the beige-carpeted corridor. The feed from the closed-circuit video probably went into archival storage and examination, rather than being viewed in real time, but there was no way to be certain.

"What's your name?" Ben demanded. "*Wie heissen Sie?*"

"Laemmel," the guard grunted. "Christoph Laemmel." He reached the end of the corridor and started to turn left.

"*No,*" Ben hissed. "*Not* that way! We're not going out the front. Take me out the back way. The service entrance. Where the trash is taken out."

Laemmel paused in momentary confusion. Ben placed the revolver near one of his beet-red ears, letting him feel the cold metal. Moving more quickly, the guard took him down the back stairs, the ugly, dented steel a dramatic contrast with the polished formality of the bank's public spaces. The gloom of the stairwell was scarcely diminished by the naked, low-wattage electric bulbs that protruded from the wall at each landing.

The guard's heavy shoes clattered on the metal stairs.

"Quiet," Ben said, speaking to him in German. "Make no sound, or I will make a very deafening one, and it will be the last thing you ever hear."

"You have no chance," Laemmel said in a low, frightened voice. "No chance at all."

Finally, they reached the wide double doors that led to the back alleyway. Ben pressed on the cross latch, made sure that the doors opened from within. "This is the end of our little trip together," he said.

Now Laemmel grunted. "Do you think you are any safer outside of this building?"

Ben stepped into the shadowy alleyway, feeling the cool air against his flushed face. "What the *Polizei* do is not your personal concern," he said, keeping his gun drawn.

"*Die Polizei?*" Laemmel replied. "I do not speak of *them*." He spat.

An eel of fear thrashed in Ben's belly. "What are you talking about?" he demanded urgently. Ben gripped the gun in both his hands and raised it to Laemmel's eyes. "*Tell me!*" he said with furious concentration. "Tell me what you know!"

There was a sudden exhalation of breath from Laemmel's throat, and a warm mist of crimson spattered Ben's face. A bullet had torn through the man's neck. Had Ben somehow lost his grip, squeezed the trigger without realizing it? A second explosion, inches away from his head, answered the question. There was a shooter in position.

Oh, Christ! Not again!

As the guard crumpled face forward, Ben lunged down the dank alley. He heard a popping noise, as if from a toy gun, then a metallic reverberation, and a pockmark suddenly appeared on the large Dumpster to his left. The shooter had to be firing from his right.

As he felt something hot crease his shoulder, he dove behind the Dumpster: temporary refuge, but any port in a storm. Out of the corner of his eye, he saw the movement of something small and dark—a rat, displaced by his arrival. *Move!* The ledge of the cement wall that separated the bank's back lot from that of its neighbor was at shoulder height; Ben stuck the gun in the waistband of his trousers and, with both hands, lifted himself up and over. A short pathway now separated him from Usteristrasse. Grasping the revolver, he fired wildly, in three different areas. He wanted the shooter to take cover, believing he was under fire. He needed the time. Every second now was precious.

There was return fire, and he could hear the slugs hitting the concrete retainer, but Ben was safely on the other side.

Now he charged, pumping his feet down the alley to Usteristrasse, fast. Faster. Faster still! "Run like your life depends on it," his track coach would tell him before competitions. Now it did.

And what if there were more than one shooter? But surely they wouldn't have had enough warning to put a whole team into position. The thoughts jostled and collided in Ben's mind. *Focus, dammit.*

A brackish smell cued him to his next move: it was a breeze from the Sihl River, the charmless narrow waterway that branched off from the Limmat at the Platz-promenade. Now he crossed the Gessner Allee, scarcely looking at the traffic, hurtling in front of a taxicab whose bearded driver honked and cursed at him before stepping on the brakes. But he'd made it across. The Sihl, banked with a declivity of blackened cinder blocks, stretched before him. His eyes scanned the water frantically until he fixed on a small motorboat. They were a common sight on the Sihl; this one had a single passenger, a plump, beer-swilling man with sunglasses and a fishing pole, though he was not yet fishing. His life jacket made his already bulky proportions look even bulkier. The river would take him to the Sihlwald, a nature preserve ten kilometers south of Zurich, where the riverbanks flattened out in the woodlands and became furrowed with brooks. It was a popular destination among the city's inhabitants.

The plump man peeled plastic wrap from a white-bread sandwich, then tossed the plastic into the waters. A notably antisocial act by Swiss standards. Ben threw himself into the water, fully clothed, and started to swim toward the boat, his clothing impeding his powerful crawl stroke.

The water was frigid, carrying the bone-chilling cold of the glacier from which it originated, and Ben felt a stiffness seep through his body even as he propelled himself through the slow-moving current.

The man in the motorboat, pushing the sandwich into his face, slurping from his bottle of Kronenberg, was aware of nothing until the small motorboat tilted abruptly leeward. First two hands were visible, the fingers faintly bluish from the cold, and then he saw the man, fully dressed, pull himself up and into the boat, river water sluicing down an expensive-looking suit.

"*Was ist das!*" he shouted. He dropped his beer in alarm. "*Wer sind Sie?*"

"I need to borrow your boat," Ben told him in German, trying to stop his teeth from chattering from the cold.

"*Nie! Raus!*" Get out! The man picked up his sturdy fishing pole and brandished it with intended menace.

"Your choice," Ben said, and then sprang toward the man, tipping him over into the water, where he bobbed comically, buoyed by his life jacket but sputtering with indignation.

"Save your breath." Ben pointed toward the nearby Zollstrasse bridge. "The tramline will take you wherever you need to go." He reached over to the engine throttle and turned it way up. The engine coughed, and then roared, the boat gaining speed as it headed south. He would not be taking it all the way to the Sihlwald, the forest preserve. Half a mile down the river bend would do it. Lying flat against the grip-textured fiberglass floor of the boat, he was still able to see the taller buildings and store-fronts along the Sihl, the immense Migros department store, a bland, boxy structure; the sooty spires of the Schwarzenkirche; the intricately frescoed walls of the Klathaus. Ben knew that he'd be vulnerable to any marksmen in position, but also that the chances of their having antici-pated his movements were slim. He felt for the envelope in his jacket pocket, and the waxy enclosure crackled reassuringly. He assumed it was waterproof, but this wasn't the time to make sure.

The motorboat moved faster, taking him beneath the algaed masonry of the Stauffacherstrasse bridge. Another fifth of a kilometer remained. Then came the unmistakable sounds of a major expressway, the whizzing noise of tires spinning along smooth-worn asphalt, of air against the carriages and contours of trucks and automobiles, the occasional bleat, treble and basso, of horns, the meshing gears of a hundred vehicles moving like the wind. It all fused into a white noise that rose and fell in intensity, the aural vibrations of industrial transportation blended into a mechanical surf.

Ben veered the thrumming motorboat toward the gently sloped retaining wall, heard the scrape of its fiberglass hull against brick as he brought it jerking to a halt. Then he sprang from the boat and toward the roadside gas station where he'd left his rented Range Rover, only minutes from the Nationalstrasse 3, the concrete river where he would merge into the swiftly coursing traffic.

Turning the steering wheel to change lanes, Ben felt a twinge in his left shoulder. He reached over with his right hand and rubbed it gently. Another twinge, sharper this time. He took his hand away. His fingers were sticky, maroon with congealing blood.

Matthias Deschner was in the same seat in front of Suchet's desk that he had occupied just an hour before. Suchet, behind the desk, was hunched forward, his face tense.

"You should have warned me in advance," the banker said angrily. "We could have stopped him from accessing the vault!"

"I had no advance notice myself!" Deschner objected. "They only contacted me yesterday. They demanded to know whether I was sheltering him. *Preposterous!*"

"You know full well the penalty for noncompliance in such matters." Suchet's face was mottled with rage and fear.

"They made it very clear," Deschner said tonelessly.

"Only just now? Then they only just learned of your possible connection to the subject?"

"Certainly. Do you think I had any idea what these brothers were involved in? I knew nothing. *Nothing!*"

"That excuse has not always been successful in sparing the Teutonic neck, if I may speak historically."

"A distant relative asked me for a favor," Deschner protested. "I wasn't apprised of its larger significance."

"And you didn't inquire?"

"Members of our profession are trained *not* to ask too many questions. I'd think you'd agree with that."

"And now you expose us *both* to danger!" Suchet snapped.

"As soon as he showed up, I was called. I could only presume they *wanted* him to access the vault!"

There was a knock at the door. Suchet's secretary entered, holding aloft a small videocassette. "This just came for you from Security, sir."

"Thank you, Inge," Suchet said sweetly. "A messenger will be arriving momentarily. I'd like you to seal the tape in an envelope and give it to him."

"Very good, sir," the secretary said, and she left the office as quietly as she had come.

CHAPTER FIFTEEN

In a modern eight-story building on Schaffhausserstrasse, not far from the University of Zurich, three men sat in a room filled with high-powered computers and high-resolution video monitors. It was a studio rented from a multimedia production company that did duplication, restoration, and editing of video for surveillance firms and corporations.

One of the group, a white-haired, scrawny man in shirtsleeves who looked a great deal older than his forty-six years, took a videocassette from a D-2 composite digital-format videotape recorder and placed it in one of the video slots in a Quantel Sapphire video-imaging computer. He had just finished making a digital copy of the surveillance tape he'd been given. Now, using this British-made video-imaging computer that had originally been developed for the Home Office, Britain's MI-5, he was going to magnify the image.

The white-haired man, who worked in silence, had been one of the top video-enhancement specialists in the Home Office until he was lured away by a private London security firm at double his old salary. These two gentlemen in the room with him had hired him, through the security firm, to do a quick job in Zurich. He had no idea who they were. All he knew was that they were paying him a generous bonus. They had flown him from London to Zurich business class.

Now the two mysterious men sat off by themselves, talking. They could have been international businessmen from any country in the world, although in fact they were speaking Dutch, which the video expert understood reasonably well.

On the other side of the room, the white-haired technician stared at the computer screen. At the bottom it said CAM 2, along with the date and the time, which flashed by in fractions of a second. He called out to his clients: "All right, now tell me what you'd like done. You want the bloke electronically compared against a photo you've got?"

"No," replied the first Dutchman. "We know who it is. We want to see what he's reading."

"I should have figured," the technician groaned. "Good God, that piece of paper he's holding is in shadow."

"How's the quality of the tape?" the second man asked.

"Not bad," the tech said. "Two frames a second, which is standard. A lot of these banks use the most god-awful equipment, but fortunately this bank used a high-performance, high-res camera. I mean, I can't say the camera was positioned terribly well, but that's not uncommon either."

The second businessman asked, "So you can zoom in on whatever he's holding?"

"Sure. The software on this Quantel compensates for all the usual problems you get from digital enlargement—the blockiness and all that. That's not the problem. The damned thing's in shadow."

"Well, you're supposed to be the best," the first man said sourly. "You're certainly the most expensive."

"I know, I know," the tech said. "All true. Well, I can bring up the contrast." He clicked on a pull-down menu that listed "Crisp," "Zoom," "Colouring," and "Contrast." By clicking on the "+" key he lightened the shadow until the paper the man in the bank vault was looking at was almost readable, then enhanced the resolution by clicking another number. He tinkered with the contrast some more, then clicked "crisp" to sharpen the image further.

"Good," he said at last.

"Can you see what he's reading?" the second man asked.

"Actually, it's a photograph."

"A *photograph*?"

"Right. An old one. A group shot. Lots of conservatively dressed men. Looks like a bunch of businessmen. A couple of German officers, too. Yes, a group shot. Mountains in the background—"

"Can you make out their faces?"

"If you give me . . . just . . . ah, here we are." He zoomed in on the photograph until it took up the entire screen. " 'Zurich, 1945,' it says here. The 'Sig' something . . . ?"

The second man glanced at the first. "Good heavens." He approached the computer monitor.

The tech said, "Sigma AG?"

The second man muttered to the first, "He's on to it."

"As I thought," the first said.

"All right," said the second man to the technician. "I want you to print out a copy of that. I also want the best head shot of this fellow you can get."

"Make fifty copies," put in the first man, rising from his chair.

The second man crossed the room to talk to his colleague. "Put out the word," he said quietly. "Our precautions have been inadequate. The American has become a serious threat."

Washington, D.C.

Anna Navarro hunched forward in her chair. Alan Bartlett's office was as immaculate as ever, the man's expression every bit as opaque.

"I've tracked Robert Mailhot's money transfers from the Nova Scotia National Bank back to an account in the Caymans, and there, I'm afraid, I've hit a dead end," Anna said. "The one source we've got there confirms that the account shows recent activity involving one of Prosperi's funds, too. But there, as I say, the money trail goes cold. It's one thing to learn where the money ends up. It's another to learn who put the money there in the first place. Should we start working through regular channels?"

"Out of the question," Bartlett said, a little peevish. "It would compromise the security of the entire operation. That means anyone with an interest in stopping the investigation can do so easily. It also means endangering the lives of others, people who may still be targets."

"I understand," Anna said. "But I don't want a repeat of Asunción, either. That's the price you pay for going through back-channels. Whoever's behind this, this—for want of a better word, this conspiracy— obviously had enough influence to stop us."

"Granted. But once we raise this thing to an A-II level, a sanctioned investigation, it's like taking out an ad in *The New York Times*, telling the subjects of our inquiries what we're up to. We can't assume there aren't people in the intelligence community working both sides on this matter."

"An A-II is still highly privileged. I don't agree—"

"No, you wouldn't," he said freezingly. "Perhaps I was wrong—perhaps you really are a loyal bureaucrat at heart."

She ignored his barb. "I've been involved in many international investigations, including homicide investigations, that have been kept quiet. Particularly when we think someone in the government might be implicated. In El Salvador, when government officials had Americans killed to cover up—"

"As you know, I'm *intimately* acquainted with your previous exploits, Agent Navarro," Bartlett said impatiently. "You're speaking of one foreign government. I'm speaking of half a dozen or more. There's a difference."

"You say there's been a victim in Oslo now?"

"That's our latest intelligence, yes."

"Then we have the Attorney General's office make a high-level, confidential appeal to the Office of the Norwegian State Prosecutor, requesting absolute secrecy."

"*No.* The risks of a direct appeal to the Norwegian authorities are far too great."

"Then I want the list. Not the list of corpses. I want the names of people with Sigma clearance files. Your 'hot list.' "

"That's impossible."

"*I see*—I only get 'em when they're dead. Well, in that case, I want off this job."

He hesitated. "Don't play games, Ms. Navarro. You've been assigned." Bartlett's carefully cultivated air of solicitude and noblesse had evaporated. Now Anna caught a glimpse of the steel that had placed Bartlett at the helm of one of the government's most powerful investigative units. "It's really not up to you."

"I can get sick, suddenly become unable to perform my job. Be unable to travel."

"You wouldn't do that."

"No, not if you gave me the hot list."

"I told you. It's impossible. This operation must abide by certain rules. If those rules sometimes amount to constraints, you must accept them as the parameters of your inquiry."

"Look," she said, "thirteen of the old men on your Sigma list are now dead under 'questionable circumstances,' let's just say. Three remain alive, right?"

"To the best of our knowledge."

"Then let me put it to you this way. Once one of these guys dies, is killed, whatever—we can't pay the body a visit without some kind of official government cooperation, on whatever level. Right? But if we get to one of them *before* he's killed . . . Listen, I realize I'm supposed to be investigating dead people, not live ones. But if we consider them potential witnesses, put them under twenty-four-hour surveillance—*discreetly*, of course. . . ."

Bartlett stared at her, conflicting imperatives evidently playing across his face. Now he walked to a floor safe taller than he was, opened it, and pulled out a folder. He handed her a sheet of paper stamped SECRET, NOFORN, and NOCONTRACT. Those classifications stipulated that, in addition to high-level secrecy constraints, it was under no circumstances releasable to foreign nationals or contract employees. "The list," he said quietly.

She quickly read down the columns of information—aliases, real names, names of any living relatives, and the numbers of the corresponding files. Three old men remained alive. Countries of origin: Portugal, Italy, Switzerland.

"No addresses?" she said.

"Just old ones. None current that we've been able to procure through the normal means. All of them have relocated in the past year."

"The past *year?* They could be anywhere in the world."

"That's a logical possibility. The probability is that they're in the same country, likely in the same general locale—at a certain point of life, one becomes subject to a sort of field of gravitation. It's difficult for old men to completely uproot themselves. Even when their safety is at risk, there is a level of personal tumult to which they will refuse to subject themselves. All the same, they haven't exactly left forwarding addresses. Evidently, they're keeping a low profile."

"Hiding," Anna said. "They're afraid."

"It would seem they have reason to be."

"It's like there's some geriatric grudge match going on. How could something that started even before the CIA was founded still have such power?"

Bartlett craned his neck, resting his gaze on the velvet-lined display case before he turned back. "Certain things grow more powerful with age. And, of course, it's a grave mistake to confuse size with influence. Today, the CIA is a vast, solid government institution with endless layers of bureaucracy. At the beginning, personal networks were where true power resided. It was true of Bill Donovan, the founder of the OSS, and even more so of Allen Dulles. Yes, Dulles is known for his role in creating the CIA, but that wasn't the most impressive of his accomplishments. For him, there was one battle, the battle against the revolutionary left."

"The 'gentleman spy,' they called him, didn't they?"

"The 'gentleman' part made him as dangerous as the 'spy' part. He was never more formidable than when he was a private citizen, back in the days when he and his brother Foster ran the international finance division of a certain law firm."

"The law firm? What did they do, double bill their clients?"

Bartlett gave her a slightly pitying look. "It's an amateur's error to underestimate the reach and range of private concerns. Theirs was more than just a white-shoe law firm. It had genuinely international reach. Dulles, traveling around the world, was able to weave a sort of spider's web across Europe. He enlisted confederates in all the major cities, finding them among the Allies, the Axis, *and* the neutrals."

"Confederates?" Anna interrupted. "How do you mean?"

"Highly placed individuals—contacts, friends, 'assets,' call them what you will—whom Allen Dulles effectively had on retainer. They served as sources of information and advice, but also as agents of influence. Dulles knew how to appeal to people's self-interest. After all, he facilitated an extraordinary number of deals involving governments and multinational corporations, and that made him an invaluable man to know. If you were a businessman, he could ensure that a large government contract was steered in your direction. If you were a government official, he might provide you with a crucial morsel of information that would further your career. Money and intelligence—Dulles understood that one could be readily converted to the other, like two currencies, albeit with constantly shifting exchange rates. And, of course, Dulles's own role as a go-between, an intermediary, depended upon him knowing just a little bit more than everyone else."

"A go-between?"

"Maybe you've heard of the Bank for International Settlement of Basel?"

"Maybe I haven't."

"It was essentially a counting house where businessmen on both sides of the war could settle down and parse the distribution of dividends. A very useful institution to have—if you were a businessman. After all, business didn't cease simply because the cannons began to fire. But the hostilities did interfere with the conduct of corporate partnerships and alliances, giving rise to all sorts of impediments. Dulles figured out ways to circumvent those impediments."

"That's not an attractive picture."

"It's the reality. Dulles, you see, believed in the 'network.' It's the key to understanding his life's mission. A network was an array of individuals—a whole, a complex configuration, that could have an influence vastly greater than the sum of its parts. It's a striking thing to contemplate. As I say, it always comes down to the crooked timber of humanity."

Anna raised an eyebrow. "It sounds a little frightening."

A vein pulsed on Bartlett's temple. "It is a little frightening, and perhaps more than a little. The nature of these networks, after all, is that they are invisible to those who are not part of them—invisible even to some who are. And they also have a tendency to survive the individuals they initially comprise. You could say they take on a life of their own. And they can have powerful effects on the organizations that they invade." He adjusted his French cuffs again. "I talked of spider's webs. There's a curious parasitic wasp, very tiny, of the genus *Hymenoepime-cis*—a clever little creature that stings a spider into temporary paralysis, and lays its eggs in the spider's abdomen. Soon the spider goes back to work, as if nothing had happened, even as the larvae grow inside him, nourished on its fluids. Then, on the night that the larvae will molt and kill the spider, they chemically induce it to change its behavior. On this night, the spider is induced to spin a cocoon web, useless to the spider but necessary for the larva. As soon as the spider has finished its work, the larvae consume the spider and hang the pupal cocoon in the special web. It's quite extraordinary, really, the parasite's fine-grained manipulation of the host's behavior. But it's nothing compared to what we humans can devise. That's the sort of thing I think about, Ms. Navarro. Who's inside of *us*? What forces might be manipulating the apparatus of civic governance into building a web that will serve their own purposes? When will the parasite decide to consume the host?"

"O.K., I'll play along," Anna said. "Let's say half a century ago, some dark conspiracy stings us, in effect—implants something that's going to grow and cause damage. Even if all that's so, how would we ever know?"

"That is an excellent question, Ms. Navarro," Bartlett replied. "Webs are hard to see, aren't they, even when they're big. Have you ever walked into an old basement or storage area in a dim light, seeing nothing in the gloom? Then you switch on a flashlight, and suddenly you realize that the empty space over your head isn't exactly empty—it's filled with layers of cobwebs, a vast canopy of glassy filaments. You direct the beam in another direction, and that canopy disappears—as if it were never there. Had you imagined it? You look straight up. Nothing. Then, directing the beam at just the right off-angle, focusing your eyes on some intermediate point, it all becomes visible once more." Bartlett's gaze searched her face for comprehension. "People like me spend our days looking for that one odd angle that brings the old webs into view. Often we look *too* hard, and we imagine things. Sometimes we see what's really there. You, Ms. Navarro, strike me as someone not prone to imagine things."

"I'll accept that at face value," Anna replied.

"I don't mean to imply that you lack imagination—only that you keep it under tight control. No matter. The point is simply that there were alliances forged among some individuals with considerable resources. That much is part of public history. And as for what became of this? I only wish we knew. All we have are these names."

"Three names," Anna said. "Three old men."

"I'd direct your particular attention to Gaston Rossignol. He'd been quite a powerful Swiss banker in his heyday. The most prominent person on the list, and the oldest."

"All right," she said, looking up. "The Zuricher. I assume you've prepared a background file on him."

Bartlett opened a desk drawer, withdrew a file festooned with classificatory warning stamps, and slid it to her across the desk. "It's fairly extensive, aside from the obvious lacunae."

"Good," Anna said. "I want to see him before they get to him, too."

"Assuming you can locate him."

"He's lived his entire life in Zurich. As you say, there's a field of gravitation there. Even if he's moved, he would have left behind friends, family members. Tributaries leading to the source."

"Or moats, protecting a fortress. A man like Rossignol has powerful friends, highly placed ones, who will do whatever they can to protect him. Friends who are, as the French say, *branché*. Powerful and plugged-in. They have the ability to remove him from the grid of visibility, the bureaucratic files and computer records. Do you have some clever subterfuge in mind?"

"Nothing like that. Subterfuge is what they'll be on guard against. Rossignol has nothing to fear from me. If his friends and confederates are as well informed as you suggest, they'll realize that and spread the word."

"So you're envisaging a simple 'I come in peace'?" The words were wry, but he looked intrigued.

Anna shrugged. "Some version of that. I suspect the best route will be the most direct one. But I'll find out soon enough." She glanced at her watch. "I'm taking the next flight I can catch to Zurich."

Mettlenberg, St. Gallen, Switzerland

A little over five hours later, Ben Hartman sat in his rented Range Rover in the staff parking lot of the Regionalspital Sankt Gallen Nord, watching people coming and going: doctors, nurses, hospital workers. The powerful engine idled softly. Fortunately, there weren't many people, even at a few minutes after five o'clock, the end of the workday for the office workers. Twilight was beginning to fall, and the outside lights were starting to come on.

From Zurich he had called the hospital and asked for Dr. Margarethe Hubli. He was put right through to Pediatrics, where he asked, in English, whether she was in.

Yes, he was told; would you like to make an appointment to see the doctor? The nurse's English was halting but comprehensible.

"No," he'd said, "I really just wanted to make sure the doctor was in the hospital. My child is ill, and I want to know whether you had a pediatrician on call in case we need one." He thanked the nurse and, after finding out how late Dr. Hubli worked, hung up.

Liesl was scheduled to be in the hospital only until four in the afternoon. He'd been waiting here over two hours; already she was more than an hour late in leaving. Ben was certain she had not yet emerged from the hospital. Moreover, he had spotted her Renault parked in the lot. He figured she was the sort of dedicated doctor who worked long hours and paid little attention to schedules.

He might be sitting here for quite some time, he realized.

The document of incorporation that Peter had referred to wasn't in the vault, so where else might it be? He had said he'd hidden it away safely. Was it possible that Liesl was telling the truth, that she really didn't know where it was? In that case was it possible that Peter had concealed it somewhere among his possessions in the cabin without Liesl knowing?

She'd answered too quickly when he'd asked her whether Peter might have hidden something there. She knew something she wasn't telling.

He had to go to the cabin.

Forty minutes later, Liesl came out of the Emergency entrance.

She was talking to someone, bantering. She gave a wave good-bye and zipped up her leather jacket. Then she half-walked, half-ran to her car, got in, and started it up.

Ben waited until she'd gone some distance down the road before he pulled out of the lot. She wouldn't recognize the Range Rover and would have no cause for suspicion, apart from her normal cautiousness. Still, it was better not to alarm her.

At a travel bookstore in Zurich he'd bought a map of the canton of St. Gallen and studied the roads in the area. Both Peter and Liesl had mentioned living in a "cabin," which likely meant that it was situated in a forest or woods. There was one wooded area about eight kilometers from the hospital, roughly north-northwest. The only other one within a two-hour drive was forty kilometers away. That was quite a distance, on back roads, for someone who had to go to work every day—sometimes even had to return to the hospital quickly in emergencies. More likely the cabin was located in the closer woods.

Having committed the roads in the area to memory, he knew that the next turnoff wasn't for two kilometers. But if she stopped somewhere along the road and turned off, he stood a chance of losing her. All he could do was hope she didn't.

Soon the road rose steeply, following the hilly topography of this part of Switzerland. It enabled him to look far ahead, and he was able to spot what he determined was her Renault, stopped at a traffic light. At the next intersection was a highway marked 10. If she took a left onto 10, she was heading toward the forest he had scoped out. If she took a right, or went beyond 10, he'd have no idea where she was going.

The Renault turned left.

He accelerated and reached the intersection with 10 just a few minutes after she had. There were enough other cars on the road that he wasn't too obvious. He felt sure she still had no idea he was tailing her.

The four-lane highway went parallel to a set of railroad tracks, past several immense farms, great fields that went on as far as he could see. Suddenly she turned off, a few kilometers before he expected she would.

Once he turned onto the narrow, winding road, he realized that his was the only car behind her. Not good. It had gotten dark, and the road was barely trafficked, and she would soon realize he was following her. How could she not? If she did, she would either slow down to see who it was behind her or, more likely, try to lose him. If she began driving strangely, he would have no choice but to show himself.

Luckily, the twisty road helped to conceal him, as long as he stayed at least one bend behind her. Now they passed a sparsely wooded area that gradually became denser. From time to time he would see the flash of her headlights, appearing and then disappearing around the bends. This enabled him to follow her at some remove, to let her gain considerable distance on him, just in case she had noticed the Rover.

But a few minutes later he could no longer see her headlights.

Where had she gone? Had she pulled off the road? He accelerated, to see whether she had herself sped up, but after a kilometer he saw no trace of her.

She had to have turned off into the woods, though he didn't seem to have passed by any roads or paths that led into the forest. He stopped, made a U-turn—no cars were coming in either direction—and reversed course, slowing down to look for any turnoffs.

It wasn't easy; it had gotten quite dark.

Soon he spotted what could barely be called a road. It was a dirt trail that looked like a footpath, but upon closer examination he saw tire ruts.

He turned onto it, and saw at once that he would have to drive slowly. It was just wide enough for the Renault, but there was not quite enough clearance for the Range Rover. Twigs and branches scraped the sides of the car. He slowed down even more: the noise might attract her attention.

The St. Gallen map had told him that the forest he had entered was not large. It surrounded a small lake—a pond, actually—and there appeared to be no other road that led into or out of the woods.

Good.

Assuming the map was accurate.

The path came to a fork, and he stopped, got out of the car, and saw that one branch of the road dead-ended a hundred feet ahead. The other branch, deeply rutted, continued. He turned down that path and navigated with some difficulty, wondering how Liesl's Renault could make it if the Range Rover was having such trouble.

It was not long before this path, too, came to an end.

And then he saw the Renault.

He parked his vehicle beside it, and got out. By now it was fully dark, and he could see nothing. Once the car's engine was shut off there was mostly silence. Rustlings now and again that sounded like small animals. The chirp and twitter of birds.

His eyes became accustomed to the dark, and he could make out another path, even narrower, canopied with branches. Ducking down under one, he entered, losing his footing a few times, his hands held out before his face to shield his eyes from the twigs.

He saw a glow, and came upon a clearing. In it was a small cabin built of split logs and rough white plaster. There were several glass windows; it clearly wasn't as rustic as it appeared. A light shone from inside. This was the back of the cabin; the entrance had to be on the other side. Treading softly, he approached the cabin and made his way around to the front, where he expected the entrance to be.

Suddenly there was a metallic click. He looked up with a jolt.

Liesl was standing before him, pointing a gun.

"*Stop right there!*" she shouted.

"Wait!" Ben called back. God, she was fearless, coming right out to confront the interloper. A split-second was all it would take for her to kill him.

"It's *you!*" she spat out with sudden realization. "What the hell are you doing here?" She lowered the gun.

"I need your help, Liesl," he said.

In the oblique moonlight her shadowed face seemed contorted with rage. "You must have followed me from the hospital! How dare you!"

"You've got to help me find something, Liesl, please." He had to make her *listen*.

She whipped her head from side to side, frantic. "You have—compromised my security! Goddamn you to hell!"

"Liesl, I wasn't followed."

"How can you possibly know? Did you rent this car?"

"In Zurich."

"Of course. *Idiot!* If they were watching you in Zurich, they'll know you rented the car!"

"But no one followed me here."

"What do you know?" she snapped. "You're an amateur!"

"So are you."

"Yes, but I am an amateur who has lived with the threat of death for four years. Now please, get out. *Go!*"

"No, Liesl," he said with quiet finality. "We need to talk."

CHAPTER SIXTEEN

The cabin was simple yet cozy, low-ceilinged, book-lined. Peter had built the bookshelves himself, Liesl said proudly. The floor was wide-board pine. There was a stone fireplace, a neat stack of split logs piled next to it, a wood stove, a small kitchen. The whole place smelled of smoke.

It was cold; she lit the wood stove for some heat. Ben took off his coat.

"You're hurt," Liesl said. "You've been hit."

Ben looked at himself, saw that the left shoulder of his shirt was stiff with dried blood. Oddly, it hadn't been painful—stress and exhaustion had somehow rendered him insensate to the injury, and he'd put it out of his mind during the long drive through the mountains.

"I'm sure it looks a lot worse than it is," Ben said.

"That depends," she said, "on what it looks like. Remove the shirt." She spoke like the doctor she was.

Ben undid the buttons of his white pinpoint Oxford cloth shirt. The fabric adhered to the top of his left shoulder, and when he tugged, there was a warning twinge of pain.

Liesl took a clean sponge, soaked it with warm water, and wet the area. Then she carefully peeled the shirt from his wounded shoulder. "You've been incredibly lucky: a bullet creased you, no more. Tell me what happened."

As Liesl tended to his wound, Ben recounted the events that happened only hours before.

"There's debris here. It must be cleansed carefully, or there will be the risk of infection." She sat him next to the sink, poured some boiling water from a kettle, and left it to cool in a porcelain bowl. She went away for a few minutes and reappeared with a quantity of gauze and a yellow plastic bottle of antiseptic.

Ben found himself wincing as she carefully washed the area, then wincing again as she daubed it with cotton saturated with the brown-colored antiseptic. "Cleaning it hurts worse than getting it did," Ben said.

Liesl applied four strips of medical adhesive tape to secure the sterile wound dressing in place. "You won't be so lucky next time," she said dryly.

"What I most need right now isn't luck," Ben said. "It's knowledge. I need to understand what the hell is going on. I need to get a fix on Sigma. They sure seem to have a fix on me."

"Luck, knowledge—trust me, you'll need both." Now she handed him a shirt. A heavy shirt of knitted cotton. One of Peter's.

Suddenly the reality of the past few days, the reality he'd tried to hold at bay, reared up and he felt a surge of vertigo, panic, sorrow, despair.

"I'll help you put it on," she said, alert to the anguish that played across his face.

He had to regain his composure, he knew, if only for her sake. He could merely guess at her own wrenching pain. When the shirt was on him, Liesl stared at him for a few moments. "You're so alike. Peter never told me. I think he never realized how alike you are."

"Twins never recognize themselves in each other."

"It was more than that. And I don't mean physically. Some people would have said that Peter was aimless. I knew better. He was like a sail, something that's slack only until it captures the wind. And then it possesses the force of the wind." She shook her head, as if frustrated by her fumbling attempts to communicate. "I mean that Peter had a larger sense of purpose."

"I knew what you meant. It's what I admired most about him, the life he came to create for himself."

"It was a passion," Liesl said, her eyes sad, gleaming, "a passion for justice, and it infused every aspect of his being."

" 'A passion for justice.' Those aren't words that mean much in the world of asset management," Ben said bitterly.

"A world you found stifling," Liesl said. "It was suffocating you by degrees, wasn't it, just as Peter said it would."

"There are quicker ways to die," Ben said. "As I've had reason to learn of late."

"Tell me about the school where you taught. In New York, Peter said. I've been to New York a couple of times, as an adolescent, and once, later, to a medical conference."

"It was in New York, yes. But not a New York any tourist ever sees. I taught in a place called East New York. About five square miles of some of the worst-off people in the whole city. You've got some auto shops, and bodegas, places that'll sell you cigarettes and booze, and places that'll cash your checks. The Seventy-fifth Precinct—what the cops call the Seven-Five, those unfortunate enough to be assigned to it. When I was teaching, there were more than a hundred homicides in the Seven-Five. Some nights, it sounded like Beirut. You'd go to sleep to the sound of Saturday Night Specials. A desperate place. Pretty much written off by the rest of society."

"And that's where you taught."

"I thought it was obscene that in America, the wealthiest nation in the world, this sort of desolation was still tolerable. Here was a place that made Soweto look like Scarsdale. Sure, there were the usual ineffectual poverty programs, but there was also the unspoken conviction of futility. 'The poor will always be with us'—nobody used those words anymore, but that's what they meant. They used other code words, talked about 'structural' this and 'behavioral' that, and, hey, the middle class was doing just fine, wasn't it? So I stuck it out. I wasn't going to save the world, I wasn't naïve. But I told myself that if I could save one kid, maybe two, maybe three, my efforts wouldn't have been wasted."

"And did you?"

"Possibly," Ben said, suddenly tired. "Possibly. I wasn't around any longer to find out, was I?" He spat out the words with distaste: "I was ordering truffled timbales at Aureole, quaffing Cristal with clients."

"Sounds like a terrible shock to the system, that kind of change," Liesl said gently. She attended to his words carefully, perhaps in need of distraction from her own pain.

"It was deadening, I think. The hell of it was, I was actually good at it. I had a knack for the game, the rituals of client courtship. If you wanted someone who could order at the city's most expensive restaurants without glancing at the menu, I was your man. And then, as often as I could, I'd go risk my neck—recreationally, of course. I was an extreme-sport junkie. I'd go climb the Vermillion Cliffs, in Arizona. Sail solo to Bermuda. Go para-skiing in Cameron Pass. Courtney—an old girlfriend of mine—used to insist I had a death wish, but that wasn't it at all. I did those things to feel alive." He shook his head. "It sounds silly now, doesn't it? The idle diversions of a pampered rich kid, someone who hadn't figured out a reason for getting dressed in the morning."

"Maybe it was because you'd been taken from your natural element," Liesl said.

"And what was that? I'm not sure that saving souls in East New York was going to be a lifelong calling, either. Anyway, I never got the chance to find out."

"I think you were a sail, like Peter. You just needed to find your wind." She smiled sadly.

"The wind found me, it would seem. And it's a goddamn monsoon. Some conspiracy that was launched half a century ago and is still claiming lives. Specializing in the people I love. Maybe you've never been in a small boat during a storm, Liesl, but I have. And the first thing you do is drop the sail."

"Is that really an option now?" She poured him a small quantity of brandy in a water glass.

"I don't even know what the options are. You and Peter have spent a lot more time thinking about it than I have. What conclusions did you come to?"

"Just the ones I told you. A great deal of conjecture for the most part. Peter did a lot of research into the period. He was disheartened by what he found out. The Second World War was a conflict that had clear rights and wrongs, and yet many of those involved were utterly indifferent to what was at stake. There were numerous corporations whose only concern was to maintain their operating margin. Some, alas, even viewed the war as an opportunity to be exploited—an opportunity to increase their profits. The victors never adequately came to grips with this legacy of corporate double-dealing. It was never convenient to do so." Her sardonic half-smile reminded Ben of his brother's banked sense of outrage, his smoldering anger.

"Why not?"

"Too many American and British industries might have had to be seized for trading with the enemy, for collaboration. Better to sweep the problem under the carpet. The Dulles brothers, you know, made sure of it. Tracking down the real collaborators—it wouldn't have looked good. It would have blurred the lines between good and evil, interfered with the myth of Allied innocence. Forgive me if I don't explain myself very well—these are stories I have heard many times. There was a young attorney in the Justice Department who dared make a speech about collaborations between American businessmen and the Nazis. He was immediately fired. After the war, German officials were called to task, some of them. And yet the citadel of Axis industrialists was never probed, never disturbed. Why prosecute German industrialists who had done business with Hitler—who had, really, made Hitler possible—given that they were just as happy now to do business with America? When overzealous officials at Nuremberg had a few of them convicted, your John J. McCloy, the American High Commissioner, had their sentences commuted. The 'excesses' of fascism were regrettable, but industrialists had to look after each other, right?"

Once again, he could almost detect Peter's passionate voice in her recountings. Dully, he said, "I still have a hard time getting my mind around it—financial partnerships when the two sides were at war?"

"Things aren't always as they seem. Hitler's senior-most intelligence officer, Reinhard Gehlen, had already begun planning his own surrender in 1944. The high command knew which way the wind was blowing, they knew Hitler was mad, irrational. So they bartered. They microfilmed their files on the U.S.S.R., buried them in watertight drums in the mountain meadows of the Alps, not a hundred miles from here, and presented themselves to the American Counterintelligence Corps to make a deal. After the war, you Americans put Gehlen in charge of the 'South German Industrial Development Organization.' "

Ben shook his head blearily. "It sounds like you both got pretty immersed in this stuff. And it sounds like I'm way out of my depths." He knocked back the rest of the brandy.

"Yes, I suppose we did get rather deep into all of this. We had to. I remember something Peter told me. He said the real question isn't where they are. It's where they aren't. That the real question isn't who can't be trusted, but who can be. Once it sounded like paranoia."

"But no longer."

"No," Liesl agreed, her voice trembling slightly. "And now they have arrayed their forces against you, through both official and unofficial channels." She hesitated. "There is something else I must give you."

Once more, she disappeared into the bedroom, and then came back with a plain cardboard box, the sort a dry cleaner might package a shirt in. She opened it on the rough-hewn table in front of them. Papers.

Laminated ID cards. Passports. The folding currency of modern bureau-cracy.

"They were Peter's," Liesl said. "The fruits of four years in hiding."

Ben's fingers quickly sorted through the identity papers as if they were playing cards. Three different names, all appended to the same face. Peter's face. And, for all practical intents, his own. " 'Robert Simon.' Smart. There must be thousands of people with that name in North America. 'Michael Johnson.' Likewise. 'John Freedman.' These look like good work, professional work, if I'm any judge."

"Peter was a perfectionist," Liesl said. "I'm sure they are flawless."

Ben continued to go through the documents and saw that the pass-ports came with matching credit cards. In addition, there were documents for "Paula Simon" and other spousal identities: if Robert Simon needed to travel with his "wife," he'd be prepared. Ben marveled, but his admiration was shadowed by a deep sadness. Peter's precautions were meticulous, obsessive, exhaustive—and yet they could not save him.

"I've got to ask, Liesl: Can we be sure that Peter's pursuers—the Sigma group or whoever they are—aren't on to them? Any of these could be flagged."

"Possibilities are not likelihoods."

"When was the last time he used 'Robert Simon'? And under what circumstances?"

Liesl closed her eyes in concentration, retrieving the details with re-markable precision. After twenty minutes, Ben had satisfied himself that at least two of Peter's aliases, unused in the last twenty-four months, were unlikely to have been detected. He tucked the papers into the ca-pacious inside pockets of his leather coat.

He placed a hand on Liesl's and looked into her clear blue eyes. "Thank you, Liesl," he said. What an astonishing woman she was, he thought once more, and how lucky his brother was to have found her.

"The shoulder wound will scab over and heal in a matter of days," she said. "You will find it considerably harder to shed your identity, though these documents will help."

Liesl opened a bottle of red wine and poured each of them a glass. The wine was excellent, deep and rich and tannic, and Ben soon began to relax.

For a few moments the two of them silently watched the fire. Ben thought: *If Peter had hidden the document here, where could it be? And if not here, where?* He'd said it was hidden away safely. Had he left it with Matthias Deschner? But that made no sense: Why would he go to such lengths to open a bank account because of the vault that came with it, and then not put the incorporation document in the vault?

Why hadn't any document been in the vault?

He wondered about Deschner. What was his role, if any, in what had happened at the bank? Had he secretly alerted the banker that Ben was in the country illegally? If so, the timing didn't track: Deschner could have done so before Ben had been admitted to the vault. Was it possible that Deschner had gotten into the vault—as he easily could have despite his claim that he could not—months or years before, taken the document, then given it to his brother's pursuers? Yet Liesl had said she trusted her cousin . . . Contradictory thoughts swirled around in his brain, warring with one another until Ben couldn't think clearly anymore.

Liesl spoke at last, interrupting his troubled ruminations. "The fact that you could so easily follow me here worries me," she said. "No offense, please, but again, you're an amateur. Think of how much easier it would have been for a professional."

Whether or not she was right, it was crucial to reassure her, Ben sensed. "But keep in mind, Liesl, that Peter had told me you two lived in a cabin in the woods, near a lake. Once I figured out which hospital it was, that narrowed things down considerably. If I didn't know as much, I'd probably have lost you pretty early on."

She said nothing, just stared with unease at the fire.

"You know how to use that thing?" Ben asked, glancing toward the revolver she'd left on a table by the door.

"My brother was in the army. Every Swiss boy knows how to fire a gun. There's even a national holiday where Swiss boys go off to shoot. My father just happened to believe that a girl is every bit the equal of a boy and should learn to use a gun too. So I'm prepared for this life." She rose. "Well, I'm famished, and I'm going to make some dinner." Ben followed her to the kitchen.

She lit the gas oven, then took a whole chicken from the tiny refrigerator, buttered it and sprinkled it with dried herbs, and put it in the oven to roast. While she boiled some potatoes and sautéed some greens, they made idle conversation about her work and his, about Peter.

After a while, Ben retrieved the photograph from his jacket pocket.

He'd verified, en route, that the wax envelope had protected it from water damage. Now he showed it to her. "Do you have any idea who these men might be?" he asked.

Her eyes suddenly registered alarm. "Oh, my God, that has to be your father! He looks so much like you two. What a handsome man he was!"

"And these others?"

She hesitated, shook her head, clearly troubled. "They look like important men, but then they all did in those heavy business suits. I'm sorry, I don't know. Peter never showed this to me. He just told me about it."

"And the document I mentioned—the articles of incorporation—did he ever mention hiding it somewhere here?"

She stopped stirring the greens. "Never." She said it with absolute certainty.

"You're sure? It wasn't in the vault."

"He would have told me if he'd hidden it here."

"Not necessarily. He didn't show you this photograph. He may have wanted to protect you, or maybe keep you from worrying."

"Well, then your guess is as good as mine."

"Would you mind if I looked around?"

"Be my guest."

While she finished making dinner, he searched the cabin methodically, trying to put himself into his brother's head. Where would Peter have hidden it? He ruled out any place that Liesl would have regularly cleaned or had any reason to look. Liesl and Peter's bedroom was one of two small rooms off the living room area, the other being Peter's study. But both rooms were spartanly furnished and yielded nothing.

He checked the floor all over for any loose planks, then inspected the log-and-plaster walls, but nothing.

"Do you have a flashlight?" Ben asked, returning to the kitchen area. "I want to look outside."

"Of course. There's a flashlight in every room—the lights go out often. There's one on the table by the door. But we'll be ready to eat in just a few minutes."

"I'll make it quick." He took the flashlight and stepped outside, where it was cold and completely dark. He made a cursory tour of the grassy area surrounding the cabin. There was a scorched place where they obviously cooked outdoors, and a large log pile covered with a tarpaulin.

The document might have been hidden in a container beneath a rock, but that would have to wait until the light of morning. He beamed the flashlight on the exterior of the cabin, made his way slowly around the walls, poking around a propane tank, but again turned up nothing.

When he went back inside, Liesl had already set out two plates and silverware on a red-and-white-checked tablecloth over a small round table against a window.

"Smells delicious," Ben said.

"Please, sit."

She poured two more glasses of wine and served both of them. The food was wonderfully flavored, and Ben devoured it. They both concentrated on eating, and only began to talk after they'd satisfied their hunger. The second glass of wine made Liesl melancholy. As she spoke about Peter and how they met, she cried. She recalled how Peter had taken such pride in furnishing their cabin, their home, building the bookcases and much of the furniture himself.

The bookcases, Ben thought. Peter had built the bookcases . . .

He got up suddenly. "Would you mind if I looked at little closer at the shelves?"

"Why not," she said with a tired wave.

The bookcases appeared to have been built as several separate units and assembled in place. They weren't open shelves; you could not see the log-and-plaster walls behind them. Instead, Peter had built a backing of wood.

Shelf by shelf, Ben removed all of the books and looked behind them.

"What are you doing?" Liesl called out in vexation.

"I'll put them all back, don't worry," Ben said.

Half an hour later, he hadn't found anything. Liesl had finished doing the dishes and announced that she was exhausted. But Ben kept at it, removing each shelf of books, looking behind them, becoming more and more frustrated. When he came to the row of novels by F. Scott Fitzgerald, he smiled sadly. *The Great Gatsby* had been Peter's favorite.

Then, behind the Fitzgeralds, he found a small compartment that had been flush-mounted, almost invisibly, into the wooden shelf backing.

Peter had done an impeccable job of carpentry: even with all the books off the shelf, you could barely see the faint rectangular outline of the compartment. He pried at it with his fingernails, but it didn't yield. He poked at it, pressed in, and then it popped open. A neat piece of crafts-manship. Peter the perfectionist.

The document was carefully rolled up. A rubber band held the roll together. Ben pulled it out, removed the rubber band, unrolled it.

It was a fragile, yellowed sheet of paper covered with mimeographed lettering. Just one page. Merely the front page of a corporate filing.

It was headed SIGMA AG. There was a date: April 6, 1945.

Then a list of what had to be the company's officers and directors.

Dear God, he thought, thunderstruck. Peter had been right: there were names he recognized. Names of corporations that still existed, that made automobiles and weapons and consumer goods. Names of moguls and corporate chairmen. In addition to the figures he'd recognized from the photograph, there was the fabled magnate Cyrus Weston, whose steel empire had exceeded even that of Andrew Carnegie's, and Avery Hen-derson, who was regarded by business historians as the twentieth cen-tury's most important financier after John Pierpont Morgan. There were the chief executive officers of the major automotive companies; of early-generation technology firms that had taken the lead in developing radar, microwave, and refrigeration technologies—technologies whose full potential wouldn't be realized for years, decades, to come. The heads of the three largest petroleum companies, based in America, Britain, and the Netherlands. Telecommunication giants, before they were called that. The mammoth corporations of the time, some as intact and as vast as ever, some of them now subsumed into corporate enti-ties even greater than themselves. Industrialists from America, Western Europe, and, yes, even a few from wartime Germany. And toward the very top of the list was the name of the treasurer: MAX HARTMAN (OBERSTURMFÜHRER, SS).

His heart was hammering away crazily. Max Hartman, a lieutenant in Hitler's SS. If this was a forgery . . . it was certainly well done. He had seen documents of incorporation many times before, and this looked very much like a page from such a document.

Liesl emerged from the kitchen. "You have found something?"

The fire was dying, and the room was beginning to get cold.

"Do you know any of those names?" Ben asked.

"The famous ones. The mighty 'captains of industry,' as Peter called them."

"But almost of all them are dead now."

"They would have heirs, successors."

"Yes. Well-protected ones," Ben said. "There are other names here, too, names that I don't recognize. I'm not a historian." He pointed to a few of those names, those that were not from the English-speaking world. "Are any of these names familiar to you? And any of them alive?"

She sighed. "Gaston Rossignol, I know, must still live in Zurich, everyone's heard of him. A pillar of the Swiss banking establishment for much of the postwar era. Gerhard Lenz was an associate of Josef Mengele, who did all those terrible medical experiments on prisoners. A monster. He died somewhere in South America many years ago. And, of course..." Her voice trailed off.

"Peter was right," Ben said.

"About your father?"

"Yes."

"It's strange. *Der Apfel fällt nicht weit vom Stamm*, my people say— the apple doesn't fall far from the tree. You and Peter are really so alike. And when I look at Max Hartman as a young man, I see you in him. Yet you're both so utterly different from your father. Appearance is an uncertain guide."

"He is an evil man."

"I'm sorry." She looked at him for a long while. Whether it was out of sorrow, or pity, or something more, Ben couldn't decide. "Just now you look more like your brother than ever before."

"How do you mean?"

"You look...haunted. As he came to look in the last—the last months." She closed her eyes, blinking back tears. After a moment, she said, "The couch in Peter's study pulls out into a bed. Let me get it ready for you."

"That's all right," he said. "I can do it."

"Let me at least get you some linens. And then I'll say good night. I'm about to drop from exhaustion and too much wine. I was never a drinker."

"You've been through some hard times recently," he said. "We both have."

He said good night, undressed, then carefully folded the document and tucked it into the pocket of his leather jacket, next to Peter's identity papers. Within moments he had fallen into a deep, almost drugged sleep.

He and his brother were packed into a sealed boxcar, jammed with other people, unbearably hot, foul-smelling, because none of the prisoners had bathed in days. He was unable to move his limbs. Soon he passed out, and the next thing he knew they were somewhere else, again in a crowd of prisoners, walking skeletons with shaved heads. But Peter looked relieved, because at last he would be allowed to take a shower, and so what if it was a communal shower? Ben was overcome with panic, because he knew. Somehow he knew. He tried to shout: "Peter! No! This is not a shower—it's a gas chamber! Get out! It's a gas chamber!" Yet his words would not come out. The others stood there like zombies, and Peter just glared at him, not understanding. A baby was crying, and then a few young women. He tried to shout again, but nothing came out. He was wild with terror. He felt suffocated, claustrophobic. He saw his brother's upturned head, welcoming the water he expected to come from the nozzles. At the same time, he could hear the knobs being turned, the rusty squeak-squeak-squeak of the valves opening, the hiss of the gas. He shouted, "No!" opened his eyes, and looked around at the pitch-dark study.

Slowly he sat up, listening. There was no rusty squeak; he had dreamed it. He was in his late brother's cabin in the woods, and he had been sleeping.

But had he heard a noise, or had he dreamed that, too?

Then he heard the thunk of a car door closing.

It was unmistakable; there is no other sound like that. And it was a big car, perhaps a truck. His Range Rover?

He bolted out of bed, grabbed the flashlight, slipped quickly into his jeans and sneakers, and threw on his leather jacket. He thought: Could it be Liesl who'd gotten into, or out of, the Range Rover for some reason? He passed by her bedroom and pushed open the door.

She was in bed, eyes closed, asleep.

Oh, God. It was someone else. Someone was out there!

He rushed to the front door, grabbed the revolver from the table, opened the door silently. He looked around the clearing, illuminated by the pale light of a crescent moon. He didn't want to switch on the flashlight, didn't want to call attention to himself or alert whoever was out there.

Then he heard an ignition turn and the roar of an engine coming to life. He raced outside, saw the Range Rover still parked there, caught the red taillights of a truck.

"Hey!" he shouted, running after it.

The truck was barreling down the narrow dirt path at maximum speed, constrained only by the closeness of the trees. Ben ran faster, gun in one hand, clutching the Mag-Lite flashlight in the other like a baton at one of his college track meets. The taillights grew farther away even as he put on a burst of speed, the branches whipping his face, though he barely noticed. He was a machine, a running machine, a track star once again, and he would not let that truck get away, and as he tore down the dirt road that connected with the path from the cabin he thought, Did they hear a noise in the cabin? Were they planning a break-and-enter but were frightened away? and he kept on going, faster and faster, and the red lights grew smaller and smaller, the truck getting away from him, and then he knew that he'd never catch it. The truck was gone. He turned around, headed back toward the cabin, suddenly remembering the Range Rover. He could try to chase them down in the Rover! There were only two directions the truck could have gone; he could race after them in his vehicle. He ran back down the path toward the cabin, and was suddenly jolted by a tremendous, ear-splitting explosion in front of him, coming from the cabin, an explosion that turned the night sky orange and red like a giant Roman candle, and then he saw with terror that the cabin was ablaze, a ball of fire.

CHAPTER SEVENTEEN

Washington, D.C.

The zipper on Anna's garment bag snagged on one of her dresses just as the taxi arrived and honked impatiently.

"All right, all right," she groaned. "Cool it."

She yanked at the zipper again, with no luck. Then the telephone rang. "Good God!"

She was late, trying to get to Reagan National Airport to catch the evening flight to Zurich. No time to get the phone. She decided to let the voice mail answer it; then she changed her mind.

"Agent Navarro, forgive me for calling you at home." She recognized the high, hoarse voice at once, though she'd only spoken to him once before. "I got your home number from Sergeant Arsenault. It's Denis Weese from the Chemistry Section of the Nova Scotia Forensic Laboratory."

He spoke excruciatingly slowly. "Yes," she said impatiently, "the toxicologist. What's up?"

"Well, the ocular fluid you asked me to look at?"

She finally worked the fabric of her dress loose from the zipper's teeth. She tried not to think of how much the dress had cost. Damage had been done, but maybe it wouldn't be too noticeable. "You find anything?"

"It's most interesting." The taxi's honking grew more insistent.

"Can you hold on a second?" she said, then dropped the phone to the carpet and ran to the window. "I'll be down in a few minutes," she shouted.

The driver yelled up, "Navarro? You called for a taxi?"

"You can put the meter on. I'll be down in a few." She ran back to pick up the phone. "Sorry. The ocular fluid, you said."

"The band showed up on electrofluoresis," the toxicologist went on. "It's not a naturally occurring protein. It's a peptide, a sort of folded chain of amino acids—"

She dropped the garment bag to the floor. "Some synthetic compound, is that what you're saying?" Not a naturally occurring protein. Something that was created in a laboratory. What could this mean?

"One that selectively binds to neuroreceptors. That explains why we didn't find any traces of it in the bloodstream. It can only be detected, in trace quantities, in the spinal and ocular fluid."

"Meaning it goes right to the brain, basically."

"Well, yes."

"What kind of compound are we talking here?"

"It's an exotic. I guess the closest thing to it found in nature is a venom peptide, like snake venom. But the molecule's clearly synthetic."

"It's a poison, then."

"An entirely new molecule, one of the new toxins that scientists are now able to synthesize. I'm guessing that what it does is induce cardiac arrest. It goes right to the brain, crossing the blood-brain barrier, but leaves no traces in the blood serum. Really quite something."

An entirely new molecule.

"Let me ask you something. What do you think this toxin is intended to be used for? Biological warfare?"

He laughed uneasily. "No, no, no, nothing of the sort. One does see such synthetic peptides created, sort of modeled, on naturally occurring poisons found in toads or snails or snakes or whatever, in basic biotech research. You see, the fact that they selectively bind to certain proteins makes them useful for tagging them. It's the same property that makes them toxic, but that's not why people concoct them."

"So this—this substance—might have been made by a biotechnology company."

"Or any company with a research arm in molecular biochemistry. Could be any of the big agricultural firms, too. Monsanto, Archer Daniels Midland, you name it. I don't know where this was created, of course."

"I'm going to ask you a favor," she said. "I'm going to ask you to fax whatever you got on this to this number, O.K.?" She gave him a fax number, thanked him, hung up, and called the ICU. If she missed the plane, so be it. Right now nothing was more important than this.

"Can you patch me in to whoever has liaison with the U.S. Patent Office?" she said. When she'd been put through, she said, "Agent Stanley, this is Agent Anna Navarro. I need you to check something for me real quick and get back to me. In a couple of minutes you're going to get a fax from the Nova Scotia Forensic Laboratory. It's a description of a synthetic molecule. I need you to do a search for me at the U.S. Patent Office. I want to know if any company has filed a patent for this thing."

Find out who makes it, and you'll find the killer. One will lead to the other.

She hoped it would be that simple.

The taxi driver was honking again, and she went to the window to tell him to cool his jets.

Switzerland

Virtually catatonic, Ben drove to Zurich. Back into the lion's den, he thought ruefully to himself. Yes, he was persona non grata there, but it was a city of nearly four hundred thousand; he'd make out so long as he kept a low profile and avoided any tripwires. And where would those be? It was a risk, a definite, calculated risk, but there was no reason to believe that safe refuge lay elsewhere. Liesl had quoted Peter's warning words: the question isn't where they are, it's where they aren't.

Oh, God. Liesl! The odor of wood smoke that permeated his clothes was a wrenching, steady reminder of her, of the once-comfortable cabin, of the explosion he had witnessed but could scarcely comprehend.

The one thing he clung to, the one thing that allowed him to keep his sanity, was that Liesl had probably been dead when the cabin had burst into flames.

Oh, Christ!

By now he had put together how it had happened; it all made a chilling kind of sense. The squeaking he had heard in the middle of the night, which had incorporated itself into his terrible dream, had come from the valve of the propane tank being turned all the way open. The cabin had quickly filled with the odorless propane—he had already stepped outside by then—which was intended to overwhelm, put to sleep, then kill the occupants of the cabin. To cover up the evidence, a timed fuse had somehow gone off. Certainly it hadn't taken much to ignite the highly flammable gas. The accident would be ascribed by the local authorities to a faulty propane tank, not an uncommon hazard in rural areas.

And then whoever had done it had gotten into his truck and stolen away.

By the time Ben returned to the Range Rover—a matter of seconds, really, after the explosion—the cabin was pretty much gone.

She had not suffered. She had surely been either asleep or dead before her little cabin became an inferno.

He couldn't stand to think of it!

For four years Liesl and Peter had lived there, lived their lives in hiding, surely always fearful, but fundamentally undisturbed. Probably they could have gone on living there for years.

Until Ben had shown up in Zurich.

And brought out these zealots, in effect luring Peter to his death.

And led these faceless, anonymous zealots to Liesl, the woman who had once saved Peter's life.

Ben was beyond grief. He no longer felt the sharp stab of guilt, because he was numb. He felt nothing anymore. The shock had turned him into a cadaver, driving through the night, staring straight ahead, a machine without emotions.

But as he approached the darkened city, he began to feel one single emotion: a slowly growing, burning anger. A fury at those who had targeted innocent and good people who'd done nothing wrong but come across a bit of information by accident.

These killers, and those who directed them, remained faceless in his mind. He could not picture them, but he was determined to unmask them. They wanted him dead; they intended to frighten him into silence. But instead of running away, instead of hiding, he had made up his mind to run *toward* them, though from a direction they could not anticipate. They wanted to operate from the shadows; he would shine light on them. They wanted to conceal; he would expose.

And if his father was one of them . . .

He needed to dig into the past now, to excavate, to learn who these murderers were, and where they came from, and above all what they were hiding. Ben knew the rational response was to be frightened, and though that he certainly was, his fear was now subordinate to his rage.

He knew he had crossed some line into an obsession beyond any rationality.

But who were these faceless attackers?

Men who had been mobilized by the board of the corporation Max Hartman had helped set up. Madmen? Fanatics? Or simply mercenaries, hired by a corporation that had been founded, decades ago, by a group of prominent industrialists and high-ranking Nazis—among them his own father—who were now trying to conceal the unlawful origins of their original wealth? Cold-blooded mercenaries without any ideology except the profit motive, the almighty dollar, the Deutschmark, the Swiss franc . . .

There were layers upon layers of interlocking possibilities.

He needed cold hard information.

Ben vaguely remembered being told that one of Switzerland's great research libraries was at the University of Zurich, in the hills overlooking the city, and that was where he now headed, the logical place to begin digging up the past.

Washington, D.C.

Anna watched queasily as the flight attendant demonstrated the flimsy thing you put over your nose and mouth to help you breathe if the plane goes down. She'd once read an article in one of those on-line magazines that said that nobody had ever survived an emergency water landing of an airplane. Never. She took a pharmacy bottle of Ativan from her purse. It was beyond the expiration date, but she didn't particularly care. This was the only way she was going to make it across the Atlantic.

She was startled to hear her ICU-issue StarTac trilling from deep in the recesses of her purse. Government-standard cryptotelephony, and hardly bulkier than the usual consumer model. She'd forgot to turn it off.

She pulled it out. "Navarro."

"Please hold for Alan Bartlett," she heard in a lightly accented Jamaican voice.

She felt a tap on her shoulder. It was a flight attendant. "I'm sorry, ma'am," he said. "You're not allowed to have any cellular phones turned on during the flight."

"We're not flying yet," Anna pointed out.

"Agent Navarro," Bartlett said. "I'm glad I caught you."

"Ma'am," the flight attendant persisted, "airline regulations forbid you from using cell phones once the aircraft has left the gate."

"Sorry, this'll just be a minute." To Bartlett she said, "What have you got for me? I'm on a plane to Zurich."

"Ma'am," the flight attendant said loudly, exasperated.

Without looking at him she took out her Justice Department ID with her free hand and flashed it at him.

"We lost another one," Bartlett said.

Another one? So soon? The murders were accelerating.

The flight attendant drew back. "My apologies, ma'am."

"You're kidding me," Anna groaned.

"In Holland. A town called Tilburg, a couple of hours south of Amsterdam. You might want to change planes in Zurich and go there."

"No," she said. "I'm going to Zurich. It's a simple matter for me to have the FBI legat in Amsterdam request an immediate autopsy. This time at least we can tell them exactly what poisons to screen for."

"Is that right?"

"I'm on my way to Zurich, Director. I'm going to catch myself a live one. Dead men don't talk. Now, what was the name of the Tilburg victim?"

Bartlett paused. "A certain Hendrik Korsgaard."

"Wait a minute!" Anna said sharply. "That name wasn't on my list."

There was silence on the other end.

"Talk to me, Bartlett, dammit!"

"There are other lists, Agent Navarro," Bartlett said slowly. "I was hoping they wouldn't prove . . . relevant."

"Unless I'm greatly mistaken, this is a violation of our understanding, Director Bartlett," Anna said quietly, her eyes darting around to verify that she wasn't being overheard.

"Not at all, Ms. Navarro. My office works like any other, by a division of labor. Information is edited accordingly. Your responsibility was to find the killers. We had reason to believe that the names on the list I gave you, from the clearance files, were being targeted. We had no reason to believe that . . . the others were in jeopardy as well."

"And did you know where the Tilburg victim resided?"

"We didn't even know he was still living. Certainly, all efforts to locate him were in vain."

"Then we can rule out the possibility that the killers have simply gained access to your files."

"It's gone far beyond that," Bartlett said crisply. "Whoever's killing these old men, they've got better sources than we do."

It was not much past four in the morning by the time Ben located the *Universitätsbibliothek* on Zähringerplatz. The library wouldn't open for another five hours.

In New York, he calculated, it was ten at night. His father would probably still be awake—he usually went to bed late and arose early, always had—and even if he were asleep, Ben wasn't much concerned about waking him. Not anymore.

Wandering down the Universitätstrasse to stretch his legs, he made sure his cell phone was switched to the GSM standard used in Europe and placed a call to Bedford.

The housekeeper, Mrs. Walsh, answered.

Mrs. Walsh, an Irish version of Mrs. Danvers from *Rebecca*, Ben had always thought, had worked for the family for over twenty years, and Ben had never got past her haughty reserve.

"Benjamin," she said. Her tone was strange.

"Good evening, Mrs. Walsh," Ben said wearily. "I need to talk to my father." He readied himself to do battle with his father's gatekeeper.

"Benjamin, your father's gone."

He went cold. "Gone where?"

"Well, that's just it, I don't know."

"Who does?"

"No one. A car came for Mr. Hartman this morning, and he wouldn't say where he was going. Not a word. He said it would be 'a while.' "

"A car? Was it Gianni?" Gianni was his father's regular driver, a happy-go-lucky sort whom the old man regarded with a certain distanced affection.

"Not Gianni. Not a company car. He's just gone. No explanation."

"I don't understand. He's never done that before, has he?"

"Never. I know he packed his passport, because it's gone."

"His passport? Well, that tells us something, doesn't it?"

"But I called his office, talked to his secretary, and she knew nothing about any international trip. I was hoping he might have said something to you."

"Not a word. Did he get any phone calls . . . ?"

"No, I don't . . . Let me look at the message book." She came back to the phone a minute later. "Just a Mr. Godwin."

"Godwin?"

"Well, actually, it says Professor Godwin."

The name took him by surprise. That had to be Ben's college mentor, the Princeton historian John Barnes Godwin. Then again, he realized, it wasn't particularly bizarre for Godwin to be calling Max: a few years ago, impressed by what Ben had told him about the famous historian, Max had given money to Princeton to set up a Center for the Study of Human Values, of which Godwin became the director. Yet his father hadn't mentioned Godwin. Why were the two of them talking on the morning before Max disappeared?

"Let me have the number," he said.

He thanked her and clicked off.

Strange, he thought. For a brief moment he imagined that his father was fleeing somewhere, because he knew his past had been uncovered or was about to be uncovered. But that made no sense—fleeing what? Fleeing where?

Ben was exhausted and emotionally depleted, and he knew he was not thinking clearly. He badly needed sleep. He was making connections now that weren't quite logical.

He thought: Peter knew things, things about their father's past, about a company Max had helped set up, and then Peter was killed.

And then . . .

And then I found a photograph of the founders of this corporation, my father among them. And I followed to Liesl and Peter's cabin, and I found a page from the incorporation document setting this company up. And then they'd tried to kill both me and Liesl and cover up the evidence by blowing up the cabin.

So is it possible that they . . . again, the faceless, anonymous They . . . had gotten to my father, informed him that the secret was out, the secret of his past, or maybe the secret of this strange corporation? Or both?

Yes, of course it was possible. Since They seem to be trying to eliminate anyone who knows about this company . . .

Why else had Max disappeared so suddenly, so mysteriously?

Might he have been compelled to go somewhere, to meet with certain people . . .

There was only one thing Ben felt sure of: that his father's sudden disappearance was in some way connected with the murders of Peter and Liesl, and with the uncovering of this document.

He returned to the Range Rover, noticed in the light of the rising sun the deep scratches that defaced its sides, and drove back to Zähringer-platz.

Then he settled back in the Rover and placed a call to Princeton, New Jersey.

"Professor Godwin?"

The old professor sounded as if he'd been asleep.

"It's Ben Hartman."

John Barnes Godwin, historian of Europe in the twentieth century and once Princeton's most popular lecturer, had been retired for years. He was eighty-two but still came into his office every day to work.

An image of Godwin came into Ben's mind—tall and gaunt, white-haired, the deeply wrinkled face.

Godwin had been not just Ben's faculty adviser but a sort of father figure as well. Ben remembered once sitting in Godwin's book-choked office in Dickinson Hall. The amber light, the vanilla-mildew smell of old books.

They'd been talking about how FDR managed to maneuver the iso-lationist United States into the Second World War. Ben was writing his senior thesis about FDR and had told Godwin that he was offended by Roosevelt's trickery.

"Ah, Mr. Hartman," Godwin replied. That was what he called Ben in those days. "How is your Latin? *Honesta turpitudo est pro causa bona.*"

Ben looked at the professor blankly.

" 'For a good cause,' " Godwin translated with a slow, sly smile, " 'wrongdoing is virtuous.' Publilius Syrus, who lived in Rome a century before Christ, and said a lot of smart things."

"I don't think I agree," Ben said, the morally indignant undergraduate. "To me that sounds like a rationalization for screwing people over. I hope I never catch myself saying that."

Godwin regarded him with what seemed to be puzzlement. "I suppose that's why you refuse to join your father's business," he said pointedly. "You'd rather be pure."

"I'd rather teach."

"But why are you so sure you want to teach?" Godwin had asked, sipping tawny port.

"Because I love it."

"You're certain?"

"No," Ben admitted. "How can a twenty-year-old be certain of any-thing?"

"Oh, I find that twenty-year-olds are certain of most things."

"But why should I go into something I have no interest in, working in a company my father built, to make even more money that I don't need? I mean, what good does our money do for society? Why should I have great wealth while others have no food on the table?"

Godwin closed his eyes. "It's a luxury to thumb your nose at money. I've had some extremely rich students, even a Rockefeller, in my class. And they all struggle with this same dilemma—not to let the money rule your life or define you, but, instead, to do something meaningful with your life. Now, your father is one of our nation's great philanthropists—"

"Yeah, wasn't it Reinhold Niebuhr who said that philanthropy is a form of paternalism? The privileged class tries to preserve its status by doling out funds to the needy?"

Godwin glanced up, impressed. Ben tried not to smile. He'd just read this in his theology class, and the line had stuck in his mind.

"A question, Ben. Is becoming a grade school teacher actually your way of rebelling against your father?"

"Maybe so," Ben said, unwilling to lie. He wanted to add that it was Godwin who had inspired him to teach, but that might sound too . . . something.

He was surprised when Godwin replied, "Bully for you. That takes guts. And you'll be a great teacher, I have no doubt of it."

Now, Ben said, "I'm sorry to be calling you so late—"

"Not at all, Ben. Where are you? The connection—"

"Switzerland. Listen, my father's disappeared—"

"What do you mean, 'disappeared'?"

"He left home this morning, went somewhere, we don't know where, and I was wondering because you called him this morning, just before that . . ."

"I was returning his call, really. He wanted to talk about another gift to the center he was planning to make."

"That's it?"

"I'm afraid so. Nothing out of the ordinary, as far as I can recall. But if he happens to call me again, is there a way I can get in touch with you?"

Ben gave Godwin his digital number. "Another question. Do you know anyone on the faculty of the University of Zurich? Someone who does what you do—modern European history."

Godwin paused for a moment. "At the University of Zurich? You can't do any better than Carl Mercandetti. A first-class researcher. Economic history's his specialty, but he's very wide-ranging in the best European tradition. The fellow also has an astounding collection of grappa, though I suppose that's neither here nor there. Regardless, Mercandetti's your man."

"I appreciate it," Ben said, and he hung up.

Then he put the car seat back and tried to doze for a few hours.

He slept fitfully, his sleep disturbed by unceasing nightmares in which he was forced to see the cabin explode time and again.

When he awoke at a few minutes after nine, he saw in the rearview mirror how unshaven and dirty he looked, saw the deep circles under his eyes, but he didn't have what it took to find a place to shave and wash.

There wasn't any time in any case.

It was time to begin excavating a past that was no longer the past.

CHAPTER EIGHTEEN

Paris

Only a small brass plaque marked the office of Groupe TransEuroTech SA, on the third floor of a limestone building on the avenue Marceau in the eighth arrondissement. The plaque, mounted on the stone to the left of the front door, was but one of seven brass plaques bearing the names of law firms and other small companies, and as such it attracted little attention.

The office of TransEuroTech never received unscheduled visitors, but anyone who happened to pass by the third floor would see nothing out of the ordinary: a young male receptionist sitting behind a glass teller's window made of a bullet-resistant polycarbonate material that looked like plain glass. Behind him, a small, bare room furnished with a few molded-plastic chairs, and a single door to the interior offices.

No one would, of course, realize that the receptionist was actually an armed and experienced ex-commando, or see the concealed surveillance cameras, the passive infrared motion detectors, the balanced magnetic switches embedded in every door.

The conference room deep inside the offices was actually a room within a room: a module separated from the surrounding concrete walls by foot-thick rubber blocks that kept all vibrations (specifically human speech) from transferring out. Immediately adjacent to the conference module was a permanent installation of antennae constantly searching for HF, UHF, VHF, and microwave transmissions—any attempt, that is, to listen in on the discussions held within the room. Attached to the antennae was a spectrum analyzer programmed to check across the spectrum for any anomalies.

At one end of a coffin-shaped mahogany conference table sat two men. Their conversation was protected against interception by both white-noise generators and a "babble tape," which sounded like the yammer of a crowded bar at happy hour. Anyone somehow able to bypass the elaborate security and listen in would be unable to separate the words of the two men at the table from the background noise.

The older of the two was speaking on a sterile telephone, a flat black box of Swiss manufacture. He was a pasty-faced, worried-looking man in his mid-fifties with gold-framed glasses, a soft jowly face, oily skin, and receding hair dyed an unnatural russet. His name was Paul Marquand, and he was a vice president of security for the Corporation. Marquand had come to the Corporation by a route common to corporate-security directors of international businesses: he had spent time in the French infantry, was forced out for wild behavior and joined the French Foreign Legion, later moving to the U.S., where he'd worked as a strikebreaker for a mining company before he was hired to do corporate security for a multinational firm.

Marquand spoke rapidly, quietly, and then hung up the phone.

"Vienna Sector is disturbed," Marquand told the man beside him, a dark-haired, olive-skinned Frenchman some twenty years younger named Jean-Luc Passard. "The American survived the propane accident in St. Gallen." He added darkly, "There can be no more errors. Not after the Bahnhofplatz debacle."

"It was not your decision to assign the American soldier," Jean-Luc said softly.

"Of course not, but neither did I object. The logic was persuasive: he'd spent time in proximity to the subject and could pick the face out of a crowd in a matter of seconds. No matter how often a stranger is shown a photograph, he could never move as quickly or as reliably as someone who has known the target personally."

"We've now mobilized the very best," Passard said. "With the Architect on the case, it will not be long before the mess is eliminated completely."

"His perfectionism leads to persistence," Marquand observed. "Still the pampered American is not to be underestimated."

"The marvel is that he is still alive, the amateur," Passard agreed. "Being a fitness freak does not give one survival skills." He snorted and spoke mockingly in heavily accented English: "He doesn't know the jungle. He knows the jungle gym."

"All the same," Marquand said, "there is such a thing as beginner's luck."

"He is no longer a beginner," Passard observed.

Vienna

The elderly, well-dressed American emerged from the gate, walking stiffly and slowly, clutching a carry-on bag. He searched the crowd until he saw a uniformed limousine driver holding up a little sign with his name on it.

The old man gave a wave of acknowledgment, and the driver, accompanied by a woman in a white nurse's uniform, hurried up to him. The driver took the American's bag, and the nurse said, "How was your flight, sir?" She spoke in English with an Austrian-German accent.

The man grumbled, "I despise traveling. I can't tolerate it anymore."

The nurse escorted him through the crowds and to the street immediately outside, where a black Daimler limousine was parked. She helped him into the interior, which was equipped with the standard appurtenances—phone, TV, and bar. Tucked unobtrusively into one corner was an array of emergency medical equipment, including a small oxygen tank, hoses and face mask, defibrillator paddles, and IV tubes.

"Well, sir," the nurse said once he was settled in the deeply cushioned leather seat, "the ride is not long at all, sir."

The old man grunted, reclined the seat back, and closed his eyes.

"Please let me know if there's anything I can do to make you more comfortable," the nurse said.

CHAPTER NINETEEN

Zurich

Anna was met at her hotel by a liaison officer from the office of the Public Prosecutor of the canton of Zurich. He was Bernard Kesting, a small, powerfully built, dark-haired young man with a heavy beard and eyebrows that joined in the middle. Kesting was unsmiling, all business, very professional: the quintessential Swiss bureaucrat.

After a few minutes of stilted introductory chat, Kesting led her to his car, a BMW 728, parked in the semicircular drive in front of the hotel.

"Rossignol is of course well known to us," Kesting said, holding the car door open for her. "A revered figure in the banking community, for many, many years. Certainly my office has never had reason to question him." She got into the car, but he stood there with the car door still open. "I'm afraid the nature of your inquiry was not made clear to us. The gentleman has never been accused of any crime, you know."

"I understand." She reached for the handle and closed the door herself. He made her nervous.

Behind the wheel, Kesting continued as he pulled out of the drive and headed down Steinwiesstrasse, a quiet residential street near the Kunsthaus. "He was, or is, a brilliant financier."

"I can't disclose the nature of our investigation," Anna said, "but I can tell you that he's not the target of it."

He was silent for a while, then said with some embarrassment, "You asked about protective surveillance. As you know, we haven't been able to locate him precisely."

"And this is customary for prominent Swiss bankers? To simply . . . disappear?"

"Customary? No. But then he is retired, after all. He is entitled to his eccentricities."

"And how are his official communications handled?"

"Received by a trust, domestic representatives of an offshore entity that remains, even to them, completely opaque."

"Transparency not being a notable Swiss value."

Kesting glanced at her quickly, apparently unsure whether she was being snide. "It seems that at some point in the past year or so, he decided he wanted to, well, keep a lower profile. Perhaps he had the delusion that he was being stalked, pursued—he's in his early nineties, after all, and mental deterioration can sometimes lead to paranoid fantasies."

"And perhaps it wasn't a delusion."

Kesting gave her a sharp look but said nothing.

Herr Professor Doktor Carl Mercandetti had warmed immeasurably when Ben mentioned that he was a friend of Professor John Barnes Godwin. "There is no inconvenience, and nothing to apologize for. I have an office in the library. Why don't you meet me there midmorning? I'll be there anyway. I hope Godwin didn't tell you—I'm supposed to be publishing a monograph as part of a Cambridge University Press series that he's editing, and already I'm two years late with it! He tells me my sense of timing is a touch Mediterranean." Mercandetti's laugh was booming even over the phone line.

Ben had been vague about what he'd wanted from Mercandetti, and Mercandetti, judging from his high jollity, had probably assumed it was as much by way of a social call as anything.

Ben spent the first part of the morning searching through every directory of corporations in Switzerland he could find, even running a computer search of all telephone listings. But he could find no record of such a corporation as Sigma AG. So far as he could see, there was no public record that it ever did exist.

Carl Mercandetti was more austere-looking in person than Ben had imagined when they spoke on the telephone. He was around fifty, slight, with a gray crew cut and oval wire-rimmed glasses. When Ben introduced himself, however, the eyes became lively, and his handclasp was welcoming.

"Any friend of God's . . ." Mercandetti said.

"And I thought it was only Princeton undergraduates who called him that."

Mercandetti shook his head, smiling. "In the years I've known him, I'd say he's only grown into his nickname. I'm quite terrified he'll be there at the pearly gates, saying, 'Now, a small query about footnote forty-three in your last article . . .' "

After a few minutes, Ben mentioned his efforts to track down a corporation named Sigma AG, one founded in Zurich toward the end of the Second World War. He didn't explain further: the scholar would doubtless assume it was the sort of thing that an international banker might well pursue, perhaps in the course of corporate due diligence. In any case, Ben knew he would not be ill-served by reticence.

When he learned of Ben's immediate concerns, Mercandetti was polite but unengaged. The name Sigma clearly meant little to him.

"You say it was established in 1945?" the historian asked.

"That's right."

"A magnificent year for Bordeaux, did you know that?" He shrugged. "Of course, we're talking well over half a century ago. Many companies that were founded during the war, or right after, failed. Our economy was not so good as it is now."

"I have reason to believe it still exists," Ben said.

Mercandetti cocked his head good-naturedly. "What sort of information do you have?"

"It's not solid information, really. It's more along the lines of—of, well, people talking. People in a position to know."

Mercandetti seemed amused and skeptical. "Do these people have any more information? The name could easily have been changed."

"But isn't there some record somewhere of corporate name changes?"

The historian's eyes scanned the vaulted ceiling of the library. "There's a place you might check. It's called the *Handelsregisteramt des Kantons Zürich*—the registry of all corporations founded in Zurich. All companies established here must file papers with the registry."

"All right. And let me ask you something else. This list here." He slid the list of directors of Sigma AG, which he had recopied in his own hand, across the sturdy oak table. "Do you recognize any of these names?"

Mercandetti put on a pair of reading glasses. "Most of these names— they are names of well-known industrialists, you know. Prosperi, here, is a sort of underworld figure—I think he just died, just recently. In Brazil or Paraguay, I forget which. These men are mostly dead or very ancient by now. Oh, and Gaston Rossignol, the banker—he must live in Zurich."

"Is he still alive?"

"I haven't heard otherwise. But if he's alive he must be in his eighties or nineties."

"Is there a way to find out?"

"Have you tried the telephone book?" An amused look.

"There were a handful of Rossignols. None of them with the right first initial."

Mercandetti shrugged. "Rossignol was a major financier. Helped restore the solidity of our banking system after the Second World War. He had many friends here. But perhaps has retired to the Cap d'Antibes, and is slathering coconut oil on his liver-spotted shoulders even as we speak. Or perhaps he now seeks to avoid any sort of attention, for some reason of his own. With the recent controversies over Swiss gold and the Second World War, there have been agitators, some of them vigilantes. Even a Swiss banker cannot live in a vault, of course. So one takes precautions."

One takes precautions. "Thanks," he said. "This is extremely helpful." Now he pulled out the black-and-white photograph he'd taken from the Handelsbank and handed it to the academic. "Do any of these men look familiar?"

"I don't know if you are a banker, at heart, or a history buff," Mercandetti said merrily. "Or a dealer in old photographs—quite a trade these days. Collectors pay fortunes for nineteenth-century tintypes. Not my sort of thing at all. Give me color any day."

"This isn't exactly a vacation snap," Ben said mildly.

Mercandetti smiled and picked up the photo. "That must be Cyrus Weston—yes, with his trademark hat," he said. He pointed with a stubby finger. "That looks like Avery Henderson, dead many years. This is Émil Ménard, who built Trianon, really the first modern conglomerate. This may be Rossignol, but I'm not sure. One always imagines him with his great bald dome, not this thatch of dark hair, but he was a much younger man here. And over here . . ." A minute passed in silence before Mercandetti dropped the photo. His smile had vanished. "What sort of prank is this?" he asked Ben, looking at him over his reading glasses. A bemused expression crossed his face.

"How do you mean?"

"This must be some sort of montage, something involving trick photography." The academic spoke with a trace of annoyance.

"Why do you say that? Surely Weston and Henderson were acquainted."

"Weston and Henderson? Surely they were. And surely they were never in the same place as Sven Norquist, the Norwegian shipping magnate, and Cecil Benson, the British automotive magnate, and Drake Parker, the head of the petrochemical giant, and Wolfgang Siebing, the German industrialist, whose family company once made military equipment and now is best known for its coffeemakers. And a dozen more of their ilk. Some of these men were archrivals, some in completely different lines of enterprise. To posit that all these people had met—now that would involve rewriting twentieth-century business history, for a start."

"Couldn't this have been a sort of mid-century economic conference, like Davos?" Ben ventured. "A precursor to the Bilderberg conferences, maybe? Some meeting of the corporate titans?"

The historian pointed to another figure. "This can only be someone's idea of a joke. A very cleverly doctored image."

"Who's that you're pointing at?"

"That, of course, is Gerhard Lenz, the Viennese scientist." Mercandetti's tone was hard.

The name sounded vaguely familiar, but Ben wasn't sure in what context he knew it. "Who is he again?"

"Was. He died in South America. Dr. Gerhard Lenz, a brilliant mind, by all accounts, was not to mention the product of Vienna's finest medical training, the epitome of Viennese civilization. Sorry, I'm being sarcastic, and that doesn't suit a historian. The fact is that Lenz, like his friend Josef Mengele, was infamous in his own right for his experiments on concentration camp prisoners, on crippled children. He was already in his late forties when the war ended. His son still lives in Vienna."

My God. Gerhard Lenz was one of the twentieth century's great monsters. Ben felt lightheaded. Gerhard Lenz, a light-eyed Nazi officer, was standing immediately next to Max Hartman.

Mercandetti fished an 8x loupe from a jacket pocket—he regularly had to resort to magnification in his archival research, Ben guessed—and scrutinized the image. Then he examined the yellowed card stock on which the emulsion was fixed. After a few minutes, he shook his head. "Indeed, it looks real. And yet it is not possible. It cannot be real." Mercandetti spoke with quiet vehemence, and Ben wondered whether he was mostly trying to persuade himself. For even as he denied the evidence of his eyes, the historian looked ashen. "Tell me," he said, and now his tone was brittle, all traces of bonhomie having evaporated. "Where did you get this?"

One takes precautions. Gaston Rossignol was alive: the death of so august a figure would not have passed without notice. And yet after another hour of research, Mercandetti and he came up empty-handed. "I apologize for a fruitless search," Mercandetti said resignedly. "But then I am a historian, not a private detective. Besides, I would have imagined that this sort of thing would be down your alley, given your familiarity with financial stratagems."

The academic was right; it should have occurred to Ben already. What Mercandetti was alluding to—financial stratagems, he called it—went by the name of asset protection, and it was something Ben had some familiarity with. Now it was his turn to sit back and think. Prominent men do not simply disappear; they create legal edifices behind which to shelter. The task of hiding one's place of residence from pursuers was not so unlike the task of hiding it from creditors or from the taxation powers of the state. Rossignol would want to retain control of his possessions while seeming to have been divested of them. It would not be easy to keep tabs on a man without property.

Ben Hartman recalled a particularly miserly client of Hartman Capital Management, who had an obsession with asset protection schemes. Ben came to dislike the man with a passion, but as much as he begrudged the time he'd spent working on the miser's account, Ben realized that what he'd learned about the subterfuges of "asset protection" would now come in handy. "Gaston Rossignol must have blood relatives in the area," Ben said to Carl Mercandetti. "I'm thinking of someone both reliable and compliant. Someone close enough to do his bidding, but decidedly younger than he is." In any variant of a gift-leaseback scheme, Ben knew, it was an undesirable complication to be predeceased by the pseudo-beneficiary. And the clandestinity of any scheme depended upon the discretion of the enlisted partner.

"You're talking about Yves-Alain, of course," the professor said.

"Am I?"

"You've just described him. Yves-Alain Taillé, the banker's nephew. A civic leader here of some distinction, thanks to his family's prominence, and a banker of no distinction at all, thanks to his intellectual mediocrity. Weak but well-meaning is the general consensus on him. Used to chair the Zurich Arts Council or some such. He has a sinecure at one of the private banks, a vice president of something or other. Easy enough to find out."

"And if I wanted to find out whether Taillé had title to property in the canton besides his primary residence? Aren't there public tax documents in connection to estate transfers?"

"There are municipal records in the Rathaus, just off the Limmat. But if it's a recent title transfer, from the past five years, you can do an on-line search. The same with the tax documents you seek. They're supposedly public documents, but they're kept on a secure server, honoring one of the two great Swiss passions—those being for chocolate and for secrecy. I myself have a user ID and password that will provide access. Not so long ago, you see, the town fathers hired me to write something for a brochure to mark the six hundred and fiftieth anniversary of Zurich's joining the Swiss Confederation. A bit more local than my usual research, but they were openhanded with the francs."

An hour later, Ben had an address, a residence decidedly more modest than Rossignol had formerly inhabited. Two hours later, after immersing himself in a series of tax documents of astounding intricacy, he had satisfied himself that it was Gaston Rossignol's. For one thing, the title was in Taillé's name, and yet it was not his primary residence. A country house? No one would have one in Zurich proper. A pied-à-terre for a mistress? But it was too grand for that. And what of the real-estate investment trust that maintained comanagement privileges? Taillé did not enjoy unilateral control over the property's disposition; he could not sell it or transfer the title without permission of the trust. And where was the trust headquartered? In one of the Channel Islands, Jersey. Ben smiled. Nicely done—a tax haven but not one of the truly infamous ones. It wasn't as notorious as Nauru, but its banking establishment was even more tightly knit, more difficult to penetrate.

Ben glanced again at the address he had jotted down. It was incredible to think that a brief car ride would take him to one of Sigma's founders. Peter had tried to hide from Sigma, and it had destroyed him. Ben took a deep breath, and felt his stores of anger burn within him. *Well, there's been a change of plans*, he thought. *Now let Sigma try to hide from me.*

CHAPTER TWENTY

Ben found Gaston Rossignol's house in the area of Zurich called Hottin-gen, a steep, hilly area overlooking the city. The houses here were situated on large lots and hidden by trees: very private, very secluded.

Rossignol's house was on Hauserstrasse, close to the Dolder Grand Hotel, the grande dame of Zurich hotels, generally considered the finest in all of Europe. The house was wide and low-slung, built of brownish stone apparently in the early part of the century.

It didn't look like any kind of safe house, Ben reflected, but perhaps that was what made it so effective. Rossignol had grown up in Zurich, but spent much of his career in Bern. He knew certain Zurichers of power and influence, of course, but it was not a place where he had casual acquaintances. Besides, the residents of the Hauserstrasse were the sort who kept to themselves; this was a neighborhood without neigh-borliness. An old man who cultivated his own garden would never at-tract notice. It would be a comfortable life, but an effectively obscure one, too.

Ben parked the Range Rover on an incline down the block and set the emergency brake to keep it from rolling. He opened the glove compart-ment and took out Liesl's revolver. There were four shells remaining in the chamber. He would have to buy more ammunition somewhere if he wanted to use the weapon for protection. Making sure the safety was engaged, he slipped it into his jacket pocket.

He rang the doorbell. There was no answer, and after a few minutes, he rang again.

Still no answer.

He tried the knob, but the door was locked.

He noticed a late-model Mercedes parked in the carport at one side of the house. Rossignol's car or someone else's, he couldn't know.

He turned to leave when it occurred to him to try all the doors, and he went around the side of the house. The lawn was newly mown, flower gardens well tended. Someone took good care of the property. The back of the house was grander than the front, a large sweep of land bordered by more flower gardens, bathed by the morning sun. A cupola sat in the middle of a large terrace at the back of the house, near an arrangement of deck chairs.

Ben approached the back entrance. He pulled open a glass storm door and then tried the knob.

The knob turned.

He opened the door, his heart hammering, and braced for an alarm to go off, but heard none.

Was Rossignol here? Or anyone else, a servant, a housekeeper, family?

He entered the house, into a dark, tiled mud room. A few coats hung on hooks, along with an assortment of wooden canes with ornamental handles. Passing through the mud room, he entered what looked like a study, a small room furnished with a large desk, a few bookcases. Gaston Rossignol, once the pillar of Switzerland's banking establishment, seemed to be a man of relatively modest tastes.

On the desk was a green blotter pad, next to it a sleek black Panasonic telephone with modern gimmicks built in: conference, caller ID, intercom, speakerphone, digital answering machine.

As he was staring at the phone, it rang. It was ear-splittingly loud, the ringer turned up to maximum volume. He froze, expecting Rossignol to enter, wondering how he would explain himself. It rang again, three times, four, then stopped.

He waited.

No one had picked up. Did that mean no one was home? He glanced at the caller ID screen, saw that the number was a long series of digits, obviously long distance.

He decided to move on farther into the house. As he walked down a corridor, he heard faint music playing—Bach, it sounded like—but where was it coming from?

Was someone in fact home?

From the far end of the hall he saw the glow of light coming from a room. He approached, and the music grew louder.

Now he entered what he immediately recognized as a formal dining room, a long table in the center of the room covered with a crisp white linen tablecloth and set with a silver coffeepot on a silver tray, a single place setting at which was a plate of eggs and sausage. Breakfast appeared to have been served by a housekeeper, but where was he or she? A port-able tape player on a buffet against one wall was playing a Bach cello suite.

And sitting at the table, his back to Ben, was an old man in a wheelchair. A tanned bald head, fringed with gray, a bull neck, round shoulders.

The old man didn't seem to have heard Ben entering. He was probably hard of hearing, Ben decided, a guess confirmed by the hearing aid in the old man's right ear.

Still, taking no chances, he slid his hand into the front pocket of his leather jacket, felt the bulk of the revolver, pulled it out, and released the safety. The old man didn't move. He had to be seriously deaf, or his hearing aid was turned off.

Suddenly Ben was jolted by the ring of the telephone, just as loud in here as it had been in the study a minute ago.

Yet the old man didn't move.

It rang again, a third time, a fourth, and stopped.

Then he heard a man's voice coming from down the hall, the tone frantic. After a moment, Ben realized that the voice was coming from the answering machine, but he couldn't make out what it was saying.

He took a few steps closer, then placed the barrel of the revolver against the old man's head. "Don't move."

The old man's head fell forward, lolling on his chest.

Ben grabbed the arm of the wheelchair with his free hand and spun it around.

The old man's chin was on his chest, the eyes wide and staring at the floor. Lifeless.

Ben's body flooded with panic.

He felt the food on the plate. The eggs and sausage were still warm.

Apparently Rossignol had died just moments ago. Had he been *killed*?

If so, the killer could be in the house right now!

He raced down the corridor from which he had come, and the tele-phone rang again. In the study, he looked at the caller ID screen: the same long series of digits, beginning with 431. Where was the call from? The numbers were familiar. A country in Europe, he felt sure.

The answering machine came on.

"Gaston? Gaston?" a man's voice shouted.

The words were in French, but spoken by a foreigner, and Ben could make out few of the heavily accented words.

Who was calling Rossignol, and why?

Another ring: the doorbell!

He raced to the back entrance, which he'd left partially open. No one was there.

Move it!

He stepped outside and ran around the side of the house, slowing when he got near the front. From behind some tall shrubbery, he could see a white police cruiser passing slowly by, patrolling the neighborhood, he guessed.

A low wrought-iron fence separated Rossignol's yard from the neighbor's. He raced to the low fence, and leaped over it into the neighbor's yard, which was roughly the same size as Rossignol's, though not as ornately landscaped. He was taking an enormous chance of being spotted by anyone in the neighbor's house, but no one called out to him, there were no shouts, and he kept running, around the far side of the house and out to Hauserstrasse. A hundred feet or so down the street was the Rover. He ran to it, leaped in, and keyed the ignition. It roared to life.

He made a quick U-turn and then drove down the steep street, deliberately slowing his pace to that of a local driving to work.

Someone had just tried to call Rossignol. Someone calling from a place whose telephone number began 431.

The digits tumbled around in his brain until something clicked.

Vienna, Austria.

The call had come from Vienna. These men have successors, heirs, Liesl had said. One of them, Mercandetti had told him, resided in Vienna: the son of the monster Gerhard Lenz. With Rossignol dead, it was as logical a lead to follow as any. Not a certainty—far from a certainty—but at least a possibility. A possible lead when there was a paucity of leads.

In a few minutes he had arrived in the heart of the city, near the Bahnhofplatz, where Jimmy Cavanaugh had tried to kill him. Where it had all begun.

He had to get on the next train to Vienna.

The Austrian Alps

There was a soft knock on the door, and the old man called out irritably, "Yes?"

A physician in a white coat entered, a short, rotund man with round shoulders and a potbelly.

"How is everything, sir?" the physician asked. "How is your suite?"

"You call this a suite?" Patient Eighteen asked. He lay atop the narrow single bed, fully dressed in his rumpled three-piece suit. "It's a god-damned monk's cell."

Indeed, the room was simply furnished, with only a chair, a desk, a reading lamp, and a television set. The stone floor was bare.

The physician smiled wanly. "I am Dr. Löfquist," he said, sitting in the chair beside the bed. "I would like to welcome you, but I must also warn you. This will be a very rigorous and difficult ten days. You will be put through the most extensive physical and mental tests you have ever had."

Patient Eighteen did not bother to sit up. "Why the hell the mental?"

"Because, you see, not everyone is eligible."

"What happens if you think I'm crazy?"

"Anyone not invited to join is sent home with our regrets."

The patient said nothing.

"Perhaps you should take a rest, sir. This afternoon will be tiring. There will be a CAT scan, a chest X-ray, then a series of cognitive tests. And, of course, a standard test for depression."

"I'm not depressed," the patient snapped.

The doctor ignored him. "Tonight you will be required to fast, so that we may accurately measure plasma cholesterol, triglycerides, lipoproteins, and so on."

"Fast? You mean starve? I'm not starving myself!"

"Sir," the doctor said, rising, "you are free to go any time you wish. If you stay, and if you are invited to join us, you will find the procedure to be lengthy and quite painful, I must be honest. But it will be like nothing you have ever experienced in your long life. Ever. This I promise you."

Kesting did not conceal his surprise when Anna returned several hours later with an address; and in truth Anna shared a measure of that surprise. She had done what she'd determined to do, and it had worked. After a few readings of the Rossignol file, she had come up with one name that could be of help: that of a Zurich civil servant named Daniel Taine. The name recurred in several different contexts, and further inquiries had confirmed her intuition. Gaston Rossignol had been Taine's first employer, and, it appeared, something of a mentor. In the seventies, Taine and Rossignol were partners in a limited liability venture involving high-yield Eurobonds. Rossignol had sponsored Taine's application to the Kifkintler Society, a men's club whose membership included many of Zurich's most powerful citizens. Now Taine, having made his small fortune, served in various honorific capacities in the canton. He was someone with precisely the sort of access and resources to ensure that his old mentor's plans ran smoothly.

Anna had dropped in on Taine at his home unannounced, identified herself, and laid her cards on the table. Her message was simple. Gaston Rossignol was in serious, imminent danger.

Taine was visibly rattled, but closemouthed, as she expected. "I cannot help you. He has moved. No one can say where, and it is no one's concern."

"Except the killers?"

"Even if there are such assassins," Taine spoke with a display of skepticism, but he acceded too readily to her stipulation, "who's to say they can find him if you cannot. Your own resources are obviously considerable."

"I have reason to believe they've already made headway."

A sharp glance: "Really? And why is that?"

Anna shook her head. "There are certain matters I can only discuss with Gaston Rossignol himself."

"And why do you suppose anyone would want to kill him? He is among the most admired of Zurichers."

"Which explains why he's living in hiding."

"What nonsense you speak," Taine said, after a beat.

Anna stared at him levelly for few moments. Then she handed him a card with her name on it, and her numbers at the Office of Special Investigations. "I will return in an hour. I have reason to think your own resources are pretty considerable. Check me out. Satisfy yourself as to my bona fides. Do whatever will help you to see that I am who I say I am, and that I'm representing myself accurately."

"How can I, a mere Swiss citizen . . ."

"You have ways, Mr. Taine. And if you don't, your friend does. I'm quite sure you'll want to help your friend. I think we understand each other."

Two hours later, Anna Navarro paid a call to Taine at his place of work. The ministry of economic affairs was located in a marble building constructed in the familiar late-nineteenth-century Beaux Arts style. Taine's own office was large, sunny, and book-lined. She was ushered in to him immediately upon her arrival; the dark-paneled door closed discreetly behind her.

Taine sat quietly behind his burled walnut desk. "This was not my decision," he stressed. "This is Monsieur Rossignol's decision. I do not support it."

"You checked me out."

"You have been checked out," Taine replied carefully, hewing to the passive voice. He returned her card to her. "Good-bye, Ms. Navarro."

The address was penciled in small print, in a blank space to the left of her name.

Her first call was to Bartlett, updating him as to her progress. "You never cease to amaze me, Ms. Navarro," he'd replied, a surprising note of genuine warmth in his voice.

As she and Kesting drove to the Hottingen address, he said, "Your request for surveillance was approved this morning. Several unmarked police cars shall be engaged for the purpose."

"And his telephone."

"Yes, we can have a tap in place within hours. An officer at the *Kantonspolizei* will be assigned to listen in at the *Mutterhaus*."

"The *Mutterhaus?*"

"Police headquarters. The Mother House, we call it."

They headed steadily uphill on Hottingerstrasse. The houses became larger and nicer, the trees denser. Finally they came to Hauserstrasse, and pulled into the driveway of a low-slung brownstone house set in the middle of a nicely landscaped yard. She noticed there were no unmarked police cruisers anywhere nearby.

"This is the correct address," Kesting said.

She nodded. Another Swiss banker, she thought, with a big house and a nice yard.

They got out and walked to the front door. Kesting rang the bell. "You do not mind, I hope, if I lead the interview."

"Not at all," Anna replied. Whatever "international cooperation" meant on paper, that was the protocol and they both knew it.

After waiting a few minutes, Kesting rang again. "He is an old man, and for some years he has been wheelchair-bound. It must take him time to move around his house."

After a few minutes more, Kesting said, "I cannot imagine he goes out very much at his age." He rang again.

I knew this was too easy, Anna thought. *What a botch.*

"He may be ill," Kesting said. Uneasily he turned the doorknob but the door was locked. Together, they walked around to the back door; it opened readily. He called into the house, "Dr. Rossignol, it is Kesting from the Public Prosecutor's office." The "Dr." seemed purely an honorific.

Silence.

"Dr. Rossignol?"

Kesting stepped into the house, Anna following. The lights were on, and she could hear classical music.

"Dr. Rossignol?" Kesting said more loudly. He ventured forward into the house. Soon they found themselves in the dining room, where the lights were on, and a tape deck played music. Anna could smell coffee, eggs, some kind of fried meat.

"Dr.— Oh, dear God!"

Horrified, Anna saw what Kesting had seen.

An old man sat in a wheelchair at the table, before a plate of breakfast. His head was on his chest, the eyes fixed and dilated. He was dead.

They'd gotten to him too! That in itself didn't surprise her. What stunned her was the timing—so soon before their arrival, it had to be. As if they knew the authorities were coming.

She tasted fear.

"Dammit," she said. "Call an ambulance. And the homicide squad. And please, don't let them touch anything."

CHAPTER TWENTY-ONE

A squad of crime-scene officers from the homicide squad of the Zurich *Kantonspolizei* arrived within the hour and took video and still photographs. The victim's house was dusted carefully for fingerprints, particularly the front and back doors and the three windows that could be accessed from the ground level. Anna asked the specialist to print both Rossignol's wheelchair and all exposed skin on the deceased's body. Elimination prints were taken from Rossignol himself before the body was removed.

Had the Americans not taken such an interest in Rossignol prior to his murder, even requesting surveillance, the old man's death would certainly have been treated as a natural occurrence. Gaston Rossignol had been ninety-one, after all.

But instead an autopsy was ordered, with special attention paid to the ocular fluid. The postmortem would be done in the facilities of the University of Zurich Institute of Legal Medicine, as was standard, since Zurich had no medical examiner.

Anna returned to her hotel. Exhausted—she hadn't slept on the plane, had decided against taking an Ativan—she drew the curtains, got into an oversize T-shirt, and climbed into the bed.

She was jarred awake by the telephone. Momentarily disoriented, she thought she was back in Washington, that it was the middle of the night. She glanced at the phosphorescent dial of her watch and saw that it was two-thirty in the afternoon, Zurich time. She picked up the phone.

"Is this Miss Navarro?" a man's voice asked.

"That's me," she croaked, then cleared her throat. "Who's this?"

"I'm Sergeant Major Schmid from the *Kantonspolizei*. I'm a homicide detective. I'm sorry, did I wake you?"

"No, no, I was just dozing. What's up?"

"The fingerprints have come back with some interesting results. Can you find your way to police headquarters?"

Schmid was an affable man with a wide face, short hair, and ridiculous little bangs. He wore a navy blue shirt and had a gold chain around his neck.

His office was pleasant, light-filled, sparsely furnished. Two blond-wood desks faced one another; she sat at one, he at the other.

Schmid toyed with a paper clip. "The fingerprints were run at the *Kriminaltechnik*. Rossignol's prints were eliminated, leaving a number of other prints, most of them unidentified. He was a widower, so we assume they belong to his housekeeper and a few others who worked at his house. The housekeeper was on duty overnight, until this morning, when she made his breakfast and then left. They must have been watching the house and saw her depart."

"He didn't have a nurse?"

"No," Schmid said, bending the wire paper clip back and forth. "You know, we now have a computerized database of fingerprints just like yours." He was referring to the Automated Fingerprint Identification Service, which stored a bank of millions of prints. "The prints were scanned in, digitized, and sent by modem to the central registry in Bern, where they were run against all available databases. The search did not take long. We got a match very quickly."

She sat up. "Oh?"

"Yes, this is why the case was assigned to me. The prints belong to an American who was detained here just a few days ago in connection with a shooting in the vicinity of the Bahnhofplatz."

"Who is he?"

"An American named Benjamin Hartman."

The name meant nothing to her. "What do you know about him?"

"A fair amount. You see, I questioned him myself." He handed her a file folder containing photocopies of Hartman's U.S. passport, driver's license, credit cards, and his Swiss police records with mug shots.

She examined the copies closely, fascinated. Could this be her man, the killer? An American? Mid-thirties, an investment banker for a financial firm called Hartman Capital Management. A family business, she assumed. That probably meant he had money. Lives in New York City. Here on a Swiss ski vacation, he had told Schmid.

But that could be a lie.

Three of the remaining Sigma victims had been killed during the time he was here in Zurich. One victim had lived in Germany, which was a train ride away, so that was a possibility. Another was in Austria; also possible.

But Paraguay? That was a long plane flight from here.

Yet the possibility could not be ruled out. Neither could the possibility that he was not working alone.

"What happened on the Bahnhofstrasse?" she asked. "He shoot someone?"

The paper clip Schmid was worrying snapped in the middle. "There was gunfire along the street and in the shopping arcade beneath the Bahnhofplatz. He was questioned in connection with that. Personally, I don't think he was the shooter. He insists someone tried to shoot him."

"Anyone killed?"

"Several bystanders. And, in his account, the guy he insists tried to shoot him."

"Hmm," she said, puzzled. A bizarre tale: How much of it was true? Who was this guy? "You let him go?"

"We had no basis on which to hold him. And there was some string-pulling from his firm. He was instructed to leave the canton."

Not in my backyard: Was that the Zurich approach to law enforcement? Anna wondered sourly. "Any idea where he is now?"

"At the time, he claimed he was planning to go to St. Moritz. The Hotel Carlton. But we've since learned that he never checked in. Then, yesterday, we received a report that he'd reappeared in Zurich, at the Handelsbank Schweiz. We tried to bring him in for further questioning, but he escaped. Another misadventure, accompanied by shooting. It follows him around."

"Surprise, surprise," Anna said. "Do you have a way of finding out whether Hartman is staying at some other hotel in Zurich, or anywhere else in the country?"

Schmid nodded. "I can contact the Hotel Control in each of the cantons. Copies of all hotel registration forms go to the local police."

"How current are they?"

"Sometimes not so current," Schmid admitted. "At least we can tell where he was."

"If he checked in under his own name."

"All legitimate hotels require foreigners to show their passports."

"Maybe he has more than one passport. Maybe he's not staying at a 'legitimate' hotel. Maybe he has friends here."

Schmid looked mildly annoyed. "But you see, I've met him, and he didn't look to me like someone who carries false passports."

"Some of these international businessmen, you know, have second passports from places like Panama or Ireland or Israel. They come in handy sometimes."

"Yes, but such passports would still have their true names on them, right?"

"Maybe yes, maybe no. Is there a way to tell if he left the country?"

"There are many different ways to leave the country—plane, automobile, train, even on foot."

"Don't the border police keep records?"

"Well, the border police are supposed to look at passports," Schmid admitted, "but often they don't. Our best bet would be the airlines. They keep records of all passengers."

"What if he left by train?"

"Then we may find no trace, unless he made a seat reservation on an international train. But I wouldn't be hopeful."

"No," Anna said, ruminating. "Can you start the search?"

"Of course," Schmid said indignantly. "It is standard."

"When can I expect the autopsy results back? I'm particularly interested in the toxicology." She knew she was probably pushing the man a little too hard. But there was no choice.

Schmid shrugged. "It could be a week. I could put in a request to speed things up."

"I have one specific neurotoxin I'd like them to search for," she said. "That shouldn't take so long."

"I can call for you."

"Would you? And bank records. I need Rossignol's bank records going back two years. Will Swiss banks cooperate, or are they going to give us that whole secrecy song-and-dance?"

"They will cooperate with the police on a homicide," Schmid said huffily.

"That's a nice surprise. Oh, and one more thing. The photocopies you took of his credit cards—think I could have those?"

"I don't see why not."

"Wonderful," she said. She was actually starting to like the fellow.

São Paulo, Brazil

The wedding reception was being held at the most ultra-exclusive private club in all of Brazil, the Hipica Jardins.

The club's members were mainly drawn from the quatrocentões, Brazil's aristocracy, descendants of the original Portuguese settlers who had been in the country for at least four hundred years. They were the land barons, the owners of paper mills and newspapers and publishing houses and playing-card factories, the hotel magnates—the richest of the rich, as the long line of Bentleys and Rolls-Royces parked in front of the clubhouse attested.

Tonight many of them had turned out, resplendent in white tie and tails, to celebrate the wedding of the daughter of one of Brazil's plutocrats, Doutor Otavio Carvalho Pinto. His daughter, Fernanda, was marrying into an equally illustrious family, the Alcantara Machados.

One of the guests was a dignified, white-haired man of almost ninety. Although he was not one of the quatrocentões—he was in fact a native of Lisbon who had immigrated to São Paulo in the fifties—he was an enormously wealthy banker and landowner, and he had been for decades a business partner and friend of the bride's father.

The old man's name was Jorge Ramago, and he sat watching the couples dance, his noisettes de veau Périgourdine untouched. One of the waitresses, a dark-haired young woman, tentatively approached the old man and said in Portuguese, "Señor Ramago, there is a telephone call for you."

Ramago turned slowly to look at her. "Telephone?"

"Yes, señor, they say it is urgent. From your home. Your wife."

Ramago at once looked worried. "Where?—where?—" he faltered.

"This way, sir," the waitress said, and she gently helped him to his feet. They walked slowly across the banquet room, for the old Lisboner was afflicted with rheumatism, though he was otherwise in excellent health.

Outside the banquet room, the waitress guided Ramago to an antique wooden telephone booth and assisted him into it, solicitously smoothing his rumpled dinner jacket.

Just as Ramago reached for the telephone, he felt a sharp pinprick in his upper thigh. He gasped, looked around, but the waitress was gone.

The pain quickly subsided, though, and he put the handset up to his ear and listened. But all he could hear was the dial tone.

"There is no one on the line," Ramago managed to say to no one just before he lost consciousness.

A minute or so later, one of the waiters noticed the old man passed out in the telephone booth. Alarmed, he called out for help.

The Austrian Alps

Patient Eighteen was awakened at midnight.

One of the nurses gently applied a tourniquet to his upper arm and began to draw blood.

"What the hell is this?" he groaned.

"I'm sorry, sir," the nurse said. Her English was heavily accented. "We are required to take venous blood samples every four hours from midnight on, throughout the day."

"Good God, for what?"

"It is to measure the levels of your serum Epo—erythropoietin."

"I didn't know I had any." All this medical stuff was unsettling, but he knew there was much more to come.

"Please, go back to sleep, sir. You have a long day ahead of you."

Breakfast was served in a lavish banquet room with the others. There was a buffet overflowing with fresh fruits, freshly baked biscuits and rolls, breakfast sausages, eggs, bacon, and ham.

When Patient Eighteen finished, he was escorted to an examination room in another wing.

There, another nurse gingerly cut into the skin of the inner part of his upper arm with a small scalpel.

He moaned.

"I'm sorry if I caused you pain," the nurse said.

"My entire damned body's one big pain. What's this for?"

"A skin biopsy to examine the elastic fibers in the reticular dermis," she replied, applying a bandage.

In the background, two white-coated physicians were quietly conferring in German. Patient Eighteen understood every word.

"His brain function is somewhat impaired," the short, rotund one said, "but nothing you wouldn't expect in a man of his age. No sign of senile dementia or Alzheimer's."

A tall, thin, gray-faced man said, "What about cardiac muscle mass?"

"Acceptable. But we measured the blood pressure at the posterior tibial artery, this time using Doppler ultrasonography, and we did find some peripheral arterial disease."

"So his blood pressure is elevated."

"Somewhat, but we expected that."

"Have you counted the number of pitted blood cells?"

"I believe that's being done in the lab right now."

"Good. I think this one is a good candidate. I suggest we accelerate the tests."

A good candidate, Patient Eighteen thought. So it would happen after all. He turned to the conferring doctors behind and smiled widely at them, feigning gratitude.

CHAPTER TWENTY-TWO

Vienna

The private investigator was almost half an hour late. Ben sat in the spacious lobby of his hotel just off the Kärntner Strasse, his mélange untouched, waiting for the detective whose name he had plucked from the yellow pages.

He knew there were far better ways to find the name of a PI than the Vienna telephone book—such as calling one of his several business contacts here and asking for a recommendation. But his instincts told him to avoid anyone he knew right now if he could possibly help it.

He'd gotten on the first train, showed up unannounced at a small hotel, and been lucky enough to get a room, registering under the name Robert Simon, one of his brother's aliases. He was asked for his passport, and held his breath as it was inspected, but it obviously looked in order, plausibly battered and stamped, as if from a few years' use.

The first thing he'd done was to look through the Vienna phone book for an investigator who seemed, from his advertisement anyway, reputable. Several were located in the first district, the heart of the city where Ben's hotel was; one in particular advertised his services in locating long-lost relatives. Ben had hired him over the phone, asking him to run a background check on an Austrian citizen.

Now he was beginning to wonder whether the PI was going to show at all.

Then a portly man of about forty plopped himself into the chair across the low table from Ben. "You are Mr. Simon?" He set down a battered leather portfolio on the table.

"That's me."

"Hans Hoffman," the PI said. "You have the money?"

"Nice to meet you too," Ben said sardonically. He took out his wallet, counted out four hundred dollars, and slid it across the table.

Hoffman stared at it for a moment.

"Something wrong?" Ben asked. "You prefer Austrian shillings? Sorry, I haven't gone to a bank yet."

"There was an additional expense involved," the detective said.

"Oh really?"

"A courtesy payment to an old buddy of mine in the HNA, the *Heeres Nachrichtenamt*—Austrian military intelligence."

"Translation, a bribe," Ben said.

Hoffman shrugged.

"I don't imagine this buddy of yours gave you a receipt?"

Hoffman sighed. "This is how we do things here. You can't get the sort of information you're looking for without exploring various channels. This friend will have to use his military intelligence ID card to get information. It will be another two hundred dollars. The number—it was unlisted, by the way—and address I can get you now."

Ben counted it out; it was the end of his cash.

The detective counted the bills. "I don't know why you wanted this person's number and address, but you must be involved in some interesting business."

"Why do you say that?"

"Your man is a very important figure in Vienna." He signaled for the waitress; when she came, he ordered a mélange and a Maximilian torte.

From his briefcase he removed a laptop computer, snapped it open, and turned it on. "The very latest in biometrics," he said proudly. "Fingertip sensor. Uses my fingerprint as a password. Without it, the computer's locked. No one does these things like the Germans."

The detective tapped at the keys for a few seconds, then turned it around to face Ben. The screen was blank except for the name and address of Jürgen Lenz.

"You know him?" Hoffman said, turning the laptop back toward himself. "He is an acquaintance of yours?"

"Not exactly. Tell me about him."

"Ah, well, Dr. Lenz is one of the wealthiest men in Vienna, a leading philanthropist and patron of the arts. His family foundation builds medical clinics for the poor. He's also on the board of the Vienna Philharmonic."

The waitress set down a coffee and pastry in front of Hoffman. The detective lunged for them before the waitress had even turned to leave.

"What kind of doctor is Dr. Lenz?"

"A medical doctor, but he gave up his practice years ago."

"How old?"

"In his fifties, I would say."

"Medicine must be something of a family tradition."

Hoffman laughed. "You're remembering his father, Gerhard Lenz. An interesting case. Our country is perhaps not the most progressive, in some ways. My compatriots would prefer to forget any such unpleasantness. It's the Austrian way: as the saying goes, we've convinced ourselves that Beethoven was an Austrian, and Hitler was a German. But Jürgen is cut from a different cloth. This is a son who seeks to make up for the crimes of the father."

"Really?"

"Oh, very much. Jürgen Lenz is resented in some circles for being so outspoken about these crimes. Even denouncing his own father. He is known to feel deep shame about what his father did." He looked at his torte impatiently. "But unlike many children of the famous Nazis, he does something about it. The Lenz Foundation is Austria's leading supporter of Holocaust studies, historical scholarship, libraries in Israel . . . they fund anything that seeks to fight hate crimes, racism, that sort of thing." He returned to his pastry, wolfing it down as if fearing it would be snatched away.

Lenz's son was a leading anti-Nazi? Perhaps they had more in common than he had supposed. "All right," Ben said, gesturing to the waitress for the check with the universal air-scrawl. "Thank you."

"Anything else I can do for you?" the detective asked, brushing crumbs off the lapels of his jacket.

Trevor Griffiths left his hotel, the Imperial, on the Kärntner Ring a few blocks from the Opera. Not only was the Imperial the finest hotel in Vienna, Trevor reflected, but it was famous as the headquarters of the Nazis during the war, the location from which they governed the city. He liked the hotel anyway.

It was a short stroll down Mariahilfer Strasse to a small bar on Neubaugasse. The garish red neon sign flashed the bar's name: BROADWAY CLUB. He sat in a booth at the back of the ill-lit basement room and waited. In his bespoke gray worsted double-breasted suit, he looked somewhat out of place here, like a businessman, a high-level executive perhaps, or a prosperous attorney.

The bar was choked with foul cigarette smoke. Trevor could not tolerate it, hated the way his hair and clothes would stink afterward. He glanced at his watch, an Audemars Piguet, top of the line, one of the few indulgences he allowed himself. Expensive suits and watches and good rough sex. What else was there, really, if you had no interest in food, art, or music?

He was impatient. The Austrian contact was late, and Trevor could not abide tardiness.

Finally, after almost half an hour, the Austrian showed up, a square, hulking troglodyte named Otto. Otto slid into the booth and placed a worn red felt bag in front of Trevor.

"You're English, yes?"

Trevor nodded, zipped open the bag. It contained two large metal pieces, a 9 mm Makarov, the barrel threaded for a silencer, and the long, perforated sound-suppressor itself. "Ammo?" Trevor asked.

"Is in there," Otto said. "Nine by eighteen. Lots."

The Makarov was a good choice. Unlike the 9 mm Parabellum, it was subsonic. "What's the make?" Trevor asked. "Hungarian? Chinese?"

"Russian. But it's good one."

"How much?"

"Three thousand shillings."

Trevor grimaced. He didn't mind spending money, but he resented highway robbery. He switched to German, so Otto, whose English was poor, would miss nothing. *"Der Markt ist mit Makarovs überschwemmt."* The market's flooded with Makarovs.

Otto became suddenly alert.

"These things are a dime a dozen," Trevor continued in German. "Everyone makes them, they're all over the place. I'll give you a thousand shillings, and you should count yourself lucky to get that."

Respect entered Otto's expression. "You're German?" he asked, amazed. Actually, if Otto were a perceptive listener, he'd have placed Trevor's German as coming from the Dresden region.

Trevor had not spoken German in quite a while; he'd had no opportunity to do so. But it came back easily.

It was, after all, his native tongue.

Anna had dinner alone at a Mövenpick restaurant a few blocks from her hotel. There was nothing on the menu that interested her, and she decided she was no connoisseur of Swiss cuisine.

Normally, she found dining alone in a foreign city depressing, but tonight she was too absorbed in her thoughts to feel lonely. She was seated by the window, in a long row of lone diners, most of them reading newspapers or books.

At the American consulate, she used a secure fax line to transmit everything she had on Hartman, including his credit cards, to the ICU and had asked that the ID unit contact each of the credit-card companies and activate an instant trace, so that they would be informed within minutes whenever he used one of the cards.

She had also asked them to dig up whatever they could on Hartman himself, and someone had called her back on the encrypted cell phone less than an hour later.

They had struck gold.

According to Hartman's office, he was on vacation in Switzerland, but hadn't checked in with the office in several days. They didn't have his travel itinerary; he hadn't provided one. They had no way to contact him.

But then the ID tech had learned something interesting: Hartman's only sibling, a twin brother, had died in a plane crash in Switzerland four years earlier. Apparently he'd been on some Swiss-gold crusade before his death. She didn't know what to make of that except that it raised all sorts of questions.

And Benjamin Hartman, the tech told her, was loaded. The company he worked for, Hartman Capital Management, managed investment funds and had been founded by Hartman's father.

Who was a well-known philanthropist and a Holocaust survivor.

Possibilities suggested themselves. Poor little rich boy, son of a survivor, gets it in his head that the Swiss bankers haven't been doing right by the Holocaust victims. Now his twin takes up the same crusade, trying for some sort of misguided revenge on a Swiss banking bigwig. A rich boy's half-cocked vendetta.

Or maybe he was in it deeper—working for whatever this Sigma outfit had morphed into. For some unexplained reason.

Then the question was, where did he get the names and addresses of all these old men in hiding?

And how was his brother's death connected—if at all?

At a little after nine o'clock in the evening she returned to the hotel and was handed a message slip by the night manager. Thomas Schmid, the homicide detective, had called.

She called him back immediately from the room. He was still in his office.

"We have some of the autopsy results back," he said. "On that poison you asked the toxicology people to screen for?"

"Yes?"

"They found that neurotoxin in the ocular fluid, a positive match. Rossignol was indeed poisoned."

Anna sat down in the chair beside the phone. Progress. She felt the pleasant tingle she always had when there was a breakthrough. "Did they find an injection mark on the body?"

"Not as yet, but they say it's very difficult to find tiny marks like that. They say they will keep looking."

"When was he killed?"

"Apparently this morning, shortly before we got there."

"That means Hartman may still be in Zurich. Are you on top of that?"

A pause, then Schmid said coldly, "I am on top of that."

"Any news on the bank records?"

"The banks will cooperate, but they take their time. They also have their procedures."

"Of course."

"We should have Rossignol's bank records by tomorrow—"

On her end of the line a beep interrupted Schmid. "One second, I think I've got another call coming in." She pressed the "flash" button. The hotel operator told her it was a call from her office in Washington.

"Miss Navarro, this is Robert Polozzi in ID."

"Thanks for calling. Turn up anything?"

"MasterCard security just called. Hartman used his card a few minutes ago. He made a charge at a restaurant in Vienna."

Kent, England

At his country estate in Westerham, Kent, Sir Edward Downey, the retired Prime Minister of England, was in the middle of a game of chess in the rose garden with his grandson when the telephone rang.

"Not again," eight-year-old Christopher groaned.

"Hold your horses, young man," Sir Edward snapped good-naturedly.

"Sir Edward, it's Mr. Holland," the voice said.

"Mr. Holland, is everything all right?" Sir Edward asked, suddenly concerned. "Our meeting is still going ahead as scheduled?"

"Oh, without a doubt. But a minor matter has come up and I wondered whether you might be able to help."

As he listened, Sir Edward gave his grandson a menacing scowl, at which Christopher giggled, as he always did. "Well, Mr. Holland, let me make a few calls and see what I can do."

Vienna

Jürgen Lenz's house was in an exclusive, densely wooded district in the southwest part of Vienna called Hietzing: an enclave of some of Vienna's wealthiest residents. Lenz's house, or, more properly, his villa, was large, modern, an intriguing and handsome mix of Tyrolean architecture and Frank Lloyd Wright.

The element of surprise, Ben thought. *I need it when I confront Lenz.* In part, it was a question of survival. He didn't want Peter's murderers to discover he was in Vienna, and, despite the seed of doubt that Hoffman had planted, the likeliest assumption was that Lenz was one of them.

Of course, he couldn't just show up on Lenz's doorstep and hope to gain admittance. The approach had to be more sophisticated. Ben ran through a mental list of the most prominent and influential people he knew personally who would vouch for him, even lie for him.

He remembered the head of a major American charity who had come to see him several times to ask for money. Each time the Hartman family, and the firm, had given generously.

Payback time, Ben thought.

The charity head, Winston Rockwell, was seriously ill with hepatitis, laid up in the hospital, last Ben had heard, and impossible to reach. This was terribly unfortunate for Rockwell—but convenient for Ben.

He called Lenz's home, asked for Jürgen Lenz, told the woman who answered the phone—Mrs. Lenz?—that he was a friend of Winston Rockwell's and was interested in the Lenz Foundation. Code language for: I have money to give you. Even rich foundations don't turn away contributions.

Mrs. Lenz replied in fluent English that her husband should be home by five, and would Mr. Robert Simon like to come by for a drink? Jürgen would be delighted to meet any friend of Winston Rockwell's.

The woman who opened the door was an elegant, fine-boned woman in her early fifties, wearing a gray sweater-dress, a pearl choker, and matching pearl earrings.

"Please come in," she said. "Mr. Simon, is it? I'm Ilse Lenz. How nice to meet you!"

"Nice to meet you, too," Ben said. "Thanks for seeing me, particularly on such short notice."

"Oh, don't be silly, we're thrilled to meet anyone Winston recommends. You're from—where, did you say?"

"Los Angeles," he replied.

"We were there years ago for some beastly technology conference. Jürgen should be right down—ah, here he is!"

A whippet-thin, athletic-looking man was bounding down the stairs. "Hallo, there!" Jürgen Lenz called out. In his blue blazer, gray flannel slacks, and rep tie he could have been an American chief executive, maybe an Ivy League college president. His smooth face glowed with health; his smile was sunny.

This was not at all what Ben had expected. Liesl's gun, holstered to his shoulder inside his sport coat and loaded with ammunition—he'd stopped at a sporting-goods shop on the Kärntner Strasse—suddenly felt bulky.

Lenz shook Ben's hand firmly. "Any friend of Winston Rockwell's is a friend of mine!" Then his voice became soft, tender. "How's he doing these days?"

"Not well," Ben said. "He's been in the George Washington University

Medical Center for weeks now, and the doctors are telling him he's not likely to go home for at least two weeks more."

"I'm so sorry to hear that," Lenz said, putting his arm around his wife's slender waist. "What a nice fellow he is. Well, let's not stand here. A drink, shall we? What's the American expression—somewhere it's got to be six o'clock, hmm?"

Trevor parked his stolen Peugeot across the street from Lenz's house in Hietzing, switched off the engine, and sat back to wait. When the target emerged from the house, he would get out of the car, cross the street, and come close to him. He did not plan to miss.

CHAPTER TWENTY-THREE

There was no time.

Certainly no time to go through channels, Anna realized.

Hartman had just made a charge at a hotel in the first district of Vienna. It was for a small amount, the equivalent of about fifteen dollars. Did that mean he had only stopped at the hotel for a drink, a coffee, a late lunch? If so, he'd be long gone. But if he was staying there, she had him.

She could go through the FBI legat in Vienna, but by the time the office had made contact with the local police through the Austrian Justice Ministry, Benjamin Hartman could well have gone on to another city.

So she had rushed to Zurich-Kloten Airport, bought a ticket on the next Austrian Airlines flight to Vienna, and then located a pay phone.

The first call she made was to a contact of hers in the Vienna police, the *Bundespolizeidirektion*. He was Dr. Fritz Weber, chief of the *Sicherheitsbüro*, the security unit of the Vienna police specializing in violent crimes. This wasn't exactly the section of the police she needed to reach, but she knew Weber would be happy to help.

She'd met Weber a few years earlier when she'd been sent to Vienna on a case involving a cultural attaché at the American embassy there who had become involved in a sex ring purveying somewhat underaged *Mädchen*.

Weber, an affable man and a smooth politician, had been grateful for her help, and her discretion, in rooting out a problem that presented potential embarrassment for both countries—and had taken her out to a festive dinner before she left. Now he seemed delighted to hear from Agent Navarro and promised to get someone on the case immediately.

Her second call was to the FBI's legat in Vienna, a man named Tom Murphy, whom she didn't know but had heard good things about. She gave Murphy an abbreviated, sanitized rundown on why she was coming to Vienna. He asked her whether she wanted him to arrange liaison with the Vienna police, but she said no, she had her own contact there. Murphy, a real by-the-book man,.did not sound happy about it but made no objection.

As soon as she arrived at Vienna's Schwechat Airport, she placed another call to Fritz Weber, who gave her the name and phone number of the District Inspector on the surveillance squad who was now working the case.

Sergeant Walter Heisler wasn't fluent in English, but they managed to muddle through.

"We went to the hotel where Hartman made the credit-card charge," Heisler explained. "He is a guest at the hotel."

The sergeant worked fast. This was promising. "Great work," she said. "Any chance of finding the car?"

The compliment seemed to warm him up. Given that the target of investigation was an American, he also realized that the involvement of a representative of the U.S. government would eliminate most of the complicated paperwork and jurisdictional issues that an apprehension of a foreign national would normally present.

"We have already the, how you say, the tail on him," Heisler said with some enthusiasm.

"You're kidding. How'd you do that?"

"Well, once we found out that he is at the hotel, we put two men in newsstand in front of the place. They saw he goes in rented car, an Opel Vectra, and they follow him to part of Vienna called Hietzing."

"What's he doing there?"

"Visiting someone, maybe. A private home. We're trying to know who it is."

"Amazing. Fantastic work." She meant it.

"Thank you," he said exuberantly. "You would like me to pick you up at airport?"

There was some small talk for a few minutes, which was stressful, since Ben's cover was only half thought out. The mythical Robert Simon ran a successful financial management firm based in L.A.—Ben figured that if he kept it close to the truth, there'd be less chance of a serious gaffe— and handled the assets of movie stars, real estate tycoons, Silicon Valley IPO paper billionaires. Ben apologized that his client list had to remain confidential, though he didn't mind mentioning a name or two they'd no doubt heard of.

And all the while he wondered: Who is this man? The sole heir of Gerhard Lenz—the notorious scientist and a principal in something called Sigma.

As he and the Lenzes chatted, all three of them drinking Armagnac, Ben furtively inspected the sitting room. It was furnished comfortably, with English and French antiques. Paintings of the Old Master school were framed in gilt, each one perfectly lighted. On a table beside the couch he noticed silver-framed photographs of what he assumed were family. Conspicuously absent was any picture of Lenz's father.

"But enough about my work," Ben said. "I wanted to ask you about the Lenz Foundation. I understand its main purpose is to promote study of the Holocaust."

"We fund historical scholarship, yes, and we give to Israeli libraries," Jürgen Lenz explained. "We give a lot of money to combat hatred. We think it's extremely important that Austrian schoolchildren study the crimes of the Nazis. Don't forget, many of the Austrians welcomed the Nazis. When Hitler came here in the thirties and gave a speech from the balcony of the Imperial, he attracted enormous crowds, women weeping at the sight of such a great man." Lenz sighed. "An abomination."

"But your father . . . if you don't mind my saying . . ." Ben began.

"History knows that my father was inhuman," Lenz said. "Yes, he certainly was. He performed the most gruesome, the most unspeakable experiments on prisoners in Auschwitz, on children—"

"Will you excuse me, please?" Ilse Lenz said, rising to her feet. "I can't hear about his father," she murmured. She walked from the room.

"Darling, I'm sorry," Lenz called after her. He turned to Ben, anguished. "I can't blame her. She didn't have to live with this legacy. Her father was killed in the war when she was a child."

"I'm sorry to have brought it up," Ben said.

"Please, not at all. It is a perfectly natural question. I'm sure it strikes Americans as strange that the son of the notorious Gerhard Lenz devotes his life to giving away money to study the crimes of his father. But you must understand, those of us who, by the accident of birth, have had to struggle with this—we, the children of the most important Nazis—we each react in very different ways. There are those, like Rudolph Hess's son Wolf, who spend their lives trying to clear their father's names. And there are those who grow up confused, struggling to make some sense of it all. I was born too late to have retained any personal memories of my father, but there are many who knew their fathers only as they were at home, not as Hitler's men."

Jürgen Lenz grew steadily more impassioned as he spoke. "We grew up in privileged homes. We drove through the Warsaw ghetto in the back of a limousine, not understanding why the children out there looked so sad. We watched our fathers' eyes light up when the Führer himself called to wish the family a merry Christmas. And some of us, as soon as we were old enough to think, learned to loathe our fathers and everything they stood for. To despise them with every fiber of our being."

Lenz's surprisingly youthful face was flushed. "I don't think of my father as my father, you see. He's like someone else to me, a stranger. Shortly after the war ended, he escaped to Argentina, I'm sure you know, smuggled out of Germany with false papers. He left my mother and me penniless, living in a military detention camp." He paused. "So you see, I've never had any doubts or conflicts about the Nazis. Creating this foundation was the very least I could do."

The room was silent for a moment.

"I came to Austria to study medicine," Lenz continued. "In some ways it was a relief to leave Germany. I loved it here—I was born here—and I stayed, practicing medicine, keeping as anonymous as I could. After I met Ilse, the love of my life, we discussed what we could do with the family money she'd inherited—her father had made a fortune publishing religious books and hymnals—and we decided I'd give up medicine and devote my life to fighting against what my father fought for. Nothing can ever efface the darkness that was the Third Reich, but I've devoted myself to trying, in my own small way, to be a force of human betterment."

Lenz's speech seemed a little too polished, too rehearsed, as if he'd delivered it a thousand times before. No doubt he had. Yet there didn't seem to be a false note. Beneath the calm assuredness, Lenz was clearly a tormented man.

"You never saw your father again?"

"No. I saw him two or three times before his death. He came to Germany from Argentina to visit. He had a new name, a new identity. But my mother wouldn't see him. I saw him, but I felt nothing for him. He was a stranger to me."

"Your mother simply cut him off?"

"The next time was when she traveled to Argentina for his funeral. She did do that, as if she needed to see that he was dead. The funny thing was, she found she loved the country. It's where she finally retired to."

There was another silence, and then Ben said quietly but firmly, "I must say I'm impressed by all the resources you've devoted to shedding light on your paternal legacy. I wonder, in this connection, if you can tell me about an organization known as Sigma." He studied Lenz's face closely as he spoke the name.

Lenz looked at him for a good long while. Ben could hear his own heart thudding in the silence.

At last Lenz spoke. "You mention Sigma casually, but I think this may be the entire reason you have come here," Lenz said. "Why are you here, Mr. Simon?"

Ben felt a chill. He had let himself be cornered. Now the roads diverged: now he could try to hold on to his false identity, or come out with the truth.

It was time to be direct. To draw out the quarry.

"Mr. Lenz, I'm inviting you to clarify the nature of your involvement with Sigma."

Lenz frowned. "Why are you here, Mr. Simon? Why do you sneak into my house and lie to me?" Lenz smiled strangely, his voice quiet. "You're CIA, Mr. 'Simon,' is that right?"

"What are you talking about?" Ben said, baffled and frightened.

"Who are you really, Mr. 'Simon'? Lenz whispered.

"Nice house," Anna said. "Whose is it?"

She sat in the front seat of a smoke-filled blue BMW, an unmarked police vehicle. Sergeant Walter Heisler was at the wheel, a beefy, hearty-looking man in his late thirties, smoking Casablancas. He was cordial enough.

"One of our more, eh, prominent citizens," Heisler said, taking a drag on his cigarette. "Jürgen Lenz."

"Who is he?"

They were both looking out at a handsome villa a hundred yards or so down Adolfstorgasse. Anna saw that most of the parked cars had black license plates with white letters. Heisler explained that you had to pay to maintain such plates; it was the old, aristocratic style.

He blew out a cloud of smoke. "Lenz and his wife are active in the social circles here, the Opera Ball and so on. I guess you'd call them, how you say, philo—philanthropists? Lenz runs the family foundation. Moved here twenty-some years ago from Germany."

"Hmmm." Her eyes were smarting from the smoke, but she didn't want to complain. Heisler was doing her a major favor. She rather liked sitting here in the smoke-filled cop car, one of the fellas.

"How old?"

"Fifty-seven, I believe."

"And prominent."

"Very."

There were three other unmarked vehicles idling on the street, one near them, the other two a few hundred yards down the block, on the other side of Lenz's villa. The cars were arranged in a classic box formation, so that no matter how Hartman chose to leave the neighborhood, they would have him trapped. The officers waiting in the cars were all highly trained members of the surveillance squad. Each of them was equipped with weapons and walkie-talkies.

Anna had no weapon. It was highly unlikely, she thought, that Hartman would put up any resistance. His records showed that he'd never owned a gun or applied for a license to carry. The murders of the old men had all been done by means of poison, by syringe. He probably had no weapon with him.

In fact, there wasn't much she knew about Hartman. But her Viennese comrades knew even less. She had told her friend Fritz Weber only that the American had left prints at the crime scene in Zurich, nothing more. Heisler, too, knew only that Hartman was wanted in Rossignol's murder. But that was enough for the Bundespolizei to agree to apprehend Hartman and, at the formal request of the FBI legat in Vienna, to place him under arrest.

She wondered how much she could trust the local police.

This was no theoretical question. Hartman was in there meeting with a man who . . .

A thought occurred to her. "This guy, Lenz," she said, her eyes burning from the smoke. "This may be a strange question, but does he have anything to do with the Nazis?"

Heisler stubbed out his cigarette in the car's overflowing ashtray. "Well, this is a strange question," he said. "His father—do you know the name Dr. Gerhard Lenz?"

"No, should I?"

He shrugged: naïve Americans. "One of the worst. A colleague of Josef Mengele's who did all kinds of horrifying experiments in the camps."

"Ah." Another idea suggested itself. Hartman, a survivor's son with an avenging spirit, was going after the next generation.

"His son is a good man, very different from his father. He devotes his life to undoing his father's evil."

She stared at Heisler, then out the windshield at Lenz's magnificent villa. The son was anti-Nazi? Amazing. She wondered whether Hartman knew that. He might not know anything about the younger Lenz except that he was the son of Gerhard, son of a Nazi. If he were really a fanatic, he wouldn't care if Lenz Junior could turn water into wine.

Which meant that Hartman might already have given Jürgen Lenz a lethal injection.

Jesus, she thought, as Heisler lit another Casablanca. *Why are we just sitting here?*

"Is that yours?" Heisler suddenly asked.

"Is what mine?"

"That car." He pointed at a Peugeot that was parked across the street from Lenz's villa. "It's been in the area since we get here."

"No. It's not one of yours?"

"Absolutely not. I can tell from plates."

"Maybe it's a neighbor, or a friend?"

"I wonder could your American colleagues be involving in this, maybe checking on you?" Heisler said heatedly. "Because if that's the case, I'm calling this operation off right now!"

Unsettled and defensive, she said, "It can't be. Tom Murphy would have let me know before sending someone in." Wouldn't he? "Anyway, he barely seemed interested when I first told him."

But if he were checking up on her? Was that possible?

"Well, then who is it?" Heisler demanded.

"Who are you?" Jürgen Lenz repeated, fear now showing on his face. "You are not a friend of Winston Rockwell's."

"Sort of," Ben admitted. "I mean, I know him from some work I've done. I'm Benjamin Hartman. My father is Max Hartman." Once more, he watched Lenz to gauge his reaction.

Lenz blenched, and then his expression softened. "Dear God," he whispered. "I can see the resemblance. What happened to your brother was a terrible thing."

Ben felt as if he'd been punched in the stomach. "What do you know?" he shouted.

The police radio crackled to life.

"*Korporal, wer ist das?*"

"*Keine Ahnung.*"

"*Keiner von uns, oder?*"

"*Richtig.*"

Now the other team wanted to know whether the Peugeot was one of theirs; Heisler confirmed he had no idea who it was. He took a night-vision monocular from the backseat and held it up to one eye. It was dark on the street now, and the unidentified car had switched off its lights. There was no street lamp nearby, so it was impossible to see the driver's face. The night-vision scope was a good idea, Anna thought.

"He has a newspaper up before his face," Heisler said. "A tabloid. *Die Kronen Zeitung*—I can just make it out."

"Can't be easy for the guy to read the paper in the dark, huh?" She thought: *Lenz Junior could be dead already, and we're sitting here waiting*.

"I do not think he's getting much reading done." Heisler seemed to share her sense of humor.

"Mind if I take a look?"

He handed her the scope. All she saw was newsprint. "He's obviously trying not to be identified," she said. What if he really was Bureau? "Which tells us something. O.K. if I use your cell phone?"

"Not at all." He gave her his clunky Ericsson, and she punched out the local number of the U.S. embassy.

"Tom," she said when Murphy came on the line. "It's Anna Navarro. You didn't send anyone out to Hietzing, did you?"

"Hietzing? Here in Vienna?"

"My case."

A pause. "No, you didn't ask me to, did you?"

"Well, someone's screwing up my stakeout. No one in your office would have taken it upon himself to check up on me without clearing it with you first?"

"They better not. Anyway, everyone's accounted for here, far as I know."

"Thanks." She disconnected, handed the phone back to Heisler. "Strange."

"Then who is in that car?" Heisler asked.

"If I may ask, why did you think I was CIA?"

"There are some old-timers in that community who have rather taken against me," Lenz said, shrugging. "Do you know about Project Paper Clip?" They had graduated to vodka. Ilse Lenz had still not returned to the sitting room, more than an hour after she had so abruptly left. "Perhaps not by that name. You're aware that immediately after the war, the U.S. government—the OSS, as the CIA's predecessor was called—smuggled some of Nazi Germany's leading scientists to America, yes? Paper Clip was the code name for this plan. The Americans sanitized the Germans' records, falsified their backgrounds. Covered up the fact that these were mass-murderers. You see, because as soon as the war was over, America turned its attention to a new war—the Cold War. Suddenly all that counted was fighting the Soviet Union. America had spent four years and countless lives battling the Nazis and suddenly the Nazis were their friends—so long as they could help in the struggle against the Communists. Help build weapons and such for America. These scientists were brilliant men, the brains behind the Third Reich's enormous scientific accomplishments."

"And war criminals."

"Precisely. Some of them responsible for the torture and murder of thousands upon thousands of concentration-camp inmates. Some, like Wernher von Braun and Dr. Hubertus Strughold, had invented many of the Nazi's weapons of war. Arthur Rudolph, who helped murder twenty thousand innocent people at Nordhausen, was awarded NASA's highest civilian honor!"

Twilight settled. Lenz got up and switched on lamps around the sitting room. "The Americans brought in the man who was in charge of death camps in Poland. One Nazi scientist they gave asylum to had conducted the freezing experiments at Dachau—he ended up at Randolph Air Force Base in San Antonio, a distinguished professor of space medicine. The CIA people who arranged all this, those few who survive, have been less than appreciative of my efforts to shed light on this episode."

"Your efforts?"

"Yes, and those of my foundation. It is not an insignificant part of the research that we sponsor."

"But what threat could the CIA pose?"

"The CIA, I understand, did not exist until a few years after the war, but they inherited operational control of these agents. There are aspects of history that some old-guard types in the CIA prefer to have left undisturbed. Some of them will go to quite extraordinary lengths to ensure this."

"I'm sorry, I can't believe that. The CIA doesn't go around killing people."

"No, not anymore," Lenz conceded, a note of sarcasm in his voice. "Not since they killed Allende in Chile, Lumumba in the Belgian Congo, tried to assassinate Castro. No, they're prohibited by law from doing such things. So now they 'outsource,' as you American businessmen like to say. They hire freelancers, mercenaries, through chains of front organizations, so the hit men can never be connected with the U.S. government." He broke off. "The world is more complicated than you seem to think."

"But that's all ancient, irrelevant history!"

"Scarcely irrelevant if you're one of the ancient men who may be implicated," Lenz pressed on inexorably. "I speak of elder statesmen, retired diplomats, former dignitaries who did a stint with the Office of Strategic Services in their youth. As they putter around their libraries and write their memoirs, they cannot avoid a certain unease." He gazed into the clear fluid in his glass as if seeing something there. "These are men accustomed to power, and deference. They would not look forward to revelations that would darken their golden years. Oh, of course, they'll tell themselves that what they do is for the good of the country, sparing the good name of the United States. So much of the wickedness men do is in the name of the commonweal. This, Mr. Hartman, I know. Frail old dogs can be the most dangerous. Calls can be made, favors called in. Mentors drawing on the loyalty of protégés. Frightened old men determined to die with at least their good names intact. I wish I could discount this scenario. But I know what these men are like. I have seen too much of human nature."

Ilse reappeared, carrying a small leather-bound book; on its spine Ben made out the name Hölderlin, lettered in gilt. "I see you gentlemen are still at it," she said.

"You understand, don't you, why we can be slightly on edge," Lenz told Ben smoothly. "We have many enemies."

"There have been many threats against my husband," Ilse said. "There are fanatics on the right who view him, somehow, as a turncoat, as the man who betrayed his father's legacy." She smiled without warmth and repaired to the adjoining room.

"They worry me less, to be frank, than the self-interested, ostensibly rational souls who simply don't understand why we can't let sleeping dogs lie." Lenz's eyes were alert. "And whose friends, as I say, may be tempted to take rather extreme measures to ensure that their golden years remain golden. But I go on. You had certain questions about the postwar period, questions you hoped I might be able to answer."

Jürgen Lenz examined the photograph, gripping it in both hands. His face was tense. "That's my father," he said. "Yes."

"You look just like him," Ben said.

"Quite the legacy, hmm?" Lenz said ruefully. No longer was he the charming, affable host. Now he peered intently at the rest of the photograph. "Dear God, no. It can't be." He sank into his chair, his face ashen.

"What can't?" Ben was unrelenting. "Tell me what you know."

"Is this genuine?" The same reaction that Carl Mercandetti, the historian, had had.

"Yes." Ben took a deep breath, and replied with the utmost intensity. "Yes." The lives of Peter, Liesl, and who knew how many others had been its guarantors of authenticity.

"But Sigma was a myth! An old wives' tale! We'd all satisfied ourselves that it was."

"Then you do know of it?"

Lenz leaned forward. "You have to remember that in the tumult following the war, there were all sorts of wild tales. One of those was the legend of Sigma, vague and shrouded as it was. That some sort of alliance was forged among the major industrialists of the world." He pointed at two faces. "That men like Sir Alford Kittredge and Wolfgang Siebing, one revered and one reviled, made common cause. That they met in secrecy, and forged a clandestine pact."

"And what was the nature of that pact?"

Lenz shook his head hopelessly. "I wish I knew, Mr. Hartman—may I call you Ben? I'm sorry. I'd never taken the stories seriously until now."

"And your own father's involvement?"

Lenz shook his head slowly. "You're exceeding my own knowledge. Perhaps Jakob Sonnenfeld would know of these things."

Sonnenfeld—Sonnenfeld was the most prominent Nazi hunter alive. "Would he help me?"

"Speaking as a major benefactor of his institute," Lenz replied, "I am certain he'll do his best." He poured himself a fortifying quantity of spirits. "We've been dancing around one issue, haven't we? You still haven't explained how you came to be involved in all of this."

"Do you recognize the man next to your father?"

"No," Lenz said. He squinted. "He looks a little like . . . but that's not possible either."

"Yes. That's my father next to yours." Ben's voice was flatly declarative.

"That makes no sense," Lenz protested. "Everyone in my world knows about your father. He's a major philanthropist. A force for good. And a Holocaust survivor, of course. Yes, it looks like him—like you, in fact. But I repeat: that makes no sense."

Ben laughed bitterly. "I'm sorry. But things stopped making sense for me when my old college buddy tried to murder me on the Bahnhof-strasse."

Lenz's eyes looked sorrowful. "Tell me how you found this."

Ben told Lenz about the events of the past several days, trying to stay as dispassionate as he could.

"Then you, too, know danger," Lenz said solemnly. "There are fila-ments, invisible filaments, that link this photograph to those deaths."

Frustration welled up in Ben as he struggled to make some sense of everything Lenz was telling him, tried to rearrange the pieces of infor-mation to make a coherent picture. Instead of becoming clearer, things were even more bewildering, more maddening.

Ben was first conscious of Ilse's return to the room from the scent of her perfume.

"This young man brings danger," she said to her husband, and her voice was like sandpaper. She turned to Ben. "Forgive me, but I cannot keep silent any longer. You bring death to this house. My husband has been menaced by extremists for so many years because of his fight for justice. I am sorry for what you have undergone. But you are careless, the way you Americans always are. You come to see my husband under false pretenses, pursuing some private vendetta of your own."

"Please, Ilse," Lenz interjected.

"And now you have brought death here with you, like an unannounced guest. I would be grateful to you if you would leave my house. My husband has done enough for the cause. Must he give his life for it, too?"

"Ilse is upset," Lenz said apologetically. "There are aspects of my life that she has never grown accustomed to."

"No," Ben said. "She's probably right. I've already put too many lives in jeopardy." His voice was hollow.

Ilse's face was a mask, the muscles immobilized by fear. *"Gute Nacht,"* she said with quiet finality.

Walking Ben to the foyer, Lenz spoke with murmured urgency. "If you want, I'll be glad to help you. To do what I can. Pull strings where I am able to, provide contacts. But Ilse is right about one thing. You can't know what you're up against. I'd advise you to be cautious, my friend." There was something familiar about the harrowed look on Lenz's face, and after a moment Ben realized that it reminded him of what he'd seen on Peter's. Within both men, it seemed, a passion for justice had been worn down by vast forces, and yet it could be mistaken for nothing else.

Ben left Lenz's house, dazed. He was far over his head: why couldn't he just admit that he was powerless, hopelessly unequipped for a task that had defeated his own brother? And the very facts he had already established now ground deeper into his psyche, like glass shards under his feet. Max Hartman, philanthropist, Holocaust survivor, humanitarian— was he, in fact, a man like Gerhard Lenz, a confederate in barbarity? It was sickening to contemplate. Might Max have been complicit in Peter's murder? Was the man behind his own son's death?

Was this why he'd suddenly disappeared? So he wouldn't have to face his own exposure? And what about the complicity of the CIA? How the hell did an *Obersturmführer* in Hitler's SS come to emigrate and settle in the States, if not with help from the U.S. government? Were allies of his, very old friends indeed, behind the horrific events? Was there some chance they were doing it on his father's behalf—to protect him and themselves as well—without the old man's knowledge?

You talk of things you cannot understand, his father had said, speaking past him as much as to him.

Ben was seized with conflicting emotions. Part of him, the devoted, loyal son, wanted to believe that there was some other explanation, had wanted to since Peter's revelations. Some reason to believe his own father was not a . . . a what? A monster. He heard his mother's voice, whispering as she died, pleading with him to understand, to try to heal the breach, to get along. To love this complicated, difficult man who was Max Hartman.

While another part of Ben felt a welcome clarity.

I've worked hard to understand you, you bastard! Ben found himself shouting inwardly. *I've tried to love you. But a deception like this, the ugliness of your real life—how can I feel anything but hatred?*

He had parked, once again, a good distance from Lenz's house. He did not want his license plates to be traced back to him; at least, that had been his thinking before, when he had assumed Lenz was one of the conspirators.

He walked down the path in front of Lenz's house. Just before he reached the street, he saw, in his peripheral vision, a light come on.

It was the interior dome light of a car, just a few yards away.

Someone was getting out of the car and walking toward him.

Trevor saw a light come on across the street and turned his head to look. The front door was open. The target was chatting with an older gentleman, whom he assumed was Lenz. Trevor waited until the two men had shaken hands and the target was strolling down the front path before he got out of the car.

CHAPTER TWENTY-FOUR

"I want you to run the plates," Heisler said on the police radio. He turned to Anna. "If is not you, and not us, then who is it? You must have some idea."

"Someone who's also staking out the house," she said. "I don't like this."

She thought: *Something else is going on here. Should I tell Heisler my suspicions about Hartman?* Yet it was such a half-baked bit of speculation—after all, what if Hartman was there simply to get information out of Lenz, information about where some of his father's old friends might be living—and not to kill him?

Still . . . they had all the legal justification they needed to storm the villa. And what if it turned out that, while they were all sitting here watching the house, one of the city's leading citizens was inside being murdered? The outcry would be enormous; it would be an international incident, and it would all be on her shoulders.

Heisler interrupted her thoughts. "I want you to walk by that car and look at the man's face," he said. It seemed an order, not a request. "Make absolute certain you don't recognize."

She agreed, wanting to see for herself.

"I need a weapon," she said.

Heisler handed her his gun. "You took this from floor of car. I must have left it. I did not give it to you."

She got out of the car and started walking toward Lenz's villa.

The front door of Lenz's house came open.

Two men were standing there, talking. One older, one younger.

Lenz and Hartman.

Lenz was alive, she saw with relief.

The two men shook hands cordially. Then Hartman started down the path toward the street.

And suddenly a light inside the Peugeot went on, and the man got out of the driver's seat, a trench coat draped over his right arm.

That was when she saw the man's face for the first time.

The face!

She knew the face. She had seen it before.

But where?

The man with the trench coat over his arm closed his car door as Hartman reached the street, not five yards away.

Just for an instant she saw the man in profile.

It stirred an old memory.

A profile shot. She had seen a profile shot of this man. Front and side views. The association was unpleasant, one of danger.

Mug shots. At work. Fairly poor-quality photos of this man, front and profile. A bad guy.

Yes, she had seen the photos once or twice in the Weekly Intelligence Briefing.

But they weren't mug shots, strictly speaking; they had been surveillance photographs taken at a distance, magnified to the point of graininess.

Yes.

Not an ordinary criminal, of course.

An assassin.

The man was an international assassin, and an extraordinarily accomplished one. Little was known about him—only fragmentary bits of evidence had ever been gathered; as to his employers, assuming he wasn't a freelancer, they had nothing at all. But the evidence they had suggested someone of uncommon resourcefulness and range. She flashed on another photograph: the body of a labor leader in Barcelona, whom he was believed to have slain. The image had lodged in her memory, perhaps because of the way blood ran down the victim's shirtfront like a neck tie. Another image: a popular political candidate in southern Italy, a man who had been leading a national reform movement. His death was originally attributed to the Mafia, but had been reclassified after snippets of information implicated a man they knew only as the Architect. The candidate, already under threats from organized crime, had been well protected, she recalled. And the assassination had been brilliantly engineered, from the perspective not merely of ballistics but of politics as well. The politician was shot dead while in a brothel staffed by illegal immigrants from Somalia, and the awkward circumstances ensured that his supporters could not transfigure his death into martyrdom.

The Architect. An international assassin of the first order.

Targeting Hartman.

She tried to make sense of it: *Hartman's on a vendetta,* she thought. *And the other man?*

Oh, my God. Now what do I do? Try to apprehend the killer?

She held the transmitter to her lips, depressed the Talk button.

"I know this guy," she told Heisler. "He's a professional assassin. I'm going to try to take him out. You cover Hartman."

"Pardon me," the man called out to Ben, striding quickly toward him.

Something seems wrong with this guy, Ben thought. *Something's off.*

The coat folded over his right arm.

The rapid pace at which he was approaching.

The face—a face he had seen before. A face he would never forget.

Ben slipped his right hand under his left jacket lapel, reached for the cold hard steel of the gun and was afraid.

She needed Hartman alive; Hartman dead did her no good.

The assassin was about to take out Hartman, she was certain. Everything was suddenly one complex calculation. As far as she was concerned, it was better for Hartman, her suspect, to flee than to be killed. In any case, she'd have to leave the pursuit of Hartman to the others.

She raised Heisler's Glock.

The assassin seemed unaware of her. He was focused only on Hartman. She knew from her training that he had fallen victim to the professional's greatest weakness: target fixation. He'd lost a sense of situational awareness. Big cats are most vulnerable to hunters precisely when they're tensing to pounce.

Maybe that would give her the advantage she needed.

Now she had to suddenly break his concentration, distract his attention.

"Freeze!" she shouted. "Halt, goddammit!"

She saw Hartman turn and look at her.

The assassin jerked his head slightly to the left but didn't turn to see where the shout had come from, didn't shift his catlike gaze away from Hartman.

Anna aimed directly at the middle of the assassin's chest, at the center of his mass. It was a reflexive gesture for her; she had been trained to shoot to kill, not to wound.

But what was he doing now? The hit man had turned back toward Hartman, who, she suddenly saw, had his own gun out.

The Architect had his target in his sights; he assumed that whoever had just shouted wasn't an immediate threat, but in any case he had made his own calculation. To turn around and engage her—whoever she was—was to lose his target, and he was unwilling to do that.

Suddenly the assassin began to turn—

She'd figured him wrong.

His movements were as preternaturally smooth as a ballet dancer's. Pivoting on the balls of his feet, he turned one hundred and eighty degrees, his gun extended and firing all the while, in precise intervals of a fraction of a second. The gun scarcely bucked in his powerful grip. Only when she turned to look did she realize what he had accomplished. Good God! A moment before, there were four armed Vienna policemen who had drawn a bead on him. Every one of them had now been shot! Each one of his shots had hit its target. The four policemen were down!

It was a breathtaking execution, displaying a level of skill she had never encountered in her life. She was filled with sheer terror.

Now she heard panicked noises, the gasping and lowing of the incapacitated gunshot victims.

The man was a professional; he had determined to eliminate all impediments before turning back to his target—and she was his final impediment.

But as he spun toward her, Anna had already aimed. She heard Hartman shout. Now it was her turn to focus single-mindedly, and she squeezed the trigger.

Bull's-eye!

The hit man tumbled to the ground, his gun clattering off to one side.

She'd dropped him.

Was he dead?

Everything was chaos. The suspect, Hartman, was tearing away down the street.

But she knew the street was blockaded in both directions by the police. She ran toward the downed man, scooped up his gun, and continued running after Hartman.

Amid the screams of the surviving gunshot victims, she heard shouts in German, but they meant nothing to her.

"Er steht auf!"

"Er lebt, er steht!"

"Nein, nimm den Verdächtigen!"

Down the block, Hartman had run directly into the clustered team of surveillance experts, all of whom had their weapons out and aimed at him, and she heard more shouting—

"Halt! Keinen Schritt weiter!"

"Polizei! Sie sind verhaftet!"

But a noise coming from behind her, from where the assassin lay, attracted her attention, and she turned around just in time to see the assassin stagger into his Peugeot and yank the door behind him.

He was wounded, but he had survived, and now he was getting away!

"Hey," she shouted to anyone, everyone, "stop him! The Peugeot! Don't let him escape!"

They had Hartman; he was surrounded by five *Polizei*. For now she could safely ignore him. Instead, she lunged toward the Peugeot just as it roared to life and barreled straight toward her.

On the few occasions when she'd permitted herself to replay in her mind her close encounter with the Lincoln Town Car in Halifax, she'd fantasized that she'd a gun in her hands and could fire at the driver. Now she did, and she squeezed off shot after shot at the man. But the windshield only pitted and spider-webbed in small areas, and the car kept bearing down on her. She threw herself to one side, out of the way, just as the Peugeot thundered by, tires squealing, down the block past two empty surveillance cars—their drivers and passengers all on the street now—and out of sight.

He'd gotten away!

"Shit!" she shouted, turning back to see Hartman with his hands up. Shaken, she ran down the block toward her newly apprehended suspect.

CHAPTER TWENTY-FIVE

Patient Eighteen was slowly jogging on a treadmill.

A snorkel-like device came out of his mouth, connected to two long hoses. His nose had been clamped shut.

Taped to his crepey, concave bare chest were twelve wires that fed into an EKG monitor. Another wire sprouted from a small device clamped onto the end of a forefinger. He was sweating and looked pale.

"How are you doing?" said the doctor, a tall gray-faced man.

The patient could not talk, but he gave a trembling thumbs-up.

"Remember, there's a panic button right in front of you," the doctor said. "Use it if you need to."

Patient Eighteen kept jogging.

The doctor said to his short, rotund colleague, "I think we're at maximal exercise capacity. He seems to have crossed the respiratory exchange ratio—he's over one. No signs of ischemia. He's strong, this one. All right, let's give him the rest of the day off. Tomorrow he'll begin the treatment."

For the first time all day, the gray-faced doctor allowed himself a smile.

Princeton, New Jersey

The grand old Princeton historian was working in his study at Dickinson Hall when the telephone rang.

Everything in Professor John Barnes Godwin's office dated from the forties or fifties, whether it was the black rotary-dial phone or the oak card-catalog drawers or the Royal manual typewriter (he had no use for computers). He liked it that way, liked the way the old things looked, the solidity of objects from the time they made things out of Bakelite and wood and steel and not plastic, plastic, and plastic.

He was not, however, one of those old men who lived in the past. He loved the world today. Often he wished his darling Sarah, his wife of fifty-seven years, were here to share it with him. They had always planned to do a lot of traveling when he retired.

Godwin was a historian of twentieth-century Europe, a winner of the Pulitzer Prize whose lectures had always been immensely popular on the Princeton campus. Many of his former students now occupied positions of great prominence in their fields. The chairman of the Federal Reserve had been one of his brightest, as were the chairman of WorldCom, both the Secretary of Defense and the Deputy Secretary of Defense, the United States ambassador to the UN, countless members of the Council on Economic Advisers, even the current chairman of the Republican National Committee.

Professor Godwin cleared his throat before answering the phone. "Hello."

The voice was immediately familiar.

"Oh yes, Mr. Holland, good to hear your voice. We're still on, I hope?"

He listened for a moment. "Of course I know him, he was a student of mine . . . Well, if you're asking for my opinion, I remember him as charming if a bit strong-headed, very bright though not really an intellectual, or at least not interested in ideas for their own sake. A very strong sense of moral purpose, I always thought. But Ben Hartman always struck me as quite reasonable and levelheaded."

He listened again. "No, he's not a crusader. He just doesn't have that temperament. And he's certainly no martyr. I think he can be reasoned with."

Another pause.

"Well, none of us wants the project disrupted. But I do wish you'd give the fellow a chance. I'd really hate to see anything happen to him."

Vienna

The interrogation room was cold and bare, with the standard furnishings of police interrogation rooms everywhere. *I'm becoming an expert*, Ben thought grimly. The one-way observation mirror, unsubtle, and as big as a bedroom window in a suburban house. The wire mesh over the window overlooking a bleak inner courtyard.

The American woman sat across the small room, in a gray suit, coiled on the metal folding chair like a clock spring. She had identified herself as Special Agent Anna Navarro of the U.S. Department of Justice, Office of Special Investigations, and flashed an ID card to prove it. She was also a serious beauty, a real stunner: wavy dark brown hair, eyes the color of caramel, olive skin; tall and slim and long-legged. Nicely dressed, too—a sense of style, which had to be rare in the Department of Justice. Yet she was all business, not a hint of a smile. No ring, which probably meant divorced, because women this gorgeous were usually snatched up early, no doubt by some gallant fellow government investigator with a square chin who'd wooed her with tales of his bravery in apprehending miscreants . . . until the stress of two high-powered government careers had taken its toll on the marriage . . .

In the folding chair next to her sat a bruiser of a cop, a beefy guy who sat silent and brooding and chain-smoking Casablanca cigarettes. Ben had no idea whether the cop understood English. He'd only said his name: Sergeant Walter Heisler of the *Sicherheitsbüro*, the major-crimes squad of the Viennese police.

Half an hour into the questioning, Ben became impatient. He'd tried being reasonable, tried to talk sense, but his interrogators were implacable. "Am I under arrest?" he asked finally.

"Do you want to be?" Agent Navarro snapped back.

Oh, good God, not this again.

"Does she have the right to do this?" Ben asked of the hulking Viennese cop, who just smoked and stared at him bovinely.

Silence.

"Well?" Ben demanded. "Who's in charge here?"

"As long as you answer my questions, there's no reason to arrest you," Agent Navarro said. "Yet."

"So I'm free to go."

"You're being held for questioning. Why were you visiting Jürgen Lenz? You still haven't explained properly."

"As I said, it was a social visit. Ask Lenz."

"Are you in Vienna for business or pleasure?"

"Both."

"You don't have any business meetings lined up. Is that the way you normally travel on business?"

"I like to be spontaneous."

"You were booked for five days at a ski resort in the Swiss Alps, but you never showed up there."

"I changed my mind."

"Why do I doubt that?"

"I have no idea. I felt like seeing Vienna."

"So you just showed up in Vienna with no hotel reservations."

"As I said, I like to be spontaneous."

"I see," said Agent Navarro, clearly frustrated. "And your visit to Gaston Rossignol, in Zurich—was that business as well?"

My God, so they knew about that, too! But how? He felt a wave of panic.

"He was a friend of a friend."

"And that's how you treat a friend of a friend—you kill him?"

Oh, Christ. "He was dead when I got there!"

"Really," Navarro said, clearly unconvinced. "Was he expecting you?"

"No. I just showed up."

"Because you like to be spontaneous."

"I wanted to surprise him."

"Instead he surprised you, huh?"

"It was a shock, yes."

"How did you get to Rossignol? Who put you in touch with him?"

Ben hesitated, a beat too long. "I'd rather not say."

She picked up on it. "Because he was no mutual acquaintance or anything like that, was he? What was Rossignol's connection to your father?"

What the hell did that mean? How much did she know? Ben looked at her sharply.

"Let me tell you something," Anna Navarro said dryly. "I know your type. Rich boy, always gets whatever he wants. Whenever you get yourself in deep doodoo, your daddy saves you, or maybe the family lawyer bails you out. You're used to doing whatever the hell you want and you think you'll never have to pay the bill. Well, not this time, my friend."

Ben smiled involuntarily, but he refused to give her the satisfaction of putting up an argument.

"Your father is a Holocaust survivor, is that right?" she persisted.

So she doesn't know everything.

Ben shrugged. "That's what I'm told." She certainly wasn't entitled to the truth.

"And Rossignol was a big-deal Swiss banker, right?" She was watching him closely now.

What was she driving at? "That's why you and all those Austrian cops were staked out in front of Lenz's house," he said. "You were there to arrest me."

"No, actually," the American woman said coolly. "To talk to you."

"You could have just asked to talk to me. You didn't need half the Vienna police force. I'll bet you'd love to pin the Rossignol murder on me. Gets the CIA off the hook, right? Or do you Justice Department guys hate the CIA? I get confused."

Agent Navarro leaned forward, her soft brown eyes gone hard. "Why were you carrying a gun?"

Ben hesitated, but just for a second or two. "For protection."

"Is that right." A statement of skepticism, not a question. "Are you registered to carry a gun in Austria?"

"I believe that's a matter between me and the Austrian authorities."

"The Austrian authorities are sitting in this chair next to me. If he decides to prosecute you for illegally carrying a gun, I won't stand in his way. The Austrians strongly disapprove of foreign visitors carrying un-registered weapons."

Ben shrugged. She had a point, of course. Though it seemed the least of his worries right now.

"So let me tell you this, Mr. Hartman," Agent Navarro said. "I find it a little hard to believe that you carried a gun to visit a 'friend of a friend.' Particularly when your fingerprints were found all over Rossignol's house. Understand?"

"No, not really. Are you accusing me of murdering him? If so, why don't you come right out and say it?" He was finding it hard to breathe, his tension steadily rising.

"The Swiss think your brother had a vendetta against the banking establishment. Maybe something in you got twisted when he died, some-thing that made you take his pursuit of them to a more lethal level. It wouldn't be hard to show motive. And then there are your fingerprints. I think a Swiss court would have no problem convicting you."

Did she genuinely believe he'd murdered Rossignol—and if so, why was this special investigator from the Department of Justice so interested? He had no idea how much power she really had here, what kind of trouble he was really in, and the uncertainty alone made him anxious. Don't be defensive, he thought. Fight back.

Ben sat back. "You have no authority here."

"Absolutely right. But I don't need authority."

What the hell did she mean? "So what do you want from me?"

"I want information. I want to know why you were really visiting Rossignol. Why you were really visiting Jürgen Lenz. What you're really up to, Mr. Hartman."

"And if I don't care to share?" He tried to project an image of confidence.

She cocked her head. "Would you like to find out what'll happen? Why don't you spin the wheel and take a chance?"

Jesus, she was good, Ben thought. He breathed deeply. The room's walls seemed to be closing in. He kept his face blank, unreadable.

She continued: "Do you know that there's a warrant for your arrest in Zurich?"

Ben shrugged. "That's a laugh." He decided that it was time for him to be aggressive, aggrieved, undefensive—as a wrongfully arrested American would be. "Maybe I know the ways of the Swiss a little better than you do. For one thing, they'll swear out a warrant if you spit out your gum on the sidewalk. For another, there's no goddamn possibility of extradition." He'd established this much from his conversations with Howie. "The canton of Zurich has a hard enough time getting cooperation from the *Polizei* of the other Swiss cantons. And the fact that the Swiss have made a name for themselves in harboring tax fugitives means that other countries ignore Swiss extradition requests as a matter of policy." These were Howie's words, and he recited them stolidly, facing her down. She might as well know that she couldn't game him. "The Zurich bulls claim they want me for 'questioning.' They don't even pretend to have a case. So why don't we cut the crap here?"

She leaned closer. "It's a matter of public record that your brother had been trying to build a case against the Swiss banking establishment. Gaston Rossignol was a preeminent Swiss banker. You visit him, and he turns up dead. Let's get back to that. Then suddenly you're in Vienna meeting with the son of an infamous Nazi. And your father was in a concentration camp. It looks an awful lot like some kind of vengeance trip you're on."

So that was it. Maybe it would look like that to someone who didn't know the truth. But I can't tell her the truth!

"That's preposterous," Ben snapped. "I don't even want to dignify your fantasies about vendettas and violence. You talk about Swiss bankers. I do deals with these people, Agent Navarro. It's my job. International finance doesn't really lend itself to murderous rampages, O.K.? In my world, the main injuries you inflict are paper cuts."

"Then explain what happened on the Bahnhofplatz."

"I can't. I've been through that with the Swiss bulls over and over again."

"And explain how you tracked down Rossignol."

Ben shook his head.

"And the others. Come on. I want to know where you got their names and their whereabouts."

Ben just looked at her.

"Where were you on Wednesday?"

"I don't recall."

"Nova Scotia, by any chance?"

"Come to think of it, I was being arrested in Zurich," he shot back. "You can check with your friends at the Zurich police. See, I like to get arrested in every country I visit. It's really the best way to appreciate the local customs."

She ignored his barb. "Tell me what got you arrested."

"You know as well as I do."

Navarro turned to her brooding sidekick, who exhaled a plume of smoke, then looked back at Ben. "Several times in the last couple of days you yourself were almost killed. Including today—"

In his dull, dazed anxiety, he was surprised to feel a warm rush of gratitude. "You saved my life. I guess I should thank you."

"Damn right you should," she replied. "Now tell me, why do you think someone was trying to kill you? Who might have known what you were up to?"

Nice try, lady. "I have no idea."

"I'll bet you have some idea."

"Sorry. Maybe you can ask your friends over at the CIA what they're trying to cover up. Or is your office involved in the cover-up, too?"

"Mr. Hartman, your twin brother was killed in Switzerland, in a suspicious plane crash. More recently, you've had some unexplained connection to shootings in that country. Death seems to follow you around like a cheap cologne. What am I supposed to think?"

"Think whatever you like. I didn't commit any crime."

"I'm going to ask you this one more time: Where did you get their names and addresses?"

"Whose?"

"Rossignol and Lenz."

"I told you, mutual acquaintances."

"I don't believe that."

"Believe what you like."

"What are you hiding? Why don't you level with me, Mr. Hartman?"

"Sorry. I've got nothing to hide."

Agent Navarro folded, then unfolded, her long shapely legs. "Mr. Hartman," she said with utmost exasperation. "I'm going to offer you a deal. You cooperate with me, and I'll do my best to get the Swiss and the Austrians to back off."

Was she sincere? His distrust had become almost a reflex. "Given that you seem to be the one pushing them to come after me, that strikes me as a hollow promise. I don't have to stay here any longer, do I?"

She watched him silently, nibbling at the inside of a cheek. "No." She took out a business card and jotted something down on the back of it, then handed it to him. "If you change your mind, here's my hotel in Vienna."

It was over. Thank God. He inhaled, felt the air reach the very bottom of his lungs, the anxiety suddenly lift.

"Nice to meet you, Agent Navarro," Ben said, rising. "And thanks again for saving my life."

CHAPTER TWENTY-SIX

The pain was intense and overwhelming; another man would have passed out. Gathering his powers of mental concentration, Trevor assigned the pain to another body—a vividly imagined doppelgänger, someone who was convulsed with agony but who was not he. By sheer force of will, he managed to find his way through the streets of Vienna to a building on Taborstrasse.

Then he remembered that the car was stolen—his thinking was sluggish, that was what alarmed him most of all—and he drove five blocks away and abandoned it, the keys dangling from the ignition. Maybe some idiot would steal it and get caught in the citywide dragnet that was sure to follow.

He limped down the street, ignoring the many glances of the passersby. He knew his suit jacket was drenched with his own blood; he had put the trench coat on over it, but even that, too, had gotten soaked through. He had lost a great deal of blood. He felt lightheaded.

He was able to get back to Taborstrasse, to the street-level office marked with a brass plaque that said DR. THEODOR SCHREIBER, INTERNIST & GENERAL SURGEON.

The office was dark, and there was no answer when he buzzed. Trevor didn't find this surprising, since it was after eight o'clock in the evening, and Dr. Schreiber kept regular hours. But he kept ringing the bell anyway. Schreiber lived in the flat behind his small office, and the bell rang in his living quarters as well, Trevor knew.

After five minutes, the light went on in the office, and then a voice came through the speaker, loud and annoyed: *"Ja?"*

"Dr. Schreiber, es is Christoph. Es ist ein Notfall."

The front door of the building unlocked electronically. Then the door off the lobby, marked with the doctor's name on another brass plaque, unlocked as well.

Dr. Schreiber was disgruntled. "You have interrupted my dinner," he said gravely. "I trust it is important—" He noticed the blood-soaked trench coat. "All right, all right, follow me." The physician turned and walked back toward the examination room.

Dr. Schreiber had a sister who lived in Dresden, in East Germany, for decades. Until the Wall came down, this simple accident of geography— he had escaped from East Berlin in 1961, while his sister had been forced to stay behind—had been enough to give East German intelligence leverage over the doctor.

But Stasi did not seek to blackmail him or to turn him into some sort of spy, as if a physician could ever be useful as a spy. No, Stasi had a far more mundane use for him: simply to serve as a doctor on call for its agents in Austria in cases of emergency. Physicians in Austria, as in many countries in the world, are required by law to report gunshot wounds to the police. Dr. Schreiber would be more discreet than that when the occasional wounded Stasi agent appeared at his office, usually in the middle of the night.

Trevor, who had lived as a Stasi illegal in London for many years before he was recruited to Sigma, had from time to time been dispatched to Vienna, under the cover of business travel, and twice he had needed to visit the good doctor.

Even now that the Cold War was long over, and Schreiber's days of covert assistance to East Germany were pretty much finished, Trevor had little doubt that the physician would cooperate. Schreiber could still be prosecuted for his covert assistance to Stasi. That he would not want.

But his vulnerability did not keep Dr. Schreiber from bristling with resentment. "You are a most fortunate man," the doctor said brusquely. "The bullet, you see, entered just over your heart. A slightly more direct angle and you would have died immediately. Instead, it appears to have entered at an oblique angle, digging a sort of trench in the skin and the fatty tissue beneath. It even tore away some of the surface fibers of the pectoralis major, your breast muscle. And exited right here, at the axilla. You must have turned just in time."

Dr. Schreiber glanced over his half-glasses at Trevor, who did not reply.

He poked with a pair of forceps, and Trevor winced. The pain was overwhelming. His body was suffused with an unpleasant prickly heat.

"It also came close to causing great damage to the nerves and blood vessels in the area of the brachial plexus. Had it done so, you'd have lost the use of your right arm permanently. Maybe even lost the arm itself."

"I'm left-handed," Trevor said. "Anyway, I don't need to know the gory details."

"Yes," the doctor said absently. "Well, you really should go to the hospital, the Allgemeines Krankenhaus, if we're going to do this right."

"That's out of the question, and you know it." A lightning bolt of pain shot down his arm.

The doctor changed into his scrubs, and injected several syringes of a local anesthetic around the wound. With a small pair of scissors and forceps he excised some blackened tissue, irrigated the wound, and then set about suturing it.

Trevor could feel a deep, tugging discomfort, but no real pain. He gritted his teeth. "I want you to make sure the wound doesn't open up if I move around," he said.

"You should take it easy for a little while."

"I'm a fast healer."

"That's right," the doctor said. "I remember now." The man was a fast healer—freakishly so.

"Time is the one luxury I don't have," Trevor said. "I want you to sew it up tight."

"Then I can use heavier suture materials—3-0 nylon, say—but it may leave a rather ugly scar."

"It doesn't concern me."

"Fine," the doctor said, turning back to his steel cart of equipment.

When he had finished, he said, "For the pain, I can give you some Demerol." He added dryly, "Or would you prefer to go without anything?"

"Some ibuprofen should be enough," Trevor said.

"As you wish."

Trevor stood, wincing. "All right then, I appreciate your help." He handed the doctor a few thousand-shilling notes.

The physician looked at him and said, quite insincerely, "Any time."

Anna splashed her face with hot water. Thirty times, her mother had trained her: her mother's only vanity. Keeps the skin vital and glowing.

Over the running water she heard the phone ringing. Grabbing a towel to dry her face, she ran to catch it.

"Anna, it's Robert Polozzi. Am I calling you too late?"

Robert Polozzi from ID Section.

"No, not at all, Robert. What is it?"

"Listen: about the patent search."

She'd forgotten about the patent search. She patted her dripping face.

He said: "The neurotoxin—"

"Oh, right. You found something?"

"So get this. May 16 of this year, patent number—well, it's a long number—anyway, a patent for this exact synthetic compound was applied for by a small Philadelphia-based biotech company called Vortex. It's a, it says, 'a synthetic analog of the venom of the conus sea snail for proposed in-vitro applications.' And then some mumbo jumbo about 'localizing ion channels' and 'tagging chemochyme receptors.'" He paused, then resumed, his voice tentative. "I called the place. Vortex, I mean. On a pretext, of course."

A little unorthodox, but she didn't mind. "Learn anything?"

"Well, not exactly. They say their stocks of this toxin are minimal and under tight control. It's hard to produce, so they don't have much, and anyway the stuff is used in ridiculously tiny quantities, and it's still experimental. I asked them whether it could be used as a poison, and the guy I talked to, the scientific director of the firm, said of course it could—the conus sea snail's venom, as found in nature, is highly deadly. He said a tiny amount could induce immediate heart failure."

She felt a growing excitement. "He told you the stuff is under tight control—that means it's under lock and key?"

"Right."

"And this guy strikes you as on the level?"

"I think so, but who knows."

"Great work, thanks. Can you find out from them whether any of their supply of this stuff has been found missing or otherwise unaccounted for?"

"Already did," the researcher said proudly. "The answer's no."

A pang of disappointment. "Can you find out for me everything you can about Vortex? Owners, principals, employees, and so on?"

"Will do."

She hung up, sat on the edge of the bed, pondered. It was possible that tugging at this thread would unravel the conspiracy behind the murders. Or unravel nothing.

The whole investigation was proving increasingly frustrating. Nor had the Vienna police had any luck chasing down the shooter. The shooter's Peugeot had previously been reported stolen—surprise, surprise. Another dead end.

This Hartman she found baffling. Against her will she also found him appealing, even attractive. But he was a type. A golden boy, born to money, graced with good looks, overconfident. He was Brad, the football player who'd raped her. The world cut men like that a break. Men like that, a blunt-speaking girlfriend of hers in college used to say, thought their shit didn't stink. They thought they could get away with anything.

But was he a killer? Somehow it seemed unlikely. She believed his version of what had happened at Rossignol's in Zurich; it jibed with the fingerprint patterns and with her own sense of him. Yet he was carrying a gun, passport control had no record of him arriving in Austria, and he'd offered no explanation for that. . . . On the other hand, a thorough search of his car hadn't revealed anything. No syringe, no poisons, nothing.

Whether he was a part of this conspiracy was hard to say. He'd thought his brother had been killed four years ago; maybe that murder had been the catalyst for those murders that came later. But why so many, and in such a short span of time?

The fact remained: Benjamin Hartman knew more. Yet she didn't have the authority, or the grounds, to hold him. It was deeply frustrating. She wondered whether her desire—all right, obsession—to get him had to do with the rich-boy thing, the old wounds, Brad . . .

She took her address book from the end table, looked up a phone number, and dialed.

It rang several times before a gravelly male voice answered, "Donahue." Donahue was a money-laundering guru at DOJ, and she'd quietly enlisted his help before she'd left for Switzerland. No context; just some account information. Donahue didn't mind being kept in the dark about the nature of her investigation; he seemed to regard it as a challenge.

"It's Anna Navarro," she said.

"Oh yeah, right, how ya doin' there, Anna?"

She found herself switching into her regular-guy voice. This she did easily; it was how her father's buddies talked, her neighbors back home. "Doin' good, thanks. How're we doin' on the money trace?"

"Na-a-ah, nothin'. We're buttin' our heads against a big brick wall. It's lookin' like each of the dead guys got regular contributions booted into their accounts from some haven country. Cayman Islands, British Virgins, Curaçao. That's where we keep hittin' the wall."

"What happens when you go to these offshore banks with an official request?"

A short bark of derision from Donahue. "They give us the finger. We give 'em an MLAT request for their financial records, they say they'll get around to it some time next few years." MLAT, she knew, was the mutual assistance treaty, which in principle obtained between the United States and many of these offshore havens. "BVI and Caymans are the worst, they tell us maybe two, three years it'll take 'em."

"Huh."

"But even if they should just open up the magic doors and show us everything, all we're going to get is where they got the money from, and you can bet your paycheck it's some other offshore. Isle of Man, Bahamas, Bermuda, Lux, San Marino, Anguilla. Probably a whole chain of offshores and shell companies. These days money can zip around the world, movin' between a dozen accounts in, like, seconds."

"Mind if I ask you something?" she said.

"Go 'head."

"How do you guys ever get anything on money-laundering?"

"Oh, we get stuff," he said, a little defensively. "It just takes years."

"Great," she said. "Thanks."

In a small room on the fifth floor of the *Sicherheitsbüro*, at Vienna police headquarters on Rossauer Lände, a young man sat before a computer screen, wearing headphones. From time to time he snubbed out a cigarette in a large gold ashtray that sat on the gray Formica table next to a No Smoking sign.

In a small box on the top left of the screen was the telephone number he was monitoring, along with the date, the start time, duration of call measured in a tenth of a second, the telephone number called. Elsewhere on the screen was a list of telephone numbers, representing each call made from this number. All you had to do was to move the cursor to any of the numbers and double-click, and the digitally recorded conversation would start playing, either on the headphones or through the external speakers. Little red bars would dance as the volume fluctuated. You could adjust not only the volume but even the speed of playback.

Every telephone call the woman had made from her hotel room was recorded onto this computer's hard disk. The technology was most impressive; it had been provided to the Vienna police by the Israelis.

The door to the little room opened and in came Detective Sergeant Walter Heisler across the institutional green linoleum floor. He, too, was smoking. He gave a little jerk of his head by way of greeting. The tech removed his headphones, put out his cigarette, looked up.

"Anything interesting?" the detective asked.

"Most of the calls have been to Washington."

"Strictly speaking, we're supposed to inform Interpol when we record any international calls." There was a twinkle in the detective's eye.

The tech raised his eyebrows in silent complicity.

Heisler pulled up a chair. "Mind if I join you?"

California

The young billionaire computer mogul Arnold Carr took the call on his cellular phone while he was strolling through a redwood forest in Northern California with his old friend and mentor the investment whiz Ross Cameron.

The two were spending a weekend in the company of some of America's richest and most powerful men at the exclusive retreat known as the Bohemian Grove. There was some sort of idiotic game called paintball going on back at the encampment, presided over by the chief executive of BankAmerica and the U.S. ambassador to the Court of St. James.

But Carr, the founder of a vastly successful software company, rarely had the chance to hang out with his billionaire buddy Ross Cameron, the so-called sage of Sante Fe. So they had spent a lot of time hiking through the woods talking about money and business, philanthropy and art collecting, their kids, and the extraordinary, highly secret project they had both been invited to join.

Carr pulled the tiny, burring phone out of the pocket of his Pendleton plaid shirt with visible annoyance. Hardly anyone had this number, and the few employees who'd dare call had been instructed not to bother him for any reason during his retreat weekend.

"Yeah," Carr said.

"Mr. Carr, I'm so sorry to bother you on a Sunday morning," the voice purred. "This is Mr. Holland. I hope I didn't wake you."

Carr recognized the voice instantly. "Oh, no way," he said, suddenly cordial. "I've been up for hours. What's up?"

When "Mr. Holland" had finished, Carr said, "Let me see what I can do."

CHAPTER TWENTY-SEVEN

Ben arrived at his hotel around nine o'clock at night, hungry but unable to eat, jittery from too much caffeine. He'd taken a cab from police headquarters, since driving the Opel Vectra was out of the question. Two of its windows had been shattered in the shootout, the leather seats covered with rounded shards of glass.

The lobby was quiet, the hotel guests either out at dinner or returned to their rooms. Several Oriental rugs overlapped one another; here and there patches of highly polished marble floor gleamed.

The concierge, a too-slick middle-aged man with alert eyes behind steel-rimmed glasses, handed him the room key before Ben said a word.

"Thanks," Ben said. "Any messages for me?" Perhaps the private detective.

The concierge tapped at his computer keyboard. "No, sir, just the one you already retrieved."

"Which one was that?" *What?* he thought, alarmed. *I haven't gotten a single message since I got to Vienna.*

"I don't know, sir. You called in a few hours ago." More tapping. "At six-twenty this evening you got a message from the hotel operator."

"Could you give it to me again?" This was either a mistake or . . .

"I'm sorry, sir, once the guest retrieves a message, it's deleted from the system." He gave Ben a feral smile. "We can't keep all messages forever, you know."

Ben took the small brass-cage elevator to the fourth floor, nervously fingering the large brass sphere that dangled from the room key. He couldn't put it past Agent Navarro to have had some male colleague call the hotel to get his messages, see whom he was in touch with.

But who had left a message? Besides Agent Navarro, only the private detective knew his whereabouts. It was surely too late to call the detective, Hans Hoffman; he wouldn't be in his office this late at night.

Navarro was suspicious about his motives, yet she couldn't seriously think he had killed Rossignol. Could she? She had to know she wasn't dealing with a serial murderer. After all, she'd mentioned she had expertise in homicide; she had to know who fit the profile and who didn't.

So what was she really after?

Was it possible she was actually working for the CIA or some gray-haired contingent thereof, mopping up, helping cover up their involvement by shifting suspicion to him?

And the fact remained: Gaston Rossignol, a founder of this mysterious corporation that might or might not have had CIA involvement, had just been murdered. As had Peter, whose single error, it seemed, was to have dug up a list of directors of this very same corporation. Had the same people killed both of them? It certainly seemed likely.

But American killers? CIA?

It was difficult to fathom. Jimmy Cavanaugh was an American . . . Yet couldn't he have been working for foreigners?

And then there was Max's baffling disappearance.

Why had he vanished? Godwin had shed no light on that mystery. Why had Max called Godwin just before leaving?

Was his father dead now, too?

It was time to place another call to Bedford.

He walked down the long corridor, struggled with the room key for a moment, and then the door came open. He froze.

The lights were off.

Yet he had left all the lights in the room on when he'd left. Had someone turned them off?

Oh, come on, he told himself. Surely the chambermaid had turned them off. The Austrians prided themselves on being environmentally conscientious.

Was he overthinking this? Was he being ridiculously paranoid? Was this what the last few days had done to him?

Still . . .

Quietly, without entering, he closed the door, turned the key to lock it again, and went back down the hall in search of a porter or bell captain. None was anywhere to be seen. He circled back and took the stairs down to the third floor. There, at the end of another long hall, he spotted a porter coming out of a room.

"Excuse me," Ben said, accelerating his stride. "Can you help me?"

The young porter turned. "Sir?"

"Listen," Ben said, "I locked myself out of my room. Can you let me in?" He palmed the porter a fifty-shilling note, about eight dollars, and added sheepishly, "This is the second time I've done it. I don't want to have to go back to the concierge. It's up one flight. Four-sixteen."

"Oh yes, certainly, sir. Ah, moment please." He searched through a ring of keys on his belt. "Yes, sir, please."

They took the elevator up to the fourth floor. The porter opened the door to 416. Feeling a little foolish, Ben stood behind him and off to one side, so that he could see into the room at an oblique angle, without being seen.

He noticed a shape, a silhouette! The figure of a man outlined against backlight from the open bathroom door. The man was crouching down, pointing a long-barreled gun toward the door!

The man turned, and his face became visible. It was the assassin who'd tried to kill him a few hours ago in front of Jürgen Lenz's villa! The assassin in the Swiss auberge.

The man who killed his brother.

The porter screamed, "No!" and ran away down the hall.

For a moment the killer was confused—he'd expected Ben, not a uniformed hotel employee. The hesitation was long enough for Ben to take off. Behind him came a series of muted spits, then the much louder explosions of bullets pocking the walls. The porter's screams became even louder, more frantic, and the gunfire came closer, and then came the racing footsteps of the gunman, and Ben put on a burst of speed. Straight ahead was the door to the stairway, and he quickly rejected it—he didn't want to be a prisoner in a stairwell with an armed killer after him. Instead he whipped around the corridor to the right, saw an open room door, a housekeeping cart in front of it, and he leaped into the room, swinging the door shut behind him. His back pressed against the door, he gasped for breath, wondering whether the killer had seen him enter the room. He heard muffled footsteps racing by: the killer had passed. He heard the porter shout, calling someone; he didn't sound as if he'd been wounded, which was a relief.

A cry from inside the room! He saw a small, dark-skinned maid in a light blue uniform cowering in the corner of the room.

"Quiet!" Ben hissed.

"Who are you?" the maid gasped, terrified. She spoke in heavily accented English. "Please don't hurt me!"

"Quiet," Ben repeated. "Get down. If you keep quiet, you won't get hurt!" ·

The maid flattened herself against the carpeting, whimpering in abject terror.

"Matches!" Ben said. "I need matches!"

"The ashtray! Please—the desk, next to the television!"

Ben found them and located the smoke/heat detector mounted on the ceiling above him. He stood on a chair, lit a match, held it to the coil. In a few seconds he could hear the Klaxon of a fire alarm sounding in the room and in the corridor outside—a rasping metallic shriek caterwauling at regular, rapid intervals. The sound was everywhere! Shouts and screams came from the hall as hotel guests ran from their rooms. In another few seconds, water began spraying from the sprinkler system in the ceiling, drenching the carpet and bed. The maid screamed again as Ben turned and opened the door, quickly looking out in either direction. The hall was chaos: people running about, some huddled in bafflement, gesturing this way and that, yelling to one another as water spewed from the sprinklers all along the ceiling the length of the corridor. Ben ran out of the room, joining the frenzied crowd in a rush to the stairwell. He knew, from the height of the main staircase that led into the hotel's front entrance, that the stairwell had to have its own exit onto the street or back alley.

The stairwell door opened onto a dark corridor, illuminated only by a flickering, buzzing fluorescent ceiling fixture, but it was enough light to make out the double doors of the hotel kitchen. He raced toward it, pushed the doors open without stopping, and saw the inevitable service entrance. He reached the door, felt the flow of cold air from the outside, slid open the heavy steel bolt, and pulled the massive door open. A ramp led down into a narrow alley crowded with trashcans. He propelled himself down, and, with fire engine sirens sounding in the distance, disappeared into the dark alley.

Twenty minutes later he came to the tall modern building overlooking the Danube canal, on the far side of the Stadtpark, a characterless American hotel that was part of an international chain. He strode purposefully through the lobby to the elevators, a hotel guest who obviously belonged.

He knocked on the door of Room 1423.

Special Agent Anna Navarro cracked open the door. She was in a flannel nightgown, her makeup was off, and yet she was luminous.

"I think I'm ready to cooperate," Ben said.

Anna Navarro fixed Hartman a drink from the honor bar: a toy bottle of Scotch, a little green bottle of mineral water, a few miniature cubes of ice from the tiny freezer. She was, if possible, even more businesslike than she'd been at the police station. Over her flannel nightgown she'd cinched a white terry-cloth robe. Probably it didn't help, Ben reflected, having a strange man in the close quarters of her hotel room when she was dressed for bed.

Ben took the drink gratefully. It was watery. She was not a drinker. But shaken as he was, he needed a drink badly, and it did the job.

Despite the sofa on which he sat, the room was not set up for visitors. She started to sit facing him, on the edge of the bed, then rejected it in favor of a big wing chair, which she pulled out at an angle to the sofa.

The plate-glass window was a black pointillist canvas. From up here, Vienna was neon-lit, its lights twinkling under the starry sky.

Navarro leaned forward, crossed her legs. She was barefoot, her feet slender and high-arched, delicate, the toenails painted.

"It was the same guy, you think?" Her abrasive edge was gone.

Ben took another sip. "Definitely. I'll never forget his face."

She sighed. "And I thought at least I'd seriously wounded him. From everything I've heard, this guy's incredibly dangerous. And what he did to those four policemen—astonishing. Like an execution machine. You were lucky. Or maybe I should say you were smart—sensing something wasn't right, using the porter to confuse him, putting our friend off balance, buying yourself time to escape. Well done."

He shrugged in self-deprecation, secretly pleased by the unexpected compliment. "You know something about this guy?"

"I've read a dossier, but it's incomplete. He's believed to live in England, probably London."

"He's British?"

"Formerly East German intelligence—Stasi. Their field agents were among the most highly trained. Certainly some of the most ruthless. Seems to have left the organization a long time ago."

"What's he doing living in England?"

"Who knows? Maybe avoiding the German authorities, like most of his ex-colleagues. What we don't know is whether he's an assassin for hire, or whether he's in the employ of some organization with diverse interests."

"His name?"

"Vogler, I think. Hans Vogler. Obviously here on some sort of job."

Some sort of job. *I am next.* Ben felt numb.

"You said he might be in some organization's employ."

"That's what we say when we haven't figured out the pattern yet." She pursed her lips. "You might be in some organization's employ, and I don't mean Hartman Capital Management."

"You still don't believe me, do you?"

"Well, who are you? What are you really up to?"

"Oh, come on," he said heatedly. "Don't tell me you guys don't have a goddamned file on me!"

She glared. "All I know about you are isolated facts without a logical explanation tying them all together. You say you were in Zurich when suddenly someone from your past pops up and tries to kill you and instead gets killed himself. And then his body disappears. Next thing I know, you've entered Switzerland illegally. Then your fingerprints turn up all over the house of a banker named Rossignol, who you claim was dead when you got there. You carry a gun, though where you got it— and why—you won't say."

Ben listened in silence, letting her go on.

"Why were you meeting with this Lenz, this son of a famous Nazi?"

Ben blinked, unsure how much to divulge. But before he could formulate a reply, she spoke again. "Here's what I want to know. What does Lenz have in common with Rossignol?"

Ben drained his Scotch. "My brother . . ." he began.

"The one who died four years ago."

"So I thought. He turned out to be hiding from some dangerous people. He didn't know who they were, exactly; I still don't know. Some conclave of industrialists, or their descendants, or maybe CIA hirelings, maybe something else entirely—who knows? But apparently he'd uncovered a list of names—"

Agent Navarro's caramel eyes grew wide. "What kind of list?"

"A very old one."

Her face flushed. "Where did he get this list?"

"He came across it in the archives of a Swiss bank."

"A Swiss bank?"

"It's a list of board members of a corporation that was founded in the last days of the Second World War."

"Jesus Christ," she breathed. "So that's it."

Ben drew a folded, grimy square of paper from his breast pocket and handed it to her. "Sorry, it's a bit soiled. I've been keeping it in my shoe. To keep it out of the hands of people like you."

She perused it, frowning. "Max Hartman. Your father?"

"Alas."

"Did he tell you about this corporation?"

"No way. My brother came across it."

"But wasn't your father a Holocaust survivor—?"

"And now we come to the sixty-four-thousand-dollar question."

"Wasn't there some physical mark—a tattoo or something?"

"A tattoo? At Auschwitz, yes. At Dachau, no."

She didn't seem to be listening. "My God," she said. "The string of mysterious homicides—every single name is here." She seemed to be speaking to herself, not to him. "Rossignol . . . Prosperi . . . Ramago . . . they're all here. No, they're not all on my list. Some overlap, but . . ." She looked up. "What did you hope to learn from Rossignol?"

What was she getting at? "I thought he might know why my brother was killed, and who did it."

"But he was himself killed before you got to him."

"So it seems."

"Did you look into this Sigma company, try to locate it, trace its history?"

Ben nodded. "But I turned up nothing. Then again, maybe it never existed, if you know what I mean." Seeing her frown, he went on. "A notional entity, like a shell company."

"What kind of shell company?"

Ben shook his head. "I don't know. Something involving American military intelligence, maybe." He told her of Lenz's worries.

"I don't think I buy it."

"Why not?"

"I work for the government, don't forget. The bureaucracy leaks like a sieve. They'd never be able to coordinate a series of murders without the world finding out."

"Then what do you figure the link is? Apart from the obvious, I mean."

"I'm not sure how much I can tell you."

"Look," Ben said fiercely, "if we're going to share information—if we're going to help each other—you can't hold back. You have to trust me."

She nodded, then seemed to come to a decision. "For one thing, they aren't, or weren't, janitors, believe me, none of them. They all had great, visible wealth, or most of them, anyway. The only one who lived modestly, at least that I saw, still had tons of money in the bank." She told him about her investigation in general terms.

"You said one of them worked for Charles Highsmith, right? So it's as if you've got your titans here, and then the guys who work for them, their trusted lieutenants and whatnot. And back in 1945 or so, Allen Dulles is running clearances on them, because they're all playing together, and Dulles doesn't like to be surprised by his playmates."

"Which still leaves the larger question unanswered. What's the game? Why was Sigma formed in the first place? For what?"

"Maybe the explanation is simple," Ben said. "Bunch of moguls got together in 1944, '45, to siphon off a huge amount of money from the Third Reich. They divided up the spoils and got even richer. The way guys like that think, they probably told themselves they were reclaiming what was properly theirs."

She seemed perplexed. "O.K., but here's what doesn't fit. You've got people who, right up until their deaths just days ago, were receiving regular, large payments. Wire transfers into their bank accounts, in amounts ranging from a quarter-million to a half-million bucks."

"Wired from where?"

"Laundered. We don't know where the money originated; we only know the very last links in the chains—places like the Cayman Islands, Turks and Caicos."

"Haven countries," Ben said.

"Exactly. Beyond that, it's impossible to get any information."

"Not necessarily," Ben said. "Depends on who you know. And whether you're willing to bend the law a little. Grease some palms."

"We don't bend the law." Agent Navarro said this with an almost haughty pride.

"That's why you don't know shit about where the money came from."

She looked startled, as if he'd slapped her face. Then she laughed. "What do you know about laundering money?"

"I don't do it myself, if that's what you're thinking, but my company does have an offshore division that manages funds—to avoid taxes, government regulations, all that good stuff. Also, I've had clients who are very good at hiding their assets from people like you. I know people who can get information out of offshore banks. They specialize in it. Charge a fortune. They can dig up financial information anywhere in the world, all through their personal contacts, knowing who to pay off."

After a few seconds, she said, "How would you feel about working with me on this? Informally, of course."

Surprised, Ben asked, "What does that mean, exactly?"

"Share information. We have an overlap of motivations. You want to know who killed your brother and why. I want to know who's been killing the old men."

Is she on the level? he wondered. Was this some kind of trick? What did she really want?

"You think the murderers are one and the same? My brother and these men on that list of yours?"

"I'm convinced of it now. All part of the same pattern, the same mosaic."

"What's in it for me?" He looked at her boldly but softened it with a grin.

"Nothing official, let me tell you that right up front. Maybe a little protection. Put it this way—they've already tried to kill you more than once. How long is your luck going to hold?"

"And if I stick close to you, I'm safe?"

"Safer, maybe. You got a better idea? You did come to my hotel, after all. Anyway, the cops took your gun, right?"

True. "I'm sure you understand my reluctance—after all, until very recently you wanted me in prison."

"Look, feel free to go back to your hotel. Have a good night's sleep."

"Point taken. You're making a generous offer. Maybe one I'd be foolish to turn down. I—I don't know."

"Well, sleep on it."

"Speaking of sleep—"

Her eyes searched the room. "I—"

"I'll call down to the front desk and get myself a room."

"I doubt you'll get one. There's some conference here, and they're booked to capacity. I got one of the last rooms available. Why don't you sleep on the couch?"

He gave her a quick look. Did the uptight Special Agent Navarro just invite him to spend the night in her room? No. He was deluding himself. Her body language, the unspoken signals, made it clear: she'd invited him here to hide out, not to slip into her bed.

"Thanks," he said.

"Just one thing: the couch is a little small, maybe a bit too short."

"I've slept on worse, believe me."

She got up, went to a closet, and found a blanket, handed it to him. "I can ask room service to bring up a toothbrush. In the morning we're going to have to retrieve your clothes, your luggage, from your hotel."

"I don't plan to go back."

"Definitely not a good idea. I'll make arrangements." She seemed to realize that she was standing a little too close, and she took a step backward, the gesture awkward. "Well, I'm going to turn in," she said.

He thought of something suddenly, an idea that had been teasing at the back of his mind since leaving Lenz's villa. "The old Nazi hunter Jakob Sonnenfeld lives in this town, doesn't he?"

She turned toward him. "That sounds right."

"I read somewhere recently he may be ancient but he's as sharp as ever. Plus, he's supposed to have extensive files. I wonder . . ."

"You think he'll see you?"

"I think it's worth a try."

"Well, be careful if you do go. Take some security precautions. Don't let anyone follow you there. For his sake."

"Hey, I'll take any advice on that you want to give me."

While she got ready for bed, he called Bedford on his digital phone.

Mrs. Walsh answered. She sounded agitated. "No, Benjamin, I haven't heard a word. Not a word! He seems to have vanished without a trace. I've—well, I've brought the police in on this. I'm at my wits' end!"

Ben felt a dull headache starting: the tension, which for a while had abated, had returned. Rattled, he mumbled a few empty words of reassurance, disconnected the call, took off his jacket, and hung it on the back of the desk chair. Then, still dressed in his slacks and shirt, he settled onto the sofa and pulled the blanket over him.

What did this mean, his father's disappearing without leaving a word? He had voluntarily gotten into a limousine; it wasn't a kidnapping. Presumably he knew where he was going.

Which was where?

He struggled to get comfortable on the couch, but Navarro was right, it was just an inch or two too short for comfort. He saw her sitting up in bed reading a file by the light of the bed lamp. Her soft brown eyes were caught by the pool of light.

"Was that about your father?" she asked. "I'm sorry, I know I shouldn't have been eavesdropping, but—"

"It's O.K. Yeah, my father vanished a few days ago. Got in a limousine to the airport and was never heard from again."

She put down the file, sat up straight. "That's a possible kidnapping. Which makes it federal business."

He swallowed, his mouth dry. Could he really have been abducted?

"Tell me what you know," she said.

The phone jangled some hours later, awakening them both.

Anna picked it up. "Yes?"

"Anna Navarro?"

"Yes, who's this?"

"Anna, I'm Phil Ostrow, from the American embassy here. I hope I'm not calling you too late." A flat Midwestern American accent with Chicagoan vowels.

"I had to get up to answer the phone anyway," she said dryly. "What can I do for you?" What State Department hack called at midnight?

"I—well, Jack Hampton suggested I call." He paused significantly.

Hampton was an operations manager for the CIA, and someone who had done Anna more than one assist on a previous assignment. A good man, as straightforward as you could be in an oblique business. She recalled Bartlett's words about the "crooked timber of humanity." But Hampton wasn't built that way.

"I have some information about the case you're working."

"What's your— Who are you, if you don't mind my asking?"

"I'd rather not get into all that over the phone. I'm a colleague of Jack's."

She knew what that meant: CIA. Hence the Hampton connection. "What's your information, or would you rather not get into that either?"

"Let's just say it's important. Can you come by the office tomorrow morning, first thing? Seven too early for you?" What could it be that was so urgent? she wondered.

"You guys do start early, don't you? Yeah, I guess I can."

"All right—tomorrow morning, then. You been to the office before?"

"Embassy?"

"Across the street from the consular section."

He gave her directions. She hung up, puzzled. From across the room Ben said, "Everything O.K.?"

"Yeah," she said unconvincingly. "Everything's fine."

"We can't stay here, you know."

"Correct. Tomorrow we should both move."

"You seem worried, Agent Navarro."

"I'm always worried," she said. "I live my life worried. And call me Anna."

"I never used to worry much," he said. "Good night, Anna."

CHAPTER TWENTY-EIGHT

It was the sound of a blow-dryer that awakened Ben; after a few groggy moments, he realized that he was in a hotel room in Vienna, and that his back ached from a night on the couch.

He craned his neck forward, heard the satisfying crack of vertebrae, felt some welcome relief from the stiffness.

The bathroom door opened and light flooded half the room. Anna Navarro was dressed in a tweedy brown suit, a little dowdy but not unbecoming, and her face was made up.

"I'll be back in an hour or so," she said crisply. "Go back to sleep."

Directly across the street from the consular section of the U.S. embassy, just as Ostrow had described, was a drab modern office building. The placard in the lobby listed a number of U.S. and Austrian business offices, and on the eleventh floor, sure enough, the Office of the United States Trade Representative—the cover for the Vienna office of the CIA. Such feelers from agencies she was investigating were far from unusual; they'd sometimes resulted in her best leads.

Anna entered an unremarkable reception area, where a young woman sat at a government-issue desk, beneath the Great Seal of the United States, answering the phone and typing at a computer keyboard. She didn't look up. Anna introduced herself, and the receptionist pressed a button and announced her.

In less than a minute a man with the pallor of a bureaucratic lifer bustled out. His cheeks were acne-scarred and sunken, his hair graying auburn. His eyes were small and gray behind large wire-rimmed glasses.

"Miss Navarro?" he said, thrusting out a hand. "I'm Phil Ostrow."

The receptionist buzzed them through the door from which he had appeared, and Ostrow guided her to a small conference room where a slender, darkly handsome man was sitting at a fake-wood-grain Formica-topped table. He had bristling, brush cut black hair salted with gray, brown eyes, long black lashes. Late thirties, maybe, Middle Eastern. Ostrow and Anna sat on either side of him.

"Yossi, this is Anna Navarro. Anna, Yossi."

Yossi's face was tanned, the lines around his eyes deeply etched, whether from squinting in the sun or from a life of great stress. His chin was square and cleft. There was something almost pretty about his face, though it was masculinized by his weathered skin and a day-old growth of beard.

"Good to meet you, Yossi," she said.

She nodded warily, unsmiling; he did the same. He did not offer his hand.

"Yossi's a case officer—you don't mind my telling her that much, do you, Yossi?" said Ostrow. "He works under deep commercial cover here in Vienna. A good setup. He emigrated to the States from Israel when he was in his late teens. Now everyone assumes he's an Israeli—which means every time he gets into trouble, someone else gets the blame." Ostrow chuckled.

"Ostrow, enough—no more," Yossi said. He spoke in a gruff baritone, his English accented with guttural Hebrew R's. "Now, we should understand each other: a number of men all around the world have been found dead in the last few weeks. You are investigating these deaths. You know these are murders, but you do not know who is behind them."

Anna gazed at him dully.

"You interrogated Benjamin Hartman at the *Sicherheitsbüro*. And you've been in close contact with him since. Yes?"

"Where are you going with this?"

Ostrow spoke. "We're making an official interagency request that you remand Hartman to our custody."

"What the hell . . . ?"

"You're over your head here, Officer." Ostrow returned her gaze levelly.

"I'm not following you."

"Hartman's a security risk. A two-woman man, O.K.?"

Anna recognized the agency slang—it referred to double agents, American assets who had been recruited by hostile parties. "I don't understand. Are you saying that Hartman's one of yours?" That was madness. Or was it? It would explain how he was able to travel through European countries without alerting passport control, among other things that had puzzled her. And wouldn't his cover as an international financier lend itself to all sorts of agency work? The named scion of a well-known financial outfit—no concocted legend could ever be as versatile and as persuasive.

Yossi and Ostrow exchanged glances. "Not one of ours, exactly."

"No? Then whose?"

"Our theory is that he's been on retainer from someone in our outfit who's been freelancing, let's say. We could be talking false-flag recruitment."

"You bring me here and talk to me about theories?"

"We need him back on American soil. Please, Agent Navarro. You really don't know who you're dealing with here."

"I'm dealing with someone who's confused about a number of things. And who's still in shock from the death of his twin brother—killed, he believes."

"We know all about it. Hasn't it occurred to you that he may have killed him, too?"

"You're joking." The imputation was incredible, and terrible; could it be true?

"What do you really know about Benjamin Hartman?" Ostrow demanded testily. "I'll ask another question. What do you know about how your list of targets started to make the rounds? Information doesn't want to be free, Agent Navarro. Information wants to command top dollar, and someone like Benjamin Hartman has the wherewithal to pay it."

Grease some palms: Hartman's words.

"But why? What's his agenda?"

"We're never going to find out so long as he's cavorting around Europe, are we?" Ostrow paused. "Yossi hears things from his former compatriots. Mossad has caseworkers in this town, too. There's a possible connection with your victims."

"A splinter group?" she asked. "Or are you talking about the Kidon?" She meant the assassination unit of Mossad.

"No. It is nothing official. It is private business."

"Involving Mossad agents?"

"And some freelancers they hire."

"But these murders aren't Mossad signature killings."

"Please," Yossi said, his face creasing with distaste. "Don't be naïve. You think my brethren all the time are leaving their business cards? When they want to be credited, sure. Come on!"

"So then they don't want to be credited."

"Of course not. Is too sensitive. Potentially can be explosive in the current climate. Israel doesn't want to be connected."

"So who are they working for?"

Yossi glanced at Ostrow, then back at Anna. He shrugged.

"Not for Mossad, is that what you're saying?"

"For Mossad to order assassinations, this is very formalized thing. There is whole internal system, 'execution list,' that the Prime Minister must sign off on. He must initial each name on the list, or it must not be carried out. People in Mossad and Shin Bet have been forced out for ordering killings without approval from top. That is why I tell you this is not authorized sanctions."

"So I ask you again: Who are they working for?"

Again Yossi looked at Ostrow, but this time his glance seemed to be a prompt, a nudge.

"You didn't hear this from me," Ostrow said.

She felt gooseflesh. Thunderstruck, she whispered, "You're kidding me."

"See, the Agency would never dirty its own hands," Ostrow said. "Not anymore. In the good old days, we wouldn't hesitate to rub out some tin-pot dictator if he looked at us the wrong way. Now we got presidential directives and congressional oversight committees and CIA directors whose balls have been lopped off. Christ, we're afraid to give a foreign citizen a head cold."

There was a knock on the door. A young man stuck his head in. "Langley on three, Phil," he said.

"Tell 'em I didn't get in yet." The door closed, and Ostrow rolled his eyes.

"Let me get this straight," Anna said, addressing Ostrow. "You guys passed intelligence on to some Mossad freelancers?"

"Someone did. That's all I know. The rumor is that Ben Hartman served as a go-between."

"You got hard evidence?"

"Yossi's come up with some suggestive details," Ostrow said quietly. "He described enough of the 'watermarks,' the 'sanitation' procedures, the interoffice markings, to tell me this came directly from CIA. I'm talking about shit that can't be made up, marks and glyphs that are rotated daily."

Anna could put two and two together: Yossi himself had to have been an American penetration agent, a deep-cover asset, spying on Mossad for the CIA. She considered asking about it directly, but decided it would be a breach of professional etiquette. "Who at Langley?" she asked.

"I told you, I don't know."

"You don't know, or you won't tell me?"

Yossi, a spectator at a bullfight, smiled for the first time. His smile was dazzling.

"You don't know me," Ostrow said, "but anyone who does knows I'm an avid enough bureaucratic gameplayer to want to screw someone there I don't like. If I had the name, I'd hand it to you just to burn the guy."

That she believed: that would be the natural response of an Agency infighter. But she was determined not to let him see that she was persuaded. "What's the motivation here? Are you talking about fanatics in the CIA?"

He shook his head. "I'm afraid I don't know anyone there who has strong feelings about anything except vacation policy."

"Then why? What possible motivation?"

"My guess? Let me tell you something." Ostrow took off his glasses, cleaned the lenses on his shirt. "You've got a list of crooks and capitalists, small fry working for big fry. When it comes to CIA and the Nazis, right after the war, that's where some serious skeletons are buried. My theory? Someone highly placed, and I do mean highly placed, saw that some names from a long time ago were about to get out."

"What does that mean?"

He put the glasses back on. "Names of old guys we used, paid off. Guys who'd mostly disappeared into the mists of history, O.K.? Suddenly a list comes out, and guess what? The names of some of the old-timers in the Agency who aided and abetted this shit are gonna come out, too. Maybe some financial shenanigans, some double-dipping into the old well. The old geezers sure as hell are gonna squeal like pigs, rat out their handlers. So who're you gonna call? Who else but some fanatical Israelis. Neat and clean. Talk about ghosts left over from the Second World War, do some hand-waving about inexplicable vengeance killings, save Old Boy asses—everybody's happy."

Yeah, she thought grimly. Everybody's happy.

"Listen to me. There's a convergence of interests here. You're trying to figure out a string of homicides. We're trying to figure out a string of

security breaches. But we can't chase this thing down without Ben Hartman. I'm not going to dump a load of supposition on you. There's a
good chance that he's being hunted by the same people he works for.
Mop-ups never end—that's the problem with them."

Mopping up: Was that what she herself was doing?

Ostrow seemed to respond to the hesitant look on her face. "We just
need to know what's true and what isn't."

"You've got paperwork?" Anna asked.

Ostrow tapped a stapled document with a blunt finger. A capitalized
section heading stood out: CUSTODIAL CONVEYANCE OF AN AMERICAN CIT-
IZEN. "Yes, I've got the paperwork. Now all I need's the body. Jack Hampton said you'd understand about these things."

"What do you have in mind for the delivery?"

"Look, there are delicate issues of extraterritoriality here . . ."

"Meaning you don't want me to bring him here."

"You got that right. We will make house calls, though. You can cuff
him, give us the signal, and we'll show up with bells on. If you want to
keep your hands completely clean, that's fine, too. Give us a time and
location, preferably someplace semisecluded, and . . ."

"And we'll handle the rest." Yossi was somber once more.

"Christ, you guys really are cowboys, aren't you?" Anna said.

"Cowboys who ride Aeron chairs, for the most part," Ostrow replied
wryly. "But, sure, we can still manage an exfiltration when we have to.
Nobody gets hurt. It's a clean snatch-and-grab—surgical."

"Surgery hurts."

"Don't overthink it. It's the right thing to do. And it means we all get
our jobs done."

"I'll take it under advisement," Anna said, grimacing.

"Then take this under advisement, too." Ostrow took out a sheet of
paper with departure times of nonstop flights from Vienna to Dulles
International Airport in Washington, and to Kennedy Airport in New
York. "Time is of the essence."

In a dark second-floor office on Wallnerstrasse, the portly *Berufsdetektiv*
Hans Hoffman slammed down the telephone and cursed aloud. It was
ten in the morning and he had already called the American four times
at his hotel, with no luck. The message he'd left the night before had

gone unanswered, too. The hotel had no other telephone number for Hartman and would not divulge whether or not he'd even spent the night at the hotel.

The private investigator needed to reach Hartman at once.

It was urgent. He had steered the American wrong, given him a dangerous lead, and whatever else people might say about Hans Hoffman, no one denied that he was a scrupulous man. It was vitally important that he reach Hartman before he went to see Jürgen Lenz.

For what the detective had discovered late yesterday afternoon was nothing less than sensational. The routine inquiries he had put out concerning Jürgen Lenz had come back with the most unexpected, the most astonishing answers.

Hoffman knew that Dr. Lenz no longer practiced medicine, but he wanted to know why. To that end he had requested a copy of Lenz's medical license from the *Arztekammer*, the archives where the licenses of all doctors in Austria are kept.

There was no medical license for a Jürgen Lenz.

There had never been one.

Hoffman had wondered: How can this possibly be? Was Lenz lying? Had he never practiced medicine?

Lenz's official biography, freely handed out at the Lenz Foundation offices, had him graduating from medical school at Innsbruck, so Hoffman checked there.

Jürgen Lenz had never gone to medical school at Innsbruck.

Driven now by an insatiable curiosity, Hoffman had gone to the Universität Wien, where the records of medical licensing examinations for all physicians in Austria are kept.

Nothing.

Hans Hoffman had furnished his client with the name and address of a man whose biography was faked. Something was very, very wrong.

Hoffman had pored over his notes, stored in his laptop computer, trying to make sense of it, attempting to assemble the facts in some other way.

Now he stared at the screen again, scrolling down the list of records he had checked, trying to think of some omission that might explain this strange situation.

A loud flat buzz jolted him. Someone was calling up to his office from the street. He got up and went over to the intercom mounted on the wall.

"Yes?"

"I'm looking for Mr. Hoffman."

"Yes?"

"My name is Leitner. I don't have an appointment, but I have some important business to discuss."

"What sort of business?" Hoffman asked. Not a salesman, he hoped.

"Some confidential work. I need his help."

"Come on up. Second floor." Hoffman pressed the button that electronically unlocked the building's front door.

He saved the Lenz file, shut off his laptop, and opened his office door.

A man in a black leather jacket, with steel-gray hair, a goatee, and a stud earring in his left ear, said, "Mr. Hoffman?"

"Yes?" Hoffman sized him up, as he did all potential clients, attempting to assess how much money the fellow might have to spend. The man's face was smooth, unlined, almost tight around his high cheekbones. Despite the steel-gray hair, he was probably no older than forty. Physically an impressive specimen, but the features were unremarkable, undistinguishable, except for the dead gray eyes. A serious man.

"Come on in," Hoffman said cordially. "Tell me, what can I do for you?"

It was only nine in the morning when Anna returned to the hotel.

As she inserted the electronic key-card into the slot above the doorknob, she could hear the sound of water running. She entered swiftly, hanging up her coat in the closet by the door, and made her way into the bedroom. An important decision lay ahead of her: she would have to rely upon her intuitions, she knew.

Presently, there was the sound of the shower being turned off, and Ben appeared in the doorway of the bathroom, evidently unaware that she had returned.

He was still dripping water, a towel draped loosely around his midriff. His body was chiseled, heavily muscled in a way that once suggested manual labor and now, she knew, suggested privilege—a personal trainer, an active sports life. With a clinical eye, she surveyed the evidence of his physical regimen—the washboard stomach, the pectorals like twin shields, the swelling biceps. Water beaded on his tan skin. He'd removed the dressing from his shoulder, where a small, angry red patch was visible.

"You're back," he said, finally taking in her presence. "What's new?"

"Here, let me take a look at the shoulder," she said, and he walked toward her. Was her interest in him purely professional? Something in the pit of her stomach made her wonder.

"It's pretty much healed," she pronounced. She ran a finger around the perimeter of the reddened area. "You don't really need the dressing anymore. A thin layer of Bacitracin, maybe. I've got a first-aid kit in my luggage."

She went to retrieve it. When she returned, he was wearing boxer shorts, and had toweled himself off, but was still shirtless.

"Yesterday you were saying something about the CIA," she said as she fumbled with the tube of ointment.

"Maybe I'm wrong about them, I don't know anymore," he said. "Lenz had his suspicions. But I can't really bring myself to believe it."

Could he be lying? Had he been deceiving her last night? It seemed incredible. It defied every instinct, every intuition she possessed. She could detect no bravado, no tension in his voice—none of the usual signals of deception.

As she rubbed the antiseptic ointment on his shoulder, their faces were close. She smelled the soap, and the green-apple fragrance of the hotel shampoo, and something more, something faintly loamy, which was the man himself. She inhaled quietly, deeply. And then, abruptly beset by a storm of emotions, she moved away.

Was her radar, her assessment of his honesty, being distorted by other feelings? That wasn't something she could afford in her position, especially under the current circumstances.

On the other hand, what if the CIA officers had been misinformed? Who were their sources, anyway? A caseworker was only as good as his assets. She knew as well as anyone how fallible the system could be. And if there were CIA involvement, would it be safe to remand him to that agency? There was too much uncertainty in her world: she had to trust her instincts, or she was lost.

Now she dialed Walter Heisler. "I need to ask you a favor," she said. "I called Hartman's hotel. He seems to have left without checking out. There was some sort of shootout. Evidently he's left his luggage there. I want to go through it, really take my time with it."

"Well, you know, that's actually our property, once an investigation is started."

"Have you started one?"

"No, not yet, but—"

"Then could you please do me a huge favor and have the luggage shipped over to me, at my hotel?"

"Well, I suppose this can be arranged," Heisler said sullenly. "Though it is . . . rather unorthodox."

"Thanks, Walter," she said warmly, and hung up.

Ben wandered over to her, still wearing nothing but boxer shorts. "Now, that's what I call full service," he said, grinning.

She tossed him an undershirt. "It's a little chilly outside," she said, her throat dry.

Ben Hartman walked out of the hotel, glancing around nervously. Showered and shaved, even though he was wearing the same now-rumpled clothes he'd slept in, he felt decently crisp. He took in the broad, heavily trafficked avenue and beyond, the green of the Stadtpark, feeling exposed, vulnerable, then he turned right and headed toward the first district.

He had spent the last half hour making telephone calls, one after another. First he had awakened a contact, a friend of a friend, in the Cayman Islands, who operated a two-man "investigative" service that supposedly did background checks for multinational corporations on potential hires. In reality, the firm was most often engaged by wealthy individuals or multinationals who once in a while had a reason to penetrate the secrecy of the banks down there.

O'Connor Security Investigations was the highly secretive enterprise of an Irish expatriate and former constabulary officer named Fergus O'Connor, who had first come to the Caymans as a security guard for a British bank there and stayed. He'd become a security officer, then chief of security. When he realized that his web of contacts and his expertise were marketable—he knew all the other chiefs of security, knew who could be paid off and who couldn't, knew how the system really operated—he'd gone into business for himself.

"This better be bloody important," Fergus had growled into the phone.

"I don't know about that," Ben replied. "But it will be awfully lucrative."

"Now we're talkin'," Fergus said, mollified.

Ben read a list of routing codes and wire-transfer numbers to him, and said he'd call back at the end of the day.

"It'll take me a hell of a lot longer than that," Fergus objected.

"Even if we double your usual fee? Does that speed things up?"

"Bloody well right it does." There was a pause. "By the way, you do know that they're saying the most appalling things about you, don't you?"

"What do you mean?"

"A whole load of bollocks. You know how the rumor mill goes. They say you've gone off on some murderous rampage."

"You're kidding."

"They say you killed your own brother."

Ben didn't respond, but felt sick. Was there not a sense in which it was true?

"Just crazy stuff like that. Not my specialty, but I know a thing or two about how people spread rumors in the financial world, just to stir things up. A load of bollocks, as I say. Still, it's interesting that someone's decided to put it out."

Jesus. "Thanks for the heads-up, Fergus," Ben said, sounding wobblier than he would have liked.

He took a few deep breaths to steady himself, and placed a second call, to a young woman in the New York office of a different sort of investigative firm. This company was large, international, legitimate, staffed with ex–FBI agents and even a few ex–CIA officers. Knapp Incorporated specialized in helping corporations conduct "due diligence" on potential business partners and solving white-collar crime, embezzlements, inside thefts—a gumshoe agency on a global scale. From time to time it was hired by Hartman Capital Management.

One of Knapp's star investigators was Megan Crosby, a Harvard Law grad who did corporate background checks like no one else. She had an uncanny knack for rooting out and then untangling Byzantine, heavily cloaked corporate structures designed to escape the scrutiny of regulators, wary investors, or competitors, and was as good as anyone at flushing out who really owned whom, who was behind what shell company. How she did it she never divulged to her clients. A magician must not divulge his tricks. Ben had taken Megan out to lunch a number of times and, since he sometimes had occasion to call her from Europe, she had given him her home phone number.

"It's three in the morning, who's calling?" was how she answered the phone.

"Ben Hartman, Megan. Forgive me, it's important."

Megan was instantly alert for her lucrative client. "No problem. What can I do for you?"

"I'm in the middle of a big-deal meeting in Amsterdam," he explained, lowering his voice. "There's a small biotech firm in Philadelphia called Vortex Laboratories I'm intrigued by." Anna, wanting his help, had mentioned Vortex to him. "I want to know who owns them, who they might have quiet partnerships with, that kind of thing."

"I'll do what I can," she said, "but no promises."

"End of the day possible?"

"Jesus." She paused. "End of which day are we talking? Yours or mine? That extra six hours will make a difference."

"Then make it the end of your day. Do what you can."

"Got it," she said.

"One more thing. There's a guy named Oscar Peyaud, based in Paris, that HCM has used for French due-diligence. Knapp has him on retainer. I need direct contact info for him."

By ten o'clock the Graben, one of Vienna's great pedestrian thoroughfares, was bustling with window-shoppers, businesspeople, tourists. He turned onto Kohlmarkt and passed Café Demel, the renowned pastry shop, where he turned to look at the lavish display windows. In its reflection, he noticed someone glancing at him and then quickly looking away.

A tall, thuggish-looking man in an ill-fitting dark blue raincoat. He had a thatch of unruly salt-and-pepper black hair, a ruddy face, and the heaviest eyebrows Ben had ever seen, a veritable wheat field of brow almost an inch thick, mostly black but salted with a little gray. The man's cheeks were covered with gin blossoms, the spiderwebs of broken capillaries that come from heavy drinking.

Ben knew he had seen the man before. He was convinced of it.

Somewhere, some time in the last day or two he had seen this same ruddy-cheeked man with the wheat-field eyebrows. In a crowd somewhere, but where?

Or had he?

Was paranoia overcoming him? Was he seeing faces, imagining that his enemies were everywhere?

Ben turned to look again, but the man had disappeared.

"My dear Ms. Navarro," Alan Bartlett said. "I wonder if we have different conceptions of what the fulfillment of your brief consists of. I must say I'm disappointed. You created high expectations."

Anna had placed a call to Robert Polozzi, of ID Section, only to be switched over, with no warning, to Bartlett.

"Listen," she protested, phone handset vised between her neck and left shoulder, "I think I'm on the verge—"

Bartlett talked over her words. "You are supposed to check in on a regular basis, Agent Navarro. And not disappear like a college student on spring break."

"If you'll listen to what I've turned up—" Anna began, exasperated.

"No, you listen to me, Agent Navarro. Your instructions are to wrap this matter up, and that's what you are going to do. We've learned that Ramago has already been taken out. Rossignol was our last, best chance. I can't speak to what means you used to reach him, but it quite clearly resulted in his death. Apparently I was misled as to your sense of discretion." Bartlett's voice was an icicle.

"But the Sigma list—"

"You spoke to me of surveillance and preemption with respect to this subject. You did not alert me that you meant to draw a large bull's-eye on him. How many times did I emphasize the delicacy of your charge? How many times?"

Anna felt as if she'd been punched in the stomach. "I apologize if anything that I did had the effect of—"

"No, Agent Navarro, I blame myself. It was I who made the assignment. I cannot say I wasn't counseled against it. It was my own mulishness, you see. Trusting you with this assignment was my mistake. I take full responsibility."

"Cut the crap," Anna said, suddenly fed up. "You don't have the data to support your accusations."

"You're already facing administrative charges. I expect you in my office no later than five o'clock tomorrow afternoon, and I don't care if you have to charter a private jet to get here."

It was a few seconds before Anna realized he had hung up. Her heart pounded, her face was flushed. Had he not ended the call when he did, she'd have gone off on him, and no doubt finished her career once and for all.

No, she told herself, you've already done that. It's over. Dupree, when he got wind that she'd run afoul of the Internal Compliance Unit, would revoke her privileges within five minutes.

Well, at least go out with a bang.

She felt a delicious sense of inevitability. It was like being on a speeding train you couldn't get off. Enjoy the rush.

CHAPTER TWENTY-NINE

The office of the legendary and world-famous Jakob Sonnenfeld—the Nazi hunter extraordinaire who had been on the cover of countless news-magazines, the subject of innumerable profiles and documentaries, had even made cameo appearances in movies—was located in a small, gloomy, relatively modern building on Salztorgasse, an inelegant street of discount stores and glum cafés. Sonnenfeld's phone number had simply been listed in the Vienna telephone directory without an address; Ben had called the number at around eight-thirty that morning and was surprised when it was answered. A brusque woman asked what his business was, why he wanted to see the great man.

Ben told her that he was the son of a Holocaust survivor and was in Vienna doing some personal research into the Nazi regime. Stick to what you know was his principle here. He was further surprised when the woman agreed to his request to meet the legend that morning.

The night before, Anna Navarro had suggested a few of what she called "evasive measures," to lose anyone who might be following. On his cir-cuitous way here, after seeing the ruddy-faced man with the wheat-field eyebrows, he had doubled back a few times, abruptly crossed the street, suddenly turned into a bookstore, and browsed and waited. He seemed to have lost the tail, or perhaps, for some reason, the man hadn't wanted to be spotted again.

Now, having reached Sonnenfeld's office building on Salztorgasse, he was buzzed in and took the elevator to the fourth floor, where a solitary guard waved him along. The door was opened by a young woman who pointed him to an uncomfortable chair in a hallway lined with plaques and awards and testaments in Sonnenfeld's honor.

While he waited, he took out his digital phone and left a message for Oscar Peyaud, the Paris-based investigator. Then he called the hotel he had so unceremoniously abandoned the night before.

"Yes, Mr. Simon," the hotel operator answered with what struck him as undue familiarity. "Yes, sir, there is a message for you—it is, if you will wait, yes, from a Mr. Hans Hoffman. He says it is urgent."

"Thank you," Ben said.

"Please, Mr. Simon, can you hold on, please. The manager has just signaled me that he would like to speak with you."

The hotel manager got on the line. Ben ignored his first instinct, which was to disconnect immediately; more important by far was to determine how much the hotel management knew, how complicit they might be.

"Mr. Simon," the manager said in a loud and authoritative basso profundo, "one of our chambermaids tells me that you threatened her, and moreover, there was an incident here last night involving gunfire, and the police wish you to return here immediately for questioning."

Ben pressed the *End* button.

It was not surprising that the manager would want to talk to him. Damage had been done to the hotel; the manager was duty-bound to call the police. But there was something about the man's voice, the suddenly bullying self-assurance of a man who is backed by the full weight of the authorities, that alarmed Ben.

And what did Hoffman, the private investigator, want so urgently?

The door to Sonnenfeld's office opened and a small, stoop-shouldered old man emerged and gestured feebly for Ben to enter. He gave Ben a tremorous handshake and sat behind a cluttered desk. Jakob Sonnenfeld had a bristly gray mustache, a jowly face, large ears, and red-rimmed, hooded, watery eyes. He wore an unfashionably wide, clumsily knotted tie, a moth-eaten brown sweater-vest under a checked jacket.

"Many people want to look at my archives," Sonnenfeld said abruptly. "Some for good reasons, some for not so good. Why you?"

Ben cleared his throat, but Sonnenfeld rumbled on. "You say your father is a Holocaust survivor. So? There are thousands of them alive. Why are you so interested in my work?"

Do I dare level with the man? he wondered. "You've been hunting Nazis for decades now," he began suddenly. "You must hate them with all your heart, as I do."

Sonnenfeld waved dismissively. "No. I'm not a hater. I couldn't work at this job for over fifty years fueled by hate. It would eat away at my insides."

Ben was at once skeptical and annoyed at Sonnenfeld's piety.

"Well, I happen to believe that war criminals should not go free."

"Ah, but they are not war criminals really, are they? A war criminal commits his crimes to further his war aims, yes? He murders and tortures in order to help win the war. But tell me: Did the Nazis need to massacre and gas to death millions of innocents in order to win? Of course not. They did it purely for ideological reasons. To cleanse the planet, they believed. It was wholly unnecessary. It was something they did on the side. It diverted precious wartime resources. I'd say their campaign of genocide hindered their war effort. No, these were most certainly not war criminals."

"What do you call them, then?" Ben asked, understanding at last.

Sonnenfeld smiled. Several gold teeth glinted. "Monsters."

Ben took in a long breath. He'd have to trust the old Nazi hunter; that was the only way, he realized, to secure his cooperation. Sonnenfeld was too smart. "Then let me be very direct with you, Mr. Sonnenfeld. My brother—my twin brother, my closest friend in all the world—was murdered by people I believe are in some way connected with some of these monsters."

Sonnenfeld leaned forward. "Now you have me very confused," he said very intently. "Surely you and your brother are much, much too young to have been through the war."

"This happened not much over a week ago," Ben said.

Sonnenfeld's brow furrowed, eyes narrowing in disbelief. "What can you be saying? You are making no sense."

Quickly Ben explained about Peter's discovery. "This document drew my brother's attention because one of the board members was our own father." He paused. "Max Hartman."

Stunned silence. Then: "I know the name. He has given much money to good causes."

"In the year 1945, one of his causes was something called Sigma," Ben continued stonily. "The other incorporators included many Western industrialists, and a small handful of Nazi officials. Those included the treasurer, who is identified by the title *Obersturmführer*, and by the name Max Hartman."

Sonnenfeld's rheumy eyes did not blink. "Extraordinary. You did say 'Sigma,' yes? Dear God in heaven."

"I'm afraid it's an old story," said the visitor in the black leather jacket.

"The wife," suggested the private detective, Hoffman, with a wink.

The man smiled sheepishly.

"She is young and very pretty, yes?"

A sigh. "Yes."

"They are the worst of all, the pretty young ones," Hoffman said, man to man. "I'd advise you to simply forget her. You'll never be able to trust her anyway."

The visitor's eye seemed to be caught by Hoffman's fancy new laptop computer. "Nice," the man said.

"I don't know how I ever used anything else," Hoffman said. "I am not so good with technical things, but this is easy. Who needs filing cabinets anymore? Everything is here."

"Mind if I take a look at it?"

Hoffman hesitated. A man come in off the street—he could easily be a thief after all. He glanced at him again, took in the man's broad shoulders, narrow waist, not a gram of body fat. Quietly he nudged open the long metal desk drawer next to his lap an inch or two and checked for the Glock.

"Maybe another time," Hoffman said. "All of my confidential files are there. So, please give me the details about your pretty young wife and the bastard she's fucking."

"Why don't you turn it on?" the visitor said. Hoffman looked up sharply. This was not a request but a demand.

"Why are you here?" Hoffman snarled, and then realized he was staring into the barrel of a Makarov attached to a silencer.

"Put the computer on," the man said softly. "Open your files."

"I will tell you one thing. This document was never meant to see the light of day," Sonnenfeld said. "It was a legalism intended for internal Swiss bank use only. For the gnomes of Zurich alone."

"I don't understand."

"Sigma has long been the stuff of legend. Not a scintilla of evidence has ever emerged to give body to the shadow of supposition. I would know. Believe me."

"Until now, correct?"

"So it would seem," he said softly. "Clearly, it is a fictional enterprise.

A front, a ruse—a means for industrialists on both sides to secure a separate peace, whatever the terms of armistice might be. The paper your brother uncovered may be the only material reality that it has."

"You say it was the stuff of legend—what was the nature of that legend?"

"Powerful businessmen and powerful politicians, meeting secretly to transfer immense, stolen state assets out of the Fatherland. Not everyone who opposed Hitler was a hero, you might as well know that. Many were cold-eyed pragmatists. They knew the war effort was doomed, and they knew who was to blame. What concerned them more was the prospect of repatriation, nationalization. They had their own empires to look after. Empires of industry. There is abundant evidence of such plans. But we've always believed that the plan remained just a plan. And almost everyone involved has since gone to their graves."

"You said 'almost everyone,' " Ben repeated sharply. "Let me ask about the few board members who fall under your professional purview. The Nazis. Gerhard Lenz. Josef Strasser." He paused before pronouncing the final name. "Max Hartman."

Sonnenfeld fell silent. He cradled his head in his large craggy hands. "Who are these people?" he said to himself, the question purely rhetorical. "That is your question. And here, always, is mine: who is asking? Why do you want to know?"

"Put your gun down," Hoffman said. "Don't be foolish."

"Close the desk drawer," the intruder said. "I am watching you very closely. One wrong move and I will not hesitate to kill you."

"Then you'll never access my files," Hoffman said triumphantly. "The computer is equipped with a biometric authentication device—a fingerprint scanner. Without my fingerprint, no one can log on. So you see, you would be very foolish to kill me."

"Oh, I don't need to go quite that far yet," said the visitor serenely.

"But do you know the truth about my father?" Ben asked. "It strikes me that you might have assembled a file on such a high-profile survivor and—forgive me—potential benefactor to your efforts. You, more than anyone, would have been in a position to see through his lies. You have all the lists of concentration-camp victims, a more exhaustive storehouse of records than anyone else. That's why I have to ask: Did you know the truth about my father?"

"Do you?" Sonnenfeld returned sharply.

"I've seen the truth in black and white."

"You have seen in black and white, yes, but you have not seen the truth. An amateur's error. Forgive me, Mr. Hartman, but these are never black-and-white matters. You're dealing with a situation whose ambiguities are very familiar to me. Your father's case, I can tell you only a little about it, but it is a sadly familiar story. You must be prepared to enter a realm of moral chiaroscuro, however. Of shadow, of ethical vagueness. Begin with the simple fact that if a Jew had money, the Nazis were willing to deal with him. This was one of the ugly secrets of the war that people seldom talk about. Often enough, the rich ones bought safe passage. The Nazis would take gold, jewels, securities, whatever. It was outright extortion, plain and simple. They even had a price schedule—three hundred thousand Swiss francs for a life! One of the Rothschilds traded his steel mills for his freedom—gave them to the Hermann Goering Works. But you won't read about any of this. No one ever talks about it. There was a very rich Hungarian-Jewish family, Weiss—they had businesses in twenty-three countries around the world. They gave their entire fortune to the SS, and in return they were escorted safely to Switzerland."

Ben was flustered. "But an *Obersturmführer* . . ."

"A Jewish *Obersturmführer*? Can that possibly be? Bear with me for a moment." Sonnenfeld paused before resuming. "I can tell you about an SS colonel, Kurt Becher, who was in charge of making deals like this for Eichmann and Himmler. Becher made a deal with a Hungarian, Dr. Rudolf Kastner—seventeen hundred Jews at a thousand dollars each. A whole train full. Jews in Budapest fought to get on that train. You know your family had money before the war, didn't you? The way it worked was very simple, if you were Max Hartman. One day *Obergruppenführer* Becher comes to see you. You make a deal. What good was your fortune if you were all going to die anyway? So you ransom your family out. Your sisters and you. This was hardly a moral conundrum. You did whatever you could to stay alive."

Ben had never thought of his father as a young man, frightened and desperate. His mind reeled. His aunt Sarah had died before he was born, but he remembered his aunt Leah, who passed away when he was in high school: a small, quiet, gentle soul, who had lived quietly as a librarian in Philadelphia. The affection she had for her brother was real, but so, too, was her recognition of his strength of character; she deferred to him in all things. If there were secrets to be kept, she would have kept them.

But his father—what else was he keeping inside?

"If what you're saying is true, why did he never tell us?" Ben asked.

"You think he wanted you to hear this?" There was a hint of scorn in Sonnenfeld's voice. "You think you would really have understood? Millions incinerated, while Max Hartman comes to America simply because he was fortunate enough to have money? People in his situation never told anyone, my friend. They often did their best to try to forget it themselves. I know these things because it is my business to know, but they are best left unexposed."

Ben didn't know how to reply, said nothing.

"Even Churchill and Roosevelt—Himmler made them an offer, you know. In May of '44. He was prepared to sell the Allies every single Jew the Nazis had, if the Allies would give them one truck for every hundred Jews. The Nazis would dismantle the gas chambers, stop murdering the Jews at once—all for some trucks they could use against the Russians. The Jews were for sale—but there were no buyers! Roosevelt and Churchill said no—they wouldn't sell their souls to the devil. Easy for them to say, no? They could have saved a million European Jews, but no. There were Jewish leaders who desperately wanted to make this deal. You see, you want to talk about morality, this wasn't so simple, was it?" Sonnenfeld's tone was bitter. "Now it's so easy to talk about clean hands. But the result is that you're here today. You exist because your father made an unsavory deal to save his own life."

Ben's mind flashed back to the image of his father, old and frail in Bedford, and the image of him, crisp and chiseled in the old photograph. What he had to go through to get here, Ben couldn't begin to imagine. Yet would he really feel compelled to hide this? How much else had he been hiding? "But still, this all leaves unanswered the matter of his name on that document," Ben prompted, "identifying him as SS. . . ."

"In name only, I'm sure."

"Meaning what?"

"How much do you know about your father?"

Good question, Ben thought. He said, "Less and less, it seems." Max

Hartman, powerful and intimidating, conducting a board meeting with gladiatorial self-confidence. Hoisting Ben, age six, way up in the air. Reading *The Financial Times* at breakfast, distant and elusive.

How I tried to earn his love, his respect! And what a warm glow his approval gave me when he so rarely granted it.

What an enigma the man has always been.

"I can tell you this much," Sonnenfeld said impassively. "When your father was still a young man, he was already a legend in German financial circles. A genius, it was said. But he was a Jew. Early in the war, when the Jews were being sent away, he was given the opportunity to work for the *Reichsbank* instead, designing intricate financial schemes that would allow the Nazis to circumvent the Allied blockades. He was given this SS title as a sort of cover."

"So in a sense he helped finance the Nazi regime," Ben said in a monotone. This was somehow no surprise, but still he felt his stomach plummet at hearing it confirmed.

"Unfortunately, yes. I'm sure he had his reasons—he was pressured, he had no choice. He would have been enlisted in this Sigma project as a matter of course." He paused again, watching Ben steadily. "I think you are not very good at seeing shades of gray."

"Odd talk for a Nazi hunter."

"Again with that journalist's tag," Sonnenfeld said. "I fight for justice, and in the fight for justice you must be able to distinguish between the venial and the venal, between ordinary and outsized wrongdoing. Make no mistake: hardship brings out the best in no one."

The room seemed to revolve slowly around him. Ben clasped his arms around himself, and breathed deeply, trying for a moment of calm, a moment of clarity.

He had a sudden mental picture of his father in his study, listening to Mozart's *Don Giovanni* as he sat in his favorite overstuffed chair in darkness. Often in the evenings after dinner Max would sit alone with the lights off, *Don Giovanni* on the stereo. How lonely the man must have been, how frightened that his ugly past would someday emerge. Ben was surprised at the tenderness he suddenly felt. *The old man loved me as much as he was able to love anyone. How can I despise him?* It occurred to Ben that the real reason Lenz grew to hate his own father was not so much the repugnance of Nazism as the fact that he had abandoned them.

"Tell me about Strasser," Ben said, realizing that only a change of subject could diminish the vertigo he was undergoing.

Sonnenfeld closed his eyes. "Strasser was a scientific adviser to Hitler. *Gevalt*, he was not a human being. Strasser was a brilliant scientist. He helped run I. G. Farben, you know this famous I. G. Farben, the big industrial firm that was controlled by the Nazis? There, he helped to invent a new gas in pellet form called Zyklon-B. You would shake the pellets and they would turn into gas. Like magic! They first tried it in the showers at Auschwitz. A fantastic invention. The poison gas would rise in the gas chambers, and as the level rose the taller victims would step on the others to try to breathe. But everyone would die in four minutes."

Sonnenfeld paused, gazed into some middle distance. In the long silence Ben could hear the ticking of a mechanical clock.

"Very efficient," Sonnenfeld at last resumed. "For this we must thank Dr. Strasser. And do you know that Allen Dulles, your CIA director in the fifties, was I. G. Farben's American lawyer and loyal defender? Yes, it is true."

Somewhere Ben had heard this before, but it still amazed him. Slowly, he said, "So both Strasser and Lenz were partners, in a sense."

"Yes. Two of the most brilliant, most terrible Nazi scientists. Lenz with his experiments on children, on twins. A brilliant scientist, far ahead of his time. Lenz took a particular interest in the metabolism of children. Some he would starve to death in order to observe how their growth slowed and stopped. Some he would actually freeze, to see how that affected their growth. He saw to it that all the children who suffered from progeria, a horrible form of premature aging, were sent to him for study." He went on bitterly: "A lovely man, Dr. Lenz. Very close to the high command, of course. As a scientist, he was better trusted than most politicians. He was thought to have 'purity of purpose.' And of course our Dr. Strasser. Lenz went to Buenos Aires too, as so many of them did after the war. Have you been there? It is a lovely city. Truly. The Paris of South America. No wonder all the Nazis wanted to live there. And then Lenz died there."

"And Strasser?"

"Perhaps Lenz's widow knows the whereabouts of Strasser, but don't even think of asking her. She'll never reveal it."

"Lenz's widow?" Ben asked, sitting upright. "Yes, Jürgen Lenz mentioned his mother had retired there."

"You spoke with Jürgen Lenz?"

"Yes. You know him, I gather?"

"Ah, this is a complicated story, Jürgen Lenz. I must admit to you, at first I found it extremely difficult to accept money from this man. Of course, without contributions we would have to close down. In this country, where they have always protected the Nazis, even protect them to this day, I get no donations. Not a cent! Here they haven't prosecuted a single Nazi case in over twenty years! Here I was for years Public Enemy Number One. They used to spit at me on the street. And Lenz, well, from Lenz this so clearly seemed to be guilt money. But then I met the man, and I quickly changed my mind. He's sincerely committed to doing good. For example, he's the sole underwriter of the progeria foundation in Vienna. No doubt he wants to undo his father's work. We mustn't hold against him his father's crimes."

Sonnenfeld's words resounded. His father's crimes. How bizarre that Lenz and I should be in a similar situation.

"The prophet Jeremiah, you know, he tells us, 'They shall say no more, the fathers have eaten a sour grape, and the children's teeth are set on edge.' And Ezekiel says, 'The son shall not bear the iniquity of the father.' It is very clear."

Ben was silent. "You say Strasser may be alive."

"Or he may be dead," Sonnenfeld replied quickly. "Who knows about these old men? I've never been able to make certain."

"You must have a file on him."

"Don't speak to me of such things. Are you in the grip of the fantasy that you will find this creature and he will tell you what you want, like some genie?" Sonnenfeld sounded evasive. "For years I have been dogged with young fanatics seeking vengeance, to slake some sense of disquiet with the blood of a certified villain. It is a puerile pursuit, which ends badly for everyone. You had persuaded me you were not one of them. But Argentina is another country, and surely the wretch is dead."

The young woman who had answered the door when Ben arrived now reappeared, and a murmured conversation ensued. "An important telephone call which I must take," Sonnenfeld said apologetically, and he withdrew to a back room.

Ben looked around him, at the huge slate-colored filing cabinets. Son-nenfeld had been distinctly evasive when the subject came to Strasser's current whereabouts. Was he holding out on him? And if so, why?

From Sonnenfeld's manner, he inferred that the telephone call was expected to be a long one. Perhaps long enough to allow a quick search of the files. Impulsively, Ben moved to an immense, five-drawer filing cabinet marked R–S. The drawers were locked but the key was on top of the cabinet: not exactly high security, Ben noted. He opened the bottom drawer, found it densely packed with yellowed file folders and crumbling papers. Stefans. Sterngeld. Streitfeld.

STRASSER. The name penned in brown faded ink. He plucked it out, and then had a sudden thought. He went to the K–M file. There was a thick file for Gerhard Lenz, but that wasn't the one he was interested in. It was the thin file next to it—the file for his widow—that he wanted.

This one was tightly wedged in. He heard footsteps: Sonnenfeld was returning, more quickly than Ben had expected! He tugged on the folder, worried it from side to side until it was slowly released from the others. Taking the trench coat he'd draped on an adjoining chair, he quickly shoved the yellowed folders under it and returned to his seat just as Sonnenfeld entered.

"It's a dangerous thing to disturb the peace of old men," Sonnenfeld announced as he rejoined him. "Maybe you think they're toothless, wiz-ened creatures. Indeed they are. But they have a powerful support net-work, even now. Especially in South America, where they have extensive loyalists. Thugs, like the *Kamaradenwerk*. They are protected the way wild animals protect their enfeebled elders. They kill whenever they must—they never hesitate."

"In Buenos Aires?"

"There more than anywhere else. Nowhere are they so powerful." He looked weary. "This is why you must never go there and ask about the old Germans."

Sonnenfeld got up unsteadily, and Ben rose, too. "Even today, you see, I must have a security guard at all times. It is not much, but it is what we can afford to pay for."

"Yet you insist on living in a city where they don't like questions about the past," Ben said.

Sonnenfeld put his hand on Ben's shoulder. "Ah, well, you see, if you are studying malaria, Mr. Hartman, you must live in the swamp, no?"

Julian Bennett, assistant deputy of operations at the National Security
Agency, sat facing Joel Skolnik, the deputy director of the Department
of Justice in the small executive dining room in the NSA's Fort Mead
headquarters. Though Skolnik, lanky and balding, held a higher bureaucratic rank, Bennett's manner was peremptory. The National Security
Agency was structured in such as way as to insulate people like Bennett
from bureaucratic oversight outside of the agency. The effect was to en-
courage a certain arrogance, and Bennett was not one to disguise it.

An overdone lamb chop and a lump of steamed spinach, mostly unea-
ten, sat on the plate in front of Skolnik. His appetite had long since
disappeared. Past a thin veneer of amiability, Bennett's manner was subtly
hectoring, and his message frankly alarming.

"This doesn't look good for you," Bennett was telling him, not for the
first time. His small, wide-spaced eyes and light-colored eyebrows gave
him a vaguely porcine look.

"I realize this."

"You're supposed to be running a tight ship here," Bennett said. His
own plate was clean; he had devoured his porterhouse in several swift
bites: plainly a man who ate simply for fuel. "And the stuff we've been
coming across is pretty damn disquieting."

"You've been clear about that," Skolnik said, hating the way it came
out—deferential, even cowed. He knew it was always a mistake to show
fear to a man like Bennett. It was like blood in the water to a shark.

"The recklessness about matters of national security your people have
shown—it compromises us all. I look at the way your staffers have conducted themselves, and I don't know whether to laugh or cry. What's
the use of bolting the front door when the back door is swinging in the
wind?"

"Let's not exaggerate the possible exposure at issue," Skolnik said. Even
to himself, the starchy words sounded defensive.

"I want you to assure me that the rot is contained with the Navarro
woman." Bennett leaned over and patted Skolnik's forearm in a gesture
that was half intimate and half menacing. "And that you'll use all means
at your disposal to bring the woman in."

"That much goes without saying," the DOJ man said, swallowing hard.

"Now stand up," the goateed man said, waving the Makarov in his left hand.

"It'll do you no good. I won't put my finger on the sensor," said the detective, Hans Hoffman. "Now get out of here, before something happens that you'll regret."

"I never have regrets," the man said blandly. "Stand up."

Hoffman stood up reluctantly. "I tell you—"

The intruder rose too and approached him.

"I tell you again," Hoffman said, "it will do you no good to kill me."

"I don't need to kill you," the man said blandly. In one lightning-swift movement he lunged.

Hoffman saw the glint of something metallic even before he felt the unbelievable pain explode in his hand. He looked down. There was a stump where his index finger had been. The cut had been perfect. At the base of where his finger had been, right next to the fatty part of the thumb, he could see a white circle of bone within a larger circle of flesh. In the millisecond before he screamed, he saw the razor-sharp hunting knife in the man's hand, and then he noticed with dazed fascination the dismembered finger lying on the carpet like a useless discarded chicken part flung there by some careless butcher.

He bellowed, a high-pitched scream of disbelief and terror and excruciating, incomprehensible pain. "Oh, my God! Oh, my God! Oh, my God!"

Trevor picked up the dismembered finger and held it aloft. At the severed end, blood still wept.

CHAPTER THIRTY

Anna put in a call to David Denneen.

"Is that you, Anna?" he said tersely, his customary warmth crimped by uncustomary wariness. "The shit's flying."

"Talk to me, David. Tell me what the hell's going on."

"Crazy stuff. They're saying you're . . ." His voice trailed off.

"What?"

"Crazy stuff. You on a sterile line?"

"Of course."

There was a pause. "Listen, Anna. The department's been ordered to place a P-47 on you, Anna—full-out mail, wire, phone intercepts."

"Jesus Christ!" Anna said. "I don't believe it."

"It gets worse. Since this morning, you've been a 12-44: apprehend on sight. Bring in by any means necessary. Jesus, I don't know what you've been up to, but you're being called a national security risk. They're saying you've been accepting money from hostiles for years. I shouldn't even be talking to you."

"What?"

"Word is the FBI's discovered all sorts of cash and jewelry in your apartment. Expensive clothes. Offshore bank accounts."

"Lies!" Anna exploded. "All goddamn lies."

There was a long pause. "I knew they had to be, Anna. But I'm glad to hear you say it, all the same. Someone's messing with you in a very serious way. Why?"

"Why?" Anna closed her eyes briefly. "So I don't get in a position to discover why. That's my guess." She rang off hurriedly.

What the hell was going on? Had "Yossi" or Phil Ostrow put poison in Bartlett's ear? She'd never called them; maybe Bartlett was angry that they'd found out about her investigation in the first place, even though she wasn't the responsible party. Or maybe Bartlett was angry that she hadn't gone along with their request to bring Hartman in.

She suddenly realized that neither agency official had mentioned Hans Vogler, the ex-Stasi assassin. Did that mean "Yossi" knew nothing about it? If so, did that mean that the Mossad freelancers had nothing to do with hiring Vogler? She retrieved Phil Ostrow's card and dialed the number. It went to automated voice mail; and she decided against leaving a message.

Maybe Jack Hampton would know something about it. She phoned him at home, in Chevy Chase. "Jack," she began. "It's—"

"Jesus Christ, tell me you're not calling me," Hampton said in a rush. "Tell me you're not jeopardizing the security clearance of your friends by a misjudged phone call."

"Is there an intercept on your end?"

"My end?" Hampton paused. "No. Never. I make sure of it myself."

"Then you're not in danger. I'm on a secure line on this end. I don't see any way by which a connection could be traced."

"Let's say you're right, Anna," he said dubiously. "You're still presenting me with a moral conundrum. Word has it you're some primo villainness—the way I've heard you described, it's like you're a combination of Ma Barker and Mata Hari. With the wardrobe of Imelda Marcos."

"It's bullshit. You know that."

"Maybe I do, Anna, and maybe I don't. The kind of sums I've heard bandied about would be awfully tempting. Buy yourself a nice spit of land in Virgin Gorda. All that pink sand, blue sky. Go snorkeling every day . . ."

"Goddamn it, Jack!"

"A word of advice. Don't take any woolen kopeks and don't whack any more Swiss bankers."

"Is that what they're saying about me."

"One of the things. One of the many things. Let's just say it's the biggest pile-on I've heard of since Wen Ho Lee. It's a bit overdone, to tell you the truth. I keep asking myself, Who's got that kind of money to throw around? Russia's so strapped for cash that most of its nuclear scientists have left to drive taxicabs in New York. And what kind of hard currency does China have—the place is Zambia with nukes. I mean, let's get real." Hampton's voice seemed to soften. "So what are you calling me for? Want our current missile codes to sell to the Red Chinese? Just let me jot down your fax number."

"Give me a break."

"That's my hot tamale," Hampton teased, relaxing further.

"Screw you. Listen, before all this shit fell from the sky, I had a meeting with your friend Phil Ostrow..."

"Ostrow?" Hampton said, guardedly. "Where?"

"In Vienna."

There was a flare of anger: "What are you trying to pull, Navarro?"

"Wait a minute. I don't know what you're talking about."

Something in her voice gave him pause. "Are you shitting me, or was somebody shitting you?"

"Ostrow's not attached to Vienna station?" she asked hesitantly.

"He's on O-15."

"Help me out here."

"That means he's kept officially on the lists, but he's really on leave. Sow confusion among the bad guys that way. Diabolical, what?"

"On leave how?"

"He's been stateside for a few months now. Depression, if you want to know. He had episodes in the past, but it got real bad. He's actually been hospitalized at Walter Reed."

"And that's where he is now." Anna's scalp became tight; she tried to quell a rising sense of anxiety.

"That's where he is now. Sad but true. One of those wards where all the nurses have security clearances."

"If I said Ostrow was a short guy, grayish-brownish hair, pale complexion, wire-rim glasses...?"

"I'd tell you to get your prescription checked. Ostrow looks like an aging surfer bum—tall, slim, blond hair, the works."

Several seconds of silence ensued.

"Anna, what the hell is going on with you?"

CHAPTER THIRTY-ONE

Stunned, she sat back on the bed.

"What's wrong?" Ben asked.

"I really can't get into it."

"If it concerns the business we're both working on—"

"It doesn't. Not this. Those *bastards!*"

"What happened?"

"*Please,*" she exclaimed. "Let me *think!*"

"Fine." Looking irritated, Ben took his digital phone from the pocket of his jacket.

She thought: No wonder "Phil Ostrow" had called her late at night—when it was too late to call the American embassy and check out his bona fides. But then who was it she'd met with at CIA station?

Was it in fact CIA station?

Who were "Ostrow" and "Yossi"?

She heard Ben speaking quickly in French. Then he fell silent, listening for a while. "Oscar, you're a genius," he finally said.

A few minutes later, he was talking on his phone again. "Megan Crosby, please."

If "Phil Ostrow" was some kind of impostor, he had to be an enormously skilled actor. And what was he doing? "Yossi" could indeed have been Israeli, or of some other Middle Eastern nationality; it was hard to tell.

"Megan, it's Ben," he said.

Who *were* they? she wondered.

She picked up the phone and called Jack Hampton again. "Jack, I need the number of CIA station."

"What am I, directory assistance?"

"It's in the building across the street from the consular office, right?"

"CIA station is in the main embassy building, Anna."

"No, the annex. A commercial building across the street. Under the cover of the Office of the United States Trade Representative."

"I don't know what you're talking about. CIA doesn't have any cover sites outside of the one right in the embassy. That *I* know of anyway."

She hung up, panic suffusing her body. If that hadn't been a CIA site where she'd met Ostrow, what was it? The setting, the surroundings— every detail had been right. *Too* right, *too* convincing?

"You've got to be kidding," she heard Ben say. "*Jesus*, you're fast."

So who was trying to manipulate her? And to what end? Obviously someone, or some group, who knew she was in Vienna, knew what she was investigating, and knew which hotel she was staying in.

If Ostrow was some kind of impostor, then his story about the Mossad had to be false. And she had been the unwitting victim of an elaborate scam. They'd planned to kidnap Hartman—and have her deliver the "package" right into their clutches.

She felt dazed and lost.

In her mind she ran through everything, from "Ostrow's" phone call, to the place she'd met him and "Yossi." Was it really possible the whole thing had been an elaborate ruse?

She heard Hartman say: "All right, let me write this down. Great work, kid. Terrific."

So the Mossad story, with all its rumors and undocumented whispers, was nothing but a tale spun by liars out of plausible fragments? My God, then how much of what she knew was wrong?

And who was trying to mislead her—and to what end?

What was the truth? Good God, *where* was the truth?

"Ben," she said.

He held up an index finger to signal her to wait, said something quickly into his phone, then flipped it closed.

But then she quickly changed her mind, decided not to reveal to Ben anything of what she'd just found out. Not yet. Instead, she asked, "Did you learn anything from Sonnenfeld?"

Hartman told her about what Sonnenfeld had said, Anna interrupting every once in a while to clarify a point or ask for a fuller explanation.

"So are you saying your father wasn't a Nazi, after all."

"Not according to Sonnenfeld, at least."

"Did he have some inkling as to the meaning of Sigma?"

"Beyond what I said, he was vague about it. And downright evasive when it came to Strasser."

"And as to why your brother was killed?"

"Obviously he was killed because of the *threat of exposure.* Someone, maybe some group, feared the revelation of those names."

"Or of the fact this corporation *existed.* Clearly someone with a major financial stake. Which tells us that these old guys were—" Suddenly she stopped. "Of course! The laundered money! These old guys were being paid off. Maybe by someone controlling the corporation they'd all helped form."

"Either paid off, as in *bribed,*" Ben added, "or else they were receiving an agreed-upon distribution, a share of the profits."

Anna stood. "Eliminate the payees, then there's no more wire transfers. No more big paydays for a bunch of doddering old men. Which tells us that whoever's ordering the murders stands to gain *financially* from them. *Has* to be. Someone like Strasser, or even your father." She looked at him. She couldn't automatically rule it out. Even if he didn't want to hear it. His father might have been a murderer himself—might have blood on his hands, might have been *behind* the murders at least.

But how to explain the intricate deception of Ostrow, the false CIA man? Might he have been somehow connected to the heirs to some vast hidden fortune?

"Theoretically, I suppose, my father could be one of the bad guys." Ben said. "But I really don't believe it."

"Why not?" She didn't know how far to push him on this.

"Because my father already has more money than he knows what to do with. Because he may be a ruthless businessman, and he may be a liar, but after talking with Sonnenfeld, I'm coming to think that he wasn't fundamentally an evil man."

She doubted Hartman was holding anything back, but surely he was hampered by filial loyalty. Ben seemed to be a loyal person—an admirable quality, but sometimes loyalty could blind you to the truth.

"What I don't get is this: these guys are old and failing," Hartman continued. "So why bother hiring someone to eliminate them? It's hardly worth the risk."

"Unless you're afraid one of them will talk, reveal the financial arrangement, whatever it is."

"But if they haven't talked for half a century, what's going to make them start now?"

"Maybe some sort of pressure by legal authorities, triggered by the surfacing of this list. Faced with the threat of legal action, any one of them might easily have talked. Or maybe the Corporation is moving to a new phase, a transition, and sees itself as peculiarly vulnerable while it's happening."

"I'm hearing a lot of conjecture," he said. "We need facts."

She paused. "Who were you talking to on the phone just now?"

"A corporate researcher I've used before. She found some intriguing background on Vortex Laboratories."

Anna was suddenly alert. "Yes?"

"It's wholly owned by the European chemicals and technology giant Armakon AG. An Austrian company."

"Austrian . . ." she murmured. "That *is* interesting."

"Those mammoth technology firms are always buying up tiny tech startups, hoping to snag the rights to stuff their own in-house research scientists haven't invented." He paused. "And one more thing. My friend in the Caymans was able to trace a few of the wire transfers."

Jesus. And her guy at the DOJ had turned up nothing. She tried to conceal her excitement. "Tell me."

"The money was sent from a shell company registered in the Channel Islands, a few seconds after it came in from Liechtenstein, from an *Anstalt*, a bearer-share company. Sort of a blind entity."

"If it came from a company, does that mean the names of the true owners are on file somewhere?"

"That's the tricky part. *Anstalts* are usually managed by an agent, often an attorney. They're essentially dummy corporations that exist only on paper. An agent in Liechtenstein might manage thousands of them."

"Was your friend able to get the name of the *Anstalt*'s agent?"

"I believe so, yes. Trouble is, barring torture, no agent will release information on any of the *Anstalts* he manages. They can't afford to sabotage their reputation for discretion. But my friend's working on it."

She grinned. The guy was growing on her.

The phone rang.

She picked it up. "Navarro."

"Anna, this is Walter Heisler. I have results for you."

"Results?"

"On the gun that was dropped by the shooter in Hietzing. The prints you asked me to run. It matched a print, a digitized print, on file at Interpol. A Hans Vogler, ex-Stasi. Maybe he doesn't expect to miss, or doesn't expect us to be there, because he wears no gloves."

Heisler's information was nothing new, but the fingerprints would be a valuable piece of evidence.

"Fantastic. Walter, listen, I need to ask you another favor."

"You don't sound surprised," Heisler said, miffed. "I said he was ex-*Stasi*, you understand? Former East German secret intelligence service."

"Yes, Walter, I do understand, and I thank you. Very impressive." She was being too brusque again, too businesslike, and she tried to soften her approach. "Thank you so much, Walter. And just one more thing . . ."

Wearily: "Yes?"

"One second." She covered the phone's mouthpiece and said to Ben, "You still haven't reached Hoffman?"

"Not a word. No answer there—it's bizarre."

She removed her hand from the mouthpiece. "Walter, can you find out for me whatever you can about a private investigator in Vienna named Hans Hoffman?"

There was silence.

"Hello?"

"Yes, Anna, I am here. Why you ask about this Hans Hoffman?"

"I need some outside help here," she replied, thinking quickly, "and his name was given to me—"

"Well, I think you may have to find someone else."

"Why is that?"

"About an hour ago a call came in to the *Sicherheitsbüro* from an employee of a *Berufsdetektiv* named Hans Hoffman. The woman, an investigator in Hoffman's office, came to work and discovered her boss dead. Shot at point-blank range in the forehead. And, curious—his right forefinger was cut off. Can this be the Hoffman you're talking about?"

Ben had stared in disbelief when Anna told him what she'd learned. "Christ, it's as if they're always just one behind us, whatever we do," he murmured.

"Maybe 'ahead of us' is the more accurate term."

Ben massaged his temples with the fingertips of both hands, and at last he spoke in a quiet voice. "The enemy of my enemy is my friend."

"How do you mean?"

"Sigma has obviously been killing its own. Those victims you're trying to find—they all have something in common with me, a shared enemy. We've observed the pattern—frightened old men going into hiding in the twilight of their lives, living under aliases. It's a virtual certainty that they have some idea what the hell's going on. That means our only hope is to establish contact with someone on the list who's still alive, who can talk. Someone with whom I can establish common ground, a conduit of sympathy, enlist his help for reasons of his own self-protection."

Anna stood, paced the room. "That's if there is anyone alive, Ben."

He stared at her a long while, saying nothing, the resolve in his eyes wavering. She could tell that he longed to trust her every bit as fervently as she hoped she could trust him. Softly, hesitantly, he replied: "I have a feeling—it's just a feeling, an educated guess—that there may be at least one still alive."

"Who's that?"

"A Frenchman named Georges Chardin."

She nodded slowly. "Georges Chardin . . . I've seen the name on the Sigma list—but he's actually been dead for four years."

"But the fact that his name was in the Sigma files means Allen Dulles had him vetted for some reason."

"Back in the fifties, yeah. But remember, most of these people have been dead for a long while. My focus was on the ones who had fallen victim to the recent spate of killings—or who were about to. Chardin isn't in either category. And he's not a *founder*, so he's not on your incorporation document." The Sigma list contains more names than just the original incorporators. She looked at Ben hard. "My question is, how did you know to ask about him? Are you holding out on me?"

Ben shook his head.

"We don't have time to play games," Anna said. "Georges Chardin—I know him as a name on paper. But he's no one famous, no one I'd ever heard of. So what's his significance?"

"The significance is his boss, a legendary French industrialist—a man who *was* one of the incorporators in the photo. A man named Émil

Ménard. In his time, one of the greatest corporate titans. Back in 1945 he was a grand old man; he's long dead."

"Him I know. He was the founder of Trianon, generally considered the first modern corporate conglomerate, correct?"

"Right. Trianon is one of the biggest industrial empires in France. Émil Ménard built Trianon into a French petrochemical giant that made even Schlumberger look like a five-and-dime."

"And so this Georges Chardin worked for the legendary Émil Ménard?"

"Worked for him? He just about did his breathing for him. Chardin was his trusted lieutenant, aide-de-camp, factotum, whatever you want to call him. He wasn't just Ménard's right-hand man, he was practically his right hand. Chardin was hired in 1950 when he was only twenty, and in a few short years the greenhorn changed the way the cost of capital was accounted for, introduced a sophisticated new way of calculating return on investment, restructured the company accordingly. Way ahead of his time. A major figure."

"In your world, maybe."

"Granted. Point is, in very short order, the old man trusted his young protégé with everything, every detail in running his vast enterprise. After 1950, Émil Ménard didn't go anywhere without Chardin. They say Chardin had all the firm's ledgers memorized. He was a walking computer."

Ben produced the yellowed photograph of the Sigma group and placed it in front of Anna, pointing out Émil Ménard's countenance. "What do you see?"

"Ménard looks pretty haggard, to tell the truth. Not well at all."

"Correct. He was pretty seriously ill at that point. Spent the last decade of his life fighting cancer, though he was an incredibly formidable man right up until the end. But he died with the supreme confidence that his corporation would remain strong, continue to grow, because he had such a brilliant young *Directeur Général du Département des Finance*—basically, his chief financial officer."

"So you're speculating that Ménard would have trusted Georges Chardin with the secret of the Sigma enterprise as well?"

"I'm virtually certain of it. No doubt Chardin was completely in the background. But he was Ménard's shadow every step of the way. It's inconceivable that Chardin wouldn't have been completely privy to the substance of Sigma, whatever its objectives and methods. And look at it from Sigma's point of view: in order to stay alive, regardless of its true purpose, Sigma had to keep bringing in new recruits to replace the original founders. So Chardin is bound to have played a significant role, likely as a member of its inner council—Ménard would have made sure of that."

"O.K., O.K., you've got me convinced," Anna put in impatiently. "But where does that get us today? We already know Chardin died four years ago. You think he might have left files, papers, or something?"

"We're told that Chardin died four years ago, sure. Right around the same time that my brother, Peter, arranged his fake death. What if he did something like what Peter did—arranged to disappear, go into hiding, escape the killers he knew were after him?"

"Come on, Ben! You're making all sorts of assumptions, jumping to unwarranted conclusions!"

Ben replied patiently, "Your list indicated that he perished in a fire, right? The old 'burned beyond recognition' ruse? Like my brother? Sorry; won't get fooled again." He seemed to recognize the skepticism in her face. "Listen to me! You said it yourself. We have a string of old men who were killed presumably because somebody viewed them as a threat. Sigma, or its heirs or controllers. So let's think this out: why might a bunch of old guys in the twilight of their lives be considered a serious enough threat to be murdered?" He stood up, began to pace. "You see, the mistake I was making all along was in viewing Sigma as merely a front organization, a false corporation—instead of a genuine one."

"How do you mean?"

"It should have been so obvious! I can give you a hundred instances from my Wall Street days. In 1992, one guy ousted another rival to become the sole CEO of Time Warner, and his first order of business was what? To purge the hostiles from the board of directors. That's what management does. You get rid of your adversaries!"

"But the Time Warner guy didn't kill his opponents, I assume," she said dryly.

"On Wall Street we have different techniques for eliminating enemies." Ben gave a twisted smile. "But he eliminated them all the same. It's what always happens when there's an abrupt change in management."

"So you're suggesting there's been a 'change in management' at Sigma."

"Exactly. A purge of what you might call dissident trustees."

"Rossignol, Mailhot, Prosperi, and the rest—you're saying they were all dissidents? On the wrong side of the new management?"

"Something like that. And Georges Chardin was known to be brilliant. No doubt he saw it coming, and so he arranged to disappear."

"Maybe yes, maybe no. But it's still all in the realm of wild speculation."

"Not quite," Ben said softly. He turned to face Anna directly. "Beginning with the time-honored principle 'Follow the money,' I hired a French investigator we've used before at Hartman Capital Management. A wizard named Oscar Peyaud. We've used him for due-diligence work in Paris, and every time he blows us away with the speed and quality of his work. And the size of his bill, but that's another matter."

"Thanks for keeping me in the loop about what you were doing," Anna said with heavy sarcasm. "So much for being partners."

"Listen to me. A man can't live without some form of financial support. So I got to thinking, what would happen if you could track down the executor to Chardin's estate—see in what form he left his assets, how he might have retained access to them." He paused, took out a folded sheet of paper from his jacket pocket. "An hour ago this arrived from Paris, from Oscar Peyaud."

The page was blank except for a brief address:

Rogier Chabot
1554 rue des Vignoles
Paris 20

Anna looked up, at once puzzled and excited. "Chabot?"

"Georges Chardin's alias, I would bet. I think we have our man. Now it's just a matter of our getting to him before Sigma does."

An hour later, the phone on Walter Heisler's desk rang. A cycle of two short rings: an internal line. Heisler was drawing deep on a cigarette— he was working through the third pack of Casablancas of the day— when he picked up, and there was a two-second pause before he spoke: "Heisler."

It was the tech from the small room on the fifth floor. "Did you get the bulletin on the American, Navarro?"

"What bulletin?" Heisler slowly let the warm smoke plume through his nostrils.

"Just came in."

"Then it's probably been sitting in the message center all morning." The *Sicherheitsbüro* message center, operating with what he regarded as third-world inefficiency, was a bane of his existence. "What's up, then? Or do I need to find out by listening to the news on the radio?" This was how he had taken to formulating the complaint. Once he really did find out the whereabouts of a fugitive from a local radio station, the messengers having misplaced the morning's faxed bulletin somewhere en route to his desk.

"She's a rogue, it seems. We've been used. The U.S. government has a warrant out for her. Not my department, but I thought somebody should give you a heads-up."

"*Christ!*" Heisler said, and let his cigarette drop from his mouth into his mug of coffee, heard the quick sizzle of the quenched butt. "*Shit!* A fucking embarrassment."

"Not so embarrassing if you're the one who brings her in, eh?" the tech said carefully.

"Checking out of Room 1423," Anna said to the harried-looking clerk at the front desk. She placed her two electronic key-cards on the black granite counter.

"One moment, please. If I can just have your signature on the final bill, *ja?*" The man was weary-looking, and fortyish, with slightly concave cheeks, and dirty-blond hair—dyed?—combed forward, flat against his skull, in a seeming attempt to simulate youth. He wore a crisp uniform jacket of some sort of brown synthetic, with slightly fraying epaulets. Anna had a sudden vision of him as she imagined he became after hours—dressed in black leather, heavily spritzed with musky cologne, haunting nightclubs where the dim light might help him get lucky with a *schöne Mädchen*.

"Of course," Anna said.

"We hope you enjoyed your stay, Ms. Navarro." He typed numbers on a keyboard, and then looked up at her, showing a toothy, yellow-tinged smile. "Apologies. It's going to take a few moments to bring the records up. A problem in the system. Computers, right?" He smiled wider, as if he had said something witty. "Wonderful labor-saving devices. When they work. Let me get the manager." He picked up a red handset, and said a few words in German.

"What's going on," asked Ben, who was standing behind her.

"A computer problem, he says," Anna murmured.

From behind the counter, a short, big-bellied man emerged in a dark suit and tie. "I'm the manager, and I'm so sorry for the delay," the man said to her. He exchanged glances with the clerk. "A glitch. It's going to take a few minutes to retrieve the records. Phone calls, all of that. We'll get it for you soon, and then you can take a look and make sure it looks right. Wouldn't want you billed for the phone calls in Room 1422. Sometimes happens with the new system. Miracle of modern technology."

Something was wrong, and it wasn't the computer system.

The manager was jovial and reassuring and effusive, and yet, despite the lobby's slight chilliness, Anna noticed the beads of sweat on his forehead. "Come and sit in my office while we get this straightened out. Take a load off your feet, yes? You're off to the airport, yes? You have transportation arranged? Why don't you let the hotel car take you—our compliments. The least we can do for the inconvenience."

"That's very kind of you," Anna said, thinking that she recognized the type well from her years of investigations—the type of person whom tension made talkative. The man was under orders to detain them. That much was clear.

"Not at all. Not at all. You come with me, and have a nice cup of coffee. Nobody makes it like the Viennese, yes?"

Most likely, he hadn't been informed why, or whether they were dangerous. He must have been instructed to notify security, but security must not have arrived yet, or he wouldn't be so anxious. She was checking out of the hotel prematurely. Which meant . . . well, there was more than one possibility. Perhaps she—he? they?—had only recently been targeted. In which case, preparations would not be fully in place.

"Listen," she said. "Why don't you just figure it out on your own time and send me the bill? No biggie, huh?"

"It will be just a few minutes," the manager said, but he was not looking at her. Instead, he was making eye contact with a guard across the lobby.

Anna looked at her wristwatch ostentatiously. "Your cousins are going to be wondering what happened to us," she said to Ben. "We'd better get a move on."

The manager stepped around the counter, and placed a clammy hand on her arm. "In just a few minutes," he said. Up close, he smelled unappetizingly of grilled cheese and hair oil.

"Get your hands off me," Anna said in a tone of low menace. Ben was startled by the sudden steel in her voice.

"We can take you wherever you want to go," the manager protested, in a tone that was more wheedling than threatening.

From across the lobby, the security guard was reducing the distance between him and them with long, fast strides.

Anna hoisted her garment bag over her shoulder and headed for the front door. "Follow me," she said to Ben.

The two made their way quickly toward the entrance. The lobby guard, she knew, would have to confer with the manager before pursuing them outside of the building.

On the sidewalk in front of the hotel, she looked around carefully. At the end of the block, she saw a police officer speaking into a walkie-talkie, presumably giving his location. Which meant that he was likely the first on the scene.

She tossed her bag to Ben, and headed straight over to the policeman. "*Christ*, Anna!" Ben snapped.

Anna stopped the policeman, and spoke to him in a loud, official-sounding voice. "You speak English?"

"Yes," the cop said uncertainly. "English, yes." He was crew-cut, athletic, and seemed to be in his late twenties.

"I'm with the U.S. Federal Bureau of Investigation," Anna said. "The Federal Bureau of Investigation, do you understand? The FBI. We're looking for an American fugitive from justice, and I've got to ask for your help. The woman's name is Anna Navarro." She flashed her OSI badge quickly while holding his gaze; he would see it without really looking at it.

"You say Anna Navarro," the policeman said with recognition and relief. "Yes. We've been notified. In the hotel, yes?"

"She's barricaded herself in her room," Anna said. "Fourteenth floor. Room 1423. And she's traveling with someone, right?"

The policeman shrugged. "Anna Navarro is the name we have," he said.

Anna nodded. It was an important piece of information. "I've got two agents in place, all right? But as observers. We can't act on Austrian territory. It's up to you. I'm going to ask you to take the service entrance, on the side of the building, and make your way to the fourteenth floor. Are you O.K. with that?"

"Yes, yes," the policeman said.

"And spread the word, O.K.?"

He nodded eagerly. "We'll get her for you. Austria is, how do you say, a law-and-order place, yes?"

Anna shot him his warmest smile. "We're counting on you."

A few minutes later, Ben and Anna were in a taxicab en route to the airport.

"That was pretty ballsy," Ben said quietly. "Going up to the cop that way."

"Not really. Those are my people. I figured they'd just got word, or they would have been better prepared. Which means they had no idea what I look like. All they know is that they're looking for an American, on behalf of the Americans. No way of knowing whether I'm the one to pursue or the one in pursuit."

"When you put it that way . . ." Ben shook his head. "But why are they after you anyway?"

"I haven't exactly figured it out, yet. I do know that somebody's been spreading the word that I've gone rogue. Selling state secrets or whatever. The question is who, and how, and why."

"Sounds to me like Sigma is going through channels. Using real police through manipulation."

"Does, doesn't it?"

"This is not good," Ben said. "The idea that we're going to have every cop in Europe on our ass, on top of whatever psycho-killers Sigma has on the payroll—it's going to put a crimp in the game plan."

"That's one way to put it," Anna said.

"We're dead."

"That's a little harsh." Anna shrugged. "How about we approach this thing one step at a time?"

ROBERT LUDLUM

"How?"

"Ben Hartman and Anna Navarro are going to book a flight from Graz, about a hundred and fifty kilometers south, to Munich."

"And what are we going to do in Munich?"

"We're not going to Munich. The thing is, I already put a trace on your credit cards. That's a genie I can't put back in the bottle. You use any card under your name, and it's going to sound an immediate alarm in Washington and God knows what branch offices we've got."

"So we're screwed."

"So we *use* that. I need you to focus, Ben. Look, your brother prepared travel documents for him and Liesl, in case they needed to take off incognito. As far as we know, the IDs are still good, and the credit card ought to be functional. John and Paula Freedman are going to book tickets from Vienna on the next available flight to Paris. Replacing Liesl's photo with mine won't be a problem. A couple of generic-looking Americans, among tens of thousands who come in and out of the airport every day."

"Right," Ben said. "Right. I'm sorry, Anna. I'm not thinking clearly. But there are still risks, aren't there?"

"Of course there are. Whatever we do has risks. But if we leave now, the chances are good that they're not going to have photographs in place, and they're not looking for Mr. and Mrs. Freedman. The main thing is to stay calm and stay smart. Ready to improvise, if need be."

"Sure," Ben said, but he didn't sound it.

She looked at him. He somehow seemed young, younger than he'd been; the cockiness was gone, and he needed, she sensed, some reassurance. "After all you've been through, I know you're not going to lose your head. You haven't yet. And right now, that's probably the most important thing."

"Getting to Chardin is the most important thing."

"We'll get to him," Anna said, gritting her teeth in resolve. "We'll get to him."

Zurich

Matthias Deschner pressed both hands to his face, hoping for a moment of clarity in the darkness. One of the credit cards that Liesl's boyfriend had, through his offices, established and maintained, had finally been put to use. The call was pro forma: because the account had not been used in quite some time, it fell to a clerk in a credit-security department somewhere to place a call and ascertain that the card had not gone missing.

Peter had provided for the automatic payment of the annual fee; the name, telephone number, and mailing address involved a corporate entity that Matthias had set up for him; all communications went to Deschner, as its legal representative. Deschner had felt quite uncomfortable with the whole thing—it seemed legally dubious, to say the least—but Liesl implored him for his help, and, well, he had done what he had done. In retrospect, he should have run, *run* in the opposite direction. Deschner believed himself to be an honorable man, but he had never had illusions of heroism.

Now a dilemma had arisen for a second time in a matter of days. *Damn* that Ben Hartman. Damn *both* the Hartman boys.

Deschner wanted to keep his word to Peter and Liesl—wanted to even though they both were now dead. But they *were* dead, and with it his oath. And there were now larger considerations.

His own survival, for one.

Bernard Suchet, at the Handelsbank, was too smart to have believed him when he said he'd been completely ignorant of what Peter Hartman was involved in. In truth, it was more a case of not wanting to know, of believing that what he did not know could not hurt him.

That was no longer true.

The more he thought about it, the angrier he became.

Liesl was a lovely girl—he got a lump in his throat when he thought about the necessary past tense—but it had been wrong of her, all the same, to have involved him in her affairs. It was an abuse of familial loyalties, was it not? He imagined himself carrying on a conversation, an argument, really, with his deceased cousin. It was wrong of her, so very wrong. He never wanted any part of her crusade. Had she any idea of the position she put him in?

Her words returned to him: *We need your help. That is all. There is nobody else we can turn to.* Deschner remembered the luminous clarity of her blue eyes, like a deep reservoir of alpine water, eyes whose righteousness seemed to expect equal righteousness in everyone else.

Deschner felt the beginnings of a throbbing headache. The young woman had asked for too much, that was all. Probably of the world, and certainly of him.

She had made enemies of an organization that murdered people with the simple indifference of a meter maid dispensing parking tickets. Now Liesl was dead, and it seemed quite possible that she would take him with her.

They would learn that the card had been activated. And then they would learn that Dr. Matthias Deschner had himself been notified of this fact but failed to report it. Soon there would be no more Dr. Matthias Deschner. He thought of his daughter, Alma, who in just two months would be getting married. Alma had talked about how much she was looking forward to walking down the aisle with her father by her side. He swallowed hard and imagined Alma walking down the aisle alone. No, it could not be. It would be not just reckless but actively *selfish* of him.

The throbbing behind his eyes was undiminished. He reached into his desk drawer, removed a bottle of Panadol, and dry-swallowed a bitter, chalky tablet.

He looked at the clock.

He would report the credit activation call. But not immediately. He would wait for several hours to pass. Then he would call.

The tardiness could be easily explained, and they would be grateful for his having volunteered the information. Surely they would.

And just maybe the delay would give the Hartman boy a running start. A few more hours on this earth, anyway. He owed him that much, Deschner decided, but perhaps no more.

CHAPTER THIRTY-TWO

Paris

The twentieth arrondissement of Paris, its easternmost, and seamiest, district, slopes on a butte adjoining the highway that rings Paris and defines its limits, the *Périphérique*. In the eighteenth century, the land supported a village of winegrowers called Charonne. Over the years, the vineyards gave way to small houses, and the houses, in turn, had largely given way to charmless, unlovely structures of concrete. Today, such street names as the rue des Vignoles seem laughably out of place in the downtrodden urban milieu.

The trip to Paris had been nerve-racking; every incidental glance seemed to hold meaning, the very impassivity of *les douaniers*, the customs officials, seemed a possible subterfuge, a prelude to arrest. But Anna had experience with the balkiness of international alerts, knew how the bureaucracies of each border authority impeded the efficient execution of security directives. She wasn't surprised that they'd slipped through. She also knew that, next time, it was a good bet they wouldn't.

Only in the near anonymity of the dense-packed RER from De Gaulle did they start to relax. Now Anna and Ben emerged from the Gambetta métro stop, walked passed the large *Mairie*, or courthouse, and down the rue Vitruve to the rue des Orteaux. They turned right. Opposite them, to either side of the rue des Vignoles, were several narrow streets that followed the precise layout of the vineyards that they supplanted.

The area around Charonne, just south of Belleville, was among the least prototypically Parisian of Parisian neighborhoods, its denizens as likely to be Africans, Spaniards, or Antilleans as French. Even before recent waves of immigration, however, it had long earned the scorn of the city's bourgeois. It was a place where the poor and the criminal classes were seen to have congregated, a place where the insurrectionists of the Paris Commune, fueled by the disarray of the Second Empire, found populist support. A place of the disaffected, and the neglected. The twentieth arrondissement's one claim to fame was the cemetery du Père Lachaise, a forty-four hectare garden of graves; starting in the nineteenth century, Parisians who would never otherwise deign to visit this arrondissement, let alone live there, agreed to consign their bodies there after death.

Dressed in the casual attire of American tourists, Anna and Ben took in their surroundings as they walked: the aroma of falafel stands, the thudding rhythm of North African pop spilling from open windows, street vendors hawking tube socks and dog-eared copies of *Paris Match*. The people on the street came in every color, and spoke in a variety of accents. There were the young artists with complicated body piercings who no doubt saw themselves as the legitimate successors to Marcel Duchamp; there were immigrants from the Mahgreb hoping to earn enough money to send to their relatives in Tunisia or Algeria. The smell of pot or hashish, rich and resinous, wafted from the occasional alleyway.

"It's hard to imagine a corporate honcho retiring to this sort of neighborhood," Anna said. "What, did they run out of beachfront properties at Côte d'Azure?"

"Actually, it's nearly perfect," Ben said, reflective. "If you wanted to disappear, there's no better place. Nobody notices anybody else, nobody *knows* anybody else. If for some reason you wanted to stay in town, it's the most heterogeneous place you'll find, thronged with strangers, new immigrants, artists, eccentrics of every persuasion." Ben knew this city, as Anna did not, and his familiarity gave him a measure of much needed confidence.

Anna nodded. "Safety in numbers."

"Plus you're still near local mass transit, a maze of streets, a fast train out of town, and the *Périphérique*. A good setup when you're planning multiple escape routes."

Anna smiled. "You're a fast learner. Sure you don't want a job as a government investigator? We can offer you a salary of fifty-five thousand dollars and your very own parking space."

"Tempting," Ben said.

They walked past La Flèche d'Or, the red-tile-roofed restaurant that was perched over a rusted ghost track. Then Ben led the way down another block to a small Moroccan café, where the air was humid and fragrant with various couscous dishes. "I can't vouch for the food," he said. "But the view has a lot to recommend it."

Through the plate glass, they could see the stone triangle that was 1554 rue des Vignoles. Seven stories high, the building occupied a freestanding island surrounded by narrow streets on three sides. Its facade was stained dark with automotive exhaust and dappled with acidic bird droppings. Squinting, Anna could make out the anomalous remains of decorative gargoyles; erosion from the elements made them look as if they had melted in the sun. The marble ledges, ornamental revetment, and parapets seemed the folly of a long-ago builder, a throwback to an era when some still harbored upmarket dreams for the arrondissement. The building, unremarkable in most ways, breathed the gentle decrepitude of neglect and indifference.

"According to my source, Peyaud, he's known as 'L'Ermite.' The hermit. He lives on the entire top floor. Makes noises from time to time, so they know he's there. That and the deliveries he gets—groceries and the like. But even the delivery boys have never seen him. They drop off the stuff in the dumbwaiter, and collect their francs when the dumbwaiter comes back down. The few people who pay him any mind at all pretty much dismiss him as a real eccentric. Then again, this place is populated with eccentrics." He tucked into his lamb tagine greedily.

"So he's reclusive."

"*Very* reclusive. It's not just the delivery boys he avoids—*nobody's* ever seen him. Peyaud talked to the woman who lives on the ground floor. She and everyone else in the building have decided he's an elderly, paranoid, morbidly shy *rentier*. A case study in advanced agoraphobia. They don't realize that he owns the building."

"And you think we're going to make an unannounced visit to this possibly unhinged, possibly paranoid, possibly dangerous, and certainly disturbed and frightened individual, and he's going to pour us some decaf and tell us whatever we want to know?"

"No, I'm not saying that at all." Ben gave her a reassuring grin. "It might not be decaf."

"You have boundless faith in your own charm, I'll give you that." Anna looked doubtfully at her vegetarian couscous. "He does speak English?"

"Fluently. Almost all French businessmen do, which is how you can tell them apart from French intellectuals." He wiped his mouth with a flimsy paper napkin. "My contribution is, I got us here. You're the professional; you're in charge now. What do the field manuals say? What do you do in a situation like this—what's the established modus operandi?"

"Let me think. The MO for a friendly visit with a psychotic whom the world believes to be dead and who you think holds the secret to a menacing global organization? I'm not so sure that one's in the field manual, Ben."

The lamb tagine started to weigh heavily in his stomach.

She took his hand as they stood up. "Just follow my lead."

Thérèse Broussard gazed sullenly out the window, down at the foot traffic on the rue des Vignoles seven stories below. She gazed as she might have gazed at a fire, if her chimney hadn't been plugged with concrete years back. She gazed as she might have gazed at her little television set, if it hadn't been *détraquée* for the past month. She gazed to sooth her nerves and alleviate her boredom; she gazed because she had nothing better to do. Besides, she'd just spent ten minutes ironing her large, baggy undergarments, and needed a break.

A heavy-set, doughy-faced woman of seventy-four with piggy features and lank black-dyed hair, Thérèse still told people she was a dressmaker, even though she hadn't cut a piece of fabric in ten years, and even though she was never particularly accomplished at it. She grew up in Belleville, left school at the age of fourteen, and was never pretty enough to count on attracting the sort of man who would support her. In short, she had to learn a trade. As it happened, her grandmother had a friend who was a dressmaker and who agreed to take the girl on as an assistant. The old woman's hands were stiff with arthritis, and her eyes had grown dim; Thérèse could be helpful, though the old woman—Tati Jeanne, Thérèse was encouraged to call her—always parted with the paltry few francs she paid her each week with an air of reluctance. Tati Jeanne's already small clientele was dwindling, and with it her earnings; it was painful to have to share even a tiny amount with someone else.

One day in 1945, a bomb fell near Thérèse as she was walking down the Porte de la Chapelle, and, though she was physically unharmed, the blast entered her dreams at night and stopped her from sleeping. Her nervous condition only worsened over time. She would start at the slightest noise, and she started to eat voraciously, whenever she could find the food to stuff herself with. When Tati Jeanne died, Thérèse took on her remaining clients, but it was scarcely a living.

She was alone, as she'd always feared, but she had also learned there were worse things: she owed Laurent that much. Shortly after her sixty-fifth birthday, she met Laurent at the rue Ramponeau, in front of the Soeurs de Nazareth, where she collected a weekly parcel of food. Laurent, another native of the Ménilmontant area, was a decade older than she was, and looked older still. Hunched and bald, he wore a leather jacket whose sleeves were too long for him. He was walking a small dog, a terrier, and she asked the dog's name, and they began to talk. He told her that he fed his dog, Poupée, before he fed himself, gave the dog first choice of everything. She told him about her panic attacks, and the fact that a magistrate for social services, *l'Assedic*, had once placed her under supervision. The magistrate also made sure that the state would provide her with five hundred francs a week. His interest in her perked up when he learned of the support she received. A month later, they were married. He moved into her flat near Charonne; to an impartial eye, it may have appeared small, spare, and dingy but it was still more appealing than his own place, from which he was about to be evicted. Soon after they were married, Laurent pressed her to return to her sewing: they needed the money, the food parcels from the Soeurs scarcely lasted them half the week, the checks from *l'Assedic* were woefully inadequate. She told people she was a dressmaker, didn't she? Why, then, didn't she make dresses? She demurred, quietly at first, holding out her pudgy, blunt fingers, and explaining she no longer had the manual dexterity. He remonstrated, less quietly. She countered with no little vehemence, pointing out that he had a knack for getting fired from even the lowliest jobs, and that she would never have married him if she'd known what a drunkard he was. Seven months later, in the heat of one of these increasingly frequent arguments, Laurent keeled over. His last words to her were *"T'es grasse comme une truie"*—You fat sow. Thérèse let a few minutes pass and her temper subside before she phoned for an ambulance. Later, she'd learn that her husband had been felled by a massive hemorrhagic stroke—an aneurysm deep in the brain. A harried physician told her something about how blood vessels were like inner tubes, and how a weakness in a vessel wall could suddenly give way. She wished Laurent's last words to her had been more civil.

To her few friends, she referred to her husband as a saint, but no one was fooled. Having been married was, at any rate, an education. For much of her life, she believed that a husband would have made her life complete. Laurent had showed her the untrustworthy nature of all men.

As she watched various figures on the street corner near her hulking, poured-concrete apartment building, she fantasized about their private deviances. Which of these men was a junkie? Which a thief? Which beat his girlfriend?

A knock at the door, loud and authoritative, jarred her from her reveries. *"Je suis de l'Assedic, laissez-moi entrer, s'il vous plaît!"* A man from the welfare department, asking to be let in.

"Why did you not buzz?" barked Madame Broussard.

"But I did buzz. Repeatedly. The buzzer is broken. As is the gate. Do you claim you didn't know?"

"But why are you here? Nothing about my status has changed," she protested. "My support . . ."

"Is under review," the man said, officiously. "I think we can straighten this all out if we just go over a few matters. Otherwise, the payments come to an end. I do not wish that to happen."

Thérèse trudged heavily over to the door and peered through the peephole. The man had the familiar haughtiness she associated with all *fonctionnaires* of the French state—clerks who imagined themselves to be civil servants, men given a thimbleful of power, and made despotic by it. Something about his voice, his accent seemed less familiar. Perhaps he came from a Belgian family. Thérèse did not like *les Belges*.

She squinted. The man from social services was attired in the thin worsted wool jacket and cheap tie that seemed to come with the job; his hair was a thatch of salt and pepper and he seemed an unremarkable specimen except for his smooth, unlined face; the skin would be babyish, if it didn't look almost tight.

Thérèse unlocked the two deadbolts and released the chain before pressing the final latch and opening the door.

As Ben followed Anna out of the café, he kept his eye on 1554 rue des Vignoles, trying to fathom its mysteries. The building was a picture of ordinary dilapidation—too distressed to excite anyone's admiration, while not so distressed as to arrest anyone's attention. But looking at it carefully—an exercise, Ben imagined, that no one had engaged in for many years—one could see the bones of a once elegant apartment building. It was evident from the oriel windows, crested with carved limestone, now randomly chipped and fractured. It was evident from the corners of the building, the quoins, where dressed stones had been laid so that their faces were alternately large and small; and the mansard roof, edged with a low, crumbling parapet. It was evident even from the narrow ledges that had once provided a balcony, before the iron rail was removed, no doubt after it had rusted to pieces and posed a hazard to public safety. A century ago, a measure of care had gone into the building's construction, which decades of indifference could not entirely efface.

Anna's instructions to him had been clear. They would join a group of passersby as they crossed the street, falling into rhythm with their stride. They would be indistinguishable from people whose destination was the nearby shop that sold cheap liquor and cigarettes, or the *shawarma* place next to it, where a large, fatty oval loaf of meat rotated, close enough to the sidewalk that you could reach out and touch it; certainly swarms of flies did. Anyone watching from the window would see no departure from the ordinary patterns of pedestrian traffic; only when they passed in front of the main door would the two stop and enter.

"Ring the bell?" Ben asked as they reached the building's main entrance.

"If we rang the bell, we wouldn't be unannounced, would we? I thought that was the plan." Glancing around quickly, Anna inserted a narrow tongue of steel into the lock and played with it for a few moments.

Nothing.

Ben felt a sense of rising panic. So far, they had been careful to blend in, to synchronize their pace with those of other pedestrians. But now they found themselves frozen in place; any casual observer would notice that something was wrong, that they did not belong here.

"Anna," he murmured with quiet urgency.

She was bent over her work, and he could see that her forehead was damp with nervous perspiration. "Take out your wallet and start counting your bills," she whispered. "Take out a phone and check for messages: Do something. Calmly. Slowly. *Languorously.*"

The faint sound of metal rattling against metal continued as she spoke.

Then finally, there was the sound of a bolt retracting. Anna turned the lever knob and opened the door. "Sometimes these locks require a little tender loving care. Anyway, it's not exactly high security."

"Hidden in plain view, I think is the idea."

"Hidden, anyway. I thought you said nobody had ever seen him."

"That's true."

"Did you stop and reflect that if he wasn't crazy when he started out, he might have become so? Total social isolation will do that to a person." Anna led him to the disheveled elevator. She pressed the call button, and they briefly listened to a rattling chain before they decided that taking the stairwell was the safer option. They made their way up seven flights, taking care to make as little noise as possible.

The hallway of the top floor, an affair of grimy white tiles, stretched before them.

Startlingly, the doorway of the sole apartment on the floor was already swinging open.

"Monsieur Chabot," Anna called out.

There was no response.

"Monsieur *Chardin!*" she called, exchanging a look with Ben.

There was a movement from within, shrouded in the gloom.

"Georges Chardin!" Anna called again. "We come with information that may be of value to you."

A few moments of silence followed—and then a deafening blast.

What had happened?

A glance at the hallway directly facing the open door made things clear: it was cratered with a deadly spray of lead pellets.

Whoever was in there was firing a shotgun at them.

"I don't know what's *wrong* with you people," Thérèse Broussard said, color rising to her cheeks. "Nothing has changed about my circumstances since my husband died. *Nothing*, I tell you."

The man appeared with a large black suitcase, and strode past her to the window, ignoring her for the moment. A very strange man.

"A nice view," the man said.

"It gets no direct light," Thérèse contradicted him scoldingly. "For most of the day, it is dark. You could develop film in here."

"For some pursuits, that can be an advantage."

Something was wrong. His accent was slipping, his French losing the straightened cadences of the social-services bureaucracy, sounding more casual, somehow less *French*.

Thérèse took a few steps away from the man. Her pulse quickened as

she suddenly remembered the reports of a rapist who had been brutal-
izing women in the vicinity of the Place de la Réunion. Some of the
women had been older, too. This man was an impostor, she decided.
Her instincts told her so. Something about the way the man moved, with
coiled, reptilian strength, confirmed her growing suspicion that he was,
in fact, the Réunion rapist. *Mon dieu!* He'd gained the trust of his victims,
she had heard—victims who had invited the assailant into their very
homes!

All her life, people had told her that she suffered from *une maladie
nerveuse*. She knew better: she saw things, felt things, that others did not.
Yet now, crucially, her antennae had failed her. How could she have been
so foolish! Her eyes darted wildly around her apartment, looking for
something she could use to protect herself. She picked up a heavy clay
pot that contained a slightly shriveled rubber plant.

"I demand that you leave at once!" she said in a trembling voice.

"Madame, your demands are meaningless to me," the smooth-faced
man said quietly. He looked at her with quiet menace, a confident predator who knew that his prey was hopelessly outmatched.

She saw a flash of silver as he unsheathed a long, curved blade, and
then she threw the heavy pot at him with all her might. But its weight
worked against her: it arced quickly downward, striking the man in the
legs, knocking him a few steps back but leaving him unharmed. *Jésus
Christ!* What else could she use to defend herself? Her little broken-down
TV! She yanked it from the countertop, hoisted it with great effort above
her head, and tossed it at him as if aiming for the ceiling. The man,
smiling, sidestepped the crude projectile. It thudded against the wall,
then dropped to the floor, its plastic casing shattered along with the
picture tube.

Dear God, no! There had to be something else. *Yes*—the iron on the
ironing board! Had she even turned it off? Thérèse dashed toward the
iron, but as she grabbed it the intruder saw what she was attempting.

"Stop where you are, you revolting old cow," called the man, a look
of disgust crossing his face. "*Putain de merde!*" With a lightning-fast
motion, he grabbed another, smaller knife and flung it across the room.
The deeply beveled steel came to a razor-sharp edge along the entire,
arrow-shaped blade; the hollowed tang provided a streamlined counter-
weight.

Thérèse never saw it coming, but she felt its impact as the blade buried itself deep into her right breast. At first she thought whatever it was had struck her and bounced off. Then she looked down and saw the steel handle protruding from her blouse. It was odd, she thought, that she felt nothing; but then a sensation—cold, like an icicle—began to grow, and an area of red blossomed around the steel. Fear drained from her, replaced with sheer rage. This man thought she was just another victim, but he had misjudged her. She remembered the nighttime visits from her drunken father, which started when she was fourteen, his breath smelling like sour milk as he worked his stubby fingers into her, hurting her with his ragged nails. She remembered Laurent, and his last words to her. Indignation flooded her like water from an underground cistern, from every time she'd ever been taunted, cheated, bullied, abused.

Bellowing, she charged the evil intruder, all two hundred and fifty pounds of her.

And she tackled him, too, slammed him to the ground by sheer momentum.

She would have been proud of what she'd accomplished, *truie grasse* or no, if the man hadn't shot her dead a split-second before her body crashed into his.

Trevor shuddered with revulsion as he pushed the obese, lifeless body off him. The woman was only slightly less off-putting in death that she'd been in life, he reflected as he returned his silenced pistol to its holster, feeling the cylinder's heat against his thigh. The twin bullet holes in her forehead were like a second pair of eyes. He dragged her away from the window. In retrospect, he should have shot her immediately upon gaining entry, but who knew she would turn out to be such a maniac? Anyway, there was always something unexpected. That was why he liked his vocation. It was never entirely routine; there was always the possibility of surprise, new challenges. Nothing, of course, he couldn't handle. Nothing had ever turned up that the Architect couldn't handle.

"*Christ,*" Anna whispered. She had avoided the shotgun spray by a couple of feet at most. "Not exactly the welcome wagon."

But where was the shooter?

A steady succession of blasts was coming from the open apartment door, from somewhere within its darkened interior. Apparently the gunman was firing through the gap between the heavy steel door and the doorjamb.

Ben's heart was thudding. "Georges Chardin," he called out, "we haven't come to harm you. We want to *help* you—and we need your help as well! Please, *listen* to us! Hear us out!"

From the dark recesses of the apartment emanated a bizarre rasping, a shuddering moan of terror, seemingly involuntary, like the night cry of a wounded animal. Still the man remained invisible, cloaked in darkness. They heard the click of a cartridge sliding into the chamber of a shotgun, and each of them raced to opposite ends of the long hallway.

Another explosion! A fusillade of pellets came through the open door, splintering the woodwork in the hall, gouging jagged crevices in the plaster walls. The air was heavy with the pungent odor of cordite. The entire hall now looked like a war zone.

"*Listen!*" Ben called out to their unseen adversary. "We're not firing back, can't you see that? We're not here to harm you in any way!" There was a pause: was the man hiding inside the apartment actually listening now? "We're here to protect you against Sigma!"

Silence.

The man was listening! It was the invocation of the name of Sigma, the shibboleth of a long-buried conspiracy thundering in its impact.

At that same instant, Ben could see Anna hand-signaling to him. She wanted him to stay where he was while she made her own way into Chardin's apartment. But *how*? With a glance, he saw the large double-hung window, saw her silently nudging open its heavy sash, felt a gust of cold air from outside. She was going to climb out the window, he realized with horror, walk along the narrow exterior ledge until she came to a window that opened directly into the Frenchman's apartment. It was *madness*! He was seized with dread. A stray gust of wind, and she would fall to her death. But it was too late for him to say anything to her; she already had the window open and had stepped onto the ledge. *Christ Almighty!* he wanted to shout. *Don't do it!*

Finally a strange, deep baritone voice emerged from the apartment: "So this time they send an American."

"There's no 'they,' Chardin," replied Ben. "It's just us."

"And who are you?" the voice came back, heavy with skepticism.

"We're Americans, yes, who have ... personal reasons why we need your help. You see, Sigma killed my brother."

Another long silence ensued. Then: "I am not an idiot. You wish me to come out, and then you will trap me, take me alive. Well, you will *not* take me alive!"

"There are far easier ways, if that's what we wanted to do. Please, let us in—let us speak with you, if only for a minute. You can keep your weapon trained on us."

"For what purpose do you want to speak with me?"

"We need your help in defeating them."

A pause. Then a short, sharp bark of derisive laughter. "In defeating Sigma? You cannot! Until just now I thought one could only hide. How did you find me?"

"Through some damned clever investigative work. But you have my utmost admiration: You did a good job covering your tracks, I must say. A damned good job. It's hard to relinquish control of family property. I understand that. So you used a *fictio juris*. Remote agency. Well designed. But then you've always been a brilliant strategic thinker. It wasn't for nothing that you got to be Trianon's *Directeur Général du Département des Finance*."

Another long silence, followed by the scrape of a chair from inside the apartment. Was Chardin preparing to show his face after all? Ben glanced down the hall apprehensively, saw Anna carefully sliding one foot after another along the ledge while clinging to the parapet with both hands. Her hair blew in the wind. Then she was out of his line of sight.

He had to distract Chardin, keep him from noticing Anna's appearance at his window. *He had to keep Chardin's attention.*

"What is it you want from me?" came Chardin's voice. His tone seemed neutral now. *He was listening; that was the first step.*

"Monsieur Chardin, we have information that could be invaluable to you. We know a great deal about Sigma, about the inheritors, the new generation that has seized control. The only protection—for either of us—is in knowledge."

"There *is* no protection against them, you fool!"

Ben raised his voice. "*Goddamn it!* Your rationality was once legendary. If you've lost that, Chardin, then they've won anyway! Can't you see how unreasonable you're being?" In a gentler tone, he added, "If you send us away, you'll always wonder what you might have learned. Or perhaps you'll never have the opportunity—"

Suddenly there was the sound of glass breaking from inside the apartment, followed immediately by a loud crash and a clatter.

Had Anna made it through a window into Chardin's apartment safely? A few seconds later he heard Anna's voice, loud and clear. "I've got his shotgun! And it's trained on him now." She obviously spoke for Chardin's benefit as well as Ben's.

Ben strode toward the open door and entered the still-darkened room. It was hard to see anything but shapes; when his eyes adjusted, after a few seconds, he made out Anna, dimly outlined against a thick curtain, holding the long-barreled gun.

And a man in a peculiar, heavy robe with a cowl rose slowly, shakily to his feet. He did not appear to be a vigorous man; he was indeed a shut-in.

It was plain what had happened. Anna, plunging through the window, had leaped onto the long, ungainly shotgun, pinioning it to the floor; the impact must have knocked him over.

For a few moments, all three of them stood in silence. Chardin's breathing was audible—heavy, nearly agonal, his face shadowed within his cowl.

Watching carefully to make sure Chardin didn't have another weapon concealed in the folds of his monklike garment, Ben fumbled for a light switch. When the lights went on, Chardin abruptly turned away from them both, facing the wall. Was Chardin reaching for another gun?

"Freeze!" Anna shouted.

"Use your vaunted powers of reason, Chardin," Ben said. "If we wanted to kill you, you'd already be dead. That's obviously *not* why we're here!"

"Turn and face us," Anna commanded.

Chardin was silent for a moment. "Be careful of what you ask for," he rasped.

"*Now*, dammit!"

Moving as if in slow motion, Chardin complied and when Ben's mind grasped the reality of what he saw, his stomach heaved and he nearly retched. Nor could Anna disguise her shocked intake of breath. It was a horror beyond imagining.

They were staring into an almost featureless mass of scar tissue, wildly various in texture. In areas it appeared crenellated, almost scalloped; in other areas, the proud flesh was smooth and nearly shiny, as if lacquered or covered in plastic wrap. Naked capillaries made the oval that had once been his face an angry, beefy red, except where varicosities yielded coils of dark purple. The staring, filmy gray eyes looked startlingly out of place—two large marbles left on a slick blacktop by a careless child.

Ben averted his gaze, and then, wrenchingly, forced himself to look again. More details were visible. Embedded in a horribly webbed and wrinkled central concavity were two nasal openings, higher than the nostrils would once have been. Below, he made out a mouth that was little more than a gash, a wound within a wound.

"*Oh, dear God.*" Ben slowly breathed the words.

"You are surprised?" Chardin said, the words scarcely appearing to come from his wound-like mouth. It was if he were a ventriloquist's dummy, one designed by a deranged sadist. A cough-laugh. "The reports of my death were quite accurate, all except for the assertion of death itself. 'Burned beyond recognition'—yes, indeed I was. I should have perished in the blaze. Often I wish that I had. My survival was a freak accident. An enormity. The worst fate a human being can have."

"They tried to kill you," Anna whispered. "And they failed."

"Oh no. I think that in most respects they quite succeeded," Chardin said, and winced: a twitch of dark red muscle around one of his eyeballs. It was apparent that the simple act of talking was painful to him. He was enunciating with exaggerated precision, but the damage meant that certain consonants remained blurry. "A close confidant of mine had suspicions that they might try to eliminate me. Talk had already begun about dispatching the *angeli rebelli*. He came by my country estate—too late. There were ashes, and blackened timber, and charred ruins everywhere. And my body, what was left of it, was as black as any of it. He thought he could detect a pulse, my friend did. He brought me to a tiny provincial hospital, thirty kilometers away, told them a tale about an overturned kerosene lamp, gave them a false name. He was canny. He understood that if my enemies knew I had survived, they would try again. Months passed in that tiny clinic. I had burns over ninety-five percent of my body. I was not expected to live." He spoke haltingly but hypnotically: a tale never before spoken. And then he sat down in a tall-backed wooden chair, seemingly depleted.

"But you survived," Ben said.

"I did not have the strength to force myself to stop breathing," Chardin said. He paused again, the memory of pain imposing further pain. "They wanted to move me to a metropolitan hospital, but of course I would not permit it. I was beyond help anyway. Can you imagine what it is like when consciousness itself is nothing other than the consciousness of pain?"

"And yet you *survived*," Ben repeated.

"The agony was beyond anything our species was meant to endure. Wound dressings were an ordeal beyond imagining. The stench of necrotic flesh was overpowering even to me, and more than one orderly would routinely vomit upon entering my room. Then, after the granulation tissue formed, a new horror was in store for me—contracture. The scars would shrink and the agony would be rekindled all over again. Even today, the pain I live with every moment of every day is of a degree I never experienced in the whole of my preceding life. When I *had* a life. You cannot look at me, can you? No one can. But then I cannot look at myself, either."

Anna spoke, clearly knowing that human contact had to be reestablished. "The strength you must have had—it's extraordinary. No medical textbook could ever account for it. The instinct for survival. You emerged from that blaze. You were saved. Something inside you fought for life. It *had* to be for a reason!"

Chardin spoke quietly. "A poet was once asked, If his house were on fire, what would he save? And he said, 'I would save the fire. Without fire, nothing is possible.'" His laughter was a low, disconcerting rumble. "Fire is after all what made civilization possible: but it can equally be an instrument of barbarity."

Anna returned the shotgun to Chardin after removing a last shell from the chamber. "We need your help," she said urgently.

"Do I look like I am in a position to help anyone, I who cannot help myself?"

"If you want to call your enemies to account, we may be your best bet," Ben said somberly.

"There is no revenge for something like this. I did not survive by drinking the gall of rage." He withdrew a small plastic atomizer from the folds of his robes, and directed a spray of moisture toward his eyes.

"For years, you were at the helm of a major petrochemical corporation, Trianon," Ben prompted. He needed to show Chardin that they had puzzled out the basic situation, needed to *enlist* him. "An industry leader, it was and remains. You were Émil Ménard's lieutenant, the brains behind Trianon's midcentury restructuring. He was a founder of Sigma. And in time you must have become a principal as well."

"Sigma," he repeated in a quavering voice. "Where it all begins."

"And no doubt your genius in accounting helped in the great undertaking of spiriting assets out of the Third Reich."

"Eh? Do you think *that* was the great project? That was *nothing*, a negligible exercise. The grand project . . . *le grand projet* . . ." He trailed off. "That was something of an entirely different order. And nothing you are equipped to comprehend."

"Try me," Ben said.

"And divulge the secrets I have spent my life protecting?"

"You said it yourself: What life?" Ben took a step toward him, forcing down his revulsion in order to maintain eye contact. "What have you left to lose?"

"At last you speak truly," Chardin said softly, and his naked eyes seemed to swivel, peering penetratingly at Ben's own eyes.

For a long moment he was silent. And then he began to talk, slowly, mesmerizingly.

"The story begins before me. It will continue, no doubt, after me. But its origins lie in the closing months of the Second World War, when a consortium of some of the world's most powerful industrialists gathered in Zurich to determine the course of the postwar world."

Ben flashed on the steely-eyed men in the old photograph.

"They were angry men," Chardin went on, "who caught wind of what the ailing Franklin Roosevelt was planning to do—let Stalin know he would not stand in the way of a massive Soviet land grab. And, of course, it's what he did do before his death. In effect he was ceding half of Europe to the Communists! It was the grossest betrayal! These business leaders knew they would be unable to derail the disgraceful U.S.-Soviet bargain at Yalta. And so they formed a corporation that would be a beachhead, a means to channel vast sums of money into fighting communism, strengthening the will of the West. The next world war had begun."

Ben looked at Anna, then stared off into space, hypnotized and astonished by Chardin's words.

"These leaders of capitalism accurately foresaw that the people of Europe, embittered and sickened by fascism, would, in reaction, turn to the left. The soil had been scorched by the Nazis, these industrialists realized, and without the massive infusion of resources at key moments, socialism would begin to take root, first in Europe, then throughout the world. They saw their mission as preserving, fortifying, the industrial state. Which meant, as well, muffling the voices of dissent. Do these anxieties seem overstated? Not so. These industrialists knew how the pendulum of history worked. And if a fascist regime was followed by a socialist regime, Europe might be truly lost, as they saw it.

"It was seen as only prudent to enlist certain leading Nazi officials, who knew which way the wind was blowing and were also committed to combating Stalinism. And once the syndicate had established its political as well as financial foundations, it began manipulating world events, bankrolling political parties as if from behind a curtain. They were successful, astonishingly so! Their money, judiciously targeted, brought to life De Gaulle's Fourth Republic in France, preserved the rightist Franco regime in Spain. In later years, the generals were placed in power in Greece, bringing to an end the leftist regime that the people had elected. In Italy, Operation Gladio ensured that a continual campaign of low-level subversion would cripple the attempt of leftists to organize and influence national politics. Plans were drawn up for the paramilitary police, the *carabinieri*, to take over radio and television stations if necessary. We had extensive files on politicians, unionists, priests. Ultra-right-wing parties everywhere were secretly bolstered from Zurich, so as to make the conservatives seem moderate by contrast. Elections were controlled, bribes paid, leftist political leaders assassinated—and the strings were pulled by the puppet masters in Zurich, in conditions of absolute secrecy. Politicians such as Senator Joseph McCarthy in the U.S. were funded. Coups were financed throughout Europe and Africa and Asia. On the left, extremist groups were created, too, to serve as *agents provocateur* and guarantee popular revulsion toward their cause.

"This cabal of industrialists and bankers had seen to it that the world was made safe for capitalism. Your President Eisenhower, who warned about the rise of the military-industrial complex, saw only the tip of the iceberg. In truth, much of the entire history of the world in the last half-century was scripted by these men in Zurich and their successors."

"*Christ!*" Ben interrupted. "You're talking about . . ."

"Yes," Chardin said, nodding his hideous faceless head. "Their cabal gave birth to the Cold War. They did. Or, as perhaps I should say, *we* did. Now do you begin to understand?"

Trevor's fingers moved swiftly as he opened his suitcase and assembled the .50 caliber rifle, a customized version of the BMG AR-15. It was, in his view, a thing of beauty, a precision-machined sniper weapon with relatively few moving parts, and a range of up to seventy-four hundred meters. At more proximate distances, its penetrative capacities were astonishing: it could pierce three inches of steel plate, would leave an exit hole in an automobile or hammer off a corner of a building. It could drive through crumbling mortar handily. The bullet would have a projection velocity of over three thousand feet per second. Resting on a bipod, and surmounted by a Leupold Vari-X scope with thermal imaging, the rifle would have the accuracy that he needed. He smiled as he seated the rifle into the bipod. He could hardly be considered underequipped for the job at hand.

His target, after all, was directly across the street.

CHAPTER THIRTY-THREE

"It's *incredible*," Anna said. "It's . . . it's too much to take *in!*"

"I have lived with it so long that it is to me a commonplace," Chardin said. "But I recognize the immense upheavals that would ensue if others realized that the public history of their times was, in no small part, *scripted*—and scripted by a cadre of men like me: businessmen, financiers, industrialists, working through their widely dispersed confederates. *Scripted by Sigma.* The history books would all have to be rewritten. Lives of purpose would suddenly seem like nothing more than the twitching at the end of a marionette's string. Sigma is a story of how the mighty have fallen, and the fallen become mighty. It is a story that must *never* be told. Do you understand that? *Never.*"

"But who would be brazen—*mad*—enough to undertake such a venture?" Ben rested his gaze on Chardin's soft brown robes. Now he understood the physical necessity of such strange, loose clothing.

"You must first understand the visionary, triumphalist sense of mission and accomplishment that suffused the midcentury corporation," Chardin said. "We had already transformed man's destiny, remember. My God, the automobile, the airplane, soon the jet: man could move along the ground at speeds inconceivable to our ancestors—man could fly through the heavens! Radio waves and sound waves could be used to provide a sixth sense, vision where vision had never been possible. Computation itself could now be automated. And the breakthroughs in the material sciences were equally extraordinary—in metallurgy, in plastics, in production techniques yielding new forms of rubber and adhesives and textiles, and a hundred other things. The ordinary landscape of our lives was being transformed. A revolution was taking place in every aspect of modern industry."

"A second industrial revolution," Ben said.

"A second, a third, a fourth, a *fifth*," Chardin replied. "The possibilities seemed infinite. The capabilities of the modern corporation seemed to be unbounded. And after the dawn of nuclear science—my God, what *couldn't* we achieve if we set our minds to it? There was Vannevar Bush, Lawrence Marshall, and Charles Smith, at Raytheon, doing pioneering work in everything from microwave generation to missile guidance systems to radar surveillance equipment. So many of the discoveries that became ubiquitous in later decades—xerography, microwave technologies, binary computing, solid-state electronics—had already been conceived and prototyped at Bell Labs, General Electric, Westinghouse, RCA, IBM, and other corporations. The material world was succumbing to our will. Why not the political realm as well?"

"And where were *you* during all this?" Ben asked.

Chardin eyes fixed on a point in the middle distance. From the folds of his cloak, he withdrew the atomizer, and moistened his eyes again. He pressed a white handkerchief to the area under his slash-like mouth, which was slick with saliva. And, haltingly at first, he began to speak.

I was a child—eight years old when the war broke out. A student at a shabby little provincial school, the Lycée Beaumont, in the city of Lyon. My father was a civil engineer with the city, my mother a schoolteacher. I was an only child, and something of a prodigy. By the time I was twelve, I was taking courses in applied mathematics at the École Normale Supérieure de Lyon, the teacher's college. I had genuine quantitative gifts, and yet the academy held no appeal for me. I wanted something else. The ozone-scented arcana of number theory held little allure. I wanted to affect the real world, the realm of the everyday. I lied about my age when I first sought employment in the accounting department of Trianon. Émil Ménard was already heralded as a prophet among CEOs, a true visionary. A man who had forged a company out of disparate parts, where no one had previously seen any potential for connection. A man who realized that by assembling once segmented operations you could create an industrial power infinitely greater than the sum of its parts. To my eyes, as an analyst of capital, Trianon was a masterpiece—the Sistine Chapel of corporate design.

Within a matter of months, word of my statistical prowess had reached the head of the department for which I worked, Monsieur Arteaux. He was an older gentleman, a man of few hobbies and a near total devotion to Ménard's vision. Some of my coworkers found me cold, but not Monsieur

Arteaux. With us, conversation flowed as if between two sports fans. We could discuss the relative advantages of internal capital markets or alternate measurements of equity risk premiums, and do so for hours. Matters that would stupefy most men, but which involved the architecture of capital itself—rationalizing the decisions of where to invest and reinvest, how risk was best to be apportioned. Arteaux, who was nearing retirement, put everything on the line by arranging for me to be introduced to the great man himself, catapulting me over endless managerial layers. Ménard, amused by my obvious youth, asked me a few condescending questions. I replied with rather serious and rather provocative responses—in truth, responses that verged on rudeness. Arteaux himself was appalled. And Ménard was, so it seems, captivated. An unusual response, but it was, in capsule form, an explanation of his own greatness. He told me later that my combination of insolence and thoughtfulness reminded him of no one so much as himself. A magnificent egotist, he was, but it was an earned egotism. My own arrogance—for even as a child I was tagged with that attribute—was perhaps not unfounded, either. Humility was a fine thing for men of the cloth. But rationality decreed that one be sensible to one's own capabilities. I had considerable expertise in the techniques of valuation. Why shouldn't it logically extend to the valuation of oneself? My own father was, I believed, handicapped by a deferential manner; he esteemed his own gifts too little, and persuaded others to undervalue them in turn. That would not be my mistake.

I became, in a matter of weeks, Ménard's personal assistant. I accompanied him absolutely everywhere. No one knew whether I was an amanuensis or a counselor. And in truth I moved, smoothly, from playing the first role to playing the second. The great man treated me far more like an adopted son than a paid employee. I was his only protégé, the sole acolyte who seemed worthy of his example. I would make proposals, sometimes bold ones, occasionally proposals that reversed years of planning. I suggested, for example, that we sell off an oil-exploration division that his managers had spent years in developing. I suggested massive investments in still unproven technologies. Yet when he heeded my advice, he almost invariably found himself pleased by the results. L'ombre de Ménard—the shadow of Ménard—became my nickname in the early 1950s. And even as he fought the disease, the lymphoma, that would ultimately claim his life, he and Trianon came to rely increasingly upon my judgment. My ideas were bold, unheard *of, seemingly mad—and soon widely mimicked. Ménard studied me as much as I studied him, with both detachment and genuine affection. We were men in whom such qualities enjoyed an easy coexistence.*

Yet for all the privileges he granted me, I had sensed, for a while, that there was one final sanctum to which I had not been granted entry. There were trips he made without explanation, corporate allocations I could not make sense of and about which he would brook no discussion. Then the day came when he decided that I would be inducted into a society I knew nothing about, an organization you know as Sigma.

I was still Ménard's wunderkind, still the corporate prodigy, still in my early twenties, and utterly unprepared for what I was to see at the first meeting I attended. It was at a château in rural Switzerland, a magnificent ancient castle situated on a vast and isolated tract of land owned by one of the principals. The security there was extraordinary: even the landscaping, the trees and shrubbery surrounding the property, was designed to permit the clandestine arrival and departure of various individuals. So on my first visit, I was in no position to see the others arrive. And no form of surveillance equipment could have survived the high-intensity blasts of high and low electromagnetic pulses, the latest technology in those days. All items made of metal were required to be deposited in containers made of dense osmium; otherwise, even a simple wristwatch would have been stopped dead by the pulses. Ménard and I came there in the evening, and were escorted directly to our rooms, he to a magnificent suite overlooking a small glacial lake, I to an adjoining chamber, less grand but exceedingly comfortable.

The meetings began the next morning. About what was said then, I actually remember little. Conversations continued from earlier ones of which I knew nothing—it was difficult for a newcomer to orient himself. But I knew the faces of the men around the table, and it was a genuinely surreal experience, something a fantasist might have tried to stage. Ménard was a man who had few peers, with respect to his own wealth, his corporate power, or his vision. But what peers he had were there in the room. The heads of two warring, mighty steel conglomerates. The head of America's leading electrical equipment manufacturers. Heavy industry. Petrochemicals. Technology. The men responsible for the so-called American century. Their counterparts from Europe. The most famous press baron in the world. The chief executives of wildly diversified portfolio companies. Men who, in combination, wielded control over assets that exceeded the gross domestic product of most of the countries in the world put together.

My worldview was shattered that day, then and forever.

Children, in history classes, are taught the names, the faces of political and military leaders. Here is Winston Churchill, here is Dwight Eisenhower, here is Franco and De Gaulle, Atlee and Macmillan. These men did matter. But they were, really, little more than spokesmen. They were, in an exalted sense, press secretaries, employees. And Sigma made sure of it. The men who truly had their hands on the levers of power were sitting around that long mahogany table. They were the true marionette masters.

As the hours passed, and we drank coffee and nibbled on pastries, I realized what I was witness to: a meeting of the board of directors of a massive single corporation that controlled all other corporations.

A board of directors in charge of Western history itself!

It was their attitude, their perspective, that stayed with me, far more than any actual words that were uttered. For these were professional managers who had no time for useless emotion or irrational sentiments. They believed in the development of productivity, in the promulgation of order, in the rational concentration of capital. They believed, in plain English, that history—the very destiny of the human race—was simply too important to repose in the hands of the masses. The upheavals of two world wars had taught them that. History had to be managed. *Decisions had to be made by dispassionate professionals. And the chaos threatened by communism— the turmoil, the redistribution of wealth it augured, made their project a matter of genuine and immediate urgency. It was a present danger to be averted, not some utopian scheme.*

They assured each other of the need to create a planet where the true spirit of enterprise would ever be safe from the envy and avarice of the masses. After all, was a world purulent with communism and fascism a world any of us wished to bequeath to our children? Modern capital showed us the way—but the future of the industrial state had to be protected, sheltered from the storms. That was the vision. And though the origins of this vision lay in the global depression that preceded the war, the vision became infinitely more compelling in the wake of the destruction wreaked by the war itself.

I said little that day, not because I was by nature taciturn, but because I was quite literally speechless. I was a pygmy among giants. I was a peasant supping with emperors. I was beside myself, and all the while it was the most I could do to maintain a look of dispassion, in emulation of my great mentor. Those were the first hours I spent in the company of Sigma, and my life would never be the same again. The daily fodder of the newspapers—a labor strike here, a party assembly there, an assassination somewhere else—was no longer a record of random events. Behind these events could now be discerned a pattern—the complex and intricate machinations of a complex and intricate machine.

To be sure, the founders, the principals, profited immensely. Their corporations, in every instance, thrived, while so many others, not fortunate enough to be part of Sigma, perished. But the real motivation was their larger vision: the West had to be united against a common foe, or it would soften and succumb. And the hardening of its battlements had to proceed with discretion and prudence. Too aggressive, too quick a push could trigger a backlash. Reform had to be titrated. One division focused on assassinations, removing thoughtful voices from the left. Another forged—the word is appropriate—the sorts of extremist groups, the Baader-Meinhofs and Red Brigades, that would be guaranteed to antagonize any moderate sympathizers.

The Western world, and much of the rest, would respond to its ministrations, and it would accept the cover stories that accompanied them. In Italy, we created a network of twenty thousand "civic committees," channeling money to the Christian Democrats. The Marshall Plan itself, like so much else, was hammered out by Sigma—very often Sigma had devised the very language of the acts that would be submitted to, and passed by the American Congress! All of the European recovery programs, economic cooperation agencies, eventually even NATO itself became organs of Sigma, which remained invisible—because it was ubiquitous. Wheels within wheels—that was the way we worked. In every textbook, you find boilerplate about the reconstruction of Europe accompanied by a photograph of General Marshall. Yet every detail had been outlined by us, mandated by us, long before.

It never crossed anyone's mind that the West had fallen under the administration of a hidden consortium. The notion would be inconceivable. Because if true, it would mean that over half of the planet was effectively a subsidiary of a single megacorporation.

Sigma.

Over time, older moguls died and were replaced with younger protégés. Sigma persisted, metamorphosing where necessary. We weren't ideologues. We were pragmatists. Sigma merely sought to remodel the whole of the modern world. To claim nothing less than the ownership of history itself.

And Sigma succeeded.

Trevor Griffiths squinted through the thermal imaging scope. The heavy room-darkening drapes were optically opaque, but to the thermal scope, they were a gauzy scrim. Human figures were hazy green forms, like blobs of mercury, visibly changing shape as they moved around pillars and objects of furniture. The seated figure would be his primary target. The others would move away from the windows, thinking themselves safe, and he would destroy them through the wall of brick itself. One bullet would clear the way; the second would destroy his target. The remaining shells would complete the job.

"If what you're saying is true . . ." Ben began.

"Men lie, for the most part, in order to save face. You can see I no longer have such motivation." The slit that was Chardin's mouth pulled up at the sides, in what was either a grimace or a smile. "I warned you that you were ill-equipped to understand what I had to say. Perhaps, though, you may now understand the situation somewhat more clearly than before. A great many powerful men everywhere—even today—have reason to keep the truth buried. More so than ever, indeed. For Sigma has, over the past several years, been moving in a new direction. In part, it was the result of its own successes. Communism was no longer a threat—it seemed pointless to continue to pour billions into the orchestration of civil acts and political forces. Not when there might be a more efficient way of achieving Sigma's objectives."

"Sigma's objectives," Ben echoed.

"Which is to say, stability. Tamping down dissent, 'disappearing' troublemakers and threats to the industrial state. When Gorbachev proved troublesome, we arranged his ouster. When regimes in the Pacific Rim proved balky, we arranged for an abrupt, massive flight of foreign capital, plunging their economies into a recession. When Mexico's leaders proved less than cooperative, we arranged for a change in government."

"My *God*," Ben said, his mouth dry. "Listen to what you're saying . . ."

"Oh yes. A session would be convened, a decision rendered and, shortly thereafter, executed. We were good at it, frankly—we could play the governments of the world like a pipe organ. Nor did it hurt that Sigma came to own an immense portfolio of companies, its ownership stakes hidden through various private equity firms. But a small inner circle came to believe that, in a new era, the answer wasn't merely to tack to the latest winds, cope with cyclical crises. It was to perpetuate a stable leadership for the long run. And so in recent years, one very special project of Sigma's came to the fore. The prospect of its success would revolutionize the nature of world control. No longer would it be about the allocation of funds, the directing of resources. It became, instead, a simple matter of who the 'chosen' would be. And I fought this."

"You had a falling out with Sigma," Ben said. "You became a marked man. And yet you kept its secrets."

"I say it again: if ever the truth were to get out, about how many of the major events of the postwar era were secretly manipulated, scripted by this cabal, the reaction would be violent. There would be riots in the streets."

"Why the sudden escalation of activity—you're describing something that has unfolded over a period of *decades!*" Ben said.

"Yes, but we are talking about *days*," Chardin replied.

"And you *know* this?"

"You wonder that a recluse like me should keep abreast of what is going on? You learn how to read the entrails. You *learn*, if you want to survive. And then there is precious little else to occupy a shut-in's hours. Years among their company have taught me to detect signals in what would sound to you like static, mere noise." He gestured toward the side of his head. Even through the cowl, Ben could tell that the man's external ear was completely absent, the auditory canal simply a hole within an outgrowth of proud flesh.

"And this explains the sudden flurry of killings?"

"It is as I explained: Sigma has, of late, been undergoing one final transformation. A change of management, if you will."

"Which you resisted."

"Long before most were attuned to it. Sigma always reserved the right to 'sanction' any members whose absolute loyalty came into question. In my arrogance, I did not realize that my exalted position conferred no protection. Quite the contrary. But the cleansing, the purging of the dissidents, only began in earnest in the last several weeks. Those who were perceived as hostile to the new direction—

along with those who worked for us—were designated as disloyal. We were called the *angeli rebelli*: rebel angels. If you recall that the original *angeli rebelli* had revolted against God Almighty himself, you grasp the sense of power and entitlement of Sigma's current overlords. Or, shall I say, overlord, since the consortium has come under the direction of one . . . redoubtable individual. In the event, Sigma has run out the clock, so to say."

"*What* clock? *Explain* it to me," Ben began. So many questions crowded his mind.

"We're talking about days," Chardin repeated. "If *that*. What fools you are, coming to me as if knowing the truth could help you anymore. Coming to me when there is no time! Surely it is already too late."

"What are you talking about?"

"It's why I had assumed you'd been sent, at first. They know that they are never more vulnerable than shortly before the final ascendancy. As I've told you, now is a time for final mop-ups, for sterilization and autoclaving, for eliminating any evidence that might point to them."

"Again, I ask you, *why now?*"

Chardin took out the atomizer and misted his filmy gray eyes again. There came a sudden explosion, bone-jarringly loud, which propelled Chardin, in his chair, backward to the floor. Both Ben and Anna sprang at once to their feet and saw with terror the two-inch round hole that instantaneously appeared in the plaster wall opposite, as if somehow put there by a large-bore drill.

"*Move!*" Anna screamed.

Where had this projectile—it seemed far too big to be a mere gunshot—come from? Ben leaped to one side of the room as Anna jumped to the other, and then he whirled around to look at the splayed body of the legendary financier. Forcing himself to survey, once more, the horrible ravines and crevices of scar tissue, he noticed Chardin's eyes had rolled back into his head, leaving only the whites visible.

A wisp of smoke arose from a charred segment of his cowl, and Ben realized that an immense bullet had passed through Chardin's skull. The faceless man—the man whose will to survive had enabled him to endure years of indescribable agony—was dead.

What had happened? *How?* Ben knew only that if they didn't seek cover immediately they would be killed next. But where could they move, how could they escape an assault when they didn't know where it came from? He saw Anna race to the far side of the room, then swiftly lower herself to the floor, lying flat, and he did the same.

And then came a second explosion, and another round punched through the solid exterior wall and then through the plaster interior wall. Ben saw a circle of daylight in the brick wall, saw now that the shots had come from outside!

Whatever their assailant was firing, the rounds had penetrated the brick wall as if it were a bead curtain. The last round had come danger-ously close to Anna.

Nowhere was safe.

"Oh, my *God!*" Anna shouted. "We've got to get out of here!"

Ben whirled and looked out the window. In a glint of reflected sun-light, he caught the face of a man in a window directly across the narrow street.

The smooth, unlined skin, the high cheekbones.

The assassin at Lenz's villa. The assassin at the auberge in Switzer-land . . .

The assassin who had murdered Peter.

Stoked by a towering rage, Ben let out a loud shout, of warning, of dis-belief, of anger. He and Anna simultaneously raced to the apartment's exit. Another hole exploded, deafeningly, in the outside wall; Ben and Anna made a dash to the staircase. These missiles would not lodge in the flesh, nor sear skin; they would tear through the human body like a spear through a spider's web. Clearly they were designed for use against armored tanks. The devastation they had done to the old building was incredible.

Ben ran after Anna, leaping and bounding down the dark stairs, as the volley of explosions continued, plaster and brick crumbling audibly behind them. Finally they staggered down to the small lobby. "This way!" whispered Anna, racing to an exit that would take them not to the rue des Vignoles but to a side street, making it far more difficult for the assassin to target them. Emerging from the building, they looked fran-tically about them.

Faces all around. At the corner of the rue des Orteaux, a blond woman, in denim and fake fur. At first glance, she looked like a hooker, or a junkie, but there was something about her that struck Ben as *off*. Again, it was a face he'd *seen* before. But where?

Suddenly he flashed back to the Bahnhofstrasse. An expensively dressed blonde, holding shopping bags from an upscale boutique. The flirtatious exchange of glances.

It was the same woman. A sentry for the Corporation? Across the street from her, a male adolescent in a ripped T-shirt and jeans: he, too, looked familiar, although Ben couldn't place him. My God! Another one?

At the opposite end of the street stood a man with ruddy, weathered cheeks and wheat-field eyebrows.

Another familiar face.

Three Corporation killers placed strategically around them? Professionals intent on making sure they'd never escape?

"We're boxed in," he said to Anna. "At least one of them's on either end of the street." They froze in place, unsure how or where to move next.

Anna's eyes searched the street, then she replied. "Listen, Ben. You said Chardin had chosen this district, this block, for good reason. We don't know what contingency plans he had, what escape routes he'd mapped out in advance, but we know that he must have had something in mind. He was too smart *not* to have arranged for path redundancy."

"Path redundancy?"

"Follow me."

She ran straight toward the very apartment building where the assassin had taken up his seventh-floor perch. Ben saw where she was headed. "That's insane!" he protested, but he followed nonetheless.

"No," Anna replied. "The base of the building is one place he *can't* reach." The alleyway was dark and fetid, the scampering of rats evidence of the quantities of refuse that had been allowed to accumulate there. A locked metal gate blocked off its egress to the rue des Halles.

"Should we climb?" Ben looked doubtfully at the top of the gate whose sharp-pointed spearlike rods loomed twelve feet above them.

"*You* can," Anna said, and unholstered a Glock. Three carefully aimed blasts, and the chain that locked the gate swung free. "The guy was using a .50 caliber rifle. There was a flood of them after Desert Storm. They were a hot commodity, because with the right ammunition they could put a hole right through an Iraqi tank. If you've got one of those monsters, a city like this might as well be made out of cardboard."

"Shit. So what do we do?" Ben asked.

"Don't get hit," Anna replied tersely, and she began running, Ben close behind.

Sixty seconds later they found themselves on the rue de Bagnolet in front of La Flèche d'Or restaurant. Suddenly Ben darted across the street. "Stay with me."

A heavyset man was just getting off a Vespa, one of those small motorized *vélocipedes* that had achieved nuisance status among French drivers.

"*Monsieur,*" Ben said. "*J'ai besoin de votre vélo. Pardonnez-moi, s'il vous plaît.*"

The bear-like man gave him an incredulous look.

Ben pointed his gun at him and grabbed the keys. The owner stepped backward, cowering, as Ben leaped onto the small vehicle and revved the motor. "Get on," Ben called out to Anna.

"You're crazy," she protested. "We'd be vulnerable to anyone in an automobile, once we get on the *Périphérique*. These things don't go any faster than fifty miles an hour. It's going to be a turkey shoot!"

"We're not going on the *Périphérique*," Ben said. "Or any other road. Climb *on!*"

Bewildered, Anna complied, taking the seat behind Ben on the motorbike.

Ben drove the Vespa around the La Flèche d'Or and then, joltingly, down a concrete embankment that led to old railroad tracks. The restaurant, Anna could now see, was actually built directly over the tracks.

Now Ben steered onto the rusted tracks. They drove through a tunnel, then back into an open stretch. The Vespa kicked up dust, but the passage of time had flattened the tracks here into the earth, and the ride became smooth and swifter.

"So what happens when we meet a train?" Anna shouted, grasping onto him tightly as they rolled over the tracks.

"There hasn't been a train on these tracks for over half a century."

"Aren't we full of surprises."

"The product of a misspent youth," Ben shouted back. "I once messed around here as a teenager. We're on a ghost railroad line known as the *Petite Ceinture*, the little belt. It runs all the way around the city. Phantom tracks. La Flèche d'Or is actually an old railroad station, built in the nineteenth century. Connected twenty stations in a loop around Paris—

Neuilly, Porte Maillot, Clichy, Villette, Charonne, plenty more. The automobile killed it off, but nobody ever reclaimed the belt. Now it's mostly a long stretch of nothing. I was thinking some more about why Chardin decided on this particular neighborhood, and then I remembered the phantom line. A useful piece of the past."

They passed through another spacious tunnel, then back into the open air.

"Where are we now?" Anna asked.

"Hard to gauge, since you can't see any of the landmarks from here," Ben said. "But probably Ford d'Obervillier. Maybe Simplon. Way the hell away. Central Paris isn't very big, of course. The whole thing is about forty square miles. If we can make our way into the métro and join a few hundred thousand Parisians there, we can begin to make our way to our next appointment."

The Flann O'Brien—the bar's name was displayed in coiled neon as well as painted in curlicued script in the window—was in the first arrondissement, on the rue Bailleul, near the Louvre-Rivoli stop. It was a dark, beery establishment, with lots of deeply grooved old wood and a dark wood floor that had soaked up sloshes of Guinness for years.

"We're meeting him at an Irish bar?" Anna asked. Her head swiveled around by something like reflex, as she scanned their surroundings, alert to any sign of threat.

"Oscar has a sense of humor, what can I say?"

"And remind me why you're so sure he can be trusted?"

Ben turned serious. "We've got to deal with probabilities, not possibilities, we're agreed on that. And so far he's been on the level. What makes Sigma a menace is the fact that it commands the loyalty of true believers. Oscar's too damn *greedy* to be a believer. Our checks have always cleared. I think that counts with Oscar."

"The honor of the cynic."

Ben shrugged. "I've got to go with my gut. I like Oscar, always have. I think he likes me."

The din in the Flann O'Brien, even at this hour, was overwhelming, and it took their eyes a while to adjust to the dim lighting.

Oscar was tucked away at a banquette toward the back, a diminutive

gray-haired man behind an enormous tankard of viscous stout. Beside
the tankard was a neatly folded newspaper, with a half-completed crossword puzzle. He had an amused expression on his face, as if he were
about to wink—Anna soon realized that this was simply his habitual
expression—and he greeted the two with a simple wave of the hand.

"I've been waiting for forty minutes," he said. He grabbed Ben's hand
in an affectionate, wrestling clasp. "Forty *billable* minutes." He seemed
to be savoring the world as it rolled off his tongue.

"A bit of a holdup at our previous engagement," Ben said tersely.

"I can imagine." Oscar nodded at Anna. "Madame," he said.
"Please, sit."

Ben and Anna slid onto the banquette on either side of the small
Frenchman.

"Madame," he said, turning his full attention to her. "You are even
more beautiful than your photograph."

"Sorry?" Anna replied, puzzled.

"A set of photographs of you was recently wired to my colleagues in
la Sûreté. Digital image files. I got a set of them myself. Came in handy."

"For his work," Ben explained.

"My *artisans*," Oscar said. "So very good and so *very* expensive." He
tapped Ben on his forearm.

"I'd expect nothing less."

"Of course, Ben, I can't say your photograph does justice to you either.
Those paparazzi, they never find the flattering angle, do they?"

Ben's smile faded. "What are you talking about?"

"I'm very proud of myself for doing the *Herald Tribune* crossword
puzzle. Not every Frenchman could do it, you'll grant. I've almost finished this one. All I need now is a fifteen-letter word for an internationally wanted fugitive from justice."

He turned the newspaper over.

" 'Benjamin Hartman'—would that do it?"

Ben looked at the front page of the *Tribune* and felt as if he had been
plunged headfirst into ice water. SERIAL KILLER SOUGHT was the headline.
Beside it was a low-resolution photograph of him, apparently taken from
a surveillance camera. His face was shadowed, the image grainy, but it
was unmistakably him.

"Who knew my friend was such a celebrity?" Oscar said, and turned
the paper over again. He laughed loudly, and Ben belatedly joined him,

realizing it was the only way one escaped notice in a bar filled with drink-fueled merriment.

From the next banquette over, he overheard a Frenchman trying to sing "Danny Boy," with uncertain pitch and an only rough approximation of the vowels. *Oh, Danny Boy, ze peeps ze peeps are caaalling.*

"This is a problem," Ben said, his urgent tone belying the soapy grin on his face. His eyes darted back to the newspapers. "This is an Eiffel Tower–sized problem."

"You *kill* me," Oscar said, slapping Ben on the back as if he had uttered a hilarious joke. "The only people who say there's no such thing as bad publicity," he said, "have never gotten bad publicity." Then he tugged a package from beneath the cushion of his seat. "Take this," he said.

It was a white plastic bag with gaudy lettering, from a tourist gift shop somewhere. *I love Paris in the Springtime,* it said, with a heart standing in for the word "love." It had the kind of stiff plastic handles that snapped shut when pressed together.

"For us?" Anna asked doubtfully.

"No tourist should be without," Oscar said. His eyes were playful; they were also intensely serious.

Oh, Danny boy, I love you sooo.

The drunken Frenchman at the next banquette was now joined, in various keys, by his three companions.

Ben sank lower in his seat, as the full weight of his predicament bore upon him.

Oscar punched him in the arm; it looked jocular, but it stung. "Don't slink down in your seat," he whispered. "Don't look furtive, don't avoid eye contact, and don't try to look inconspicuous. That's about as effective as a movie star putting on sunglasses to shop at Fred Segal, *tu comprends?*"

"*Oui,*" Ben said weakly.

"Now," Oscar said, "what's that charming American expression you have? 'Get the fuck out of here.'"

After acquiring a few items at some small side-street stalls, they returned to the métro, where they were just another couple of moony-eyed tourists to the casual spectator.

"We've got to make plans—plans for what the hell to do next," Ben said.

"Next? I don't see what choice we have," Anna said. "Strasser's the one surviving link we know about—a member of Sigma's board of incorporators who's still alive. We've got to reach him somehow."

"Who says he's still alive?"

"We can't afford to assume otherwise."

"You realize they're going to be watching every airport, every terminal, every gate."

"It's occurred to me, yes," Anna replied. "You're beginning to think like a professional. A real fast learner."

"I believe they call this the immersion method."

On a long underground journey to one of the *banlieues*, the downtrodden areas that ringed Paris proper, the two conversed in low voices, making plans like lovebirds, or fugitives.

They got out at the stop at La Courneuve, an old-fashioned working-class neighborhood. It was only a few miles away, but a different world—a place of two-story houses and unpretentious shops that sold things to use, not to display. In the windows of the bistros and convenience stores, posters for Red Star, the second-division soccer team, were prominent. La Courneuve, due north of Paris, wasn't far from Charles De Gaulle airport, but that was not where they'd be heading.

Ben pointed to a bright red Audi across the street. "How about that one?"

Anna shrugged. "I think we can find something less noticeable." A few minutes later, they came across a blue Renault. The car had a light coating of grime, and on the floor inside there were yellow wrappers from fast-food meals, and a few cardboard coffee cups.

"I'll put my money on the owner being home for the night," Ben said. Anna set to work with her rocker pick, and a minute later had the car door unlocked. Disassembling the ignition cylinder on the steering column took a little more time, but soon the motor roared to life and the two took off down the street, driving at the legal speed limit.

Ten minutes later, they were on the A1 highway, en route to the Lille-Lesquin airport in Nord–Pas de Calais. The trip would take hours, and involve risks, but they were calculated ones: auto theft was commonplace in La Courneuve, and the predictable police response would be to make perfunctory inquiries among the locals known to be involved in the activity. The matter would almost certainly not be referred to the *Police Nationale*, which patrolled the major thoroughfares.

They drove in silence for half an hour, lost in their own thoughts.

Finally, Anna spoke. "The whole thing Chardin talked about—it's just impossible to absorb. Somebody tells you that everything you know about modern history is wrong, upside down. How can that be?" Her eyes remained fixed on the road in front of her, and she sounded as utterly drained as Ben felt.

"I don't know, Anna. Things stopped making sense for me that day at the Bahnhofplatz." Ben tried to stave off a profound sense of enervation. The rush of their successful escape had long since given way to a larger sense of dread, of terror.

"A few days ago, I was essentially conducting a homicide investigation, not examining the foundations of the modern age. Would you believe?"

Ben did not directly reply: what reply could there be? "The homicides," he said. He felt a vague unease. "You said it started with Mailhot in Nova Scotia, the man who worked for Charles Highsmith, one of the Sigma founders. And then there was Marcel Prosperi, who was himself one of the principals. Rossignol, likewise."

"Three points determine a plane," Anna said. "High-school geometry."

Something clicked in Ben's mind. "Rossignol was alive when you flew off to see him, but dead by the time you arrived, right?"

"Right, but—"

"What's the name of the man who gave you the assignment?"

She hesitated. "Alan Bartlett."

"And when you'd located Rossignol, in Zurich, you told him, right?"

"First thing," Anna said.

Ben's mouth became dry. "Yes. Of course you did. That's why he brought you in, in the first place."

"What are you talking about?" She craned her neck and looked at him.

"Don't you see? You were the cat's-paw, Anna. *He was using you.*"

"Using me *how?*"

The sequence of events cascaded in Ben's mind. "*Think*, dammit! It's just the way you might prepare a bloodhound. Alan Bartlett first gives you the scent. He knows the way you work. He knew the next thing you'd demand . . ."

"He knew I'd ask him for the list," Anna said, her voice hollow. "Is this possible? That damned show of reluctance on his part—a piece of theater for my benefit, knowing it would only steel my resolve? The same with the goddamn car in Halifax: maybe he knew a scare like that would make me that much keener."

"And so you get a list of names. Names of people connected with Sigma. But not just any names: these are people who are *in hiding*. People whom Sigma *cannot find*—not without alerting them. Nobody connected with Sigma could possibly reach these people. *Otherwise they would have been dead already.*"

"Because . . ." Anna began slowly. "Because all of the victims were *angeli rebelli*. The apostates, the dissidents. People who could no longer be trusted."

"And Chardin told us that Sigma was approaching a delicate transitional phase—a time of maximum vulnerability. It *needed* these people eliminated. But *you* could find somebody like Rossignol precisely because *you were who you said you were*. You really *were* trying to save his life. And your bona fides could be verified in meticulous detail. Yet you had been unknowingly *programmed!*"

"Which is why Bartlett gave me the assignment in the first place," Anna said, her voice growing steadily louder, a realization dawning. "So that I would locate the remaining *angeli rebelli*." She banged a hand on the dashboard.

"Whom Bartlett would then arrange to have killed. *Because Bartlett is working for Sigma*." He hated himself for the pain that his words had to be causing her, but everything was now coming into sharp focus.

"And in effect so was I. God*damn* it to hell! *So was I*."

"*Unwittingly*," Ben emphasized. "As a *pawn*. And when you were becoming too hard to control, he tried to pull you off the case. They'd already found Rossignol, they didn't need you anymore."

"*Christ!*" Anna said.

"Of course, it's no more than a theory," Ben said, though he felt certain he was speaking the truth.

"A theory, yes. But it makes too much damned *sense*."

Ben didn't reply. The demand that reality make sense seemed now an outlandish luxury. Chardin's words filled his mind, their meaning as hideous as the face of the man who spoke them. *Wheels within wheels—that was the way we worked . . . organs of Sigma, which remained invisible . . . Every detail had been outlined by us . . . long before . . . it never crossed anyone's mind that the West had fallen under the administration of a hidden*

consortium. The notion would be inconceivable. Because if true, it would
mean that over half the planet was effectively a subsidiary of a single me-
gacorporation. Sigma.

Another ten minutes of silence elapsed before Ben said flatly, "We've
got to work out an itinerary."

Anna studied the article in the *Herald Tribune* again. " 'The suspect is
believed to have used the names Robert Simon and John Freedman in
his travels.' So those IDs are blown."

How? Ben recalled Liesl's explanation of how the credit accounts were
kept current, how Peter had made the arrangements through her impeccably trustworthy second cousin. "Deschner," Ben said tightly. "They
must have gotten to him." After a moment, he added, "I wonder why
they didn't release my real name. They've supplied aliases, but not the
name 'Benjamin Hartman.' "

"No, it's the smart thing to do. Look, they knew you weren't traveling
under your real name. Bringing your true identity into it might have
muddied the waters. You'd get your Deerfield English teacher opining
that the Benny she knew would never do such a thing. Plus the Swiss
have gunshot residue analysis that puts you in the clear—but it's all filed
under Benjamin Hartman. If you're running a dragnet, it makes sense
to keep it simple."

Near the town of Croisilles, 'they saw a sign for a motel and pulled
into a modern low-slung concrete building, a style Ben thought of as
International Ugly.

"Just one night," Ben said, and counted out several hundred francs.

"Passport?" the stone-faced clerk asked.

"They're in our bags," Ben said apologetically. "I'll bring them down
to you later."

"Just one night?"

"If that," Ben said, giving Anna a theatrically lascivious look. "We've
been touring France on our honeymoon."

Anna stepped over and put her head on Ben's shoulder. "This is such
a beautiful country," she told the clerk. "And so sophisticated. I can't get
over it."

"Your honeymoon," the clerk repeated, and, for the first time, smiled.

"If you don't mind, we're in a hurry," Ben said. "We've been driving
for hours. We need a rest." He winked.

The clerk handed him a key attached to a heavy rubberized weight.

"Just at the end of the hall. Room 125. You need anything, just call."

The room was sparsely furnished; the floor was covered with dull, mottled green carpeting and the brashly cherry-scented air freshener did not conceal the faint, unmistakable smell of mildew.

Once the door closed behind them, they emptied the plastic bag Oscar had given them on the bed, along with their other recent purchases. Anna picked up an EU passport. The photograph was of her, although digitally altered in various ways. Anna said her newly assigned name aloud a few times, trying to get accustomed to the unfamiliar sounds.

"I still don't see how this is going to work," Ben said.

"Like your Oscar said, they categorize you before they really look at you. It's called profiling. If you don't belong to the suspect genus, you get a free pass." Anna took out a tube of lipstick and, looking into a mirror, applied it carefully. She wiped it off a few times before she was confident that she had done it correctly.

By then, Ben was already in the bathroom, his hair slick with syrupy, foamy hair dye, which gave off a tarry, ammoniac smell. The instructions said to wait twenty minutes before rinsing. It also cautioned against dyeing eyebrows, at the risk of blindness. Ben decided to take that risk. With a cotton swab, he applied the thick fluid to his brows, pressing a wad of tissue paper against his eyes to prevent it from dripping down.

The twenty minutes felt like two hours. Finally, he stepped into the shower, blasted himself with water, and opened his eyes only when he was certain the peroxide had all been washed down the drain.

He stepped out of the shower and looked at himself in the mirror. He was a plausible blond.

"Say hello to David Paine," he said to Anna.

She shook her head. "The hair's too long." She held up the multi-cut electric clippers, chrome-clad except for the clear rubberized grip. "That's what this baby is for."

In another ten minutes, his curls were flushed away, and he was ready to put on the neatly creased U.S. Army fatigues that Oscar Peyaud had provided him. Blond, crew cut, he looked like an officer, consistent with the insignia, patches, and overseas service bars on his green uniform coat. U.S. Army officers wore identifying badges when traveling by air, he knew. It wasn't an inconspicuous way to travel; but being conspicuous in the right way could amount to a life-saving distraction.

"Better make tracks," Anna said. "The faster we can get out of this country, the safer we'll be. Time's on *their* side, not ours."

Carrying their belongings with them, the two walked to the end of the hall and stepped out into the parking lot.

They tossed Anna's garment bag in the backseat of the blue Renault, along with the white plastic sack that Oscar had given them. It contained the spent bottle of hair dye, and a few other pieces of garbage they didn't want to leave behind. At this point, the smallest detail could give them away.

"As I said, we're down to our last card, our last play," Anna said, as they made their way back on the highway heading north. "Strasser was a founder. We've got to find him."

"*If* he's still alive."

"Was there any indication either way in Sonnenfeld's file?"

"I reread it this morning," Ben said. "No, to be honest. And Sonnenfeld thought it was entirely possible that Strasser died, maybe even *years* ago."

"Or maybe not."

"Maybe not. You're an incurable optimist. But what makes you think we're not going to get arrested in Buenos Aires?"

"Hell, like you've said, there were notorious Nazis living there openly for decades. The local police are going to be the least of our troubles."

"What about Interpol?"

"That's what I was thinking—they might be able to help us locate Strasser."

"Are you crazy? Talk about going into the lion's den. They're going to have your name on some watch list, aren't they?"

"You obviously don't know anything about the way the Interpol office is run down there. Nobody checks IDs. You are who you claim you are. Not the most sophisticated operation, let's just say. You got a better idea?"

"Sonnenfeld said Gerhard Lenz's widow may be alive," Ben said broodingly. "Wouldn't she be in a position to know?"

"Anything's possible."

"I'll try to remember that," Ben said. "You really think we've got a shot at getting out of this country undetected?"

"There aren't going to be any transatlantic flights at this airport. But we can get to some of the European capitals. I suggest that we both travel separately. There's a decent chance they're looking for a man and a woman traveling together."

"Of course," he said. "I'll go via Madrid; you take Amsterdam."

They settled into another silence, less tense and more companionable. From time to time, Ben found his gaze drifted toward Anna. Despite all they had been through today, she was extravagantly beautiful. At one point, their glances met; Anna defused the faint awkwardness with a crooked grin.

"Sorry, I'm still trying to get used to your new Aryan officer look," she said.

Some time later, Anna fished her cell phone out of her handbag and punched in a number.

David Denneen's voice had the tinny, artificial clarity conferred by decrypted telephony. "Anna!" he said. "Everything O.K.?"

"David, listen. You've *got* to help me—you're the only one I can trust."

"I'm listening."

"David, I need whatever you can get me on Josef Strasser. He was like Mengele's smarter older brother."

"I'll do whatever I can," Denneen replied, his voice tentative, baffled. "Of course. But where do you want the material sent?"

"BA."

He understood the abbreviation for Buenos Aires. "But I can't exactly send the file care of the embassy, can I?"

"How about care of the American Express office?" Anna gave him a name to use.

"Right. Low profile's a good idea down there."

"So I hear. How bad is it?"

"Great country, great people. But some long memories. Watch your back down there. Please, Anna. I'll get right on to it." And with that Denneen clicked off.

The main border-control security room of the *aéroport* Lille-Lesquin was a drab, windowless interior space, with low acoustic-tiled ceilings, a white projection screen at one end of the room. Color photographs of internationally sought criminals hung beneath a black-and-white sign that read DÉFENSE DE FUMER. Nine immigration and border-control officials sat on folding chairs of tube metal and beige plastic while their boss,

Bruno Pagnol, the director of security, filled them in on the new advisories of the afternoon. Marc Sully was one of them, and he tried not to look as bored as he felt. He had no love for his job, but wasn't eager to lose it, either.

Just in the past week, Pagnol reminded them, they had arrested seven young Turkish women arriving from Berlin with illicit cargo in their bellies: having been recruited as "mules," they had swallowed condoms packed with China White. Finding the seven was partly a matter of luck, but credit had to go to Jean-Daniel Roux (Roux gave a slit-eyed nod when the boss singled him out, pleased but determined not to look it), who was alert enough to catch the first of them. The woman had looked visibly woozy to him; as they later learned, one of the knotted condoms in her colon had started to leak. In fact, the woman almost overdosed on the contraband. In the hospital, they'd retrieved fifteen small balls, double-wrapped in latex, tied off with fishing line, each containing several grams of extremely pure heroin.

"How'd they get it out of her?" one of the officers asked.

Marc Sully, sitting in the back, farted audibly. "Rear extraction," he said.

The others laughed.

The red-faced director of airport security frowned. He saw nothing funny. "The courier nearly died. These are desperate women. They'll do anything. How much money do you think she was paid? A thousand francs, nothing more, and she almost died for it. Now she's facing a very long jail sentence. These women are like walking suitcases. Hiding drugs in their own shit. And it's our job to keep that poison out of the country. You want your kids hooked on it? So some fat-ass Asian can get rich? They think they can promenade right past us. Are you going to teach them better?"

Marc Sully had been a member of the *police aux frontières* for four years, and sat through hundreds of briefings just like this one. Every year Pagnol's face got a little redder, his collar a little tighter. Not that Sully was anyone to talk. He himself had always a little weight on him, wasn't ashamed of it. Bit his nails to the quick, too, had given up trying to stop. The boss once told him he looked "sloppy," but when Marc asked him how, he just shrugged. So nobody was going to put him on a recruitment poster.

Marc knew he wasn't popular with some of his younger colleagues, the ones who bathed every single day, afraid of smelling like a human being instead of a walking bar of deodorant soap. They'd walk around with their quiffs of freshly shampooed hair, smiling nicely at the prettier female passengers, as if they were going to find dates on the job. Marc thought they were fools. It was a dead-end job. Giving strip searches might be a way to get a sniff, especially if you were into third-world *cul*, but you weren't going to bring anybody home that way.

"Now two advisories fresh from *la DCPAF*." The *Direction centrale de la police aux frontière* was the national bureau that gave them their orders. Pagnol pressed a few switches, and was able to project photographs directly from a computer. "Highest priority. This one's an American. Mexican ancestry. She's a professional. You find her, you be very careful. Treat her like a scorpion, right?"

Grunts of assent.

Sully squinted at the images. He wouldn't mind giving her a taste of his baguette.

"And here's another one," the security director said. "White male in his mid-thirties. Curly brown hair, green or hazel eyes, approximately one and three-quarters meters in height. Possible serial killer. Another American, they think. Very dangerous. There's reason to believe he's been in the country today, and that he'll be trying to make his way out. We'll be posting photographs at your stations, but I want you to take a careful look right now. If it turns out that they left through Lille-Lesquin and that the people here let them slip through, it won't just be *my* job on the line. Everybody understand?"

Sully nodded with everyone else. It annoyed Sully that Roux, that apple-cheeked hard-on, was still riding high for having lucked out with that *Gastarbeiter* whore. But who knew? Maybe it was Sully's day to get lucky. He took another look at the photographs.

Ben dropped off Anna by an airport shuttle bus stop, and deposited the blue Renault at the long-term parking lot at the *aéroport* Lille-Lesquin. They'd enter the airport separately, and take different flights.

They agreed to meet in Buenos Aires within ten hours.

Assuming nothing went wrong.

Anna looked at the blond, crew-cut American officer, and felt confident that he'd elude detection. But despite her brave words to Ben, she felt no such confidence herself. Her hair was neither cut nor colored. It was combed out, and she had changed her garb, but otherwise she was entrusting her camouflage to something very small indeed. She felt a knot of fear in the pit of her stomach, and the fear fed on itself, for she knew nothing would betray her faster than the appearance of fear. She had to focus. Her usual hyperattentiveness to her surroundings could now be her undoing. Before she stepped into the terminal, she had to let every bit of fear and anxiety wash from her. She imagined herself traipsing through meadows filled with Bermuda grass and dandelions. She imagined holding hands with somebody constant and strong. It could be anybody—it was simply a mental exercise, as she was perfectly aware—but the person she kept imagining was Ben.

Sully kept a sharp eye out at the incoming passengers by his station, alert for signs of anxiety or agitation, for customers traveling with too few bags or too many, for customers who fit the description they'd received from *DCPAF.*

The man, third from the front of the line, caught his attention. He was the approximate height of the man they were looking for, had curly brown hair, and kept jingling the change in his pocket, a nervous tic. From his dress, he was almost certainly an American. Perhaps he had reason to be nervous.

He waited until the man showed his ticket and passport to the airline security officer, and then stepped forward.

"Just a few questions, sir," Sully said, his eyes boring in on him.

"Yeah, all right," the man said.

"Come with me," Sully said, and drew him to a station post near the ticket counter. "So what took you to France?"

"Medical conference."

"You're a doctor?"

A sigh. "I work in sales for a pharmaceutical company."

"You're a drug dealer!" Sully smiled, though his eyes remained wary.

"In a matter of speaking," the man replied wanly. He had a look on his face like he'd smelled something bad.

Americans and their obsession with hygiene. Sully scrutinized his face for a moment longer. The man had the same angular cast to his face, square chin, curly hair. But the features didn't look quite right—they were too small. And Sully didn't hear real stress in the man's voice when he answered questions. Sully was wasting his time.

"O.K.," he said. "Have a good trip."

Sully went back to scrutinizing the check-in line. A blond-haired woman with swarthy skin caught his eye. The suspect could have dyed her hair; the other specifics matched. He drifted toward her.

"Could I see your passport, madame," he said.

The woman looked at him blankly.

"*Votre passeport, s'il vous plaît, madame.*"

"*Bien sûr. Vous me croyez être anglaise? Je suis italienne, mais tous mes amis pensent que je suis allemande ou anglaise ou n'importe quoi.*"

According to her passport, she resided in Milan, and Sully thought it unlikely that an American could speak French with such an egregious Italian accent.

No one else on line just then looked terribly promising. A dot-head with two bawling children was ahead of the blond Italian. As far as Sully was concerned, her kind couldn't leave the country fast enough. Chicken vindaloo was going to end up being the national dish at the rate the goddamn dot-heads were immigrating. The Muslims were worse, of course, but the dot-heads with their unpronounceable names were pretty awful. Last year, when he'd dislocated his arm, the Indian doctor at the clinic had flatly refused to give him a real painkiller. Like maybe he was supposed to do some fakir-style mind control. If his arm wasn't half out of its socket, he would have punched the guy.

Sully glanced at the woman's passport without interest and waved her and her sniveling brood through. The dot-head whore even smelled like saffron.

A young Russian with acne. Last name was German, so probably a Jew. *Mafiya?* Not his problem just now.

An honest-to-goodness Frenchman and his wife, off to a vacation.

Another goddamn dot-head in a sari. Gayatri was the name, and then something unpronounceable. Curry *cul.*

None of the other men fit the profile: too old, too fat, too young, too short.

Too bad. Maybe it wasn't going to be his lucky day after all.

————

Anna settled into her coach-class seat, adjusting her sari and mentally repeating her name: Gayatri Chandragupta. It wouldn't do to stumble over it if anyone were to ask. She was wearing her long black hair straight back, and when she'd caught a glimpse of her reflection in a window, she hardly recognized herself.

CHAPTER THIRTY-FOUR

Buenos Aires

Anna looked anxiously through the plate glass of the American Express office at sedate, tree-lined Plaza Libertador General San Martín. The park, once a bull ring, once a slave market, was now dominated by the great bronze statue of General José de San Martín astride his horse. The sun blazed fiercely. Inside it was air-conditioned, ice-cold, and quiet.

"Señorita Acampo?"

She turned to see a slender man in a close-fitting blue blazer, stylish heavy black-framed glasses. "I am very sorry, señorita, but we cannot locate this package."

"I don't understand." She switched to Spanish so there would be no mistake: *"Está registrado que lo recibió?"*

"We received it, yes, madam, but it cannot be found."

Maddening, but this at least was progress. The last employee had adamantly denied a package had ever been received in her name.

"Are you saying it's lost?"

A quick reflexive shrug like a nervous tic. "Our computers show it was sent from Washington, D.C., and received here yesterday, but after that, I cannot say. If you'll fill out this form, we'll begin a search throughout our system. If it's not located, you're entitled to full replacement value."

Damn it! It seemed unlikely to her that the envelope had been lost. More likely it had been stolen. But by whom? And why? Who knew what was inside? Who knew to look? Had Denneen given her up? She could scarcely credit it. Possibly his phone was tapped, unknown to him. In truth, there were too many potential explanations, and none of them changed the basic fact: if it *had* been stolen, whoever had done it now knew who she was—and why she was here.

The office of Interpol Argentina is located within the headquarters of the *Policía Federal Argentina* on Suipacha. Interpol's man in Buenos Aires was Miguel Antonio Peralta, the *Jefe Seccion Operaciónes*. A plaque on his door read SUBCOMISARIO DEPARTAMENTO INTERPOL. He was a round-shouldered, bulky man with a large, round head. Strands of black hair matted across the top of his pate advertised his baldness instead of disguising it.

His wood-veneered office was jammed with tributes to Interpol's work. Plaques and commemorative plates from grateful police forces around the world crowded the walls, along with crucifixes and diplomas and images of saints and a framed apostolic benediction on his family from the Pope himself. An antique silver–framed sepia photograph of his policeman father was almost as prominent.

Peralta's lizard eyes were sleepy behind his perfectly round tortoise-shell glasses. A holstered pistol sat atop his gleaming bare desk, the leather holster old but lovingly cared for. He was genial and flawlessly courteous. "You know we are always eager to help in the cause of justice," he said.

"And as my assistant explained, we at CBS find ourselves in a rather competitive situation right now," Anna said. "The people at *Dateline* are apparently on the verge of locating and exposing this man. If they reach him first, so be it. But I didn't get where I am today by being a pushover. I'm working with an Argentine field producer who thinks we can get the story, with a little assistance from you."

"In Argentina, football—soccer, I think you say—is our national sport. I gather network TV plays that role in the States."

"You could say that." Anna rewarded him with a wide smile, and crossed her legs. "And I'm not at all putting down my colleagues at *Dateline*. But we both know what sort of story they'll do, because it'll be the same old tune. Argentina as a backward country that harbors these bad, bad people. They'll do something very exploitative, very cheap. We're not like that. What we have in mind is much more sophisticated and I think much more accurate. We want to capture the *new* Argentina. A place where people like yourself have been seeing that justice is done. A place with modern law enforcement, yet respect for democracy"—she wiggled a hand vaguely—"and like that." Another wide smile. "And certainly your efforts would be handsomely compensated with a consultant's fee. So, Mr. Peralta. Can we work together?"

Peralta's smile was thin. "Certainly if you have proof that Josef Strasser is living in Buenos Aires, you must only to tell me. Produce the evidence." He jabbed the air with a silver Cross pen to emphasize how simple it all was. "That is all."

"Mr. Peralta. Someone is going to do this story, whether it's my team or the competition." Anna's smile faded. "The only question is how the story will be done. Whether it's a story of one of your successes, or one of your failures. Come on, you must have a file of leads on Strasser— some sort of indication that he's here," Anna said. "I mean, you don't *doubt* he's living in Buenos Aires, do you?"

Peralta leaned back in his chair, which squeaked. "Ms. Reyes," he said, his tone that of a man with a delicious piece of gossip to impart, "a few years ago my office received a credible tip from a woman living in Belgrano, one of our wealthiest suburbs. She had seen Alois Brunner, the SS *Hauptsturmführer*, on the street, coming out of a neighboring house. Immediately we have a round-the-clock surveillance on this man's house. Indeed she was correct, the old man's face matched our file photos of Brunner. We moved in on the gentleman. Indignant, he produced his old German passport, you know, imprinted with the eagles of the Third Reich—and a big J, for Jew. The man's name was Katz." Peralta came forward in his chair until he was upright again. "So how do you apologize to a man like this, who had been in the camps?"

"Yes," Anna agreed equably, "that must have been terribly embarrassing. But our intelligence on Strasser is solid. *Dateline* is filming their second-unit footage—background shots—even as we speak. They must be very confident."

"*Dateline, 60 Minutes, 20/20*—I am familiar with these investigative programs. If you people were so very sure Josef Strasser was, as you Americans like to say, alive and living in Argentina, you would have found him long ago, no?" His lizard eyes were fixed on her.

She could not tell him the truth—that her interest was not in his Nazi past, but in what he may have been involved in when he parted company with his Führer, and joined forces with the invisible architects of the postwar era. "Then where would you suggest I begin looking?"

"Impossible to answer! If we knew there was a war criminal living here, we would arrest him. But I must tell you, there *are* no more." He dropped his pen onto his desk definitively.

"Really." She made some meaningless marks on her yellow pad.

"Times have changed in Argentina. The bad old days, when a Josef Mengele could live openly here, under his own name, they are gone. The days of the Perón dictatorship are over. Now Argentina is a democracy. Josef Schwammberger was extradited. Erich Priebke was extradited. I cannot even recall the last time we arrested a Nazi here."

She crossed out her doodle with a slash of her pen. "What about immigration records? Records of people who entered the country in the forties and fifties?"

He frowned. "Maybe there are records of entries, arrivals. The National Registry, the Migrations Department—it is index cards, everything entered by hand. But our coastline is thousands of kilometers long. Who knows how many tugboats and rowboats and fishing trawlers landed decades ago at one of the hundreds of *estancias*—the ranches—and were never detected? Hundreds of kilometers of coastline in Patagonia, no one is there to see."

He again jabbed the air. "And then in 1949, Perón issued a blanket amnesty for anyone who had entered the country under a false name. So it is unlikely there will be any immigration record of Josef Strasser even if he really is here. Maybe you can go down to Bariloche, the ski resort, and ask around. The Germans love Bariloche. It reminds them of their beloved Bavaria. But I would not hold out much hope. I am terribly sorry to disappoint you."

Anna Navarro was not gone from Miguel Antonio Peralta's office two minutes before the Interpol man picked up his telephone. "Mauricio," he said. "I've just had a most interesting visitor."

In a modern office building in Vienna, a bland-looking middle-aged man watched without interest as the plasterboard walls that had enclosed a carpeted "reception area" and "conference room" were dismantled and wheeled away toward a freight elevator by a team of construction workers. Next came a Formica conference table, a plain metal desk, and assorted office equipment including a dummy telephone system and a working computer.

The bespectacled man was an American who for the last decade or so had been engaged to perform a variety of services around the world, the significance of which was invariably obscure to him. He had never even met the company's chief, had no idea who he was. All he knew was that the mysterious head of the firm was a business associate of this building's owner, who'd been happy to lend use of the eleventh floor.

It was like watching a stage set being struck. "Hey," called out the bespectacled American, "someone's gotta take down the sign in the lobby. And leave that U.S. seal with me, will ya? We might need it again."

New York

Dr. Walter Reisinger, the former Secretary of State, took the call in the back of his limousine as it inched through morning rush-hour traffic on Manhattan's East Side.

Dr. Reisinger disliked the telephone, which was unfortunate, since these days he spent virtually every waking moment on the phone. His international consulting firm, Reisinger Associates, was keeping him even busier than his days at State.

Secretly he had been afraid that, after retiring from the government and writing his memoirs, he'd be gradually marginalized, treated as an éminence grise, invited to appear on *Nightline* once in a while, and to write the occasional thumb-sucker for the *New York Times* Op-Ed page.

Instead, he had become more famous, and certainly far richer. He found himself globe-hopping more now than during his shuttle-diplomacy days in the Middle East.

He pressed the speaker button. "Yes?"

"Dr. Reisinger," said the voice on the other end of the phone, "this is Mr. Holland."

"Ah, good morning, Mr. Holland," Reisinger said jovially. The two men chatted for a minute or so, and then Reisinger said, "This shouldn't be a problem. I have good friends in just about every government in the world—but I think the most direct route would be to go right to Interpol. Do you know its Secretary-General? A most interesting man. Let me give him a call."

Patient Eighteen lay on a hospital bed with his eyes closed, an IV feeding tube in his left arm. He was shaking, as he had done constantly since the treatments began. He was also nauseated, and periodically retched into a bedpan placed beside the bed. A nurse and a technician stood watch nearby.

A doctor, whose name was Löfquist, came into the examination room and went up to the nurse. "How is the fever?" he asked. They spoke in English, because his English was still better than his German, even after working here in the clinic for seven years.

"It hasn't broken," the nurse replied tensely.

"And the nausea?"

"He's been vomiting regularly."

Dr. Löfquist raised his voice to address Patient Eighteen. "How're you feeling?"

The patient moaned. "My goddamned *eyes* hurt."

"Yes, that's normal," Dr. Löfquist said. "Your body is trying to fight it off. We see this all the time."

Patient Eighteen gagged, leaned over to the bedpan, and was sick. The nurse wiped his mouth and chin with a damp washcloth.

"The first week is always the most difficult," Dr. Löfquist said cheerily. "You're doing wonderfully well."

CHAPTER THIRTY-FIVE

Our Lady of Mercy, Nuestra Señora de la Merced, was an Italianate basilica perched on the swarming Calle Defensa, across from a disconcertingly contemporary branch office of the Banco de Galicia. The church's granite facade was crumbling. A wrought-iron fence enclosed a forecourt paved with worn and cracked black-and-white harlequin stone tiles, where a Gypsy mother and her brood begged for alms.

Ben watched the mother in her jeans, black hair tied back, sitting on the steps against the ruins of a column's pedestal, kids spilling out of her lap and at her feet. Deeper into the courtyard an old man in coat and tie dozed, one arm locked in a crutch, the top of his bald pate tanned.

At one-fifteen exactly, as instructed, Ben entered the church's foyer, and walked through swinging wooden doors into the loamy darkness of the narthex, which smelled of beeswax candles and sweat. The interior, once his eyes accustomed to the dark, was immense, daunting, and shabby. The Romanesque ceilings were high and vaulted, the floor paved with ancient encaustic tiles, beautifully inlaid. A priest's singsong Latin chant, electronically amplified, echoed in the cavern, and the congregants responded dutifully. Call and response. All rise.

One o'clock weekday Mass and it was, impressively, almost half full. *But then Argentina is a Catholic country*, Ben thought. Here and there the trilling of cell phones. He oriented himself, spotted the chapel on the right.

A few rows of benches were arrayed before a glassed-in tabernacle containing the bloodied figure of Christ and bearing the words HUMILIDAD Y PACIENCIA. To its left, another statue of Jesus, this one in the open, beneath the words SAGRADO CORAZÓN EN VOS CONFIO. Ben sat on the front bench, also as instructed, and waited.

A priest in his vestments sat praying by a bottle-blond young woman in miniskirt and high heels. The swinging doors squeaked and slammed, and when they opened, the throaty blare of a motorcycle intruded. Each time Ben turned to look: Which one was it? A businessman with a cell phone entered the narthex, crossed himself, then turned into the alcove—was it him?—but then touched the figure of Jesus, closed his eyes, and prayed. More unison chanting, more electronically amplified Latin, and still Ben waited.

He was afraid but determined not to show it.

A few hours earlier he'd dialed a number he'd pilfered from Sonnenfeld's files, one that had, so it appeared, once belonged to Lenz's widow.

It still did.

The woman obviously wasn't in hiding, but she hadn't come to the phone herself. A brusque, hostile baritone answered: her son, he'd said. Lenz's brother? Half brother?

Ben had identified himself as a trusts-and-estates lawyer from New York, come to Buenos Aires to settle a huge bequest. No, he could not identify the deceased. He would only say that Vera Lenz had been left a good deal of money, but he would first have to meet with her.

A long silence ensued while the son decided what to do. Ben interjected one more piece of irrelevant-seeming information, which probably turned out to be the deciding one. "I've just come from Austria," he said. No names, no mention of her son—nothing specific to hang on to or object to. Less said the better.

"I don't know you," the son at last replied.

"Nor I you," Ben came back smoothly. "If this is inconvenient for you or for your mother . . ."

"No," he said hastily. He would meet Ben—"Mr. Johnson"—at a church, in a certain chapel, a certain bench.

Now he sat with his back to the entrance, turning with each squeak of the doors, each gust of noise from the outside.

Half an hour went by.

Was this a setup? The priest looked at him, wordlessly offered a couple of beeswax candles to light. "No, thanks," Ben said, turning back to the door.

A group of tourists with cameras and green guides. He turned back to Jesus in his display case and saw the priest move close to him. He was swarthy, tall, and strong-looking, fiftyish, balding, barrel-chested.

He spoke to Ben in a hushed baritone. "Come with me, Mr. Johnson."

Ben rose, followed him out of the chapel and down the nave, then a sharp right across an empty row to a narrow passage that ran parallel to the nave, along a stone wall, until they were almost at the apse.

A small, almost concealed wooden door. The priest opened it. The room was pitch-black, dank and musty. The priest flicked a switch and a wan yellow light illuminated what appeared to be a dressing room. A coatrack with priestly garb. A few scuffed wooden chairs.

The priest was pointing a gun.

Ben felt a jolt of fear.

"Do you have anything on you?" the priest asked with unexpected courtesy. "Weapon of any kind, any electronic devices?"

Fear gave way to anger. "Just my cell phone, if you consider that a deadly weapon."

"May I have it, please?"

Ben handed it over. The priest ran his free hand down the front and back of Ben's suit jacket, beneath the shoulders, at the waist, the legs and ankles. A swift and expert frisking. He then examined the cell phone carefully and returned it to Ben.

"I need to see your passport, some form of identification."

Ben produced his Michael Johnson passport and slipped out a business card as well. Earlier in the morning he had taken the precaution of stopping at a printing-and-copy shop on Avenue 9 de Julio and ordering fifty of them, surcharge for rush. An hour later he had plausible-looking cards for Michael Johnson, partner in a fictional Manhattan law firm.

The priest examined it.

"Look," Ben said, summoning high dudgeon, "I really don't have time for this. And put the damn gun away."

Ignoring his request, the priest indicated the exit. "This way."

He pulled the door open to the dazzling sun, a tiny courtyard, and the sliding side doors of a windowless black van.

"Please." A wave of the gun barrel. He meant: into the van.

"Sorry," Ben said. So this was the widow's son? He could scarcely credit it: he didn't look anything like Jürgen, who would have to be his half brother at least. "Nothing doing."

The priest's eyes blazed. "Then you are, of course, free to go. But if you wish to see my mother you must go my way." His tone softened. "You see, people still come to Buenos Aires to talk to her. Journalists sometimes, but sometimes also bounty hunters, crazy people with guns.

Maybe agents from the Mossad. They used to threaten her to make her
tell where is Lenz. For a long time people did not believe he was dead.
Like with Mengele, they thought he made a trick. Now I will not let her
see anyone she does not know unless I clear it."

"You say 'Lenz'—he's not your father?"

A scowl. "My father married Lenz's widow. But she has outlived both
husbands. A strong woman. I take care of her. Please, get in."

Everything is a chance. He had not come this far to back out now. This
man could finally lead him to the truth. After studying the enigmatic
priest for a moment, he climbed into the back of the van.

The priest slid the doors closed with the rumble of thunder. Now the
only illumination came from a dim roof light. Except for pull-down seats
the van was entirely empty.

Everything is a chance.

Ben wondered: *What have I done?*

The engine started up, then protested all the way into first gear.

This is how they execute people, Ben thought. *I don't know this man,
genuine priest or not. Maybe he's from one of those groups Sonnenfeld
mentioned who defend and protect the old Nazis.*

After some twenty minutes, the van came to a halt. Its doors slid open,
revealing a cobblestone street in dappled light that filtered through a
canopy of trees. The length of the journey told him they were still in
Buenos Aires, but the street looked entirely different from the city he
had seen so far. It was serene and quiet but for birdsong. And, just barely
audible, piano music.

No, I'm not about to be killed.

He wondered what Anna would think. No doubt she'd be appalled at
the risk he'd taken. And she'd be right.

They were parked in front of a two-story brick house with a roof of
barrel tiles, not particularly large, but graceful. Wooden shutters on all
the windows were closed. The piano music seemed to be coming from
within the house, a Mozart sonata. A tall, serpentine wrought-iron fence
enclosed the house and its small patch of yard.

The priest took Ben by the elbow and helped him out of the van.
Either his gun was now concealed or, less likely, it had been left in the
van. At the front gate he keyed a code into a number pad, unlocking the
gate with an electrical buzz.

Inside, the house was cool and dark. The Mozart recording was coming

from a room straight ahead. A note was bungled, the passage begun
again, and Ben realized that this was no recording; someone was playing
the piano with great skill. The old woman?

He followed the priest into the room from which the piano music
emanated. It was a small sitting room, book-lined, Oriental carpets on
the floor. A tiny, birdlike old woman was hunched over a Steinway grand.
She did not seem to notice when they entered. They sat down on a
coarse, uncomfortable couch and waited in silence.

When the piece was finished, she kept her hands frozen in the air,
poised over the keys, then brought them slowly to her lap. The affecta-
tions of a concert pianist. Slowly she turned. Her face was prune-like,
her eyes sunken, her neck crepey. She had to be ninety.

Ben clapped a few times.

She spoke in a quavering, hoarse small voice. *"¿Quién es éste?"*

"Mother, this is Mr. Johnson," the priest said. "Mr. Johnson, my stepmother."

Ben went over to her and took her fragile hand.

The priest continued, to Ben, "And I am Francisco."

"Póngame en una silla cómoda," the old woman said.

Francisco put an arm around his stepmother and helped her into a
chair. She said in decent English, "You come from Austria?"

"I was just in Vienna, yes."

"Why have you come?"

Ben began to speak, but she interrupted, fearful, "You are from the
company?"

The *company?* Did she mean Sigma? If so, he had to make her talk.
"Frau . . . Frau Lenz, I'm afraid I've come here under false pretenses."

Francisco swiveled his head toward Ben, furious. "I'll kill you!"

"You see, Jürgen Lenz asked me to see you," Ben said, ignoring him.
He offered no explanation. Mention Austria, suggest that he had gained
the trust of Jürgen Lenz. If pressed, he would improvise. He was getting
good at that. "He asked me to meet with you and warn you to be especially careful, to tell you that your life may be in danger."

"I am *not* Frau Lenz," she said haughtily. "I have not been Lenz for
over thirty years. I am Señora Acosta."

"My apologies, señora."

But the old woman's hauteur had given way to fear. "Why does Lenz
send you? What does he want?"

"Señora Acosta," Ben began, "I've been asked—"

"Why?" she asked, raising her quavering voice. "*Why?* You come here from Semmering? We've done nothing wrong! We've done nothing to break the agreement! Leave us alone!"

"*No! Silence*, Mother!" the priest shouted.

What was she referring to? *The agreement* . . . Was *this* what Peter had stumbled on to?

"Señor Acosta, your son specifically asked me—"

"My son?" the old woman rasped.

"That's right."

"You say my son in *Vienna?*"

"Yes. Your son Jürgen."

The priest rose. "Who are you?" he asked.

"Tell him, Francisco," the old woman said. "Francisco is my *step*son. From my second marriage. I never had any children." Her face was contorted with fear. "*I have no son.*"

The priest loomed menacingly over Ben. "You're a liar," he snapped. "You say you're a lawyer for an estate, and now you lie to us again!"

Head reeling, Ben attempted a quick recovery. "You have no son? Then I'm glad I'm here. Now I see I haven't wasted my time, or my firm's money, in coming down here to Buenos Aires."

The priest glowered. "Who sent you here?"

"He is not from the company!" his stepmother croaked.

"This is exactly the sort of fraud I need to clear up," Ben said, feigning a sense of triumph. "So this Jürgen Lenz of Vienna—he says he is your son, but he is *not* your son? *Then who is he?*"

The priest turned to his stepmother, who looked as if she were about to speak. "Say nothing!" he ordered. "Do *not* answer him!"

"I cannot talk about him!" the old woman said. To her stepson, she added, "Why does he ask me about Lenz? Why do you invite him here?"

"He is a liar, an impostor!" the priest said. "Vienna would send word ahead first before sending a messenger!" He reached behind him and produced his revolver, aiming it directly at Ben's forehead.

"What kind of a priest are you?" Ben asked in a hush. *Not a priest. A priest would not put a gun to my head.*

"I'm a man of God who protects my family. Now leave here at once."

A sudden thought occurred to Ben, the obvious explanation, and he said to the old woman, "Your husband had another family. A son with another wife."

"You're not welcome in this house," the priest said with a wave of his weapon. "Out."

"*Gerhard Lenz had no children!*" the old woman cried.

"*Silence!*" the priest thundered. "*Enough!* Say nothing more!"

"He pretends to be the son of Gerhard Lenz," Ben said, half to himself. "Why in the world would he pretend to be the son of . . . a monster?"

"Stand up!" the priest commanded.

"Gerhard Lenz didn't die here, did he?" Ben said.

"What are you *saying?*" the stepmother gasped.

"If you don't get out of here, I'll kill you," the priest said.

Ben rose obediently, but looked at the old woman, sunk deep within her easy chair. "The rumors were true, then," he said. "Gerhard Lenz wasn't buried in Chacarita cemetery in 1961, was he? He escaped from Buenos Aires, evaded his pursuers—"

"He died *here!*" the old woman said frantically. "There was a funeral! I myself flung dirt on his coffin!"

"But you never saw his body, did you?" Ben said.

"*Out!*" the priest barked.

"Why is he saying these things to me?" she cried.

She was interrupted by the ring of the telephone on a sideboard behind the priest. Without moving his revolver he reached to his right and snatched up the receiver. "*Sí?*"

He seemed to be listening intently. Ben took advantage of the priest's momentary inattention to sidle ever so subtly in the priest's direction. "I need to reach Josef Strasser," he said to the old woman.

She spat out her reply, "If you're really sent from Austria, you *know* how to reach him. You're a *liar!*"

Then Strasser *was* alive!

Ben inched closer to the priest and continued talking to the stepmother. "I myself was lied to—set up!" There was in fact no logic in what he said, not without a fuller explanation, but he wanted only to confuse the old woman, rattle her further.

"That confirms it," the priest said, hanging up the phone. "That was Vienna. This man's a fraud." He looked at Ben. "You lied to us, Mr. *Hartman!*" he said, glancing behind him for an instant, and Ben immediately lunged. He grabbed the priest's right wrist, the one holding the gun, twisting it with all his strength, and at the same time slammed his other hand into the priest's throat, forefinger and thumb in a rigid V. The old woman screamed with terror. Caught by surprise, the priest cried out in pain. The revolver fell from his hand and clattered to the floor.

With one immense movement Ben forced the priest to the floor, closing his grip around the priest's neck. He could feel the bony cartilage of the larynx shift to one side. The man's cry grew strangled as he sprawled against the tiled floor, his head at an unnatural angle, trying to rear up, trying to reach his free, left hand around, but it was vised beneath his rib cage. He struggled with great strength, gasping for breath. The old woman flung the backs of her hands against her face in a strange protective gesture.

The gun! Must get the gun!

Ben jammed his left hand more forcefully into the man's throat, and thrust a knee into his stomach, aiming for the solar plexus. The priest's sudden, involuntary exhalation of breath told Ben that he'd hit the mark. The priest's dark eyes rolled upward so that only the whites were showing. He was momentarily paralyzed by the blow. Ben snatched the revolver from the floor, swung it around, and shoved it against the man's forehead.

He cocked the trigger. "Make a move, and you're dead!"

Immediately the priest's body fell slack. "No!" he choked out.

"Answer my questions! Tell the truth if you want to live!"

"Don't, please don't! I'm a man of God."

"Right," Ben snapped disdainfully. "How do I reach Josef Strasser?"

"He is—I don't know—*please*—my *throat!*"

Ben eased the pressure a bit, enough to allow him to breathe and to speak. "*Where's Strasser?*" he thundered.

The priest gulped air. "Strasser—I don't know how to reach Strasser— he lives in Buenos Aires, that's all I know!" A small rivulet of urine appeared on the floor between the man's legs.

"Bullshit!" Ben shouted. "You give me an address or a phone number, or your stepmother will have *no one* to take care of her!"

"No, please!" the old widow said, still cowering in her chair.

"If—if you kill me," the priest gasped, "you won't get out of Buenos Aires alive! They'll track you down—they'll do things—you'll wish—*wish* you were dead!"

"Strasser's *address!*"

"I don't have it!" the priest said. "Please! I have no way to reach Strasser!"

"Don't lie," Ben said. "You all know each other. You are all tied together in a network. If you had to reach Strasser you have ways."

"I'm nothing! You kill me, I'm nothing to them! They'll find you!"

Ben wondered, who were "they"? Instead, he asked: "Who's Jürgen Lenz?" He pressed the barrel of the gun against the priest's forehead. There were a few drops of blood; he had broken the skin.

"He—please, he's powerful, he controls—he owns her house, her property, the man who calls himself Jürgen Lenz—"

"Then who is he really?"

"Put the gun down and get away from him."

The voice—low, calm, Spanish-accented—came from the doorway behind Ben. A tall man stood there holding a sawed-off shotgun. He was dressed in heavy green slacks and a denim work shirt, and he looked to be in his late twenties or early thirties, broad-chested and powerful.

"Roberto, help!" the widow cried. "Save my Francisco! Get this man out of here at once!"

"Señora, should I kill this intruder?" Roberto asked.

The man's demeanor told Ben he would fire without remorse. Ben hesitated, unsure what to do. The priest was a hostage, with the revolver to his forehead, yet Ben knew he could not bring himself to pull the trigger. And even if he did, the man with the sawed-off shotgun would kill him in the blink of an eye.

But I can still bluff, he realized.

"Roberto!" the old woman croaked. "Now!"

"Put the gun down or I'll fire," said the young man. "I don't care what happens to this scumbag." He indicated the priest.

"Yes, but the señora does," Ben said. "We will lower our weapons at the same time."

"All right," the young man agreed. "Take the weapon away from his head, stand up, and get out of here. If you want to live." He lowered the shotgun's barrel, pointing it toward the floor, as Ben pulled the revolver away from the priest's forehead. He got up slowly, the gun still lowered.

"Now move toward the door," the man said.

Ben backed away, his right hand gripping the revolver, his left patting the air behind him, feeling for obstacles as he moved. The young man moved with him into the hall, his rifle still lowered.

"I just want you out of this house," the man said calmly. "If you ever come near this house again, you'll be killed on sight." The priest had sullenly raised himself to a sitting position, looking drained and humiliated. Ben backed out of the open door—either the priest had left it open or Roberto had entered this way—and then pulled it shut.

In a few seconds he was running.

Anna paid the cabdriver and entered the small hotel, located on a quiet street in the district of Buenos Aires called La Recoleta. It was not, she thought uneasily, the sort of place where a single young woman traveling alone would easily go unnoticed.

The concierge greeted her by name, which disturbed her. Earlier in the day she and Ben had checked in, separately and several hours apart. They'd also called in their reservations separately and at different times. Staying in the same hotel made logistical sense, but it also increased certain risks.

The chambermaid's cart was parked outside her room. Inconvenient. She wanted to be alone, go over the files, make phone calls; now she'd have to wait. As she entered she saw the maid, hunched over her open suitcase.

Taking files out of Anna's leather portfolio.

Anna stopped abruptly. The maid looked up, saw Anna, and dropped the files and portfolio back into the suitcase.

"What the hell are you doing?" Anna said, advancing on her.

The maid protested indignantly in Spanish, a mix of haughty denials. Anna followed her out into the hall, demanding to know what she was doing. *"Eh, ¿qué haces? ¡Ven para acá! ¿Qué cuernos haces revisando mi valija?"*

Anna tried to read the woman's name tag, but the woman suddenly bolted, running down the corridor at top speed.

The maid hadn't been just pilfering. *She had been going through Anna's papers.* Whether she read English or not was beside the point; most likely she had been hired to steal any documents, papers, files, notes.

But hired by whom?

Who could possibly know Anna was here, or what she was investigating? She was being watched—but by whom?

Who knows I'm here? Denneen, yes, but had he told someone, some associate?

Had Peralta, the Interpol representative, figured out who she was? Was that possible?

Just as she reached for the bedside phone, it rang. The manager, calling to apologize? Or Ben?

She picked it up. "Hello?"

There was only dead air. No, not dead air: it was the familiar hiss of a surveillance tape. Then the sounds of faint, indistinct voices, becoming sharper, amplified.

A surge of adrenaline. "Who is this?"

She made out a voice: *"What about immigration records? Records of people who entered the country in the forties and fifties?"* It was her own voice. Then the voice of a male interlocutor. Peralta.

On the telephone, someone was playing back a tape recording of the conversation between Peralta and herself.

They had heard everything, and they—whoever "they" were—knew precisely where she was and what she was after.

She sat on the edge of the bed, stunned and terrified. Now there could be no question her presence was known, despite all the precautions. The pilfering maid was no isolated player.

The phone rang again.

Prickly all over with terror, she snatched up the receiver. "Yes?"

"We want to capture the new Argentina. A place where people like yourself have been seeing that justice is done. A place with modern law enforcement, yet respect for democracy . . ." Her own voice, tinnily but crisply rendered through whatever eavesdropping equipment had been in place.

A click.

In her haste, she had left the room door open; she ran to close it. No one was in the corridor. She shut the door, double-locked it, seated the slide bolt of the safety chain in its socket.

She ran to the window, its heavy drapes open, realizing she was exposed, a target for a shooter stationed in a window of any of the tall buildings across the street. She yanked the drapes closed to block the line of sight.

The phone rang again.

She walked to it slowly, put the handset to her ear, said nothing.

"I didn't get to be where I am today by being a pushover..."

"Keep calling," she finally forced herself to say into the phone, feigning calm. "We're tracing the calls."

But no one was listening. There was only the dull hiss of a surveillance recording.

She depressed the phone's plunger and, before it could ring again, called down to the front desk. "I've been getting obscene calls," she said in English.

"Obscene...?" the switchboard operator repeated, not comprehending.

"Amenazas," she said. *"Palabrotas."*

"Oh, I'm very sorry, señorita, would you like me to call the police?"

"I want you to hold all calls."

"Yes, ma'am, certainly."

She brooded for a minute, then retrieved a slip of paper from her purse, torn from a notepad in the Schiphol departure lounge. On it she had scrawled the phone number of a local private investigator that Denneen had recommended. Someone reliable, highly skilled, well connected with the authorities, but entirely honest, Denneen had assured her.

She punched out the number, let it ring and ring.

An answering machine came on. Sergio Machado identified himself and his agency. After the beep, she left her name and number, mentioned Denneen's name. Then she called the hotel switchboard operator again and told her she would accept a call only from a Sergio Machado.

She needed someone knowledgeable and resourceful and most of all trustworthy. You couldn't hope to get anywhere, learn anything, without someone like that, unless you had a reliable contact in the governmental bureaucracy, and that she did not have.

She went to the bathroom, splashed her face at the sink, first cold water, then hot. The telephone rang.

Thickly, in a stupor, she walked to the bedside table.

The phone rang again, then again.

She stood over the phone, stared at it, considered what to do.

She picked it up.

Said nothing, waited.

There was silence.

"Hello?" a male voice said finally. "Is anyone there?"

Quietly, mouth dry, she said: "Yes?"

"Is this Anna Navarro?"

"Who's this?" She tried to keep her tone neutral.

"It's Sergio Machado—you just called me? I went out to get the mail, now I'm returning your call."

Relieved, she sighed, "Oh, God, I'm sorry. I've just been getting a bunch of obscene calls. I thought it might be the caller again."

"What do you mean, obscene calls—like heavy breathing, that sort of thing?"

"No. Nothing like that. It's too complicated to get into."

"You in some kind of trouble?"

"No. Yes. I don't know, probably. Anyway, listen, thanks for calling back. David Denneen thought you might be able to help me."

"Sure, you want to get a cup of coffee? Not like the shit you drink in America. Real coffee."

"Yeah, sure, I'd like that." Already the anxiety was beginning to ebb.

They agreed to meet early that evening in front of a café/restaurant not too far from his office. "I'll do what I can," he said. "I can't promise anything more than that."

"That's good enough for me," she said.

She hung up and stood over the phone for a moment, looking at it as if it were some alien life-form that had invaded the room.

Ben and she would have to change hotels. Perhaps she had been followed from her visit with Peralta. Perhaps she had been followed from the airport. But her location and her mission were known: that was the real message of those calls. She knew better than to take them as anything other than threats.

A knock at the door.

Adrenaline propelled her to a position beside it. The safety chain was securely looped from the slide bolt in the door plate to the doorjamb.

The door could not be opened with just a key.

Could it?

There was no peephole.

"Who is it?" she said.

The voice that replied was male, familiar. She never would have thought she'd be so glad to hear it.

"It's Ben," the voice said.

"Thank God," she muttered.

CHAPTER THIRTY-SIX

He was bedraggled, shirt and tie askew, hair wild.

"What's with the door chain?" he said. "You used to live in East New York, too?"

She stared. "What happened to you?"

After they'd each recounted the events of the last few hours, she said, "We have to get out of here."

"Damn right," Ben said. "There's a hotel downtown, in the *centro*— sort of a fleabag, but supposed to be kind of charming. Run by British expatriates. The Sphinx." He'd bought a South America guide at the airport. He thumbed through it, found the entry. "Here we go. We can either show up or call from the street, on my cell phone. Not from here."

She nodded. "Maybe we should stay in the same room this time. Husband and wife."

"You're the expert," he said. Was there a glint of amusement in his eyes?

She explained: "They're going to call around looking for an American man and woman traveling together but staying in separate rooms. How long do you think it'll take them to locate us?"

"You're probably right. Listen—I have something." He produced a folded sheet of paper from his inside jacket pocket.

"What's that?"

"A fax."

"From?"

"My researcher in New York. It's the names of the board of directors of Armakon AG of Vienna. Owners of that little biotech startup in Philadelphia that made the poison that killed the old men."

He handed it to her. "Jürgen Lenz," she breathed.

"One of the directors. Is that an intriguing coincidence or what?"

Once again, Arliss Dupree returned to the paperwork in front of him and once again he found it impossible to focus. It was a long report prepared by the deputy director of the Executive Officer for U.S. Trustees, which oversees bankruptcy estates; the report detailed allegations of corruption involving the federal bankruptcy courts. Dupree read the same sentence three times before he set it aside and got himself another cup of the near-rancid coffee produced by the sputtering machine down the hall.

He had other things on his mind—that was the trouble. The developments involving Agent Navarro were annoying. Worse than annoying. They spelled major aggravation. He didn't give a damn what happened to her. But if she'd been guilty of security breaches, it reflected badly on him. Which was totally unfair. And he couldn't help thinking that it all started with that goddamn liver-spotted spook at the Internal Compliance Unit, Alan Bartlett. Whatever the hell *that* was about. Several times he'd made inquiries—proper, interdepartmental inquiries—and each time he had been rebuffed. As if he had some lowly custodial capacity at the Office of Special Investigations. As if the OSI itself weren't worthy of a civil word. Whenever Dupree thought about it for too long, he had to loosen his tie. It was *galling*.

First that bitch Navarro was cherry-picked from his team to go gallivanting off God only knew where. Next thing, word came down that she was rotten, had been selling off information to traffickers and hostiles and whoever else. If so, she was Typhoid Mary, which—he kept coming back to it—was bad news for the person she'd reported to, namely, Arliss Dupree. If Dupree had any sense of which way the wind was blowing— and his career was based on his having that sense—a shit storm was coming his way.

And he was damned if his career was going to be dented by Navarro's misconduct or—since the charges mostly sounded like bullshit to him— by Bartlett's double-dealing. Dupree was, above all, a survivor.

Sometimes surviving meant that you took the bull by the goddamn horns. Dupree had friends of his own—friends who would tell him stuff he needed to know. And maybe paying a visit on the Ghost might help concentrate the old guy's mind. Bartlett looked like a goddamned vapor trail, but he was a major power in the department, a mini J. Edgar Hoover. Dupree would have to deal with him carefully. Even so, Bartlett had to learn that Dupree wasn't somebody to mess with. The Ghost spent his days directing investigations into his colleagues; when was the last time anybody looked into what *he* was up to?

Dupree tore open a couple of envelopes of sugar and dumped it into his coffee. It still tasted foul, but he slurped it down anyway. He had a lot of work ahead of him. With any luck at all, Alan Bartlett would be getting a dose of his own medicine.

The rooms at the Sphinx were large and light-filled. There was one double bed, which they each glanced at warily, deferring any decisions on sleeping arrangements until later.

"What I still don't understand," she said, "is how anyone knew I was here and *why*."

"The Interpol man—"

"Except that I saw him *after* the package was stolen from American Express." She was standing by the tall windows, fiddling with the sheer, gauzy curtains. "Once the package was stolen, the bad guys knew I was looking for Strasser. Question is, how did anyone even know to take it? You didn't tell anyone you were traveling to Buenos Aires with me, right?"

He didn't like her implication, but he ignored it. "No. But did you make any phone calls from the hotel?"

She was silent a moment. "Yeah, I did. One to Washington."

"Not hard to tap hotel phones if you have the proper contacts, right?"

She looked at him, visibly impressed. "That might also explain the fake CIA man. Yes. Did you give Jürgen Lenz any indication—"

"I never told Lenz I was even thinking of going to Buenos Aires, because at that point I *wasn't*."

"I wish there was a way to get Lenz's fingerprints, run 'em through a bunch of databases, see what we turn up. Maybe there's even a criminal record. Did he give you anything—a business card, anything?"

"Nothing, as far as I can recall—well, actually, I gave him the photograph to look at, the one I got from Peter's bank vault in Zurich."

"How many people have you shown it to?"

"You. A historian at the University of Zurich. Liesl. And Lenz. That's all."

"He handled it?"

"Oh yeah. Front and back, turned it over. His fingers were all over it."

"Great, I'll have a copy made and send the original off to AFIS."

"How? I get the impression your DOJ privileges have been revoked."

"But Denneen's haven't. If I can get it to him, he can pass it along to a friend in another agency, probably FBI. He'll figure it out."

He hesitated. "Well, if it enables us to get something on Lenz. Or to find Peter's killers . . ."

"Excellent. Thank you." She glanced at her watch. "Let's continue this over supper. We're meeting this detective, Sergio whatever, in a part of the city called La Boca. We can grab something to eat there."

The cabdriver was a middle-aged woman with flabby arms, wearing a tank top. On the dashboard was a framed color photo of a child, presumably her own. A tiny leather moccasin dangled from the rearview mirror.

"A gun-toting priest," Anna mused. "And I thought the Dominican nuns in church were scary." She'd changed into a gray pleated skirt and white blouse, a pearl choker around her swan neck, and smelled of something floral and crisp. "He told you that Jürgen Lenz actually owns her house?"

"Actually, he used the phrase, 'the man who *calls* himself Jürgen Lenz.' "

They entered a seedy working-class barrio on the southernmost tip of Buenos Aires. On their left was the Riachuelo Canal, a stagnant body of water in which rusting dredges and scows and hulks were half-submerged. Along the waterway were warehouses and meat-packing plants.

"She told you Gerhard Lenz *had* no children?" Anna's brows were knit in concentration. "Am I missing something?"

"Uh-uh. He's Lenz, yet he's *not* Lenz."

"So the man you met in Vienna, who everyone knows as Jürgen Lenz, is an impostor."

"That would be the implication."

"Yet whoever he really is, this old woman and her stepson obviously fear him."

"No question about it."

"But why in the world would Jürgen Lenz pretend to be the son of someone so infamous if he's *not?*" she said. "It makes no sense."

"We're not talking about an Elvis impersonator here, granted. The thing is, we don't really understand much about how succession works at Sigma. Maybe it was his way of gaining a foothold there. Representing himself as the direct descendant of one of the founders—that might have been the only way he could worm his way in."

"That's assuming that Jürgen Lenz is Sigma."

"At this point, it seems safer than assuming the contrary. And, going from what Chardin said, the question with Sigma isn't what they control, but what they *don't* control."

Darkness had settled. They were entering an area that was crowded, ill-lit, dangerous-seeming. The houses here were constructed of sheet metal, with corrugated metal roofs, painted pink and ocher and turquoise.

The cab pulled up in front of a restaurant-bar bustling with rowdy patrons at creaky wooden tables or gathered at the bar, talking and laughing. Prominently displayed behind the bar was a color portrait of Eva Perón. Ceiling fans turned slowly.

They ordered *empanadas* and a San Telmo cabernet sauvignon and a bottle of *agua mineral gaseosa*. The wineglasses had the perspirant smell of old sponge. The napkins were slick squares of deli paper.

"The widow thought you were from 'Semmering,'" Anna said when they were settled. "What do you think she meant—a place? A company?"

"I don't know. A place, I suppose."

"And when she mentioned 'the company'?"

"I took that to be Sigma."

"But there's another company. Jürgen Lenz—whoever he really is—is on the Armakon board."

"How much are you going to trust this Machado guy with what we know?"

"Not at all," she replied. "I simply want him to find Strasser for us."

They finished with a couple of *humitas*, creamy sweet-corn paste in cornhusk packets, and coffee.

"I assume the Interpol guy wasn't much help," Ben said.

"He denied the possibility that Strasser might live here. Highly suspicious. Interpol was controlled by the Nazis for a time, just before the Second World War, and some people think it never really purged itself. It wouldn't surprise me at all if this guy's in the pocket of one of these Nazi protection rackets. Now, your gun-toting priest—"

"My gun-toting priest insisted he had no way to reach Strasser, but I don't believe him."

"I'll bet he got on the phone to Strasser the moment you were out the door."

Ben reflected. "If he called Strasser . . . What if we could somehow get the widow's telephone records?"

"We can ask Machado. He may be able to do it, or know who to reach out to."

"Speaking of reaching out, do you know what this guy looks like?"

"No, but we're meeting him right in front."

The street was crowded and raucous and electric—rock music blaring from speakers set out on sidewalks, an opera's aria, tango music from a nearby cantina. *Porteños* strolled down the cobblestones of the Caminito, a pedestrian thoroughfare, browsing at the stalls of an open-air market. People came in and out of the restaurant, repeatedly colliding with Ben and Anna without apology.

Ben noticed a gaggle of young boys in their late teens or early twenties, a roving gang of eight or more toughs, heading toward him and Anna, talking loudly, laughing, drunk on alcohol and testosterone. Anna muttered something to Ben out of the side of her mouth, something he couldn't quite understand. Several of the guys were staring directly at him and Anna with something more than idle curiosity, and in an instant the gang surrounded them.

"Run!" he shouted, and he was slugged in the stomach by a fist.

He protected his abdomen with both arms, as something slammed into his left kidney—a foot!—and he lunged forward to ward off the attack. He heard Anna scream, but it seemed to come from a great distance. He was blocked, hemmed in; his assailants, though evidently teenagers, seemed to be trained in combat. He couldn't move, and he was being pummeled. In his peripheral vision he could see Anna flinging one of the attackers aside with surprising strength, but then several more grabbed her. Ben tried to break free, but was overwhelmed by a barrage of fists and kicks.

He saw the glint of knife blades, and a knife slashed against his side. A hot line of sensation exploded into vast pain, and he grabbed the hand holding the knife, twisted it hard, and heard a yelp. He kicked at his attackers, slammed wildly with his fists, connecting a few times, and he felt an elbow jabbed into his rib cage, then a knee in his stomach. Breath left him, and he gasped helplessly, then a foot kicked him in the testicles and he doubled over in pain.

He heard the whoop of a siren, and he heard Anna shout, "Over here! Oh, thank God!" A foot kicked him hard on the side of his head, and he could taste blood. He flung his hands out, half protectively, half in an attempt to grab whatever he could, to stop the pummeling; he heard shouting, new voices, and he lurched to his feet to see a couple of policemen shouting at his accosters.

One of the cops grabbed him, yelled, "*¡Vamos, vamos por acá, que los vamos a sacar de acá!*" Come on, get over here, we'll get you out of here! Another cop pulled Anna toward the cruiser. Somehow he made it to the police car, saw the door open, felt a shove, and he was inside. The door slammed behind him, and all the shouts and screams of the crowd were muted.

"You all right?" one of the cops said from the front seat.

Ben groaned.

Anna said, "*Gracias!*" Ben noticed that her blouse was torn, her pearl choker was gone. "We're American . . ." she began, then seemed to think for a moment. "My purse," she said. "Shit. My money was in there."

"Passport?" Ben managed to croak out.

"Back in the room." The car was moving. She turned to him. "My God, what was that? You O.K., Ben?"

"I'm not sure." The screaming pain in his groin was beginning to subside. There was a sticky warmth where he'd been slashed by the knife. He touched his side, felt the blood.

The car swung into traffic, barreling down the road. "That was no random attack," Anna said. "That was deliberate. Planned, coordinated."

Ben looked at her dully. "Thank you," he said to the policemen in the front seat.

There was no reply. He realized that there was a Plexiglas barrier between the front and back seats, and he heard Anna say, "The partition—?"

The Plexiglas had not been there before; it had just come up. Ben did not hear a police radio, or maybe the sound wasn't coming through the Plexiglas.

Anna seemed to notice the same thing at the same moment, for she leaned forward and banged on the Plexiglas, but the two policemen didn't respond.

The back doors locked automatically.

"Oh, my God," Anna breathed. *"They're not cops."*

They pulled at the door handles, which did not yield. They grabbed at the door lock buttons, but they would not move.

"Where's your gun?" Ben whispered.

"I don't *have* one!"

Headlights flashed by as the car accelerated down a four-lane highway. They were now clearly outside the city limits. Ben hammered at the Plexiglas partition with both fists, but neither the driver nor the passenger in the front seat seemed to notice.

The car swerved onto an exit ramp. In a few minutes they were on a dark, two-lane road, lined with tall trees, and then without warning they turned off the road into an unlit cul-de-sac within a copse of tall trees.

The engine was switched off. For a moment there was silence, interrupted only by the sound of an occasional car passing by.

The two men in the front seat seemed to be conferring. Then the passenger got out and went around to the back of the car. The trunk popped open.

In a moment he returned to his side of the car, clutching in his left hand something that looked like a piece of cloth. In his right he held a handgun. Then the driver got out, taking a gun from a shoulder holster. The back doors unlocked.

The driver, apparently in charge, yanked open the door on Anna's side and waved the gun at her. She got out slowly, put her hands up. He stepped back and, with his free left hand, slammed the car door shut, leaving Ben alone in the backseat.

The deserted country road, the weapons . . . this was a classic execution.

The other false policeman—or perhaps they were real ones; did it make any difference?—walked to where Anna stood, her hands in the air, and began frisking her for weapons, beginning with her underarms. His hands lingered on her breasts.

He ran his hands down her side, moving them into her crotch, his fingers spending too much time there as well, then moved down the inside of her legs to her ankles. He pulled back, seemed to determine her safe. Then he took a burlap sack and placed it over her head, tightening it around her neck.

The driver barked something, and she fell to her knees and clasped her hands behind her back.

Ben saw with horror what was about to happen to her. *"No!"*

The driver shouted another order, and the younger cop opened the car door, pointing his weapon at Ben. "Step out slowly," he said in fluent English.

There was no hope of making a dash for the road, nor of grabbing Anna and taking her to safety. Not faced with two men with guns. He got out of the car, thrust his hands in the air, and the younger one began frisking him too, this time more roughly.

"No está enfierrado," the man said. He's clean.

To Ben, he said conversationally, "Any sudden movements and we'll kill you. Understand?"

Yes, I understand. They'll kill us both.

A burlap sack went over his head. It stank of a horse barn, and was cinched tight at his neck, too tight, choking him. Everything was dark. He croaked, "Hey, watch it!"

"Shut the hell up," one of the men said. It sounded like the older man's voice. "Or I kill you and no one find your body for days, hear me?"

He heard Anna whisper, "Go along with them for now. We don't exactly have a choice."

He felt something hard pressed against the back of his head. "Kneel," a voice said.

He knelt, and without being asked, he clasped his hands behind his back. "What do you want?" Ben said.

"Shut the hell up!" one of them shouted. Something hard cracked against the back of his head. He groaned in pain.

His abductors didn't want to talk. They were going to die in this godforsaken field off a dark road in the middle of a country he didn't know. He was thinking of how it all began, at the Bahnhofplatz in Zurich, with his near-death, or did it really begin with Peter's disappearance? He recalled the agony of Peter's murder in the country inn in rural Switzerland, but instead of demoralizing him, the memory gave him resolve. If he were killed here, at least he would have the satisfaction of knowing that he had done everything he could to find his brother's murderers, and if he had failed to bring them to justice, or to discover what their reasons were, at least he had come close. He would leave behind no wife, no child, and in time he would be mostly forgotten by his friends, but in the history of the world all our lives are as brief as the winking of a firefly on a summer night, and he would not feel sorry for himself.

He thought of his father, wherever he'd vanished to, and regretted only that he'd never know the entire truth about the man.

Out of the darkness came a sudden voice. The older man.

"Now you answer some questions. What the hell you want with Josef Strasser?"

So they wanted to talk after all.

These goons were protecting Strasser.

He waited for Anna to speak first, and when she didn't, he said, "I'm an attorney. An American lawyer. I'm probating an estate—that means I'm trying to get him some money that's been left to him."

Something cracked hard against the side of his head.

"I want the truth, not your *bullshit!*"

"I'm *telling* you the truth." Ben's voice was shaky. "Leave this woman out of it—she's just my girlfriend. She's got nothing to do with it. I dragged her along, she'd never been to Buenos Aires—"

"Shut *up!*" one of them bellowed. Something slammed into his right kidney, and he tumbled to the ground, his face inside the burlap flat against the dirt. The pain was so acute he could not even groan. Then came a blinding pain as something cracked into the side of his face, perhaps a foot, and he smelled and tasted blood. Everything was bleached out.

He screamed, "*Stop!* What do you want? I'll tell you what you want!"

He hunched forward, brought his hands around to protect his face, gasping from the unfathomable pain, and he felt blood seeping from his mouth. He braced himself for the next blow, but for a moment nothing happened.

Then came the voice of the older one, quiet and matter-of-fact, as if making a reasonable point in a pleasant conversation. "The woman is not 'just' your girlfriend. She is Agent Anna Navarro, and she is on the payroll of the United States Justice Department. This we know. You, we want to know about."

"I'm helping her," he managed to get out, cringing, and it came, a swift blow to the other side of his head. A lightning bolt of pain pierced his eyes. The pain was so great now, so constant and overwhelming, that he thought he could not possibly survive it.

Then a pause, a momentary intermission in the torture session, and there was silence, the men seemingly waiting for him to speak again.

But Ben's mind was sluggish. Who—where were these men from? The man called Jürgen Lenz? Sigma itself? Their methods seemed too home-spun for that. The *Kamaradenwerk?* That was more plausible. What answer would satisfy them, end the beatings, forestall the execution?

Anna spoke. His ears were plugged, probably with blood, and he could barely hear what she said. "If you're protecting Strasser," she said in a voice that was surprisingly steady, "you'll want to know what I'm doing here. I've come to Buenos Aires to warn him—not to seek his extradition."

One of the men laughed, but she kept speaking. Her voice seemed so far away. "Do you know that a number of Strasser's comrades have been murdered in the last few weeks?"

There was no response. "We have information that Strasser is about to be killed. The U.S. Justice Department has no interest in trying to seize him, or we'd have done it long ago. Whatever terrible things he's done, he's not wanted for war crimes. I'm trying to keep him from being murdered, so I can talk to him."

"Liar!" one of the men screamed. There was a thud, and Anna cried out.

"Stop!" she shouted, her voice cracking. "There are ways you can check that I'm telling you the truth! We need to get to Strasser to warn him! If you kill us, you'll be harming *him!*"

"Anna!" Ben yelled. He needed to connect with her. "Anna, you O.K.? Just tell me you're O.K."

His throat felt as if it were going to burst. The exertion of yelling made his head throb excruciatingly.

Silence. Then her muffled voice: "I'm O.K."

It was the last thing he heard before everything vanished.

CHAPTER THIRTY-SEVEN

Ben awoke in a bed in a large, unfamiliar room with high ceilings, and tall windows that looked out over a city street he didn't recognize.

Evening, traffic noise, twinkling lights.

A lanky woman with dark brown hair and brown eyes, in a T-shirt and black Lycra bicycle shorts, languidly curled in a chair, watching him. *Anna.*

His head throbbed.

In a sedate voice, she said, "Hey."

"Hey," he said. "I'm alive." The nightmarish scene began to come back to him, but he couldn't remember when he lost consciousness.

She smiled. "How're you feeling?"

He thought about this for a moment. "Sort of like the guy who falls from the top of a skyscraper, and someone sticks his head out of a tenth-floor window and asks how he's doing, and the guy says, Well, so far I'm fine."

Anna chuckled.

"I have kind of a low-grade headache." He turned his head from side to side, felt the pain sear and sparkle behind his eyeballs. "Maybe not so low-grade."

"Well, you got bashed up pretty bad. For a while I thought you might have a concussion, but I guess not. Not from what I can tell." She paused. "They kicked me around a little, but they seemed to be focusing on you."

"Real gentlemen." He thought a moment, still disoriented. "How'd I get back here?"

"I guess they got tired of beating on you, or maybe they got scared when you passed out. At any rate, they brought us back to town, dropped us off somewhere in La Boca."

The only light in the room came from a lamp beside the bed where he lay. He became aware of bandages, on his forehead and side. "Who did this?"

"What do you mean—who were they? Or who bandaged you up?"

"Who fixed me up?"

"*Moi,*" she said, bowing her head modestly. "Medical supplies courtesy the Sphinx, mostly peroxide and Betadine."

"Thank you." His thinking was muzzy and slow. "So who *were* those guys?"

"Well, we're alive," she said, "so I'm guessing they're local muscle. *Pistoleros*, they're called, guns for hire."

"But the police car . . ."

"The Argentine police are famous for corruption. A lot of them moonlight as *pistoleros*. But I don't think they were connected with Sigma. *Kamaradenwerk*, or something along those lines—thugs who look out for the old Germans. The local network could have been alerted lots of ways. My Interpol friend—I gave him a fake name, but he might have seen an ID photo. Maybe it was the stolen package at American Express. Maybe it was my investigator guy, Machado. Maybe your pistol-packin' priest. But enough questions. I want you to take it easy."

He tried to sit up, felt a pain in his side, lay back down. Now he remembered being kicked in the stomach, the groin, the kidneys.

His eyelids kept drooping, the room going in and out of focus, and soon he succumbed to sleep.

When he awoke again, it was still night, and the room was mostly dark. The only light came from the street, but it was enough to see the shape in bed next to him. He could smell her faint perfume. He thought, *Now she's willing to share a bed.*

The next time he awoke, the room was bright. It hurt his eyes to look around. He heard the sound of water running in the bathroom, and struggled to sit up.

Anna emerged in a cloud of steam, wrapped in a bath towel.

"He's awake," she said. "How's it feel?"

"A little better."

"Good. You want me to order some coffee from room service?"

"They have room service here?"

"Yeah, you're feeling better," she said with a laugh. "The old sense of humor's starting to come back."

"I'm hungry."

"Understandable. We didn't have a chance to eat dinner last night." She turned back toward the bathroom.

He was in a clean T-shirt and boxer shorts. "Who changed my clothes?"

"Me."

"My shorts, too?"

"Mm-hmm. You were soaked in blood."

Well, well, he thought, amused. *Our first moment of intimacy and I slept through it.*

She began brushing her teeth and reemerged a few minutes later, makeup applied, wearing a white T-shirt and violet gym shorts.

"What do you think happened?" he asked. His head was beginning to clear. "You think your call to that private detective, what's-his-name, was intercepted?"

"Possibly."

"From now on we use my digital phone only. Let's assume even the Sphinx's switchboard is tapped."

She placed two pillows behind him. She wore no perfume now but smelled pleasantly of soap and shampoo. "Mind if I use it now to call our last hotel? My friend in Washington thinks I'm staying there, and might be trying to reach me." She tossed him a copy of the *International Herald Tribune.* "You take it easy. Read, sleep, whatever."

"Make sure it's charged. You might have to plug it in."

He leaned back and idly flipped through the pages. An earthquake in the Gujarat state in India. A California utilities company facing a shareholders' lawsuit. World leaders set to gather at the International Children's Health Forum. He put the paper aside and shut his eyes, but only to rest. He'd had enough sleep. He listened to her talk to the hotel in La Recoleta, her voice lulling. She had a lively, infectious laugh.

She appeared to have lost her sharp edge, her defensiveness. Now she seemed confident and assured, but without the brittleness. Maybe it was his weakness that allowed her to be strong. Maybe she liked to nurture. Maybe it was the shared adventure they had just been through, or his concern for her, or maybe it was pity for what had happened to him, or misplaced guilt. Maybe it was all these things.

She ended the phone conversation. "Well, this is interesting."

"Hmm?" He opened his eyes. She was standing beside the bed, her hair tousled, her breasts outlined beneath the white cotton T-shirt. He felt the tug of arousal.

"I got a message from Sergio the private eye, apologizing for being late, he was tied up on a case. Sounds entirely innocent."

"Call was intercepted at the hotel, probably."

"I'm going to meet him."

"Are you crazy? Haven't you had enough traps for one lifetime?"

"On my terms. My arrangement."

"Don't."

"I know what I'm doing. I may screw up—I *do* screw up sometimes—but you know, I'm actually considered pretty good at what I do."

"I don't doubt it. But you don't do organized crime or drugs, you don't do shoot-'em-up stuff. I think we're *both* in over our heads."

He felt oddly protective of her, even though she was no doubt a far better shot than he, more equipped to defend herself. Yet at the same time—even more perplexing—he felt safer with her around.

She came over and sat on the bed next to him. He edged over a bit to give her room. "I appreciate your worrying about me," she said. "But I've been trained, and I *have* been a field agent."

"I'm sorry, I didn't mean to imply—"

"No apology necessary. No offense taken."

He stole a quick glance at her. He wanted to say, *My God, you're beautiful*, but he didn't know how she might take it. She still seemed pretty defensive.

She said, "Are you doing this for your brother or for your father?"

The question caught him by surprise. He hadn't expected such bluntness. And he realized the answer wasn't simple. "Maybe both," he said. "Mostly for Peter, of course."

"How well did you and Peter get along?"

"Do you know any twins?" he asked.

"Not well."

"I suspect it's the closest relationship there is, closer than many husbands and wives. Not that I know about *that* firsthand. But we protected each other. We could almost read each other's mind. Even when we fought—and we did, believe me—afterward we each felt more guilty than angry. We competed with each other in sports and such, but not really in any other way. When he was happy, I was happy. When something good happened to him, I felt like it had happened to me. And vice versa."

To his surprise he saw tears in her eyes. For some reason that brought tears to his own.

He continued, "When I say we were close, that seems so inadequate. You don't say you're 'close' to your leg or your hand, right? He was like a part of my body."

It all came back to him suddenly, a jumble of memories, or really, images. Peter's murder. His mind-boggling reappearance. The two of them, as kids, running through the house, laughing. Peter's funeral.

He turned away in embarrassment, covered his face with his hand, unable to stanch the sob that welled up.

He heard a low keening and realized that Anna was crying too, which surprised him and, most of all, moved him. She took his hand in hers and squeezed tight. Her cheeks glistening with tears, she put an arm gently around his shoulders, then both of her arms, and she embraced him, seemingly careful of his wounds, and laid her face damply on his shoulder. It was a moment of intimacy that at once startled him and felt natural, part of the complex, passionate Anna he was slowly coming to know. He took solace from her, and she from him. He could feel her heart thudding against his chest, her warmth. She raised her head off his shoulder and slowly, tentatively at first, placed her lips against his, her eyes closed tight. They kissed slowly, tenderly at first, then deeply and with abandon. His arms encircled her lithe body, his fingers exploring her as his mouth and tongue did the same. They had crossed a line each of them had invisibly and firmly drawn some time ago, a boundary, a high wall between natural impulses, containing and isolating the powerful electrical charges that now crackled back and forth between them. And somehow, when they made love, it didn't seem as awkward as he'd imagined it might be, when he'd allowed himself to imagine it.

Finally, exhausted, they napped for half an hour or so, entwined in each other.

When he awoke, he saw that she was gone.

The gray-haired man parked his rented Mercedes and walked several cobblestone blocks down Estomba until he located the house. He was in the heart of a barrio of Buenos Aires called Belgrano, one of the wealthiest residential sections. A young man passed by walking six dogs at once. The gray-haired man, in a well-tailored blue suit, gave him a neighborly smile.

The house was a Georgian-style mansion built of red bricks. He walked past it, seeming to admire the architecture, then he turned back, having noted the security booth on the sidewalk in front of the house: an off-white windowed sentry box in which stood a uniformed man wearing an orange Day-Glo reflective vest. There seemed to be one of these security booths on every block around here.

A very quiet, very safe neighborhood, Trevor Griffiths thought. Good. The security guard looked him over. Trevor nodded in a neighborly manner, and approached the booth as if to ask the guard a question.

Anna carefully packaged Ben's photograph and brought it to a DHL office, paying to get it to Denneen's home address in Dupont Circle as quickly as possible. Everything she did now involved some degree of risk, but she hadn't mentioned DHL on the phone or even to Ben in the room, and she made sure that no one followed her there. She was reasonably certain the photo would arrive safely.

Now she stood in a doorway of a shop beneath a red Lucky Strike sign, watching the windows of a café at the corner of Junin and Viamonte, just down the street from the *Facultad Medecina*. The café's name, Entre Tiempo, was painted on the plate glass in jumbled letters, presumably signifying wacky fun within. Couples strolled by absorbed in each other, gaggles of students wearing backpacks. A slew of passing yellow-and-black taxis.

This time there would be no surprises.

She'd reconnoitered this site in advance, arranged to meet Sergio Machado here at six-thirty precisely, arrived a full forty-five minutes beforehand. A public place in broad daylight. She'd asked him to take a seat at a table in the window, if one was available, or as close to the window as possible. And to bring his cell phone. Machado seemed more amused than annoyed by her precautions.

At twenty-five after six, a silver-haired man in a blue blazer and open-neck button-down blue shirt, fitting the description he'd supplied over the phone, entered the café. A minute or so later he appeared at a table by the window and looked out onto the street. She pulled back into the shop so she couldn't be seen and continued to watch through the glass door. She'd already explained to the shopkeeper that she was waiting here for her husband.

At six thirty-five, Machado hailed a waiter.

A few minutes later the waiter set down a bottle of Coca-Cola.

If Machado had been complicit in last night's kidnapping, there would surely be others stationed nearby, but she saw no sign of anyone. No one lingering, pretending to window-shop, dawdling at a newsstand, sitting in a car idling by a curb. She knew what to look for. Machado was alone.

Were there others in place in the café awaiting her arrival?

Perhaps. But she was prepared for the possibility.

At six forty-five, she switched on Ben's phone and called Machado's cell.

It rang once. "*Sí?*"

"It's Anna Navarro."

"You get lost somewhere?"

"God, this city's so *confusing*," she said. "I guess I got the wrong place—would you mind terribly meeting me here, where I am now? I just *know* I'll get lost *again!*" She gave him directions to a café a few blocks away.

She watched as he got up, left some change, and, without appearing to signal to, or consult with, anyone inside the café, emerged. She knew what he looked like, but presumably he wouldn't recognize her.

He crossed the street and walked past her, and she got a better glimpse of him. The silver hair was premature; he was a man in his forties with soft brown eyes and a pleasant look about him. He carried no briefcase or file, just his phone.

She waited a few seconds, then followed him.

He located the café easily, and went inside. She joined him a minute or so later.

"You mind explaining what all this was about?" Machado asked.

She related what had happened to her and Ben the night before. She watched his face closely; he seemed appalled.

Machado had the saturnine look of an Italian film star of the 1960s. He was deeply and meticulously tanned. Around his neck was a thin gold chain, and another gold chain encircled his left wrist. A vertical worry line was scored deeply between his close-set fawn's eyes. He wore no wedding band.

"The police here, they are totally corrupt, you are absolutely right," he said. "They hire me to do investigative work for them, as an outside consultant, because they don't trust their own people!"

"I'm not surprised." The fear left over from the abduction had become anger.

"You know, we have no cop shows here in Argentina like you have in America, because here cops aren't heroes. They're scum. I know. I was in Federal Police for twenty-one years. Got my pension and left."

A long table nearby, some sort of student study group by the look of them, burst into laughter.

"Everyone here is afraid of the police," he went on heatedly. "Police brutality. They charge for protection. They shoot to kill whenever they want. You like their uniforms?"

"They look like New York City cops."

"That's because their uniforms were copied *exactly* from the NYPD. And that's *all* they copied." He flashed an endearing smile. "So what can I do for you."

"I need to find a man named Josef Strasser."

His eyes widened. "Ah, well, you know, this old bastard lives under a false name. I don't know where he lives, but I can ask some questions. Not so easy. You gonna extradite?"

"No, actually, I need to have a talk with him."

He straightened. "Really?"

"I may have a way to locate him, but I'll need your help." She related Ben's meeting with Lenz's widow. "If Vera Lenz or her stepson are in touch with Strasser, and they called to warn him, say—could you find out what number they dialed?"

"Ah," he said. "Very nice. Yes of course, but only if you can get Señora Lenz's telephone number."

She handed him a slip of paper with the number on it.

"The phone companies in Argentina, they record the beginning and end of all telephone conversations, the number called and how long the call. It is the Excalibur system, they call it. My friends in the police, for the right price, they will get for me all calls made from that number."

And as if to demonstrate how easy it was, he placed a call, spoke briefly, read off the number on the scrap of paper.

"No problem," he said. "We'll know soon. Come, I buy you a steak."

They walked a few blocks to his car, a white Ford Escort whose back-seat had for some reason been removed. He took her to an old-style restaurant near the Cementerio de la Recoleta called Estilo Munich, its walls adorned with stuffed boar's and stag's heads. The floor was marble but looked like drab linoleum; the ceiling was acoustic tile. Weary waiters shuffled slowly between the tables.

"I will order for you *bife de chorizo*," Machado said. "With *chimichurri* sauce. *Jugoso*, it is O.K.?"

"Rare is how I like it, yes. Any symbolism in the fact that you brought me to a restaurant called Munich?"

"They serve one of the best steaks in Buenos Aires, and we are a city that knows steaks." He gave her a complicit glance. "Used to be a lot of restaurants in BA called Munich—very fashionable once. Not so fashionable now."

"Not so many Germans."

He took a pull of the Carrascal. His cell phone rang; he spoke briefly, put it back. "My girlfriend," he apologized. "I thought we might have some results on our search, but no."

"If Strasser has managed to live here for so long without anybody finding him, he must have some good false ID."

"People like him got excellent false papers. For a long time only Jakob Sonnenfeld was able to trace them. For years, you know, there was a rumor that Martin Bormann was still alive in Argentina, until his skull turned up in Germany. Nineteen seventy-two, in Berlin. They were building a bridge, they dug up the ground, and they found a skull. Identified it as Bormann's."

"Was it?"

"A couple of years ago they finally did the DNA test. It was Bormann's skull, yes."

"What about the rest of his body?"

"Never found. I think he was buried here, in Bariloche, and someone brought the skull to Germany. To mislead the pursuers." His eyes sparkled with amusement. "You know Bormann's son lives here. He's a Catholic priest. Really." Another swig of Carrascal. "It's true. Always rumors about Bormann. It is like with Josef Mengele. After he was buried everyone thinks he faked his own death. With Lenz the same thing. For years after his death was announced, there was rumors that he's still alive. Then they found his bones."

"Were they DNA-tested, too?"

"I don't think."

"No one found his skull anywhere."

"No skull."

"Could he still be alive somewhere?"

Machado laughed. "He'd be more than one hundred twenty."

"Well, only the good die young. He died of a stroke, didn't he?"

"This is the public line. But I think Lenz was murdered by Israeli agents. You know, when Eichmann came here, he and his wife took false names, but their three sons—they used the name Eichmann! At school everyone knew the boys as Eichmann. But no one came to find them, you see. No one came to look for them until Sonnenfeld."

Their steaks arrived. Amazingly delicious, Anna thought. She was not much of a meat-eater, but this could convert her.

"Mind if I ask why you want to talk to Strasser?" Machado asked.

"Sorry. Can't say."

He seemed to accept it with good grace. "Strasser was one of the inventors of Zyklon-B."

"The gas used at Auschwitz."

"But it was his own idea to use it on human beings. A clever fellow, this Strasser. He came up with the way to kill Jews so much more expeditiously."

After dinner they walked a few doors down to a large café called La Biela, on Avenue Quintana, which at after eleven o'clock at night was crowded and loud.

Over coffee she asked, "Can you get me a weapon?"

He looked at her slyly. "It can be arranged."

"By tomorrow morning?"

"I'll see what I can do."

His phone rang again.

This time he jotted down notes on a little square napkin.

"His phone's listed under the name Albrecht," Machado said when he'd hung up. "The right age, too. He used his real birthdates on his application forms. I think you've found your man."

"So someone did call him from Lenz's house."

"Yes. With the phone number it was a simple thing to get the name and address. I think he must have been out of town for a long time, because no outgoing calls were made from his home for the last five weeks. Two days ago the calls started up again."

That would explain why Strasser hadn't yet been reported killed like all the others, she thought. *He was out of town.* That's how he had stayed alive. "Your contact," she said. "Whoever got this information for you— why does he think you're interested?"

"Maybe he believes I'm planning some sort of extortion."

"He wouldn't let Strasser know you've been looking?"

"My police contacts are too stupid to play those sorts of games."

"Let's hope so." But her worry was not so easily allayed. "What about the sorts of thugs who kidnapped us . . ."

He frowned. "The sons and grandsons of the fugitives, they won't mess with me. I have too many friends in the police. It is dangerous for them. Sometimes when I do this sort of job, I go home and I find Wagner on my answering machine, a veiled threat. Sometimes they walk by me on the street, take flash photographs of me. But that's all they do. I never worry." He lit another cigarette. "You have no reason to worry either."

No, no reason to worry, she thought.

Easy for you to say.

"I'm afraid Mr. Bartlett isn't able to see any visitors right now, and I don't see an appointment for you." The receptionist spoke with icy authority.

"I'm *making* an appointment—for right now," Arliss Dupree said. "Tell him he'll *want* to see me. It's about a matter of mutual concern. Interdepartmental business, O.K.?"

"I'm very sorry, Mr. Dupree, but . . ."

"Save you the trouble, I'll just mosey on down and knock on his door. You can give him a head's up, or not. His office is down that way, right?" A grin played across Dupree's ruddy moon face. "Don't trouble yourself, girl. We're going to be fine."

The receptionist spoke hurriedly, softly, into the microphone of her headset. After a moment, she stood up. "Mr. Bartlett said he'd be pleased to see you. I'll show you to him."

Dupree looked around the director's spartan office and for the first time felt a twinge of alarm. It wasn't the comfortable burrow of the typical career officer—of the lifer who surrounded himself with photos of loved ones and stacks of unfiled paper. It barely showed signs of human habitation at all.

"And how can I help you today, Mr. Dupree?" Alan Bartlett stood behind a large desk, so uncluttered it might have been a floor model at an office-furniture store. There was something glacial, Dupree thought, about the man's polite smile, something unreadable about the gray eyes behind the aviator glasses.

"Lotsa ways, I suppose," Dupree said, and sat himself down unceremoniously on the blond-wooden chair facing Bartlett's desk. "Starting with this whole Navarro business."

"Most unfortunate, the recent revelations," Bartlett said. "Reflects poorly on all of us."

"As you know, I wasn't pleased by the TDY you arranged," he said, referring to the cross-departmental assignment of temporary duties.

"That much you made clear. Perhaps you knew something about her that you chose to be less than forthcoming about."

"Naw, that wasn't it." Dupree forced himself to meet Bartlett's steady gaze. It was like talking to an iceberg. "Frankly, it undermines my authority when a member of my staff gets shifted around like that, without my knowledge or consent. Some of the staffers will always assume it's some sort of promotion."

"I suspect you didn't come here to discuss your personnel difficulties or management style, Mr. Dupree."

"Hell, no," Dupree said. "Here's the thing. The rest of us at Justice always give you guys at ICU a wide berth. You get up to your stuff, and most of the time we're just as happy not to know about it. But this time, you started something that's leaving jelly stains on my carpet, you see what I'm saying? Putting me in a tight spot. I'm not making any accusations, I'm just saying that it got me thinking."

"An unaccustomed activity for you, no doubt. You will find it grows easier with practice." Bartlett spoke with effortless mandarin disdain.

"I may not be the sharpest tool in the shed," Dupree said. "But you'll find I can still cut."

"How reassuring."

"It's just that something about the whole thing smelled bad to me."

Bartlett sniffed. "Aqua Velva, would that be? Or Old Spice? Your aftershave arrives before you do."

Dupree just shook his head, in a show of good-natured confusion. "So I poked around a little. Learned a little more about you, about where you've been. I hadn't realized before that you owned a huge piece of property on the Eastern Shore. Not your typical federal employee, I guess."

"My mother's father was one of the founders of Holleran Industries. She was one of the heirs to the estate. That's not a secret. Nor is it something I choose to draw attention to, I'll admit. I have little interest in the high life. The life I've decided to lead is a rather plain one, and my tastes are, on the whole, modest. Anyway, what of it?"

"Right, your mother was a Holleran heiress—I found that out, too. Came as a surprise, I got to say. Way I see it, it's kind of flattering that a multimillionaire would deign to work among us."

"All of us must make decisions in our lives."

"Yup, I guess that's true. But then I'm thinking, how much else is there about Alan Bartlett that I don't know about? Probably a lot, right? Like, what's with all those trips to Switzerland. Now, Switzerland—I guess because at the OSI we're always dealing with money-laundering, that place always sets off alarm bells. So it gets me wondering about these trips of yours."

A beat. "Excuse me?"

"Well, you do head over to Switzerland a bunch, am I right?"

"What gives you that idea?"

Dupree pulled a sheet of paper from the breast pocket of his jacket. It was slightly crumpled, but he laid it flat on Bartlett's desk and smoothed it out. On it was a series of dots, in a roughly circular array. "Sorry it's so crude, I drew it myself." He pointed to the topmost dot. "Over here, we got Munich. Just under it, Innsbruck. Moving southeast, Milan. Turin. Then, a little more easterly and a little further north Lyon. Dijon. Freiburg."

"And this would be an adult-education course in geography that you're taking?"

"Naw," Dupree said. "Took me a long time to get this stuff. I had to go through the computers at passport control and the major airlines, too. Major pain in the ass, I can tell you. But these are all airports that you traveled through at some point over the past fifteen years. A lot of them direct from Dulles, some of them with a connecting flight through Frankfurt or Paris. So here I am, and I'm looking at this scatter of points. All these dreary goddamn airports and what do they have in common?"

"I expect you're going to tell me," Bartlett said, a look of chilly amusement in his eyes.

"Well, Christ, take a look at the scatter. What would you conclude? It's obvious, isn't it? They're in a circle of points within a two-hundred-mile radius of Zurich. They're all a hop and a skip from Switzerland—that's what these places got in common. They're all places you'd go if you wanted to go to Switzerland and maybe didn't want to have 'Switzerland' stamped on your passport. *Either* of your passports, in *your* case: I was impressed to see you have two authorized passports."

"Which is not uncommon among officials in my particular line of work. You're being absurd, Mr. Dupree, but I'll play along. Let's say I have indeed visited Switzerland—so what?"

"Right, so what? No harm, no foul. Only, why'd you tell me you didn't?"

"You're really being deliberately dense, Mr. Dupree, aren't you? If I choose to discuss my vacation plans with you, you'll be the first to know. Your behavior today calls into question your fitness to discharge your official responsibilities. It also, if I may say so, verges on insubordination."

"I don't report to you, Bartlett."

"No, because seven years ago, when you sought transfer to our unit, you were turned down. Judged *not* to be of ICU caliber." Bartlett's voice remained cool, but his cheeks had colored. Dupree knew he had rattled him. "And now, I'm afraid, I'll have to call this conversation to an end."

"I'm not finished with you, Bartlett," Dupree said, standing up.

A death's-head smile: " 'Great works are never finished. Only abandoned.' So said Valéry."

"Harper?"

"Good-bye, Mr. Dupree," Bartlett said serenely. "Your commute home to Arlington is a long one at this time of day, and I know you'll want to beat the rush hour."

Ben awoke, aware first of the soft early-morning light, then of Anna's soft breathing. They had slept in the same bed. He sat up slowly, feeling the dull ache in his limbs, his neck. He could feel warmth radiating from her nightgown-clad body a few inches away.

He walked slowly to the bathroom, the pain now awakening too. He realized he'd slept through an entire day and night. Ben knew he was badly battered, but it was better to move around, stay as limber as possible, than to confine himself to bed. Either way it would take time to recover.

He returned to the bedroom, quietly picking up his phone. Fergus O'Connor in the Caymans was expecting his call. But when he tried to switch the phone on, he discovered that the battery was dead. Anna had apparently forgotten to charge it. He heard her stirring in the bed.

He slipped the phone into its charger cradle and called Fergus.

"Hartman!" Fergus exclaimed heartily, as if he'd been waiting for Ben's call.

"Give me some news," Ben said, hobbling to the window and looking out over the traffic.

"Well, I've got good news and bad news. Whaddaya want first?"

"Always the good first."

There was a beep on the line—another call coming in—but he ignored it.

"Right. There's one shady lawyer in Liechtenstein who came to his office this morning and discovered there'd been a break-in."

"Awful sorry to hear that."

"Yes. Particularly since one of his files is missing—the folder on an *Anstalt* he manages for some unnamed party or parties who reside in Vienna."

"Vienna." His stomach tightened.

"No names, unfortunately. A set of wire instructions, ID codes, and all that shit. But definitely Vienna-based. The owners were careful to keep their names secret, even from this guy. Who, by the way, probably isn't going to be calling the Liechtenstein cops about a missing file. Not with all the illegal shite he's into."

"Well done, Fergus. So what's the bad news?"

"You've run up quite a bill. The job in Liechtenstein alone cost me fifty grand. You think those guys come cheap? They're fucking *thieves!*" Even for Fergus, that was a significant charge. But given the information he'd turned up—which no law-enforcement agency could ever have gotten—it was worth it.

"I don't suppose you've got any receipts for me," Ben replied.

As soon as he disconnected the call, the phone rang. "Yes?"

"Anna Navarro, please!" a man's voice shouted. "I need to talk to her!"

"She's—who is this?"

"Just tell her it's Sergio."

"Ah, yes. Yes. Just a moment."

Anna was awake; the ringing had awakened her. "Machado?" she murmured, her voice raspy from sleep. Ben gave her the phone.

"Sergio," she said. "I'm sorry, I had the phone turned off, I think . . . All right, sure, that's . . . What? . . . *What?* . . . Sergio, hello? Are you *there?* Hello?"

She pressed the Off button. "How weird," she said.

"What is it?"

She stared at him, obviously mystified. "He said he'd been trying to reach me all night. He was calling from his car, in a part of town called San Telmo. He wants to meet at the Plaza Dorrego Bar, I think he said— he's got a gun for me."

"Why did he sound so frantic?"

"He said he didn't want any part of this investigation any longer."

"They got to him."

"He really sounded frightened, Ben. He said—he said he'd been contacted by people, threatened—that these weren't the usual locals who watch out for the fugitives." She looked up, shaken. "And the call ended in midsentence."

They could smell the fire even before they entered Plaza Dorrego. As their cab pulled up to the side of the Plaza Dorrego Bar, they saw a large crowd, ambulances and police cars and fire trucks.

The cabdriver spoke quickly.

"What's he saying?" Ben asked.

"He says he can't go any farther, there's been some kind of accident. Come on."

She asked the driver to wait for them, then she and Ben leaped out of the car and raced into the square. The smoke had mostly dissipated, but the air smelled of sulfur and carbon and combusted gasoline. Peddlers had temporarily abandoned their tables in the park at the center of the plaza, leaving their cheap jewelry and perfumes untended while they gathered to watch. Residents huddled in the doorways of the ancient tenements, to stare in fascinated horror.

It was immediately obvious what had happened. A car had been parked directly in front of the Plaza Dorrego Bar when it exploded, shattering the window of the bar, and blowing out windows across the street. Apparently it had burned for quite a while before the fire trucks were able to put it out. Even the white zebra stripes painted on the road near the wreck had been blackened.

A white-haired old woman in a brown print blouse was screaming, over and over, *"Madre de Dios! Madre de Dios!"*

Ben felt Anna grab his hand and squeeze it tight as they watched the emergency medical workers hacksawing at the burnt-out carcass of the once-white Ford Escort, trying without success to extricate the charred body.

He felt her shudder when one of the workers managed to wrench back a chunk of metal, revealing the black incinerated arm, the wrist encircled by the blackened gold chain, the scorched claw of a hand gripping the little cell phone.

CHAPTER THIRTY-EIGHT

They sat, stunned, in the back of the cab.

Not until they had gone several blocks did either one speak.

"Oh, my God, Ben. Dear God." Anna leaned back against the seat, eyes closed.

He put a hand on her shoulder, nothing more than a moment of comfort. There was nothing he could say to her, nothing that would mean anything.

"When Machado and I had dinner last night," she said, "he told me that in all his years of investigations, he was never afraid. That I shouldn't be afraid either."

Ben didn't know how to reply. He couldn't shake the horror of seeing Machado's incinerated body. The hand clutching the cell phone. *Some say the world will end in fire.* Shuddering, he flashed on Chardin's faceless countenance, the man's testimony that the horrors of surviving could be far greater than those of perishing. Sigma seemed to have a fondness for incendiary solutions. As gently as he could, he said, "Anna, maybe I should do this alone."

"*No*, Ben," she said sharply. Ben saw her steely resolve. She was staring straight ahead, her face tense, her jaw clenched.

It was as if what they'd just witnessed had fueled her determination instead of deterring her. She was intent on visiting Strasser, no matter what, and getting to the bottom of the conspiracy that was Sigma. Maybe it was crazy—maybe they were *both* crazy—but he knew he wasn't going to turn back either. "Do you think either of us can just go back to our lives after what we've learned? Do you think we'd be *allowed* to?"

Another long silence elapsed.

"We'll make a circuit," she said. "Make sure no one's staking out the house, waiting for us. Maybe they assume that since they've eliminated Machado, there's no more threat." There seemed to be relief in her voice, but he couldn't be sure.

The cab barreled through the crowded streets of Buenos Aires toward the wealthy barrio of Belgrano. It occurred to Ben what a strange and terrible irony it was that a good man had just died so that they could try to save the life of an evil one. He wondered whether the same notion had occurred to her. *Now we're about to risk our lives to save the life of a world-historic villain*, he reflected.

And the true scope of his villainy? Was there any way of knowing?

The harrowing words returned to him.

Wheels within wheels—that was the way we worked. . . . It never crossed anyone's mind that the West had fallen under the administration of a hidden consortium. The notion would be inconceivable. Because if true, it would mean that over half of the planet was effectively a subsidiary of a single megacorporation—Sigma.

In recent years, one very special project of Sigma's had come to the fore. The prospect of its success would revolutionize the nature of world control. No longer would it be about the allocation of funds, the directing of resources. It became, instead, a simple matter of who the "chosen" would be.

Was Strasser himself one of the "chosen"? Or maybe he, too, was dead.

Ben said, "I talked to Fergus, in the Caymans. He's traced the wire transfers all the way back to Vienna."

"Vienna," she repeated without inflection.

She said nothing further. He wondered what she was thinking, but before he could ask, the cab pulled to a stop in front of a red-brick villa with white shutters. A white station wagon was parked in the small driveway.

Anna said something to the driver in Spanish, then turned to Ben. "I told him to circle the block. I want to look for parked cars, loiterers, anything suspicious."

Ben knew it was time, once again, to defer to her. He'd simply have to trust that she knew what she was doing. "What's our approach going to be?" he asked.

"All we have to do is get in the door. Warn him. Tell him his life's in danger. I've got my DOJ credentials, which should be enough to make us legitimate in his eyes."

"We've got to assume that he's been warned—by the *Kamaradenwerk* thugs, by Vera Lenz, by whatever other sort of early-warning systems he has in place. And then what if his life *isn't* in danger? What if he's the one *behind* the killings? Have you considered *that?*"

After a beat of silence, she conceded, "It's a real risk."

A real risk. That was a colossal understatement.

"You don't have a weapon," Ben reminded her.

"We only need his attention for a moment. Then if he chooses to listen further, he can."

And if he was the one behind the killings? But it was useless to argue.

When they had made a complete circuit, the cab stopped, and they got out.

Although it was a warm, sunny day, Ben felt a chill, no doubt from fear. He was sure Anna was frightened, too, but she didn't show it. He admired her strength.

Twenty-five feet before Strasser's house there was a security booth on the sidewalk. The guard was a stooped old man with wispy white hair and a drooping mustache, a blue cap perched almost comically atop his head. If ever there were a serious incident on the street, this guard would be useless, Ben thought. Still, it was best not to alert him, so the two of them continued their determined stride as if they belonged here.

They stopped before Strasser's house, which was surrounded, like most of the houses on this street, by a fence. This one was of dark-stained wood, not wrought iron, and it was no higher than Ben's chest. It was purely ornamental and seemed to send the message that the inhabitant of this house had nothing to hide. Anna unlatched the wooden gate, pulled it open, and they entered a small, well-kept garden. From behind they heard footsteps on the pavement.

Nervously, Ben turned. It was the security guard approaching, maybe twenty feet away. He wondered whether Anna had an alibi prepared; he didn't. The guard smiled. His dentures were ill-fitting and yellow. He said something in Spanish.

Anna muttered, "He wants to see our identification." To the old man she said, "*¡Cómo no, señor!*" Certainly.

The guard reached into his jacket, oddly, as if to offer identification of his own.

Ben noticed a slight movement across the street, and he turned to look.

There was a man standing across the street. A tall man who had a ruddy face, a thatch of black hair going gray, and thick wheat-field eyebrows.

Ben felt a jolt of recognition. The face was horribly familiar.

Where have I seen him before?

Paris—the rue des Vignoles.

Vienna. The Graben.

And somewhere before that.

One of the killers.

He was aiming a gun at them.

Ben shouted, "Anna, *get down!*" He flung himself onto the concrete garden path.

Anna dove to her left, out of the line of fire.

There was a spit, and the guard's chest erupted, a gusher of crimson, and he fell backward to the flagstone sidewalk. The ruddy-faced man raced toward them.

They were trapped inside Strasser's yard.

The assassin had shot the guard! Ben and Anna had ducked, and the poor guard had been caught in the line of fire.

Next time the killer would not miss.

Even if I could run, Ben thought, it would be *toward* the killer.

And both of them were unarmed!

He heard the man shout in English, "It's O.K.! It's O.K.! I'm not going to shoot!"

Ruddy-face had his gun at his side as he raced toward them.

"Hartman!" he yelled. "Benjamin Hartman!"

Ben looked up, startled.

Anna screamed, "I've got a gun! Back off!"

But the ruddy-faced man still did not raise his weapon. "It's O.K.! I'm not going to shoot!" The man flung his gun to the pavement in front of him, his hands outstretched. "He was about to kill you," the ruddy-faced man said as he ran up to the body of the old man. "Look!"

Those were the last words the ruddy-faced man spoke.

Like a mannequin twitching with incipient life, the ancient guard moved an arm, yanking a slim, silenced revolver from his trousers, and pointing it at the ruddy-faced man who stood over him. There was a *phut* and then a soft-nosed slug slammed into his forehead and blew out the back of his skull.

What the hell was going on?

The ancient guard now began to sit up, even as blood still dribbled from his shirtfront. He had been wounded, perhaps mortally, but his firing arm was absolutely steady.

An impassioned bellow came from behind them: *"No!"*

Ben turned to see another man, stationed by an oak tree, at a diagonal from them: their side of the street, but twenty yards to their left. This man was holding a large rifle with a sniper scope, a marksman's special.

The ruddy-faced killer's backup?

The barrel was directed in their general direction.

There was no time to escape its deadly aim.

Immediately, Ben heard the blast of the high-powered rifle, too paralyzed with fear even to flinch.

Two, then three bullets hit the ancient guard in the center of his chest and he slumped back to the ground.

Once again they had been spared. Why? With the scoped rifle, there was no way the sniper could have missed his intended target.

The man with the rifle—a man with glossy black hair and olive skin—raced over to the crumpled, bloodied body of the watchman, ignoring them.

It made no sense. Why were the gunmen so intent on killing the old guard? Who was their real target?

Ben stood up slowly, and saw the man reach inside the jacket of the old man's uniform, and pull out another weapon: a second slim automatic revolver, silencer screwed on to the barrel.

"Oh, dear God," Anna said.

The olive-skinned man grabbed a fistful of the guard's wispy white hair and tugged at it, and it came off in one floppy piece, like the pelt of a rabbit, revealing the steel-gray hair underneath.

He yanked at the white mustache, which came off just as easily, then grabbed at the loose skin of the old man's face, lifting off wrinkled, irregular patches of flesh-colored rubber.

"Latex prostheses," the man said. He pulled off the nose, then the wrinkled bags under the old man's eyes, and Ben recognized the smooth, unlined face of the man who had tried to kill him in front of Jürgen Lenz's house in Vienna. The man who tried to kill them all in Paris.

The man who killed his brother.

"The Architect," Anna gasped.

Ben froze.

Gaped, disbelieving, but it was true.

"He was going to kill you both when he got within point-blank range," the man said. Ben focused on his tawny skin, oddly long lashes, and square jaw. The man spoke with a vaguely Middle Eastern accent. "Which he would easily have done, since his appearance deceived you."

Ben recalled the odd gesture, the image of the frail old man reaching into his jacket, the almost apologetic expression.

"Wait a minute," Anna said. "You're 'Yossi.' From Vienna. The Israeli CIA guy. Or so you pretended."

"*Dammit,* tell me who you are!" Ben said.

"My name isn't important," he replied.

"Yeah, well it is to me. Who are you?"

"Yehuda Malkin."

The name meant nothing. "You've been following me," Ben said. "I saw your partner in Vienna and in Paris."

"Yeah, he screwed up and got spotted. He'd been following you for the entire last week. I was doing backup. You may as well know: your father hired us, Ben."

My father hired them. For what? "Hired you . . . ?"

"Max Hartman bought our parents' way out of Nazi Germany more than fifty years ago. And the man who was killed wasn't just my partner. He was my cousin." He closed his eyes for a moment. "*Goddammit* to hell. Avi wasn't meant to die. It wasn't his time. Goddammit to hell." He shook his head hard. His cousin's death evidently hadn't sunk in, and right now he wouldn't let it—it wasn't the moment. He looked hard at Ben, saw the confusion playing across his face. "Both of us owed your father everything. I guess he must've had some kind of in with the Nazis, because he did that for a bunch of other Jewish families in Germany too."

Max ransomed Jews—bought their way out of the camps? Then what Sonnenfeld said was true.

Anna broke in, "Who trained you? You're not American-trained."

The man turned to her. "I was born in Israel, on a kibbutz. My parents moved to Palestine after they escaped from Germany."

"You were in the Israeli army?"

"Paratrooper. We moved to America in '68, after the Six Day War. My parents were fed up with the fighting. After high school I joined the Israeli army."

"This whole CIA ruse in Vienna—what the hell was it about?" Anna demanded.

"For that, I brought in an American comrade of mine. Our orders were to spirit Ben away from danger. Get him back in the States, and under our direct protection. Keep him safe."

"But how did you . . ." Anna started.

"Look, we don't have time for this. If you're trying to interrogate Strasser, you'd better get in there before the cops show up."

"Right," Anna said.

"Wait," Ben interrupted. "You say my father hired you. *When?*"

The man looked around impatiently. "A week or so ago." He called Avi and me, told us you were in some kind of danger. Said you were in Switzerland. He gave us names and addresses, places he thought you might turn up. He wanted us to do what we could to protect you. He said he didn't want to lose another son." He looked around quickly. "You were almost killed on our watch in Vienna. Again in Paris. And you sure had some kind of close call here."

Ben's mind swirled with questions. "Where did my father go?"

"I don't know. He said Europe, but he didn't specify, and it's a big continent. He said he'd be out of contact with everyone for months. Left us a pile of money for travel expenses." He smiled grimly. "A whole lot more than we'd ever need, frankly."

Anna, meanwhile, was leaning over Vogler's body and had taken a weapon from a nylon shoulder holster. She unscrewed the silencer, put it in the jacket of her blazer and tucked the gun into the waistband of her skirt so it was hidden by the jacket. "But you didn't follow us *here,*" she said, "did you?"

"No," he conceded. "Strasser's name was on the list Max Hartman gave me, along with his address and cover identity."

"He knows what's going on!" Ben said. "He knows who all the players are. He figured I'd eventually track Strasser down."

"But we were able to tail Vogler, who wasn't much concerned about being followed himself. So once we knew he was flying to Argentina, and we had Strasser's address . . ."

"You've been watching Strasser's house for the last couple of days," Anna said. "Waiting for Ben to show up."

He glanced around again. "You guys ought to move it."

"Right, but first tell me this," she went on. "Since you've been doing surveillance: did Strasser just recently return to Buenos Aires?"

"Apparently so. Back from some vacation, it looked like. He had a lot of luggage."

"Any visitors since his return?"

The man thought a moment. "Not that I saw, anyway. Just a nurse who got here maybe a half hour ago . . ."

"A nurse!" Anna exclaimed. She looked at the white station wagon that was parked in front of the house. The car was emblazoned with the words PERMANENCIA EN CASA. "Come *on!*" she shouted.

"Oh, man," Ben said, following her as she rushed to the front door and rang the bell repeatedly.

"Shit," she groaned. "We're too late." Yehuda Malkin stood back and to one side.

In less than a minute, the door slowly came open. Before them stood an ancient man, withered and stooped, his deeply tanned, leathery face a mass of wrinkles.

Josef Strasser.

"*¿Quién es éste?*" he said, scowling. "*Se está metiendo en mis cosas—ya llegó la enfermera que me tiene que revisar.*"

"He says his nurse is here for his checkup," Anna said. She raised her voice. "No! Herr Strasser—stay away from this nurse, I warn you!"

A white shape came into view behind the German. Ben said, "Anna! Behind him!"

The nurse approached the door, speaking quickly, chidingly it seemed, to Strasser. "*¡Vamos, Señor Albrecht, vamos para allá, que estoy apurada! ¡Tengo que ver al próximo paciente todavía!*"

"She's telling him to hurry up," Anna told Ben. "She's got another patient to see. Herr Strasser, this woman isn't a real nurse—I suggest you ask her for her credentials!"

The woman in the white uniform grasped the old man's shoulder and pulled him half toward her in one violent gesture. "*¡Ya mismo,*" she said, "*vamos!*"

With her free hand she grabbed the door to pull it closed, but Anna bent forward to block the door's arc with her knee.

Suddenly the nurse shoved Strasser aside. She reached into her uniform, and in one swift motion took out a gun.

But Anna moved even more quickly. "Freeze!"

The nurse fired.

At the same moment, Anna spun her body sideways, slamming Ben to the ground.

As Ben rolled to one side he heard a gunshot, followed by an animal-like roar.

He realized what had happened: the nurse had shot at Anna, but Anna had dodged out of the line of fire, and it was the Israeli protector who had been hit.

A red oval appeared in the middle of the man's forehead, and there was a spray of blood where the bullet exited his skull.

Anna got off two quick shots, and the fake nurse arched backward and then slumped to the floor.

And suddenly, for the briefest moment, everything was quiet. In the near-silence Ben could hear the distant singing of a bird.

Anna said, "Ben, you O.K.?"

He grunted yes.

"Oh, Jesus," she said, turning to see what had happened. Then she spun back around toward the doorway.

Strasser, crouched on the floor in his pale blue bathrobe, shielding his face with his hands, keened and keened.

"Strasser?" she repeated.

"*Gott im Himmel*," he moaned. "*Gott im Himmel. Sie haben mein Leben gerettet!*" Good God in heaven. You saved my life.

Images. Shapeless and unfocused, devoid of significance or definition, outlines blurring into plumes of gray, disintegrating into nothingness like a jet's exhaust tracks in a windy sky. At first, there was only awareness, without even any defined object of awareness. He was so cold. So very cold. Save for the spreading warmth on his chest.

And where there was warmth, he felt pain.

That was good. Pain was good.

Pain was the Architect's friend. Pain he could manage, could banish when he needed to. At the same time, it meant he was still alive.

Cold was not good. It meant that he had lost a great deal of blood.

That his body had gone into shock to lessen the further loss of blood: his pulse would have slowed, his heart beating with lessened force, the vessels in his extremities constricting to minimize the flow of blood to nonvital parts of the body.

He had to do an inventory. He was on the ground, motionless. Could he hear? For a moment, nothing disturbed the profound silence within his head. Then, as if a connection had been established, he could hear voices, faintly, muffled, as if inside a building . . .

Inside a house.

Inside *whose* house?

He must have lost a great deal of blood. Now he forced himself to retrieve the memories of the past hour.

Argentina. Buenos Aires.

Strasser.

Strasser's house. Where he had expected Benjamin Hartman and Anna Navarro and where he had encountered . . . *others.* Including someone armed with a marksman's rifle.

He had taken several gunshots to the chest. Nobody could survive that. *No!* He banished the thought. It was an unproductive thought. A thought such as an amateur might have.

He had not been shot at all. He was fine. Weakened in ways he could compensate for, but not out of the running. They *thought* he was out of the running, and that would be his strength. The images wavered before his mind, but for a brief while he was able to fix them, the images, like passport photos, of his three targets. In order: Benjamin Hartman; Anna Navarro; Josef Strasser.

His mind was as thick and opaque as old crankshaft oil, but, yes, it would function. Yet again, it was a matter of mental concentration: he would *assign* the injuries to another body—a vividly conceived doppelgänger, someone who was bloodied and in shock but *who was not he.* He was fine. Once he had gathered his reserves, he would be able to move, to stalk. To kill. His sheer force of will had always triumphed over adversity, and it would again.

Had an observer been keeping a close watch on Hans Vogler's body, he might possibly have detected, amid this furious gathering of mental fortitude, the barest flicker of an eyelid, nothing more. Every physical movement would now be planned and measured out in advance, the way a man dying of thirst in a desert might ration swallows from a canteen. There would be no wasted movement.

The Architect lived to kill. It was his area of unexampled expertise, his singular vocation. Now he would kill if only to prove that he still lived.

"Who are you?" asked Strasser in a high-pitched, hoarse voice.

Ben glanced from the nurse-impostor in her blood-drenched white uniform, sprawled on the floor, to the assassin who had almost killed them both, to the mysterious protectors his father had hired, both now lying murdered on the red clay tiles of the patio.

"Herr Strasser," Anna said, "the police will be here any moment. We have very little time."

Ben understood what she was saying: the Argentine police weren't to be trusted; they couldn't be here when the police arrived.

They would have very little time to learn what they needed from the old German.

Strasser's face was deeply creased and striated, etched with countless crisscrossing lines. His liver-colored lips stretched downward in a grimace, and they were wrinkled too, like elongated prunes. Seated on either side of his creviced, wide-nostriled nose were deep-sunk dark eyes like raisins in a ball of dough. "I am not Strasser," he protested. "You are confused."

"We know both your real name and your alias," Anna said impatiently. "Now tell me: the nurse—was she your regular one?"

"No. My usual nurse was sick this week. I have anemia and I need my shots."

"Where have you been for the last month or two?"

Strasser shifted from one foot to another. "I have to sit down," he wheezed. He moved slowly down the hallway.

They followed him down the hall, to a large, ornate, book-lined room. It was a library, a two-story atrium with walls and shelves of burnished mahogany.

"You live in hiding," Anna said. "Because you're a war criminal."

"I am *no* war criminal!" Strasser hissed. "I'm as innocent as a baby."

Anna smiled. "If you aren't a war criminal," she replied, "why are you hiding?"

He faltered, but only for a moment. "Here it has become fashionable to expel former Nazis. And yes, I was a member of the National Socialist party. Argentina signs agreements with Israel and Germany and America—they want to change their image. Now they only care what America thinks. They'd expel me just to make the American President smile. And you know, here in Buenos Aires, tracking down Nazis is a business! For some journalists it's a full-time job, how they make their living! But I was never a Hitler loyalist. Hitler was a ruinous madman—that was clear early in the war. He would be the destruction of all of us. Men like me knew that other accommodations had to be reached. My people sought to kill the man before he could do further damage to our industrial capacities. And our projections were correct. By the war's end, America had three-quarters of the world's invested capital, and two-thirds of the world's industrial capacity." He paused, smiled. "The man was simply bad for business."

"If you'd turned against Hitler, why are you still protected by the *Kamaradenwerk?*" Ben asked.

"Illiterate thugs," Strasser scoffed. "They are as ignorant of history as the avengers they seek to thwart."

"Why did you go out of town?" Anna interrupted.

"I was staying at an *estancia* in Patagonia owned by my wife's family. My late wife's family. At the foot of the Andes, in Río Negro province. A cattle and sheep ranch, but very luxurious."

"Do you go there regularly?"

"This is the first time I go there. My wife died last year and . . . Why do you ask these things?"

"That's why they couldn't find you to kill you," Anna said.

"Kill me . . . But *who* is trying to kill me?"

Ben looked at Anna, urging her to continue speaking.

She replied, "The company."

"The company?"

"Sigma."

She was bluffing, Ben knew, but she did it with great conviction. Chardin's words came to his mind, unbidden. *The Western world, and much of the rest, would respond to its ministrations, and it would accept the cover stories that accompanied them.*

Now Strasser was brooding. "The new leadership. Yes, that is it. Ah, yes." His raisin eyes gleamed.

"What is the 'new leadership'?" Ben prompted.

"Yes, of course," Strasser went on as if he hadn't heard Ben. "They are afraid I know things."

"Who?" Ben shouted.

Strasser looked up at him, startled. "I helped them set it up. Alford Kittredge, Siebert, Aldridge, Holleran, Conover—all those crowned heads of corporate empires. They had contempt for me, but they needed me, didn't they? They needed my contacts high up in the German government. If the venture wasn't properly multinational, it had no hope of succeeding. I had the trust of the men at the very top. They knew I had done things for them that forever placed me beyond the pale of ordinary humanity. They knew I had made that ultimate sacrifice for them. I was a go-between trusted by all sides. And now that trust has been betrayed, exposed for the charade it always was. Now it has become clear that they were using me for their own ends."

"You talked about the new leaders—is Jürgen Lenz one of them?" Anna asked urgently. "Lenz's son?"

"I have never met this Jürgen Lenz. I didn't know Lenz had a son, but then I wasn't an intimate of his."

"But you were both scientists," Ben said. "In fact, you invented Zyklon-B, didn't you?"

"I was one of a *team* that invented Zyklon-B," he replied. He pulled at his shabby blue bathrobe, adjusted it at the neck. "Now all the apologists attack me for my role in this, but they do not consider how elegant was this gas."

"Elegant?" Ben repeated. For a second he thought he'd misheard. *Elegant.* The man was loathsome.

"Before Zyklon-B, the soldiers had to shoot every prisoner," Strasser said. "Terrible bloodbaths. Gas was so clean and simple and elegant. And you know, gassing the Jews actually spared them."

Ben echoed: "Spared them." Ben was sickened.

"Yes! There were so many deadly diseases that went around those camps, they would have suffered much longer, much more painfully. Gassing them was the most humanitarian option."

Humanitarian. I'm looking in the face of evil, Ben thought. *An old man in a bathrobe uttering pieties.*

"How nice," Ben said.

"This is why we called it 'special treatment.'"

"Your euphemism for extermination."

"If you wish." He shrugged. "But you know, I didn't hand-pick victims for the gas chambers like Dr. Mengele or Dr. Lenz. They call Mengele the Angel of Death, but Lenz was the real one. The real Angel of Death."

"But not you," Ben said. "You were a scientist."

Strasser sensed the sarcasm. "What do you know of science?" he spat. "Are you a scientist? Do you have any idea how far ahead of the rest of the world we Nazi scientists were? Do you have any *idea?*" He spoke in a high tremulous voice. Spittle formed at the corners of his mouth. "They criticize Mengele's twin studies, yet his findings are still cited by the world's leading geneticists! The Dachau experiments in freezing human beings—those data are still used! What they learned at Ravensbrück about what happens to the female menstrual cycle under stress—when the women learned they were about to be executed—scientifically this was a breakthrough! Or Dr. Lenz's experiments on aging. The famine experiments on Soviet prisoners of war, the limb transplants—I could go on and on. Maybe it's not polite to talk about it, but you still use our science. You'd rather not think about how the experiments were done, but don't you realize that one of the main reasons we were so advanced was precisely *because* we were able to experiment on live human beings?"

Strasser's creased face had gotten even paler as he spoke, and now it was chalk-white. He had grown short of breath. "You Americans are disgusted by how we did our research, but you use fetal tissue from abortions for your transplants, yes? This is acceptable?"

Anna was pacing back and forth. "Ben, don't debate with this monster."

But Strasser would not stop. "Of course, there were many crackpot ideas. Trying to make girls into boys and boys into girls." He chortled. "Or trying to create Siamese twins by connecting the vital organs of the twins, a total failure, we lost many twins that way—"

"And after Sigma was established, did you continue to keep in touch with Lenz?" Anna asked, cutting him off.

Strasser turned, seemingly perturbed at the interruption. "Certainly. Lenz relied on me for my expertise and my contacts."

"Meaning what?" Ben said.

The old man shrugged. "He said he was doing work, doing research—*molecular* research—that would change the world."

"Did he tell you what it was, this research?"

"No, not me. Lenz was a private, secretive man. But I remember he said once, 'You simply cannot fathom what I'm working on.' He asked me to procure sophisticated electron microscopes, very hard to get in those days. They had just been invented. Also, he wanted various chemicals. Many things that were embargoed because of the war. He wanted everything crated and sent to a private clinic he had set up in an old *Schloss*, a castle, he had seized during the invasion of Austria."

"Where in Austria?" Anna asked.

"The Austrian Alps."

"Where in the Alps? What town or village, do you remember?" Anna persisted.

"How can I possibly remember this, after all these years? Maybe he never told me. I only remember Lenz called it 'the Clockworks'—because it had once been some kind of clock factory."

A scientific project of Lenz's. "A laboratory, then? Why?"

Strasser's lips pulled down. He sighed reproachfully. "To continue the research."

"What research?" he said.

Strasser fell silent, as if lost in thought.

"Come *on!*" Anna said. "*What* research?"

"I don't know. There was much important research that began during the Reich. Gerhard Lenz's work."

Gerhard Lenz: what was it Sonnenfeld had said about Lenz's horrific experiments in the camps? Human experimentation . . . but what?

"And you don't know the nature of this work?"

"Not today. Science and politics—it was all the same to these people. Sigma was, from the beginning, a means of funneling support to certain political organizations, subverting others. The men we're talking about— these were already men of enormous influence in the world. Sigma showed them that if they pooled their influence, the whole could be far, far greater than the sum of its parts. Collectively, there was very little they couldn't affect, direct, orchestrate. But, you know, Sigma was a living thing. And like living things, it evolved."

"Yes," Anna said. "With funds provided by the largest corporations in the world, along with funds stolen from the state *Reichsbank*. We know who the founding board members were. You're the last living member of that original board. But who are your successors?"

Strasser looked down the hall, but he seemed to be staring at nothing.

"Who controls it *now*? Give us *names!*" Ben shouted.

"I don't *know!*" Strasser's voice cracked. "They kept people like me quiet by sending us money regularly. We were lackeys, finally excluded from the inner councils of power. We should all be billionaires many, many times over. They send us millions, but it is crumbs, table scraps." Strasser's lips curled up in a repellent smile. "They give me table scraps, and now they wish to cut me off. They want to kill me because they don't want to pay me anymore. They're greedy, and they're ashamed. After all I did for them, they regard me as an embarrassment. And a danger, because even though the doors have been shut to me for years, they still think I know too much. For making possible everything they do, how am I repaid? With *contempt!*" A growing sense of rage—the pent-up grievance of years—made his words hard, metallic. "They act as if I am a poor relation, a black sheep, a foul-smelling derelict. The swells gather in their fancy-dress forum, and their biggest fear is that I will crash their party, like a skunk at a kaffeeklatsch. I know where they gather. I am not such a fool, such an ignoramus. I would not join them in Austria had they *asked* me to."

Austria.

"What are you talking about?" Ben demanded. "Where are they gathering? Tell me."

Strasser gave him a look that combined wariness and defiance. It was clear that he would say no more.

"Goddammit, answer me!"

"You are all the same," Strasser spat. "You would think somebody my age would be treated with respect! I have nothing more to say to you."

Anna was suddenly alert. "I hear sirens. This is it, Ben. We're out of here."

Ben stood directly in front of Strasser. "Herr Strasser, do you know who I am?"

"Who you are . . . ?" Strasser stammered.

"My father is Max Hartman. I'm sure you remember the name."

Strasser squinted. "Max Hartman . . . the Jew, our treasurer . . . ?"

"That's right. And he was an SS officer as well, I'm told." *But Sonnenfeld had said that would merely have been a cover, a ruse.* His heart was pounding, he dreaded hearing Strasser's confirmation of Max's ugly past.

Strasser laughed, flashing his ruined brown teeth. "SS!" he laughed. "He was no SS. We gave him fake SS papers so ODESSA would smuggle him out of Germany into Switzerland, with no questions asked. That was the deal."

Blood roared in Ben's ears. He felt a wave of relief, a physical sensation.

"Bormann chose him personally for the German delegation," Strasser went on. "Not just because he was skilled at moving money around, but because we needed a . . . a false head—"

"A figurehead."

"Yes. The industrialists from American and elsewhere were not so comfortable with what the Nazis had done. A Jewish participant was necessary to provide legitimacy—to show that we weren't the wrong kind of Germans, to show that we were not zealots, not Hitler disciples. For his part, your father got for himself a good deal—he got his family out of the camps, and a lot of other Jewish families as well, and he was given forty million Swiss francs—almost a million dollars U.S. A lot of money." A horrible smile. "Now he calls himself 'rags to riches story.' Is a million dollars rags? I don't think."

"Ben!" Anna shouted. Quickly she flashed the leather wallet that held her Department of Justice credentials. "Now you want to know who *I* am, Herr Strasser? I'm here on behalf of the U.S. Justice Department's Office of Special Investigations. I'm sure you know who they are."

"Oh ho," Strasser said. "Well, I'm sorry to disappoint you, but I'm an Argentine citizen and I don't recognize your authority."

The sirens were louder, just a few blocks away it seemed.

Anna turned back to him. "So I guess we'll see how serious the Argentine government is about extraditing war criminals. Out the back way, Ben."

Strasser's face flashed with rage. "Hartman," he said hoarsely.

"Come *on*, Ben!"

Strasser crooked a finger at Ben, beckoning him. Ben could not resist. The old man began to whisper. Ben knelt down to listen.

"Hartman, do you know your father was a weak little man?" Strasser said. "A man without a spine. A coward and a fraud who pretends to be a victim." Strasser's lips were inches from Ben's ear. His voice was singsong. "And you are the fraud's son, that's all. That is all you are to me."

Ben closed his eyes, fought to control his anger.

The fraud's son.

Was this true? Was Strasser right?

Strasser was clearly enjoying Ben's discomfort.

"Oh, you'd like to kill me right now, isn't that right, Hartman?" Strasser said. "Yet you don't. Because you're a coward, like your father."

Ben saw Anna starting down the hall.

"No," he said. "Because I'd much rather you spend your remaining
life in a stinking jail cell in Jerusalem. I'd like your last days to be as
unpleasant as possible. Killing you is a waste of a bullet."

He ran down the corridor, following Anna to the back of the house,
as the sirens grew louder.

Crawl, don't walk. The Architect knew that the effort to maintain or-
thostatic blood pressure in his head would be made much more difficult
by standing erect, when there was as yet no absolute need to do so. It
was a rational decision, and his ability to make it was almost as reassuring
as the Glock he had retained in an ankle holster.

The front door was open, the hallway deserted. He crawled, in a standard infantry crawl, indifferent to the wide smear of blood he was leaving
as his shirtfront draped against the blond flooring. Every yard seemed
like a mile to him. But he would not be deterred.

You're the best. He was seventeen, and the drill instructor told him so,
in front of the entire battalion. *You're the best.* He was twenty-three, and
his commanding officer at Stasi had said so in an official report that he
showed young Hans before forwarding it to his superior. *You're the best.*
These words from the head of his Stasi directorate: he had just returned
from a "hunting trip" in West Berlin, having dispatched four physicists—
members of an internationally distinguished team from the University of
Leipzig—who had defected the day before. *You're the best*: a top-level
Sigma official, a white-haired American in flesh-toned glasses, had spoken those words to him. It was after he had stage-managed the death of
a prominent Italian leftist, shooting him from across the street while the
man was in the throes of passion with a fifteen-year-old Somali whore.
But he would hear those words again. And again. Because they were true.

And because they were true, he would not give up. He would not
succumb to the nearly overpowering urge to surrender, to sleep, to stop.

With robotic precision, he moved hand and knee and propelled himself down the hallway.

Finally, he found himself in a spacious, double-height room, its walls lined with books. Lizardlike eyes surveyed the area. His primary target was not present. A disappointment, not a surprise.

Instead, there was the wheezing, sweating weakling Strasser, a traitor who, too, was deserving of death.

How many more minutes of consciousness did the Architect have left? He eyed Strasser avidly, as if extinguishing his light might help to restore his own.

Shakily, he rose from the floor into a marksman's crouch. He felt muscles in his body trying to spasm, but he held his arms completely still. The small Glock in his arms had now acquired the weight of a cannon, yet somehow he managed to raise the firearm until it was at the precisely correct angle.

It was at that moment that Strasser, perhaps alerted by the old-penny odor of blood, finally became aware of his presence.

The Architect watched the raisin-like eyes widen momentarily, then fall closed. Squeezing the trigger was like lifting a desk with one finger, but he would do so. *Did so.*

Or did he?

When he failed to hear the gun's report, he first worried that he had not executed his mission. Then he realized that it was his sensory awareness that was beginning to shut down.

The room was swiftly darkening: he knew that brain cells starved of oxygen ceased to function—that the aural and optical functions shut down first, but that sentience itself would soon follow.

He waited until he saw Strasser hit the ground before he allowed his own eyes to close. As they did so, there was a fleeting awareness that his eyes would never open again; and then there was no awareness of anything at all.

Back in the hotel room, Ben and Anna rifled through a stack of papers that they'd hurriedly purchased at a newsstand on the way. Chardin had referred to an imminent development. And the "fancy-dress forum" in Austria that Strasser had mentioned chimed with an item they'd recently come across: but what was it?

The answer was within their grasp.

It was Anna who came across the item in *El País*, Argentina's leading newspaper. It was another brief article about the International Children's Health Forum—a convocation of world leaders to discuss matters of pressing mutual concern, especially with respect to the developing world. But what caught her eye this time was the city where the meeting was to be held: Vienna, Austria.

She read on. There was a list of sponsors—among them, the Lenz Foundation. Translating from the Spanish, she read the article out loud to Ben.

A shiver ran down his spine. "My God," he said. "This is it! It has to be. Chardin said only *days* remained. What he was talking about has to be related to this conference. Read me the list of sponsors again."

Anna did so.

And Ben started to make a few phone calls. These were calls to foundation professionals, people who were delighted to hear from one of their contributors. Slipping into a familiar role, Ben sounded hale and hearty when he spoke to them, but what he learned was profoundly dismaying.

"They're great people, the folks from the Lenz Foundation," Geoffrey Baskin, programs director for the Robinson Foundation, told him in his dulcet New Orleans accent. "It's really their baby, but they just wanted to keep a low profile. They put it together, footed most of the bill—it's hardly fair that we're getting any of the glory. But I guess they wanted to make sure it had an international feeling. Like I say, they're really selfless."

"That's nice to hear," Ben said. His kept his tone upbeat even as he felt a rising sense of dread. "We may be partnering with them on a special project, so I just wanted to get your sense of them. Really nice to hear."

Dignitaries and leaders from around the world would be gathering in Vienna, under the auspices of the Lenz Foundation . . .

They had to get to Vienna.

It was the one place in the world they shouldn't be showing their faces, and the one place where they had no choice but to go.

Anna and he paced the hotel room. They could take precautions— precautions that now came as second nature: disguise, falsified identities, separate flights.

But the risks seemed much greater now.

"If we're not just chasing a will-o'-the-wisp, we've got to assume that every commercial flight into Vienna is going to be scrutinized very carefully," Anna said. "They're going to be on full alert."

Ben felt the flicker of an idea. "What did you say again?"

"They're going to be on full alert. Border control isn't going to be a cakewalk. More like a gauntlet."

"Before that."

"I said we've got to assume that every commercial flight into Vienna . . ."

"That's *it*," Ben said.

"What's it?"

"Anna, I'm going to take a risk here. And the calculation is that it's a smaller risk than we'd otherwise be facing."

"I'm listening."

"I'm going to call a guy named Fred McCallan. He was the codger I was supposed to go skiing with in St. Moritz."

"You were going to St. Moritz to go skiing with a 'codger.' "

Ben blushed. "Well, there was a granddaughter in the picture."

"Go on."

"More to the point, though, there's a private *jet* in the picture. A Gulfstream. I've been in it once. Very red. Red seats, red carpeting, red TV set. Fred will still be at the Hotel Carlton there, and the plane will probably be at the little airport in Chur."

"So you're going to call him up and ask for the keys. Kind of like borrowing someone's station wagon to pick up groceries, right?"

"Well . . ."

Anna shook her head. "It's true what they say—the rich really are different from you and me." She shot him a look. "I mean, of course, just me."

"Anna . . ."

"I'm scared as shit, Ben. Bad jokes come with the territory. Listen, I don't know this guy from Adam. If you think you can trust him—if that's what your gut is telling you—then I can live with it."

"Because you're right, it's the *commercial* flights they'll be watching . . ."

Anna nodded vigorously. "So long as they're not coming from places like Colombia, private flights get pretty much a free pass. If this guy's pilot can move the Gulfstream to Brussels, let's say . . ."

"We go directly to Brussels, assuming nobody's onto the IDs Oscar made for us. Then transfer to Fred's private jet and fly to Vienna that way. That's the way the Sigma principals travel. Chances are, they're not going to be expecting a Gulfstream with two fugitives on board."

"O.K., Ben," Anna said. "I call this the beginning of a plan."

Ben dialed the number of the Hotel Carlton and waited a minute for the front desk to connect him.

Fred McCallan's voice boomed even through the international phone lines. "My God, Benjamin, do you have any idea of the hour? Never mind, I suppose you're calling to apologize. Though I'm not the one you should apologize to. Louise has been devastasted. *Devastated*. And you two have *so* much in common."

"I understand, Fred, and I . . ."

"But actually I'm glad you finally called. Do you realize they're saying the most *preposterous* things about you? A guy called me up and gave me an earful. They're saying that . . ."

"You've got to believe me, Fred," Ben said urgently, cutting him off, "there's no truth to those reports whatever—I mean, whatever they're accusing me of, you've got to believe me when I say that . . ."

"And I *laughed* in his face!" Fred was saying, having talked over Ben's interjection. "I told him, maybe that's what you get from your creepy English boarding schools, but I'm a Deerfield man myself, and there's no way on God's green earth that . . ."

"I appreciate the vote of confidence, Fred. The thing is . . ."

"Top-seeded in tennis, I told him. You were, weren't you?"

"Well, actually . . ."

"Track and field? I was a track and field man myself—did I ever show you my trophies? Louise thinks it's ridiculous that I'm still boasting about them fifty years later, and she's right. But I'm *incorrigible*."

"Fred, I've got a really, really, really big favor to ask."

"For you, Benny? You're practically family, you know that. One day you might actually *be* family. Just say the word, my boy. Just say the word."

As Anna said, it was the beginning of a plan, no more. But foolproof would take more time than they had. Because the one thing that was certain was that they had to make their way to Vienna as fast as possible, or it would be too late.

Unless it was, as Chardin had suggested, already too late.

CHAPTER THIRTY-NINE

The hotel was in Vienna's seventh district, and they had selected it because it appeared to be suitably anonymous, catering mostly to German and Austrian tourists. Traveling to Brussels in uniform as David Paine, Ben arrived first, by several hours; Anna, using the Gayatri Chandragupta alias for one last time, had traveled on a separate flight, connecting through Amsterdam. McCallan's pilot, a genial Irishman named Harry Hogan, was perplexed by the odd garb of his guests, and further perplexed that they'd refused to tell him in advance where they planned on going, but the old man had been vehement in his instructions: whatever Ben wanted, Ben would get. No questions asked.

Compared to the luxury of the Gulfstream, and the open-faced companionability of Harry Hogan, the hotel seemed drab and depressing. All the more so because Anna hadn't arrived yet: they agreed that traveling together from the airport was a risk best avoided. They'd travel separately, and by different routes.

Alone in the room, Ben felt caged and anxious. It was noontime but the weather was foul; rain spattered against the room's small windows, deepening his sense of gloom.

He thought about Chardin's life, about the incredible ways in which the governance of the Western world had been molded and directed by these corporate managers. And he thought about his father. A victim? A victimizer? Both?

Max had hired people to watch out for him—minders, *baby-sitters*, for God's sake. In a way, that was typical of the man: if Ben wouldn't let old secrets stay buried, then Max would try to control him his own way. It was both infuriating and touching.

When Anna arrived—they were sharing the room as Mr. and Mrs. David Paine—he embraced her, placing his face next to hers and feeling some of his sense of anxiety ebb.

Feeling grimy from the long flight, they each showered. Anna took a long time, emerging from the bathroom in a terry-cloth robe, her dark brown hair combed straight back, her skin glowing.

As she went to her suitcase to pick out clothes, Ben said, "I don't want you to see Lenz alone."

She didn't look up. "Oh, is that right?"

"Anna," he said, exasperated, "we don't even know who Jürgen Lenz really *is*."

Holding a blouse in one hand and a navy skirt in the other, she turned to face him. Her eyes flashed. "At this point, it doesn't matter. I *have* to talk to him."

"Look, whoever he is, we can assume that he was at least involved in the murder of eight old men around the world. My brother, too. And it's a plausible assumption that he's become a principal in a conspiracy that, if Chardin is right, has no real outer bounds. Lenz knows my face, and now he no doubt knows where I've been. So it's a fair assumption that he knows I've been traveling with you, which means he may well have seen a photograph of you. It isn't *safe* for you to go see this man."

"I'm not disputing that, Ben. We don't have the luxury of choosing between the safe thing and the dangerous thing: whatever we do at this point will involve danger. Even doing nothing. Besides, if I'm killed shortly after asking him questions about a series of murders around the world, he'd immediately be the focus of suspicion—and I seriously doubt he wants that."

"What even makes you think he'll see you?"

She set the clothes down on the edge of the bed.

"The best way to play him is not to play him."

"I don't like the sound of this."

"This is a man who's used to being in control, used to manipulating people and events. Call it arrogance or call it curiosity, but he'll *want* to see me."

"Listen to me, Anna . . ."

"Ben, I can take care of myself. I really can."

"Obviously," he protested. "It's just that—" He stopped. She was looking at him strangely. "What?"

"You're the protective type, aren't you?"

"I don't know about protective, exactly. I'm just—"

She approached him, examining him as if he were an exhibit in a museum. "When we met, I just assumed you were another rich, spoiled, self-centered preppy."

"You were probably right."

"No. I don't think so. So was that your role in the family—the caretaker?"

Embarrassed, Ben didn't know how to reply. Maybe she was right, but for some reason he didn't want to say it. Instead, he drew her close. "I don't want to lose you, Anna," he said quietly. "I've lost too many people in my life."

She closed her eyes and hugged him tight; both of them were agitated, nervous, exhausted, and yet as they embraced a moment of calm passed between them. He inhaled her delicate floral scent, and something in him melted.

Then, gently, she withdrew. "We have a plan, and we've got to follow it, Ben," she said, her voice soft but resolute, and she dressed quickly. "I have to make a pickup at the DHL office, and then make a business call."

"Anna," Ben said.

"I've got to go. We can talk later."

"*Oh, sweet Jesus,*" said Officer Burt Connelly. He had been on the I66 Virginia highway patrol for only six months, and he still wasn't accustomed to the sight of roadside carnage. He felt his stomach heaving, scurried to the side of the road, and vomited. A splash got on his crisp blue uniform, and he wiped it off with a tissue. Then he tossed the tissue out, too.

Even in the low light of the early evening, he could see only too clearly the blood spattered across the windscreen and the man's head on the dashboard. It had been severed from the body and horribly flattened by the impact—the "second collision," as they called it, which was the collision of the passenger inside the crashed vehicle itself.

Connelly's partner, Officer Lamar Graydon, had been on highway patrol for more than a year. He'd seen a few gruesome accidents before, and he knew how to keep his lunch down.

"It's a bad one, Burt," Graydon said, walking over and patting his partner's back. A sort of weary bravado played in his brown eyes. "But I've come across worse."

"Did you see the guy's head!"

"At least there's no little kids involved. Let me tell you, last year, I was at an accident scene where a baby got ejected through the open window of an Impala, thrown thirty feet in the air. Like a goddamn rag doll. Now, *that* was horrible."

Connelly coughed a few times, and straightened up. "Sorry," he said. "It's just that guy's face . . . I'm O.K. now. Ambulance on the way?"

"Should be here in ten minutes. Not that *he's* feeling any pain." Graydon nodded toward the decapitated accident victim.

"So what's the situation here? SVF?" Statistically, a single-vehicle fatality was the most common sort.

"Not a chance," Graydon said. "No guardrail does that. This is what happens when you slam into one of those Kenworth car haulers, and there are plenty of 'em on this highway. With monsters like that, the back hangs low, and it's one flat steel edge—like a blade. If you're behind one of those things and it stops short, either you duck or it takes your head off. I'll betcha that's what you're looking at."

"Then what happened to the other guy? Where's the goddamn truck?" Connelly was starting to regain a sense of self-possession. Oddly, he even felt a little hungry again.

"Looks like he decided not to stick around," Graydon said.

"Well, are we going to find it?"

"I've radioed it in. Dispatcher's got the info. Between you and me, though, I wouldn't bet money on it. Thing to do right now is try to ID the guy. Search the pockets."

Though the top of the red Taurus was smashed in, the door on the driver's side opened easily. Connelly put on latex gloves before rummaging through the headless man's pockets; that was procedure when clothing was blood-soaked.

"Give me a name, and I'll radio that in, too," Graydon called out.

"Driver's license says Dupree, Arliss Dupree," Connelly said. "Lives on Glebe Road, in Arlington."

"That's all we need to know," Graydon said. "And you don't have to freeze your ass off, Burt. We can wait in the patrol car now."

———

The building that housed the Lenz Foundation was, Bauhaus style, all glass and marble. The lobby was flooded with light, furnished simply with white leather chairs and sofas.

Anna asked the receptionist to call the office of the director. That he was at the foundation she'd already verified with an earlier phone call.

"Who shall I say wishes to see Dr. Lenz?" she inquired.

"My name is Anna Navarro. I'm an agent with the U.S. Department of Justice."

She'd earlier considered and rejected the idea of approaching him under some false alias. But as she'd told Ben, she'd decided that the best way to play him was not to play him. If Lenz did even a cursory background check, he'd learn of her outlaw status. But would that make him less likely to see him, or more? If their theories about Alan Bartlett were correct, Jürgen Lenz might already know a fair amount about her. But he wouldn't know—couldn't know—precisely what she had learned, and might have conveyed to others. She had to rely upon his curiosity, his arrogance, and, most of all, his desire to control the situation. He would want to know whether she posed a threat to him, and he would want to assess that himself.

The receptionist picked up her desk phone and spoke quietly, then handed Anna the handset. "Please."

The woman on the phone was courteous but firm. "I'm afraid Dr. Lenz has a full schedule today. Perhaps you'd like to make an appointment for another day? I'm afraid that with the International Children's Health Forum, all the people here have their hands full."

He had to be evading her, but was that because he'd heard her institutional affiliation, or because he already knew her name? Maybe the woman hadn't even bothered to convey the message.

"It really can't wait," Anna said. "I need to see him as soon as possible on an extremely urgent matter."

"Can you tell me what you wish to speak with Dr. Lenz about?"

She hesitated. "Please tell him it's a personal matter."

She put the phone down and paced nervously around the lobby.

Here I am in the lair of the beast, she thought. *The heart of darkness, airy and full of light.*

The white Carrara marble walls were bare except for a line of large blowups of photographs depicting the wide range of humanitarian causes supported by the Lenz Foundation.

There was a picture of several generations of a refugee family—a toothless, hunched old woman, a weathered and beaten-down husband and wife, their ragged children. This was entitled simply KOSOVO.

Meaning what? What did the Lenz Foundation have to do with refugees?

There was a portrait of a peculiarly wizened girl with a beaked nose, parchment skin, prominent eyes, long hair that was obviously a wig. She was smiling with crowded, irregular teeth, at once a young girl and an old woman. This photograph was labeled HUTCHINSON-GILFORD PROGERIA SYNDROME.

There was the famous stark and shocking photograph of emaciated concentration-camp inmates looking curiously at the camera from their bunk beds. THE HOLOCAUST.

A strange array of causes. What connected them?

Anna sensed a presence and looked up. A matronly woman had appeared in the lobby, a pair of reading glasses hanging from a chain around her neck. "Ms. Navarro," she said. "You're quite fortunate. Dr. Lenz has managed to free up a few minutes to see you."

At a security station on the floor above, a technician hunched over a control panel. Manipulating a joystick, he swiveled and zoomed in one of the wall-mounted cameras. The visitor's light brown face now filled the flat screen plasma display. The press of a button froze the image. By means of a thirty-seven point physiognomic metric, the face could be digitally compared with a set of image files in the system's extensive database. Somehow the technician suspected that it would not take long to come up with a match.

He was right. A quiet electronic chirp alerted him that the image matched a file from the watch list. As a column of information scrolled down the monitor, he picked up the phone and called Lenz, dialing a number that rang directly on his desk.

Jürgen Lenz was just as Ben had described him: whippet-thin, silver-haired, elegant, and charming. He wore a perfectly cut suit of dark gray flannel, a neatly pressed white shirt, a foulard tie. He sat in a Chippendale-style chair facing her, his hands folded in his lap.

"Well, you've got me," he said as he handed her credentials back to her.

"Excuse me?"

"You've piqued my curiosity. I'm told a woman is here to see me from the American government in connection with a 'personal matter'—how could I possibly resist such a lure?"

She wondered how much he knew about her. She could see already that he was as smooth and hard as polished stone.

"Thank you for seeing me," Anna returned courtesy with courtesy. "I've been on special assignment, investigating a series of murders around the world—"

"*Murders?*" he said. "What in heaven's name can I tell you about murders?"

She knew she had one chance, and she'd have to hit him hard. Any weakness, any hesitation, any uncertainty, and the game was over. She would stick to one issue of narrow concern: the Sigma homicides.

"The murder victims were all involved in a corporation known as Sigma, of which Gerhard Lenz was a founder. We've established a direct connection between the deaths and a subsidiary of the chemical giant Armakon, on whose board you sit . . ."

Lenz seemed to relax. He laughed deeply, mellifluously. "Ms. Navarro, in all my years of crusading against the evil that my father did, I've been accused of many terrible things—disloyalty to family, disloyalty to my country, opportunism, insincerity, you name it—but no one has *ever* accused me of murder!"

Anna had known what to expect. He would be poised, nonconfrontational, evasive. So she had tried to anticipate his every response, and she was ready with a reply. "Dr. Lenz," she said, "I hope you're not denying that you're on the board of Armakon."

"It's purely honorary."

She hesitated, then said, "I don't want to waste your time. As you know, Armakon is the secret owner of a biotech start-up in Philadelphia called Vortex."

She watched his face. His eyes were neutral, guarded. "I'm sure Armakon owns many inconsequential start-ups around the world. So?"

"Vortex," she went on, "is the inventor and manufacturer of a synthetic substance that's used in basic research, for molecular tagging. It's also a deadly poison that, once injected into a person's bloodstream, induces immediate death by heart failure, and is then undetectable in the blood."

He replied in a flat voice, "How interesting."

"That particular toxin was found in the ocular fluid of several of these murder victims."

"Do you have a point?"

"I do," she said quietly, eyes locked on his. She was momentarily startled by what she saw there: absolute searing contempt. "I have evidence linking you directly to those murders."

For a moment there was only the ticking of a clock. Somberly, Lenz clasped his hands. He looked like a Lutheran minister. "Agent Navarro, all these terrible charges you hurl at me. These terrible things you say I've done. I took time out of an extremely busy day—time I can scarcely afford to squander—because I thought we could help each other in some way. Perhaps a friend of mine was in trouble. Perhaps someone needed my help, or vice versa. Instead, you come here on what I believe is called a 'fishing expedition.'" He rose from his chair. "I'm afraid you'll have to leave."

Heart hammering, she thought: *Not so fast, you bastard.* "I'm not done yet," she said with a firmness that she could see surprised him.

"Agent Navarro, I really don't have to talk to you. Correct me if I'm wrong, but anyone who visits me as an agent of American law enforcement is here as a guest of my country. If you wish to interrogate me because of who my father was, you must ask permission of the Austrian government, yes? Have you done that?"

"No," she admitted, flushing. "But let me be clear—"

"*No*, madame," he said, raising his voice. "Let *me* be clear. You haven't done that because you are no longer in the employ of your country. In fact, you are yourself a fugitive from justice. Let us *both* put our cards on the table. Your investigations have taken you outside the boundaries of lawful conduct. My secretary conveys the insistent requests of an American agent to see me. At my behest, she makes a few phone calls to verify your identity." His eyes didn't leave her face. "She discovers that you are a wanted woman. But then you must have expected we would take such precautions. And yet you came to see me all the same. Which piqued my curiosity further."

"Anything to alleviate the dull tedium of your days," Anna said.

"Put yourself in my position, Ms. Navarro. A rogue U.S. agent takes a very peculiar interest in me—this isn't something that happens every day. Naturally I wonder: Have you come across someone or something that is a threat to me? Have you broken ranks and come to tell me about some hostile intrigue within American intelligence? I know our investigations of Operation Paper Clip have earned me enemies in some American circles. Have you come to warn me of some imminent menace? The imagination whirls. The mind boggles. So how could I resist meeting with you? You knew I could not."

"We're getting off the subject," Anna broke in. "None of this—"

Lenz talked over her. "So you'll appreciate how sorely disappointed I was when I learned that you're here only to hurl absurd, unfounded, and easily discredited accusations. From all indications, you're not only off the reservation, as your countrymen like to say—you're out of your mind." He pointed to his desk. "I need only pick up this phone and call a friend of mine in the Justice Ministry and you would be remanded to the tender mercies of the U.S. authorities."

You want a fight, she thought, *you got it*. He was not going to intimidate her. Not with what she knew about him.

"You're perfectly right," she said calmly. "You could pick up that phone and do that. But I wonder whether it would best serve your interests."

Lenz had turned his back on her and was heading toward the exit. "Miss Navarro, your silly games really don't interest me. Now would you please leave my office this moment, or shall I be forced to—"

"Just before I came here I stopped at the local DHL office, where a document was waiting for me. It contained the results of a search I requested. I had submitted a set of your fingerprints and asked the lab to identify them. It took a long time. Our Latent Fingerprints Section had to dig deep to find a match. But they did." She took a breath. "Dr. Lenz, I know who you are. I don't understand it. I really can't fathom it, to be quite honest. But I know who you really are."

She was terrified, more frightened than she'd ever been before. Her heart was hammering; blood rushed in her ears. She knew she had no backup.

Lenz stopped short, a few feet from the exit, and closed the door. When he turned around, his face had gone dark with rage.

CHAPTER FORTY

Ben joined the modest crowd of journalists and cameramen assembled outside the Wiener Stadthalle Civic Center, the large, beige stone structure where the International Children's Health Forum was to be hosted. He made eye contact with a cold and miserable-looking man—paunchy, middle-aged, dressed in a fraying tan trench coat. Ben extended a hand. "I'm Ron Adams," he said. "With *American Philanthropy* magazine. Been standing out here long?"

"Too damn long," the rumpled man said. He spoke with a cockney accent. "Jim Bowen, *Financial Times*. European correspondent and pathetic wretch." He shot Ben a comic, mock-baleful glance. "My editor sweet-talked me into going with promises of schnitzel and strudel and *Sachertorte*, and I thought to myself, 'Well, that's a bit of all right then.' Higgins will *never* hear the end of it: there's a solemn vow. Two days of standing around in this lovely frigid rain, my little piggies turning into popsicles, down to practically my last fag, and all we get are the same damn press releases they're faxing all the bureaus."

"But you must be seeing some pretty grand poobahs sauntering in and out. I've looked at the guest list."

"Well, that's the thing—wherever they are, they're not here. Maybe they're just as bored with the program as everybody else. Probably all decided to nip out and take a quick skiing vacation. Strictly B-list, the only people I've caught sight of. Our photographer's taken to drink, he has. I think he's got the right idea, too. I've got half a mind to pop down the corner for a pint, except they serve the ale too damn cold in this country. Ever notice that? Plus which, the stuff they make tastes like piss."

The big names weren't here? Did that mean that the Sigma conclave was taking place elsewhere? Ben's stomach plummeted: Had he been misled? Perhaps Strasser had been mistaken. Or perhaps he and Anna had made a false assumption somewhere along the line.

"Any rumors about where the muckety-mucks are hanging out?" Ben kept his tone light.

The cockney scribe snorted. "Bloody hell. Know what it is? It's like one of those sodding nightclubs where all the really hip people get shown to a special room, and the squares get stuck in a pen with hay on the floor." He rummaged through a badly squashed and nearly empty pack of Silk Cuts. "Bloody hell."

Ben's mind raced. Jürgen Lenz was clearly calling the shots here. Just as clearly, the real action wasn't taking place at the conference at all. The answer was no doubt to be found in the Lenz Foundation's activities. And here, an indirect approach would probably yield the quickest results. Back at the hotel, he worked the phones, keeping one eye on his watch. He wanted to collect as much information as possible before he and Anna compared notes at the end of the day.

"Cancer Foundation of Austria."

"I'd like to speak with the administrator in charge of fund-raising, please," Ben said. There was a click, several seconds of hold music— "Tales from the Vienna Woods," naturally—and then another woman's voice: "Schimmel."

"Frau Schimmel, my name's Ron Adams, and I'm an American journalist in Vienna, working on a profile of Jürgen Lenz for *American Philanthropy* magazine."

The administrator's voice changed instantly from wary to exuberant: "Yes, certainly! How may I help you?"

"I guess I'm really interested—especially in light of the International Children's Health Forum—in documenting his generosity, the extent of his support for your foundation, his involvement, that sort of thing."

The vague question elicited an even vaguer reply. She went on at length, then he hung up, frustrated. He had called the Lenz Foundation and asked a low-level staffer for a list of all charities they funded. No questions were asked: as a tax-exempt institution, the Lenz Foundation was obligated to divulge all of its gifts.

But what he was looking for specifically, he had no idea. He was probing mindlessly. There had to be a way to penetrate the facade of Jürgen Lenz, philanthropist. Yet there seemed to be no logic to the type of grants

Lenz made, no commonality, no organizing principle. Cancer—Kosovo—
Progeria—The German-Jewish Dialogue? Those were the main ones. But
if there was a connection, he had yet to find it, even after calling three
different charities.

One more try, he told himself, and then move on. He got up from
the desk in the hotel room, got a Pepsi from the little refrigerator, returned to the desk, and dialed another number from the list.

"Hello, Progeria Institute."

"May I speak to the administrator in charge of fund-raising, please?"

A few seconds went by.

"Meitner."

"Yes, Frau Meitner. My name is Ron Adams . . ."

Without much hope he went through his now-standard interview. The
woman was, like all the administrators he talked to, a great fan of Jürgen
Lenz and delighted to sing his praises.

"Mr. Lenz is really our chief benefactor," she said. "Without him, I
think we could not exist. You know, this is a tragic and exceedingly rare
disorder."

"I really don't know anything about it," he said politely. He realized
he was wasting time when there was none to spare.

"To put it simply, it's premature aging. The full name is Hutchinson-
Gilford Progeria Syndrome. It causes a child to age seven or eight times
faster than he should. A ten-year-old child with progeria will look like
an eighty-year-old man, with arthritis and heart problems and all the
rest. Most of them die by the age of thirteen. Seldom do they grow taller
than the height of the average five-year-old."

"My God," Ben said, genuinely appalled.

"Because it's so rare, it is what is called an 'orphan disease,' which
means it gets very little funding for research, and the drug companies
have no financial incentive to find a cure. That's why his help is so
terribly important."

Biotech companies . . . Vortex.

"Why do you think Mr. Lenz takes such a personal interest?"

A hesitation. "I think perhaps you should ask Mr. Lenz."

He sensed the sudden chill in her voice. "If there's anything you'd like
to tell me off the record . . ."

A pause. "Do you know who Jürgen Lenz's father was?" the woman
said carefully.

Did anyone? "Gerhard Lenz, the Nazi doctor," Ben replied.

"Correct. Off the record, Mr. Adams, I'm told that Gerhard Lenz did some ghastly experiments on children with progeria. No doubt Jürgen Lenz simply wishes to undo what his father did. But please don't print that."

"I won't," Ben promised. *But if Jürgen Lenz was not Gerhard's son, why the interest in the same causes? What sort of bizarre masquerade was this?*

"You know, Mr. Lenz even sends a few of these poor children to a private sanatorium in the Austrian Alps that his foundation runs."

"Sanatorium?"

"Yes, I think it's known as the Clockworks."

Ben bolted upright. The Clockworks: the place where Strasser had sent the senior Lenz electron microscopes. If Jürgen *was* Gerhard's son, he would have inherited it. But was he really using it as a sanatorium?

He attempted a breezy tone. "Oh, where's that?"

"The Alps. I don't know exactly where. I've never been there. It's exclusive, private, very luxurious. A real escape from the bustle of the city."

"I'd love to talk to a child who's been there." *And find out what's really going on.*

"Mr. Adams," she said somberly, "the children who are invited are usually at the very end of their brief lives. Frankly, I don't know of any who might still be living. But I'm sure one of the parents wouldn't mind talking to you about Mr. Lenz's generosity."

The man's apartment was a fourth-floor walk-up in a dismal apartment building in Vienna's twelfth district, a small and dark place that smelled of stale cigarette smoke and cooking grease.

After the death of their beloved son at the age of eleven, the man explained, he and his wife had divorced. Their marriage had not survived the stress of their son's illness and death. Prominently displayed next to the sofa was a large color photograph of their boy, Christoph. It was hard to tell his age; he could have been eight or eighty. He was completely bald, with a receding chin, a large head with a small face, bulging eyes, the wizened countenance of a very old man.

"My son died at the sanatorium," the man said. He had a full gray beard, bifocal glasses, a scraggly fringe around a bald pate. His eyes were filled with tears. "But at least he was happy at the end of his life. Dr. Lenz is a most generous man. I'm glad Christoph could die happy."

"Did you ever visit Christoph there, at the Clockworks?" Ben asked.

"No, parents are not permitted. It's a place only for children. All of the children's medical problems are taken care of by an expert medical staff. But he sent me postcards." He got up and returned a few minutes later with a picture postcard. The handwriting was a large, childish scrawl. Ben turned the card over and saw the color photograph of an alpine mountain. The caption beneath the photograph said SEMMERING.

Lenz's widow had mentioned Semmering.

Strasser had talked about Gerhard Lenz's research clinic in the Austrian Alps.

Could it be the same place?

Semmering.

He had to find Anna immediately, get this information to her.

He looked up from the card and saw the father weeping silently. In a minute the man was able to speak. "This is what I always tell myself. My Christoph died happy."

They had arranged to meet back at the hotel no later than seven o'clock that evening.

If she was unable to return by then, Anna said, she'd call. If for some reason she was unable to call, or thought it was unsafe to do so, she had specified a fallback meeting place: nine o'clock at the Schweizerhaus in the Prater.

By eight o'clock she hadn't returned to the hotel, and there was no message.

She'd been gone for almost the entire day. Even if Lenz had agreed to see her, Ben couldn't figure out how she could spend more than an hour or two at the foundation. But she'd been gone almost twelve hours.

Twelve hours.

He was beginning to worry.

At eight-thirty, when she still hadn't called, he left for the Schweizerhaus, on Strasse des Ersten Mai 2. By now he was beyond nervous; he was fearful that something had happened to her. He asked himself, *Am I overreacting?* She doesn't have to account for her whereabouts at all times.

Still . . .

It was a lively place, renowned for its roasted pork hocks served with mustard and horseradish sauce. Ben sat alone at a table for two, waiting, nursing a Czech Budweiser beer.

Waiting.

The beer didn't calm his nerves. All he could think about was Anna, and what might have become of her.

By ten o'clock there was still no sign of her. He called the hotel, but she had neither arrived nor left a message. He repeatedly checked his phone to make sure it was on so she could reach him if she tried.

He ordered dinner for two, but by the time the food arrived he'd lost his appetite.

Around midnight he returned to the empty hotel room. He tried to read for a while but was unable to concentrate.

The sandpaper of Chardin's voice: *Wheels within wheels—that was the way we worked. . . .* Strasser: *a cabal within a cabal . . . Lenz said he was doing work that would change the world.*

He fell asleep on top of the bed, in his clothes, with all the room lights on, and slept fitfully.

He and Peter were strapped to two gurneys, side by side; above them was Dr. Gerhard Lenz, gowned and masked in full surgical garb. His light eyes, however, unmistakable. "We will make the two of them one," he was saying to a hatchet-faced assistant. "We will connect their organs so that neither will be viable without the other. Together, both will survive—or together, both will die." A gloved hand wielded a scalpel like a violin bow, pressing it against flesh in bold, confident strokes. The pain was beyond endurance.

Struggling against the restraints, he turned to see his brother's face, staring, frozen in horror.

"Peter!" he called out.

His brother's mouth gaped open, and under the harsh overhead lights, Ben could see that Peter's tongue had been removed. The heavy smell of ether filled the air, and a black mask was forcibly placed over Ben's face. But it didn't produce unconsciousness; if anything, he grew more alert, more aware of the horrors being done to him.

He awoke at three in the morning.

And still Anna hadn't returned.

A long, sleepless night followed.

He tried to doze but was unable to. He hated not having anyone to call, or anything he could do to locate her.

He sat, tried to read, couldn't focus. He could think only of Anna.

Oh, God, he loved her so.

At seven, groggy and disoriented, he called down to the front desk, for the fifth time, to see whether Anna might have called from somewhere in the middle of the night.

No message.

He took a shower, shaved, ordered a room service breakfast.

He knew something had happened to Anna; he was certain of it. There was no way in the world she would have voluntarily gone off someplace without calling in.

Something had happened to her.

He drank several cups of the strong black coffee, then forced himself to eat a hard roll.

He was terrified.

In Währinger Strasse, there is an "Internet café," one of several such places listed in the Vienna telephone book. This one called itself an Internet Bar/Kaffehaus and turned out to be a garishly fluorescent-lit room with a few iMacs on little round Formica tables, and an espresso machine. The floor was sticky and the place smelled of beer. It charged fifty Austrian shillings for thirty minutes of Internet access time.

He typed the word *Semmering* in several different search engines and came up with the same entries each time: home pages for ski resorts, hotels, and general chamber-of-commerce-type descriptions of a village and ski resort in the Austrian Alps about ninety kilometers from Vienna.

Desperate, knowing he could be making a terrible mistake, he found a public telephone and called the Lenz Foundation. This was the last place he knew she'd gone. It was crazy, almost pointless, to ask there, but what else was there to do?

He asked for Jürgen Lenz's office, and then asked Lenz's executive assistant whether a woman named Anna Navarro had been in.

She seemed to know Anna's name immediately, without hesitation. But instead of answering his question, she demanded to know his name.

Ben identified himself as being an "attaché" from the U.S. embassy.

"Who is this calling?" the woman demanded to know.

He supplied a false name.

"Dr. Lenz has asked me to take a number, and he'll call you back."

"Actually, I'm going to be out of the office the whole day. Let me talk to Dr. Lenz, if I could," he said.

"Dr. Lenz is not available."

"Well, do you have any idea when he'll be free to talk? It's important that we speak."

"Dr. Lenz is out of the office," she said coldly.

"All right, I've got his home phone number, I'll try him there."

The secretary hesitated. "Dr. Lenz is not in Vienna," she offered.

Not in Vienna. Smoothly: "It's just that the ambassador himself asked me to speak to him. A matter of great urgency."

"Dr. Lenz is with a special delegation from the International Children's Health Forum—he's taken them on a private tour of some of our facilities. That's no secret. Did the ambassador want to join them? If so, I'm afraid it's too late."

Too late.

After a pause, the secretary said, "You must be reachable at the U.S. embassy general telephone number, yes?"

He hung up.

CHAPTER FORTY-ONE

The train to Semmering left Vienna's Südbahnhof at a few minutes after nine. Ben had left Vienna without checking out of the hotel.

He was wearing jeans and sneakers and his warmest ski parka. The ninety-kilometer journey would be brief, much faster than renting a car and driving along the twisting alpine roads.

The train cut through the dense terrain, plunged into long tunnels and skirted high above steep mountain passes. It passed gently rolling green farmland, whitewashed stone buildings with red roofs, the iron-gray mountains rising up behind; then it climbed slowly, over narrow viaducts, and sliced through breathtaking limestone gorges.

The train compartment was mostly empty, its interior amber-lit, the high-backed seats upholstered in ugly orange twill. He thought about Anna Navarro. She was in some kind of peril. He was sure of it.

He felt he knew her well enough to be certain that she'd never simply vanish of her own accord. Either she'd abruptly gone somewhere from which she couldn't call, or she'd been forcibly *taken* somewhere.

But where?

After they'd rejoined each other in the Vienna hotel, they had spent a long time discussing Lenz. Ben recalled what Gerhard Lenz's widow had blurted out—*why does Lenz send you? You come here from Semmering?* And Strasser had told them of having electron microscopes shipped to an old clinic in the Austrian Alps known as the Clockworks.

But what was in Semmering now that the old woman was so afraid of? Obviously something ongoing, perhaps connected to the string of murders.

Anna was determined to locate that clinic in the Alps. She was convinced she'd find answers there.

Which suggested that she might have gone looking for the Clockworks. And if he were wrong—if she wasn't there—then at least maybe he'd be a step closer to finding her.

He studied the Freytag & Berndt map of the Semmering-Rax-Schneeberg region he'd picked up in Vienna before he left, and tried to devise a plan. Without knowing where the clinic or research facility was, though, he had no idea how to get inside.

The Semmering station was a modest two-story structure in front of which stood only a green bench and a Coke machine. As soon as he stepped off the train he was hit by an icy wind; the climate difference between Vienna and the Austrian Alps to the south was striking. Here it was bracingly cold. After a few minutes of hiking up the steep, winding road into the town, his ears and cheeks stung from the chill.

And as he walked he began to feel misgivings. *What am I doing?* he asked himself. *What if Anna's not here, then what?*

The village of Semmering was tiny. It was one street, Hochstrasse, lined with *Gasthauses* and inns, set into the south face of a mountain, above it a couple of sprawling luxury resort hotels and sanatoriums. To the north was Höllental, Hell's Valley, a deep gorge carved out by the Schwarza River.

Above the bank on Hochstrasse was a small tourist office presided over by a plain young woman.

Ben explained that he was interested in hiking around the Semmering region and asked for a more detailed *Wanderkarte.* The woman, who clearly had nothing else to do, provided one and spent a good deal of time pointing out particularly scenic trails. "You can go, if you want, along the historic Semmering Railway—there is a panoramic vista where you can watch the train go through the Weinzettlwand Tunnel. There is also a wonderful place to stop where they took the picture for the old twenty-shilling banknote. And a magnificent view of the ruins of the castle of Klamm."

"Really," Ben said, feigning interest, and then added casually, "I'm told there is some sort of famous private clinic around here in an old *Schloss.* The Clockworks, I think it's called."

"The Clockworks?" she said blankly. "*Uhrwerken?*"

"A private clinic—maybe more of a research facility, a scientific insti-tute, a sanatorium for sick children."

There seemed to be a quick flash of recognition in the woman's eyes—or did he imagine it?—but she shook her head. "I don't know what you're talking about, sir, I'm sorry."

"I think someone said this clinic was owned by Dr. Jürgen Lenz . . . ?"

"I am sorry," she repeated, too quickly. She had suddenly turned sullen. "There is no such clinic."

He continued down Hochstrasse until he came to what appeared to be a combination *Gasthaus* and pub. In front was a tall black chalkboard topped with a green placard for Wieninger Bier and an invitation on a painted scroll beneath it: *"Herzlich Willkommen"*—A Hearty Welcome. The day's specials were advertised in bold white chalk letters.

It was dark inside and smelled of beer. Although it was not yet noon, three portly men were sitting at a small wooden table drinking from glass steins of beer. Ben approached them.

"I'm looking for an old *Schloss* around here that houses a research clinic owned by a man named Jürgen Lenz. The old Clockworks."

The men gazed up at him suspiciously. One of them muttered something to the others, who murmured back. Ben heard "Lenz" and *"Klinik."* "No, nothing here."

Again, Ben sensed unmistakable antagonism. He was certain that these men were concealing something, and slipped several thousand-shilling notes on the table, toying with them idly. No time for subtlety. "All right, thank you," he said, turning halfway to leave. Then, as if he'd forgotten something, he turned back. "Listen, if any of you guys have any friends who might know something about this clinic, tell them I'll pay for the information. I'm an American entrepreneur looking for some investment opportunities."

He left the pub and stood for a moment in front of the building. A cluster of men in jeans and leather jackets strolled by, hands in pockets, speaking Russian. No sense in asking them.

A few seconds later he felt a tap on his shoulder. It was one of the men from the pub. "Em, how much will you pay for this information?"

"I'd say if the information is accurate, it's worth a couple thousand shillings to me."

The man glanced around furtively. "The money first, please."

Ben regarded him for a moment, then handed him two banknotes. The man led him down the road a few meters and then pointed up toward the steep mountain. Set into the side of the snow-covered peak and surrounded by tightly packed, snow-frosted fir trees as dense as crabgrass, was an ancient medieval castle with a baroque facade and a gilded clock tower.

Semmering.

The clinic where Hitler's science adviser, Josef Strasser, had shipped sophisticated scientific equipment decades ago.

Where Jürgen Lenz invited a few lucky children afflicted with a terrible disease.

Where—piecing together what he'd learned with what Lenz's secretary had said—a delegation of world leaders and dignitaries had come to visit.

And where Anna might have gone. Was it possible?

Certainly it was possible; in any case, it was all he had.

The Clockworks had been there all along, hidden in plain sight, and he had seen it walking up from the train station. It was by far the biggest property visible anywhere around.

"Magnificent," Ben said softly. "Do you know anyone who's ever been inside?"

"No. No one is allowed. There is much security there. It is very private, you can never go in."

"Well, they must hire local workers."

"No. All workers are flown in by helicopter from Vienna, and they have living quarters there. There is a helipad, you can see it if you look closely."

"What do they do there, do you know?"

"I only hear things."

"Like what?"

"They do strange things there, people say. You see strange-looking children arriving in buses . . ."

"Do you know who owns it?"

"Like you say, this Lenz. His father was a Nazi."

"How long has he owned it?"

"A long time. I think maybe his father owned it after the war. During the war the *Schloss* was used by the Nazis as a command center. It used to be called the Schloss Zerwald—this is the old name for Semmering from the Middle Ages. It was built by one of the Esterházy princes in the seventeenth century. For a while at the end of last century it was, how you say, abandoned, then it was used for about twenty years as a clock factory. The old-timers around here still call it the *Uhrwerken*. How do you say—?"

"Clockworks." Ben took out another thousand-shilling note. "Now, just a few more questions."

A man was looming over her, a man in a white coat whose face kept
going in and out of focus. He had gray hair and was speaking softly,
even smiling. He seemed friendly, and she wished she could understand
what he was saying.

She wondered what was wrong with her that she couldn't sit up: had
she been in an accident? Had a stroke? She was overtaken by a sudden
panic.

She heard *". . . to have to do that to you, but we really had no choice."*
An accent, perhaps German or Swiss.

Where am I?

Then: *"dissociative tranquilizer . . ."*

Someone speaking English to her with some sort of Middle European
accent.

And *". . . as comfortable as possible while we wait for the ketamine to
leave your system."*

She began to recall things now. The place she was in was a bad place,
a place she had been very curious about once but now wished she
wasn't in.

She had vague memories of a struggle, of being grabbed by several
strong men, of being jabbed with something sharp. After that, nothing.

The gray-haired man, who she now felt was a very bad man, was gone,
and she closed her eyes.

When she opened them again, she was alone. Her head had cleared.
She felt bruised all over, and she realized that she was tied down to
a bed.

She lifted her head as much as she could, which was not very far
because there was a belt around her chest.

But it was enough to see the cuffs and belts in which she was locked
and fastened to a hospital gurney. They were polyurethane medical restraints, the kind that also came in leather and were used in mental
hospitals for their most violent and dangerous patients. They were called
"humane restraints," and she had used them herself back in her training days.

Her wrists were cuffed and locked and attached by a long chain to a
waist belt that was also locked. The same for her ankles. Her arms were
chafed and painful, indicating that she had struggled mightily.

The restraints were color-coded: red for the wrists, blue for the ankles. These were of more recent vintage than the leather ones she had used, but surely the lock hadn't changed. The key, she remembered, was small and flat with no teeth on it, straight on one side, tapered on the other to a wedge-shaped point.

She remembered that hospital restraints were actually quite easy to pick if you knew how, but she would need a paper clip or something like it, a straight and rigid piece of metal wire.

She craned her head to one side and examined the bulky anesthesia machine on one side of her bed, and, on the other side, the metal cart just a few tantalizing feet away.

It had eight drawers. On top of it were scattered medical supplies, bandages and forceps, scissors, and a sterile package of safety pins.

But there was no way to reach it.

She tried to shift her body to the left, toward the gleaming cart, hoping for slack in the restraints, but there was almost none. She shifted to the left, this time violently, a sudden hard jerk that did nothing; the only thing that moved at all was the bed itself, which had to be on wheels.

Wheels.

She was silent for a moment, listening for approaching footsteps. Then she lurched against the restraints again and felt the wheels give what she imagined was another inch or two.

Encouraged by the movement, tiny as it was, she lurched again. The wheels moved another minuscule distance.

But the cart still looked as distant and unreachable as the mirage of a lake to a thirsty man in a desert.

She rested a moment, her neck spasming in pain.

Then she summoned her strength again and, trying to ignore how far away the cart was, she *jerked* at the restraints and gained maybe an inch.

An inch, out of several feet, felt like a single step in the New York Marathon.

She heard footsteps in the hallway and voices that grew louder, and she froze, resting her strained neck while she waited, and the voices passed.

A *lunge* to the left and the gurney gave up another couple of inches.

She did not want to think about what she would do once she reached the cart; that was another challenge entirely. She would have to take this a step at a time.

An inch at a time.

Another inch or so. Another. The cart was not much more than a foot away. She jerked again and gained another inch and the silver-haired man entered the room.

Jürgen Lenz, as he called himself. But now she knew the astonishing truth.

Jürgen-Lenz-who-was-not-Jürgen-Lenz.

CHAPTER FORTY-TWO

At the end of Hochstrasse Ben found a sporting goods store that featured a wide variety of equipment for the tourist and sportsman. He rented a pair of cross-country skis and asked where he could rent a car.

No place for miles.

Parked at the side of the shop was a BMW motorcycle that looked old and decrepit but still functional. He struck a deal with the young man who managed the place, and owned the bike.

With the skis strapped to his back he set off across the ridge of the Semmering pass until he came to a narrow unmarked dirt road that wound steeply uphill through a ravine to the *Schloss*. The road was rutted and icy; it had evidently been used recently by trucks and other heavy vehicles.

When he had managed to climb perhaps a quarter of a mile, he came to a red sign that said BETRETEN VERBOTEN—PRIVATBESITZ: No Trespassing—Private Property.

Just ahead of the sign was a barrier gate whose arm was striped in yellow-and-black reflective paint. It appeared to be electronically controlled, but Ben was easily able to hop over it and then wheel the bike underneath, tipped at an angle.

Nothing happened: no Klaxon, no alarm bells.

He continued up the road, through dense snow-covered woods, and in a few minutes reached a high, crenellated stone wall. It looked centuries old, though recently restored.

From atop the wall rose several feet of thin, horizontally strung wire. At a distance, this addition was not visible, but Ben saw it clearly now. It was probably electrified, but he did not want to scale the wall and find out the hard way.

Instead, he followed the wall for a few hundred feet until it came to what appeared to be the main gate, about six feet wide and ten feet high, constructed of ornately scrolled wrought iron. Upon closer examination,

Ben realized that the fence was in fact steel painted to look like iron, entirely backed with a screen of woven wire fabric. This was certainly high-security, designed to foil intruders.

He wondered whether it was made to keep people out—or in.

Had Anna somehow gotten inside? he wondered. Was it possible? Or was she being held prisoner?

The dirt road came to an end another few hundred meters from the gate. Beyond it was glistening virgin snow. He parked the motorcycle, put on his skis, and set off across the snow, staying close to the wall.

His idea was to survey the entire perimeter of the property, or at least as much as was possible to examine, in hopes of discovering any holes in the security, any possible points of entry. But it did not look promising.

The snow was soft and deep, so he sank into the powder, and the even deeper drifts and dunes made maneuvering difficult. It was no easier once he got the hang of it, because the terrain became steeper, the skiing ever more arduous.

The ground next to the wall became higher, and pretty soon Ben could see over it.

Glare coming off the snow forced him to squint, but he could now make out the *Schloss*, a great rambling stone structure, more horizontal than vertical. At first glance this could have been a tourist attraction, but then he saw a couple of guards in military-style tunics, carrying submachine guns, patrolling the property.

Whatever was happening inside these walls was not simple research.

What he saw next was a profound shock. He didn't understand it, but within the enclosed area were children, dozens and dozens of ragged-looking children, milling outside, in the cold. He peered again, squinting against the snow glare.

Who were they?

And why were they there?

This was no sanatorium, that was for sure; he wondered whether they were prisoners.

He skied uphill a short distance, close enough to get a better look, but not so close that he lost his line of sight behind the high stone wall.

Inside, next to the wall, was a fenced-in area the size of a city block. Within it were several large military-style tents jammed with children. It seemed to be a makeshift shantytown, a tent city, its inhabitants youth from some Eastern European country. The steel fence that enclosed it was topped with coils of razor wire.

It was a strange vision. Ben shook his head as if to clear it of an optical illusion, then looked again. Yes. They were children, some toddlers, some teenagers, unshaven and rough-looking, smoking and shouting to one another; girls in headscarves, shabby peasant dresses, and tattered coats, children swarming all around.

He had seen news footage of people like this. Whoever they were, wherever they were from, they had that unmistakable look of impoverished youth driven out of their homes by war—Bosnian refugees, escapees from the conflicts in Kosovo and Macedonia, ethnic Albanians, perhaps.

Was Lenz sheltering war refugees here, on the grounds of his clinic?

Jürgen Lenz, humanitarian, giving shelter to refugees and ailing children?

Unlikely.

For this was hardly a shelter. These peasant children were packed into their tent city, inadequately dressed, freezing in the cold. And there were the armed guards. This looked like some kind of internment camp.

Then he heard a shout from the encampment, an adolescent boy's voice. Someone within had spotted him. The shout was soon joined by others, the wretched inmates suddenly waving at him, beckoning to him, calling to him. He understood at once what they wanted.

They wanted to be released.

They wanted his help. They saw him as a savior, someone outside who could help them escape. His stomach turned, he shivered, and not from the cold.

What was being done to them?

Suddenly a shout arose from another direction, and one of the guards pointed his weapon toward Ben. Now several of the guards were shouting at him, waving him away.

The threat was clear: get off the private property or we'll shoot.

He heard a blast of gunfire and turned to see a fusillade of bullets pock the snow a few feet to his left.

They weren't kidding, and they weren't patient.

The refugee children were prisoners here. And Anna?

Was Anna inside there too?

Please, God, I hope she's all right. I hope she's alive.

He didn't know whether to wish she was inside—or to pray she wasn't. Ben turned around and headed back down the mountainside.

"Well, I see you're more aware now," Lenz said, smiling brightly. He stopped at the foot of her bed and clasped his hands in front of him. "Perhaps now you'd like to say to whom you've told my real identity."

"Screw you," she said.

"I thought not," he said equably. "Once the ketamine has worn off"— he glanced at his gold watch—"which will be in no more than another half an hour, certainly, you'll be infused intravenously with about five milligrams of a powerful opioid called Versed. You have had this before? During surgery, perhaps?"

Anna gazed at him blankly.

He continued, unruffled. "Five milligrams is about the proper dose to make you relaxed but still responsive. You'll feel a little rush, but this passes in ten seconds or so, and then you'll feel calmer than you've ever felt before in your life. All your anxiety will seep out of you. It's a wonderful feeling."

He cocked his head to one side like a bird. "If we were to inject you with one single bolus of this drug, you'd stop breathing and very probably die. So we must titrate it slowly over eight to ten minutes. We certainly don't want anything to happen to you."

Anna gave a grunt that communicated, she hoped, both skepticism and sarcasm at once. Despite her chemically induced calm, she was at the same time deeply frightened.

"Rather, you'll be found dead in your wrecked rental car, another victim of drunk driving—"

"I didn't rent a car," she slurred.

"Oh, in fact you did. Or rather, it was done for you, using your credit card. You were arrested last night in a neighboring town. Your blood-alcohol level was measured at two-point-five, which is surely why you got into an accident. You were kept overnight in a holding cell and then released. But you know how it is with problem drinkers—they never learn."

She displayed no reaction. But her mind raced, desperate to find a way out of the maze. There *had* to be flaws in his plan, but where?

Lenz continued, "Versed, you see, is the most effective truth serum ever invented, even though it was not intended for this use. All the drugs the CIA has tried, like sodium pentothol or scopolamine, they never worked. But with the correct dose of Versed you'll become so free of inhibitions that you'll tell me anything I want to know. And here's the magical thing: afterward you'll remember nothing. You'll talk and talk quite lucidly and yet, from the moment you're put on the IV, you'll have no memory of what happened. It's really quite remarkable."

A nurse entered the room, wide-hipped and squat and middle-aged. She rolled in a cart of equipment—tubes, blood-pressure cuffs, syringes— and began setting up. She watched Anna suspiciously as she filled a few of the syringes from little vials and then applied preprinted labels to them.

"This is Gerta, your nurse-anesthetist. She is one of our best. You are in good hands." Lenz gave Anna a little wave as he left the room.

"How are you feeling?" Gerta asked perfunctorily, in a stern con- tralto, as she hung a bag of clear liquid on the IV stand to the left of Anna's bed.

"Pretty . . . groggy . . ." Anna said, her voice trailing off, her eyes flut- tering closed. But she was hyper-vigilant; now she had a tentative plan.

Gerta did something with what sounded like plastic tubing. After a few moments she said, "All right, I'll come back. Doctor wants to wait until the ketamine is mostly out of your system. If we start the Versed now you may stop breathing. Anyway, I have to go to the anesthesia workroom. This sat probe is no good." She closed the door behind her.

Anna opened her eyes and flung her body hard to the left, as hard as she could, augmenting the push by throwing her manacled arms into it. It was a movement she was beginning to master. The bed seemed to jump several inches toward the supply cart. There was no time to rest. One more try, and she was there.

She lifted her shoulders as far as the restraining belt would allow and pressed her face against the cold top edge of the cart. Out of the corner of her left eye she could see the safety pins, used to secure bandages, in their little square blister-wrap sterile packaging, just an inch or two away.

Yet still out of reach.

If she turned her neck to the left as far as it would go, she could almost look at the pack of safety pins straight on. The tendons on her neck and along her upper back were so strained they began to tremble. The ache quickly became excruciating.

Then, like a jeering child, she stuck her tongue all the way out. Tiny pinpoints of pain jabbed the underside of her tongue at its root.

Finally she lowered her distended tongue to the surface of the cart as if it were a steam shovel. It touched the plastic of the package, and she slowly pulled her head backward, edging the pack along as she did, right to the edge of the cart. Just before it could teeter off the edge she clenched it between her teeth.

A footfall, and the door to her room came open.

Quick as a rattlesnake she lay back on the bed, the little blister-pack concealed under her tongue, its sharp edges poking at its base. *How much had she seen?* The nurse was coming toward her. Anna gagged but kept the packet in her closed mouth in a pool of saliva.

"Yes," Gerta said, "ketamine can make you nauseated sometimes, it will do that. You're awake, I see."

Anna made a complaining *mmmmph* through her shut mouth and shut her eyes. Saliva pooled behind her front teeth. She forced herself to swallow.

Gerta came around to Anna's right and began fumbling at the head of the bed. Anna shut her eyes and tried to make her breathing sound regular.

A few minutes later Gerta left the room again and closed the door quietly behind her.

She would be back much sooner this time, Anna knew.

There was blood in her mouth from where the packet had cut into soft tissue, and Anna moved it to her lips with her tongue and then spit it out, forward. It landed squarely on the back of her left hand. She moved her hands together and reached her right index finger over, pulling the safety-pin packet into her fist.

Now she moved quickly. She knew what she was doing, because she had picked these locks on more than one occasion when she had misplaced the key and was too embarrassed to ask for a replacement.

The wrapping came off with some difficulty, but then it was an easy thing to bend the safety pin's point away from its clasp.

The left cuff first. She inserted the pinpoint into the lock, pushed the inner pins to the left, then to the right, and the lock clicked open.

Her left hand was free!

She felt exhilarated. Even more quickly now she freed her right hand, then the restraining belt, and then the door came open again with a low squeak. Gerta had returned.

Anna drew her hands back into the polyurethane cuffs so that they appeared still to be fastened and closed her eyes.

Gerta approached the bed. "I could hear you moving in here."

Heart pounding so loud it had to be audible.

Anna opened her eyes slowly and made them look unfocused.

"I say enough is enough," Gerta said menacingly. "I think you are making pretend." Under her breath she added, "So we will have to take our chances."

God, no.

She applied a rubber tourniquet to Anna's left arm until the vein popped out, and inserted the intravenous needle, then turned her back to adjust the flow clamp on the IV tubing. In one snapping-turtle motion Anna pulled her hands free of the unlocked cuffs and tried silently to undo the tourniquet, *quiet, must be quiet*, but Gerta heard the snap of the rubber and turned around, and as she did Anna raised herself up off the bed as far as the chest belt would allow and caught the nurse's neck with the crook of her right elbow, a strange gesture of affection. Pulled back hard on the rubber tube, *hard* against Gerta's fleshy neck..

A yelp.

Gerta flailed her hands, reached for her neck, tried to claw her fingers under the garrote, could not get a purchase, her fingernails scratching at her own neck, wriggling madly. Her face purpled. Her mouth gasped and sucked for breath. Gerta's fluttering hands slowed; she was probably losing consciousness.

Within a few minutes Anna, almost numb from exertion, had the nurse gagged and cuffed to the bed rail. Springing open the ankle cuffs, she slipped off the bed, her body feeling buoyant, and cuffed Gerta to the anesthesia machine as well, which would not easily move.

She removed Gerta's key ring from her belt, and glanced at the anesthesia cart.

It was full of weapons. She scooped up a handful of packaged hypodermic needles and several small glass ampules of various drugs, then remembered she was wearing a hospital johnny with no pockets.

In the supply closet hung two white cotton doctor's jackets. She put one on, stuffed the pilfered supplies in both slash pockets, and ran from the room.

CHAPTER FORTY-THREE

The records office for the Semmering area occupied a small basement room in a Bavarian-style building housing a scattering of municipal workers. There were rows of green filing cabinets, arranged by the number of the parcel of land.

"The Schloss Zerwald is not accessible to the public," the white-haired woman who ran the office said flatly. "It is part of the Semmering Clinic. Strictly private."

"I understand that," Ben said. "It's actually the old maps themselves that I'm interested in." When Ben went on to explain that he was a historian researching the castles of Germany and Austria, she looked vaguely disapproving, as if she'd just smelled something fetid, but ordered her trembling teenage assistant to snap-to and pull out the property map from one of the drawers along the side wall of the room. It was a complicated-looking system, but the white-haired woman knew exactly where to find the documents Ben wanted.

The map had been printed in the early nineteenth century. The owner of the parcel of land, which in those days took up much of the mountainside, was identified as J. Esterházy. A cryptic series of markings ran through the parcel.

"What does this mean?" Ben asked, pointing.

The old woman scowled. "The caves," she said. "The limestone caves in the mountain."

Caves. It was a possibility.

"The caves run through the *Schloss's* property?"

"Yes, of course," she said impatiently.

Under the *Schloss*, that meant.

Trying to contain his excitement, he asked, "Can you make a copy of this map for me?"

A hostile look. "For twenty shillings."

"Fine," he said. "And tell me something: is there a floor plan of the *Schloss* anywhere?"

The young clerk at the sporting goods shop examined the property map as if it were an insoluble algebra problem. When Ben explained that the markings indicated a network of caves, he quickly agreed.

"Yes, the old caves run right underneath the *Schloss*," he said. "I think there even used to be an entrance into the *Schloss* from the caves, but that was long time ago and it must be blocked off."

"Have you been in the caves?"

The young clerk looked up, appalled. "No, of course not."

"Do you know anyone who has?"

He thought a moment. "*Ja*, I think so."

"Do you think he might be willing to take me there, be my guide?"

"I doubt it."

"Can you ask?"

"I'll ask, but I don't value your chances."

Ben hadn't expected a man in his late sixties, but that was who entered the shop half an hour later. He was small and wiry, with cauliflower ears, a long misshapen nose, a pigeon chest, ropy arms. He spoke rapidly and irritably in German to the clerk as he entered, then fell silent when he met Ben.

Ben said hello; the man nodded.

"He's a little old, frankly," Ben told the salesman. "Isn't there someone younger and stronger?"

"There is younger but not stronger," the older man said. "And no one who knows the caves better. Anyway, I am not so sure I want to do this."

"Oh, you speak English," Ben said, surprised.

"Most of us learned English during the war."

"Do the caves still have an entrance into the *Schloss*?"

"There used to be. But why should I help you?"

"I need to get inside the *Schloss*."

"You can't. It is now a private clinic."

"Still, I must get inside."

"Why?"

"Let's just say it's for personal reasons that are worth a great deal of money to me." He told the old Austrian what he was willing to pay for his services.

"We'll need equipment," the man said. "You can climb?"

His name was Fritz Neumann, and he had been caving around Semmering for longer than Ben had been alive. He was also immensely strong, yet nimble and graceful.

Toward the end of the war, he said, when he was a boy of eight, his parents had joined a Catholic workers' Resistance cell that was secretly fighting the Nazis, who had invaded their part of Austria. The old Clockworks had been seized by the Nazis and turned into a regional command post.

Unknown to the Nazis who lived and worked in the *Schloss*, there was a crawl space off the basement of the old castle with a slot entrance to a limestone cave that ran beneath the castle's property. The *Schloss* had in fact been built over this mouth quite deliberately, because the original inhabitants, concerned about attacks on their stronghold, had wanted a secret exit. Over the centuries the cave mouth had largely been forgotten.

But during the war, when the Nazis had commandeered the Clockworks, the members of the Resistance realized they were in possession of a crucial piece of knowledge that would enable them to spy on the Nazis, to commit sabotage and subversion—and, if they were quite careful about it, to do it without the Nazis even realizing how it was done.

The Resistance had spirited dozens of prisoners out of the *Schloss*, and the Nazis had never figured out how.

As an eight-year-old boy, Fritz Neumann had helped his parents and their friends, and he had committed the cave's intricate passages to memory.

Fritz Neumann was the first off the ski lift, Ben close behind. The ski area was on the north face of the mountain. The *Schloss* was on the opposite side, but Neumann had judged it easier to reach the mouth of the cave this way.

Their skis had Randonee bindings, which allow the heel to go free for cross-country skiing but can be locked in for downhill. Even more important, the bindings allowed them to wear mountaineering boots instead of ski boots. Neumann had outfitted them both: flexible twelve-point crampons favored by Austrian climbers on hard ice; Petzl headlamps; ice axes with wrist leashes; climbing harnesses; pitons; and carabiners.

All easily obtained at the shop.

The guns Ben wanted were not so easily found. But this was hunting country, and quite a few of the old man's friends had handguns as well as shotguns, and one of them was willing to make a deal.

Wearing woolen balaclavas, windproof pants and gaiters, alpine climbing packs, and thin polypropylene gloves, they cross-country skied to the summit, then locked in their bindings for the long downhill stretch on the south face. Ben considered himself a good skier, but Neumann was a phenomenon, and Ben found it difficult to keep up as the older man negotiated the virgin snow. The air was frigid, and Ben's face, the exposed part anyway, quickly began to smart. Ben found it amazing that Neumann was able to lead the way through paths that were barely paths, until he saw the dashes of red paint on the occasional fir tree, which seemed to mark the way.

They had been skiing for twenty minutes when they came to a crevasse at the beginning of the timberline, and shortly thereafter a steep gorge. They stopped about ten feet from the edge, removed their skis, and concealed them in a copse.

"The cave, as I tell you, it is very difficult to get to," Neumann said. "Now we rope down. But you say you know how, yes?"

Ben nodded, inspecting the cliff. He estimated the drop at about a hundred feet, maybe less. From here he could see Lenz's *Schloss*, so far down the mountain that it seemed an architect's model.

Neumann set out a neat butterfly coil of rope. Ben was relieved to see it was dynamic kernmantle rope, made of twisted nylon threads.

"It is eleven millimeters," Neumann said. "It is O.K. for you?"

Ben nodded again. For a drop like this, that was just fine. Whatever it took to reach Anna.

From this angle, he couldn't see the mouth of the cave. He assumed it was an opening on the cliff face.

Neumann knelt near the cliff edge by an outcropping of rock, and began driving the pitons in with a hammer he took from a holster. Each piton gave off a reassuring ringing sound that rose in pitch the deeper it was driven in, indicating that it was sunk in solidly.

Then, looping the rope around the largest rock, he pulled it through the pitons.

"This is not so easy to do, getting into the cave mouth," he announced. "We'll rappel down and swing a little, maneuver into the cave. Now we put on the crampons and the harnesses."

"What about the ice axes?"

"Not for here," he said. "There's very little ice here. For the cave."

"There's ice in the cave?"

But Neumann, busy unpacking, did not reply.

Ben and Peter used to go caving near the Greenbriar, but the caves there were little more than crawl holes. He'd never had to deal with ice.

For a moment he felt his stomach knot. Until this point he had been propelled by adrenaline and anger and fear, focusing on one thing only: getting Anna out of Lenz's clinic, where he was convinced she'd been taken.

Now he wondered whether this was the best way. Climbing wasn't particularly risky if you did it right, and he was confident of his climbing skills. But even very experienced cavers had been killed.

He had weighed storming the main gate, counting on the guards to seize him, and thereby attracting Lenz's attention.

But it was just as likely that the guards would shoot to kill.

Hard as it was to accept, this cave was the only alternative.

The two of them lashed the crampons' neoprene straps over the Vibram soles of their weathered mountaineering boots. These affixed twelve sharp spikes to the bottoms and toes of their boots, giving them serious traction on the cliff side. Then they attached the nylon climbing harnesses to their waists and they were ready to go.

"We use the *dulfersitz*, yes?" Neumann said, using the Austrian argot for rappelling without a rack, using only one's body to control the descent.

"No rappel rack?"

Neumann smiled, enjoying Ben's discomfort. "Who needs it?"

Without a rappel rack the descent would be unpleasant, but it saved them having to bring racks. Also, they wouldn't be tied to the rope, making the rappel more dangerous.

"You will follow," Neumann said as he tied a double figure-eight knot at one end of the rope and then wrapped the rope around his shoulder, around his hip, and through his crotch. He walked backward toward the edge, lifting the rope a bit, his feet spread widely, and then he went over the side.

Ben watched the older man dangling free, swinging slowly back and forth, facing the cliff, until he found a foothold. From there, tensioning the rope, Neumann moved his feet down the cliff face. He descended a little farther, dangling in free space again, swaying back and forth, then there was a crunching sound, followed by a shout.

"O.K., come on, now you!"

Ben straddled the rope in the same manner, walked backward to the edge, held his breath, and dropped over the side.

The rope immediately slid against his crotch, the friction creating a painful burn even through the windproof pants. Now he remembered why he hated the *dulfersitz*. Using his right hand as a brake, he descended slowly, leaning back, his feet against the cliff, groping for footholds, maneuvering downward, playing the rope. In what seemed like seconds, he spotted his target: a small, dark ellipse. The mouth of the cave. Moving his feet down a few more meters, he came to the opening, and swung his feet inward.

This wasn't going to be as easy as he'd hoped. It wasn't a matter of simply dropping into the cave mouth; it was more complicated than that. The opening was flush with the sheer cliff face.

"Move *in* a little!" Neumann shouted. "Move *in!*"

Ben saw at once what he meant. There was a narrow inset ledge on which he would have to land.

There was very little room for error. The ledge was no more than two feet wide. Neumann was crouched on it, gripping a handhold in the rock.

As Ben moved his body forward, into the cave, he began to sway backward and forward as well. He felt unstable, and he forced himself to hang until the swaying slowed.

Finally he played out the rope, braking with his right hand, swaying into the cave and then out again. Finally, when he was both forward just enough and far enough down, he dropped to the ledge, cushioning the impact by bending his knees.

"Good!" Neumann shouted.

Still gripping the rope, Ben leaned forward into the darkness of the cave and peered down. Enough sunlight streamed in at an oblique angle to illuminate the peril just below.

The first hundred or so feet of the entrance to the cave, a steep downhill slant, was thickly coated with ice. Worse, it was watered ice, slick and treacherous. It was like nothing he had ever seen before.

"Well," Neumann called to him after a few seconds, sensing Ben's reluctance. "We can't stand here on this ledge all day, hmm?"

Experience or no, negotiating that long icy slope was unnerving to contemplate. "Let's go," Ben said with all the enthusiasm he could muster.

They donned their lightweight helmets and Velcro-strapped them into place, then their headlamps. Neumann handed Ben a couple of high-tech carbon-fiber ice axes with curved picks. One axe looped over each wrist by means of a leash. They dangled from Ben's hands like useless appendages.

With a nod, Neumann turned his back to the cave mouth, and Ben followed suit, his stomach fluttering. Each took one backward step, and they were off the narrow ledge, their crampons crunching into the ice. The first few steps were awkward. Ben tried to maintain his balance, driving his crampons deep into the ice, steadying himself until he had backed down far enough to grab the ice axes in each hand and chop into the glossy surface. He saw Neumann scrambling down the steep slope as if he were walking down a staircase. The old man was a goat.

Ben continued unsteadily, spider-crawling down, stomach to the ice, leaning his body weight on the wrist loops of the axes. The crunch of a boot, the chop of the ice axe, then again, and again, and by the time he had begun to achieve some sort of rhythm, he had reached the bottom, where the ice had given way to limestone.

Neumann turned, slipped off his ice axes and crampons, and began to negotiate the gentler downward slope. Ben followed close behind.

The descent was gradual, a spiral staircase through rock, and as they went the beam of Ben's headlamp illuminated any number of passages that diverged to either side of them, branches he might easily have taken were it not for Neumann. There were no slashes of red paint here, nothing to separate the right path from the many wrong ones. Fritz Neumann was obviously navigating from memory.

The air felt warmer than it had outside, but Ben knew this was deceptive. There was permanent ice on the walls of the cave, which indicated the temperature was below freezing, and the water that ran underfoot would soon make it feel even colder. It was also extremely humid.

The floor of the cave was strewn with rubble and coursed with running water. Here and there, Ben almost lost his footing as the debris on the cave floor shifted. Soon the passage broadened into a gallery, and Neumann stopped for a moment, turning his head slowly, his helmet lamp illuminating the breathtaking formations. Some of the stalactites were fragile soda straws, slender and delicate, tapering to points as sharp as knitting needles; too, there were the banded calcite stumps of stalagmites, the occasional column formed by the meeting of a stalactite and a stalagmite. Water oozed down the walls and seeped down the stalactites, the steady drip-drip-dripping into water on the cave floor the only noise in the eerie silence. Hardened flowstone formed terraces, and translucent sheets of calcite hung down from the ceiling like drapery, their edges serrated and sharp. Everywhere was the acrid ammonia stench of bat guano.

"Ah, look!" Neumann said, and Ben turned to see the perfectly preserved skeleton of a bear. There arose a sudden papery thunder of hundreds of batwings; a cluster of hibernating bats had been awakened by their approach.

Now Ben began to feel the chill. Somehow, for all his precautions, water had seeped into his boots, dampening his socks.

"Come," Neumann said, "this way."

He led them into a narrow passage, one of several corridors off the gallery barely distinguishable from the others. The ground gradually rose up before them, the walls growing closer together, almost to a bottleneck. The ceiling was barely head-high; had Ben been any taller than his six feet, he would have had to stoop. The walls here were icy, the seep water at their feet frigid.

Ben's toes had begun to go numb. But lithe Neumann scrambled up the steep crevice with astonishing ease, and Ben followed more gingerly, stepping over the jagged rocks, knowing that if he lost his footing here, the tumble would be nasty.

Finally the ground seemed to level off. "We're about on the same level as the *Schloss* now," Neumann said.

Then without warning the narrow passage came to a dead end. They stopped at what appeared to be a blank wall, in front of which was a pile of rubble, evidently the remains of a long-ago cave-in.

"Jesus," Ben said. "Are we lost?"

Without a word, Neumann scraped some of the rubble aside with his boot, exposing a rusty iron rod about four feet long, which he hoisted with a flourish.

"It's undisturbed," Neumann said. "This is good for you. It has not been used for many years. They have not discovered it."

"What are you talking about?"

Neumann took the iron rod, wedged it underneath a boulder, and leaned his weight on it until the rock began to dislodge, revealing a small irregular passageway no more than two feet high and three or four feet wide.

"During the war we'd move this rock back and forth to hide the final passage." He pointed out grooves in the rock scored, Ben assumed, decades earlier. "Now you're on your own. I'll leave you here. This is a very narrow crawlway, and very low, but you can get through it, I believe."

Ben leaned closer and examined it with horrified fascination. He felt a wave of panic.

This is a goddamned coffin. I don't think I can do it.

"You'll travel about, oh, maybe two hundred meters. It's most of the way level, but then it goes uphill at the very end. Unless it's caved in since I was here as a boy, you'll come to a keyhole slot opening."

"It opens right into the *Schloss*?"

"No, of course not. The entrance is gated. Maybe even locked. Probably so."

"*Now* you tell me."

Neumann drew a rusty-looking skeleton key from a pocket of his old green parka. "I can't tell you for sure if this will work, but the last time I tried it, it did."

"The last time being fifty years ago?"

"More than that," Neumann admitted. He extended his hand. "Now I say good-bye," he said solemnly. "I wish you much luck."

CHAPTER FORTY-FOUR

It was a formidably tight squeeze. It must have taken real courage and determination for the Resistance fighters to make this final approach to the *Schloss*, and do it repeatedly, Ben thought. No wonder they had made use of a boy like the young Fritz Neumann, who could slip through this space easily.

Ben had wriggled through crawl holes like this before, in the caves of White Sulphur Springs, but never for more than a few feet before they broadened out. This, however, appeared to be hundreds of yards long. Only now did he fully understand what veteran cavers meant when they insisted that their subterranean pursuit allowed them to face down primordial terrors—the fear of darkness, of falling into the void, of being trapped in a maze, of being buried alive.

But there was no choice, certainly not now. He thought only of Anna and summoned up the will.

He entered the hole, headfirst, feeling a cold rush of air. At its opening, the passage was about two feet high, which meant that the only way to move through it was to slither on his stomach like an earthworm.

He removed his pack and pushed off with his feet, pulling with his arms, nudging his pack ahead of him. There was an inch or two of frigid water on the tunnel floor. Quickly his pants became soaked through. The tunnel angled sharply one way, then another, forcing him to contort his body.

Then, at last, the passageway began to widen, its ceiling rising to four feet, enabling him to lift his numbed belly out of the ice water, get to his feet, and stoop-walk.

It was not long, though, before his back began to ache, and rather than continue he stopped for a moment and set down the pack, resting his hands on his thighs.

When he was able to go farther, he noticed that the ceiling was low-

ering again, back to two, maybe three feet high. He got onto his hands
and knees and began scuttling along like a crab.

But not for long. The rocky floor bruised his kneecaps. He attempted
to ease the stress by putting his weight on his elbows and toes instead.
When he wearied of that, he continued crawling. The ceiling became
lower still, and he turned onto his side, pushing with his feet and pulling
with his arms along the winding tunnel.

Now the ceiling height had diminished to no more than eighteen
inches, scraping against his back, and he had to stop for a moment to
suppress a wave of panic. He was back to belly-crawling again, only this
time there was no end in sight. His headlamp shone a beam for twenty
feet or so, but the coffin-sized, even coffin-shaped tunnel seemed to go
on and on. The walls seemed to narrow.

Through the scrim of his fear, he observed that the passage appeared
to be winding slowly uphill, that water no longer pooled on the floor,
though it was still damp, and that, horribly, rock was now scraping
against both his stomach and his back.

He continued pushing his pack ahead of him. The tunnel was now
barely twelve inches high.

Ben was trapped.

No, not trapped, not yet, exactly, but it certainly felt that way. Terror
overwhelmed him. He had to *squeeze* himself through. His heart raced,
his body flooded with fear, and he had to stop.

The worst thing, he knew, was to panic. Panic caused you to freeze
up, lose flexibility. He breathed slowly in and out a few times, then
exhaled completely to reduce his chest diameter so he could fit through
the passage.

Sweating and clammy, he forced himself to squirm ahead, trying to
focus on where he was going and why, how crucial it was. He thought
ahead, to what he would do once he got into the *Schloss*.

The uphill slope was becoming steeper. He inhaled and felt the walls
press in on his chest, keeping him from filling his lungs with air. This
prompted a surge of adrenaline, which made his breathing fast and shallow, made him feel as if he were about to suffocate, and he had to stop
once again.

Don't think.

Relax.

No one else knew he was down here. He would be buried alive here in this pitch-black hell where there was no day or night.

Ben found himself listening to this voice with skepticism, as his braver, better self now assumed command of his brain. He began to feel his heart slow, felt the delicious cold air hit the bottom of his lungs, felt calm spread through his body like ink on a blotter.

Steadily now, with an inner serenity, he urged his body along, earth-wormed, wriggled, ignoring the chafing of his back.

Suddenly the ceiling soared upward and the walls widened, and he got to his aching hands and knees and crawled up the incline. He had arrived at a sort of twilit grotto, where he was able to stand fully, blessedly, upright.

He was aware of the faintest glimmering of light.

It was a very dim and distant light, but to him it seemed almost as bright as day, as joy-inspiring as sunrise.

Directly ahead of him was the cave exit, and it was indeed shaped a little like a keyhole. He scrambled up a scree pile, then sort of half-mantled himself into the lip of the opening, pushing down with both hands until he could support his body on rigid arms.

There he saw the close-set rusted iron bars of an ancient gate that was fitted into the irregular cave mouth as tightly as a manhole cover. He could not make out what lay behind the gate but he could see an oblong shaft of light, as if from under a door.

He drew out the skeleton key Neumann had given him, inserted it into the lock, and turned it.

Tried to turn it.

But it would not turn. The key would not *move*.

The lock was rusted shut. That had to be it; the old lock hadn't been replaced, at least not for decades. The entire thing, he saw, was one solid mass of rust. He wriggled the key back and forth again, but it would not turn.

"Oh, my God," Ben said out loud.

He was done for.

This was the one thing neither he nor Neumann had anticipated.

He could see no other way in. Even if he had the tools, there was no way to dig around the gate; it was embedded in solid rock. Would he now have to somehow climb back *out?*

Or maybe . . . Maybe one of the bars was so rusted through that he could push it out. He tried that, banging his gloved fist against the iron bars until the pain was too great, but no: the gate was solid. The rust was only on the surface.

In desperation, he grabbed the bars and rattled them, like an enraged lifer in San Quentin, and suddenly there was a metallic clatter.

One of the hinges had broken off.

He rattled again, harder, until another hinge popped off.

He kept rattling, exuberantly, and finally the third and last hinge fell to the ground.

He grabbed the gate with both hands, lifted it up and pushed it forward, and gently lowered it to the ground.

He was inside.

CHAPTER FORTY-FIVE

Ben felt something hard and smooth and dusty: it was a solid iron door, secured by a heavy latch. He lifted the latch and pushed at the door, and the door gave a brief high screech. Obviously it hadn't been opened in decades. He pushed with all his weight. With a moan, the door gave way.

He found himself in a larger space of some sort, though it was still small. His eyes, used to the dark, began to discern shapes, and he followed the narrow shaft of light to another door, where he felt around on either side for a light switch.

He found the switch, and a light came on from a single bulb mounted on the ceiling.

He was, he could see, in a small storage closet. The stone walls were lined with steel shelves painted an indeterminate beige, holding old cardboard boxes, wooden crates, and cylindrical metal tanks.

He removed his helmet and woolen cap, then the pack from his back, from which he took both of the semiautomatic pistols, placing everything but the weapons on one of the shelves. He slipped one of the weapons under the waistband of his heavy pants, at the small of his back. The other he held while he studied the photocopied floor plan. No doubt the place had been restored since its clock factory days, but it was unlikely that the basic plan had been much changed, or that the massive walls had been moved.

He tried the doorknob. It turned easily, and the door opened.

He emerged into a brightly lit corridor with stone floors and vaulted ceilings. There was no one in view.

Arbitrarily, he turned right. The Vibram soles of his mountaineering boots muffled his footsteps. Except for the slight squish of wet leather, his walk was silent.

He had not gone far before someone appeared at the end of the hall, striding directly toward him.

Keep calm, he told himself. *Act as if you belong.*

This was not easy, dressed as he was in his wet, mud-crusted climbing attire and heavy boots, his face still bruised and scratched from the incident in Buenos Aires.

Quickly, now.

On his left was a door. He stopped, listened for a moment, and then opened it, hoping what lay beyond was unoccupied.

As he ducked into the room, the figure passed by, a man dressed in a white tunic or jumpsuit. A handgun was holstered at his waist. Obviously a guard.

The room was perhaps twenty feet long and fifteen feet wide. By the light from the corridor he could see that this was another storeroom, also lined with metal shelves. He located a switch and turned on the light.

What he saw was too horrific to be real, and for a moment he was sure his eyes had been deceived by some sort of nightmarish optical illusion.

But it was no illusion.

God in heaven, he thought. *This can't be.*

He could barely stand to look, yet he couldn't turn his eyes away.

On the shelves were rows of dusty glass bottles, some as small as the Mason canning jars Mrs. Walsh used to preserve fruit in, some two feet tall.

Each bottle held a fluid of some kind, which Ben assumed to be a preservative such as formalin, slightly cloudy with age and impurities.

And floating in them, like pickles in brine, one to a bottle . . .

No, this could not be.

He felt his skin erupt in gooseflesh.

In each bottle was a human baby.

The bottles were arrayed with ghastly precision.

In the smallest were tiny embryos, at the earliest stage of gestation, little pale pink prawns, translucent insects with grotesque large heads and tails.

Then fetuses not much longer than an inch: hunched, stubby arms and oversized heads, suspended in the shrouds of their amniotic sacs.

Fetuses not much bigger but looking more human, bent legs and waving arms, eyes like black currants, floating in perfectly round sacs surrounded by the ragged halo of the chorionic sac.

Miniature infants, eyes closed, sucking thumbs, a tangle of tiny perfectly formed limbs.

As the bottles increased in size so did their contents, until in the largest bottles floated full-term babies, ready to be born, eyes closed, arms and legs splayed, little hands waving or clenched, severed umbilical cords floating loose, swathed in translucent wisps of amniotic sac.

There must have been a hundred embryos and fetuses and babies.

Each bottle was labeled in German, in neat calligraphy, with a date (the date ripped from the womb?), prenatal age, weight in grams, size in centimeters.

The dates ranged from 1940 to 1954.

Gerhard Lenz had done experiments on human babies and children.

It was worse than he'd ever imagined. The man was inhuman, a monster . . . *But why were these ghastly exhibits still here?*

It was all he could do not to scream.

He stumbled toward the door.

On the facing wall were glass tanks, from a foot to almost five feet tall and two feet around, and in them floated not fetuses but small children.

Small wizened children, from tiny newborns to toddlers to children seven or eight years old.

Children, he guessed, who had been afflicted with the premature-aging syndrome known as progeria.

The faces of little old men and women.

His skin prickled.

Children. Dead children.

He thought of the poor father of Christoph in his gloomy apartment. *My Christoph died happy.*

A private sanatorium, the woman at the foundation had said.

Exclusive, private, very luxurious, she'd said.

He turned, lightheaded, to leave the room, and heard footsteps.

Carefully peering out of the doorway he saw another white-suited guard approaching, and he backed into the room, concealed himself behind the door.

As the guard passed, he cleared his throat loudly, and he heard the footsteps halt.

The guard, as Ben had expected, entered the room. Swift as a cobra, Ben lunged, slamming the butt of his revolver into the back of the guard's head. The man collapsed.

Ben shut the door behind him, placed his fingers on the guard's neck and felt the jugular vein pulse. Alive but unconscious, though undoubtedly for a good long while.

He removed the man's holster and pulled out the Walther PPK, then stripped off the white jumpsuit.

He removed his clammy clothes and donned the uniform. It was too large for him, but acceptable. Fortunately the shoes fit. With his thumb he flicked at the left of the Walther's slide and removed the magazine. All eight brass cartridges were there.

Now he had three handguns, an arsenal. He checked the pockets of the guard's jumpsuit and found only a pack of cigarettes and a key-card, which he took.

Then he returned to the corridor, pausing only to make sure no one else was in sight. Farther down the hall he came on the brushed steel double-doors of a large elevator, modern for this ancient building. He pressed the call button.

A ping, and the doors opened immediately to reveal an interior lined with protective gray quilting. He entered, inspected the panel, and saw that a key-card had to be inserted before the elevator would move. He inserted the guard's card, then pressed the button for the first floor. The doors closed rapidly, the elevator jolted upward, and opened a few seconds later onto another world entirely.

It was a brightly lit, ultramodern-looking corridor that could have been in any prosperous corporate headquarters.

The floors were carpeted in neutral industrial gray, the walls not the ancient stone of the floor below but smooth white tile. A couple of men in white coats, doctors or clinicians perhaps, passed by. One was pushing a metal cart. The other glanced at Ben but seemed to look through him.

He strode purposefully down the hall. Two young Asian women, also in white jackets, stood by an open door to what appeared to be a laboratory, speaking a language Ben did not recognize. Absorbed in conversation, they paid no attention to him.

Now he entered a large atrium, well lit by a combination of soft incandescent light and amber late-afternoon sun that filtered in through cathedral windows. This looked like it was once the grand entrance hall of the *Schloss*, artfully converted to a modern lobby. A graceful stone staircase wound upstairs. There were a number of doors in the lobby. Each was marked, in black type on white placards, with a number and letter, each accessible only by inserting a card into a card-reader. Each door probably led to a corridor.

A dozen or so people were passing through, to and from the hallways, up or down the stairs, to the bank of elevators. Most wore lab coats, loose-fitting white pants, white shoes or sneakers. Only the guards, in their jumpsuits, wore heavy-duty black shoes. A man in a white coat passed by the two Asian women and said something; the two women reversed course, back toward the laboratory. Obviously the man was someone senior, someone in charge.

Two orderlies carried a stretcher across the lobby, on which an old man in a pale blue hospital gown lay still.

Another patient in a hospital johnny came through the lobby, moving from corridor 3A to corridor 2B. This was a vigorous-looking young-middle-aged man of around fifty who hobbled as if he were in great pain.

What the hell was all this?

If Anna was indeed here, where was she?

This clinic was far larger, far busier, than he had imagined. Whatever they were doing—whatever the purpose was of those nightmarish specimens in the basement, if indeed they had any bearing on the work being done here—there were a lot of people involved, both patients and doctors or laboratory researchers.

She's in here somewhere, I know she is.

But is she safe? Alive? If she'd discovered whatever horrible thing was being done here, would they have *let* her live?

Must go. Must *move it.*

He walked through the atrium hurriedly, his face stern, a security guard dispatched to check out a disturbance. He stopped at the entrance to corridor 3B and inserted his key-card, hoping it gave him access to this area.

The door lock clicked. He entered a long white corridor that could have been in any hospital anywhere.

Among the many people passing by was a white-uniformed woman, presumably a nurse, who appeared to be walking a small child on a leash.

It was as if she were walking a large, obedient dog.

Ben looked at the child more closely and realized from the papery skin, the wrinkled and wizened face, that this was a little boy afflicted with progeria, looking very much like the child in the photographs in the father's apartment he had so recently visited. He also looked like the full-grown children, preserved in formaldehyde, in that nightmarish basement room.

The boy walked like an old man, his gait wide-legged and rickety.

Ben's fascination cooled to an icy anger.

The boy stopped in front of a door and waited patiently while the woman holding the leash unlocked the door with a key on a loop around her neck. The door led into a large glassed-in area fully visible from the hall.

The long room behind the plate glass could have been a hospital nursery, except that everyone inside was a progeric. There were seven or eight little wizened children here. At first glance, Ben thought they were on leashes, too; on closer inspection, he saw that each was connected to some sort of clear plastic tube coming from his or her back. The tubes were connected to shiny metal columns. It appeared that each child was being kept on an intravenous drip through the tubing. They had no eyebrows or eyelashes, their heads were small and shriveled, their skin crepey. The few who were walking shuffled like old men.

Some squatted on the floor, quietly absorbed in games or puzzles. Two of them were playing together, their tubes entangled. A little girl with a long blond wig wandered aimlessly about the floor, chanting or talking to herself, her words inaudible.

The Lenz Foundation.

A few selected progeric children were invited each year to the clinic. No visitors were allowed.

This was no summer camp, no retreat. The children were being treated like animals. They were, they *had* to be, human subjects in some sort of experiment.

Children in the basement pickled in formaldehyde. Children being treated like dogs.

A private sanatorium.

This was neither a sanatorium nor, he was sure, a clinic.

Then what was it? What kind of "science" was being done here?

Nauseated, he turned and continued down the hall until it came to an end. To his left was a red door, locked, accessible only by key-card. Unlike most of the other hallway doors he'd seen here, this door had no window.

The door was unmarked. He knew he had to find out what lay behind it.

Ben inserted the guard's key-card, but this time it did nothing. Apparently this door required a different level of access.

Just as he turned away, the door came open.

A man in a white coat emerged, clutching a clipboard, a stethoscope dangling out of one pocket. A doctor. The man glanced incuriously at Ben, nodded, and held the door open for him. Ben passed through the doorway.

He was not prepared for what he saw.

He was in a high-ceilinged room as big as a basketball court. The vaulted stone ceiling and leaded stained-glass cathedral windows appeared to be all that remained of the original architecture. The floor plan indicated that this enormous chamber had originally been a grand private chapel as big as a church. Ben wondered whether it had later been used as the main factory floor. He estimated it was more than a hundred feet long, maybe a hundred feet wide, the ceilings easily thirty feet high.

Now it was clearly an immense medical facility. Yet at the same time it looked almost like a health club, at once well equipped and spartan.

In one area of the room was a line of hospital beds, each separated from the other by a curtain. Some of the beds were empty; on others, maybe five or six of them, patients lay supine, connected to some sort of monitor and IV stand.

In another area was a long row of black treadmills, each equipped with an EKG monitor. On a few of them elderly men and women were running in place, electrodes or probes sprouting from their arms and legs, necks and heads.

Here and there were nurses' stations, respirators, anesthesia equipment. A dozen or so doctors and nurses observed, assisted, or bustled about. All the way around the enormous room ran a catwalk, roughly twenty feet above the floor and ten feet from the ceiling.

Ben realized that he had been standing at the room's entrance for too long. In a guard's uniform, he had to act as if he were on assignment. So he walked, slowly and purposefully, into the room, checking one side and then another.

Sitting in a modern black-leather-and-steel chair was an old man. A plastic tube was attached to one arm and connected to an IV stand. The man was speaking on a phone, a folder of papers in his lap. Obviously he was a patient, but he was clearly engaged in some kind of business.

In a few places the man's hair had the downy look of a newborn's. Around the sides the hair was coarser, denser, and more luxuriant, white or gray at the ends, but growing in black or dark brown.

And the man looked familiar. His face was often on the cover of *Forbes* or *Fortune*, Ben thought. A businessman or investor, someone famous.

Yes! It had to be Ross Cameron, the so-called "sage of Santa Fe." One of the richest men in the world.

Ross Cameron. There was no question about it now.

Seated next to him was a much younger man whom Ben recognized right away. This was unquestionably Arnold Carr, the fortyish software billionaire and founder of Technocorp. Cameron and Carr were known to be friends; Cameron was sort of Carr's mentor or guru, kind of a father-son relationship. Carr, too, was hooked up to an IV; he also was speaking on the phone, obviously conducting business, though without any papers.

Two legendary billionaires, sitting side by side like a couple of guys in a barbershop.

In a "clinic" in the Austrian Alps.

Being infused with some kind of fluid.

Were they being studied? Treated for something? Something bizarre was taking place here, something secret and important enough to require fully armed security, important enough to kill people over.

A third man walked over to Cameron, said a few words in greeting. Ben recognized the chairman of the Federal Reserve, now in his seventh decade and among the most revered figures in Washington.

Nearby, a nurse adjusted a blood pressure cuff on—well, it had to be Sir Edward Downey, but he looked the way he had when he was England's Prime Minister, three decades ago.

Ben kept walking until he reached the treadmills, where a man and a woman were running next to each other, talking, out of breath. They each wore gray sweatpants and sweatshirts and white running shoes, and both had electrodes taped to their foreheads, the backs of their heads and necks, their arms and legs. The threadlike wires coming out of the electrodes rose neatly behind each of them, out of the way, connected to Siemens monitors that seemed to be recording their heart rates.

Ben recognized both of them, too.

The man was Dr. Walter Reisinger, the Yale professor turned Secretary of State. In person, Reisinger looked healthier than he seemed on TV or in photographs. His skin glowed, though that might have been a result of the running, and his hair seemed darker, though it was probably dyed.

The woman he was talking to on the next treadmill resembled Supreme Court Justice Miriam Bateman. But Justice Bateman was known to be nearly crippled with arthritis. During State of the Union addresses, when the Supreme Court filed in, Justice Bateman was always the slowest, walking with a cane.

This woman—*this* Justice Bateman—was running like an Olympic athlete in training.

Were these people look-alikes of famous world figures? Ben wondered. Doubles? Yet that wouldn't explain the infusions, the training.

Something else.

He heard the Dr. Reisinger clone voice saying something to the Justice Bateman clone about "the Court's decision."

This *was* no clone. This had to be Justice Miriam Bateman.

So then what *was* this place? Was this some sort of health spa for the rich and famous?

Ben had heard of such places, in Arizona or New Mexico or California, sometimes Switzerland or France. Places where the elite went to recover from plastic surgery, from alcoholism or drug dependency, to lose ten or twenty pounds.

But this—?

The electrodes, the IV tubes, the EKG screens . . . ?

These famous people—all, except Arnold Carr, old—were being closely monitored, but what for?

Ben came upon a row of StairMasters, on one of which an ancient man was moving up and down at top speed, just as Ben regularly did at his health club. This man, too—no one Ben recognized—was clad in gray sweats. The front of his sweatshirt was darkened with sweat.

Ben knew young athletes in their twenties who couldn't sustain such a grueling pace for more than a few minutes. How in the world was this old man, with his wrinkled face and liver-spotted hands, able to do it?

"He's ninety-six years old," a man's voice boomed. "Remarkable, isn't it?"

Ben looked around, then up. The person speaking was standing on the catwalk, just above Ben.

It was Jürgen Lenz.

CHAPTER FORTY-SIX

A soft, low chime filled the air, melodic and sedate. Jürgen Lenz, resplendent in a charcoal suit, blue shirt, and silver tie, under a neatly pressed white doctor's coat, strolled down wrought-iron stairs to the main floor. He glanced over at the treadmills and StairMasters. The Supreme Court Justice and the former Secretary of State and most of the others were beginning to finish their exercise sessions, dismount from the machines, nurses removing the wires from their bodies.

"That's the signal for the next helicopter shuttle to Vienna," he explained to Ben. "Time to return to the International Children's Health Forum they were so kind as to depart. Needless to say, they're busy people despite their age. In fact, I'd say *because* of their age. They all have much to give the world—which is why I've selected them."

He made a subtle hand gesture. Both of Ben's arms were suddenly grabbed from behind. Two guards held him while another expertly frisked him, removing all three weapons.

Lenz waited impatiently as the weapons were confiscated, like a dinner-table raconteur whose tale has been interrupted by the serving of the salad course.

"What have you done with Anna?" Ben asked, his voice steely.

"I was about to ask you the very same thing," Lenz replied. "She insisted on inspecting the clinic, and of course I couldn't refuse. But somehow, along the way, we lost her. Apparently she knows something about evading security systems."

Ben studied Lenz, trying to determine how much of this was truth. Was that his way of stalling, of refusing to bring him to her? Was he negotiating? Ben felt a surge of panic.

Is he lying? Fabricating a story he knows that I'll believe, that I'll want to believe?

Have you killed her, you lying bastard?

Then again, that Anna might have disappeared to investigate what was happening in the clinic was plausible. Ben said, "Let me warn you right now, if anything happens to her—"

"But nothing will, Benjamin. Nothing will." Lenz put his hands in his pockets, head bowed. "We are in a clinic, after all, that is devoted to life."

"I'm afraid I've already seen too much to believe that."

"How much do you really *understand* of whatever you've seen?" Lenz said. "I'm sure that once you truly grasp the work we're doing, you'll appreciate its importance." He motioned for the guards to let Ben go. "This is the culmination of a lifetime's work."

Ben said nothing. Escaping was out of the question. But in fact he wanted to remain here.

You killed my brother.

And Anna? Have you killed her, too?

He became aware that Lenz was speaking. "It was Adolf Hitler's great obsession, you know. The Thousand-Year Reich, and all that nonsense— though it lasted, what, twelve years? He had a theory that the bloodlines of the Aryans had been polluted, adulterated, because of interbreeding. Once the so-called 'master race' was purified it would be extremely long-lived. Rubbish, of course. But I'll give the old madman credit. He was determined to discover how he and the Reich's leaders could live longer, and so he gave a handful of his brightest scientists free rein. Unlimited funds. Do your experiments on concentration-camp prisoners. Whatever you like."

"Made possible by the generous sponsorship of the greatest monster of the twentieth century," Ben said, biting off his words.

"A mad despot, let us agree. And his talk of a thousand-year Reich was laughable—a deeply unstable man, promising an epoch of lasting stability. But his pairing of the two desiderata—longevity and stability— was *not* ill-founded."

"I'm not following."

"We human beings are singularly ill-designed in one respect. Of all the species on the planet, we require the longest period of gestation and childhood—of development. And really, we must think about intellectual as well as physical development. Two decades for complete physical mat- uration, often another decade or more to attain full professional mastery in our area of specialization. Somebody with a highly involved craft, such as a surgeon, may be well into his fourth decade before he has achieved full competence at his vocation. The process of learning and progressive mastery continues—and then, just as he reaches its height, what happens? His eyes begin to dim, his fingers to lose their precision. The depredations of time begin to rob him of what he spent half a lifetime acquiring. It's like a bad joke. We're Sisyphus, knowing as soon as we have rolled the boulder toward the top of the hill, it will start hurtling back down. I'm told you once taught schoolchildren. Think how much of human society is devoted simply to reproducing itself—transmitting its institutions, its knowledge and skills, the struts and gearings of civilization. It's an extraordinary tribute to our determination to win out over time. And yet how much farther would our species have been able to advance if only its leadership, political and intellectual, had been able to focus on advancement, rather than simply self-replacement! How much farther we'd all be if some of us were able to stay the course, mount the learning curve and stay there! How much farther we'd be if the best and the brightest of us could keep that boulder rolling uphill, rather than fending off the nursing home or the grave by the time the crest came into view!"

A doleful smile. "Gerhard Lenz, whatever we think of him, was a brilliant man," Lenz went on. Ben made a mental note: was Jürgen Lenz really Gerhard's son? "Most of his theories never amounted to anything. But he was convinced that the secret to how and why human beings age was in our cells. And this was even before Watson and Crick discovered DNA, all the way back in 1953! A remarkable man, really. So farsighted in so many ways. He knew the Nazis would lose, and Hitler would be gone, and the funds would dry up. He simply wanted to make sure his work would continue. Do you know why that was important, Benjamin? May I call you Benjamin?"

But Ben was transfixed, looking around the cavernous laboratory in stupefaction, and did not answer.

Because he was there and not there.

He was entwined with Anna, their bodies slick and warm. He was watching her cry after he'd told her about Peter.

He was sitting in a rural Swiss inn with Peter; he was standing over Peter's blood-soaked body.

"An extraordinary undertaking required extraordinary resources. Hitler prattled about stability while contributing to its destruction, and so it went with other tyrants in other parts of the world. But Sigma really could contribute to the pacification of the planet. Its founders knew what was necessary. They were devoted to a single creed: rationality. The remarkable advances we'd seen over the past century in technology had to be matched with advances in the management of our race—the *human* race. Science and politics could no longer be relegated to separate dominions."

Gradually Ben focused. "You're not making sense. Technology proved an *aid* to the madness. Totalitarianism depended on mass communication. And scientists helped make the Holocaust possible."

"All the more reason why Sigma was necessary—as a bulwark against that sort of madness. You can understand that, can't you? A single madman had driven Europe to the brink of anarchy. On the other side of a great land mass, a small band of agitators had turned an empire secured by Peter the Great into a seething cauldron. The insanity of the mob amplified the insanity of the individual. That's what the century had taught us. The future of Western civilization was too important to rest in the hands of the mobs. The aftermath of the war had left a vacuum, a powerful one. Civil society was everywhere in disarray. It fell upon a small group of powerful, well-organized men to impose order. Indirect rule. The levers of power were to be manipulated, even as that manipulation would be carefully camouflaged by the official instrumentalities of governance. Enlightened leadership was necessary—leadership behind the scenes."

"And what was to guarantee that the leadership was going to be enlightened?"

"I told you. Lenz was a farsighted man, and so were the industrialists he allied with. Again, it comes down to the marriage of science and politics: one would have to heal and strengthen the other."

Ben shook his head. "That's something else that doesn't make sense. These businessmen were folk heroes, many of them. Why would they agree to consort with the likes of Strasser or Gerhard Lenz?"

"Yes, this was an extremely inclusive group. But perhaps you forget your own father's indispensable role."

"A Jew."

"Doubly indispensable, one could say. Substantial sums were transferred out of the Third Reich, and to do so without detection was a challenge of mind-numbing complexity. Your father, who was quite a wizard in such financial matters, rose to the challenge. But, equally, the

fact that he was Jewish was exceedingly helpful in reassuring our counterparts in Allied nations. It helped establish the fact that this wasn't
about furthering the Führer's insanity. This was about business. And
about betterment."

Ben gave him a frankly skeptical look. "You still haven't explained
Gerhard Lenz's special appeal to these businessmen."

"Lenz had something to offer them. Or, at that point, I should say
that he had something to *promise*. The word had spread among the
moguls that Lenz had made some extremely suggestive scientific breakthroughs in an area of direct personal interest to all of them. Based on
some preliminary successes, Lenz had, at the time, thought he was nearer
than he in fact was. He was flush with excitement, and the excitement
was infectious. As things turned out, the founders didn't survive to benefit from his researches. But all of them deserve credit for making it
possible. Billions of dollars invisibly went to support the research—a level
of support that made the Manhattan Project look like a high school lab
class. But now we touch on matters that may lie beyond your grasp."

"Try me."

"No doubt your inquiries are purely disinterested, yes?" Lenz said
dryly. "Like Ms. Navarro's."

"What have you done with her?" Ben asked again, turning toward Lenz
as if coming out of a stupor. He was beyond anger now. He was in
another, calmer place. He was thinking about killing Jürgen Lenz, realizing with peculiar satisfaction that he did in fact have it in him to kill
another person.

And he was thinking about how he would find Anna. *I'll listen to you,
you bastard. I'll be civil and obedient and I'll let you talk until you take
me to her.*

And then I'll kill you.

Lenz looked at him, unblinking, and then continued his explanation.
"I expect you've figured out the basic scenario. Quite simply, what his
work promised was the opportunity to explore the limits of mortality. A
man lives for a hundred years if he's lucky. Mice only get two years.
Galápagos tortoises can live *two hundred* years. Now, why in the world
is that? Has nature dictated these arbitrary limits?"

Lenz had begun pacing slowly back and forth in front of Ben, his
guards standing watch. "Even though my father was forced to move to
South America, he continued to direct his research institute here long-

distance. Traveled back and forth several times a year. In the late fifties one of his scientists made an intriguing discovery—that every time a human cell divides, its chromosomes, those tiny spindles of DNA, become shorter! Microscopically shorter, yes, but still, measurably so. So what *was* it, exactly, that was getting shorter? It took years to discover the answer." He smiled again. "Father was right. The secret really was in our cells."

"The chromosomes," Ben said. He was beginning to understand.

Father was right.

He had an idea now where Max had gone.

"Just one tiny part of the chromosomes, really. The very tip of them—looks a little like those plastic tips at the end of shoelaces. Way back in 1938 those little caps had been discovered, named 'telomeres.' Our team found that every time a cell divides, those little caps get shorter and shorter, until the cell starts to die. Our hair falls out. Our bones get brittle. Our spines curve. Our skin wrinkles and sags. We get old."

"I saw what you're doing to those children," Ben said. "The progerics. I take it you're experimenting on them." *And who else are you experimenting on?* "The world believes you invite them in for a vacation. Some vacation." No, he chided himself, must remain calm. He struggled to control his rage, keep from showing it.

Listen to him. Lead him on.

"True, it's no vacation for them," Lenz agreed. "But these poor children do not need vacations. They need a cure! It's really fascinating, you know, these little young-old people. They're *born* old. If you took a cell from a newborn progeric child and put it side by side, under a microscope, with one from a ninety-year-old man—why, even a molecular biologist couldn't tell the difference! In a progeric, those little tips start out short. Short telomeres, short lives."

"What are you *doing* to them?" Ben asked. He realized his jaw ached from clenching it so hard so long. A mental image flashed of the progeric children in the bottles.

Dr. Reisinger and Justice Miriam Bateman, Arnold Carr, and the others were straggling out of the room, conversing.

"Those little shoelace tips, they're like tiny odometers. Or timing devices, say. We have a hundred trillion cells in our bodies, and each cell has ninety-two telomeres—that makes ten *quadrillion* little clocks telling our body when it's time to shut down. We're *preprogrammed* to die!"

Lenz seemed unable to contain his excitement. "But what if we could somehow reset the clocks, hmm? Keep them from getting shorter? Ah, that was the trick. Well, it turns out that some cells—certain brain cells, for instance—make a chemical, an enzyme, that fixes up their little telomeres, rebuilds them. All of our cells have the ability to make it, but for some reason they don't—it's just switched off most of the time. So . . . what if *we* could turn that switch on? Keep those little clocks ticking? So elegant, so simple. But I'd be lying to you if I said this was easy to do. Even with all the money in the world, and some of the world's most brilliant scientists to choose from, it still took decades, and a number of scientific advances, like gene splicing."

This was what the killings were about, wasn't it?

A neat little irony, Ben thought. People die so that others can live far beyond their natural life span.

Keep him talking, explaining. Bury the rage. Keep sight of the goal.

"When did you make your breakthrough?" Ben asked.

"Around fifteen, twenty years ago."

"And why hasn't anybody else caught up with you?"

"Others are working in the field, of course. But we've got an advantage they lack."

"Unlimited funding." Credit Max Hartman, he thought.

"That helps, certainly. And the fact that we've been working on it pretty much nonstop since the forties. But that's not the whole story. The big difference is human experimentation. Every 'civilized' country in the world has outlawed it. But how much can you really learn from rats or fruit flies, for God's sake. We made our earliest advances by experimenting on children with progeria, a condition that doesn't exist elsewhere in the animal world. And we still use progerics, as we continue to refine our understanding of the molecular pathways involved. One day we won't need them anymore. But we still have so much to learn."

"Human experimentation," Ben said, scarcely concealing his revulsion. There was no difference between Jürgen Lenz and Gerhard Lenz. To them, human beings—sick children, refugees, camp inmates—were nothing more than lab rats. "Like those refugee children in their tents, fenced in out there," Ben said. "Maybe you brought them in under the guise of 'humanitarianism.' But they're expendable too, aren't they?" He recalled words that Georges Chardin had spoken to him, and he said them aloud: "The slaughter of the innocents."

Lenz bristled. "That's what some of the *angeli rebelli* called it, but it's a rather inflammatory description," he said. "As such, it only impedes rational deliberation. Yes, some must die that others may live. A disquieting idea, no doubt. But put away the veil of sentimentality for one moment and face the brutal truth. These unfortunate children would otherwise be killed in war, or die from the diseases of poverty—and for what? Instead, they are *saviors*. They'll change the world. Is it more ethical to bomb their homes, let them be machine-gunned down, let them die senselessly, as the 'civilized world' permits? Or to give them the chance, instead, to alter the course of history? You see, the form of telomerase enzyme that our treatment requires is most readily isolated from the tissues of the central nervous system—the cells of the cerebrum and cerebellum. The quantities are far richer in the young. Unfortunately, it cannot be synthesized: it's a complex protein, and the shape, the conformation, of the protein is crucial. As with many such complex proteins, they cannot be produced by artificial means. And so . . . we must harvest it from human beings."

"The slaughter of the innocents," Ben repeated.

Lenz shrugged. "The sacrifice troubles you, but it has not unduly troubled the world at large."

"What do you mean?"

"You've no doubt heard the statistics—the fact that twenty thousand children disappear every year. People know, and they shrug. They've come to accept it. Perhaps it would provide a measure of consolation to know that these children haven't perished for no reason. It has taken us years to perfect our assays, techniques, dose levels. *There was no other way*. Nor will there be in the foreseeable future. We need the tissue. It must be human tissue, and it must be from juveniles. A seven-year-old's brain—a quart and a half of quivering jelly—is hardly smaller than a grown-up's, but its yield of telomerase enzymes is ten times as great. It is the greatest, most valuable natural resource on earth, yes? As your countrymen say, a terrible thing to waste."

"And so you 'disappear' them. Every year. Thousands and thousands of children."

"Typically from war-torn regions where their life expectancy would be paltry, anyway. This way, at least, they do not die in vain."

"No, they don't die in vain. They die for vanity. They die so that you and your friends can live forever, isn't that it?" *This is not a man you argue with*, Ben thought, but he was finding it increasingly difficult to contain his outrage.

Lenz scoffed, "Forever? Please, none of us will live forever. All we're doing is arresting the aging process in some cases, reversing it in others. The enzyme enables us to repair much of the damage to the skin, the integument. Reverse the damage caused by heart disease. As yet, this therapy can only occasionally restore us to the prime of our youth. And even to give someone my age his forty-year-old body back is time-consuming . . ."

"These people," Ben said, "they all come here to . . . to become younger."

"Only a few of them. Most of them are public figures who can't change their appearance drastically without attracting attention. So they come here, at my invitation, to *halt* their aging, maybe undo some of the damage that age has inflicted."

"Public figures?" Ben shot back mockingly. "They're all rich and powerful!" He was beginning to understand what Lenz was doing.

"No, Benjamin. They're the great ones. The leaders of our society, our culture. The few who advance our civilization. The founders of Sigma came to understand this. They saw that civilization was fragile, and that there was only one way to ensure the continuity that it required. The future of the industrial state had to be protected, sheltered from the storms. Our societies would only advance if we could push back the horizon of human mortality. Year by year, Sigma used whatever tools it had at its disposal, but now the original goals can be advanced by other, more effective means—good God, we're talking about something far more effective than throwing billions of dollars at coups and political action groups. We're talking about the formation of a stable, lasting elite."

"So these are the leaders of our civilizations . . ."

"Precisely."

"And you're the man who leads the leaders."

Lenz responded with a thin smile. "Please, Benjamin. I have no interest in boss-man theatrics. But in any organization, there must be a . . . co-ordinator."

"And there can only be one."

A pause. "Ultimately, yes."

"And what of those who oppose your 'enlightened' regime? I suppose they're purged from the body politic."

"A body *must* purge toxins if it is to survive, Benjamin." Lenz spoke with surprising gentleness.

"What you're describing isn't some utopia, Lenz. It's a slaughter-house."

"Your reproach is as glib as it is vacuous," Lenz returned. "Life is a matter of trade-offs, Benjamin. You live in a world where vastly greater sums are spent on medications for erectile dysfunction than are spent on tropical diseases that claim the lives of millions every year. And what of your own *personal* decisions? When you buy a bottle of Dom Perignon, you have spent a sum of money that could have vaccinated a village in Bangladesh, spared lives from the ravages of disease, yes? People will *die*, Benjamin, as a result of the decisions, the priorities, entailed by your purchase. I'm quite serious: Can you deny that the ninety dollars a bottle of Dom Perignon costs could have easily saved half a dozen lives, perhaps more? Think about it. The bottle will yield seven or eight glasses of wine. Each glass, we can say, represents a life lost." His eyes were bright, a scientist having solved an equation and moved on to another one. "That is why I say that such trade-offs are inevitable. And once you understand that, you start to ask higher order questions: qualitative questions, not quantitative ones. Here we have the opportunity to vastly extend the useful life span of a great humani-tarian or thinker—someone whose contribution to the commonweal is inarguable. Compared to this good, what is the life of a Serbian goat-herd? Of an illiterate child who would have otherwise been destined to a life of poverty and petty criminality. Of a Gypsy girl who would oth-erwise spend her days picking the pockets of tourists visiting Florence, her nights picking lice out of her hair. You have been taught that lives are sacrosanct, and yet every day you make decisions signifying an awareness that some lives are more valuable than others. I *mourn* for those who have given their lives for the greater good. I truly do. I gen-uinely wish that the sacrifice they made was unnecessary. But I also know that every great achievement in the history of our species has come at the cost of human lives. 'There is no document of civilization that is not simultaneously a document of barbarism': a great thinker said that, a thinker who died too young."

Ben stood blinking, speechless.

"Come," Lenz said, "there's someone who wants to say hello to you. An old friend of yours."

Ben gaped. "Professor Godwin?"

"Ben."

It was his old college mentor, long since retired. But his posture seemed straighter, his once wrinkled skin was now smooth and pink. He looked younger by several *decades* than his eighty-two years. John Barnes Godwin, emeritus historian of Europe in the twentieth century, was vigorous. His handshake was firm.

"Good Lord," Ben said. If he hadn't known Godwin, he'd have put his age in the early fifties.

Godwin was one of the elect. Of course: he was a behind-the-scenes kingmaker, he was powerful and extremely well connected.

Godwin stood before him as mind-boggling proof of Lenz's achievement. They stood in a small antechamber off the great hall, which was comfortably furnished with couches and easy chairs, throw pillows and reading lamps, and racks of newspapers and magazines in a variety of languages.

Godwin seemed pleased at Ben's astonishment. Jürgen Lenz beamed.

"You must not know what to make of all this," Godwin said.

It took Ben a few seconds before he could think of a response. "That's one way of putting it."

"It's extraordinary, what Dr. Lenz has achieved. We're all deeply grateful to him. But I think we're also aware of the significance, the *gravity*, of his gift. In essence, we've been given our lives back. Not our youth so much as—as another chance. A reprieve from death." He frowned thoughtfully. "Is it against nature? Maybe. The way curing cancer is against nature. Emerson, remember, told us that old age is 'the only disease.' "

His eyes gleamed. Ben listened in stunned silence.

In college, Ben had always addressed him as Professor Godwin, but now he chose not to address him by name at all. He said simply, "Why?"

"Why? On a personal level? Do you have to ask? I've been given another lifetime. Perhaps even another *two* lifetimes."

"Will you gentlemen excuse me?" Lenz interrupted. "The first helicopter is about to leave, and I must say good-bye." He bustled, almost sprinted, out of the room.

"Ben, when you get to be my age, you don't buy green bananas,"

Godwin resumed. "You don't take on book projects you don't think you'll live to complete. But think of how much I can *do* now. Until Dr. Lenz called, I'd felt as if I'd struggled and worked and learned for decades to get where I am, to learn what I know, to gain the *understanding* I have—yet at any moment everything might be snatched away: 'If youth but knew, if old age but could,' right?"

"Even if all this is true—"

"You have *eyes*. You can see what's in front of you. Look at me, for God's sake! I used not to be able to climb the stairs at Firestone Library, and now I can *run*." Godwin, Ben realized, was not just a successful experiment, he was *one of them*—a conspirator with Lenz. Didn't he know about the cruelty, the murders?

"But have you *seen* what's going on here—the child refugees on the lawn? Thousands of abducted children? *That* doesn't bother you?"

Godwin looked visibly uncomfortable. "I'll admit there are aspects of all this that I prefer not to know about, and I've always made that clear."

"We're talking about the ongoing murder of thousands of children!" Ben said. "The treatment *requires* it. Lenz calls it 'harvesting,' a pretty word for systematic slaughter."

"It's . . ." Godwin faltered. "Well, it's morally complex. '*Honesta turpitudo est pro causa bona.*' "

" 'For a good cause, wrongdoing is virtuous,' " Ben translated. "Publilius Syrus. You taught me that."

Godwin, too. He'd gone over; he'd joined Lenz. "What's important is that the cause has genuine merit." He ambled over to a leather sofa. Ben sat facing him on the adjacent sofa.

"And were you involved in Sigma's cause in the old days as well?"

"Yes, for decades. And I feel so privileged to be around for this whole new phase. Under Lenz's leadership, things are going to be very different."

"I gather not all your colleagues agreed."

"Oh yes. The *angeli rebelli*, Lenz calls them. Rebel angels. There *were* a handful of people who wanted to put up a fight. Out of vanity or shortsightedness. Either they never trusted Lenz, or they felt demoted by the fact that new leadership had emerged. I guess a few of them had qualms about the . . . sacrifices that had to be made. Any time there's a shift in power, you've got to expect some forms of resistance. But a few years ago, when Lenz allowed that his project would soon be ready for actual trials, he made it clear the collective would have to recognize his leadership. He didn't do it out of any sense of self-interest, either. It's just that some difficult decisions would have to be made about who was going to be—well, admitted into the program. Inducted into the permanent elite. The risk of factionalism was too great. Lenz was the leader we needed. Most of us recognized that. A few didn't."

"Tell me, does your plan ultimately call for making this treatment available to everyone, to the masses? Or just what he calls 'the great ones'?"

"Well, you raise a serious point. I was flattered that Jürgen selected me to be a kind of recruiter, as it were, for this august group of world . . . luminaries, I suppose. The *Wiedergeborenen*, as Dr. Lenz calls us—the Reborn. We're reaching out far beyond the Sigma rump group. I brought Walter in, you know, and my old friend Miriam Bateman—Justice Miriam Bateman. I've been charged with helping choose those who seem deserving of it. From around the world—China, Russia, Europe, Africa—everywhere, without prejudice. Except for a prejudice in favor of greatness."

"But Arnold Carr's not much older than I am . . ."

"In fact, he's really at the perfect age to begin these treatments. He can stay forty-two for the rest of his very, very long life, if he chooses. Or become the biological equivalent of thirty-two again." The historian widened his eyes in wonderment. "There are forty of us by now."

"I understand," Ben interrupted, "but—"

"*Listen* to me, Ben! Good Lord, the other Supreme Court Justice we've chosen, a great jurist who's also black, he's a sharecropper's son who's lived through segregation and desegregation both. The wisdom he's accumulated in his lifetime! Who could ever replace him? A painter whose work is already transforming the art world—how many more spectacular canvases might be in him? Imagine, Ben, if history's greatest composers and writers and artists—take Shakespeare, take Mozart, take—"

Ben leaned forward. "This is insanity!" he thundered. "The rich and powerful get to live twice as long as the poor and powerless! It's a goddamned conspiracy of the elite!"

"*And what if it is?*" Godwin shot back. "Plato wrote of the philosopher-king, of the rule of the wise. He understood that our civilization advances and retreats, advances and retreats. We learn lessons only to forget them. History's tragedies repeat themselves—the Holocaust, and then the genocides that followed, as if we'd all forgotten. World wars. Dictatorships. False messiahs. Oppression of minorities. We don't seem to *evolve*. But now, for the first time, we can change all that. We can *transform* the human species!"

"How? Your numbers are tiny." Ben folded his arms on his chest. "That's another problem with elites."

Godwin stared at Ben for a moment, then chuckled. " 'We few, we happy few, we band of brothers'—yes, it all sounds hopelessly inadequate to the grand tasks, right? But humanity doesn't progress through some process of collective enlightenment. We progress because an individual or small team somewhere makes a breakthrough, and everyone else benefits. Three centuries ago, in a region with a very high rate of illiteracy, one man discovers calculus, or two men do—and the course of our species is changed forever. A century ago, one man discovers relativity, and nothing is ever the same. Tell me, Ben, do you know exactly how an internal combustion engine works—could you assemble one even if I gave you the parts? Do you know how to vulcanize rubber? Of course not, but you benefit from the existence of the automobile all the same. That's how it works. In the primitive world—I know we're not supposed to use those words anymore but indulge me—there's no great chasm between what one tribesman knows and another. Not so in the Western world. The division of labor is the very mark of civilization: the higher the degree of division of labor, the more advanced the society. And the most important division of labor is the intellectual division of labor. A minuscule number of people worked on the Manhattan Project—and yet the planet was changed by it forever. In the past decade, you had a few small teams decoding the human genome. Never mind that most of humanity can't remember the difference between Nyquil and niacin— they'll benefit all the same. People everywhere are using personal computers—people who couldn't understand a scrap of computer code, don't know the first thing about integrated circuitry. The mastery belongs to the happy few, and yet the multitudes benefit. The way our species advances isn't through vast, collective exertions—the Jews building the Pyramids. It's through individuals, through very small elites, who discover fire, the wheel, or the central processing unit, and thereby change the very landscape of our lives. And what's true in science and technology can be true of politics, as well. Except the learning curve here takes place over a far longer period of time. Which means that by the time we've learned from our errors, we've been replaced by younger upstarts who make those errors all over again. We don't learn enough, because we're not around long enough. The people who founded Sigma recognized this as an inherent limitation, one that our species would eventually have to overcome if we were to survive. Are you starting to see, Ben?"

"Keep going," Ben said, like a hesitant student.

"The efforts of Sigma—our attempt to *moderate* the politics of the postwar era—were only the beginning. Now we can change the face of the planet! Ensure universal peace, prosperity, and security, through the wise management and marketing of the planet's resources. If that's what you call a conspiracy of the elite—well, is it really such a bad thing? If a few miserable war refugees have to meet their maker ahead of schedule in order to save the world, is that really such a tragedy?"

"It's only for the ones you judge worthy, right?" Ben said. "You want to keep it from everyone else? There will be two classes of human being."

"The ruled and the rulers. But that's inevitable, Ben. There will be the Wise Men and the ruled masses. That's the only way to engineer a viable society. The world's already overpopulated. Much of Africa doesn't even have clean drinking water. If everyone lives twice or three times longer, think of what this will do! The world would collapse! That's why, in his wisdom, Lenz knows it must only be available to the few."

"And what happens to democracy? The rule of the people?"

Godwin's cheeks colored. "Spare me the sentimental rhetoric, Ben. The history of man's inhumanity to man has been history itself: *mobs* destroying what the *nobility* had painstakingly constructed. The main task in politics has always been saving the people from themselves. This wouldn't go down well with the undergraduates, but the *principle* of aristocracy was always correct: *aristos, kratos*—rule of the best. The problem was that aristocracy often didn't give you the best. But imagine if for the first time in human history, you could rationalize the system, create a hidden aristocracy based on merit—with *Wiedergeborenen* serving as the custodians of civilization."

Ben stood up and paced. His head spun. Goodwin, spinning his giddy justifications, had been hooked by the irresistible lure of near-immortality.

"Ben, you're what, thirty-five, thirty-six? You imagine you will live forever. I know I did at your age. But I want you to imagine being eighty-five, ninety, God willing you live so long. You have a family, you have children and grandchildren. You've had a happy life, your work is meaningful, and although you have all the normal afflictions of old age—"

"I'll want to die," Ben said curtly.

"Correct. If you're in the condition of most people at that age. But you don't ever have to *be* ninety. If you begin this therapy now, you'll always be in your prime, in your mid-thirties—God, what I'd give to be your age! Please don't tell me you have some ethical objection to it."

"I'm not sure what to think at this point," Ben said, watching Godwin closely.

Godwin seemed to believe him.

"Good. You're being open-minded. I want you to join us. Join the *Wiedergeborenen.*"

Ben sank his head into his arms. "It's certainly a tempting offer." His voice was muffled. "You make some very good points—"

"Are you still here, John?" interrupted Lenz's voice, loud and enthusiastic. "The last helicopter's about to leave!"

Godwin rose swiftly. "I need to catch the shuttle," he apologized. "I want you to think about what we discussed."

Lenz entered with his arm around a stoop-shouldered old man.

Jakob Sonnenfeld.

"Did you have a good talk?" Lenz inquired.

No. Not him, too. "You—" Ben blurted out to the old Nazi hunter, revolted.

"I think we may have a new recruit," Godwin said somberly, and gave Lenz a brief but significant look.

Ben turned to face Sonnenfeld. "They knew where I was going in Buenos Aires because of you, isn't that right?"

Sonnenfeld looked pained. He averted his eyes. "There are times in life when one must choose sides," he said. "When my treatment begins—"

"Come, gentlemen," Lenz interrupted again. "We must hurry."

Ben could hear the roar of a helicopter outside, as Godwin and Sonnenfeld moved toward the exit.

"Benjamin," Lenz said without turning around. "Please stay right there. I'm so glad to hear you may be interested in our project. So now you and I must have a little talk."

Ben felt something slam him from behind, and steel clamped against his wrist.

Handcuffs.

There was no way out.

The guards dragged him through the great hall, past the exercise equipment and the medical monitoring stations.

He screamed at the top of his lungs and let himself go limp. If any of the *Wiedergeborenen* remained, they'd see him being abducted, and surely they'd object. These were not evil people.

But none of them remained, at least no one he could see.

A third guard took his upper arm and joined the others. His legs and knees slid painfully against the stone floor, the abrasions excruciating. He kicked and struggled. A fourth arrived, and now they were able to hold Ben by each limb, though he torqued himself back and forth to make it as difficult for them as possible, and he kept shouting.

They trundled him into an elevator. A guard pressed the second-floor button. In seconds the elevator opened on to a stark white corridor. As the guards carried him out—he'd ceased resisting; what was the point?— a passing nurse gaped at him, then looked away quickly.

They brought him into what looked like a modified operating room and hoisted him onto a bed. An orderly who appeared to have been expecting him—had the guards radioed ahead?—fastened colored restraints to his ankles and wrists, and then, once he was secured to the table, removed the handcuffs.

Exhausted, he lay flat, his limbs immobile. All of the guards but one filed out of the room, their work done. The remaining guard stood watch by the closed door, an Uzi across his chest.

The door opened, and Jürgen Lenz entered. "I admire your cleverness," he said. "I'd been assured that the old cave was sealed or at least impassable, so I thank you for pointing out the security risk. I've already ordered the entrance dynamited."

Ben wondered: Did Godwin really invite him to join them? Or was his old mentor simply trying to neutralize him? Lenz was far too suspicious to trust him anyway.

Or was he?

"Godwin asked me to join the project," Ben said.

Lenz wheeled a metal cart over next to the bed and busied himself with a hypodermic needle.

"Godwin trusts you," Lenz said, turning around. "I myself do not."

Ben watched his face. "Trusts me about what?"

"About respecting our need for confidentiality. About who you or your investigative friend might have already talked to."

Here was his vulnerability! "If you release her unharmed, you and I can strike a bargain," Ben said. "We each get what we want."

"And, of course, I can trust you to keep your word."

"It'd be in my own best interests," Ben said.

"People do not always act in their own self-interest. If I were ever to forget it, the *angeli rebelli* were there to remind me."

"Let's keep it simple. My interest is in having you release Anna Navarro. Yours is to keep your project secret. We have a mutual interest in striking a deal."

"Well," Lenz said dubiously. "Perhaps. But first I'll need a little chemically inspired honesty, in case you don't come by it naturally."

Ben tried to suppress the wave of panic. "What does that mean?"

"Nothing harmful. A pleasant experience, in fact."

"I don't think you have time for this. Especially with law-enforcement agents due to arrive at any second. This is your last chance to deal."

"Ms. Navarro is here on her own," Lenz said. "She hasn't called in anyone else. She told me so herself." He held up the hypodermic. "And I assure you she was speaking the truth."

Keep conversing. Keep him diverted.

"How do you know you can trust the scientists on your team?"

"I don't. Everything, all the materials, the computers, the sequencers, the slides, the formulas for the infusions—they're all here."

Ben pressed. "You're still vulnerable. Somebody could get access to whatever offsite storage arrangements you've got for the data files. And no encryption is unbreakable."

"Which is precisely why there *is* no offsite storage," Lenz said, with evident satisfaction in demonstrating the fallacies in Ben's suppositions. "That represents a risk I cannot afford. In all honesty, I did not get where I am by placing excessive trust in my fellow man."

"As long as we're both being honest, let me ask *you* something."

"Yes?" Lenz tapped Ben's left forearm until a vein popped up.

"I'd like to know why you had my brother killed."

Lenz jabbed a needle into the vein with what seemed unnecessary force. "It should never have happened. It was done by fanatics among my security people, and it's something I deeply regret. A terrible mistake. They were concerned that his discovery of Sigma's original board would imperil our work."

Ben's heart thudded, and again he fought to control himself. "And my father? Did your 'fanatics' kill him, too?"

"Max?" Lenz looked surprised. "Max is a genius. I very much admire the man. Oh no, I wouldn't harm a hair on his head."

"Then where is he?"

"Did he go somewhere?" Lenz asked innocently.

Move on.

"Then why kill all those other old men . . . ?"

There was a slight twitch under Lenz's left eye. "Housecleaning. For the most part, we're talking about individuals with personal involvement in Sigma who sought to resist the inevitable. They complained that Sigma had fallen under my sway, felt displaced by my emerging role. Oh, all our members were treated generously . . ."

"Kept on a string, you mean. Given payments to fortify their discretion."

"As you like. But it was no longer enough, not now. What it came down to was a failure of vision. The point remains that they declined to, shall we say, get with the program. Then there were those who became importunate, possibly indiscreet, had long since ceased to have anything to offer. They were loose threads, and the time had come to snip them. Perhaps it seems harsh, but when there's this much at stake, you do not simply give people a firm talking to, or spank their wrists, or put them in 'time-out,' yes? You take more definitive measures."

Don't give up, Ben told himself. *Keep him engaged.*

"Murdering these old men in itself seems a foolish risk, don't you think? The deaths were bound to attract suspicion."

"Please. All the deaths appeared to be natural, but even if the toxin were discovered, these were men with plenty of worldly enemies—"

Lenz heard the sound at the same moment Ben did.

A burst of machine-gun fire not far away.

And then another, even closer.

A shout.

Lenz turned toward the door, hypodermic needle in one hand. He said something to the guard standing by the door.

The door burst open in a hail of bullets.

A scream, and the guard collapsed in a pool of his own blood.

Lenz dropped to the floor.

Anna!

Ben's relief was enormous. *She's alive, somehow she's alive.*

"Ben!" she shouted, flinging the door shut behind her and turning the lock. "Ben, you all right?"

"I'm all right," he called.

"Stand up!" she screamed at Lenz. "You goddamned son of a bitch."

She advanced, machine gun leveled. She was wearing a doctor's short white coat.

Lenz stood. His face was flushed, his silver hair mussed. "My guards will be here any second." His voice quavered.

"Don't count on it," Anna replied. "I've sealed off the entire wing, and the doors are jammed from the outside."

"You've killed that guard, I think," Lenz said, bravado returning to his voice. "I thought the United States trained its agents only to kill in self-defense."

"Haven't you heard? I'm off duty," Anna said. "Hands away from your body. Where's your weapon?"

Lenz was indignant. "I have none."

Anna approached. "You don't mind if I look, do you? Hands *away* from your body, I said."

Slowly she took a step toward Lenz, slid her free hand inside his jacket. "Let's see," she said. "I sure hope I can do this without setting off the damned machine gun. I'm not too familiar with these little guys."

Lenz paled.

She produced a small handgun from inside Lenz's suit with a flourish, like a conjurer pulling a rabbit out of a top hat.

"Well, well," she said. "Pretty slick for an old man, Jürgen. Or do your friends still call you Gerhard?"

CHAPTER FORTY-SEVEN

Ben gasped, "Oh, my God."

Lenz pursed his lips, and then, oddly, he smiled.

Anna pocketed Lenz's handgun. "For the longest time it baffled me," she said. "The federal ID lab ran the prints but turned up nothing, no matter how many databases they used. They tried the army intelligence files, but still nothing. Until they went back to the old ten-print cards from the war and a few years after, which haven't yet been digitized, why should they be, right? Your SS prints were included in the Army's files, I guess because you escaped."

Lenz watched her, amused.

"The techies speculated that maybe the prints on the photo I'd sent them were old, but the strange thing was, the fingerprint oil, the perspiration residue they call it, was fresh. Made no sense to them."

Ben looked at Lenz. Yes, he resembled the Gerhard Lenz who appeared in the picture with Max Hartman. Lenz in that 1945 photo was in his mid-forties. That made him, what, over a hundred years old.

It seemed impossible.

"I was my own first successful subject," Gerhard Lenz said quietly. "Almost twenty years ago I was for the first time able to arrest, then reverse, my own aging. Only a few years ago did we devise a formulation that works reliably on everyone." He was looking off in the distance, his gaze unfocused. "It meant that everything that Sigma stood for could now be made secure."

"All right," Anna interrupted. "Give me the key to the restraints."

"I don't have the key. The orderly—"

"Forget it." She shifted the machine gun to her right hand, pulled a straightened paper clip out of a jacket pocket, and freed Ben, handing him a long plastic object, which he glanced at and understood at once.

"Don't move a muscle," Anna shouted, thrusting the Uzi in Lenz's direction. "Ben, take those restraints and lock this bastard to something immobile." She quickly looked around. "We've got to get out of here as fast as possible, and—"

"No," Ben said, steely.

She turned, startled. "What are you—?"

"He's holding prisoners here—young people in tents outside, sick kids in at least one of the wards. We've got to let them out first!"

Anna understood immediately. She nodded. "Fastest way is to shut down the security system. De-electrify the fences, unlock . . ." She turned to Lenz, adjusted the machine gun in her hands. "There's a master control panel, an override, in your office. We're taking a little walk."

Lenz looked phlegmatic. "I'm afraid I don't know what you're talking about. All security for the clinic is controlled from the central guard station on the first level."

"Sorry," Anna said. "I've already 'debriefed' one of your guards." She pointed with the Uzi toward a closed door, not the one through which they'd entered. "Let's *go*."

Lenz's office was immense, dark, cathedral-like.

Glimmers of pale light filtered in through slot windows cut into the stone walls high above their heads. Most of the room was in shadows, except for a small circle of light from a green-glass-shaded library lamp in the middle of Lenz's massive walnut desk.

"I assume you don't object to my putting on the lights so I can see what I'm doing," Lenz said.

"Sorry," Anna said. "We don't need it. Just go around to the other side of your desk and push the button that raises the control panel. Let's make this easy."

Lenz hesitated but a moment, then followed her directions. "This is a pointless exercise," he said with weary contempt as he walked around to his side of the desk. She followed, sidling, the weapon always leveled at him.

Ben came just behind her. A second set of eyes in case Lenz attempted something, as he was sure Lenz would do.

Lenz pushed a recessed button at the front edge of the desk. There was a mechanical rumble, and a long, flat section arose from the middle of the desktop like a horizontal tombstone: a brushed-steel instrument panel, strange-looking atop the Gothic desk.

Set into the steel was what appeared to be a flat plasma screen, on which nine small squares, glowing ice blue, were arranged in rows of three. Each square display showed a different view of the interior and exterior of the *Schloss*. Below the screen was an array of silver toggle switches.

In one display the progeric children played, tethered to their poles; in another, refugees milled about around their tents on the snow, smoking. Guards stood by various entrances. Other guards patrolled the grounds. Winking red lights every few feet along the electrified fences atop the ancient stone walls, presumably showing that the system was still operational.

"Move it," Anna commanded.

Lenz bowed his head indulgently, and began toggling each switch off in order from left to right. Nothing happened, no sign of the security system shutting down. "We will find other progerics," Lenz said as he switched them off, "and there's an endless supply of youthful war refugees, displaced children the world doesn't miss—there always seems to be a war somewhere." This thought seemed to amuse him.

The winking red lights had gone out. A cluster of refugee children was playing a game near one of the tall iron gates. One of them pointed— noticing that the red power lights had stopped blinking?

Another of them ran up to the gate, tugged at it.

The gate slowly came open.

Tentatively the child walked through the gate, looking back at the others, beckoning. Slowly another joined him, passing through the gate to freedom. They appeared to be shouting to the others, though there was no sound.

Then a few more of the children. A bedraggled-looking girl with matted curly hair. Another young boy.

More children.

Frenetic movement. The children began to scramble out, pushing and shoving.

Lenz watched, his expression inscrutable. Anna's attention was riveted on him, the Uzi still pointed.

In another screen, a door to the children's ward was now wide open. A nurse appeared to be waving the children out, looking around furtively.

"So they are escaping," Lenz said, "but for you it will not be so easy. Forty-eight security guards have been trained to shoot any intruders on sight. You will never make it outside." He reached for a large ornate brass lamp to switch it on, and Ben snapped to attention, sure that Lenz was about to pick the lamp up to hurl or swing it, but instead Lenz tugged at a protruding section of the base and pulled out a small oblong object that he instantly pointed at Ben. It was a compact, brass-plated pistol, cleverly concealed.

"Drop it!" Anna shouted.

Ben was a few feet to Anna's side, and Lenz could not cover them both. "I suggest you put down your weapon at once," Lenz said. "That way no one will be hurt."

"I don't think so," Anna said. "We're not exactly evenly matched."

Lenz, unfazed, said blandly, "But you see, if you begin to fire at me, your friend here will be killed, too. You must ask yourself how important it is to kill me—whether it's really worth it."

"Drop the goddamn toy gun," Anna said, although Ben could see it was no toy.

"Even if you succeed in killing me, you change nothing. My work will continue even without me. But your friend Benjamin will simply be dead."

"*No!*" came a hoarse shout.

An old man's voice.

Lenz spun around to look.

"*Lassen Sie ihn los! Lassen Sie meinen Sohn los!* Let him go!"

The voice came from a corner of the great room that was hidden in shadows. Lenz pointed his weapon toward the voice, then seemed to reconsider, and swung it back toward Ben.

The voice again: "Let my son go!"

In the dim light Ben could just make out the seated figure.

His father. In his hand was a gun, too.

For a moment Ben couldn't speak.

He thought it might be a trick of the strange oblique light, and he looked again, and knew that what he saw was real.

Quieter now, Max's voice: "Let them both go."

"Ah, Max, my friend," Lenz called, in a loud and hearty voice. "Perhaps you can talk reason to these two."

"Enough of the killing," Max said. "Enough bloodshed. It's over now."

Lenz stiffened. "You are a foolish old man," he replied.

"You're right," Max said. He remained seated, but his gun was still trained on Lenz. "And I was a foolish young man, too. I was beguiled by you then, just as now. All my life I've lived in fear of you and your people. Your threats. Your blackmail." His voice rose, choked with rage. "No matter what I built or what I became, you were always there."

"You can lower your gun, my friend," Lenz said mildly. His weapon was still pointed at Ben, but for a split-second he turned to Max.

I can rush him, tackle him to the floor, Ben thought. *The next time his attention is diverted.*

Max continued as if he hadn't heard, and as if there were no one in the room but Lenz. "Don't you see I'm not afraid of you any longer?" His voice reverberated against the stone walls. "I will never forgive myself for what I did, for helping you and your butcher friends. For making my deal with the devil. Once I thought it was the right thing to do, for my family, for my future, for the world's. But I was lying to myself. What you did to my son, my Peter—" His voice broke.

"But you *know* that should never have happened!" Lenz protested. "It was the work of overzealous security people who exceeded their authority."

"Enough!" Max bellowed. "No more! Enough of your goddamned lies!"

"But the *project*, Max. My God, man, I don't think you understand—"

"No, you don't understand. You think I care about your dreams of playing God? You think I ever did?"

"I invited you here as a favor to you, to make amends. What are you trying to tell me?" Lenz's voice was controlled, but only barely.

"Amends? But this is only a continuation of the horror. For you, everything and everyone were sacrificed to your dream of living forever." A labored breath. "You're about to take my only remaining child from me! After everything else you've taken from me."

"Then your overtures were merely a ploy. Yes, I'm beginning to see. When you joined us it was always with the intention of betraying us."

"It was the only way I could gain entrance to a walled city. The only way I could hope to monitor from within."

Lenz spoke as if to himself. "My mistake is always to imagine that others are as philanthropic as I am—as concerned with the greater good. How you disappoint me. And after all we've been through together, Max."

"Ach! You pretend to be interested in human progress," Max shouted.

"And you call *me* a foolish old man! You talk of others as subhuman, but you are yourself not human."

Lenz briefly turned his gaze toward Max, seated in the dim corner, and at the same instant that Ben coiled to spring forward, he heard the hollow pop, the retort of a small-caliber pistol, and Lenz looked more surprised than stricken as a small but widening red circle appeared on the breast pocket of his white lab coat near his right shoulder. Aiming in Max's general direction, Lenz squeezed the trigger three times, returning fire wildly.

Then a second blotch of red appeared on Lenz's chest. His right arm dangled uselessly at his side as his pistol clanked to the floor.

Anna lowered the Uzi slightly, watched him.

Suddenly Lenz lunged at Anna, knocking her to the floor, the Uzi clattering.

His hand was at her throat, squeezing her larynx in an iron clutch. She tried to rear up, but he slammed her head back against the floor with an audible crack.

Again he slammed her head against the stone, and then Ben, enraged, leaped on top of Lenz, gripping the plastic cylinder she'd handed him earlier. Ben roared with exertion and fury as he swung his right hand up and jabbed the hypodermic needle directly into Lenz's neck.

Lenz howled in pain. Ben had hit the internal jugular vein, he could tell, or had at least come very close to it, and he depressed the plunger.

Lenz's expression of horror seemed frozen on his face. His hands flew to his neck, found the syringe, yanked it out, and he saw the label. *"Verdammt nochmal! Scheiss Jesus Christus!"*

A bubble of saliva formed at his mouth. Suddenly he fell backward like an upended statue. His mouth opened and shut as if he were trying to scream, but instead he only gasped for air.

Then he went rigid.

Lenz's eyes stared in fury, but the pupils were fixed and dilated.

"I think he's dead," Ben gasped, short of breath.

"I *know* he's dead," Anna said. "That's the most potent opioid there is. They keep some pretty powerful stuff in their locked medicine cabinets. Now let's get *out* of here!" She glanced at Max Hartman. *"All of us."*

"Go," Ben's father whispered from his chair. "Leave me here, but you two must go *now*, the guards—"

"No," Ben said. "You're coming with us."

"Dammit," Anna said to Ben. "I heard the helicopter taking off, so that's out. How did you get in, anyway?"

"A cave—under the property—opens into the basement. But they've found it."

"Lenz was right, we're done for, there's no way out—"

"But there *is* a way," Max said, his voice faint.

Ben ran over to him, stricken by what he saw.

Max, dressed in a pale blue hospital johnny, was feebly holding his hands to the base of his throat, where, as Ben now realized, a bullet had lodged. Blood was spreading insistently beneath his trembling fingers. The thin cotton garment was stenciled with the black numeral eighteen.

"No!" Ben shouted.

The man had taken a bullet in order to kill Lenz—and protect his only surviving son.

"Lenz's private helicopter," Max whispered. "You reach the bay through the back passage on the far left . . ." He murmured instructions for a few moments longer. Finally he said, "Tell me you understand." Max's eyes were imploring. In a voice barely audible he repeated the words: "Tell me you understand."

"Yes," Ben said, hardly able to speak himself. *Tell me you understand*—his father meant the instructions to the bay, of course, but Ben couldn't help thinking that he meant something more, too. *Tell me you understand:* tell me you understand the difficult decisions I made in life, however mistaken.

Tell me you understand them. Tell me you understand who I really am.

As if in resignation, Max pulled his hands from his throat, and blood began to spurt, with the slow, regular pulse of his heartbeat.

Tell me you understand.

Yes, Ben had told him, and just then, at least, he did. *I understand.*

Within a few moments, his father slumped backward, lifeless.

Lifeless, and yet the picture of health. Blinking away tears, Ben could see that his father looked decades younger, his hair beginning to grow in glossy and dark, his skin smooth, firm, toned.

In death, Max Hartman had never looked more alive.

CHAPTER FORTY-EIGHT

Ben and Anna raced down the corridor, gunfire audible all around. The bandolier swung against the barrel of her Uzi as she ran, producing a dull rattle. At any moment, they could be set upon, but the guards realized they were heavily armed, would have to approach with caution. Anna knew that no paid sentry, however loyal, would endanger his life needlessly.

Max's directions had been clear and accurate.

Another right turn brought them to a stairwell.

Ben opened the steel-plated door, and Anna directed a burst of gunfire into the landing area: anyone present would instinctively dive for cover. As they entered, there was a deafening return burst: a guard located on the level below, shooting in the narrow space between the stairs. It was not an angle that afforded any accuracy; the biggest danger was being hit by a ricochet.

"Run upstairs," Anna whispered to Ben.

"But Max said the bay level is downstairs," Ben protested in a low voice.

"Do what I say. Start running upstairs. Loudly."

He immediately understood, and did so, making sure that his shoes thundered against the stairs as he mounted them.

Anna flattened herself against the wall, just out of the sight line from the lower landing. Within a few moments, she detected the guard's movements: hearing Ben's ascent, he was scrambling to catch up with his quarry.

The seconds became hours. Anna could picture the guard bounding up to the lower landing: she'd have to work with a mental image, assembled from sounds of the man's movements. Once she was visible to the guard, she would have no advantage over him other than swiftness. She would keep out of sight until the last possible moment; and then her reflexes would have to be instantaneous.

Now she leaped into the air and fired where she pictured the guard in her mind, squeezing the trigger even as she was at last able to confirm his position visually.

The guard had a submachine gun aimed directly at her. Victory or defeat would be measured in milliseconds. Had she waited until she could see him before firing, the advantage would have been his.

Instead, she watched as his tunic erupted into blood and his weapon fired harmlessly above her, then fell noisily down the stairs.

"Anna?" Ben called out.

"*Now!*" she replied, and he sprinted down the two flights of stairs, joining her at the bay level, at a gate-latch door, also of gray-painted steel, which pushed out.

As they entered Bay Number 7, they felt a gust of cold, and there it was—the helicopter glinting in the waning light, a great gleaming metallic creature. It was a large, sleek, black Agusta 109, brand new. Italian-made, with wheels instead of skids.

"Can you really fly this thing?" Anna asked, after they'd both clambered into it.

Ben, seated in the cockpit, grunted assent. In truth he had flown a helicopter only once before, a training vehicle, with a licensed pilot at the twin set of controls. He had flown planes many times, but this was entirely different, counterintuitive. He scanned the dim cockpit for the controls.

For an instant, the complexities of the instrument panel dissolved into a blur. The image of his father's crumpled body seemed to hover before his eyes. He flashed on a Max Hartman just young enough that he could glimpse how he once must have looked. He could glimpse the youthful financier who found the country around him erupting into a lethal blaze of hatred. Who raced around, entering into loathsome accommodations with a loathsome regime in order to save as many families as he could. A man accustomed to mastery turned into a pawn.

He could glimpse the man—an émigré, a harrowed man, a man with secrets—whom his mother met and fell in love with. Max Hartman, his father.

Ben shook his head hard. He had to focus.

He had to focus or they would both be dead. And everything would be for nothing.

THE SIGMA PROTOCOL 521

The bay was open to the elements. Outside the gunfire seemed to be coming closer.

"Anna, I want you ready with the Uzi in case any of the guards try to shoot us down," Ben said.

"They won't shoot," Anna said, a wish expressed as a declaration. "They know it's Lenz's helicopter."

A voice from the back, cultivated and precise: "Quite so. Did you suppose that Lenz had no passengers waiting for him, Ms. Navarro?"

They weren't alone.

"A friend of yours?" Ben asked Anna quietly.

They both turned around and saw the passenger crouched in the rear compartment, a white-haired but vigorous-looking man wearing large glasses with translucent flesh-toned frames. He was immaculately attired in a King Edward–style Glenn Urquhart suit, a crisp white shirt, and a tightly knotted olive silk tie.

In his hands was a short-barreled automatic weapon, the one inelegant touch.

"Alan Bartlett," Anna breathed.

"Toss me the gun, Ms. Navarro. My gun is trained on you, and yours is hardly in position. I'd very much regret having to squeeze the trigger, you know. The discharge would surely blow out the windshield and possibly damage the fuselage as well. Which would be unfortunate, since we'll be needing this vehicle as a means of conveyance."

Slowly, Anna let the Uzi slide to the floor, and pushed it toward Bartlett. He did not lean over to retrieve it, but seemed satisfied that it was out of her reach.

"Thank you, Ms. Navarro," said Bartlett. "My debt of gratitude toward you only grows. I don't know that I adequately expressed my thanks for your having located Gaston Rossignol for us, and so swiftly. The wily old bird really was poised to cause us a great deal of trouble."

"You bastard," Anna said in a low voice. "You evil, manipulative son of a bitch."

"Forgive me, I realize this is hardly the time or place for a fitness report, Ms. Navarro. But I must say, it's terribly unfortunate that, having given us such excellent service, you've started to undo all the good you've achieved. Now, where is Dr. Lenz?"

Ben answered for her: "Dead."

Bartlett was silent for a moment. There was a flicker in his gray, expressionless eyes. "Dead?" His grip tightened on his automatic rifle as he digested the information. "You *idiots!*" His voice flared abruptly. "You *destructive* idiots! Vicious children seeking to ruin something whose beauty you could never comprehend. What gave you the *right* to do that? What made you think this was your decision to make?" He fell silent again, and was visibly shaking with anger when he resumed. "Damn you both to hell!"

"After you, Bartlett," Ben snapped.

"You're Benjamin Hartman, of course—I'm sorry we meet under these circumstances. But then I have only myself to blame. I should have ordered you killed at the same time as your brother: *that* shouldn't have taxed our capabilities. I must have grown sentimental in my old age. Well, my young lovers, I'm afraid the two of you have left me with some difficult decisions to make."

Faintly reflected in the windshield of the cockpit was the wide barrel of Bartlett's assault weapon. Ben kept his eyes on it.

"First things first," Bartlett went on, after a pause. "I'm going to have to rely upon your piloting skills. There's a landing strip outside Vienna. I'll direct you to it."

Ben glanced again at Bartlett's automatic weapon and toggled up the battery switch.

There was the clicking sound of the spark plugs firing, then the whine of the starter motor, which gradually deepened. It was fully automatic, Ben realized, which would make it much easier to fly.

In ten seconds there was ignition, and the engine thundered to life. The rotors began turning.

"Belt yourself in tight," Ben murmured to Anna. He pulled up on the collective's twist grip with his left hand, heard the sound of the rotors slowing.

Then some kind of horn sounded, and the engine slowed.

"Damn," he said.

"Do you know what you're doing?" Bartlett asked. "Because if you don't, you're of no use to me at all. I needn't spell out what that means."

"Just a little rusty," Ben replied. He grabbed the throttles, the two sticks that came down from the top of the windshield, and pushed both of them forward.

Now the engine and both the tail and the main rotors roared again. The helicopter lurched forward, then yawed left and right.

Ben abruptly yanked back on the throttle: the helicopter came to an abrupt jarring halt. Both he and Anna pitched forward against the restraint belts; Bartlett, as Ben had hoped, was hurtled against the metal grid that backed the cockpit.

Even as he heard the clatter of the assault rifle smashing into the partition, Ben unbelted himself and sprang into action.

Bartlett, he could see, had been temporarily stunned by the impact; a rivulet of blood descended from his left nostril. Now, with the suddenness of a leopard, Ben hurled himself around his seat and pounced on Bartlett with both hands, slamming the man's shoulders to the grip-textured steel flooring. Bartlett put up no resistance.

Had the impact of the partition knocked him unconscious? Was he already dead?

It was too risky to make any assumptions.

"I've got an extra set of restraints on me," Anna said. "If you can bring his wrists together . . ."

Within moments, she had manacled both his hands and legs, leaving her old employer trundled in the back like a rolled-up carpet.

"*Jesus*," Anna said. "There's no time. We've got to get a move on. The guards—they're on their way!"

Ben pushed the two sticks forward, then twisted the collective up while maintaining his grip on the cyclic. The collective controlled the helicopter's lift; the cyclic controlled its lateral direction. The helicopter's nose moved to the right, the tail to the left, and then it started rolling out of the bay and onto the snow-covered lawn, coolly illuminated by the moonlight.

"*Shit!*" Ben shouted, pushing the collective down to reduce power, trying to stabilize the craft.

Slowly he pulled the collective up, adding power slowly, and felt the aircraft getting light.

He pushed the stick forward an inch or two, felt the nose pitch down, then added a bit more power with the collective.

They were rolling now.

The helicopter taxied forward across the snow.

The collective was now halfway up.

Suddenly, at a speed of twenty-five knots, the chopper jumped into the air.

They'd lifted off.

He pulled back on the stick to gain more power, and the nose went right. They kept rising.

Bullets clattered against the cabin.

Several guards were running, their submachine guns pointed at the helicopter, shouting.

"I thought you said they wouldn't shoot at Lenz's helicopter."

"Word must have got out about the good doctor," Anna said. "Hey, better to travel hopefully, right?" She thrust the barrel of her Uzi out the open side window and fired off a burst. One of the guards fell to the ground.

Then she fired another, more sustained burst.

The other guard was down.

"O.K.," she said, "I think we're all right for a little while."

Ben brought the collective back past center, and the nose corrected.

Higher, then higher still.

They were directly above the *Schloss* now, and the craft felt more stable. Now he could fly it like an airplane.

Ben became aware of a sudden movement, and just as he turned, he felt a jabbing, searing pain at the base of his neck and shoulders. What he felt had some resemblance to the sensation of a pinched nerve but a hundred times worse.

Anna shrieked.

From the hot moist breath near his face, Ben realized what had happened. Bartlett, his arms and legs shackled, had thrown himself at Ben, attacking him with the only thing left at his disposal—his jaws.

A guttural vocalization, like the growl of a jungle creature, rose from Bartlett's throat as he sank his teeth farther into Ben's exposed neck and shoulders.

As Ben released the collective in order to grab hold of Bartlett, the helicopter started to yaw perilously to one side.

It wasn't over! Anna knew that to fire her gun at him would be to risk killing Ben. She seized handfuls of Bartlett's lank white hair and pulled with all her might. Pulled until the hair came out, exposing bloodied pink ovals of scalp.

And still Bartlett would not let up.

It was as if he were directing all his vital force into his jaws, pushing his teeth down into Ben's flesh with the muscular strength of his entire body.

It was all he had left. A wounded animal's one chance to survive—or, at least, to ensure that his enemy did not.

Ben, obviously convulsed by agony, pounded at Bartlett's head with his fists, but to no effect.

Was it possible—to have come so far, survived so much, only to be destroyed in the midst of escape?

Bartlett was maniacal, insensible to pain—a man of elegance and supernal ambition now reduced to the most elemental posture of any vertebrate. He could have been a hyena on the Serengeti plains, sinking his incisors into another creature, hoping that only one of them would make it to another day.

Even as his mouth vised on Ben's neck and shoulders, Bartlett's body was writhing, flailing, thrashing—kicking at Anna with both feet, jolting her out of position, weakening her grasp on him. A blast of cold air suddenly filled the helicopter. Bartlett's wild, eel-like movements had kicked open the door on Anna's side.

Another violent movement of his jarred the pedals, which controlled the tail rotors, and the helicopter began to rotate left, first spinning slowly and then more swiftly. As the centrifugal force gained in power, Anna began to slide precariously toward the open door. She clawed at Bartlett's face, her nails in his flesh providing her sole purchase. What she was doing sickened her, but it was the only way: she dug deeper, harder, forcing her finger into his orbital cavity.

"Open wide, you son of a bitch!" she shouted, gouging into the yielding flesh until, at last, with a blood-curdling scream, Bartlett released his mandibular grip.

What happened next was a blur: both Anna and Bartlett were thrown toward the open door, toward the yawning drop to the earth far beneath them.

Then she felt an ironlike grip on her wrist. Ben's hand had shot out, grabbing her, holding her back as the helicopter continued to spin at a forty-five degree incline and Bartlett, bellowing, finally succumbed to gravity and slid out of the helicopter.

His bellows became fainter as he plunged to the *Schloss* far below them. But would the helicopter follow him down? Unlike an airplane, a he-

licopter that had moved beyond the limits of correct angular position
would simply drop like a stone. And the rotating helicopter continued
to tilt, horrifyingly, as the loss of lift became sickeningly apparent.

Regaining proper position would require both hands and feet. Ben
frantically adjusted the cyclic and the collective as his feet worked the
pedals, coordinating the tail rotor with the main rotor.

"Ben!" she yelled, only just managing to latch the door. "Do something!"

"*Jesus!*" he roared over the straining rotors. "I don't know if I can!"

The helicopter suddenly plunged, and Anna's stomach lurched upward, but she noticed that even as it fell, it was starting to right itself.

If it righted itself in time—found the angle required for lift—they'd
stand a chance.

Ben manipulated the controls with furrowed intensity. Viscerally, they
knew that the rotorcraft had only seconds remaining before the descent
velocity became unrecoverable: any wrong decisions would be fatal.

She felt it before she saw it—felt the lift before she saw, from the
horizon line, that the helicopter had returned to even keel.

For the first time in a long while, she experienced a small but growing
abatement of panic. Deftly, she tore off a piece of her blouse and pressed
it to the area of Ben's lower neck that had been attacked. The area was
deeply grooved with tooth marks, but the compression wounds left very
little blood, which was fortunate. No major vessels had been breached.
Ben would need medical attention before too long, but it wasn't an emergency.

Now she looked down out of the window. "Look!" she called out.
Directly below them she could see the toy-model castle surrounded by
its serpentine fence. And at the base of the mountain a dense crowd of
people was surging, streaming.

"That's them!" she shouted. "It looks like they got out!"

They heard an explosion from below, and a great crater suddenly appeared in the ground next to the *Schloss*.

A small section of the ancient stone fortress nearest the blast crumbled
like a fragile confection of spun sugar.

"The dynamite," Ben said.

They were more than a thousand feet up now, cruising at 140 knots.
"The idiots dynamited the mouth of the cave. Way too close to the
building—look at what the explosion's done. *Jesus!*"

She saw what looked like a white cloud forming near the summit of the mountain, rolling like dense fog down the mountainside.

A white cloud of snow, a great wave, the avalanche a cruel fact of nature in the Austrian alps.

It was a strangely beautiful sight.

Apart from scores of children who managed to flee the grounds of the *Schloss*, there were no survivors.

Thirty-seven people around the world, many of them great men and women, all of them leaders in their field, were shocked to read the obituaries of the Viennese philanthropist Jürgen Lenz, in the avalanche that buried the Alpine *Schloss* he had inherited from his father.

Thirty-seven men and women, all of whom were in remarkable health.

CHAPTER FORTY-NINE

A gleaming throwback to a more elegant age, the Metropolis Club occupied the corner of a handsome block on East Sixty-eighth Street in Manhattan. It was a grand McKim, Mead & White building from the late nineteenth century, adorned with limestone balustrades, trimmed with intricate modillion courses. Inside, the curved wrought-iron railings of the double staircase led past marble pilasters and plaster medallions to the spacious Schuyler Hall. Three hundred chairs were now assembled on its black-and-white harlequinade floor. Ben had to admit, for all his misgivings, that it wasn't an inappropriate venue for his father's memorial service: Marguerite, Max Hartman's executive assistant for twenty years, had insisted on organizing the event and her efforts were, as always, beyond reproach. Now he blinked hard and looked at the faces in front of him, until the collectivity came into focus as individuals.

Seated in all those chairs was a curious community of mourners. Ben saw the careworn faces of older men from New York's banking community, grizzled, jowly, stoop-shouldered men who knew that banking, the profession to which they had devoted their lives, was now changing in ways that exalted technical competence over the cultivation of personal relationships. These were bankers who had made their biggest deals on the fairways—gentlemen of the green who glimpsed that the future of their industry belonged to callow men with bad haircuts and doctorates in electrical engineering, callow men who did not know a putter from a nine iron.

Ben saw the elegantly attired leaders of major charitable causes. He made fleeting eye contact with the executive director of the New-York Historical Society, a woman who wore her abundant hair in a tight bun; her face looked slightly stretched, in a diagonal that ran from each corner of her mouth to an area behind each ear—the familiar sign of a recent face-lift, marks of the surgeon's crude craft. In the row behind her, Ben recognized the white-haired, navy-suited head of the Grolier Society. The soigné president of the Metropolitan Museum. The neo-hippyish chair-woman of the Coalition for the Homeless. Elsewhere were provosts and deans of several major educational institutions, each keeping the others at a careful distance, each regarding Ben somberly. In the first row was the charismatic national director of the United Way charities, slightly rumpled, his brown basset-hound eyes looking genuinely moved.

So many faces, dissolving briefly and then resolving into particularity once more. Ben saw striving couples, tight-bodied wives and soft-bellied men, who had helped secure their position in New York society by en-listing Max Hartman's support in their ceaseless fund-raisers for literacy, AIDS, freedom of expression, wildlife conservation. He saw neighbors from Bedford: the softball-playing magazine mogul with his trademark bold-striped shirt; the slightly tatty-looking, long-faced scion of a distin-guished old family who once directed an Egyptology program at an Ivy League university; the youngish man who had launched, and sold to a conglomerate, a company that made herbal teas with colorful New Age names and progressive box-top homilies.

Worn faces, fresh faces, familiar ones and strange ones. There were the people who worked for Hartman Capital Management. Prized clients, like good old Fred McCallan, who'd dabbed at his eyes with a handker-chief once or twice. Former colleagues of his from his days teaching in East New York; newer colleagues of his from the job he'd just taken at an equally poor high school in Mount Vernon. There were people who had helped him and Anna in their time of need. Above all, there was Anna, his fiancée, his friend, his lover.

Before all of these people, Ben stood before a rostrum at the raised platform at the end of the hall and tried to say something about his father. In the previous hour, a very fine string quartet—one that Max Hartman had helped sponsor—had played an adagietto by Mahler, adapted from his Fifth Symphony. Erstwhile business colleagues and ben-eficiaries of Max had evoked the man they knew. And now Ben found himself speaking, and wondering as he spoke, whether he was really ad-dressing the assembled or himself.

He had to speak of the Max Hartman *he* knew, even as he wondered how much he ever did know or *could* know him. His only certainty was that it was his task to do so. He swallowed hard and continued speaking: "A child imagines that his father is all-powerful. We see the pride and the broad shoulders and the sense of mastery and it's impossible to think that this strength has limits. Maybe maturity comes of recognizing our error." Ben's throat constricted, and he had to wait a few moments before resuming.

"My father was a strong man, the strongest man I've ever known. But the world is powerful, too, more powerful than any man, however bold and determined he may be. Max Hartman lived through the darkest years of the twentieth century. He lived through a time when mankind revealed how very black its heart could be. In his mind, I think, the knowledge defiled him. I know that he had to live with that knowledge, and make a life and raise a family, and pray that his knowledge would not shadow our lives as it did his own. After such knowledge, what forgiveness?" Again Ben paused, took a deep breath, and pressed on.

"My father was a complicated man, the most complicated man I have ever known. He lived through a history of astonishing complexity. A poet wrote:

"*Think now*
History has many cunning passages, contrived corridors
And issues, deceives with whispering ambitions,
Guides us by vanities.

"My father liked to say that he only looked forward, never behind. That was a lie, a brave, defiant lie. History was what my father was shaped by, and what he would always struggle to overcome. A history that was anything but black and white. The eyesight of children is very sharp. It dims with age. And yet there is something that children really don't see too well: the intermediate tones. Shades of gray. Youth is pure of heart, right? Youth is uncompromising, resolute, zealous. That is the privilege of inexperience. That is the privilege of a moral cleanliness untested and untroubled by the messiness of the real world.

"What if you have no choice but to deal with evil in order to fight evil? Do you save those you love, those you can, or do keep yourself pure and unsullied? I know I never had to make that call. And I know something else. A hero's hands are chapped, scuffed, chafed and callused, and only rarely are they clean. My father's were not. He lived with the sense that, in fighting the enemy, he had also done work that served their purposes. In the end, his broad shoulders would be bowed with a sense of guilt that none of his good deeds could ever erase. He could never forget that he had survived when so many he had cherished did not. Again: After such knowledge what forgiveness? The effect was that he redoubled his efforts to do what was right. Only recently have I come to understand that I was never truer to him and his own sense of mission than when I thought I was rebelling against him, and his expectations for me. A father wants, above all, to keep his children safe. But that is the one thing that no father can do."

Ben's eyes met Anna's for a long, lingering moment, and he found solace in the steady, answering gaze of her liquid brown eyes.

"One day, God willing, I will be a father, and no doubt I will forget this lesson and have to relearn it. Max Hartman was a philanthropist—in the root sense of the word, he loved people—and yet he was not an easy man to love. Every day, his children would ask themselves whether they made him proud or ashamed. Now I see that he was burdened by this question, too: would he make us, his children, proud or ashamed?

"Peter, above all else, I wish you were here with me at this very moment, to listen and to talk." Now his eyes welled. "But, Peter, this you've got to file under 'strange but true,' as you used to say. Dad lived in fear of *our* judgment."

Ben bowed his head for a moment. "I say my father lived in fear that I would judge him—and yet it seems incredible. He feared that a child bred of luxury and indolence would judge a man who had to endure the annihilation of everything he held dear."

Ben squared his shoulders, and, his voice hoarse and thickened with sadness, spoke a little louder. "He lived in fear that I would judge him. *And I do.* I judge him mortal. I judge him imperfect. I judge him a man who was mulish and complicated and hard to love and forever scarred by a history that left its mark on everything it touched.

"And I judge him a hero.

"I judge him a good man.

"And because he was hard to love, I loved him all the harder . . ."

Ben broke off, the words strangled in his throat. He could say no more, and perhaps there was nothing more that needed to be said. He looked at Anna's face, saw her cheeks glistening with tears, saw her weeping for them both, and he slowly walked away from the rostrum, and toward the back of the hall. Soon Anna joined him, standing by his side while countless guests shook his hand as they filed out through the hall and talked among themselves in an adjoining room. There were words of condolence and of affectionate reminiscence. Kindly old men squeezed his shoulder, clearly remembering him as a child, one half of the adorable Hartman twins. Ben steadily regained his composure. He'd felt wrung out, but part of what had been wrung out of him was the heaviness of grief.

Ten minutes later, when someone—the head of the tax division at HCM—told a fond, funny anecdote about his father, Ben found himself laughing out loud. Somehow he felt lighter than he had in weeks, maybe years. As the crowd thinned, a tall, square-jawed, sandy-haired man clasped his hand.

"We've never properly met," the man said, and then he glanced at Anna.

"Ben, this is someone who has been a good friend to us both," Anna said warmly. "I'd like you to meet the new director of the Internal Compliance Unit, at Justice—David Denneen."

Ben shook his hand vigorously. "I've heard a lot about you," he said. "And can I say thanks for saving our ass? Or is that just part of your job description?" Ben knew that Denneen had been chiefly responsible for clearing Anna's name; the word had been artfully "leaked" that she'd been working for a sting operation, those reports of her misdeeds faked in order to draw out some genuine malefactors. Anna had even received an official governmental letter of thanks for her "dedicated service and valor," although the letter discreetly left the circumstances of that valor unspecified. Still, it served a turn in helping her land a job as vice president in charge of risk-avoidance at Knapp Incorporated.

Now Denneen bent down and kissed Anna on the cheek. "The debt runs the other way," he said, turning back to Ben. "As you very well know. Anyway, these days at the ICU I'm in the downsizing business. Someday, when my mother asks me what I do for a living, I'd like to be able to tell her."

"And Ben?" Anna presented the diminutive, brown-skinned man accompanying Denneen. "One more dear friend of mine I'd like you to meet: Ramon Perez."

Another vigorous handshake. Ramon smiled, showing very white teeth. "An honor," he said, bobbing his head a little.

He was still smiling when he and Anna drifted off to a corner to talk.

"You look like the cat that ate the canary," Anna said. "What is it? What's so funny?" Her moist eyes gleamed with amusement.

Ramon just shook his head. He glanced at her fiancé across the room and then at her, and still he was smiling.

"Ah," she said at last. "I know what you're thinking. 'What a waste,' right?"

Ramon shrugged but didn't deny it.

Anna looked over toward Ben until their eyes met. "Well, let me tell you something," she said. "He ain't wasted on me."

Afterward, Ben and Anna found a HCM Lincoln Town Car waiting for them in front of the Metropolis; the driver, seeing them emerge, stood stiffly in front of the car, ready to open the rear door. Ben held Anna's hand in his gently as the two walked toward the vehicle that would take them away. A faint drizzle made the streets gleam in the evening dusk.

Then Ben started, felt a twinge of adrenaline: the driver looked curiously youthful, almost adolescent, yet compactly, powerfully built. A kaleidoscope flashed before his mind, nightmarish images from a time not long in the past. Ben grasped Anna's hand fiercely.

The driver turned to face Ben, and the glow from the arched windows of the Metropolis illuminated his face. It was Gianni, Max's driver for the last two years of his life, a gap-toothed, boyish, high-spirited fellow. Gianni took off his taupe cap, waved it.

"Mr. Hartman," he called out.

Ben and Anna entered the car, and Gianni closed the door with an efficient thunk before settling into the driver's seat.

"Where to, Mr. Hartman?" Gianni asked.

Ben glanced at his watch. The night was young, and tomorrow wasn't a school day, anyway. He turned to Anna. "Where to, Ms. Navarro?" Ben asked.

"Anywhere at all," she said. "As long as it's with you." Her hand found his again, and she rested her head on his shoulder.

Ben inhaled deeply, sensed the warmth of her face next to his, and felt at peace. It was an odd, unaccustomed feeling.

"Just drive," Ben said. "All right, Gianni? Anywhere, nowhere—just drive."

CHAPTER FIFTY

USA TODAY

INSIDERS SPECULATE ABOUT
NEXT SUPREME COURT NOMINEE

Declaring that he "deeply regretted but fully understood" Justice Miriam Bateman's decision to step down from the U.S. Supreme Court at the conclusion of the spring term, President Maxwell said that he and his advisers would take their time and make a "considered, deliberate" decision about who would be proposed as her successor. "Living up to Justice Bateman's probity and wisdom will be a heavy burden on any nominee, and we approach this task with humility and with open minds," the President said in a press conference. However, insiders have already produced a short list of names believed to be under active consideration . . .

THE FINANCIAL TIMES

MERGER TALKS BETWEEN ARMAKON, TECHNOCORP

In what would be an unusual pairing of two New Economy pow-
erhouses, officials at both the Vienna-based agricultural and biotechnology giant Armakon and the Seattle-based software giant
Technocorp acknowledged that the corporations had entered into
preliminary merger negotiations. "Biotech is increasingly about
computing, and software is increasingly about applications," Arnold
Carr, Technocorp's CEO, told reporters. "We've been strategic partners in the past, but a more formal consolidation would, we believe,
ensure the long-term growth of both our companies." One prominent member of Technocorp's board of directors, former Secretary
of State Dr. Walter Reisinger, said that the boards of both companies
fully supported management in the decision. According to Reinhard
Wolff, the managing director of Armakon, the merger would ob-
viate the need for costly outsourcing of programming and potentially represent billions in savings. He credited the "truly wise and
distinguished directors" of both companies with having facilitated
the negotiations.

Large shareholders in both companies seemed to approve of the
merger talks. "There is strength in unity," Ross Cameron, whose
Sante Fe Group holds 12.5 percent of Technocorp's series A stock,
said in a prepared statement, "and we believe that together these
companies have a tremendous amount to offer the world."

A joint press release issued by the companies said that the combined corporation would be able to take a position of leadership in
the health sciences.

"Given Armakon's record of extensive research in biotechnology,
and Technocorp's enormous resources," Wolff stated, "the merged
companies will be able to push back the frontiers of the life sciences
in ways we cannot simply foresee."

On Wall Street, analysts had sharply divided reactions to the proposed merger . . .